PENGUIN CLASSICS

THE MYSTERIES OF PARIS

EUGÈNE SUE was born in 1804 to a doctor in Napoléon's army. Following his disappointing performance as a medical student, he enrolled in the French navy as a surgeon's assistant. Upon his discharge in 1829, he moved to Paris, where he proceeded to write nautical and adventure novels. Sue inherited a large fortune on the death of his father in 1830 but ran through it quickly. He took to the writing of serial novels in newspapers in order to support himself. One of the most widely read novels of the nineteenth century, *The Mysteries of Paris* first appeared in the conservative *Journal des Débats* from June 1842 through October 1843. While the novel was met with great popular success, it was perceived by many of Sue's contemporaries to be dangerously socialist in its political agenda. Other novels with controversial themes followed, including the hugely popular *The Wandering Jew* (1844–45), an anticlerical melodrama. In 1849, Sue began his massive *The Mysteries of the People*, a fictionalized history of the working classes throughout French history. Sue won election to the National Assembly in 1850 as a Socialist delegate. After speaking out against Louis-Napoléon's coup d'état, he was briefly imprisoned in 1851 and, after his release, went into exile in Annecy, in the French Alps. He died in Annecy in 1857, just after completing *The Mysteries of the People*, which was immediately banned by the French government.

CAROLYN BETENSKY received her doctorate in French and Comparative Literature at Columbia University. She is an associate professor of English at the University of Rhode Island and the author of *Feeling for the Poor: Bourgeois Compassion, Social Action, and the Victorian Novel.*

JONATHAN LOESBERG is a professor emeritus of literature at American University. He is the author of *Fictions of Consciousness: Mill, Newman, and the Reading of Victorian Prose* and *Aestheticism and Deconstruction: Pater, Derrida, and de Man.* He has been a fellow at the Rutgers Center for the Critical Analysis of Contemporary Culture, where he completed *A Return to Aesthetics: Autonomy, Indifference, and Postmodernism.*

PETER BROOKS taught for many years at Yale, where he was Sterling Professor of Comparative Literature, and currently teaches at Princeton. He is the author of *The Melodramatic Imagination, Reading for the Plot,* and *Henry James Goes to Paris*. His reviews and essays have appeared in *The New York Times, New York Review of Books, Times Literary Supplement*, and elsewhere.

EUGÈNE SUE

The Mysteries of Paris

Translated with an Introduction and Notes by
CAROLYN BETENSKY *and* JONATHAN LOESBERG

Foreword by
PETER BROOKS

PENGUIN BOOKS

PENGUIN BOOKS
An imprint of Penguin Random House LLC
375 Hudson Street
New York, New York 10014
penguin.com

This translation published in Penguin Books 2015

LIBRARY OF CONGRESS CATALOGING-IN-PUBLICATION DATA
Sue, Eugène, 1804–1857.
[Mystères de Paris. English]
The mysteries of Paris / Eugene Sue; translated with an introduction and notes by Carolyn Betensky and Jonathan Loesberg; foreword by Peter Brooks.
pages cm
Originally published in French as Les mystères de Paris. Nouv. éd. rev. par l'auteur.
Paris : C. Gosselin, 1843–44.
ISBN 978-0-14-310712-5
1. Working class—Fiction. 2. Paris (France)—Fiction. I. Betensky, Carolyn, 1962– translator, writer of added commentary. II. Loesberg, Jonathan, 1950– translator, writer of added commentary. III. Brooks, Peter, 1938– writer of foreword. IV. Title.
PQ2446.M7E5 2015
843'.7—dc23
2015023155

Printed in the United States of America
3 5 7 9 10 8 6 4 2

Set in Sabon

Contents

THE MYSTERIES OF PARIS

BOOK I

BOOK II

BOOK III

BOOK IV

BOOK V

BOOK VI

BOOK VII

BOOK VIII

Acknowledgments

The translators would like to acknowledge the following people for their invaluable assistance in completing this project: Robert Callahan, Gail Grella, Priscilla Parkhurst Ferguson, and Susan Hiner. Thanks are due as well to the Center for the Humanities at the University of Rhode Island.

Foreword

We're plunged from the start into the lowest depths of Paris-by-night, entering the *tapis-franc*, sinister low-life tavern on the Île de la Cité, the inner circle of Paris crime, prostitution, poverty, exploitation. Right away, we have a violent encounter of Slasher and Songbird, and the providential arrival of Rodolphe to rescue Songbird, alias Fleur-de-Marie, prostitute with a pure heart, who's been tortured by her guardian, the Owl, imprisoned, and sold by the ogress. Slasher, Songbird, and Rodolphe then enter the tavern together, to trade stories (everyone in this novel has a story to tell), where they are served by the ogress and spied on by the arch-villain, the Schoolmaster.

With this new complete English translation we can now summon up the joy felt by readers when on June 19, 1842, the newspaper *Journal des Débats* began publishing *Les Mystères de Paris* on the "ground floor"—the bottom quarter—of the front page. The novel held that place until October 15, 1843, unfolding over some sixteen months and 150 installments its breathless and lurid tale. It was certainly the runaway bestseller of nineteenth-century France, possibly the greatest bestseller of all time. It's hard to estimate its readership, since each episode was read aloud, in village cafés and in workshops and offices throughout France. Diplomats were late to meetings, countesses were late to balls, because they had to catch up on the latest episode. It was a truly national experience, riveting in the way certain celebrity trials have been in our time, breathlessly maintained from one installment to the next in a manner we now know through the television serial. The novel was such a success that it saved the staid and respectable *Journal des Débats* from looming bankruptcy. The emergence of the mass-circulation newspaper in fact depended on the popular fiction it featured on page one.

The novel of course triggered endless imitations and reworkings by others, in novels and stage melodramas: *The Mysteries of London, The Mysteries of Naples, The Mysteries of Lisbon, The Mysteries of New York*—the list goes on. Once the newspaper serialization was over, the ten volumes of the published book sold edition after edition. It made its author more than a celebrity: he became a hero to working-class French and their political leaders. He was elected to the National Assembly in 1850, after the Revolution of 1848 created a short-lived republic, and then suffered the suppression and pulping of his final novel, *The Mysteries of the People*, and exile from France when Emperor Napoléon III grabbed power and silenced all opposition.

Sue, before *The Mysteries of Paris*, was the moderately successful author of seafaring tales and sentimental fiction. When he began *The Mysteries of Paris*, he had only a bare outline of the plot (any alert reader will guess that Rodolphe and Fleur-de-Marie will turn out to have some deep mysterious tie that calls them to each other) and let one episode lead him to the next, under the imperative of closing each installment at a cliff-hanging moment, followed by the sacramental "la suite à demain": continued tomorrow. Since newspaper subscriptions renewed quarterly, the end of each quarter needed to stage a particularly dire moment. He began his exploration of low-life Paris largely from sensationalistic motives: this, as his fellow novelist and rival Balzac also understood, was colorful stuff. He might be accused of slumming, like his hero Rodolphe, but with less benevolent motives. But as he went on, particularly in creating Rigolette, the virtuous seamstress whose earnings are scarcely sufficient to keep her from dire poverty and the slide into prostitution, and the unfortunate jewel-cutter Morel, on whose family disaster after disaster accumulates, he began to deal with the realities of contemporary society. Reader reaction was intense, and it changed the course of the novel. The letters written to Sue demonstrate how he altered its themes and its scope as he began to discover that there was a true melodrama to the precarious existence of the working classes.

Many readers wanted to see Sue's characters as real: they wanted Rodolphe to help them; they wanted to rescue Morel. But other letters reached Sue from readers who had tales that mirrored those of Morel and Fleur-de-Marie, who recognized themselves in the excruciating circumstances Sue had created for his characters. Socialist reformers, too, began to bombard Sue with ideas and tracts, including serious sociological studies of the worker's condition—this was a moment of several remarkable inquiries into economic and social destitution in France, into prostitution, its causes and management, into the underside of nascent capitalist wealth and expansion. Sue began responding by way of his novel, introducing such reformist schemes as a nationally organized pawnshop that would provide credit to the poor, public defenders for the accused, and a hospice for the children of convicts. A real dialogue developed, and by the time the novel drew to its close, Sue was ready to proclaim himself a socialist. Though Marx and Engels would ridicule the unscientific and utopian brand of socialism endorsed by Sue and those he inspired, and who in turn inspired him, for many *The Mysteries of Paris* was a gospel of humanitarianism.

The Grand Duke Rodolphe of Gerolstein (this identity is mostly hidden when he's out and about) travels in the underworld of Paris in search of opportunities to exercise his benevolence. He engages in "virtue policing" (a notion many readers thought should be instituted in the real world), rewarding those who deserve better than their fate, in a gesture of top-down charity. He finds his female counterpart in the society lady Clémence d'Harville, who comes to succor the prisoners at Saint-Lazare, where female thieves and prostitutes were locked up. This appears a bit condescending at first, but a contemporary reviewer of the novel caught the importance of what was going on: "Up till now, the novel, almost exclusively lordly, had kept proudly to the social summits, not deigning to look down. . . . This is the first time that it has penetrated so deeply into the miseries of the people; it is the first time that it has stirred up so profoundly the social slime, and that it has descended into these somber abysses where human suffering seems forever cast away from the pity of man and the justice of God." Rarely has a novel had such an impact.

The pleasures awaiting the reader of *The Mysteries of Paris* are multiple and varied. Sue has created a rich cast of characters, from the villainous to the virtuous, and he manages their entries and exits expertly, interweaving five or six different plotlines in order to maintain suspense and keep the reading experience one of high tension. His characters act out their psychic lives in the heightened words and gestures of melodrama. Writing in France, he can permit himself a dose of the erotic that was unavailable to English novelists such as Dickens or Wilkie Collins or Mary Braddon. The plot that uses the creole Cecily to put an end to the malefactions of the evil notary Jacques Ferrand is masterfully over the top. The taming of the fierce She-Wolf touches on questions of female sexuality unaddressed by more decorous novelists. Rodolphe's attempt to re-virginize Fleur-de-Marie is a more complex matter that evokes all the ambivalences of male understandings of women and their bodies. Sue, you might say, earns his melodramatic presentation of reality by bringing to light emotions and issues often repressed, in reality and in more self-censoring novels.

Sue's message was all the more important because the *Journal des Débats* was politically moderate and pro-government. He gave voice to truths about the social order that may have been dimly known but were not acknowledged. Well before Victor Hugo focused his long-standing social concern in *Les Misérables*, Sue asks us to pay attention. Joseph Conrad famously wrote that the task of the novelist is "by the power of the written word, to make you hear, to make you feel—it is, before all, to make you see." Sue does that, and he keeps you highly entertained along the way.

PETER BROOKS

Translators' Introduction

Eugène Sue's *Les Mystères de Paris* appeared in serial form for the first time between 1842 and 1843 in the *Journal des Débats*. It was translated in England in 1843, and twice in the same year, in two different versions, in the United States. The novel was wildly successful on both sides of the Atlantic, and in the years following its publication it was imitated by numerous authors around the world, including George Reynolds and Ned Buntline, whose *Mysteries of London* and *Mysteries and Miseries of New York*, respectively, came also to dominate the popular literary market.

All three of the 1843 translations have considerable shortcomings and inaccuracies. None of the translations have been available in book form since the early twentieth century (all current e-book translations reproduce the British translation, which is characterized by significant omissions). It is thus unsurprising that the novel itself is only very slightly known to the English-reading public, despite its international success in the nineteenth century and its ongoing importance for French literary and historical studies. Indeed, it is probably not going too far to say that *The Mysteries of Paris* is the most important work of nineteenth-century French fiction that is virtually unread in English.

The lack of a readable translation thus poses a serious challenge to scholarship—the novel is surely as significant, in French social and cultural history, at least, as *Les Misérables*, on which it had a profound influence—but it also deprives the many readers who enjoy nineteenth-century melodrama of a genuine source of pleasure. In France, contemporary readers have no such trouble purchasing the novel, as it is available in several editions. The two French film adaptations of the novel that have appeared since the silent period, along with one French television serial, also testify to its ongoing popularity.

It is our hope that this new translation will serve to introduce contemporary English-speaking readers to Sue's work. There are, we think, three problems that hampered nineteenth-century translations of *The Mysteries of Paris* and that, in contrast to the case of nineteenth-century translations of Dumas, for instance (which are sometimes equally faulty and which are nevertheless still in circulation), have hampered the novel's reception in English. The first problem for the translator, peculiar to this novel, is its inclusion of a criminal argot, a specialized thieves' slang that Sue did not expect his contemporary readers to understand. The second difficulty for Sue's translators is the more common problem of translating the tone of voice, ranging from the sententious to the flippantly casual, of various characters. While the translation of tone will always pose a challenge to translation, Sue's novel is particularly rich in dialogue that operates at several different levels of speech. Sue's diverse registers of tone and terminology frequently bump up against each other, and many of the text's comic and melodramatic effects depend, for better or worse, on capturing such differences. Finally, recognizing the continuing popularity of Victorian melodramatic fiction—not merely of works by Dickens, but of those by Collins and Braddon, as well—the translator needs to find a way to render Sue's melodramatic narrative voice that, while not making it falsely contemporary or masking any of the frequently dated and awkward narrative intrusions, makes it at least as accessible to current readers as the voices of these Victorian writers.

The problem of translating the criminal argot in the book may be described in terms of Walter Benjamin's distinction, in "The Task of the Translator," between "the intended object" and "the mode of intention"—or, in less phenomenological language, between what a sentence means and how it means it. One might think that translating the seemingly artless prose of *The Mysteries of Paris* would present much less of the problem of translating mode of intention than, say, translating a novel by Flaubert, but Sue's use of criminal argot makes the problem of mode of intention quite pointed. For as we've mentioned above, numerous phrases in the novel are clearly intended *not* to be understood by the average French reader. We know this, first of all, because these phrases are themselves translated into conventional French in the footnotes Sue himself supplied within the original text; and second, because Sue makes a point of announcing, in the opening of the novel, that this language will not be understood by the uninitiated. Thus, the narrator tells us, "These men have their own moral code, their own women, their own language—a mysterious language, full of morbid imagery and metaphors steeped in blood. And like savages, these individuals generally refer to themselves by nicknames that derive from their energy or cruelty, or from particular physical strengths or deformities."

With regard to the translation of nicknames, the mandate of this passage is fairly clear. The "savages" Sue references here refer to characters in the works of James Fenimore Cooper. In keeping with Cooper's "translations" of the names of his characters, we have translated almost all nicknames from French to English. *Le Chourineur* thus becomes "the Slasher," and *la Chouette* is translated as "the Owl." Occasionally, however, a nickname is more suggestive than strictly referential, even in the original French. A literal translation of *Pique Vinaigre*, for instance, would be "Vinegar Bite" or

"Vinegar Sting." As we are told, the character had earned his nickname because "he was endowed . . . with a great wealth of irony, which had won him his nickname, as his witticisms were often sardonic or humorous." His nickname derives, accordingly, from something like a stinging sense of humor. We have called this character "Bitters"; this is not a literal translation, obviously, but one that captures the meaning of the name with a metaphor in English that suggests something with a bite. Alas, not all nicknames sound felicitous when translated literally into English, but leaving them untranslated would be the same as leaving "Pathfinder" or "Hawkeye" untranslated into French if one were translating Fenimore Cooper.

In the case of the footnoted criminal argot, our choices were less straightforward. One possibility, sometimes employed in the nineteenth-century translations, would be to leave the words in French (since French speakers wouldn't have understood them anyway) and to translate the footnotes. Another option was to translate the footnotes directly into the text—that is, we could remove the footnotes altogether and provide the translation of the strange term in the text, as if it had not been footnoted to begin with. We rejected the second approach since it would have stripped the novel entirely of its peculiar quality of hosting a mysterious and unfamiliar language within it. And we never really considered the first solution: what Benjamin calls the mode of intention, the way the meaning is expressed, is part of the meaning, since the fact that "these men" speak a language special to them is part of who they are. Moreover, many of the slang expressions, although presumably unfamiliar to Sue's original French readership, do nonetheless turn out to have metaphorical significance that warrants translation, just like the nicknames. Our solution was to find—and sometimes, to invent—slang terms in English that retained, as much as possible, the implications of the French argot, all the while identifiably functioning as elements in a criminal language.

The passage in which the Schoolmaster threatens Rodolphe with a knife offers an example of the problem we faced of maintaining a metaphor. In this scene, Rodolphe answers him dismissively (here, rendered more or less literally), "Put your larding needle away. There are no chickens here to lard. I'm an old rooster and I have spurs." The problem in this case is that not only do American cooks no longer have larding needles in their kitchens—since American meat and fowl is already too fatty to need larding—but also that "larding needle" hardly seems tough-guy talk in English. We could have translated it as "toothpick," but then we would have lost Rodolphe's metaphorical extension of the slang into the realm of chickens and old roosters. Drawing on the word "pigsticker," we have invented the term "chicken sticker" to carry the dismissive element of *lardoir*, which also allows Rodolphe to draw out the metaphor with his claim about chickens, roosters, and spurs.

The word *lardoir*, however, is still understandable to a French speaker.

The most daunting challenge for us in translating *The Mysteries of Paris* occurred when we were faced with phrases we knew to be incomprehensible in standard French. The problem is particularly evident in one scene that involves a character using argot that another noncriminal character does not understand, thereby leading to a discussion of the argot and making the mode of intention part of the referential meaning. In that scene, the character known as the Slasher is talking to Tom, an upper-class foreigner, who nevertheless speaks standard French perfectly. Tom is visiting the Île de la Cité, the neighborhood in which the novel's criminal characters are concentrated, in search of Rodolphe. In the course of the conversation, the name of another criminal, Red-Arm, comes up. Tom asks who Red-Arm is and the Slasher answers that he "*pastiquait les maltouzes.*" The phrase means that he sells contraband, but this meaning is clear only to one who understands the criminal argot. If we translated the Slasher's first phrase into standard French directly—saying, simply, that Red-Arm sells contraband—it would make no sense when Tom tells the Slasher that he cannot understand him. And since the Slasher then translates the phrase into conventional French in the text to explain to Tom what he has said, the exchange would become meaningless. To put it plainly: the Slasher would tell Tom that Red-Arm sells contraband, Tom would ask what it means "to sell contraband," and the Slasher would answer that it means "to sell contraband." The usual etymology offered by slang dictionaries for the phrase *pastiquer les maltouzes* speculates that *maltouze* comes from *maltôte*, a tax, and *pastiquer* means "to pass by." But had we resorted exclusively to using this etymology, we would only have arrived back at a self-evidently meaningful phrase—and lost the metaphor. But *maltouze* also derives, according to the French slang dictionaries, from *malle*, a valise or packing trunk. With this meaning as our inspiration, we invented "he fakes packing trunks," a phrase neither self-evidently meaningful in English nor, once translated, utterly meaningless. Occasionally, as an alternative, we translated the criminal into actual English slang, an approach that often required the same sort of annotation as Sue provided his own readers. Hence, "beak" for "judge," and "onion" for "pocketwatch."

Translating the different levels of slang, formality, jauntiness, high melodramatic sentiment, low comedy, etc., in the dialogue calls for less special comment. A translator of Zola's *L'Assommoir*, with its narrative constructed from the free indirect discourse of its working-class characters, surely has an equally difficult task in this regard. But there is more slang, perhaps, in Sue, and more disparity from register to register. Furthermore, the clashes in genre, tone, and language occur in the service of various narrative effects, which need preservation. The dialogue between the comic couple of Madame and Monsieur Pipelet, for instance, in which Madame Pipelet sounds like a kindhearted lower-class shopkeeper from a Warner Bros. crime movie and her husband speaks with the perpetually aggrieved formality of Oliver Hardy, demands some effort from the translator who wishes to preserve even the fairly broad comic effects those interchanges mean to achieve.

Capturing an author's narrative voice is perhaps both the most significant part of any translation and the part about which little may be said beyond the translation itself. Nineteenth-century translations from French into English—and not just of Sue—frequently have a tone of quaintness that must have sounded marked even to nineteenth-century English ears. Sue's narrative voice had the easy moral judgment, the range of historical and intellectual reference (however inaccurate it might have been), and the melodramatic sentiment familiar to English readers of Anthony Trollope, Thomas Hardy, Wilkie Collins, and Charles Dickens. In this translation, our goal has been neither to make Sue sound like our contemporary nor to make him sound like a resurrected artifact; our intention has been to give this novel the opportunity to appear before English readers as it now does to contemporary French readers: a novel not only important for its historical and literary influence, but one that remains compulsively readable.

Footnotes in the text that are by Sue are so noted as [SN]. We have annotated references we expect not to be familiar to contemporary American and English readers, and these footnotes are marked as translators' notes [TN].

CAROLYN BETENSKY
JONATHAN LOESBERG

The Mysteries of Paris

BOOK I

CHAPTER I

THE JOINT

In the slang of murderers and thieves, a "joint" is the lowest sort of drinking establishment. Ex-cons, called "ogres," generally run these taverns; or, when it is an equally debased woman, she is known as an "ogress." Serving the scum of Paris, inns of this variety are packed with freed convicts, swindlers, thieves, and assassins. Whenever a crime has been committed, the police first cast their nets in this mire, so to speak. And here they almost always find their man.

This opening should alert readers to the sinister scenes that await them. If they proceed, they will find themselves in strange places, foul urban abscesses that teem with criminals as terrifying and revolting as swamp creatures.

We have all read the legendary work of the American Walter Scott, James Fenimore Cooper, whose pages describe the brutal ways of savages, their quaint and poetic language, the countless tricks they use to pursue or flee their enemies. Their readers tremble for the welfare of colonists and town-dwellers when they consider how they are surrounded by these wild tribes whose bloody ways mark them off from all things civilized. For our own readers, we are going to attempt to depict some episodes from the lives of *French* savages who are as far removed from civilization as the Indians Cooper so vividly depicts. And these barbarians are all around us. We will spend time with them in the dens in which they get together to plan murders and robberies, in the holes where they divvy up their victims' spoils among themselves.

These men have their own morality, their own women, their own language—a mysterious language, full of morbid imagery and metaphors steeped in blood. And like savages, these individuals generally refer to each other by nicknames that derive from their energy or cruelty, or from particular physical strengths or deformities.

We will approach some of the scenes of this story with the utmost caution. First of all, we fear being accused of seeking out only the basest, most repellent episodes. But even if they accept the setting, some readers may consider us unequal to the task of representing such unusual behaviors with accuracy and vigor. Indeed, while writing some of these passages, we have almost frightened ourselves. At times, our hearts have stopped beating. We have felt what we would call the pain of anxiety—the anxiety that stems from the fear of looking ridiculously presumptuous.

When we reflect that perhaps our readers might feel the same repulsion, we have wondered whether perhaps it might be best to turn back from the path we have taken. And, to some extent, we still have our doubts. If we had not felt that the story you are about to read needed so urgently to be heard, we would have regretted placing it in such shocking surroundings. In the end, we rely on the fearful curiosity that terrible spectacles sometimes elicit. In addition, we believe in the power of contrasts. It is perhaps a good idea to make certain characters, existences, and faces speak, in a work of art, in all their grimness, energy, and even crudeness. Such representations of evil might serve to repulse the reader and propel him toward experiences of a completely different kind.

Thus forewarned, readers may wish to follow us on the journey we are inviting them to take among the denizens of the infernal race that fills our prisons and whose blood stains the scaffolds. We do not doubt this investigation will be new for them. Let us reassure our readers that once they begin this story, with each step on its way, the air becomes purer.

On a rainy, cold evening on the thirteenth of December 1838, a sturdy-looking man in a shabby worker's shirt crossed the Pont au Change and entered the Cité, that maze of obscure, narrow, twisted streets that stretches from the Palais de Justice to the Cathedral of Notre-Dame.

Despite the fact that it is kept under strict surveillance, the area around the Palais de Justice serves nonetheless as safe haven and meeting place for the evildoers of Paris. Is it not odd that an irresistible attraction tends to lure criminals toward the very tribunal that will eventually condemn them to prison, the galleys, or the gallows?

On this particular night, the wind was blowing fiercely through the alleys of the gloomy quarter. Buffeted by its gusts, streetlamps projected their weak gleam upon streams of blackish water running down the muddy cobblestones. Mud-colored houses were studded here and there with the odd window with no glass in it, usually surrounded by a worm-eaten frame. One dark, pestilential alley led to another one that was still darker and more diseased. They were connected by stairways so steep that one could barely climb them, even with the help of the ropes attached by iron clamps to the fetid walls.

The ground floor of some of these houses was occupied by the storefronts of colliers, tripe vendors, and retailers of bad meat. Despite the poor quality of these commodities, iron bars covered the fronts of almost all of these miserable shops. Such was the mistrust the shopkeepers harbored toward the bold thieves of the quarter.

The man of whom we speak slowed his pace considerably as he turned onto rue aux Fèves, at the center of the Cité. He felt himself on home ground.

The night was dark, the rain falling in torrents. Strong gusts of wind and rain whipped at the walls. In the distance, the clock of the Palais de Justice chimed ten. Sheltered under awnings deep and dark as caverns, women sang refrains of popular songs in soft voices. The man of whom we were speaking clearly recognized one of these creatures. Stopping abruptly in front of her, he took hold of her arm.

"Good evening, Slasher."

This man, an ex-con, had been given this moniker in prison.

"Hey, Songbird," said the man in the worker's shirt. "Stand me a drink, or I'll make you dance to the music!"

"I don't have any money," replied the girl, trembling. This man terrified everyone in the neighborhood.

"If you have holes in your pockets, go ask the ogress at the joint to lend you some as an advance on your pretty mug."

"Good Lord! I owe her already for the shirt on my back."

"So you talk back, now?" the Slasher shouted. In the dark, out of nowhere, he gave her such a blow that she cried out in pain. "That's nothing, my girl. That's just to give you fair warning."

No sooner had the thug uttered these words than he let out a bloodcurdling curse: "My wing's slashed! You've scratched me with your scissors."

Furious, he lunged after Songbird in the dark alley.

"Keep away from me, or I'll cut your lights with my clippers," she said in a confident voice. "Why did you hit me? I didn't do anything to you."

"I'll tell you," returned the bandit as he groped around in the dark. "Ah! I've got you! And you're going to dance to that music now!" he added, grabbing her tiny, frail wrist in his large, strong hands.

"No: you're the one who will be dancing!" said a man in a deep voice.

"A man! Is that you, Red-Arm? Answer me already and stop holding me so tight. This is the alley by your house. It must be you."

"I am not Red-Arm," said the voice.

"Good, because he's no friend of mine. There's going to be some blood spilled around here," said the Slasher. "But who owns this little paw I've got ahold of?"

"Here's the other one." Under the delicate and soft skin of the hand that had just seized him brusquely by the neck, the Slasher could feel nerves and muscles of steel.

Songbird was hiding deep in the alley. She had nimbly climbed up several steps in the stairway; she stopped for a moment and called out her thanks to her unknown savior: "Thank you, sir, for helping me. The Slasher had been beating me because I didn't want to pay for his liquor. I got some of my own back, but I couldn't do much against him with my little scissors. Now that I'm safe, let him be. Be careful—it's the Slasher you're dealing with!" It was clear that this man inspired her with overwhelming fear. "Didn't you hear me? Don't you understand? I'm telling you that he's the Slasher!" repeated Songbird.

"Well, I don't get the chills so easily," said the stranger.

Then all was silent. For a few seconds the sounds of a mortal struggle could be heard. "Do you want me to beat you to a pulp?" asked the Slasher, making a violent effort to rid himself of this adversary, whom he found surprisingly strong. "Good, good. I'll make you pay for Songbird and for yourself, too," he added, gnashing his teeth.

"I'll give you back your change with my fists," answered the stranger.

"Hands off my tie or I'll bite your nose off," stammered the Slasher, gasping for air.

"My nose is too small for that, my good man, and you can hardly see it."

"All right. Let's go under the streetlamp."

"Let's go," responded the man. "Let's look each other in the eye." He threw himself upon the Slasher, whom he had still in his tight grip. He shoved him toward the opening of the alley and then pushed him violently into the street, barely lit by the glow of the streetlamp.

The bandit stumbled, but immediately regaining his balance, he jumped in fury upon the stranger, whose lithe, slight figure held no hint of the incredible strength he possessed.

Although the Slasher was athletic and highly skilled at savate,[1] he had met his *master*, as they say. The stranger hooked his leg around him (effectively tripping him) and, with remarkable dexterity, flipped him over twice. Not ready to admit the superiority of his opponent, the Slasher charged again, bellowing with anger. At this point, Songbird's defender, abruptly changing his approach, showered the Slasher's head with a hail of blows that fell on him as brutally as if they were dealt with an iron gauntlet.

These blows, worthy of the envy and admiration of Jack Turner, one of the most celebrated boxers of London, were so much more forceful than the parries of the ordinary street fight that the Slasher was doubly stunned. For the third time now, he fell like an ox on the cobblestones, muttering, "My goose is cooked."

"If he gives up, don't kill him! Have mercy on him!" cried Songbird, who had ventured during this battle toward the entrance to the alley of Red-Arm's house. Then she asked, in astonishment, "Who are you, anyway? Besides the Schoolmaster, there's no one from rue Saint-Éloi to Notre-Dame who can beat the Slasher. I must thank you, sir. Alas! If not for you, he would have knocked my brains out."

Instead of answering the young woman, the stranger listened attentively to her voice. Never had he heard a voice so soft, so delicate, so

1. A French form of kickboxing developed in the late eighteenth and early nineteenth century; in some styles, only use of the feet was allowed. [SN]

silvery; he tried to make out her features, but he could not see her in the darkness. The light of the streetlamp was too dim.

After remaining still for a few minutes, the Slasher began to move his legs and arms. Finally, he sat up.

"Be careful!" shouted Songbird, retreating again down the alley and taking her protector by the arm. "Watch out! He may want to get back at you!"

"Don't worry, my girl—if he wants another piece of me, I have more to give him."

The hoodlum heard these words. "I've had crab apples enough. I've had my fill for today and don't need more to eat," he said to his opponent. "Another time, who knows? If I find you . . ."

"You're not satisfied, then, with what you've gotten? Are you complaining?" asked the man in a menacing tone. "Have I cheated you of something?"

"No, no, I'm not complaining. You're the kid with all the trumps," he said with the surly but grudging respect that physical strength always brings out in this kind of man. "You beat me, and other than the Schoolmaster, who can eat three Hercules for lunch, no one has ever been able to boast of putting his foot on my neck."

"So, then?"

"So, then, I've met my master—that's that. You'll meet yours one of these days. Everyone meets his master someday. If not down here, you always have the big guy up in heaven there to deal with, as the priests say. The only thing I know for sure is that now that you've beaten the Slasher, you can sow your wild oats where you want in the Cité. All the ladies of the night will be your slaves; all the ogres in the dives will let you drink on credit. But who are you, anyway? You speak the lingo like one of us. If you're a thief, I don't want anything to do with you. I've stabbed people, it's true; when the blood comes into my head, I see red, and I have to strike someone. But I've put in fifteen years in the galleys to pay for my slashing. I've done my time, I don't owe anything anymore to any beaks,[2] and I've never stolen anything—just ask Songbird," he said.

"It's true. He's not a thief," she agreed.

"So let's go and get ourselves a drink, and you'll find out who I am," said the stranger. "Let's go—no hard feelings."

"You're a decent fellow. You're my master, I admit it. You sure know how to use those fists. Especially that storm of punches at the end there—thunder and lightning raining down on my head. I've never seen anything

2. Judges. Sue supplies footnotes to translate much of the thieves' slang he includes in the novel. We have tried to stay as faithful to his slang as English allows, but we have not kept each of his original translation footnotes. [TN]

like it. You were hammering away at me like a forge. It's a whole new game—you'll have to teach me how to do that."

"I'll do it again whenever you like," said the stranger.

"No, not on me, thanks—I've had enough. I've seen enough stars. But do you know Red-Arm, whose alley you were in a moment ago?"

"Red-Arm!" said the stranger in puzzlement. "I don't understand. Is he the only one living there?"

"You've got it, my boy. He has his reasons for not liking neighbors around," said the Slasher with a knowing grin.

"So much the better for him, then," said the stranger, who seemed uninterested in pursuing this line of conversation. "I don't know Red-Arms from Black-Arms. I was just looking for shelter from the rain when I entered that alley. You wanted to beat this poor girl, I beat you up, and that's all there is to it."

"That's fine—it's none of my business. People who need Red-Arm's services don't go shouting it about. We don't have to talk about it anymore."

Then, turning to Songbird, he said, "Well, you're a good girl. I give you a pounding, you give me a jab with your scissors. That's how it goes. The thing you did that was really nice tonight was that you didn't tell this crazy guy to keep on walloping me after I'd had enough. Come have a drink with us! This guy's paying. While we're at it," he said, turning to the stranger, "what would you say if we had a bite at the White Rabbit instead of just drinking?"

"Fair enough. I'll pay for dinner. Want to come, Songbird?" asked the stranger.

"I was hungry before," she answered, "but after watching you two pummel each other, I got sick to my stomach and lost my appetite."

"Come on! Eating will bring your appetite back," said the Slasher. "The food's great at the White Rabbit."

Now in perfect agreement, the three made their way over to the tavern together.

During the fight between the Slasher and the stranger, a huge collier, hiding in another alley, had been watching the course of the battle anxiously, without, as far as anyone could tell, giving the least help to either side. This man followed the stranger, the Slasher, and Songbird toward the tavern.

The ruffian and Songbird entered the tavern first. The stranger was walking behind them, when the collier came up to him and said to him, in English, in a quiet and respectfully disapproving tone, "Take care, my lord!"

The stranger shrugged his shoulders and rejoined his companions. The collier stayed close to the door of the establishment. Listening carefully, he looked from time to time through a little hole in the thick coat of whitewash that always covers the insides of the windows of such places.

CHAPTER 2

THE OGRESS

The White Rabbit Inn is about halfway down rue aux Fèves. This tavern occupies the ground floor of a tall house whose facade has two windows in what is called guillotine-style. Over the door of a dark, vaulted alley hangs an oblong lantern. On its cracked glass, in red letters, are the words "Rooms for the Night Here." The Slasher, the stranger, and Songbird entered the tavern. The inn was a large, low room, with a smoky ceiling, crisscrossed with black beams. A decrepit oil lamp suffused the place with a reddish glow. The patched-up, whitewashed walls had vulgar drawings on them in places, as well as bits of wisdom written in thieves' jargon. The battered, saltpetered floor was caked with mud. An armful of straw was strewn to function as a carpet below the ogress's counter, which was situated to the right of the door, under the oil lamp. On each side of this room, there were six tables. They were attached to the wall at one end, as were their accompanying benches. At the back of the room was a door to the kitchen. To the right, next to the counter, was an exit to an alley that led to the ratty rooms where one could sleep for three sous a night.

But now, a few words about the ogress and her guests. Her name was Old Lady Ponisse. She had three professions: innkeeper, cabaret proprietor, and renter of clothing to the wretched souls who swarmed the streets of the foul quarter. She was about forty years old; tall, strong, stout, and ruddy, with a slight beard. Her husky, masculine voice, massive arms, and large hands all proclaimed her unusual strength. On her bonnet she wore an old red and yellow scarf. A rabbit's-hair shawl covered her torso and was knotted in back. Her green wool dress left visible her black clogs, which her foot-warmer had frequently singed. She had a coppery complexion that had been enflamed by her long abuse of hard drink.

The lead-surfaced counter had jugs with iron hoops and tin measuring cups on it. On a little table attached to the wall were several glass flasks shaped into life-size replicas of the emperor's face. These bottles contained adulterated pink and green liquids that went by the names of "Perfect Love" and "Consolation." A fat black cat with yellow pupils who crouched near the ogress appeared to be the sinister mascot of the house. In a contrast that will seem hard for people to believe if they don't know what an unfathomable mystery the human soul can be, a holy branch of Easter wood[3] that the ogress had bought at church was placed behind the box of an antique cuckoo clock.

Two men with sinister faces and bristling beards, dressed practically in rags, hardly touched the jug of wine that they had been served. They were speaking quietly and seemed nervous. One of them, a very pale, almost ghastly man, kept pulling the shabby fez he was wearing down over his eyes. He kept his left hand hidden most of the time, taking care to behave as naturally as he could when he had to use it.

Farther down sat a young man no older than sixteen. His face was beardless, haggard, hollow, and leaden; his gaze was dead. His long black hair hung around his neck. This precociously corrupt adolescent smoked a short white pipe. With his back leaning up against the wall, his two hands in the pockets of his smock, his legs stretched out on the bench, he smoked, never taking his pipe out of his mouth except for when he drank from the bottle of brandy in front of him.

The other men and women who frequented the joint were unremarkable. Their faces were ferocious or brutish, their cheerful behavior vulgar or licentious, their silence morose or stupid. Such were the guests of the joint when the stranger, the Slasher, and Songbird walked in.

These three individuals play too important a role in this story, and their faces display too much character besides, for us not to spend time describing them. The Slasher, a very tall and muscular man, had pale, almost whitish-blond hair, thick eyebrows, and full, bright russet sideburns. The sun, hunger, and the hard manual labor of prison had tanned his skin to the ghoulish, greenish hue so typical for convicts. Despite his terrible nickname, the features of this man expressed more a brutish daring than any real ferocity. But the singularly well-developed posterior portion of his skull made it clear that he was dominated by murderous and carnal appetites. He was wearing a shabby blue smock and a pair of coarse velvet pants in a primitive shade of green—though one could hardly tell what their real color was under the thick coat of mud that covered them.

By some strange anomaly, Songbird presented an open and angelic countenance that preserved its purity even in the midst of depravity, as if her creature sins were powerless to erase the noble imprint that God puts on the forehead of a few select beings. She was sixteen and a half years old. The purest, whitest forehead rose above a perfect oval of a face. Eyelashes so long they curled slightly half veiled her big blue eyes. Her round, rosy cheeks shone with all the bloom of youth. Her little scarlet mouth, her delicate, straight nose, and her dimpled chin all took adorably sweet forms.

3. Wood blessed for Palm Sunday. [TN]

From each of her satiny temples a plait of ash-blond hair caressed her cheeks and looped behind her ears, whose pinkish-ivory lobes remained visible. The plaits then disappeared beneath the folds of a blue-checked cotton kerchief that tied at the top, in what is vulgarly called a squirrel style.

A coral necklace showcased her dazzling white neck. Though it was much too big for her, her brown damask dress hinted, nonetheless, at a delicate figure, round and supple as a reed. She wore a tattered little orange shawl fringed with green wrapped across her chest.

The charm of Songbird's voice had struck her unknown protector. Her sweet, vibrant, harmonious voice was so irresistible that the crowd of scoundrels and fallen women among whom she lived often begged her to sing for them. They listened to her with such delight that they had given her the nickname Songbird.

She had been given another nickname, owing no doubt to the virginal simplicity of her features: she was also called Fleur-de-Marie.[4] In street slang, this name refers to the Holy Virgin.

If only I could make my reader understand my surprise at encountering such a name amid the constant stream of foul language in which the words that signified theft, blood, and murder are even more hideous and frightening than the hideous and frightening things they represent. Here was a metaphor, a sweet bit of poetry, so tenderly pious: Fleur-de-Marie! She was like a beautiful lily raising its fragrant, snowy calyx above a field of carnage.

What a peculiar contrast, what a strange accident of fate! The inventors of this appalling language had also risen to the level of sacred poetry. They had ended up making the chaste thought they were trying to express sound even more charming. Together with other contrasts that break up the monotony of the most criminal lives, don't these reflections give credence to the possibility that certain principles of morality and piety that one might almost call innate might cast glimmers once in a while in the darkest souls?

Songbird's protector (we'll give this stranger the name Rodolphe) seemed to be between thirty and thirty-six years of age. His average, slender, perfectly proportioned build did not suggest the surprising strength of the man who had just defeated the athletic Slasher in a struggle. It would be very difficult to ascribe a particular character to Rodolphe's face. It combined the strangest contrasts. His features were regular and beautiful—too beautiful for a man, perhaps. His pale, delicate complexion, his large, burnt-orange irises that were ringed with blue in eyes that were almost always half closed, his nonchalant bearing, distracted gaze, and ironic smile all seemed to betoken a blasé man whose constitution was, if not broken, at least weakened by the aristocratic excesses of an

4. Literally, "Flower-of-Mary." [TN]

opulent life. Nonetheless, with his elegant white hand, Rodolphe had just taken down one of the strongest, most feared criminals in this neighborhood of criminals. We say "aristocratic excesses" for the same reason that the drunkenness one experiences from a great wine is completely different from the drunkenness that comes from adulterated swill. To the careful observer, the excesses differ in their symptoms in the same way they differ in nature and kind.

Certain lines in Rodolphe's brow revealed him to be a profound thinker, a man given to contemplation. The firmness of his mouth's contours, however, and the sometimes imperious and bold angle at which he held his head, betrayed a man of action whose physical force and daring always exercised an irresistible influence on a crowd. Often his gaze took on a melancholy cast, and the most human commiseration and touching pity could be read on his face. At other times, on the other hand, Rodolphe's gaze became hard and vicious. His features expressed so much disdain and cruelty that one would never believe him capable of gentle feelings.

What follows in this narrative will show the kinds of events and ideas which evoked in him such contrary passions.

In his fight with the Slasher, Rodolphe had betrayed neither anger nor hatred toward his adversary, who had been no match for him. Confident in his power, skill, and agility, he had demonstrated only bemused disdain for the primitive animal he had just taken down.

To complete the portrait of Rodolphe, let us say that his hair was of a light chestnut color, as were his nobly arched eyebrows and his fine and silky little mustache. His slightly prominent chin was carefully shaven. In every other way, the manners and language that he used so naturally made Rodolphe fit in perfectly with the ogress's other patrons. Around his slender neck, as elegantly turned out as that of an Indian Bacchus, he wore a casually knotted tie whose ends fell on the collar of his blue smock. The bleached-out smock looked as if it had seen better times. His big shoes were equipped with a double row of nails. In all, the only material evidence that he didn't belong in this joint was his delicate hands. And yet, his resolute demeanor and audacious calm, if one can say such a thing, put a great distance between him and the others.

Upon entering the joint, the Slasher, clapping one of his big, hairy hands on Rodolphe's shoulder, cried out, "Here's to the Slasher's master! Yes, you guys, this young guy just did me in. A word to the wise for all you so-called experts who might be thinking about getting their kidneys crushed or their skulls dented—I'm talking about the Schoolmaster, too, who would meet his master in this guy, also—I guarantee it! I'll bet on it!"

With these words, everyone from the ogress to the joint's regulars looked with fearful respect at the Slasher's victor. Some of them moved their glasses and jugs to the end of the table they were sitting at, eager to make room for Rodolphe in case he wanted to sit next to them. Others came up to the Slasher to ask him in lowered tones for details about this stranger who had made such a striking entrance into their world.

Finally, the ogress gave Rodolphe one of her most gracious smiles. She got up from her counter to take Rodolphe's order and to find out what the gentleman desired. This was an unheard-of event, an extravagant and legendary occurrence in the White Rabbit's usual feastings. Not even the notorious Schoolmaster, the terrible villain who made even the Slasher tremble with fear, managed to get such attention from the ogress.

One of the two men with sinister faces that we've already mentioned (the pale one who was hiding his left hand and pulling the brim of his fez down over his forehead) leaned toward the ogress as she was carefully wiping down Rodolphe's table and said to her in a hoarse voice, "The Schoolmaster hasn't come in today?"

"No," said Old Lady Ponisse.

"And yesterday?"

"He was here."

"With his new dame?"

"Are you kidding? You think I'm going to spill the beans on him? You think I'm going to rat on my regulars?" the ogress said, roughly.

"I have a meeting with the Schoolmaster," the thief repeated. "We have some business to discuss."

"That must be something, your business. You're just a bunch of killers!"

"Killers?" the bandit repeated, irritated. "Only the kind of killers who let you earn your living!"

"Enough already! Leave me alone!" the ogress cried, menacingly, holding the jug she had in her hand over the head of the man who was questioning her.

The man went back to his seat, muttering to himself.

Fleur-de-Marie, entering the tavern on the heels of the Slasher, had exchanged a friendly nod with the adolescent with the withered face. The Slasher said to the young man, "Hey, Fishhook, are you still downing the hard stuff?"

"You bet! I'd rather starve and wear old rags than go without putting liquor in my gullet or tobacco in my pipe," said the young man in a hoarse voice without shifting his position, blowing out huge mouthfuls of smoke.

"Good evening, Old Lady Ponisse," said Songbird.

"Good evening, Fleur-de-Marie," the ogress answered while getting closer to her in order to inspect the clothes on her back, clothes that she had rented out to the unhappy young woman. After getting a good look at her, the ogress said with a surly sort of satisfaction, "It's a pleasure to rent things to you. You're as tidy as a little cat. I wouldn't have trusted trash like Dervish or Death's Head to wear that beautiful orange shawl.

That's why I was the one who took you under my wing after you got out of prison—and to do you justice, I've never had a better pupil than you in all my time in the Cité."

Songbird lowered her head and didn't seem to take any pride in the ogress's praise.

"Hey, are those holy branches there on your cuckoo clock, Ma?" asked Rodolphe. He pointed his finger in the direction of the branch from Palm Sunday behind the old clock.

"What of it? We can't be expected to live like pagans," the horrible woman said, naively. Then, turning to Fleur-de-Marie, she added, "Tell me, Songbird, when are you going to warble us some of your tunes?"

"After we finish eating, Old Lady Ponisse," said the Slasher.

"What can I get you, my good man?" the ogress asked Rodolphe, wanting to make him feel welcome and hoping to be able to call on his aid if need be.

"Ask the Slasher, Ma. He's ordering, I'm paying."

"Fine!" said the ogress, turning to the bandit. "What do you want to eat, you filthy cur?"

"Two liters of twelve-sou wine, three pieces of unstale bread, and a harlequin,"[5] said the Slasher, after perusing the menu.

"I see that you're still quite a boozer and that you still like your harlequin."

"Sure do. Now, Songbird," said the Slasher, "are you hungry?"

"No, Slasher."

"Would you like something other than a harlequin, my girl?" asked Rodolphe.

"Oh, no, I'm not hungry anymore."

"But look at the boss, my girl!" said the Slasher, laughing loudly and gesturing at Rodolphe with his eyes. "Are you afraid to put your eyes on him?"

Songbird blushed and lowered her eyes without saying a word.

After a few moments, the ogress came back to put a jug of wine on Rodolphe's table along with some bread and the harlequin. We won't go into any detail about this meal except to say that the Slasher found it eminently to his taste, for he exclaimed, "What a meal! Lord, what a meal!! It's like a smorgasbord! There's something here for everyone—for those who like the fat and for those who like the lean, people who like sugar and people who like pepper . . . Poultry drumsticks, fish tails,

5. A harlequin is a collection of meat, fish, and various other leavings from the servants' provisions of wealthy homes. We are ashamed to mention these details, but they complement the picture of these strange manners. [SN]

For the value of French monetary terms, see the Note on Currency at the end of the book. [TN]

meat bones, crusts from pâtés, fried foods, cheese, vegetables, heads of woodcocks, crackers and salad. Go ahead, Songbird. Eat! You need to take care of yourself. Have you eaten your fill today?"

"Eaten my fill? Oh, yes. I ate the same meal I always do this morning, a penny's worth of milk and a penny's worth of bread."

The entrance of a new individual into the inn interrupted every conversation and made everyone turn their heads. This individual was a middle-aged man, alert and robust, wearing a hat and a jacket, perfectly at ease with the joint's rituals. He used the language of the customers to ask for a meal. Although this stranger was not one of the joint's usual patrons, everyone soon stopped paying attention to him. He had been sized up. Just like honest people, bandits have a knack for recognizing one of their own. This new arrival had positioned himself in such a way as to be able to observe the two men with sinister faces, one of whom had asked after the Schoolmaster. He didn't take his eyes off of them. From their position, however, the men could not tell that they were under his surveillance.

The conversations that had been interrupted when the man walked in resumed. Despite his brashness, the Slasher displayed a sort of deference toward Rodolphe. He did not dare to address him familiarly.

"Word of honor!" he said to Rodolphe. "Even though you made me dance to the music, I am still honored to have met you."

"Because you like the harlequin?"

"Well, yes, but also because I'm itching to see you go head-to-head with the Schoolmaster. He's always done me in, so to see you do him in in turn would do me good."

"Oh, really? You think I'd take on a bulldog like the Schoolmaster just to amuse you?"

"No, but he'll jump you as soon as he hears that you're stronger than he is," responded the Slasher, rubbing his hands together.

"I've got enough small change left over to pay him his due!" said Rodolphe, nonchalantly. Then he said, "The weather is so lousy. Let's have some grog. Maybe that would get Songbird to sing."

"Fine by me," said the Slasher.

"And to get to know each other, let's tell each other who we are," added Rodolphe.

"The Albino," said the Slasher. "Freed con, stevedore on the floating wood at the quai Saint-Paul. I freeze in the winter and roast in the summer—that's me, in a nutshell," said Rodolphe's companion as he gave him a military salute with his left hand. "All right," he added. "What about you, boss? It's the first time we've seen you around here. I'm not blaming you, but you've really gotten into my head and under my skin. Honestly, what a rumble that was! Especially that volley of fists at the end. I'll always remember that, how you got me good! Do you have another profession besides clobbering the Slasher?"

"I paint fans! And my name is Rodolphe."

"Fan-painter! So that's why your hands are so white," said the Slasher. "That's fine. If all your friends are like you, you must have to be pretty strong to do that job. But if you're a worker, and obviously an honest worker, what are you doing in a joint where there are only thieves, murderers, and ex-cons like myself who can't go anywhere else?"

"I'm here because I like good company."

"Hmm . . ." said the Slasher, shaking his head in doubt. "I found you in Red-Arm's alley. Okay . . . that's enough. You say you don't know him?"

"Are you going to bore me again with your Red-Arm? May he rot in hell, if Lucifer will have him!"

"Listen, boss, you may not trust me, and you wouldn't be wrong, but I'm going to tell you my story on the condition that you teach me those knockout blows you used on me. I want to learn how to do that."

"It's a deal, Slasher. You tell me your story, and Songbird will tell me hers, too."

"Fine," said the Slasher. "The weather is so foul that even a soldier wouldn't go outside. It'll be fun. Want to tell your story, Songbird?"

"All right. But it's not very long," said Fleur-de-Marie.

"And you'll tell us yours, comrade Rodolphe?" added the Slasher.

"Yes, I'll start."

"Being a fan-painter must be a nice way to make a living," said Songbird.

"How much do you earn, tiring yourself out doing that?" asked the Slasher.

"I do piecework," said Rodolphe. "On good days I earn four francs, sometimes five, but that's in the summer, because the days are long then."

"And you go wandering around like a beggar a lot?"

"Yes, when I have money. First I need six sous for my night's lodging."

"Excuse me, my lord . . . You pay six sous a night for your room?" asked the Slasher, touching his cap with his hand.

The ironic tone the Slasher used when he said "my lord" brought a slight smile to Rodolphe's face. He continued, "Well, convenience and cleanliness matter a great deal to me."

"Look here, we've got one of the Peers of France! A banker! A rich guy!" exclaimed the Slasher. "He pays six sous for his lodging!"

"On top of that," Rodolphe continued, "four sous for tobacco, which makes ten; four sous for lunch; that's fourteen; fifteen for dinner; one or two sous for liquor, that makes for about thirty pops a day. I don't need to work all week. The rest of the time I go out on the town."

"And your family?" Songbird asked.

"The cholera took them," said Rodolphe.

"What did your parents do for a living?" Songbird asked.

"Rag sellers under the columns of Les Halles, dealers in old rags."

"And how much did what they left behind bring you?" asked the Slasher.

"I was too young, it was my guardian who sold it. When I came of age, I owed him a balance of thirty francs. That was my whole inheritance."

"And who's your boss now at the factory?" asked the Slasher.

"My boss? His name is Monsieur Borel. He lives on rue des Bourdonnais. He's stupid, but brutal. A thief, but stingy. He would rather lose an eye than pay his workers. That's what he's like. If he wanders off, I hope he gets good and lost. Don't bring him back to the factory. I was apprenticed to him when I was fifteen years old. I had a good number in the draft.[6] I live on rue de la Juiverie, on the fourth floor in the back; my name is Rodolphe Durand. And that's my story."

"Now it's your turn, Songbird," said the Slasher. "I'll save my story for dessert."

6. The army, after the Restoration, was largely volunteer but was filled out by conscription, mostly from the lower classes. This limited draft was determined by lottery. [TN]

CHAPTER 3

SONGBIRD'S STORY

"Let's begin at the beginning," said the Slasher.

"Yes. Who were your parents?" asked Rodolphe.

"I never knew them," replied Fleur-de-Marie.

"Hmph!" grunted the Slasher.

"Never saw them, never knew them. Brought by the stork, like they tell children."

"Now that's funny, Songbird. We're from the same family."

"Really? You, too, Slasher?"

"Paris street orphan, just like you, my girl."

"And who raised you, Songbird?" asked Rodolphe.

"I don't know. As far back as I can remember, from the age of seven or eight, I think, I lived with a one-eyed old hag they called the Owl because of her hooked nose and her one round green eye. She looked like an owl with one eye put out."

"Ah, I can see the Owl as if she were right here in front of me!" said the Slasher, roaring with laughter.

"That one-eyed hag," Fleur-de-Marie continued, "made me sell barley sugar on the Pont Neuf every evening as a way of begging. When I didn't bring her back at least ten sous, the Owl would beat me instead of giving me dinner."

"I get it, my girl," said the Slasher. "A kick for bread, with a blow to butter it."

"Lord, yes."

"And you're sure that this woman wasn't your mother?" asked Rodolphe.

"I'm sure of it. The Owl made me feel bad often enough for having no mother or father. She always told me that she had picked me up off the street."

"So you got the runaround for your stew when you didn't make your ten sous?"

"A glass of water to top it off, and then I would go off to shiver all night on a bed of straw in a hole in the ground that the Owl stuffed me into. You know, people think straw is warm. Well, people are wrong."

"And that's what they call our stuffed mattresses!" cried the Slasher. "You're right, my girl—it's like sleeping on ice. Sleeping on a dunghill would be a hundred times better. But they say that's just what we want: 'Riffraff, that's what comes naturally to them.'"

This joke made Fleur-de-Marie smile. She continued: "The next morning the Owl would give me the same ration for lunch as for supper, and I would go to Montfaucon to look for some earthworms to use as fish bait. During the day the Owl ran a bait and tackle stand under the Notre-Dame bridge. For a seven-year-old child who was dying of hunger and cold, it's a long way from rue de la Mortellerie to Montfaucon."

"That exercise made you grow up as straight as a reed, my girl; shouldn't complain about that," said the Slasher, lighting his pipe.

"Finally, I would return exhausted with a basketful of worms. At noon, the Owl would give me a nice hunk of bread, and I wouldn't leave a crumb of it uneaten, I'll tell you."

"From not eating, you've got a wasp's waist, my girl. Shouldn't complain about that, either," said the Slasher, puffing noisily on his pipe. "But what's wrong, pal? No, I mean, Master Rodolphe? You look a little strange. Is it because this kid had such a hard childhood? Hey, haven't we all?"

"Oh, I doubt you've been as unhappy as I have, Slasher," said Fleur-de-Marie.

"Me, Songbird? Your childhood was like a queen's compared to mine! At least, when you were little, you slept on straw and got some bread to eat. Me, on good nights, I slept like a real hobo in the pottery kilns at Clichy, and I fed myself on the cabbage leaves I found at the city limits. Most of the time, though, since it was too far to go to get to the Clichy pottery kilns, and seeing as no grub made my legs give out, I slept under the big stones of the Louvre. In the winter, I got to sleep in nice white sheets . . . when it snowed, that is."

"Well, men are tougher than women. But I was a poor little girl. And on top of that, a weakling," said Fleur-de-Marie.

"You remember all that?"

"I sure do! When the Owl beat me, I would always drop at the first blow. After that, she would stomp all over me, crying, 'This little tramp doesn't even have a penny's worth of strength! She can't even take two whacks!' Then she would call me 'Miss Lowlife.' That's the only name I had. That was my Christian name."

"Sounds just like me. I had the baptism you give a stray dog. They called me Thing, Whatchamacallit, or Albino. It's really astonishing how much we're alike, my girl," said the Slasher.

"It's true," said Fleur-de-Marie, addressing her remarks mainly to the Slasher. Feeling, in spite of herself, a sort of shame in the presence of Rodolphe, she barely dared to raise her eyes, even though he appeared to belong to the class of people she usually associated with.

"And when you were done looking for worms for the Owl, what did you do?" asked the Slasher.

"The half-blind hag would send me begging around her until nightfall. In the evenings she would fry up some fish on the Pont Neuf. Oh, dear! Lord, by then my piece of bread was long gone; but if I had the bad luck to ask the Owl for something to eat, she would beat me, saying, 'Go make ten sous begging, Miss Lowlife, and then you'll have supper!' Since I was hungry, and on top of that she was hurting me, I would cry out every tear I had in my body. The hag would put my tray of barley sugar around my neck and plant me on the Pont Neuf. How I used to sob and shiver from hunger and cold!"

"Me, too, my girl, just like you," said the Slasher, interrupting Songbird. "People wouldn't believe it, but hunger makes you shiver just like the cold."

"In the end, I would stay on the Pont Neuf until eleven at night, crying my eyes out with my store of barley sugar around my neck. Often the sight of me crying touched the passersby, and sometimes they gave me ten or even fifteen sous, all of which I turned over to the Owl."

"A pretty good haul for a weakling!"

"But that's how it was that the hag, who was watching everything—"

"Out of one eye," said the Slasher, laughing.

"Out of one eye, as you say, since she only had one. But that's how it was that the hag took care to give me a beating before setting me up on the Pont Neuf. She knew I'd be crying in front of people passing by and make more money that way."

"Well, that's not so dumb!"

"You really think so, Slasher? Well, I ended up getting a lot tougher from all her blows. I could see that the Owl got angry when I didn't cry, so to get even with her I decided that the more she hurt me, the more I would laugh. At night, instead of sobbing while selling my barley sugar, I sang like a lark, even though I didn't feel much like singing."

"Hey, those barley sugar candies must have been pretty tempting for you, poor Songbird!"

"They sure were, Slasher, but I never got to taste any of them. I wanted to taste that barley sugar, and it was that desire that got me in trouble, as you'll see. One day, when I was returning with my worms, some kids beat me and stole my basket. I came back, knowing full well what was in store for me. I got 'paid back for my troubles,' so to speak, and received no bread. That night, before going to the bridge, the hag, who was furious at me for not having done good business during the day, let me have it. Instead of just beating me as usual to get me to start crying, she went so far as to torture me, making me bleed by tearing my hair out at the temples, where it's most sensitive."

"Now, that's going too far!" cried the bandit, pounding his fist on the table and frowning. "To beat a child, that's one thing, but to torture her, that's going too far!"

Rodolphe had been listening attentively to Fleur-de-Marie's story. He looked at the Slasher in astonishment. This flash of sensitivity took him by surprise.

"What is it, Slasher?" he asked him.

"What is it? What, her story meant nothing to you? That monster Owl torturing this child? You must be as hard as your fists!"

"Go on, my girl," said Rodolphe to Fleur-de-Marie, without responding to the Slasher's interruption.

"I was telling you that the Owl was torturing me to make me cry. That just made me dig in my heels even more. To enrage her, I started laughing and then set off for the bridge with my barley sugars. The hag was at her frying pan. From time to time, she shook a fist at me. Then, instead of crying, I sang louder. Even as all of this was going on, I was so hungry! For the six months I had been carrying around those barley sugars, I had never tasted one of them. Goodness, that day, I couldn't stand it. As much from hunger as from my desire to enrage the Owl, I took one of the barley sugars and ate it."

"Bravo, my girl!"

"Then I ate another."

"Bravo! Long live the Charter!"[7]

"Good Lord, it was delicious. But no sooner had I eaten them than an orange merchant started yelling at the hag, 'Hey, Owl, Miss Lowlife is eating up your wares!'"

"Oh, my God, this story's getting hot. It's getting bad," said the Slasher, especially interested. "Poor little rat! You must have been trembling when the Owl found out, huh?"

"How did you get yourself out of that, my poor Songbird?" asked Rodolphe, just as interested as the Slasher.

"Oh, Lord, it was hard. But there was one funny thing," said Fleur-de-Marie, laughing. "And that was that even though she was full of rage from seeing me eat her barley sugars, she couldn't leave her frying pan, because the stuff she was frying in it was boiling."

"Ha, ha! Isn't that how it goes! Now that's what I call a tough spot!" cried the Slasher between bursts of laughter.

After this moment of shared laughter, Fleur-de-Marie continued, "Oh, dear! I was thinking about the blows that were waiting for me, when I said to myself, 'So what? I'm not going to be beaten any worse for eating three of them than for one.' I took a third piece, and before I ate it, like

---

7. This was a rallying cry during the Revolution of 1830. The charter decreased the powers of the monarch (Louis-Philippe d'Orléans, known as the "bourgeois king") and instituted certain other democratic changes to state policy, such as the elimination of censorship of the press, a limited expansion of the voting pool, and the demotion of Catholicism from official state religion to the religion of the majority. [TN]

that, the Owl threatened me from afar with her big iron fork. I swear, just as sure as this is a plate here in front of me, I held up the barley sugar and I munched on it right under her nose."

"Bravo, my girl! That shows me how it was that you used your scissors against me a little while ago. It's true, what I said—you've got grit. But the Owl must have roasted you alive after that?"

"When she finished her frying, she came after me. People had given me three sous in alms and I had eaten six sous' worth. When the hag took me by the hand to lead me away, I thought I would drop right there, I was so afraid. I remember it as if I was still there. It was just around New Year's. You know how there are all those toy shops on the Pont Neuf? All evening long they had been making my head spin. Just from looking at all those beautiful dolls, all those cute little sets of doll furniture . . . Think what it was like, for a child."

"And you never had any toys, Songbird?" asked the Slasher.

"Me? Are you nuts? Who would have given me any? Finally, the evening was over. Even though it was the middle of winter, I only had a horrible tattered cloth dress to wear. No socks, no shirt, and only clogs on my feet! Not much there to swelter in, right? Well, when the one-eyed hag took my hand, I broke out in a sweat. The thing that terrified me the most was that instead of swearing or blowing up at me, the Owl just muttered the whole way between her teeth. But she didn't let me go, and she made me walk so fast—so fast—that with my little legs I had to run to keep up with her. While running I lost one of my clogs. I didn't dare tell her. I just followed her with one bare foot. When we arrived, it was covered in blood."

"That horrible bitch of a one-eyed hag!" exclaimed the Slasher, pounding the table again in anger. "That's some picture, this child trotting alongside this old thief, with her poor little foot all bloodied up."

"We had landed in a storehouse on rue de la Mortellerie. Next to the gate to the alley, there was a liquor store. The Owl went in, still holding me by the hand. She downed a half pint of brandy at the counter."

"Good Lord! I couldn't drink that without getting as drunk as a skunk."

"That was her usual serving. She always fell asleep drunk. That's maybe why she beat me so much. Finally, we got home. It was no picnic, I'll tell you. We arrived at our door. The Owl double-locked it. I threw myself at her feet, asking her to forgive me for eating her barley sugars. She didn't respond, and I heard her mutter as she walked into the bedroom, 'What am I going to do tonight to this Miss Lowlife, to this barley sugar thief? Let's see, what should I do to her?' And she stopped to look at me with her green eye. I was still on my knees. Suddenly, the hag went to a cupboard and took out a pair of tongs."

"Tongs!" cried the Slasher.

"Yes, tongs."

"What for?"

"To hit you with?" asked Rodolphe.

"To pinch you with?" asked the Slasher.

"Not even close!"

"To tear out your hair?"

"You're still not there. Swear not to tell?"

"I give you my word."

"We both do."

"Well, then: she used it to rip out one of my teeth!"[8]

The Slasher let out such a formidable stream of curses that all the patrons of the joint looked at each other in alarm.

"What's up with him?" asked Songbird.

"What's up with me? I would carve her up, I would, if I could lay hold of her, that one-eyed hag! Where is she? Tell me! If I ever find her, I'll put her in the deep freeze!" The bandit's face darkened.

Rodolphe had shared the Slasher's horror at the cruelty of the hag, but he was wondering at the phenomenon of a cutthroat getting angry just by hearing about a wicked old woman driven by sheer malice to tear a tooth out of a child's mouth. But we think this feeling of pity is possible and indeed probable in an otherwise ferocious character.

"And so she yanked your tooth out, my poor little one?" asked Rodolphe.

"Yes, did she ever yank it out! And not on the first try, either. My God, how hard she had to work at it! She was holding my head between her knees like a vise. Eventually, half with the tongs, half through the work of her fingers, she pulled out the tooth. Then she said to me, to scare me, of course, 'I'm going to pull out another one of these every day, Little Miss Lowlife, and when you don't have any teeth left, I'm going to throw you in the water, where you'll be eaten by the fish. They're going to get revenge on you for finding the worms that got them hooked.' I remember that because it seemed so unjust. Really, as if I went collecting worms out of pleasure!"

"Ah! That wretch! Breaking and yanking out the teeth of a poor little child!" cried the Slasher with renewed anger.

"Oh, well, what's done is done. Can you see anything of it now?" asked Fleur-de-Marie. She smiled, her slightly parted pink lips revealing two rows of pearly white little teeth.

Was this carefree attitude forgetfulness or rather an instinctive generosity on the part of this unfortunate creature? Rodolphe noted that he had heard not a single word of hatred in her story toward the atrocious woman who had tortured her.

---

8. We ask those of our readers who find this cruelty exaggerated to recall the almost daily sentences passed on the savage beings among us who beat and abuse children. There have been fathers and mothers who have not refrained from committing these abominable acts. [SN]

"So then what did you do?" asked the Slasher.

"Good Lord, I had had enough of her. The next day, instead of looking for worms, I escaped by way of the Panthéon. I walked all day around there, I was so afraid of the Owl. I would have walked to the ends of the earth before letting myself fall into her clutches again. As I found myself walking through abandoned neighborhoods, I never ran into anyone I could beg for money, and in any case I wouldn't have dared to ask. At night, I slept in a work site, under a stack of wood. I was no bigger than a rat. Sliding under an old door, I hid in the middle of a heap of bark. Hunger was eating me up. I tried to chew on a bit of wood bark to trick my hunger pangs, but I couldn't do it. I could only bite a little birch bark, because it was the only thing soft enough. Eventually I fell asleep. On daybreak, hearing a sound, I hid myself deeper down in the woodpile. It was almost warm down there, like in a cave. If I had had something to eat there, it would have been the best I could have felt in winter."

"That's what it was like for me in the pottery kiln."

"I didn't dare leave the timber yard. I figured that the Owl was looking for me everywhere to rip out my teeth and throw me to the fish, and I figured that she would find me out if I moved."

"Hey, no more talk about that old wretch. You're making my blood boil!"

"Finally, the second day, I had chewed a bit more birch bark and I'd started to fall asleep when I heard a large dog barking. That woke me right up. I listened . . . the dog kept barking as he came closer to the woodpile. So here was another reason to be scared. Fortunately, I don't know why, but the dog never came closer—but you're going to laugh, Slasher."

"With you, there's always something to laugh at. You're a good girl, all the same. Listen, you know, I'm sorry now for hitting you—I swear," said the Slasher.

"Why shouldn't you have hit me? I had no one to defend me."

"What about me?" asked Rodolphe.

"You are a very good man, Monsieur Rodolphe, but the Slasher didn't know that you would be there. Neither did I."

"All the same, I really meant what I just said. I'm sorry I hit you," the Slasher repeated.

"Go on with your story, child," said Rodolphe.

"I was huddling under the woodpile when I heard the dog bark. While the dog was yapping, a loud voice was saying, 'My dog is barking! There's someone hiding in the work site.' 'It must be thieves,' answered another voice. Then I heard, 'Retrieve!' They were setting their dog on me, yelling, 'Get him! Get him!'"

"The dog ran at me. I was afraid of being bitten, so I cried out as loud as I could. 'Hey!' said the man. 'That sounds like a child's voice.' One called off the dog, one went to look for a lantern, I got out of my hole. I found myself face-to-face with a fat man and a boy in a worker's smock. 'What are you doing in my timber yard, little thief?' the fat man asked in a mean tone of voice. 'Please, sir, I haven't eaten in two days. I ran away from the Owl, who had pulled a tooth out of my mouth and wanted to throw me to the fish. I didn't know where to sleep, so I slipped under your door and spent the night sleeping in your bark pile, under the wood stacks. I didn't think I was doing anyone any harm.' Then the merchant said to his boy, 'I'm not going to fall for that. She's a little thief, and she's going to take my logs.'"

"Ah! The old beggar! The old piece of rubbish! Steal his logs? You were eight years old!"

"It was pretty stupid. The boy answered him, 'You think she's stealing your logs, boss? How would she do that? She's smaller than your littlest log.'"

"'You're right,' the wood merchant said. 'But even if she isn't here on her own, it comes to the same thing. Thieves use children to spy things out and then to hide and open the door for others. We need to bring her to the police.'"

"What a rotten beast, that wood merchant."

"They brought me to the police. I told them everything and ended up admitting to being a vagrant. They sent me to prison. I was brought to court, still for vagrancy, and sentenced to stay in prison until I was sixteen. I thanked the judges for their kindness. Good Lord! To think of it: in prison, I had food to eat, and they didn't beat me. It was like paradise compared to the Owl's storehouse. Even better, in prison, I learned to sew. But there's the rub. I was always lazy and enjoyed wandering around. I liked singing better than working, especially when the sun was out. Oh! When it was nice out in the prison courtyard, I couldn't keep myself from singing. It's funny to think it, but singing made me feel like I was no longer a prisoner."

"It appears you're a born nightingale, my girl," Rodolphe said with a smile.

"You're very nice, Monsieur Rodolphe. Since then, I've been called Songbird instead of Miss Lowlife. Finally, I got to be sixteen, and I was released from prison. At the gate I found the ogress from here and two or three old women who came from time to time to see my fellow prisoners. They had told me that they could give me work when I got out."

"Good, good. I see how this is going to go," said the Slasher.

"'My darling, my beautiful angel, my pretty little one,' the ogress and her friends said to me. 'Would you like to stay with us? We'll supply you with nice dresses, and you'll have nothing to do but have fun.' Well, you know very well, Slasher, that you don't spend eight years in prison without understanding what their talk really meant. I sent them away from me, those old pimps. I said to myself, 'I know how to sew, I have three hundred francs here in front of me, I'm still young . . .'"

"And you still have the beauty of youth, my girl!" said the Slasher.

"Here I was, eight years in prison, and I was going to have a little fun without hurting anyone else. The work would come when my money was gone, and I sure made those three hundred francs fly. That was my big mistake," Fleur-de-Marie added with a sigh. "What I should have done, first of all, was to make sure I had work. But I had no one to advise me. Well, what's done is done. I put myself to work spending my money. First I bought myself some flowers to put in my room—I love flowers so much! And then I bought a dress and a pretty shawl. I took a donkey ride through the Bois de Boulogne, and then another on the boulevard Saint-Germain."

"With a lover, my girl?" asked the Slasher.

"Good Lord, no. I wanted to be my own mistress. I had my fun with one of my prison friends who had grown up in an orphanage, a really good girl named Rigolette.[9] They gave her that name because she was always giggling."

"Rigolette? Rigolette? I don't know her," said the Slasher, seeming to search his memory.

"Of course you don't know her. She's an honest girl, that Rigolette. She's a very good worker. Now she's earning at least twenty-five sous a day. She's set up her own little household. Alas, I've never dared to go back to see her. In the end, after frittering away my money, I only had forty-three francs left to my name."

"You should have bought a bunch of jewelry with that," said the Slasher.

"Good Lord, I did better than that. I had a laundress they called 'the woman from Lorraine,' a little lamb of God. At the time, she was very pregnant, but still had her hands and feet in the water. Think of it! She couldn't work anymore, so she asked to be allowed to enter the Mire.[10] There was no room, they turned her down, and she couldn't earn any more money. There she was, ready to give birth, and she didn't have the money for a bed in a furnished room. Fortunately, by chance, she met Goubin's wife on the corner of the Notre-Dame bridge one evening. She had been hiding for four days in the cellar of a house behind the Hôtel-Dieu that was being demolished."

"Huh? Why was Goubin's wife hiding during the day?"

"To escape from her husband, who was trying to kill her! She only went out at night to buy her bread. That's how she met the poor Lorraine woman, who had no idea what to do and who was about to give birth at any moment. When Goubin's wife saw her, she brought her back to the cellar she was hiding in. It was at least a shelter."

"Wait a minute . . . Goubin's wife, is that Helmina?" asked the Slasher.

---

9. Rigolette will explain later in the novel how she came by this name, which comes from the verb *rigoler*, which means "to laugh" or "to joke around." [TN]

10. A confinement hospital for the poor. [TN]

"Yes, she's a great gal," answered Songbird. "She's a seamstress who had worked for me and Rigolette. Lord, she did what she could, giving half of the cellar, half her straw, and half her bread to the woman from Lorraine, who had given birth to a poor little child on nothing but a bed of straw. Goubin's wife couldn't stand seeing that. At the risk of getting knocked off by her husband, who was looking for her everywhere, she left the cellar in broad daylight and went out to find me. She knew that I still had a little money left and that I wasn't mean. I was about to get in a carriage with Rigolette to finish off the last of the forty-three francs on a trip to the country, through the fields—how I love fields, trees, and prairies!—well, anyway, when Helmina told me the woman from Lorraine's sad story, I sent the carriage back and ran to my room to fetch all the bed linens I had, along with my mattress and my quilt. I sent them over on the back of a hired man, and I walked along at a good pace with Goubin's wife to the cellar. Oh, you should have seen how happy that poor Lorraine woman was! We both watched over her. When she could get up, I helped her with the rest of my money until she was well enough to return to her laundry business. Now she's earning a living, but I can't stop bringing her my laundry order. I can tell she wants to repay me that way. If it goes on this way, I'll stop giving her my business," Songbird said, meaningfully.

"And Goubin's wife?" asked the Slasher.

"What! You don't know?" asked Songbird.

"No, what happened?"

"Oh, that poor woman! Goubin found her! He stabbed her three times between the shoulders. Someone told him she was prowling around the Hôtel-Dieu, and one night when she was leaving her cellar to find milk for the woman from Lorraine, he killed her."

"I guess that's why he got the brain fever.[11] He's going to be pruned[12] in a week," said the Slasher.

"Exactly," returned Songbird.

"And when you gave your money to the woman from Lorraine, what did you do next, my girl?" asked Rodolphe.

"Good Lord, I searched for work. I was good at sewing and I was confident and knew what to do. I went into a clothing store on rue Saint-Martin. I didn't want to deceive anyone, so I told them that I had gotten out of prison two months before and that I really wanted to work. They showed me the door straightaway. I asked for piecework that I could do at home, but they told me that I must be kidding if I thought they would entrust me with a single shirt. I went off feeling very depressed. I ran into the ogress and one of the old women who were always hovering around me

11. Condemned to death. [SN]

12. He will be executed. [SN]

since I got out of prison. I didn't know how I was going to live. They led me away and forced some brandy on me. And here I am."

"I understand," said the Slasher. "I know you now as if I were your father and mother and as if you had never left my lap. Oh, well. That's the whole story, I hope."

"It seems as if it's made you sadder to have told your life's story, my girl," said Rodolphe.

"The fact is that it pains me to look back on it all. This is the first time since my childhood that I've recounted all of these things at one time. It's not a pretty picture, is it, Slasher?"

"That's how it is," said the latter, with an ironic tone. "Maybe you regret not being the kitchen maid in some low-class chop house, or the domestic servant to the family of some stupid old people?"

"That would be fine by me. It would be nice to be a respectable woman," said Fleur-de-Marie, sighing.

"Respectable? That's so stupid!" cried the bandit, guffawing loudly. "Respectable! And why not throw in a wreath of flowers, while you're at it, to honor your father and mother whom you never met?"

The girl's face had lost for a moment its usual carefree expression. She said to the Slasher, "Listen, I'm no crybaby. My father or mother got rid of me as if I were a dog no one wanted. I don't hold it against them—they probably didn't have anything to eat for themselves. That doesn't mean that there aren't happier fates than mine, Slasher, you see?"

"But what do you need? You're as gorgeous as Venus, you're seventeen years old, you sing like a nightingale, you have a maidenly air, they call you Fleur-de-Marie, and you're complaining! What are you going to say when you have a foot-warmer under your dogs and a moth-eaten chinchilla wrap around you, like the ogress here?"

"Oh, I'll never get that old."

"Maybe you have a patent on an invention that prevents aging?"

"No, but I won't live long with such a hard life. I already have a bad cough."

"Okay, sure, I can see you in the hearse already. Come on—don't be silly!"

"Do you think often of these things, Songbird?" asked Rodolphe.

"Sometimes. Listen, Monsieur Rodolphe, maybe you understand. In the morning, when I go to buy my milk from the dairywoman at the corner of rue de la Vieille-Draperie and see her go off in her little cart with her donkey, I often envy her. I say to myself, 'She's going back to the country, into the fresh air, to her house, to her family . . . and I am going back all alone to the ogress's kennel, where it's so dark you can't see your hand in front of your face in broad daylight.'"

"All right, then—be respectable, my girl, if you want to try that farce. Be respectable!" said the Slasher.

"Respectable! Good Lord, how am I going to do that? The clothes on my back belong to the ogress. I owe her for my room and board. I can't move from here. She would get me arrested as a thief. I belong to her. I need to pay off my debt to her."

Saying these last horrible words, the poor girl could not keep herself from shivering.

"So stay the way you are, and don't compare yourself anymore to any country girls," the Slasher said. "Do you want to go crazy? But think about it: you shine in the capital, while the milkmaid goes home to make dinner for her kids, milk the cows, find plants to feed the rabbits, and get smacked around by her husband when he comes home from the bar. Now there's a fate to brag about! A real nice one."

"Give me more to drink, Slasher," said Fleur-de-Marie brusquely after a long silence. She held out her glass. "No, not wine, brandy. It's stronger," she said in a soft voice, waving away the jug of wine that the Slasher was about to pour into her glass.

"Brandy! All right! That's how I like you, my girl! You've got pluck!" said the man, neither understanding Songbird's gesture nor noticing the tear that was trembling on the girl's eyelashes.

"It's too bad that brandy is so hard to drink, because it really knocks you out," said Fleur-de-Marie as she put her glass on the table. She had drunk its contents with as much repugnance as disgust.

Rodolphe had listened to this sad and naive story with growing interest. It was more poverty and abandonment than evil tendencies that had led to the downfall of this miserable girl.

CHAPTER 4

THE SLASHER'S STORY

The reader has not forgotten that two of the dive's patrons were being watched avidly by a third person who had recently arrived. One of these two men was wearing a fez and keeping his left hand hidden. He insistently asked the ogress whether the Schoolmaster had come in yet. During Songbird's story, which they couldn't hear, these two men spoke several times to each other in low voices, anxiously watching the door all the while. The man with the fez said to his friend, "The Schoolmaster isn't showing, unless it's because his pal knocked him off to keep his part of the loot."

"That would be just great for us, after we cooked up the plan for this job," answered the other.

The most recent arrival, who was observing these two, was too far away from them for their conversation to reach his ears. After discreetly consulting a small piece of paper several times that he had hidden in the bottom of his hat, he seemed satisfied with what it said. He got up from the table and said to the ogress, who was dozing at her counter with her feet atop the foot-warmer and her fat cat on her knees, "Listen, Old Lady Ponisse, I'll be right back. Watch out for my jug and my plate; you can't be too careful with these drunks."

"Don't worry, pal," said Old Lady Ponisse. "If your plate's empty and your jug, too, no one will touch them."

The man laughed at the ogress's joke and made off without anyone noticing his departure.

As this man was leaving, before the door closed, Rodolphe glimpsed in the street the collier with a black face and huge physique whom we've already mentioned. Rodolphe had the chance to show the collier, with an impatient gesture, how inconvenient to him this protective surveillance was. The latter, however, ignoring Rodolphe's wishes to the contrary, stayed stationed outside the joint.

Despite the glass of brandy she had drunk, Songbird did not recover her cheerfulness. Under the influence of this stimulant, her expression grew instead sadder and sadder. Leaning with her back against the wall, hanging her head down on her chest, her big blue eyes wandering mechanically around her, the unfortunate creature seemed as if she were overwhelmed by the darkest of thoughts.

Two or three times Fleur-de-Marie, encountering Rodolphe's pointed gaze, had looked away. She didn't understand the impression this stranger had made on her. Put out and oppressed by his presence, she reproached herself for having shown so little gratitude toward the man who had saved her from the Slasher's grasp. She almost regretted having told her story to Rodolphe so candidly.

The Slasher, on the other hand, couldn't have been in better spirits. He ate up the harlequin all on his own. The wine and liquor made him very talkative. The shame of having "met his master," as he'd put it, had faded in view of Rodolphe's generous behavior, and, moreover, he recognized in Rodolphe so great a superiority that his humiliation had given way to a feeling of mixed admiration, fear, and respect.

This absence of rancor, the savage candor with which he had admitted having killed and been justly punished for it, the fierce pride with which he denied ever having stolen, proved at least that despite what he had done, the Slasher wasn't a completely hardened criminal. This detail had not escaped Rodolphe's discriminating notice. He was curious to hear the Slasher's story.

This man's ambition was so insatiable, so peculiar in its infinite claims, that Rodolphe actually looked forward to the arrival of the Schoolmaster, this terrible thief whom he had nearly dethroned. For this reason he invited the Slasher to distract him with the story of his adventures.

"Go on, my boy," he said to him. "We're listening."

The Slasher emptied his glass and started: "You, my poor Songbird, you were at least picked up by the Owl—may she burn in hell! You had shelter over your head until you were put in prison as a vagrant. Me, I don't remember having slept in a real bed until I was nineteen years old, a fine age, when I enlisted."

"You served in the military, Slasher?" asked Rodolphe.

"For three years, but I'll get to that in a moment. The stones of the Louvre, the pottery kilns of Clichy, and the quarries of Montrouge: those were the houses I grew up in. You see, I had nothing less than a Paris residence and a home in the country!"

"What was your trade?"

"Lord, sir, I have a foggy memory of having tramped around in my childhood with an old ragpicker who used to beat me unconscious with his hook. It must be true, because I've never been able to see one of those junkmen with wicker baskets without wanting to fall on him—proof that they must have beaten me in my childhood. My first trade was to help slaughter horses in Montfaucon. I was ten or twelve years old. When I started slashing those poor old beasts, I didn't feel right about it. After a month, I didn't notice it anymore. On the contrary, I started to enjoy my job. No one had knives as sharp or pointed as I did. Those knives made me want to use them! When I slaughtered my animals, they threw me a bit of the rump of a horse dead from disease. The horses they slaughtered were sold to the stew-mongers of the medical school neighborhood who made them into beef, lamb, veal, game, all depending on the taste of the buyer. Ah! But when I had gotten my bit of horseflesh, I was my own man at least! I made away with my meat back home to my pottery kiln, like a wolf returning to its den. There, with the permission of the furnace workers, I grilled it up nicely over the coals. When the furnace workers weren't working, I gathered dry wood in Romainville, I lit a fire, and I made my roast in the corner of one of the walls of the charnel house. Man! That meat was bloody and almost raw, but that way, I didn't always have to eat the same thing."

"And your name? What was it?" asked Rodolphe.

"At the time my hair was more straw colored than now, and my eyes already got red. Because of that, they used to call me the Albino. Albinos are the white rabbits of the human race. They have red eyes," Slasher added gravely, in a physiological aside.

"And your parents, your family?"

"My parents? Living where Songbird's do. My place of birth? The first corner of any old street, on the left- or right-side curb, toward or away from the gutter."

"Do you curse your father and mother for having abandoned you?"

"That would do me a lot of good! But it's all the same to me—they played a dirty trick on me when they brought me into the world. I wouldn't complain if they had made me the way the Big Guy[13] should make all lowlives: without cold, thirst, or hunger. It wouldn't cost him a thing and it wouldn't be as hard for criminals to be honest people."

"You were hungry, you were cold, and still you didn't steal, Slasher?"

"No! But I was plenty miserable all the same. I went sometimes for two days without a crumb to eat, more than my share of the time. Well, I never stole."

"Because you were afraid of prison?"

"Are you kidding me?" said the Slasher, his shoulders shaking with laughter. "That would be like not stealing bread out of fear of having bread! As an honest man, I was dying of hunger. As a thief, I would have been fed in prison. No, I didn't steal because . . . because . . . well, I guess because it's just not in me to steal things."

The Slasher did not understand the full significance of this truly beautiful response. Rodolphe was profoundly moved. He sensed that the poor

13. God. Isn't it strange and noteworthy that the name of God should be found even in the setting of this corrupt language? [SN]

man who had stayed honest amid even the cruelest privations was doubly respectable because the punishment for the crime could have brought him some security. He held out his hand toward this unfortunate savage of our civilization whom poverty had not completely destroyed. The Slasher looked at his host in astonishment, almost with respect. He hardly dared touch the hand he was being offered. He had the intuition that a huge abyss lay between himself and Rodolphe.

"Good, good!" Rodolphe said to him. "You still have heart and honor."

"Lord, I don't know anything about that," said the Slasher, clearly moved. "But what you're saying to me . . . look . . . I've never felt anything like it . . . and the blows that finished me off . . . and those blows were so many, they could have gone on until tomorrow, and instead you pay for my dinner . . . well, all I can say is it's cradle to grave for us: you can count on the Slasher."

Rodolphe responded with more restraint, not wanting him to see how moved he was. "Did you remain an assistant slaughterer for a long time?" he asked.

"Sure did. At first, slaughtering those poor old beasts made me sick to my stomach. Later, I enjoyed it, but when I turned about sixteen and my voice changed, it became something like an obsession for me, a passion for slaughtering! I forgot to eat and drink. I could only think of slaughtering. You should have seen me at my job: except for an old pair of cloth trousers, I was totally naked. When I stood there with my big, sharp knife in my hand, with up to fifteen or twenty horses waiting in line for their turn (I'm not bragging about this) . . . Man! When I set about slitting their throats, I don't know what came over me. It was like some kind of fury. There was buzzing in my ears! I saw red, all red, and I slashed! And I slashed . . . and I slashed, until the knife fell out of my hands! Man! That was ecstasy! If I was a millionaire I would have paid to do that work."

"So that's how you got into the habit of slashing," said Rodolphe.

"That may well be. But when I was sixteen, the fury ended up getting so strong that one time, while slashing away, I went crazy in the middle of the slaughter and I ruined the job . . . Yes, I spoiled the hides from slashing every which way. Finally, they showed me the door of the slaughterhouse. I wanted to work with the butchers. I still had a taste for that kind of work. Yeah, right! They stuck up their noses. They showed the same kind of disdain for me that a bootmaker would show a cobbler. Seeing this—and also my passion for killing fading by the end of the year—I looked for my bread elsewhere. I didn't find anything right away, so I stuck my head in my shell and waited it out. Finally, I worked in the Montrouge quarries. But after two years I got sick of squirreling around in the pits, hauling out the stone, averaging twenty sous a day. I was big and strong, so I enlisted in a regiment. They asked me for my name, my age, and my papers. My name? Albino. My age? Look at my beard. My papers? Here's the certificate of my quarry master. I could be a first-rate grenadier. They signed me up."

"With your strength, courage, and passion for knifework, you could have become an officer if there had been a war."

"Damn! Do you think you need to tell me that? To knife Englishmen or Prussians would have suited me much better than slashing at old nags. But unfortunately, there was no war, and there *was* military discipline. If an apprentice tries to give his boss a licking, that's one thing. If he's weaker, he gets what's coming to him. If he's stronger, he dishes it out. He loses his job, sometimes he gets locked up, nothing more. In the military, it's a different story. One day my sergeant knocked me over in order to make me obey him more quickly. He was right, because I was moving like a snail. It annoyed me, so I balked. He pushed me, so I pushed him back. He grabbed me by the collar, so I punched him. Everyone jumped me, and the fury came back to me. Blood came into my eyes, I saw red. I had my knife in my hand, I was in the kitchen, and off I went. I started into slashing, slashing . . . like at the slaughterhouse. I cut that sergeant into pieces. I wounded two soldiers! A real bloodbath. Eleven stabs to the three of them—yes, eleven! Blood, blood, like in a slaughterhouse!" The bandit lowered his head, looking somber and haggard. He stayed silent for a moment.

"What are you thinking about, Slasher?" asked Rodolphe, watching him with interest.

"Not a thing, nothing," he answered, brusquely. Then he resumed his brutal carelessness. "Finally, they knocked me out, they hauled me up in front of a beak, and they sentenced me to lose my head."

"So you escaped?"

"No, but they sent me to the galleys for fifteen years instead of chopping my head off. I forgot to tell you that in the regiment I fished two guys out who were drowning in the Seine. We were at a garrison in Melun. Another time—you'll laugh and say that I'm an amphibian that can live in the fire and the water and rescue men and women!—another time, at the garrison in Rouen, some wooden houses, real hovels, caught fire in one area. It was burning up in there like a box of matches. I was on fire duty. We got to the fire. Someone called out that there was an old woman who couldn't come down from her room, and it was getting hot. I ran to get her. Damn! It was getting hot, so it brought back to me the pottery kilns on a good day. Finally, I rescued the old lady. My prison rat[14] managed to do such a good job of weaseling around with his four paws and tongue that he got my sentence changed. Instead of going to the Abbey of Mount Regret,[15] I got off with fifteen years in the

14. Lawyer. [SN]

15. The scaffold. [SN]

fields.[16] When I saw that I wasn't going to be killed, my first impulse was to hurl myself onto my mouthpiece to strangle him. Do you understand, sir?"

"You were sorry to see your sentence commuted?"

"Yes. For those who live by the knife, the executioner's blade is a just end. For thieves, leg irons: each to his own deserts. But to force you to go on living when you've killed people, well, the beaks don't know what it does to you at first."

"You felt remorse then, Slasher?"

"Remorse? No, because I did my time," said the savage man. "But there's hardly a night that passes without a nightmare in which I see the sergeant and soldiers I slashed. They aren't alone, in this nightmare," the bandit added with a sort of terror. "There are dozens, hundreds, thousands waiting their turn in a kind of slaughterhouse, like the horses waiting their turn that I used to slaughter at Montfaucon. In the nightmare, I would see red, and I would start to slash away . . . to slash away at those men, the way I used to do it with the horses. But the more I slashed at the soldiers, the more there were of them. While dying they gave me such a tender look—such a tender look!—that I cursed myself for having killed them, but I couldn't help myself from doing it. That's not all. I never had a brother, and all the people I was slaughtering were my brothers, brothers for whom I would have thrown myself into a fire. In the end, when I couldn't stand it anymore, I would wake up drenched in a sweat as cold as melted snow."

"That's a hard dream, Slasher."

"That's for sure. Well, in the beginning of my time in the galleys, I had that dream . . . every night. You see, I was going to go crazy or mad. I tried to kill myself twice, once by swallowing verdigris, another by trying to strangle myself with a chain. I was strong as a bull, however. The verdigris just made me thirsty. The chain that I'd put around my neck just ended up giving me a natural blue necktie. After that, the habit of living got the upper hand, my nightmares became less frequent, and I did what everyone else did."

"You were at a good school for learning to steal."

"Yes, but I never had the taste for it. The other cons teased me about that, but I beat them back with a chain. That's how I got to know the Schoolmaster. But watch out for that guy's grip. He gave me my due the way you just did a little while ago."

"So he's a freed convict?"

"Say instead he's a lifer who freed himself."

"He escaped? And no one has turned him in?"

"I wouldn't be the one to turn him in. I'd always live in fear of him."

---

16. Galleys. [TN]

"How is it that the police don't know about him? Don't they have his description?"

"His description? Oh, you better believe it! A long time ago he altered the sweet little mug that the Big Guy put on him. Now it's just the baker of souls[17] can recognize the Schoolmaster."

"How did he do it?"

"He started by grinding down his nose, which was as long as an alder tree. Then he shaved off his beard with acid."

"Are you joking?"

"If he comes in here tonight, you'll see. He had a big parrot's beak, but now he's got a nose as flat as Death's own, and besides, he's got lips as fat as a fist and an olive-colored face that's as patched together as a ragpicker's jacket."

"So he's that unrecognizable!"

"In the six months since he escaped from Rochefort,[18] stoolies have run into him a hundred times without recognizing him."

"Why was he in prison?"

"For being a counterfeiter, a thief, and an assassin. They call him the Schoolmaster because he has beautiful handwriting and because he's very educated."

"And is he feared?"

"He won't be, once you've done for him the way you did for me. And damn, I would like to see that."

"What does he do for a living?"

"They say he brags about having killed and robbed a livestock merchant three weeks ago on the Poissy road."

"They'll arrest him sooner or later."

"They'll need more than two men to do that, because he always carries two loaded pistols and a dagger under his shirt. The reaper is waiting for him, and they can only prune him once, so he'll kill everyone he can kill to escape. Oh, he's not hiding from it, and since he's twice as strong as you and me, it will be hard to get him."

"And when you got out of prison, what did you do, Slasher?"

"I asked for work from the master stevedore on the quai Saint-Paul, and that's how I make a living."

"But if you're not a thief after all, why do you live in the Cité?"

"Where do you want me to live? Who do you think would want to pass the time with an ex-con? And then, I get bored on my own. I like to have some company, and here I live with people like me. I get into brawls sometimes . . . People fear me like fire in the Cité, and the bulls have nothing on

17. The devil. [SN]

18. Rochefort is a port town in southwestern France, formerly the location of a penal colony. [TN]

me, except for the brawls, and those just get me twenty-four hours in the pen."

"And how much do you earn a day?"

"Thirty-five sous. That will last as long as I have the arms to bear it. When I don't, I'll pick up a hook and a wicker rake, like the ragpicker I can just barely remember from my childhood."

"And with all of this to deal with, you're not unhappy?"

"There are plenty worse off than me. Except for my dreams about the sergeant and the soldiers with their throats cut—I still have those dreams—I could die in peace like some other person on some corner on the outskirts of town, or in a hospital. But the dream . . . Listen, damn it! I can't stand thinking about that!" said the Slasher. And he emptied his pipe on the corner of the table.

Songbird had listened only distractedly to the Slasher. She seemed to be absorbed in a sad reverie of her own.

Rodolphe sat pensively. The two stories he had just heard were giving him food for thought.

Then a tragic event occurred that reminded these three people what kind of place they were in.

CHAPTER 5

THE ARREST

The man who had left for a moment after asking the ogress to keep watch over his jug and plate came back in shortly, accompanied by another broad-shouldered individual with a lively face. He said to the other, "What luck, running into you here, Borel! Come on in and we'll drink a glass of wine."

Quietly, gesturing toward the newcomer, the Slasher said to Rodolphe and Songbird, "Storm's brewing. He's a police spy. Watch out!"

The two bandits—including the one who was wearing the fez pushed down over his eyebrows and who kept asking for the Schoolmaster—exchanged a hurried glance, got up simultaneously from the table, and made directly for the door. But the two agents leapt on them, hurling a battle cry.

A terrible struggle ensued.

The door of the tavern opened. Other officers rushed into the room, and the gleam of the police firearms could be seen outside. Taking advantage of the tumult, the collier of whom we have spoken moved toward the doorway of the joint. Meeting Rodolphe's gaze accidentally, he put his right index finger to his lips. In a quick, imperious gesture, Rodolphe ordered him to withdraw. Then he continued to watch what was happening in the tavern.

The man in the fez was shouting angry epithets. Partly stretched out on the table, he struggled so violently that three men could hardly control him.

Overwhelmed, sullen, with a livid face, white lips, and a fallen, trembling lower jaw, his companion offered no resistance. He held out his hands to be put in cuffs.

Well accustomed to such scenes, the ogress sat by impassively at the counter. She kept her hands in her apron pocket.

"So what did those two guys do, Monsieur Borel?" she asked one of the officers, whom she knew.

"Yesterday they killed an old woman on rue Saint-Christophe while robbing her room. Before dying, the poor woman said that she had bit one of her attackers on the hand. We've had our eye on these two villains. My partner came here a little while ago to verify their identities, and now we've nabbed them."

"Good thing they paid for their pints in advance," said the ogress. "Wouldn't you like something to drink, Monsieur Borel? Maybe a little glass of Perfect Love, a nip of Consolation?"

"Thanks, Old Lady Ponisse, but I've got to lock these two bandits in the hole. And this one's still struggling." It was true: the assassin in the fez was fighting in a rage. When it came time to put him in the carriage waiting out on the street, he resisted so much that they had to carry him.

His accomplice, seized with nervous trembling, could hardly hold himself up. His purple lips were moving as if he would speak. They threw his inert mass into the wagon.

"Oh, by the way, Old Lady Ponisse," said the agent, "be careful of Red-Arm. He's crafty. He's capable of getting you into trouble."

"Red-Arm? I haven't seen him around here for weeks, Monsieur Borel."

"It's always when he's someplace that you can't see him—you know how it goes. Just don't take any kind of package or bundle from him to keep or hold on to. You'll be receiving stolen goods."

"Don't worry, Monsieur Borel, I'm as scared of Red-Arm as I am of the devil. You never know where he's going or where he's been. The last time I saw him, he told me he'd just come back from Germany."

"All right, but I'm warning you. Watch out."

Before leaving the joint, the agent surveyed the other customers carefully, and said to the Slasher, in an almost affectionate manner, "You're here, troublemaker? We haven't heard a peep from you in a long time. You haven't gotten yourself into any new fistfights, have you? You've decided to be nice?"

"As humble as a minister, Monsieur Borel. You know that I hardly ever break anyone's skull unless they ask for it."

"With your strength, all we need is for you to go and start provoking people."

"But here's my better, Monsieur Borel," said the Slasher, clapping his hand on Rodolphe's shoulder.

"Hey, I don't know this guy," the officer said, looking Rodolphe over.

"And we're not going to get to know each other, my friend," the latter answered.

"I hope that's true, for your sake, my boy," said the agent. Then, addressing the ogress, he said, "Good evening, Old Lady Ponisse. Your joint is a veritable mousetrap for us. This is the third murderer I've found here."

"And I hope he won't be the last, Monsieur Borel. Happy to be at your service," the ogress said graciously, bowing to him deferentially.

After the police left, the young man with the leaden face who was smoking while drinking his liquor reloaded his pipe and said to the Slasher in a husky voice, "Didn't you recognize the guy in the fez? He works for the Fat Man. They call him Shaggy. When I saw the agents walk in, I said to myself, 'Something's happening tonight.' And Shaggy was hiding his hand under the table."

"All the same, the Schoolmaster sure is lucky that he didn't turn up here," said the ogress. "The man in the fez asked for him several times because of some business they had together. But I never rat out the people I deal with. If they get arrested, fine. Every man to himself. But I wouldn't sell them out. Well, speak of the devil," added the ogress. At that moment, a man and a woman entered the joint. "There's the Schoolmaster and his woman."

The joint's customers all shivered in terror.

Even the naturally daring Rodolphe couldn't overcome the slight unease he felt at the sight of the feared bandit. He contemplated him for a few moments with a curiosity mixed with horror. The Slasher had told the truth. The Schoolmaster had mutilated himself horrendously.

A more gruesome sight than the face of this villain could not be found. It was furrowed all over with deep red scars. The corrosive action of the acid had bloated his lips. With the top of his nose cut off, two uneven holes remained where his nostrils used to be. His gray eyes—very bright, very small, very round—sparkled ferociously. His forehead, flat as a tiger's, half disappeared under a fur hat made of long animal hair. It looked like the mane of a monster.

The Schoolmaster was barely five feet, two or three inches tall. His head, disproportionately large, was sunk between two broad, powerful, arching, meaty shoulders that you could see even under the folds of his unbleached shirt. He had long, muscular arms, and short, fat hands that were hairy right up to the tips of their fingers. His legs were a bit bowed, but their huge calves evidenced their great athletic strength.

In a word, this man was the very picture of the short, squat, and stocky Farnese Hercules.[19] One can't even begin to depict the ferocious expression of his cruel face and the restless, mobile gaze that made him look as fierce as a wild, stalking beast.

The woman who accompanied the Schoolmaster was old, neatly attired in a brown dress, a black and red plaid tartan shawl, and a white bonnet. Rodolphe saw her in profile. She had a round green eye, a hooked nose, thin lips, and a jutting chin, a face at once wicked and sly: all of this made him think of the Owl.

He was about to share this observation with Songbird when he looked at the girl and saw her grow pale. She was looking at the Schoolmaster's hideous companion in mute terror. Finally, seizing Rodolphe's arm, her

19. A Roman copy from the third century CE of a Greek sculpture made in the fourth century BCE by Lysippus. [TN]

hand trembling, Fleur-de-Marie said to him in a low voice, "The Owl! Good Lord! The Owl! The one-eyed hag!"

At that moment, the Schoolmaster, quietly exchanging a few words with the joint's regulars, made his way slowly toward the table where Rodolphe, Songbird, and the Slasher sat.

Then, in a voice that sounded as husky and hollow as a tiger's roar, he said to Fleur-de-Marie, "Hello, there, blondie. Time for you to leave these two jerks and come with me."

Songbird did not answer him. She was huddled up against Rodolphe, her teeth chattering from fright.

"Don't worry about me! I won't get jealous!" said the horrible Owl, laughing uproariously. She didn't recognize in Songbird her old victim, Miss Lowlife.

"Listen, little one, didn't you hear me?" said the monster as he came closer. "If you don't come with me, I'll take your eye out and give it to the Owl to match the one she has. And you, fellow with the mustache"—he was talking to Rodolphe—"if you don't toss me that blond girl over the table, I'll kill you."

"My God! My God! Save me!" Songbird cried out to Rodolphe, putting her hands together in prayer. Then, upon reflecting that she was putting him in great danger, she continued in a low voice, "No, no, don't move, Monsieur Rodolphe. If he gets closer, I'll yell for help, and out of the fear of a commotion that would attract the police, the ogress will back me up."

"Don't worry, my girl," said Rodolphe, looking intrepidly at the Schoolmaster. "You're with me. You're not going anywhere. And since this hideous animal is frightening you and me, too, I'm going to show him the door."

"You?" said the Schoolmaster.

"Me!" answered Rodolphe.

And despite Songbird's efforts, he got up from the table.

The Schoolmaster took a step backward when he saw the terrible ferocity in Rodolphe's face. Fleur-de-Marie and the Slasher were also struck by this expression of malevolence, of diabolical rage that was at this moment distorting the noble face of their companion. He had become unrecognizable. In his fight with the Slasher, he had been disdainful and mocking. Facing the Schoolmaster, however, he seemed possessed of a fierce hatred. With his pupils dilated from anger, his eyes shone with a strange glow.

Certain gazes have an irresistible magnetic power. Some famous duelists are said to owe their bloody victories to the compelling effect of a gaze that demoralized and struck down their enemies. Rodolphe was gifted with this terrifying, fixed, and piercing gaze. Those who were caught in its power could not evade it. This gaze would obsess and overpower them. They could feel it almost physically, and in spite of themselves, it held them. They could not look away.

The Schoolmaster shuddered, took another step backward, and no longer trusting in his tremendous strength, reached under his shirt for his dagger.

A murder might have stained the joint with blood if the Owl, seizing the Schoolmaster by the arm, had not cried, "Wait a minute—wait a minute, Killer, let me say something. You can get rid of these jerks in just a moment. They're not going anywhere."

The Schoolmaster looked at the one-eyed hag in wonder.

For the past few minutes, the Owl had been looking at Fleur-de-Marie, searching her memory. Finally, she was free of any doubt: she recognized Songbird.

"Is it possible?" cried the hag as she clasped her hands in astonishment. "It's Miss Lowlife, the barley sugar thief. Where have you come from? Must be the baker[20] who sent you!" she said, showing her fist to the girl. "So, you're going to fall back into my clutches? Oh, don't worry, if I don't tear out any more of your teeth, I'll squeeze all the tears out of your body. Ah, think you're going to get all angry at me? You must not know, then! I know who your parents are. In prison, the Schoolmaster has seen close up the man who gave you to me when you were little. He told me the name of your mother. They're in clover, your parents."

"My parents? You know them?" cried Fleur-de-Marie.

"Yes, my man knows your mother's name. But I'd rip out his tongue before I'd let him tell you. He saw the guy who brought you to my dump because they weren't paying your wet nurse anymore. Since she couldn't care less about you, your mother would just as soon have seen you croaked, for sure, but it's all the same. If you knew her name now, you could blackmail her very nicely, my little foundling. The man I told you about has some papers. Yes, Miss Lowlife, he has some letters from your mother. And if he doesn't make good use of them, he has his reasons. Hmm, you're angry. You're crying, Miss Lowlife. Well, no, you'll never know your mother. You'll never know her."

"I'd just as soon she thought me dead," said Fleur-de-Marie, wiping her eyes.

Rodolphe, forgetting the Schoolmaster, had listened attentively to the Owl, whose story he found interesting. Meanwhile, the bandit, no longer under the power of Rodolphe's gaze, had gotten his courage back up. He could not believe that this young, slender man of average build could contend with him. Sure of his herculean strength, he came up to Songbird's protector and said to the Owl, with authority, "Enough of this chitchat. I want to slice the mug off this handsome jerk and remove his cute little features. That way the pretty blonde will find me better looking than him."

In a single leap, Rodolphe jumped over the table.

20. The devil. [SN]

"Watch my plates!" the ogress exclaimed.

The Schoolmaster put himself in a defensive crouch, with his two hands in front of him, holding his upper body back, planted on his robust haunches, his weight buttressed, so to speak, by one of his gigantic legs that looked like a stone baluster.

At the moment Rodolphe lunged at him, the door of the joint opened violently. The collier we've mentioned, who was almost six feet tall, rushed into the room. He tossed the Schoolmaster aside roughly, came up to Rodolphe, and said into his ear, in English, "Sir, Tom and Sarah are here, at the end of the street."

At these mysterious words, Rodolphe looked angry, threw a louis on the counter of the ogress, and ran toward the door.

The Schoolmaster tried to block Rodolphe's exit, but Rodolphe turned around and gave him two such harshly dealt blows in the face that the beast staggered, stunned. He fell backward heavily, facedown on a table.

"Long live the Charter! Those are the blows that finish you," the Slasher exclaimed. "A few more lessons like that, and I'll be able to do it myself."

Regaining consciousness after a few seconds, the Schoolmaster ran out in pursuit of Rodolphe. The latter had disappeared with the collier into the somber maze of the Cité's streets. Finding them would be impossible.

When the Schoolmaster returned, foaming with rage, two men, running from the opposite direction from the one in which Rodolphe had disappeared, hurried into the joint, panting, as if they had run a long way, quickly. Their first action was to look around the tavern.

"I'm done for!" said one of them. "He got away from us again!"

"Be patient! The day has twenty-four hours, and life is long," answered the other person.

These two newcomers spoke to each other in English.

CHAPTER 6

THOMAS SEYTON AND COUNTESS SARAH

The two individuals who had just entered the joint were of a higher class than that of most customers of the tavern. One of them was tall and slim and had hair that was nearly white, black eyebrows and side whiskers, and a bony brown face with a hard, severe expression. There was a ribbon on his round hat. His long black waistcoat had buttons on it all the way up to the neck. Over his gray, clinging pants, he wore the kind of boots that used to be called Suwarow-style.[21]

His companion was very small, and like him, dressed in mourning. This person was pale and handsome. The companion's long hair, eyebrows, and deep black eyes brought out her pallor. From her gait, her build, and the delicacy of her features, it was easy to see that this was a woman disguised as a man.

"Tom, ask for something to drink, and ask these people about *him*," Sarah said, still speaking in English.

"Yes, Sarah," answered the man with the white hair and black eyebrows.

Sitting at a table while Sarah was wiping her forehead, he said to the ogress in excellent French with nearly no accent, "Madame, please give us something to drink."

The entrance of these two people in the joint had roused everyone's attention. Their clothing and their manners suggested that they never frequented such plebeian taverns as this one. From their preoccupied and anxious expressions, it was not hard to guess that they had good reasons for coming to this neighborhood.

The Slasher, the Schoolmaster, and the Owl watched them with avid curiosity. Songbird, terrified from her encounter with the one-eyed hag and fearing the threats of the Schoolmaster, who had expressed the desire to take her with him, took advantage of their distracted attention. She slipped out of the tavern through the door, which was ajar.

The Slasher and the Schoolmaster, each for his own reason, had no interest in starting any new brawls.

---

21. Alexander Suwarow (1729–1800) was a Russian general and military hero. He is associated with a particular style of slouching boots. [TN]

Surprised at the appearance of such unusual patrons, the ogress shared everybody else's interest in them. Tom said to her a second time, impatiently, "We asked you for something to drink, madame. Would you please be so kind as to serve us?"

Old Lady Ponisse, flattered by such courteous treatment, got up from her counter and came up to lean over Tom's table in a gracious manner. "Would you like a liter of wine or a sealed bottle?" she asked.

"Give us a bottle of wine, some glasses, and some water."

The ogress served them, and Tom tossed her a hundred sous. Refusing the change she brought him, he said, "Keep it, madame. Won't you have a glass with us?"

"You are a good man, sir," said Old Lady Ponisse, looking at Tom more in astonishment than in gratitude.

"But tell me," he went on. "We were supposed to meet one of our friends in a bar on this street. Maybe we've made a mistake."

"This is the White Rabbit. At your service, monsieur."

"That's the name, all right," said Tom, giving Sarah a pointed look. "Yes, it was the White Rabbit where he was supposed to be waiting for us."

"There's only one White Rabbit on this street," the ogress said proudly. "But what did your friend look like?"

"Tall and thin, with light chestnut-colored hair and mustache," said Tom.

"Wait, wait . . . He was just here, that one. A very tall collier came in to get him, and they left together."

"That's them," said Tom.

"Were they alone here?" asked Sarah.

"Well, the collier was only here for a moment. Your other friend ate here with the Slasher and Songbird." And with a glance, she indicated Rodolphe's guests who remained in the bar.

Tom and Sarah turned toward the Slasher. After a few minutes of looking at him, Sarah said in English to her companion, "Do you know this man?"

"No, Karl had lost Rodolphe's trail at the entrance of these back streets. When he saw Murph disguised as a collier prowling outside this bar and peering continually through its windows, he suspected something and came to warn us."

As this conversation was going on in low voices and in a foreign tongue, the Schoolmaster said quietly to the Owl, looking at Tom and Sarah, "The big thin guy dropped a hundred sous on the ogress. It's going to be midnight soon. It's raining and windy. When they leave, let's follow them. I'll knock out the tall one and take his money. He's with a woman, so he won't dare make a sound."

"If the little one calls for help, I have some acid in my pocket. I'll break the bottle and throw it in her face," said the one-eyed hag. "You always have to give babies something to drink to keep them from crying." Then she added, "Hey, Killer, when we find Miss Lowlife, we have to show her who's boss. Once we have her back at our place, we'll rub her muzzle with some acid. That'll make her less proud of her pretty little mug."

"You know, Owl, I'm going to end up marrying you," said the Schoolmaster. "You have no equal in shrewdness or courage. The night with the livestock merchant, I took your measure. I said, 'Here's the woman for me. She'll work better than any man.'"

After reflecting for a moment, Sarah said to Tom, with a gesture toward the Slasher, "If we question this man about Rodolphe, maybe we'll know what brought him here."

"We can try," said Tom. Then, addressing the Slasher, he said, "Hey, pal, we were supposed to meet one of our friends in this bar. He dined here with you. Since you know him, can you tell us whether you know where he went?"

"I know him because he knocked me out two hours ago to defend Songbird."

"And you had never seen him before?"

"Never. We met in the alley behind Red-Arm's house."

"Hostess! Another sealed bottle here, the best you have," said Tom.

Sarah and he had hardly touched their glasses, which were still full. Old Lady Ponisse, doubtless merely for the honor of her establishment, had drained her own glass several times.

"And please serve us at Monsieur's table, if he doesn't object," added Tom as he went with Sarah to sit next to the Slasher, who was as amazed as he was flattered by this politeness. The Schoolmaster and the Owl were still discussing their sinister plans in lowered tones. Once the wine was served, when Tom and Sarah were seated with the Slasher as well as the ogress, who regarded a second invitation as unnecessary, the interview continued.

"You were telling us, good man, that you had met our friend Rodolphe at Red-Arm's house?" said Tom, clinking his glass with the Slasher's.

"Yes, my good man," answered the latter as he downed his glass in short order.

"What a curious name, Red-Arm! Who is this Red-Arm?"

"He fakes packing trunks," said the Slasher, negligently. Then he added, "This is some great wine, Old Lady Ponisse!"

"That's why you shouldn't have an empty glass, my good man," said Tom as he refilled the Slasher's glass.

"To your health," said the Slasher, "and to the health of your small friend who . . . well, anyway, if my aunt was a man, she would be my uncle, like the proverb says. So go at it, joker. I get you."

Sarah blushed imperceptibly. Tom continued, "I didn't understand what you said about Red-Arm. Rodolphe was leaving his place, surely?"

"I told you that Red-Arm fakes packing trunks."

Tom looked at the Slasher in surprise. "What do you mean, he fakes packing trunks? What does that mean?"

"Fakes packing trunks. He sells contraband goods. It seems you don't speak the lingo."

"My good man, I don't understand you."

"I'm telling you that you don't speak slang like Monsieur Rodolphe."

"Slang?" said Tom, looking at Sarah in surprise.

"Come on, you guys are a couple of mugs. Rodolphe, though, he's a real pal. Even though he's a fan-painter, he's as fluent as I am in street slang. Well, since you don't speak this beautiful tongue, I'll tell you in plain French that Red-Arm is a contraband dealer. I'm not giving anything away when I say that. He doesn't hide it. He flaunts his wares in front of the customs officers. Catch him if you can, but Red-Arm is a shrewd one."

CHAPTER 7

YOUR MONEY OR YOUR LIFE

The noise of the closing door jolted Tom and Sarah out of their reverie. They rose and thanked the Slasher for the information he had given them. The latter inspired less confidence in them once he had so crudely yet so sincerely expressed his coarse admiration for Rodolphe.

As the Slasher left the joint the wind had become twice as violent, and the rain was coming down in torrents.

Hiding in an alley across from the joint, the Schoolmaster and the Owl watched as the Slasher kept his distance from the side of the street on which a house was being demolished. Soon his footsteps, a little heavier than usual because of the libations he had indulged in so frequently over the course of the evening, could no longer be heard amid the whistling of the wind and the noise of the rain whipping against the high walls.

Tom and Sarah exited the tavern in spite of the heavy downfall. They walked in the opposite direction from the Slasher.

"They're done for!" said the Schoolmaster in a low voice. "Get your acid ready. Look out!"

"Let's take off our shoes so they don't hear us walking behind them," said the Owl.

"You're right, Owl, just like you always are. I wouldn't have thought of that. Let's walk on cat's paws."

The hideous couple took off their shoes and slipped into the shadows, holding to the sides of the houses. Thanks to this stratagem, the sound of the Owl's and the Schoolmaster's footsteps were so muted that they could follow Tom and Sarah closely enough almost to touch them without their victims being able to hear them.

"Fortunately, our carriage is on the street corner," said Tom. "The rain is going to drench us. Aren't you cold, Sarah?"

"Maybe we can learn something from that smuggler, Red-Arm," Sarah said pensively without answering Tom's question. Suddenly, Tom stopped short. They were only a small distance away from the spot the Schoolmaster had chosen for his crime.

"I've got the wrong street," said Tom. "We should have turned left upon leaving the cabaret. We need to go back by the house that's being demolished to get back to our carriage. Let's turn around." The Schoolmaster and the Owl ducked into the recess of a door so as to avoid being noticed by Tom and Sarah, who were so close they nearly brushed up against them.

"In fact, I prefer that they walk by the ruins," said the Schoolmaster, quietly. "If the patsy fights back, I'll know what to do."

Tom and Sarah, after having passed the joint a second time, walked near the house in ruins. The open cellar of this half-demolished hovel formed a sort of abyss along the side of the road. The Schoolmaster leapt forward with the vigor and agility of a tiger. With one of his big hands he seized Tom by the throat and said to him, "Give me your money or I'll throw you in this hole." Pushing him from behind, the bandit made him lose his balance. With one hand he let Tom dangle over the pit, while with the other hand he grabbed Sarah's arm in a vise grip. Before Tom could make a move, the Owl had robbed him with marvelous dexterity.

Sarah did not call out, not seeking to get involved in a struggle. She said in a calm voice, "Tom, give them your wallet." And to the bandit, she said, "We won't scream; don't hurt us."

After having gone through the ambush victims' pockets carefully, the Owl said to Sarah, "Let's see your hands to find out if you're wearing any rings. No, you're not," grumbled the old woman. "No one to give you rings? How wretched!"

Tom's sangfroid did not flag during this scene, as rapid as it was unexpected. "Would you like to make a deal? My wallet contains papers that will be useless to you. Give them back to me, and tomorrow I'll give you twenty-five louis," he said to the Schoolmaster, whose hand was gripping him less roughly now.

"Sure, to lay a trap for us!" answered the bandit. "Come on, start walking, and don't look behind you. You're lucky to get away this cheaply."

"Wait a moment," said the Owl. "If he's a good boy, he'll get his wallet back. I've got a plan." Then, turning to Tom, she said, "Are you familiar with the Saint-Denis plain?"

"Yes."

"Do you know where Saint-Ouen is?"

"Yes."

"Across from Saint-Ouen, at the end of the chemin de la Révolte, the plain is flat. You can see a long distance away on that field. Go there tomorrow morning all alone, hand over the money, and you'll find me with your wallet. Fair exchange and I'll give it back to you."

"But he'll get you pinched, Owl!"

"I'm not so stupid! There's no way. You can see too far from there. I have only one eye, but it's a good one. If the patsy comes with anyone else, he won't find me. I'll be long gone."

Sarah seemed to be struck with a new idea. She asked the criminal, "Would you like to make some money?"

"Yes."

"Did you see in the cabaret we were in—you see, now I recognize you—did you see the man that the collier came looking for?"

"A thin guy with a mustache? Yes, I was going to take a piece out of that rotter, but he didn't give me the chance. He knocked me out with two punches that left me hanging upside down off the table. That's the first time it's ever happened to me. Oh, I'll get back at him."

"Good, then. It's him we want," said Sarah.

"Him?" cried the Schoolmaster. "Give me a thousand francs and I'll kill him for you."

"Sarah!" cried Tom, horrified.

"You miserable rat, I don't want him killed," Sarah said to the Schoolmaster.

"So what, then?"

"Come to the Saint-Denis plain tomorrow, and you'll find my companion there," she said. "You'll see that he's all alone. He'll tell you what to do. It's not one thousand francs I'll give you but two—if you succeed."

"Killer," said the Owl in a low voice to the Schoolmaster, "there's money to be made here. These people are flush and they want to get back at an enemy. The enemy is the same creep you wanted to do in. Let's do it. If I were you, I'd do it. Two thousand smackers! My boy, that's worth the trouble."

"Well, then, my woman will go," said the Schoolmaster. "You'll tell her what has to be done, and I'll see."

"That's it, then. Tomorrow at one o'clock."

"At one o'clock."

"On the Saint-Denis plain."

"On the Saint-Denis plain."

"Between Saint-Ouen and the chemin de la Révolte, at the end of the road."

"It's a deal."

"And I will bring you your wallet."

"And you will have the five hundred francs I've promised, along with an advance on the other job if things work out."

"Now turn right, and we'll turn left. Don't follow us, or else . . ." And the Schoolmaster and the Owl went off quickly.

"The devil comes to our aid," said Sarah. "That bandit may be useful to us."

"Sarah, I'm afraid now," said Tom.

"Well, I'm not afraid. On the contrary, I have hope. But come on, I see where we are. The carriage can't be far from here." And the two individuals walked quickly toward the Notre-Dame square.

An invisible witness had watched this whole scene. It was the Slasher, who had been crouching in the ruins to take shelter from the rain. The proposition that Sarah had made the bandit concerning Rodolphe was of vital interest to the Slasher. Afraid of the dangers that threatened his new friend, he regretted not being able to do anything to protect him. His hatred for the Schoolmaster and the Owl may well have had something to do with this worthy sentiment. The Slasher resolved to warn Rodolphe of the danger he was facing. But how would he manage to find him? He had forgotten the address of this man who had identified himself as a fan-painter. Perhaps Rodolphe wouldn't return to the joint. How would he find him?

As he reflected on this problem, the Slasher followed Tom and Sarah without thinking about it. He watched as they got into the carriage that was waiting for them in front of the Notre-Dame square. The carriage was departing. A stroke of genius came to him. He mounted the back of the carriage.

At one in the morning, this carriage stopped on the boulevard de l'Observatoire, and Tom and Sarah disappeared onto one of the little streets that end there. The night was very dark. The Slasher could not mark out for himself any landmark that might assist him the next day in recognizing precisely all the places he had been. Then, with the wisdom of a savage, he took out his pocketknife and made a long and deep cut in one of the trees near the place the coach had stopped. Then he went home, which was very far from where he had ended up.

For the first time in a long while, the Slasher experienced deep slumber in his miserable little room. His dreams were not once interrupted by the horrible vision of the sergeants' slaughterhouse, as he referred to it in his rough tongue.

CHAPTER 8

A WALK

The day after the evening whose events we have just recounted, a radiant autumn sun was shining in the middle of a pure blue sky. The night's torrent had passed. Although it was still darkened by the height of the houses, the hideous quarter we have visited seemed less horrible in the light of a bright day.

Either because Rodolphe was unafraid of meeting the two people he had avoided the day before or because he was eager to face them, he entered to rue aux Fèves at about eleven in the morning and walked toward the ogress's tavern.

Rodolphe was still dressed like a worker, but you could see that he had chosen his clothes with care. His brand-new smock, open at the chest, revealed a red wool shirt that was fastened with several silver buttons. The collar of another shirt of white linen was folded down over a black silk tie that was carelessly knotted around his neck. From his shiny-brimmed sky-blue velvet cap escaped a few stray chestnut-brown curls. Two perfectly polished boots replacing the crude studded shoes of the day before suited his well-formed feet, which seemed all the smaller for emerging from underneath a pair of wide olive velvet pants. This outfit did not in any way reduce the elegance of Rodolphe's appearance. His was a rare mix of grace, agility, and strength. Our everyday clothing tends to be so ugly that we can only improve our appearance, even when we exchange it for the coarsest apparel.

The ogress was lazily passing the time in the doorframe of the joint when Rodolphe showed up. "At your service, young man! You've returned no doubt in order to collect the change from your twenty francs!" she said deferentially, not daring to forget that the night before the man who had vanquished the Slasher had thrown a louis onto her counter. "I owe you seventeen pounds and ten sous . . . and that's not all. Somebody came asking for you yesterday—a large, well-dressed man. He was wearing full-grained leather boots, like the ones a drum major wears when he's out of uniform, and he had a small woman disguised as a man on his arm. They drank some high-quality wine with the Slasher."

"Ah! They drank with the Slasher! And what did they say to him?"

"When I say that they drank, that's wrong. They barely touched their glasses, and—"

"I asked you what they told the Slasher."

"They talked to him about this and that. About Red-Arm, the rain, the weather."

"Do they know Red-Arm?"

"No, not at all. The Slasher explained to them who he was and how you had beaten him."

"That's nice, but not quite accurate."

"You want your change?"

"Yes. I'm going to take Songbird for a day in the country."

"Oh, that's impossible, my boy."

"Why?"

"What if she didn't come back? I own her clothes, plus she still owes me two hundred and twenty francs before she's repaid her debt to me for her room and board since I took her in. If she wasn't as honest as she is, I wouldn't let her go any further than the street corner."

"Songbird owes you two hundred and twenty francs?"

"Two hundred and twenty francs and ten sous. But what difference is it to you, my boy! You're not going to pay for her, are you? Go ahead, milord!"

"Here you go," said Rodolphe, tossing eleven louis onto the ogress's tin counter. "Now, how much is the hand-me-down clothing worth that you rent her?"

The old woman, stunned, stared at the louis, one after the other, in a defiant and suspicious manner.

"What, do you think I would give you counterfeit money? Go get it changed, and let's be done with it. How much are the hand-me-downs you're renting to the poor girl?"

Torn between her desire to make a good profit, her astonishment at seeing a worker have so much cash in his possession, her fear of being duped, and her hope of earning even more money, the ogress remained silent for a moment, and then said, "Her clothes are worth at least . . . a hundred francs."

"Rags like that? Come on! You can keep the change from yesterday and I'll give you another louis, nothing more. Paying you ransom is stealing from the poor who need my alms."

"Fine, my boy. I'll keep the clothes. Songbird is not going anywhere. I'm free to sell my belongings for the price I want."

"May you burn in hell someday for this! Here's your money. Go and get me Songbird."

The ogress pocketed the gold, thinking that the worker must have committed a robbery or come into money. She said to him, with a horrible smile, "Why don't you go up yourself to look for Songbird, my son? That would make her very happy, because—Old Lady Ponisse's word—she had her eyes on you yesterday!"

"Go and get her and tell her that I'm taking her into the country, nothing more than that. Whatever you do, do not tell her that I paid up her debt."

"Why not?"

"What do you care?"

"Actually, it's fine with me. I would rather have her think she's still under my thumb."

"Will you be quiet? Go up and get her!"

"Oh, what a mean man! I pity the people you get angry at. All right, I'm going, I'm going."

And the ogress went upstairs.

A few minutes later she came back downstairs. "Songbird didn't want to believe me. She turned crimson when she heard you were here. But when I told her that I would permit her to have a day in the country, I thought she was going mad. For the first time in her life, she wanted to throw her arms around my neck."

"That was her joy at leaving you."

Fleur-de-Marie entered the room at this moment, dressed as she was the day before. She wore a brown Aleppo silk dress, an orange shawl knotted at the back, and a red checkered kerchief that revealed only two thick blond braids. She blushed when she saw Rodolphe and lowered her eyes in confusion.

"Would you like to spend the day in the country with me, child?" asked Rodolphe.

"With all my heart, Monsieur Rodolphe, since the ogress is permitting me."

"I am allowing this trip, my little kitten, on account of your good behavior, which you are displaying right now. Come, give me a kiss."

The shrew leaned her blotchy face toward Fleur-de-Marie. The poor girl, overcoming her repugnance, offered her forehead to the ogress's lips, but suddenly a violent shove from Rodolphe's elbow pushed the old woman back onto the counter. He took Fleur-de-Marie's arm and left the joint to the sound of Old Lady Ponisse's imprecations.

"Be careful, Monsieur Rodolphe," said Songbird. "The ogress could throw something at your head—she's so nasty!"

"Don't worry, child. But what's wrong? You seem embarrassed or sad. Are you bothered by coming with me?"

"On the contrary. But . . . but . . . you've given me your arm."

"So?"

"You're a worker. Someone could tell your boss that he ran into you with me. That would damage your reputation. Masters don't like their workers to stray." And Songbird gently disengaged her arm from Rodolphe's, adding, "Walk ahead by yourself. I'll follow you to the edge of town. Once we get into the fields, I'll walk next to you again."

"You have nothing to fear," said Rodolphe, moved by her delicate tact. He took Fleur-de-Marie's arm again. "My boss doesn't live in this neighborhood, and in any case we're going to hire a carriage on the quai aux Fleurs."

"As you wish, Monsieur Rodolphe. I'm just telling you this to keep you from coming into any harm."

"I believe you, and I thank you for it. But tell me honestly, do you care where we go in the countryside?"

"It's all the same to me, Monsieur Rodolphe, so long as it's the countryside. It's so nice out. The air is so good to breathe! Did you know that I haven't been further than the flower market for the past five months? And, if the ogress let me leave the Cité, it's only because she trusted me."

"And when you came to this market, was it to buy flowers?"

"Oh, no! I didn't have any money. I just came to see them and inhale their perfume. For the half hour the ogress let me walk on the pier on market days, I would be so happy that I forgot everything!"

"And when you went back to the ogress's place, back onto these wretched streets?"

"I returned sadder than when I'd left—and I choked back my tears so she wouldn't beat me. Listen: at the market, the thing that gave me the most longing—such longing—was to see all the little female workers so nicely dressed and proper, walking along happily with a pretty flowerpot in their arms."

"I'm sure that if you had had only a few flowers on your windowsill, you would have considered them good company."

"It's true what you say, Monsieur Rodolphe. Would you believe that one day the ogress, on her birthday, knowing how much I like flowers, gave me a little rosebush. If you knew how happy it made me! I was never bored anymore. I amused myself by counting its leaves, its flowers. But the air is so foul in the Cité that after two days it started to turn yellow. So . . . but you're going to make fun of me, Monsieur Rodolphe."

"No, no, go on."

"Well, I asked the ogress for permission to go out and take my rosebush for a walk. Yes, the way I would have taken a child for a walk. I would take it to the pier, thinking it would do it good to be with other flowers in the good, sweet air. I would dip its poor wilted leaves into the clear water of the fountain, and then, to dry it out, I would put it in the sun for a quarter of an hour. Dear little rosebush, it didn't get any sun in the Cité, because on our street the sun doesn't reach any lower than the rooftops. Finally, I would come back. And I am sure, Monsieur Rodolphe, that thanks to the walks I took it on, the rosebush lived perhaps ten days longer than it would have without them."

"I believe you. But when it died, you must have felt a great loss."

"I cried over it, and I felt real sorrow. Listen, Monsieur Rodolphe, since you understand all about loving flowers, I can tell you something. Well, then, I also felt grateful to that plant for . . . oh, this time you'll really make fun of me."

"No, no! I love—I adore flowers. That's why I understand all the crazy things they inspire people to do."

"All right. Well, I was grateful to that poor rosebush for flowering so kindly for me even though . . . well . . . in spite of what I was." And Songbird bowed her head and turned red from shame.

"Unhappy child! With your awareness of your horrible position, you must have often—"

"Wanted to end it all, you were going to say, Monsieur Rodolphe?" Songbird said, interrupting her companion. "Oh, yes! More than once I looked at the Seine from over the parapet . . . but then I would look around at the flowers and the sun . . . And then I would say to myself, 'The river will always be there. I'm not seventeen years old yet. Who knows?'"

"When you said, 'Who knows,' were you hoping for something to happen?"

"Yes."

"What were you hoping for?"

"I don't know. I just hoped . . . I hoped for something, almost despite myself. In those moments, it seemed to me that I didn't deserve what had become of me, that there was something good in me. I said to myself, 'I've been tortured, but at least I haven't done any harm to anyone else. If I had had someone to give me advice, I wouldn't be where I am!' That thought would drive away my sadness for a while. I must say that those thoughts came to me the most after I lost my rosebush," added Songbird with a solemnity that made Rodolphe smile.

"You still feel bad about it."

"Yes. Look, here it is."

And Songbird pulled a little wooden box out of her pocket. It was carefully carved and fastened with a pink ribbon.

"You preserved it?"

"Of course. It's the only thing I own in the world."

"What? You don't have anything else that's your own?"

"Nothing."

"What about that coral necklace?"

"It belongs to the ogress."

"What? You don't own a single scarf or bonnet or handkerchief?"

"No, nothing . . . nothing but the dried branches of my poor rosebush. That's why it matters so much to me."

With each word, Rodolphe's astonishment grew. He could not understand this appalling slavery, this horrible sale of body and soul in exchange for a sordid shelter, a few rags, and some wretched food.[22]

Rodolphe and Songbird arrived at the quai aux Fleurs. A carriage awaited them therc. Rodolphe helped Songbird into it. He followed her and said to the driver, "To Saint-Denis. I'll tell you later which way to go."

The car departed. The sun was shining, and the sky was cloudless. The cool air had a slight nip to it. The breeze felt lively and refreshing through the lowered windows.

"Look! A woman's coat!" said Songbird upon noticing that she had sat on this garment without seeing it.

"Yes, it's for you, child. I brought it along because I thought you might get cold. Wrap yourself up in it, snugly."

Little accustomed to such thoughtful behavior, the poor girl looked at Rodolphe with surprise. The kind of intimidation that he evoked from her grew stronger, along with a vague sadness of which she seemed unaware.

"My God! Monsieur Rodolphe, you are so good! I am so ashamed!"

"Because I'm good to you?"

"No, but . . . it seems to me that you aren't talking the way you were yesterday. You seem very different."

"Listen, Fleur-de-Marie. Which do you prefer? Yesterday's Rodolphe, or today's?"

"I like you much better now. But yesterday, I felt I was closer to being your equal." Then, correcting herself out of fear of having insulted Rodolphe, she said, "When I say 'your equal,' Monsieur Rodolphe, I know that can't be."

"Something about you surprises me, Fleur-de-Marie."

"What's that, Monsieur Rodolphe?"

"You seem to have forgotten what the Owl told you yesterday about your parents, that she knows your mother."

"Oh! I haven't forgotten. I thought about it last night, and I cried a lot. I'm sure it's not true, though. The one-eyed hag must have invented that story to make me feel bad."

---

22. If we allowed ourselves to provide the details that we shrink from offering, we would prove that this servitude exists, that our laws are designed such that a poor creature, often sold by her relatives and thrown into this abyss of infamy, is condemned to live in it forever. Repentance and regret are useless. It is almost impossible, from a material perspective, for such a young woman to extricate herself from this life in the gutter. (The reader may consult the invaluable work of Dr. Parent-Duchâtelet, the great philosopher and philanthropist.) [SN]

Alexandre Parent du Châtelet (1790–1836) was a doctor and researcher in the area of public hygiene. Sue refers to his posthumous book *De la prostitution dans la ville de Paris, considérée sous le rapport de l'hygiène publique, de la morale et de l'administration* (Prostitution in the City of Paris: Considered in Terms of Public Hygiene, Morality and Administration). Sue's footnote is as near as he approaches to making Songbird's prostitution explicit. [TN]

"It's possible that the Owl might know more than you think. If that's true, wouldn't you be happy to find your mother again?"

"Alas! Monsieur Rodolphe, if my mother never loved me, what good would it do to find her? She wouldn't even want to see me. If she loved me, what shame I would cause her! She might even die from it."

"If your mother loved you, Fleur-de-Marie, she would take pity on you, she would forgive you, and she would love you still. If she abandoned you, her shame when she saw the hideous fate to which she condemned you by abandoning you would be your revenge."

"What's the good of revenge? If I were to get revenge on her, it seems to me I would no longer have the right to feel I was unhappy. And sometimes that's a consolation to me."

"Perhaps you're right. Let's not talk about it anymore."

At that moment, the car approached Saint-Ouen, at the crossing of rue Saint-Denis and the chemin de la Révolte. Despite the monotony of the landscape, Fleur-de-Marie was so transported by seeing "fields," as she put it, that her charming face was beaming. She forgot the sad thoughts that the memory of the Owl had just awoken in her. She leaned on the carriage door, clapping her hands and crying, "Monsieur Rodolphe, I'm so happy! Grass! Fields! Can I get out? It's so beautiful! I would so love to run through these meadows."

"Let's get out and run, my child. Driver, stop here!"

"What? You, too, Monsieur Rodolphe?"

"Me, too. I'm on holiday!"

"I'm so happy, Monsieur Rodolphe!"

At this, Rodolphe and Songbird took each other by the hand and ran until they were out of breath across a vast field of recently mown hay. To recount Fleur-de-Marie's little leaps, cries of joy, and expressions of ecstasy would be impossible. Poor gazelle! She had been held as a prisoner for so long that the fresh air was intoxicating for her. She went to and fro, stopping herself for a moment and then taking off again in new raptures. At the sight of some patches of daisies and some buttercups that had been spared by the first frost, Songbird couldn't keep herself from exclaiming anew with this latest pleasure. Leaving not a single flower behind, she picked the whole field clean.

After having thus run through the fields, the girl tired quickly, having lost the habit of regular exercise. Stopping to catch her breath, she sat on the trunk of a fallen tree at the edge of a deep pit.

Fleur-de-Marie, ordinarily so pale, now showed hints of a more vivid color. Her large blue eyes shone sweetly. Her ruby lips, panting, revealed two rows of moist pearls, and her breast heaved under her old skimpy orange shawl. She brought one hand up to her heart to restrain its beating, while, with the other hand, she offered Rodolphe the bouquet of flowers that she had picked. Nothing could have been more charming than the innocent and pure expression of joy that shone on her earnest face.

When Fleur-de-Marie could talk, she said to Rodolphe, with profound happiness and almost religious gratitude, "How good the good Lord is to have given us such a beautiful day!"

A tear came into Rodolphe's eye as he heard this poor, scorned, fallen, abandoned creature who had no safe home and no bread cry out in happiness and ineffable gratitude toward the Creator, just because she had enjoyed a ray of sunlight and the view of a meadow.

Rodolphe was drawn out of his meditation by an unforeseen incident.

CHAPTER 9

THE SURPRISE

As we said, Songbird was sitting on a fallen tree trunk next to a deep ditch.

Suddenly, a man, rising up from the bottom of the trench, shook the covering under which he had been crouching and let out a roar of laughter. Songbird turned around and cried out in fear. It was the Slasher.

"Don't be afraid, my girl," said the Slasher, seeing the girl's fright as she shrank back next to her companion. "Funny meeting you this way, huh? You weren't expecting that, Monsieur Rodolphe, were you? Me, neither." Then, in a more serious tone, he added, "Listen, boss, you can say whatever you like, but something's in the air . . . up high, over our heads. The Big Guy is a sly one. He seems to be saying to us, 'Go where I send you.' And when you think that he sent you here, too, it's damned amazing."

"What are you doing here?" asked Rodolphe, very surprised.

"I'm keeping watch out for you, boss. But thunder and lightning, what a joke that you came right by my country house. You know, there's something going on up there. There's really something going on."

"But again, what are you doing here?"

"You'll know soon enough. Just give me the chance to get a lookout from the height of your horses." The Slasher ran toward the carriage, parked a short distance away, and looked sharply here and there over the field. He returned quickly to rejoin Rodolphe.

"Will you tell me what all this means?"

"Be patient, boss! Just one more thing: what time is it?"

"Half past noon," said Rodolphe, looking at his watch.

"Good. We've got some time. The Owl won't be here yet for another half hour."

"The Owl!" cried Rodolphe and Songbird in unison.

"Yes, the Owl. In short, boss, here's what happened. Yesterday, after you left the joint, a man came—"

"A tall man with a woman dressed in men's clothes; they asked for me. I know about that. And so?"

"Then they paid for my drink, and wanted me to blab about you. I didn't want to say anything, since you hadn't said anything beyond that thrashing you had the courtesy of giving me. I don't know anything more about any of your secrets. And even if I did know anything, it would have been the same. It's cradle to grave for us, Monsieur Rodolphe. Devil take me if I know why I feel so attached to you—it's like a bulldog and his master. It's all the same to me. I can't figure it out and I've given up trying. You make of it what you want."

"Thank you, my friend, but go on with your story."

"Since they weren't getting anything out of me, the tall gentleman and the little woman dressed like a man left the ogress's place, and so did I; they went toward the Palais de Justice, and I went toward Notre-Dame. When I got to the end of the street, I realized that it was raining cats and dogs—a real flood! Nearby, there was a house that was being torn down. I said to myself, 'If that downpour goes on, I can sleep there just as well as I can at my place.' I crawled into a kind of cellar for shelter; I made a bed out of an old beam, a pillow out of some old plaster debris, and there I was, bedded down like royalty."

"And then?"

"We'd had a bit to drink together, Monsieur Rodolphe. I drank some more with the big one and the little one dressed like a guy. Which is to say that my head was feeling a little heavy. When that happens, there's nothing like the sound of falling rain to lull me to sleep. I started to snooze. I hadn't been out for long when a noise jerked me awake. It was the Schoolmaster who was talking in a friendly way with someone else. I listened . . . good God! Who did I recognize? The voice of the tall one who had been at the joint with the little one dressed like a guy."

"They were talking with the Schoolmaster and the Owl?" asked Rodolphe, astonished.

"With the Schoolmaster and the Owl. They were saying that they would see each other the next day."

"That's today!" cried Rodolphe.

"At one o'clock."

"That's now!"

"At the junction of the Saint-Denis and Révolte roads."

"That's here!"

"As you say, Monsieur Rodolphe. It's here!"

"The Schoolmaster! Be careful, Monsieur Rodolphe!" cried Fleur-de-Marie.

"Calm down, my girl. He isn't supposed to come. Only the Owl."

"How did that man manage to fall in with those two wretches?" asked Rodolphe.

"I swear I have no idea. And maybe I only woke up at the end of things, because the tall man was talking about getting back his wallet, which the Owl was supposed to bring here—for five hundred francs. Probably the Schoolmaster had begun by robbing them and then afterward they'd ended up talking like old pals."

"This is strange!"

"I'm frightened for you, Monsieur Rodolphe," said Fleur-de-Marie.

"Monsieur Rodolphe is not a child, my girl, but as you say, things could get hot for him, and so here I am."

"Go on please, my boy."

"The tall one and the little woman promised the Schoolmaster two thousand francs to make you—I don't know what. It's the Owl who is supposed to come here around now to bring the wallet and to find out what's going on, so she can go tell it to the Schoolmaster, who's taking care of everything else."

Fleur-de-Marie shuddered.

Rodolphe smiled with disdain.

"Two thousand francs to do something to you, Master Rodolphe! It makes me think (not that I'm comparing the two cases) of times I've seen posters for five-hundred-franc rewards for a lost dog. I would tell myself, modestly enough, 'You could get lost, you animal, and no one would offer even a hundred sous to get you back.' Two thousand francs to do something to you? So who are you, anyway?"

"I'll tell you in a moment."

"Fine with me, boss. When I heard the deal made with the Owl, I said to myself, 'I have to find the nest of those filthy rich types who want to put the Schoolmaster on Monsieur Rodolphe's heels. It could be good for something.' When they went away, I got out from my pile of debris and followed them on tiptoe. The big and the little one picked up a carriage at the square in front of Notre-Dame. They got in and I followed right after. We got to the boulevard de l'Observatoire. It was dark as a dungeon, and I couldn't see a thing. I marked a tree so I could find the place again the next day."

"Well done, my boy."

"This morning, I returned. Ten steps from my tree, I saw a little alley blocked by a barrier. In the mud of the alley, prints of big strides and little ones. At the end of the alley, a house. The nest of the big one and the little one must be there."

"Thank you, my good man. Without suspecting it, you have done me a great service."

"Excuse me, Monsieur Rodolphe, but I did suspect it. And that's why I did it."

"I know, my boy, and I would like to repay you more than by just saying thank you. Unfortunately, I am just a poor devil of a worker, even though they're offering two thousand francs to do something to me, as you've said. Now, I'll tell you why."

"All right, if you want, but it's all the same to me. They plot something against you, I'm there to fight them. Reasons don't concern me."

"I can guess what they want. Listen to me carefully: I have a secret for carving ivory for fans by machine. But the secret doesn't belong to me alone. I'm waiting for my associate to put the procedure into practice, and it must be the working model of the machine, which I have at home, that they want to get hold of, at any cost. There's a lot of money to be made with this discovery."

"So the tall one and the little one? Who are they?"

"They are the manufacturers I work for. I didn't want to give them my secret."

This explanation seemed enough for the Slasher, whose intelligence was less than remarkable. "I understand now," he said. "What wretches! And they don't even have the courage to do their own dirty work. But to finish my story: here's what I said to myself this morning. 'I know about the meeting between the Owl and the tall one, and I'm going to wait for them. I have good legs. The head docker will just have to wait for me, and too bad for him.' I got here, I saw this ditch, I was going to take an armful of compost and hide under it up to my eyes. And then, poor Songbird came and sat down next to my hideout. That's when I decided to play a joke on you and shout out like I was on fire and jump out of my spot at the same time."

"And now what's your plan?"

"I'm going to wait for the Owl. She'll definitely get here first. I'm going to try to hear what she says to the tall one because it might help you. There's nothing here in this field besides that overturned tree trunk. From there, you can see everything across the plain—it's as if it was put there on purpose to sit on. The Owl's meeting is four steps away from there, at the junction of the roads. You can bet they'll sit there. If they don't come over there, if I can't hear anything, then when they're separated, I'll jump the Owl. That's what I'll do. I'll pay her what's owed her on Songbird's account, and I'll wring her neck until she tells me the names of the poor girl's parents. What do you think of my plan, Monsieur Rodolphe?"

"It sounds good enough, my boy, but we have to fix one part."

"Oh! First, Slasher, you shouldn't start a nasty fight for me. If you hit the Owl, the Schoolmaster—"

"Enough, my girl. The Owl will have to get past me. Good God! I'll double her dose just because she has the Schoolmaster to defend her!"

"Listen, my boy, I have a better way to avenge Songbird for the Owl's wickedness. I'll tell you what to do later. As for now," said Rodolphe, moving several paces away from Songbird and lowering his voice, "as for now, would you like to do me a real service?"

"Anything, Master Rodolphe."

"The Owl doesn't know you, does she?"

"I saw her for the first time yesterday at the joint."

"Here's what you have to do. First, you should hide. But when you see her close by, you should leave your hole."

"To wring her neck?"

"No. Save that for later! Today, we just have to keep her from talking to the tall one. If he sees someone with her, he won't dare come up to her. If he does, don't leave her for a minute. He can't make any plans with her while you're there."

"If he thinks I don't belong here, I'll handle it. He's no Schoolmaster, nor a Monsieur Rodolphe."

"I know that swell. He won't have anything to do with you."

"Good. I'll stick to the Owl like her shadow. The man won't say a word I can't hear, and he'll end up taking off."

"If they set up another appointment, you'll know it, because you won't leave their side. In any case your presence will be enough to get rid of the swell."

"Good, good. And then I can give a good round of punches to the Owl? That's what I really want."

"Not yet. The one-eyed hag doesn't know if you're a thief or not, right?"

"No. Unless the Schoolmaster told her it wasn't my thing."

"If he told her that, you'll give out you've had a change of heart."

"Me?"

"You!"

"Good Lord! Monsieur Rodolphe, you know, well . . . I don't like the sound of that game."

"Don't do anything you don't want to. You'll see soon enough whether I'm asking anything crooked of you."

"Oh! Well, then, I'm okay with it."

"And you're right to feel that way."

"You tell me, boss, and I'll do it."

"Once the man leaves, I want you to sweet-talk the Owl."

"Me? That old hag? I'd rather fight the Schoolmaster. I just don't know how I'll keep from jumping down her throat."

"If you do that, you'll wreck everything."

"So what should I do?"

"The Owl will be furious about the windfall she's just lost. You'll try to calm her down by telling her you have a good job to pull off. Tell her you're there to wait for your accomplice and that if the Schoolmaster wants in, there's lots of loot to be had."

"I get it, I get it."

"After waiting an hour, you'll say to her, 'My friend isn't coming, it's off for now.' And you'll make an appointment with the Owl and the Schoolmaster for early tomorrow. You understand?"

"I understand."

"And tonight, you'll show up at ten o'clock at the corner of the Champs-Élysées and the allée des Veuves. I'll meet you there and tell you the rest."

"If it's a trap, take care! The Schoolmaster is crafty. You've beaten him. He'll kill you as soon as he looks at you."

"Don't worry."

"Heavens, this is a crazy scheme, but you do what you want with me. It's not so hard, but something tells me that there's going to be trouble with the Schoolmaster and the Owl. But . . . one more thing, Monsieur Rodolphe."

"What?"

"It's not that I think you're likely to trap the Schoolmaster for the police. He's bad enough, and he should die a hundred deaths for what he's done, but to get him arrested—count me out. That's not something I want to be part of."

"Me, neither, my boy. But I have a score to settle with him and with the Owl because they're plotting with people who are after me. The two of us, we'll get to the bottom of this, if you help me."

"Oh, for that, one thing's as good as another. I'm in."

"If we succeed," added Rodolphe in a more serious, almost solemn tone that the Slasher found striking, "you will be as proud of yourself as if you had saved the man and woman who brought you into the world from fire and water!"

"Whatever you say, Monsieur Rodolphe! I've never seen that look from you before. But quick, quick!" cried the Slasher. "I see a white spot down there. That must be the Owl's bonnet. Get out of here! I'm going back into my hole."

"See you tonight, at ten."

"At the corner of the allée des Veuves and the Champs-Élysées it is."

Fleur-de-Marie had not heard the last part of the conversation between the Slasher and Rodolphe. She got back into the carriage with her travel companion.

CHAPTER 10

THE FARM

After his discussion with the Slasher, Rodolphe remained preoccupied for a few moments, lost in thought.

Fleur-de-Marie looked on in sadness at her companion, not daring to interrupt his silence.

Lifting his head, Rodolphe smiled at her beneficently. "What are you thinking about, my child? Our meeting with the Slasher wasn't very pleasant for you, was it? And we'd been enjoying ourselves so much!"

"No, on the contrary, it was a good thing for us, Monsieur Rodolphe, because the Slasher can be useful to you."

"For someone who's one of the lot that hangs out at the joint, that man still seems to have a good heart, don't you think?"

"I don't know, Monsieur Rodolphe. Before yesterday, I'd seen him often enough, but I hardly ever talked to him. I thought he was as bad as the others."

"Let's not think any more about it, my little Fleur-de-Marie. I'll feel bad if I make you sad, after I'd hoped to arrange a nice day for you."

"Oh, I'm so happy! It's been so long since I set foot outside Paris!"

"Since your fabulous outings with Rigolette."

"Dear Lord, yes, Monsieur Rodolphe. It was in the spring, but even though it's almost winter, I'm just as happy now. How sunny it is! Look at those little pink clouds over there, and that hill! And those pretty white houses among the trees . . . Look at how many leaves are left! Isn't that incredible, in the middle of November, Monsieur Rodolphe? In Paris the leaves fall so quickly. And over there, look! That flock of pigeons swooping down over the roof of a windmill . . . In the countryside, you never get tired of looking at things. Everything is so interesting."

"It's a pleasure to see how sensitive you are to these little things that make the countryside so charming, Fleur-de-Marie."

Indeed, the more the girl contemplated the calm and cheerful vista that spread out before her, the more her face glowed anew.

"And over there, that burning straw in the plowed fields—what beautiful white smoke it's sending into the sky! And that plow with the two nice large gray horses . . . If I was a man, how I'd like to be a farmworker! To be in the middle of a silent field, following a plow . . . seeing the tall forest in the distance on a day as beautiful as today, for instance! Right now, it makes you want to sing melancholy songs, the kind that bring tears to your eyes, like 'Geneviève de Brabant.'[23] Do you know that one, Monsieur Rodolphe?"

"No, child, but be nice and sing it to me when we get to the farm."

"How exciting! We're going to a farm, Monsieur Rodolphe?"

"Yes, to a farm run by my nurse, the good woman who raised me."

"And can we have some milk?" cried Songbird, clapping her hands.

"Oh, milk! We'll have excellent cream, if you please, and butter that the farmer will make in front of us, and some nice fresh eggs, too."

"That we'll take from the nests ourselves?"

"Certainly."

"And will we get to see the cows in their stable?"

"I don't see why not."

"And can we go into the dairy, too?"

"Into the dairy, too."

"And into the pigeon coops?"

"The pigeon coops as well."

"Oh, you know, Monsieur Rodolphe, I can't believe it. I'm going to have so much fun. What a great day. What great day!" exclaimed the girl, completely enchanted.

Just then, taken by a sudden turn of thought, remembering that after these hours of freedom in the countryside she would have to return to her filthy hovel, the poor girl hid her head in her hands and burst into tears.

Surprised, Rodolphe asked Songbird, "What's wrong, Fleur-de-Marie? What's making you sad?"

"Nothing, nothing, Monsieur Rodolphe." She wiped her eyes and tried to smile. "I apologize for being sad. Don't pay any attention to me. It's nothing, I swear. It's just a passing idea. I'm going to be cheerful."

"But you were so happy a moment ago!"

"That's just it," Fleur-de-Marie answered innocently. She looked at Rodolphe, her eyes still wet with tears.

These words cleared things up for Rodolphe. He understood everything.

In an attempt to lift the girl's spirits, he said to her, smiling, "I bet you're thinking about your rosebush. You feel sorry that you can't share our trip to the farm with it. Poor little rosebush! You would have even tried to feed it a little bit of cream!"

Songbird took this bit of gentle teasing as an excuse to smile. Bit by

---

23. In a medieval legend, Geneviève de Brabant is a chaste wife falsely accused by a spurned suitor. It's not clear what song Songbird refers to. There is an Offenbach operetta by the same title, but it was first performed years later, in 1859. [TN]

bit, the cloud of her sadness lifted; she decided to think about nothing but the present and not to give a fig for the future.

The carriage approached Saint-Denis. The tall spire of the church could be seen from afar.

"Oh, what a beautiful steeple!" cried Songbird.

"That's the steeple of Saint-Denis, a fine church. Would you like to see it? We'll stop the carriage."

Songbird lowered her eyes. "Since I've been living at the ogress's place, I haven't entered a church. I haven't dared to. In prison, on the other hand, I so enjoyed singing at mass! And at Corpus Christi, we made such gorgeous bouquets for the altar!"

"But God is good and merciful; why would you be afraid of praying or entering a church?"

"Oh, no, no, Monsieur Rodolphe, it would be an act of sacrilege. It's bad enough to offend God in all the other ways."

After a moment of silence, Rodolphe said to Songbird, "Have you ever loved anyone?"

"Never, Monsieur Rodolphe."

"And why not?"

"You've seen the kind of people who hang out at the joint. And then to love, you have to be respectable."

"What do you mean?"

"To depend only on yourself—on your abilities—for your living. But listen, if you don't mind, Monsieur Rodolphe, let's talk about something else."

"As you wish, Fleur-de-Marie, we'll speak about other things. But why are you looking at me that way? There are your beautiful eyes, all full of tears again. Have I done something wrong?"

"No, not at all! But you're so good to me that it makes me want to cry. You treat me with respect. And then you seem so pleased to see me happy, you'd think you'd taken me out today merely for my own pleasure. As if it wasn't enough to have defended me yesterday—now you've arranged such a wonderful day with you."

"Are you really happy?"

"It will be a long time before I forget how happy I have been."

"Happiness is so rare for you?"

"So rare."

"You know, because of what I don't have, I amuse myself by dreaming of what I wish I had. I say to myself, 'This is what I wish I could be. This is the fortune I aspire to.' And you, Fleur-de-Marie, do you ever have dreams like that, of castles in the air?"

"I used to, in prison, yes; before I lived with the ogress, I spent my life daydreaming and singing. Since then, though, I don't often indulge in daydreams. What about you, Monsieur Rodolphe? What are your dreams?"

"As for me, I'd like to be rich, very rich. I would like to have servants, a retinue, a mansion. I'd like to go out into the fashionable world every day, and go to the theater. What about your dreams, Fleur-de-Marie?"

"I'm not that hard to please. I'd like to pay back the ogress and have some extra money so I can have the time to find a job. I'd like to have a pretty, clean room where I could see trees while I worked."

"Lots of flowers on your windowsill."

"Oh, of course! To live in the country would be nice if it worked out that way. And that's it."

"A little room, a decent job—those are necessities. But if it's ask and have, you're allowed to think about extras. Wouldn't you like to have carriages, diamonds, pretty clothing?"

"I wouldn't want so much. To have my freedom, to live in the country, not to worry about dying in a hospital . . . Oh, most of all that—not to die there! You know, Monsieur Rodolphe, I often find myself thinking about that. It's frightening!"

"Unfortunately, for us poor people . . ."

"It's not because of the wretchedness there. It's just that after . . . when you're dead . . ."

"What about it?"

"Do you know what they do with you when you're dead?"

"No."

"I knew a girl in prison who died in the hospital. They let the surgeons have her body," whispered the poor girl, shuddering.

"That's horrible! Do you think about bleak things like that often, poor child?"

"It surprises you, Monsieur Rodolphe, doesn't it, that I still have shame—for after my death? Alas, dear God, that's all they've left me."

These painful and bitter words struck Rodolphe. He buried his head in his hands, quivering. He thought of the terrible luck that weighed down on Fleur-de-Marie. He thought of the poor creature's mother. Could her mother have been happy, rich, respectable, perhaps? Respectable, rich, happy . . . and her child, whom she had no doubt atrociously sacrificed out of shame, had left the Owl's garret for prison and then left prison for the ogress's den. And from there, she might end up dying on a pauper's pallet in a hospital. And after her death . . .

It was awful.

Poor Songbird, observing how somber her companion looked, said to him sadly, "Excuse me. I shouldn't have ideas like that. You took me with you today to be happy, and I keep saying these sad things to you—such sad things! I don't know how that happens. I'm really not trying to do it. I've never been happier than I've been today, yet at every turn I keep getting tears in my eyes. You're not angry at me for that, are you, Monsieur Rodolphe? Anyway, you see, the sadness goes away. Just like it came, it leaves. Listen, I'm not thinking about those things anymore. I'm going to be a good girl. Look, Monsieur Rodolphe, look at my eyes."

And Fleur-de-Marie, after blinking two or three times to get rid of a last, rebellious tear, opened her eyes wide and gave Rodolphe a look full of innocent charm.

"Fleur-de-Marie, I beg of you. Don't hold yourself back. Be happy if you feel happy, and sad if you're sad. Lord knows, I sometimes have gloomy thoughts like you do, too. I wouldn't like it if I had to pretend to feel cheerful when I wasn't."

"Really, Monsieur Rodolphe? You get sad sometimes?"

"Absolutely. My future is hardly any brighter than yours. I don't have a father or mother. If I get sick tomorrow, how will I live? Each day, I spend what I earn."

"That's a mistake, you know—a big mistake, Monsieur Rodolphe," said Songbird in a grave tone of remonstrance that made Rodolphe smile. "You should save your money in a bank account. My awful fate has befallen me because I didn't save money. When a worker has two hundred francs stashed away, he's never at anyone's mercy, never in want. And it's so often want that leads you astray."

"What you've said is very wise, very sensible, my little financial manager. But two hundred francs? How do you manage to put together two hundred francs?"

"It's very simple, Monsieur Rodolphe. Let's look at your finances, and you'll see. You earn as much as five francs a day sometimes, right?"

"Yes, when I work."

"You'll just have to work every day. There's no reason to pity you, you know. You have a good position. A fan-painter! That must give you pleasure. Really, Monsieur Rodolphe, you're not being very reasonable," Songbird added, with some severity. "A worker can get by, even live well, on three francs. You have forty sous left if you live on that, which leaves you sixty francs of savings a month. Sixty francs a month! That's real money!"

"Yes, but it's so much fun to wander about the town and do nothing."

"Monsieur Rodolphe, I'll tell you one more time: you are no more reasonable than a little child."

"All right. I'll be reasonable, you little scold. You're giving me some things to think about. I never thought about things like that."

"Really?" asked the girl, clapping her hands with joy. "If you only knew how happy that makes me! You'll set aside forty sous a day, truly?"

"I promise."

"You'll see how proud you'll be when you set aside your first savings. And that's not all. If you promise me not to get angry—"

"Do I seem that mean?"

"No, not at all, but I don't know if I should tell you—"

"You have to tell me everything, Fleur-de-Marie."

"All right, then. Can't you see that you are above . . . Well, what are you doing hanging about places like the ogress's tavern?"

"If I hadn't gone to the joint, I wouldn't have had the pleasure of taking you into the countryside today, Fleur-de-Marie."

"Well, that's true enough, but still, Monsieur Rodolphe. Listen, I'm as happy as can be from this outing, but, still, I would give up any chance of doing it again without a second thought if that would keep you from doing anything that might harm you."

"On the contrary, you've given me some very good financial advice."

"And you'll follow it?"

"I've given you my word of honor. I will put aside at least forty sous a day."

CHAPTER II

WISHES

At this moment Rodolphe said to the driver, who had passed the village of Sarcelles, "Take the first road on your right. Go through Villiers-le-Bel, then turn left, and then go straight."

Then, turning to Songbird, he said, "Now that you're happy with me, Fleur-de-Marie, we can amuse ourselves building castles in the air, as we were doing before. It doesn't cost much, so you can't complain about the expenses."

"And I won't. So let's build your castles in the air, then."

"Yours first, Fleur-de-Marie."

"Let's see if you can guess what I like, Monsieur Rodolphe."

"Let's try. I will imagine that this road—I say this one because it's the one that we're on."

"That's true. One shouldn't start by looking far off."

"I will imagine that this road, then, leads us to a charming village, far away from the main road."

"Good, that's much quieter."

"It's halfway up the hill and full of trees."

"There's a little river right nearby."

"Indeed, there is a little river. At the end of the village you can see a nice, pretty farm; on one side of the house there's an orchard, and on the other there's a beautiful garden full of flowers."

"I can see it all from here, Monsieur Rodolphe!"

"On the ground floor there's a big kitchen for the farmhands and a dining room for the mistress of the farm."

"The house has green shutters. That's so cheerful, isn't it, Monsieur Rodolphe?"

"Green shutters? I agree. There's nothing more cheerful than green shutters. Naturally, the mistress of the farm would be your aunt."

"Of course. And she would be a very good woman."

"Excellent. She would love you like a mother."

"What a good aunt! It must be so nice to be loved by someone!"

"And you would love her, too?"

"Oh!" Fleur-de-Marie exclaimed, clasping her hands and gazing upward with an expression of happiness that is beyond the ability of words to render. "Oh! Yes, I would love her, and I would help her to work, to sew, to wash and sort the clothes, to preserve fruits for the winter, indeed to do all the housework . . . She wouldn't complain of my laziness, I can promise you that. In the mornings—"

"Hold on, Fleur-de-Marie! You're so impatient! Let me finish describing the house for you."

"Go ahead, Mister Painter, I can tell you're practiced in painting lovely landscapes on your fans," said Songbird, laughing.

"Little chatterbox, let me finish telling you about my house."

"It's true, I do chatter. But it's so much fun! Monsieur Rodolphe, I'm all ears. Finish describing the farmhouse."

"Your room is upstairs, on the first floor."[24]

"My own room! What a privilege. Let's see my own room, let's see it."

And the girl snuggled up against Rodolphe, her eyes wide open and full of curiosity.

"Your room has two windows that overlook the flower garden and a field at the end of which the little river flows. On the other side of the river there's a hillside all planted with old chestnut trees, and amid the trees you can see the bell tower of the church."

"It's all so beautiful—so beautiful, Monsieur Rodolphe! It makes you wish you were there."

"Three or four nice cows are grazing in the field, which is separated from the garden by a hedgerow of hawthorn bushes."

"And from my window I can see the cows?"

"Yes, easily."

"There's one who's my favorite, right, Monsieur Rodolphe? I'll make her a beautiful collar with a bell on it, and I'll train her to eat out of my hand."

"The cow won't be lacking. She's pure white and very young. Her name is Musette."

"What a lovely name! Sweet little Musette! How I love her!"

"Let's finish seeing your room, Fleur-de-Marie. It's decorated with a pretty Persian wall hanging and matching drapes. A large rosebush and an enormous honeysuckle cover the walls of the farm on that side and surround your casement windows, so every morning you have only to stretch out your hand to pick a beautiful bouquet of roses and honeysuckle."

"Oh, Monsieur Rodolphe, what a talented painter you are!"

"Now let's talk about how you'll spend your days."

"Yes, let's see what my days are like."

"First, your kind aunt comes in to wake you up with a tender kiss on the

---

24. The first floor, in this case and throughout the book, is what the French and other Europeans call the first floor but what Americans call the second floor. Likewise, the French second floor corresponds to the American third floor, and so on. [TN]

forehead. She brings you a bowl of hot milk, because you've got weak lungs, poor child! You get out of bed, and you make the round of the farm, visit Musette, the chickens, your friends the pigeons, the flowers in the garden. At nine in the morning, your writing tutor arrives."

"My tutor?"

"You do realize that you need to learn how to read, write, and do sums so that you can help your aunt manage the books for the farm, don't you?"

"That's true, Monsieur Rodolphe—I never think of anything. I need to learn how to write in order to help my aunt," the poor girl said in a serious tone, so absorbed by the cheerful picture of this peaceful life that she had begun believing in its details.

"After your lesson, you'll do some mending, or you'll embroider a pretty peasant's bonnet. At two, you'll work on your writing, and then you'll go with your aunt on a good, long walk to see the harvesters in the summer and the plowmen in the fall. You'll get nice and tired, and you'll bring a choice handful of grass from the fields back for your sweet Musette to eat."

"That's because we come home through the meadow, right, Monsieur Rodolphe?"

"Absolutely. There's a wooden bridge over the river. When you return, my goodness, it must be six or seven o'clock. By this time, there's a nice roaring fire in the farm's big kitchen. You go in there to warm yourself and to talk with the good people who are having their supper after their work. Then you dine with your aunt. Sometimes the priest or some old friends of the family dine with you. After that, you read or you work while your aunt plays cards. At ten, she kisses your forehead and you go back up to your room; and the next morning, it all starts over again."

"You could live like that for a hundred years, Monsieur Rodolphe, and never think of being bored."

"But that's nothing yet! There are still Sundays, and holidays!"

"And what happens on those days, Monsieur Rodolphe?"

"You dress up in pretty clothing, you put on a charming peasant dress and a very cute round bonnet that suits you perfectly. You ride in an open wicker cart with your aunt and Jacques, the farmhand, to go to mass in the village. In the summertime, after mass, you and your aunt never miss any of the festivals at the nearby parishes. You're so sweet, so gentle, such a good housekeeper, your aunt loves you so much, and the priest says so many nice things about you, that all the young farmers who live in the area want to dance with you, because that's how marriages start. Little by little, you'll notice one of the farmers, and—"

Rodolphe, startled by the silence of Songbird, looked at her. The unfortunate girl was trying desperately to keep herself from sobbing. Caught up, for a brief moment, in the illusion of Rodolphe's words, she had forgotten the present. And the contrast between that present and the dream of a sweet and cheerful existence had reminded her of the horror of her true condition.

"Fleur-de-Marie, what's wrong?"

"Oh, Monsieur Rodolphe, I know you didn't mean it, but you've made me so unhappy. For a moment, I believed in that paradise."

"But, my poor child, the paradise exists. Look around you. Driver, stop the carriage!"

The carriage came to a halt. Songbird lifted her head without thinking. She saw that she was at the summit of a small hill. She was astonished—indeed, stunned. The pretty village on the hillside, the farm, the field, the nice cows, the little river, the chestnut grove, the church in the distance . . . the entire picture stretched out before her eyes. Nothing was missing, right down to Musette, a beautiful white heifer and Songbird's future pet. Upon this charming countryside shone a warming November sun. The yellow and purple leaves of the chestnut trees remained on their branches and were outlined against the bright blue sky.

"Well, Fleur-de-Marie, what do you think? Am I a good painter or not?" Rodolphe asked, smiling.

Songbird looked at him with a mixture of surprise and anxiety. All of this seemed nearly supernatural to her.

"How did this happen, Monsieur Rodolphe? Good Lord, is it a dream? It almost frightens me. How can this be true? What you told me . . ."

"Nothing is simpler, my dear. The mistress of the farm is my old nurse. I was brought up here. I wrote to her very early this morning to let her know that I would be coming to see her. I was painting from real life."

"Indeed, you were, Monsieur Rodolphe!" said Songbird, sighing deeply.

CHAPTER 12

THE FARM

The farm to which Rodolphe brought Fleur-de-Marie lay outside and at the far end of the village of Bouqueval, a small, isolated, little-known parish buried in the countryside, about two leagues away from Écouen.

Following Rodolphe's directions, the driver took the car down a short path and onto a long avenue lined with cherry and apple trees. The carriage traveled silently upon a carpet of fine, short grass of the sort that covers most of the roads in the area.

Fleur-de-Marie, melancholy and silent, remained sorrowful, in spite of her best efforts. Rodolphe almost reproached himself for having made her feel this way.

After a few minutes, the carriage drove up in front of the large gate leading to the farm's courtyard. It continued on its way along a thick arbor and stopped in front of a small, rustic wood porch that was partially hidden beneath a healthy vine stock with leaves on it that had been turned purple by the autumn.

"Here we are, Fleur-de-Marie," said Rodolphe. "Are you happy?"

"Yes, Monsieur Rodolphe, but I'm worried that I'm going to feel too ashamed to face the farm mistress. I won't be able to look her in the eye."

"Why is that, my child?"

"You're right, Monsieur Rodolphe. She doesn't know me." And Songbird suppressed a sigh.

People had no doubt been watching out for the arrival of Rodolphe's carriage. The driver opened the door. A woman of about fifty, dressed as a rich farm mistress does when she is from the environs of Paris, had a face that was both sad and kind. She appeared on the porch and came up to Rodolphe with a respectful eagerness. Songbird blushed deep red and got out of the carriage after a moment's hesitation.

"Hello, my good Madame Georges," said Rodolphe to the farm mistress. "You see, I'm on time."

Then, turning toward the driver and putting money in his hand, he said, "You can go back to Paris now."

The driver, a small, stocky man, had his hat pulled down over his eyes and his face almost entirely hidden by the collar of his coachman's overcoat. He pocketed the money without saying anything, got back into his seat, whipped up his horse, and disappeared rapidly into the green passage.

"After such a long ride, that silent driver must be in an awful hurry to get going," Rodolphe thought at first. "Bah! It's only two o'clock. He wants to get back to Paris so he can make good use of the rest of the day." And thus Rodolphe decided that there was no basis for any suspicions.

Fleur-de-Marie came up to him with an anxious, troubled, almost alarmed look. She said to him quietly, so as not to be heard by Madame Georges, "My goodness! Monsieur Rodolphe, pardon me, but you sent back the carriage, and I have to get back to the ogress by tonight. If I don't, she'll think I'm a thief. The clothes I'm wearing belong to her, and I owe her—"

"Don't worry, my child. I should be apologizing to you."

"Apologizing to me? For what?"

"For not having told you earlier that you owe nothing more to the ogress and that you can take off these rags and put on the clothing that my good Madame Georges will give you. She has some that are more or less your size. She will be happy to lend you something to wear. You see, she's already starting to assume her role as your aunt."

Fleur-de-Marie thought she was dreaming. She looked first at the farm mistress, then at Rodolphe, unable to believe what she was hearing.

"Is this possible," she said, in a voice palpitating with emotion, "that I don't have to go back to Paris? I can stay here? Madame will let me? Can it be possible, this castle in the air from just a few minutes ago?"

"This was the farm. Your dream has come true."

"No, no, it can't be. It would be too beautiful, it would make me too happy."

"You can never have enough happiness, Fleur-de-Marie."

"Oh, for pity's sake, Monsieur Rodolphe! Don't trick me. It would be too painful."

"My dear child, believe me," said Rodolphe in a voice that was still affectionate but with a tone of dignity that Fleur-de-Marie had not noticed before. "Yes, from this day onward, if you like, you may stay with Madame Georges and lead the peaceful life that made you so happy when you pictured it. Even though Madame Georges isn't really your aunt, when she comes to know you, she will feel the tenderest affection for you. You will pass for her niece in the eyes of the farm people. This little fiction will make your position a bit more natural. So, again, if it pleases you, Fleur-de-Marie, you may live the dream of a moment ago. As soon as you're all dressed like a farm girl," he added, smiling, "we'll take you to meet your future pet, Musette. She's a pretty little heifer who's just waiting for that collar you promised her. We'll also take a look in at your friends the pigeons, and then we'll go to the dairy. We'll walk around the whole farm. I mean to keep my promise."

Fleur-de-Marie clasped her hands tightly. Surprise, joy, gratitude, and respect all shone on her resplendent face. Her eyes brimming with tears, she exclaimed, "Monsieur Rodolphe, you must be an angel sent from God, doing so much good for the unfortunate without even knowing them! You deliver them from shame and misery!"

"My poor child," answered Rodolphe with a smile of deep sadness and indescribable goodness, "even though I am still young, I have already suffered greatly in my life. That should explain to you my compassion for those who suffer. Fleur-de-Marie—or rather, Marie—go with Madame Georges. Yes, Marie. From now on, use this name. It's as sweet and pretty as you are. Before I leave, we'll talk some more. I'll leave here very happy to know that you're happy."

Fleur-de-Marie spoke no more. She went up to Rodolphe, performed a slight curtsy, and took his hand, bringing it respectfully to her lips in a gesture full of grace and modesty. She then followed Madame Georges, who was contemplating her with deep interest.

CHAPTER 13

MURPH AND RODOLPHE

Rodolphe headed toward the courtyard of the farm and there met up with the large man who, the day before, disguised as a coal miner, had come to warn him of the arrival of Tom and Sarah.

Murph—for that is the name of this character—was about fifty years old. A few white strands stood out within the two little clumps of bright blond hair that framed his nearly bald head. His broad ruddy face was completely shaven except for the very short, vivid blond sideburns that stopped at the level of his ears and widened over his chubby cheeks. Despite his age and stoutness, Murph was quick and strong. His face, though somewhat phlegmatic, was both kind and resolute. He wore a white tie, a long waistcoat, and a great black coat with wide tails. His knee breeches were made from a greenish-gray fabric, the same material as the mother-of-pearl-buttoned gaiters he wore that didn't quite come up to his garters, leaving a gap that revealed his beige woolen traveling stockings. Murph's clothing and masculine comportment gave him the appearance of a quintessential English gentleman-farmer. We hasten to add that Murph was indeed an English gentleman (a squire), but not a farmer.

As Rodolphe entered the courtyard, Murph took a pair of pistols that he had just finished polishing meticulously and put them back into the compartment of a small carriage.

"Why the devil do you need those pistols?" asked Rodolphe.

"That's my affair, Your Lordship," said Murph as he got down from the footboard. "You do what you have to, I'll do what I have to."

"For what time did you order the horses?"

"According to your orders, I ordered them for nightfall."

"You arrived this morning?"

"At eight o'clock. Madame Georges had plenty of time to get everything ready."

"You're in some kind of mood. Are you angry with me over something?"

"I am only too content with you, Your Lordship, too content. One day or another, these risks will end up costing you your life."

"You're a fine one to talk! If I let you have your way, you'd take all the risks and—"

"And if you did good deeds without risking your life, why would that be so terrible, Your Lordship?"

"Where would the pleasure be in that, Master Murph?"

"You!" said the squire, shrugging his shoulders. "To think of you, going into that kind of tavern!"

"Oh, there you go again. You're a regular John Bull, with your aristocratic scruples. You believe the great lords to be somehow better than you. Poor little sheep, proud of your butchers!"

"If you were an Englishman, Your Lordship, you would understand it. You honor those who give honor. In any case, even if I were Turkish, Chinese, or American, I would still think you were wrong to take risks like that. Last night, as I walked through that abominable neighborhood on rue de la Cité with you in order to dig up that Red-Arm—the devil take him!—the only thing that kept me from going to your aid in your struggle with that bandit you found in the alley of that hovel was my fear of displeasing and disobeying you."

"So you're saying you doubt either my strength or courage, Mr. Murph?"

"Unfortunately, you've shown me a hundred times that I have no cause to doubt either the one or the other. Thank goodness, Crabb of Ramsgate taught you how to box. In Paris, Lacour[25] taught you how to fight with a cane, but he also taught you savate, and just for the fun of it, street slang. The remarkable Bertrand taught you fencing. In your matches against these teachers, you often managed to win. You can shoot doves flying in the sky with an army pistol. You have muscles of steel. Even though you're slender and trim, you could beat me as easily as a racehorse could beat a brewer's horse. It's true."

Rodolphe listened indulgently to this enumeration of his gladiatorial skills and said, with a smile, "So, then, what are you afraid of?"

"Your Lordship, I contend that it's not a good idea for you to face down every lout who happens to come your way. I'm not saying that because of how unseemly it is for an honorable gentleman of my place in the world to blacken his face with coal and act like a savage. In spite of my gray hair, my stoutness, and my dignity, I would dress up like a tightrope dancer if it helped you in some way. But I hold to what I've said."

"Oh, I know too well, old Murph, that when an idea gets riven into that ironclad head of yours, when faithfulness gets planted in your trusty, valiant heart, the devil himself would have to use his teeth and nails to pry them out."

"You're flattering me, Your Lordship. Are you considering—"

"Don't be embarrassed."

"Are you considering some mad act, Your Lordship?"

"My poor Murph, you're wasting your time giving me lectures."

25. Lacour was a famous teacher of savate. [SN]

"Why?"

"This is, in fact, one of my greatest moments of pride and joy. I'm here—"

"In a place where you've done good?"

"It's a place of refuge against your homilies. It's my Temple Bar."[26]

"If that's the way it is, what the devil do you want me to do, Your Lordship?"

"Master Murph, you flatter me. You want to keep me from committing some mad act."

"Your Lordship, there are some mad acts that I can put up with."

"Extravagant expenditures of money?"

"Yes, because, after all, with almost two million francs of income . . ."

"One can often feel quite pinched, my poor Murph."

"Who do you think you're talking to, Your Lordship?"

"And yet, there are pleasures that are so vivid, so pure, so profound, that cost so little! What can compare to the feeling I experienced a short time ago when that poor creature found herself to be safe here and kissed my hand? That's not all: my happiness has a long future, because tomorrow, the next day, and many days after that, I'll be able to think with delight about how that poor child will feel upon waking up in this tranquil haven in the company of that excellent Madame Georges. Madame Georges will love her tenderly, because unhappy people sympathize with each other."

"Oh, no good deeds were ever better invested than in Madame Georges. She is a noble, courageous woman. A virtuous angel—an angel! I don't get emotional, but I have been moved by the trials of Madame Georges. But your new protégée—well, let's not talk about that, Your Lordship."

"Why not, Murph?"

"Your lordship always does what seems best to you."

"I do what is just," said Rodolphe with a hint of impatience.

"What is just according to you."

"What is just before God and my conscience," Rodolphe responded, severely.

"Listen, Your Lordship, we will never agree about this. So I say again, let's not talk about it."

"On the contrary, I order you to talk about it!" Rodolphe cried, imperiously.

"I am not accustomed to being ordered by my lord to be silent; I should hope that he would not order me to speak," responded Murph, proudly.

---

26. Temple Bar is a significant crossing in London. According to tradition, monarchs approaching London from Westminster stop at Temple Bar before entering the city to receive the blessings of the Lord Mayor. It is not clear, though, how Rodolphe's allusion is relevant here. [TN]

"Mr. Murph!" shouted Rodolphe in growing irritation.

"Your Lordship!"

"You know, Murph, that I do not care for reticence."

"It suits me to be reticent just now," said Murph, brusquely.

"Understand, sir, that if I condescend to talk with you familiarly, it's on the condition that you yourself rise to the level of candor." It is impossible to depict the regal haughtiness of Rodolphe's face as he pronounced these last words.

"Your Lordship, I am fifty years old. I am a gentleman. You should not speak to me in that manner."

"Silence!"

"Your Lordship!"

"Silence!"

"Your Lordship, it is unworthy of you to force a man of good faith to remind you of the services he has performed."

"Your services? Do I not repay them in every case?"

It must be said that Rodolphe had not meant to give these cruel words the humiliating sense they had of placing Murph in the position of a hireling. Unfortunately, the latter interpreted them that way. He flushed in shame and carried his two clenched fists up in front of his bald forehead in an expression of pained indignation. Then, suddenly, in an abrupt change of demeanor, he looked over at Rodolphe, whose noble face was contorted and made ugly by the violence of ferocious disdain. Murph suppressed a sigh and looked at the young man with tender compassion, and said to him in a gentle voice, "Your Lordship, take control of yourself. You're not being reasonable."

These words brought Rodolphe's agitation to a peak. His eyes glared with a savage brilliance, his lips went bloodless, and, advancing on Murph with a threatening gesture, he cried, "Do you dare?"

Murph backed away from Rodolphe and said sharply, as if despite himself, "Your Lordship, REMEMBER THE THIRTEENTH OF JANUARY!!"

These words had a magical effect on Rodolphe. His face, clenched in anger, began to soften. He gave Murph a steady glance, then lowered his head. And then, after a moment of silence, he murmured, in an altered voice, "Ah, sir, you are cruel. And yet I believed . . . and even you . . . you!" Rodolphe could not finish his sentence. His voice died out. He fell onto a stone bench and hid his head in his hands.

"Your Lordship!" cried Murph, sadly. "My good sir, please forgive me! Forgive your old and faithful Murph! It's only because you pushed me to my breaking point, and I feared the consequences of your temper—not for me, alas, but for you—that I said that. I said it without anger, without reproach. I said it against my own wishes and with compassion. Your Lordship, I was wrong to be so sensitive. Good Lord! Who knows you if not I—I, who have never left you since your childhood! Please, have mercy, tell me that you forgive me for having reminded you of that dreadful day. Alas! You've done everything to expiate—"

Rodolphe raised his head. He was very pale. In a soft and sad voice, he said to his companion, "Enough, enough, my old friend. I thank you for having damped down that fatal temper of mine. I won't make any excuses for the hard things that I said to you. You know full well that it is a long way from the heart to the lips, as the good people say where I come from. I was mad. Let's not talk about it anymore."

"Alas! Now you'll be unhappy for a long time. I'm so sorry. I want nothing more than to see you get out of your dark mood, and here I plunge you back into it by being so stupidly sensitive. Heavens! What's the good of being an honest man with gray hair if you can't withstand undeserved reproaches patiently? No," Murph continued with a comic excitement that contrasted with his usual phlegmatic behavior, "no, you have to flatter me all day long. You have to say, 'Mr. Murph, you are a model servant. Mr. Murph, no one is more loyal than you. Mr. Murph, you are an admirable man! Mr. Murph, you are so devilishly handsome. Good Mr. Murph. Brave Mr. Murph! Come on, old parrot, let's get your old gray head scratched.'" Then, remembering the affectionate words Rodolphe had said at the beginning of their conversation, he cried out, in a crescendo of grotesque temper, "But he did call me his good old faithful Murph! And I respond like a boor, just because of a thoughtless outburst! At my age! Heavens, it's enough to make you want to tear your hair out." At this, the worthy gentleman lifted his hands up to his temples.

These words and this gesture signaled, in Murph, a desperation that bordered on a fit. Unfortunately for Murph—or perhaps fortunately—he was almost completely bald. This condition rendered his attack upon his own coiffure somewhat ineffective, to his great and sincere regret. When he tried to do what he proclaimed, his clenched fingers met the surface of a polished scalp that shone as if made of marble. The worthy squire was confused and ashamed of his presumptuousness. He felt like a braggart, a swaggerer. I should hasten to say, in order to exculpate him from any charge of boastfulness, that he had formerly had the thickest, most golden head of hair that had ever graced the scalp of a Yorkshire gentleman.

Ordinarily, Murph's disappointment over the state of his hair would have amused Rodolphe greatly, but his thoughts at the moment were serious and painful. Nevertheless, not wishing to add to the regrets of his companion, he said to him, with a gentle smile, "Listen to me, good Murph. You seemed to praise the good that I'd done for Madame Georges without reservation."

"Your Lordship . . ."

"And yet you were surprised at my interest in that poor, lost girl?"

"Your Lordship, please, have mercy. I was wrong. I was wrong."

"No. I understand, appearances could have fooled you. But since you know my life, since you have aided me with as much loyalty as courage in the project I have undertaken, it is my duty, or, if you prefer, a matter of my gratitude to you, to convince you that I do not act lightly."

"I know that you do not, Your Lordship."

"You know my ideas about the good that people can do. Saving good, unfortunate people who are to be pitied is a fine thing to do. Learning about those who struggle without losing their honor and energy and coming to their aid, sometimes without their knowledge, and preventing misery or temptation from taking hold of them and leading them into crime—that's even better. Rehabilitating people in their own eyes, taking people who have managed to hold on to the purity of their good hearts in the midst of the sort of contempt that withers it, in the midst of poverty that gnaws at them, in the midst of corruption that surrounds them, and making them completely respectable—and, to that end, braving contact oneself with that poverty, that corruption, that filth—that's better still. Pursuing vice, infamy, and crime with single-minded hatred and implacable vengeance, whether they crawl in the mud or lounge in silk upon a throne—that's what I call justice. But blindly rescuing people from a misery they deserve, degrading alms and pity, staining these pure and pious consolations to my wounded soul, prostituting them to those who are unworthy and base—now that would be horrible, impious, sacrilegious. It would make people lose faith in God. And the person who gives needs to make people believe in Him."

"Your Lordship, I didn't mean to say that you had performed your good deeds for unworthy people."

"One more word, my old friend. Madame Georges and the poor girl whom I have placed in her care have come from two extreme points on the spectrum to fall into the common abyss that is unhappiness. One, happy, rich, loved, respected, graced with every virtue, saw her existence withered, broken, and annihilated by the hypocritical scoundrel to whom her oblivious parents married her off. I say with joy that if it weren't for me, that unhappy woman would have perished of poverty and need, for her shame kept her from asking anyone for help."

"Ah, Your Lordship, when we got to that attic, what frightful poverty we saw! It was horrible—horrible! And when after her long illness she woke up, so to speak, right here, in this calm house, what a surprise it was for her! She was so grateful! You are right, Your Lordship, it makes one believe in God to see people in such unfortunate circumstances rescued."

"And so, to rescue them is to do honor to God. I am grateful to Him. Nothing is more heavenly than serene and thoughtful virtue. Nothing is more respectable than a woman like Madame Georges, who, raised by a pious and good mother and trained to do her duty intelligently, has never faltered—not once! And she courageously overcomes the most terrible trials. But isn't pulling from the mire one of those rare beings it pleased him to have graced another way of honoring that which is most divine in God? Doesn't the unhappy child who, left to her own devices, who, tortured, imprisoned, demeaned, soiled, has, in a holy way, kept guard, in the depths of her heart, over the noble seeds that God had planted there—doesn't she also deserve our pity, interest, and respect—yes, respect? If you had heard, from the first glimmer of interest that I showed in that poor creature, from the first honest and friendly word she had ever heard, how the most charming instincts, the purest tastes, the most delicate and poetic thoughts, emerged all at once from her innocent soul, as in spring a thousand wildflowers of the field open in the first rays of the sun—without knowing it! In the hour I spent with her dressed as a poor laborer, I discovered in Fleur-de-Marie troves of goodness, of wisdom—yes, of wisdom, my old Murph. A smile came to my lips and a tear to my eye when she told me, in her gentle prattling way, that I should be setting aside forty sous a day to protect myself from need or temptation. Poor little girl, she said all of that in such a serious, such a meaningful way! She was so sweetly satisfied for having given me good advice, so sweetly happy when I promised her I would follow it! I was moved to tears—oh, moved to tears, I tell you. And people accuse me of being jaded, hard, and rigid? Oh, no, no, thank God! Sometimes I can still feel my heart beating with warmth and generosity. But even you, you've been moved, my old friend. Come on. Fleur-de-Marie won't make Madame Georges jealous. You can interest yourself in her well-being, too."

"It's true, Your Lordship. That request that you save forty sous a day . . . thinking that you were a laborer, instead of trying to get you to spend money on her—yes, that gesture touched me perhaps more than it should have."

"And when I think that the poor child has a rich, respected mother who abandoned her in such an unworthy way! Oh, if that's true—I'll find out the truth, I hope. And I'll tell you how. Oh! If this is true . . . A curse—a curse on that woman! She will have a terrible atonement to undergo. Murph—Murph, I have never felt greater hatred than I do now toward this woman I don't even know. You know, Murph—you know all too well that there are some kinds of revenge that are very dear to me. Some kinds of suffering are precious. I thirst for certain kinds of tears!"

"Alas, Your Lordship!" cried Murph, pained at the expression of infernal viciousness that had appeared on Rodolphe's face as he spoke in this way. "I know it all too well. People who deserve attention and compassion often say of you, 'He's an angel!' But those who deserve contempt and hatred cry out in their despair as they curse you, saying, 'He must be the devil!'"

"Say no more now. Here are Madame Georges and Marie . . . Prepare for our departure. We have to get to Paris early."

CHAPTER 14

SAYING FAREWELL

Thanks to the efforts of Madame Georges, Marie (let us henceforth give Songbird that name) looked like a different person. A pretty, round peasant's bonnet and two thick blond plaits framed the girl's innocent face. A wide muslin shawl covered her breast and disappeared partly underneath the high square flap of a small multicolored taffeta apron. Its blue and pink reflections played off the somber background of the Carmelite's dress she wore, a dress that looked as if it had been made for her.

Her face looked deeply contemplative. There are some kinds of happiness that throw one's soul into an ineffable sadness, a holy melancholy. Rodolphe wasn't surprised at Marie's seriousness; indeed, he had expected it. Had she babbled cheerfully, he would not have thought as highly of her. With perfect tact, he gave her no compliments as to her beauty, even though it had become very striking. He sensed something solemn or august in this form of redemption in which a human soul is torn from the grip of vice.

Madame Georges's serious and resigned features revealed her long suffering and deep troubles; she looked at Marie with a gentleness and compassion that were nearly maternal. The girl's grace and sweetness filled her with great sympathy.

"Here is my child. She would like to thank you for your kindness, Monsieur Rodolphe," said Madame Georges as she presented Marie to him.

At the words "my child," Songbird turned her big eyes slowly toward the woman who was her guardian and gazed upon her for a few moments with an indescribable expression of gratitude on her face.

"Thank you on Marie's behalf, my dear Madame Georges; she is worthy of your tender care, and she will always be worthy of it."

"Monsieur Rodolphe," Marie said in a wavering voice, "you do understand, don't you, that I am at a loss for words?"

"Your emotions tell me everything, Marie."

"Oh! She knows just how providential the happiness is that has come to her," said Madame Georges, who was deeply affected. "Her first act, upon entering my room, was to throw herself onto her knees before my crucifix."

"Because, thanks to you, Monsieur Rodolphe, I can now dare to pray," said Marie, looking at her friend.

Murph suddenly turned away. His phlegmatic English nature and country squire's dignity forbade him to let anyone see how moved he was by Marie's simple words.

Rodolphe said to the girl, "My child, I must have a few words with Madame Georges. My friend Murph will take you on a tour of the farm and introduce you to your future animal friends. We will see you again shortly. So, then, Murph—did you hear me, Murph?"

The good gentleman turned away from them and pretended to blow his nose, making a great honking noise as he did so. He put his handkerchief back in his pocket, pulled his hat down over his eyes, and, turning halfway back toward them, offered his arm to Marie. Murph had cleverly managed to keep both Rodolphe and Madame Georges from noticing his face. Taking the girl's arm, he took her directly toward the farm buildings, walking so quickly that Songbird had to run to keep up with him, just as, earlier in her childhood, she had had to run after the Owl.

"So, Madame Georges, what do you think of Marie?" asked Rodolphe.

"Monsieur Rodolphe, as I told you, no sooner had she walked into my room than, seeing my cross, she ran over and knelt down. I cannot tell you how spontaneous and naturally pious that gesture was. I understood instantly that her soul had not been degraded. And also, Monsieur Rodolphe, nothing about her gratitude toward you is exaggerated or forced. She is entirely sincere. One more example will prove to you how powerful her religious instinct is: I said to her, 'You must have been shocked and delighted when Monsieur Rodolphe told you that you would be staying here permanently. What a deep impression that must have made on you!' And she answered me, 'Oh, yes. When Monsieur Rodolphe told me that, something happened to me, I can't explain it, but I felt arise within me a kind of pious happiness, the holy awe that I used to feel when I went to church—when I could go to church, that is,' she added, 'because you understand, madame—' I didn't let her finish her sentence, seeing her face so full of shame. 'I know, my child—and I will always call you my child if you're willing to let me—I know that you have suffered a great deal, but God blesses those who love and fear him, those who have been unhappy and those who repent.'"

"Well, then, my good Madame Georges, I am doubly happy about what I've done. That poor girl will make you care for her. You have only to sow, and so shall you reap. Your intuitions are correct. Her instincts are excellent."

"The thing that affected me even more, Monsieur Rodolphe, is that she hasn't let herself ask the slightest question about you, even though she had to have been extremely curious. Struck by her incredibly tactful reserve, I wanted to know how conscious it was. I asked her, 'You must be very curious to know who your mysterious benefactor is, aren't you?' 'I know who he is,' she answered with a charming innocence. 'His name is *my benefactor.*'"

"So, then, you will come to care for her. You're a fine woman. Her company will be good for you, too. She'll take your mind off of your heart's troubles."

"Yes, I'll take care of her the same way I would have taken care of *him*," said Madame Georges, in a heartbreaking tone.

Rodolphe took her hand. "There, there, don't be discouraged. Even though our search hasn't turned anything up yet, maybe one day . . ."

Madame Georges shook her head sadly and said, bitterly, "My poor son would have been twenty years old by now!"

"Say, rather, he *is* twenty years old."

"From your lips to God's ear, Monsieur Rodolphe!"

"I dearly hope God will grant my wish! Yesterday I had gone looking for a fellow who goes by the name of Red-Arm. I was told that he might be able to give me some information on the whereabouts of your son. I didn't find him, but as I left his place and then got into a little tussle, I found that unfortunate child."

"Alas! And also so much the better! At least your resolution to help me ended up putting you in the way of rescuing another unlucky person."

"I had long wanted to explore the world of our impoverished classes. I was nearly certain that I could find a few souls among them to carry off from old Scratch. I like to thwart Satan now and then," said Rodolphe, smiling. "I enjoy making away with some of his best prizes." Then he continued, in a more serious tone, "You haven't had any news from Rochefort?"

"None at all," said Madame Georges in a low, quavering voice.

"So much the better! That monster will have perished on the mud banks, trying to escape. His description has been circulated far and wide. He's a dangerous enough criminal to warrant a full-scale search to find him, and it's been about six months since he got out of the penal—"

Rodolphe stopped himself from pronouncing this horrible expression.

"Penal colony! Oh! You can say the word. Penal colony!" cried the unhappy woman with horror and in an almost demented voice. "The father of my son! Ah! If the unhappy child is still alive—if he, like myself, hasn't changed his name—how shameful! And that's nothing. Maybe his father has kept his horrible promise. Ah! Monsieur Rodolphe, forgive me, but despite your good deeds, I'm still dreadfully unhappy!"

"Poor woman, try to stay calm."

"Sometimes I feel terribly afraid. I figure that my husband has escaped from Rochefort safe and sound. I fear that he will hunt me down and kill me, just as he might have killed our son. For in the end, what else did he do with him?"

"This mystery will be the death of me," said Rodolphe, pensively. "For what reason did that scoundrel carry off your child—it was fifteen years ago, you said? He was trying to get away through a foreign country. A child of that age could only have made his escape more difficult."

"Alas, Monsieur Rodolphe, when my husband"—the poor woman shuddered as she said this word—"was arrested at the border, brought to Paris, and thrown into the prison, and they let me in to see him, he uttered these horrible words to me: 'I kidnapped your child because you love him, and it's a way to make you send me money that he may or may not benefit from, depending on my whim. Whether he lives or dies won't change anything for you. But if he lives, he will be in good hands. You will drown in the shame of your son as you have in that of his father.' Alas! A month later, my husband was sentenced to life in prison. Since then, all of the earnest solicitations and prayers that my letters contained have been in vain. I have managed to learn nothing of the fate of my child. Ah! Monsieur Rodolphe, where is my son right now? Those horrifying words keep coming back into my mind: 'You will drown in the shame of your son as you have in that of his father.'"

"But that would be a senseless atrocity. Why would he want to infect your child with vice? Why would he want to corrupt him? Why, most of all, would he want to carry him off?"

"I've just told you, Monsieur Rodolphe: in order to force me to send him money. Although he ruined me, I still have a few last resources for him to drain. Despite his wickedness, I can't believe he wouldn't use at least a portion of them to raise our poor son."

"And your son doesn't have any mark or special feature that would serve to identify him?"

"The only one is the sign I told you about, Monsieur Rodolphe. It's a little lapis lazuli cross that hangs around his neck on a silver chain. That relic, blessed by the pope, came down to me from my mother. She wore it when she was little and was very attached to it. I wore it, too. I put it around the neck of my son! Alas! That talisman has lost its power."

"Who knows, dear woman? God is all-powerful."

"Providence did put me on your path, Monsieur Rodolphe."

"Too late, my good Madame Georges, too late. I would have spared you years of sorrow, perhaps."

"Ah, Monsieur Rodolphe, my cup runneth over, thanks to you."

"What have I done? I bought this farm. Back when you were prosperous, you liked to make the most of your belongings. You agreed to serve as my manager here. Thanks to your excellent care, to your intelligent stewardship, this little farm earns me an income of—"

"Earns *you* what, monsieur?" said Madame Georges, interrupting him. "Am I not the one who hands over the rent to our good Father Laporte? And doesn't he distribute that whole sum in alms, according to your orders?"

"Well, isn't it an excellent arrangement? But you've let the dear priest know that I've arrived, haven't you? I need to recommend my protégée to him. He's received my letter?"

"Mr. Murph brought it over to him this morning when he got here."

"In that letter, I told our good priest, in a few words, the story of that poor child. I wasn't sure I would be able to come here today. If I hadn't been able to come myself, Murph would have brought her here."

A farmworker interrupted this conversation, which had taken place in a garden. "Madame, the priest is waiting to see you."

"Have the post-horses arrived yet, my boy?" asked Rodolphe.

"Yes, Monsieur Rodolphe. They are being harnessed." The worker left the garden.

Madame Georges, the priest, and the inhabitants of the farm knew Fleur-de-Marie's protector only under the name of Monsieur Rodolphe. Murph's discretion was impeccable. As punctiliously as he referred to Rodolphe as "Your Lordship" in private meetings with him, he was careful to call him nothing but "Monsieur Rodolphe" among strangers.

"I forgot to warn you, my dear Madame Georges," said Rodolphe as he neared the house. "Marie has weak lungs. The deprivation and poverty she has endured have weakened her health. This morning, at the height of the day, I was taken aback by how pale she is, even though her cheeks were bright pink. Her eyes seemed to me also to shine rather feverishly. We'll need to take very good care of her."

"Count on me, Monsieur Rodolphe. But thank God it's nothing serious. At her age, in the countryside, with some fresh air, some rest, and some happiness, she'll recover quickly."

"I believe she will. Nevertheless, I don't trust your country doctors. I'll tell Murph to send a skilled doctor here, and he'll tell us the best course to follow. You will give me frequent news of Marie's health. In a while, once she's fully rested and calm, we will begin to think about her future. Perhaps it might be best for her to remain here with you permanently, if her character and conduct suit you."

"That would be my wish, Monsieur Rodolphe. She would take the place of the child I still ache for every day."

"Well, then, let's hope so for you and for her."

As Rodolphe and Madame Georges approached the farm, Murph and Marie were arriving from a different direction. Marie was animated from the walk. Rodolphe pointed out to Madame Georges the color in her cheeks. Though they glowed vividly, their rosiness was limited to a small area and contrasted greatly with her general pallor.

The good gentleman let go of Songbird's arm and whispered into Rodolphe's ear, in an almost confused manner, "That little girl has bewitched me. I can't say whose plight affects me more, hers or Madame Georges's. I was an unfeeling beast before."

"Don't pull your hair out over that, old Murph," said Rodolphe, smiling as he shook the squire's hand. Madame Georges, leaning on Marie's arm, entered the small salon on the ground floor where Father Laporte was waiting. Murph went to see to the preparations for their departure, while Madame Georges, Marie, Rodolphe, and the priest remained in the room.

Simple but very comfortable, the small living room was draped and furnished in chintz, like the rest of the house—just as Rodolphe had described it to Songbird. A thick carpet covered the floor, a good fire burned in the fireplace, and two enormous bouquets of asters of every color, placed in two crystal vases, infused the room with their light balsamic fragrance. Through the partially closed green shutters, one could see the field, the little river, and, beyond that, the riverbanks covered with chestnut trees.

Father Laporte, sitting next to the chimney, was eighty years old. He had served this poor parish since the last years of the Revolution. There was nothing in the world more venerable or more gently imposing than his elderly, gaunt, and slightly suffering face, framed by long white hair that fell on the collar of his black cassock, which was mended in more than one place. The priest preferred, he said, to put two or three poor children in warm clothing over playing the dandy, which is what he called keeping his cassocks for less than two or three years. The good priest was so old that his hands trembled constantly. There was something touching in this movement. And when, from time to time, he lifted them as he spoke, it looked as if he were giving his blessing.

Rodolphe watched Marie with interest. If he had known her less well, or if, rather, he had divined less accurately who she was, he might have been astonished to see her approach the priest in a sort of pious serenity. Marie's admirable instinct told her that shame ends where repentance and expiation begin.

"Father," Rodolphe began, respectfully. "Madame Georges wishes to take this girl into her care. I ask you to give her your blessing."

"She has the right to it, sir, as do all who come to us. God's clemency is inexhaustible, my dear child. He proved it to you by not abandoning you in your many painful experiences. I know all about it." He took Marie's hand in his trembling, venerable hands. "This generous man who saved you has embodied the words of the Holy Scripture: 'The Lord is nigh unto all of them that call upon him. He will fulfill the desire of them that fear him; he will also hear their cry and save them.'[27] Now, it is up to you to merit his goodness by your conduct. You will always be able to find me for encouragement and sustenance, on the righteous path upon which you enter. You will have in Madame Georges a daily example, and in me a vigilant counselor. The Lord will fulfill his work."

27. Psalms 145:18–19. [TN]

"And I will pray for those who have taken pity on me and who have led me to him, my father," said Songbird. In an almost involuntary movement, she fell on her knees before the priest. Her emotion was overpowering; she was overcome with sobbing. Madame Georges, Rodolphe, and the priest were all profoundly touched.

"Get up, my dear child," said the priest. "You will soon merit absolution from the great sins of which you were more the victim than the transgressor. For once again, as the prophet said, 'The Lord upholdeth all that fall and raiseth up those that he bowed down.'"[28]

"Farewell, Marie," said Rodolphe to Marie as he gave her a little gold Jeannette cross[29] attached to a black velvet ribbon. He added, "Keep this little cross to remember me by. I've had the date of your deliverance—of your redemption—engraved on it this morning. Soon, I will return to you."

Marie took the cross to her lips.

At this moment, Murph opened the door to the living room. "Monsieur Rodolphe, the horses are ready."

"Farewell, Father. Farewell, good Madame Georges. I commend this child to you. Farewell again, Marie."

The venerable priest, leaning on the arms of Madame Georges and Songbird, who were supporting his unsteady steps, left the living room to watch Rodolphe depart. The last rays of the sun were casting a vivid color on this interesting and sad group. Here were an old priest, a symbol of charity, forgiveness, and eternal hope; a woman who had endured all the trials that could befall a wife or a mother; and a young woman, barely more than a child, formerly thrown into the abyss of vice by poverty and by the squalid persistence of crime.

Rodolphe got into the carriage. Murph took his place at his side. The horses took off at a gallop.

---

28. Psalms 145:14. [TN]

29. This is a pendant in the form of a heart with a Latin cross hanging from it. [TN]

CHAPTER 15

THE MEETING

The day after he had left Songbird in the care of Madame Georges, Rodolphe, still dressed in worker's clothes, showed up precisely at noon at the door of the Flower-Basket cabaret, not far from the Bercy barrier. The day before, at ten in the evening, the Slasher had gone right to the meeting, as Rodolphe had asked him to do. What follows will make known the consequences of that meeting.

It was noon. The rain was coming down in torrents. The Seine, swollen with the almost continuous rainfall, had reached an enormous height and was flooding part of the pier. Rodolphe looked out impatiently from time to time from the side of the gate. Finally, spotting in the distance a man and a woman who were coming toward him sheltered by an umbrella, he recognized the Owl and the Schoolmaster.

These two characters had undergone complete transformations. The criminal had left behind his foul clothing and brutal, ferocious swagger. He wore a long waistcoat of green beaver cloth and a round hat. His tie and his shirt were immaculately white. If not for the appalling hideousness of his features and the savage gleam in his always sharp and shifting glance, one would take this man, with his calm and confident step, for an upright citizen. Also decked out in her Sunday best, the one-eyed hag was wearing a white bonnet and a large shawl made with silk thread in the manner of cashmere, and had in her hand a large shopping basket.

The rain had stopped for a moment. Rodolphe overcame a twinge of disgust and walked straight over to the dreadful couple. The Schoolmaster had substituted for the jargon of the joint a way of speaking that was nearly learned—which was all the more horrible as it suggested that he had a cultivated intelligence and also made his speech contrast with the criminal's bloodcurdling boasting. When Rodolphe approached him, the Schoolmaster greeted him with a deep bow. The Owl curtsied to him.

"Sir, I am your very humble servant," said the Schoolmaster. "To render you my obligations, I am honored to make your acquaintance, or rather, to make it once again, since the day before yesterday you bestowed upon me two blows that would have felled a rhinoceros. But let us not talk about that right now. It was just a joke on your part, I'm sure—a little joke. Let's not think about it again, for serious business brings us together. I saw the Slasher last night at eleven at the joint. I told him to come here this morning to meet me, in case he wanted to collaborate with us. It seems his refusal is a decided one."

"You accept my terms, then?"

"If you wish, monsieur. What is your name?"

"Rodolphe."

"Monsieur Rodolphe, we were on our way into the Flower-Basket. Neither I nor the lady has had our lunch yet. Let's talk about our business over a snack."

"With pleasure."

"And we can always continue our discussion as we walk. Without casting blame, you and the Slasher owe my wife and me compensation. You made us lose more than two thousand francs. The Owl had a meeting near Saint-Ouen with an important gentleman in mourning who had come looking for you the other night at the joint. He offered us two thousand francs to do something to you. The Slasher fairly explained this to me. But, now that I think of it, Finette, go and get us a booth at the Flower-Basket and order us some lunch: some cutlets, a piece of veal, a salad, and two bottles of the finest Beaune. We'll meet you in there."

The Owl did not let Rodolphe out of her sight for an instant. She left them after exchanging a glance with the Schoolmaster. The latter continued: "I was telling you, Mr. Rodolphe, that the Slasher had edified me on the matter of the two thousand francs."

"What does 'edify' mean?"

"Oh, that's right. My language is perhaps a little elevated for you. I meant that the Slasher had more or less explained to me what the tall man in mourning wanted to do to you for his two thousand francs."

"Good, good."

"It's not so good, young man. After the Slasher met the Owl near Saint-Ouen yesterday morning, he didn't leave her for a second once he saw that tall man in mourning approaching. Because of him, the tall man didn't dare come over to her. That's why you need to help me make up the two thousand francs, and that's not counting the five hundred francs for the wallet we were supposed to return, which we wouldn't have given back in any case, seeing as there were papers in there that looked as if they were worth even more."

"So there were valuable papers in there?"

"The wallet contained documents that looked decidedly peculiar, although most of them were written in English. I've got them in here," said the bandit, tapping one of the side pockets of his waistcoat.

Rodolphe was delighted to learn that the Schoolmaster still had in his possession the papers seized from Tom the day before. They were very valuable to him, indeed. His instructions to the Slasher had been only to prevent Tom from connecting with the Owl. That meant that the

Owl still had the wallet, and Rodolphe hoped to take possession of it himself.

"I'll keep these papers, just in case they might be worth something," the criminal said. "For I've discovered the address of the man in mourning, and one way or another I'll meet up with him again."

"We can do some business right here, if you like. If our plan works, I'll buy those papers from you. I know that guy, so they will mean more to me than to you."

"We'll see. In the meantime, let's get back to getting our ducks all in a row."

"All right. So I had made an excellent proposition to the Slasher. At first he accepted it, but then he reconsidered."

"He's always had his own way of thinking."

"Well, between you and I, as he changed his mind, he pointed out to me—"

"You mean, 'between you and me.'"

"Well, you are up on your grammar."

"The Schoolmaster, at your service."

"So, between you and me, he pointed out to me that even if he didn't like hot bread, that was no reason to make others turn their noses up at it. He said you could give me a hand."

"And would it be indiscreet of me to inquire why you wanted to grant the Slasher an interview yesterday morning at Saint-Ouen? That was the basis of his opportunity to meet the Owl. He seemed uncomfortable discussing that subject."

Rodolphe bit his lips imperceptibly and answered the Schoolmaster with a shrug of his shoulders. "I'm not surprised. I had only told him half of my plan. You understand. I wasn't sure he would want in on it."

"That was prudent of you."

"All the more prudent, since I had two strings to my bow."

"No, really?"

"Absolutely."

"You are a cautious man. So you granted the Slasher an interview at Saint-Ouen because . . ."

After hesitating for a moment, Rodolphe fortunately came up with a plausible cover story to explain away the Slasher's clumsiness. "Here's the plan. The job I propose is quite a good one, because the owner of the house in question is in the countryside. My only fear is that he would have returned. In order to be sure, I said to myself, 'There's just one thing I need to do.'"

"That was to ascertain that the said home owner was in point of fact in the countryside."

"You said it. So I left for Pierrefitte, where he has his country house. My cousin is a servant there—you understand?"

"Perfectly, you slyboots. And so?"

"So my cousin said that her master wouldn't be returning to Paris until the day after tomorrow."

"The day after tomorrow?"

"Yes."

"Very good. But to return to my question: why did you grant the Slasher an interview at Saint-Ouen?"

"You're not too swift, are you? How far is it from Pierrefitte to Saint-Ouen?"

"About a league."

"And from Saint-Ouen to Paris?"

"The same."

"So? If I hadn't found anyone home in Pierrefitte, that is, if I'd found the house empty, there would be a good haul to be made there, too—not as much to be had as in Paris, but still pretty good. I was coming back to Saint-Ouen to find the Slasher, who was waiting for me there. We were going back to Pierrefitte on a back road I know and—"

"I understand. If, on the other hand, the robbery were to be in Paris?"

"We would have gotten to the Étoile barrier via the chemin de la Révolte, and from there we'd take the allée des Veuves."

"It's right close by. Quite simple. At Saint-Ouen, you were prepared for either of the two separate plans. That was very clever of you. Now I understand why the Slasher was present at Saint-Ouen. So the house on the allée des Veuves will be empty until the day after tomorrow."

"Empty, except for the doorkeeper."

"That goes without saying. And it will be a profitable affair?"

"My cousin speaks of sixty thousand francs in gold in her master's office."

"And you know the comings and goings of these people?"

"Like the back of my hand. My cousin has been there for a year. Hearing her talk about the amounts of money her master took out of the bank to invest elsewhere, that's when I got this idea. Since the doorkeeper's a big guy, I talked with the Slasher. After hemming and hawing, he agreed, but then he balked. But at least he'd never sell out a friend."

"No, he's not a bad guy. But now we come to the point. I don't know if you feel the way I do, but this morning air has given me an appetite."

The Owl was right at the threshold of the cabaret. "Come this way," she said. "This way! I've ordered our lunch."

Rodolphe wanted to let the bandit go in before him. He had his reasons for this, but the Schoolmaster was so insistent on declining this courtesy that Rodolphe went in first.

Before sitting down at the table, the Schoolmaster tapped lightly on both partitions of the booth so as to get a sense of how thick and soundproof they might be.

"We won't have to speak too quietly," he said. "The partition isn't too thin. They'll serve us in a minute, and then we'll be able to have our conversation without any interruption."

A cabaret waitress brought them their lunch. Before the door was closed, Rodolphe saw the collier, Murph, solemnly seated at a table in a neighboring booth.

The room in which the scene we are recounting occurred was long, narrow, and illuminated by the window that looked out on the street and faced the door. The Owl had her back turned away from the casement window, the Schoolmaster was on one side of the table, and Rodolphe was on the other. The waitress left the room. The bandit got up, took his place setting, and moved over to sit next to Rodolphe so as to block the door quite effectively.

"We'll talk better this way," he said, "and we won't have to speak so loudly."

"And you can put yourself between me and the door in order to prevent me from leaving," Rodolphe answered, icily.

The Schoolmaster nodded. Then, taking a stiletto as long and thick as a goose's plume, with a wooden handle that disappeared under his hairy fingers, partway out of his pocket, he said, "You see this?"

"Yes."

"Consider it a warning for amateurs."

And, frowning in such a way as to wrinkle his broad, flat forehead, which looked like a tiger's, he gestured meaningfully.

"Watch out for me, too. I'm my man's knife-sharpener," added the Owl.

With an easy motion, Rodolphe slid his hand underneath his shirt and drew out the double-barreled pistol he had there. He showed it to the Schoolmaster and the Owl, and then slid it back into the pocket under his shirt.

"We should be able to come to terms, I see," the criminal said. "But you still don't understand me fully. Let's suppose the impossible. If I were to get arrested—I don't care whether you set the trap or not—I'll ice you with this pick!" And he glared ferociously at Rodolphe.

"And I would jump on him to help you, Killer!" cried the Owl.

Rodolphe did not bother to reply. He merely shrugged his shoulders, poured himself a glass of wine, and drank it down. This sangfroid impressed the Schoolmaster.

"I was just warning you."

"Yeah, yeah. Put your chicken sticker away. There are no chickens here. I'm an old rooster, and I've got spurs, my boy," said Rodolphe. "Now, let's get back to business."

"Indeed, let's get back to business. But don't speak ill of my chicken sticker. It doesn't make any noise, it doesn't get anyone's attention."

"And we do nice, clean work with it, don't we, Killer?" added the Owl.

"By the way, is it true that you know who Songbird's parents are?"

"My man put two letters that mention that in the wallet of that tall gent in black. But she'll never see them, that little morsel. I would sooner rip out her eyes with my own two hands. Oh! When I find her back at the joint, I'll settle her account."

"Oh, that again? Finette, we're talking and talking, but business isn't progressing."

"Can we chat in front of her?" asked Rodolphe.

"With complete confidence. She's tried and true, and she can be of great help to us when we need a lookout or need information, or when we need a fence to hold or sell the things we steal. She has all the qualities of an excellent housewife. Good old Finette!" the bandit added, holding his hand out to the horrible old woman. "You have no idea how helpful she has been to me. But take off your shawl, Finette, or you might catch a chill when you leave. Put it on the chair with your shopping bag." The Owl took off her shawl.

Despite his presence of mind and self-control, Rodolphe couldn't restrain a surprised start when he saw, hanging around the old woman's neck from a thick chain of imitation gold on a silver ring, a little lapis lazuli cross that perfectly matched the description of the one that Madame Georges's son was wearing around his neck when he disappeared.

Upon making this discovery, a sudden idea occurred to Rodolphe. According to the Slasher, the Schoolmaster had escaped from prison six months ago. And he had evaded all police investigations by disfiguring himself. And it was six months ago that Madame Georges's husband had disappeared from prison, with no one having any idea as to his whereabouts. Thinking about this strange coincidence, Rodolphe considered that the Schoolmaster could well be the husband of the unfortunate woman. That wretch had belonged to the leisure classes—and the Schoolmaster expressed himself as if he were very well educated. This memory recalled another: Rodolphe remembered further that a trembling Madame Georges, telling him one day of her husband's arrest, spoke of the violent resistance the monster had offered and of his near escape, thanks to his herculean strength. If this criminal were indeed Madame Georges's husband, he would certainly know what had become of his son. In addition, the Schoolmaster was keeping some papers relating to Songbird's birth in the wallet he had stolen from the foreigner known as Tom. Rodolphe thus had new and serious motives for persevering in his projects.

Fortunately, the criminal, who was serving the Owl, did not notice his preoccupied state of mind. Rodolphe said to the one-eyed hag, "My, that's a beautiful chain you have on."

"Beautiful, and cheap," said the old woman, laughing. "It's fool's gold. I'm waiting for my man to give me a real one."

"It depends on this fellow, Finette. If everything works out, we'll have no need to worry."

"It's remarkable what a good imitation it is," said Rodolphe, persisting in his query. "And what's that little blue thing at the bottom?"

"It's a gift from my man, a placeholder for the onion[30] he's going to give me. Right, Killer?"

Rodolphe found his suspicions partly confirmed. He waited anxiously to hear the Schoolmaster's reaction. The latter answered, his mouth full of food, "You have to keep this even when you get the onion, Finette. It's a talisman. It brings good luck."

"A talisman?" Rodolphe asked, nonchalantly. "You believe in talismans? But where the devil did you find this one? Give me the address of the maker so I can get one."

"They're not making these anymore, my friend. The shop is closed. The jewel, as you can see, is very old. It goes back three generations. I am very attached to it. It's a family heirloom," he added with a hideous smile. "That's why I've given it to Finette. It's to bring her good luck in the enterprises she aids me in so skillfully. You'll have the chance to see her on the job—you'll see her in action if we conduct a commercial operation together. But to get back to our business: you've said that on the allée des Veuves . . ."

"There's a house—it's number seventeen—that a guy with deep pockets lives in. His name is . . . Monsieur . . ."

"I won't be so indiscreet as to ask his name. There are, you say, sixty thousand francs in gold in an office?"

"Sixty thousand francs in gold!" said the Owl.

Rodolphe nodded.

"And you know the comings and goings of this house?"

"Very well."

"And will it be difficult to get in?"

"There's a seven-foot wall on the allée des Veuves side, a garden, the windows all on one floor. The house only has one level."

"And there's only one doorkeeper to guard this treasure?"

"Yes!"

"And what would be your plan of attack, young man?" asked the Schoolmaster, carelessly.

"It's very simple. Climb up from the wall in the back, pick the lock of the door of the house or force the exterior shutters."

"And if the doorkeeper wakes up?" asked the Schoolmaster, looking closely at the young man.

"It'll be his problem," said the latter, making a gesture that spoke volumes. "Does this suit you?"

---

30. Watch. [TN]

"You will understand if I say that I cannot give you an answer before I have examined the matter thoroughly myself, or rather, with the assistance of my woman. But if everything you've told me is correct, it seems like a good idea to strike while the irons are hot—tonight." And the bandit looked closely at Rodolphe.

"Tonight is impossible," said the latter, coldly.

"Why not, since the owner is not returning until the day after tomorrow?"

"Yes, but I can't tonight."

"Really? Well, I can't make it tomorrow night."

"Why not?"

"For the same reason you can't make it tonight," the criminal said, snickering.

After a moment's reflection, Rodolphe answered him, "All right! Let's get it done. It's on for tonight. Where will we meet?"

"Meet? We'll never be apart," said the Schoolmaster.

"What do you mean?"

"What good would it do to separate now? If the weather clears up a bit, we can have a stroll over to have a look at the allée des Veuves. You'll see how my woman knows her way around. Once we've finished, we'll come back to play a hand of cards and grab a bite in a cellar I know on the Champs-Élysées, right by the river. Since the allée des Veuves empties out early, we can wind our way back over there around ten."

"So I'll join up with you at nine."

"Do you want to do this business together or not?"

"Yes. Of course."

"All right, then. We won't leave each other's side before this evening, or else . . ."

"Or else?"

"I'll think you're trying to roll me in some way, and that that's the reason you want to take off."

"If I wanted to lay a trap for you, what's to keep me from doing it tonight?"

"Everything. You weren't expecting me to propose doing the job so early. And if we stay together, you won't have the chance to warn anyone."

"You don't trust me?"

"Not one bit. But it could be possible that there's some truth to what you're telling me, and half of sixty thousand francs is worth the risk. I'd like to give it a try, but it's tonight or never. If it's never, I'll know how much I can depend on you, and one of these days, I'll serve you a dish of my own making."

"And I'll return the courtesy—you may count on that."

"This is all cheap patter," said the Owl. "I agree with Killer. It's tonight or never."

Rodolphe found himself in a cruel bind: if he let this chance to seize the Schoolmaster slip away from him, no doubt he would never have such an opportunity again. In the future, the criminal would be on his guard, or he could even be recognized, arrested, and taken back to prison. He would take with him all the secrets that Rodolphe so much wanted to know. Trusting in his fate, his skills, and his courage, he said to the Schoolmaster, "It's a deal. We won't leave each other's side from now until this evening."

"Then I'm your man. But look, it's almost two o'clock. It's a long way to go from here to the allée des Veuves. And it's pouring rain. Let's pay the bill and get a cab."

"If we take a cab, I'll be able to smoke a cigar first."

"Certainly," said the Schoolmaster. "Finette doesn't mind the smell of tobacco."

"Good! I'm going to go out to find some cigars," said Rodolphe, getting up.

"Don't trouble yourself," said the Schoolmaster, blocking him. "Finette will go."

Rodolphe sat down again. The Schoolmaster had figured out his intent. The Owl went out.

"What a great lady I've got here, huh?" said the scoundrel. "And she's so indulgent! She'd see herself burned alive for me."

"Speaking of fire, isn't it very hot in here?" said Rodolphe as he hid his hands under his shirt. Then, as he continued talking with the Schoolmaster, he took a pencil and a piece of paper from his vest pocket and, so that no one could see, he wrote out a few hasty words. He was careful to space the letters so as not to superimpose them on each other, for he was writing inside his shirt and without being able to see. This letter got by the Schoolmaster's watchfulness. But Rodolphe still had to get it to its address. He got up, went up to the window mechanically, and began to hum, accompanying himself by tapping on the glass.

The Schoolmaster came over to look through the window and said nonchalantly to Rodolphe, "What's that song you're singing?"

"I'm singing 'You Won't Get My Rose.'"

"It's a very pretty tune. I was just wondering whether it would have the effect of getting passersby to turn around."

"I wouldn't claim to have such talent."

"You're wrong, young man. You're drumming away pretty loudly on the windowpanes. But I'm thinking about tonight. The guardian at the house in the allée des Veuves might be a determined type. If he kicks back, all you have is a pistol. And that's pretty noisy, whereas a tool like mine (and he showed Rodolphe the handle of his dagger) doesn't make a ruckus. It won't bother a soul."

"Are you saying that you're going to kill him?" Rodolphe exclaimed. "If that's what you're thinking, forget about it. Nothing doing. Count me out."

"But if he wakes up?"

"We'll run away."

"That's better. I hadn't understood you. It's better to sort things out now, in advance. So we're talking about a simple breaking and entering."

"Nothing more."

"That's how we'll do it, then."

"And since I won't leave your side for a second," thought Rodolphe, "I can keep you from spilling blood."

CHAPTER 16

PREPARATIONS

The Owl returned to the booth with the tobacco.

"It looks like it's not raining anymore," said Rodolphe, lighting his cigar. "Let's go find a cab ourselves. It would give us a chance to stretch our legs."

"What do you mean, it's not raining?" responded the Schoolmaster. "Are you blind? Do you think I'm going to let Finette catch cold? To risk such a precious life—and ruin a brand-new shawl?"

"You're right, my man. It's not fit for a dog outside."

"All right, then. When the waitress comes back and we pay her, we'll have her hail us a cab," said Rodolphe.

"Now you have said something prudent, young man. We can go wander a bit around the allée des Veuves."

The waitress entered. Rodolphe gave her a hundred sous.

"Ah, sir, you are taking advantage. I can't allow it," cried the Schoolmaster.

"Come on, it's my turn!"

"Well, in that case, I assent. But it's on the condition that something equal is on me at a little tavern I know on the Champs-Élysées. It's an excellent spot."

"Fine, it's a deal."

After having paid the waitress, they left. Rodolphe wanted to be polite and let the Owl walk out in front of him. The Schoolmaster wouldn't allow it and followed on his heels, watching his slightest movements.

The innkeeper also kept a wine bar. Among several customers, a collier with a dirty face and a hat pulled low over his eyes was paying his tab at the counter as our three characters appeared. Despite the Schoolmaster's and the Owl's careful surveillance, Rodolphe, who was walking ahead of the hideous couple, exchanged a rapid and imperceptible glance with Murph.

The door of the cab was open. Rodolphe stopped, determined this time to get in last, inasmuch as the collier was slowly approaching him. Ultimately, the Owl went first, but only after much coaxing. Rodolphe was obliged to follow her, for the Schoolmaster whispered in his ear, "Do you really want me to be suspicious of you?"

Rodolphe got into the car. The collier advanced, whistling at the threshold of the door, and looked at Rodolphe with a surprised and anxious glance.

"Where to, boss?" asked the driver.

Rodolphe answered, in a loud voice, "Go to the allée des—"

"To the allée des Acacias, in the Bois de Boulogne," cried the Schoolmaster, interrupting him. Then he added, "You will be well paid, driver."

The door was closed. "Why the devil did you say where we were going in front of those street idlers?" asked the Schoolmaster. "Should everything come out tomorrow, that kind of clue can be the death of us! Ah, young man, young man, you're not very careful!"

The coach began to move. Rodolphe responded, "It's true, that hadn't occurred to me. But my cigar is going to turn the two of you into smoked kippers. Do you mind if we open a window?" And Rodolphe, putting his words into action, let a tiny little piece of folded paper fall out of the car. This was the piece of paper on which he had had a moment to write a few words in pencil under his shirt.

The Schoolmaster's gaze was so perceptive that, in spite of Rodolphe's impassive expression, the criminal must have managed to spot a momentary glint of triumph, because he stuck his head out of the window and called to the driver, "Stop! There's someone behind your car."

Rodolphe trembled, but he joined the Schoolmaster in calling out to the driver.

The coach stopped. The driver got onto his seat, looked around, and said, "No, boss, there's nobody there."

"Damn it, I'm going out to make sure," said the Schoolmaster as he jumped down into the street. He didn't see anyone or anything amiss. Since the moment at which Rodolphe had tossed his note out the window, the car had traveled several feet. The Schoolmaster decided he had been mistaken. "You may laugh at me, but I could swear that there was someone following us."

At that moment, the cab turned onto a cross street. As the coach disappeared, Murph, who had not let it out of his sight and who had perceived Rodolphe's action, ran over and grabbed the little note hidden in the crack between two cobblestones.

After a quarter of an hour, the Schoolmaster said to the cabdriver, "You know, driver, we've changed our mind. Take us to the Place de la Madeleine!"

Rodolphe looked at him in amazement.

"Indeed, young man, you see that from this place one could go in a thousand different directions. If anyone suspected us, the cabdriver's deposition would be useless."

As the cab approached the gate, a tall man with a swarthy-looking face who was wearing a long, whitish frock coat and a hat pulled down over his eyes passed quickly along the road. He was bent over the mane of a large and magnificent hunting horse that ran at a great speed.

"A beautiful horse and a good rider!" said Rodolphe as he leaned into the window, following Murph with his eyes. "What a pace that big guy is going at. Did you see?"

"Heavens, he went by so quickly," the Schoolmaster said, "that I didn't even notice him."

Rodolphe managed to disguise his joy. Murph had deciphered the nearly hieroglyphic signs in which he had written his note. Now certain that the cab was not being followed, the Schoolmaster relaxed. Wanting to emulate the Owl, who was napping—or rather, who seemed to be napping—he said to Rodolphe, "Excuse me, young man, but the motion of a carriage always does the same thing to me. It makes me sleep like a baby."

Under cover of this false nap, the bandit planned to examine the face of his companion, to see whether it would betray any emotion. Rodolphe saw through this ruse and answered, "I got up early this morning. I'm sleepy, too. I'll do the same thing as you." And he closed his eyes.

Soon the loud breathing coming from the Schoolmaster and the Owl, who were snoring in unison, took Rodolphe in so completely that he believed that his companions were sound asleep. He opened his eyelids partially. The Schoolmaster and the Owl, despite their loud snoring, had their eyes open wide, and they were exchanging mysterious signs by means of their fingers, which they were folding or placing in the palms of their hands in a peculiar manner.

Suddenly, the symbolic speech came to a halt. The bandit, sensing no doubt from some imperceptible clue that Rodolphe was not sleeping, called out in laughter, "Ah-ha, my friend! You're testing your partners, aren't you?"

"It shouldn't surprise you, you who snore with your eyes open."

"It's different with me. I'm a sleepwalker."

The cab stopped at the Place de la Madeleine. The rain had stopped for a moment, but the clouds, blown by the violent winds, were so black and so low that it was as dark as night. Rodolphe, the Owl, and the Schoolmaster headed over toward the Cours-la-Reine.

"Young man, I have an idea that isn't half bad," said the bandit.

"What is it?"

"A way to assure myself that what you told us about the inside of the house on the allée des Veuves is correct."

"Would you like to go there now under some pretext? That would make people suspicious."

"I wasn't born yesterday, young man. Why do you think I keep a woman named Finette?"[31]

31. The name Finette contains the word *fin* ("fine," in English), which suggests cleverness. [TN]

The Owl raised her head.

"Do you see her, young man? She looks like a cavalry horse who hears the call to charge, doesn't she?"

"You intend to send her to scout out the terrain?"

"Exactly."

"It's number seventeen on the allée des Veuves—right, my man?" cried the Owl, impatiently. "Don't worry. I have only one eye, but it's a good one."

"Do you see her, young man? Do you see her! She's already champing at the bit!"

"If she's careful about entering, it's not a bad idea."

"Hold on to the umbrella, Killer. In a half hour I'll be back, and you'll see what I can do," said the Owl.

"Wait a moment, Finette. We're going to go over to the Bleeding Heart. It's only two steps away. If little Gammy is there, bring him along with you. He can stay outside the door and keep watch while you're in there."

"Good idea. He's as sly as a fox, that little Gammy. He's not even ten years old yet, but the other day—"

The Schoolmaster interrupted the Owl with a sign.

"What is the Bleeding Heart? That's a strange name for a tavern," said Rodolphe.

"You'll have to lodge a complaint about that with the innkeeper."

"What's his name?"

"The innkeeper of the Bleeding Heart?"

"Yes."

"He doesn't ask his customers what their names are."

"Still . . ."

"Call him anything you like. Pierre, Thomas, Christopher, or Barnaby—he answers to anything. But here we are, and it's about time, too, since it's started to pour again. How that river is rumbling. It sounds like a torrent. Hey, look! If it rains for two more days, the water is going to be higher than the arches of the bridge."

"You said we were here, but where the devil is the tavern? I don't see any houses here."

"If you look around you, of course not."

"And where are you proposing that I look?"

"At your feet."

"My feet?"

"Yes."

"Where at my feet?"

"Look, over there. You see that roof? Be careful not to walk on top of it."

Rodolphe had not, in fact, noticed one of those underground taverns that you used to be able to find a few years ago around the Champs-Élysées, particularly near the Cours-la-Reine. A stairway had been dug into the wet, slimy earth that led to the bottom of this large ditch. On one of its walls leaned a squat, sordid, cracked hovel cut out with a pick. Its roof, covered with mossy tiles, barely came up to the level of the ground where Rodolphe was standing. Two or three sheds made of worm-eaten boards served as a storeroom, a rabbit hutch, and a lean-to. Together, they made up this miserable dump. A very narrow alley crossing the length of the pit led from the stairway to the door of the establishment. The rest of the site disappeared under a bower of trellises that sheltered two rows of coarsely made tables planted in the ground. The wind was making an ugly sheet metal plate groan on its hinges. Through the rust that covered it you could still make out a red heart pierced by an arrow. The sign swayed on a post pitched atop the den. It was a veritable burrow for humans.

A thick, wet fog was now mixing in with the rain. Night was approaching.

"What do you think of this mansion, young man?" asked the Schoolmaster.

"Thanks to the rain that's been falling for the past two weeks, it's wet enough for a pond. There must be good fishing. Let's go on in."

"Just a second. I need to see if the host is there. Careful."

And the bandit, vigorously rubbing his tongue against his palate, let out a unique cry, a sort of prolonged, sonorous guttural rumbling. It sounded like this: "*Prrrr!*"

The same cry answered him from the depths of the hovel.

"He's in," said the Schoolmaster. "Pardon me, young man. Treat the ladies with respect. Let the Owl go in first. I'll follow you. Be careful not to fall—it's slippery."

CHAPTER 17

THE BLEEDING HEART

The innkeeper of the Bleeding Heart, after having answered the Schoolmaster's signal, came up affably to the doorway. This character, whom Rodolphe had been looking for in the Cité and whom he still did not know under his real name, or rather under his usual nickname, was Red-Arm. Small and thin, weak and stunted looking, this man looked to be about fifty years old. His face combined the features of a weasel and a rat. His pointy nose, his receding chin, his bony cheeks, and his darting, piercing little black eyes all gave his face an inimitable expression of deceptiveness, shrewdness, and intelligence. An old blond, or rather yellow, wig that matched his bilious complexion was perched atop his skull; underneath, his graying neck was visible. He wore a lined jacket and one of those grimy, long kinds of aprons that wine store merchants wear.

Our three characters had hardly come to the end of the stairway when a very small, clever-looking, but sickly, lame, slightly deformed boy, who was at most ten years old, came over and joined Red-Arm. He looked so much like Red-Arm that one could not mistake him for anyone other than his son. He had the same penetrating and astute gaze. The child's forehead was half hidden underneath a forest of straight yellowish hair that was as stiff as a horse's mane. A pair of brown pants and a shirt cinched with a leather belt completed Gammy's look. He was named Gammy because of his deformity. He stayed by his father's side, standing on his good leg like a heron at the edge of a marsh.

"Here's just the kid we were looking for," said the Schoolmaster. "Finette, time is passing and night is coming. We need to make the most of the rest of the day."

"You're right, dear. I'll go ask his father for the little brat."

"Hello there, old pal," said Red-Arm to the Schoolmaster in a tart and sharp little falsetto. "What can I do for you?"

"Can you lend your kid to my wife for a quarter of an hour? She's lost something near here, and he can help her find it."

Red-Arm winked, signaled to the Schoolmaster that he was in the know, and said to his son, "Gammy, go with the lady."

The hideous child, attracted by the ugliness and wicked look of the

Owl the way other people are charmed by a benevolent appearance, ran off, limping, to take the one-eyed hag's hand.

"What a little love he is. Now there's a child," said Finette. "Look how he comes right up to you right away! He's nothing like that little Miss Lowlife. She always seemed heartsick whenever she came near me, that little beggar!"

"Let's go. Hurry up, Finette. Keep your eyes peeled and look out for squalls. I'll wait for you here."

"I won't be long. You first, Gammy!" And the Owl and the little lame boy mounted the slippery staircase.

"Finette, take the umbrella!" cried the criminal.

"It would get in my way, dear," said the old woman, soon disappearing with Gammy amid the accumulating mists of nightfall and the sad murmurings of the wind that shook the black, leafless branches of the Champs-Élysées' great elms.

"Let's go in," said Rodolphe.

He had to crouch down to pass under the door of the tavern. The tavern had two rooms; in one there was a bar and a worn-out billiard table, while in the other stood garden tables and chairs that had once been painted green. Two narrow casement windows with cracked panes, covered with cobwebs, allowed a small amount of light to illuminate these rooms with their greenish walls whose humidity made saltpeter ooze out from them.

Rodolphe was alone for barely a minute. Red-Arm and the Schoolmaster took the time to exchange a few words and some mysterious signs.

"Will you have a beer or a glass of brandy while we wait for Finette?" asked the Schoolmaster.

"No, I'm not thirsty."

"Suit yourself. I'm going to have a glass of brandy," answered the criminal. And he sat down at one of the little green tables in the second room.

The lair had begun to get so dark that one could not see, in one of the corners of the second room, the gaping entrance to the kind of cellar you enter through a double-paneled trapdoor, one panel of which always remained open for ease of entry. The table where the Schoolmaster was sitting was right next to this deep, black hole, to which he turned his back, hiding it completely from Rodolphe's view.

The latter was looking out the windows in order to keep his expressions in check and to mask his anxiety. The sight of Murph hurrying toward the allée des Veuves didn't completely reassure him. He feared that the worthy squire had not understood the full meaning of his note, which had been, of necessity, so terse that it read simply: "For this evening at ten o'clock."

Determined not to show up at the allée des Veuves before that time, nor to let the Schoolmaster out of his sight until then, he was afraid nonetheless of losing this rare occasion to possess the secrets that he was so determined to know. Although he was very strong and well armed, this would be a struggle of wit and wile with a dangerous murderer who was capable of anything.

Need it be said? Such was the energetic temper of this strange personality, who hungered after strong and violent feelings, that he found a sort of terrible charm in the worries and obstacles that had just thrown a monkey wrench into the plan he had put together the night before with his faithful Murph and the Slasher. Not wanting nonetheless to allow his thoughts to be understood, he went to sit down at the Schoolmaster's table and asked for a glass, for the sake of appearances.

Having exchanged a few quiet words with the criminal, Red-Arm looked Rodolphe over with a curious, sardonic, and distrustful attitude.

"Seems to me, young man," said the Schoolmaster, "that if my woman tells us that the people we want to see are at home, we can go visit them around eight o'clock."

"That would be two hours too early," said Rodolphe. "We would be disturbing them."

"You think?"

"I'm sure of it."

"Nonsense! Among friends you don't need to wait on appearances."

"I know them. I'm telling you again, we shouldn't get there before ten o'clock."

"Aren't you the stubborn one!"

"It was my idea, and I'll be damned if I leave here before ten o'clock!"

"Don't worry, I never close my establishment before midnight," said Red-Arm in his falsetto. "That's when my best customers come in, and my neighbors never complain about the noise we make in here."

"Since we must give in to everything you ask, young man," answered the Schoolmaster, "so be it. We won't go on our visit until ten o'clock."

"That's the Owl!" said Red-Arm upon hearing and answering the same secret cry that the Schoolmaster had given before going down into the underground establishment.

One minute later, the Owl came into the billiard room alone.

"It'll work, my dear! We've got it in the bag!" cried the one-eyed woman as she entered. Red-Arm withdrew discreetly without asking where Gammy was. He probably had not expected to see him come back. The old woman's clothing was soaked with rain. She sat down in front of Rodolphe and the criminal.

"So?" asked the criminal.

"This guy has told the truth up to now."

"You see!" cried Rodolphe.

"Let the Owl explain herself, young man. Let's see what she says. Go on, Finette."

"I arrived at number seventeen after leaving Gammy huddled in a hole on the lookout. It was still daylight. I rang the chimes at a small side door that had its hinges on the outside, with two inches of space over the threshold, which is to say none to speak of. I rang, and the guard opened the door. He was a tall, fat man, in his fifties. He looked sleepy and good-natured, with red sideburns and whiskers, and a bald head. Before ringing, I had put my bonnet in my pocket in order to look like a neighbor. When I saw the guard, I started sobbing as hard as I could, crying that I had lost my parakeet, Cutie, who I adored. I told him that I lived on the avenue de Marboeuf, and that I had been going from garden to garden looking for Cutie. And I ended up begging the man to let me look for my pet."

"Huh!" said the Schoolmaster in proud satisfaction as he gestured toward Finette. "What a woman you are!"

"Very clever," said Rodolphe. "But what happened next?"

"The guard let me look for my pet, so there I am in the garden calling, 'Cutie! Cutie!' and looking up, down, and everywhere. Inside those walls," the old woman went on, continuing in her description of the home, "inside those walls, there are trellises everywhere, a veritable stairway. In the corner of the wall, at the left, there's a pine tree that's like a ladder. A pregnant woman could get down it. The house has six windows on the ground floor, and there is no other floor. There are four basement windows without any bars over them. The windows on the ground floor lock with shutters. There's a latch below, and a spring latch up above. Press on the column, pull the iron cord . . ."

"And presto," said the Schoolmaster, "it's open!"

The Owl continued: "The glass entrance door has two blinds on the outside."

"What a memory," said the criminal.

"Exactly like that, just as if we were right there," said Rodolphe.

"On the left," the Owl continued, "near the courtyard, there's a well. A rope would be useful if our escape was blocked on the door side, because there's no trellis on the wall there. When I went into the house—"

"You got into the house? She got in, young man!" said the Schoolmaster, beaming with pride.

"Of course I got in. Since I didn't find Cutie, I moaned so much that I could simulate being out of breath. I asked the guard for permission to sit on the doorstep. The good man told me to enter, and he offered me a glass of water and some wine. 'Just a glass of water,' I said, 'just a glass of water, my good sir.' Then he had me walk into an antechamber. There was carpeting everywhere. A good thing to know in advance: you can't hear anyone walking or the sound of windows breaking, if we had to take out a pane. Left and right, doors and locks with lever handles. They open if you breathe on them hard. At the back, there's a strong door that's locked with a key. It had the look of a safe. You could smell the money! I had my wax in my shopping basket . . ."

"She had her wax, young man. She never goes anywhere without her wax!" said the criminal.

The Owl continued, "I had to go by the door that smelled like money. Then I acted as if I had been taken by such a strong fit of coughing that I had to lean against the wall. Hearing me cough, the guard said to me, 'I'm going to get you a sugar cube.' He probably went to look for a teaspoon, because I heard the jingling of silverware. Silverware in the room on the right—don't forget that, Killer. So anyway, while I was coughing and whining, I walked up to the door at the back. I had my wax in the palm of my hand. I leaned against the lock, just like nothing. Here's the wax imprint. If it doesn't help us today, it might another time." And the Owl gave the criminal a piece of yellow wax upon which could be clearly seen the imprint of the lock.

"That's so you can tell us if it's actually the safe door," said the Owl.

"That's it! That's where the money is," said Rodolphe.

And he said to himself under his breath, "Was Murph taken in by this old wretch? It's possible. He's not expecting to be attacked until ten o'clock. At that time, all of his defenses will be up."

"But that's not where all of the money is!" continued the Owl, with a gleam in her green eye. "As I went up to the windows, still looking for Cutie, to the left of the door, there were sacks of coins on a desk. I saw them as clearly as I see you, my dear. There were at least a dozen of them."

"Where is Gammy?" asked the Schoolmaster, suddenly.

"He's still in his hole, two steps away from the garden door. He sees in the dark like a cat. That's the only way into number seventeen. When we go there, he'll tell us if anyone has come."

"Good work."

Hardly had he pronounced these words when the Schoolmaster pounced suddenly upon Rodolphe, seized him by the throat, and pushed him into the open cellar behind the table. This attack was so quick, so unexpected, and so vigorous that Rodolphe had no chance to anticipate or evade it. The Owl, frightened, gave a piercing cry, for she had not seen at first how this rapid struggle would come out.

When the sound of Rodolphe's body rolling down the steps had subsided, the Schoolmaster, who knew the subterranean ins and outs of this establishment very well, walked slowly into the cellar, listening carefully.

"Be careful, Killer!" cried the one-eyed woman as she leaned on the opening of the trapdoor. "Take out your dagger!"

The criminal said nothing and disappeared. At first they couldn't hear anything, but after a few moments, the distant sound of a rusty door that was creaking on its hinges resonated hollowly in the depths of the cellar, and there was silence again.

It was now totally dark out.

The Owl riffled through her shopping bag, lit a match, and then lit a small candle whose glow spread out in the gloomy room.

At that moment, the monstrous face of the Schoolmaster appeared at the opening of the trapdoor. The Owl could not hold back an exclamation of fright at the view of the pale, stitched-up, mutilated, horrible head, which seemed, with its almost phosphorescent eyes, to creep along the floor out of the darkness that the candle barely illuminated.

Pulling herself together, the old woman exclaimed, with a frightful sort of flattery, "That's how horrifying you look, Killer! You actually scared me there—me!"

"Quickly, quickly, let's go to the allée des Veuves," said the criminal as he fastened the two panels of the trapdoor with an iron bar. "In an hour it will be too late! If it's a trap, it's not laid yet. If it's not one, we'll do this job alone."

CHAPTER 18

THE VAULT

Under the stairway of the cellar, Rodolphe remained unconscious and motionless from the blow of his horrible fall. Dragging him from the entrance to a second and much deeper vault, the Schoolmaster had lowered him into it and locked him behind a thick, hinged door. Then he had rejoined the Owl to go with her to commit a robbery, and possibly a murder, in the allée des Veuves.

After about an hour, Rodolphe began slowly to recover his senses. He was lying on the ground amid dark shadows. He reached his arm around and touched some steps made of stone. Feeling something distinctly cool at his feet, he brought his hand there: it was a pool of water. With a painful effort he managed to sit up on the last step of the stairway. His grogginess faded away slowly, and he moved around a bit. Fortunately, none of his limbs was broken. He listened but heard nothing—nothing but a soft lapping sound that was muted and weak, and continuous.

He did not at first suspect what caused the sound. As his thinking became more lucid, the circumstances of the surprise to which he had fallen victim started coming back to him, but only slowly and incompletely. He was on the verge of gathering together his memories of what had happened when he felt anew the impression of something cool at his feet. He crouched down and felt below him: he had water just up to his ankles.

And amid the gloomy silence that surrounded him, he could hear even more distinctly that soft, muted, continuous lapping noise. Now he understood the cause: water was pouring into the cellar. The Seine was rising at a formidable rate, and this underground cavern was at river level. This danger brought Rodolphe completely back to consciousness. As quick as lightning, he climbed the wet stairway. When he arrived at the top of the stairs, he collided with a door. He tried in vain to shake it, for it sat immobile on its iron hinges.

In this desperate situation, his first concern was for Murph. "If he's not on guard, that monster is going to kill him—and it's I who will have been the cause," he exclaimed. "Poor Murph!"

This cruel thought was a goad to Rodolphe's strength. Buttressing himself on his feet and bending his shoulders into the task, he used all his strength in a superhuman effort to break down the door. But his effort was in vain. The door did not budge on its iron hinges.

Hoping to find a lever in the vault, he walked back down again. At the second-to-last stair, two or three soft, round objects were rolling around and fleeing under his feet: these were rats that the water was forcing out of their holes. Rodolphe groped his way across the cellar and felt in all directions, with the water coming midway up his leg. He found nothing. He slowly walked up the stairs again in deep despair.

He counted the steps: there were thirteen. Three of them were already underwater. Thirteen! A fatal number! In some situations, even the strongest minds cannot avoid falling into superstitious thinking. He saw in that number a bad omen. Murph's possible fate returned to his thoughts. He searched in vain for some kind of opening between the floor and the door, but the humidity had clearly caused the wood to swell, for the door formed a hermetic seal with the wet and slimy ground.

Rodolphe yelled at the top of his lungs, thinking that his cries would reach the ears of the tavern hosts, and then he stopped to listen. He heard nothing—nothing but the soft, muted, weak, continuous lapping sound of the water that kept climbing higher, higher, higher . . .

Overcome, Rodolphe sat down, his back supported by the door. He wept over the fate of his friend, who was perhaps already facing a murderer's knife. At that moment, he regretted bitterly having undertaken his imprudent and audacious projects, however generous their motive might have been. His heart breaking, he remembered the thousands of acts of devotion that Murph had performed for him—Murph, who had been rich and respected, who had left a wife and a beloved child, as well as his own deepest concerns, to follow and assist Rodolphe in the valiant but strange expiation the latter had imposed upon himself.

The water continued to rise. There were no more than five dry steps left. Standing up by the door, Rodolphe touched the vault of the ceiling with his forehead. He could calculate how long his agony would last. This would be a slow, silent, dreadful death. He remembered the pistol he had with him. At the risk of injuring himself by shooting at the door point-blank, he could perhaps break it down. But no! No luck! In his fall, the weapon had been lost or it had been taken from him by the Schoolmaster.

If not for his fears for Murph's safety, Rodolphe would have met death calmly. He had lived a rich life; he had been ardently loved; he had done good in the world—and wished he could do more, God knows! Without any complaint against this death sentence, he saw in this destiny a just punishment for a fatal action he had not yet expiated. His thoughts grew loftier and more expansive with the danger he faced.

A new kind of torture arrived to test Rodolphe's stoicism. The rats, trying to escape the rising waters, had fled from stair to stair, without finding an exit. Since they could hardly climb the perpendicular walls or door, they took to clinging onto Rodolphe's clothing. When he felt them swarming upon him, his disgust and horror were unspeakable. He tried to chase them away; their sharp and cold bites made his hands bleed. His shirt and jacket had come open in his fall, and now he felt on his naked chest the sensation of icy little paws and furry bodies. He threw the appalling creatures as far as he could after prying them off his clothing, but they kept swimming back to him.

Rodolphe cried out again, but no one heard him. In a few moments, he would not be able to cry out any longer, for the water had reached his neck and would soon be at his mouth.

The compressed air of the tight space in the cellar was now in short supply. Rodolphe felt the first symptoms of asphyxia overwhelming him; the arteries in his temples were throbbing violently and he felt dizzy. He was going to die. Thinking one last time of Murph, he offered his soul to God—not in hopes of being saved from the danger, but rather in the hope that God would accept his suffering as expiation.

At this pivotal moment, on the verge of leaving not only everything that makes a life happy, brilliant, and desirable, but also a nearly royal title, a sovereign power, forced to give up an enterprise that, in satisfying his two passions—the love of the good and the hatred of evil—might one day have weighed against his sins, preparing to die a painful death, Rodolphe manifested none of the impulses of rage or impotent frenzy that mark the last moments of weak souls as they accuse or curse man, fate, and God, one after another.

No: as long as his mind remained lucid, Rodolphe submitted to his fate with humility and respect. When his agony obscured his thought process, he struggled physically, so to speak, purely out of an instinct to live, but he did not struggle morally against death.

Vertigo carried off Rodolphe's thinking into a rapid and frightening vortex; the water was churning away at his ears. He thought he was swirling around in an eddy. The last vestiges of his consciousness were about to be extinguished when the sound of hurried footsteps and voices rang out near the door to the cellar.

Hope reanimated his waning strength. With a final effort of mind, he perceived the following words—the last words he heard or understood: "You see? No one's here."

"Damn! It's true!" the sad voice of the Slasher responded. And the footsteps moved away.

Rodolphe, overcome, did not have the strength to hold on any longer. He slid down the stairs.

Suddenly, the door of the cellar opened violently outward. The water that had been held back underground escaped as if a floodgate had opened. The Slasher was able to grab the nearly drowned Rodolphe, who was still clinging to the doorframe in a final autonomic act, by both of his arms.

CHAPTER 19

THE SICK NURSE

Torn from the maw of death by the Slasher and transported back to the house on the allée des Veuves that the Owl had gone off to explore before the Schoolmaster's attempt to rob it, Rodolphe lay in a comfortably furnished bedroom. A big fire roared in the fireplace, and a lamp sitting on a chest of drawers cast a warm light through the apartment. Rodolphe's bed remained in darkness behind a veil of thick green damask drapery.

A black man of average height held a gold watch in his left hand that he seemed to be consulting as he took Rodolphe's pulse with his right hand. He had white hair and eyebrows and was dressed with care. He wore an orange and green ribbon in the buttonhole of his blue suit. This black man was sad and pensive. He glanced at the sleeping Rodolphe with an expression of the most tender care.

The Slasher, dressed in rags, covered in mud, stood motionless at the foot of the bed. His arms hung down with his hands crossed before him. His red beard was long. His thick head of hair, the color of oakum, was tangled and soaked with water. His coarse features were hard and sunbaked. From under this ugly and unpromising shell, however, an ineffable expression of caring and pity shone through. Hardly daring to breathe, he let himself exhale only with the greatest restraint. Anxious at the contemplative attitude of the black doctor and fearing a bad diagnosis, he allowed himself to make the following philosophical observation in an undertone as he looked at Rodolphe: "Who would ever say, looking at him all weak like that, that he was the guy who gave me such a proud whopping? He won't take long to get his strength back, right, Doctor? I swear, I would be happy if he beat his convalescence out of my back. It would cure him, don't you think, Doctor?"

Without answering, the black man made a gentle sign with his hand.

The Slasher became silent.

"The potion?" asked the black man.

Immediately, the Slasher, who had left his hobnailed shoes by the door out of politeness, walked over toward the chest as lightly as he could on his tiptoes. The way that he contorted his limbs, swayed his arms, and pushed out his shoulders to achieve this end would have been highly amusing under different circumstances. The poor devil seemed to want to carry all his weight on the parts of his body that weren't touching the floor. Despite the carpeting, however, the parquet floor groaned under the Slasher's hulking stature. Unfortunately, in his eagerness to help and out of fear of dropping the translucent vial that he was carrying so carefully, he squeezed the neck of the bottle so hard in his big hand that it broke, and the potion spilled onto the carpet.

In the wake of this clumsiness, the Slasher stood motionless with one of his meaty legs in the air, his toes nervously contracting. He looked back and forth in confusion between the doctor and the neck of the flask that remained in his hand.

"You devilish oaf!" cried the black man, impatiently.

"Damned imbecile!" cried the Slasher, apostrophizing himself.

"Ah!" the Aesculapius[32] said, looking over at the chest. "Fortunately, you got the wrong one. I wanted the other vial."

"The little pinkish one?" the unlucky sick nurse said, meekly.

"Indeed, since it's the only one left."

In turning quickly on his heels, an old habit he had picked up in the military, the Slasher crushed the debris from the broken flask. A more delicate pair of feet would have been cruelly torn up, but this master of survival owed to his profession the special quality of having feet that were like natural sandals, as tough as horseshoes.

"Be careful! You're going to hurt yourself!" cried the doctor.

The Slasher paid no attention whatsoever to this advice. He was deeply preoccupied with his new mission, which he wished to perform with glory so as to wipe out the memory of his earlier clumsiness. The delicacy, conscientiousness, and light touch with which he took the thin crystal vial between his two big fingers was a sight to behold. A butterfly could not have left an atom's worth of golden dust from its wings between the Slasher's thumb and index finger.

The black doctor shuddered at the prospect of a new accident that might occur from this excess of caution. Happily, the potion crashed upon no new reef of clumsiness.

Approaching the bed, the Slasher went back to pulverizing the remains of the other flask under his feet.

"You crazy man, are you trying to mutilate yourself?" said the doctor in a quiet voice.

The Slasher looked at him with surprise.

"Huh? How would I mutilate myself, Doctor?"

"That's the second time you've walked on glass."

32. The god of medicine in Greek mythology, hence a moniker for a doctor. [TN]

"If that's all, don't worry. The bottoms of these dogs are cured tougher than wheelbarrows."[33]

"Bring me a teaspoon!" ordered the doctor.

The Slasher returned to his sylphlike motions and brought the doctor what he had requested.

After taking a few spoonfuls of this potion, Rodolphe moved slightly and his hands fluttered weakly.

"Good! Good! He is regaining consciousness," said the doctor. "The bloodletting helped him. Soon he'll be out of the woods."

"Saved! Bravo! Long live the Charter!" cried the Slasher in a burst of joy.

"Can you please calm down?"

"Yes, Doctor."

"The pulse is coming back to normal. This is wonderful. Wonderful."

"And Monsieur Rodolphe's friend, Doctor? Damn, when he knows. Fortunately—"

"Silence."

"Yes, Doctor."

"Sit down."

"Yes, D—"

"Sit down already. You disturb me with your incessant buzzing about. You're distracting me. Please, sit down!"

"Doctor, I am as filthy as a floating log that's about to be hauled off from the water. I would mess up the furniture."

"All right, then—sit on the floor."

"I would get the carpet dirty."

"Do whatever you want, but good Lord, stay still," said the doctor, impatiently. And, collapsing into an armchair, he put his head in his hands.

After a moment of deep thought, the Slasher took hold of a chair. He did this less out of a need to rest than out of a wish to obey the doctor. With the greatest care, and looking perfectly pleased with himself, he turned the chair over, so its back was on the floor. He intended, in all goodwill, to sit neatly and primly on its outer rungs so as to keep everything unsoiled. He proceeded to do this with the most delicate of preparations. Unfortunately, the Slasher was less than familiar with the laws of leverage and the proper balancing of weight. The chair tipped over. Then the poor man swung his arm around in an involuntary movement and toppled a pedestal table upon which rested a tray, a cup, and a teapot.

Reacting to this frightful noise, the black doctor lifted his head and then jumped from the chair.

---

33. The soles of his feet are as thick as if they were covered in wood. [SN]

Rodolphe, awakening suddenly, sat straight up in his bed. He looked around him anxiously, tried to collect his thoughts, and cried, "Murph! Where's Murph?"

"Your highness may be reassured that there is considerable hope," said the black man, respectfully.

"He's wounded?" cried Rodolphe.

"Alas! Yes, Your Lordship."

"Where is he? I want to see him."

And Rodolphe tried to get up. However, he fell back down to the bed, vanquished by the pains of the bruises, which he suddenly felt.

"I demand that I be carried this instant to see Murph, since I cannot walk to see him myself!" he exclaimed.

"He is resting, Your Lordship. It would be dangerous to stir up his emotions at this time."

"Ah! You are deceiving me! He's dead! He's been murdered! And it's my fault! I am the cause of his death!" cried Rodolphe in a wrenching voice, raising his hands to the heavens.

"Your lordship is well aware that I am incapable of lying. I affirm to you on my honor that Monsieur Murph is alive. He is quite seriously injured, it is true, but he is almost certain to recover."

"You're saying this to prepare me for some terrible news. He must be in a critical condition."

"Your Lordship—"

"I'm sure of it. You are deceiving me. I demand to be taken to him this moment. The sight of a friend always makes one feel better."

"Once again, Your Highness, I swear to you on my honor that Monsieur Murph will soon be getting better unless something unforeseen happens."

"Is this really true, my dear David?"

"It's really true, Your Lordship."

"Listen, you know how much I respect you. Since you joined my household, you have always had my confidence. Never have I had any doubt about your unmatched wisdom. But for the love of God, if an outside consultation is necessary—"

"That was my first thought, Your Lordship. For the moment, a consultation is completely unnecessary. You can trust me about this. In any case, I didn't want to bring any outsiders here before knowing whether the orders you gave yesterday—"

"But how did all of this happen?" asked Rodolphe, interrupting the black man. "Who rescued me from the cavern in which I was drowning? I have a dim memory of the sound of the Slasher's voice. Am I wrong?"

"No! No! That brave fellow can tell you all about it, Your Lordship, because he did everything."

"But where is he? Where is he?"

The doctor glanced around to see where the improvised sick nurse had gone. Rattled by his fall, the Slasher had hidden behind the bed drapery.

"Here he is," said the doctor. "He seems completely embarrassed."

"Come over here, you brave man!" said Rodolphe as he held out his hand to his rescuer.

CHAPTER 20

THE SLASHER'S STORY

The Slasher was even more confused when he heard the black doctor call Rodolphe "his lordship" several times.

"Come over here already! Give me your hand!" said Rodolphe.

"I'm sorry, monsieur . . . I meant to say 'Your Lordship,' but . . ."

"Call me Monsieur Rodolphe, the way you've been doing. I like that better."

"And it would make things easier for me. But as for my hand, please excuse me. I've been doing a lot of dirty work lately." And he timidly held out his black and calloused hand. Rodolphe shook it cordially.

"So sit down and tell me everything. How did you discover the vault? But I just realized—where is the Schoolmaster?"

"He's under lock and key," said the black doctor.

"Him and the Owl, all wrapped up like two plugs of tobacco. When I think what ugly faces they must be making at each other, if they do look at each other, I'll bet they're both feeling good and disgusted with each other by now."

"And my poor Murph! My God, I've only thought of him just now! David, where are his injuries?"

"On the right side, Your Lordship . . . fortunately, toward the last floating rib."

"Oh! Revenge will be mine, and it will be terrible! David, I am counting on you."

"Your lordship knows that I belong to him, body and soul," responded the black man, coldly.

"But how did you manage to get there in time, my good man?" Rodolphe asked the Slasher.

"If you want, your lord—I mean, Monsieur Rodolphe. I'll start at the beginning."

"That's right. I'm listening."

"You know how you told me yesterday, when you came back from the countryside where you had gone with poor Songbird: 'Try to find the Schoolmaster in the Cité; tell him that you know of a good job to pull off that you don't want a part of. Tell him if he wants to take your place he should show up the next day (that's this morning) at the Bercy barrier, at the Flower-Basket. That's where he would see the one who cooked up the plan.'"

"And so?"

"When I left you, I went over to the Cité. I go to the ogress's place—no sign of the Schoolmaster. I check on rue Saint-Éloi, rue aux Fèves, rue de la Vieille-Draperie—no one. Finally, I get ahold of him with that slug of an Owl in the square of Notre-Dame Cathedral at a shop run by a little guy who's a tailor, a retailer, a fence, and a thief. They wanted to get rid of all the money they had stolen off the tall guy in black who wanted to do something to you. They were buying cast-off clothing of any kind. The Owl was haggling over a red shawl. Old monster! I said my little speech to the Schoolmaster. He said that that worked for him, and that he would be there for the meeting. So far, so good! This morning, I came over here like you asked me yesterday to tell you what he'd said. You said to me, 'My boy, come back tomorrow morning before dawn. You'll spend the day in the house, and at night you'll witness something that will be worth your while.' You wouldn't spill any more of the beans to me, but I understood plenty. I said to myself, 'This is an act to fool the Schoolmaster tomorrow, to bait him into getting him involved in something. He's a real scoundrel. He murdered the livestock merchant, I am cer—'"

"And my error was in not telling you everything, my boy. This horrible misfortune might never have happened if I had."

"That was your business, Monsieur Rodolphe. What was *my* business was serving you . . . because, you know, well, I don't know how it happened, and I already told you about this, but I feel like your bulldog. So . . . enough already. I said, 'Tomorrow's the big event, today I have the day off, Monsieur Rodolphe paid me for two days that I've wasted, and two others in advance, too, because I haven't been at work at the dock for three days, and since I'm not a millionaire, work is how I earn my bread.' I also said to myself, 'You know, Monsieur Rodolphe has paid for my time, so my time belongs to him. I'm going to use it to serve him.' And then I thought: 'The Schoolmaster is crafty, so he must be on his guard against a trap. Monsieur Rodolphe has proposed a heist for tomorrow, it's true, but that wretch is capable of coming around here in the daytime to get the lay of the land, and if he doesn't trust Monsieur Rodolphe, he's capable of bringing another henchman into it, or even of saying, "See you tomorrow," and robbing the house on his own today.'"

"You guessed right. That's what happened—and Providence ordained that I should owe you my life!"

"It's amazing, Monsieur Rodolphe, the way that things seem to keep getting rigged by something up there since I've known you. And I keep having ideas that I've never had before since you told me, 'My boy, you have heart and honor.' Heart! Honor!! Hell, those words make you feel something in your belly. You understand, Monsieur Rodolphe, you get used to hearing people warn each other that you're a wolf or a rabid dog—when you just want to get to know honest people."

"So in the past few days you've had some ideas that you've never had before?"

"Well, sure, Monsieur Rodolphe. Just think, now I would say to myself, 'If I knew someone who had done something wrong, through drink or anger, whatever, I would say to him, "My man, you did something wrong, that's true. But that's not the end of things. The good Lord doesn't create people who are drowning, burning, or dying of hunger just to please the king of Prussia. Be my friend, and if you earn forty sous, give twenty of them to old poor people, or to little children—to anyone who's more miserable than you and who has neither bread nor strength with which to earn it. Most of all, don't forget, my good man, that if there's someone who needs to be saved, even if you have to risk your hide to do it, that's your job! On that condition, and if you don't start doing the stupid things you were doing before, I'll always be there for you."' But I'm just babbling away here, Monsieur Rodolphe. I'm sorry. You have things you want to know."

"No, I like hearing you talk that way. And anyway, I'll find out soon enough how my poor Murph became the victim of this terrible misfortune. I thought I could make sure not to leave the Schoolmaster's side for a single minute during that dangerous business. And then he would have killed me a thousand times before laying a hand on Murph. Alas! Fate decided otherwise. Please continue, my boy."

"Since I wanted to use my time on your behalf, Monsieur Rodolphe, I said to myself, 'I'd better go stash myself somewhere where I can see the walls. The garden door—there's only one entrance there . . . If I find a good spot . . . Even if it rains, I'll stay there all day long, all night long, more importantly, and tomorrow morning I'll be good and ready.' I was telling myself this on the stroke of two o'clock at Batignolles, where I had a bite to eat after leaving you, Monsieur Rodolphe. I come back to the Champs-Élysées, look for a place to nest. What do I see? A little bar about ten steps away from your door. I sit myself down on the ground floor next to the window, I ask for a liter of wine and a quarter pound of nuts, and I say I'm waiting for some friends, a hunchback and a tall woman—it seems perfectly natural that way. I get all settled, and here I was, watching your door. It was raining and everything. No one came by, night was approaching—"

"But," said Rodolphe, interrupting the Slasher, "why didn't you go to my place?"

"You told me to come back the next morning, Monsieur Rodolphe. I didn't dare return before that. I would have seemed like a wise guy or what the soldiers call a flunky. After all, I know what I am, a freed convict, and when someone like you treats me like you do, Monsieur Rodolphe, you don't go to him until he says, 'Come!' After that, if I saw a spider crawling on the collar of your coat, I'd take it off and crush it without troubling you.

Do you understand what I'm saying? So I was at the window of the bar, cracking my nuts and drinking my wine, when through the fog I saw the Owl dart by with Red-Arm's kid, little Gammy."

"Red-Arm! So he's the owner of the underground tavern at the Champs-Élysées?" cried Rodolphe.

"Yes, Monsieur Rodolphe. You didn't know that?"

"No, I thought he lived in the Cité."

"He lives there, too. He lives everywhere, that Red-Arm. He's a sly, proud villain, you know, with his yellow wig and pointy nose! So finally, when I see the Owl and Gammy run by, I say to myself, 'All right, good, things are starting to heat up!' Gammy was basically crouching in one of the gulleys in the alley, facing your door as if he were a mole looking for shelter from the flood. As for the Owl, she takes off her bonnet, puts it in her pocket, and rings the doorbell. Poor Monsieur Murph, your friend, opens the door to the hag, and she goes running around the garden with her arms wide open. I couldn't figure out for the life of me what the Owl was up to. Finally, she comes back out, puts her bonnet back on, says something to Gammy, who goes back into his hole, and she takes off. I tell myself: 'Wait! Let's not mix things up,' I say to myself. Gammy came with the Owl; that means that the Schoolmaster and Monsieur Rodolphe are at Red-Arm's. The Owl came to spy on the house. That means they're going to rob the place tonight. If they do it tonight, that means that Monsieur Rodolphe, who thinks they're doing it tomorrow, is getting one put over on him. If Monsieur Rodolphe is getting one put over on him, I need to go over to Red-Arm's place to see what's going on. Yes, but if during this time the Schoolmaster arrives, yeah, that's a problem. Well, too bad. I'm going to go into the house to tell Monsieur Murph, 'Watch out!' Yes, but that little vermin Gammy is right next to the door and he'll hear me ring and see me, and then he'll let the Owl know. If she comes back, that will spoil everything, especially if Monsieur Rodolphe has arranged things differently for tonight. Hell! All those yeses and nos were fluttering around my brain. I was flabbergasted, completely flummoxed. I didn't know what to do. I say to myself, 'I'm going out, maybe the fresh air will give me some ideas.' I leave, and it does. I take off my shirt and my tie, I go to the ditch Gammy is in, I take the little kid by the scruff of his neck. He tries kicking, scratching me, and squawking, but I wrap him up in my shirt as if it was a sack and I knot the sleeves together at one end and use my tie to secure him at the other end. He could still breathe. I carry this little packet under my arm. I see a vegetable garden nearby with a little wall around it, and I toss Gammy in the middle of a carrot planter. He was making low grunting sounds like a suckling pig, but you couldn't hear him from further than two feet away. I get out of there—it was about time! I climb one of the large trees of the alley, right in front of your door, over Gammy's ditch.

Ten minutes later, I hear someone walking. It was still raining. It was so dark out—so dark that the devil would have stepped on his own tail. I listen; it was the Owl. 'Gammy! Gammy!' she said, in a low voice. Go ahead, look for your Gammy! 'It's raining, the kid must have gotten tired of waiting,' says the Schoolmaster, cursing him. 'If I catch him, I will skin him alive!!!' 'Be careful, Killer,' says the Owl. 'Maybe he went to warn us about something. What if it was a trap! The other guy didn't want to do this until ten o'clock.' 'That's why we're here now,' answers the Schoolmaster. 'It's just seven. You saw the silver. Nothing ventured, nothing gained. Give me the crowbar and the cold chisel.'"

"Those tools?" asked Rodolphe.

"They came from Red-Arm's place. Oh! He's got a well-stocked house. In two shakes, he's got the door forced open. 'Stay there,' says the Schoolmaster to the Owl. 'Pay attention, and yell to the high heavens if you hear anything.' 'Put your dagger in a buttonhole in your vest so you can get at it right away,' said the hag. And the Schoolmaster went into the garden. I say to myself suddenly, 'Monsieur Rodolphe isn't there. He's either dead or alive at this precise moment. I can't do anything, but the friends of our friends are our—' Oh, pardon me, Your Lordship! I didn't mean . . ."

"It's all right. And? Go on."

"I say to myself, 'The Schoolmaster might murder Monsieur Murph, Monsieur Rodolphe's friend, who's not expecting anything.' That's where things start to heat up. I jump out of my tree and pounce on the Owl. I knock her out with two choice punches. She falls without a sound. I go into the garden. But hell! Monsieur Rodolphe! It was too late."

"Poor Murph!"

"When he heard a noise at the door, he must have walked out of the vestibule. He was wrestling with the Schoolmaster on the little flight of steps. Even though he was already wounded, he kept going strong, without crying out for help. Good man! He's like a good dog. 'He bites more than he barks,' I say to myself. And I throw myself head over heels onto the both of them, seizing the Schoolmaster by a leg, the only thing handy at that moment. 'Long live the Charter! It's me, the Slasher! We're a team, Monsieur Murph!' 'Ah, you ruffian! What are you doing here?' the Schoolmaster yells at me, stunned to see me. 'Get out of here with your questions,' I answer him, wrenching one of his legs between my knees and grabbing his wing, the one that was holding the dagger, the right one. 'And . . . Rodolphe?' Monsieur Murph cries out, helping me all the while."

"What a fine, courageous man!" murmured Rodolphe, sadly.

"'I don't know what happened to Rodolphe,' I answered him. 'Maybe this scoundrel killed him.' Then I turned back to the Schoolmaster. He was trying to stick me all over with his dagger, but since I was lying on top of him with my chest on his arm, the only thing free was his wrist. 'You're all alone, right?' I asked Monsieur Murph, all the while continuing to wrestle with the Schoolmaster. 'There are people nearby, but they wouldn't be able to hear me yell.' 'Are they far from here?' 'They're ten minutes away.' 'Let's call out for help. If there are any passersby, they'll come to help us.' 'No; now that we've got him, we need to keep him here. But I'm feeling weak—I've been wounded,' Monsieur Murph told me. 'Well, damn! Go and run for help, if you can make it. I'll try to hold him down. Take his knife away from him; just help me get on top of him. Even though he's twice as strong as I am, I can do it once I've got him in my grips.' The Schoolmaster wasn't saying anything. The only noise he made was to snort like a bull, but Lord, what strength! Monsieur Murph couldn't get the dagger out of his hand. The grip of that man was like a vice. Finally, with the full weight of my body on his right arm, I put my two hands behind his neck and held them clasped there as if I wanted to kiss him. Keeping him hooked like that was all I wanted in life at that moment. So I said to Monsieur Murph, 'Hurry! I'll wait for you. If you find yourself with any extra company, go get the Owl from behind the garden door. I knocked her out.' I stay on my own with the Schoolmaster. He knew what was waiting for him."

"No, he didn't! Nor do you, my good man," said Rodolphe, somberly, his features contracted into the hard, nearly ferocious mask we described earlier.

Surprised, the Slasher said to Rodolphe, "I thought that the Schoolmaster knew what he had coming to him, because—well, hell—not to brag or anything, but there was a moment there that wasn't exactly a picnic. We were half on the ground, half on the last step of the stairway. I had my arm around his neck, my cheek against his cheek. I could hear him grinding his teeth. It was getting dark out. It was still raining, and the lantern in the vestibule was lighting things up a bit. I had clamped one of his legs between mine. Nevertheless, he had such a strong back that he lifted us both a foot off the ground. He wanted to bite me, but he couldn't. I never felt so strong before. Damn, my heart was pounding, but in a good way. I said to myself, 'I'm like someone who's trying to nab a rabid dog in order to keep him from attacking the public.' 'Let me escape, and I won't do anything to you,' said the Schoolmaster. 'You're such a coward!' I said to him. 'So you're only brave when you're the strong one, right? You wouldn't have dared murder the cattle merchant at Poissy to rob him if only he'd been as strong as me, huh?' 'No,' he said to me, 'but I'm going to kill you just as I killed him.' After he said that, he jumped so violently, stiffening his legs at the same time, that he threw me to the side. But I still had my hands clasped under his head and his right arm underneath me. As soon as he had his two legs free, he made good use of them. That gave him some spirit. He half turned back to me. If I hadn't had a good hold on his dagger arm, I'd be finished. In that moment, my left wrist started to give out; I had to unlace my fingers. Things were going badly. I said to myself, 'I'm on the bottom, he's on the top; he's going to kill me. It's all right, though: I wouldn't want to trade places with him. Monsieur Rodolphe told me that I had heart and honor. I feel that it's true.' That's what I was thinking when I saw the Owl, with her goggle eye and red shawl, standing upright on the stairs. Damn! I thought I was in a nightmare. 'Finette!' the Schoolmaster called out to her, 'I dropped my knife. Pick it up, over there, under him, and stab him in the back, between the shoulders.' 'Wait, wait, Killer, let me collect myself.' And the Owl circled around us like the bird of prey that she is. Finally, she saw the dagger and tried to jump on it. I was flat on my stomach. I gave her a kick in the stomach that knocked her down, but she got up again, and kept at it. I couldn't take it any longer. I was still bearing down on the Schoolmaster, but he was punching me so hard in the jaw from below that I was going to lose my grip. I was starting to go numb, when suddenly I see three or four armed fellows clambering down the staircase, along with Monsieur Murph, who was totally pale and barely supported by the doctor. They seized the Schoolmaster and the Owl and tied them up. But things weren't over yet. I needed to find Monsieur Rodolphe. I jumped on the Owl, remembering poor Songbird's tooth, and I grabbed her arm and twisted it. 'Where is Monsieur Rodolphe?' I asked. She wouldn't say, but on the second try, she cried out, 'At Red-Arm's place, in the cellar, at the Bleeding Heart.' Good, I thought. As I passed him, I wanted to take Gammy in his carrot patch; that was the way to go. I looked; there was nothing left but my shirt. He had gnawed himself out of it with his teeth. I arrived at the Bleeding Heart, I pounced on Red-Arm and took him by the neck. 'Where is the young man who came here tonight with the Schoolmaster?' 'Let go your grip, I'll tell you: they wanted to play a trick on him, so they locked him in my cellar. We'll open it up and let him out.' We went down . . . but no one there. 'He must have left when I wasn't looking,' said Red-Arm. 'You can see that there's no one here.' I was going away, all sad, when the glow of a lantern showed another door. I ran over to it, I pulled it toward me, and I got something like an enormous bucket of water right in the mug. I saw your two poor arms in the air. I fished you out and I carried you here on my back since there wasn't anyone who could go to fetch a carriage. So, Monsieur Rodolphe, that's what happened, and if I may say it without bragging, I'm damned happy."

"My boy, I owe my life to you. It's a debt that I will repay, you can be sure, and in every way. You have so much heart that you will share the feeling that I can't let go of right now. I'm terribly anxious about my friend whom you saved so valiantly, and I also feel the need to exact a terrible revenge against the one who almost killed the two of you."

"I understand that, Monsieur Rodolphe. Jumping on you like a traitor, throwing you in a cellar, and dragging you into a vault after you've passed out in order to drown you—that Schoolmaster deserves what's coming to him. He told me that he'd killed the livestock merchant. I'm no chicken, but hell! At this point, I'd be happy to go fetch the police myself to get that villain into handcuffs."

"David, would you please go to find out how Murph is doing?" Rodolphe asked, without responding to the Slasher. "Come right back to let me know." The black man left the room. "Do you know where the Schoolmaster is, my boy?"

"In a room below, with the Owl. You're going to get the police, Monsieur Rodolphe?"

"No."

"You're not thinking of letting him go! Ah, Monsieur Rodolphe, don't even think of being generous with this guy. Let me repeat what I've already said: he's a rabid dog. 'Passersby, beware!'"

"Rest assured: he's not going to bite anyone ever again."

"Are you going to lock him up somewhere?"

"No. In half an hour, he'll walk out of here."

"The Schoolmaster?"

"Yes."

"Without the police?"

"Yes."

"What? He's going to walk out of here a free man?"

"A free man."

"On his own?"

"Yes, all on his own."

"But he'll go—"

"Wherever he wants," interrupted Rodolphe, with a smile that sent chills down the Slasher's spine.

The black man returned to the room.

"Well, David? How is Murph?"

"He is dozing, Your Lordship," said the doctor, soberly. "His breathing is still labored."

"Is he still in danger?"

"His condition is very grave, Your Lordship. However, we can still hope."

"Oh, Murph! I will avenge you! Yes, I will avenge you!" cried Rodolphe, in a cold and intense show of fury. Then he added, "David, I need to have a word with you." And he whispered into the black man's ear. The latter trembled. "You hesitate?" Rodolphe asked him. "Yet I've often discussed this with you before. The moment for applying the idea is now."

"I'm not hesitating, Your Highness. I approve of your idea. It embodies a whole philosophy of penal reform that should be studied by the greatest scholars of criminality, for this sentence will be at once simple, terrible, and just. In the present case, this measure is appropriate. Besides the many crimes that led to this criminal's being sent away for life, he's responsible for three murders or attempted murders: the cattle merchant, Murph, and you. This is just."

"And this way, he'll still have endless days ahead to repent what he's done," said Rodolphe. "Good, David. We understand each other."

"Yes, we are of one mind on this action, Your Lordship."

After a moment of silence, Rodolphe added, "Would you say that five thousand francs would be enough for him, David?"

"That should be perfectly sufficient, Your Lordship."

"My boy," said Rodolphe to the flabbergasted Slasher, "I need to talk a little more with this gentleman. While I'm speaking with him, would you please go into the room next door and look for a large red wallet on the desk? Take five one-thousand-franc bills out of it and bring them to me."

"And who is this five thousand for?" asked the Slasher, unable to restrain himself.

"For the Schoolmaster. Tell him while you're there that we're bringing him in here."

CHAPTER 21

THE PUNISHMENT

The scene takes place in a brilliantly lit red sitting room. Wearing a long black velvet dressing gown that enhances his facial pallor, Rodolphe sits in front of a large table, covered with a carpet. Two wallets are resting on this table: the one the Schoolmaster had stolen from Tom in the Cité and the other belonging to the bandit. Also on it are the Owl's imitation gold chain with the lapis lazuli cross, the stiletto (still bloodstained) that had been used to attack Murph, the crowbar used to break down the door, and, finally, the five one-thousand-franc notes that the Slasher had gotten from the adjoining room.

The black doctor is seated on one side of the table, the Slasher on the other. The Schoolmaster, tightly bound and unable to move, sits in a wheelchair in the middle of the sitting room. Those who brought the man in have left the room. Only Rodolphe, the doctor, and the Slasher remain. Rodolphe is no longer angry: he remains calm, sad, collected; he is going to accomplish a solemn and formidable task. The doctor is thoughtful. The Slasher is vaguely apprehensive; he cannot wrest his eyes from Rodolphe's gaze.

The Schoolmaster is white with fear. Perhaps he might have found a legal arrest less frightening. His daring would not have abandoned him before a normal tribunal. But, here, everything around him both surprised and frightened him; he was in Rodolphe's power—Rodolphe, a man he had deemed a worker capable of betraying him or of flinching at the moment of the crime, the same man he had intended to sacrifice to his suspicion and in the hope of profiting all alone from the heist. And at this moment, Rodolphe seemed to him as awesome and imposing as justice itself.

Outside, all is completely silent. The only sound to be heard is the noise of the rain falling from the roof onto the cobblestones.

Rodolphe addresses the Schoolmaster. "You escaped from the penal colony to which you were condemned for life for the crimes of counterfeiting, theft, and murder. You are, in fact, Anselme Duresnel."

"That's false, let anyone who can, try to prove it!" the Schoolmaster said in a distorted voice, looking around wildly and nervously.

"What?" cried the Slasher. "Weren't we together at Rochefort?"

Rodolphe made a sign to the Slasher, who then became silent. Rodolphe continued: "You are Anselme Duresnel. You will admit to that in due time. You robbed and murdered a livestock merchant on the Poissy road."

"That's false!"

"You will admit it in due time."

The criminal looked on Rodolphe with wonder.

"You broke in here tonight in order to steal; you stabbed the master of this house."

"You are the one who gave me the idea to do it," said the Schoolmaster, beginning to regain a little of his confidence. "I was attacked, so I defended myself."

"The man you struck did not attack you; he was unarmed! It is true that I proposed this theft to you and I will tell you why in just a moment. The day before, after having robbed a man and a woman in the Cité, after having stolen this very wallet, you made them an offer to kill me for one thousand francs!"

"I heard it myself!" cried the Slasher.

The Schoolmaster shot him a look of fierce hatred.

Rodolphe continued, "So you see, you did not need me to tempt you into doing evil!"

"You are not the public prosecutor. I have no more to say to you."

"Here is why I proposed this heist to you. I knew you had escaped the penal colony. You knew the parents of an unfortunate girl whose tortures were caused almost entirely by the Owl, your accomplice. I wanted to lure you here with the promise of a theft, the only lure capable of attracting you. Once you were in my power, I would have given you the choice either of being turned over to the law, which would have made you pay with your life for the murder of the livestock merchant."

"That's false! It wasn't me."

"Or to be taken, by my own means, outside of France to a place where you would be imprisoned for life, but on the condition that you give me the information that I wanted. You were condemned for life to a penal colony and you had escaped and violated the condition of your imprisonment. By seizing you and putting you somewhere where you couldn't hurt anyone else I would have been serving society, and, with the confession you could have made to me, I could have returned to his family a poor creature who is more unfortunate than guilty. Such was my project, at first. It was not legal; but, considering your escape and your new crimes, you have put yourself outside the rule of law. Yesterday, Providence revealed your true name to me."

"That's false! My name is not Duresnel."

Rodolphe picked up the Owl's chain from the table, and, showing the Schoolmaster the lapis lazuli cross, he exclaimed, in a menacing tone: "This is sacrilege! You have debased this holy relic—three times holy because your child had it as a pious gift from his mother and his grandmother—by giving it to a filthy creature!" The Schoolmaster, dumbfounded by this discovery, lowered his head in silence. "Yesterday, I learned that fifteen years ago you abducted your own son from his mother and that you alone knew where and whether he still lived. This new misdeed has been one reason the more for me to take you captive, not even considering my own personal reason. That is not the reason I seek revenge. Tonight you have spilled blood yet again for no reason. The man you attacked approached you in all trust, not suspecting your murderous madness. He asked you what you wished. 'Your money and your life!'—and you struck him down with your dagger."

"Monsieur Murph gave me the same report when I came to his aid," said the doctor.

"It's false—he lies."

"Murph never lies," Rodolphe said, coldly. "Your crimes call out for an extraordinary expiation. You entered this garden with a weapon, and you stabbed a man to rob him. You have committed another violent crime. You are going to die here. Out of pity for your wife and child, we will spare you the humiliation of the scaffold. We will put it out that you were killed in an armed attack. Prepare yourself. Our weapons are loaded and ready." Rodolphe's expression was implacable.

The Schoolmaster had noticed two men armed with rifles in the next room. His captors knew who he was. He really did think that they were going to do away with him in order to bury in darkness his latest crimes and save his family from fresh opprobrium. Like others of his kind, this man was as cowardly as he was fierce. Believing that his time had come, he trembled convulsively; his lips whitened; in a strangulated voice, he cried, "Mercy!"

"There will be no mercy for you," said Rodolphe. "If we do not blow your brains out here, the scaffold awaits you."

"I prefer the scaffold. At least that way I would live for two or three months longer. Why would you care, since I will still be punished either way in the end? Mercy! Mercy!"

"But your wife . . . your son . . . they bear your name."

"My name is already dishonored. Even if I live only eight more days, have mercy!"

"He doesn't even demonstrate the disdain for life you can find sometimes in great criminals," said Rodolphe, with disgust.

"And, anyway, the law forbids taking justice into your own hands," the Schoolmaster continued, feeling more confident.

"The law!" Rodolphe cried. "The law? You dare invoke the law, you who have lived for these last twenty years in open and armed rebellion against society?"

The thief hung his head without responding, and then said in a humble voice, "For pity's sake, at least let me live!"

"Will you tell me where your son is?"

"Yes, yes, I'll tell you everything I know."

"Will you tell me who the parents are of that girl whose childhood was made a living hell by the Owl?"

"In my wallet there are papers that will put you on their tracks. It seems that her mother was a great lady."

"Where is your son?"

"You will let me live?"

"First, confess."

"But when you know . . ." said the Schoolmaster, hesitating.

"You have killed him!"

"No, no, I placed him with one of my accomplices who, when I was arrested, managed to escape."

"What did he do with him?"

"He took him away; he gave him the necessary training to enter into our business, so we could make use of him. But I won't tell you any more unless you promise not to kill me."

"You dare to bargain with me, you wretch?"

"Well, okay, then, no I won't. But have pity; just have me arrested for today's crime; don't speak of the other. Give me at least the chance to save my life."

"So you want to live?"

"Oh, yes, yes! Who can tell? One never knows what might happen," the criminal let out involuntarily. He was already pondering the possibility of another escape.

"You want to live at any price—to live?"

"Yes, to live, even in chains, even for a month, even for a week. Oh! I don't want to die right now!"

"Confess all your crimes and you'll live."

"I'll live! Truly? I'll live?"

"Listen, out of pity for your wife and your son, I will give you a bit of wise advice: die—die today!"

"Oh, no! Don't go back on your word—let me live. The most degraded, the most frightening existence is nothing compared to death."

"That's what you want?"

"Oh, yes, yes!"

"That's what you want?"

"Yes, I'll never complain about any of this."

"So what have you done with your son?"

"The friend of whom I spoke to you had him taught to keep books in order to place him in a bank so that he could give us information about . . . certain things. We arranged it between us. Even when I was at Rochefort and waiting to escape, I was directing the scheme. We communicated by code."

"This man terrifies me!" cried Rodolphe, shivering. "There are crimes that I didn't suspect. Confess! Confess! Why did you want to have your son placed with a banker?"

"For . . . well, you understand . . . being in an agreement with us . . . without seeming to . . . to inspire confidence in the banker . . . to help us . . . and . . ."

"Oh, my God! His son—his own son!" cried Rodolphe in horror and pain, hiding his head in his hands.

"But it was only a question of counterfeiting!" cried the criminal. "And even then, when we revealed to him what we expected of him, my son became indignant. After a violent scene with the person who had carried him off in order to help with our plans, he disappeared. That was eight months ago. Since then, no one knows what's become of him. You will find in my wallet evidence of all the steps that this person took to find him, fearing that he would denounce our conspiracy, but in Paris, we lost all trace of him. The last place he lived was at fourteen rue du Temple, under the name of François Germain; the address is also in my wallet. You see, I have told you everything. Keep your promise and have me arrested only for this night's robbery."

"And the livestock merchant from Poissy?"

"No one can find out about that—there's no evidence. I am willing to admit it to you to show my goodwill, but before the judge I will deny everything."

"You admit it, then?"

"I was completely wretched, I didn't know how I would live. It was the Owl's suggestion. Now, I'm sorry for it, you see, since I admit it. Oh, if you would just turn me in to the law, I would give you my word of honor that I would never take up this way of living again."

"You will live, and I will not turn you in to the law."

"You are going to forgive me?" cried the Schoolmaster, not believing his ears. "You are going to forgive me?"

"I judge—and I punish!" Rodolphe thundered. "I will not turn you in to the law, because from there you will go either to the penal colony or to the scaffold, and that cannot happen. No, that cannot happen. To the penal colony, to rule over that cesspool once again by your strength and your villainy? To slake your instinct for brutal oppression once again, perhaps abhorred and feared by all, for crime has its pride and you rejoice in your monstrosity? To the penal colony? No, no! Your iron body is invulnerable to the galley slave's work and the screw's club. And then, chains may be broken, walls broken through, ramparts scaled, and one of these days you would manage once again to escape your sentence to throw yourself on society, like a wild, rabid animal, leaving murder and rapine in your wake, because nothing is safe from your herculean strength and your knife. This must not be—no, this must not be! In the penal colony you will break your chains. What can be done to keep society safe from your madness? Should you be turned over to the executioner?"

"So it's my death that you want?" cried the bandit. "It's my death, then?"

"Death? Don't even hope for it! You are such a coward, you fear death so much that you would never believe it was about to befall you! In your determination to live, in your obstinate hope, you would escape the anguish of its formidable approach! A stupid, insane hope! But what does that matter? It would obscure the expiating horror of your final torment; only under the blade of the executioner would you believe it was upon you! And then, senseless from terror, you would be no more than an inert mass offered as a sacrifice to the spirits of your victims. That cannot happen. You would believe you could save yourself until the last minute. You, monster, left with some hope? What? To have hope come and hang its sweet and consoling illusions on the walls of your cell, right up to the point at which death clouds your vision? No, indeed! Old Satan would laugh too much. If you do not repent, I will not allow you any more hope in this life—I will not."

"What can I have done to this man? Who is he? What does he want from me? Where am I?" cried the Schoolmaster, almost in delirium.

Rodolphe continued: "If, on the other hand, you faced death brazenly, still it would be imperative not to deliver you to the executioner. For you, the scaffold would be a bloody platform where you, like so many others, could make a showcase of your ferocity. It would be a place where you would damn your soul with one final blasphemy out of indifference to your wretched life! That must not happen, either. It is not good for the common people to see a condemned man mocking the guillotine, flouting the executioner, and chuckling as he exhales the last divine spark the Creator has placed in us. The saving of a soul is something sacred. Every crime may be expiated, may be atoned for. So says our Savior. But one must sincerely desire that expiation and atonement. There is not enough space between judgment and the scaffold for that. You must not die like that."

The Schoolmaster was crushed. For the first time in his life, there was something that scared him more than death—his fear was vague, but horrible. The black doctor and the Slasher looked upon Rodolphe anxiously. They quivered as they listened to the reverberations of his voice, as cutting and pitiless as the edge of an ax. They could feel their hearts beating painfully in their chests.

Rodolphe continued: "So, Anselme Duresnel, you will not go to the penal colony, and you will not die."

"But what do you want from me? Have you been sent for me by the devil?"

"Listen," said Rodolphe, rising solemnly in a way that lent him a menacing authority, "you have criminally taken advantage of your strength: I will paralyze that strength. The strongest trembled before you: you will tremble before the weakest. Murderer, you have plunged God's creatures into an eternal night: the eternal darkness will begin for you in this life—today!—in a moment. Finally, your punishment will fit your crimes. However," Rodolphe added with heartbreaking pity, "this horrible punishment will at least open before you an endless horizon for expiation. I would be as much a criminal as you if, in punishing you, I merely exacted my revenge, as justified as that would be. Far from being a merely sterile death, your punishment will be fertile. Far from damning you, it might redeem you. If, to remove from you any further ability to cause harm, I also dispossess you forever of the splendors of creation—if I plunge you into utter darkness, alone, with only the memory of your crimes, it is so that you will ceaselessly think upon their enormity. Yes, isolated forever from the external world, you will be forced to look forever inward upon yourself—and then, I hope, your face, darkened by infamy, will redden with shame. Your soul, hardened now by ferocity, corrupted by crime, will be softened then by commiseration. Every word you speak now is a blasphemy, every word you speak later will become a prayer. You are bold and cruel now because you are strong; later, you will be gentle and humble because you will be weak. Your heart is closed now to repentance, but later you will weep for your victims. You have degraded the intelligence that God gave you and reduced it to its instincts for pillage and murder. You have turned yourself from a man into a savage beast. One day your intelligence will be reignited by remorse and will be lifted up by expiation. You have not even given the respect that wild beasts give to their females and their young; after a long life consecrated to the redemption of your crimes, your final prayer will be to beg God to grant you the unmerited happiness of dying in the midst of your wife and child." In speaking these last words, Rodolphe had become sad and deeply emotional.

The Schoolmaster had almost ceased to be frightened. He believed that Rodolphe had wanted merely to frighten him in order to arrive at his moral message. Almost reassured by his judge's gentle tones, the criminal, becoming more insolent as he lost his fear, said with a coarse laugh: "So, are we going to play charades now, or will we be attending a catechism?" The black man looked at Rodolphe anxiously, expecting a return of his rage. But nothing of the sort happened. The young man shook his head with an ineffable expression of sadness and said to the doctor, "Proceed, David! Let God punish me if I am in error!" And Rodolphe hid his face in his hands.

At the words "Proceed, David!" the black man rang a bell. Two men entered, dressed in black. With a gesture, David pointed to the door of an adjoining office. The two men rolled the Schoolmaster's chair into the office. He had been so securely bound that he could not make the slightest movement. His head was affixed to the back of the chair with a scarf that went around his neck and shoulders.

"Secure his forehead to the chair with a handkerchief and gag him with another one," said David, without going into the office.

"You want to cut my throat now? Have mercy!" said the Schoolmaster. "Mercy!" And then nothing more than confused murmuring could be heard.

The two men reappeared. The doctor signaled to them, and they left. "My lord?" the black man said, verifying his intentions one last time.

"Proceed," Rodolphe responded, without moving. And David walked slowly into the office.

"Monsieur Rodolphe, I'm frightened," said the Slasher, completely pale and in a trembling voice. "Monsieur Rodolphe, say something to me. I'm frightened. Am I dreaming? What is the black man going to do to the Schoolmaster? I can't hear anything, Monsieur Rodolphe—and that makes me even more frightened."

David left the office. He had become pale in the manner of blacks. His lips were white. He rang. The two men reappeared. "Bring the chair back in." They brought the Schoolmaster back in. "Remove his gag." They removed it.

"So you want to torture me?" the Schoolmaster cried out, more in anger than in pain. "Why do you amuse yourself by pricking at my eyes? That was painful. Have you put out the lights here to torture me further in the darkness as you did there?"

There was a moment of terrifying silence.

"You are blind," David said, finally, in a voice full of feeling.

"That's not true! It's not possible! You are making it dark here on purpose!" the Schoolmaster cried out, making a violent effort to get out of the chair.

"Untie him. Allow him to get up and walk," said Rodolphe. The two men removed the Schoolmaster's bonds. He quickly got up, made a step while holding his hands in front of him, and then fell back in the chair, raising his arms to the heavens.

"Give him this wallet, David," said Rodolphe.

The doctor placed a small wallet into the trembling hands of the Schoolmaster.

"There is enough money in that wallet to give you food and shelter until you end your days in solitude somewhere. Now you are free. Go and repent. God is merciful!"

"Blind," the Schoolmaster repeated, mechanically grasping the wallet in his hand.

"Open the doors. Get him out of here!" said Rodolphe. The doors were opened with much noise.

"Blind! Blind! Blind!" the Schoolmaster repeated, crushed. "My God! It's really true!"

"You are free, you have money. Leave!"

"But I can't leave. What would you have me do? I can't see anything anymore!" he cried out in despair. "Really, it's an unspeakable crime to take advantage of your power in this way to—"

"It's an unspeakable crime to take advantage of your power," Rodolphe repeated, interrupting him in a solemn tone. "And you, what did you do with your power?"

"Oh, death! Yes, I would have preferred death!" the Schoolmaster cried out. "To be at the mercy of the whole world! To fear everything! A child could defeat me now! What can I do? My God! My God! What can I do?"

"You have money."

"Someone will rob it," the criminal said.

"Someone will rob it! Do you understand these words that you speak in fear—you, who have robbed so many? Leave!"

"For the love of God," the Schoolmaster said in supplication, "give me someone to guide me! How am I to get by in the streets? Oh! Kill me! I ask you to kill me! For pity's sake—kill me!"

"No. One day, you will repent."

"Never, never, I will never repent!" the Schoolmaster cried out in rage. "But I will avenge myself. Oh, yes, I will avenge myself!" And grinding his teeth in fury, he threw himself out of the chair, his fists closed and threatening.

And at the first step, he tripped. "No, no, I can't do it! But I am still so strong. Oh, I am to be pitied, but no one will pity me—no one." And he broke down in tears.

The Slasher's fear and stupor during these events cannot be described: his rude and savage face expressed compassion. He came near Rodolphe and said quietly, "Monsieur Rodolphe, this may be no more than he deserves—he is a notorious wretch! And it's true he wanted to kill me just a moment ago. But he's blind now, and he's weeping. Well, by God! It makes me feel sorry for him. He doesn't know how to get out of here. He could get himself run over in the streets. Do you want me to take him somewhere where he can rest quietly at least?"

"That's a fine idea," said Rodolphe, moved by this generosity and taking the Slasher's hand. "Good, go with him."

The Slasher came up to the Schoolmaster and put his hand on his shoulder. The Schoolmaster started. "Who is touching me?" he asked in a dull voice.

"Me."

"Who is me?"

"The Slasher."

"So you want to get back at me, too."

"You don't know where to go. Take my arm. I'll guide you."

"You? You?"

"Yes, you make me feel sorry for you. Come on, now!"

"You want to set some trap for me, don't you?"

"You know well enough that I'm no coward. I wouldn't take advantage of your misfortune. Now let's go; let's get out of here. It's daylight."

"Daylight!!! Oh, there's no more daylight for me!" the Schoolmaster cried.

Rodolphe could bear this scene no longer. Quickly, he went back in, followed by David. He gestured to the two servants to withdraw.

The Slasher and the Schoolmaster remained alone together.

"Is it true that there's money in the wallet he gave me?" the criminal asked after a long silence.

"Yes, I myself put five thousand francs in it. With that you can let a room somewhere in some part of the countryside to live out your days—or would you rather that I took you to the ogress?"

"No, she would rob me."

"To Red-Arm?"

"He would poison me in order to rob me!"

"So where should I take you?"

"I don't know. At least you're no thief, Slasher. Here, hide my wallet deep in my jacket so that Owl doesn't see it. She'd lift it from me."

"The Owl? They took her to the clinic at Beaujon. In my fight with the two of you tonight, I bent up one of her legs."

"What will become of me? My God, what will become of me, with this black curtain always drawn in front of me? And what if, on this black curtain, I saw the pale and dead faces of those . . ." He trembled, and said to the Slasher in a hollow voice, "The man from tonight—is he dead?"

"No."

"That's good, at least!" And the criminal stayed silent for a bit. Then, suddenly, he cried out, bursting forth in anger, "But it's your fault—you got me into this, Slasher! Thief! If not for you, I would have iced the man and carried off the money. If I'm blind, it's your fault! Yes, it's your fault!"

"Stop thinking like that. It will just make you feel rotten. So, are you coming or not? I'm tired and I want to sleep. I've had enough fun for one day. Tomorrow, I'm going back to my hole. I'll take you where you want and then I'm going to bed."

"But I have no idea where to go. I don't dare return to my hideout, I have to say—"

"Well, then, listen: do you want to stay in my hole for a day or two? I could maybe find some honest people who didn't know who you were and who would be willing to let you a room with them as a disabled person. I have just the thing: I know a dockworker at the Saint-Nicolas port whose mother lives at Saint-Mandé; she's a good woman who hasn't been so lucky. She might well be willing to take you in. Are you coming or not?"

"A person can trust you, Slasher. I'm not frightened to go to your place with my money. You've never robbed people. You aren't mean—you're generous."

"Come on. That's enough of those epitaphs."

"It's just that I'm grateful because you're willing to do me a good turn, Slasher. You harbor no hatred and no bitterness," the criminal said, humbly. "You're a better man than I am."

"Well, damn, I daresay it's true! Monsieur Rodolphe said I had heart."

"But what kind of man is he anyway, this man? He isn't a man," the Schoolmaster cried, with a returning surge of fury and desperation, "he's a hangman! A monster!"

The Slasher shrugged his shoulders and said, "Are we going?"

"We're going to your place, right, Slasher?"

"Yes."

"You don't bear me any ill will from tonight—you swear it, right?"

"Yes."

"And you're sure he didn't die . . . that man?"

"I'm sure of it."

"Well, there's that, at least," said the bandit in a hollow voice. And, leaning on the Slasher's arm, he left the house in the allée des Veuves.

BOOK II

CHAPTER I

L'ÎLE-ADAM

One month had passed since the events we have just recounted. We will now take our reader to the small city of L'Île-Adam, which is in a beautiful location on the banks of the Oise river, at the edge of a forest.

The most trivial occurrences take on outsize significance in the provinces. Thus the idlers of L'Île-Adam, who were walking about this morning in the church square, were greatly concerned to know when the person who had purchased the town's fanciest butcher shop, which the Widow Dument had recently sold, would arrive. There could be no doubt that the purchaser was wealthy. After all, he had had the shop richly painted and decorated. Workers had been at the job day and night for three weeks. A beautiful gilded bronze grille stretched out over the opening of the stall, enclosing it while allowing the air to circulate. On either side of the grille stood large rectangular columns topped by two large bull's heads, each with golden horns. These columns supported the vast entablature that would hold the store's sign. The rest of the two-storied building was painted the color of stone. Its shutters were a light gray. Except for the hanging of the sign, all of the work had been completed. The town's idlers impatiently awaited the sign so that they might know the name of the owner who would succeed the widow.

Finally, the workers carried over a large placard on which the curious could read in gold letters against a black background, "Francoeur, Merchant and Butcher." This information only partially satisfied the curiosity of L'Île-Adam's busybodies. Who was this Monsieur Francoeur, anyway? One of the most impatient of them went to find out this information from the cheerful and friendly butcher's assistant, who was busy putting the last touches on the display.

Asked about his employer, Monsieur Francoeur, the assistant said that he did not know him yet since the man had bought the business by proxy. But the boy had no doubt that his boss would make every effort to deserve the patronage of the worthy clients of L'Île-Adam. This slight compliment, made in a welcoming and friendly way, disposed the curious in Monsieur Francoeur's favor. Many even promised their patronage to the assistant right then and there.

The house had a carriage entrance that opened on the Church road.

Two hours after the opening of the store, a brand-new wicker cart, harnessed to a good, strong draft horse, entered the courtyard of the butcher shop. Two men got out of this cart. One was Murph, who, though still pale, was completely cured of his wound. The other was the Slasher.

At the risk of retailing commonplaces, we will say that mode of dress is such a powerful sign of prestige that the habitué of the Cité's joints could hardly be recognized in the clothing he now wore. His facial expression had undergone the same metamorphosis: along with his rags, he had thrown off his savage, brutal, and stormy manner. If you saw him walking along, with his hands in the pockets of his long, warm, brown beaver-hair overcoat, his chin freshly shaven and ensconced in a white tie with embroidered edges, you would have taken him for the most mild-mannered member of the bourgeoisie.

Murph tied the horse's reins to an iron ring attached to the wall and signaled to the Slasher to follow him. They came into into an attractive entrance hall furnished in walnut. This was the back room of the store. Its two windows looked out onto the courtyard, where the horse was impatiently stamping. Murph seemed to feel at home there, opening a cupboard, taking out a bottle of brandy and a glass, and saying to the Slasher:

"Since it is so frightfully chilly this morning, perhaps you will have a glass of brandy, my boy?"

"If you don't mind, Monsieur Murph, I'd rather not."

"You decline?"

"Yes. I'm already so happy, and joy has a way of warming you up. But you know, well, when I say 'happy'—well, maybe."

"What do you mean?"

"Yesterday, you came to find me at the Saint-Nicolas gate, where I was working hard at unloading to warm myself up. I had not seen you since that night when the black man with white hair blinded the Schoolmaster. It's true enough that it was the only time he didn't steal something, but still—damn! That did make me feel sorry for him. And Monsieur Rodolphe, what an expression he had on his face! Him, who seemed such a gentle guy, he frightened me at that moment."

"Well . . . and so?"

"So you said to me, 'Hello, Slasher.' 'Hello, Monsieur Murph. And so you're up on your feet? Damn, that's for the better—that is! And how's Monsieur Rodolphe?' 'He had to leave a few days after the business in the allée des Veuves, and he forgot you, my boy.' 'Well,' I answered you, 'I would really be sorry if Monsieur Rodolphe has truly forgotten me.'"

"I meant to say, my loyal friend, that he had forgotten to compensate you for your services, but he will remember them always."

"And those words cheered me up immediately, Monsieur Murph. Damn! I'm not one to forget it, you can be sure. He said to me that I had heart and honor—and that's all I needed."

"Unfortunately, my boy, his lordship left without leaving any further instructions as to what to do for you. I possess nothing myself except that which his lordship gives me, so I cannot show my gratitude as I would like to, given all I owe you for my own part."

"Oh, come on, Monsieur Murph! You've got to be kidding."

"But why the devil didn't you come back to the allée des Veuves after that deadly night? His lordship would not have left town without thinking of you."

"Well, Monsieur Rodolphe didn't ask for me. I thought he didn't have any more need of me."

"You surely must have thought at least that he needed to show you his gratitude."

"Well, didn't you just tell me that Monsieur Rodolphe has not forgotten me, Monsieur Murph?"

"Well, then. Very well, we won't talk any more about it. But I must say that I had a lot of trouble finding you. You don't go to the ogress's place anymore?"

"No."

"Why not?"

"For personal reasons, really. Nothing special."

"I think it's splendid. But let's get back to what you were saying to me."

"About what, Monsieur Murph?"

"You were saying, 'I'm happy to have run into you,' and then you said, 'Happy—maybe.'"

"I'll give it to you straight, Monsieur Murph. Yesterday, when you came to my hole, you said, 'My boy, I'm not rich, but I might be able to find you a position that would be easier on you than your work at the docks and that would allow you to earn four francs a day.' Four francs a day! Long live the Charter! I couldn't believe it. That's the pay of an assistant sergeant! So I answered, 'That works great for me, Monsieur Murph.' 'But,' you said, 'you can't go dressed like a beggar, because that would frighten the respectable people where I am taking you.' So I answer, 'I don't have any other kind of clothing.' So you say, 'Come to the Temple.' So I follow you. I choose the sharpest duds I can find at Old Lady Hubart's store. You lend me money to pay and in a quarter of an hour I'm cinched up like a proprietor or a dentist. You set a meeting for this morning at the Saint-Denis gate, at daybreak; I find you there with your cart and here we are."

"So! What is there in all this for you to feel sorry about?"

"Well, there's this . . . to be well dressed, you see, Monsieur Murph, it spoils you. When I put my worker's smock and rags back on, they won't feel right. And then, earning four francs a day when before you only made two, and so suddenly—it all just seems too good to be true, like something that can't last. So I'd rather spend my life on the dirty straw bed in my hole than sleep in a comfortable bed for five or six nights. That's just how I am."

"There's some logic to what you're saying. Still, it would be even better to sleep in a comfortable bed every night."

"It's clear that it's better to have your fill of bread than to fall over from hunger. But look over here! Isn't this a butcher shop?" asked the Slasher when he heard the blows from the assistant's cleaver and glimpsed beef quarters through the curtains.

"Yes, my loyal friend. It belongs to one of my friends. Would you like to have a look around while my horse is catching its breath?"

"You bet! It brings me back to my youth, if it weren't for the fact that I had Montfaucon for a slaughterhouse and old nags for livestock. It's funny, you know. If I had any money, being a butcher is a life I could really have liked. Going out on your hack to buy cattle at the fairs, coming home to your fireplace to warm up when it's cold or dry out when the weather is wet, finding your woman there, a plump, fresh, happy mama with a whole bunch of children who search your pockets to see if you've brought them home any treats. And then, in the morning, taking hold of a steer by its horns . . . especially when it's acting up—of course it would act up—tying it to the ring, slaughtering it, cutting it up, dressing it . . . Damn! That would have been my dream, just like Songbird's was to eat barley candy when she was little. Speaking of that poor girl, Monsieur Murph, when I didn't see her anymore at the ogress's place, I suspected that Monsieur Rodolphe had gotten her out of there. Now that would be a good thing to do, Monsieur Murph. Poor girl! She never wanted to do anything bad. She was so young! And then later—you get used to it. Well, Monsieur Rodolphe did a good thing."

"I am much of your opinion. But would you like to visit the shop while we wait for our horse to catch its breath?"

The Slasher and Murph went into the shop. Then they went to the stable in which three magnificent steers and around twenty sheep were enclosed. Then they visited the horse stables, the shed, the slaughterhouse, the barn, and all the outbuildings of the establishment. The care with which everything was maintained suggested an environment of order and ease.

When they had seen everything but the upper floor, Murph said: "You have to admit, my friend is one lucky fellow. He owns this establishment and everything in it, not to mention a thousand crowns he has on hand for his trade needs. And on top of that, he's just thirty-eight years old and strong as a bull; he has an iron constitution and enjoys his occupation. The loyal and honest assistant that you saw below can hold his place down competently when he goes to fairs to buy livestock. As I said, isn't he lucky, my friend?"

"You bet, Monsieur Murph. But that's how it is. Some of us are lucky, some aren't. When I think that I'm going to earn four francs a day while others earn only half of that, or even less . . ."

"Would you like to go upstairs to see the rest of the house?"

"I'd be glad to, Monsieur Murph."

"Good, since the proprietor who wants to hire you is upstairs."

"The proprietor who wants to hire me?"

"Yes."

"Well, why didn't you tell me that sooner?"

"I'll explain it all in a bit."

"Wait a moment," said the Slasher, looking sad and embarrassed, holding Murph's arm to stop him. "Listen, I have to tell you something . . . that Monsieur Rodolphe maybe didn't tell you, but that I can't hide from the proprietor who wants to hire me. Since it might disgust him, it's better for him to find out right away rather than later."

"What do you want to say?"

"I want to say . . ."

"Well?"

"That I'm an ex-con—that I was in a penal colony," said the Slasher, quietly.

"Ah!" said Murph.

"But I've never done anything bad to anybody," the Slasher cried out, "and I'd rather pitch over dead from hunger than steal. But I did worse than stealing," the Slasher added, lowering his head. "I killed, in anger. And that's not all," he continued after a moment of silence. "Proprietors don't want to employ convicts, and they're right. You don't crown those types with roses. That's what always got in the way of my finding any work other than unloading timber rafts at the docks. Because I always said when I went for a job, 'Here's how it is—do you want me or not?' I prefer being turned down on the spot than having them find out later. I just want to tell you that I'm going to lay it all out for the proprietor. You know him. If he's going to turn me down, spare me the scene and tell me, and I'll turn tail right now."

"No, come along anyway," said Murph.

The Slasher followed Murph, they climbed a staircase, a door opened, and both of them found themselves in the presence of Rodolphe.

"My good Murph, you may leave us now," said Rodolphe.

CHAPTER 2

RECOMPENSE

"Long live the Charter! I am so happy to see you again, Monsieur Rodolphe, or, I should say, Your Lordship," cried the Slasher. He felt real joy in seeing Rodolphe again, for bighearted people feel as close to those to whom they have given as they do to those from whom they have received.

"Hello, my boy; I am delighted to see you again, as well."

"And Monsieur Murph said you were gone. What a joker he is. But wait, Your Lordship—"

"Call me Monsieur Rodolphe, I like that better."

"Well, then, Monsieur Rodolphe! Forgive me for not having been to see you after the night with the Schoolmaster. I can see now that I lacked courtesy—but, well, you won't hold that against me, will you?"

"I forgive you," Rodolphe said, smiling. And then he added: "Has Murph shown you the house?"

"Yes, Monsieur Rodolphe. It's a beautiful place to live, a beautiful shop. It's well cared for and high end. Speaking of high end, that's what I'm going to be, Monsieur Rodolphe: four francs a day for a job Monsieur Murph has found for me—four francs a day!"

"I have something better to offer you, my boy."

"Better than that? I don't want to contradict you, but that would be hard. Four francs a day!"

"I have something better to offer you, I tell you. Because this house—everything in it, the shop, and the one thousand crowns in this wallet—all of this belongs to you."

The Slasher smiled stupidly and crushed his beaver-hair hat between his knees, which he pressed together mechanically. He did not understand what Rodolphe had said to him, even though his words were quite clear.

Rodolphe continued, with affection: "I understand how you may be surprised. But I'm going to say it again: this house and this money are yours. They are your property."

The Slasher's face turned crimson, he ran his calloused hand over his forehead, which was bathed in sweat, and he stammered in a husky voice: "So that means . . . that means . . . it's mine?"

"Yes, it's yours. I am giving you all this. Do you understand? I am giving all this to you."

The Slasher fidgeted in his chair, scratched his head, coughed, lowered his eyes, and didn't say a word. He felt he could not hold on to his train of thought. He understood perfectly what Rodolphe was saying to him and, for just that reason, he couldn't believe what he had heard. Between the extreme wretchedness, the degradation that had been his life, and the position Rodolphe had just offered him lay an abyss that even the service he had performed for Rodolphe could not bridge. Not wishing to hasten the moment at which his protégé's eyes would open to the reality before him, Rodolphe took full pleasure in his astonishment, in the vertigo of his happiness.

With a mixture of joy and indescribable bitterness, he recognized that some people become so accustomed to suffering and unhappiness that they cannot rationally entertain the possibility of a future that, for many, would have little in it to envy. He thought that if man had ever succeeded like Prometheus in procuring some spark of the divine, surely it was in a case like this one, in these moments in which he had done (if one will pardon the blasphemy!) what divine justice ought to do once in a while for the world's edification. He had proven to the good and the evil alike that there is reward for the one and punishment for the other. After having enjoyed the Slasher's happy stupefaction for a little while longer, Rodolphe went on, "Does what I have given you really seem so far beyond your expectations?"

"Your Lordship," the Slasher said, springing up suddenly, "you are offering me this house and all that money—to tempt me. But I can't do it."

"You can't do what?" Rodolphe asked, with astonishment.

The Slasher became animated, and he ceased to be ashamed. He said in a firm tone of voice, "You aren't offering me all this money to pay me to steal, that I know well. In any case, I've never stolen in my life. Maybe it's to pay me to kill, but I've had enough dreams of that sergeant," the Slasher added, darkly.

"Oh, how unhappy people can be!" Rodolphe cried out bitterly. "They see compassion so rarely, then, that they can only understand generosity as an extension of crime?" Then, turning to the Slasher, he said to him gently, "You misjudge me. You are mistaken. I will never demand anything of you that is anything but honorable. What I give you, I give you because you have deserved it."

"Me?" the Slasher cried, his dumbfoundedness beginning again. "What have I done to deserve it?"

"I will tell you: without any notion of good and evil, left only to your savage instincts, imprisoned for fifteen years in a penal colony with the most frightening criminals, harried by misery and hunger, forced by the stain of your past and by the reprobation of honest people to remain in the company of the dregs of society, not only have you stayed honest, but the remorse you have shown for your crime has gone beyond any expiation that human justice could have asked of you."

This simple, noble speech was a new source of astonishment for the Slasher. He looked upon Rodolphe with a respect that was a mixture of fear and gratitude. But he couldn't yet be persuaded by the evidence.

"How do you figure, Monsieur Rodolphe, because you beat me, because thinking you to be a worker like me—since you spoke slang like you learned it at your mother's knee—I told you about my life over a glass of wine, and because after that, I stopped you from drowning, how do you figure it? Me, I mean . . . a house . . . money . . . me, a property owner? Really, Monsieur Rodolphe, I still say that this can't be."

"Thinking me to be another like yourself, you told me about your life, quite naturally and without pretense, without hiding any of your guilty or generous acts. I have judged you—and judged you well—and it pleases me to reward you."

"But, Monsieur Rodolphe, this doesn't happen. No, really, there are poor workers who are honest all their lives and who—"

"I know that, and perhaps I have done for many of them more than I am doing for you. But if the man who lives honestly amid honest people, supported by their esteem, deserves my care and support, then don't you think that the man who, despite being separated from good people, stays honest amid the most abominable villains in the world, also deserves care and support? And, moreover, that's not all you have done: you have saved my life. You have also saved the life of Murph, my dearest friend. What I do for you, then, owes as much to my own gratitude as it does to my desire to pull out of the mire a good and strong soul who has perhaps gone astray, but who is not lost. And that's not all."

"So what else do you think I've done, Monsieur Rodolphe?"

Rodolphe grasped his hand in friendship and said, "Filled with commiseration for the misery of a man who, up to that point, had wanted to kill you, you offered him your support. You even offered him a place to stay in your poor home, number nine in the Notre-Dame cul-de-sac."

"You know where I live, Monsieur Rodolphe?"

"Just because you forget all you have done for me doesn't mean I forget it. When you left my house, I had you followed and you were seen to come back to your place with the Schoolmaster."

"But Monsieur Murph told me that you didn't know where I lived, Monsieur Rodolphe."

"I wanted to put you to one last trial. I wanted to see if you were disinterested and generous. And, sure enough, after your generous action, you returned to your hard, everyday work, asking nothing, hoping nothing, not even having a bitter word on your lips for the apparent ingratitude with which I responded to your services. And when, yesterday, Murph offered you a position that earned you only slightly more than your usual work, you accepted his offer with joy, with gratitude!"

"Now listen, Monsieur Rodolphe, as for that, four francs a day are four francs a day, however you figure it. As to whatever I have done for you, it's me that should be thanking you."

"Why do you think that?"

"Yes, indeed, Monsieur Rodolphe," he went on, sadly, "I've still been thinking things over, because since I have known you, and since you said just a handful of words—'You still have HEART AND HONOR'—it's surprising how much I have been reflecting on it. It's pretty funny, when you think about it, how a handful of words—a handful of words—has done so much. But, really, you plant a handful of grains of wheat in the earth, and big stalks of the stuff will grow."

Rodolphe found this just and almost poetic comparison striking. After all, it had turned out that a mere handful of words, but powerful and magic words for those who understood them, had almost immediately cultivated in this passionate soul the good and generous instincts that were already latent there.

"So you see, Your Lordship," the Slasher went on, "it's true I saved Monsieur Rodolphe, and Monsieur Murph, a little, too, but I could have saved hundreds and thousands of people, and that wouldn't bring back to life those—" The Slasher lowered his head somberly.

"The remorse you show is a good thing, but your good deeds still make a difference."

"And then what you said to the Schoolmaster about criminals, Monsieur Rodolphe—there were things there that spoke to me, both for good and for ill."

Wanting to break the Slasher's train of thought, Rodolphe said to him, "You are the one who found the Schoolmaster a place at Saint-Mandé?"

"Yes, Monsieur Rodolphe. He had me change the notes into gold and buy a belt that I sewed around him. We put the loot in it and sent him on his way. He has room and board there for thirty sous a day, with good people who will make his life a little easier."

"I need you to perform yet another service for me, my boy."

"Whatever you say, Monsieur Rodolphe."

"In a few days, go find him, and bring him this paper. It's a title for placement in perpetuity at the Bons-Pauvres Hospice.[34] He will give them forty-five hundred francs and he will be admitted for life upon presentation of this title. Everything is arranged. I have reflected on things and I think this is a better way. It assures him of food and shelter for the rest of his days, and he will have nothing to concern himself with except repentance.

---

34. The Bons-Pauvres Hospice, located at Bicêtre, was, at various points in its history dating back to 1634, a hospital, an orphanage, an old-age home, an asylum for the mentally ill, and a prison. Here, Rodolphe is suggesting that the Schoolmaster might be cared for at the hospice, but later in the novel the same institution will appear in its guises of asylum and prison. [TN]

I am sorry not to have gotten him this situation at first, rather than having given him the money, which could have been squandered or stolen. But he made me feel such horror that I just wanted to be out of his presence. Make him this offer and take him to the hospice. If, by chance, he turns the proposal down, we'll think of something else we can do. So, you agree, you'll go find him?"

"I would be more than happy to do what you ask, Monsieur Rodolphe, but I don't know if I'm at liberty to. Monsieur Murph has got me a job for four francs a day."

"What? And what about your shop and your house?"

"Come on, Monsieur Rodolphe, stop teasing me. You've already had enough fun testing me, as you call it. 'Your house and your shop': you're just making fun of me again. You are saying to yourself: 'Let's see if this beast of a Slasher is enough of a goose to believe that . . .' Enough already, Monsieur Rodolphe. You're funny, but enough already."

"What do you mean? I just explained it all to you."

"To make it seem more believable, right. You sure made me bite, a little bit. I must have been one dumb bird!"

"My boy, you are being crazy!"

"No, no, Your Lordship. Listen, let's talk about Monsieur Murph. Even if it's already pretty shocking, four francs a day, one can just about understand that. But a shop, a house, a large pile of money—what a joke! Damn, what a joke!" And he began laughing—a loud, sincere belly laugh.

"But, again—"

"Listen, Your Lordship, frankly you had me going there a little bit for a moment. I said to myself, 'Monsieur Rodolphe, he's a playful one, there aren't many guys like that around. He maybe has something he needs someone to go to the baker of souls to find, he gives me the job, and he wants to grease my palm, so I don't suspect things.' But then I thought that I was wrong to think that of you and I realized you were putting me on, because if I were enough of an old fool as to think that you would give me a fortune for absolutely nothing, that would be the end of it, my lord. You would say: 'Poor Slasher! Scram already, you are bothering me. Have you lost your mind?'"

Rodolphe began to wonder how he could convince the Slasher. He spoke to him in a grave, imposing, almost severe tone of voice: "I never treat lightly the gratitude and interest that noble conduct inspires in me. I have told you, this house and the money are yours. It is I who give them to you. And since you won't believe me, since you force me to take an oath, I swear on my honor that all this belongs to you, that I give it to you for the reasons that I have stated to you."

In view of Rodolphe's firm, elevated tone and the serious expression on his face, the Slasher no longer doubted the truth of what he heard. For a few moments, he looked at him in silence, and then he said, without emphasis, but in a way that showed how profoundly moved he was, "I believe you, Your Lordship, and I thank you very much. A poor man like me doesn't know how to make beautiful speeches. But, again, I thank you very much. All I can say, I guess, is that I won't ever refuse aid to someone who's down, because hunger and misery are monsters as real as the ogress that caught that poor Songbird, and once you're in the gutter, there isn't a grip in the whole world strong enough to pull you out."

"You couldn't find a better way to thank me, my boy—you understand me. You will find in this desk titles to the property, acquired for you in the name of Monsieur Francoeur."

"Monsieur Francoeur?"

"You don't have a name, so I gave you that one. It presages well and I am sure you will honor it."[35]

"I promise that to you, Your Lordship."

"Take heart, my boy. You can help me to do a good deed."

"Me, Your Lordship?"

"You. In the eyes of the world, you will be a salutary living example. The happy place divine justice gives you will show that people can fall very far and still pull themselves up. And they can be of good hope if they are repentant and if they preserve certain important qualities. When people see how happy you are because you stayed honest, courageous, and generous even after you had to expiate the crime you committed by serving a terrible sentence, those who have fallen will try to become better. I wish that nothing of your past go unremembered. Sooner or later people will know about it. It's better to be up front about these things before they are discovered. In just a few minutes, we will go and find the mayor of this district. I have informed myself about him; he is a man worthy of participating in my work. I will tell him who I am, and I will be your security. And to establish, from this moment, upright relationships between you and the two people who are the moral representatives of the social life in this city, I will pledge a monthly sum of one thousand francs to be given over the next two years to the poor. I will send you this sum each month and, with the mayor and the priest, you will determine how it should be spent. If either of these two has the least scruple about being associated with you, the necessities of the charitable work will soon erase it. Once these relations are secure, it will depend only on you to deserve the esteem of these worthy people, and you won't fail to do so."

"My lord, I understand you. It isn't me, the Slasher, to whom you do all this good; it's the unfortunates who, like me, have been caught in trouble and in crime and who have gotten themselves out of it, as you say, with

35. Since Francoeur is a proper name, we have not translated it as we have the epithetic nicknames. But *Francoeur* suggests the meaning "honest heart," and Rodolphe has chosen it for that reason. [TN]

courage and honor intact. With all due respect, it's like in the army: when a whole battalion has faced death, you can't give medals to every soldier. You can give only four crosses and there are five hundred worthy men, but those who don't get the medal say to themselves: 'Okay, I'll get it the next time,' and the next time, they charge right into death again."

Rodolphe listened to his protégé with happiness. By giving this man back his self-esteem, by raising him up in his own eyes, by giving him, so to speak, an awareness of his own worth, he had almost in one stroke developed in his heart and mind thoughts full of good sense, honor, and even, one might almost say, a certain delicacy of sensibility.

"What you have said, Francoeur," Rodolphe resumed, "is a new way of showing me your gratitude, and I, in turn, give you thanks for it."

"So much the better, Your Lordship, because I would be hard-pressed to show it in any other way."

"Now let's go visit your house. Good old Murph has already had the experience of this pleasure, and I want to have it as well."

Rodolphe and the Slasher went downstairs. As they entered the courtyard, the assistant came up to the Slasher and said to him respectfully, "Since you are the proprietor, Monsieur Francoeur, I'm here to tell you that we've had business. We are out of both cutlets and lamb legs, and we will have to slaughter one or two sheep right away."

"My word!" said Rodolphe to the Slasher. "Here's the moment to put your skill to use—and I'll get the benefit of it. The morning air has given me an appetite, and I'm going to taste your cutlets, even if they are, as I fear, a little tough."

"You are truly a good person, Monsieur Rodolphe," said the Slasher, happily. "You flatter me; I'll do my best."

"Should we bring two sheep to the slaughterhouse, boss?" asked the boy.

"Yes, and bring a well-sharpened knife, one that doesn't have too thin an edge but has a strong blade."

"I have just the ticket, boss, don't worry. You could shave with it, you could."

"Damn! Monsieur Rodolphe," the Slasher said, as he took off his coat eagerly and rolled up his shirtsleeves, making visible his muscular arms. "It reminds me of my youth at the slaughterhouse. You'll see how well I cut things up. God, I want to be at it. Your knife, boy, your knife! That's the one—you understand what's needed. Now there's a blade! What more could you want? With a sticker like this, I could fell a mad bull." And the Slasher brandished the knife. His eyes began to get blood in them. The beast took over and his instinct, his sanguinary appetite, reappeared in all its frightening energy.

The slaughterhouse was in the court. It was a dark, vaulted room with rock flooring, lit from the top by a narrow opening. The boy brought a sheep up to the door: "Should I tie him to the ring, boss?"

"Tie him up, damn! Don't I have my knees! Don't you worry, I'll hold it between them as if it was in a vise. Just bring the animal over here and go back to the shop."

The boy went back. Rodolphe remained along with the Slasher. He watched him attentively, almost anxiously. "So, let's see it. To work!" he said.

"And, damn, it won't take long! You'll see if I can handle a knife or not. My hands are burning and my ears are buzzing. The blood is beating in my head like it did when I saw red. Come here, sheep. Hey, Madelon, I'm going to slash you up good!" His eyes ablaze with a savage gleam, the Slasher no longer paid any heed to the fact that Rodolphe was present. He grabbed the sheep effortlessly and carried it into the slaughtering area in a fierce ecstasy.

One would have thought him a wolf in the sheep pen, carrying off his prey. Rodolphe followed him, pressing against one of the panels of the door and closing it. The slaughterhouse was dark. The Slasher's rough face, blond hair, and rust-colored sideburns were lit, in the manner of Rembrandt, by one bright ray of light coming straight down. Bent over double, holding the knife, which gleamed in the low light, between his teeth, he pulled the ewe between his knees. When he had it under control, he took it by the head, exposed its neck, and slit its throat.

At the moment the ewe felt the blade, it let out a slight, gentle, plaintive bleat and turned its dying gaze toward the Slasher. Two spurts of blood struck the butcher in the face. The cry, the look, the blood, which disgusted him—all made a frightening impression on the man. The knife fell from his hands. His face became livid, tense, and frightening under the blood that covered it. His eyes were wide open and his hair stood on end. Then, backing away suddenly in horror, he cried out, breathlessly, "Oh! The sergeant! The sergeant!"

Rodolphe ran to his side.

"Snap out of it, my boy."

The Slasher kept repeating, "Look there . . . there . . . the sergeant." He backed up, haggardly, one step after another, his eyes transfixed as he pointed at some invisible ghost. Then, with a frightening cry, as if the ghost had touched him, he ran to the back of the slaughterhouse, to the darkest part, and there, pounding his chest against the wall, as if he wanted to break it down and escape a horrible vision, he repeated again and again, in a heavy and tormented voice, "Oh! The sergeant! . . . The sergeant! . . . The sergeant!"

CHAPTER 3

DEPARTURE

Through their care, and with great effort, Murph and Rodolphe calmed the agitated Slasher. He returned to his senses completely, but only after a long struggle with himself. He found himself alone with Rodolphe in a room on the first floor of the butcher shop.

"Your Lordship," he said, despondently, "you have been very good to me, but, after all, as you can see, I'd rather be a thousand times more unfortunate than I was before than to accept the position you're offering me."

"All the same, think it over."

"Really, Your Lordship, when I heard that poor beast's cry, and it did nothing to defend itself, when I felt the blood spurt on my face—and it was hot blood—it seemed to be alive. Oh! You don't know what that's like. And then my dream returned, the sergeant, and those poor young soldiers I slashed up, who didn't defend themselves and died looking at me in such a gentle way . . . so gentle . . . as if they were pitying me! Oh! Your Lordship, it could drive you mad!" And the unfortunate man hid his face in his hands with a convulsive movement.

"Come now, pull yourself together."

"Pardon me, Your Lordship, but now the sight of blood—of a knife—I couldn't bear it. At any moment, it would revive the dreams that I had begun to forget. To have my hands and feet in blood, every day . . . to slit the throats of poor animals who don't defend themselves . . . Oh! No, no, I couldn't do it. I'd rather be blind, like the Schoolmaster, than to be forced to take that job." The forcefulness of the Slasher's body language, tone of voice, and facial expression as he said this cannot be described.

Rodolphe felt himself profoundly moved. He was now persuaded of the horrible sensation that the sight of blood caused his protégé. In a single moment, the Slasher had been overcome by the wild animal in him, the instinct for blood, but remorse had overcome the instinct. That was indeed beautiful. That was indeed instructive. It must be said in praise of Rodolphe that this remorse was not for him unexpected. It was his wish, not mere chance, that had brought on the scene in the slaughterhouse.

"Excuse me, Your Lordship," said the Slasher timidly. "This is a poor reward for your goodness toward me, but—"

"Far from it. You have exceeded my greatest hopes. But, I admit, I wasn't sure I would find your remorse to be this holy and exalted."

"What do you mean, Your Lordship?"

"Listen," said Rodolphe, "here was what I was thinking: I had chosen the occupation of butcher for you because your instincts and your preferences led you that way."

"Alas, Your Lordship, it's true. Putting aside what you now know, it would have made me very happy. I was just saying as much to Monsieur Murph."

"I knew that, and, my well-named Francoeur, if you had accepted the offer I made you—and you could have done it without having lost any of my respect—everything here would belong to you since I was paying a sacred debt. I would have removed you from a thankless life, I would have made of you a good, striking, and salutary example for others, and I would have continued to take a personal interest in your future. If, on the contrary, the sight of blood—which you would ordinarily have to be ready to spill, as a matter of course—had reminded you of your crime, if the kind of involuntary reaction you displayed showed me that your remorse was still active in the depths of your soul, my intentions for you would change. The occupation that I offered you would then have become a daily torture."

"Oh! That's only too true, Monsieur Rodolphe, a terrible torture."

"Now here is what I propose. I believe you will accept it, and I have acted upon this conviction. A person I know who owns considerable property in Algeria[36] has transferred to me on your behalf (there is nothing more to do than to sign the deed) a vast farm intended for the raising of livestock. The lands connected with it are extremely fertile and fully cultivated. But I won't hide from you, knowing as I do your courage and your need to exercise it, that I have acquired this property conditionally, even though they are at the edges of the Atlas, which is to say at the outposts, and exposed to frequent Arab attacks. You will have to be as much of a soldier as a farmer. The place is both fortress and farmland. The man who runs this property in the owner's absence will catch you up on everything you need to know. They say that he is honest and loyal. You will keep him with you as long as you need him. Once you get settled there, you will have the ability not only to increase your wealth through your industry and intelligence, but also, with your courage, to do a real service to your country. The colonists are forming militias. The extent of your property and the number of tenants on it will make you the leader of an armed band of considerable size. If this armed band follows your courageous lead in enthusiasm and discipline, it could become

36. France invaded Algeria in 1830. The French annexation, colonization, and occupation of the country lasted until Algeria achieved independence in 1962. [TN]

extremely useful for protecting properties scattered across the plain. Let me tell you again: I have chosen this situation for you despite the danger, or rather because of it, because I wanted to put your natural intrepidity to good use. For even though you have paid for and almost redeemed your crime, your rehabilitation will be nobler, more complete, and more heroic for having been achieved in the midst of an untamed country and its perils rather than in the midst of the peaceful inhabitants of a small town. If I did not give you this choice at first, it's because it seemed to me more than likely that the other one would have made you content. And this one was so risky that I did not want to expose you to it without having given you the choice. And you still don't have to choose this alternative. If this position doesn't suit you, just tell me honestly, and we'll look for something else . . . Otherwise, tomorrow all the papers will be signed and I will give you the titles to your property, and you will go to Algiers with the representative of the prior owner of the farmland, who will put you in possession of your goods. Two years' worth of rent will be due to you and you will take possession of it upon your arrival. The land brings in three thousand francs. Work it, improve it, be active and vigilant, and you will easily enhance your well-being and that of the colonists. You will also be a savior to them, because I have no doubt that you will always show yourself to be charitable and generous. You will remember that being rich means giving much. Even though we will be separated from each other, I will not lose sight of you. I will never forget that both my best friend and I owe our lives to you. The one proof of attachment and gratitude I ask of you is that you learn as quickly as you can to read and write so that you will be able to keep me informed, by writing once a week, of what you are doing, and so that you can reach me directly if you have any need of advice or support."

It is hardly necessary to describe the Slasher's extreme joy. Knowing the man's character and his instincts as he does, the reader will have no trouble understanding that no proposition could have suited him more.

And so, the next day, the Slasher left for Algiers.

CHAPTER 4

INVESTIGATIONS

The house Rodolphe possessed in the allée des Veuves was not his principal residence. He lived in one of the largest mansions in the neighborhood of Saint-Germain, at the end of rue Plumet. To avoid being shown the honors due to his sovereign rank, he had kept incognito since his arrival in Paris. His chargé d'affaires to the court of France had announced that his sovereign would make all necessary official visits under the name and title of the Count of Duren. Thanks to this custom, a frequent one in the northern courts, a prince could travel both freely and agreeably, without having to incur the obligation of participating in oppressively boring ceremonies. Despite this transparent disguise, Rodolphe kept a grandly appointed house, as was suited to him.

We take our reader into the mansion on rue Plumet on the day after the Slasher's departure for Algeria. It was just ten o'clock in the morning. In the middle of a large room on the ground floor leading to Rodolphe's study, Murph was sitting at a desk and sealing numerous dispatches. A butler, dressed in black with a gold chain around his neck, opened the two panels of the waiting room's door and announced: "His excellency, the Baron de Graün!"

Without looking up from his work, Murph greeted the baron with a gesture that was both cordial and familiar. "Monsieur the chargé d'affaires," he said, smiling, "please warm yourself up. I will be with you in a moment."

"Sir Walter Murph, private secretary to his serene highness. I await your orders," Monsieur de Graün responded gaily, and, jokingly, he made a deep and respectful bow to the worthy squire.

The baron was about fifty years old, with sparse gray hair that was lightly powdered and teased. His slightly pointed chin was half buried in a high, dazzlingly white tie made of weighty muslin. He wore an intelligent expression and his bearing showed him to be quite distinguished. From behind the lenses of his golden binocles showed a gaze that was both sly and penetrating. Even though it was ten o'clock in the morning, Monsieur de Graün wore a black suit as etiquette demanded. A striped ribbon of striking colors was knotted in his buttonhole. He put his hat down on a chair and walked up to the fireplace while Murph continued his work.

"His highness has clearly been up for part of the night, my dear Murph, if one is to judge from the considerable correspondence there."

"His lordship went to bed at six o'clock this morning. He wrote, among other letters, one of eight pages to the grand marshal, and he dictated another one of equal length to the chief of the Supreme Council."

"Should I wait for his highness to get up so that I can impart to him the information I bring?"

"No, my dear baron. His lordship has ordered that he not be awakened before two or three o'clock in the afternoon. He wishes you to have these dispatches sent this morning by special courier, rather than wait until Monday. You will give me the information you have discovered and I will make it known to his lordship upon his awakening. Those are his orders."

"Perfect! I think his highness will be content with what I have to tell him. But I hope, my dear Murph, that the use of a special courier has no undesirable significance. The last dispatches that I had the honor to transmit to his highness—"

"Announced that everything was going well there, and it is precisely because his lordship wants to convey his happiness to the chief of the Supreme Council and the grand marshal at the soonest possible moment that he desires you to send the courier this very day."

"Completely in character for his highness. If it were a matter of a reprimand, he would never be in such a hurry, and, in any case, our interim government operates in complete unity. It is clear," added the baron with a smile, "the master has calibrated the watch perfectly. One has only to keep it wound so that its invariable and perfect operation marks each day the work of each hour and each person. An orderly government always inspires confidence and tranquility in its people. And hence the good news that you give me."

"And here, is there nothing new, dear baron? There is no gossip circulating about us? Our mysterious adventures . . ."

"No one has any knowledge of them. Since his lordship has come to Paris, people have become used to seeing him only rarely on those few occasions on which he allows himself to be introduced to someone. Everyone believes that he prefers seclusion, that he makes frequent trips to the countryside around Paris. His highness was wise in dismissing, for a time, the chamberlain and the aide-de-camp that he brought from Germany."

"And who would have been highly inconvenient for us."

"And so no one, with the exceptions of Countess Sarah MacGregor, her brother Tom Seyton of Halsbury, and their henchman Karl, knows about the disguises of his highness, and, moreover, neither the countess and Tom nor Karl has any interest in betraying this secret."

"Ah, my dear baron," said Murph with a smile, "how unfortunate that this cursed countess should be a widow right now!"

"Wasn't she married in 1827 or 1828?"

"In 1827, shortly after the death of that unfortunate little girl who would today be sixteen or seventeen years old. His lordship still grieves for her, although he never speaks of it."

"And his grief is even more understandable since his highness has never had a child from his marriage."

"And, indeed, my dear baron, I believe that, apart from the pity that poor Songbird inspires in him, his lordship's interest in this unfortunate creature derives most of all from the fact that the girl he grieves for so bitterly (and whose mother, the countess, he so detests) would now have been the same age."

"It is truly an evil fate that this Sarah, from whom we had thought ourselves delivered forever, finds herself free just eighteen months after his highness lost the best of wives, and this, after only a few years of marriage. I am sure that the countess believes herself fortune's favorite as a result of their both being widowed."

"And these insane hopes have become more ardent than ever, despite the fact that she knows that his lordship has an aversion toward her that is as deep as it is deserved. Wasn't she responsible for . . . Ah! Baron," said Murph, without finishing his sentence, "that woman is evil. Please God that she bring us no further grief."

"What has one to fear from her anymore, my dear Murph? Once she had the kind of influence over his lordship that intriguing and skillful women can have over a young man who loves for the first time in his life. And that influence was even more powerful because of circumstances of which you are aware. But it has been destroyed by the discovery of her despicable maneuverings, and even more by the frightening memory of the horrible event that she set in motion."

"Speak more quietly, my dear de Graün, speak more quietly," said Murph. "Alas, it is now that the ill-fated month and the no less ill-fated day, January 13, approaches. This terrible anniversary always makes me uneasy about his lordship."

"And yet if one can expiate errors and be pardoned for them, surely his highness will be absolved."

"Please, my dear de Graün, let us speak no more of this. It would ruin my entire day."

"So I was saying a moment ago that the aims of the Countess Sarah are absurd. The death of the girl about whom you were just speaking has destroyed any remains of an attachment that his lordship might have had for this woman. She is mad if she persists in her hopes."

"Yes! But she is a dangerous madwoman. Her brother, as you know, shares these ambitious and stubborn illusions, even though this worthy couple has as many reasons to despair now as they had reasons to hope eighteen years ago."

"Oh! How many misfortunes has that infernal Father Polidori caused through his criminal complicity!"

"Speaking of that wretch, I hear that he has been here for the past year or two. He is either living immersed in poverty or involved in some nefarious new project."

"What a fall for him, a man of such knowledge, such wit, such intelligence."

"But also of such abominable perversity. Heaven forbid that he and the countess ever meet! The union of these two evil spirits would be truly dangerous."

"Once again, my dear Murph, as unreasonable as her ambition is, her own self-interest will stop the countess from ever taking advantage of his lordship's taste for adventure. She won't attempt any evil actions in that regard."

"I hope not, as well. Still, only luck undid I don't know what detestable proposition that woman wanted to make to the Schoolmaster. That frightening scoundrel is now no longer able to harm anyone, living as he is, unknown, perhaps in a state of repentance, among the honest inhabitants of Saint-Mandé. Alas, I am sure that it was mostly to avenge me that his lordship risked putting himself in a very dangerous position by inflicting that terrible punishment upon him."

"Dangerous! Hardly, my dear Murph. After all, all told, here is the issue: an escaped prisoner, a known murderer, breaks into your house and stabs you with his dagger. You would be within your rights to kill him in self-defense or to send him to the scaffold. Either of these choices would doom the villain to death. Now, instead of killing him or delivering him to the executioner to face the terrible punishment he richly deserves, you have made this monster incapable of harming society ever again. Who would accuse you of anything? Would the law prosecute you on the part of a criminal like that? Would you be culpable for having done less than the law would have permitted you to do, for having merely deprived him of his sight when you could legally have killed him? Do you think that if this society recognizes my right over the life and death of my fellow man in the cases of self-defense or flagrant adultery—a formidable right, without oversight or appeal, which makes me judge, jury, and executioner—why, then, would I not be able to use my discretion to modify the capital punishment that I could have inflicted with impunity? And more especially in the case of the criminal of whom we are speaking? That, after all, is the issue. I won't even mention his lordship's position as the sovereign prince of the German Confederation.[37] I know that as a matter of law, his position

---

37. The German Confederation was established in 1815 by the Congress of Vienna as a loose union of the German states that had composed the Holy Roman Empire. The purpose of the congress was to create a buffer state between Austria and Prussia. The confederation ended in 1866 with the Austro-Prussian War, which connected all those states to Prussia, ultimately leading to German unification. [TN]

means nothing, but in practice, it gives him strong immunity. And besides, even supposing that such a trial took place, how many generous actions would plead in his favor! How much charity, how many good deeds would come to light! Finally, considering the conditions under which all this took place, let us suppose such a strange charge was brought before a court of law—what do you think would be the result?"

"His lordship has always told me that he would accept responsibility in the case of any accusation and would not take advantage of any immunity from prosecution that his position could provide. But who would make that unfortunate event known? You know how imperturbably discreet David is, and the same is true of the four Hungarian servants in the house on the allée des Veuves. The Slasher, to whom his lordship has been very generous, hasn't said a word about the Schoolmaster's punishment for fear of finding himself compromised. Before leaving for Algiers, he swore to me never to speak about it. As for the Schoolmaster himself, he knows that to issue a complaint would be to deliver his own head to the scaffold."

"And really neither you nor I will ever speak of it, right? My dear Murph, for all the people who know this secret, it will nevertheless be a well-kept one. At the worst, we might have some minor difficulties to fear. And then, such noble and great things would come to light in relationship to this strange event that such an accusation, as I have said, would be a triumph for his highness."

"All this makes me feel much better. But you bring me, you say, information you have obtained from the letters found on the Schoolmaster and from declarations the Owl, who was released from the hospital several days ago once her broken leg healed, made during her stay in the hospital."

"Here is the information," said the baron, taking a piece of paper out of his pocket. "It concerns research pertaining to the birth of the girl they call Songbird and to the current place of residence of François Germain, the Schoolmaster's son."

"Would you read me these notes, my dear de Graün? I know his lordship's intentions and I will be able to see if this information will suffice. You still have confidence in your agent?"

"He is a very valuable man, a man of unimpeachable intelligence, skill, and discretion. It has even been necessary upon occasion to rein him in slightly because, as you know, his highness likes to keep certain discoveries for himself."

"And he is completely ignorant of the role his lordship plays in all this?"

"Absolutely. My diplomatic position serves as an excellent pretext for the investigations I have undertaken. Monsieur Badinot (that is the man's name) is very deft at working with people, and he maintains open or hidden social connections with individuals from practically every walk of life. He was once an attorney, but he was forced to give up his practice as a result of serious acts of embezzlement. He has, nonetheless, remembered in detail the fortunes and positions of his former clients. He knows many secrets and he boasts shamelessly of formerly having trafficked in them. He has made and lost his own fortune two or three times in business and is now too well known to attempt any new forms of speculation. He is thus reduced to getting by day to day, by any means necessary, and usually these are more or less illicit. He is a sort of Figaro—an interesting person to get to know. So long as it is in his interest, he will do the bidding of anyone who pays him, and he has no interest in cheating us. Moreover, I keep him under surveillance without his knowing it. And so we have no reason to distrust him."

"The information he has given us up to now is, in any case, very accurate."

"He has integrity—in his fashion—and, I assure you, my dear Murph, that Monsieur Badinot is the very type of an original and mysterious kind of person one almost never runs into and whom one finds only in Paris. He would amuse his highness greatly if any relationship between them were not completely impossible."

"Ought we to raise Monsieur Badinot's pay? Do you think such an enhancement necessary to keep him loyal to us?"

"Five hundred francs a month and incidental expenses, which come to almost as much, seem to me quite sufficient: he seems happy. We will find out in due time."

"And he has no shame in his occupation?"

"Him? On the contrary, he glories in it. Whenever he gives me a report, he never fails to assume a certain pompous attitude. I would say that he acts almost as if he were a diplomat. This character seems to believe that what he does is a matter of great political importance. He seems to marvel at the hidden connections that may exist between the most diverse interests and the destiny of empires. Indeed, he has the impudence to tell me from time to time, 'What unknown and banal complications lie beneath the surface in the government of a state! Truly, who would think that the notes that I submit to you, my lord baron, surely play a part in the affairs of Europe.'"

"Well, scamps always like to have illusions that they are important; it's even flattering for honest people. But to these notes, my dear baron."

"Here they are, almost entirely taken from the report of Monsieur Badinot."

"I'm listening."

Monsieur de Graün read the following:

NOTES IN CONNECTION TO FLEUR-DE-MARIE

Around the beginning of the year 1827, a man named Pierre Tournemine, currently a prisoner in the penal colony of Rochefort for the crime of counterfeiting, proposed to Gervaise, the woman known as the Owl, that she take permanent charge of a girl of about five or six years old in exchange for an immediate payment of one thousand francs.

"Alas, my dear baron," said Murph, interrupting Monsieur de Graün, "1827—that is exactly the year that his lordship learned of the death of that unfortunate child for whom he has grieved so painfully. For that reason as well as a number of others, that was a black year for our master."

"Happy years are rare enough, my poor Murph. But let me continue."

The bargain concluded, the child stayed with this woman for two years, at the end of which, wanting to escape the woman's oppressive treatment, the little girl disappeared. The Owl had not heard her spoken of for several years when she saw her for the first time in a cabaret in the Cité, about six weeks ago. The child, having become an adolescent, was at that time known by the nickname of Songbird.

A few days after this encounter,[38] the man named Tournemine, whom the Schoolmaster had become acquainted with in the penal colony at Rochefort, had submitted to Red-Arm (a secret and habitual correspondent of prisoners detained in penal colonies or liberated from them) a detailed letter concerning the child once confided to the woman Gervaise, known as the Owl. From this letter and from the declarations of the Owl, we know that one Madame Séraphin, housekeeper for a solicitor named Jacques Ferrand, had, in 1827, charged Tournemine with finding him a woman who, for one thousand francs, would consent to take charge of a child of five or six whom someone wanted to abandon, as was said above. The Owl accepted this proposition.

Tournemine's aim, in giving this information to Red-Arm, was to allow the latter to give a third party the means to blackmail Madame Séraphin by threatening to make noise about this long-since-forgotten affair. Tournemine affirmed that this Madame Séraphin was merely the intermediary for persons unknown.

Red-Arm had confided this letter to the Owl, for some time the Schoolmaster's partner in crime. This explains how this information was found in the bandit's possession and how, at the time of the meeting in the White Rabbit cabaret, the Owl was able to torment Fleur-de-Marie by telling her: "We have found your parents, but you will never know who they are."

38. Since we learn below that the Owl knew the information that follows when she encountered Songbird, Sue may have meant "before." [TN]

The question was to determine if Tournemine's letter concerning the child given by him, a long time ago, to the Owl, contained the truth. Investigations into Madame Séraphin and the solicitor Jacques Ferrand have shown that both of them exist. The solicitor resides at number forty-one rue du Sentier. Everyone thinks he is austere and pious; at the very least, he goes to church a lot. He conducts his business with such excessive correctness that people consider him rigid. His practice is very profitable. He is so cheap that one could almost consider him a miser. Madame Séraphin still works as his housekeeper.

Monsieur Jacques Ferrand, who was extremely poor, bought his practice for three hundred and fifty thousand francs, the funds having been furnished by means of a note countersigned by Monsieur Charles Robert, an upper-level officer in the administrative office of the National Guard of Paris, a very handsome young man much in fashion in certain circles. He divides with the solicitor the profits of his practice, which are estimated to be around fifty thousand francs a year. He never gets involved in the affairs of the law practice, naturally. Some of his detractors claim that, as a result of fortunate speculations or spectacular stock market deals, made in concert with Monsieur Charles Robert, the solicitor should now be able to repay the price of his practice. But Monsieur Jacques Ferrand's reputation is so well established that most people agree that this is just malicious gossip. Thus, it appears that Madame Séraphin, this pious man's governess, should be able to furnish important information on the circumstances of Songbird's birth.

"Wonderful, dear baron," said Murph. "This Tournemine's report seems scrupulously accurate. Perhaps at the solicitor's we will find the means to discover the parents of this unfortunate child. Now, is the information you received on the Schoolmaster's son as helpful as the work he did on Songbird?"

"It's perhaps less precise, but it's also satisfactory."

"This Monsieur Badinot is truly a treasure."

"You will see that Red-Arm is the lynchpin in all of this. At the time of his lordship's first attempts to find the son of Madame Georges Duresnel, that monster the Schoolmaster's unfortunate wife, Monsieur Badinot, who must have some connections with the police, had already marked Red-Arm out to us as the intermediary for several prisoners."

"Doubtless. And it was when he went to search for Red-Arm in his hole in the Cité at number fifteen rue aux Fèves that his lordship encountered the Slasher and Songbird. His highness was determined to make use of his pursuit of Red-Arm to visit these hideous dens, thinking that he might find some unfortunate souls there whom he might pull from the mire. His intuitions were completely accurate, but at what cost? Good heavens!"

"You courageously shared the dangers he ran, my dear Murph."

"Have I not been called on to serve as his highness's collier in residence?" the squire answered, smiling.

"Say rather that you have been called on to serve as his fearless bodyguard, my worthy friend. But it gets tiresome to speak continually of your courage and devotion, so I will go on with my report. Here is the note concerning François Germain, son of Madame Georges and the Schoolmaster, the man also known as Duresnel."

CHAPTER 5

INFORMATION RELATING TO FRANÇOIS GERMAIN

Monsieur de Graün continued:

About eighteen months ago, a young man named François Germain came to Paris from Nantes, where he had been employed in the banking house of Noël and Company. We know from the Schoolmaster's statements as well as several letters found in his possession that he left his son with a scoundrel who was to pervert him so that they could make use of him in their crimes one day. This scoundrel revealed their dreadful intentions regarding this young man by asking him to abet them in a theft and counterfeiting operation that they wanted to commit against the house of Noël and Company, which is where François Germain worked.

François Germain rejected this suggestion with indignation. Not wanting to denounce the man who had raised him, however, he wrote an anonymous letter to his employer informing him of the type of plot that was being woven. He then secretly left Nantes to escape the people who had attempted to make him an accomplice and instrument of their crimes.

When these wretches learned of Germain's departure, they came to Paris and got in contact with Red-Arm. They then set themselves in pursuit of the Schoolmaster's son, doubtless with sinister intentions since the young man knew of their plots. After a long and extensive search, they managed to discover his address. But they were too late. Germain had run into the man who had attempted to corrupt him a few days before, and, realizing what must have brought him to Paris, he quickly changed his residence. Thus, the Schoolmaster's son once again escaped his persecutors.

Nevertheless, about six weeks ago, these people came to know that he was now residing at number seventeen rue du Temple. One night as he was returning home, he was nearly taken in an ambush (the Schoolmaster had hidden this event from his lordship). Germain realized who was behind the attempt and left rue du Temple. We do not know his new place of residence. This is where our investigations had led us at the moment the Schoolmaster was punished for his crimes.

It was at this time, as well, that his lordship ordered us to begin our search anew. And here is the result:

François Germain lived for around three months at number seventeen rue du Temple—a house, incidentally, which is quite unusual because of the good morals and the hardworking habits of most of the people who live there. They were very fond of Germain because of his cheerful, open, helpful personality. Although he seemed to live on a very modest income or salary himself, he had taken great pains to nurture an indigent family who lived in the attic of the house. Attempts to ascertain François Germain's new residence or the position he holds at his former address have been in vain. It may be supposed that he is employed in some office or commercial house, because each day he left in the morning and returned at around six o'clock in the evening.

The only person who knows with certainty where this young man is now living is a young woman who is also a tenant in the house at rue du Temple. This young woman, who seemed to have an intimate connection with Germain, is an extremely pretty seamstress[39] named Mademoiselle Rigolette. She lives in the room next to the one that Germain occupied. This room, empty since the young man's departure, is currently for rent. It is under the pretext of being interested in its rental that we have come by this information.

"Rigolette?" Murph said all of a sudden. For the last few moments, he had seemed to be reflecting on something. "Rigolette? I know that name!"

"What? Sir Walter Murph," the baron continued, laughing, "how is it that you, the worthy and respectable head of a family, has come to know seamstresses? How could it be that the name Rigolette is not new to you? Really, now!"

"Well, my word! His lordship has brought me into contact with so many strange acquaintances that you hardly have the right to be surprised by this one, Baron. But wait a minute. Yes, now I have it. I remember perfectly: his lordship, when he told me Songbird's history, could not stop himself from laughing at the grotesque name Rigolette. As far as I remember, it was the name of one of poor Fleur-de-Marie's friends in prison."

"Well, at this point, Mademoiselle Rigolette may turn out to be extremely useful to us. I will now end my report":

39. The word Sue uses is *grisette*, which originally just referred to a working-class young woman. By 1835, the dictionary of the Académie Française added that the working-class woman was coquettish and flirtatious, and so the word entered English, where it could also mean a part-time prostitute. [TN]

Perhaps it might be advisable to rent the vacant room in the house on rue du Temple. We have not been ordered to proceed any further in our investigations. But, as a result of certain remarks that the doorkeeper let slip, we have reason to believe not only that we might discover new information in this house about the Schoolmaster's son from Mademoiselle Rigolette, but also that his lordship might be able to observe the moral fiber, hardworking behaviors, and above all the extreme poverty of these people, a poverty he could never begin to imagine without seeing it for himself.

CHAPTER 6

THE MARQUIS D'HARVILLE

"So you see, my dear Murph," said Monsieur de Graün, finishing the reading of the report, which he then deposited with the squire, "according to our information, we must go to Jacques Ferrand's residence for information on Songbird's parents, and we must ask Mademoiselle Rigolette where François Germain currently resides. It seems to me a fair amount to have achieved already. We know where to look for the information we are seeking."

"Certainly, Baron. And, furthermore, I'm sure his lordship will harvest a bountiful crop of observations in that house. But that's not all: have you obtained information concerning the Marquis d'Harville?"

"Yes, and at least as far as money is concerned, his highness's fears are without cause. Monsieur Badinot attests that the marquis's fortune has never been better protected and is wisely administered. And I believe Monsieur Badinot knows whereof he speaks."

"Having searched in vain for the cause of the profound grief that was tormenting Monsieur d'Harville, his lordship imagined that the marquis was perhaps experiencing some financial difficulty: he would then have come to his aid with that mysterious tact you know so well. Since he guessed incorrectly in this case, however, he will have to give up trying to solve this puzzle, albeit with considerable regret since he has such great affection for Monsieur d'Harville."

"It's easy enough to understand. His highness has never forgotten all that his father owes to the marquis's father. You know, my dear Murph, that in 1815, at the time of the reorganization of the German Confederation, his highness's father was in considerable danger of being expelled from the confederation because of his known attachment to Napoléon. The late old Marquis d'Harville performed an immense service for our master's father on this occasion, thanks to the friendship the Emperor Alexander felt for him. This friendship, which dated from the marquis's emigration to Russia, and which the marquis called upon, had a powerful influence on the deliberations of the congress in which the princes of the German Confederation discussed their interests."

"And you see, Baron, how often one noble action is linked to another. In '92, the marquis's father was banished from France. He was received with the most generous hospitality in Germany by his lordship's father. After a stay of three days in our court, he left for Russia. There he earned the goodwill of the czar and, with the aid of that goodwill, he was able to be of great service to the prince who had so nobly received him earlier."

"Wasn't it in 1815, during the visit of the old Marquis d'Harville to the then reigning grand duke, that the friendship between his lordship and young Harville began?"

"Yes, they have only the sweetest memories of this happy period when they were young. But that is not all there is to their friendship. His lordship feels such profound reverence for the memory of the man who was so helpful to his father that anyone belonging to the family of Harville may depend on his highness's benevolence. The ceaseless goodness of his lordship to Madame Georges, for instance, owes as much to her family connections as to her misfortunes and her virtues."

"Madame Georges! The wife of Duresnel, the prisoner we know as the Schoolmaster?" the baron cried out.

"Yes, the mother of François Germain, for whom we are looking and whom, I hope, we will find . . ."

"She is related to Monsieur d'Harville?"

"She was his mother's cousin and her close friend. The old marquis was also Madame Georges's devoted friend."

"But why did the Harville family allow her to marry that monster, Duresnel, my dear Murph?"

"Monsieur de Lagny, the unfortunate woman's father, was a steward in Languedoc before the Revolution and possessed considerable wealth. He managed to avoid being exiled. In the first moment of calm after that terrible period, he turned his attention to finding a husband for his daughter. Duresnel put himself forward. He belonged to a prominent parliamentary family. He was rich, and he hid his perverse inclinations behind the manners of a hypocrite. He married Mademoiselle de Lagny. The man's formerly hidden vices soon emerged and flourished. Dissipated, an out-of-control gambler who was addicted to the basest villainies, he made his wife absolutely miserable. She never complained. She hid her sorrows and, after the death of her father, withdrew to a farm that she worked in order to distract herself. Soon enough, her husband had sunk their common fortune in gambling and debauchery; the property was sold. And so she took her son and returned to her relation, the Marquise d'Harville, whom she loved like a sister. Duresnel, having devoured his own wealth and his wife's fortune, found himself reduced to living by his wits: he sought new resources in crime, becoming a counterfeiter, a thief, and a murderer. He was condemned to the penal colonies for life and kidnapped his son from his wife in order to apprentice him to a wretch after his own kind. And you know the rest."

"But then how did his lordship come in contact with Madame Duresnel?"

"When Duresnel was thrown into prison, his wife, reduced to deepest penury, took the name of Georges."

"If she was in such a terrible predicament, why didn't she ask the Marquise d'Harville, her relative and best friend, to help her?"

"The marquise had died before Duresnel was condemned to prison, and after that, Madame Georges's deep shame was such that she didn't dare ask for help from the marquise's family, even though they would certainly have shown her the care due such an unfortunate woman. Notwithstanding her shame, she had been made so desperate by poverty and illness that she managed to steel herself one single time to ask Monsieur d'Harville, her best friend's son, for assistance. And that was how his lordship met her."

"Tell me the details."

"One day, when he was going to see Monsieur d'Harville, a poor woman was walking a few steps in front of him. She was wearing ragged clothes, and she was pale, despondent, and clearly in pain. Standing before the door of the Harville mansion, just as she was about to knock after hesitating for a long while, she suddenly turned around and retraced her steps, as if she had lost heart. His lordship, quite surprised by all this, and feeling a vibrant interest in her gentle and suffering appearance, decided to follow her. She entered a sad-looking dwelling. His lordship made inquiries about her, and all he heard about her was praiseworthy. She had been supporting herself by working, but at that time she had neither her health nor a job. She was in a desperate state. The next day, I went with his lordship to visit her. We arrived just in time to prevent her from starving to death.

"After a long illness, during which his lordship showered on her every possible care, Madame Georges, in her gratitude, told his lordship the story of her life. She did not yet know either his name or his rank, but she told him about her life, Duresnel's prison sentence, and the kidnapping of her child."

"And was that how his highness learned that Madame Georges was a member of the Harville family?"

"Yes, and once he found out that she was, his lordship, who had come to appreciate Madame Georges's qualities more and more, established her on the Bouqueval farm, where she currently resides with Songbird. In this peaceful retreat, she has found tranquility, if not happiness. She distracts herself from her troubles by managing the affairs of the farm. His lordship left Monsieur d'Harville ignorant of the fact that he had saved his relation from terrible distress, both out of sympathy for Madame Georges's extreme sensitivity and because he does not like to have his good deeds proclaimed from the rooftops."

"And now I understand the dual interest his lordship has in following the traces of this poor woman's child."

"You may also judge from all this, my dear baron, the affection his highness feels for the entire family and how sharp his grief is to see the young marquis so sad when he has so many reasons to be happy."

"Indeed, what is it that troubles Monsieur d'Harville? He has everything: a noble birth, fortune, youth, intelligence; his wife is charming, and she is as good as she is beautiful."

"True enough. And his lordship didn't dream of making inquiries until he had tried, in vain, to see what lay beneath Monsieur d'Harville's melancholy. Harville showed how profoundly touched he was by his highness's concern, but he always maintained complete silence on the subject of his sadness. Perhaps it has to do with troubles of the heart?"

"And yet he seems completely in love with his wife and she does not give him any reason to be jealous. I meet her frequently in society and she always has many people about her, as does any young and charming woman; but there has never been the least question about her reputation."

"Yes, the marquis has always thought himself very fortunate in his wife. There has been only one small disagreement between them. It was on the subject of the Countess Sarah MacGregor."

"She knew her, then?"

"By the most unfortunate stroke of bad luck, seventeen or eighteen years ago, the Marquis d'Harville's father knew Sarah Seyton of Halsbury and her brother Tom when they were staying in Paris with the wife of the English ambassador. When he learned that the brother and sister were going to Germany, the old marquis gave them letters of introduction to his lordship's father, with whom he maintained an ongoing correspondence. Alas, my dear de Graün, without that introduction, we might perhaps have avoided so much misfortune, since his lordship would doubtless never have known this woman. Later, when Countess Sarah returned here, knowing the friendship between his highness and the marquis, she had herself invited to the Harville mansion in the hope of running into his lordship there. She is as relentless in pursuing him as he is persistent in fleeing her."

"To disguise herself as a man to hunt down his highness in the Cité! Only she could come up with an idea like that."

"Maybe she hoped in that way to get through to his lordship and force him into a meeting that he has always refused and avoided. But to come back to Madame d'Harville: her husband, to whom his lordship had spoken about Sarah, as might be expected, advised his wife to see her as little as possible. But the young marquise, who was seduced by the countess's hypocritical flattering, rebelled a little against Monsieur d'Harville's advice. That has resulted in a little dissension between the two, but that can hardly be the cause of the marquis's great sadness."

"Ah! Women—women! My dear Murph, I dearly regret Madame d'Harville's acquaintance with this Sarah. Such a young and charming little marquise can only be hurt by having anything to do with such a diabolical creature."

"Speaking of diabolical creatures," said Murph, "here is a dispatch relating to Cecily, the unworthy spouse of the worthy David."

"Just between us, my dear Murph, that daring *métisse*[40] would have deserved the punishment that her husband, our beloved black doctor, inflicted on the Schoolmaster on his lordship's orders. She has also caused blood to be spilled, and she is frightfully corrupt."

"Nevertheless, she is so beautiful and seductive! I always find a perverse soul with such a gracious external appearance to be doubly horrifying."

"From this perspective, Cecily is doubly odious, but I hope this dispatch cancels the lordship's last orders with regard to this wretch."

"On the contrary, Baron."

"His lordship still wants us to help her to escape the fortress where she has been sentenced to life imprisonment."

"Yes."

"And he still wants her ostensible abductor to bring her to France? To Paris?"

"Yes, and much more. This dispatch commands us to hasten as much as possible Cecily's escape and to expedite her journey so that she arrives no later than two weeks from now."

"I don't understand it. His lordship had always displayed the greatest horror of her."

"And he displays it even more now, if that is possible."

"And yet he is having her brought to him! Well, at least it will always be easy enough, as his highness knows, to get Cecily extradited if she does not do what he wishes. We have commanded the son of the jailer of the Gerolstein fortress to abduct this woman and to feign that he has fallen under her spell. We have given him all he needs to accomplish this project. Only too happy to escape, the *métisse* will follow her supposed abductor and come to Paris. This is all well and good, but she still has her sentence hanging over her head; she is still an escaped prisoner and I am completely within my powers, as soon as it pleases his lordship, to reinstate an order for her extradition and to have it put into effect."

"Time will tell, my dear de Graün. I will also ask you, in accordance

---

40. A Creole child from a white and a quadroon slave. *Métisses* do not differ from whites except by the most imperceptible of signs. [SN]

In French, the word *métis* as well as its feminine form, *métisse*, means merely someone of a mixed-race heritage. It has no specific proportional significance of the kind that Sue's footnote declares. In order to mark his rather idiosyncratic usage, we have kept the French word as a special term, and his footnote defining it. [TN]

with his lordship's command, to write to our chancellery to request that a verified copy of David's marriage license be relayed to us in the earliest post. Owing to his position as an officer of his lordship's house, he was, after all, married in the ducal palace."

"Writing by today's courier, we will have the license in one week, at the latest."

"When his lordship informed David of Cecily's imminent arrival, he was petrified with fear; then he cried out, 'I hope your highness does not demand that I see this monster?' 'Don't worry,' his lordship responded, 'you won't see her—but I need her for certain projects.' David felt unburdened of an enormous weight. Nevertheless, I'm sure that this has reawakened in him some very painful memories."

"That poor black man! It may be that he still loves her. She is said still to be very pretty!"

"Charming—only too charming. Only the practiced eye of a Creole could discover her mixed blood from the nearly imperceptible brownish color just lightly present on the tips of this *métisse*'s fingernails. Our freshest northern beauties cannot boast a clearer complexion, whiter skin, or chestnut-colored hair with more golden glints in it."

"I was in France when his lordship returned from America, bringing with him David and Cecily. I have always known this excellent man to be, since that time, attached to his highness by the most intense gratitude, but I still don't know what events led to his devoting himself to the service of our master and how he came to marry Cecily, whom I saw for the first time about a year after his marriage. God knows the scandal she had already caused by then."

"I can tell you everything you wish to know, my dear baron. I was with his lordship during his voyage to America. It was there that he tore David and the *métisse* from the grips of the most appalling of fates."

"You are too good, my dear Murph. I'm all ears," said the baron.

CHAPTER 7

THE STORY OF DAVID AND CECILY

"Monsieur Willis, a rich American plantation owner in Florida," said Murph, "had recognized that one of his young black slaves named David, who worked in the estate infirmary, was remarkably intelligent and demonstrated great sympathy for the poor patients he cared for. David fulfilled the doctors' orders for these patients with the most loving attention. In addition, he showed a singular vocation for the study of botany as it applies to medicine. Without having had any formal education, he had composed and catalogued a taxonomy of the flora on the estate and its neighborhood. Monsieur Willis's property was situated on the oceanfront and was fifteen or twenty leagues away from the nearest city. The local doctors, who were not very knowledgeable in any case, used to find it very difficult to travel such a long distance on such uncomfortable forms of transport. The colonist[41] thought it wise to remedy a situation that was not merely inconvenient, but dangerous in a territory subject to violent epidemics. In order to have a skillful practitioner, he had the idea of sending David to France to learn surgery and medicine. Delighted by this offer, the young black man left for Paris. The plantation owner paid the cost of his studies, and, after eight years of hard work, David received his medical degree with the highest distinction. He returned to America to put his learning to his master's service."

"But David must have realized that he was a free man both in fact and by law as soon as he set foot in France."

"But David is extraordinarily loyal. He had promised Monsieur Willis he would return, and so he did. Furthermore, he did not regard his education as his own, so to speak, since his master had paid for it. And finally, he hoped to alleviate the moral and physical suffering of those who had been his fellow slaves. He had resolved to be not only their doctor but their supporter and defender before the colonist."

"He truly must have been endowed with the rarest integrity and the saintliest love for his fellow men if he could return to his master after

41. Since Florida became a territory of the United States in 1822, Willis could not have been precisely a colonist. [TN]

living in Paris for eight years and rubbing elbows among the most democratic youth in all Europe."

"This trait tells you what kind of man he is. So there he is in Florida, treated by Monsieur Willis with, one must say, kindness and consideration. He ate at his table and slept under his roof. It remains to say that this colonist, who was stupid, evil, and a sensualist, despotic as some Creoles[42] are, thought himself very generous in giving David a salary of six hundred francs. After a few months, a severe typhus epidemic broke out on the plantation. Monsieur Willis was infected, but he was quickly cured by David's excellent care. Only two of the thirty slaves who were seriously ill perished. Monsieur Willis, delighted with David's work, doubled his salary to twelve hundred francs. The black doctor thought himself the happiest man in the world and his brothers thought of him as their savior. Albeit with great difficulty, he had obtained from his master some improvement in their lot and he hoped to do more in the future. While waiting, he preached and commiserated with these poor people, recommending resignation. He spoke to them of a God who watched over the black man and the white man alike, and of a world to come whose inhabitants would not be divided into masters and slaves, but rather into the just and the wicked. He spoke of a next life. In the life to come, an eternal life, human beings would no longer be treated like cattle and property, and those who were now the victims would be so happy that they prayed in heaven for their tormentors. What can I tell you? Unlike the rest of mankind, these unfortunate beings derived a bitter joy from their knowledge that each day brought them closer to the tomb, and to them, David offered the hope of immortal freedom. And so, their chains seemed to them less heavy, their labor less painful. David was their idol. A year passed in this way. A *métisse* of fifteen years old named Cecily was among the prettiest of the plantation's slaves. Monsieur Willis took a sultan's fancy to this girl. And he encountered, perhaps for the first time in his life, frustration and stubborn resistance. Cecily was in love—in love with David, who, during the last epidemic, had cared for her with complete devotion and had cured her. In time, gratitude led to love, a very pure love. David was too sensitive to gossip about his happiness before he could marry Cecily. He was waiting for her to reach her sixteenth birthday. In the manner of a sultan, Monsieur Willis, ignorant of their mutual affection, arrogantly tossed his handkerchief, so to speak, before the object of his desire. In tears, the pretty *métisse* came to David to tell him of these brutal approaches, which she had

42. In nineteenth-century French (as in nineteenth-century English), the term *créole* could refer to an individual of European descent who had been born in the island colonies, or it could refer to a person of mixed racial heritage. [TN]

barely escaped. The black man comforted her and went immediately to Monsieur Willis to ask for her hand in marriage."

"Damn! My dear Murph, I can guess only too well what would be the response of this American sultan—he denied his consent?"

"He denied his consent. He told him he fancied this slave, and that he had never in his life submitted to a refusal from a slave. He wanted her and he would have her. David could choose another wife or another mistress, whichever he preferred. There were at least ten mulattoes or *métisses* on the plantation who were as pretty as Cecily. David spoke of the love that he and Cecily had felt for each other for quite some time. The plantation owner shrugged his shoulders. David insisted, but in vain. The Creole was imprudent enough to say that a master giving way to a slave would set a bad example, and moreover, that he would not set such an example merely to satisfy David's whim. David begged and the master began to become impatient. Ashamed to humiliate himself further, David reminded his master, in a firm tone, of the services he performed and of his disinterestedness, inasmuch as he was satisfied with the most paltry salary. Irritated, Monsieur Willis responded with disdain that he was treated a thousand times better than any slave ought to expect. Hearing this, David burst out in indignation. For the first time he spoke like a man who recognized the rights that his stay in France had given him. Furious, Monsieur Willis treated him as a rebellious slave and threatened to chain him up. David's response was curt, bitter, and violent. Two hours later, David was chained to a post, his flesh torn to shreds by the whip, while Cecily was dragged before his eyes to the plantation owner's seraglio."

"The plantation owner's conduct was as stupid as it was disgusting. Cruelty always turns out to be foolish. He needed this man, after all . . ."

"Indeed he did, and the need became clear that very day. The brute's attack of rage, combined with the drunken stupor he fell into every night, led to an extremely dangerous inflammation whose symptoms broke out with the speed particular to such diseases. The plantation owner took to his bed with a burning fever. He sent by messenger for a doctor, but no doctor could come to the plantation any faster than thirty-six hours."

"This really seems to be a case of divine poetic justice. That man fully deserved to be at death's door."

"The disease developed with frightening speed. Only David could cure the colonist; but Willis, like all scoundrels, trusted no one and was certain that the black man would get revenge on him by poisoning him with some kind of potion. After all, David had been whipped and locked in a cell. Finally, terrified by the progress of the disease, racked with pain, he thought that, all things considered, there was at least a small chance that his slave might be generous. Albeit with great reservations, Willis had David released from his chains."

"And David saved the plantation owner!"

"For five days and nights he watched over the man as he would have watched over his own father. With impressive knowledge and skill, he fought the disease at every turn. In the end, he won the battle, to the surprise of the doctor who had been sent for and who did not arrive until two days later."

"And when he was returned to health, what did the colonist do?"

"Because he recognized David's admirable generosity, he was unable to bear his shame before the slave. So the colonist managed to engage for his plantation, at significant cost, the doctor whom they had gone in search of. He had David sent back to his cell."

"But that's terrible. Still, it doesn't surprise me. David would have been a living reminder of his guilt."

"Moreover, this barbarous conduct was not solely dictated by vengeance and jealousy. Monsieur Willis's blacks, as a result of their ardent gratitude, loved David as their savior, both of body and of soul. They knew the intense care he had given to the colonist when he was ill. And then, miraculously, these unfortunate beings emerged from the animal-like apathy to which slavery normally reduced them and made an open show of their indignation, or rather their sorrow, upon seeing David brutally whipped. Monsieur Willis thought he saw in this demonstration the beginnings of a rebellion, and this rebellion, he thought, was a result of the influence David exercised over them. And he thought David capable of leading a slave uprising that would avenge the appalling ingratitude his master had shown him. This absurd fear provided a further motive for the colonist to overwhelm David with harsh treatment. He would thus keep from him any opportunity to carry out the sinister designs he suspected him of."

"From the perspective of his savage terror, this conduct was not entirely foolish, even if it was completely barbaric."

"We arrived in America only a little after these events had taken place. His lordship had chartered a Danish ship in Saint Thomas. Incognito, we visited all the coastal areas along our way. Monsieur Willis welcomed us with superb generosity. On the evening of our second day there, after drinking, and as much from cynical boasting as from the effects of the wine, Monsieur Willis told us the story of David and Cecily, complete with horrible witticisms (I forgot to tell you that he had also thrown the unfortunate girl into the cell to punish her for her earlier resistance). His highness thought this terrible story had its origins in either delusional bragging or drink. The man was certainly drunk, but he wasn't merely bragging. To dispel his lordship's disbelief, the colonist rose from the table, called for a slave to light their way, and took us to David's prison cell."

"And so?"

"I have never seen such a disturbing sight in my life. Pale, skeletal, half naked, covered with wounds, David and that unfortunate girl were chained about their waists, opposite each other, one at each end of the cell. They looked like ghosts. The lantern that lit our way lent an even gloomier hue to this scene. David didn't say a word when he saw us. His gaze was frighteningly fixed.

"The colonist said to him cruelly, 'Well, Doctor, how are you? You who are so skilled in your field, save yourself, if you can!'

"The black man responded with a single word and a sublime gesture: he slowly raised his right hand, his index finger extended toward the ceiling, and, looking straight at the colonist, in a solemn tone, he said: '*GOD!*' And then he was quiet.

"'*God?*' responded the plantation owner, breaking out laughing. 'Go tell God to come here and take you from me! I defy him to do it.' Then Willis, out of his mind with rage and drunkenness, cried out, blaspheming, 'Yes, I defy God to carry off my slaves before their death. If he doesn't do it, then I deny his existence!'"

"What a complete fool!"

"It made our stomachs turn with disgust. His lordship didn't say a word. We left the prison cell. This den, like the entire plantation, was located right on the sea. We returned to our ship, anchored a small distance away. At one o'clock in the morning, when everyone on the plantation was deep asleep, his lordship came back on land with eight well-armed men, went straight to the prison cell, forced it open, and carried off David as well as Cecily. The two victims were carried aboard before anyone knew of our expedition. Then his lordship and I went to the plantation owner's house.

"It's extremely strange, but these people who torture their slaves take no precautions against them: they sleep with their windows and doors entirely open. We easily got into the plantation owner's bedroom, which was lit by a skylight. He rose up in his bed, his brain still fogged with drunkenness.

"'You have defied God to carry off your slaves before their death. He has carried them off,' his lordship said. Then, taking a sack I was carrying, which contained twenty-five thousand francs in gold, he threw it on the man's bed and added, 'This will compensate you for the loss of your two slaves. I am countering the kind of murderous violence you practice with a different kind of violence, one that saves people. To your violence that kills, I oppose a violence that saves. God will judge between us!' And we disappeared, leaving Monsieur Willis stupefied, motionless, believing himself to be dreaming. A few minutes afterward, we reached our ship and set sail."

"It seems to me, my dear Murph, that his highness compensated that wretch for the loss of his slaves too generously. Strictly speaking, after all, David no longer belonged to him."

"We more or less calculated the expense of David's medical education for eight years, then at least tripled his and Cecily's value as simple slaves. I realize that our conduct offended human law. But if you had seen the horrible conditions in which these two unfortunate people were kept, almost dying in agony, if you had heard this drunken, raging man spitting sacrilegiously in God's face, you would understand why his lordship chose, as he said at the time, 'to play the role of divine justice, at least a little bit.'"

"This action was exactly as legally actionable as the punishment of the Schoolmaster, my worthy squire. But did your adventure not lead to any consequences?"

"It could hardly have had any. The ship flew under a Danish flag. His highness's incognito was strictly maintained; we passed for rich English people. Assuming Monsieur Willis would have dared to lodge a complaint, to whom could he have addressed his accusations? In fact, he had said himself—and the doctor and his lordship could both have testified as much in a trial—that these two slaves could not have lived eight more days in that frightening cell. The greatest medical care was necessary to wrest Cecily from the grip of almost certain death. Finally they recovered. Since that time, David has remained attached to his lordship as his doctor, and he serves him with the deepest devotion."

"And David of course married Cecily when they arrived in Europe?"

"The marriage, which seemed to promise such happiness, took place in his lordship's palace temple. But, in an extraordinary turn of events, once in possession of her unhoped-for happiness, Cecily forgot everything David had suffered for her and that she herself had suffered for him. In this new milieu, she was ashamed to be married to a black man. She was soon seduced by a completely depraved man and thus committed her first sin. It appears that her naturally perverse bent, which had been until then lying dormant within her, was merely biding its time. The right catalyst came along and developed it with frightening vigor. You know the rest of the story and the scandal of her adventures. After two years of marriage, David, who trusted as much as he loved, learned of all of her infamies. This thunderbolt tore him from his deep blindness."

"They say that he wanted to kill his wife."

"Yes. But thanks to his lordship's insistence, he consented to have her confined for life in a fortress. And it is this prison cell that his lordship has now opened, to your great surprise and, I won't hide it from you, to mine as well, my dear baron."

"Frankly, his lordship's decision surprises me that much more because the governor of the fortress has warned his highness many times that this woman is irredeemable. Nothing has managed to cure her of her bold temperament, hardened as it is in vice. And despite that, his lordship persists in having her sent here. What is his purpose? Why is he doing it?"

"I am just as ignorant as you are in that respect, my dear baron. But it is getting late and his highness wishes that your courier leave as soon as possible for Gerolstein."[43]

"He will be on his way in two hours. And so, my dear Murph, until we meet again this evening!"

"This evening?"

"Have you forgotten that there is a grand ball at the embassy of ***, and that his highness has to be there?"

"That's right. I keep forgetting that, since the departures of Colonel Warner and of the Count d'Harneim, I am fulfilling the functions of chamberlain and aide-de-camp."

"Speaking of the colonel and the count, when will they be returning to us? Have they nearly completed their missions?"

"As you know, his lordship has kept them away as long as possible in order to have more liberty and time to himself. As to the mission his highness gave them, sending one to Avignon and the other to Strasbourg in order to get rid of them—well, I'll tell you about it one day when we are both in a black mood. I defy the gloomiest hypochondriac not to break out laughing when he knows not only about the mission he gave them, but also about certain passages in the dispatches these worthy gentlemen have sent. They take their fraudulent missions unbelievably seriously."

"Really, I never completely understood why his highness employed the colonel and the count in his private service."

"How can you say that? Isn't Colonel Warner the perfect image of a military man? Is there in the whole German Confederation anyone with a better build, a more beautiful mustache, a more martial comportment? When he is cinched up, saddled, harnessed, plumed, is there a more triumphant, more glorious, prouder, more beautiful . . . beast?"

"It's true, but that beauty gets in the way of his seeming overly intelligent."

"Well, then, his lordship says that, thanks to the colonel, he can tolerate the dullest of people. Before appearing among certain deathly boring people, he shuts himself up for a half hour with the colonel and he leaves there scintillating and cheerful—ready to defy boredom incarnate."

"The way Roman soldiers used to put on leaden sandals before a forced march so that when they took them off they found anything else light by comparison. Now I understand the usefulness of the colonel. But what about the Count d'Harneim?"

"He also performs a great service to his lordship: when he listens to the incessant, showy, booming noise this empty old rattle makes by his side

43. There is a real Gerolstein, but it is merely a town in Germany and not a grand duchy. Offenbach nevertheless wrote an operetta, *The Grand Duchess of Gerolstein*, which premiered in Paris in 1867, over twenty-five years after this novel was published. [TN]

and watches this soap bubble, filled with . . . nothing, when he sees him so magnificently ornamented, so representative of the theatrical and infantile side of sovereign power, his lordship recognizes all the more poignantly the vanity of pomp and formalities. By contrast, the chamberlain often leads his lordship to grave and serious contemplation."

"Anyway, my dear Murph, to be just, in what court could one find, if you please, a more perfect model of a chamberlain? Who knows better than Harneim the innumerable rules and traditions of etiquette? Who can wear the enamel cross around his neck with greater gravitas and the golden keys on his back more majestically?"

"On that subject, Baron, his lordship says that the back of a chamberlain has a physiognomy all its own: it has, he says, an expression that is at once both constrained and rebellious, one that is painful to see, because—oh, dear!—it is on the back of the chamberlain that the solemn sign of his duty shines. And, according to his lordship, this worthy Harneim seems always tempted to show himself in retreat so that one can know his importance immediately."

"It's certainly the case that the one subject that the count cannot stop thinking about is the question of why it is that, by some terrible caprice, the chamberlain's key is placed on his back. Because, as he says, very sensibly, in a mock sort of wrath: 'What the devil! One does not open a door with one's back, after all!'"

"Baron! The courier, the courier!" said Murph, pointing to the clock.

"Curses on you for making me chat. It's your fault. Give my respects to his lordship," said Monsieur de Graün, running to get his hat. "I'll see you tonight, my dear Murph."

"Tonight, my dear baron. We will be a little late because I'm sure his lordship will want to visit the mysterious house in rue du Temple this very day."

CHAPTER 8

A HOUSE ON RUE DU TEMPLE

In order to make use of the information Baron de Graün had acquired about Songbird and Germain, the Schoolmaster's son, Rodolphe had to go to rue du Temple and then to see the solicitor Jacques Ferrand. A visit to the solicitor's establishment would allow him to see whether Madame Séraphin could give him any leads regarding Fleur-de-Marie's family. At the house on rue du Temple, on the other hand, he hoped to discover from Mademoiselle Rigolette where Germain, who had lived there until recently, had gone. This task would likely be difficult to accomplish, given the probability that the seamstress knew that the Schoolmaster's son had very good reasons for keeping people from knowing the location of his new place of residence. By renting the room in the house on rue du Temple that Germain had been living in, Rodolphe could make his inquiries more easily. At the same time, he would be able to observe from close up the behaviors of people in different walks of life.

At around three o'clock on a mournful winter day—the very same day as the one on which the discussion between the Baron de Graün and Murph took place—Rodolphe showed up at rue du Temple. Located in the middle of a busy commercial area, this house had nothing special about its appearance. It had a ground floor which was occupied by a liquor shop, four further floors, and additional rooms in the attic. A dark, narrow alley led to a small court or, rather, a well of about five to six feet in width, completely bereft of air and light. It was a filthy receptacle containing all of the house's refuse, which rained down from the upper floors. Each landing had small glassless windows that opened over lead gutters.

At the foot of a dark, dank stairway, a reddish glow indicated the location of the doorkeeper's living quarters. That room was smoky from the burning of a lamp that was necessary even at midday to illuminate this somber den. Here we follow Rodolphe, who was dressed more or less in a salesman's weekday clothing. He wore a coat of indeterminate color, a hat that had been squashed out of shape, and gigantic hinged clogs. He carried an umbrella. To complete his disguise, he held a large roll of carefully packed fabrics under his arm.

He went into the doorkeeper's lodgings to ask him if he could see the vacant room. These living quarters were lit by an oil lamp placed behind a water-filled glass bowl, which served as its reflector. At the back of the room could be seen a bed that was covered with a multicolored counterpane sewn together from many different fabric scraps of every kind and color. On the left was a chest of drawers made of walnut. Atop the marble surface of the chest, the following ornaments were arranged:

A small wax figure of Saint John, with his white sheep and blond hair, sitting under a cracked glass case, with its cracks ingeniously plugged with blue paper; two candle holders in old gold plate, which held, instead of candles, two sequined oranges, no doubt recently given to the doorkeeper as New Year's gifts; two boxes, one made of different colors of straw, the other covered with small seashells. One could smell the prison or penal colony where these two decorative boxes had been made from a mile away (let us hope, for the sake of the morality of rue du Temple's doorkeeper, that these were not tokens of gratitude given to him by their creators).

Finally, between the two boxes, and under a glass-covered pendulum, stood a small pair of full-grained boots in fancy red leather. These were veritable doll's boots, though they were meticulously and skillfully crafted and covered with ornamentations and perforations. Together with the rank odor of rancid leather and the arabesque-like arrangement on the walls made up of innumerable pairs of old shoes, this masterwork (as artisans of old used to call such things) made it clear that this house's doorkeeper had made new shoes before having been reduced to repairing old ones.

When Rodolphe ventured into this hole, Monsieur Pipelet, the doorkeeper, had stepped out for the moment. His place was held down by Madame Pipelet. She sat by a cast-iron stove and listened gravely to the singing of the pot (that is the accepted expression). The French Hogarth, Henri Monnier,[44] has so perfectly captured the essence of the female doorkeeper that we will merely ask the reader, if he wishes to depict Madame Pipelet for himself, to recall the ugliest, most withered, most pimpled, most squalid, shabbiest, meanest, most poisonous of female doorkeepers immortalized by this artist. The only trait that we would add to this stereotype, which is all too real, would be her strange head covering, a wig in the style of Titus. The wig was originally blond, but time had transformed it into a mass of rusty, yellowish, brown, and fawn-colored hues that congealed, so to speak, into an indistinguishable tangle of hard, stiff, bristled, tangled locks. Madame Pipelet never appeared without this unique and timeless ornament poised atop her sexagenarian skull.

Upon seeing Rodolphe, the doorkeeper's wife rudely accosted him with these sacramental words: "Where are you going?"

---

44. Henri Monnier (1799–1832) made lithographs between 1827 and 1832 depicting and satirizing the French lower and middle classes. [TN]

"Madame, I believe there is a room with an office for rent in this house?" asked Rodolphe, stressing the word *madame.*

Madame Pipelet was more than a little flattered by this title. She responded, slightly less sharply, "There is a room for rent on the fourth floor, but it can't be shown at the moment. Alfred has gone out . . ."

"Your son, I take it, madame? Will he be back soon?"

"No, monsieur, he's not my son, but my husband! Why can't Pipelet be named Alfred?"

"He has a perfect right to be named Alfred, madame, but if you will allow me, I will wait a moment for him to come back. I am very interested in renting this room. The neighborhood and the street suit me. I like the house since it seems very well maintained. But before I visit the room, I would like to know, madame, if you will accept serving as my housekeeper. I prefer to employ only concierges, at least when they agree to it."

This offer, posed in such flattering terms—concierge!—completely won Madame Pipelet over.

"But of course, monsieur . . . I will be your housekeeper . . . it would be an honor, and for six francs a month, you would be treated like a prince," she responded.

"Done for six francs a month. Madame . . . what is your name, please?"

"Pomone-Fortunée-Anastasie Pipelet."

"Well, then, Madame Pipelet, we are agreed on six francs a month for your wages. And if the room suits me, how much will it cost?"

"With the office, one hundred and fifty francs, monsieur. And you won't get it for a penny less. The principal renter is a skinflint and a dog."

"And his name is?"

"Monsieur Red-Arm."

This name and the memories it awakened in Rodolphe made him quiver slightly. "The name of the principal renter, you say, Madame Pipelet, is . . . what?"

"As I said, Monsieur Red-Arm."

"And where does he live?"

"Thirteen rue aux Fèves. He also has a bar in the trenches along the Champs-Élysées."

There was no longer any doubt. It was the same man. This seemed to Rodolphe a strange coincidence.

"If Monsieur Red-Arm is the principal renter, who is the owner of the house?"

"Monsieur Bourdon, but I've never had anything to do with anybody but Monsieur Red-Arm."

Wanting to put the doorkeeper's wife at ease, Rodolphe said, "Listen, I'm a bit tired, my dear Madame Pipelet. The cold has turned me into a block of ice. Would you do me a great favor and go to the liquor salesman who lives in the house and bring back a bottle of cassis and two glasses—no, make that three glasses, since your husband will be coming back." And he gave her a hundred sous.

"Oh, sir! Really, you are going to make everybody love you here!" Madame Pipelet cried out, as the pimples on her nose seemed to light up with all the fires of bacchic desire.

"Good, Madame Pipelet, because I want everyone to love me here."

"You and I will get along like cherry pie. But I'll only bring two glasses. Alfred and I always drink from the same one. Poor dear, he has such a soft spot for women."

"So go on, Madame Pipelet, and we'll wait for Alfred."

"But what if someone comes? Will you keep watch?"

"Don't worry."

And the old woman went out. Left alone, Rodolphe reflected on this strange circumstance that brought him back to Red-Arm. He was surprised only that François Germain would have been able to stay in this house for three months before being found out by the Schoolmaster's accomplices, given the Schoolmaster's relationship with Red-Arm.

At this moment, a mail carrier knocked on the tiles of the doorkeeper's room, put his arm in, and held out two letters, saying, "Three sous!"

"Six sous. There are two letters," said Rodolphe.

"One is franked," said the letter carrier.[45]

After paying the mail carrier, Rodolphe at first glanced merely mechanically at the two letters that he had just been given. But soon enough they seemed to him to merit a much closer look. One, addressed to Madame Pipelet, exuded the strong scent of musk perfume through the calendered paper of its envelope. The two letters *C.R.* could be seen on its red wax seal, over which was a helmet. The letters rested on the pedestal of the cross of the Legion of Honor. The address was written in a firm hand. The heraldic pretention of the helmet and the cross made Rodolphe smile and confirmed his notion that the letter was not written by a woman. But who was this perfumed, herald-adorned correspondent . . . of Madame Pipelet?

The other letter, on plain gray paper, closed with a sealing wafer pricked with a needle, was addressed to "Monsieur César Bradamanti, Dentist." This address, clearly written in disguised handwriting, was composed entirely in capital letters. Whether it was his intuition, a flight of fancy, or in fact reality, Rodolphe thought this letter had a sad look to

---

45. Franked mail is stamped or otherwise prepaid. Rodolphe is asked to pay only for the unfranked mail. [TN]

it. He noticed that some of the letters of the address were half rubbed out and that the paper was lightly crumpled. A tear had fallen there.

Madame Pipelet returned with the bottle of cassis and two glasses.

"I have dawdled, haven't I, monsieur? But once you're in old Joseph's shop, it's hard to get out. The old lecher! Would you believe that even with a woman of my age, he still likes to play at hanky-panky?"

"You don't say! What if Alfred knew about that?"

"Don't even say that! My blood runs cold at the mere thought of it. Alfred is as jealous as a Turk; but on old Joseph's part, it's all joking. He doesn't really mean anything by it."

"Here are two letters the mail carrier brought," said Rodolphe.

"Oh, heavens. Pardon me, monsieur—you paid for them?"

"Yes."

"You are too good. Well, I'll take that out of the change I've brought back. How much is it?"

"Three sous," said Rodolphe, who smiled at the singular way Madame Pipelet had of reimbursing people.

"How could it be three sous? For two letters, it's six sous."

"I could take advantage of you by making you withhold six sous of the change you brought back instead of three, but I can't do that kind of thing, Madame Pipelet. One of the letters is franked. And without wishing to be indiscreet, I have to say that your correspondent sends you love letters that have a beautiful perfume."

"Let me see that," said the doorkeeper's wife, taking the letter in calendered paper. "My lord, it's true. This has the look of a love letter! Really, monsieur, a love letter! Well! Really! So who is the joker who would dare?"

"And if Alfred had found that, Madame Pipelet?"

"Don't say such things. I'll faint in your arms!"

"I won't say another word, Madame Pipelet!"

"But what a fool I am. Now I've figured it out," said the doorkeeper's wife, shrugging her shoulders. "I know—I know—it's from the commandant. What a fright that gave me! But that shouldn't stop us from settling up. Let's see, it's three sous for the other letter, right? So, as we said: fifteen sous for the cassis, and the letter is three sous, which I will hold back, that makes eighteen. Eighteen and two and that's twenty, and four francs makes one hundred sous. Short debts make long friendships."

"And here's twenty sous for you, Madame Pipelet. Your way of reimbursing the advances one gives you is so remarkable that I feel I must encourage it."

"Twenty sous! You're giving me twenty sous! Why are you doing that?" Madame Pipelet cried out, at once alarmed and surprised at this generosity that seemed to come straight out of a fairy tale.

"That will be a down payment on the good faith money if I take the rooms."

"I'll accept it on those terms. But I'll tell Alfred about it."

"Of course. But here's another letter. It's addressed to Monsieur César Bradamanti."

"Oh, yes . . . the dentist on the third floor. I'll go put it in the letter boot."

Rodolphe thought he had misheard, but he saw Madame Pipelet deposit the letter gravely into an old inside-out boot attached to the wall. Rodolphe watched this with surprise. "What are you doing?" he asked her. "You put that letter—"

"Yes, monsieur, I put it in the letter boot. Like that, nothing gets misplaced. When the renters come back in, either Alfred or I shake the boot, things get sorted, and each one gets what's his."

"This house is so well ordered that I really do want to live here. I'm especially taken by this letter boot."

"My goodness, it's really quite simple," Madame Pipelet responded modestly. "Alfred had an old boot that didn't have a match and thought he might as well use it for the renters."

After saying that, the doorkeeper's wife unsealed the letter addressed to her and turned it every which way. After a few moments of embarrassment, she said to Rodolphe, "Alfred is always in charge of reading because I don't know how. Would you be so good, monsieur, as to . . . do for me what Alfred does?"

"Insofar as reading this letter, with pleasure," said Rodolphe, who was very curious as to who Madame Pipelet's correspondent was. He read what followed on the letter's calendered paper, in the corner of which were reprinted the helmet, the letters *C.R.*, the heraldic pedestal, and the cross of honor.

"Tomorrow, Friday, at eleven o'clock, light large fires in the two rooms, clean the mirrors well, take off all the slipcovers, and take care not to scratch the gilding of the furniture when you dust it.

"If, by chance, I have not yet arrived by the time a woman comes strolling by around one o'clock and asks for me under the name of Monsieur Charles, have her shown upstairs to the apartment and bring the key back down, so that you can give it to me when I arrive."

Despite the somewhat vague phrasing of this letter, Rodolphe understood completely what it was about. He asked the doorkeeper's wife, "So who lives on the first floor?"

The old woman put her yellowed, wrinkled finger to her blubbery lips and answered with a sly chuckle, "Mum's the word . . . this concerns affairs of the heart."

"I'm asking about it, my dear Madame Pipelet, because before I live in a house, I would like to know—"

"Well, I understand that. Show me who you want to ditch and I'll show you who likes you. Right?"[46]

"That's what I was going to say."

"And anyway, I can tell you all I know about that, since it's not very much. About six weeks ago, an upholsterer came here, looked at the first-story apartment, which was for rent, asked the price, and the next day he returned with a handsome young blond-haired man with a pencil mustache, a cross of honor, and fine clothing. The upholsterer called him 'Commandant.'"

"So he's a military man?"

"A military man!" Madame Pipelet answered, raising an eyebrow. "I think not. That would be like Alfred deciding to call himself a concierge."

"What do you mean?"

"He's just in the headquarters of the National Guard. The upholsterer called him 'Commandant' to flatter him, just the same as it would flatter Alfred if someone called him a concierge. So, when the commandant (that's the only name we know for him) had seen everything, he said to the upholsterer, 'This is good, it suits me. Go arrange things with the owner.' 'Yes, Commandant,' says the other guy. And the next day, the upholsterer signed the lease in his own name with Monsieur Red-Arm and paid him six months in advance. It seems that the young man doesn't want his identity known. Right after that, workers came and gutted the first-floor apartment. They brought in sofas, silk curtains, gilded mirrors, fancy furniture. The apartment looked as beautiful as the cafés on the boulevards! And that's not even mentioning the carpets everywhere—carpets so thick and soft that you feel like you're walking on animal skins. When all the work was finished, the commandant came back to see everything. He said to Alfred, 'Could you take charge of maintaining everything in this apartment? I won't be here often. Light a fire from time to time and make everything ready for me when I tell you by letter that I'll be coming.' 'Yes, Commandant,' that flatterer, Alfred, said. 'And what will you ask to do that?' 'Twenty francs a month, Commandant.' 'Twenty francs! You must be joking, doorkeeper.' And so here is this young dandy, bargaining like a tightwad, skinning the poor people. And all that for one or two lousy hundred-sou coins after he spent fortunes on an apartment where he wouldn't even be living! Finally, after fighting tooth and nail, we got him to agree to twelve francs. Twelve francs! Can you believe it? That two-penny commandant! You're a different story, monsieur!" the doorkeeper's wife added in a flattering tone to Rodolphe. "You don't tell me to call you

46. Madame Pipelet is punning on a French expression, "Show me the company you keep and I'll tell you who you are." [TN]

'Commandant,' you don't have your nose in the air, and you agreed to pay me six francs on the spot."

"And has this young man returned since then?"

"Wait till I tell you—that's the funniest part. Someone's really making the commandant beg for it. He has written three times before this, just like today, to light the fire, get everything ready, he'd be coming with a lady. Right! Go see if anyone comes!"

"No one's ever showed up?"

"Here's the story. The first of the three times, the commandant came dressed to kill, whistling between his teeth, holding his chest out. He waited two full hours . . . no one shows. When he came back past our room, we were watching, Alfred and me, to see his expression and to get his goat by talking to him. 'Commandant, no little lady, no little lady at all, came asking for you,' I say to him. 'That's all right,' he says, but he looks humiliated and furious, and he leaves right away, biting back his anger. The second time, before he came, a messenger brings a little letter addressed to Monsieur Charles. I suspect that this time things were going up in flames, too. Pipelet and me were going to get our laugh out of this one and then the commandant comes. 'Commandant,' I say, putting the back of my left hand to my wig, saluting like a real army man, 'here's a letter; it seems there's another problem today.' He gives me a look, proud as any king, opens the letter, and turns red as a shrimp. Then, making as if nothing has bothered him at all, he says to us, 'I knew she wasn't coming; I came here to ask you to keep a careful watch over everything.' It wasn't true. It was to hide from us that someone made him come that he said that. And then he wriggled away, forcing himself to sing, but he was good and irritated, you can be sure. Well done! Well done, two-penny commandant! That'll teach you to only give twelve francs a month for your housekeeping."

"And the third time?"

"Ah! The third time I really thought would be the charm. The commandant arrived dressed to the nines. He seemed so happy and sure of himself that his eyes were popping out of his head. A really good-looking young man all the same—well turned out, smelling like a bottle of perfume. He was so pumped up with his own importance that he was floating. He took the key, and as he went upstairs he said to us, puffed up and mocking, as if to get back at us for the other times, 'Please tell the lady that the door is close by.' Good! We two Pipelets were so curious to see the little lady, even though we didn't much count on it, that we left our room to be on watch at the door to the street. This time, a little blue carriage with lowered shades stopped in front of the house. 'Good! It's her,' I said to Alfred. 'Let's get out of the way a little so we don't frighten her.' The coachman opens the door. And so we see a little lady with a muff on her knees and a black veil hiding her face. She was also holding a handkerchief to her mouth. She seemed to be crying. But then it turns out that the moment the steps for getting off the coach are lowered, instead of climbing out, the lady says a few words to the coachman, who is all surprised, but then closes the doors again."

"And she didn't come out?"

"No, monsieur. She threw herself back into the coach, putting her hands over her eyes. So I jump up and, before the coachman can get back on his seat, I say to him, 'So, my honest man, you are going back, then?' 'Yes,' he says to me. 'And where is that?' I ask him. 'Where I came from.' 'And where do you come from?' 'Rue Saint-Dominique, at the corner of rue de Belle-Chasse.'"

At these words, Rodolphe trembled. The Marquis d'Harville, one of his best friends, who had been overcome with sadness for some time, lived on rue Saint-Dominique at the corner of rue de Belle-Chasse, as we have said. Was it the Marquise d'Harville who was courting her own fall? Did her husband suspect her of some misdeed? Some misdeed on her part might be the sole cause of the grief that seemed to be eating him up.

These doubts crowded in on Rodolphe. But he knew all of the marquise's inner circle and he didn't recall ever having seen anyone who looked like the commandant. The young woman in this case might, after all, have taken a coach from that location without residing on that street. There was nothing that could prove to Rodolphe that it was the marquise. Nevertheless, he still had vague and tormenting suspicions.

The doorkeeper's wife did not fail to notice his anxious and absorbed mood. "So, monsieur, what are you thinking about?" she asked.

"I'm trying to think why this woman, who came right up to the door, suddenly changed her mind."

"It could be anything, monsieur—an idea, something that frightened her, a moment of superstition. We poor women are so weak, such cowards," said the horrible doorkeeper's wife in a timid and frightened manner. "I guess that if I had acted like that, trying to two-time Alfred on the sly, I don't know how many times I would have had to keep pushing at myself to keep myself going. But not me—never on your life! Poor dear. Not a living soul can boast of—"

"I believe you, Madame Pipelet. But this young woman—"

"I don't know if she's young. You couldn't see one bit of her face. All the same, as I said, she left as she came, no trumpet, no drumroll. You could have given ten francs to each of us, Alfred and me, and we couldn't have been happier."

"Why is that?"

"Thinking about the face the commandant would make, we could have died laughing, that's why. First, instead of telling him right away that the woman had left, we let him stew in his juices for a good long hour. Then I went up. I was only wearing cloth slippers on my poor feet.

I came to the door, which was nearby. I pushed it and it screeched. The stairway is as black as an oven; so is the inside of the apartment. And so the moment I came in, the commandant takes me in his arms, saying tenderly, 'My angel! How late you are!'"

Despite the seriousness of the thoughts that occupied him, Rodolphe couldn't keep himself from laughing, particularly as he looked at the grotesque wig and the severely withered and pimpled face of the heroine of this ridiculous scene of mistaken identity.

Madame Pipelet continued with a grimacing leer that made her even more hideous. "Ha, ha, ha! There's a good one! But just wait and see what happens next. Me, I don't say anything, I just hold my breath and surrender to the commandant. But suddenly, here he is crying out and pushing me away, the rotter, as disgusted as if he'd found a spider in his bed. 'But who the devil is it?' 'It's me, Commandant, Madame Pipelet, the doorkeeper's wife. So you should just keep your hands to yourself, don't hold me around the waist, don't call me your angel, and don't tell me I'm late. If Alfred had been here, what then?' 'What do you want?' he said to me, furious. 'Commandant, the little lady just came in a coach.' 'So then have her come up. Are you stupid? Didn't I tell you to have her come up?' I let him go on like this. 'Yes, Commandant, it's true, you told me to have her come up.' 'And so?' 'Well, it's just that the little lady . . .' 'So tell me what already!' 'It's just that the little lady left again.' 'Go on—you must have said or done something stupid,' he cried out, even more furious. 'No, Commandant. The little lady never got down from the coach. When the coachman opened the door, she told him to take her back to where she had come from.' 'The coach can't be far away!' the commandant cried out, running to the door. 'Well, yes, it's more than an hour since she left,' I say back to him. 'An hour! An hour! And why have you waited so long to tell me?' he cried out, getting more and more angry. 'Well, honestly, because we were afraid to get you that upset for still not having gotten what you'd paid for.' So take that! I say to myself. You fop, that will teach you to get sick to your stomach when you touch me. 'Get out of here. You do nothing but say and do stupid things!' he cried out in rage, taking off his Tartar-style dressing gown and throwing his gold-embroidered velvet fez to the ground. It was a nice cap, actually. And that dressing gown! It was quite a beauty. The commandant looked like a shiny worm."

"And since then, neither he nor the lady has returned?"

"No. But wait until you hear the end of the story," said Madame Pipelet.

CHAPTER 9

THE THREE FLOORS

"So here's the end of the story," Madame Pipelet went on. "I hurried down the stairs to get back to Alfred. The doorkeeper's wife from number nineteen and the oysterwoman who stations her cart in front of the liquor store happened to be in our rooms at the time. I told them about how the commandant had called me his angel and put his arm around my waist. And, boy, did we laugh! And Alfred, even though he was pretty melan—yes, melancholy is the word—even though he was pretty melancholy because of the remarks that monster Cabrion made."

Rodolphe looked at the doorkeeper's wife, baffled.

"Yes, I'll tell you all about that one day when we know each other better. Anyway, that's how it was that Alfred, despite his melancholia, started to call me his angel. Then the commandant left his apartment and closed the door, getting ready to leave. But when he heard us laughing, he didn't have the guts to come down. He was afraid we'd make fun of him and he couldn't avoid going by our rooms. We figured out what was happening and so the oysterwoman, in her loud voice, starts crying out, 'Pipelet, how late you are, my angel!' Hearing that, the commandant went back inside his place and slammed the door with a loud noise. That showed just how furious he was—he must have been as furious as a tiger. He was white to the tip of his nose. Before it was all over, he must have opened his door ten times to see if anyone was still in our rooms. And there sure was, because we weren't going anywhere. In the end, figuring that no one was leaving, he put on a bold front, came down the steps in long strides, threw the key in my face without saying anything, and made off, completely in a rage. We were still dying with laughter all the while, and the oysterwoman kept repeating, 'How late you are, my angel!'"

"But weren't you afraid that the commandant wouldn't want you to go on working for him?"

"Not likely! He wouldn't dare. We had him but good. We know where the floozy lives. And if he said anything, we could always threaten to let the cat out of the bag. And besides, for his lousy twelve francs, who else would do his housekeeping? Someone from outside the building? We would make her life too hard. Lousy miser, let him try! Really, monsieur, would you believe it, he was so petty that he inspected his woodpile and scratched out the number of logs burned while we waited for him. He's some Johnny-come-lately, you can bet, some nobody who's made a pile of dough. That kind has his nose in the air and his body in rags. He spends a little over here and skimps a lot over there. I don't wish him any real harm, but it really is fun to watch his fancy woman give him the air. I'll bet tomorrow it'll be the same thing all over again. I'll go tell the oyster-woman who was here the last time—it'll be entertaining. If the little lady comes, we'll see whether she's a brunette or a blondie and if she's nice. It's really pretty funny, isn't it? You know, monsieur, there's got to be one ninny of a husband in the background somewhere. But that's his business, poor guy. Anyway, we'll see the little lady tomorrow and, veil or no veil, she'll really have to keep her head down for us not to see what color her eyes are. And that's really a double shame, as we say where I come from; she comes to a man's house and then she makes a show of being too frightened. But excuse me a moment while I take my pot off the stove. It's finished whistling and that means the grub's ready to eat. It's tripe, and that'll cheer Alfred up, at least a little bit. He says it himself: for tripe, he'd betray France—his beloved France—the poor old dear."

While Madame Pipelet took care of these domestic considerations, Rodolphe gave himself over to sad reflection. The woman in question (whether it was the Marquise d'Harville or not) had certainly hesitated. She had struggled with herself at length before granting the first and then the second rendezvous. Then, probably frightened by the consequences of her imprudence, she had been kept from dangerous commitment because of a salutary remorse. Here she is, giving in to an irresistible temptation; she arrives in tears at the doorstep of this house; but at the moment she is about to allow herself to become forever a fallen woman, she hears the voice of duty and she avoids dishonor one more time. And for whom did she risk so much shame, so much danger?

Rodolphe knew the world and the human heart very well. He could tell, with some accuracy, what kind of man the commandant was merely from hearing a few of his traits depicted with naive coarseness by the doorkeeper's wife. Here was someone who was so filled with a petty pride that he was vain about a title that had absolutely no real military significance; a man so lacking in tact that he did not take the care to disguise himself sufficiently so as to cloak in complete mystery the guilty actions of a woman who risked everything for him; a man so foolish, so miserly in the end that he didn't even understand that his desire to save a few louis had exposed his mistress to the coarse, insolent mocking of the inhabitants of this house! And so, the next day, impelled by a fatal attraction, but at the same time recognizing the immensity of her sin, this unfortunate young woman would come trembling and lost to this rendezvous. All she had to support her in this terrible torment was a blind faith in the honor of the man to whom she gave more than her life. And she would have to endure the bold and prurient gazes of this crew of wretches and perhaps even overhear their filthy witticisms. How shameful! What a lesson it would be! What a warning for a lost woman who, up to now, would have experienced only the most poetic and charming of love's illusions!

And the man for whom she faces such opprobrium, so many dangers—will he at least be moved by the heart-wrenching agony he causes?

No.

Poor woman! Passion blinds her and tosses her once more to the edge of the abyss. One last courageous effort of virtue saves her one more time. And what will this man feel at the thought of this painful, holy struggle? Nothing but spite, anger, and rage. He will think only that he has put himself out three times, all for nothing, and that his idiotic vanity has been seriously insulted—in the eyes of his doorkeeper, no less. And worst of all, the last sign of his remarkable and enormous blunder: this man had spoken and dressed for their first assignation in such a way as to make the woman die of shame and confusion—if her shame and confusion hadn't already been enough to crush her.

"Oh!" Rodolphe thought. "How crushing a realization it would be were this woman (whom I hope I do not know) to overhear the hideous terms they used to describe what she was doing. Her actions were no doubt guilty, but how much love did they cost her, how many tears, how much terror, how much remorse?"

And then Rodolphe thought about the fact that the Marquise d'Harville might be the sad protagonist of this story. He asked himself what quirk of fate could have led her to dishonor Monsieur d'Harville, who was young, intelligent, devoted, generous, and—more than all that—tenderly in love with his wife—all for this clearly greedy, selfish, and ridiculous ninny. Could the marquise have simply been taken with the face of this man who was said to be so very handsome?

And yet Rodolphe knew Madame d'Harville to be a woman of feeling, wit, and taste, a woman of the most elevated character. Never had her reputation been tainted with the least slander. Where could she have met this man? Rodolphe was in her company with some frequency and he could not remember anyone in the Harville mansion who fit the commandant's description. After considerable thought, he was almost able to convince himself that the woman in question could not be the marquise.

Madame Pipelet, having finished her culinary obligations, once more picked up her discussion with Rodolphe.

"Who lives on the second floor?" he asked the doorkeeper's wife.

"That would be Old Lady Burette, a really good fortune-teller. She can read your hand like it was a book. There are very high-society types who visit her to have her tell their fortune. And she makes more money than she can shake a stick at. And being a fortune-teller is only one of her occupations."

"What else does she do?"

"She keeps what they call a pawnbroker's establishment."

"What?"

"I'm telling you this because, since you're a young man, this could make you want to be a tenant here even more."

"Why would that be?"

"Let's just consider: here we are coming up on Mardi Gras, the time when the streets fill up with dockworkers and streetwalkers, Turks and savages; that's the time when even the steadiest can get in a little trouble. Well, then! It's always a help to have a place to go in the house, rather than having to go to my aunt. That's much more humiliating because the whole world knows what you're doing."

"Your aunt lends people money on the basis of their salary?"

"What, you mean you don't know? Get on with you, you joker! Playing the innocent at your age!"

"How am I playing the innocent, Madame Pipelet?"

"Asking me if my aunt lends money on the basis of people's salary."

"And that's playing the innocent because . . ."

"Because any young person beyond the age of reason knows that giving something as surety to a pawnbroker is called 'going to my aunt.'"

"Ah! Now I understand. So you're saying the second-floor renter is also a pawnbroker?"

"Get on with you, Mr. Slyboots. Yes, she's a pawnbroker and she gives better rates than the official ones. Plus, it's not a big deal at all. You aren't weighed down with papers, notes, numbers, all that stuff. Just think about it: you bring a shirt that's worth three francs to Old Lady Burette. She lends you ten sous; after a week, you owe her twenty, otherwise she keeps the shirt. That way everything's easy, isn't it? Always nice round sums. Even a child can understand it."

"It's perfectly clear now. But I thought it was illegal to lend people money against their salary."

"Ha, ha, ha!" Madame Pipelet shrieked in bursts of laughter. "Did you just get here to the big city, young man? Pardon me, but I'm talking to you as if I were your mother and you were my child."

"And you are very good to treat me that way."

"Well, of course it's illegal to lend money against wages, but if you only did what the law allowed, well, really, you'd spend most of your time just sitting around doing nothing. Old Lady Burette doesn't write anything down and doesn't give receipts. There's nothing to prove she's doing anything and she couldn't care less about the police. The strange stuff people bring to her, it's downright funny to see. You wouldn't believe the things she advances money against sometimes. I've seen her lend money against a gray parakeet that swore like a sailor, the scoundrel."

"Against a parakeet? But what could a parakeet be worth?"

"Just listen. It was a well-known parakeet. It belonged to a letter carrier's widow, a Madame d'Herbelot, who lives near here on rue Sainte-Avoye. Everybody knew that she valued her parakeet like she valued her own life. Old Lady Burette said to her, 'I'll lend you ten francs against your bird, but if in one week at noon I don't have my twenty francs—'"

"Her ten francs."

"With interest, that made twenty francs—always round numbers, remember. 'If I don't have my twenty francs and the cost of feeding it, I'll give little Jaquot a parsley salad seasoned with arsenic.' See, she really knew her business. She put a real scare in Madame d'Herbelot. Old Lady Burette had her twenty francs at the end of seven days. Madame d'Herbelot took back her filthy bird, who continues to fill the air with its swearing. It makes Alfred, who is really quite prudish, blush. But it's easy enough to understand why: his father was a parish priest during the Revolution. You understand—there were parish priests who married nuns."

"And Old Lady Burette doesn't have any other occupations, I'm guessing?"

"Well, she doesn't have any others to speak of. Still, she gets into some kind of scheming sometimes in a room that no one goes into except Monsieur Red-Arm and an old one-eyed hag called the Owl."

Rodolphe looked at the doorkeeper's wife with astonishment. She interpreted his surprise according to her own lights and said, "Owl, that's a funny name, isn't it?"

"Indeed . . . and does that woman come here often?"

"She hadn't been here for six weeks. But we saw her again the day before yesterday; she was limping a little."

"And what was she doing at this fortune-teller's?"

"Well, that's more than I can say. I do know this much about the scheming in the little room I was talking about, the one where only the Owl and Monsieur Red-Arm go. I've noticed, at least, that on those days the one-eyed hag always brings a package in her basket and Monsieur Red-Arm always brings a package under his coat, and neither of them ever carries anything away."

"And what do the packages contain?"

"I don't know anything about that, unless they're making some kind of the devil's own stew, because you can smell something like sulfur, charcoal, and melted tin when you pass them on the stairway. And then you hear them blowing, blowing, blowing—like a blacksmith's bellows. Well, of course, Old Lady Burette plays tricks when she tells fortunes or does magic. At least that's what Monsieur César Bradamanti says—he's the lodger on the third floor. Now there's someone special, that Monsieur

César. When I say someone special, well, he's Italian but he speaks French as good as you and me, except for the heavy accent. But that's all the same—he's a real scholar! He knows about medicinal herbs and he pulls out your teeth without charging you, just for the honor of it. Really, just for the honor of it. You could have six bad teeth and he says it for anyone to hear, that he'll pull out the first five teeth for nothing and only charge you for the sixth. It's not his fault if all you have is the sixth one."

"That's really generous."

"And in addition to that, he sells a really good kind of water that stops hair from falling out, cures eye problems, corns on your feet, and stomach problems. And it kills rats without arsenic."

"The same water cures stomach problems!"

"The same water."

"And it also kills rats?"

"It's never failed to kill a single one. After all, what's healthy for human beings is bad for animals."

"That's right, Madame Pipelet, I hadn't thought of that."

"And the proof that it's very good water is that it's made from medicinal herbs that Monsieur César gathered in the mountains of Lebanon, right next to American herbs. He also brought a horse home from there, a horse that looks like a tiger: it's all white but speckled with bay spots. I'll tell you, when Monsieur César Bradamanti is up on that beast, wearing his red coat with the yellow lining and his feathered hat, well, anyone would pay to see it. With all due respect, he looks like Judas Iscariot, with his big rust-colored beard. For the last month, he hired Monsieur Red-Arm's son, little Gammy, who he dresses up as if he were a troubadour. He wears a black cap, a ruff, and an apricot-colored jacket. He beats a drum near Monsieur César to attract customers. And on top of that, the little kid takes care of the dentist's speckled horse."

"It seems to me that your principal renter's son has one humble job there."

"His father wants to teach his child to make money as best he can, because otherwise he'll end up on the scaffold. And, really, he's one sly monkey—and wicked. He's tricked Monsieur César Bradamanti more than once. And Monsieur César is the most honest of honest people. When you think that he's cured Alfred of rheumatism, well, you understand that we have a special place for him in our hearts. Well, then, monsieur, there are people who are unnatural enough—but that's enough. It would make your hair stand on end. Alfred says that if it were true, it would be a case for the prison ships."

"What are you talking about?"

"I really can't say—I could never talk about it."

"Well, then, let's drop the subject."

"The thing is—for a respectable woman to say such things to a young man . . ."

"Let's drop the subject, Madame Pipelet."

"Well, but since you are going to be our renter, it's better that you know in advance the lies people spread. You are in a position to be friends with Monsieur Bradamanti, to be part of his circle, right? If you believed the stuff people said about him, you would be disgusted at the idea of getting to know him."

"Go ahead, then. I'm listening."

"People say that when . . . sometimes a girl does something foolish . . . you know what I'm saying, right? . . . and she fears the consequences . . ."

"What then?"

"Well, this is the part I really shouldn't talk about."

"But what is it?"

"No, I can't . . . and besides, it's all silliness . . ."

"Tell me anyway."

"But it's lies."

"Tell me anyway."

"It's just what gossips say."

"But what is it?"

"People who are jealous of Monsieur César's speckled horse."

"Great, but what do they say?"

"I'm ashamed to say it."

"But what's the connection between a girl who's fallen and the charlatan?"

"I didn't say it was true!"

"But, in the name of heaven, what is it, after all?" Rodolphe cried out, impatient with Madame Pipelet's strange reticence.

"Listen, young man," the doorkeeper's wife started up again, in a solemn tone, "you must promise on your honor never to repeat this to anybody."

"When I know what we are talking about, I either will or I won't make that promise."

"If I tell you, it won't be because of the six francs you promised me or because of the cassis you bought."

"Yes, that's fine."

"It's because you inspire trust."

"Good."

"And to help out poor Monsieur César Bradamanti by proving his innocence."

"You have only the best intentions. I don't doubt it. And so?"

"Well, people say . . . but this doesn't get out of here, at least."

"Of course. So what do people say, then?"

"But really, I still don't like to speak about it. Well, I'll whisper it in your ear. That will cause me less trouble—just as if I were a child, eh?" And the old woman whispered a few words to Rodolphe, who recoiled in horror.

"But that's shocking!" he cried out, jumping up reflexively and looking around him in terror, as if the house had had a curse put on it. "God," he murmured in a half whisper, in an anguished stupor, "are such abominable crimes really possible? And this hideous old woman seems almost not to care about the horrible revelation she has just made."

The doorkeeper's wife didn't hear Rodolphe, and she went on, while she continued to attend to her housekeeping, "Isn't that just a pile of evil gossip? Really! A man who cured Alfred's rheumatism, a man who brought a speckled horse back from Lebanon, a man who offers to pull five out of six teeth for free, a man who has degrees from all over Europe, a man who pays his rent down every month on the nose. I tell you. I'd rather die than believe that!"

While Madame Pipelet was expressing her indignation against the scandalmongers, Rodolphe recalled the letter written to the charlatan. It had been written on coarse paper, in a disguised handwriting that was half erased by the trace of a tear. Rodolphe saw a tragedy in that tear, in that mysterious letter addressed to that man, a terrible tragedy. An involuntary premonition told him that the atrocious gossip about the Italian was well founded.

"Listen, Alfred will tell you," the doorkeeper's wife cried out. "He'll say the same thing as me, that it's just malicious gossips who accuse Monsieur César Bradamanti of such abominations. And him having cured Albert of rheumatism and all."

CHAPTER 10

MONSIEUR PIPELET

The reader should recall that these events took place in 1838.

Monsieur Pipelet entered his rooms in a serious and magisterial manner. He was around sixty years old. He had an enormous nose, a respectable plumpness, and a fat face with sharp features that was lit up like those nutcracker men from Nuremberg.[47] This strange visage was topped off by a brownish, worn-out old stovepipe hat with a wide brim. Alfred would no sooner think of removing this hat than his wife would think of removing her monstrous wig. He lounged about in an old green coat with immense coattails and lapels that had a rather metallic look to them, since the stains it bore gleamed a shiny gray in various spots. Despite his stovepipe hat and green coat, which was not lacking in a certain dignity, Monsieur Pipelet had not stopped wearing the humble emblem of his occupation: a leather apron in the shape of a fawn-colored triangle, worn over a waistcoat as multicolored as Madame Pipelet's patchwork bedspread.

The doorkeeper greeted Rodolphe with some friendliness, but there was something very bitter, alas, about his smile. One could see the deep melancholy in it that Madame Pipelet had told Rodolphe about.

"Alfred, this gentleman wishes to rent the room and the office on the fourth floor," said Madame Pipelet, introducing Rodolphe to Alfred, "and we have been waiting for you to drink the glass of cassis that he ordered for you."

This tactful touch put Rodolphe in Monsieur Pipelet's confidence instantly. The doorkeeper brought his hand to the brim of his hat and said in a deep voice that would have done credit to a cantor in a cathedral, "We will satisfy your needs in a doorkeeper just as you will satisfy ours in a renter. Birds of a feather flock together." Then, cutting himself off, Monsieur Pipelet said to Rodolphe anxiously, "Unless Monsieur is a painter."

"No, I'm a salesperson."

47. Probably a reference to Hoffmann's tale "Nutcracker and Mouse King," written in 1816. The Tchaikovsky ballet *The Nutcracker* is based on the adaptation of the tale in 1844 by Alexandre Dumas. Sue would have known only the Hoffmann tale, however. [TN]

"Well, then, monsieur, your humble servant. I thank God that you are not like those monstrous artists!"

"Artists are monsters?" Rodolphe asked.

Rather than responding, Monsieur Pipelet raised his hands toward the ceiling and moaned in anguish.

"Painters have poisoned Alfred's life. They have caused the melancholy I talked to you about," Madame Pipelet whispered to Rodolphe. Then she went on in a normal voice and an affectionate tone, "Come on, now, Alfred, calm down. Don't give any more thought to that rogue. You'll make yourself sick and you won't be able to eat your dinner."

"No, I will take heart and be calm," responded Monsieur Pipelet, with a sad and resigned dignity. "He wronged me grievously; he persecuted and tortured me for a long while. But now I feel nothing but contempt for him." And then he turned to Rodolphe and added, "Painters. Ah! Monsieur, they are the plague of a house; they bring it to rack and ruin."

"You rented a room to a painter?"

"Alas, yes, monsieur, we rented a room to one!" said Monsieur Pipelet, bitterly. "A painter named Cabrion." Monsieur Pipelet, despite his seemingly restrained manner, clenched his fists at the mere memory.

"Was he the prior tenant of the room I am interested in renting?" asked Rodolphe.

"No, no, the prior tenant was an honest, worthy young man named Monsieur Germain. But the one before him was Cabrion. Ah, monsieur, since he has left, this Cabrion has almost driven me crazy—he has almost even made me lose my mind."

"You miss him that much?" asked Rodolphe.

"Do I miss Cabrion?" the doorkeeper retorted, flabbergasted. "I should miss Cabrion! But just imagine, monsieur! Monsieur Red-Arm paid him two months' rent just to get him out of here, because he had made the unfortunate mistake of giving him a lease. What a pest he was! You have no idea, monsieur, of the horrible tricks he played on us and the other renters. Just to mention one of these games, there was no kind of wind instrument that he didn't scheme with to make the renters miserable! Yes, monsieur, from the hunting horn to the serpent,[48] he put all of them to bad use, carrying his meanness so far as to play out of key, and then the same note for hours on end, on purpose. You could go crazy from it. There were more than twenty petitions to Monsieur Red-Arm, the principal renter, to get rid of that beggar. Finally, monsieur, it came to buying him off with two months' rent. It sounds funny, doesn't it? A renter getting paid two months' rent? But we would have paid three months' rent to shake ourselves loose from him. So he leaves . . . And you think that's maybe the last we'd hear of Cabrion. Well, just wait. The next night at eleven o'clock, I was in bed.

48. An ancient curved wind instrument. [TN]

Bam, bam, bam! I pull the bell rope and someone comes to the rooms. 'Good evening, doorkeeper,' a voice says, 'would you be so kind as to give me a lock of your hair?' My wife says to me, 'It's someone who's come to the wrong place.' And I answer the stranger, 'You have the wrong place; try one of the neighboring houses.' 'But isn't this number seventeen? And the doorkeeper's name is Pipelet?' responded the voice. 'Yes,' I say, 'my name is Pipelet, all right.' 'Well, then, Pipelet, my friend, I am here to ask you for a lock of your hair for Cabrion. He's got a hankering for it and he means to have it.'"

Monsieur Pipelet looked at Rodolphe, shaking his head and crossing his arms as if posing for a sculpture. "You understand, monsieur. He asked me, his mortal enemy—me, whom he had showered with endless outrages—he came to me, of all people, to ask shamelessly for a lock of my hair. That's the kind of request that ladies often refuse even to their beloved!"

"But what if this Cabrion had been a good renter, like Monsieur Germain?" said Rodolphe, keeping a straight face.

"Even if he had been a good renter, I still wouldn't have granted him that lock of hair," the man in the stovepipe hat said majestically. "That's something I neither think right nor am given to doing. But I would have made a point of turning him down politely."

"And that's not all," the doorkeeper's wife went on. "Would you believe, monsieur, that since that day until now, morning, noon, and night, at any moment, a swarm of starving painter types, all coming from that frightful Cabrion, pops up, one after the other, asking Alfred for a lock of his hair, always for Cabrion!"

"And you can guess whether I gave in or not!" Monsieur Pipelet said in a firm voice. "You could drag me to the scaffold first, monsieur! After three or four months of their obstinacy and my resistance, my strength triumphed over the relentlessness of these wretches. They saw that they were up against a stone wall and they were forced to give up their insolent requests. But all the same, monsieur. I was struck here." Alfred put his hand over his heart. "I could have committed the most frightening crimes and my sleep would not have been more restless. At any moment, I would wake up with a jolt, thinking I had heard the voice of that accursed Cabrion. I distrusted everybody. Everywhere I looked, I saw enemies. I was losing my normal congeniality. I couldn't see a stranger show up at our rooms without trembling at the thought that it was another one of Cabrion's pack. And even now, monsieur, I am suspicious, sullen, moody, as nitpicky as the nastiest man . . . I'm afraid to open myself up to any new acquaintance for fear of seeing one of Cabrion's pack pop up. I've lost my zest for life."

Madame Pipelet put her index finger to her left eye, as if to wipe away a tear, and nodded her head.

Alfred went on, lamenting ever more dramatically, "I shrank into myself more and more, and I could see a future in which my life force would go on slipping away from me. Was I exaggerating, monsieur, when I told you that that infernal Cabrion had poisoned my existence?" And Monsieur Pipelet, letting out a deep sigh, bowed his stovepipe down under the weight of his terrible misfortune.

"I understand now why you don't like painters," said Rodolphe. "But at least this Monsieur Germain you've talked about has made up for Monsieur Cabrion."

"Oh, yes, monsieur. There's a good and worthy young man, a real straight shooter, helpful and not proud. And cheerful, but he's cheerful in a good way that doesn't harm other people. He's not an insolent prankster like that Cabrion, devil take his soul!"

"Come now, calm down, my dear Monsieur Pipelet. Don't mention that name. And now who is the landlord lucky enough to have Monsieur Germain, that pearl of renters, lodging with him?"

"Nobody has any idea. No one knows where Monsieur Germain lives now, or even knows how to go about looking for him. When I say nobody . . . I mean nobody except Mademoiselle Rigolette."

"And who is this Mademoiselle Rigolette?" asked Rodolphe.

"A little working girl, the other renter on the fourth floor," Madame Pipelet went on. "And she's another pearl. She pays her rent in advance and is so neat in her little room and so nice to everybody, and so cheerful—one of God's creatures, gracious and content! And she works like a busy beaver. She sometimes makes up to two francs a day, but Lord, what an effort it takes."

"But why is Mademoiselle Rigolette the only one who knows where Monsieur Germain resides?"

"When he left the house," Madame Pipelet answered, "he said to us, 'I don't expect any letters, but if, by chance, any come for me, give them to Mademoiselle Rigolette for me.' And she's worthy of his trust, even if the letter had things important inside. Isn't that right, Alfred?"

"The fact is that there would be nothing to say against Mademoiselle Rigolette," the doorkeeper said severely, "if she hadn't been weak enough to allow herself to be sweet-talked by that awful Cabrion."

"Well, as far as that goes, Alfred," responded the doorkeeper's wife, "you know that that's not Mademoiselle Rigolette's fault. It comes with the territory. It was the same with the traveling salesman who occupied the room before Cabrion, just like it was Monsieur Germain who sweet-talked her after that rotten painter. It never works any other way. It comes with the territory."

"So," said Rodolphe. "So one of the obligations of renting this room is to flirt with Mademoiselle Rigolette?"

"An absolute obligation, monsieur, and you'll see why. You are neighbors with Mademoiselle Rigolette. The two rooms are adjoined, and, well, when two young people are near each other . . . there's a light that needs lighting, a burning ember to borrow, or maybe you need water. Oh! As for water, you can always find that at Mademoiselle Rigolette's; she is never short of it. That's her one luxury and she takes to it like a little duck. As soon as she has a moment to spare, there she is washing her floor, her hearth. And so her place is always so clean—you'll see."

"And so Monsieur Germain respected the rules of the territory and was, as you say, on good neighborly terms with Mademoiselle Rigolette."

"Yes, monsieur. And you have to say that they were made for each other. So nice, so young, it was a pleasure to see them coming down the stairs together on Sundays, the only day off those poor children had! She would be dressed up in a pretty bonnet and a pretty dress made of fabric costing twenty-five sous a yard, a dress that she'd made herself but that suited her as if she were a little queen. And he would be dressed up like a real dandy!"

"And Monsieur Germain hasn't seen Mademoiselle Rigolette again since he left this house?"

"No, monsieur, not unless on Sundays. Because Mademoiselle has no time for thinking about lovers on any other day. She gets up at five or six o'clock and works right up to ten and sometimes eleven o'clock at night. She never leaves her rooms except in the morning to buy food for herself and her two canaries, and the three of them together hardly eat anything at all. What do they live on? Two sous' worth of milk, a little bread, a little birdfeed, some salad, some millet, and some good, clean water. And that doesn't stop them from babbling and tweeting, all three of them, the little one and the two birds. What a blessing it is. And on top of that, she's good and generous with what she has, which is to say her waking hours and her care, because even with working sometimes more than twelve hours a day, she barely makes just enough to live on. You know the unfortunate people who live in the attic, the ones Monsieur Red-Arm is going to throw out on the street in no more than three or four days? Well, Mademoiselle Rigolette and Monsieur Germain looked after their children for several nights!"

"So there's an unfortunate family living here?"

"Unfortunate, monsieur! God knows it's only too true! Five very young children, the mother bedridden and at death's door, a senile grandmother, and to support all of these people, a man who certainly does not eat his fill laboring away like a galley slave, because he works like the dickens! He never gets more than three hours of sleep each day. And not a real sleep—woken up by children crying out in hunger, by a sick wife moaning on her straw mat, or by a senile old woman who decides every so often to howl like a wolf—and howl in hunger at that, being no more in control of herself than an animal. When she is hungrier than she can bear, you can hear her howling on the stairs."

"That's horrible!" Rodolphe cried out. "Doesn't anyone try to help them?"

"Lord, monsieur, we do what we can, poor as we are. Ever since the commandant has been paying us twelve francs a month for his housekeeping, I make a stew once a week and give the poor people in the attic the stock. Mademoiselle Rigolette works during the night for them, and, Lord, that costs her. She has to buy fuel for light to turn little scraps of fabric into baby clothes and hats for the little ones. That poor Monsieur Germain, who wasn't that much better off, pretended that he had been given some nice wine from time to time and Monsieur Morel—that's the worker's name—would drink one or two good-size hits of it, which would warm him up a little and lift his spirits."

"And the charlatan, didn't he do anything for these poor people?"

"Monsieur Bradamanti?" said the doorkeeper. "It's true he cured my rheumatism, and I am truly grateful for that. But ever since that day, I said to my wife, 'Anastasie, that Monsieur Bradamanti . . .' Well? Well, didn't I say that to you, Anastasie?"

"It's true, that's what you said, but he does like to laugh, that one does! In his fashion, anyway, because he never opens his mouth to really laugh."

"So what did he do?"

"It's like this, monsieur. When I told him about the misery of the Morels after he complained that he couldn't sleep with the senile old woman howling in hunger all night, he said to me, 'In deference to their poverty, if they have teeth that need pulling, I won't even make them pay for the sixth one, and I'll give them a bottle of my water at half price.'"

"Well, then!" Monsieur Pipelet cried out. "Even if he cured my rheumatism, I think that that joke was in poor taste. But he doesn't make any other kind of jokes—and even so, if they were only in poor taste!"

"You have to take into account, Alfred, that he's Italian and that maybe they have a different sense of humor."

"I have to say, Madame Pipelet," said Rodolphe, "that I don't think well of this man, and I will not be, as you put it, one of his friends or one of his circle. And the pawnbroker, has she been more charitable to the Morels?"

"Well, in the same way Monsieur Bradamanti is charitable," said the doorkeeper. "She lends them money on the scraps of things they have, and now she has everything but their last mattress—not that she's gotten so many mattresses from them, since they only had two to begin with."

"And now she doesn't give them any more help?"

"Old Lady Burette? Yeah, right! She's as much of a skinflint in her own way as her lover is in his. Because, you know, Monsieur Red-Arm and Old Lady Burette—" Madame Pipelet added, winking and nodding maliciously.

"Really!" Rodolphe said.

"Yes, sir. I'd stake my life on it. You know, things heat up in the summer here just like they do everywhere else. Isn't that right, deary?"

Monsieur Pipelet's only response was to shift his stovepipe hat in a melancholy gesture.

Madame Pipelet had begun to seem less repulsive to Rodolphe once she showed some charitable feelings toward the unfortunates in the attic. "What is the poor worker's job?" he asked.

"He makes costume jewelry. He does piecework and as hard as he works at the job, and as many pieces as he makes—well, you'll see. A man is only a man, after all, and you can't do what you can't do—isn't that right? And when you have to feed a family of seven, not counting himself, it's hard! His older daughter helps him as much as she can, but that's not much."

"How old is that daughter?"

"Seventeen. And she's a real beauty—as beautiful as daylight. She's a servant at an old miser's. He's a solicitor and rich enough to buy Paris. His name is Monsieur Jacques Ferrand."

"Monsieur Jacques Ferrand!" said Rodolphe, surprised at coming upon this name again. It was from this solicitor, or at least from his housekeeper, that he had to get information regarding Songbird. "The Monsieur Jacques Ferrand who resides in rue du Sentier?" he asked.

"The very same! You know him?"

"He's the solicitor for the sales house I work for."

"Well, then, you must know that he's one notorious penny-pincher. Although you have to give him his due: he's honest and pious, every Sunday at mass and vespers taking communion and going to confession. If he messes around with anyone, it's only with priests. He drinks only holy water and eats only communion wafers—a real holy man! The strongbox for common people who invest their savings with him! But, Lord, he's a miser, and hard as a rock on himself, as well as on everybody else. Louise, the costume jewelry maker's daughter, has been working there for eighteen months. She does everything over there for eighteen francs a month, no more, no less. She keeps six francs a month to maintain herself and gives the rest to her family. And she always comes through, but when seven people have to eat off of that!"

"But what about the father, does he work hard?"

"Does he work hard? That man's never been drunk a day in his life. He's orderly and as gentle as Jesus. And he never asks anything from God except to make the day last forty-eight hours so he can earn some more food for his little ones."

"So his work doesn't bring in very much?"

"He was bedridden for three months and that got him behind. His wife ruined her health caring for him and now she's dying. It was for those three months that they had to live on Louise's twelve francs and on what they could borrow from Old Lady Burette as well as the bit of money the costume jewelry broker he worked for lent him. But eight people, it keeps coming down to that. And if you saw the hole they lived in! But really, monsieur, let's stop talking about it. Here's dinner, all cooked, and just thinking about their attic turns my stomach. Fortunately, Monsieur Red-Arm is going to throw them out of the house. When I say 'fortunately,' I don't mean to sound hard-hearted. But since these poor Morels are so miserable, and we really can't help them much, they might as well be miserable somewhere else. It's one less heartbreak."

"But if he throws them out, where will they go?"

"Lord, that's more than I know."

"And how much a day can this poor worker make?"

"If he didn't have to take care of his mother, his wife, and his children, he would make at least four or five francs, because he really sticks to it. But what with losing three quarters of his time taking care of his household, the most he makes is forty sous."

"That's really not much. Poor souls!"

"Poor souls—you can say that again! But there are so many poor people, and since you can't do anything about it, the best you can do is console yourself with the thought that you can't do anything about it—right, Alfred? But, speaking of consolation, we've got some cassis to consume here."

"Frankly, Madame Pipelet, what you just told me makes me heartsick. Please, you and Monsieur Pipelet, drink to my health."

"You are a good man, monsieur," said the doorkeeper. "But do you still want to see the room upstairs?"

"Yes, please. If it suits me, I'll give you the good faith money."

The doorkeeper left his lair and Rodolphe followed him.

CHAPTER II

THE FOUR UPPER FLOORS

The gray winter day made the lightless, humid stairway seem even darker than it would otherwise. The entryway of each of the apartments in the house offered a unique physiognomy, so to speak, to the keen observer. Thus the door of the lodging that the commandant used as his place of rendezvous was freshly painted in a grained brown that imitated rosewood. A gilded brass button sparkled in the lock and a beautiful bellpull tufted with red silk stood out against the worn, dank walls.

The door on the second floor, where the fortune-teller-cum-pawnbroker lived, had an even more singular appearance. A stuffed owl—a bird of the highest symbolic and cabalistic significance—was nailed to the doorframe by its claws and wings. A small peephole, with iron wire grilling, enabled the occupant to inspect any visitors before allowing them in.

The lodging of the Italian charlatan who was rumored to engage in an abominable practice also stood apart because of its strange entryway. His name could be read on the door, where it was written out in horses' teeth embedded in a type of black wood placard. Rather than sporting the usual rabbit's foot or mountain goat's paw for a knob, the bellpull was attached to the forearm and hand of a mummified monkey. This dried-out arm, with its tiny hand and its five fingers articulated by their bones and tapering off into fingernails, was a hideous sight. It looked very much like a child's hand.

As Rodolphe walked by this sinister-looking door, he thought he heard some stifled sobbing. Then suddenly a painful cry echoed in the silence of the house. It was a convulsive, horrible cry that seemed to have been torn from someone's innards. Rodolphe quivered. With a movement faster than thought, he ran to the door and rang the bell violently.

"What's wrong with you, monsieur?" asked the surprised doorkeeper.

"That cry," Rodolphe said. "Didn't you hear it?"

"Sure I did, monsieur. It's probably one of Monsieur César Bradamanti's customers. He's probably pulled out a tooth or two."

This explanation seemed likely enough, but it didn't satisfy Rodolphe. The cry he had just heard didn't seem merely one of physical pain. It was a cry of moral distress as well, if such a thing exists.

He had rung the bell quite violently. At first, no one answered. Several doors closed, one after the other. Then behind the glass of a peephole placed next to the door, to which he had attached his gaze thoughtlessly, Rodolphe saw a face, though obscurely. It appeared to be gaunt with a cadaverous pallor. A tangle of gray-streaked, rust-colored hair crowned this hideous face, which ended in a long beard that matched the hair in color. This apparition disappeared almost immediately.

Rodolphe stood there, petrified. Although he had glimpsed the face for only a moment or two, he thought he recognized some of its very particular features. Those sparkling, seaweed-green eyes that shone under large, bristling, fawn-colored eyebrows, that livid pallor, that thin, jutting nose that looked like an eagle's beak, with its strangely dilated nostrils that pulled away to reveal part of the nasal wall: all of these features strikingly recalled one Father Polidori. This was the same Father Polidori whom Murph had cursed during his interview with the Baron de Graün.

Even though Rodolphe had not seen Father Polidori for sixteen or seventeen years, he had only too many reasons not to have forgotten him. But one thing put him off and made him less sure that the priest and the Italian charlatan were one and the same. The priest's hair had been dark brown, and not at all rust colored.

Rodolphe (supposing his suspicions were correct) was not surprised, moreover, to see a man who wore a mantle of holiness, a man he knew to be possessed of deep intelligence, wide-ranging knowledge, and unusual wit, fallen to such a degree, maybe even fallen so far as into infamy. He knew that that unusual wit, that deep intelligence, that wide-ranging knowledge went hand in hand with deep perversity, unruly conduct, indecent desires, and, most of all, cynical pride and withering disdain for all men and for all things. Such a man, reduced to the penury he deserved, would have been capable of—no, would almost have to have looked for—the most dishonorable of ways to make a living. He would have taken ironic and sacrilegious satisfaction in seeing himself, someone truly distinguished by the gift of intelligence and thought to be saintly, engage in the lowly occupation of an obnoxious mountebank. But we must remind the reader that, even though Rodolphe had last seen Father Polidori in the prime of his life and he would now be the same age as the charlatan, there were certain differences between the two that were so marked that Rodolphe was very uncertain as to their identity. Nevertheless, he asked Monsieur Pipelet, "Has Monsieur Bradamanti lived here for a long time?"

"Well, about a year, monsieur. Yes, a year. He came here at the end of January. He's a very punctual tenant. And he cured my terrible rheumatism. But, as I was just telling you, he has one fault: he's too much of a joker and he shows no respect for anything in the jokes he tells."

"What do you mean by that?"

"Well, monsieur," Monsieur Pipelet said gravely, "I'm no blushing maiden, but there's laughter and then there's laughter."

"So he's really cheerful?"

"It's not that he's cheerful. On the contrary, he's like a walking dead man. He never really laughs—he only laughs in what he says. For him there are no mothers, no fathers, no God, no devil. He makes jokes about everything—even his water, monsieur, even his own water! I won't lie, his jokes make me afraid. They make my flesh creep. After a quarter of an hour in his rooms, listening to him jabber on about all the barely dressed women he's seen in the different uncivilized countries he's been to, when I'm back alone with Anastasie, well, then, monsieur, even I, who for thirty-seven years have made it my practice, even made it my law to cherish Anastasie—well, then! Sometimes it seems to me that I don't cherish her quite as much. You're going to laugh at me. But, again, sometimes when Monsieur César leaves the building, after he has described princely feasts he's been at to watch the princes use the teeth he's fitted in their mouths, well, food tastes bitter to me and I lose my appetite. After all, I like my occupation, monsieur, and I am honored to serve at it. I could have been just another shoemaker like all the rest, but I thought resoling old shoes was more useful. Well, monsieur, on my word of honor, there are days when that devil of a Monsieur César, with his ironies, almost makes me regret not having been a normal bootmaker! And then, finally . . . he has a way of talking about those uncivilized ladies he knew . . . Well, really, monsieur, like I said, I'm no blushing maiden, but sometimes—well, good gosh, I blush crimson," Monsieur Pipelet added in a tone of offended chastity.

"And Madame Pipelet puts up with all this?"

"Anastasie is unreasonably fond of wit. And Monsieur César, despite his deplorable tone, certainly has a lot of it, so she lets him get away with everything."

"She also spoke to me of certain horrifying rumors."

"She spoke to you about . . . ?"

"Don't worry. I am very discreet."

"Well, then, monsieur, I don't believe that rumor and I never will. But I can't stop thinking about it and that adds to the uncomfortable effect that Monsieur Bradamanti's jokes have on me. Really, monsieur, all things considered, I truly hate Monsieur Cabrion, and that hatred will go with me to the grave. But then sometimes I think I would prefer the degraded practical jokes that he had the effrontery to perform in the house over the kind of wit Monsieur César retails in that deadpan manner of his, with his lips pinched up in that disgraceful way. It reminds me of the final torment of my uncle Rousselot, who pinched up his lips just like Monsieur Bradamanti when he was giving up his last gasp on his deathbed."

Some of what Monsieur Pipelet said about the perpetual irony with which this charlatan treated everybody and everything, withering the purest joys with his bitter mockery, confirmed Rodolphe in his suspicions about him. The priest, when he dropped his hypocritical mask, had always displayed the most audacious and revolting skepticism. Rodolphe had determined firmly to clear away his doubts one way or the other on this matter since the presence of the priest in this house could get in his way. And he felt more and more inclined to a gloomy interpretation of the horrible cry that had struck him so forcefully. Rodolphe followed the doorkeeper to the next floor, where the room he wanted to rent was located.

Mademoiselle Rigolette's lodgings, which were next to the rooms Rodolphe wanted to rent, were easily recognizable, thanks to a charming bit of gallantry created by the painter who was Monsieur Pipelet's mortal enemy. A half dozen chubby little cupids, skillfully and wittily painted after the style of Watteau,[49] hovered around a kind of sign. Together, they formed an allegory. One bore a thimble, another a pair of scissors, a third a clothes iron, a fourth a mirror. In the middle of the sign, against an azure blue, in pink letters, appeared the words "Mademoiselle Rigolette, Dressmaker." The whole design was framed by a garland of flowers, which stood out marvelously against the pale green of the door. This panel was really very pretty and again contrasted strikingly with the ugliness of the stairway.

At the risk of further aggravating Monsieur Pipelet's still open wound, Rodolphe said to him, gesturing toward Mademoiselle Rigolette's door, "This is surely Monsieur Cabrion's handiwork."

"Yes, monsieur. He went so far as to ruin the painting on the door with this indecent splattering of completely naked children which people call cupids. If it had not been for Mademoiselle Rigolette's requests and Monsieur Red-Arm's weakness, I would have painted all this over as well as the palette that that monster painted to block off the door of your rooms." And, indeed, a palette, bearing an assortment of paints of different colors, seemingly attached to the door by a nail, was painted on the door in trompe l'oeil. Rodolphe followed the doorkeeper into this fairly spacious room into which led an office, lit by two windows opening onto rue du Temple. Monsieur Germain had scrupulously maintained some fantastical sketches that Monsieur Cabrion had painted on the second door.

Rodolphe had only too many reasons for wanting to live in this house, and so he booked the rooms immediately. He humbly gave the doorkeeper forty sous and said to him, "This room suits me perfectly. Here's a good faith down payment. Tomorrow I'll send over my furniture. There's no need for me to see the principal renter, Monsieur Red-Arm, is there?"

---

49. Jean-Antoine Watteau (1684–1721), a painter who transitioned from Baroque to Rococo and was famous for painting scenes of pastoral romance and flirtation. [TN]

"No, monsieur. Except to plot things with Old Lady Burette, he rarely comes here. People always handle these things directly with me. And I only need to know your name."

"Rodolphe."

"Rodolphe . . . what?"

"Just Rodolphe, Monsieur Pipelet."

"Well, that's different, monsieur. I won't press just for curiosity's sake. We have free will, and so we can choose our names."

"Tell me, Monsieur Pipelet: tomorrow, as a new neighbor, shouldn't I go ask Monsieur Morel if I can help him in any way? I know that Monsieur Germain, the prior renter, did what he could for them."

"Yes, monsieur, you could do that. It's true that it won't do them much good since they're going to be evicted, but it always makes them feel better." Then, as if struck by a sudden thought, looking at his renter in a proud and mischievous way, Monsieur Pipelet cried out, "Now I get it. That's the way you'll begin and you'll end, by being neighborly to your little female neighbor in the adjoining rooms."

"Indeed, I was planning on it."

"There's nothing wrong with that. It's the custom here. And, really, I'm sure that Mademoiselle Rigolette heard us visiting the rooms and will be on the lookout to see us go downstairs. I'll make a noise on purpose when I lock the door and just you watch when we go by the landing."

And indeed, Rodolphe saw that the door so elegantly ornamented with the Watteau cupids was ajar, and, through the narrow aperture, he could just about make out the end of a rose-colored, upturned nose and a lively, curious dark eye. But the moment he slowed down, the door abruptly closed.

"I told you she'd be watching," the doorkeeper said. Then he added, "Pardon me, excuse me, monsieur! I'm going to my small observatory."

"What's that?"

"At the top of this ladder, there's a landing. The Morels' attic door opens on it. There's a little black hole behind the paneling where I keep junk. Given how worn the wall is, when I'm in my hole, I can see into their place and hear everything as if I were there. It's not that I'm spying on them, heaven knows! But I do go to watch them sometimes in the way one watches gloomy melodramas. When I get back down to my rooms, I feel like I'm in a palace. If you want to, monsieur, if you are so inclined, before they have left . . . It's sad but it's interesting. Because when they see you, like wild animals, that disturbs them."

"That's very kind of you, Monsieur Pipelet. Maybe another day I'll take advantage of your hole. Maybe tomorrow."

"As you wish, monsieur. But I need to go up to my observatory. I need a bit of tinder. If you want to go down, monsieur, I'll meet you downstairs." And Monsieur Pipelet began to climb up the ladder to the attic. This was a fairly dangerous climb for him at his age.

Rodolphe took a last look at Mademoiselle Rigolette's door, thinking that the girl, poor Songbird's old friend, probably knew where the Schoolmaster's son was staying. Suddenly, one floor down, he heard someone come out of the charlatan's apartment. He recognized the light step of a woman and made out the sound of silk brushing against something. He paused a moment, discreetly. When he no longer heard anything, he went down.

When he got to the second floor, he saw a handkerchief on the last steps and picked it up. It must have belonged to the woman who had left the charlatan's rooms. Rodolphe walked up to one of the narrow windows that allowed light on the landing and looked the handkerchief over. It was magnificently ornamented with lace, and embroidered in one of its corners were the letters *L* and *N* under a ducal crown. The handkerchief was literally wet with tears.

Rodolphe's first thought was to run after the woman who had dropped the handkerchief in order to give it back to her. But then he thought that that step, under the circumstances, might seem motivated by an embarrassing curiosity. So he kept it and thus, without intending to, found himself on the track of a mysterious and sinister set of events.

When he got down to the doorkeeper's wife, he asked her, "Did a woman just come downstairs?"

"No, monsieur. It was a beautiful, tall, thin lady with a black veil. She came from Monsieur César's. Little Gammy had gone to search for a carriage and she just got into it. What really surprised me is that that little beggar got up to sit on the back of the carriage. Maybe he wants to see where she goes, because he's as curious as a cat, that one is. And faster than a whippet, despite his bad leg."

And so, Rodolphe thought, the charlatan would soon know the name and address of this woman, assuming he had ordered Gammy to follow her.

"Well, then, monsieur, does the room suit you?"

"It suits me to a T. I've booked it and I'll send my furniture over tomorrow."

"God be thanked for sending you to our door, monsieur! We will have one more remarkable renter. You seem to be well behaved; Pipelet will like you right away. You'll make him laugh like Monsieur Germain did. He always had some funny story to tell him. The poor dear man, all he wants in life is to laugh. So I think you'll be fast friends in a month's time."

"Come on, you're flattering me, Madame Pipelet."

"Not at all. When I say that, I'm just opening my mind up to you. And if you're nice to Alfred, you'll see how grateful I'll be. Your place will look great. I'm fierce about cleanliness. And if you'd like to dine here on Sundays, I'll cook things up for you that will have you licking your fingers."

"So we're agreed, Madame Pipelet, that you'll be my housekeeper.

Tomorrow, someone will bring over the furniture and I'll come to oversee setting the place up." And Rodolphe left.

The visit to the house had brought significant progress both toward finding the answer to the mystery he was trying to solve and toward finding ways to satisfy his noble search for occasions to do good and prevent evil.

This much he had come to know: Mademoiselle Rigolette certainly knew the location of the new residence of François Germain, the Schoolmaster's son.

A young woman who, on the basis of some evidence, was perhaps the Marquise d'Harville, had granted a rendezvous tomorrow to the commandant, a rendezvous that might destroy her honor forever. For many reasons, Rodolphe cared deeply for Monsieur d'Harville, whose tranquility and honor seemed to be so cruelly threatened.

Crushed by the most horrible poverty, an honest and hardworking laborer was going to be thrown out onto the streets with his family, on Red-Arm's orders.

Lastly, Rodolphe had accidently discovered evidence of some event in which the principal actors were a woman who most probably belonged to the highest levels of society and the charlatan, Monsieur César Bradamanti (possibly Father Polidori).

And over and above all that, the Owl, who had recently gotten out of the hospital after the events in the allée des Veuves, had very suspicious connections with Old Lady Burette, the fortune-teller and pawnbroker who lived on the second floor.

Having gathered all this information, Rodolphe returned to his house on rue Plumet, putting off until the next day his visit to Jacques Ferrand, the solicitor.

That very night, as we know, Rodolphe had to make an appearance at a grand ball, at the house of the ambassador of ***.

Before following our hero on this new adventure, we will go backward in time to cast a retrospective glance on Tom and Sarah, who both play significant roles in this story.

CHAPTER 12

TOM AND SARAH

Sarah Seyton, at this time the widow of Count MacGregor, was about thirty-seven or thirty-eight years old. She came from an excellent Scottish family. She was the daughter of a baronet and a country gentleman. An accomplished beauty, orphaned at seventeen, Sarah had left Scotland with her brother, Tom Seyton of Halsbury.

Her nurse, an old Highlander, had absurdly predicted for her, with an unbelievable tenacity of conviction, the most exalted destiny . . . why not say it? That she would be a queen. This prophecy had aggravated Sarah's two capital vices, pride and ambition, to the point of insanity. The young Scottish woman had surrendered herself to her nurse's prophecy, making her repeat endlessly, as a corroboration, that a fortune-teller had also promised a crown to that good and beautiful Creole who would one day occupy the French throne and who had been a queen by her grace and goodness as others were by their grandeur and majesty.[50]

And here's a strange thing: Tom Seyton, as superstitious as his sister, encouraged her insane expectations. He had resolved to devote his life to the realization of Sarah's dream, a dream as dazzling as it was mad. Nevertheless, neither the brother nor the sister was sufficiently blind as to believe the Highlander's prediction in absolute detail. They did not limit their aim to a throne of the first order, disdaining secondary realms or ruling principalities. No, provided that the beautiful Scot could place some kind of ruling crown atop her imperial forehead, the proud couple would close their eyes to the importance of that crown's possessions. With the aid of the *Almanac of Gotha* for the year of our Lord 1819, just as they were leaving Scotland, Tom drew up a sort of synoptic chart listing, according to their ages, all the kings and royal highnesses of Europe who were still unmarried.[51]

---

50. An allusion to the Empress Joséphine, Napoléon's first wife. Sue's high opinion of her may be related to the fact that he was her godson. [TN]

51. Between 1763 and the end of the Second World War, the *Almanac of Gotha* was the principal reference book listing noble and royal families of Europe. Published each year in Germany, it appeared in French and German. [TN]

Absurd as it was, the ambition of both brother and sister was devoid of any intention to have recourse to shameful expediencies. Tom would aid Sarah in weaving the conjugal web in which they would entrap any crown-bearer they could. He would take part in any tricks or any intrigues that could bring about that result. But he would have killed his sister before he would see her the mistress of a prince, even with the certitude that there would ensue a marriage that would make an honest woman of her.

The matrimonial inventory produced by Tom and Sarah's research into the *Almanac of Gotha* was a satisfactory one. The German Confederation, above all, offered numerous presumptive young sovereigns. Sarah was Protestant. Tom was not unaware of how easily a marriage the Germans called "left-handed" could be arranged. It was a legitimate marriage, after all.[52] And, as a last resort, he was prepared to accept such a marriage for his sister. So it was decided between them to go to Germany first to begin trying to snare a bird who wore a crown.

If this project seems improbable and its expectations insane, it must be noted first of all that unbridled ambition, enhanced by superstitious belief, rarely prides itself on being reasonable in its aims. Only the impossible is any temptation to it. Furthermore, if we recall certain contemporary events, starting with august and respectable morganatic marriages between sovereigns and subjects and extending right up to that odyssey of love, the marriage between Miss Penelope and the Prince of Capua, we cannot say that there was no possibility that Tom and Sarah's fantasies would not lead to a happy outcome.[53]

It must also be noted that Sarah combined dazzling beauty with the gifts of many different talents and an extraordinary power to seduce. That power was particularly dangerous because Sarah had a hard, logical mind, a skilled intellect that would stop at nothing, a profound ability to disguise her true feelings, and a stubborn and absolute temperament. These aspects of her character lurked behind what seemed to be an open, ardent, and passionate nature. Her body lied in its appearances as shamelessly as her mind did in its calculations.

Under their ebony eyebrows, her large black eyes, at one moment sparkling and at another languorous, could feign the fires of sensual pleasure. Yet love's burning desires would never make her icy breast heave. No jolt

52. Also known as a morganatic marriage. This was a legal marriage between people of unequal social rank. It was called "left-handed" because the titled husband held his wife's right hand in his left hand, rather than his right hand. Since these marriages prohibit the husband's title and privileges from passing to the wife or children, it's hard to see how such a marriage would have fulfilled Tom and Sarah's ambitions. [TN]

53. In 1836, against the wishes of his brother, the king, the Prince of Capua married the commoner Penelope Smyth, in Scotland. Since the prince was not a sovereign and, as a result of the marriage, was dispossessed of his wealth and lived in exile, this example should not have been an encouraging one for Tom and Sarah. [TN]

from the heart or the senses would ever throw off her pitiless calculations, cunning, egotistical, and ambitious as she was.

Upon arriving on the continent, Sarah, following her brother's advice, put off beginning her project in favor of a stay in Paris. She wanted to complete her education there. The idea was to soften her British rigidity by mixing in a society known for its elegance, its charms, and its naturally good taste. Letters of introduction, along with the benevolent patronage of the English ambassador's wife and of the old Marquis d'Harville, who had known Tom and Sarah's father in England, assured Sarah's introduction into the best and highest circles of Parisian society.

People who are hypocritical, cold, and deliberate are able to assimilate themselves with uncanny speed to languages and mores that are at complete variance with their characters. To them, everything is external, surface, appearance, polish, shell. As soon as one sees past that and realizes who they are, they are lost. Thus they are granted a kind of instinct for self-preservation that makes them particularly adept at disguising who they are. They paint their faces and don costumes as easily and cleverly as the most consummate actors.

All of this is to say that after six months in Paris, Sarah vied with the most Parisian of Parisian women in her gracious and biting wit, her charming brightness, the fashion of her dress, and the naive enticement in her glance, which she could make simultaneously chaste and passionate.

Approving of his sister's finish, Tom left with her for Germany, armed with only the best letters of introduction. The Grand Duchy of Gerolstein was the first state in the German Confederation on their itinerary. The infallible and diplomatic *Almanac of Gotha* for the year 1819 describes its ruling family thus:

GENEALOGIES OF THE SOVEREIGN CROWNS
OF EUROPE AND OF THEIR FAMILY
GEROLSTEIN

Grand Duke: MAXIMILIEN-RODOLPHE, born December 10, 1764. Succeeded to the throne of his father CHARLES-FRÉDÉRIK-RODOLPHE, April 21, 1785. Widowed, January 1808, by LOUISE, daughter of Prince JEAN-AUGUSTE DE BURGLEN.

Son: GUSTAVE-RODOLPHE, born April 17, 1803.

Mother: Grand Duchess JUDITH, dowager, widow of Grand Duke CHARLES-FRÉDÉRIK-RODOLPHE, April 21, 1785.

Tom, showing some good sense, had written the names of the youngest princes from whom he'd hoped to find a brother-in-law first on his list. He thought that someone very young would be easier to seduce than someone more mature. In addition, as we have said, Tom and Sarah had particularly good introductions to the reigning Grand Duke of Gerolstein from the old Marquis d'Harville, who had been, like the rest of the world, quite taken with Sarah. He could not admire her beauty, her grace, and her natural charm enough. It is unnecessary to add that the heir presumptive of the Grand Duchy of Gerolstein was Gustave-Rodolphe. He was just eighteen when Tom and Sarah were presented to his father.

The young Scottish woman's arrival into this small, simple, calm, rather patriarchal German court was an event of the first order. The grand duke, the best of men, governed his state with wise firmness and paternal affection. It was, both materially and morally, the happiest of principalities. Its hardworking and serious, sober and pious people embodied the ideal of the German character. These honest people enjoyed such profound contentment and were so completely satisfied with their lot in life that the grand duke's enlightened care was hardly necessary to guard them from the current mania for constitutional innovation. The grand duke kept himself abreast of modern discoveries and practical ideas that might have a healthy influence on the well-being or the moral tone of his people, and he put them to work constantly. His stays in other European states had only one goal: he wanted to keep himself current on all scientific progress particularly as it related to public utility and political practice.

As recounted above, the grand duke felt both great affection for the old Marquis d'Harville and as great a debt of gratitude for his invaluable aid in 1815. Consequently, thanks to the recommendation of the old marquis, Tom and Sarah Seyton of Halsbury were granted an especially distinguished and warm reception at the court of Gerolstein.

Within two weeks of her arrival, Sarah, a gifted and sharp observer, had easily read the firm, honest, and open character of the grand duke. In her wisdom, she knew very well that, before seducing the son, she needed to know how the father would react. At first Sarah thought that he loved his son so completely that he would even assent to a misalliance rather than see his son forever heartbroken. But soon the Scottish woman became convinced that the father, affectionate as he was, would never vary from certain principles and ideas about the duties of princes. This was not pride on his part but conscience, reason, and dignity. And moreover a man of such a temper, energetic as it was affectionate, a man who was as good as he was because he was firm and strong, would never give way in anything concerning his conscience, reason, or dignity.

Considering these insurmountable obstacles, Sarah was on the verge of abandoning her project. Then she considered that, on the other hand, Rodolphe was very young indeed, that everybody praised his sweetness, his goodness, his simultaneously timid and dreamy personality. She considered the young prince, therefore, to be weak and irresolute. And so she persisted in her project and in her hopes.

On this occasion, her and her brother's conduct was a masterpiece of subtlety. The girl figured out how to make friends of everyone, and especially of those who had the most reason to be jealous or envious of her advantages. She made everybody forget her beauty and her elegance, veiling them with a modest simplicity. Soon she was idolized not only by the grand duke but by his mother, the dowager grand duchess, who, despite her ninety years, or perhaps because of them, was madly in love with all things young and charming.

Tom and Sarah spoke any number of times about leaving, but the sovereign of Gerolstein would not permit it. To keep the brother and sister at the court, he begged the Baronet Tom Seyton of Halsbury to accept the position, which was open at the moment, of first equerry, and he also implored Sarah not to leave the grand duchess, Judith, who could no longer do without her. After considerable hesitation, confronted by insistent requests, Tom and Sarah accepted these brilliant offers and, two months after their arrival, they became fixtures at the court of Gerolstein.

Sarah was an accomplished musician, and knowing the taste of the grand duchess for old masters, and especially for Gluck, she had all his works sent for. She fascinated the old princess with the simple, expressive beauty with which she sang these old arias, thus adding to their impression of her inexhaustible kindness a further impression of her extraordinary talent.

Tom, for his part, figured out how to make himself indispensable in the position the grand duke had offered to him. The Scot had a perfect understanding of horses; he was both orderly and firm, and in no time at all he had almost completely transformed the workings of the grand duke's stables, workings which prior negligence and routine had left in a fairly sad state.

Both brother and sister were equally loved, celebrated, and spoiled at the court. Where a ruler prefers, the preferences of those beneath him will follow. Moreover, Sarah needed as much help as she could get in support of her project and so she employed her powers of seduction in winning partisans to her cause. Her hypocrisy, decked out in the most attractive ways, easily deceived most of these loyal Germans, and a general affection for her soon confirmed the grand duke's excessive kindness.

Here, then, is our couple established at the court of Gerolstein in perfectly stable and honorable positions, without Rodolphe having yet for a moment entered into any consideration with regard to their rise. By a happy bit of luck, a few days after Sarah's arrival, Rodolphe, with an aide-de-camp and the faithful Murph, had left the court to inspect the troops. This absence was particularly favorable to Sarah's purposes because it allowed her to put in place the first threads in the plot she was weaving without being bothered by the presence of the young prince whose attraction to her at that time, especially if it had been too obvious, would perhaps have awakened the suspicions of the grand duke. Instead, in the absence of his son, the grand duke, unfortunately, didn't even dream that he had just admitted into his circle of intimates a girl of rare beauty and charming wit who would, perforce, be in Rodolphe's presence every moment of the day.

Sarah was at heart completely insensible to the touching and generous welcome she had been granted and to the open and noble confidence with which she had been received into the heart of this ruling family. Neither she nor her brother hesitated an instant in the face of their malicious scheme. They had just knowingly brought trouble and sadness into a peaceful and happy court. They coldly calculated the probable results of the cruel division that they were going to cause between a father and son who, until that moment, had been tenderly united.

CHAPTER 13

SIR WALTER MURPH AND FATHER POLIDORI

As a child, Rodolphe had a weak constitution. His father decided on a course of action that might seem strange but that was fundamentally quite sound. "English country gentlemen," he reasoned to himself, "generally have remarkably robust constitutions. Their fitness results in large part from the physical vigor of their simple, hard, rustic upbringing, which cultivates their strength. Rodolphe needs to be removed from the care of the women who have brought him up. He is delicate. By teaching this child to live more or less like the son of an English farmer, perhaps I will strengthen his constitution."

The grand duke had his people look throughout England for a man both worthy of such a charge and able to oversee this physical education. Sir Walter Murph, the kind of athletic country gentleman one finds in Yorkshire, was entrusted with this important task. The training he gave the young prince was precisely what his father had had in mind. Murph and his student lived for several years on a charming farm amid field and forest. A few leagues from the city of Gerolstein, the spot was both beautiful and conducive to physical health.

Free from all court etiquette, Rodolphe worked with Murph at farming tasks suited to his age. He lived the sober, regular, manly life of farming. He amused himself with vigorous exercises: wrestling, boxing, horseback riding, and hunting. In the fresh air of field, wood, and mountain, the young prince seemed to become a different person. He grew strong like a young oak; his somewhat sickly pallor gave way to a bright, healthy color. Though he was still slender and wiry, he endured the most tiring physical challenges. Skill, energy, and courage supplemented what he lacked in pure muscle. By the time he was sixteen or seventeen, he could defeat young men much older than he at wrestling.

His intellectual education, up to this point, had necessarily suffered from the preference given to his physical cultivation. Rodolphe was quite ignorant at this time. But the grand duke wisely considered that if one were to demand much of the intellect, that intellect would need the support of a strong physical organization. And so, even though his intellectual education had a late start, Rodolphe's mental faculties demonstrated rapid progress.

Honest Walter Murph was no scholar. He could give Rodolphe only the most basic intellectual education. But there was no one better to inspire in his student an awareness of what was just, honest, and generous, and a hatred for all that was base, cowardly, and wretched. This hatred of evil and the energetic and healthy admiration of the good took permanent root in Rodolphe's soul. Later, the storms of passion shook these principles violently, but they were never uprooted from his heart. Lightning may strike a tree, split it, and tear it apart, but the sap still runs through its roots, and a thousand green shoots will spring soon enough from the trunk that had seemed dried out and dead.

Murph gave Rodolphe a sound mind in a sound body, as they say. He made him strong, resourceful, and daring, sympathetic with everything good, angered by everything evil. Having so admirably fulfilled his charge, Murph was suddenly called back to England by pressing personal concerns. Rodolphe, who loved him dearly, deeply regretted his departure from Germany. Murph was expected to return with his family permanently once he had taken care of these pressing concerns. He hoped his absence would not last longer than a year.

Now assured of his son's health, the grand duke turned seriously to the intellectual education of his cherished child. A certain Father Polidori—a renowned philologist, a distinguished physician, an erudite historian, a scholar of wide knowledge in the objective and physical sciences—took on the task of cultivating and sowing the rich but fallow mental soil Murph had so well prepared. This time, the grand duke's choice was an unfortunate one. Or rather, his religious principles were cruelly deceived by whoever introduced him to the priest and persuaded him to accept a Catholic priest as the teacher of a Protestant prince. This seemed to many people a startling innovation and one that did not augur well for Rodolphe's education.

Chance—or rather the priest's abominable character—was responsible for the partial fulfillment of these predictions. The priest was the worst teacher one could find for a young man. He was impious, deceitful, and hypocritical. He had sacrilegious contempt for everything human beings hold most sacred. Skilled in deception, he could hide the most dangerous immorality and the most terrifying skepticism under an austere and pious appearance. He exaggerated a false Christian humility to hide an ingratiating flexibility, just as he put on a manner of expansive generosity and naive optimism to hide the perverse self-interest behind his constant flattery. He was profoundly knowledgeable about human beings, or at least he was vastly experienced in their shameful passions and their worst actions.

Leaving the vigorous independent life he had hitherto led with Murph for the pale existence of book learning and submission to the ceremony and etiquette of his father's court, Rodolphe felt an immediate aversion to the priest. It was bound to happen. Upon leaving his student, the poor squire had compared him, not without some accuracy, to a wild, strong, beautiful colt that had been allowed to roam free on the wild prairies. There, it had cavorted in joyous freedom, but now it would be broken to the bit and the spur. It would need to learn to control and direct its strength, which it had used up to then only to run and jump any way it pleased.

Rodolphe began by stating to the priest that he felt no inclination for learning. He needed most of all to move his limbs, to breathe the fresh air of the fields, to run through woods and over mountains. He thought a good rifle and a good horse far preferable to the best books the world had to offer.

The priest responded to his student that there was nothing more tedious than study, but there was also nothing more vulgar than the pleasures he preferred to studying. They were pleasures fit only for stupid German farmers. And the priest drew such a clownish, mocking picture of that simple, rustic life that Rodolphe grew ashamed of having loved it so much. And so he asked the priest, in all innocence, how one passed one's time if not in studying, in hunting, or in the free life of the countryside. The priest answered mysteriously that he would learn that soon enough.

After his fashion, the priest had hopes as ambitious as those of Sarah. Although the Grand Duchy of Gerolstein was a state of only secondary importance, the priest had the idea of making himself its Richelieu[54] one day and of raising Rodolphe to become an idling, good-for-nothing prince. So he began by trying to make himself agreeable to his student and, through condescension and obsequiousness, to make him forget Murph. Rodolphe continued to be a recalcitrant student, but the priest hid the young prince's aversion to study from the grand duke. Indeed, the priest praised Rodolphe's assiduity and his surprising progress. To preserve the grand duke's blind confidence (and one must say that he was not that well educated), the priest and his student planned a few highly rehearsed intellectual exchanges that they presented as having occurred by chance.

Little by little, Rodolphe's initial aversion to the priest was replaced by a cavalier familiarity that stood in complete contrast to the solemn attachment he felt to Murph. Little by little, Rodolphe found himself acting as if he and the priest were two accomplices in a plot (even though his reasons for acting that way were entirely innocent). Sooner or later, however, Rodolphe would come to despise a man of the priest's age and character, who lied shamelessly to excuse his student's laziness. And the priest

54. Cardinal Richelieu (1585–1642) known as the Red Eminence, was Louis XIII's prime minister and essentially governed France until his death, though his official policy was to strengthen royal power. [TN]

knew that. But he also knew that if you don't immediately distance yourself in disgust from corrupt creatures, you gradually get used to their often quite attractive wit. And by small steps, you begin to hear things you held dear mocked and ridiculed without experiencing shame or indignation.

Finally, the priest was too shrewd to confront directly certain of Rodolphe's convictions that had taken root as a result of Murph's education. After ramping up his mockery of the vulgarity of Rodolphe's early pastimes, he lowered his austere mask slightly. He had piqued Rodolphe's curiosity vividly with allusions to the enchanted lives of certain princes from times past. With infinitely patient care and constant witty remarks about the ceremonial solemnity of the grand duke's court, he elicited Rodolphe's urgent desire that he explain his allusions. Then, seeming to give in to that desire, he fired up the young prince's imagination with brightly colored and exaggerated tales of the pleasures and seductions that characterized the reigns of Louis XIV, the Regency, and—above all—of Louis XV, César Polidori's hero.

He told this unfortunate child, who listened to him with an ill-fated eagerness, that pleasures, even carried to excess, far from making a truly gifted prince less moral, would on the contrary make him even more generous and merciful; this was because beautiful souls were even more given to charity and affection when they were happy. The example of Louis XV, the well beloved, proved this assertion beyond any doubt. And then, the priest noted, how many great men from both ancient and recent history had practiced the most refined epicureanism! From Alcibiades to Maurice de Saxe, from Antony to the Grand Condé, from Caesar to Vendôme![55]

Such discussions could only have the most terrible and destructive effects on a young, ardent, virginal soul. The priest went so far as to translate eloquently to his student those odes of Horace in which that rare genius, with enticing charm, exalted the sweet pleasure of a life given over to love and exquisite sensuality.[56] To mask the dangers of these theories,

55. It's hard to know what to make of this list. Most of these men were successful military leaders. Alcibiades (450–404 BCE) was a student of Socrates who at various times was a general for both sides in the Peloponnesian Wars. He did take part in Plato's *Symposium* on love, and is represented there as something of a playboy. Marc Antony (83–30 BCE) might plausibly be argued to have been an epicurean to the extent that he is identified with his love for Cleopatra. The same might conceivably be said about Julius Caesar (100–44 BCE) if one sees his assassination as resulting from lax ambition. There are more than one Maurice de Saxe and Comte de Vendôme, numbers of whom were successful military leaders. Louis de Bourbon, the Prince of Condé (1621–1686) was known as the Grand Condé for his military prowess and acumen. None of them have particular reputations as sensualists. [TN]

56. Horace (65–8 BCE) famously wrote *Odes*. Some deal with love, others with friendship and poetry. Polidori would have done better to teach Rodolphe the poetry of Catullus. [TN]

however, and to appeal more effectively to Rodolphe's basically generous character, the priest also lulled him now and then with accounts of charming utopias. To hear him tell it, an intelligently voluptuous prince could improve the human condition through pleasure, make people better through happiness, and bring the most skeptical to religious belief by exalting their gratitude to the Creator, who, in the order of things, showered pleasures down upon man with inexhaustible prodigality. To indulge in all pleasures at all times was, according to the priest, to glorify the magnificence of God and the eternal life of his gifts to us.

These theories had their desired effects. Amid this orderly and virtuous court, which, following the example of its master, sought only honest pleasures and innocent distractions, under the priest's tutelage Rodolphe was already dreaming of the mad nights of Versailles, the orgies of Choisy, the extreme sensuality of Parc-aux-Cerfs, and also, now and then, for contrast, certain love stories that were just like the ones in novels.[57]

The priest hastened to add that a prince of the German Confederation could have no other military ambition than to put his army at the service of the Diet.[58] And, in any case, the spirit of the age was not a warlike one.

The priest encouraged Rodolphe to spend his days in delicious and idle pleasure, surrounding himself with women and refined sensuality, varying the drunkenness of sensual pleasure with the pleasing recreation of aesthetic pleasure, even taking up hunting from time to time, not in the manner of a savage Nimrod, but searching there, as an intelligent epicurean, for a momentary fatigue that would intensify the charm of indolence and laziness. This was, according to the priest, the only suitable life for a prince who—if he were that fortunate!—could find a prime minister capable of bravely devoting himself to the demanding and heavy burden of the affairs of state. Rodolphe, giving himself over to suppositions that were hardly criminal as they were in the order of the normal course of events, determined that, when God called his father, the grand duke, to the next life, he would devote himself in this life to the pleasures Father Polidori depicted in such bright and cheerful colors. Of course, he would also make the priest his prime minister. It bears repeating that Rodolphe loved his father dearly and he would miss him deeply, even if his death allowed him to make of himself a second, miniature Sardanapalus.[59]

57. Versailles was the palace built by Louis XIV that became famous for sensuality under Louis XV. Louis XV gave Choisy to his mistress Madame de Pompadour. She hired women to live in the Parc-aux-Cerfs, which was attached to Versailles, to serve the king's pleasures. [TN]

58. A diet is a German legislative assembly. [TN]

59. Sardanapalus was the last king of Assyria, famous for his decadence. He was supposed to have lived in the seventh century BCE. [TN]

Needless to say, the prince kept the unfortunate hopes that grew within him entirely to himself.

Rodolphe knew that the heroes the grand duke was partial to were Gustavus Adolphus, Charles XII, and Frederick the Great (Maximilien-Rodolphe was proud to be closely related to the Royal House of Brandenburg).[60] He had good reason to think that his father, who expressed deep admiration for these warrior-kings, forever in boots and spurs, sitting astride their horses and making war, would consider his son hopelessly lost if he thought him capable of wanting to exchange his grave German court for the easy and licentious manners of the Regency. One year, then eighteen months passed this way. Murph had not yet returned, even though he said he would be arriving soon.

Having overcome his initial aversion to book learning, thanks to the priest's obsequiousness, Rodolphe managed to learn something from his teacher's scientific instruction. If he was not really learned, and neither deeply nor widely read, he at least attained a smattering of knowledge. That little bit of knowledge, combined with his naturally lively and intelligent mind, allowed him to appear much more learned than he really was. And so his education redounded to the priest's honor.

Murph returned from England with his family and wept for joy as he embraced his old student. But, after a few days, the worthy squire was deeply troubled. Without understanding the reason for Rodolphe's change, he found his old student cold and constrained toward him and almost ironic when he referred to his hard, rustic upbringing. Murph knew the young prince's naturally good heart and he guessed where the trouble lay. He believed that Rodolphe had been momentarily perverted by Father Polidori's influence. He instinctively detested the priest on first sight and determined to watch over him carefully. For his part, the priest was no less annoyed by Murph's return. He feared the squire's honest good sense and insight, and he immediately decided to poison Rodolphe's mind against him.

It was at this point that Tom and Sarah were presented at the court of Gerolstein and welcomed with honor and distinction. A short time after they arrived, accompanied by an aide-de-camp and Murph, Rodolphe left to inspect the troops and various garrisons. Since this trip was entirely military in its purposes, the grand duke saw no reason for the priest to be one of the party. Thus, to the priest's great regret,

60. Gustavus Adolphus was the king of Sweden from 1611 to 1632. He was known for his military leadership. Charles XII was also a Swedish monarch and military tactician, reigning from 1697 to 1718. Frederick the Great was the king of Prussia from 1740 to 1786; known as a military strategist and conqueror, he was also credited with the implementation of important bureaucratic and other civil policies. [TN]

at least for a few days, Murph would resume his prior relationship to the young prince.

The squire counted on this chance to clear up once and for all what had brought about Rodolphe's coldness toward him. Unfortunately, Rodolphe had become trained in the art of dissimulation and he thought it would be dangerous to let his old teacher in on his new ambitions for the future. Rodolphe accordingly treated the squire with warm affection and pretended to miss the times of his youth and their rustic pleasures. And so he laid Murph's fears almost completely to rest.

We say "almost" because for some people loyalty is accompanied by a sharp instinct. Despite the affection the prince showed toward him, Murph had a vague feeling that Rodolphe was keeping something from him. He tried to clear up his suspicions, but his attempts were in vain. Rodolphe's talent at duplicity withstood all his efforts.

The priest had not remained idle during this period.

Schemers can always sense each other, or perhaps they recognize each other by certain mysterious signs. At any rate, they learn to watch each other until they know whether their interests should lead to an alliance or open war. Within a few days of Sarah's and his establishment at court, Tom had allied himself most particularly with Father Polidori. The priest, meanwhile, admitted to himself, with revolting cynicism, that he had a natural and almost involuntary affinity for duplicity and evil. Consequently, he recognized, without knowing precisely what Tom and Sarah were after, that he was drawn to them by a sympathy so strong that he knew that they had some diabolical design.

Various questions that Tom asked about Rodolphe's character and history, questions that would have meant nothing to someone less alert than the priest, immediately informed him of what the brother and sister were after. His only error was that he could not believe that the young Scottish woman's aims were both so ambitious and so honest.

The arrival of this charming young woman seemed to the priest a fateful stroke of luck. Here was Rodolphe, his mind inflamed with amorous fantasies. Sarah was made to play the role of the ravishing reality that would take the place of all those charming dreams. In the priest's view of things, before you come to the point of choosing among pleasures and seeking variety in sensual experience, you almost always start with a single romantic attachment. Marie Mancini and Rosette d'Arey were perhaps the only real loves of Louis XIV and Louis XV.[61] The priest thought things would proceed in the same fashion for Rodolphe and the beautiful Scot. There could be no doubt that she would have an enormous influence on the prince, whose heart would be in thrall to the enchanting charms of

61. Marie Mancini (1639–1715) was Louis XIV's first love. We can't trace any Rosette d'Arey. [TN]

a first love. And so the priest planned to direct and make use of that influence to rid himself of Murph forever.

An achieved schemer, the priest easily made the ambitious brother and sister understand that they needed him since, as far as the grand duke was concerned, he was the only one in charge of the young prince's private life. And that wasn't all. They needed to distrust entirely one of the prince's old teachers who was at that moment accompanying him on a military inspection. This stiff, vulgar man, bristling with absurd prejudices, had once held great sway over Rodolphe's mind, and he could become a dangerous opponent. And far from excusing or tolerating the charming follies and extravagances of youth, Murph would think himself obliged to denounce them to the grand duke and his strict morality.

Even though they had told the priest nothing of their aims, Tom and Sarah understood him at his first hint. And so, when Rodolphe and the squire returned, Tom, Sarah, and the priest had become firm allies as a result of their common interests. All three were tacitly leagued against Murph, who was their most feared enemy.

CHAPTER 14

FIRST LOVE

That which had to happen, happened. Upon his return, seeing Sarah every day, Rodolphe was madly smitten with by her. Soon enough, she confessed to him that she also loved him. But, she noted, this would undoubtedly lead to heartbreak for them. They could never be happy; their lots in life were too far apart. And so she counseled the greatest discretion so as to avoid, at all costs, awakening the grand duke's suspicions. He would surely be inexorably opposed to their love and would deprive them of their only happiness, the opportunity to see each other every day.

Rodolphe promised to watch over himself and hide his love. The Scot was too ambitious and had too much control over herself to compromise her position by revealing their love to the court. And the young prince did see the need for dissimulation. He imitated Sarah's prudence. They kept their love perfectly secret, at least for a little while.

Rodolphe's unbridled passion soon came to its climax, its anguished exaltation. It became more difficult day by day for him to contain himself. He was on the point of bursting out and ruining everything. When Tom and Sarah saw this, they made their most daring move. The priest's personality encouraged Tom to confide in him, and in any case, what he would demand was entirely moral. So Tom made his first overtures to the priest regarding the necessity of Rodolphe and Sarah marrying. If they did not, he added in all sincerity, he and his sister would leave Gerolstein immediately. Sarah shared the prince's love, but she preferred death to dishonor and would never be anything to his highness if not his wife.

The priest was flabbergasted by this demand. He would never have believed Sarah's ambition to be so audacious. Such a marriage would entail innumerable difficulties and every danger imaginable. The priest thought it was impossible and listed to Tom frankly all the reasons for thinking that the grand duke would never consent to such a union.

Tom acknowledged these reasons and recognized their gravity. He proposed instead a secret marriage as a *mezzo termine*[62] that might resolve all their problems. Such a marriage, legal and duly entered into by both

62. A compromise. Literally, a "middle term." [TN]

parties, did not need to be revealed until after the death of the current grand duke. Sarah was of a noble and ancient family; there were sufficient precedents for such a marriage. So Tom gave the priest, and thus the prince as well, one week to decide. His sister would not be able to hold up any longer against the cruel anguish of uncertainty. If she had to renounce Rodolphe's love, she would rather take that painful step as soon as possible.

As a cover for the rapid departure that might ensue, Tom, providing for all eventualities, had addressed a letter to a friend in England, which would, he said, be sent from London to Germany; this letter would contain reasons demanding Tom and Sarah's return that were powerful enough to necessitate their immediate departure from the grand duke's court, at least for a little while.

This time at least, the priest's low opinion of humanity served him well, and he figured out the truth. Always seeking an ulterior motive to explain the most seemingly honest sentiments, once he saw that Sarah wanted to legitimize her love by marriage, rather than seeing this as a proof of her virtue, he recognized it as an indication of her ambition. He would barely have believed in the young woman's disinterest if she had sacrificed her honor to Rodolphe, as he thought her capable of doing. He would have merely supposed her to have intended to become his student's mistress. According to the priest's principles, selling oneself at a good price was a duty and it had nothing to do with love. "It's a weak and watery love," he said, "that hesitates before heaven and earth." Certain that he was not mistaken about Sarah's intentions, the priest nevertheless was extremely confused. After all, the demand Tom had forwarded in his sister's name was an entirely honorable one. What were they asking for? Either a separation or a legitimate marriage. Despite his cynicism, the priest would not have dared to reveal to Tom his suspicion that Tom's motives were not entirely honorable. He would never have said crudely and openly that Tom and his sister had cleverly plotted to bring the prince to a marriage of unequals.

The priest could take one of three actions:

He could alert the grand duke to this matrimonial conspiracy.

He could open Rodolphe's eyes to Tom and Sarah's plotting.

He could lend a hand to the marriage.

But alerting the grand duke meant alienating forever the affections of the presumptive heir to the throne.

On the other hand, revealing Sarah's ulterior motives to Rodolphe made him risk meeting the kind of reception that lovers always give to those who criticize the object of their love. And more, what a terrible blow it would be for the prince's vanity, to reveal to him that she wanted to marry him only because he was a sovereign ruler! And finally, it would surely be strange for a priest to find fault with the conduct of a young woman who wanted to remain chaste and not give to anyone but a husband the rights of a lover.

If, on the contrary, he promoted the marriage, the priest would be linked to the prince and his wife by their profound gratitude, or at least by the solidarity demanded by participation in a dangerous conspiracy. Of course, the whole thing might be discovered and he would be at the mercy of the grand duke's anger. But the marriage would have been solemnized, it would be legal, the storm would have to pass, and the future sovereign of Gerolstein would find himself that much more obliged to the priest, given the risks the priest would have run in his service. And so, after considerable reflection, the priest decided to aid Sarah. He imposed one restriction, nevertheless, which we will discuss later.

Rodolphe's passion had reached the breaking point. He was completely exasperated both by the constraints he was under and by Sarah's subtle seduction: she seemed to him to suffer even more than he did from the insurmountable obstacles that honor and duty placed in the way of their happiness. Any day now, the prince would betray his feelings. The reader should bear in mind that this was a first love, a love as ardent as it was innocent, as trustful as it was passionate. Sarah had employed the most infernal modes of refined flirtatiousness to spark that passion. Never had the virginal emotions of an openhearted young man, who was both imaginative and passionate, been more artfully and knowingly inflamed. Never had a woman been more dangerously seductive than Sarah. One moment foolishly gay, then melancholy; one moment chaste, then passionate; first modest, then enticing: her great, languorous black eyes lit an inextinguishable flame in Rodolphe's bright, young soul.

When the priest gave Rodolphe the choice of either never seeing this intoxicating girl again or making her his through a secret marriage, Rodolphe threw himself on the priest's breast, calling him friend, savior, father. If the church and the minister had been ready, the young prince would have married her on the spot.

For reasons of his own, the priest wanted to take care of everything. He found a minister and witnesses. The marriage ceremony (whose forms and legalities Tom carefully oversaw) took place secretly when the grand duke was absent for a short period to attend a meeting of the German Diet.

The old Scottish Highlander's prediction had come true: Sarah was married to the heir to a crown.

Without dampening the fire of his love, possession made Rodolphe more circumspect and calmed the violence of his passion, a violence that threatened to reveal the secret of his love for Sarah. The young couple, overseen by Tom and the priest, got on so well together and showed so much reserve in their relationship that they escaped all suspicion.

For the first three months of the marriage, Rodolphe was the happiest man alive. When tranquil reflection followed his first passion, he considered his position calmly and found he had no regrets at having bound himself irrevocably to Sarah. He abandoned, without regrets, the dreams of a future life of affairs and lax sensual pleasures that he had at first so ardently desired. He and Sarah made the most beautiful plans imaginable for their future reign.

In these far-off hypothetical plans, the role of prime minister, which the priest had destined for himself *in petto*,[63] was considerably diminished. Sarah kept for herself the direction of the government. She was too imperious not to covet power and domination; she hoped to reign in Rodolphe's stead.

An event that Sarah had impatiently awaited soon brought on the storm that always follows the calm. Sarah was going to be a mother. And this woman then started making completely new demands, thus terrifying Rodolphe. Bursting into hypocritical tears, she declared that she found the constraints of their current life unbearable. And her pregnancy was making those constraints only that much more painful. In their current crisis, she demanded firmly to Rodolphe that they reveal everything to the grand duke. He, like the dowager grand duchess, was becoming fonder and fonder of Sarah. He would, almost certainly, be indignant at first and be overcome by anger, she added, but he loved his son so tenderly and so blindly and he had so much affection for her, Sarah, that little by little his paternal anger would calm and she would finally assume the rank that was proper to her at the court of Gerolstein. Indeed, that rank was hers that much more fittingly since she would bear the future heir presumptive to the throne.

This claim truly frightened Rodolphe. He knew that his father loved him deeply, but he also knew the inflexibility with which the grand duke held all principles regarding the duties of a prince.

Immovable, Sarah answered all his objections the same way: "I am your wife before God and man. Before long, I will no longer be able to hide my pregnancy. I will not blush because of something that I am in fact proud of. I have every right to shout it to the rooftops."

His upcoming fatherhood had intensified the tender affection Rodolphe felt for Sarah. Caught between wanting to grant her wishes and fearing his father's anger, he was torn apart by conflicting desires.

Tom took his sister's part in the argument: "The marriage can't be dissolved," he said to his serene highness, his brother-in-law. "The most the grand duke can do is exile you and your wife from his court. He can't do anything more than that. But he loves you too much to carry out any such sentence. He will prefer to put up with what he cannot do anything about."

63. In secret. Used to describe the appointment of a cardinal that is not made public. [TN]

This argument—and really it was a good one—did little to calm Rodolphe's fears. At this point, the grand duke requested that Tom visit various stud farms in Austria. He could hardly refuse this mission and, in any case, it would last only two weeks, at the most. But he left his sister at this critical moment with considerable reluctance.

Sarah was both pained and happy at her brother's departure. She would lose the aid of his counsel, but, if all were discovered, he would be protected from the grand duke's anger. Meanwhile, Sarah was to provide Tom with daily updates describing each phase of an operation that was so critical for both of them. In order for the correspondence to be more secret and more secure, they arranged a code between them.

This precaution, by itself, shows that Sarah had more to discuss with her brother than just her love for Rodolphe. And in fact, this cold, egotistical, ambitious woman's icy heart had not melted one bit before the fires of passion that she had lit up. Maternity was nothing more to her than an even more sure way of controlling Rodolphe and did nothing to soften her steely heart. She had no sympathy for Rodolphe's youth, his mad love, his almost childish innocence, which she had played upon to entrap him inextricably. In her intimate correspondence with Tom, she complained with bitter disdain of Rodolphe's weakness. What a boy, to tremble before the most fatherly of German princes! And that father had a long life ahead of him! In short, this correspondence between brother and sister clearly revealed their egotistic self-interest, their calculated ambition, their almost homicidal impatience. It laid bare all the elements of the dark web by which they had entrapped Rodolphe into marriage.

A few days after Tom's departure, Sarah was sitting with the grand duchess and her ladies. Several of the women looked at her with surprised glances and whispered to their neighbors. The Grand Duchess Judith, despite her ninety years, had excellent hearing and sharp eyesight. She did not miss this merry-go-round of whispering. She signaled to one of her ladies in waiting to come over to her and she was told that they thought Sarah was less slender and willowy than usual. The old princess adored her young protégée and would have taken her oath on Sarah's chastity. Indignant with these malicious observations, she shrugged her shoulders and, from her end of the room, said at the top of her voice:

"Sarah, my dear, come here!"

Sarah got up. To reach the princess, she had to walk through the circle of her ladies in waiting. The princess had foreseen this and had entirely kindly intentions. She meant Sarah's walk to give the lie to the gossips and prove to them triumphantly that her figure had lost none of its grace and delicacy. Alas! The most evil-intentioned enemy could not have imagined a greater trial than the princess imagined to defend her protégée.

Sarah came to her. Only the respect owed to the grand duchess could restrain a general murmur of surprise and indignation when the girl walked through the circle of the ladies in waiting. Even the least clear-sighted could see what Sarah herself had no interest in hiding. She could have kept her pregnancy hidden for somewhat longer yet, but the ambitious woman had arranged this outburst as a means of forcing Rodolphe to reveal their marriage.

The grand duchess, who was not yet ready to believe her own eyes, whispered to Sarah: "My dear child, you are frightfully dressed today. You, whose waist can fit between two hands? You're barely recognizable."

Later, we will recount the results of this discovery. It had large and terrible consequences. We will merely note now what the reader has already doubtless figured out: the child of this unfortunate marriage was Songbird. Fleur-de-Marie was the daughter of Sarah and Rodolphe. And both of them thought she was dead.

The reader has certainly not forgotten that Rodolphe, after having visited the house in rue du Temple, had returned home and had that very night to go to the ball given by the wife of the ambassador of ***. To this party, we will duly follow his highness, the reigning Grand Duke of Gerolstein, traveling in France under the name of the Count of Duren.

CHAPTER 15

THE BALL

At eleven o'clock at night, a Swiss guard in expensive livery opened the doors of the mansion in rue Plumet to allow a magnificent blue sedan to exit. It was harnessed to two superb large horses of a pure gray hue. An enormous coachman was ensconced on a large covered seat with silk-lined fringes. His blue fur-lined coat, with its sable pilgrim collar edged all around in silver, made him look even more enormous. The coat was covered with a breastplate of decorative cording. Behind the carriage a giant, powdered footman in blue daffodil and silver livery sat right next to a messenger with a formidable mustache. The messenger was decked out like a drum major and his large, embroidered hat was almost hidden by tufts of yellow and blue feathers. The lamps threw a vivid light into the satin-lined interior of the coach. There, Rodolphe sat on the right. To his left was the Baron de Graün and in front of him was loyal Murph. In deference to the ruler represented by the ambassador whose ball he was attending, Rodolphe wore on his clothing only the diamond-adorned badge of the order of ***. Around Murph's neck was the orange ribbon that carried the enameled cross of the Grand Commander of the Silver Eagle of Gerolstein. The Baron de Graün was decorated with the same insignias. Only as a matter of accurate notation must it be mentioned how innumerable were the crosses from every country that swayed on a golden chain hanging between the first two buttonholes of his suit.

"I am very happy," said Rodolphe, "with the good news Madame Georges sends about my poor little protégée at the farm at Bouqueval. David's care has worked miracles. Relieved of the sadness that was overwhelming her, the poor girl is getting much better. And speaking of Songbird, you have to admit, Sir Walter Murph," Rodolphe added with a smile, "that if one of the bad company you keep in the Cité saw the brave collier they knew so disguised as you are, they would be completely dumbfounded."

"Well, I think, my lord, that your highness would evoke the same surprise if he decided to go to rue du Temple tonight and pay a friendly visit to Madame Pipelet in hopes of cheering up poor Alfred in his melancholy. After all, he wants only to be your friend, as the estimable wife of the doorkeeper told your highness."

"His lordship has so perfectly depicted Alfred, with his majestic green suit, his academic air, and the stovepipe hat he never removes," said the baron, "that I can almost see him there in his place of honor in his dark, smoky rooms. And so may I dare to hope that your highness is satisfied with the information my private agent provides? Was this house in rue du Temple all that his lordship hoped?"

"Yes," Rodolphe said. "I even found more than I hoped for." Then, after a moment of mournful silence and to chase away the painful thoughts brought on by his fears about the Marquise d'Harville, he went on in a more cheerful tone, "I hardly dare admit to such childishness, but I really am tickled by these contrasts: one day I'm a fan-painter seated in a low-life bar in rue aux Fèves; this morning I'm a salesman proposing a glass of cassis to Madame Pipelet; and tonight, by the grace of God, one of those privileged to rule in this world. The man with forty crowns refers to his investment income exactly as a millionaire does," Rodolphe added, parenthetically, alluding to the small extent of his lands.

"But most millionaires don't have the uncommon and admirable good sense of the man with forty crowns," said the baron.

"Ah! My dear de Graün, you are too good, really too good. I am overcome," said Rodolphe, acting as if he were both delighted and embarrassed at the same time. The baron looked at Murph like someone who realizes too late that he has made a faux pas. "Truly," Rodolphe went on with imperturbable gravity, "I don't see, my dear de Graün, how to express my gratitude for the good opinion you have of me or, even more, how to return it in kind."

"I beg his lordship not to give himself the trouble," said the baron, who had forgotten for a moment how much Rodolphe detested flattery and how he returned it with pitiless scorn.

"Now really, Baron, I can't leave things there with you. Unfortunately the best I can come up with at the moment is, on my honor, you don't look a day over twenty. Antinous is no match for your charms."[64]

"Please, Your Lordship, enough!"

"Look at him, Murph. Does the Apollo Belvedere have a figure any more slender, more elegant, more youthful than this one?"[65]

"Your Lordship, it's so long since I've made such a mistake."

"And the purple coat. How well it suits him!"

---

64. Antinous was a Greek who lived in the second century CE. He was the lover of the Emperor Hadrian, who, upon his lover's death at the age of twenty, commissioned numbers of statues, many of which still exist, to commemorate his beauty. [TN]

65. The Apollo Belvedere was a Greek statue discovered in Italy in the fifteenth century. Throughout the nineteenth century, to a great extent because of the high opinion the eighteenth-century German art critic Johannes Winkelmann had of it, it was thought to represent ideal classical beauty. [TN]

"Please, Your Lordship, I'll mend my ways."

"And that golden circle that holds the curls of his beautiful black hair floating around his divine neck without hiding them."

"Please, Your Lordship, forgive me. I'll never do it again," said the unfortunate diplomat with an expression of comic desperation. (The reader has not forgotten that he was fifty years old, with grizzled, powdered gray hair, a large white tie, a thin face, and gold binocles.)

"Great God! Murph, he only lacks a silver quiver on his shoulders and a bow in his hand or he could stand for the conqueror of the serpent Python!"[66]

"I beg Your Lordship's pardon for him. Please don't bury him under the weight of all this mythology," the squire said, laughing. "I will be his guarantor to your highness that it will be a long time before he tries any flattery again, since, in the vocabulary of Gerolstein, that is how one translates the word 'truth.'"

"Not you, too, my old Murph? Even you dare—"

"Your Lordship, poor de Graün's situation pains me and I want to share his punishment."

"Sir Collier in Ordinary, here is a devotion to friendship that does you honor. But really, my dear de Graün, how could you forget that I tolerate flattery only from d'Harneim and his like? Because—you have to be fair—they don't know how to say anything else. That's the way those birds sing. But a man of your wit and taste? For shame, Baron!"

"Well, then, Your Lordship," the baron said, bravely, "there's more than a little pride—may your highness pardon me!—in your aversion to praise."

"Well, it's about time, Baron. I like this better! Explain yourself."

"Well, it's exactly as if a pretty girl said to one of her suitors, 'God, I know I'm charming. Your praise is completely pointless and boring. Why belabor the obvious? Does one walk down the streets announcing that the sun is shining?'"

"Now this is cleverer and more dangerous, Baron. So I will vary your punishment. I must confess that not even the infernal Father Polidori could have found a better way to disguise how poisonous flattery is."

"Your Lordship, I will not say another word."

"So," said Murph, speaking seriously now, "your highness no longer has any doubts that the charlatan you met is really the priest?"

"Once you told me that he had come to Paris a while ago, there could no longer be any room for doubt."

66. The Apollo Belvedere depicts Apollo having just shot an arrow, and he is thought to have slain the serpent Python. It is also called the Pythian Apollo for that reason. [TN]

"I had forgotten to speak about him to you, Your Lordship, or rather I had failed to do so," said Murph sadly, "because I know how much your highness detests even the memory of that priest."

Rodolphe's expression once again became somber. Immersed in sad contemplation, he remained silent right up until the moment his carriage entered the ambassador's courtyard. Every window of that immense mansion was lit up against the dark night. A veritable hedgerow of servants in elegant livery stretched from the columns of the courtyard and the entryway right up to the waiting rooms. And there footmen were waiting. It was an imposing, even royal reception.

The Count *** and the Countess *** had taken care to be in the first reception hall to greet Rodolphe. He soon entered, followed by Murph and Monsieur de Graün. Rodolphe was at this time thirty-six years old.[67] But, even though he was now just past middle age, he still was imposing. The perfect regularity of his features—perhaps too attractive, as we have noted, for a man—and the friendly, dignified manner that characterized everything he did would have made him stand out even if they were not enhanced by the august effect of his rank. When he appeared in the ambassador's first reception hall, he was completely transformed from the Rodolphe we have seen. No longer did one see the rowdy expression, the brisk, fearless manner of the fan-painter who beat the Slasher; no longer did one see the gay, ironic salesman who sympathized with such good humor with the misfortunes of Madame Pipelet. He was a prince, in the full, poetic meaning of the word.

Rodolphe held his head high, with pride. His naturally curly chestnut hair framed his open and noble forehead. His look was both gentle and dignified. When he spoke to someone with the witty kindness which came to him so naturally, his charming and graceful smile revealed enameled teeth which the deep color of his light mustache made even more dazzling. Brown sideburns, which went down to his slightly jutting chin, framed a perfectly oval, fair face.

Rodolphe was dressed very simply. He had on a white vest and tie. His blue coat was buttoned up. A badge ornamented with diamonds gleamed on its left side. This coat set off a figure that was as fine as it was elegant and lithe. Finally, something manly and resolute in his attitude counterbalanced what might have seemed too easygoing and graceful in his carriage.

Rodolphe was seen so rarely in society and he was so princely in his manner that his arrival could not fail to elicit some notice. All eyes were upon him when he came into the ambassador's first reception

67. In Book II, Chapter 12, the *Almanac of Gotha* lists Rodolphe as having been born in April 1803, which would make him thirty-five in 1838, which is, according to Book II, Chapter 10, when the novel takes place. [TN]

hall, accompanied by Murph and the baron, who remained a few steps behind him.

As soon as he appeared, a servant charged with watching for his arrival alerted the Countess ***. She immediately approached Rodolphe, along with her husband, and said, "I cannot express to your highness the gratitude we feel for the honor you deign to do us today."

"Madame Ambassador knows well that I am always eager to attend her and always happy to have the opportunity to tell the ambassador in what esteem I hold him. We are, after all, old acquaintances, are we not, Count?"

"Your highness is only too good in recalling that and thereby giving me one more reason never to forget his kindnesses."

"It is not my fault, I swear, Count, if I cannot forget some things. I have the good fortune of having a very good memory for that which I take pleasure in."

"That is a rare gift, Your Highness," the Countess *** said, with a smile.

"Isn't it just, madame? In the same way, in years to come, I hope I will have the pleasure of recalling this night to you and the taste and high elegance of everything about this ball. Because truly, although I must whisper it to you, you are the only hostess who really knows how to throw a party."

"My lord!"

"But that's not all. Tell me, Ambassador, why women always seem prettier here than elsewhere."

"That is because his majesty extends even to them the goodness with which he graces us."

"You will permit me to disagree, Count. I believe it is due to Madame Ambassador."

"Would his majesty have the goodness to explain whence this effect?" asked the countess with a smile.

"But it's really quite simple, madame. You know how to surround yourself with beautiful women with perfect manners and exquisite grace, you speak to each of them with such charm and flattery that those who are not worthy at first . . . at first of such praise," said Rodolphe with a mischievous smile, "are made more radiant by your notice, while those who are worthy are certainly not made less radiant by your appreciation. Such innocent pleasures illumine any face; happiness makes the least prepossessing attractive and, so, Countess, women seem always prettier here than elsewhere. I feel certain that the ambassador would say no less."

"His highness reasons so well that I cannot but submit to his views."

"As for myself, Your Lordship," said Countess ***, "at the risk of becoming as pretty as those beautiful women who are not worthy at first . . . at first of the praise they receive, I accept the flattering explanation with as much gratitude and pleasure as if it were the truth."

"In order to convince you, madame, that nothing could be more true, let us observe the effects of praise on people's faces."

"Ah, my lord! That would be setting a terrible trap," the ambassador's wife said with a laugh.

"Well, then, Madame Ambassador, I will abandon the experiment on one condition only, and that is that you permit me to offer you my arm. People speak of a flower garden that is truly magical in the month of January. Would you be kind enough to take me to see this wonder from *The Arabian Nights*?"

"With the greatest pleasure, my lord. But the account his highness has heard is greatly exaggerated. In any case, you will be the judge, at least unless your usual indulgence doesn't impede your perception."

Rodolphe offered his arm to the ambassador's wife and walked with her through the other rooms while Count *** stayed to talk to the Baron de Graün and Murph, whom he had known for a long time.

CHAPTER 16

THE WINTER GARDEN

Indeed, nothing could have been more magical or more worthy of *The Arabian Nights* than the garden Rodolphe had spoken of to the Countess ***. Imagine at the end of a long, splendid gallery, a space eighty yards long and sixty wide.[68] A very light glass enclosure, vaulted and fifty feet high, encloses this parallelogram. Its walls are covered with an infinite number of mirrors, which are covered over with the green diamond patterns of a trellis made of tightly linked rushes. Because of the light reflected from the mirrors, they resemble an arbor bathed in daylight. There is a row of orange trees as large as those in the Tuileries and another of camellias of the same size. The former are filled with shining fruit like so many golden apples against a background of luscious green; the latter are enameled with purple, white, and pink flowers that cover the whole stretch of the walls.

That was the garden's peripheral area. Five or six enormous clusters of trees or bushes from India or the tropics planted in large containers of peat were surrounded by walkways marbled with a charming seashell mosaic. These pathways were so wide that two or three people could walk abreast.

It is impossible to describe the effect this exotic garden and its rich, brilliant vegetation created in the setting of this ball, at the height of winter.

Here were enormous banana trees, almost reaching the glass panes in the vault and mixing their large, gleaming green palms with the tapered leaves of giant magnolias. Many of these were already covered with large flowers as perfumed as they were beautiful. From their bell-shaped calyxes, which were purple on the outside and silvered within, shot out golden stamens. Palm and date trees like those of the Levant, red fan palm trees, and fig trees from India, vibrant, blooming, and leafy, completed this immense bank of natural, shining greenery. It shone like vegetation of the tropics and seemed to gleam like emeralds, so decked out in bright and sparkling colors were the thick, fleshy, varnished leaves of these trees.

---

68. Sue uses an archaic French measure, *toise*, which corresponds roughly with a yard but is approximately six inches shorter. [TN]

All along these trellises, between the orange trees, among the tree banks, weaving across the trees one after another, here in garlands of leaf and flower, there surrounded in spirals, farther on in endless webs, an infinite number of climbing plants ran, twined, and climbed right up to the glass vaults. Falling from the top of the vault like colossal garlands were the branches of winged pomegranate trees, passifloras with large purple flowers that were striated with blue and crowned with a tuft of dark violet. The way they were throwing their delicate twines around the arrows of giant aloes made them look like they wanted to climb back up.

Farther on, an Indian bignonia with long, lightly leaved, saffron-yellow-colored calyxes, was surrounded by a stephanotis with fleshy white flowers that gave off a sweet smell. These two interlaced vines ornamented the large velvety leaves of an Indian fig tree with their green fringe and golden and silver bellflowers.

Yet farther on, asclepias stems beyond number burst out and fell back in a multicolored, flowery cascade. Their leaves and umbels, with fifteen or twenty starred flowers, were so thick and polished that one would have thought they were bouquets of pink enamel, surrounded by little green porcelain leaves.

The edges of the banks were made up of heather from Capetown, tulips from Thol, narcissi from Constantinople, hyacinths from Persia, cyclamens, and irises. They formed a natural carpet in which all colors and shades mixed together in the most splendid way.

Chinese lanterns of transparent silk, some blue, others the palest pink, half hidden here and there among the foliage, gave light to the garden. It is impossible to put into words the mysterious and gentle light that arose from the mixture of these two shades. It was charming and otherworldly. It suggested the limpid blue of a beautiful night, made slightly pink by the vermilion gleam of an aurora borealis.

One entered this immense hothouse, two or three feet lower than ground level, through a long gallery gleaming with gold, crystal, mirrors, and lights. This flaming light nearly framed the shadows in which the large trees of the winter garden were vaguely outlined. These could be seen through a large bay window half closed by crimson velvet door curtains. The giant window looked as if it were opening on some beautiful Asian landscape during a serene sunset.

Seen from the garden's immense divans that sat under a dome of foliage and flowers, the gallery made a striking contrast with the gentle darkness of the hothouse. It looked, from a distance, like a golden, luminous mist in which the striking, varied colors of the women's dresses and the glinting prisms of diamonds and other rare stones sparkled and shimmered like animated embroidery. The sounds of the orchestra, muted by distance and by the dull, happy buzzing of the gallery, died melodiously in the motionless foliage of the giant, exotic trees.

One automatically spoke in whispers in this garden. In it, one could just barely hear the light noise of steps and the light touch of silk. Together, the warm, light air, filled with a thousand sweet scents of perfumed flowers, and the vague, faraway music filled the senses with a gentle, soft tranquility.

Two lovers, happy in the first bloom of passion, seated on silk in some shady corner of this Eden, intoxicated with love, harmony, and perfume, would surely not be able to find a more enchanting place for their ardor, still at its sunrise. (Alas, one or two months of serene love will churlishly transform these two lovers into a cold married couple.)

As he came into this ravishing winter garden, Rodolphe could not contain a surprised exclamation and said to the ambassador's wife, "Truly, madame, I would never have believed such a wonder possible. More than great luxury rendered in exquisite taste, it is poetry in motion: rather than writing like a poet or painting like a grand master, you create what they would hardly dare to dream of."

"Your highness is much too kind."

"Admit it. Anyone who could faithfully represent this enchanting scene, with the charm of its colors and contrasts—here a dazzling tumult, there delicious repose—either in painting or in poetry, would have created a masterpiece. And he would merely be reproducing your own masterpiece."

"The praise your highness indulges me in is even more dangerous because I can't help being charmed by its intelligence and, much as I might try, I can't help but be very pleased to hear it. But look over there, my lord. What a charming young woman! Your highness will at least admit that the Marquise d'Harville is pretty no matter where she goes. Isn't her elegance ravishing? Doesn't she look even more beautiful in contrast with the austere beauty who is with her?"

At that moment, Countess Sarah MacGregor and the Marquise d'Harville came down the steps of the gallery leading to the winter garden.

CHAPTER 17

THE MEETING

The ambassador's wife's praise for Madame d'Harville was no exaggeration. It is impossible to describe her enchanting face. It bloomed with a rare beauty, one which owed more to the charm of her expression than to any regularity of feature. One might almost say that her touching expression of goodness modestly veiled the charm of her face. We insist on this goodness because usually it is not precisely goodness that figures most in the expression of a young, twenty-year-old woman as beautiful, witty, sought after, and petted as was Madame d'Harville. And so the contrast between her indescribable sweetness and the success she had in the social world—not to mention her advantages of birth, name, and fortune—made Madame d'Harville particularly attractive.

We will try to explain more clearly what we mean. Madame d'Harville was too worthy and too supremely gifted to court praise directly. And yet, she was as warmly grateful for any praise she received as she would have been if she had hardly merited it. Never proud of compliments she received, they always made her happy nonetheless because, while she was indifferent to the praise, she was very sensitive to kindness and could tell the difference between flattery and sympathy perfectly well.

Her wit was sharp and refined, mischievous without being ill-natured; it took aim particularly at those who were entranced by their own charms. She trained her inoffensive, mocking humor on the sort of people who always wanted to draw attention to themselves or to show themselves off, radiating foolish contentment and puffed up with foolish pride. "Such people," Madame d'Harville said in her winning manner, "always seem to be dancing alone in front of a mirror only they can see and smiling at it in satisfaction." Because, in contrast, she was both timid and almost proud in her reserve, Madame d'Harville always evoked people's interest.

This short description will help the reader understand the intelligence, as one might put it, of the marquise's beauty.

Her dazzlingly clear complexion was enhanced by its subtle, fresh, rosy shading. Her long chestnut curls just grazed her round, firm shoulders, which gleamed with the beauty of white marble. The angelic beauty of her large gray eyes, fringed with long black lashes, can hardly be described.

Her adorably soft, ruby mouth complemented her charming eyes, just as her inexpressibly touching way of speaking complemented her sad, gentle gaze. We will leave undescribed both her perfect figure and the exquisite distinction of her bearing. She wore a white crepe dress, ornamented with real pink camellias. Diamonds, half hid here and there in the leaves of those flowers, gleamed like so many drops of sparkling dew. On her pure white forehead, she wore a garland made of the same flowers.

Countess Sarah MacGregor's beauty was of a type that made the Marquise d'Harville's beauty stand out even more. Now thirty-five years old, Sarah hardly looked more than thirty. Nothing is better for one's physical health than cold egotism; everything keeps better on ice. There are hard, dry souls such as Sarah's that are impervious to the emotions that wear out our hearts and age our features. They feel only the inconveniences of pride and the miscalculations of disappointed ambitions. Such grief has little effect on the body. Sarah's youthful appearance proves what we are saying here.

Her figure, larger and less slender than Madame d'Harville's, had a slight plumpness that gave her a voluptuous grace that was the sole exception to her otherwise youthful brilliance. Few gazing upon her could bear the deceptive fire of her passionate black eyes. Her moist red (partially painted) lips expressed both determination and sensuality. The transparency of her fine, milky white flesh revealed the blue networks of her veins around her temples and her neck.

Countess MacGregor wore a straw-colored moiré dress under a crepe tunic of the same color. A crown of natural, emerald green leaves encircled her head and went beautifully with the braids of her hair, which were as black as ink. Her hair was parted in the middle, above her forehead and aquiline nose with flared nostrils. This austere hairstyle lent a classic air to her imperious and passionate profile.

Often people take on the character of their own facial features, finding it impossible to resist the direction their own physiognomy seems to suggest. One man looks rather warlike, so he becomes a warrior; another looks like a rhymester, so he writes rhyming couplets; a man who looks like a conspirator conspires; one who looks like a politician politicks; a man who looks like a preacher preaches. Sarah had taken on, not without reason, a supremely regal air. She had accepted the half-realized predictions of the Highland fortune-teller as gospel truth and thus persisted in her belief in her own sovereign destiny.

Sarah and the marquise had seen Rodolphe as soon as they walked into the winter garden. The prince had not seen them, however, because he was standing at the bend of a path just as the two women walked in.

"The prince is paying so much attention to the ambassador's wife," said Madame d'Harville to Sarah, "that he doesn't even notice us."

"Don't believe it, my dear Clémence," responded the countess, who had become a trusted intimate of Madame d'Harville. "The prince certainly saw us. But he is frightened of me. He is still sulking."

"I've never understood why he persists in staying away from you. I often criticize him for how strange his conduct is toward you—an old friend. 'Countess Sarah and I are mortal enemies,' he joked. 'I have sworn never to speak to her.' And he added, 'You must believe that I take that oath as a holy one since I deprive myself of the conversation of such a kind person.' And as singular as that answer seemed to me, my dear Sarah, I could hardly fail to accept it."[69]

"I can assure you that this mortal tiff, which is half serious, half a joke, is completely harmless. If there weren't a third party involved in it, I would have told you the whole story of this secret a long time ago. But what's wrong with you, my dear child? You seem preoccupied."

"Oh, it's nothing. It was just so hot in the gallery a moment ago that I felt a slight migraine coming on. Let's sit down here for a moment. It will pass, I hope."

"You're right. Stay right here in this dark corner. You'll be completely hidden from those who will miss you most," Sarah added, smiling and emphasizing her last words. They both sat down on a couch. "I said 'those who will miss you most,' my dear Clémence. Aren't you grateful for my discretion?" The young woman blushed slightly and lowered her head, but she didn't say anything. "Now you're being silly," Sarah said to her, in a tone of friendly reproach. "Don't you trust me, my child? And you are my child, since I'm almost old enough to be your mother."

"Not trust you?" said the marquise to Sarah, sadly. "On the contrary, haven't I told you what I shouldn't even have admitted to myself?"

"Yes, you have, perfectly well. So, then, let's see . . . let's talk about him. So have you decided to let him die from despair?"

"Oh!" Madame d'Harville cried out in fear. "What are you saying?"

"You don't really know him yet, my poor dear child. He is a man of cold determination, and life means little to him. He's always been so unhappy—and one would think that you like to torture him."

"Is that what you think? Heavens!"

"You may not mean to, but that's what you are doing. Oh! If you only knew how painfully sensitive and impressionable people can be when they have been devastated by long suffering! Really, only a little while ago, I saw him weeping."

"Is that really true?"

"No mistake—in the middle of a ball, no less. And at the risk of

---

69. Rodolphe's and Sarah's love affair and the events that resulted from it took place seventeen or eighteen years ago. No one knew anything about their relationship since both Sarah and Rodolphe had every reason to keep it secret. [SN]

being horribly ridiculed if anyone saw him suffering such bitter sorrow. You know, you must really love someone when you suffer like that—and especially if you don't even try to hide your suffering from anyone."

"Please don't say any more about that," Madame d'Harville responded, with great emotion in her voice. "You are causing me great pain. I know that expression of resigned and gentle suffering only too well. Alas! It's the pity I felt for him that made me stray," Madame d'Harville said, despite herself.

Sarah seemed not to have understood the implications of that last word. "What an exaggeration! Straying merely for having toyed with a man who carries discretion and reserve to the point of refusing to meet your husband out of fear of compromising you! Isn't Monsieur Charles Robert the very soul of honor, delicacy, and sentiment? If I insist on defending him, it's because you met him and came to know him in my home and because he respects you as much as he loves you."

"I have never doubted the nobility of his character. You always speak so well of him! But, you know, it's his misfortunes that have made me feel for him."

"And you have to admit, such misfortunes should make you feel for him. And then, also, how could such a worthy face not be the image of his soul? With his tall, handsome bearing, he reminds me of knights in the age of chivalry. I saw him once in uniform: no one could have looked more impressive. It's a sure thing that if one granted nobility on the grounds of merit or beauty, he would be a duke or a peer, instead of being just plain Monsieur Charles Robert. Wouldn't he really be worthy of one of the greatest names in France?"

"You forget how little I care about noble birth, you who sometimes criticize me for being a republican,"[70] said Madame d'Harville, with a smile.

"Well, I certainly do think that Monsieur Charles Robert has no need of titles to be attractive. And what talent! What a charming voice! What an addition he has been to our little morning concerts! Do you remember? The first time you sang together, what expression he put into that duet, what emotion!"

"Please, I beg of you," said Madame d'Harville, after a long silence, "let's change the subject."

"Why?"

"What you told me just now about his despairing manner makes me deeply sad."

"I can tell you that a person as passionate as that, when he feels too much sorrow, might well consider death to put an end to—"

---

70. The word "republican" refers to one who subscribes to the principles of the French Republic, as opposed to the rule of a monarch. [TN]

"Oh! I beg of you, be quiet, be quiet!" said Madame d'Harville, interrupting Sarah. "I have already thought of that." Then, after a long silence, the marquise said, "Once more, let's talk about something else—about your mortal enemy," she added, with feigned good humor. "Let's speak of the prince, whom I have not seen for such a long time. Do you know, he is always charming, even though he's almost a king. As much of a republican as I am, I find few men as nice as he is."

Sarah threw a quick disguised look of inquiry and suspicion at Madame d'Harville. Then she went on, cheerfully, "Really, you have to admit, Clémence, that you are nothing if not capricious. I have seen you one moment full of admiration for the prince, and the next I see you take a singular aversion to him. Only a few months ago, when he came here, you were so enthusiastic about him that, just between us, for a while, I was afraid your heart was no longer whole."

"Thanks to you, at least," Madame d'Harville said with a smile, "my admiration didn't last very long. You play your role of mortal enemy all too well. You have told me such things about the prince—well, I confess, distance has replaced the enthusiasm that made you fear for the safety of my heart. If your mortal enemy has troubled my heart's tranquility, in any case, it's hardly anything he meant to do, because only a little before what you told me about him, while continuing to have the closest relationship with my husband, he almost entirely stopped honoring me with his visits."

"Speaking of your husband, is he here tonight?" asked Sarah.

"No, he didn't want to go out," Madame d'Harville responded, with some discomfort.

"It seems to me that he goes out into society less and less."

"Yes, sometimes he prefers to stay at home."

The marquise was visibly uncomfortable. Sarah saw it and then went on, "The last time I saw him, he looked paler than usual."

"Yes . . . he was a little ill . . ."

"Really, my dear Clémence, may I be frank with you?"

"Please."

"When it comes to your husband, you often seem unusually anxious."

"Me? That's crazy!"

"Sometimes when you talk about him, despite yourself, your expression shows— God! How should I say this to you?" Sarah emphasized the following words, looking as if she were reading into the bottom of Clémence's soul: "Yes, your expression speaks of a sort of—frightened repugnance."

Madame d'Harville's impassive features at first resisted Sarah's inquiring gaze, but finally Sarah saw an almost imperceptible, light nervous trembling in the young woman's lower lip. Not wanting to push things any farther, and especially not wanting to awaken her friend's suspicion, the countess hastened to add, so as to change the meaning of what she had just said, "Yes, a frightened repugnance, the sort of repugnance someone might normally feel for a surly, jealous husband . . ."

Taking what Sarah said this way, Madame d'Harville dropped the light convulsive movement of her lip. A tremendous weight seemed to have been lifted from her and she answered, "Really, no, Monsieur d'Harville is neither surly nor jealous." Then, seeking, doubtless, a pretext for dropping a subject that weighed on her, she cried out suddenly, "Oh, God! Isn't that that unbearable Duke de Lucenay, one of my husband's friends? Let's hope he doesn't see us! But where can he have come from? I thought he was a thousand miles from here!"

"It's true, people said that he had left for a one- or two-year trip to the Orient, and it's hardly been five months since he left Paris. That's a pretty sudden return and it must have really put out the Duchess de Lucenay, even though the duke hardly gets in her way," Sarah said with a wicked smile. "And she won't be the only one to curse this irritating return. Monsieur de Saint-Remy will share her sadness."

"Don't gossip maliciously, my dear Sarah. Say instead that this return will irritate . . . everybody. Monsieur de Lucenay is sufficiently disagreeable to merit your remark being generalized."

"Malicious? Certainly not! I am only echoing what others say. People persist in saying that Monsieur de Saint-Remy, a model dandy who has dazzled all Paris with his splendor, has almost ruined himself, even though he seems to have given up hardly any of his expenditures. And it is true that Madame de Lucenay is remarkably wealthy . . ."

"Really, that's frightful!"

"Again, I'm just being an echo. Oh, dear! The duke has seen us. He's coming this way. We'll just have to put up with it. It's really too bad. I don't know anyone in the whole world more unbearable than that man. He's really terrible company. He laughs so loudly at stupid jokes, and he is so noisy about it, that it's quite deafening. If you value your flask or your fan, hold on to them for dear life around him, for he has one other bad habit: he breaks everything he touches. And he does it in such a playful and self-satisfied way."

His grace, the Duke de Lucenay belonged to one of the greatest families in France. And his face would not have been disagreeable were it not for his grotesque and exaggeratedly long nose. But in this man were combined a turbulent demeanor and perpetual agitation; his shouts and his loud laughter at jokes that were in deplorable taste were matched by a cavalier and unexpected nonchalance. You had to constantly remind yourself of his noble name so as not to be astonished to see him in the most distinguished Parisian homes and to understand why anyone tolerated his bizarre language and comportment. But people had gotten used to it, and so he now met with a kind of indulgence or impunity. People flew from him like the plague, although you did have to admit that there was some real wit that popped up here and there among his incredibly exuberant remarks. He was a vengeful type, and you always hoped to see the hateful and the ridiculous run afoul of him.

Madame de Lucenay was one of the most pleasant of women and also one of the most fashionable in Paris, even though her thirtieth birthday was now behind her. She often caused people to talk about her, but everyone forgave her actions, as lacking in prudence as they were, in light of Monsieur de Lucenay's unbearable eccentricities.

One last trait of this irritating character was his amusement at attributing to people whimsical indispositions or unlikely and absurd illnesses. He described these illnesses in exaggerated, cynical, and unheard-of ways, pitying their ostensible victims at the top of his lungs before crowds of people. Moreover, since he was completely without fear, he always accepted the consequences of his tasteless witticisms: he had given as good as he got in numbers of duels without changing his ways one bit.

Having explained all this, we will now make our readers' ears resonate with Monsieur de Lucenay's sharp, piercing voice at the moment that he saw Madame d'Harville and Sarah from a distance and commenced to shout, "Oh, well, now! And what's that? What's that I see there? What can this be? The prettiest woman at the ball is hiding herself in a corner. Is that even allowed? Do I really have to come back from the ends of the earth to put a stop to such a scandal? First of all, if you persist in hiding so that no one can admire you, Marquise, I'll howl out like someone in agony, I'll scream about the disappearance of this ball's most charming ornament." And as a conclusion to this tirade, Monsieur de Lucenay threw himself backward onto the couch beside the marquise. Then he crossed his left leg over his right thigh and held his foot in his hand.

"So, monsieur, you've already come back from Constantinople?" Madame d'Harville said, pulling back from him impatiently.

"Already, you say! And I can tell that's what my wife thinks, too, since she didn't want to come with me tonight for my reentry into society. So you come back to give your friends a surprise, and this is what you get!"

"Well, that's easily explained. It was so easy to make people like you—from far away," Madame d'Harville said, with a half smile.

"Which is to say, stay away, isn't it? That's really horrible—that's a terrible thing for you to say," Monsieur de Lucenay howled. And then he uncrossed his legs and beat on his hat as if it were a tambourine.

"For the love of heaven, Monsieur de Lucenay, don't shout like that. And sit still or you'll force us to get up and leave," Madame d'Harville said, with some ill temper.

"Get up and go! So you can give me your arm, I hope, and take a walk with me around the gallery."

"With you? Absolutely not. Look, please don't touch my bouquet, and leave my fan alone, too. You're going to break it, just like you always do."

"Well, that's nothing. I've broken hundreds, you know. There was a beautiful Chinese one that Madame de Vaudémont gave to my wife."

With these reassuring words, Monsieur de Lucenay started to pick at a web of climbing vines, which he pulled and shook. Finally, he pulled them off the tree they were holding on to. They fell on him, and the duke found himself crowned with them. And then he broke out in screeching, mad laughter that was so deafening that Madame d'Harville would certainly have fled this bothersome and irritating man if she had not seen Monsieur Charles Robert (or as Madame Pipelet would call him, the commandant). He was walking toward her from the other end of the alley. The young woman was afraid that she might seem to be running to meet him and so stayed next to Monsieur de Lucenay.

"So tell me, Madame MacGregor, don't I look just like the god Pan, or a naiad, a faun, or a savage under these leaves?" Monsieur de Lucenay said to Sarah, beside whom he had suddenly stretched himself out. "Speaking of savages, I really should tell you a completely improper story. Imagine that in Tahiti—"

"Duke!" Sarah said to him in an icy tone.

"Oh, well, then, I won't tell you my story. I'll save it for Madame de Fonbonne over there." Madame de Fonbonne was a fat little fifty-year-old woman whose chin hung down to her cleavage. She was pretentious and ridiculous, always rolling up her fat eyes as she spoke of her soul—of her soul's languors, her soul's needs, her soul's desires. This night, she was wearing an atrocious copper-colored cloth turban sprinkled with small green designs. "I'm saving it for Madame de Fonbonne!" the duke cried out.

"What are we talking about, Duke?" Madame de Fonbonne said, simpering, cooing, and making eyes, as they say in popular parlance.

"We're talking about a completely improper story, madame, an indecent, unsuitable, unseemly story."

"Oh, my God! Who would dare? Who would let themselves tell such a story?"

"Me, madame. And it would make a sailor blush. But I know the kind of thing you like, so listen to this one."

"Monsieur!"

"Well, then, I won't tell you my story after all! Because for someone who always dresses so well, with so much taste and elegance, your turban tonight, I have to tell you, looks like an old pie tin that's been eaten away by verdigris." And the duke burst out laughing.

"If you've come back from the Orient just to start telling your awful jokes again—which people only put up with, by the way, because you're half mad—everybody will be sorry you ever returned, monsieur," said the fat lady, with some irritation. And she walked haughtily away.

"I really have to hold myself back so I don't tear the hat off of that vile, pretentious woman," said Monsieur de Lucenay. "But I do respect her. She's an orphan." And the duke broke out laughing again, "Ha, ha, ha! Look, here's Monsieur Charles Robert," he said. "I ran into him at one of the baths in the Pyrénées. He's a charming boy, and he sings like a swan. You watch, Marquise, how I confuse him. Do you want me to introduce you?"

"Sit still and leave us alone," Sarah said.

As Monsieur Charles Robert walked slowly toward them, seeming to admire the flowers in the hothouse, Monsieur de Lucenay managed cleverly to get his hands on Sarah's flask and he busied himself silently in taking apart the opening of the little knickknack.

Monsieur Charles Robert continued to come toward them. His tall figure was perfectly proportioned. His features were as regular as one could ask for. And he was dressed with the most complete elegance. But his face and his carriage lacked charm, grace, or distinction. He walked stiffly and clumsily. His hands and feet were large and vulgar. When he saw Madame d'Harville, his usual blank expression disappeared and was replaced by one of deep sadness. The change was too sudden for the expression not to have been feigned. But the pretense was a very good one nevertheless. Monsieur Robert seemed to be desperately unhappy, so unfeignedly in despair that Madame d'Harville couldn't stop thinking about Sarah's menacing speech about the extremes to which his despair might carry him.

"Well, hello there, my dear sir!" Monsieur de Lucenay said to him, stopping him as he walked toward them. "I haven't had the pleasure of your company since we were at the baths. But what's wrong with you? You look like you're in pain!"

Monsieur Charles Robert here gave Madame d'Harville a long, melancholy glance and said to the duke in a plaintive voice, "It's true, monsieur, I am in pain."

"My God, my God, so you haven't been able to get rid of your phlegm?" Monsieur de Lucenay asked him, with an air of grave concern.

For a moment, Monsieur Charles Robert was flabbergasted into silence by this question, as whimsical as it was absurd. Then his face went red with anger and he turned to Monsieur de Lucenay and said, in a curt, firm tone, "Since you take such an interest in my health, monsieur, I hope you will visit me tomorrow to ask after my response."

"What do you mean, my dear sir? Well, certainly, I'll send my second—" said the duke, loftily.

Monsieur Charles Robert acknowledged this, just barely, and walked away.

"The thing about it is that he no more has phlegm than the Grand Turk," said Monsieur de Lucenay, heaving himself back down next to Sarah, "unless that was just a lucky guess. What would you say, Madame MacGregor—do you think he seemed to have phlegm?"

Sarah immediately turned her back to Monsieur de Lucenay without saying a word. All this happened in an instant. Sarah could hardly contain her laughter.

Madame d'Harville had really felt terrible, thinking of the horrible position Monsieur Charles Robert had been put in, being cross-examined so absurdly before the woman he loved. She was terrified to think that a duel might take place. And so, under the influence of an irresistible feeling of pity, she quickly got up, took Sarah's arm, and walked over to Monsieur Charles Robert, who was still beside himself with rage. As she walked by, she whispered to him, "Tomorrow at one o'clock. I'll be there." Then she went back to the gallery with the countess and left the ball.

CHAPTER 18

HOW LATE YOU ARE, MY ANGEL!

Rodolphe had come to this party as a matter of social obligation. But he also wanted to see if he could find out whether his fears about Madame d'Harville had any foundation. Could she really be the protagonist of Madame Pipelet's story?

After having left the winter garden with Countess ***, Rodolphe went through several rooms, hoping to run into Madame d'Harville alone. But he had no luck. He returned to the hothouse and stopped for a moment on the first step of the stairs. There he saw the rapid exchange between Madame d'Harville and Monsieur Charles Robert that followed the Duke de Lucenay's deplorable joke. Rodolphe saw them exchange meaningful glances. He instinctively felt that this tall, handsome young man was the commandant. He went back to the gallery so that he could make sure.

A waltz was beginning. After a few minutes, he saw Monsieur Charles Robert standing in a doorway. He looked quite happy with himself, satisfied both with his response to Monsieur de Lucenay (despite how ridiculous he was, Monsieur Charles Robert was in fact very brave) and with the rendezvous Madame d'Harville had given him for the next day. He was certain that this time she would show up.

Rodolphe went to find Murph. "Do you see that young man with blond hair in the middle of that group over there?"

"The tall one who seems so happy with himself? Yes, my lord."

"Try to get close to him—close enough so that, without his seeing you, you can whisper so only he hears, 'How late you are, my angel!'"

The squire looked at Rodolphe, dumbfounded. "Are you really serious, my lord?"

"Absolutely serious. If he turns around when you say it, keep that calm composure of yours I've so admired so often. Don't allow the gentleman to figure out who said the words."

"I don't have the slightest idea what you have in mind, my lord, but I'll do what you ask." Before the end of the waltz, the worthy Murph had found a place immediately behind Monsieur Charles Robert. Rodolphe, perfectly positioned so as not to miss the result of his experiment, followed Murph carefully with his eyes. After a second, Monsieur Charles Robert suddenly turned around as if he were astonished.

The calm squire didn't so much as twitch. This big, bald man with his imposing and serious face would obviously be the last person the commandant would have thought would have uttered these words since they recalled the unpleasant misunderstanding that Madame Pipelet had caused and in which she had been the primary figure.

Once the waltz was finished, Murph came back to Rodolphe. "Well, my lord, that young man spun around as if something had bitten him. So are the words a magic spell?"

"Indeed they are, my old Murph. They told me just what I wanted to know."

Rodolphe could only pity Madame d'Harville for her error. It seemed to him an even more dangerous one since he had the vague feeling that Sarah was involved in it, as an accomplice, perhaps, or maybe as a confidante. He was struck by the pain of this discovery. He now no longer had any doubts about the cause of Monsieur d'Harville's sorrows. And he had the deepest friendship for Monsieur d'Harville. There could no longer be any doubt that he was suffering from jealousy. His wife, who was gifted and charming, was going to throw herself away on a man who in no way was worthy of her. Having discovered this secret by chance, Rodolphe was unwilling to act on the knowledge it gave him. He could hardly use it to bring Madame d'Harville to her senses, especially since she was in the grip of a blind passion. Rodolphe seemed to himself condemned to be a helpless witness to this young woman's fall.

Monsieur de Graün interrupted these reflections: "If your highness will grant me a moment of his time in the little room, where we will be alone, it will be my honor to bring him up-to-date on the information he ordered me to seek out." Rodolphe followed Monsieur de Graün, who continued, "The only duchess to whose name the initials *N* and *L* can refer is her grace, the Duchess de Lucenay, whose birth name is Noirmont. She is not here tonight. I just saw her husband, Monsieur de Lucenay. He left five months ago on a trip to the Orient that was supposed to last for a year. He came home suddenly two or three days ago."

The reader will remember that Rodolphe, during his visit to the house on rue du Temple, had found a handkerchief on the landing of the stairs next to the charlatan César Bradamanti's apartment. That handkerchief, which was wet with tears, had rich lacework on it, and in the corner of it he had noted the letters *N* and *L* under a ducal crown. Without knowing any of the details, Monsieur de Graün, following Rodolphe's orders, had learned the names of all the duchesses currently in Paris and had thus uncovered the information he had just passed on to Rodolphe.

Rodolphe now understood everything. He had no reason to care about Madame de Lucenay, but he could not stop himself from trembling at the thought that she had actually visited the charlatan. That wretch, who was none other than Father Polidori, now knew her name, since he had had her followed by Gammy. And the priest was certainly capable of using that information to his own ends, thus putting the duchess at his mercy.

"Chance certainly works in strange ways sometimes, my lord," Monsieur de Graün went on.

"What do you mean by that?"

"Monsieur de Grangeneuve just told me about Monsieur and Madame de Lucenay. He added, wickedly enough, that Monsieur de Lucenay's unexpected return must have exasperated Madame de Lucenay and a certain very handsome man quite a bit. That man was the Viscount de Saint-Remy, the most wonderful dandy in Paris. At the same moment Monsieur de Grangeneuve was telling me all this, Monsieur the ambassador came up to ask me if I thought that your majesty would like to be introduced to the viscount, who was here tonight. He has just joined the legation to Gerolstein and would be only too happy to take advantage of this occasion to pay his respects to your majesty."

Rodolphe could not suppress an impatient gesture. He said, "This is really a complete bother, but I can't refuse. Let's go tell Count *** he may introduce Monsieur de Saint-Remy to me." Despite his irritation, Rodolphe knew the duties of a prince too well to show himself to be less than genial on this occasion. And, in any case, Monsieur de Saint-Remy was rumored to be the Duchess de Lucenay's lover, and that was enough to pique Rodolphe's curiosity a little.

The Count *** brought Monsieur de Saint-Remy up to Rodolphe. He was a charming young man, twenty-five years old, slender, willowy, with the most distinguished figure and the most becoming face imaginable. His complexion was quite brown, but that velvety, transparent, amber-colored brown one finds in Murillo's portraits.[71] He had black hair with glints of blue in it. It was parted on the left; smooth over the forehead, it fell in curls around his face, mostly covering his pale earlobes. The deep black of his pupils stood out against the rest of his eyes, which, instead of being white, shone with that light nuance of azure that gives such a charming expression to the look of Indians. In one of those freaks of nature, the silky thickness of his mustache stood out against the juvenile beardlessness of his chin and cheeks, which were as bare as those of a girl. In a flourish of dandyism, he wore a tie of deep, dark satin. This allowed one to see the base of his neck, which possessed an elegance worthy of an ancient Greek statue of a flutist. Pinned to the folds of his tie was one single pearl, but it was a pearl of great price to judge by its size, the purity of its shape, and its striking iridescence—an iridescence to rival that of any opal. Monsieur de Saint-Remy's attire set off this magnificently simple jewel in perfect

71. Bartolomé Esteban Murillo (1618–1682), a Spanish Baroque painter known for portraits of working-class women and children. [TN]

taste. His whole bearing was so different from that of the usual dandy as to make him unforgettable.

His coach and horses were extremely opulent. He gambled generously for large stakes, and his bets on racing amounted to two or three thousand louis a year. His house on rue de Chaillot was spoken of as a model of sumptuous elegance. When one went there, one dined magnificently, and then one gambled like the devil. He frequently lost considerable sums of money and did so with the most hospitable nonchalance. And yet everyone was quite sure that the viscount's wealth had long since been frittered away.

To explain his unbelievable expenditures, gossips and scandalmongers spoke as Sarah had of the Duchess de Lucenay's great wealth. But, setting aside the contemptuousness of this supposition, it ignores the fact that the Duke de Lucenay of course had control over his wife's fortune and that Monsieur de Saint-Remy must have been spending fifty thousand crowns or two hundred thousand francs a year. Others spoke of imprudent moneylenders, since Monsieur de Saint-Remy no longer expected any inheritance. Still others, finally, said he was TOO fortunate at the turf[72] and whispered about trainers and jockeys he bribed to make sure that the horses he bet a lot of money against lost. But most of society didn't really care much how Monsieur de Saint-Remy paid for his opulence.

His birth admitted him to the best and most distinguished society. He was cheerful, brave, a good companion, witty, and easy to get along with. He gave good bachelor dinners and afterward took on any bets that anyone offered him. Who could ask for anything more?

Women adored him. One could hardly count all of his conquests. He was young and handsome, gallant and splendid, in all the ways that a man could be with women of the world. Indeed, the infatuation for him was such that it even lent a mysterious charm to his secrecy about the source of wealth that he drained with such openhandedness. People smiled carelessly and said, "That devil Saint-Remy must have found the philosopher's stone." When they learned that he had been assigned to France's legation to the Grand Duchy of Gerolstein, some people thought that Monsieur de Saint-Remy had decided to make an honorable retreat from the world of fashion.

The Count *** introduced Monsieur de Saint-Remy to Rodolphe and said, "I have the honor of introducing to your highness the Viscount de Saint-Remy, assigned to the French legation to Gerolstein."

The viscount bowed deeply and said to Rodolphe, "I hope your highness will deign to excuse my impatience to come to pay him my respects.

72. A racecourse where wagers are made. [SN]
Sue footnotes this because he uses the English word "turf" in the French text. [TN]

It is possible that I may be in too much haste to enjoy an honor to which I attach such value."

"It will be a pleasure to see you again at Gerolstein, monsieur. Do you expect to go there soon?"

"Your highness's stay in Paris makes my departure less pressing."

"The tranquility of our German courts will shock you, monsieur, given how much you are used to Parisian life."

"I think I may assure your highness that the kindness he deigns to show me—and will be so good, perhaps, as to continue to show me—would be sufficient by itself to prevent me from ever missing Paris."

"It will not be merely my doing, monsieur, if you do not feel this way for as much time as you spend in Gerolstein." And Rodolphe nodded slightly, announcing to Monsieur de Saint-Remy that his audience had ended. The viscount bowed deeply and withdrew.

Rodolphe was an accomplished reader of physiognomies and had immediate sympathies and aversions that almost always turned out to be accurate. After this very short exchange with Monsieur de Saint-Remy, without being able to explain why, he experienced a sort of involuntary distaste. He found him to have a perfidiously deceitful look, and there was something about his expression that he considered dangerous.

We will meet Monsieur de Saint-Remy again in circumstances that will form a frightening contrast with his prominent place in the world at the time of his introduction to Rodolphe. The reader will judge whether Rodolphe's instincts were accurate or not.

Once this introduction was completed, Rodolphe went down into the winter garden, contemplating the strange meetings chance had brought about. Dinner had been announced and nearly all the rooms were empty. The most hidden corner of the hothouse was to be found at the foot of a bank in the angle of two walls. An enormous banana tree, covered with climbing plants, hid it almost entirely. Not far from this tree, a small servant's entrance, hidden behind trellises, remained ajar. Via a long corridor, it led to the buffet room. Here Rodolphe sat down, sheltered by the windbreak of the tree's leaves. He had been sitting for a few moments, immersed in deep thought, when he shuddered at the sound of a well-known voice pronouncing his name.

Seated on the other side of the tree that hid Rodolphe entirely, Sarah was speaking in English with Tom. Tom was dressed in black. Even though he was only a few years older than Sarah, his hair was almost completely white. His face showed a passionless but stubborn willfulness. His tone of voice was sharp and curt, his look somber, his voice hollow. Great sorrow or great hatred must have been eating away at him.

Rodolphe listened closely to the following discussion:

"The marquise has gone to the Baron de Nerval's ball; fortunately, she left without running into Rodolphe, who was looking for her. I am still afraid of the influence he has over her. I have taken great pains to oppose that influence and eliminate even a small part of it. Finally this rival, whom I have always instinctively feared and who later might have gotten in the way of my plans—this rival will have lost everything tomorrow. Listen, now—this is important, Tom."

"You are mistaken. Rodolphe has never thought of the marquise in that way."

"Now is the time to explain some of these things to you. Much has happened since your last trip, and since we have to act sooner than I thought—in fact, this very night, when we leave here—this discussion is absolutely necessary. Fortunately, here we are alone."

"I'm listening."

"Before she met Rodolphe, I'm sure this woman had never loved anyone. I don't know why, but she has an invincible aversion to her husband, even though he worships her. There is some deep secret there that I have tried to plumb, but I've failed. Rodolphe's presence stirred many new emotions in Clémence's heart. I snuffed out this nascent love with damning revelations about the prince. But the marquise's need to love had been awakened. When she met Charles Robert at my place, she was struck by his beauty in the way one is struck by the sight of a painting. Unfortunately, this man, handsome as he is, is also a complete ninny. But there is something touching about his look. I praised his noble soul and elevated personality to the skies. Knowing Madame d'Harville's natural kindness, I endowed Monsieur Robert with the most touching sorrows. I counseled him to act as if he was always heartsick, never to breathe without sighing and saying 'alas,' and, above all, to speak as little as possible. He followed my advice. Thanks to his talent as a singer, to his pretty face, and above all to his appearance of inconsolable grief, he has almost made Madame d'Harville fall in love with him. And so she has filled the need for love that the mere sight of Rodolphe had awakened in her. Do you understand now?"

"Completely. Go on."

"Robert and Madame d'Harville were never alone together except at my place. Twice a week, the three of us played music together in the mornings. The handsome, gloomy man sighed, whispered a few tender words, and slid her two or three notes. I was more afraid of the writing than of the speech. But a woman always looks indulgently at the first declarations of love made to her. Those my protégé made did not upset her at all. But the important thing was to get her to grant him a rendezvous. This little marquise had principles that were stronger than her love, or rather, she did not yet love him enough to make her forget her principles. Without her knowing it, she still had a memory of Rodolphe deep in her heart. It watched over her, one might say, and opposed her weak inclination for Monsieur Charles Robert. This inclination was always more artificial than real in any case, but it was kept alive by her deep feeling for Monsieur Charles Robert's imaginary sorrows and by my incessantly exaggerated praise of this brainless Apollo. Finally, overcome by her sorrowful worshipper's appearance of profound despair, Clémence came around one day and granted him the rendezvous he so much desired."

"So she made you her confidante?"

"She confessed her feelings for Charles Robert to me, but that's all. I didn't do anything to find out more—that could have made for problems. But, head over heels with happiness—or with pride, anyway—he shared the good news with me. He didn't tell me the time or place of the rendezvous, though."

"So how did you find out?"

"On my orders, both the next day and the day after, starting early in the morning, Karl kept watch over Monsieur Robert's door and followed him. The second day, around noon, our lovebird took a carriage to an obscure section of town, rue du Temple. He got off at a shabby house, stayed there for about an hour and a half, and then left. Karl waited a long time to see if someone left after Charles Robert, but no one did. The marquise had broken her promise. The lovebird told me the next day, and he was angry as much as he was disappointed. I advised him to intensify the despair. Clémence felt even more pity—gave him a second rendezvous—but she didn't keep that one, either. But the last time she made it to the door, which is something at least. You see how much this woman resists. And why? I'm sure it's because, without knowing it, she still has a memory of Rodolphe deep in her heart and—how I hate that man!—it seems to protect her. Finally, tonight, the marquise gave this Robert fellow a rendezvous for tomorrow and, this time, I'm sure she'll show up. The Duke de Lucenay ridiculed this man in the grossest way and the marquise was so overcome by her lover's humiliation that she granted to him out of pity what she would never have granted without it. This time, I tell you, she'll keep her promise."

"What are your plans?"

"This woman responds to a sort of exalted charitable instinct rather than to love. Charles Robert is so little suited to the delicate sentiment that dictated the marquise's resolution tonight that tomorrow he will want to take advantage of the rendezvous and Clémence will lose all respect for him. She has only given in to this step through pity. Neither attraction nor passion plays any role. I have no doubt that, in a word, she'll go there to demonstrate her brave feeling for him, but she'll be perfectly calm and completely certain not to forget her obligations for a single moment. This fool, Charles Robert, won't be able to understand that at all; the marquise will develop a deep aversion to him. Her illusion destroyed, she'll fall back under the influence of Rodolphe's memory. It still flourishes at the bottom of her heart, I'm sure of it."

"And so?"

"And so I want her lost forever as far as Rodolphe is concerned. I don't doubt that Rodolphe would have betrayed his friendship for Monsieur d'Harville sooner or later and given in to Clémence's love. But if he knows her to have been guilty of a weakness that wasn't for him, he will be horrified. That's the one unpardonable crime for a man. And, under the pretext of the affection that binds him to Monsieur d'Harville, he'll abandon forever this woman who treated this friend whom he holds so dear so badly."

"So you are going to warn the husband?"

"Yes, this very night, unless you advise otherwise. According to Clémence, he has vague suspicions but he doesn't suspect anyone in particular. It's midnight, and we're going to leave the ball. You'll go into the first café we come upon and you'll write to Monsieur d'Harville that his wife is going to seventeen rue du Temple tomorrow at one o'clock in the afternoon for a lovers' rendezvous. He is jealous. He'll catch Clémence there. You can figure out the rest."

"This is a disgusting thing to do," the gentleman said coldly.

"Tom, you have scruples?"

"I will shortly do exactly what you request. But, I repeat, this is a disgusting thing to do."

"But you still agree to it?"

"Yes. Tonight Monsieur d'Harville will know everything. And . . . but . . . I think there's someone behind this bank!" Tom whispered suddenly, after having broken off what he was saying. "I think I heard something move."

"So go look," said Sarah, nervously.

Tom got up and walked around the bank, but he didn't see anyone. Rodolphe had just left by the small door mentioned above.

"I was wrong," Tom said, returning. "There's no one there."

"That's what I thought."

"Listen, I don't think this woman endangers your plans as much as you do. Rodolphe has certain principles that he will never violate. The girl he brought to the farm six weeks ago when he was disguised as a worker is another matter. This little girl, whose care he watches over, for whom he provides an excellent education, whom he has visited several times—she gives us much better reasons for fear. We don't know who she is, even if she seems to belong to the lowest class of society. But the unusual beauty people attribute to her, the disguise Rodolphe assumed to take her to the village, the obvious care he has for her, all prove that this is not some insignificant affection. And so, I've done something on my own. To get this obstacle, which is, I think, more real, out of our way, I needed to get information about the people on the farm and about the girl's daily activities, and I needed to do so with the utmost caution. Now I have that information, and the moment to act is upon us. By a stroke of good luck, the horrible old woman who kept my address has turned up again. Her connection with people like the thief who attacked us on our outing in the Cité will be extremely useful to us. I've planned for everything. There won't be any evidence of our involvement. And, anyway, if this creature belongs to the lower classes, as she seems to, she won't hesitate between what we offer her and whatever brilliant end she might dream of for herself, since the prince has completely disguised his identity. Well, tomorrow we'll know one way or the other. Otherwise . . . well, let's see what the future brings."

"Once we've gotten rid of these two problems, Tom, then our great plan—"

"There are still difficulties, but it has a chance at success."

"You have to admit that the chances will be a lot better if we carry it out just when Rodolphe is overwhelmed both by the scandal of Madame d'Harville's affair and by the disappearance of this little girl he cares for so much."

"I think so. But if this last attempt fails—then I will be free," Tom said, looking at Sarah darkly.

"You'll be free?"

"You will never renew the demands on me that, despite myself, have kept me twice already from getting my revenge!" Then, indicating the crepe around his hat and the black gloves that covered his hands, Tom added, smiling sinisterly, "I'm still waiting my turn. I've worn this mourning for sixteen years, as you well know, and I'll never take it off unless—"

Sarah, with an expression of fear she couldn't control, quickly interrupted her brother, saying to him anxiously, "I've said you'll be free, Tom, because then my supreme confidence, which has kept me going in the face of so many different situations, because it has shown itself to be merited beyond what any human being could expect—well, then, I will have lost it entirely. But until then, there is no danger, however slight it seems, that I won't want to deal with at any price. Success hangs so often on the slightest of chances. Even the smallest obstacle might block my path at the moment I near my goal; I want my path free, and I will destroy those obstacles. My methods are odious? So be it! Have I ever stopped at anything?" Sarah cried, raising her voice without realizing it.

"Be quiet! People are coming back from dinner," said Tom. "Since you seem to think it a good idea to warn the Marquis d'Harville about tomorrow's rendezvous, let's get going. It's late."

"Receiving this warning at a late hour will prove its seriousness to him."

Tom and Sarah left the ambassador's ball.

CHAPTER 19

RENDEZVOUS

Wishing above all to warn Madame d'Harville of the danger she was in, Rodolphe left the embassy without waiting for Tom and Sarah to finish their conversation. He thus had no idea of the plot they were hatching against Fleur-de-Marie, nor of the imminent danger she faced.

Despite his best efforts, Rodolphe was unfortunately incapable of saving the marquise as he had hoped. She had agreed to make an appearance at Madame de Nerval's party after leaving the embassy. Overcome by emotion, however, Madame d'Harville lacked the strength to appear at a second party, and she returned home. This unexpected turn of events spoiled Rodolphe's plan.

The Baron de Graün, like almost everybody else in the Countess ***'s circle, was invited to Madame de Nerval's party. Rodolphe took him there in all haste and ordered him to find Madame d'Harville at the ball. He was to tell her that the prince would be found in front of the Harville residence this evening, on foot, wishing to give her a message of the greatest importance. He would approach the window of the marquise's carriage in order to speak with her as her attendants were waiting for the door to open.

After losing a great deal of time in search of Madame d'Harville at the ball, the baron returned. She had never been there. Rodolphe was in despair. He had wisely figured that he needed first and foremost to warn the marquise of the betrayal of which she was the intended victim. He couldn't stop Sarah from informing on the marquise, but if he was successful, her message would seem like vile slander. But it was too late. The vile letter had reached the marquis at one in the morning.

The next morning, Monsieur d'Harville was walking slowly around his bedroom, which was furnished with an elegant simplicity, ornamented only with a display of modern arms and a shelf full of books. The bed had not been slept in, but the silk bedspread was lying in shreds. A chair and a small ebony table with bowed legs had been overturned and were lying next to the chimney. Elsewhere in the room could be seen the broken shards of a crystal glass, half-crushed candles, and a two-branched candelabra that had toppled out of its place. A violent struggle seemed to have caused this mess.

Monsieur d'Harville was approximately thirty years old. His manly face, ordinarily gentle and friendly, was at this moment tense, pallid, and almost blue. He still had on the clothes he had been wearing the day before. His neck was bare, his waistcoat open. His ripped shirt appeared to be stained with blood in various places. His brown hair, normally curled, fell in a wiry tangle over his blanched forehead.

After having paced back and forth for a long while around the room with his arms crossed, his head lowered, and his gaze unwavering and inflamed, Monsieur d'Harville stopped abruptly in front of the fireplace. There was no fire burning in it, despite the night's freezing temperatures. He took the following letter from atop the marble mantelpiece and reread it with voracious attention in the weak light of this winter day: "Tomorrow, at one o'clock, your wife will come to 17 rue du Temple for an amorous tryst. Follow her, and you will know all. Happy husband!"

As he read these words, even though he had already read them so many times, his lips, which were turning blue from the cold, seemed to be convulsively spelling out the fatal message, one letter at a time.

At this moment the door opened and a valet entered. This aged servant had gray hair and a kind, honest face. The marquis turned his head brusquely without moving, holding the letter in his hands. "What do you want?" he asked the servant, roughly.

Instead of answering him, the servant took in the disorder of the room and was momentarily dazed by sadness. Then, looking carefully at his master, he exclaimed, "Blood on your shirt! Heavens! Sir, you must have hurt yourself! You were all alone. Why didn't you ring for me as you usually do when you feel—"

"Get out of here!"

"But, sir, you're not thinking; your fire is out. It is colder than the devil in here, and most of all, after your—"

"Be still. Leave!"

"But, sir," the valet responded, trembling, "you told Monsieur Doublet to be here this morning at ten thirty. It's now ten thirty, and he's here with the solicitor."

"That's right," said the marquis, bitterly, as he recovered himself. "When one is rich, one must attend to one's affairs. How delightful it is to be wealthy!" Then he added, "Ask Monsieur Doublet to come into my office."

"He's there already, sir."

"Help me find my clothes. I will be going out shortly."

"But, sir—"

"Do as I tell you, Joseph," said Monsieur d'Harville, in a softer tone. Then he added, "Has anyone attended my wife yet today?"

"I don't believe the marquise has rung yet."

"Let me know the moment she does."

"Yes, sir."

"Tell Philippe to come and help you here. You will never finish."

"But, sir, let me tidy up a bit here," insisted Joseph, in a sad tone. "People will see this mess and won't be able to understand what could have happened last night to Monsieur the marquis."

"And if they understood, it would be pretty terrible, wouldn't it?" responded Monsieur d'Harville in a voice of painful mockery.

"Oh, sir!" cried Joseph. "Thank God, no one has any idea—"

"No one? No, no one!" replied the marquis, gloomily.

As Joseph busied himself with the task of putting his master's room back in order, the marquis walked directly to the display of arms that we have already noted. He examined the weapons in it attentively for a few minutes and made a gesture of sinister satisfaction before saying to Joseph, "Surely you have forgotten to have the rifles that I have up there in my hunting kit cleaned?"

"Monsieur the marquis has not asked me to do so," responded Joseph, surprised.

"I have, but you have forgotten."

"I must object, sir—"

"They should be in perfect condition!"

"It's been hardly a month since they were taken to the gunsmith's."

"No matter. As soon as I'm dressed, go and get me that hunting kit. I may go out hunting tomorrow or sometime soon. I want to have a look at those rifles."

"I'll bring them down for you right away."

Once the room was put back in order, a second servant came to help Joseph.

After he finished dressing, the marquis entered the office. Monsieur Doublet, his manager, was waiting for him there, along with a legal clerk. "Here is the deed that is to be read to you, sir," said the manager. "It awaits your signature."

"You've read it, Monsieur Doublet?"

"Yes, sir."

"That's good enough for me. I'll sign it." He signed the document, and the clerk left the room.

"With this latest acquisition, sir," said Monsieur Doublet triumphantly, "your investment income, from solid land holdings, will be no less than one hundred and twenty-six thousand francs in bank notes. Do you realize how beautiful it is, sir, to have an income of one hundred and twenty-six thousand francs in real estate income?"

"What a lucky man I am, Monsieur Doublet, no? One hundred and twenty-six thousand francs in income from real estate. There's nothing better than that!"

"And that doesn't include the rest of your fortune . . . it doesn't include—"

"No, it certainly doesn't. It doesn't include all the other . . . good fortune I enjoy!"

"The Lord be praised! Monsieur the marquis, you lack for nothing. You have youth, wealth, kindness, good health—you have been showered with every kind of happiness, basically. Among them," said Monsieur Doublet, smiling agreeably, "or rather, I should say chief among them, I count your being married to the marquise and having a charming little girl who looks like a cherub."

Monsieur d'Harville glared at the manager balefully.

We will restrain ourselves from recording the tone of savage irony with which he spoke to Monsieur Doublet as he gave him a familiar pat on the shoulder. "With one hundred and twenty-six thousand francs of real estate income and a wife like mine . . . and a child who looks like a cherub, who could ask for anything more, right?"

"Oh, sir," the manager returned naively, "you can still wish to live as long as possible, to see Mademoiselle, your daughter, married, and to see yourself become a grandfather. What I hope for Monsieur the marquis is for him to become a grandfather, and for Madame the marquise to become a grandmother, and then a great-grandmother."

"Good old Monsieur Doublet is thinking of Philemon and Baucis.[73] He always has something relevant to add."

"Monsieur le Marquis is only too good. Is there anything else you wish me to do?"

"Nothing. Oh, yes—actually, there is. How much money do you have available in the coffers?"

"Nineteen thousand, three hundred francs and change at the moment, sir, not counting the money you have in the bank."

"Bring me ten thousand francs this morning in gold, and give them to Joseph if I have already left."

"This morning?"

"This morning."

"In an hour, the funds will be here. Does Monsieur the marquis have nothing more to tell me?"

"No, Monsieur Doublet."

"One hundred twenty-six thousand francs of rent in bank notes—in bank notes!" the manager repeated on his way out. "This is a great day

73. Philemon and Baucis are characters in Ovid's *Metamorphoses*. A poor, faithfully married couple, they famously offered exceptional hospitality to the strangers—divinities in disguise—who had come to visit them to test their fabled generosity. They were rewarded for their hospitality by having various wishes granted to them, including dying at the same moment. [TN]

for me: I was so afraid that that farm that suited us so well was going to slip out from our fingers! Your servant, sir."

"Good-bye, Monsieur Doublet."

The manager was scarcely out the door when Monsieur d'Harville collapsed into a chair, overcome. He put his elbows on the desk and hid his face in his hands.

For the first time since he had received Sarah's fatal missive, he could cry. "Oh!" he said. "What a colossal joke my wealth is! What do I put in this gold frame now? My shame? Clémence's disgrace? A disgrace that will taint my daughter's reputation, perhaps. That scandal—should I just accept it? Or should I take pity on—"

Then, rising from his seat—his eyes inflamed, his teeth gnashing convulsively—he cried out in a strangulated voice, "No! No! There must be blood! Terror cleanses us of ridicule. Now I understand her aversion—the wretch!

"Her aversion—I know only too well where it comes from. I horrify her. I frighten her!" And then, after a long silence, he continued. "But is it my fault? Does this warrant her betrayal? Instead of hating me, shouldn't she be pitying me?" he asked, becoming more animated. "No, no—there must be blood! Both of them! Both of them! For she has no doubt told everything to the OTHER MAN."

This thought only intensified the marquis's anger. He lifted his clenched fists to the heavens. Then, holding his burning hand in front of his eyes, he remembered that he had to stay calm before his servants. He returned to his bedroom in apparent tranquility. There he found Joseph.

"So, you have the guns?"

"Here they are, sir. They are in perfect condition."

"I'll make sure. Has my wife rung?"

"I don't know, sir."

"Go and find out."

The valet left the room.

Monsieur d'Harville hastened to remove from the rifle box a small powder flask, a few bullets, and some firing caps; then he closed the kit and kept the key. He proceeded to the arms display, taking from it a pair of half-size Manton pistols,[74] which he loaded before sliding them easily into the pockets of his long morning jacket.

At this moment Joseph returned. "Sir, you can go into Madame the marquise's room."

"Did Madame d'Harville request her carriage?"

"No, sir. I heard Mademoiselle Juliette telling the marquise's driver, who had come to take his orders for the morning, that since the weather

---

74. Pistols made by Joseph Manton (1766–1835), a famous English gunsmith. [TN]

was cold and dry, Madame would go out on foot—if she did indeed go out."

"Very good. Ah! I forgot. If I go out hunting, it will be tomorrow or later. Tell Williams to inspect the little green britska this morning. Do you understand?"

"Yes, sir. You don't want your cane?"

"No. Is there a cabstand near here?"

"Very close by, on the corner of rue de Lille."

After a moment of hesitation and silence, the marquis continued, "Go and ask Mademoiselle Juliette if Madame d'Harville will see me."

Joseph left the room.

"Let's see. It's a performance like any other. Yes, I'd like to go into her room and observe the sweet and perfidious mask that vile woman wears as she dreams, no doubt, of her most recent adulteries. I will hear the lies come out of her mouth as I read the crime in her already corrupted heart. Yes, it's curious to see how a woman looks at you, speaks to you, and answers you when, moments later, she will soil your name with the ridiculous and horrible sort of stain that can only be cleansed with blood. What a fool I am! She will look at me the way she always does, with a smile on her lips and an honest face! She will look at me the way she looks at her daughter when she kisses her on the forehead and makes her say her prayers. And they say the eyes are the mirror of the soul!" (He shrugged his shoulders in derision.) "The sweeter and more chaste a look is, the falser and more corrupt it is! She proves it, and I've been made a fool. I can't bear this! What kind of cold and insolent contempt she must have had for me behind that phony mirror, at the very moment perhaps that she was going out to be with the other man. I used to shower her with proofs of my esteem and affection. I used to speak to her as if she was a young mother who was chaste and serious. I had put in her all of my hopes for my entire life. No! No!" cried Monsieur d'Harville, as he felt his rage growing. "No! I will not see her. I do not want to see her! Nor my daughter, either! I would give myself away and endanger my revenge."

Instead of going into Madame d'Harville's rooms after leaving his own, he merely said to the marquise's chambermaid, "Tell Madame d'Harville that I would like to speak with her this morning but that I am obliged to leave for a short while. If by chance it would suit her to have lunch with me, I will be back at about noon. If not, she need not concern herself with me."

"If she thinks that I'm going to return, she will believe herself to be at greater liberty," Monsieur d'Harville said to himself. And he went over to the cabstand near the house.

"Driver, right now!"

"Yes, boss, it's eleven thirty. Where to?"

"Rue de Belle-Chasse, at the corner of rue Saint-Dominique, along the wall of a garden that's there—you will wait there."

"Yes, boss."

Monsieur d'Harville lowered the blinds. The cab departed and soon arrived almost right in front of the marquis's house. From here, no one would be able to leave his home without his seeing them.

The rendezvous his wife had granted was for one o'clock. With his gaze fixed steadfastly upon the door to his home, he sat in wait.

His thoughts were caught up in such frightening and vertiginous torrents of rage that the time seemed to pass with incredible speed.

The bells of Saint Thomas of Aquinas were ringing noon when the door to the Harville mansion opened slowly and the marquise walked out.

"Already! Ah, how thoughtful she is! She's afraid of making the other wait!" the marquis said to himself with savage irony.

The cold was biting; the road was dry. Clémence wore a black hat draped with a luminous veil of the same color and a purple quilted overcoat made of silk. Her large cashmere shawl of dark blue fell down to the flounce of her dress, which she lifted lightly and gracefully to cross the street.

Thanks to this movement, her narrow, high-arched little foot, beautifully shod in a Turkish satin boot, could be seen just up to her ankle.

What was strange was that even with the terrible ideas that were causing him such distress, Monsieur d'Harville noticed his wife's foot. Never had it seemed prettier or more alluring to him. The sight made him more furious. The sharp bite of sensual jealousy wounded him to the quick. He could see the other on his knees, bringing that charming foot to his lips in a drunken ecstasy. In the space of one second, every kind of ardent expression love could take—passionate love, that is—burned hellishly in his imagination.

And then, for the first time in his life, he felt a terrible physical pain in his chest—a shooting pain that was deep, sharp, and penetrating, causing him to utter a dull moan. Up until that point, only his soul had suffered, for until then he had thought only of the dishonor done to their sacred vows.

This new thought was so cruel that he could barely manage to disguise his voice to speak to the driver through the partly raised blind. "You see that woman in the blue shawl and black hat who's walking along the wall over there?"

"Yes, boss."

"Keep up with her, and follow her. If she goes over to the cabstand where I hired you, stop there and follow the cab she gets into."

"Sure, boss. Hey, this is getting interesting!"

Madame d'Harville did indeed head for the cabstand and entered one of the cabs. The coachman and Monsieur d'Harville followed it, and the two cabs departed.

After a while, to the great astonishment of the marquis, his driver took the road toward the Church of Saint Thomas of Aquinas, and soon came to a stop.

"So? What are you doing?"

"Boss, the lady just went into the church. Good Lord! Nice pair of legs on her, if it's all the same to you. This is pretty interesting!"

A thousand different thoughts churned in Monsieur d'Harville's mind. He believed at first that his wife had noticed that she was being followed and that she had intended to foil her pursuers. Then it occurred to him that perhaps the letter he had received was an outrageous slander. If Clémence was guilty, what good would be served by a false front of piety? Wouldn't that be a sacrilegious joke?

For one moment Monsieur d'Harville had a flash of hope, so great was the contrast between this appearance of piety and the conduct of which he was accusing his wife.

This consoling illusion did not last for long.

His driver leaned over toward him and said, "Boss, the little lady is getting back into the car."

"Follow her."

"Yes, boss! Very, very interesting!"

The cab passed by the quais, the city hall, rue Sainte-Avoye, and finally it arrived at rue du Temple.

"Boss," said the driver as he turned back toward Monsieur d'Harville, "my buddy has just stopped in front of number seventeen. We're at number thirteen. Do you want me to stop here, too?"

"Yes!"

"Boss, the little lady just entered the walkway for number seventeen."

"Open the door for me."

"Yes, boss."

A few seconds later, Monsieur d'Harville followed his wife's footsteps down the walkway.

CHAPTER 20

AN ANGEL

Madame d'Harville entered the house. Dying of curiosity, Madame Pipelet, her husband, and the oysterwoman were gathered at the threshold of the doorkeeper's rooms. The stairway was so dark that it was hard to see it when you came in from outside. The marquise had to ask Madame Pipelet for directions. She said to her in a strange, almost faltering voice, "Monsieur Charles, madame?"

"Monsieur who?" repeated the old woman, pretending not to have heard her so her husband and the oysterwoman had the chance to get a good peek at her face through her veil.

"I would like to see Monsieur Charles, madame," said Clémence again, her voice trembling. She kept her head lowered in an attempt to hide her face from the insolent curiosity of these prying eyes.

"Ah! Monsieur Charles! Now I get it. You spoke so quietly I couldn't hear you. Well, then, little lady, since it seems you are going to see the handsome Monsieur Charles, go right up the stairs. It will be the door right in front of you."

The marquise, overwhelmed and confused, set foot on the first step.

"Hee, hee, hee!" added the old woman, snickering. "It looks like it's on for today! On with the party! Up you go!"

"That commandant knows how to pick 'em after all," commented the oysterwoman. "Nothing shabby about that dolly of his."

If she hadn't had to pass by the doorkeeper's rooms and by this crowd again, Madame d'Harville, dying of shame and fear, would have come right back down the stairs at once. She forced herself to keep going and reached the landing.

And then, suddenly . . . there was Rodolphe, right in front of her. Putting a bag of money into her hands, he quickly said to her, "Your husband knows everything. He's following you."

At this moment, Madame Pipelet shouted out in her grating voice, "Where are you going, monsieur?"

"It's him!" said Rodolphe, adding hastily as he fairly shoved Madame d'Harville toward the stairway to the second floor, "Go up to the fifth floor. You've come here to help an impoverished family named Morel."

"Monsieur, if you don't tell me where you're going, you won't get anywhere unless it's over my dead body!" cried Madame Pipelet, blocking Monsieur d'Harville's passage.

Standing at the end of the alley, he had seen his wife talking with Madame Pipelet, and so he had stopped for a moment. "I'm with that woman who just came in," said the marquis.

"That's different. Go on then."

When he heard an unfamiliar noise, Monsieur Charles left his door ajar. Rodolphe entered his room abruptly and shut the door behind him as Monsieur d'Harville was reaching the landing. Despite the overall darkness of the stairway, Rodolphe feared being recognized by the marquis. He took this opportunity to make a safe escape.

Monsieur Charles Robert, magnificently done up in his floral dressing gown and his embroidered velvet fez, was astonished to find himself in the presence of Rodolphe, whom he had not noticed the night before at the embassy and who was dressed much more humbly in any case.

"Monsieur, what does this mean?"

"Silence!" Rodolphe said in a low voice. He sounded so upset that Monsieur Charles Robert kept his mouth shut.

A frightening sound, like that of a fallen body tumbling down several steps, echoed in the silence of the stairway. "The miserable wretch has killed her!" cried Rodolphe.

"Killed? Who? What is going on here, anyway?" asked Monsieur Charles Robert in a low voice. He had become pale. Without answering him, Rodolphe opened the door slightly. He saw little Gammy going down the stairs in a rush, limping. In his hand he held the red silk money bag that Rodolphe had just given to Madame d'Harville.

Gammy disappeared.

The light step of Madame d'Harville could be heard as she went up to the higher floors, followed by the heavier step of her husband.

Not understanding how Gammy could have procured the money bag but feeling a bit relieved all the same, Rodolphe said to Monsieur Robert, "Don't leave here. You almost ruined everything."

"Really, now, monsieur," said Monsieur Robert in an impatient and angry tone. "Will you tell me what's going on? Who are you and what right do you have to—"

"What's going on, monsieur, is that Monsieur d'Harville knows everything. He followed his wife to your door, and he is still following her upstairs!"

"Oh, no!" cried Charles Robert, clutching his palms in terror. "But what is she going to do upstairs?"

"None of your business. Stay in here, and don't go out until the doorkeeper's wife tells you to."

Leaving Monsieur Robert both terrified and bewildered, Rodolphe went down to the doorkeeper's lodgings.

"Well, now!" said Madame Pipelet, aglow. "Things are really getting hot. There's a man following the little lady. That toff must be her husband. I guessed it right away. I told him he could go up. He's going to get himself killed along with the commandant. This'll get all over the neighborhood—they'll be lining up to see this house like they did to see number thirty-six, after there was a murder there."

"My dear Madame Pipelet, would you like to do me a great favor?" Rodolphe put five louis in the doorkeeper's wife's hand. "When that little lady comes downstairs, ask her how the poor Morel family is doing. Tell her that she'll be doing a good thing by helping them as she promised to do when she came to find out about them."

Madame Pipelet looked at the money and Rodolphe in a stupor. "What? Monsieur, this gold, it's for me? And the little lady, she isn't at the commandant's place, then?"

"The man following her is her husband. Because she was tipped off in time, the poor woman knew to go up to see the Morels, so it would look like she was here to help them. Do you understand?"

"Don't I ever! I have to help you keep the husband in the dark. I like that. It suits me to a T! Heh, heh, heh! You could say I've spent my whole life doing this sort of thing, you know?"

At this point the stovepipe hat of Monsieur Pipelet could be seen standing up at attention in the shadows of the lodgings. "Anastasie," Alfred said, gravely, "you have no respect for anything on this earth, just like Monsieur César Bradamanti. There are some things you don't make a game of, even among friends."

"Look, my dear, stop being such a prude, and lose those goggle eyes. You know I'm joking. Don't you know that there's no one in the world who can say about me that— All right, forget it. If I help these youngsters, it's just to be nice to our new renter, who is such a good fellow." Then, turning back to Rodolphe, she said, "Watch me go to work! Wait there in the corner, behind the curtain. And here they are now."

Rodolphe hid himself hurriedly.

Monsieur and Madame d'Harville were coming down the stairs. The marquis had given his wife his arm. As they stood in front of the doorkeeper's lodgings, Monsieur d'Harville's face was a mix of beatific joy, astonishment, and confusion. Clémence was calm and pale.

"So, my good little lady!" said Madame Pipelet, leaving the lodgings. "Did you see those poor Morels? It breaks your heart, doesn't it? Heavens, the good you are doing there . . . I told you that they were in terrible shape the last time you came to inquire about them. Rest assured: nothing you could do for these good people would be too much. Isn't that so, Alfred?"

Alfred's prudery and natural uprightness made him disgusted at the very idea of having anything to do with this anticonjugal plot, so he just grunted in a vaguely negative way.

Madame Pipelet said, "Alfred has a cramp in his pyloric sphincter. That's why you can't hear what he says. Otherwise, he'd be telling you just like me that those poor people are going to bless you in their prayers, my worthy lady!"

Monsieur d'Harville looked at his wife in admiration and repeated, "An angel! An angel! What slander!"

"An angel? You are so right, monsieur, and a good angel from the good Lord at that!"

"Let's go, darling," said Madame d'Harville, who was suffering horribly from the constraints she had been under since entering this house. She felt as if she was about to collapse.

"Let's leave," said the marquis. He added, as they were leaving the entryway, "Clémence, I must beg your forgiveness and pity."

"Who does not need forgiveness and pity?" said the young woman, sighing.

Rodolphe left his hiding place, deeply moved by this scene that mixed terror with the absurd and the vulgar—the peculiar denouement of a mysterious drama that had aroused so many different passions.

"So?" asked Madame Pipelet. "I hope I did a good job of handling the toff! Now he'll put his wife on a pedestal. Poor, dear man. And your furniture, Monsieur Rodolphe? It never arrived."

"I'm going to take care of it. You can tell the commandant that he can come out now."

"That's right. Hey, what a comedy this has been! You'd have thought he was renting an apartment for the king of Prussia. It was a good job—with his lousy twelve francs a month."

Rodolphe left.

"Say, Alfred," said Madame Pipelet, "it's the commandant's turn now. This is going to be a laugh." And she went upstairs to see Monsieur Charles Robert. She rang, and he opened the door.

"Commandant," said Anastasie, giving him a military salute with her hand held up next to her wig, "I have come to release you from prison. They left arm in arm, the husband and his wife, right under your nose. It's not too bad, though—you got out of a real scrape there, thanks to Monsieur Rodolphe. You owe him big time!"

"That thin gentleman with a mustache, that's Monsieur Rodolphe?"

"The very same."

"Who is that man, anyway?"

"That man," cried Madame Pipelet, angrily, "is the best of men. He's better than two of any other man! He's a traveling salesman, a tenant in the house. He only rents one room, but he's no tightwad. He gave me six francs to do his housekeeping. Six francs, and that was right away! Six francs, without any haggling!"

"That's good . . . that's good. Here, take the key."

"Will you be needing a fire tomorrow, Commandant?"

"No!"

"What about the day after tomorrow?"

"No! No!"

"So, Commandant, remember? I told you you wouldn't get your money's worth!"

Monsieur Charles Robert glared at the doorkeeper's wife and walked out of the house, unable to understand how a traveling salesman, Monsieur Rodolphe, had come to know about his assignation with Madame d'Harville. As he was leaving the entrance, he ran into little Gammy, who was hobbling in.

"There you are, you little brat," said Madame Pipelet.

"Did the one-eyed hag come looking for me?" he asked the doorkeeper's wife, without answering her greeting.

"The Owl? No, you nasty little monster. Why should she come looking for you?"

"To take me to the countryside," said Gammy, steadying himself in the doorway to her lodgings.

"And your boss?"

"My father asked Monsieur Bradamanti to give me the day off today, so I could go out into the countryside, the countryside, the countryside!" chanted Red-Arm's son, humming and tapping on the windowpanes of the doorkeeper's lodging.

"Cut that out, you little rascal! You'll break my windows! Hey, here's a cab."

"Oh, good! It's the Owl," said the child. "I get to go in a carriage!"

Indeed, reflected in the mirror, on the red window blind opposite, the sickly smooth profile of the hag could be seen. She signaled to Gammy, and he ran out to her. The coachman opened the door for him, and he hopped into the cab.

The Owl was not alone. In the other corner of the cab, wrapped in an old coat with a fur collar, his features partly hidden by a black silk cap pulled down over his eyes, sat the Schoolmaster. His red eyelids revealed two white eyes that did not move and had no pupils in them. These eyes made his slashed-up face look all the more frightening. The cold had marbled the scars, turning them purplish and ghastly.

"Come on, kid, lie down on my man's pegs. You'll warm him up," said the one-eyed hag to Gammy, who crouched down like a dog between the legs of the Schoolmaster and the Owl.

"On to the Bouqueval barnyard now—right, Owl?" asked the driver of the cab. "You'll see I know how to make this rattletrap move!"

"And you're especially good at keeping your nag warm," said the Schoolmaster.

"Take it easy, no-peeps, he'll hotfoot it to the fork."[75]

"You want me to give you a prescription?"[76] asked the Schoolmaster.

"Sure, go ahead," responded the driver.

"You give the moneytakers the air;[77] they might recognize you. You've prowled around the tollgates for a long time."

"I'll keep my eyes open," said the other man as he took his seat.

We preserve this hideous language in order to show that this supposed driver was really a criminal and one of the Schoolmaster's worthy associates.

The carriage left rue du Temple.

Two hours later, as the sun set, this cab containing the Schoolmaster, the Owl, and Gammy stopped before a wooden cross that marked the turnoff for a deserted, sunken road that led to the farm at Bouqueval. Here Songbird lived under Madame Georges's care.

---

75. Calm down, no-eyes (another word that is almost graceful in this appalling lexicon), he'll run all the way to the crossroads. [SN]

76. Some advice. A person who gives advice: a doctor. [SN]

77. Go quickly as you pass by the clerks at the tollgate. [SN]

CHAPTER 21

AN IDYLL

The church bells struck five in the little village of Bouqueval. It was bitterly cold and the sky was clear. The sun was slowly setting behind the large, bare woods that crown the heights of Écouen. The horizon had turned scarlet. Pale, oblique rays of the remaining sunlight fell on vast plains hardened by the frost.

In the fields, every day of each season almost always has its own special charm to offer.

At times, the dazzling snow turns the countryside into great landscapes of alabaster that display their immaculate splendors against a gray-pink sky. Then, sometimes, at dusk, the farmer makes a late return to his home, climbing the hill or descending into the valley. Horse, coat, hat—everything is covered in snow. The cold is bitter, the northern wind is glacial, the night that approaches is somber; but over there, amid the barren trees, the little windows of the farm are gaily illuminated. The high brick chimney sends a thick column of smoke up into the sky, a sign to the farmer that his family awaits him. A crackling hearth, a rustic supper—then, after an evening chattering away, a peaceful and warm night while the wind whistles outside and the dogs of the few farms that dot the plains bark and answer each other from afar.

At other times, in the morning, the frost hangs off the trees like crystal chandeliers. The winter sun makes it sparkle with the diamond-like gleam of a prism. The plowed land is wet and slimy; long rows are furrowed into it, and the wild hare makes his home here, along with gray partridges that run lightly by. Here and there, one hears the melancholy clanging of the lead ram's bell. His large flock of sheep is spread across the green and grassy slopes along the sunken roads. Meanwhile, well swaddled in his gray coat with black stripes, the shepherd sits at the foot of a tree, singing as he weaves a basket of rushes.

Sometimes the scene heats up. The faint sounds of a horn and the yelps of a pack of dogs echo back and forth. A frightened deer suddenly jumps out from the forest, emerging onto the plain in terrified flight before heading over the horizon to hide in the bushes. The horns and the barking get closer; the white and rust-colored dogs now exit the forest. They run across the brown earth, over the fallow fields; avidly tracking the deer's scent with their noses, they follow it, howling all the way. The hunters, dressed in red, follow them; they are bent over the neck and wither of their fast horses. They urge the dogs on, shouting and blasting their horns. This chaotic whirlwind thunders by. The noise gets further away, and, little by little, the silence returns. Dogs, horses, hunters alike: all disappear into the distance in the woods behind the fleeing deer.

Then the calm is reborn. The droning song of the shepherds is the only thing that interrupts the deep silence of the open countryside and the tranquility of the wide horizons.

These scenes, these rural sights could be found in abundance around the village of Bouqueval. Despite its proximity to Paris, the village was situated in an isolated place that could be reached only by means of side roads. Hidden in summer like a nest in the foliage, the farm where Songbird had retreated was in this season denuded of its green cover. It was entirely visible.

The path of the little river, frozen by the cold, looked like a long silver ribbon that had been sloppily unwound within the still green fields. Across these fields, some comely cows were passing by on their way back to their stable. Called back with the approach of night, flocks of pigeons landed in succession on the steep roof of the dovecote. The immense oaks that, in the summertime, lent their shade to the courtyard and the farm buildings were barren of all leaves now. Through them one could see roofs covered with emerald-colored moss, some tiled and some thatched.

A heavy wagon was bringing back sheaves of wheat from one of the mills on the plain. Three strong, stocky horses with thick manes and lustrous coats pulled the wagon along. The horses wore blue collars ornamented with bells and red wool tufts. This large vehicle arrived in the courtyard by the carriage gateway as a large flock of sheep was thronging at one of the side entrances.

Beasts and humans alike seemed impatient to escape the nighttime cold and to enjoy the sweet rewards of rest. The horses were whinnying joyously at the sight of the stable, the sheep were bleating as they cleared the gate of the warm sheepfolds, and the laborers cast hungry glances through the ground-floor windows at the kitchen. There, a supper was being prepared for them to sate a Rabelaisian appetite.

A rare and meticulous order reigned on this farm. It was scrupulously and unusually clean. Instead of being caked in dry mud, splattered, and exposed to the vagaries of the seasons, the harrows, plows, and other farming instruments (of which several were of recent invention) were lined up, clean and painted, in a vast hangar where the plowmen also came to arrange the harnesses of their horses in a symmetrical fashion. Large, neat, and nicely planted, the sandy courtyard did not offer the observer the typical view of the manure heap or the stagnant pools of water that mar the most beautiful farms of Beauce or Brie. Surrounded by a green trellis, the poultry yard sheltered and took in all of the fine feathered individuals that came home at night by means of a little door that opened onto the fields.

Without dwelling overly long on these important details, let us say that in every way this place justly passed for a model farm, not only because of its orderliness or the excellence of its agricultural techniques or its harvests, but also because of the happiness and the high morale of the many employees whose labor made this land bring forth its wealth.

We will explain shortly why this farm was so prosperous and advanced. In the meantime, we will take the reader to the trellised door of the poultry yard. This yard was no less impressive than the rest of the farm with respect to the rural elegance of its roosts, its henhouses, and the little stone-lined canal that ran through it. The water of this canal flowed unobstructed, sparkling and clear; any ice that might have formed in it had been carefully removed.

Some kind of revolution took place all of a sudden among the winged denizens of this poultry yard. The hens left their roosts, clucking; the turkeys gobbled; the guinea fowl squawked; and the pigeons, cooing, abandoned the roof of the dovecote and swooped down to the sand.

Fleur-de-Marie's arrival had set off all of this mad gaiety.

If only poor Songbird's cheeks had been rounder and pinker, neither Greuze nor Watteau could ever have imagined such a charming model. Nevertheless, despite her pallor and the oval thinness of her face, her expressive features and her overall demeanor, the gracefulness of her attitude would still have been worthy of inspiring the brushes of these great painters.

Fleur-de-Marie's little round bonnet revealed her forehead and her crown of blond hair. Like almost all of the peasant women on the outskirts of Paris, she wore a large headscarf of Indian red atop this bonnet (the bottom and tufts of which could still be seen). The ends of this scarf fell squarely on her shoulders. How Switzerland and Italy must envy us this picturesque and graceful millinery style!

A cambric shawl, worn across her chest, was partly hidden by the high and wide strap of her ecru apron. A blue blouse made out of coarse cloth with tight sleeves revealed her delicate waist; it contrasted with her thick skirt of gray fustian striped with brown. Hidden away in little black clogs that were embellished at the instep with a square of lambskin, some very white stockings and buskin socks completed this outfit of rustic simplicity. Fleur-de-Marie's natural charm lent this clothing an extraordinary grace.

Holding her apron up by the two corners with one hand, she was taking fistfuls of grain from it and scattering it to the winged mob that was surrounding her.

A handsome silvery-white pigeon with crimson beak and feet, bolder and more familiar than its companions, finally landed on Fleur-de-Marie's shoulder after flying around her for a short while.

The girl, no doubt accustomed to these cavalier ways, did not stop throwing handfuls of grain, but, partly turning her sweet face with its charming profile, she raised her head slightly and offered her smiling pink lips to the little pink beak of her friend.

The last rays of the setting sun beamed a pale and golden light on this innocent scene.

CHAPTER 22

WORRIES

As Songbird was tending to her work on the farm, Madame Georges and Father Laporte, the parish priest of Bouqueval, were sitting in a corner by the fire in the farm's small living room. They were speaking of Fleur-de-Marie, a subject that was always a matter of interest to them.

Thoughtful and contemplative, his head lowered and elbows perched atop his knees, the old priest stretched his two trembling hands automatically toward the hearth. Madame Georges, busy with her sewing, gazed at the priest from time to time. She seemed to be waiting for him to answer her. After a moment of silence, he said, "You are right, Madame Georges. We must warn Monsieur Rodolphe. She is so grateful to him that perhaps, if he asks her, she will tell him, as her benefactor, what she's been keeping from us."

"I think so, too, Father. I've made up my mind: I will write this very evening to the address he gave me, at the allée des Veuves."

"Poor child!" the priest went on. "She should be so happy. What sorrow can be eating away at her now that she's here?"

"Nothing manages to take her mind off her sadness, Father. Not even the effort she puts into her studies."

"She has truly made extraordinary progress in the short time since we took her under our wing."

"It's true, isn't it, Father? She has learned to read and write almost perfectly, and she has also learned enough math to be able to help me keep up with the farm's accounts. And the little dear helps me with such devotion in everything that I'm both touched and astonished. She has been working herself so hard—almost against my wishes—that I fear for her health!"

"Fortunately, the black doctor has reassured us that that worrisome little cough she has is nothing to fear."

"He is such a good man, that Monsieur David! He is so concerned for her well-being. But Lord, so is everyone who gets to know her. Everyone cherishes and respects her here. It's not surprising, considering that Monsieur Rodolphe's generous and enlightened views prevail around here, so the people who work at the farm are the very best the country has to offer. But even the most vulgar and insensitive people would respond to her angelic and timid gentleness, that way she has of always seeming to ask for mercy. Poor child! As if she were the only sinner that ever was!"

The priest spoke again after a few minutes of reflection. "Haven't you told me that Marie's sadness dates back to the visit, after All Saints' Day, of Madame Dubreuil, the Duke de Lucenay's farmer at Arnouville?"

"Yes, Father, I believe I noticed it then, even though Madame Dubreuil and her daughter Clara, the very picture of innocence and goodness, were completely taken by her. Both of them showered her daily with marks of their affection. You know that every Sunday either our friends from Arnouville come to visit us or we go there. Well, it seemed that each visit made our dear child sadder, even though Clara already loves her like a sister."

"Truly, Madame Georges, it's a strange mystery. What can be the cause of her hidden sorrow? She ought to be so happy! Between the life she leads at present and the life she used to lead, it's the difference between heaven and hell. You certainly can't accuse her of ingratitude."

"Her? Gracious, no! She, who has been so grateful to us for all our care? She, in whom we have witnessed only the rarest and most delicate of instincts? Doesn't that poor little girl do everything she can to earn her bed and board? Doesn't she try to compensate us for our hospitality by trying to do things for us? That's not all: every day except on Sunday, when I insist that she dress up a bit to go to church with me, she always wants to wear the same common clothing country girls wear. Even when she's dressed like that, you can see through to her real grace and distinction. Those old clothes make her even more charming. Don't you think so, Father?"

"Ah, now I hear a mother's pride," he said, smiling. But upon hearing those words, Madame Georges's eyes welled up with tears. She was thinking of her son.

The priest guessed the cause of her sorrow and said to her, "Be of good heart. God has sent you this poor child to help you to wait until you find your son again. And a sacred bond will soon tie you closer to Marie. A godmother, when she understands the full extent of her mission, is almost the same as a mother. As for Monsieur Rodolphe, he brought her soul back to life, so to speak, when he rescued her from the abyss. He fulfilled his duties as godfather beforehand."

"Do you think she's learned enough to receive the sacrament that she's almost certainly never received before, poor girl?"

"In a moment, when I return to the rectory with her, I will tell her that the ceremony will probably take place within two weeks."

"Perhaps, Father, you will preside over yet another sweet and solemn ceremony on her behalf."

"What are you getting at?"

"If someone falls in love with Marie, as she well deserves, if she chooses a faithful and honest man, why should she not get married?"

The priest shook his head with sadness and answered, "Marry her? Think about it, Madame Georges. Honesty demands that you reveal everything to anyone who might want to marry Marie. And despite all the care we might take, what kind of man would be willing to take on the sordid past of that poor child's youth? No one will want her."

"But Monsieur Rodolphe is so generous! He will do more for his protégée than he's done already. A dowry—"

"Alas!" said the priest, interrupting Madame Georges. "It would be no kindness to Marie if someone married her because his greed outweighed his scruples! That would be the worst fate that could befall her. A union like that would surely lead to the cruelest kind of recriminations."

"You're right, Father. That would be terrible. Ah! What an unhappy future awaits her, then!"

"She has great sins to atone for," the parish priest said, gravely.

"Heavens! Father, how could she not have fallen, given the fact that she was abandoned at such a young age, without any resources, without any support, hardly knowing the difference between right and wrong, led along the path of vice against her will?"

"A good moral compass should have sustained and enlightened her. In any case, did she try to escape her horrible fate? Are charitable souls so rare in Paris, then?"

"Surely not, but where should she have gone to find them? Before one finds such a soul, how many rejections, how much indifference must one encounter? And then again, if anyone wanted to help Marie, a single handout wouldn't have done much good. Only a sustained interest in her that might have helped her earn her living honorably would have made a difference. Plenty of mothers would no doubt have taken pity on her, but she would have had to have been lucky enough to meet one. Ah! Believe me, I've known what misery is. Without a stroke of providential luck similar to the one that—too late, alas!—brought Marie into contact with Monsieur Rodolphe—without the benefit of such luck as that, the unfortunate don't believe in pity, because they are almost always brutally repulsed the first time they ask for help. When they are oppressed by hunger—hunger, which has such power over us—sometimes they look to vice for the aid they despair of finding in sympathy."

At that moment, Songbird came into the parlor. "Where have you been, child?" asked Madame Georges, sympathetically.

"I've been in the fruit storeroom, madame, after I closed the gates to the poultry yard. The fruit is holding up well in there, except for a few of them that I removed."

"Why didn't you ask Claudine to take care of that, Marie? You have surely overexerted yourself."

"No, not at all, madame. I love being in my fruit storeroom! The perfume of ripe fruit is so sweet!"

"You must visit Marie's fruit room someday, Father," said Madame Georges. "You cannot imagine how tastefully she has arranged it. Garlands of grapes separate every kind of fruit, and the different kinds of fruit are themselves separated further into compartments with borders of moss."

"Oh, Father, I am sure you would love it!" said Songbird, with innocent joy. "You'll see how nice the moss looks around the red apples and the beautiful golden pears. The lady apples are the best of all. They are so lovely, with their charming pink and white colors, that they look like little cherub heads in a green, mossy nest," the girl added, with the enthusiasm of the artist for her artwork.

The priest smiled at Madame Georges and said to Fleur-de-Marie, "I've already admired the dairy that you supervise, my child. It would be the envy of even the most demanding manager. One of these days I will stop by to see your fruit storeroom as well—those beautiful red apples and golden pears, and most of all those pretty little cherub apples in their mossy bed. But just now, the sun has set. You'll only have the time to bring me to the rectory and to return here before nightfall. Take your mantle and let's go, child. No, on second thought—it's bitter cold out. You stay here. Someone from the farm will take me back."

"Ah! Father, you will make her unhappy," said Madame Georges. "It brings her such satisfaction to take you home every evening!"

"Father," added Songbird, raising her great, timid blue eyes to look at the priest, "I'll think I've done something to offend you if you don't let me accompany you tonight, as usual."

"Me? Poor child. Go, get your mantle, then, quickly, and wrap yourself up tight."

Fleur-de-Marie rushed to throw a hooded, fur-lined cloak of off-white wool over her shoulders. The cloak had a black velvet border running around it. She offered her arm to the priest. "Happily," he said, "we don't have far to go, and it's a safe road."

"Since it's a little later than usual tonight," Madame Georges said, "would you like to have someone from the farm come with you, Marie?"

"You would think I was a scaredy-cat," said Marie, smiling. "Thank you, madame, but please don't trouble anyone on my behalf. It only takes a quarter hour to get from here to the rectory. I'll be back before dark."

"I won't insist because—thank God!—I've never heard any reports of vagabonds in these parts."

"Otherwise, I would never allow this dear child to accompany me along the way, however much I might need the help."

Soon the priest left the farm, supported on the arm of Fleur-de-Marie. She adjusted the pace of her light footsteps to match the slow, difficult walk of the old man.

A few minutes later, the priest and Songbird arrived at the sunken road where the Schoolmaster, the Owl, and Gammy were lying in ambush.

BOOK III

CHAPTER I

THE AMBUSH

Bouqueval's church and rectory were built halfway up a hill in the middle of a chestnut grove overlooking the village. Crossing the sunken road that cut this hill diagonally, Fleur-de-Marie and the priest reached a twisting path that led to the priest's house. The Owl, the Schoolmaster, and Gammy, hidden in one of the crevices of this road, saw the priest and Songbird climb down in the gully and leave it by a sharp incline. Because the hood of her cape hid the girl's face, the one-eyed hag couldn't recognize her old victim.

"Silence, my boy," the old woman said to the Schoolmaster. "The chicky and the boar have just passed the bend in the road. Judging from the description the tall man in mourning gave us, it really must be her: dressed like a farm woman, middle height, striped dress, woolen coat with a black border. Every day she takes the boar to his hole like that and then comes back all alone. When she comes back to the end of the road, we'll jump her, carry her off, and put her in the carriage."

"But what if she cries for help?" asked the Schoolmaster. "They'll hear her from the farm. You said it yourself: you can see its buildings from here. Because all of you can see," he added in a hollow voice.

"Sure, you can see the buildings from here, right close by," Gammy said. "Just now, I climbed up to the top of the hill, dragging myself on my stomach. I heard a wagon driver speaking to his horses in that court over there."

"All right, then, here's how we'll do it," the Schoolmaster went on after a moment of silence. "Gammy will stand watch at the beginning of the path. When he first sees the little girl from far off, he'll run up to her, crying out that he's the son of a poor old woman who hurt herself falling into the sunken road. He'll ask the girl to come help them."

"I get you, Killer. The poor old woman, that'll be your little Owl. The real profs couldn't have come up with a better plan. My boy, you're still sharper than any snake. So then what do I do?"

"You'll burrow into the sunken road on the same side where Fishhook is waiting with the cab. I'll be hiding right nearby. When Gammy brings the little girl to the middle of the gully, stop moaning and jump on her, one hand around her gullet and the other down her piehole so you can hold her flapper still and stop her from crying out."[78]

"Got it, Killer—like we did with the woman at the Saint-Martin canal who we pushed into the deep end after we lifted the black box she was carrying under her arm, right?"

"Yes, just the same. While you keep a tight hold on the little girl, Gammy will run and get me. The three of us will pack the girl up in my coat, we'll carry her to Fishhook's coach, and from there we'll go to the Saint-Denis plain, where the man in mourning is waiting for us."

"Now that's how to snatch somebody. Really, you know, Killer, there's no one like you. If I could do it, I'd send up fireworks of your noodle and I'd light you up in colored glass to Saint Charlie, the patron saint of hangmen. You listen up, brat, if you want to become a real tough guy, you just watch my sly old snake. There's a real man!" the Owl said proudly to Gammy. Then, turning to the Schoolmaster, she said, "While we're on the subject, you don't know but Fishhook is scared stiff that he's gonna be snuffed by the law."

"Why's that?"

"A little while ago, he offed a guy in a fight. The guy was the husband of a milkmaid who came from the countryside every morning in a cart with a donkey to sell milk in the Cité, on the corner of rue de la Vieille-Draperie, near the ogress's place at the White Rabbit."

Red-Arm's son, who didn't understand the slang, listened to the Owl with a sort of frustrated curiosity.

"You probably want to know what we're talking about, don't you, brat?"

"That's for sure!"

"If you're nice, I'll teach you the slang. Soon you'll be old enough for it to do you some good. Would you like that, deary?"

"You bet I would! And I'd like to stay with you rather than with that old swindler of a charlatan I work for, grinding his drugs and grooming his horse. If I knew where he kept his human rat poison, I'd put it in his soup so I could stop slaving away for him."

That set the Owl off laughing and she pulled Gammy to her and said, "Come here now and give your mama a kiss, deary. Aren't you a sweety? But how do you know your boss has rat poison for humans?"

"Listen. I heard him say it when I was hiding in his room's back closet, the one where he keeps his bottles and his steel contraptions and where he fiddles around with his pots."

"What did you hear him say?" the Owl asked.

"I heard him say it to a man when he gave him some powder in a piece of paper: 'Whoever swallows this three times will be sleeping six feet

78. One hand around her neck and the other in her mouth to hold her tongue. [SN]

under—and no one will know why or how it happened, and it doesn't leave a trace.'"

"And who was this man?" the Schoolmaster asked.

"A handsome young man with a black mustache and a face as pretty as a lady's. He came another time, but that time Monsieur Bradamanti told me to follow him to find out where he hung out. The pretty guy went into a nice house on rue de Chaillot. My boss told me, 'No matter where this man goes, follow him and keep a watch on his door. If he leaves again, follow him again until he goes somewhere and doesn't come back out again. The last place he goes will tell us where he lives. So, Gammy, my boy, you take that twisted leg of yours and twist around until you know his name—or else, I'll twist your ears good and proper, I will.'"

"And so?"

"And so I twisted around and I found out the pretty guy's name."

"And how did you do that?" the Schoolmaster asked.

"Look, I'm not so dumb. The place this guy didn't come back out of was the one on rue de Chaillot, so I went to the doorkeeper there. He had powdered hair and a handsome brown suit with a yellow collar edged in silver. So I say to him like this, 'My good sir, I've come to get a hundred sous that the owner of this place promised me because I found his dog, a little black thing called Trumpet. And to prove it, the gentleman has brown hair, a black mustache, a whitish frock coat, and light blue pants, and he told me he lived at eleven rue de Chaillot and that his name was Dupont.' 'You're talking about my boss, but he's named Viscount de Saint-Remy, and the only dog here is you, you filthy street urchin. So get yourself out of here or I'll beat you up good and proper to teach you not to try to filch a hundred sous from me,' the doorkeeper says, and he kicks me one for good measure. But it's all the same to me," Gammy went on, philosophically. "I found out the name of the pretty guy with the black mustache who came to my boss to get human rat poison. His name was the Viscount de Saint-Remy—mee, mee, Saint-Remy," Red-Arm's son added, humming the last words, as he habitually did.

"You're so sweet, I could just eat you up, you little squirt," the Owl said, giving Gammy a kiss. "Isn't he a sly one? Really, you could be my own son, you scoundrel!"

These words impressed the little lame boy deeply. His wicked, sly, crafty expression suddenly became sad. He seemed to be taking the Owl's maternal gestures seriously and he said to her, "And I love you, too, I do, because the first time you came to look for me at my father's place, the Bleeding Heart, you kissed me. No one since my dead mama has ever held me. Everybody either kicks me or chases me away like a mangy dog. Everybody—even Old Lady Pipelet, the doorkeeper's wife."

"That old bag of bones, I'll teach her to act disgusted," the Owl said, giving out that she was revolted and taking Gammy in with the act.

"To throw a child's love back in his face like that . . ." And the one-eyed hag kissed Gammy again, with grotesque affection.

Red-Arm's son was deeply moved by this new demonstration of affection. He responded to it expansively, declaring gratefully, "You can tell me to do anything and you just watch how I'll do it! I'm really going to work for you!"

"Really? You do that and you won't be sorry for it."

"Oh! How I'd like to stay with you!"

"You be good and we'll see about that. You won't leave us two, my man."

"Right," said the Schoolmaster. "You'll lead me around like a poor blind man, you'll say you're my son, we'll sneak into homes. And then, by damn!" the murderer went on in a fit of anger. "I'll show that devil of a Rodolphe who put my eyes out that I'm not at the end of my rope yet! He took away my sight but he didn't take away my evil ways. I'll be the head, Gammy the eyes, and you, Owl, you'll be the hand. You'll help me, won't you?"

"I'm yours till the hangmen get us, Killer. When I got out of the hospital and I heard at the ogress's that you had sent for me from that dope from Saint-Mandé, didn't I come running to where you were staying with those country bumpkins, telling them I was your skirt?"

The one-eyed hag's words brought back a bad memory to the Schoolmaster. Suddenly changing his tone with the Owl, he cried out in rage, "God, I was bored, all alone with those honest types. At the end of a month, I couldn't stand it anymore. I was afraid. And then I had the idea to send for you to come get me. And look what good came of it!" he went on, getting more and more angry. "The day after you came, someone lifted the rest of the money that that devil in the allée des Veuves gave me. Yes, someone stole my belt full of gold while I was sleeping. Only you could have done that, and so here I am at your mercy. Really, every time I think about that, I don't know why I don't kill you where you stand, you old thief!" And he took a step toward the one-eyed hag.

"You watch out if you try to hurt the Owl," Gammy cried out.

"I'll crush both of you, you and her, like the evil vipers you are!" the bandit howled in rage. And, hearing Red-Arm's son talking next to him, he struck out blindly with his fist, a furious blow that would have killed Gammy if it had reached him.

Gammy, to get back at him both for himself and for the Owl, picked up a rock, took aim, and hit the Schoolmaster with it in the forehead. The blow wasn't dangerous but the pain it caused was sharp enough. The bandit rose up as terrible as a wounded bull. He took a few chance steps forward, but then he fell down.

"Reckless fool!" the Owl howled, laughing so hard she brought tears to her eyes. Although she was attached to this monster with ties of blood, she had good reasons for taking a sort of savage joy in the powerlessness of this man who had once been so fearsome and so proud of his herculean strength. The one-eyed hag, in her fashion, gave meaning to La Rochefoucauld's frightening adage that we always take some satisfaction in the suffering of our best friends.[79]

The hideous, yellow-haired, weasel-faced boy shared the one-eyed hag's mirth. When the Schoolmaster tripped again, he shouted out, "Open your eyes, old man, open your eyes! You're walking sideways, you're lurching about. Can't you see clearly? You need to clean your glasses better!"

When he found he couldn't reach the child, the murderer, with all his herculean strength, just stopped and stamped his foot with rage. He put his two enormous, hairy fists over his eyes and gave out a hollow growl like a muzzled tiger.

"You're coughing, old man!" Red-Arm's son said. "Wait, here's some delicious licorice that will help soothe your throat. A policeman gave it to me, so don't turn your nose up at it!" And he gathered up a fistful of fine sand and threw it in the face of the criminal.

This rain of gravel lashing his face was a new outrage, and the Schoolmaster suffered from it even more than he had from the rock hitting his forehead. Turning white with rage under his livid scars, he suddenly crossed his arms and stretched them out in a gesture of indescribable despair, and, lifting his terrifying face to the sky, he cried out, as if he were pleading, "My God! My God! My God!" Coming from someone who bore the taint of every kind of crime, before whom the most determined criminals had once trembled, this appeal for divine sympathy seemed almost poetic justice.

"Ha, ha! The scary killer with the big arms," the Owl cried out, snickering. "You're tongue-tied, my boy. You should be calling out to the baker of souls to help you."

"Give me a knife at least so I can kill myself. Since everyone is deserting me, at least a knife!" the wretch howled, biting his fists with savage fury.

"A knife? You have one in your pocket, Killer, and it's got a sharp edge. The old man in rue du Roule and the livestock merchant are telling the worms all about it, that's for sure."

Recognizing that he could carry out what he had threatened, the Schoolmaster suddenly changed his tone and went on in a hollow, whining voice, "The Slasher at least was good. He didn't steal from me. He pitied me."

"What makes you think I'm the one who made off with your loot?" the Owl went on, hardly able to stop herself from laughing.

"You're the only one who was in my room," said the bandit. "I was

---

79. François VI, Duke de la Rochefoucauld (1613–1680). He is the author of *Réflexions ou sentences et maximes morales*, usually translated into English simply as *Maxims*. [TN]

robbed the night you came back. Who do you think I should suspect? Those country people wouldn't do something like that."

"Why can't country people make off with things just like anyone else? Just because they drink milk and get their rabbits from the fields?"

"Well, after all is said and done, it's still the case that someone robbed me."

"And why is that the Owl's fault? Well, let's think this one over. If I had filched your stuff, why would I have stuck around afterward? You're a fool. Sure, I'd have cleaned you of your money if I could have, but, word of honor, once I'd used up every penny, I'd have come right back, because, after all, you're so pretty with your all-white eyes! So be nice and stop gnawing your chompers like this."

"You'd think he was cracking nuts," Gammy said.

"Ha, ha, ha! The little kid's right. So calm down, old boy, and let him laugh. It's what kids do. And admit it, you're not being fair. Here's the tall guy in mourning who looks like a gravedigger, who comes to me and says, 'Here's a thousand francs for you if you kidnap a girl on a farm in Bouqueval and if you bring her to me where I tell you to in the Saint-Denis plain.' So tell me, Killer, didn't I ask you in on the job right away when I could have chosen someone who can still see? Anyone would say I'm giving you a handout. Except for holding the little girl while Gammy and us pack her up, you're about as good to me as a fifth wheel on a wagon. But that's fine with me. Even though I would have stolen from you if I could, I like to be nice to you. I like it that you owe everything to your dear old Owl. 'Cause that's just who I am! We'll give two hundred smackers to Fishhook for driving the cart and for having come here once before with one of the servants of the big man in mourning so he could learn where we had to hide to wait for the little girl. And that leaves us eight hundred smackers for us two to make merry with. So what do you say about that? Are you still angry at your old lady?"

"Who's to say you'll pay up once the job's done?" the criminal said, still gloomy and suspicious.

"I could give you nothing, it's true, because I've got you like a chicken in the oven, my boy, just like I once had Songbird. So you're just going to have to fry the way I want you to until the baker of souls puts you in his oven, hee, hee, hee! So, Killer, are you still going to sulk at your old Owl?" the one-eyed hag added, clapping the criminal on the shoulder. He stood there, silent and overcome.

"You're right," he said, sighing in deep anger. "That's what's left to me. Me! Me! At the mercy of an old woman and a little kid who I could once have crushed like bugs. Oh, if only I weren't so afraid of dying!" he said, falling back on the embankment.

"So you're gutless now! You're gutless!" the Owl said, scornfully. "Pretty soon you'll be talking about the little goody-two-shoes voice in your head. That'd be even funnier. Really, if you haven't any more courage than that, I'll just pick up and leave you."

"So I'll never be able to avenge myself against that man who tortured me this way and left me in this awful state, and I'm stuck in it forever!" The Schoolmaster howled, his rage intensifying. "Oh, I really am afraid of death! It's true, it scares me. But if someone came and said to me, 'I'll deliver this man into your hands—into your hands—and then, afterward, I'll cast you into a pit,' I'd say, 'Go ahead and throw me in, yes, because I'd make sure not to let him go before hitting bottom.' And while we were falling, I'd tear the flesh from his face with my teeth; I'd get my teeth into his neck too and I'd eat out his heart. I'd kill him with my teeth because I wouldn't want to leave the job to a mere knife!"

"That'll be great, Killer. That's how I like to see you. Calm down. We'll find him again, that wretch of a Rodolphe, and the Slasher, too. When I got out of the hospital, I wandered around the allée des Veuves. Everything's closed up. So I said to the tall man in mourning, 'A while ago, you wanted to pay us to do something to that monster of a Rodolphe. After this job with the girl, couldn't we cook something up against him?' 'Maybe,' he told me. Did you hear that, Killer? Maybe. Take heart, my boy, we'll eat Rodolphe's heart out, you take my word for it. We'll eat it out of him!"

"Really? You won't desert me?" the criminal said to the Owl, submissive but still distrustful. "Because if you desert me now, what will become of me?"

"That's how it is. So you think about it, Killer. What a good joke it would be if the two of us, Gammy and me, made off with the cart and left you here in the middle of the fields tonight! The cold's gonna bite hard! That would be really funny—wouldn't it, tough guy?"

The Schoolmaster trembled at this threat. He came up to the Owl and said to her, cowering, "No, no, you wouldn't do that, Owl—not you, not Gammy. That would be too mean."

"Ha, ha, ha! Too mean! What a simpleton! And the little old man in rue du Roule! And the livestock merchant! And the woman in the Saint-Martin canal! And the man in the allée des Veuves! Do you think they thought you such a loving fellow, you with your big knife? Why shouldn't it be your turn to be the butt of the joke?"

"Okay, I'll admit it," the Schoolmaster said in a hollow tone. "Let's see: I was wrong to suspect you, I was also wrong to want to beat Gammy. I ask your pardon, do you hear? And you, too, Gammy. Yes, I ask you both to pardon me."

"Well, I think he should be on his knees when he asks forgiveness for having wanted to beat Owl," said Gammy.

"What a little beggar! He is funny!" the Owl said, laughing. "But, all the same, he makes me want to see what your mug would look like if you had to do that, my man. Get going, get on your knees. Make like you were whispering sweet nothings to your old Owl. And hurry up or we'll leave you here. And in half an hour it'll be nighttime, I can tell you."

"What difference does night or day make to him?" Gammy said, taunting him. "This one always has his shutters closed. He's scared of ruining his milky complexion."

"Here I am on my knees. I ask your pardon, Owl, and you, too, Gammy. Well, then, are you happy now?" said the criminal, kneeling in the middle of the road. "So now you won't leave me here, right?"

Framed by the gulley's embankment, lit by the orange-red of the setting sun, this strange group was a hideous sight. On his knees begging in the middle of the road, the Schoolmaster was stretching out his two powerful hands toward the Owl. His thick, wiry hair was falling across his pallid forehead like the mane of a horse. His red eyelids, completely open in fear, left his motionless, dull, glassy dead pupils partially visible. It was like a corpse looking at you. His powerful shoulders were hunched in humility. This Hercules knelt, trembling, at the feet of an old woman and a child.

Wrapped in her red tartan shawl, wearing an old black tulle hat, with a few strands of gray hair hanging out from under it, the one-eyed hag stood tall over the Schoolmaster. This old woman's face, with its hooked nose, in all its bony, weathered, wrinkled, sagging glory, was lit up with a savage and disdainful joy. Her one wild eye glinted like a hot coal. A sinister grimace pulled her lips back, revealing some long facial hairs and three or four loose yellow teeth.

Gammy, his shirt cinched by a leather belt, leaned on the Owl's arm to keep his balance as he stood on one foot. The child's sickly, sly face, with its color as yellow as his hair, at this moment showed a devilish, mocking ill will.

The gully's steep slope cast a shadow that only intensified the horror of this scene, which the night's growing darkness had started to obscure.

"So at least promise me that you won't leave me here!" the Schoolmaster repeated. The Owl and Gammy were enjoying his fear, and their silence only frightened him more. "Are you still here?" the murderer went on, leaning forward and automatically stretching out his arms.

"Yes, yes, my boy, we're still here. Don't be frightened. Abandon you! I'd rather kiss the reaper. Once and for all, I want to convince you, so I'll tell you why I won't ever leave you. So listen up. I've always loved having someone who can feel the pain of my nails—animal or human. Before Miss Lowlife (and let me get my hands on her again, I know what I'll do—I'll clean her face with acid)—before Miss Lowlife, I had a kid, and the pain I dealt him made him a little too cold, so I got the cooler for six years. While I was there, I tortured birds. I tamed them and then pulled their feathers off while they were alive. But it was hardly worth it, they barely lasted long enough. When I left prison, I got my claws into Songbird. But that little beggar escaped while she still had enough life left in her to be entertaining. After her, I got a dog and I made it suffer as much as she had. In the end, I cut off one back paw and one front paw. That made it look so funny that I almost split my gut laughing."

"I've got to try that on a dog I know that bit me," Gammy said to himself.

"When I met you, my boy," the Owl went on, "I was tearing apart a cat, slowly. And so now you're gonna be my cat, my dog, my bird, my Miss Lowlife. You're gonna be the thing I torture now. Get it, my boy? Instead of a bird or a child to torment, I've got like a wolf or a tiger, and that's really the cat's whiskers, isn't it?"

"You old witch!" the Schoolmaster howled, getting up in a rage.

"Here you go again, sulking at your old woman! So get up and leave—you can do what you want! I'm not tricking you into anything."

"Yeah, there's the door. Run away without seeing. Just keep going straight!" Gammy said, breaking out in laughter.

"Oh, I wish I would die!" the Schoolmaster moaned, his arms writhing.

"Now you're just going on and on. You already said that. But really, you can't be serious, you're as sturdy as an iron bridge. So give it a rest. You're gonna live to make your Owl happy. I'll torture you a bit from time to time because that's my joy in life and you have to earn your keep from me. But if you're nice, you'll get to help me pull off good jobs like now. And there'll be better ones where you can make yourself useful. But you're my dog now. When I say 'Come!' you'll come. When I say 'Bite!' you'll bite. But look, my boy, I won't force you into anything. If you don't want the life I'm offering, just choose another: do you want an income? Wanna roll along in big carriages with a pretty little woman, be awarded the Cross of Honor, be named high court judge, see clearly instead of being blind? Well, don't get upset. It's easy—all you have to do is ask and we'll serve it for you piping hot. Right, Gammy?"

"Hot, boiling hot, and right away!" Gammy answered, snickering. But then he bent down on the ground and said in a low voice, "I hear steps in the path. Let's hide. It's not the girl, because whoever it is is coming from the same direction she came in."

And in fact, after a few minutes, a vigorous country woman, in the prime of life, appeared, carrying a basket on her head and followed by a large dog. She crossed the gully and took the same path that Songbird and the priest had followed.

We will return to Songbird and the priest now, leaving our three plotters hiding out in ambush on the sunken road.

CHAPTER 2

THE RECTORY

The sun's last rays slowly flickered out behind the imposing hulk of the château of Écouen and the woods that surrounded it; the immense plains, whose brown furrows were hardened by the cold, stretched out as far as the eye could see. The hamlet of Bouqueval seemed to be an oasis in this vast wasteland. A perfectly calm sky was streaked with the purple rays of sunset, a sure sign that wind and cold were in the offing. First bright red, these tints turned violet as the twilight advanced. The slender crescent moon, as thin as the half of a silver ring, began shining gently in the middle of the shadowy blue sky. At this solemn hour, an absolute silence reigned.

The priest stopped on the hill for a moment to enjoy the view of this beautiful night. After a few minutes of meditation, stretching his hand out to the depths of a horizon partially veiled with the night fog, he said to Fleur-de-Marie, who walked next to him, deep in thought, "Look, my child, at this limitless immensity. You can't hear a sound. It seems to me that this silence and infinite view give us some notion of eternity. I'm telling you this, Marie, because you are sensitive to the beauties of creation. I have often been touched by the religious awe they inspire in you—you who were denied them for so long. Aren't you as struck as I am by the overwhelming calm that rules over everything at this moment?"

Songbird didn't answer. Surprised, the priest looked at her and saw that she was crying. "What's wrong with you, my child?"

"Father, I am so unhappy!"

"Unhappy? You are unhappy right now?"

"I know I shouldn't be complaining about what has happened to me after everything you all have done for me . . . and yet . . ."

"And yet?"

"Oh, Father, pardon my sadness. I know it might show ingratitude toward my benefactors."

"Listen, Marie, we have often asked you the reasons for the sadness that overcomes you sometimes. It really worries your foster mother. You avoid answering us, and we respect your secret, even though it sorrows us not to be able to comfort you in your pain."

"Alas, Father, I can't explain what I feel. A moment ago, I was moved, just like you, at the sight of this calm, sad night. And it broke my heart and I started to cry."

"But what's wrong, Marie? You know how much we all love you. Come now, tell me everything. Moreover, I can tell you that the day is coming soon when Madame Georges and Monsieur Rodolphe will take you before the baptismal fountain to vow to be your protectors forever."

"Monsieur Rodolphe? The man who saved my life?" Marie cried out, clasping her hands together. "He would really do that for me! Now I can't hold anything back from you—I could never be such an ingrate!"

"An ingrate? What do you mean?"

"To explain, I have to go back to the first days after I came to the farm."

"I'm listening. We can talk about this as we walk along."

"You will be indulgent with me, won't you, Father? What I'm going to tell you may be really very sinful."

"The Lord has shown you how merciful he is. Take heart."

"After I came here, when I knew that I would never have to leave the farm and Madame Georges," Fleur-de-Marie said, after a moment of thoughtfulness, "I thought I was living in a dream. At first my happiness was intoxicating. I kept thinking about Monsieur Rodolphe. Often, when I was alone, despite myself, I looked up into the heavens to try to see him there and thank him. In the end—and I know it was sinful, Father—I thought more about him than about God; because, after all, he had done more for me than God ever had. I was happy—happy like someone who had escaped something terrible forever. You and Madame Georges were so good to me that I thought myself more to be pitied than at fault." The priest looked at Songbird with surprise. Then she went on, "Little by little, I got used to this sweet life. When I woke up, I no longer was afraid that I was still at the ogress's place. I felt I could sleep safely, if you understand what I mean. All my joy in life was to help Madame Georges in the work around the farm and to study hard at the lessons you gave me, Father—and also to become better because of your encouragement. Except for when I felt shameful every now and then, when I thought of the past, I felt myself as good as anybody else in the world, because everyone was good to me. Then, one day—" And Fleur-de-Marie broke off in tears.

"Come along, calm yourself, my poor child. Take heart and go on with your story."

Songbird wiped her eyes and continued, "You remember, Father, that around the time of All Saints' Day, Madame Dubreuil, who manages the Duke de Lucenay's farm in Arnouville, came to visit here with her daughter?"

"Of course. And it gave me the greatest pleasure to see you make the acquaintance of Clara Dubreuil; she has so many good qualities."

"She's an angel, Father, an angel. When I knew that she was going to stay on the farm for a few days, I was happy beyond all measure. I thought of nothing else except when I would see this friend I wanted so much. Finally, she came. I was in my room, the room I was going to share with her. I dressed myself in my best; I was sent for. As I came into the room, my heart was beating. Madame Georges pointed to this pretty young person, who seemed so gentle and modest and good, and she said to me, 'Marie, here is a friend for you.' 'And I hope that you and my daughter will be like sisters to each other soon,' Madame Dubreuil added. Hardly were these words out of her mother's mouth than Mademoiselle Clara came running up to kiss me. Well, Father," said Fleur-de-Marie, crying, "I don't know what came over me . . . but, suddenly, when I felt Clara's pure, fresh face press up against my withered cheek, my cheek became so hot with shame—with remorse—I remembered what I had been. Me! Me, receiving the affection of this young person who was so pure! Oh! It seemed to me the worst kind of trickery, a terrible travesty."

"But, my child—"

"Oh, Father," Fleur-de-Marie cried, interrupting the priest with a pained sigh, "when Monsieur Rodolphe took me out of the Cité, I was already vaguely aware of how degraded I was. But can you really believe when you and Madame Georges enlightened me with the education you gave me, the advice you gave me, the examples you were for me, can you really believe, alas, that that wouldn't also make me understand that I was more guilty than merely unfortunate? Before Clara came, when such thoughts tortured me, I made myself forget by trying to make you and Madame Georges happy with me, Father. If I blushed at my own past, it was only in my own eyes. But then this young person, who was exactly my age, came, and she was so young and so virtuous that I could immediately see the gulf that would exist forever between her and me. For the first time, I came to feel that there are stains that can never be washed away. Since then, I can't stop thinking about it. Despite myself, I can't stop dwelling on it; since that day, really, I haven't had a moment of rest." And Songbird wiped away the tears that were filling her eyes.

After looking with tender sympathy at her for a few moments, the priest said, "But consider, my child, if Madame Georges wanted to see you and Mademoiselle Dubreuil become friends, it's because she knew that the life you were now leading made you worthy of such a connection. The reproaches you are making of yourself amount to reproaches of your foster mother."

"I know that, Father, and I must be wrong. But I haven't been able to get over my shame and my fear. And that's not all—but it's hard to tell everything."

"Go on, Marie. Up to now, your scruples, or rather your remorse, only do you credit."

"Once Clara was settled on the farm, I was as sad as I had at first been happy when I thought about the pleasure of having a friend of my own age. Clara, on the other hand, was all smiles. We made up a bed for her in my room. The first night, after she got into bed, she kissed me and told me that she felt so close to me already, that she already loved me; she told me to call her Clara and she would call me Marie. And then she started to pray, telling me that she was adding my name to those she prayed for and asking me if I would pray for her as well. I could hardly refuse her that. After we talked for a little while, she went to sleep. I hadn't gotten into bed yet; I walked up to her; crying, I looked at her angelic face; and then, at the thought that she was sleeping in the same room as me, me who had slept under the ogress's roof, with thieves and murderers, I shivered as if I had committed some sin. I had vague fears . . . it seemed to me that God would punish me one day. When I went to bed, I had terrible dreams. I saw once more those awful faces that I thought I had forgotten: the Slasher, the Schoolmaster, the Owl, that one-eyed woman who tortured me when I was a child. God, what a night! What a night! The dreams I had!" Songbird said, still trembling at the memory of it.

"Poor Marie!" responded the priest, who had been deeply moved. "Why didn't you tell me these things earlier? I would have comforted you. But go on."

"It was very late before I got to sleep. Mademoiselle Clara came to wake me up with a kiss. To overcome what she called my reserve and to prove her friendship for me, she wanted to tell me a secret: when she reached the age of eighteen, she was supposed to marry the son of one of Goussainville's farmers, a young man she loved dearly. The two families had agreed upon the marriage a long time ago. And then, in a few words, she told me the story of her life. It was a simple, calm, happy life; she had never been apart from her mother and she never would be since her fiancé would join Monsieur Dubreuil in the management of their farm. 'Now, Marie,' she said, 'you know me like a sister would; so tell me about your life.' When she said this, I thought I would die of shame. I blushed, I stuttered. I didn't know what Madame Georges had said about me and I was afraid of contradicting her. I said vaguely that I was an orphan and had been raised by cruel people and so my childhood had not been a happy one. I told her I had only begun to be happy when I started to live with Madame Georges. And then, more from sympathy than from idle curiosity, Clara asked where I had been raised, in the country or the city? Who was my father? And she asked especially whether I remembered my mother. Each of these questions hurt and embarrassed me because I could only answer them with falsehoods, and you have taught me, Father, how great a sin lying is. But Clara couldn't imagine that I would try to deceive her. Clara believed me; she thought I was slow to answer because my childhood memories were so sad and she pitied me with a goodness that broke my heart. Oh, Father! You'll never know how much I suffered during this talk. It was so painful not to be able to say anything that wasn't hypocritical and false."

"You poor girl! God's anger will surely come down heavily on all those who forced you into that abominable life of sin. It's because of them that you may well suffer your entire life from the inexorable consequences of one early false step!"

"Oh, yes, Father! They were really wicked," Fleur-de-Marie responded bitterly, "because I will never lose my shame. And that's not all. When Clara spoke to me of the happiness that awaited her, of her marriage, of her loving family, I couldn't stop comparing my future to hers; because despite all the good things I have been given recently, I will always be wretched in the end. In teaching me what virtue means, you and Madame Georges have also taught me how debased my past was. Nothing can change the fact that I belonged to the vilest dregs of society. Alas! If the knowledge of good and evil must be so horrible for me, why didn't you all leave me to my fate!"

"Oh, Marie, Marie!"

"Didn't I tell you, Father? What I am telling you is sinful, isn't it? Alas! This is what I have never been able to admit to you. Yes, sometimes I am such a wretch that I misjudge the goodness that has befallen me and say, 'If only no one had removed me from that evil life! Then the wretchedness and the torment would have killed me quickly enough and at least I would have died not knowing anything about the purity I will now always lament having lost.'"

"Alas, Marie! This is the fate of us all! Any person sunk even for one day in the mire you were pulled out of—even a person to whom the Creator has been the most generous in his endowments—will always bear the marks of the experience. That is how God's eternal justice works!"

"So you understand, Father," Fleur-de-Marie cried out in pain, "I can look forward only to despair until the day I die."

"You can never hope to erase that horrible experience from your life," said the priest in a grave and sad voice, "but you must always hope for the infinite mercy of the All-Powerful One. Here on earth, my poor child, there may be only tears, remorse, and expiation, but one day, up there, above," he added, raising his hand to the heavens in which the stars were beginning to gleam, "there, above, there will be forgiveness and eternal joy."

"Take pity on me, my lord, take pity! I am so young and I may live for such a long time!" Songbird cried in a heart-wrenching voice as she fell unself-consciously to her knees before the priest.

The priest stood at the top of the hill over which the rectory hovered. His black cassock and his venerable face, framed by long gray hair, were gently lit up by the last rays of sunset. They stood out against a deep, limpid, transparent horizon, which was golden at the bottom, sapphire at the top. He raised one of his trembling hands to heaven and gave the other to Fleur-de-Marie, who covered it with tears. With the hood of her gray mantle lying back on her shoulders, the girl's enchanting profile was visible along with her charming, prayerful gaze bathed in tears. Her beautiful blond hair fell on her dazzlingly white neck.

By a strange coincidence, this grand and simple scene occurred at almost the same moment as the dreadful one between the Owl and the Schoolmaster was going on in the depths of the sunken road. The contrast between the two scenes was remarkable. Hidden in the shadows of a dark gulley, assailed by cowardly terrors, a fearful, violent criminal, already punished for his crimes, was also on his knees, but he kneeled before his partner in crime, a vengeful, mocking fury who tortured him mercilessly and goaded him toward further crimes—his partner in crime and the first tormentor of Fleur-de-Marie—Fleur-de-Marie, who was still in the grip of her unending remorse.

Is it not easy enough to comprehend her exaggerated misery? She had grown up since childhood among wicked, vile, degraded creatures. She left prison for the ogress's den and thus entered another dreadful prison. Never leaving the courtyard of this new jail or the labyrinthine streets of the Cité, this unfortunate girl had lived up to that point in complete ignorance of the good and the beautiful. She was as ignorant of noble and religious feelings as she was of the magnificent splendors of nature. And now, suddenly, she escapes her filthy sewer for a rustic and charming retreat; she escapes her foul existence to share a happy and peaceful life with people who are virtuous and who feel only the tenderest sympathy for her misfortunes.

In a word, everything admirable about humanity and about the world was suddenly revealed, all at once, to her startled soul. Her mind expanded before this imposing revelation, her intelligence grew, her noble instincts awakened. And from this expansion of mind, this growth of intelligence, this awakening of noble instinct, she became aware of her prior degradation and felt for her past life a painful and incurable horror. She understood—alas!—as she had said, that there are some stains that can never be cleansed.

"Oh, the horror of it!" Songbird moaned desperately. "Even if I were to live as long as you, Father, my entire life will be branded by my knowledge and memory of my past life. The horror of it!"

"On the contrary, the joy of it for you, Marie, the joy of it for you to whom the Lord sends this bitter but saving remorse. It shows that your soul is ripe for religious belief. If they were in your place, so many others less susceptible to these feelings than you would have forgotten their past life all too quickly so that they could attend only to their present good luck. A sensitive soul like yours suffers torments where ordinary people have no sense of pain. But each of these torments will count in your favor in heaven. Trust me, God left you only for a moment on that terrible path so that you could experience the glory of repentance and the eternal reward that expiation earns. Hasn't he himself said, 'Those who do good without a fight and who come to me with a smile on their lips, they are my elect; but those who, wounded from the struggle, come to me bleeding and bruised, those are the elect among my elect'?[80] So take heart, my child. You will lack for nothing. Help, support, advice—you will have them all. I am very old, but Madame Georges and Monsieur Rodolphe all have long lives ahead of them. Especially Monsieur Rodolphe, who has shown you so much sympathy, who follows your progress with such wise care. Can you really say, Marie, that you could ever regret having met him?"

Songbird was about to respond when she was interrupted by the country woman we mentioned before. She had followed the same road as the girl and the priest and had just caught up with them. She was one of the farmworkers.

"Please excuse me, Father," she said to the priest. "Madame Georges told me to bring this basket of fruit to the rectory. And that way, I can accompany Mademoiselle Marie back to the farm, because it's getting late. But I've got Turk with me," said the farm girl, patting a dog enormous enough to have braved a bear in a fight. "Even though you never run into trouble in this area, it's always good to be careful."

"You have done well, Claudine. Here we are at the rectory, in any case. Please thank Madame Georges for me." Then, turning to Songbird, he whispered to her gravely, "Tomorrow, I have to go to a meeting at the diocese, but I will be back at five o'clock. If you would like, my child, I will wait for you at the rectory. I can see from the state you're in that you still need to have a long talk with me."

"I thank you, Father," Fleur-de-Marie answered. "Since you are good enough to allow it, I'll come again tomorrow."

"Here we are already at the garden entry," said the priest. "Leave the basket there, Claudine. My housekeeper will get it. Go back to the farm with Marie quickly; night is almost here and it's getting colder by the moment. I'll see you tomorrow at five, Marie!"

"Until tomorrow, Father."

The priest went back into his garden. Songbird, Claudine, and Turk returned to the road leading back to the farm.

80. Although the priest's prior quotations have been from the Bible, we cannot trace this one. [TN]

CHAPTER 3

THE MEETING

A clear, cold night had fallen. The Owl, following the Schoolmaster's advice, had gone with him to a part of the sunken road that was farther away from the path and closer to the crossroad where Fishhook was waiting with the cab.

Gammy, stationed in advance of them, watched for Songbird's return. His role was to draw her into the ambush by begging her to come help him give aid to a poor old lady. Red-Arm's son had taken only a few steps outside the gulley to go to his post when, pricking up his ears, he heard Songbird in the distance talking to the country woman, who was walking along with her. Now that Songbird was not alone, the plan would no longer work. Gammy made haste to go back down into the gulley and run to Owl to warn her. "There's someone with the girl," he gasped, out of breath, in a whisper.

"I wish the guillotine would harvest the head of that beggar!" the Owl howled in fury.

"Who is she with?" the Schoolmaster asked.

"It must be the country woman who went down the path a moment ago, followed by the big dog. I recognized a woman's voice," said Gammy. "Listen . . . do you hear it? Do you hear the sound of their clogs?" And indeed, in the quiet night, one could hear the wooden soles clattering on the frozen earth from a long way off.

"There are two of them . . . I can take care of the little girl in the gray cloak, but what about the other one! What should we do? Killer here can't see, and Gammy isn't strong enough to muzzle the companion, devil take her! What should we do?" the Owl repeated.

"I may not be strong. But if you want, I'll throw myself between the legs of the country woman with the dog. I'll hang on to them with my hands—with my teeth if I have to. You'll see, I won't let her go! While I do that, you can carry off the little girl, Owl."

"And if they cry out or struggle, they'll be able to hear them from the farm," said the one-eyed hag, "and they'll have the time to get here and save them before we can reach Fishhook and his cab. It's not all that easy to carry off a woman while she's struggling with you."

"And they have that big dog with them!" said Gammy.

"Oh, bah! If that was all there was, I'd crack their dog's skull open with one good kick," said the Owl.

"They're getting closer," said Gammy, pricking up his ears anew at the footsteps, which were no longer far off. "They're coming down into the gulley."

"Well, say something, Killer," said the Owl to the Schoolmaster. "What do you think we should do, my crafty snake? Have you become dumb as well as blind?"

"There's nothing we can do today," the criminal responded.

"And the thousand francs from the guy in mourning," the Owl cried out. "They just go up in smoke? Sooner than that, your knife! Your knife, Killer! I'll kill the companion so she doesn't get in our way. As for the little girl, Gammy and me, the two of us will manage well enough to gag her."

"But the guy in mourning isn't paying us to kill anybody."

"Well, we'll just have to add it to the bill as an extra. He'll have to pay us since he's our accomplice."

"There they are! They're coming down into the sunken road," Gammy whispered.

"Give me your knife, I tell you!" the Owl repeated in a whisper, taking off her shoes as quickly as she could and ignoring Gammy. "I'll take off my shoes," she went on, "so I can take them by surprise, coming up silently behind them. It's already dark, but I'll recognize the little girl by her cloak and I'll ice the other one."

"No!" the criminal said. "This won't work today. We can always do it tomorrow."

"You're afraid, you coward!" the Owl said, with bitter scorn.

"No, I'm not frightened," the Schoolmaster answered, "but you might not pull it off, and then you'll ruin everything."

The dog with the country woman must have scented the people waiting in ambush in the sunken road. He started to bark ferociously and paid no attention to Songbird's repeated commands.

"Do you hear their dog? Here they are. Quick, your knife—or else!" the Owl screamed, threatening him.

"Come here and take it—just try!" the Schoolmaster said.

"It's all over—it's too late!" the Owl cried, after she had listened carefully for a moment. "They've already gone by. You'll pay for this! Go to the devil!" she added in a rage, shaking her fist at her partner. "We've lost a thousand francs because of you!"

"Say, instead, we'll make a thousand, two thousand, maybe three thousand," the Schoolmaster said in an authoritative tone. "Just listen to me, Owl, and you'll see whether I was wrong not to give you my knife. You go back to Fishhook. Then the two of you will go in his coach to keep the appointment with the guy in mourning. You'll tell him that we couldn't manage it today but that, tomorrow, she'll be kidnapped."

"And what about you?" the Owl murmured, still angry.

"Just keep listening. The little girl takes the priest back every night all by herself. It was just chance that she ran into someone tonight. More than likely, we'll have better luck tomorrow. So tomorrow you and Fishhook, with his coach, will come back to this crossroad."

"Sure, but what about you? What about you?"

"Gammy will take me to the farm where the little girl lives. He'll say that we're lost, that I'm his father, a poor mechanic blinded in an accident; he'll say we're going to Louvres, to someone in our family who has offered to help us, and that we got lost in the countryside looking for a shortcut. We'll ask to spend the night there in some corner of the barn. No one ever turns down a request like that. The farmers will believe us and give us a place to sleep. Gammy will carefully go over all the doors, windows, and other entrances to the house. People like this always have money in the house when the farm rents are due. I once owned property like that," he added bitterly, "and I know all about it. It's the middle of January now, and that's the right time. Now is when the rent's come due. You say the farm is in an isolated location. Once we know all the entrances and exits, we can come back here with friends. This is a job that needs to be cooked up carefully."

"Always the wise old serpent—always the prof!" the Owl said, softening up. "Go on, Killer."

"Tomorrow morning, instead of leaving the farm, I'll complain of some kind of pain that would stop me from walking. If they don't believe me, I'll show them the sore I've had ever since I broke my shackle, which really still does cause me trouble. I'll say it's a burn I gave myself with a red-hot iron bar, working as a mechanic—they'll believe me. That way, I'll stay at the farm for a good part of the day and Gammy will have more time to look things over carefully. When night comes and it's time for the little girl to go out, I'll say that I'm better and that I'm in shape to leave the farm. Gammy and I, we'll follow the girl from a distance and we'll come back here, outside the gulley, to wait for her. She'll know us and she won't suspect anything when she sees us. We'll jump her—me and Gammy—and once she's in my reach, she's sunk, I can tell you, and we'll have our thousand francs. And that's not all. In two or three days, we can hand over the farm job to Fishhook and the others, and we'll all divvy it up afterward, if there's anything to be had. After all, we cooked the plan up."

"You know, no-eyes, there's no one like you," said the Owl, kissing the Schoolmaster. "But what if, by chance, the little girl doesn't bring the priest back tomorrow night?"

"We'll start all over again the day after tomorrow. This is a dish you eat cold and slowly. And besides, all that will just add charges to the bill we give to the guy in mourning. Also, once I'm at the farm, I'll be able to figure out from what I hear whether the plan we've worked out for kidnapping the little girl will work. If it won't, we can figure out another one."

"This will work, my boy. That plan is a really sharp one! You know, Killer, even if you became completely disabled, you'd just have to make yourself a consulting crook and you'd still make as much money as a jailhouse mouthpiece. So come kiss your Owl and then get going. These farmer types go to sleep as early as chickens. I'll manage to catch up with Fishhook again. Tomorrow at four o'clock, we'll be here at the crossroad with him and his wheels—unless he's arrested for knocking off the dairymaid's husband on rue de la Vieille-Draperie. But if we're not here with him, it'll be here with someone else, that's all. After all, the fake cab belongs to the guy in mourning, and he's already used it. Fifteen minutes after we get to the crossroad, I'll be waiting for you here."

"It's agreed, then. Until tomorrow, Owl."

"But I've completely forgotten to give Gammy some wax. What if there's something on the farm we need an impression of! Do you know how to use it, deary?" the one-eyed hag asked as she gave Gammy a small piece of wax.

"Yeah, sure, of course—my dad showed me how. I got the impression off a little iron box for him, one my boss the charlatan kept in his black office."

"Well, that works out well, then. And don't forget to wet the wax after you've warmed it up in your hands so it doesn't stick."

"Yeah, I know all that!" Gammy answered. "But, look, I'm doing everything you tell me because—well, because you love me a little bit, don't you, Owl?"

"Of course I love you! I love you as if you were my child by the late, great Napoléon!" the Owl said, kissing Gammy, who was pleased beyond all measure by this imperial comparison. "Until tomorrow, Killer."

"Until tomorrow," the Schoolmaster answered.

The Owl went to find the cab. The Schoolmaster and Gammy climbed out of the sunken road and went in the direction of the farm, guided by the light shining from its windows.

What a strange fate that brought together Anselme Duresnel and the wife he hadn't seen since he had been condemned to hard labor!

CHAPTER 4

THE NIGHT BEFORE

Is there anything more pleasing to the eye than a large farm's kitchen at the moment of the evening meal, especially in wintertime? Is there anything that better shows the calm and well-being of rustic life? The sight of the farm at Bouqueval's kitchen is proof enough of this claim.

Its gigantic fireplace—six feet high and eight feet wide—looked like a large picture window opening onto a roaring fire. A veritable pyre of beechwood and oak blazed on its black hearth. This fiery inferno not only heated the kitchen but lit up every corner of it. It made the lamp that hung from the main beam crossing the room completely superfluous.

Large pots and red copper saucepans, scrubbed to a bright shine, stood next to each other on the shelves. An old-style shone, also of red copper, water jug like a dazzling mirror. Next to it, a carefully polished bread box sent forth the appetizing smell of freshly baked bread, still hot from the oven. In the middle of the room stood a heavy table, covered with a meticulously clean, rough canvas tablecloth. Each worker's place was marked by an earthenware bowl that was brown on the outside, white within, and by iron utensils that shone like silver.

In the middle of the table, a large tureen filled with vegetable soup steamed like the mouth of a volcano. Under that savory cloud rested a gigantic dish of sauerkraut and ham and a no less gigantic bowl of lamb and potato stew. Finally, the spread was completed by a quarter of a roasted veal, flanked by two winter salads pushing up against two baskets of apples and two more of cheese. Two or three jars of sparkling cider and as many round loaves of brown bread, large as millstones, lay within easy reach of each worker.

A black griffin of an almost toothless old sheepdog, the reigning elder of the canine species on the farm, lay down by the corner of the fireplace. Having earned this privilege by reason of his great age and long service, he nevertheless took only modest and discreet advantage of it, lying there with his head on his two forepaws and watching carefully the various culinary activities that preceded the supper. This venerable animal responded to the very unbucolic name of Lysander.

This normal evening meal, simple as it was, may seem more than usually sumptuous for farmworkers like these, but Madame Georges, following Rodolphe's policies, worked to improve the life of her workers as much as possible. She chose them exclusively from among the most honest and industrious of the workers in the neighborhood, paying them generously and making their days enviably happy. As one might expect, all the best workers in the area had the ambition to become tenants of the Bouqueval farm. An innocent enough ambition, it was even more praiseworthy in that it sparked a competition among all the local workers that redounded to the benefit of all their masters since only the best references would serve to gain one of the vacant positions on the Bouqueval farm.

Thus, on a very small scale, Rodolphe had created a model farm whose benefits, according to his aims, were not merely the improvement of the stock and the modes of cultivation, but, most important, of the people of the area. And he had achieved this end by giving these people a reason to be honest, active, and intelligent.

Having finished all the preparations for the supper, the cook put a jug of wine to accompany the dessert on the table and rang the dinner bell. On hearing this welcome call, field hands, house servants, milkmaids, and girls who worked in the farmyard, twelve to fifteen in all, cheerfully came into the kitchen. The men were manly and openhearted, the women healthy and attractive, the girls lively and happy. All their peaceful expressions radiated good humor, serenity, and contentment with their place in life. They sat down with the simple sense of doing honor to this meal which they had earned by the hard work they had done that day.

An old white-haired worker sat at the head of the table. He had an honest face, a frank and open look, and a slightly mocking tone: he was the epitome of the farmer who is endowed with good sense and an intelligence at once firm and straightforward, clear and precise, rustic and sly. One could tell from a mile off that he was a Gaul of the old stock. Old Châtelain, which was this Nestor's name, had worked on this farm since his childhood, and was now the head field hand. When Rodolphe bought the farm, the old worker had come highly recommended, and rightly so; Rodolphe kept him on and made of him something of a chief, under the orders of Madame Georges, of all the agricultural work. As a result of his age, his knowledge, and his experience, Old Châtelain exercised considerable influence over all the workers on the farm.

All the farmworkers took their seats at the table. After having said grace, Old Châtelain, following an old and sacred custom, outlined a cross on one of the loaves of bread with a knife and then cut off a piece. This bit represented "the Virgin's share," or the share of the poor; with the same invocation, he poured a glass of wine and then put the bread and wine on a plate and placed it, piously, in the middle of the table.

At this moment, the watchdogs started barking furiously. Old Lysander answered with a low growl and lifted his lip to bare a couple of still respectable-looking fangs.

"There's someone at the courtyard walls," said Old Châtelain, and the words were hardly out of his mouth when the bell of the large door rang out. "Who could be there this late?" the old worker wondered. "Everyone is within the walls. Well, go see who it is, Jean-René." Jean-René, a young farmworker, left the kitchen after putting down his soup spoon with some regret. He had been blowing on it with a force that would have put Aeolus to shame.

"This is the first time in a long while that Madame Georges and Mademoiselle Marie haven't sat by the fire to be with us during our dinner," Old Châtelain said. "I'm plenty hungry, but I'll eat with less appetite because of it."

"Madame Georges is upstairs with Mademoiselle in her room. When she returned from taking the priest home, she felt a little ill and went to bed," answered Claudine, the strong girl who had brought Songbird back from the rectory and had thus, without knowing it, overturned Owl's sinister plan.

"I hope our good Mademoiselle Marie is just a little under the weather and not really ill," the old worker said in a worried tone.

"No, no, thank God, Old Châtelain! Madame Georges said it was nothing," Claudine said. "Otherwise she would have sent to Paris to call for Monsieur David, the black doctor who first took care of Mademoiselle Marie when she was ill. Say what you like, a black doctor is really odd! If I were the patient, I wouldn't be so sure of him. A white doctor, now we're talking—that's Christian."

"Didn't Monsieur David cure Mademoiselle Marie the last time when she was in such a weak state?"

"Indeed he did, Old Châtelain."

"Well, then?"

"Say what you will, I still think a black doctor has something frightening about him."

"Didn't he get old Annie back on her feet after she'd injured her legs? Remember, she hadn't even been able to get out of bed for three years?"

"That's true, Old Châtelain."

"Well, then, my girl?"

"I agree, Old Châtelain. All the same, a black doctor—think about it. Black, black all over."

"Listen, young woman. What color is your heifer Musette?"

"She's white, Old Châtelain, white as a swan, and she gives a remarkable amount of milk. You can say that and not have to blush."

"And your heifer Rosette?"

"Black as a crow, and she also gives a remarkable amount of milk. You have to be fair to everyone."

"And what color is the milk your black heifer gives?"

"It's white, of course, Old Châtelain. What else would it be but white as snow?"

"Even though Rosette is black?"

"Even though Rosette is black. What does it matter to the color of the milk whether the cow is black, brown, or white?"

"It doesn't matter at all?"

"Not one little bit, Old Châtelain."

"Well, so, then, my girl! Why don't you think a black doctor can't be as good as a white one?"

"Well, really, Old Châtelain, it's a matter of skin color," the girl said after a moment of profound concentration. "But really, in fact, since black Rosette gives milk as good as white Musette's, the skin must not mean much."

Jean-René's return interrupted Claudine's anatomical analyses on the differences between the white and black races. He was blowing on his fingers with the same force with which he'd blown on his soup. "It sure is cold! It's one cold night! It's freezing enough to break rocks," he said, coming in. "You really want to be inside rather than out in weather like this. It's cold out there!"

"A frost that begins with an east wind is always hard and long. You should know that, my boy. But who is ringing?" the chief worker asked.

"A poor blind man and a child leading him, Old Châtelain."

CHAPTER 5

HOSPITALITY

"So what does this blind man want?" Old Châtelain asked Jean-René.

"That poor man and his son have gotten lost trying to go to Louvres by the shortcut. Since it's so cold out, the night's so dark and the sky so cloudy, the blind man and his son are asking if they can spend the night at the farm in the stable somewhere."

"Madame Georges is too kind ever to refuse hospitality to someone in want. She will certainly want to give those poor people a place to sleep, I'm sure, but we'll have to let her know. Go and tell her, Claudine." And Claudine left.

"Where is this good man waiting?" asked Old Châtelain.

"In the small barn."

"Why did you put him in the barn?"

"If he stayed in the yard, the dogs would have eaten him alive, him and his kid. Sure, Old Châtelain, I tried to say, 'Good dog, Rex. Here, Turk. Down, Sultan!' For all the good it did. Such a bunch of badly behaved dogs I've never seen! And yet, on this farm, we don't train them to attack poor people, the way they do in lots of other places."

"Indeed, friends, it's come to us to take care of these people for good and all tonight. Move a little closer together—good! Let's put two more place settings at the table, one for the blind man, the other for his son. Surely Madame Georges will let them spend the night here."

"Still, it's odd that the dogs should be so riled up," said Jean-René. "Especially Turk, the one Claudine brought with her on the way to the rectory—he was barking like he was possessed. When I petted him to calm him down, I could feel his hair literally standing up on his back, like he was a porcupine. What do you think about that, Old Châtelain? You know everything!"

"My boy, I may know everything, but animals know even more. After this autumn's hurricane turned the little river into a raging torrent, I was returning in the dark of night with my workhorses. Sitting on the old roan horse, I had no idea where the ford in the river was, since you couldn't see any more than you would in an oven! Well, I let go of the bridle on the old roan horse's neck, and he managed to find the way all on his own. No human being could have found it. Who taught him that?"

"Good question, Old Châtelain. Who could have taught that old roan horse to know that?"

"The same one who teaches swallows to build their nests on rooftops and wagtails to make theirs amid reeds, my boy. Well, Claudine," said the old oracle to the dairymaid who was returning with two sets of clean white sheets that smelled of sage and verbena. "I guess Madame Georges must have told you to give the poor blind man and his son some supper and let them sleep here, didn't she?"

"Here are some sheets to make their beds. They can sleep in the little bedroom at the end of the corridor," said Claudine.

"Go and get them, Jean-René. You, my girl, pull a couple of chairs up to the fire so they can warm up a bit before sitting down to eat. It's really cold out tonight."

And then the dogs started barking furiously all over again, and Jean-René tried to calm them down all over again. The door of the kitchen opened suddenly: the Schoolmaster and Gammy hurried in, as if they were being chased.

"Take care of your dogs!" the Schoolmaster cried out in fear. "They almost bit us!"

"They tore a piece out of my shirt!" said Gammy, still pale with terror.

"Please forgive us, my good man," said Jean-René as he closed the door. "I have never seen our dogs act up like this before. I'm sure it's the cold that's got them out of sorts. The poor animals don't have any reason. Maybe they thought it'd warm them up to take a bite out of you!"

"Hey, now it's the other one!" said the laborer, holding Lysander back just when, with a threatening growl, he was about to lunge upon the newcomers. "He heard the other dogs barking like crazy, now he wants to join in. Lie down, you bad dog! Lie down!"

At these words of Old Châtelain's, accompanied by a meaningful kick, Lysander returned, still growling, to his favored spot by the corner of the hearth. The Schoolmaster and Gammy stayed in the doorway to the kitchen, too scared to advance further.

Wrapped in a blue coat with a fur collar, his hat pulled down over the black cap that almost completely hid his forehead, the bandit held Gammy's hand. The boy was pressing up against him and looking askance at the peasants. The honesty of these faces disoriented and nearly frightened Red-Arm's son. Perverted characters have their own kinds of aversions and sympathies, too.

The Schoolmaster's features were so hideous that the inhabitants of the farm were instantly struck, some with disgust, some with fear. This impression did not escape Gammy; the fear of these peasants reassured him. He was proud of the dread his companion inspired in them. Once this first moment passed, Old Châtelain, thinking only of fulfilling the duties of the host, said to the Schoolmaster, "My good man, come and sit close by the fire. You can warm up a bit first and then eat with us. You came just as we were about to sit down to eat. Please, sit down there. But what was I thinking?" added Old Châtelain. "I should be talking to your son, not to you, because, alas, you're blind. Here, my child, bring your father to sit over by the fireplace."

"Yes, my good sir," answered Gammy, talking in a high-pitched, unctuous, and hypocritical tone. "May the good Lord reward you for your blessed charity! Follow me, poor Papa . . . follow me . . . be careful." And the boy guided the criminal.

The two reached the area near the fireplace. First Lysander emitted a low growl. But then, after catching the scent of the Schoolmaster, he suddenly released the sort of lugubrious howl that everyone knows means that the dogs are baying at the presence of death.

"Damnation!" said the Schoolmaster to himself. "Is it the blood they're smelling, these cursed beasts? These are the pants I was wearing the night I killed the livestock merchant."

"You know, it's weird," Jean-René said in a low voice. "Old Lysander is howling as if he's smelling death when he sniffs that man!"

Then something strange happened. Lysander's cries were so piercing, so plaintive, that the other dogs heard him (the farmyard was separated from the kitchen only by a glass window), and, as is common among the canine species, they outdid each other in choruses of lamentation. Even though they were not given to superstition, the farmworkers looked at each other with something approaching fear. And in fact, what was happening wasn't normal.

A man that they could not look upon without horror had set foot on the farm. Then the normally calm animals had become furious and were clamoring in the most sinister way—in a way that, according to popular beliefs, presaged the approach of death.

Even the criminal himself, in spite of his hardened character, in spite of his hellish daring, found himself shivering for a moment in fear as he heard the funereal, deathly howls that broke out upon his arrival—the arrival of a murderer.

Corrupted at his mother's breast, so to speak, Gammy, the skeptical, jaded child of Paris, was the only one who was unaffected by this scene. Once he was no longer afraid of being bitten, the mocking runt made fun of the scene that had stunned the farm's inhabitants and made the Schoolmaster shudder.

His first moment of shock gone by, Jean-René left the room, and soon the crack of his whip could be heard, letting Turk, Sultan, and Rex understand that their gloomy prognostications were no longer welcome. Gradually, the saddened faces of the laborers became calm once again. After a few moments, they ceased to fear the Schoolmaster's horrifying ugliness as much and began to pity it more. They pitied the little limping boy his infirmity and found his cunning face rather interesting. Most of all, they praised the tender care he showered on his father.

Forgotten momentarily, the laborers' appetite returned with a vengeance. For a few moments, the only sound to be heard was the noise of busy forks. As they did valiant battle with their country meal, the farm-workers, men and women alike, remarked with tenderness the way the child anticipated the blind man's needs. He had seated himself right next to the Schoolmaster. With seeming filial care, Gammy cut his food into bite-size pieces, sliced his bread, and kept his glass full.

That was the beautiful side of the coin. Here is the other side: Gammy's attentions came as much from cruelty as from the pleasure of acting that comes so naturally to boys his age. He took a sadistic pleasure in tormenting the Schoolmaster. In this, he followed the Owl's example. He was proud to imitate her, for he loved her with a kind of devotion. How could this perverse child feel the need to be loved? How could he feel happy to receive the semblance of affection the old hag displayed for him? How, finally, could he be moved by a distant memory of his mother's caresses? This was another one of the frequent and numerous anomalies that manage happily once in a while to militate against the monolithic quality of vice.

As we've said, like the Owl, the puny Gammy found exquisite charm in having a muzzled tiger at his disposal to abuse. Seated at the laborers' table, Gammy wanted, maliciously, to refine his pleasure by forcing the Schoolmaster to endure his abuse without flinching. Thus, he matched each of his ostensible attentions to his father with a sharp kick under the table aimed directly at an old wound the Schoolmaster, like many convicts, had on his right leg. This was the place where he had worn the leg iron that attached to his chains during his time in the penal colony.

Since, in order to make his position even more difficult, the little monster chose to kick him precisely when the Schoolmaster took a drink or tried to speak, the criminal needed that much more stoic courage to hide the suffering he felt at each attack. And still, his imperturbable calm did not betray him. Miraculously, he contained his anger and pain, thinking (and Red-Arm's son knew this very well) that it would put their plot in great danger if the laborers guessed what was going on under the table.

"Here, my poor Papa—here's a walnut. I got it all nice and clean for you," said Gammy as he put on the Schoolmaster's plate a morsel that he had carefully removed from its shell.

"Good, my child," said Old Châtelain. Then, turning to the bandit, he said, "You are surely much to be pitied, my good man, but your son is such a good boy that he must provide you with some consolation."

"Yes, yes, I am in a lot of pain; without the tenderness of my dear child . . . I . . ." The Schoolmaster could not keep himself from crying out sharply. Red-Arm's son had found the center of the wound, and the pain was intolerable.

"Oh, no! What's wrong, my poor Papa?" cried Gammy, tearfully. And, rising from his seat, he threw his arms around the Schoolmaster's neck.

In his first reaction of anger and rage, the criminal wanted to suffocate the little lame boy between his herculean arms. He pressed him so violently against his chest that the child, unable to breathe, let out a low moan. But upon remembering that he couldn't do without Gammy, the Schoolmaster stopped himself and threw him back into his chair.

As all of this was going on, the peasants saw only a tender exchange of love between a father and his son. Gammy's pallor and apparent inability to breathe seemed to them to be caused by the poor child's emotions.

"What's wrong with you, good man?" asked Old Châtelain. "Your cry just now made your child turn pale. Poor little kid. Hey, he's having trouble breathing!"

"Oh, he's fine," answered the Schoolmaster, regaining his composure. "I'm a locksmith and mechanic by profession, and a little while ago, while I was hammering a red-hot bar of iron, I dropped the iron on my legs, and I burned myself so badly that it still hasn't healed over. Just a moment ago I bumped into the table leg and I couldn't keep from shouting in pain."

"Poor Papa!" said Gammy, recovered from his fear and casting a diabolical gaze upon the Schoolmaster. "Poor Papa! It's true, good sirs, they were never able to fix his leg. Alas, never, never! Oh! I wish it could have been me who was suffering instead of him. If only he didn't have to suffer any more, poor Papa!"

The women looked tenderly at Gammy. "Well, my good man," said Old Châtelain, "it's too bad you didn't come to the farm three weeks ago instead of tonight."

"Why is that?"

"Because we had a doctor here with us for a few days, a doctor from Paris who has the very best remedy for leg problems. A sweet old woman from the village had been having trouble walking for three years; the doctor put his ointment on her wounds, and now she runs as fast as a Basque. She has sworn that she is going to make a pilgrimage on foot to the allée des Veuves to thank her savior. You know that's pretty far from here. But what's wrong with you now? Is that cursed wound acting up again?"

Those words, "allée des Veuves," brought back such terrible memories for the Schoolmaster that he could not keep from shuddering and contorting his hideous facial features. "Yes," he answered, pulling himself together. "Another shooting pain."

"Good old Papa, it's all right. Stay calm, and I'll wash your wound out carefully tonight," said Gammy.

"Poor little guy!" said Claudine. "He loves his father so much!"

"It's really a pity," said Old Châtelain, turning to the Schoolmaster, "that the worthy doctor isn't here right now. But I think he's just as charitable as he is wise. When you get back to Paris, have your little boy bring you to him at number seventeen on the allée des Veuves. He'll heal you, I'm sure. His address isn't difficult to remember: number seventeen, allée des Veuves. If you forget the number, I'm sure it doesn't matter. There can't be so many doctors in the area, especially not black doctors, because—can you believe it?—he's black, that excellent doctor, David."

The Schoolmaster's features were so covered with scars that no one could see how pale he had become. He had gone pale, however, frightfully pale, at the first mention of the address of Rodolphe's house, and then, when he heard David spoken of . . . David, the black doctor . . . the black doctor who, on Rodolphe's orders, had inflicted a dreadful torture upon him which continued to make his every moment an agony.

This had been a hard day for the Schoolmaster. In the morning, he had had to endure the torments inflicted on him by the Owl and Red-Arm's son. Then he got to the farm, and the dogs barked bloody murder at his homicidal look and wanted to eat him alive. Finally, fate had led him directly into a house in which his torturer had been staying a few days before.

Separately, these circumstances would have been enough, one after the other, to elicit either the criminal's rage or his fear. But coming so quickly over the course of a few hours, they dealt him a real blow. For the first time in his life he felt a sort of superstitious terror coming over him. He wondered whether such strange incidents could possibly be the result of mere chance.

Not noticing the Schoolmaster's condition, Old Châtelain went on. "In any case, my good man, when you leave, we'll give the address of the doctor to your son. And, moreover, Monsieur David always takes it as a favor when he can help someone. He's such a very kind man! It's too bad he seems so sad all the time, though. But let's drink to the health of your future savior!"

"Thank you, but I'm not thirsty anymore," said the Schoolmaster darkly.

"Oh, come on, drink, dear old Papa! Come on and drink—it'll do your poor stomach good!" Gammy added as he put the glass in the blind man's hand.

"No, no, I don't want to drink anymore," said the latter.

"I didn't fill your glass with cider this time. Instead I filled it with a good, old wine," said the laborer. "There are plenty of well-off types who've never had anything as good as this. Hey, this isn't just any old farm. What do you think of our daily fare?"

"It's very good," the Schoolmaster answered automatically, increasingly absorbed in his sinister thoughts.

"Well, then! We dine like this every day. Good work, good meals, a good conscience, and a good bed—that's our life, in a nutshell. There are seven of us farmers here, and—not to brag, but we do as much work as fourteen. But they pay us as if there were fourteen of us, too. They pay field hands one hundred and fifty crowns a year. The dairy girls and the farm girls get sixty crowns! And we all get to share a fifth of the farm's production. Lord! You can bet we don't leave a single stalk on the ground. The more old mother nature produces, the more we get!"

"Your boss must not be making much money if he pays you that well," said the Schoolmaster.

"Our boss! Oh! He's not a boss like the others. He's got his own way of getting rich."

"What do you mean by that?" asked the blind man, wanting to keep the conversation going in order to escape the dreadful ideas that were hounding him. "Your boss sounds pretty unusual!"

"He's unusual in every way, my good man. But listen—since this village is so far from any major road, it's pure chance that's brought you here. You'll surely never come back here. You won't leave here without learning what our boss is like and what he's doing with this farm. I'll tell you about it, in a couple of words, on condition that you spread the word. You'll see, it's as pleasant to talk about as it is to hear of."

"I'm all ears," said the Schoolmaster.

CHAPTER 6

A MODEL FARM

"You won't be sorry for listening," Old Châtelain said to the Schoolmaster. "So imagine this: One day, the owner of the farm said to himself, 'I'm very rich, which is all well and good. But, with all that money, I can't eat more than my fill. What if I helped others who don't get anything to eat to have a meal? What if I helped those good people who do get to eat but don't get enough to eat their fill—Lord, I like that idea! Let's get to work!' And so the owner got to work. He bought this farm, which wasn't being worked well at the time—it barely had use for more than two plows. I know all about it because I was born here. The owner bought more land—I'll tell you why in a moment. He put a worthy woman who was both respectable and unfortunate in charge of the farm. That's the way he always chooses his people. He said to her, 'This house will be like God's own house, open to the good and closed to the wicked. We will send lazy beggars packing, but we will always give people with the right attitude the gift of work. That kind of help doesn't humiliate its recipient and brings profit to the donor. Any rich man who doesn't give this kind of help is not a good man.' The owner said this, and, by God, he's right! But he does more than talk: he acts. There used to be a direct road from here to Écouen that shortened the distance by a good league, but Lord, it had collapsed so badly that no one could use it anymore. It was breaking down horses and carriages alike. A little hard labor and a bit of money from each of the farmers of the area would have been enough to put the road back in working order, but, as much as everyone wanted the road to be repaired, each one shied away from paying money or providing labor. Seeing this, the owner said, 'The road will be remade. But those who could contribute to remaking it won't because they don't need it. Even though, one day, it will benefit those people who have horses and carriages, before that, it will benefit those who have only their two arms, a good outlook, and no work.' So let's say a strapping young fellow comes by the farm and says, 'I am hungry and out of work.' 'My boy,' I say, 'here's a good bowl of soup, a pickax, and a shovel. We'll take you over to the Écouen road. Every day you'll make two fathoms of broken stones, and every night you'll get forty sous—twenty sous a fathom, ten sous a half fathom—otherwise, nothing.' I go over myself at dusk on my way from the fields to see how the road is going. I look to see how much each one has accomplished."

"And if you can believe it, there were actually two good-for-nothings who were crooked enough to eat the soup and then steal the pickax and the shovel!" said Jean-René, indignantly. "It makes you want to give up on doing good deeds."

"It's true," said a few of the laborers.

"Come on, fellows!" Old Châtelain answered. "So, we shouldn't plant or sow just because there are caterpillars, boll weevils, and other nasty pests that eat the leaves and munch on the grain? No, no, what you do is get rid of the vermin. The good Lord is not stingy. He makes new buds grow, new ears of grain shoot up. The damage gets repaired, and no one even notices that the malicious little beasts were there. Isn't that true, my good man?" the old laborer asked the Schoolmaster.

"No doubt, no doubt," responded the latter, who seemed, for the last few moments, to be deep in thought.

"As for the women and children, there's work for them also, suited to what they can do," Old Châtelain added.

"Nevertheless, the road isn't coming together quickly," said Claudine, the dairymaid.

"Lord, what that proves, my girl, is that fortunately there's plenty of work for good people around here!"

"But for infirm people—like myself, for example," the Schoolmaster said, suddenly, "would I be given the charity of a place in some corner of the farm, a piece of bread, and some shelter, for the little time I have remaining to live on this earth? Oh! If only it were possible, my good people, I would spend the rest of my life thanking the owner."

The criminal was speaking sincerely at this moment. He did not repent his crimes for all that, but the frightening future that the Owl had in mind for him made him regard the peaceful and happy existence of the laborers as that much more an enviable one. He never would have imagined such a future for himself, and as he turned toward his accomplice next to him, it made him regret even more that the possibility of living among the honest people with whom the Slasher had placed him was forever to be denied him.

Old Châtelain looked at the Schoolmaster in astonishment. "But, my poor man," he said to him, "I didn't think you were so destitute."

"God, yes, alas! I lost my sight in an accident at work. I'm going to Louvres to look for help from a distant relative. But, you know, sometimes people are so selfish, so hard," said the Schoolmaster.

"Oh, selfishness won't get in your way," Old Châtelain answered. "A good and honest worker such as yourself, unfortunate as you are, with such a nice child—it would melt a heart of stone. But the boss you were working for before you had your accident—why isn't he doing anything to help you?"

"He's dead," said the Schoolmaster, after a moment's hesitation. "And he was my only protector."

"What about a home for the blind?"

"I'm not old enough for that."

"Poor man! You're in a bad situation!"

"Well, if I don't find the help I'm hoping for in Louvres, do you think that the owner—whom I respect already without even knowing him—might have pity on me?"

"Unfortunately, you see, the farm isn't a home. Ordinarily, here, we let infirm people spend a night or a day on the farm, and then we give them assistance and hope that the good Lord helps them."

"So I have no hope of making your owner sympathize with my sad story?" the criminal asked with a sigh of regret.

"I've told you how it works here, my good man, but the owner is so compassionate, so generous, that he's capable of anything."

"Do you think so?" exclaimed the Schoolmaster. "Could he possibly agree to let me live here in a corner? It would take so little to make me happy!"

"Like I said, the owner is capable of anything. If he agrees to keep you on the farm, you won't have to hide yourself away in a corner. You'll be treated like the rest of us, the way you're being treated today. We would find some work for your child that would be appropriate for someone his age. He wouldn't go without good advice and good role models here. Our venerable priest would teach him, along with the other village children. He would grow up on the right path, like people say. But before we can talk about this, really, you'll have to speak with complete honesty tomorrow with Our Lady of Good Works."

"What?" said the Schoolmaster.

"That's what we call our mistress around here. If she finds your case compelling, you're in good shape. When it comes to charity, the owner never refuses anything our lady requests."

"Oh! I'll talk with her, I will!" the Schoolmaster cried joyously, imagining himself already delivered from the Owl's tyranny. Gammy did not share this hope. He felt no desire to benefit from the old laborer's offers or to grow up on the right path, under the tutelage of a venerable priest. Red-Arm's son had no taste for rural experience and he was not at all disposed toward country pleasures. Furthermore, faithful as he was to the Owl's training, he found the idea of the Schoolmaster's escaping their ill usage disagreeable in the extreme. Thus, as the criminal lost himself in his absurd bucolic delusions, Gammy decided to recall him to reality.

"Oh, yes," repeated the Schoolmaster. "I'll talk to her—to Our Lady of Good Works—she'll have pity on me and—"

At this moment, Gammy aimed a cunning and vigorous kick at the Schoolmaster, hitting him in just the right spot. The bandit's suffering made him interrupt and shorten the sentence he repeated after a painful spasm: "Yes, I hope this good woman will take pity on me."

"Poor, good, Papa," answered Gammy. "Aren't you forgetting how much my dear aunt, Madame Owl, loves you? Poor Aunt Owl! Oh, she would never abandon you that way, you know? She would probably come here with our cousin Monsieur Fishhook to pick you up and take you away."

"This good fellow has fish and birds for relatives," said Jean-René in a low voice as he mischievously gave Claudine, who was sitting next to him, a nudge with his elbow.

"You have no heart, come now! Laughing at these unfortunate people?" answered the farm girl, returning Jean-René's nudge with one of her own that was strong enough to crack three ribs.

"Madame Owl is one of your relatives?" the laborer asked the Schoolmaster.

"Yes, she is one of our relatives," he answered, overcome with gloom and sadness.

Even if he were to find an unexpected refuge on the farm, he feared that the one-eyed hag would come and denounce him out of sheer malice. He feared also that the strange names of his supposed relatives Gammy had named, Madame Owl and Monsieur Fishhook, might raise people's suspicions. Here, however, his fears were unfounded. Even Jean-René saw in these names only something to joke about in whispers, and Claudine certainly had not welcomed the joke.

"Is that the relative you're going to look for in Louvres?" asked Old Châtelain.

"Yes," the criminal said, "but I believe my son is wrong to be counting on her."

"Oh, my poor Papa! I'm not wrong! Auntie Owl is so kind! You know that she's the one who sent the special water I bathe your leg in. She also told me how to do it. She's the one who told me, 'Do for your papa just what I would do for him, and the good Lord will bless you for it.' Oh! My aunt Owl loves you! She loves you so much that—"

"All right, all right," said the Schoolmaster, interrupting Gammy. "Anyway, that won't stop me from talking tomorrow morning with the nice lady from this place and asking her to help me win the support of the respectable owner of this farm. But," he added in order to change the subject and to put an end to Gammy's imprudent remarks, "speaking of the owner of this farm, you promised to tell me what's so special about the way the farm we're on is organized."

"I promised," said Old Châtelain, "and I'll keep my word. The owner, after having thought up what he calls the 'alms of work,' said to himself, 'There are institutions and prizes that nurture the improvement of horses, cattle, plows, and many other things. My Lord! It seems to me it's high time to work toward improving people. Good animals are good, yes, but good people—that's even better. But it's harder to achieve. If you offer horses and cattle good oats and thickly planted meadows, flowing water and pure air, constant care and safe shelter—they'll come out just the way you want them to and they will make you happy. But when it comes to men, it's a completely different story. You can't make a man more virtuous the way you can fatten an ox. Grass improves the ox because it tastes good and pleases him, fattening him up. Well! It seems to me that for good advice to improve people, they have to see that there's something in it for them if they follow it.'"

"The same way the ox gets something by eating good grass, right, Old Châtelain?"

"Exactly, my boy."

"But, Old Châtelain," said another laborer, "people used to talk about a kind of farm on which young thieves who behaved very well in spite of their past learned agriculture. They were cared for and coddled as if they were little princes."

"It's true, my children. There's some good in that. It's human and charitable to never lose faith in the wicked. But you also have to give hope to the good. Suppose an honest young man, robust and hardworking, wanted to do good work and learn. He comes to this farm of ex-thieves, and they say to him, 'My friend, have you stolen a little something and been a vagabond?' 'No,' he says. 'Well,' they would say, 'there's no place here for you.'"

"That's really true what you say, Old Châtelain," said Jean-René. "People do things for rogues that they don't do for honest people. We raise livestock so they're healthy, but not men."

"As I was telling this good man here, it was in order to set an example and fix this problem, my boy, that the owner established this farm. 'I know,' he said, 'that up above, there are rewards that come to honest people, but up above, Lord—it's pretty high and pretty far! Some people (we should feel sorry for them), my children, can't see that far or climb that high. And then, where are they going to find the time to look up there? During the day, from dawn to dusk, hunched over the earth, they dig and dig for their boss. At night, they toss and turn in their sleep on their pallets. On Sundays they go drinking in bars to forget the weariness they felt yesterday and the weariness they'll feel tomorrow. Even their fatigue doesn't do them any good, poor people! After their forced labor, they still get just black bread, their beds are still hard, their children are still sickly, their wives are still incapable of nursing their babies.

Nursing their babies! Those women, who are almost starving themselves! No! No! No! I know full well, my friends, that their bread is black, but it's bread. Their pallet is hard, but it's a bed. Their children are weak, but they're alive. The poor would bear their fate more lightly, perhaps, if they thought that everyone lived the same way. But then they go into town on market day, and there they see white bread, thick and warm bedding, children who are flourishing like rosebushes in the month of May, and so well fed—so well fed—that they throw the dogs some of their cake. Lord! Then, when they return to their mud huts and their black bread, their pallets, when they see their little half-starved, scrawny, famished children, to whom they would have gladly brought one of the cakes that the little rich children were throwing to the dogs, then these people say to themselves, "Since it is ordained that there be rich and poor, why were we not born rich? It's unfair. Why does each person not get a turn at it?" Certainly, my friends, what they say is foolish, and doesn't help them make their yoke any lighter. But their yoke is hard and heavy and it sometimes wounds and crushes. And still they have to bear it without ever putting it down, without any hope of rest, or of experiencing the joy of ease for one day—just one single day. Their whole lives are like that—Lord! Such a life seems endless, like a rainy day without the tiniest ray of sunshine. So they go to work sad and disgusted with their life. In the end, most wage earners say to themselves, "What good does it do me to work harder or longer? Whether the stalk is heavy or light, it's all the same to me. What good does it do me to knock myself out trying to do a good job? Let's be totally honest: evil is punished, so let's not do evil, but the good goes unrewarded, so let's not bother doing good. Let's be like the best beasts of burden: work with patience, strength, and docility." These thoughts are unhealthy ones, my friends; there's not much difference between heedlessness and idleness, and even less between idleness and vice. Unfortunately, these people, the ones who are neither good nor wicked and do neither good nor evil, are the most numerous. So,' says the owner, 'these are the ones who stand in need of improvement, no less than if they had the privilege of being horses, or horned or woolly animals. Let's make it in their interest to be active, wise, hardworking, educated, and devoted to their duties. Let's show them that if they improve themselves, they will become happier in material terms. Everyone wins this way. So that these good principles benefit them, let's give them a little taste down here of what they can look forward to up above if they're just.'

"Once his plan was drawn up, the owner let it be known in the neighborhood that he needed six laborers and the same number of women or farm girls, but that he wanted to select these people from among the best citizens of the area, according to recommendations he would receive from local mayors or priests, or from elsewhere. They would have to be paid as we are, that is to say, like princes, and fed like people who are comfortably off. All the laborers would share among themselves one fifth of the product of the harvest. They could stay on the farm for only two years, so as to make room for other laborers to be chosen under the same conditions. After five years away, former laborers could come back to work there again, if there were any vacancies. Thus, since the beginning of the farm, laborers and dayworkers in the area have said to each other, 'Let's be active, honest, hardworking. Let's get noticed for how well we behave, and one day we'll get one of the positions at the Bouqueval farm. There we can live as if we were in paradise for two years. We'll perfect our skills, we'll set aside some savings, and then, after that, when we leave, we'll get hired by someone, because working here attests to one's excellent character.'"

"I've already gotten an offer to work at the Arnouville farm, for Monsieur Dubreuil," said Jean-René.

"And I've been hired to work for Gonesse," said another laborer.

"You see, my good man, everyone wins this way. The farmers around here benefit twofold, because there are only twelve places to fill with men and women, but there are always maybe fifty good citizens who are in the canton to claim them. Now, those who don't manage to secure positions won't be any less good for all that, will they? And, as they say, once good, always and forever good, because if they don't have any luck the first time, they hope to have better luck the next time. In the end, there are always many good people to be had. Listen—with all due respect, when a horse or other animal wins the prize for speed, strength, or beauty, there are a hundred young animals that are capable of disputing this prize. Well? The ones among those hundred that haven't won the prize yet aren't any less fine or strong for not having won it, right? My good man, didn't I tell you that our farm was not an ordinary one and that the owner wasn't an ordinary boss?"

"Oh, certainly!" cried the Schoolmaster. "The greater his kindness and his generosity appear, the more I hope he'll take pity on me for my sorry fate. A man who does so much good, in such noble spirit, and with such intelligence won't think twice about doing another good deed more or less."

"On the contrary, he does think twice, my good man," said Old Châtelain. "But this would be to glory in a new good deed. It seems to me that we'll see each other again, for sure, at the farm, and that this won't be the last time you sit down to eat at this table!"

"I hope it's true! You know, in spite of myself, I'm beginning to have hope. Oh! If you only knew how happy and grateful I am!" the Schoolmaster exclaimed.

"I have no doubt. The owner is so kind."

"Can I know his name at least, and that of Our Lady of Good

Works?" the Schoolmaster asked eagerly. "I'd like to be able to bless their noble names in advance."

"I understand your impatience," said the laborer. "Lord, I'll bet you were expecting to hear some fancy names? Well, it would seem likely. But their names are as simple and sweet as the names of saints. Our Lady of Good Works is named Madame Georges, and the owner is named Monsieur Rodolphe."

"My wife! My torturer!" murmured the criminal, staggered by this revelation.

CHAPTER 7

NIGHT

Rodolphe! Madame Georges!

The Schoolmaster didn't believe for a moment that he was being misled merely by a coincidental resemblance of names. Before subjecting him to his terrible torture, Rodolphe had told him he was deeply concerned for Madame Georges. Finally, the recent presence of David, the black man, on this farm proved to the Schoolmaster that there was no mistake about this.

He recognized that there was something providential, even fated, in this latest encounter of his. The hopes he had pinned on the generosity of the farm's owner were now completely overturned. His first thought was to flee: Rodolphe inspired in him an invincible terror. Perhaps he was even now somewhere on the farm! Barely recovered from his daze, the criminal got up from the table, took Gammy's hand, and cried out in a distraught manner, "Let's go! Take me away! Let's get out of here!"

The laborers looked at each other in surprise. "You're taking off—right now? You can't be thinking of doing that, my poor man," said Old Châtelain. "Really, what's gotten into you? Have you gone crazy?"

Gammy adroitly seized on this last possibility and let out a meaningful sigh. Gesturing toward his forehead with his index finger, he indicated to the laborers that the man he claimed to be his father was not entirely sane.

The old laborer answered him with a sign of comprehension and compassion.

"Come, come, let's go!" repeated the Schoolmaster as he sought to take the child away.

Gammy had decided that there was absolutely no way he would leave a warm lodging in exchange for passing a frigid night in the fields. He said, dolefully, "My God! Poor Papa, your brain fever is getting the better of you. You've got to calm down. We can't go out on this cold night. It would make you sick. I would rather anger you by disobeying you than take you out now." Then, turning to the laborers, he said, "Won't you help me to keep my father from leaving, good sirs?"

"Yes, of course. Don't worry about it, child," said Old Châtelain. "We won't let your father out the door. We will force you to stay here on the farm!"

"You can't force me to stay here!" cried the Schoolmaster. "And, anyway, it would bother the owner, Monsieur Rodolphe. You told me that the farm isn't a home. So—once again—let me out of here!"

"Bother the owner? You don't have to worry about that. Unfortunately, he doesn't live on the farm and doesn't come here as often as we'd like. But even if he were here, you certainly wouldn't bother him. This house isn't a home, it's true, but as I've told you, infirm, pitiable people such as yourself can spend a day and a night here."

"The owner isn't here tonight?" asked the Schoolmaster, less terrified.

"No. He'll probably be here, as usual, in five or six days. So you see, you have nothing to fear. By now, it's unlikely that our good lady will come down, but if she did, she'd reassure you. Didn't she tell us to make you a bed here? In any case, if you don't see her this evening, you'll speak with her tomorrow before you leave. You can make your little request to her so she can tell the owner about you and interest him in your story—maybe he'll keep you on the farm."

"No, no!" said the criminal in terror. "I've changed my mind! My son is right! My relative in Louvres will take pity on me. I'll go and find her."

"As you like," said Old Châtelain in an easygoing manner. He thought he was dealing with someone who was a little cracked in the head. "You can leave tomorrow morning. As for going on your way tonight with this poor little boy, forget about it. We'll work things out."

Rodolphe's absence at the moment from Bouqueval did little to calm the Schoolmaster's fears. He still feared that his wife might recognize him, even horribly disfigured as he was. She could come in at any moment. If she did, he was convinced that she would denounce him and have him arrested. He had always thought that the reason Rodolphe had inflicted such a terrible punishment on him was that he had wanted to satisfy Madame Georges's hatred and avenge her. But the criminal couldn't leave the farm. He found himself at Gammy's mercy, and thus resigned himself to his fate. In order to avoid being surprised by his wife, he said to the laborer, "Since you assure me that I won't be an imposition on your master or your lady, I accept your hospitality. But as I'm very tired, I'm going to go to sleep, if you don't mind. I would like to leave tomorrow at daybreak."

"Oh! Tomorrow morning is fine—whenever you want! We all get up early around here. We'll make sure to point you in the right direction so you don't get lost again."

"If you like, I'll drive this poor man to the end of the road myself," said Jean-René. "Madame asked me to take the carriage out to pick our money up from the lawyer, in Villiers-le-Bel."

"You can take this poor blind man on his way, but you'll be doing it on foot," said Old Châtelain. "Madame has just changed her mind. She decided rightly that it didn't make sense to have such a great sum of money on the farm so early. Next Monday will be the day to go to Villiers-le-Bel. Until then, the money may as well be at the lawyer's office as here."

"Madame knows her business better than I do, but why is she worried about keeping the money here, Old Châtelain?"

"She's not, my boy, thank God. And it's really six of one, half a dozen of the other. I'd just as soon have five hundred sacks of wheat around here as ten sacks of coins," said Old Châtelain. Then he turned to the criminal and Gammy. "Come, my good man, and you, my little child, follow me," he said, taking a torch. Then, walking before the farm's two guests, he led them into a little bedroom on the ground floor. They arrived there after walking through a long corridor that had several doors opening off of it.

The laborer put the light on the table and said to the Schoolmaster, "Here's your room. May the good Lord grant you a good night's sleep, my good man! As for you, my child, you'll sleep well. You're young!"

The criminal went to sit down on the edge of the bed Gammy had led him to. He was in a somber and thoughtful mood. The little lame boy made a sign to the laborer as the latter left the room, and he rejoined him in the corridor. "What do you need, my child?" asked Old Châtelain.

"Good sir, I'm in a bad way! Sometimes my father has attacks during the night. They're like convulsions. I can't help him on my own. If I need help, will someone hear me from here?"

"Poor child!" said the laborer sympathetically. "Don't worry. You see that door over there next to the staircase?"

"Yes, good sir, I see it."

"Well, one of the servants in the house always sleeps there. All you have to do is wake him up. The key is in the door. He'll help you with your father."

"Alas, sir, it's possible that farm boy and I won't be strong enough to take care of my poor papa if his convulsions get the better of him. Couldn't you come, too, since you seem so very nice?"

"My boy, I sleep like the other laborers in a barracks at the back of the yard. But don't worry: Jean-René is strong. He could knock a bull out with one blow. And if you still needed someone to help, he would go tell our old cook. She sleeps on the first floor next to Madame and our young lady. If you need her, that good woman can take care of the sick. She's very caring."

"Oh, thank you, thank you, my worthy sir! Because you have cared enough to take pity on my poor papa, I'll keep you in my prayers."

"Very good, my child. Good night. I hope you won't need anyone's help to restrain your father. Go back in there—he might need you."

"I'm going right back in. Good night, sir."

"May God keep you, my child!" And the old laborer left.

No sooner was his back turned than the little lame boy made the supremely mocking and rude gesture in his direction that the children of Paris are prone to making: it consists of repeatedly tapping the back of the neck with the palm of the left hand while making a forward motion each time with an open right hand.

With diabolical cunning, this dangerous child had just managed to uncover some of the information he needed to be able to help the Owl and the Schoolmaster achieve their sinister plans. He already knew that the central wing of the house, where he was going to sleep, was inhabited only by Madame Georges, Fleur-de-Marie, an old cook, and a farm boy.

Upon returning to the bedroom he shared with the Schoolmaster, Gammy was careful not to get too close to him. The latter heard him and said to him in a low voice, "Where are you coming from now, you little scoundrel?"

"You're pretty curious, no-eyes!"

"Oh, you're going to have to pay for everything you made me suffer and put up with tonight, you miserable little imp!" cried the Schoolmaster. Furious, he got up and felt around for Gammy, holding himself up against the walls and feeling his way along them. "I'll smother you, you evil snake!"

"Poor Papa! Aren't we jolly, playing blind man's bluff with our dear little child?" said Gammy, laughing as he easily eluded the Schoolmaster's pursuit. The latter, though at first carried away by an uncontrollable rage, was soon obliged, as always, to give up on his attempts to seize Red-Arm's son. Forced to put up with this brazen persecution until he had the opportunity to avenge himself without danger, the criminal suppressed his impotent anger and threw himself on his bed, cursing.

"Poor Papa, do you have a toothache? What's making you swear like that? What would the priest say if he heard you? He would make you do penance!"

"Go ahead," said the criminal, after a long silence, in a quiet, restrained voice. "Jeer at me, make fun of my misery, you coward. That's really nice. That's kind."

"Oh! That's great! 'Kind'! You've got some nerve!" Gammy cried out, convulsed with laughter. "Excuse me! Next thing we know, you're going to be putting on boxing gloves to swat at everything that flies, as if you didn't have both your eyes gouged out."

"But what have I ever done to you? Why are you tormenting me like this?"

"Because you've said foolish things to the Owl, for starters. And when I think that Monsieur wants to find a way to hang around here by making nice to the peasants . . . Would Monsieur like to take a bath in donkey milk?"

"Scoundrel! If I could have stayed at this farm—may lightning strike it now—you would have made it almost impossible with your insolence."

"You? Stay here? That's a good one! Who would be Madame Owl's beast of burden, then? Me, maybe? Thanks, but you can forget about it!"

"You vicious monster!"

"Monster, huh? That's one reason the more for doing what I do. I agree with my aunt Owl that there's nothing more entertaining than getting you worked up. You, who could kill me with one punch! It's a much more refined kind of entertainment than if you were weak. You were so funny this evening at the table. Good Lord! What a show I put on, all for myself, a real tour of the Gaïté![81] Every time I gave you a kick in secret, you got so angry your blood rose and your white eyes got red at the borders. All they needed was a little blue in the center, and you'd have the French flag! Two ribbons for a sergeant in the guard, don't you think?"

"All right, look. You like to laugh, you like to have fun—bah! You're a kid. I'm not angry at you," said the Schoolmaster in an affectionate and relaxed voice, hoping to win Gammy's sympathy. "It would be better, though, if, instead of staying here and making fun of me, you remembered what the Owl you love so much told you. You should be checking everything out and taking wax impressions. Did you hear them talking about a big sum of money that they'll be getting on Monday? We can come back here with some friends and we'll pull off a good job. Bah! I was stupid to want to stay here. I would have had enough of these simple-minded peasants within a week. Isn't that true, my boy?" said the criminal, trying to flatter Gammy.

"It would have been a real problem if you had done that, I swear!" said Red-Arm's son, laughing.

"Yes, yes, there's a good job to be pulled off here! And even if there's nothing to steal, I'd come back to this house with the Owl to get revenge," said the criminal, his voice transformed by rage and hatred. "Because you can bet it's my wife who drove that infernal Rodolphe to torture me. Didn't he put me at the mercy of everyone when he blinded me? At the Owl's mercy, at the mercy of a little brat like you? All right! Since I can't avenge myself on him, I'll do it to my wife! Yes! She'll pay for it all. Even if I have to burn this house down and bury myself in the ashes. Oh, I'd like that! I'd like that!"

"You'd like to get your hands on your wife again, wouldn't you, old man? What if I said that she was only ten steps away from you? That must drive you crazy! If I wanted to, I could lead you to the door of her bedroom. I could, because I know where her bedroom is. I know, I know, I know where!" added Gammy in his habitual singsong voice.

"You know where her bedroom is?" cried out the Schoolmaster with savage joy. "You know where it is?"

81. The Théâtre de la Gaïté was, in Sue's time, a popular theater on rue du Temple. [TN]

"I can see you coming," said Gammy. "I'm going to make you stand up on your hind legs like a dog who's being offered a bone. Here, old Fido!"

"You know where my wife's bedroom is?" repeated the criminal, turning toward Gammy's voice.

"Yes, I do. And what's even better is that there's only one farm boy sleeping in the wing we're in. I know where his door is, and the key. Click! One turn, and it's locked. Let's go, stand up and beg, old Fido!"

"Who told you this?" cried the criminal, rising involuntarily.

"Good, Fido. Next to your wife's bedroom there's an old cook. Another turn of a key, and we're masters of the house, masters of your wife and the girl in the gray mantle we were going to kidnap. Now give me your paw, old Fido, be a good boy for your master! Now!"

"You're lying! You're lying! How would you know that?"

"I'm lame, but I'm not stupid. Just a little while ago, I made up a story to tell that old laborer guy. I said that you sometimes have convulsions at night, and I asked him where I could get help if you had one of your attacks. So he told me that if you had an attack I could wake up the valet and the cook, and he told me where they sleep. One is downstairs, one is upstairs, on the first floor, next to your wife—your wife, your wife!" And Gammy repeated his monotonous chant.

After a long silence, the Schoolmaster said to him calmly, with sincere and frightening determination, "Listen. I've had enough of this life. Just a while ago, I admit it, I had a hope that makes my fate look even more horrifying than it did before. Prison, the penal colony, the guillotine—none of them is anything compared to what I have had to put up with since this morning. And I will have to put up with this forever. Bring me to my wife's bedroom. I have my knife over here. I'll kill her. They'll kill me afterward, but I don't care. I'm being suffocated by hatred. I will be avenged, and that will make me feel better. What I've had to endure is just too much—too much! For me, before whom all trembled. Listen, do you understand? If you knew what I'm suffering you'd have pity on me. I've been feeling for the last minute that my skull was going to explode. My veins are pounding so hard they're going to burst. My brain is overloaded."

"Brain fever, old man? I understand. Have a good sneeze, it'll get rid of everything," said Gammy, breaking into laughter again. "Want a pinch of snuff?" And, thwacking him on the back noisily with his closed left hand the way he might bang on the top of a snuffbox, he chanted, "I've got some good tobacco in my snuffbox! I've got some good tobacco, and you'll get none!"

"Oh, my God, my God, they're making me crazy!" cried the criminal. He had truly become nearly deranged by a sort of feverish desire for a bloody, burning, implacable revenge. It was a fever that he was seeking in vain to assuage.

The exuberance of this monster's strength could be matched only by his current impotence. Imagine, if you will, a famished, furious wolf, rabid, and harassed all day through the bars of his cage by a child. Two steps away, he scents a victim who would in one fell swoop satisfy his hunger and his rage.

At Gammy's last sarcastic taunt, the criminal almost lost his head. In his frenzy, since he couldn't put his hands on someone else, he wanted to spill his own blood, which was suffocating him. Once he decided to kill himself, he wouldn't have hesitated, if he had had a loaded pistol in his hand. He riffled around in his pocket, took out a long dagger, opened it, and raised it to stab himself with it. But as rapid as the gesture was, he was hindered by reflection, fear, and the instinct to live. The murderer lacked courage. His arm fell back onto his knees.

Gammy followed these movements attentively. When he saw the harmless denouement of this tragic impulse, he cried out in laughter, "Waiter, a duel! Strip the feathers from the ducks!"[82]

The Schoolmaster was afraid that he might lose his sanity in one last and futile explosion of anger. And so, if one may put it this way, he refused to hear this new insult from Gammy, who was insolently mocking the cowardice of this murderer who flinched at the idea of killing himself. Despairing of escaping what he called, with vengeful resignation, the cruelty of this cursed child, the criminal decided to make one last effort, appealing to the greed of Red-Arm's son. "Oh!" he said to him, nearly begging. "Just bring me to my wife's door. You can take anything you want from her bedroom, and then you can save yourself and get out of here. I'll stay here on my own. You can cry out, 'Murder!' if you want. They'll arrest me, they'll kill me on the spot. So much the better! This way, even though I don't have the courage to kill myself, at least I'll die and die avenged. Take me there! I'm sure there's gold and jewels in her room, and I tell you, you can take it all. Do you understand? You can keep it all to yourself. All I ask is that you take me to her door, take me near her."

"Yes, I understand. You want me to take you to her door. And then to her bed . . . and then you'll want me to tell you where to strike her, and then you'll ask me to guide your arm, right? In short, you want to make me the handle of your knife, you old monster!" said Gammy with an expression of contempt, anger, and horror. For the first time all day, his weasel face—until then always mocking and brazen—wore a serious expression. "Listen, you'd have to kill me before you could make me take you to your wife."

82. A "duck without feathers" (*canard sans plumes*) is French slang for a club or cudgel. Gammy is mocking the Schoolmaster by attending to the literal meaning of the expression and thus asking a waiter for a weapon to use in a duel against the Schoolmaster's knife. [TN]

"So you refuse?"

Red-Arm's son didn't answer. He came up barefoot and soundlessly behind the Schoolmaster, who was sitting on his bed still holding his large knife in his hand. Then, with marvelous speed and deftness, Gammy took the weapon away from him and bounded to the other side of the room.

"My knife! My knife!" cried the criminal, stretching out his arms.

"No, you can't have it, because you could ask someone tomorrow to speak with your wife so you could throw yourself on her and kill her. After all, as you said, you've had enough of life and you're too much of a coward to kill yourself."

"Now he's protecting my wife from me!" cried the criminal. His thoughts were getting more and more confused at this point. "Is this little brat the devil himself? Where am I? Why is he protecting her?"

"Just to get your goat," said Gammy. And his face resumed its mask of impudent mockery.

"Oh, so that's how it is," murmured the Schoolmaster, completely unhinged. "All right. I'll burn the house down. We'll burn everyone! Everyone! I'd as soon burn that way as another. Where's the candle? The candle?"

"Ha, ha, ha!" Gammy shouted, exploding into laughter once again. "If they hadn't snuffed out your lights forever, you'd be able to see that our candle has been out for an hour." And he chanted, "My candle is out, my fire is gone . . ."

The Schoolmaster groaned softly, stretched out his arms, and fell from his full height onto the tile floor, facedown on the ground, struck by an apoplectic fit. He lay there motionless.

"I know your game, old man!" said Gammy. "It's a trick to make me come near you so you can catch me a good one. Once you've had enough making a raft of the tiles, you'll get up again."

And Red-Arm's son, having decided against sleeping for fear of being surprised by the Schoolmaster's groping around, stayed seated in his chair, his eyes fixed on the criminal. He was sure that the latter was laying a trap for him. He did not think the criminal was really ill at all.

In order to pass the time agreeably, Gammy mysteriously pulled a little red silk wallet out of his pocket. With a greedy and joyful expression, he slowly counted the seventeen pieces of gold that it contained.

Here's how Gammy acquired his ill-gotten gain. The reader will remember that Madame d'Harville was going to get caught by her husband during the fatal rendezvous she had given to the commandant. When he gave this wallet to the young woman, Rodolphe had told her to go up to the fifth floor to see the Morel family, on the pretext that she was there to help them out. Madame d'Harville was rapidly climbing the staircase when Gammy, leaving the charlatan's rooms, spied the wallet out of the corner of his eye.

He pretended to fall as he was passing Madame d'Harville, gave her a push, and in the ensuing tumult quickly took the wallet away from her. Madame d'Harville, panicked and hearing the steps of her husband, rushed to the fifth floor without having a chance to protest against the audacious theft committed by the little lame boy.

After having counted and recounted his gold, Gammy could hear no noise coming from anywhere on the farm. Barefoot, ears on alert, shielding his light with his hand, he went to take impressions of the four doors that opened on the corridor. If anyone surprised him outside of his bedroom, he was prepared to say that he was looking for help for his father.

Upon his return, Gammy found the Schoolmaster still stretched out across the floor. Worried for a moment, he listened carefully to his chest. He heard the criminal breathing freely and thought that he was still feigning after all this time. "Still up to your tricks, old man?" he said to him.

A lucky chance had saved the Schoolmaster from a cerebral congestion that would doubtless have ended his life. His fall had provoked an abundant nosebleed that acted as a countermeasure. Afterward, he fell into a sort of febrile torpor in which he was half asleep and half delirious. He had the following strange and terrifying dream.

CHAPTER 8

THE DREAM

Here is the Schoolmaster's dream:

He sees Rodolphe again at the house on the allée des Veuves. Nothing has changed in the salon where the bandit underwent his horrible torture. Rodolphe is seated behind the table, atop which are the Schoolmaster's papers and the little lapis cross he had given to the Owl. Rodolphe's face is serious and sad. To his right stands the black man, David, imperturbable and silent; at his left is the Slasher, who looks upon the scene in shock. The Schoolmaster is no longer blind but rather sees through a film of clear blood that fills the cavities of his eye sockets. Everything looks to him as if it is tinted red.

In the manner of birds of prey that hover immobile in the air above their victims, mesmerizing them before devouring them, a monstrous owl with the hideous face of the one-eyed hag hovers over the Schoolmaster. She keeps her round, greenish, blazing eye fixed on him. Her continuous gaze weighs down on his chest with an immense heaviness. Just as, when one gets used to the darkness, one can distinguish objects there that were at first imperceptible, the Schoolmaster perceives that an immense lake of blood separates him from the table at which Rodolphe is seated.

Little by little, this inflexible judge, along with the Slasher and the black man, grows to colossal size. As they get larger, these three phantoms reach the friezes at the edge of the ceiling, which rise to accommodate them. The lake of blood is calm and as smooth as a red mirror. The Schoolmaster sees his own hideous image reflected in it. But soon this image disappears with the bubbling up of the swelling waves. From their agitated surface arises something like the fetid exhaust of a swamp—a mist with the livid, violet color particular to the lips of a corpse. But even as this mist mounts and mounts, the faces of Rodolphe, the Slasher, and the black man continue to grow and grow incomprehensibly, continuing to dominate the sinister vapor.

Amid this vapor, the Schoolmaster sees pale specters appearing, along with violent scenes in which he played a part. In this fantastic mirage, he sees first of all a little old man with a bald head. He wears a brown waistcoat and a green silk eyeshade. In a shabby room, by the light of a lamp, he is busy counting gold pieces and organizing them into piles. The Schoolmaster can see himself through the window, which is illuminated by a pale moon that whitens the tops of a few tall trees blowing in the wind. He sees himself outside, pressing his horrible face to the glass of the window.

With eyes all agleam, he follows the smallest movements of the little old man. Then he breaks a windowpane, opens the window, leaps in one bound upon his victim, and stabs him between the shoulders with a long knife. The action is so rapid, the blow so abrupt and so accurate, that the old man's corpse remains seated in his chair.

The murderer wants to remove his knife from the dead body. He can't do it. He redoubles his efforts . . . they are in vain. He then decides to abandon his knife—impossible. The handle of the knife holds on to the murderer's hand just as much as the victim's body holds on to its blade. The murderer then hears spurs clanging and sabers reverberating on the tiles of a neighboring room. Feeling he must escape at any cost, he decides to take the puny body of the old man along with him, since he can't free the knife or his hand. He can't do this, however, because the frail little corpse weighs as much as lead. Despite his herculean shoulders, despite his desperate efforts, the Schoolmaster cannot lift this enormous weight.

The sound of reverberating steps and dangling swords gets closer and closer . . . The key turns in the lock. The door opens . . . The vision disappears.

And then the owl flaps its wings, shrieking, "That was the old rich guy from rue du Roule . . . Your first time as a murderer, murderer, murderer!"

Although the vapor covering the lake was thick for a moment, it becomes transparent again, allowing another specter to appear. The day is beginning to break; the mist is thick and dark. A man who is dressed like a livestock merchant is lying dead on the edge of a highway. The trampled earth and the torn grass testify to the fact that the victim had put up a desperate resistance. This man has five wounds bleeding from his chest. He is dead, yet he is whistling for his dogs. He calls for help, crying, "Come to me! Come to me!" But he is whistling and calling through his five large wounds; the sides of these gaping wounds are moving around like lips that speak . . . These five calls and five simultaneous whistles, coming out of this corpse through the mouths of his wounds, are terrifying to hear.

At this moment, the owl flaps its wings and mocks the dismal groans of the victim by cackling five times. Its cackle is strident and ferocious like the laughter of the insane, and it cries out, "The livestock merchant from Poissy . . . Murderer! Murderer! Murderer!"

At first, prolonged subterranean echoes repeat the sinister laughter of the owl at a high volume; then they seem to dissipate into the earth's entrails. This noise provokes two large dogs that are as black as ebony and with eyes gleaming like firebrands, and always fixed on the Schoolmaster. They begin to bark and to turn . . . turn . . . turn around him with dizzying speed. They almost touch him, and yet their barks are so distant that they seem to be carried off with the morning wind.

Little by little, the specters get pale and fade away, disappearing like shadows and melting into the livid vapor that continues to mount. New fumes cover the lake of blood's surface and superimpose themselves onto it. These fumes are a sort of greenish, transparent mist. They look like a vertical cross section from a canal full of water. First, one sees the base of the canal covered with a thick slime composed of numerous reptiles that are ordinarily imperceptible to the human eye; here, however, they are enlarged as if one were looking at them under a microscope. They take on a monstrous aspect and enormous proportions relative to their real size. Now it's not the mire anymore—it's a compact, living, swarming mass, an inextricable tangle that's milling and pullulating. This mass is packed so tight that a dull sounding and imperceptible undulation barely lifts the level of this slime—or rather, of this bank of impure animals.

Above, filthy, thick, dead water flows slowly, slowly, carrying along with it the refuse that is incessantly vomited up by the sewers of a large city: debris of all sorts, the corpses of animals. Suddenly, the Schoolmaster hears the sound of a body falling heavily into the water. In a rapid reaction, the water splashes up and hits him in the face. Through a crowd of air bubbles that are coming up to the surface of the canal, he sees a woman getting rapidly swallowed up in the water . . . she is floundering, floundering in the water . . .

And he sees himself, himself and the Owl, saving themselves in the nick of time on the banks of the Saint-Martin canal. They carry a safe wrapped in black canvas. Nevertheless, he remains to hear all of the stages of agony of the victim whom he and the Owl have just thrown into the canal. After her first immersion, he sees the woman get up to water level and wave her arms around headlong like someone who doesn't know how to swim but is trying in vain to save herself. Then he hears a great cry. This desperate cry in extremis ends in the dull, choppy sound of involuntary submersion . . . and the woman sinks a second time below the water's surface.

The owl, still hovering immobile, parodies the convulsive death rattle of the drowned woman, just as it parodied the groans of the cattle merchant. In the midst of its funereal bursts of laughter, the owl repeats, "Glug . . . glug . . . glug . . ." The subterranean echoes say this over and over again.

Submerged a second time, the woman, suffocating, in spite of herself, inhales violently. Instead of air, however, she inhales water. Then she throws her head backward, the blood runs to her head and her face turns blue, her neck becomes livid and swollen, her arms grow rigid, and, in a last convulsion, the drowning woman in her death throes moves her legs, which were lying in the slime. She is then surrounded by a cloud of blackish mud that surfaces with her to the top of the water. The drowned woman has hardly breathed her last when she is already covered with all sorts of microscopic reptiles, the voracious and horrible vermin of the mire . . . The corpse stays afloat for a moment, oscillates a little more, then sinks slowly, horizontally, with her feet lower than her head, and, immersed in the water, starts to follow the current of the canal. Sometimes the corpse turns over and the Schoolmaster sees her face directly in front of his own. Then the specter stares at him intently out of her two big sea-green, glassy, opaque eyes . . . her violet lips are moving . . .

The Schoolmaster is some distance from the drowned woman, yet she murmurs in his ear: "Glug, glug, glug," accompanying these peculiar words with the sound that a pitcher held underwater makes as it fills up with water. The owl repeats, "Glug . . . glug . . . glug . . ." It flaps its wings, crying, "The woman from the Saint-Martin canal! Murderer! Murderer! Murderer!" The subterranean echoes answer it, but instead of dissipating into the entrails of the earth, they reverberate more and more strongly and seem to get closer. The Schoolmaster seems to hear these bursts of laughter resonating from one end of the earth to the other.

The vision of the drowned woman disappears. The lake of blood, beyond which the Schoolmaster can still see Rodolphe, turns a bronzed black. Then it turns red and changes soon into a liquid furnace like molten metal. Then this lake of fire rises, rises, rises toward the sky, like an enormous whirlpool. Soon, the horizon is as incandescent as white-hot iron. This immense, infinite horizon dazzles and burns the Schoolmaster's eyes at the same time. Nailed to his spot, he can't avert his gaze. Then, against this background of burning lava that is devouring him with its reflected heat, he sees one by one, passing by again and again, slowly, the black and gigantic specters of his victims.

"The magic lantern of remorse . . . remorse . . . remorse!" the owl cries out, flapping its wings amid bursts of laughter.

In spite of the intolerable pain that his continuous contemplation causes him, the Schoolmaster has his eyes fixed on the specters that move across the burning plain of lava. Then he experiences something terrifying: passing through all the stages of a nameless torture, as a result of staring into this roasting fire, he feels his pupils, which have replaced the blood with which his eye sockets were filled, heat up. Burning, smoking, bubbling, they melt in this furnace. Finally, they burn away to ashes in their cavities as if these cavities were two crucibles of red iron. As a result of a terrifying perceptual ability, after having seen as well as felt the successive transformation of his pupils into ashes, he falls back into the darkness of his first blindness.

But then, suddenly, his intolerable pain is calmed through enchantment. An aromatic breeze of delicious freshness has passed over his still burning eye sockets. This breeze is a pleasant mixture of the springtime scents country flowers emit when bathed in wet dew. The Schoolmaster hears a light rustling around him like that of a breeze playing in the shrubbery, like the sound of a fresh spring that trickles and murmurs on its bed of pebbles and moss.

Now and then, thousands of birds warble the most melodious fantasies; when they are silent, childlike voices of angelic purity sing strange, unknown words, words that could be called winged. Shivering lightly, the Schoolmaster hears them ascend into the sky.

Little by little, a feeling of moral well-being, an indefinable softness and languor, comes over him. The opening out of his heart, the rapture of his spirit, the shining of his soul—no physical impression, no matter how intoxicating, could possibly be compared to it. The Schoolmaster feels himself floating sweetly in a luminous, ethereal sphere. It seems to him that he has risen a great distance above the rest of humanity.

After having tasted this nameless felicity for a few moments, he finds himself back in the gloomy abyss of his usual thoughts. He still dreams, but he has become once more merely the muscular bandit who curses and damns himself in fits of impotent rage. A sonorous, solemn voice reverberates: the voice of Rodolphe!

The Schoolmaster shivers from fright. He is vaguely aware that he is dreaming, but the fear that Rodolphe inspires in him is so overwhelming that he tries—though in vain—to escape this new vision. The voice speaks, and he listens. Rodolphe's tone is not angry: it is full of sadness and compassion.

"Poor wretch," he says to the Schoolmaster. "The moment when you will repent has not yet come. God only knows when it will. The punishment for your crimes is not yet over. You have suffered, but you haven't expiated your crimes. Destiny pursues its work of higher justice. Your accomplices have become your tormentors; a woman and a child subjugate and torture you. When I inflicted a punishment upon you that was as terrible as your crimes, I told you it would happen . . . I told you so! Remember what I said: 'You have criminally abused your strength: I will paralyze that strength. The strongest and most ferocious men trembled before you: you will tremble before the weakest.' You left the hidden retreat where you could have lived in repentance and expiation. You were afraid of silence and solitude. Just now, you envied the peaceful existence of the laborers of this farm for a moment, but it was too late—too late! Almost defenseless, you fall back into your old milieu, a bunch of villains and murderers, and you're afraid to stay any longer with the honest people among whom you found yourself. You wanted to numb your pain by committing new crimes.

You ferociously defied the person who wanted to keep you from hurting your fellow beings, and your criminal defiance was in vain. Despite your audacity, despite your villainy, despite your strength, you are in chains. Your thirst for crime devours you, but you can't satisfy it. A moment ago, in a frightening and bloodthirsty mania, you wanted to kill your wife. She's there, under the same roof as you, sleeping, defenseless. You have a knife, her bedroom is two steps away. No obstacle stands between you and her—nothing can protect her from your rage. Nothing but your own impotence! The dream you have just had, the one you are dreaming now, can serve as a great lesson to you. These dreams can save you. The mysterious images of this dream have deep meaning. The lake of blood in which your victims appeared is the blood that you've spilled. The burning lava that replaced it is the gnawing remorse that should consume you so that one day God, pitying your long torments, will call you to Himself and allow you to taste the ineffable sweetness of forgiveness. But that's not how it will be. No! No! All of these warnings will be useless. Far from repenting, every day you will miss those days when you used to commit your crimes, cursing their absence blasphemously. Alas! The ongoing struggle between your bloodthirstiness and the impossibility of satisfying it, between your habits of ferocious oppression and the necessity of submitting to people who are as weak as they are cruel—it will result for you in a fate that is so appalling, so horrible! Oh, you poor wretch!"

And then Rodolphe's voice changed. He was quiet for a moment, as if his emotion and fear prevented him from continuing. The Schoolmaster felt the hair on his brow stand on end. What kind of fate was this, then, that would make even his torturer feel pity for him? "The fate that awaits you is so dreadful," Rodolphe went on, "that if God, in His inexorable and omnipotent revenge, had wanted to make you expiate, you alone, all the crimes of all people, He would not have imagined a more frightening torture than the one that awaits you. You are cursed, cursed! Fate wants you to know the frightening punishment that awaits you, and it wants you to do nothing to prevent it from happening. It wants you to know your own future!"

It seemed to the Schoolmaster that his sight was restored. He opened his eyes . . . he saw . . .

But what he saw struck him with such terror that he let out a piercing cry and woke up in a jolt from this horrible dream.

CHAPTER 9

THE LETTER

The clock was chiming nine o'clock in the morning on the Bouqueval farm when Madame Georges came quietly into Fleur-de-Marie's room. The girl was sleeping so lightly that she awoke in an instant. A brilliant winter sun, darting its rays through the blinds and double-layered pink chintz gingham curtains, spread a vermilion glow through Songbird's bedroom and gave her pale and sweet face the color it was lacking.

"Well, my child?" said Madame Georges as she sat on the girl's bed and kissed her on the forehead. "How are you feeling?"

"Much better, madame. Thank you."

"You didn't wake up very early this morning?"

"No, madame."

"I'm glad of that! That unfortunate blind man and his son, whom we allowed to sleep here yesterday, wanted to leave at daybreak. I was afraid that the noise they made opening the doors might have woken you up."

"Poor people! Why did they leave so early?"

"I don't know. Last night, after you looked a little calmer and I left you, I went down to the kitchen to see them, but they were both so tired that they had asked permission to go to bed. Old Châtelain told me that the blind man seemed not to be entirely sane. And all of our people were struck by how touchingly the child of this unfortunate man cared for him. But listen, Marie, you have a bit of a fever. I don't want you to go out into the cold today. You will not leave the living room."

"Madame, pardon me—I must visit the rectory this evening at five o'clock. The priest will be waiting for me."

"That wouldn't be prudent. I am sure you have had a bad night. Your eyes look tired. You haven't slept well."

"It's true. I still have some frightening dreams. I saw once again in my dreams the woman who tormented me when I was little. I woke up with a start, terrified. I'm embarrassed by this foolish weakness."

"But the weakness troubles me because it makes you suffer, my poor little one!" said Madame Georges tenderly as she saw Songbird's eyes fill with tears.

The latter, throwing her arms around her adoptive mother, hid her face in her bosom.

"Heavens! What's wrong with you, Marie? You frighten me!"

"You are so good to me, madame, that I am sorry for not having told you what I told the priest. Tomorrow he will tell you everything himself. It would be too hard for me to repeat my confession to you myself."

"Come, come, child, don't worry. I'm sure that there's more to praise than to blame in this great secret you told our good priest. Don't cry like that, you're making me feel terrible."

"I'm sorry, madame, but for some reason, I don't know why, my heart has been breaking for the last two days. In spite of myself, the tears just come. I'm having some bleak premonitions. I feel that something horrible is going to happen to me."

"Marie, Marie! I'm going to scold you if you give in to these imaginary fears. Don't we have enough real sorrows weighing down on us?"

"You're right, madame. I'm wrong, and I'll try to overcome my weakness. God, if only you knew how much I blame myself for not always being joyous, smiling, and happy, the way I should be! Alas! My sadness must seem to you like the height of ingratitude!"

Madame Georges was going to reassure Songbird when Claudine entered the room, after having knocked on the door.

"What do you want, Claudine?"

"Madame, Pierre has just arrived from Arnouville in Madame Dubreuil's carriage. He has a letter for you, and he says it's very urgent."

Madame Georges read the following letter aloud:

> My dear Madame Georges, you will do me a great service, and you will save me from great trouble, if you come right away to the farm. Pierre will bring you here and take you back home after dinner tonight. I really don't know where to turn. Monsieur Dubreuil is at Pontoise to sell wool; you and Marie are the only people I can turn to. Clara sends kisses to her good little sister and awaits her impatiently. Try to come by eleven o'clock for lunch.
>
> Very sincerely, your friend,
> Madame Dubreuil.

"I wonder what could possibly be the matter?" said Madame Georges to Fleur-de-Marie. "Fortunately, the tone of Madame Dubreuil's letter proves that it can't be anything too serious."

"Shall I accompany you, madame?" asked Songbird.

"It might not be a good idea, because it's so cold out. But after all," Madame Georges went on, "it might distract you. If we get you all bundled up, the little trip can only do you good."

"But, madame," said Songbird, "the priest will be waiting for me tonight at five at the rectory."

"You're right. We'll be back before five o'clock, I promise."

"Oh, thank you, madame! I will be so happy to see Mademoiselle Clara again!"

"There you go again!" said Madame Georges in a tone of gentle reproach. "Mademoiselle Clara? Does she say 'Mademoiselle Marie' when she speaks of you?"

"No, madame," answered Songbird, lowering her gaze. "It's just that, well, I . . ."

"You! You're a cruel child who only thinks of tormenting yourself. You have already forgotten what you promised me just now. Get dressed quickly, and make sure you're dressed warmly. We can get to Arnouville before eleven o'clock."

Then, as she left the room with Claudine, Madame Georges said to her, "Have Pierre wait a moment. We will be ready in a few minutes."

CHAPTER 10

A RECOGNITION

Half an hour after this conversation, Madame Georges and Fleur-de-Marie were getting into one of those large cabs used by rich farmers who live in the vicinity of Paris. This carriage, harnessed to a robust horse driven by Pierre, was soon traveling quickly along the grassy road that led from Bouqueval to Arnouville. The many buildings and numerous adjoining structures on Monsieur Dubreuil's farm attested to the importance of the magnificent property that Mademoiselle Césarine de Noirmont[83] had brought the Duke de Lucenay when she married him.

The echoing crack of Pierre's whip informed Madame Dubreuil that Fleur-de-Marie and Madame Georges had arrived. These ladies descended from their carriage to a joyous welcome from the farmer's wife and her daughter.

Madame Dubreuil was about fifty years old. Her face was sweet and friendly. Her daughter, a pretty brunette with blue eyes and pink cheeks, had a face that bespoke innocence and goodness. When Clara came over to embrace her, Songbird noticed, to her great astonishment, that her friend was dressed as she was, in simple country garb, instead of in the fashionable clothing she usually wore.

"You, too, Clara? Are you, too, disguising yourself as a country lass?" asked Madame Georges as she embraced the girl.

"It's just another way that she has imitated her sister Marie," said Madame Dubreuil. "She wouldn't stop at anything, including wearing that broadcloth blouse or that fustian skirt, just like your Marie. These little girls have such unpredictable whims, my poor Madame Georges!" she said, sighing. "Come, let me tell you about the fix I'm in."

Following her mother and Madame Georges into the living room, Clara sat next to Fleur-de-Marie and gave her the best place next to the fire. She asked her a thousand times what she could do to make her more comfortable, took her hands in her own to warm them up, kissed her again, and called her her bad little sister, reproaching her quietly for waiting so long to come visit her again. If the reader remembers the discussion poor Songbird had with the priest, he will understand that she could only have

---

83. Sue everywhere else identifies this character as Clotilde. [TN]

greeted these tender and naive caresses with a mixture of humility, happiness, and fear.

"And so, what is going on, my dear Madame Dubreuil?" asked Madame Georges. "How can I help you?"

"Heavens! Where do I start? I will explain everything to you. I believe you don't know that this farm actually belongs to the Duchess de Lucenay herself. She is the person we have direct dealings with. We don't deal with the duke's manager."

"Indeed, I didn't know that."

"You'll understand soon why that matters. So we pay our rent to the duchess or to Madame Simon, her principal chambermaid. The duchess is so good, so good—although a little brisk—that it's a real pleasure to do business with her. Dubreuil and I would walk through fire for her. It's not hard to understand why this is so! I knew her when she was a little girl, when she used to come here with her father, the late Prince de Noirmont. So, lately, she asked us for six months of rent in advance. Forty thousand francs doesn't grow on trees, as they say. But we had that sum in reserve for Clara's dowry, so within twenty-four hours the duchess had her money in good, solid gold coins. These great ladies have an endless need for finery! Still, it's only in the last year that the duchess has wanted the rent precisely on the due date. Before, she used to never seem to need the money. But now, it's a different story!"

"I don't see, based on what you're saying, how I can be of any help to you, my dear Madame Dubreuil."

"I'm getting there, I'm getting there. I told you this to let you know that the duchess has complete trust in us. Not to mention that when she was twelve or thirteen, she was Clara's godmother and her father was Clara's godfather. She has always heaped kindness on Clara. So last night I received a letter by mail from the duchess. It read, 'It is absolutely imperative, my dear Madame Dubreuil, that the little pavilion in the orchard be ready to be occupied by the evening of the day after tomorrow. Have all necessary furniture, carpets, curtains, etc., etc., brought over there. Nothing must be lacking; it must be as *comfortable* as possible.' Comfortable! You understand, Madame Georges? And it's underscored, to boot!" said Madame Dubreuil, looking at her friend in a manner that was both meditative and troubled. Then she continued, "'Have a fire going day and night in the pavilion in order to reduce its humidity, for it's been unoccupied for a long time. You will treat the person who comes to stay there exactly as you would treat me. A letter that this person will give you will tell you what I expect from your usual attention and zeal. I am counting on you this time as well, and I have no fear you will fail me. I know how good and loyal you are. Adieu, my dear Madame Dubreuil. Give my goddaughter a kiss for me. Yours affectionately, Duchess Noirmont de Lucenay. P.S. The person in question will arrive the day after tomorrow in the evening. Above all, do not forget, I beg of you: make the pavilion as *comfortable* as possible.' You see? Again, this accursed word is underscored!" said Madame Dubreuil as she put the Duchess de Lucenay's letter back in her pocket.

"So? Nothing easier," said Madame Georges.

"Seriously? Nothing easier? Have you not understood? The duchess wants above all for the pavilion to be as *comfortable* as possible. That's why I asked you to come here. Clara and I put our heads together and tried to figure out what *comfortable* meant, and we couldn't do it. Even Clara, who has lived in a pension at Villiers-le-Bel and won I don't know how many prizes in history and geography—well, all the same, she had no more idea than I do as to what that baroque word means. It must be a word they use in the court or in the fashionable world. But you must understand how embarrassing this is. The duchess wants above all for the pavilion to be *comfortable.* She underscores the word, she repeats it twice, and we have no idea what she means!"

"Lord have mercy! I can resolve this great mystery for you," said Madame Georges, smiling. "*Comfortable* means, in this context, a suitable apartment that is very tidy, snug, and warm. In short, it should be a place where there's everything you need and nothing excessive."

"Oh, Lord! I understand now! But now I'm in even more trouble!"

"Why?"

"The duchess speaks of carpets, furniture, and of a lot of et ceteras, but we don't have any carpets here, our furniture is of the most common kind, and then, also, I have no idea whether the person who's coming is a gentleman or a lady. Everything is supposed to be ready for tomorrow night! What should I do? What should I do? I have no one to turn to here. Truly, Madame Georges, I am going mad."

"But, Mama," said Clara, "if you took the furniture in my bedroom, I could spend three or four days in Bouqueval with Marie while it was being refurnished."

"Your bedroom? Your bedroom? My child, is it beautiful enough?" asked Madame Dubreuil, shrugging her shoulders. "Is it . . . is it . . . *comfortable* enough, as the duchess says . . . Heavens! How do they come up with words like that?"

"So, normally, no one lives in this pavilion?" asked Madame Georges.

"No, no one at all. It's the little white house that stands all alone at the back of the orchard. The prince had it built for the duchess before she was married. When she used to come to the farm with her father, that was where they would rest. There are three pretty rooms in it, and at the back of the garden there's a Swiss dairy where the duchess used to play milkmaid when she was a child. Since her marriage, we've only seen her twice on the farm. Each time she was here, she spent a few hours in the little pavilion. The first time was six years ago, she came on horseback with—"

Then, as if the presence of Fleur-de-Marie and Clara prevented her from saying any more, Madame Dubreuil said, "But I just keep chattering away, and this doesn't help me out of my trouble. Please help me, my poor Madame Georges! Come to my rescue!"

"All right. Tell me how this pavilion is furnished right now."

"It's hardly furnished at all. In the main room, there's a straw mat on the floor, a rattan sofa, some matching armchairs, a table, a few chairs—that's it. That's a far cry from being comfortable, as you can see."

"All right! If I were you, here's what I would do. It's eleven o'clock. I would send an intelligent man to Paris."

"Our jack-of-all-trades![84] There's no one sharper than he."

"Excellent. In two hours at most he'll be in Paris. He can go to see an upholsterer on the chaussée d'Antin—any one of them will do. He should give him the list that I'll make for you after I see what's missing in the pavilion. He should tell the man that whatever it costs—"

"Oh, of course! If the duchess is happy, it doesn't matter."

"He should say that whatever the cost, everything on the list must be delivered this evening or overnight, along with three or four assistants to put everything in place."

"They can come in the Gonesse carriage. It leaves Paris at eight o'clock in the evening."

"And since all we have to do is arrange for the furniture to be transported, for the carpets to be laid down and curtains to be hung, there should be no problem getting everything done by tomorrow evening."

"Ah, my good Madame Georges, what a fix you've gotten me out of! I never thought of doing that. You are my salvation. Will you be so good as to make the list of what the pavilion needs in order to be . . ."

"Comfortable? Yes, of course."

"Oh, no, there's another difficulty I almost forgot about! We still don't know if this is a gentleman or a lady. In her letter, the duchess only said 'a person.' It's all a muddle!"

"Act as if you were expecting a woman, my dear Madame Dubreuil. If it's a man, he'll only be the better for it."

"You're right! You're always right."

A farm servant came to announce that lunch was served. "We'll have lunch in a moment," said Madame Georges. "But while I go to write the list of necessary items, go to measure the three rooms for their height and area so we can know what sizes of curtains and rugs we need."

"Good, good! I'll go tell all of this to my jack-of-all-trades."

"Madame," the farm servant went on, "that dairymaid from Stains is also here. Her whole household is contained in a wagon drawn by an ass. Not that there's much to carry there, Lord knows!"

---

84. A sort of property manager employed by large agricultural properties around Paris. [SN]

"Poor woman!" said Madame Dubreuil in a concerned voice.

"So who is this woman?" asked Madame Georges.

"She's a peasant from Stains who used to have four cows and ran a little business selling her milk every morning in Paris. Her husband was a blacksmith. One day, needing to buy iron, he accompanied his wife on her trip, arranging with her to come pick her up at the corner of the street where she usually sold her milk. Unfortunately, the dairymaid had set up her stand in a bad neighborhood, it seems. When her husband returned, he found her in the grips of some drunken creeps who had had the wicked idea of spilling her milk into the brook. The blacksmith tried to reason with them, but they knocked him about. He defended himself, and in the ensuing scuffle he was stabbed to death."

"How horrible!" cried Madame Georges. "Did they catch the murderer?"

"Unfortunately not. In the tumult, he escaped. The poor widow swears that she would recognize him because she had seen him many times with his companions who used to hang out in the neighborhood. But up until now, all attempts to find him have led nowhere. In any case, since her husband's death, the dairymaid has had to sell her cows and the few bits of land she possessed in order to pay off her many debts. The farmer from the Stains château recommended this good woman to me as an excellent person who is as honest as she is unfortunate. She has three children of whom the oldest is no older than twelve. I happened to have a vacant position here, so I hired her, and she's coming to live here on the farm."

"Your kindness doesn't surprise me, my dear Madame Dubreuil."

"Tell me, Clara," said the farm woman, "could you help this good woman to set up her living quarters while I go tell the jack-of-all-trades to prepare to depart for Paris?"

"Yes, Mama. Marie will come with me."

"Of course. Can either one of you do without the other?" said the farm woman.

"And I," said Madame Georges, sitting at a table, "I will start my list so we don't lose any time. We have to be back at Bouqueval by four o'clock."

"Four o'clock! Why the hurry?" asked Madame Dubreuil.

"Marie needs to be back at the rectory at five."

"Oh, it's for that good Father Laporte. It's a sacred duty, then," said Madame Dubreuil. "I'll give the appropriate orders, in that case. Those two children have a lot to say to each other. We need to let them have time to talk."

"We will leave then at three o'clock, my dear Madame Dubreuil?"

"Understood. But I really can't thank you enough. What a good idea it was to ask for your help!" said Madame Dubreuil. "Run along, Clara! Run along, Marie!"

While Madame Georges was writing, Madame Dubreuil left the room in one direction and the girls in another with the servant who had announced the arrival of the dairymaid from Stains.

"Where is the poor woman?" asked Clara.

"She is with her children, her little wagon, and her ass, in the barnyard, mademoiselle."

"Let's go see her, Marie. Let's go see that poor woman," said Clara, taking Songbird's arm. "She's so pale! She looks so sad in her widow's clothing! The last time she came to see my mother, she really broke my heart. She was weeping so much as she spoke of her husband, and then suddenly her tears stopped and she went into a fit of rage against the murderer. Then she scared me, she looked so mean. But her resentment is perfectly natural, in fact. Poor woman! Some people are so unfortunate! Isn't it true, Marie?"

"Oh, yes, yes, it's certainly true," responded Songbird, sighing distractedly. "Some people are so very unfortunate, you are right, mademoiselle—"

"Hey!" cried Clara, stomping her foot in irritated impatience. "You spoke formally to me again,[85] and you called me 'mademoiselle'! Are you angry at me for some reason, Marie?"

"Me? Good God!"

"So? Why, then, did you speak to me so formally? You know that my mother and Madame Georges have scolded you for that. I'm warning you: I'm going to get you in trouble again, and it'll just be too bad for you."

"Clara, I beg your pardon. I was distracted—"

"Distracted? When it's a week since the last time you saw me?" said Clara, sadly. "Distracted? That's bad enough. But no, no, that's not it. Listen, Marie: I'm going to end up thinking you're too proud to be my friend."

Fleur-de-Marie turned as pale as death and didn't answer her . . .

Upon seeing her, the woman in mourning had let out a cry of anger and horror.

This woman was the dairymaid who used to sell milk to Songbird each morning when she lived at the ogress's place in the joint.

85. She has used the French *vous* instead of the more familiar *tu*. [TN]

CHAPTER II

THE DAIRYMAID

The scene we are about to recount took place in one of the farmyards in the presence of the field hands and women servants who were coming back from work to have their midday meal. Within a shed stood a little wagon drawn by an ass. The wagon contained the paltry, crude furniture that belonged to the widow. A little boy of twelve, assisted by two other, younger children, was starting to unpack the wagon.

The dairymaid was dressed completely in black. She was about forty years old and had a rugged, masculine face that showed her to be a woman of firm resolve. Her eyelids were red from recent weeping. Upon seeing Fleur-de-Marie, she first let out a scream of fear, but then her features contracted into an expression of pain, indignation, and anger. She threw herself upon Songbird, took her brutally by the arm, and cried as she pointed her out to the people of the farm, "Here's a wretched young woman who knows my poor husband's murderer. I must have seen her talking with that criminal twenty times. When I sold milk at the corner of rue de la Vieille-Draperie, she used to come to buy it from me every morning for a sou. She must know the thug who killed him. She's like all the rest, a member of that pack of criminals. Oh, you won't get away from me, you little devil!" The dairymaid shouted these words, exasperated by unfair suspicions. She seized Fleur-de-Marie's other arm. Trembling, bewildered, the girl wanted to flee.

Shocked by this sudden attack, Clara found herself incapable of speaking until now. At this intensification of violence, however, she faced the widow and cried out, "You must be crazy! You are being driven mad by your sorrows! You are mistaken!"

"I'm mistaken?" repeated the peasant woman in a bitterly ironic tone. "I'm mistaken! Oh, no, I'm not mistaken. Look, look how pale she is already, the wretch! See how her teeth are chattering? Justice will make you speak, all right! I'm taking you with me to see the mayor, do you understand? Oh, don't bother resisting. I've got a good right hook. I think I'll pick you up and carry you myself, come to think of it."

"How can you be so insolent?" cried Clara. "Leave here at once! How dare you insult my friend, my sister, in this way!"

"Your sister? Please, mademoiselle, be serious. You're the one who's crazy here!" said the widow in a coarse manner. "Your sister! She's a streetwalker I saw hanging around in the Cité for six months!"

Hearing these words, the laborers began to grumble about Fleur-de-Marie. Naturally, they took the part of the dairymaid, who was, after all, from their own class. They sympathized with her grief.

Upon hearing their mother raise her voice, the three children rushed up to her and gathered around her, crying. They didn't know what was going on. The sight of these poor little children, dressed like their mother in mourning, amplified the sympathy that the widow was eliciting. The peasants' indignation against Fleur-de-Marie was growing.

Afraid of their almost threatening gestures, Clara said to the farm people in an emotional voice, "Please take this woman away from here. I repeat, her sorrows have made her lose her wits. Marie, Marie, I'm so sorry! Dear God, the crazy woman doesn't know what she's saying."

Songbird was pale; she hung her head down to avoid the eyes of those around her. She remained silent, crushed, and rooted to the spot, and made no attempt to escape the harsh grip of the powerful dairywoman. Clara attributed her friend's dejection to the fear such a scene must have caused her. She said once again to the workers, "Didn't you hear me? I order you to get rid of this woman. To punish her for her insolence, since she persists in her insults, she won't have the place my mother promised her here. She will never set foot on this farm again as long as she lives."

Not a single worker made a move to obey Clara's orders. One of them even said, "Mademoiselle, if that's a girl of the streets who knows the murderer of this poor woman's husband, she should have to appear before the mayor."

"I repeat: you will never enter this farm," said Clara to the dairymaid, "unless you apologize to Marie for your insults."

"You're getting rid of me, mademoiselle? Well, that's just great," said the widow, bitterly. "Come, my poor little fatherless children, repack the cart, we're going to have to earn our bread somewhere else. The good Lord will have pity on us. But at least if we have to go, we'll take this wretched girl along with us to see the mayor. She'll have to tell him who murdered my husband because she knows the whole pack of them! Just because you're rich, mademoiselle . . ." she said, looking at Clara insolently, "just because you have friends like this doesn't mean you should be so unkind to the poor!"

"It's true," said a field hand. "The dairymaid's right."

"Poor woman!"

"She's within her rights!"

"They killed her husband. Is she supposed to be happy about it?"

"You shouldn't stop her from trying to do everything she can to find out who the criminals were who did it."

"It's wrong to send her away."

"Is it her fault if Mademoiselle Clara's friend turns out to be a street-walker?"

"You don't throw out an honest woman, a mother of three, because of such a wretch as that!"

The murmurings were becoming more and more threatening when Clara cried, "Thanks be to God, there's my mother!" And indeed, Madame Dubreuil was walking across the yard, returning from the pavilion in the orchard.

"What's going on, Clara? Marie?" said the mistress of the farm as she approached the group. "Aren't you coming in for lunch? Come along, children, it's getting late!"

"Mama," exclaimed Clara, pointing to the widow, "you need to protect my sister against this woman's insults. Please, have mercy. Send her away from here. If you knew all the insolent things she had the audacity to say to Marie . . ."

"What? She dared to insult her?"

"Yes, Mama. Look, poor little sister, look how she's trembling! She can hardly stand up. Oh! It's scandalous that such a scene should have taken place at our home. Marie, forgive us, I beg of you!"

"But what is going on here?" asked Madame Dubreuil, looking around her anxiously after observing how crushed Songbird looked.

"Madame will be fair, for sure. She will," murmured the workers.

"Here's Madame Dubreuil. You're the one who's going to get thrown out of this place," said the widow to Fleur-de-Marie.

"So it's true!" cried Madame Dubreuil at the dairymaid, who was still holding Fleur-de-Marie by the arm. "You dare to speak like that to my daughter's friend! Is that how you repay my kindness? Will you leave that girl alone!"

"I respect you, madame, and I am grateful to you for your kindness," said the widow as she let go of Fleur-de-Marie's arm. "But before you accuse me of things and send me and my children away, go ahead and ask this wretch if it's true. I don't think she'll be shameless enough to deny that I know her and that she knows me, too."

"My God, Marie, do you hear what this woman is saying?" Madame Dubreuil asked in utter amazement.

"Your name is Songbird—yes or no?" asked the dairymaid to Marie.

"Yes," said the unhappy girl in a low voice, crushed. She did not look at Madame Dubreuil. "Yes, that was what they used to call me."

"You see?" exclaimed the workers in anger. "She admits it! She admits it!"

"She admits it, but what does she admit?" cried Madame Dubreuil, half frightened at Fleur-de-Marie's answer.

"Let her answer, madame," said the widow. "She'll tell us that she lived in a notorious house on rue aux Fèves in the Cité. I sold her milk there every morning for a sou. She will also admit that she used to talk about me to the murderer of my poor husband. Oh, she knows him only too well, I'm sure. He's a pale young man who's always smoking, wears a hat and a smock, and has long hair. She must know his name. Isn't this true? You're going to answer me, you wretch!" cried the dairymaid.

"It's possible that I talked to your husband's murderer, because there is unfortunately more than one murderer in the Cité," said Fleur-de-Marie almost deliriously. "But I don't know which one you're talking about."

"What? What did she say?" cried Madame Dubreuil, frightened. "She was talking about murderers!"

"That's the only kind of people creatures like her know," answered the widow.

At first astonished to hear Fleur-de-Marie confirm such a strange revelation, Madame Dubreuil now understood everything. She recoiled in disgust and horror, pulling her daughter Clara toward her brusquely and forcefully. Clara had approached Songbird to support her.

"Ah! What an abomination! Clara, take care! Keep away from that wretched girl! But how could Madame Georges have thought it appropriate to allow her in her home? How dared she introduce her to me—how could she have allowed my daughter . . . ? Heavens! It's too horrible! I can hardly believe my eyes! But no, Madame Georges is incapable of such an indignity! She must have been mistaken, like us. Otherwise—oh, what a crime that would be!"

Saddened, frightened by this cruel scene, Clara thought she must be dreaming. In her naive ignorance, she didn't understand what her friend was being accused of. Her heart was broken, and, seeing Songbird in shock, mute, and crushed like a criminal before her judges, her eyes filled with tears.

"Come away right now, daughter," said Madame Dubreuil to Clara. Then, turning to Fleur-de-Marie, she said, "As for you, you unworthy creature, the good Lord will punish you for your criminal hypocrisy. How dare you allow my daughter—an angel of purity—to call you her sister? Her friend! Her sister! You, the lowest of all scum in the world! What effrontery! You dare to mix with honest people when you deserve no doubt to be thrown in prison like the rest of your ilk!"

"Yes! Yes!" the workers shouted out. "She should go to prison! She knows the murderer!"

"She might even be his accomplice!"

"You see, there is justice in heaven!" said the widow, brandishing her fist at Songbird.

"As for you, my good woman," said Madame Dubreuil to the dairymaid, "far from sending you away, I will reward you for having exposed this wretched girl."

"Finally! Our mistress is just!" murmured the laborers.

"Come, Clara," said the mistress of the farm. "Madame Georges will explain her behavior, or else I'll never speak to her again in my life. If she wasn't being deceived, then she has been acting horribly toward us."

"But, Mother, look at poor Marie . . ."

"Let her die of shame if she likes—so much the better! You must spurn her. I don't want you to spend a single moment in her company. She is one of those creatures a proper girl like you can't talk to without dishonoring yourself."

"My God, my God, Mama!" said Clara, resisting her mother, who was trying to take her away. "I don't know what all this means! Marie may well be guilty, since you say so, but look—she's about to collapse. Have pity on her, at least."

"Oh, Mademoiselle Clara, you are good! You forgive me! It was truly against my will that I deceived you. I blamed myself for it all the time," said Fleur-de-Marie, casting a look of ineffable thanks in the direction of her protector.

"Mother, how can you be so without pity?" cried Clara in a heart-rending voice.

"Pity for her? Please! If we didn't have Madame Georges to take her off our hands, I would just put this wretch at the door of the farm as if she had the plague," said Madame Dubreuil, harshly.

As Madame Dubreuil led her daughter away, Clara turned around one last time to see Songbird and cried, "Marie, my sister! I don't know what they're accusing you of, but I'm sure you're not guilty, and I will love you forever!"

"Be quiet! Be quiet!" said Madame Dubreuil, clamping her hand over her daughter's mouth. "Be quiet! Fortunately, everyone here has seen that you didn't spend a single moment alone with that fallen creature after her odious revelation. Isn't that true, my friends?"

"Yes, yes, madame," said a field hand. "We are all witness to the fact that Mademoiselle Clara did not spend a moment with that girl—who is certainly a thief since she knows murderers."

Madame Dubreuil dragged Clara away. Songbird remained alone in the midst of the threatening group that had formed around her. In spite of the insults Madame Dubreuil had showered on her, the presence of the woman and Clara had reassured Fleur-de-Marie to some extent as to her safety. Once these two women were gone, however, she found herself at the mercy of these peasants, and her strength failed her. She had to support herself on the parapet of the deep drinking trough provided for the farm's horses.

Nothing could be more touching than the sight of this unfortunate girl.

Nothing could be more threatening than the words and attitude of the peasants who were surrounding her.

Barely sitting down on the hard edge of the trough, her head lowered and hidden in her hands, her neck and breast veiled by the square ends of the red Indian scarf that was wrapped around her little lined bonnet, the motionless Songbird bore an unimaginably overwhelming expression of pain and resignation.

Several paces away from her, the murderer's widow, triumphant and still angry at Fleur-de-Marie for the nasty things Madame Dubreuil had said to her, pointed the girl out to her children and the workers with gestures of hatred and scorn. The farm people stood in a circle and did not try to disguise the hostile sentiments they were harboring. Their rough and coarse faces expressed indignation, anger, and a sort of brutal and insulting mockery all at once. The touching beauty of Fleur-de-Marie was no small cause for the relentless rage they were feeling against her. Men and women alike could not pardon Fleur-de-Marie for having been treated up until that point as an equal by their masters. And furthermore, some of the workers of Arnouville had not been able to come up with good enough references to obtain one of the sought-after positions at the Bouqueval farm. These people thus felt a smoldering resentment against Madame Georges that her protégée would suffer from as well.

The first impulses of uneducated people like this are always extreme: either excellent or abominable. But they quickly become horribly dangerous when a multitude believes its brutality to be authorized by the real or apparent faults of those who are the targets of their hatred or anger. Although the majority of the farm's workers might not have had every right, strictly speaking, to display such savage sensibility to Songbird's failings, they seemed to feel themselves soiled by the contagion of her mere presence. Their modesty rose up in revolt as they imagined what set of people this unfortunate girl must belong to. After all, she had admitted to consorting often with murderers. What more did these country folk, still excited by the example of Madame Dubreuil, need to push their anger over the edge?

"We have to take her to the mayor," shouted one.

"Yes, yes! And if she doesn't want to walk, let's drag her!"

"Can you believe that creature dares to dress like us honest country girls?" asked one of the ugliest, most slovenly women on the farm.

"With her holier-than-thou attitude," said another, "you'd think she wouldn't need to confess to take communion."

"Do you think she had the shamelessness to go to mass?"

"What a bold hussy! Why don't we give her communion right here?"

"And she had the nerve to mix with the masters, too!"

"As if we were too lowly for her to socialize with!"

"It's a good thing everyone gets what's coming to him."

"You need to talk and say who the murderer is!" cried the widow. "You run in the same crowd. I'm not even sure that I don't remember seeing you there that day with them. Come now, come now, don't be a crybaby now that you've been exposed. Show us your face—it's pretty enough to look at!" The widow brutally pushed down the girl's hands. They had been hiding her tearstained face.

At first crushed by shame, Songbird started to tremble from fear upon finding herself all alone at the mercy of this frenzied mob. She put her hands together, turned toward the dairymaid with fear and supplication in her eyes, and said to her in a soft voice, "Please, madame, I arrived at the Bouqueval farm two months ago. I could not have been present when the terrible thing you speak of took place and—"

Furious cries drowned out Fleur-de-Marie's timid voice:

"Take her to the mayor . . . she can explain things there!"

"Let's go, cutie, forward march!"

And as the menacing group got closer to Songbird, she crossed her hands in an automatic gesture and looked from side to side in terror, seeming to beg for help.

"Oh, you may as well stop looking around you," said the dairymaid. "Mademoiselle Clara isn't here to protect you anymore. You're not going to get away from us."

"Alas, madame, I don't want to get away from you," she said, trembling violently. "I only want to be able to answer the questions you're asking, since I might be able to help you. But what have I done to all these people who are surrounding me and threatening me?"

"What you did was to have the nerve to hang around with our employers while we, who are worth a thousand times what you're worth, never get that opportunity. That's what you've done to us."

"And also, why did you want them to send this poor widow and her children away?" said another.

"It wasn't me, it was Mademoiselle Clara who wanted—"

"Oh, spare us," said the laborer, interrupting her. "Not only did you not ask for mercy for her, but you were happy enough to see the bread snatched right out of her mouth."

"No, no, she didn't ask for mercy!"

"She's a bad one!"

"A poor widow, too! The mother of three children!"

"If I didn't ask for mercy for her, it was only because I didn't have the strength to say anything at all," said Fleur-de-Marie.

"You sure had the strength to talk with murderers!"

As is typical in the emotional life of the common people, these peasants—who were more ignorant than they were malicious—got irritated, then excited, then intoxicated by the sound of their own voices, and then more excited still, the more they lavished insults and threats on their victim. This is how, through growing excitement, the masses sometimes unwittingly end up committing the most unjust and brutal actions.

The threatening circle of farmworkers was getting closer and closer to Fleur-de-Marie. They were all gesticulating as they spoke. The blacksmith's widow had lost all possession of herself.

Separated from the deep drinking trough only by the parapet on which she sat, Songbird feared falling back into the water. She cried, extending her hands toward them in supplication, "Dear God! What do you want of me? For pity's sake, don't hurt me!"

And as the dairymaid came closer and closer to her, still gesturing and putting her fists right up into her face, Fleur-de-Marie cried in fear as she began to fall backward, "I beg of you, madame, give me some space! You're pushing me into the water!"

Fleur-de-Marie's words gave these rough people a cruel idea. Thinking only of playing one of those tricks peasants like to play that leave you half dead on the spot, one of the most violent ones exclaimed, "Let's dunk her! Come on, let's dunk her in the water!"

"Yes, yes, into the water! Into the water!" they repeated, laughing uproariously and applauding in a frenzy.

"That's a good idea, dunking her! It won't kill her!"

"It'll teach her to mix with honest people!"

"Yes! Yes! Into the water! Into the water!"

"We just broke up the ice this morning."

"This streetwalker will remember the good people from the Arnouville farm!"

As she heard these inhuman cries and these barbarous taunts, and as she saw the exasperated, stupid, and angry expressions of the crowd coming toward her to seize her, Fleur-de-Marie thought she was about to die. This moment of fright was followed by a sort of bitter satisfaction: she saw her future in such bleak colors that she was mentally thanking the heavens for bringing her suffering to an end. She no longer said anything to protest their actions; she let herself fall to her knees and crossed her hands over her chest religiously, and then closed her eyes, waited, and prayed.

The farmworkers, surprised by Songbird's attitude and silent resignation, hesitated a moment before carrying out their savage plan. Chided, however, for their weakness by the women of the party, they took up their shouting again to give each other the courage to accomplish their shameful goal. Two of the most furious men were about to seize Fleur-de-Marie when a booming voice, full of emotion, rang out: "Stop!"

At the same instant, Madame Georges, who had made her way through this crowd, reached Songbird. Songbird was still on her knees. Madame Georges took her in her arms, lifted her up, and cried, "Stand up, my child! Stand up, my cherished daughter! We only kneel before God."

Madame Georges's tone of voice and attitude were so courageous and imperious that the crowd retreated and went silent. Her normally pale face had turned red with indignation. She looked at the farmworkers with a stern gaze and said to them loudly and in a threatening manner, "You wretches! Have you no shame, acting so violently, and against this unfortunate child!"

"But she's a—"

"She's my daughter!" cried Madame Georges, cutting off one of the farmworkers. "Father Laporte, whom everyone blesses and respects, loves and protects her, and anyone he esteems should be respected by all."

These simple words affected the laborers greatly. People in the area regarded Bouqueval's priest as a saint. And several peasants were not unaware of the interest he took in Songbird. However, a few quiet mutterings could still be heard. Madame Georges picked up on what they were saying, and exclaimed, "Even if this unfortunate girl was the least of all people, even if everyone else had abandoned her, your conduct toward her would be no less odious. What are you punishing her for? And what is your right to do so, in any case? What is your authority? Merely your might? Isn't it cowardly and shameful for men to make a defenseless girl their victim? Come, Marie; come, my beloved child, let's go home. There at least you are known and valued."

Madame Georges took Fleur-de-Marie's arm. The confused workers, now recognizing how brutally they had acted, moved away respectfully. Only the widow came forward to say resolutely to Madame Georges, "This girl is not leaving here until she makes a deposition at the mayor's office on the subject of my poor husband's murder."

"My dear friend," said Madame Georges, restraining herself, "my daughter has nothing to say here. Later, if the legal authorities believe it appropriate to request her testimony, they can do so, and I will accompany her to the inquiry. Until then, no one has the right to interrogate her."

"But, madame, I'm telling you—"

Madame Georges interrupted the dairymaid, saying to her, severely, "The tragedy of which you have been the victim hardly serves to excuse your behavior. One day you will surely come to regret the violence you have so unwisely instigated here. Mademoiselle Marie lives with me on the farm at Bouqueval. Tell this to the judge who heard your first testimony. We will await his orders."

The widow could say nothing in the face of this wise counsel. She sat down on the parapet of the drinking trough and began to cry bitterly, her children in her arms.

A few minutes after this scene, Pierre brought the carriage by, and Madame Georges and Fleur-de-Marie got inside it to return to Bouqueval. As they passed by the mistress of Arnouville's house, Songbird caught a glimpse of Clara. She was crying, half hidden behind a partially opened set of blinds. She bade Fleur-de-Marie adieu with her handkerchief.

CHAPTER 12

CONSOLATION

"Oh, madame, how shameful for me, and how painful for you!" said Fleur-de-Marie to her adoptive mother as soon as they were alone in the little living room back at the Bouqueval farm. "Now you'll probably be angry with Madame Dubreuil forever, and it's all my fault. Oh, I had a feeling this was going to happen! God has punished me for deceiving that lady and her daughter. I have come between you and your friend."

"My friend . . . is an excellent woman, my dear child, but she's a little foolish. Still, she has a very good heart, and I am sure that tomorrow she'll regret the thoughtless outburst of anger she showed today."

"Alas, madame, please don't think that I'm trying to justify her behavior by blaming you—God forbid! But your generosity toward me may have blinded you to reality. Put yourself in Madame Dubreuil's shoes. If you learned that her cherished daughter's companion was . . . what I am—what would you say? Can you blame her for feeling a mother's indignation?"

Alas, Madame Georges had nothing to say in response to Fleur-de-Marie's question. Getting increasingly agitated, the girl went on: "That horrible scene that I went through in front of all those people will be the talk of the whole region tomorrow. I'm not worried about anything, as far as I'm concerned. But I'm worried about Clara. She may have stained her reputation forever. She called me her friend, her sister! I should have followed my instinct and resisted the feeling that drew me to Mademoiselle Dubreuil. I shouldn't have worried about making her hate me; I should have just rejected her friendship. But I forgot the distance that separated me from her. So you see, I've been punished—oh, cruelly punished!—since I may have done irreparable harm to that young woman who is so virtuous and so good."

"My child," said Madame Georges, after a few moments of thought, "you are wrong to blame yourself so harshly. You have a guilty past—it's true, a very guilty past. But does it mean nothing to have earned the protection of our venerable priest, thanks to your sincere repentance? Was it not under his auspices and mine that you were introduced to Madame Dubreuil? Wasn't it your own goodness that made her like you of her own free will? Wasn't she the one who told you to call Clara your sister? And finally, as I told her just a while ago, because I neither wanted to nor would hide anything from her: certain as I was of your repentance, could I really make your past known and so make your rehabilitation even more painful? Indeed, if I made you despair by opening you to the scorn of people—who, if they had been abandoned or as unfortunate as you, would have never been able to preserve their innate instinct of honor and virtue as you did—your rehabilitation would have perhaps been impossible. That woman's revelation was distressing and awful. But should I have forestalled it by sacrificing your future peace on the highly unlikely chance that something like that was going to happen?"

"Oh, madame, the thing that proves that my position is an impossible one and I will be wretched forever is that, because of your affection for me, you were right to hide the past—and Clara's mother was also right to heap scorn on me on account of that same past. She was right to humiliate me—the way everyone will from now on when the scene from the Arnouville farm gets around. Everyone will know about it. Oh! I will die of shame. I won't be able to look anyone in the eye!"

"Not even me? Poor child!" said Madame Georges as she melted into tears and held Fleur-de-Marie in her arms. "And yet you will never find anything in my heart for you but tenderness and the devotion of a mother. Take heart, Marie! Know that you have repented. You are surrounded by friends here, right? This house will be your world. We will get out in front of the revelation you're afraid of: our good priest will assemble all the people on the farm who already love you so much, and he will tell them the truth about the past. Believe me, my child, his word holds so much power with everyone that this revelation will only make people sympathize with you even more."

"I believe you, madame, and I will resign myself to my fate. Yesterday, when we talked, the priest warned me that there was much painful atonement ahead of me. I should not be surprised that it has begun. He told me also that my suffering would someday be counted in my favor. I hope it's so! I won't complain, so long as I am supported in these trials by you and him."

"And you will be seeing him in a few moments. Surely no one has ever needed his help more than you do now. It's already four thirty. Get ready to go to the rectory, my child. I'll write to Monsieur Rodolphe to tell him what happened at the Arnouville farm. I'll send him the letter by express messenger. Then I'll join you at the rectory, since it's important that the three of us talk together."

A few moments later, Songbird left the farm to go to the rectory by way of the sunken road where the Schoolmaster and Gammy had agreed to wait the day before.

CHAPTER 13

REFLECTIONS

As can be seen from her conversations with Madame Georges and the priest of Bouqueval, Fleur-de-Marie had benefited so nobly from her benefactors' counsel and had taken in their principles so thoroughly that, as she reflected on her abject past life, she increasingly despaired about her present one. Even more unfortunately, her intelligence had developed to the same extent that her elevated instincts were flourishing, in the atmosphere of honor and purity in which she now lived. If she had been any less intelligent, her sensibility any less refined, her imagination any less vivid, Fleur-de-Marie could easily have consoled herself. She had repented; a revered priest had pardoned her. She could have forgotten the horrors of the Cité amid the sweetness of the rural life she shared with Madame Georges. She would even, in the end, have accepted, without fear, the friendship Mademoiselle Dubreuil was offering her—not out of any carefree attitude regarding the sins she had committed, but out of total confidence in the advice of those whose goodness she recognized. They said to her, "Now your good conduct makes you the equal of any respectable person"; and so she would have ceased to see any difference between herself and other honest folk.

The painful scene at the Arnouville farm had affected her terribly, but had she not foreseen it in advance? Why else had she shed bitter tears and felt a vague sense of remorse as she gazed upon Clara asleep, innocent and pure, and sharing a room with the former tenant of the ogress? Poor girl! Had she not accused herself far more harshly, as she lay sleepless in her bed during the long nights, than even the inhabitants of the farm who had heaped such dire recriminations on her? Her own analysis, her own incessant examination of what she was reproaching herself for, was killing Fleur-de-Marie by slow degrees. Most of all, it was her constant comparison of the future that her inexorable past imposed on her and the future that she would have hoped for, were it not for that past.

The spirit of analysis, criticism, and comparison almost always appears in people of superior intelligence. Among the haughty and the proud, such a spirit makes them doubt and rebel against others. Among the meek and the delicate, on the other hand, such a spirit leads to self-doubt and to rebellion against themselves. One condemns the former and they absolve themselves. One absolves the latter and they condemn themselves.

The priest of Bouqueval, in spite of his holiness, and Madame Georges, in spite of her virtues—or rather, in both cases, one because of his holiness and the other because of her virtues—could not imagine how profoundly Songbird suffered once her soul, detached from what had polluted it, could contemplate the depth of the abyss into which it had formerly been immersed. They did not know that Songbird's horrifying memories had nearly the force, the vividness of reality. They could not understand the strength of this girl's exquisitely refined perceptions, her poetic and otherworldly imagination, all of which made her especially vulnerable to painful sensations. They could not know that this girl did not go a single day without remembering and feeling a painful suffering that combined disgust and horror at the shameful misery of her former existence.

Imagine a girl of sixteen, honest and pure, who is conscious of her honesty and her purity, thrown by means of some demonic power into the vile tavern the ogress ran. Imagine her subjected to the power of that shrew, without any hope of getting away! That was how Fleur-de-Marie's past affected her experience of the present. Can we thus understand the sort of retrospective feeling, or rather moral backlash, that Songbird was suffering from so cruelly, that she regretted—more often than she dared admit to the priest—that she had not died in the mire?

Anyone who reflects even a little, or who has any experience of life, will not take what we are about to say as a paradox: the thing that made Fleur-de-Marie merit care and pity was not only that she had never loved, but that her senses had always remained dormant and frozen. If it is the case so often among women perhaps less endowed with delicacy than Fleur-de-Marie that they feel chaste repulsion for a long time after their marriage why then should we be surprised that this unfortunate girl, intoxicated by the ogress and thrown into the horde of savage and ferocious beasts that infested the Cité, had felt only horror and fear, and had left this sewer morally pure?

The innocent confessions that Clara Dubreuil had made on the subject of her honest love for the young farmer she was to marry had broken Fleur-de-Marie's heart. She felt that she, too, could have loved valiantly, that she could have experienced everything noble, sacred, pure, and great that love can offer. And yet, she would never be permitted to inspire or experience this sentiment. For if she loved, she would choose her beloved on account of the elevation of his soul—and the worthier such a choice might appear to her, the less worthy of him she would believe herself to be.

CHAPTER 14

THE SUNKEN ROAD

The sun was setting on the horizon; the plain was silent and deserted. As Fleur-de-Marie was approaching the entrance to the sunken road she had to take in order to reach the rectory, she saw a little lame boy leaving the gulley. He was dressed in a gray tunic and a blue hat; he looked tearful, and as soon as he saw Songbird, he ran up to her.

"Oh, good lady, take pity on me, please!" he cried as he joined his hands in a gesture of prayer.

"What do you want? What's wrong, my child?" asked Songbird, sympathetically.

"Alas, good lady, my poor grandmother, who is very, very old, fell over there as she was going down into the gulley. She's badly hurt. I'm afraid she's broken her leg. I'm too weak to help her get up. Heavens, what will I do if you don't help me? Poor Grandmother! She might even die!"

Touched by the pain of this young lame boy, Songbird exclaimed, "I'm not very strong, either, my child, but I'll try to help you save your grandmother. Let's go to her right away. I live on the farm over there. If we can't get the poor old woman there ourselves, I'll get people to help her."

"Oh, bless you, my good lady! Come this way. It's two steps down, in the sunken road, like I told you. She fell as she was going down the bank."

"You're not from around here, are you?" asked Songbird as she followed Gammy, whom the reader has no doubt already recognized.

"No, good lady, we're from Écouen."

"And where were you headed?"

"To see a good priest who lives on the hill over there," said Red-Arm's son, to increase Fleur-de-Marie's trust in him.

"To Father Laporte, perhaps?"

"Yes, good lady, to Father Laporte. My grandmother knows him well—very, very well."

"That's just where I was going. What a coincidence!" said Fleur-de-Marie as she climbed down into the sunken road.

"Grandma! Here I am! Here I am! Be patient—I'm bringing help!" cried Gammy in order to alert the Schoolmaster and the Owl to get ready to fall upon their victim.

"Your grandmother hasn't fallen far from here, has she?" asked Songbird.

"No, good lady, she's behind that big tree over there, by the turn in the road, twenty feet away from here."

Suddenly Gammy stopped in his tracks. The sound of a galloping horse was echoing in the silence of the plain. "The jig's up now," he said to himself.

There was a very sharp turn in the road a few paces away from where Red-Arm's son was standing with Songbird. A horseman arrived at this spot. When he came near the girl, he stopped. Then the trot of another horse became audible, and a few moments later a servant dressed in a brown waistcoat with silver buttons, white leather breeches, and top boots appeared. A narrow fawn-colored leather belt cinched his master's mackintosh behind his waist. This master was dressed simply in a thick bronze-colored waistcoat and light gray trousers. He sat gracefully astride an exceptionally beautiful purebred bay horse. Despite the long journey the horse had just completed, the shining luster of its coat, with its golden highlights, bore no sign of even the slightest sweat. The groom's horse, standing immobile a few paces from his master, also showed its distinguished breeding.

Gammy recognized this horseman, with his tanned and charming face, to be the Viscount de Saint-Remy, the man assumed to be the Duchess de Lucenay's lover.

"My charming girl," said the viscount to Songbird, whose beauty had struck him, "would you be so good as to show me where the road to the village of Arnouville is?"

Lowering her eyes under the bold and searching gaze of this young man, Marie answered, "When you leave the sunken road, sir, take the first path on your right. That path will take you to a road lined with cherry trees, and that road will take you directly to Arnouville."

"Many thanks, beautiful child. You have given me better directions than an old woman I saw a little ways off. She was lying down at the foot of a tree. The only thing I got out of her was groaning."

"That was my poor grandmother!" murmured Gammy in a mournful voice.

"Now, just one more thing," said Monsieur de Saint-Remy, addressing Songbird. "Can you tell me if it's easy to find Monsieur Dubreuil's farm once I get to Arnouville?"

Songbird couldn't help trembling at these words, as they reminded her of the morning's painful scene. "The farm buildings border the road that takes you to Arnouville, monsieur," she answered.

"Thank you once again, my pretty child!" said Monsieur de Saint-Remy. At this, he galloped away, followed by his groom.

The viscount's charming features had relaxed slightly as he spoke with Fleur-de-Marie, but once he was alone again, his brow again became furrowed and his face showed a deep anxiety.

Fleur-de-Marie remembered the unknown person for whom the pavilion at the Arnouville farm was being prepared on Madame de Lucenay's orders. She was sure that this young and attractive horseman must be that guest.

For some moments, the galloping of the horses shook the ground, hardened by the cold. Then it grew fainter, and finally it stopped . . . Everything returned to silence.

Gammy took a deep breath.

Wishing to reassure and alert his accomplices, one of whom, the Schoolmaster, had been hidden from the sight of the horsemen, Red-Arm's son cried, "Grandmother, here I am with a good lady here who's coming to help you!"

"Quickly, quickly, my child! That man on the horse made us lose precious time," said Songbird, quickening her pace to get to the turn in the sunken road.

As soon as she arrived at the spot, the Owl, who was hiding there, said in a low voice, "Come help me now, Killer!" Then, jumping on Songbird, the one-eyed hag seized her by the neck with one hand and covered her mouth with the other. Gammy, in the meantime, threw himself at the girl's feet and held on to her legs to keep her from moving.

All of this happened so quickly that the Owl had had no time to look at Songbird's face. But in the few moments it took the Schoolmaster to get out of the ditch he had been squatting in and to grope his way over, with his cloak, the old woman had recognized her old victim.

"Miss Lowlife!" she exclaimed, at first astonished. Then she added, in ferocious joy, "It's you again! The baker of souls has sent you back to me! It's your fate to keep falling into my talons. I have that acid in the carriage—this time, I'm going to make sure to get it all over your pretty little mug, because that virginal face of yours really bugs me. She's all yours, my man! Watch that she doesn't bite you, and hold on to her tightly while we get her all gift-wrapped."

With his two powerful hands, the Schoolmaster seized Songbird, and, before she could even cry out, the Owl threw the cloak over her head and muffled her tightly. In an instant, Fleur-de-Marie was bound and gagged and thus prevented from moving or calling for help.

"Here you go, Killer—here's a little package for you," said the Owl. "Hee, hee! At least she's not quite as heavy as the woman all wrapped in black who we drowned in the Saint-Martin canal, eh? Right, dear?" And when the bandit shivered at these words that reminded him of his frightening dream from the night before, the one-eyed hag said again, "Oh, Killer, what's got into you now? It looks like you've got the shivers! Since this morning, your teeth have been chattering now and again as if you had a fever. And you keep looking into the air like you were searching for something."

"Big faker! He's watching the flies buzzing around," said Gammy.

"Come on, let's get going, my man! You've got to get little Miss Lowlife all wrapped up already!" the Owl added as she observed the bandit taking Fleur-de-Marie in his arms as if he were holding a sleeping child. "Come on, we've got to get over to the carriage!"

"But who's going to lead me?" asked the Schoolmaster in a dull voice, grasping his soft, light bundle in his herculean arms.

"Old snake! He thinks of everything," said the Owl. Removing her shawl, she unknotted the red scarf that had been covering her scraggly neck. She twisted the scarf in half lengthwise and said to the Schoolmaster, "Open your gullet and take the end of this scarf in your chompers. Bite down hard—Gammy will take the other end in his hand, and all you'll have to do is follow him. Good blind men get good seeing-eye dogs! Over here, brat!"

The little lame boy leapt over toward her, imitating a grotesque barking sound in a low voice as he did so. He took the other end of the scarf in his hand and led the Schoolmaster along with it as the Owl rushed ahead to alert Fishhook of their approach.

We could not begin to depict the terror Fleur-de-Marie felt when she found herself in the clutches of the Owl and the Schoolmaster. She felt herself giving way and saw the futility of putting up the slightest resistance.

A few minutes later, Songbird was being transported in a carriage driven by Fishhook. Although it was night, the carriage blinds were carefully shut, and the three accomplices, with their nearly expiring victim, set out for the plain of Saint-Denis, where Tom was waiting for them.

CHAPTER 15

CLÉMENCE D'HARVILLE

The reader will forgive us for abandoning one of our heroines in such a critical situation—a situation whose denouement we will recount later. The requirements of this multipart story—its unity, unfortunately a too variegated one—force us to move constantly from one character to another so that we may, as much as our abilities allow, develop the general concern of the work—that is, if this work, difficult, conscientious, and impartial as it is, can be said to have a general concern.

We have still to follow some of the protagonists of this story into attic apartments, where poor wretches shiver with cold and hunger in a timid, resigned, upright, and hardworking poverty.

We will have to follow them into women's prisons—some of them seductive prisons decorated with flowers, others black and somber—vast schools of perdition all, with nauseating and vicious atmospheres in which innocence withers and dies, each a hellish pandemonium where the accused may enter in a pure state, but from which she almost always leaves corrupted . . .

We will follow them into hospitals in which the poor, treated at times with touching humanity, also sometimes miss the solitary pallets on which they bathed in the cold sweat of their fever . . .

We will follow them into those mysterious asylums where the girl who has been seduced and abandoned gives birth to the child she bathes in bitter tears but will never see again . . .

We will follow them into those terrible places in which madness—touching, grotesque, stupid, hideous, or ferocious—shows itself in its most terrifying aspects, from the peaceful madman who chuckles sadly with a laughter that makes you cry, to the frenzied creature who roars like an angry beast and clings to the bars of his cage.

We still have many places to explore. But what good does this overly long enumeration serve? Ought we not worry that we might frighten the reader? He has already given us the benefit of the doubt in following us into some rather strange places; perhaps he will hesitate to accompany us in our new wanderings.

All of that being said, let us continue with our tale.

The reader will remember that the day before the events we just finished recounting took place (the kidnapping of Songbird by the Owl), Rodolphe had rescued Madame d'Harville from an imminent danger that Sarah had manufactured out of jealousy, by alerting Monsieur d'Harville to the rendezvous that the marquise had granted so unwisely to Monsieur Charles Robert.

Rodolphe, profoundly moved by this scene, had returned to his home on rue du Temple, putting off until the next day the visit he was planning to make to Mademoiselle Rigolette and the family of unfortunate artisans whom we have mentioned. He believed that their immediate needs had been taken care of, thanks to the money that he had given the marquise to distribute to them. This money had allowed her to claim, with some likelihood, that her visit had been a charitable one. Unfortunately, Rodolphe did not know that Gammy had made off with the wallet (the reader already knows how the little lame boy had committed this bold theft).

Around four o'clock, an elderly woman had delivered the following letter to the prince and then left without waiting for his response:

My Lord,

I owe you more than my life. I would like to express my gratitude to you this very day; tomorrow my shame may prevent me from doing so. If you could do me the favor of visiting me this evening, you would complete this day as you began it, my lord—with a generous act.

D'Orbigny-D'Harville

P.S. You need not respond, my lord. I will be at home all evening.

Although Rodolphe was happy to have been so importantly helpful to Madame d'Harville, the intimacy these circumstances suddenly forced upon him and the marquise made him uneasy. Incapable of betraying the friendship of Monsieur d'Harville but profoundly moved by the spiritual grace and beauty of Clémence, Rodolphe was troubled by his attraction to her and had decided, after a month of attentiveness, to avoid seeing her again. He also remembered, with emotion, the discussion between Tom and Sarah that he had overheard at the embassy of ***. Although motivated by hatred and jealousy, Sarah had affirmed—not without reason—that Madame d'Harville still felt a deep affection for Rodolphe, even if she was unaware of it herself. Sarah was too clever, too discerning, too experienced in matters of the human heart to overlook the fact that Clémence believed herself to be neglected and perhaps disdained by a man who had made a deep impression on her. Sarah was too smart not to know that it was only out of resentment that Clémence had given in to the obsessions of a perfidious friend and allowed herself almost by surprise to sympathize with the imaginary sorrows of Monsieur Charles Robert. And she would not, for all that, completely forget her feelings for Rodolphe.

Other women, faithful to the memory of the man they had first favored with their attention, would have remained indifferent to the sighs of the commandant. Clémence d'Harville was thus doubly guilty, even though she had only given in to the seduction of unhappiness, and even though a strong, healthy sense of duty (accompanied, perhaps, by a memory of the prince) that kept watch over her heart had managed to prevent her from compromising herself irreparably.

Thinking about his conversation with Madame d'Harville, Rodolphe felt himself torn in many directions. He was quite firm in his resolve to resist his attraction to her. And, at times, he thought himself fortunate in having overcome his affection for her by blaming her for her regrettable weakness for Monsieur Charles Robert. But, at other times, he was bitterly sorry to have to see her fall from the great height she had always occupied in his esteem.

Clémence d'Harville also awaited this meeting with trepidation. The two feelings she experienced most profoundly were a painful confusion she had when she thought of Rodolphe—and a deep aversion when she thought of Monsieur Charles Robert. There were many reasons for this aversion, this hatred that she felt. A woman may risk her peace of mind and her honor for a man, but she will never forgive him for placing her in a humiliating or ridiculous situation.

Now, Madame d'Harville had almost died of shame at finding herself the butt of Madame Pipelet's sarcastic comments and insulting looks. But that was not all. When she received the warning from Rodolphe of the danger she was in, Clémence had run quickly up to the fifth floor. The placement of the stairway had allowed her, in climbing it, to glimpse Monsieur Charles Robert in his dazzling dressing gown. At that moment, recognizing the woman he awaited, he had partially opened the door and stood there with the confident, expectant smile of one who has made a conquest. The insolent fatuousness of the commandant's suggestive apparel had let the marquise understand how terribly wrong she had been about this man. Led along by the goodness of her heart, by the generosity of her character, into an act that could ruin her, she had granted this rendezvous not out of love, but only out of commiseration. She had wanted to console him for the ridiculous position that the Duke de Lucenay, with his odious manners, had put him in when they were at the embassy of ***. Imagine Madame d'Harville's mortification and disgust when she saw Monsieur Charles Robert all decked out like a conqueror!

The clock had just chimed nine in the little salon where Madame d'Harville usually received her guests. Decorators and innkeepers have overused the Louis XV and Renaissance styles so much that the marquise, with her excellent taste, did not allow any furnishings of such a sort into her apartment. Décor of this luxurious variety—now so vulgar seeming—was relegated to the part of the Harville mansion reserved for grand receptions.

There could be nothing more elegant or more distinguished than the furnishings of the salon in which the marquise awaited Rodolphe. The tapestries and curtains fell naturally and were made of an Indian fabric the color of straw. Against this brilliant background were arabesques embroidered in simple silk of the same color. These whimsical designs were in the most charming taste. Double curtains made of Alençon lace hid the windows completely.

The rosewood doors were decorated with very delicately engraved gilded silver moldings. In each panel, they framed an oval medallion of Sèvres porcelain that was almost a foot across in diameter. These medallions depicted birds and flowers rendered in admirable detail and splendor. The frames of the mirrors and the curtain rods were also made of rosewood and bore the same ornamentation of gilded silver. The friezes of the white marble fireplace and its two caryatids were of an antique beauty and an exquisite grace. These were the work of Marochetti's magisterial chisel; the eminent artist had agreed to sculpt this extraordinary masterpiece, remembering, no doubt, that Benvenuto had not disdained the sculpting of ewers or armor.[86]

Two candelabras and two vermeil torches, fashioned with minute attention by Gouthière, flanked the clock.[87] The clock was made out of a square block of lapis lazuli and was elevated on a plinth of oriental jasper. It was covered with a large and magnificent dome of enameled gold, ornamented with pearls and rubies. This piece had been made during the most beautiful period of the Florentine Renaissance.

Several excellent though average-size paintings of the Venetian school completed an interior decoration of unsurpassed magnificence.[88]

The lamp that softly illuminated this pretty salon was distinguished

86. Carlo Marochetti (1805–1867), an Italian sculptor who lived in France between 1832 and 1848. Benvenuto Cellini (1500–1571), famous sculptor of the Italian Renaissance, also famous for a vibrantly written autobiography that candidly admits several crimes. [TN]

87. Pierre Gouthière (1732–1813), a French metalworker. [TN]

88. School of painting centered in Venice in the fifteenth century, sometimes called the school of Giorgione after one of its most influential practitioners. Other famous members of the school were Titian and, later, Tintoretto. The style of painting was characterized by vividness of light and color as well as by the sensuality of the treatment of subject matter. [TN]

by its charmingly innovative design: its frosted crystal dome disappeared in part amid a cluster of natural flowers contained in a deep and immense Japanese porcelain cup of blue, scarlet, and gold that was suspended from the ceiling like a chandelier by three thick chains of vermeil. Around these chains twined the green shoots of several climbing plants; a few of their branches, swaying and in full flower, overflowed the cup. The branches fell graciously, like a fringe of fresh greenery, on the porcelain enameled in gold, scarlet, and azure.

We emphasize these really picayune details in order to give a sense of Madame d'Harville's naturally good taste—a taste that is almost always the sign of someone with a good heart. We do so also because hidden suffering and mysterious unhappiness seem all the more poignant when contrasted with what appears to everyone to be a happy and enviable life.

Sitting deep in a great armchair totally covered in a straw-colored fabric, like the other chairs in the room, Clémence d'Harville, bareheaded, wore a high-necked dress of black velvet against which stood out the marvelous artistry of its large collar and its flat, pointed, English-style cuffs. The collar and cuffs kept the black velvet from contrasting too violently against the glowing whiteness of her hands and neck.

As the moment of her meeting with Rodolphe drew nigh, the marquise grew more and more uneasy. Nevertheless, her confusion had given way to a resolution: after long reflection, she had decided to reveal a great and cruel secret to Rodolphe, hoping that her extreme candor would win back the esteem he had had for her, one which she had prized highly.

Revived by her gratitude, her earlier attraction to Rodolphe had reawakened with new energy. One of the presentiments that rarely lead hearts that love astray told her that it was not an accident that had led the prince to be there at that precise moment to save her, and that if he had stopped seeing her for the past few months, it was not because the sentiment that determined his actions was aversion. A vague instinct also cast doubt in Clémence's mind as to the sincerity of Sarah's affection.

After a few minutes, after knocking discreetly on the door, a servant entered and said to Clémence, "Would the marquise like to see Madame Asthon and Mademoiselle d'Harville?"

"But of course," answered Madame d'Harville. "I am always happy to see them."

Her daughter slowly walked into the room. She was a child of four who would have had a charming face were it not for her sickly pallor and extreme thinness. Madame Asthon, her governess, held her by the hand. Despite her weakness, Claire (this was the child's name) rushed over to her mother, holding out her arms. Two knots of cherry-red ribbon held her curly brown hair in plaits at each temple. Her health was so frail that she was wearing a little brown quilted silk overcoat instead of one of those pretty white muslin dresses, decorated with ribbons that match those in a child's hair, the kind of dress cut to leave visible the pink arms and smooth, fresh shoulders that are so pleasing to see in healthy children.

The great black eyes of this child seemed enormous in contrast with the hollowness of her cheeks. In spite of her sickly appearance, a smile full of gentleness and grace spread on Claire's face when she sat on her mother's knees. Her mother kissed her with a tenderness that was both sad and passionate.

"How has she been lately, Madame Asthon?" Madame d'Harville asked the governess.

"Well enough, my lady, although for a moment I was afraid—"

"Again?" cried Clémence, holding her daughter tightly to her chest in an involuntary movement of fright.

"Fortunately, madame, I was wrong," said the governess. "The fit did not occur. Mademoiselle Claire calmed down. She had only a momentary weakness. She slept very little after dinner, but she didn't want to go to sleep without coming to kiss her mother."

"Poor little beloved angel!" said Madame d'Harville as she covered her daughter with kisses.

The little girl was returning her kisses with a childish joy when the servant opened the doors of the salon and announced, "His Most Serene Royal Highness, His Lordship, the Grand Duke of Gerolstein!"

Sitting on her mother's knees, Claire had thrown her two arms around her neck and was holding her tightly. At the sight of Rodolphe, Clémence blushed. She put her daughter gently down on the carpet, signaled to Madame Asthon to take the child to bed, and rose.

"You will permit me, madame," said Rodolphe, smiling after having greeted the marquise respectfully, "to renew my acquaintance with my little friend of old who, I fear, has forgotten me." And bending over slightly, he held out his hand to Claire.

At first, Claire stared at him curiously with her large black eyes. Then, recognizing him, she nodded her head sweetly to him and blew him a kiss from her thin little hand.

"Do you remember his lordship, my child?" Clémence asked Claire. She nodded her head in the affirmative and blew him another kiss.

"Her health seems improved since I last saw her," he said sympathetically, as he turned to Clémence.

"She is doing a bit better, my lord, although she is still quite ill."

The marquise and the prince, both embarrassed to think of their impending conversation, were almost glad to have an opportunity to postpone it for a few minutes because of Claire's presence. But once the governess had taken the child discreetly out of the room, Rodolphe and Clémence found themselves alone.

CHAPTER 16

CONFESSIONS

Madame d'Harville's armchair was placed to the right of the fireplace. Rodolphe had remained standing there and was leaning lightly against it, propping himself up on his elbow. Clémence had never before been so struck by how noble and gracious the prince's features were. Never had his voice seemed gentler or more sonorous.

Sensing how painful it was for the marquise to speak first, Rodolphe said to her, "You were the victim of a terrible act of betrayal, madame. Countess Sarah MacGregor's despicable accusation nearly ruined you."

"So it's true, my lord?" cried Clémence. "My intuitions were correct, then . . . And how did my lord manage to find this out?"

"Yesterday, by accident, at the Countess ***'s ball, I uncovered the secret of this vile plot. I was sitting in an isolated spot in the winter garden. Sarah and her brother came to discuss their plans and the trap they were laying for you, little knowing that only a bank of hedges separated them from me and that I could hear them. Thinking you would be at Madame de Nerval's ball, I rushed over there to tell you about the danger you were in, but you never showed up. If I had written to you here that morning, my letter might have fallen into the marquis's hands, and his suspicions must already have been aroused. I preferred to wait for you at rue du Temple in order to foil Sarah's treasonous plan. You will pardon me, will you not, for speaking with you at such length on a topic that must be disagreeable to you? Except for the letter you had the kindness to write me, I never in my life would have mentioned any of this to you."

After a moment of silence, Madame d'Harville said to Rodolphe, "I only have one way to show you my gratitude, my lord, and that is to tell you something that I have told no one. The confession I will make to you will not justify my conduct in your eyes, but it may make it look less blamable."

"Frankly, madame," said Rodolphe, smiling, "my position with regards to you is rather embarrassing."

Taken aback by his almost breezy tone, Clémence looked at Rodolphe with surprise. "I beg your pardon, my lord?"

"Thanks to a circumstance you will no doubt guess, I am obliged to act something like an old uncle regarding an adventure that, once you escaped the countess's odious trap, no longer merited being taken seriously. But," said Rodolphe with a nuance of gentle gravity and affection in his voice, "your husband is almost a brother to me. My father swore his most affectionate gratitude to his father. Thus it is with great seriousness that I congratulate you for having restored your husband's sense of well-being and security."

"And it's also because you honor Monsieur d'Harville with your friendship, my lord, that I insist on telling you the entire truth, about a choice that will surely seem to you as unhappy as, in fact, it is, and about my conduct, which offends the man your highness says is nearly his brother."

"I will always be happy and proud, madame, to receive the least token of your trust. However, please allow me to say, with respect to the choice of which you speak, that I know that you gave in as much to a feeling of sincere pity as to Countess Sarah MacGregor's obsession and her desire, for reasons of her own, to ruin you. I also know that you hesitated for a long time before making the decision you now regret so much."

Clémence looked at the prince with surprise.

"You're surprised? I'll tell you my secret another time so you won't think I'm trying to make myself out to be a sorcerer," Rodolphe replied, smiling. "But is your husband's peace of mind assured now?"

"Yes, my lord," said Clémence, lowering her eyes in confusion. "And I must say that it's painful to hear him asking my forgiveness for having suspected me and to hear him exult at my pursuing my good works so quietly and modestly."

"He's living in a happy illusion; don't begrudge him that. Instead, try to keep him happy in his sweet illusion. If it weren't forbidden for me to speak lightly of your adventure, and if it weren't you who was involved in it, madame, I would say that a woman is never more charming in her husband's eyes than when she is trying to hide something she's done wrong. People have no idea of the seductively sly things a guilty conscience can inspire one to do. They cannot imagine all the ravishing flowers that a perfidious act can bring into full bloom. When I was young," Rodolphe added, with a smile, "I always felt, in spite of myself, a vague distrust rise in me after certain moments of increased tenderness. And as I never felt more at my best than when I had something I needed someone to forgive in me, as soon as someone would behave toward me in a way that is as deceptively amiable as I try to seem myself, I have always been very sure that this charming coincidence of our mutual appearance hid a mutual infidelity."

Madame d'Harville was more and more astonished to hear Rodolphe speak in such mocking humor of an adventure that could have had such horrible consequences for her. But soon she realized that the prince was trying to downplay the importance of the service he had rendered her by pretending to make light of everything. Profoundly touched by his delicacy, she said, "I understand your generosity, my lord. You are permitted to make light of the peril you rescued me from and to forget it. But what I have to tell you is so serious, so sad, and has so much to do with the events of this morning—and your counsel can really be of such use to me—that I beg you keep in mind that you saved my honor and my life. Yes, my lord—my life. My husband was armed. He told me so when his desire for my forgiveness was at its height. He actually wanted to kill me!"

"Good God!" cried Rodolphe, full of emotion.

"It was his right to do so," Madame d'Harville replied, bitterly.

"I must tell you, madame," Rodolphe responded in great seriousness now. "You must believe me: I cannot be indifferent to anything that concerns you. If I was joking a moment ago, it was because I did not want to weigh you down with bleak thoughts about this morning—which must have been a highly emotional one for you. Now, madame, since you honor me by saying that my advice might help you in some way, I will listen with the greatest attention."

"Oh! It will help me immensely, my lord! But before asking you for it, permit me to tell you a few things about my past you do not know about—things from the years that preceded my marriage with Monsieur d'Harville."

Rodolphe inclined his head. Clémence continued. "When I was sixteen years old, I lost my mother," she said, unable to hold back a tear. "I won't tell you how much I adored her. Imagine, monsieur, the ideal of goodness on earth. She always acted toward me with the most exquisite tenderness. She found that it consoled her for bitter troubles. She cared little for society, was of delicate health, and was sedentary by nature. Her greatest pleasure was to take sole charge of my education, for her firmly grounded and wide-ranging knowledge made her better suited than anyone else to this task she set herself.

"Imagine her astonishment, and my own, my lord, when at sixteen, at the moment my education was almost complete, my father, using my mother's delicate health as a pretext, announced that a young and very distinguished widow, whose great suffering merited charitable treatment, was going to finish the job my mother had begun. My mother refused at first to go along with my father's wishes. And I, myself, begged him not to put a stranger between my mother and myself. He was inexorable, however, in spite of our tears. Madame Roland, the widow of a colonel who had died in India, she said, came to live with us and was appointed to be my tutor."

"What? Is that the same Madame Roland whom your father married right after your own marriage?"

"Yes, my lord."

"So she was very beautiful?"

"She was pretty, in an average way, my lord."

"Very intelligent, then?"

"As far as dissimulation and trickery—nothing more. She was about twenty-five years old, with very pale blond hair, eyelashes that were nearly white, and big, round, light blue eyes. Her expression was humble and unctuous; her character, perfidious to the point of cruelty, seemed kind to the point of self-abasement."

"And her teaching?"

"Utterly worthless, my lord. I could not understand how my father, who had been until then an utter slave to convention, had not considered how this woman's lack of intellectual capacity would scandalously betray the real motive of her presence in his home. My mother made him recognize Madame Roland's profound ignorance, but he responded in a manner that did not admit of a reply. He said that this young widow, who merited our sympathy, would occupy the position he had put her in, whether she was knowledgeable or not. I only figured it out later, but my mother understood everything from that point onward. She was deeply disturbed, but she deplored my father's infidelity less, I think, than the internal disorder this liaison was likely to lead to. She also worried that rumors of it would reach my ears."

"But in fact, even from the point of view of his unreasonable passion, your father made an error in calculation when he invited this woman to stay in his home."

"You will be even more astonished, my lord, when I add that my father is a man of the stiffest and most uncompromising character I have ever known. To make him so forgetful of all convention, Madame Roland's influence must have been very great. It was all the more effective in that she hid it behind the appearance of a violent passion for him."

"But how old was your father then?"

"About sixty years old."

"And he believed that this young woman loved him?"

"My father had been one of the most fashionable men of his time. Madame Roland, obeying either her intuition or the clever advice she was getting—"

"Advice? Who was giving her advice?"

"I will tell you in a moment, my lord. Recognizing that a man of some wealth, when he reaches old age, enjoys being flattered on his appearance even more than most men because it reminds him of the happiest moments of his life, this woman—can you believe it, my lord?—flattered my father on his gracefulness, on the charm of his face, on the inimitable elegance of his figure and appearance. And he was sixty years old! Everyone recognizes his great intelligence, and yet he fell blindly into this vulgar trap. That was, and that still is, I'm sure, the source of that woman's influence over him. You know, my lord, I can't keep from smiling, in spite of my sad worries, when I remember having so often heard Madame Roland in the days before my marriage going on and on about how 'real maturity' was the most beautiful age in life. She explained that this real maturity rarely began, truly, before a man had reached the age of fifty-five or sixty."

"Your father's age?"

"Yes, my lord. Only then, Madame Roland said, did wit and experience reach the height of their development. Only then did a man who was eminently placed in society enjoy all of the consideration he deserved. Only then did the overall look of his features and the grace of his manners come together in all their perfection, with his face offering at this time of his life a rare and divine mixture of gracious serenity and gentle gravitas. Finally, a slight tinge of melancholy—caused by the deceptions that experience always brings with it—completed the irresistible charm of this 'real maturity.' This charm could only be appreciated, Madame Roland hastened to add, by women of real discernment and feeling who have the good taste to shrug with indifference at the youthful extravagances of those little dunces who are only forty years old. The character of such men offers no security whatsoever and their features are insignificant and juvenile, since they have yet to be rendered poetic by the majestic expression that a deep knowledge of life lends them."

Rodolphe could not keep himself from smiling at the ironic verve with which Madame d'Harville sketched the portrait of her stepmother.

"There's one thing that I can never forgive in absurd people," he said to the marquise.

"What's that, my lord?"

"It's their wickedness. It gets in the way of just laughing at them, without any second thoughts."

"They've probably taken that into account," said Clémence.

"I think you're right, and it's a pity. For if I could forget, for example, that this Madame Roland had necessarily been quite harmful to you, I would really be amused by her invention of 'real maturity,' in opposition to those forty-year-old starlings who, according to that woman, seem hardly to have completed their apprenticeships, as our grandparents would have said."

"At least, I believe, my father is happy in the illusions in which my stepmother keeps him immersed."

"No doubt, at this point, punished for her falseness, she is having to endure the consequences of her feigned passionate love. Your father took her at her word; he surrounds her with solitude and love. Now, if I may be so bold, the life of your stepmother must be as intolerable as her husband's is happy. Imagine the proud joy of a man of sixty, habituated to success, who believes himself still so passionately adored by a young woman that he inspires in her the desire to shut herself off from the world with him and live in utter isolation."

"And so, my lord, since my father is happy, I should perhaps not complain about Madame Roland. But her despicable behavior to my mother—and the unfortunately too active role she played in my marriage—cause my aversion toward her," said Madame d'Harville after a moment of hesitation.

Rodolphe looked at her with surprise.

"Monsieur d'Harville is your friend, my lord," Clémence went on in a firm voice. "I know the seriousness of the words I have just uttered. In a moment you will tell me if they are merited. But to return first to Madame Roland: she was installed as my tutor, despite her obvious unsuitability. My mother had a painful exchange of words with my father on the subject and told him that, wanting at least to manifest her objection to the intolerable position of this woman in the household, she would no longer appear at meals in the future if Madame Roland did not leave the house on the instant. My mother was sweetness and goodness itself. But she had an unshakeable firmness in the face of challenges to her personal dignity. My father was inflexible; she kept her promise. From that moment on, we lived in complete isolation from him in her chambers in the house. From that time onward, my father displayed as much coldness toward me as he did toward my mother. Madame Roland, meanwhile, became the mistress of the house almost openly, always in the role of being my tutor."

"See how a mad passion will overcome the most distinguished intellect! Especially since we pride ourselves more on qualities or advantages we don't have or no longer have than we do on those we have. To prove to a man of sixty that he's only thirty years old, that's how you flatter people! And the more vulgar the flattery, the further it gets you. Alas, we princes know all about that."

"So people have tried this often on you, my lord."

"In this matter, at least, your father has been treated like a king, but your mother must have suffered terribly."

"More on my account than on her own, my lord, because she was thinking about the future. Her health, which was already very delicate, became even worse. She fell gravely ill. Fate had it that our house doctor, Monsieur Sorbier, died. My mother had complete confidence in him and was very sorry to lose him. Madame Roland had a doctor and friend who was an Italian of considerable skill, she claimed. My father, persuaded by her, consulted him sometimes and felt better as a result. He proposed that my mother consult him, and she did—alas!—and thus it was this man who was caring for her during her last illness." As she said these words, Madame d'Harville's eyes welled up with tears. "I am ashamed to admit my weakness to you, my lord," she added, "but the very fact that this doctor had come to my father by way of Madame Roland, without any other reason, made me feel an involuntary revulsion for him. I watched in fear as my mother put her trust in him. However, as far as his knowledge went, Doctor Polidori—"

"What did you say, madame?" Rodolphe exclaimed.

"What's wrong, my lord?" said Clémence, bewildered at the change in Rodolphe's expression.

"No, it couldn't be possible!" said the prince to himself. "I must be wrong. That was five or six years ago, and I've been told that Polidori has only been in Paris for about the last two years, living under an assumed identity. It was him I saw yesterday—that charlatan Bradamanti. Still, two doctors with the same name[89] . . . what a coincidence!" Turning to Madame d'Harville, he said, "I need to ask you a few things about this Doctor Polidori." She looked at him with increasing surprise. "How old was this Italian man?"

"About fifty."

"What was his face like—how did he look?"

"Sinister. I will never forget his light green eyes, nor his nose, hooked like an eagle's beak."

"That's him! It's really the same man!" exclaimed Rodolphe. "Do you believe, madame, that Doctor Polidori is still living in Paris?" he asked Madame d'Harville.

"I don't know anything about that, my lord. About a year after my father's marriage, he left Paris. One of my friends who was also a patient of this Italian at the time, Madame de Lucenay—"

"The Duchess de Lucenay!" cried Rodolphe.

"Yes, my lord. Why are you so shocked?"

"I beg your permission to remain silent about that for the moment. But at that time, what did Madame de Lucenay say about that man?"

"That he wrote to her frequently, after he had left Paris, very witty letters about the countries he visited—he did a lot of traveling. It comes back to me now that a month ago, when I asked Madame de Lucenay if she was still hearing from Monsieur Polidori, she answered me in a troubled way that no one had heard anything of him for a long while, that people had no idea what had become of him, and that some people even thought he might have died."

"That's odd," said Rodolphe, remembering Madame de Lucenay's visit to the charlatan Bradamanti.

"You know this man, then, my lord?"

"Unfortunately for me, I do. But please, go on with your story. Later I'll tell you who this Polidori really is."

"What? That doctor—"

"Say, rather, 'that man who has committed the vilest crimes.'"

"Crimes," Madame d'Harville cried out, in fear. "That man committed crimes? The friend of Madame Roland and my mother's doctor?

---

89. We will remind the reader that Polidori was a distinguished doctor when he took over as Rodolphe's tutor. [SN]

My mother died in his care, a few days after she took ill! Ah! My lord, you terrify me! You are either telling me too much or not enough!"

"Without accusing that man of another crime, without accusing your stepmother of a horrifying complicity in it, I can tell you that you should perhaps thank God that your father has not needed the medical attention of Polidori since marrying Madame Roland."

"My God!" cried Madame d'Harville with a heartrending wail. "So my intuitions weren't wrong, then!"

"Your intuitions?"

"Yes . . . a moment ago, I was telling you about the revulsion I felt toward that doctor because he had been brought into the household by Madame Roland. I haven't told you everything, my lord."

"What else?"

"I was afraid of accusing an innocent person, of being unduly influenced by my own bitter sorrows. But I'll tell you everything, my lord. My mother's illness lasted five days. I had watched over her all that time. One evening I went out for a breath of fresh air on the terrace of our house. I returned after a quarter of an hour by way of a long, dark hallway. In the faint light that came from Madame Roland's rooms, I saw Monsieur Polidori leaving. Madame Roland accompanied him. I was in the shadows, so they didn't see me. Madame Roland said a few words to him in a low whisper that I couldn't hear. The doctor answered in a slightly louder voice, 'The day after tomorrow.' And when Madame Roland whispered something else to him, he answered her again, in a peculiar way, 'The day after tomorrow, I told you. The day after tomorrow.'"

"What did he mean?"

"What did that mean, my lord? Well, on Wednesday night, Monsieur Polidori said, 'The day after tomorrow.' On Friday, my mother was dead!"

"Oh! That's shocking!"

"When I thought back and reflected on the words 'the day after tomorrow,' which seemed to have predicted the time of my mother's death, they kept coming back to me. I thought that Monsieur Polidori, with his medical knowledge, having recognized how little time my mother had left to her, had rushed over to see Madame Roland to keep her informed. Madame Roland had only too many reasons to rejoice at the prospect of my mother's death. This alone made me hold these two in horror. But I would never have dared to think that—oh! No, no—I still can't believe they could have committed a crime like that!"

"Was Polidori the only doctor who cared for your unfortunate mother?"

"The day before she died, that man brought in one of his colleagues for a consultation. According to what my father told me later, this doctor found my mother in a very dangerous state. After this sad event, I was taken to stay with one of our relatives. She had loved my mother dearly.

Forgetting the discretion she owed to one of my young age, this relative made it only too clear to me how many reasons I had to hate Madame Roland. She made clear to me the ambitious hopes this woman henceforth must have had. This revelation overwhelmed me. I finally understood how much my mother must have suffered. When I saw my father again, my heart was broken. He came to pick me up to take me to Normandy. We were supposed to spend the beginning of our period of mourning there. Along the way, he wept frequently and told me that only I could help him bear up under this grief. I answered him, with profound emotion, that he was all I had left after the loss of the most beloved of mothers. After a few words about how troubling it would be if he had to leave me alone during the absences that his business affairs forced upon him from time to time, he told me—abruptly, and as if it was the most natural thing in the world—that, happily for him and for me, Madame Roland had consented to take up the management of the household and to serve as my guide and friend.

"Astonishment, pain, and indignation—all rendered me speechless. I wept in silence. My father asked me the cause of my tears. I exclaimed, too bitterly, I'm sure, that I would never live in the same house as Madame Roland, that I despised that woman as much as I hated her for the sorrows she had brought upon my mother. He remained calm and argued against what he called my 'childishness.' Then he told me coldly that this was his final decision and that I would have to submit to it.

"I begged him to let me go to the Sacré-Coeur convent, where I had some friends. I would remain there until he thought it was time for me to marry. He informed me that the time had gone by when girls got married right upon leaving the convent. He said that my eagerness to leave him would be very hurtful to him if he didn't know that a forgivable but irrational overexcitement motivated my speech. He was sure that I would calm down, he said. Then he kissed my forehead and called me a foolish girl.

"Alas! Indeed, I had to give in. Imagine, my lord, how painful it was for me! I had to live every day with a woman I all but blamed for my mother's death. I foresaw the most painful scenes between my father and myself, since I knew I would never be able to hold back the aversion I felt for Madame Roland. It seemed to me that only by showing my hatred could I avenge my mother, and that the smallest sign of affection given to that woman would be an act of sacrilegious cowardice on my part."

"That existence must have been painful for you. How little I knew how much you had already suffered when I had the more frequent pleasure of your company! You never said a word that led me to suspect that—"

"That's because then, my lord, I had no need to excuse myself in your eyes for having behaved with unpardonable weakness. If I am speaking at length to you about this period of my life, it is to make you understand the position I was in when I got married—and why, despite a warning I received that should have made things clear to me, I married Monsieur d'Harville.

"When we arrived at Aubiers (that's the name of my father's property), the first person who came to see us was Madame Roland. She had gone to set herself up there the day my mother died. In spite of her humble and sweet appearance, she was already allowing herself to display a poorly hidden triumphant joy. I will never forget the look she gave me upon my arrival. It was at once ironic and wicked. She seemed to be saying to me, 'I am here in my own home. It is you who are the stranger.' A new sorrow arose for me: either through an inexcusable want of tact or a shameless impudence, that woman was now occupying my mother's quarters. In my indignation, I complained to my father that it was highly unconventional. He responded with severity that it would surprise me less if I could get accustomed to considering and respecting Madame Roland as a second mother. I said to him that such a prospect profaned the sacred name of my mother. To his great distress, I lost no opportunity to display my aversion toward Madame Roland. Several times he got carried away with his anger and reprimanded me harshly in front of her. He scolded me for my ingratitude, my coldness toward the angel of consolation that fate had sent us. 'I beg you, dear father, to speak for yourself only,' I said to him one day. He treated me cruelly. Madame Roland, with her honeyed voice, interceded on my behalf with deep hypocrisy. 'Be gentle with Clémence,' she said, 'the grief she is feeling for the excellent person we are all mourning is so natural, so praiseworthy that we should show consideration for her sadness and even pity her when she is overcome by her emotions.' 'Well, then!' said my father, gesturing at Madame Roland in admiration. 'Did you hear that? Isn't she incredibly good and incredibly generous? You should throw yourself into her arms to show her your thanks.' 'That would be pointless, Father. She hates me and I hate her.' 'Ah! Clémence! You're hurting me terribly, but I forgive you,' said Madame Roland as she raised her gaze to the heavens. 'My friend! My noble friend!' cried my father in an emotional voice. 'Calm down, I beg of you! Out of consideration for me, have pity on a mad girl who is to be pitied for misjudging you so badly in this way!' Then, glaring at me irritably, he said, 'You had better be afraid for yourself if you dare once again to insult the most beautiful soul in the world. Tell her you're sorry this instant!' 'My mother sees me and hears me. She wouldn't forgive me such cowardice,' I said to my father. I left, leaving him to comfort Madame Roland and to dry her phony tears. Pardon me, my lord, for stressing these childish scenes, but I need to do so in order to give you an idea of the life I was leading at that time."

"I feel as if I had been present during these scenes in your home—they are so sad and human in their truthfulness. How many families have experienced such scenes, and how many more will experience them in the future? There is nothing more vulgar, but at the same time nothing more clever, than Madame Roland's conduct. It's so easy to be treacherous that the means of treachery are at the fingertips of many unintelligent people. And even then, that woman wasn't so clever—it was your father, rather, who was blind. But in which capacity did Madame Roland present herself to the community?"

"As my tutor and friend. And they accepted her that way."

"I need not ask you whether he lived in the same conditions of isolation?"

"Except for a few rare visits that were necessary due to relations with the neighbors or business associates, we never saw anyone. My father, completely dominated by his passion and giving in no doubt to Madame Roland's insistence, stopped dressing in mourning for my mother after barely three months—on the pretext that his mourning was taking place internally, in his heart. His coldness toward me increased more and more; his indifference grew to the point that he gave me unimaginable liberty for a girl of my age. I would see him at lunchtime. He would return to his rooms then with Madame Roland, who acted as his secretary for his business correspondence. Then he would go out with her by car or on foot, and he wouldn't return until an hour before dinner. Madame Roland dressed herself up in a fresh and charming manner, while my father dressed with a care that was strange for someone of his age. Sometimes, after dinner, he received people he couldn't avoid seeing. After that, he would play a game of backgammon with Madame Roland until ten o'clock, and then he would offer her his arm in order to lead her to my mother's room, kiss her hand respectfully, and finally withdraw to his own rooms. As for me, I could do whatever I wanted with my days. I could ride my horse with a servant or take long walks as I pleased in the woods that surrounded the château. Sometimes, overwhelmed with sadness, I didn't appear at lunch. My father wasn't in the slightest bit concerned."

"What peculiar obliviousness! What neglect!"

"After meeting one of our neighbors several times in a row in the woods in which I ordinarily rode my horse, I stopped my promenades and never left the grounds again."

"But how did that woman treat you when you were alone with her?"

"She avoided such meetings as much as she could, just as I did. One time only, she alluded to some harsh things I had said to her the day before. She said to me coldly, 'Be careful. You want to fight me, but I'll break you.' 'The way you did with my mother?' I said. 'It's too bad Monsieur Polidori isn't lurking around to promise you that it would be—the day after tomorrow.' These words made a deep impression on Madame Roland, but she quickly overcame it. Now that I know, thanks to you, my lord, the kind of person Doctor Polidori is, and what he is capable of, the fear Madame Roland displayed when she heard me reminding her of those mysterious words may well confirm the horrible suspicions I had . . . But no, no, I don't want to believe that. I would be too horrified to think that my father is at this moment at the mercy of that woman."

"And what did she say to you when you recalled Polidori's words to her?"

"She blushed at first. Then, overcoming her emotion, she asked me what I meant. I answered, 'Think about it, madame, when you are alone. You know what I'm talking about.' A little while after that, a scene took place that basically decided my fate. In the salon where we assembled in the evenings hung a portrait of my mother, among many other paintings. One day I noticed that it was gone. Two of our neighbors had dined with us. One of them, Monsieur Dorval, a country barrister, had always had the greatest admiration for my mother. When he arrived in the salon, I asked, 'Where did my mother's portrait go?' 'Seeing that painting was too painful for me,' said my father, embarrassed; he glanced quickly at the outsiders who were witness to this conversation. 'And where is the portrait now, Father?' He turned to Madame Roland and gave her a querying and impatient look. 'Where was the portrait put?' he asked her. 'In the furniture warehouse,' she answered, looking at me this time in defiance, figuring that the presence of our neighbors would prevent me from responding. 'I understand, madame,' I said to her coldly, 'that my mother's gaze must be difficult for you to countenance, but that is no reason to relegate to the storehouse the portrait of a woman who, when you were poor, was charitable enough to allow you to live in her home.'"

"Well done!" exclaimed Rodolphe. "You must have crushed her with your glacial disdain."

"'Mademoiselle!' exploded my father. 'But you yourself know,' I said, interrupting him, 'that a person who insults the memory, in a cowardly way, of a woman who gave alms to her merits only scorn and aversion.' My father was momentarily stunned. Madame Roland became scarlet with shame and anger. The neighbors were very embarrassed. They lowered their gazes and stayed silent. 'Mademoiselle!' continued my father. 'You forget that Madame is the friend of your mother. You forget that Madame has tended—and still tends—to your education with a maternal interest. You are forgetting finally that I have the greatest esteem for her. And since you have allowed yourself to lash out in such an unconventional manner before these gentlemen, I myself will tell you that I call ingrates and cowards those who, forgetting the most tender care shown them, dare to reproach a person who deserves care and respect for having suffered a noble misfortune.' 'I will refrain from arguing about this matter with you, Father,' I said in a submissive voice. 'Perhaps, mademoiselle, I will be happier that way myself!' cried Madame Roland, the limits of her habitual equanimity for once overcome by her anger. 'Perhaps you will do me the kindness not only not to argue about it,' she went on, 'but further, to acknowledge that, far from owing your mother the slightest gratitude, I need only remember the distance she always kept from me. It was very much against her will that I—' 'Ah, madame!' I said to her, interrupting her. 'Out of respect for my father, out of modesty for yourself, please restrain yourself from making these shameful revelations! You will make me regret having exposed you to such humiliating declarations!' 'What? Mademoiselle!' she cried, almost apoplectic with rage. 'You dare to say—' 'I am saying, madame,' I said, interrupting her again, 'I am saying that my mother, in deigning to allow you to live in her home instead of sending you packing, as was her right, must have proven to you, by her scorn, that her tolerance in your regard was forced.'"

"Better and better!" exclaimed Rodolphe. "Perfect execution! And that woman?"

"Madame Roland cut off our conversation in a very vulgar but very convenient way. She cried, 'Good Lord!' and fell ill. Thanks to that incident, the two witnesses to this scene departed, on the pretext of going to get help. I imitated them by leaving while my father made a great show of caring for Madame Roland with the utmost zeal."

"How angry your father must have been when you saw him again!"

"He came to my quarters the next morning and said to me, 'In order to prevent scenes such as the one you made yesterday from repeating themselves, I am hereby informing you that, as soon as our period of mourning is over, I am going to marry Madame Roland. You will thus have to treat her from this time onward with the respect and esteem that are owed to—my wife. For complicated reasons, it is necessary for you to marry before me. Your mother's fortune is more than a million francs: that is your dowry. From this day onward I will be actively looking for a suitable union for you. I will be pursuing several propositions that have been made to me with regard to you. The persistence with which you have attacked a person who is so dear to me, even though I have begged you to stop, allows me to see just how little affection you have for me. Madame Roland can ignore these attacks, but I will not tolerate such scenes to be repeated in my own home in front of outsiders. From now on, you will not enter or stay in the salon except for when we are there alone.'

"After that last conversation, I lived in even greater isolation. I saw my father only during meals, and those meals took place in gloomy silence. My life was so sad that I was impatient for the moment that my father would give me the chance to get married, no matter to whom. Madame Roland stopped speaking ill of my mother but got her revenge by making me suffer from a constant torture: purely in order to exasperate me, she decided to use things that had belonged to my mother. Her armchair, her tapestry frame, books from her private library—even a table-screen I had embroidered for her with her monogram in the middle of it. That woman profaned everything."

"Oh! I can only imagine the horror that must have caused you."

"And the isolation made everything so much worse."

"You had no one to whom you could turn?"

"No one. However, I did receive evidence of caring that moved me, evidence that should have helped me to understand what was in store for me. One of the two witnesses to the scene in which I had treated Madame Roland so badly was Monsieur Dorval, an old and honest lawyer. My mother had helped him with regard to one of his nieces. In accordance with my father's decree, I did not go into the salon anymore when there were guests there. I had thus not seen Monsieur Dorval again when, to my great surprise, he came by one day mysteriously to find me on a path in the park where I took my daily walk. 'Mademoiselle,' he said to me, 'I fear that the count will know that I am here. Read this letter and burn it immediately afterward. There is some very important information for you in it.' And he disappeared.

"In this letter, he told me that I was set to be married to the Marquis d'Harville. This prospect seemed agreeable in every way. Monsieur d'Harville was said to have good qualities: he was young, very rich, of a distinguished intelligence, and with an attractive face. Yet the families of the two young women he was supposed to have married had abruptly called off the marriage, one after the other. The lawyer could not tell me the reason for the ruptures, but he said he thought it was his duty to warn me of them, without claiming that the reason for these ruptures had anything to do with any fault of Monsieur d'Harville. The two young women concerned were the daughters of Monsieur de Beauregard, a French peer, and of Lord Boltrop. Monsieur Dorval was confiding this secret to me because my father seemed very impatient to marry me off and did not appear to be attaching as much importance to the circumstances as they might indicate."

"In fact," said Rodolphe after thinking for a few moments, "I remember now that, over the course of a year, your husband announced two upcoming marriages to me that were abruptly broken off at the last moment. He wrote to me that they were broken off because of some financial disagreements."

Madame d'Harville smiled with bitterness and said, "You will know the truth soon enough, my lord. After having read the old lawyer's letter, I felt as much curiosity as anxiety. Who was Monsieur d'Harville? My father had never spoken of him. I searched my memory in vain; I could not remember having heard that name. Soon, Madame Roland left for Paris, to my great astonishment. Her journey was supposed to last at most one week, but my father was terribly upset over this brief separation. His character became sharper, and he behaved even more coldly toward me. He even allowed himself to tell me, one day when I asked him how he was doing, 'I'm suffering, and it's all your fault.' 'My fault, Father?' 'Yes. You know how much I depend on Madame Roland, and that admirable woman whom you've insulted has gone on a journey purely on your behalf, and that journey has taken her far away from me.'

"That sign of Madame Roland's interest in me scared me. I had a vague intuition that it had something to do with my marriage. I will leave you to imagine my father's joy, my lord, when my future stepmother returned. The day after she did, he asked me to come to his chambers. He was alone with her. 'For a long time,' he said to me, 'I have been thinking of your future. Your period of mourning will end in a month. Tomorrow Monsieur d'Harville will be coming here. He is an extremely distinguished young man; he is very rich, and he will be able to bring you happiness in every respect. He has seen you in society, and he has a strong desire to marry you. All of the financial matters have been taken care of. You will have to be married within six weeks. If, on the other hand, some caprice on your part that I'd rather not imagine makes you decide to reject this almost unhoped-for offer, I will still get married, as I said I would, once the period of mourning is over. If that happens, I must tell you that I will tolerate your presence in my home only if you promise to display to my wife the affection and respect she deserves.' 'I understand you well, Father. If I do not marry Monsieur d'Harville, you will get married anyway. So, as far as you and . . . Madame are concerned, there's no reason I should not retire to the Sacré-Coeur convent.' 'None at all,' he answered me, coldly."

"Ah, that's no longer mere weakness—that's outright cruelty!" exclaimed Rodolphe.

"You know, my lord, the thing that always prevented me from harboring any resentment against my father was that I had a kind of presentiment that he would pay dearly one day for this blind passion he had for Madame Roland. Thank God, that day has not yet arrived."

"And you told him nothing about what the old lawyer told you about the two marriages that had been so abruptly called off by the families with whom Monsieur d'Harville was to ally himself?"

"Yes, I did, my lord. That very day, I asked my father to give me the chance to speak with him privately. 'I have no secrets from Madame Roland. You can talk to me in front of her,' he said. I remained silent. He went on, with severity in his voice: 'Once again, I have no secrets from Madame Roland. Tell me clearly what this is all about.' 'Please allow me, Father, to speak with you alone.' Madame Roland got up abruptly and left the room. 'Are you satisfied now?' he asked me. 'So? Talk.' 'I feel no antipathy toward the union you have proposed for me, Father; I just wanted to say that I have heard that Monsieur d'Harville was about to get married two other times and—' 'Fine, fine,' he interrupted me, 'I know what happened there. Those breaks took place because of arguments over finances in which, by the way, Monsieur d'Harville's privacy was completely safeguarded. If that's the only objection you have, you're as good as married already—and happily married, because all I want is for you to be happy.'"

"No doubt Madame Roland was thrilled with this marriage?"

"Thrilled? Yes, my lord," said Clémence, bitterly. "Oh, she was thrilled, all right—for this marriage was all her doing. She had given my father the idea to pursue it. She knew what the real reason was that Monsieur d'Harville's other marriages were called off. That's why she was so interested in having me marry him."

"But to what end?"

"She wanted to avenge herself on me by delivering me to a terrible fate."

"But your father—"

"He was deceived by Madame Roland. He believed that it was true that the only reason Monsieur d'Harville's plans didn't work out was that there were financial disagreements."

"What a horrible conspiracy! But what was this mysterious reason?"

"I will tell you in just a moment, my lord. Monsieur d'Harville arrived in Aubiers. I liked his manners, his intellect, and his face. He seemed kind. His character was sweet, a little sad. I noticed in him a contrast that surprised and pleased me at the same time. His intellect was cultivated, his fortune was the envy of all, his pedigree illustrious; and yet sometimes his face, normally full of energy and resolve, expressed a sort of almost fearful timidity and abjection, a sort of self-doubt that touched me very much. I also liked the way he treated the old valet who had brought him up; he was charming and good to him, and this valet was the only person he would allow to tend to him. After he had been with us for a little while, Monsieur d'Harville stayed in his room for two days. My father wanted to see him. The old servant was opposed to this prospect, giving the pretext that his master had such a violent migraine that he could see absolutely no one. When Monsieur d'Harville reappeared, he looked very pale, very different. Later he seemed to be impatient in an almost peevish way whenever anyone mentioned his brief period of indisposition. The more I got to know Monsieur d'Harville, the more numerous were the qualities I discovered in him that I found to my liking. He had so many reasons to be happy that I was grateful to him for his modesty in his happiness. The date of our marriage was arranged. He always went above and beyond satisfying my slightest wishes for our future plans. If sometimes I asked him the cause of his sadness, he spoke to me of his mother and father, who would have been so proud and thrilled to see him marry someone so dear to his heart and so greatly to his liking. I would have been ungracious if I didn't accept such a flattering explanation. Monsieur d'Harville guessed the relations in which I had lived at first with Madame Roland and my father, even though the latter, happy that I was getting married because it allowed him to get married sooner, had become very affectionate with me again.

In several conversations, Monsieur d'Harville let me understand, with great tact and restraint, that he loved me perhaps even more on account of my past sorrows. On this matter, I thought it was my duty to let him know that my father wished to remarry. When I spoke to him about the way that marriage would affect my fortune, he wouldn't let me finish what I was saying, proving to me his noble disinterestedness. The families he had been on the verge of marrying into must have been quite greedy, I thought at the time, if they had had such serious financial disagreements with him."

"That's the way I have always known him," said Rodolphe, "full of devotion and tact. But did you never speak with him about those two broken-off marriages?"

"I swear to you, my lord, when I saw how honest and kind he was, the question was on the tip of my tongue several times—but soon, out of fear of insulting that honesty, that kindness, I didn't dare broach such a topic. The closer the date of our marriage came, the happier Monsieur d'Harville claimed he was. Even so, I did see him overwhelmed with a gloomy sadness two or three times. One of those days, he looked at me, and a tear fell from his eye. He seemed oppressed; he looked like he wanted to tell me an important secret but didn't dare to do so. What I remembered hearing about those two broken-off marriages came back into my mind. I admit, I was afraid. A secret intuition warned me that it was something that might make me unhappy for my whole life, but I was so tormented living in my father's house that I overcame my fears."

"And Monsieur d'Harville didn't tell you anything?"

"Nothing. When I asked him why he was melancholy, he answered, 'Forgive me; I am happy in a sad way.' Those words, pronounced in such a touching way, reassured me a little. And then, how could I dare? At that very moment, when his eyes were full of tears, how could I challenge him in such an insulting way about his past?

"Monsieur d'Harville's witnesses, Monsieur de Lucenay and Monsieur de Saint-Remy, arrived at Aubiers a few days before my marriage. My closest relatives were the only ones invited to it. We were supposed to go directly to Paris right after the mass. I didn't feel love for Monsieur d'Harville, but I did care for him. His character inspired me with esteem for him. If the events that followed that fatal marriage hadn't happened, I would, no doubt, have more tender feelings for him. The marriage took place."

As she said these words, Madame d'Harville turned slightly pale. Her determination to tell Rodolphe her story seemed to wane. Then she continued: "Right after my marriage, my father held me tenderly in his arms. Madame Roland embraced me, too. I couldn't escape this new kind of hypocrisy, in front of everyone as we were. With her dry, white hand, she squeezed my own hand so hard it was clear she wanted to hurt me. She said in my ear, in a sickeningly sweet and treacherous voice, the words I will never forget: 'Think of me sometimes when you're enjoying your happy marriage, because I'm the one who arranged it for you.'

"Alas! I was far from understanding at that time what those words really meant. Our marriage took place at eleven o'clock; we got into our carriage right after that, followed by my own servant and Monsieur d'Harville's old valet. We were traveling so fast that we should have gotten to Paris before ten o'clock in the evening.

"I would have been taken aback by Monsieur d'Harville's silence and melancholia if I hadn't been given to understand that he was prone to what he called 'sad happiness.' I was terribly emotional myself because I was returning to Paris for the first time since my mother's death. Also, even though I hardly had any cause to miss my father's home, that was the home I had known, and I was leaving it for a house in which everything would be new and unfamiliar. I was going to arrive there alone with my husband, whom I had known for scarcely six weeks, a man who the day before had said nothing to me that wasn't phrased in a formal and respectful way. Perhaps people don't realize how frightening the abrupt change is for women in the tone and manners of even well-bred men once we women belong to them. No one thinks about the fact that a young woman can't forget her timidity, her young girl's scruples, in just a few hours."

"Nothing has ever seemed more barbaric or more savage than the custom of brutally carrying a young woman off as if she were prey. Marriage should be only the consecration of the right to make use of all of love's resources, to make use of all the seductions of passionate tenderness to endear oneself to one's beloved."

"You understand, then, my lord, the heartbreak and the vague terror I felt as I returned to Paris, the city in which my mother had died hardly a year before. We arrived at the Harville mansion."

The young woman became more emotional; her cheeks had turned bright red, and she went on, in a heartrending voice: "It is essential that you know everything. If you don't, you will think me detestable." She went on, resolute in her desperation. "I was taken to the rooms that had been assigned to me. I was left alone. Monsieur d'Harville came to join me. Even though he insisted that he only had tender feelings for me, I was utterly terrified. I was sobbing so hard that I nearly choked. I was his; I had to resign myself to my fate. But soon my husband let out a terrible cry and took me so hard by the arm that it almost broke. I tried in vain to escape from his iron grip; I begged him to have mercy on me, but he did not hear my pleas. His face contracted in frightening convulsions. His eyes were rolling in their sockets with a rapidity that was mesmerizing. His misshapen mouth was full of bloody foam. His arm was still constraining me. I made a desperate effort, and his stiff fingers fell away, finally, from my arm. I fainted away just as Monsieur d'Harville was struggling in the paroxysm of that horrible attack. That was my wedding night, my lord! That was Madame Roland's revenge!"

"Poor woman!" said Rodolphe, overcome with pity. "Now I understand . . . he's an epileptic! Oh, how dreadful!"

"And that's not all," added Clémence in a voice that was painful to hear. "Oh! May that fatal night be forever cursed! My daughter—my poor little angel—has inherited her father's horrifying illness!"

"Your daughter as well? Really? Is that why she is so pale, so weak?"

"That's why . . . God! That's why, and the doctors all think that the condition is incurable because it is hereditary."

Madame d'Harville hid her head in her hands. Overcome by her painful revelation, she no longer had the courage to say a single word. Rodolphe remained silent as well. His mind recoiled at the thought of the terrible mysteries of that wedding night. He imagined what it must have been like for a young woman who was already saddened to be returning to the city in which her mother had died. She had arrived in this unfamiliar house, alone with a man for whom she felt caring interest and esteem but no love—nothing of that unsettling feeling that troubles people so delightfully, none of that sense of intoxication that makes a chaste woman forget her fear completely in the midst of her enjoyment of a legitimate, mutual passion.

No, no—trembling in modesty and fear, Clémence had arrived sad, cold, heartbroken, blushing with shame, her eyes filled with tears. She had resigned herself, and then, instead of hearing words of acknowledgment, love, and tenderness, words that would console her for the happiness she was giving him, she had watched as her husband rolled around at her feet—disoriented, writhing, foaming at the mouth, bellowing as he underwent the appalling convulsions caused by one of the most frightening and incurable maladies humans can be struck with!

And that was not all. Her daughter—poor little innocent angel—was withering already with the disease, even at the moment of her birth.

These painful and sad confessions produced bitter reflections in Rodolphe. The law in this country ordains, he said to himself, that if a beautiful, young, pure woman who is loyal, trusting, and the victim of a cynical fraud who unites her destiny to that of a man who has a terrible disease, a fatal inheritance that he must pass on to his children—if this woman uncovers this horrible mystery, what can she do? Nothing at all . . . she can do nothing but suffer and cry; nothing but try to transcend her disgust and her fear; nothing but spend her days in anguish, in infinite terror; nothing but search, perhaps, to console herself with guilty pleasures outside the bounds of the desolate existence to which she has been condemned.

Once again, thought Rodolphe, these strange laws sometimes force people into shameful compromises that make humanity weep. According to these laws, animals always seem to make out better than humans when one considers the care they are given, the improvements that are sought for them, the protection they are granted, the guarantees that are made to assure their well-being. Thus, if you buy any animal, if the animal has an infirmity covered by the law, the purchase is null and void. Of course, what an indignity, what an outrage against society it is to force a man to keep an animal that coughs, wheezes, or limps! It's considered a scandal, a crime, an unparalleled monstrosity! Imagine, then, being forced to keep—to keep forever—for its whole life—a mule that coughs, a horse that wheezes, a donkey that limps! What sort of terrible consequences would it not imply for the health of all of humanity! Thus, there can be no deal in such a case that holds, no words that bind, no contract that engages the parties. The law in all its power can undo all of the transactions that were completed.

But if it is a creature made in God's image instead of an animal, if it is a young woman who, in her innocent faith in a man's honesty, unites with him and realizes that she is in the company of an epileptic, of an unfortunate person struck by a terrible disease with frightening moral and physical consequences, a disease that can create disorder and aversion in the family, perpetuate itself horribly, and afflict generations—oh! The law that is so inexorable when it comes to lame or wheezing or coughing animals—such a farsighted law that sees to it that an unsound horse does not mate—that law does nothing to help the victim of such a union. These bonds are sacred and indissoluble. To break them is to offend man and God alike.

Truly, mused Rodolphe, humans sometimes manifest a shameful blend of humility and obscenely proud selfishness. They reduce themselves to a level beneath the beast by covering the animal with guarantees they refuse to offer themselves. They impose the most challenging infirmities on themselves and dedicate themselves to perpetuating them by placing these diseases under the protection of an immutable divine and human law.

CHAPTER 17

CHARITY

Rodolphe considered Monsieur d'Harville to be much to blame for what happened, but he took it upon himself to excuse his friend in Clémence's eyes, even though he well knew that, considering the sadness she had revealed to him, the marquis had forever alienated her affections.

Rodolphe's thought process was as follows:

"As a matter of duty, I have kept myself apart from a woman I loved, and who may well already, although unaware of it, have had some feeling for me. Either because her heart was unoccupied or through pity, she very nearly sacrificed her honor, indeed her life, for a fool she thought to be suffering. If instead of keeping myself apart, I had showered her with attention, love, and respect, still my self-constraint would have been such that there would have not been the slightest shadow cast on her reputation and her husband's suspicions would never have been awakened. Instead, she is at this very moment at the mercy of Monsieur Charles Robert's stupidity, and I fear, given that he has no reason for discretion, he will hardly exercise any.

"And then, even despite the dangers she has run, who knows whether Madame d'Harville's heart will remain forever her own? There is no chance that it will ever turn back to her husband. Young, beautiful, possessed of a personality that will always feel sympathy for all who suffer—how many dangers will she face, how many reefs will she skirt? As for Monsieur d'Harville, how much anguish, how much sorrow is in store for him! Both in love with his wife and jealous of her, he will never be able to overcome the estrangement, the fear, that that sad wedding night has awakened in her. What a future awaits him!"

So much had her revelation cost her that Clémence, her forehead resting in her hands, her eyes wet, her cheeks burning with confusion, did all she could to avoid Rodolphe's eyes.

"So! Now," Rodolphe went on after a long silence, "I understand the reasons for Monsieur d'Harville's sadness. Up to now, I never could figure out what they were . . . now I understand his sorrows."

"His sorrows!" Clémence protested. "Say rather his remorse, my lord—if he in fact experiences any—since never has a like crime been so coldly calculated."

"A crime, madame?"

"And what else can one call it, my lord? Attaching yourself with unbreakable chains to a young woman who trusts in your honor, even as you know yourself to be fatally stricken with a disease that inspires nothing but fear and horror—what is that but a crime? What would you call it to condemn an unfortunate child to the same wretchedness? Who forced Monsieur d'Harville to create two new victims of his disease? A blind and reasonless passion? Not at all. He found my birth, my fortune, and my person to his liking. He had likely become bored with the bachelor's life and simply wanted to make a suitable marriage."

"Madame, do you not feel any pity?"

"Pity! Do you know who deserves my pity? My daughter, the innocent victim of this revolting marriage! How many days, how many nights, have I spent by her side, how many tears have I shed over her suffering!"

"But her father suffers the same undeserved misery!"

"But that very father has condemned her to a sickly childhood, a withered-up youth, and, if she lives, a life of loneliness and sorrow, since certainly she will never marry. No! I could never expose her to the pain of mourning for her own child, fatally stricken, as I mourn for her. His betrayal has been far too painful for me to make me cause or participate in any crime like it!"

"Oh, you're right! Your mother-in-law's revenge was truly terrible. But be patient . . . perhaps your turn will come," Rodolphe said after a moment of meditation.

"What do you mean to say, my lord?" Clémence asked, in surprise at his tone of voice.

"I have nearly always had, let us say, the good fortune, of seeing the wicked I have known punished—and cruelly punished, I assure you," he added in a tone that made Clémence tremble. "But, the day after that terrible wedding night, what did your husband say to you?"

"He confessed to me, with a strange innocence, that the families with which he had tried to ally himself had discovered the secret of his illness and had all broken off the planned marriages. Thus, having been twice rejected, he again tried—oh, that was truly vile! And yet, in our society, this is what we call a gentleman, a man of honor and feeling!"

"You are always so kind and now you are too cruel!"

"I am cruel because I have been unjustly deceived. Monsieur d'Harville knew me to be kind. Why didn't he appeal to my kindness and tell me the whole truth!"

"You would have turned him down."

"Your own words condemn him, my lord. If he feared that rejection, then he betrayed me, despicably."

"But he loved you!"

"If he loved me, shouldn't he have given up his selfishness? God knows,

I was in so much pain, I wanted so much to leave my father's house, maybe I would have been touched, moved by his condition, the reprobation to which he was condemned, and the loneliness that his horrible fate had in store for him. Yes, seeing him at once so honest and so unhappy, perhaps I would not have been able to turn him down: and if that had been how I took the holy vow to suffer the consequences of my giving myself to him, I would fearlessly have kept my promise. But to try to compel my sympathy and pity, while first making me dependent upon him—indeed, to demand that sympathy and pity in the name of my duties as a woman, at the same moment that he was betraying his own duties as an honest man—that was madness, and it was cowardly. Now, my lord, you be the judge of my life, you be the judge of the cruel deceptions practiced upon me. I put my faith in Monsieur d'Harville's honesty and he shamefully took advantage of me: his sweet and timid melancholy evoked my sympathy; and that melancholy that he said was caused by pious memories was nothing but his awareness of his incurable disease."

"But, really, were he a stranger to you, indeed an enemy, you would surely have pitied the spectacle of his suffering: you have such a noble and generous heart."

"But can I do anything to alleviate that suffering? If he could even hear my voice, if he could even respond to my look of tender care with any sign of recognition! But that can never be. Oh, my lord, you don't know how terrifying these attacks are. When they strike, the man struggles in savage madness; he sees nothing, he hears nothing, he feels nothing. And when the frenzy finally falls away, it leaves him in a sort of animal-like despondency. When my daughter falls prey to one of these attacks, there is nothing for me to do but suffer; my heart breaks; weeping, I kiss her arms, rigid from the murderous convulsions. And it's my daughter, my daughter! And when I see her suffer like that, I curse her father a thousand times over again each time. If my daughter's suffering would abate, so would my anger against my husband abate; then . . . yes, then, because I am kind, I would pity him and my distaste for him would be replaced by a feeling of pity for his pain. But finally, did I get married at seventeen only to experience forever either hatred or a painful compassion, to weep for an unfortunate child who may well not be long for this world? And speaking of my daughter, my lord, please allow me to forestall a reproach that I may well merit and that you may not feel you ought to make. She is so pitiable that she should be enough to occupy my heart, and I do love her passionately; but this heartbreaking love is mixed with so much bitterness for her present and so much fear for her future that my tender feelings for my daughter always end in tears. Seeing her, my heart is continually broken again, tormented, rendered desperate because I am unable to conjure away that illness that people tell me is incurable. And so, to get away from my overwhelming and sinister life, I dreamed of an attachment that would be for me sweet refuge and repose. Alas, I was deceived, I admit it, I was despicably deceived, and so here I am again, fallen back into the miserable existence to which my husband has condemned me. So you tell me, my lord, is this the life I had a right to expect? Was I alone guilty of the wrong for which, that morning, Monsieur d'Harville wanted to make me pay with my life? I have wronged greatly, I know it, that much more greatly in that my choice of men is one I can only blush for. Luckily for me, my lord, you overheard Sarah and her brother plotting about Monsieur Charles Robert and thus spared me the shame of this new confession. But at least now I hope that you will see me as someone as much to be pitied as blamed, and that you will consent to advise me in the cruel position in which I find myself."

"I cannot begin to say, madame, how much your story moves me; from the time your mother died to the time your daughter was born, you have had nothing but heartrending sorrow and hidden sadness—you, so alive, so admired, so envied!"

"Believe me, my lord, there are some pains from which you can suffer that make it terrible to hear said about yourself, 'She is so happy!'"

"It's true, isn't it? There is nothing more puerile. Well, then, know that you are not alone in suffering from this cruel opposition between what is and what appears to be."

"What do you mean, my lord?"

"In the eyes of the world, your husband must seem even happier than you since you belong to him. And yet, isn't he also very much to be pitied? Is there an existence in the world more atrocious than his? He has wronged you greatly. But he has also been horribly punished for it! He loves you as you deserve to be loved—and he knows that you can feel for him only an insurmountable aversion. His suffering and sickly child is a constant reproach to him. And then, to top it all, comes jealousy to torture him further."

"And what can I do about that, my lord? Remove from him the right to be jealous? With all my heart. But because my heart doesn't belong to anyone, that hardly means that it will belong to him. And he knows that. Since the terrible scene I told you about, we have lived separately. But as far as the world is concerned, I have all the feelings for him that one expects in a wife. And except to you, my lord, I have never breathed a word of this terrible secret."

"And, madame, I must tell you that if I have done you any service that merits any reward, I think myself paid back a thousand times over by the trust you have shown in me. But since you ask my advice, I ask first your permission to speak to you frankly."

"My lord, please, I ask for nothing better."

"Let me tell you, then, that because you do not put to use one of your most precious gifts, you are denying yourself great joys that would not only meet your heart's demands, distract you from your domestic troubles, and respond to your need for lively, poignant sentiment, but, I would almost daresay (if you will pardon my bad opinion of women), would respond to that taste for mystery and intrigue that has so much power over the female sex."

"What do you mean, my lord?"

"I mean that if you chose to entertain yourself by doing good deeds, nothing would give you more pleasure; nothing would engage you more." Madame d'Harville looked at Rodolphe with amazement. "You understand," he went on, "that I'm not suggesting that you send some generous contribution in any careless or almost disdainful way to unfortunate people you know nothing of and who may well not deserve your generosity. But if you entertained yourself as I do by playing the role of divine justice from time to time, you would find that certain good deeds can sometimes be as engaging as novels."

"I had never thought, my lord, of seeing charity from the point of view of being entertaining," Clémence said, smiling in her turn.

"It's a discovery I owe to my aversion toward anything that's boring, an aversion that political discussions with my ministers, more than anything else, inspire in me. But to return to our entertaining good deeds, I do not, alas, possess that virtue of the disinterested who place the care of dispensing their alms in the hands of others. If it were simply a matter of sending my chamberlains with some hundreds of louis to each Parisian arrondissement, I confess to my shame that I would not have much taste for the business. Doing good the way I mean it, however? Well, there's nothing more entertaining in the world than that. I insist on that word because for me it suggests . . . all that is pleasing, all that is charming, all that makes us attached to something. And truly, madame, if you would like to become my accomplice in various shadowy intrigues of this genre, you will see, I repeat, that, even putting aside the nobleness of the action, there is often nothing more curious, more attractive, more seductive—even sometimes more diverting—than these charitable adventures. And then, think what mysteries one has to engage in to hide one's good deeds! What care one has to take not to be found out! What contrary and powerful emotions one feels at the spectacle of poor, good people weeping with joy upon your arrival! Well, really! It almost makes up for the pouting face of some jealous, unfaithful lover—since jealous lovers are almost always unfaithful in their turn. But hold on! The emotions I'm describing are much like those you felt this morning when you went to rue du Temple. When you left your home, clothed simply so as not to be noticed, your heart would beat every bit as much as it did this morning. You would be just as nervous as you climbed into your modest hackney cab, whose shutters you would close so no one could see you, and then, glancing here and there, fearing to be seen, you would enter just as furtively into some wretched-looking house—just like this morning, I tell you. The only difference is that where before you would say, 'If I'm found out, all is lost,' in this case you would say, 'If I'm found out, people will bless me.' But since one of your lovable traits is modesty, you will surely employ the most perfidious and diabolical ruses to avoid anyone blessing you."

"Oh, my lord!" Clémence cried out, emotionally. "You have saved my life! I can't tell you what new ideas, what consolation and hope your words bring me. You speak truly when you say that putting your heart and soul into making yourself adored by those who suffer is almost like loving. Indeed, it's better than loving. When I put this new existence that I'm catching a glimpse of up against the one that shameful straying would have made for me—well, I reproach myself even more bitterly."

"Now that would make me unhappy," Rodolphe said, smiling, "because all I wanted to do was to help you forget the past and merely show you how many ways there are to distract you from your troubles. Good means and evil ones are so frequently nearly identical—only their ends are different. In a word, if good is as seductive and as entertaining as evil, why not prefer the former? Look, I'll make a completely vulgar comparison. Why do women take for lovers men who aren't worth their husband's little finger? Because love's greatest charm is the tasty attraction of forbidden fruit. Admit it, if you took away from love affairs their fears, anguish, dangers, and tribulations, there wouldn't be much left to them; that's to say, you'd be left with nothing but the lover as he really is. It's more or less like the case of the man to whom his friends say, 'Why don't you marry this widow who is your mistress?' 'Alas! I've thought about it, but then I wouldn't know what to do with my evenings.'"

"It's only too true, my lord," Madame d'Harville said, smiling.

"Well, then, if I can find the means of allowing you to feel this fear, anguish, and nervousness that attract you, if I make use of your natural taste for mystery and adventure, your tendency toward dissimulation and trickery (there's my execrable opinion of women, again; you see how it always comes out, despite my best efforts)," Rodolphe added gaily, "won't I be taking those imperious, inexorable instincts—instincts which are so excellent if used well and so dreadful if used badly—and turning them into impulses toward generosity? So let's think about this. Tell me, wouldn't you like us to cook up between us all sorts of machinations for doing good, charitable treacheries whose victims will always be good people? We'll have to have assignations, intimate correspondence, secrets—and, above all, we'll have to hide everything from the marquis, since your visit this morning has already awakened his suspicions. In sum, if it pleases you, we'll have a complete intrigue, following all the established rules of the genre."

"I accept this shadowy association gratefully and with great pleasure, my lord," Clémence answered in the same bantering tone. "And to begin our novel, let's go back as soon as we can, tomorrow, to those poor people to whom I was only able to give a few words of sympathy this morning. The purse you gave me, you should know, I lost when a lame boy, taking advantage of my fear, stole it from me. Oh, my lord!" Clémence added, her features losing the expression of gentle gaity that had animated them momentarily, "If you could see what wretchedness . . . what a horrible sight! No, I could hardly have believed that such misery existed! And here I am, feeling sorry for myself and complaining against my fate!"

Rodolphe did not want to let Madame d'Harville see how much her reflections, which showed her soul's beauty, touched him. So he began, again, in the same bantering tone, "If you will allow me, I will exclude the Morels from our community and will take care of them on my own. You must promise me especially not to return to this sad house. I live there, after all."

"You, my lord? Surely you're joking!"

"I've never been more serious. It's a humble enough place, it's true—only two hundred francs a year. And then, on top of that, six francs a month, which I pay, liberally enough, for housekeeping to the doorkeeper's wife, Madame Pipelet, that old horror you know only too well. Add to the account that my neighbor is the prettiest seamstress in the whole neighborhood of rue du Temple, Mademoiselle Rigolette, and you really have to agree that for a salesman who makes eighteen hundred francs (I'm passing for a salesman, there), it's not a bad arrangement."

"Your presence there on that dreadful morning—which I could hardly have expected—is proof enough that you mean what you say about living there, my lord. Some charitable affair brings you there, no doubt. But what good work do you have set aside for me, then? What role do you have in store for me?"

"You will be an angel of consolation and, if you will permit me the questionable phrase, a devil of subtlety and deception. Some delicate and painful wounds can only be nursed and cured by the hand of a woman. In the same way, some poor people are so proud, so touchy, so hidden away, that only rare penetration can find them and only irresistible charm can elicit their trust."

"And when will I get to put this penetration and skill that you attribute to me into practice?" Madame d'Harville asked, impatiently.

"Soon, I hope. The time approaches when you will need to make a conquest worthy of your abilities, but you will need your most Machiavellian resources."

"And when do you plan to unfold this great secret to me, my lord?"

"You see, already we need to plan an assignation. Would you do me the kindness of letting me come here in four days?"

"As far away as that!" Clémence said, naively.

"And what about the mystery of it, its affront to suitability? Think about it! If people thought we were conspiring, they would distrust us. But I may need to write to you. Who was the elderly woman who brought your letter this evening?"

"One of my mother's old chambermaids. The very soul of discretion."

"Then I'll send my letters to her and she'll give them to you. If you do me the kindness of responding, address the letter 'To Monsieur Rodolphe, rue Plumet.' Your chambermaid will post your letters."

"I'll post them myself, my lord, when I go for my usual walk."

"You go out alone, on foot?"

"When it's nice out, almost every day."

"Perfect! Now there's a practice all women should take up as soon as they're married. It gives excuses to good women—and bad ones. As judges say, it creates a precedent, and when the time comes, these walks, taken as usual, don't give any basis for dangerous interpretations. If I had been a woman (and, just between the two of us, if I had been, I'm afraid I would have been both very charitable and all too easy), the day after I got married, I would have taken up, in all innocence, the most mysterious of practices. I would have, with complete ingenuousness, taken on the most compromising appearances, all to establish the precedent I referred to, so that one day I could visit poor people—or my lover."

"Now that's real treachery, my lord!" Clémence said, with a smile.

"Fortunately for you, madame, you've never had to have either the wisdom or the humility to engage in forethought like that."

Madame d'Harville stopped smiling, lowered her eyes, blushed, and said sadly, "That is hardly gallant, my lord."

At first, Rodolphe gave the marquise a look of surprise. Then he went on: "I understand, madame. But once and for all, let's come to an understanding about your position with regard to Monsieur Charles Robert. One day, a woman, one of your friends, comes to you to show you one of those poor beggars who roll their eyes languorously and play the clarinet in an imploring tone to make passersby pity them. 'He's a deserving, poor man,' your friend says to you. 'He has seven children at least, a wife who's a blind deaf-mute, etc., etc.' 'Oh, what terrible luck,' you say, charitably giving him some money. And every day you run into the beggar, as soon as he sees you, no matter how far away, his eyes implore, his clarinet gives out the most mournful sounds, and your contribution falls into his money sack. One day, when your friend, who is taking advantage of your kindness, makes you feel more and more sorry for this poor man, you agree, charitably, to go visit him in the midst of his wretchedness. You arrive and—alas—no more melancholy clarinet, no more piteous and imploring looks. Instead here's a funny fellow—alert, jovial, fresh as a daisy, tooting out a song from the cabarets. And just as quickly, pity gives way to scorn, because you've taken a conniving poor man for a deserving one, nothing more, nothing less. Wasn't that the case?"

Madame d'Harville couldn't stop herself from smiling at this singular way of putting the case, and she said to Rodolphe, "Much as I might like this justification, my lord, it seems to me a little too facile."

"But after all, the most that can be said about what you did is that it was noble, generous, and imprudent. You have plenty of ways to make up for it and show your regret. But will I see Monsieur d'Harville tonight?"

"No, my lord. What happened this morning affected him so much that he is . . . indisposed," the marquise said quietly.

"Ah! I understand," Rodolphe said, sadly. "But take heart! You needed something to desire, to give you a goal to work toward, a distraction from your sorrows, as you said. Let's hope that you will discover that distraction in the future activities I've described. If that happens, the sweet consolation that will fill your soul won't leave any space for bad feelings toward your husband. You'll feel for him something like the sympathy you have for your child. And as for that little angel, now that I know why she is such a sickly child, I would even almost tell you to have a little hope there."

"Is that possible, my lord? What hope is there?" Clémence cried out, clasping her hands together in gratitude.

"I have as my attending physician a man who, though completely unknown, is extremely knowledgeable. He was in America for a long time and I remember him speaking to me of two or three nearly miraculous cures he effected among slaves suffering from this terrible disease."

"Oh, my lord, if only it were possible . . ."

"Don't hope for too much; the disappointment would be too painful. But, on the other hand, don't despair completely."

Clémence regarded Rodolphe's noble features with profound gratitude. He seemed to her almost a king, consoling her as he did with so much grace, intelligence, and kindness. She wondered how she could ever have looked upon Monsieur Charles Robert with interest. The very idea seemed horrible to her. "I owe you so much, my lord," she said in a voice that expressed deep emotion. "You calm me, you give me hope that my daughter might have the future she deserves, which would be for me both a consolation and a pleasure. I was right, after all, wasn't I, when I wrote you that if you would be so kind as to come here, you would finish the day as you began it—with a good deed?"

"I'll agree with you, as long as you also call it, madame, one of those good deeds that, in my selfishness, I love the most since it is so charming, so attractive, so full of pleasure," said Rodolphe as he got up, as the clock in the room rang eleven thirty.

"Good-bye, my lord. Please don't forget to tell me about those poor people in rue du Temple as soon as possible."

"I will go see them tomorrow morning. Unfortunately, I didn't know the little lame boy stole that purse from you. Those poor unfortunate people may well be in a terrible state by now. In four days—don't forget, I beg of you—I will apprise you of the role you have been so kind as to accept. But I must warn you that a disguise may be indispensable for you."

"A disguise! What fun! What will I disguise myself as, my lord?"

"I can't say at the moment. I'll leave the choice to you."

On returning home, the prince congratulated himself on the general tenor of his talk with Madame d'Harville. Here is what they had established:

They would occupy with charity the mind and heart of this young woman, who had become emotionally separated from her husband by an insurmountable distance; they would awaken in her sufficient novelistic curiosity and indulgence in mystery unconnected with love to satisfy her imaginative needs, her soul, and, in this manner, they would keep her safe from any new love affair.

In addition, they would inspire in Clémence d'Harville a passion of such depth, a passion that was so incurable and that was at once so pure and so noble, that this young woman would never again be able to feel any love less elevated. She would thus never again disturb the peace of mind of Monsieur d'Harville, whom Rodolphe loved like a brother.

CHAPTER 18

DESTITUTION

We hope that the reader has not forgotten the unfortunate family that lives in the attic of the house on rue du Temple or its father, the gem-cutter named Morel. We will now lead our reader into this depressing abode. It is five o'clock in the morning. Outside, the deep silence of an icy cold black night reigns. It is snowing.

A candle is supported by two thin pieces of wood, which stand on a square plank. Its pale yellow flame barely lights up the shadows of the attic. The tiny room is narrow and low, two thirds of it covered by the wood of the steeply sloping roof, which meets the floor at a sharp angle. Greenish tiles cover the entire floor.

Covered over by plaster that has been blackened by time and fissured all over with numerous cracks, the partitions reveal the worm-eaten slats that make up these thin walls. A door hangs askew on one of these walls and opens onto the stairway. The floor is sticky and foul, its color indeterminate. Rotting bits of straw lie scattered about it alongside filthy rags and the large bones that the poor buy from the most lowly merchants of rotten meat so that they can chew on the bits of cartilage that remain on them.[90] Such appalling disorder is always the sign either of carelessness or of an honest poverty that is nonetheless so desperate and so crushing that the poor man, reduced to nothing, no longer feels the will, the strength, or the need to pull himself out of that mire; he just wallows there like a beast in its den.

During the day, this hovel is lit by a narrow, oblong skylight built into the roof's incline. Its glass frame opens by means of a chain hook hanging from it. At this moment a thick layer of snow covers the skylight. The candle, placed more or less at the center of this attic room on the gem-cutter's workbench, creates an area of pale light that diminishes little by little until it fades into the shadows that engulf the garret. Amid these shadows, one can make out the vague forms of several people.

The workbench is a heavy square table made of coarsely cut unfinished oak stained with fat and wax. In a heap on the table, a handful of

90. One can find, in neighborhoods where the masses live, sellers of stillborn calves, livestock that has died of diseases, etc. [SN]

impressively sized diamonds and rubies glitter and gleam with remarkable brilliance. Morel worked in real gems—not in paste, as he gave out and as the people in the house on rue du Temple thought. Thanks to this innocent lie, the jewels with which he was entrusted seemed so valueless that he could keep them in his room without fear of their being stolen. So much wealth put in the charge of such poverty renders needless any discussion of Morel's integrity.

Seated on a backless stool, overcome by fatigue, cold, and sleepiness, having worked through this long winter's night, the gem-cutter let his heavy head and benumbed arms drop to rest on his workbench. His forehead was leaning on a grindstone placed horizontally across the table, which, under normal circumstances, operated by means of a small handwheel. Scattered around him were a saw of fine steel and various other tools. The craftsman, his bald head encircled with gray hair, wore an old brown knit jacket over his bare torso, and cheap canvas pants. His slippers, worn through at the edges, barely covered his feet, which were blue from the cold and resting on the tiles.

It was so icy cold in this attic room that the craftsman's body, despite the trancelike state to which he had been reduced from sheer exhaustion, still shivered, now and then, from top to bottom. The length and blackness of the candlewick indicated that Morel had been sleeping for some time. The only sound to be heard was his labored breathing, for none of the six other occupants of the attic room were asleep.

Yes, seven people lived in this cramped room. There were five children, of whom the youngest was four and the eldest barely twelve. Then came their ill mother, and finally, the mother of their mother, a woman in her eighties who had sunken into senility.[91] The cold must have been bitter indeed since the natural heat of seven people, piled one atop another in this small space, could not warm up the frigid air. It must be observed, however, that these seven stunted, frail, shivering, exhausted bodies emitted little caloric energy, as a scientist might put it.

No one slept except for the father of the family, who, his strength having reached its limit, had dozed off for a moment. No one slept because cold, hunger, and illness kept them wide awake. Few of us are aware how rare and precious that deep and healthy sleep that restores our strength and allows us to forget our pains is for the poor. One wakes from such beneficent sleep feeling so fresh, so unburdened, so courageously disposed to face the hardest kinds of work that even the least religious, in the catholic sense of the word, experience a vaguely recognized gratitude—if not toward God, then at least toward sleep itself. To bless the effect is, after all, to bless the cause.

91. Although Sue tells us that seven people lived in the room, he describes eight people: five children, their mother, father, and grandmother. [TN]

The contrast between the sight of this craftsman's appalling poverty and the value of the jewels with which he was entrusted was striking in a way that both saddens and uplifts our souls. This man had continuously before his eyes the wrenching spectacle of his family's suffering. His family was beset by every kind of misery, from hunger to madness, yet he guarded those jewels safely—even though a single one of them would have wrested his wife and children from the privation that was slowly killing them. Doubtless he was merely doing his duty, the obvious duty of any honest man; but because a duty is obvious, does that make fulfilling it any less great, any less beautiful? And moreover, doesn't the context in which one fulfills one's duty make doing so even more meritorious?

And, furthermore, doesn't this craftsman, who was so miserable and yet so honest before the temptation of this treasure, exemplify that immense and impressive majority of people who, condemned to endless privation, remain peaceful, hardworking, and resigned even as they see every day, without hatred or bitter envy, the riches of the world spread before their eyes? And finally, isn't it both ennobling and consoling to think that it is neither strength nor terror but rather their good sense of morals that keeps this ocean of people under control? And how much more so when one considers that this ocean's overflowing would drown our whole society, tossing its laws about on its powerful waves, just as an enraged sea tosses dikes and ramparts about! Ought we not then to sympathize, in our hearts and in our minds, with these generous souls who ask for so little, a mere place in the sun, in exchange for so much misfortune, so much courage, and so much resignation?

But let us return to this, alas, all too real example of appalling poverty that we will try to depict in all its heartbreaking nakedness.

The gem-cutter possessed only one thin mattress and a bit of bedcover, all of which had fallen to the senile grandmother, who, in her idiocy and savage selfishness, refused to share her pallet with anyone. She had gone into a rage when, at the beginning of winter, they had tried to put the youngest child next to her. She had nearly strangled the child, a little girl of four who had been afflicted, for some time, with consumption. She suffered bitterly from the cold, on the straw mattress she shared with her brothers and sisters. In a moment, we will explain this mode of bedding so commonly used among the poor. Compared to them, we treat our livestock like royalty; at least we change their bedding.

Such is the picture, in its entirety, presented to us by this attic room once our eyes adjust to the shadows that have just swallowed the last of the candle's light.

The senile old woman's mattress sat on the tiles along the weight-bearing wall, which was less damp than the other partitions. Since she could not stand to have anything on her head, her short-cropped white hair outlined the shape of her skull, with its flattened forehead. Her gray eyebrows shadowed deep-set eyes that gleamed with a savage light. Her hollow, pale cheeks, creased with many wrinkles, hung from her cheekbones and the sharp angles of her jaw. Lying on her side, curled up, her chin almost touching her knees, she shivered beneath a gray wool blanket, which was too small to cover her whole body. It left visible her bony legs and the bottom of an old skirt she had on, which had worn away to rags. The pallet gave off a fetid smell.

A little distance from the head of the grandmother's pallet, also parallel to the wall, was the straw mattress that served as a bed for the five children. And here is how that bed was put together. They made a lengthwise slit on both ends of a canvas and then slid the children inside with the damp and nauseating straw. In this way, the canvas could serve as both sheet and cover. Two little girls, one of whom was gravely ill, shivered on one side, and three little boys shivered on the other. Both the boys and the girls slept in their clothing, if one could call a few miserable rags clothing.

Their wan, worn-down, suffering faces were half hidden by their dull, pale, disheveled, and bristling hair, which their mother let grow to give them a little extra protection against the cold. One of the boys, his fingers stiff, pulled the covering of the straw mattress right up to his chin, trying to cover himself better. The second, fearing to expose his hands to the cold, held the canvas between his chattering teeth. The third huddled up against his two brothers. The second of the two daughters, weakened by consumption, languidly held her poor little face, which already had a deathly blue pallor, against her sister's icy chest. The older girl, only five years old, tried in vain to warm her little sister in her arms and watched over her with nervous solicitude.

The craftsman's wife was lying down, stretched out on another straw mattress, like that of the children, but at the back of the hovel. She was worn out by a slow fever and painful illness that, for the last few months, had not let her get up on her feet. Madeleine Morel was thirty-six years old. An old blue cotton handkerchief, wrapped around her depressed forehead, accentuated the bilious pallor of her bony face. Each of her dull, sunken eyes had a brown circle around it; her pale lips were cracked and bleeding. Her saddened, beaten-down expression and unremarkable features revealed a personality that was gentle but without resistance or energy, a personality that never struggled against misfortune but bowed beneath it and became ever weaker as it bemoaned its fate.

Weak, listless, narrow-minded, she stayed honest because her husband kept her honest. Had she been left to her own resources, her misery might have corrupted her and pushed her to evildoing. She loved her husband and her children, but she had neither the strength nor the courage to keep to herself her bitter complaints about their common misfortune. The gemcutter, whose hard labor was the family's sole support, often had to interrupt his work to pacify and console the poor, sickly woman.

To keep his wife warm, Morel had placed a few scraps of clothing over a nasty brownish-gray sheet filled with holes. That clothing had been so patched and repatched that even their pawnbroker wanted nothing to do with them.

All the possessions of the family can be quickly itemized: a stove, a casserole and an earthenware pot with a deformed opening, two or three cracked cups scattered over the floor, a tub, and a washboard. A large stoneware jug sat under the sloping roof near the door that hung askew and which the wind battered about constantly.

This is the desolate picture revealed by the candle, whose flame, flickering in the breeze that blew through the cracks between the tiles, alternated between casting a pale and vacillating light on this poverty and illuminating the pile of diamonds and rubies lying on the workbench where the gem-cutter slept, making them glitter as if they were aflame, as if they were exploding into all the colors of the rainbow.

Without thinking, all these poor people, lying silent and awake, from the old woman to the littlest child, looked instinctively to the gem-cutter, their sole hope, their sole support. In their thoughtless self-centeredness, they became anxious as they noticed that he was motionless, worn down by the burden of his work. The mother thought of her children. The children thought about themselves. The senile old woman didn't seem to be thinking about anyone or anything. Nevertheless, she suddenly sat up in bed, crossed her arms—which were dry and yellow as boxwood—across her bony chest, looked, blinking at the candle, and then slowly got up, the shreds of her bedcover trailing after her like a shroud. She was very tall and her shaved head seemed small out of all proportion to her. Her thick, pendulous lower lip twitched with a spasmodic movement. The hideous mask her face offered presented the very essence of a wild, bestial stupidity.

The senile old woman walked slyly toward the workbench, like a child about to engage in some mischief. When she was within reach of the candle, she put her two shaking hands around its flame. Her hands were so thin that the light they sheltered gave them a sort of whitish transparency.

From her pallet, Madeleine Morel watched every one of the senile old woman's gestures. While continuing to warm her hands at the candle's flames, the old woman lowered her head and looked, with imbecilic curiosity, at the shimmering of the rubies and diamonds that glittered on the table. Absorbed in this meditation, the senile old woman didn't keep her hands far enough from the flame; it burned her and she let out a hoarse yelp.

This sound abruptly awakened Morel, who quickly raised his head. He was forty years old and had an open face. It was the face of a worker: an intelligent and gentle face, but one that was withered and hollowed out by poverty. A gray beard of several weeks' growth covered the bottom of his face, which was scarred with pockmarks. His forehead was furrowed with premature wrinkles beneath his already bald head, and his inflamed eyelids were red from working through too many nights.

As is too frequently the case with workers whose constitution is weak and who engage in a sedentary labor that constrains them all day in an almost changeless position, his weak posture had become deformed. Continuously forced to keep himself bent over his workbench, while at the same time having to lean to his right in order to keep his grindstone moving, the gem-cutter had become petrified, ossified into the pose he held for twelve or fifteen hours a day. His body was arched and twisted to one side. Likewise, his right arm, constantly in motion and moving the handwheel with difficulty, had become very muscular. At the same time, his left hand and arm were thin and had horribly atrophied muscles from remaining continuously motionless, poised in place on the workbench in order to hold the diamond edges up to the grindstone. His frail legs, which a complete lack of exercise had rendered almost useless, could hardly hold up his exhausted body. The entire substance, vitality, and strength of his body seemed concentrated in the one part of it that his labor exercised ceaselessly. As Morel said, with poignant resignation, "If I eat, it's not so much for myself as for the arm that turns the grindstone."

The gem-cutter, who had been jolted awake, found himself face-to-face with the senile old woman. "What's wrong with you? What's wrong, Mother?" Morel said to her. And then he added, with his voice lowered, fearing as he did to awaken his family, which he believed to be asleep, "Go lie down, Mother. Don't make noise; Madeleine and the children are sleeping."

"I'm not sleeping; I'm trying to keep Adèle warm," said the oldest of the little girls.

"I'm too hungry to sleep," one of the boys piped up. "It wasn't my turn to eat supper with Mademoiselle Rigolette, like my brothers did."

"You poor children," Morel said, overwhelmed. "I thought you, at least, were sleeping."

"I was afraid of waking you up, Morel," his wife said. "Otherwise, I would have asked for some water. My fever has come on again and I'm awfully thirsty."

"Right away," the worker said. "Except first I've got to get your mother back to bed. Come on, now, leave the stones alone," he said to the old woman, whose attention was caught by the shimmer of a ruby that she wanted to carry off. "Go lie down, Mother," he repeated.

"This one, this one," said the senile old woman, pointing to the precious stone she had her eye on.

"Now we're going to get angry," said Morel, raising his voice to frighten his mother-in-law as he pushed her back gently with his hand.

"God, Morel! I'm dying of thirst," Madeleine murmured. "Go get me something to drink!"

"And how do you expect me to do that, too? I can't leave your mother alone with the stones or she'll make me lose a diamond, like last year. And, God knows, that diamond cost us plenty and it may well cost plenty more." And the gem-cutter put his hand to his forehead in a dark mood. Then he turned to one of his children and said, "Félix, since you're not sleeping, go and get your mother some water."

"No, no, I'll wait. He'll get cold," Madeleine answered.

"I won't be any colder than I am here in the straw mattress," said the child, getting up.

"Oh, now enough—stop it already!" Morel cried in a menacing tone to shoo away the senile old woman, who didn't want to leave the work-bench and was fixated on making off with one of the stones.

"Mama, the water in the jug is frozen over," Félix exclaimed.

"Break the ice, then," Madeleine said.

"It's too thick. I can't."

"Morel, you go and break the ice in the jug," Madeleine said in a doleful and impatient voice. "If I can get nothing but water to drink, let me at least have some water. You're making me die of thirst."

"For God's sake! A little bit of patience! What do you expect me to do? I have your mother to deal with," the unfortunate gem-cutter yelled. He couldn't manage to get the senile old woman out of his way, and she began to become irritated with the resistance she was running into and let loose an angry growl.

"Please, call her away," said Morel to his wife. "She listens to you sometimes, at any rate."

"Mother, go lie down. If you're good, I'll give you coffee. You always like that."

"This one, this one," the senile old woman repeated, this time trying to make off violently with the ruby she was coveting. Morel tried to push her away without harming her, but he couldn't.

"For God's sake, you know that you'll never control her unless you frighten her with the whip," Madeleine cried. "There's no other way to make her keep quiet."

"I know it's what I have to do. But even though she's mad, threatening an old woman with a whip still rubs me the wrong way," Morel said. Then, turning to the old woman, who was trying to bite him and whom he was holding back with one hand, he shouted in his most menacing tone, "If you don't go lie down right now, watch out for the whip!" But the threat was again made in vain. He took the whip out from under his work-bench and cracked it violently, threatening the senile old woman and saying, "Go lie down, now! Go lie down!"

The old woman, hearing the echoing sound of the whip, first jumped back from the workbench, but then she stopped, snarled between her teeth, and looked angrily at her son-in-law.

"Get to bed! Get to bed!" he repeated, coming toward her, cracking the whip as he approached.

Then the senile old woman slowly backed up, returning to her bed but brandishing her fist at the gem-cutter. But he wanted to end this cruel scene so that he could give his wife water and so he came right up to the old woman, cracked his whip one last time, though still without touching her with it, and repeated in his threatening tone, "To bed, now!"

The old woman, in her fear, began to howl in a terrible way. She threw herself on her bed and huddled there like a dog in its kennel, but she didn't stop howling.

The frightened children, who thought their father had struck the old woman, cried out to him, in tears, "Don't beat Grandma, don't beat her!"

It would be impossible to describe the sinister effect of this nocturnal scene, with the prayerful cries of the children, the furious howling of the old woman, and the doleful moan of the gem-cutter's wife.

CHAPTER 19

THE DEBT

Morel, the gem-cutter, had only all too often participated in scenes as sad as the one we have just described. In a sudden attack of despair, though, he threw his whip on the workbench and cried out, "Oh! What a life! What a life!"

"Is it my fault my mother is senile?" Madeleine asked, crying.

"Is it mine?" retorted Morel. "What do I ask of life? Just to kill myself working for all of you. Day and night I slave away. I don't complain; as long as I'm strong enough to do it, I'll do it. But I can't do my job and at the same time care for a lunatic, a sick person, and children! Really, the world is unjust. It's unjust! It's too much for one man to handle on his own!" said the gem-cutter in a heartrending fashion. And then, overcome, he fell back onto his stool, hiding his head in his hands.

"They didn't want to accept my mother in the home because they decided she wasn't crazy enough—what do you want me to do about it?" said Madeleine, her voice listless, sorrowful, and plaintive. "What good is it to torture yourself over things you can't control?"

"None," said the artisan, wiping his eyes, which had filled with tears. "None. You're right. But when everything is beating you down, you sometimes lose control of yourself."

"Oh! I'm so thirsty! I'm shivering, and I'm burning with fever," said Madeleine.

"Wait, I'll get you something to drink."

Morel went to take up the pitcher that was sitting under the roof. With some difficulty, he broke the ice that had formed on the water, filled a cup with this frigid liquid, and approached his wife's pallet. She was holding out her hands toward him impatiently.

But after a moment of reflection, he said to her, "No, it's too cold. If your fever goes up, it might make your condition worse."

"It will make me sicker? So much the better—give it to me right away, then," said Madeleine bitterly. "It will all be over faster, and I won't be any more trouble to you. You'll only have to look after the old woman and the children. There'll be one less sick person to worry about."

"Why are you talking like that to me, Madeleine? I don't deserve it," said Morel, sadly. "Listen: don't make me feel bad. It's a wonder I have the strength and sanity to go on working. My mind isn't that strong, it won't stand up to much more. And then what would become of all of you? I'm saying this for your own good—if I only had to worry about myself, I'd hardly think about what was going to happen tomorrow. Thank God! In time the river carries us all out to sea."

"Poor Morel!" said Madeleine, touched by her husband's words. "It's true, I was wrong to talk in anger like that and say that I wanted to help you get rid of me. Don't be mad at me for it—I meant well. Yes, because I'm useless to you and our children. It's been sixteen months I've been bedridden. God! I'm so thirsty! I beg of you, give me something to drink!"

"In just a minute. I'm trying to warm the cup in my hands."

"You're so good to me! And to think that I was saying such mean things to you just now!"

"Poor woman, you're suffering! Suffering makes people bitter. Say whatever you like to me, but don't tell me that you want me to be rid of you."

"But what am I good for?"

"What good are our children for, then?"

"To load you down with work."

"Certainly! But also, thanks to all of you, I find the strength to go on working sometimes for twenty hours a day, even to the point of becoming deformed and crippled. Do you think that if it weren't for you, I'd carry on like this for the pure pleasure of it? Oh, no, life isn't that beautiful. I'd sooner be done with it."

"That's the way I feel," answered Madeleine. "If it weren't for the children, I would have said to you a long time ago, 'Morel, you've had enough of it all, and so have I. All it would take is lighting a coal heater and we'd be done with our poverty. But those children—our children!'"

"You see? They are good for something," said Morel with admirable naiveté. "Come on, then. Drink, but take little sips. It's still pretty cold."

"Oh, thank you, Morel!" said Madeleine, drinking greedily.

"Enough, enough . . ."

"It was too cold! I'm shivering even more now!" said Madeleine as she returned the cup to him.

"Oh, God, I told you so. Now you're in pain."

"I don't have the strength to shiver anymore. I feel like I'm trapped from all sides in a giant ice cube—that's how I feel."

Morel took off his jacket, put it on his wife's feet. This left him naked from the waist up. The poor man had no shirt.

"But you're going to freeze, Morel!"

"I'll take my jacket back in a minute if I get too cold."

"Poor man! Ah! How right you are—fate is unjust. What have we done to be so unhappy, while others . . ."

"Everyone has problems, the rich as well as the poor."

"Yes, but the rich have problems that don't leave them starving from want and shivering in the cold. My gorge rises when I think that with the price of one of the diamonds that you polish, you and I and our children could have enough to live on comfortably. Why does anyone need diamonds?"

"If all we had to do was ask, 'Why do other people need this?' we could solve a lot of problems. It's as if you said: 'Why did that man that Madame Pipelet calls the commandant need to have rented and furnished the first floor of the house, where no one goes? Why did he need a good mattress and nice linens there, if he lives somewhere else?'"

"It's too true. There must have been enough in there to deck out more than just one poor household like ours . . . and that's before you even take into account the fact that Madame Pipelet lit a fire every day in there to keep the furniture from getting ruined by mildew. So much good heat wasted, while we and our children freeze in here! But now you'll tell me that we're not furniture. Oh, those rich people! They're so heartless!"

"No more heartless than other people, Madeleine. They just don't know what poverty is, you see. They're born happy, live happy, and die happy. Why should they think of us? And then, you know what? They just don't know. How would they have any idea of the degradation we live in? When they get hungry, they're just that much happier because their dinner is that much more satisfying. When it's very cold, so much the better—they think the winter is beautiful. And you can see why. If they go out on foot, they come back to sit by a nice fireplace, and the cold makes them enjoy the fire all the more. That's why they don't have more pity for us, because, for them, hunger and cold only make for more pleasure. They don't know, you see? They don't know! If we were in their place, we'd be just like them."

"The poor are better people than all of them, then, because they help each other out. That nice little Mademoiselle Rigolette has looked in on me and the children so often and helped us when we were sick. She invited Jérôme and Pierre yesterday to share her supper. And her supper hardly amounts to much—a cup of milk and some bread. At her age people have a big appetite. She must have gone hungry herself."

"Poor girl! Yes, she is good. And why? Because she knows what it means to be in need. As I always say, 'If the rich only knew! If they only knew!'"

"And that little lady who came to see us the day before yesterday?[92] The one who seemed so frightened and asked us if we needed anything? Now she knows what it's like to be unfortunate. But you see, she hasn't come back to see us."

---

92. A couple of pages down, they will refer to Madame d'Harville as having come yesterday, rather than the day before, which seems more likely. [TN]

"Maybe she will. Even though she seemed upset, she had a kind and respectable face."

"Oh, you! In your books, if someone's rich, they're always right. You'd think the rich were cut from a different cloth from us."

"I wouldn't say that," said Morel, gently. "I'd say, on the contrary, that they have their faults, just like we have ours. The sad thing is that they don't know about us. The sad thing is that there are plenty of policemen, for example, to look for wretches who have committed crimes, and no policemen to look for honest workers with needy families at their last gasp. Because they don't get any help at the right time, they sometimes get led into temptation. Punishing crime is good, but preventing it would maybe be better. Say you've been honest up to the age of fifty, but extreme poverty and hunger turn you to crime—there's one more criminal. If they only knew . . . But what good does it do to think about this? The world is what it is. I'm poor and desperate, so I talk this way. If I were rich, I'd be talking about parties and pleasures. So, my poor wife, are you doing any better?"

"Still the same. I can't feel my legs any longer. But you—you're shivering. Take your jacket back and blow out the candle. We don't need it anymore. It's daytime."

Indeed, a pallid glow, coming in weakly through the snow that was covering the pane of the skylight, was beginning to bring the interior of this hovel into sad definition, making it look even more sordid. The dark of night covered over at least part of this wretchedness.

"I'll wait until it's light enough to start working again," said the gemcutter as he sat at the edge of his wife's pallet and held his forehead in his hands.

After a few moments of silence, Madeleine said to him, "When is Madame Mathieu supposed to come to pick up the stones you're working on?"

"This morning. I only have one more facet of a fake diamond to polish."

"A fake diamond! You, who never cut anything but fine gems, despite what they think in this house!"

"What? You don't know? That's right, you were sleeping the other day when Madame Mathieu came by. She gave me ten fake diamonds, ten rhinestones to cut to exactly the same size and in exactly the same manner as the same number of fine gems she brought me, the ones that are over there with the rubies. I've never seen diamonds of a more beautiful water. Those ten stones there are surely worth more than sixty thousand francs."

"And why did she want you to make imitations of them?"

"A wealthy lady they belong to—a duchess, I believe—asked Monsieur Baudoin, the jeweler, to sell her set of jewels and to make her a set of fake ones to wear in their place. Madame Mathieu, Monsieur Baudoin's gem broker, told me this when she brought me the genuine stones so I could cut the fake ones to look the same. Madame Mathieu has given the same order to four other gem-cutters because there are forty or fifty stones to cut. I couldn't do them all, and they were supposed to be done this morning. Monsieur Baudoin needs the time to remount the fake jewels. Madame Mathieu says that these ladies often do this kind of thing in secret, replacing their diamonds with rhinestones."

"You see! Fake jewels do just as good as real ones, and those great ladies who put them on just to dress up would never think of giving a diamond away to help poor wretches like us!"

"Poor woman! Think a moment; your sorrows make you unjust. Who do you think even knows that we, the Morels, are wretched?"

"Oh, you are exasperating! If they cut you up into little pieces, you'd say thank you."

Morel shrugged his shoulders with compassion.

"How much does Madame Mathieu owe you this morning?" asked Madeleine.

"Nothing. I got an advance of one hundred and twenty francs from her."

"Nothing? But we went through our last twenty sous yesterday!"

"Yes," said Morel, looking beaten.

"What are we going to do?"

"I don't know."

"And the baker won't give us any more credit."

"No, and yesterday I borrowed a quarter loaf of bread from Madame Pipelet."

"Old Madame Burette won't lend us anything?"

"Lend us anything? Now that she has all our belongings in hock, what would she lend us money on? Our children?" said Morel with a bitter smile.

"But my mother, the children, and you together only ate a pound and a half of bread yesterday! You can't starve. And it's your fault. You didn't want to register this year at the charity office."[93]

"They only take poor people who have furniture, and we don't have any anymore. They consider us to be living in lodgings. It's the same way it works if you want to be admitted to a workhouse. The children need to have at least a shirt, and ours have only rags to wear. And also, for the charity office, if I'd wanted to register, I would have had to return to the

93. Charity offices were lay agencies run independently by each municipality in France. Every charity office operated under different rules and regulations. As it was considered highly desirable, according to nineteenth-century authorities on charity, to keep the poor in their homes, the specifications Morel names probably derive from policies favoring those who could prove they had a place to live. Without furniture, the Morels would have a harder time claiming permanent residency. [TN]

office about twenty times because we don't have any sponsors. I would have lost more time than it was worth."

"So what can we do, then?"

"Maybe that little lady who visited us yesterday won't forget us."

"Sure, count on that. But Madame Mathieu will surely lend you a hundred sous, won't she? You've been working for her for ten years. She can't mean to leave an honest worker like you with a family in such conditions."

"I don't think she'll be able to lend us anything. She did all she could by giving me that hundred and twenty francs in small advance payments. That's a lot of money for her. Even though she's a diamond broker and sometimes has fifty thousand francs in her basket, she's not rich. She thinks she's done well when she makes a hundred francs in a month. She has two nieces to raise. A hundred sous for her is just as big a deal as it is for us, you see. Sometimes you just don't have it. Since she's already given me these advances, it would be like taking bread out of her mouth and the mouths of her relatives."

"That's what happens when you work for brokers instead of working for powerful jewelers. Sometimes they're less stingy. But you let everybody walk all over you. It's your fault."

"It's my fault?" cried the unhappy man, exasperated by this absurd reproach. "It's your mother, isn't it, who got us into this mess? If I didn't have to pay for the diamond your mother lost, we would be in the black. We would be able to benefit from my days' work, we would have the eleven hundred francs that we took out of the savings bank in order to combine them with the thirteen hundred francs we borrowed from that Monsieur Jacques Ferrand, God damn his name!"

"You're still too obstinate to ask that guy for anything. He's so greedy that it probably wouldn't do any good. Still, it wouldn't hurt to try."

"You want me to ask him for something? Him?" cried Morel. "I'd rather be slowly roasted to death over coals. Please don't talk to me about that guy. You'll make me crazy."

As he said these words, the gem-cutter's face, ordinarily so gentle and resigned, became fierce and somber. His pale face reddened slightly. He got up abruptly from the pallet where he had been sitting and walked around in the garret in an agitated manner. Despite his frail and deformed appearance, the attitude and expression of this man could still show profound indignation.

"I'm not a bad man!" he exclaimed. "All my life, I've never done anything bad to anyone. But that solicitor—you know![94] Oh! I wish him all the evil he brought on me." Then, putting his hands on his forehead, he

94. The reader will perhaps remember that when Fleur-de-Marie was a baby, she was entrusted to this solicitor and that his housekeeper had abandoned the child to the Owl, giving her a onetime payment of a thousand francs to take care of her. [SN]

murmured in a mournful voice, "God! What have I done to deserve getting me and my family put in the clutches of that hypocrite! Why does he have the right to use his wealth to destroy, corrupt, and make miserable anyone he feels like destroying, corrupting, and making miserable?"

"Oh, right, go ahead," said Madeleine. "Go up against him. A lot of good it'll do you when he gets you thrown in prison. He could do that any day he liked on account of that letter of credit for thirteen thousand francs over which he won that suit against you. He's keeping you like a dog on a leash. I hate him as much as you, but since we're living at his mercy, we need to—"

"What, we need to let our daughter dishonor herself? Is that what you mean?" cried the gem-cutter in a thunderous voice.

"God! Be quiet! The children are awake. They'll hear you."

"Fine—so much the better," Morel responded with a chilling irony. "It will be a good lesson for our two little girls. It will prepare them for what's coming. All it takes is for that solicitor to take a fancy to one of them one of these days. Aren't we at his mercy, as you keep telling me? Can't he put me in prison, as you keep telling me? So let's talk frankly: we should let him have our daughter, isn't that what you're saying?"

Then this unhappy man finished his lament by bursting into tears. His honest and decent nature could not sustain this tone of painful sarcasm for very long.

"Oh, my children!" he cried, sobbing. "My poor children! My Louise! My good, beautiful Louise! Too beautiful, too beautiful! It's because of that that we have all these problems. If she hadn't been so beautiful, that man would never have offered to lend me that money. I work hard and I'm honest. The jeweler would have given me time, I wouldn't have had this obligation to this old monster, and he wouldn't be taking advantage of the favor he did us by trying to dishonor my daughter. I wouldn't have let her stay a day at his place. But it's what we have to do. What we have to do. He has me in his clutches. Oh! Poverty! Poverty! What outrages poverty leads to!"

"But what can we do? He said to Louise, 'If you leave my home, little girl, I'll throw your father in prison.'"

"Yes, he talks down to her like that as if she were the least of creatures."

"If that were all, we could do as we pleased. But if she leaves the solicitor, he'll have you arrested, and then, while you're in prison, what would become of me—and of my mother and our children? If Louise earned twenty francs in another position, would all six of us be able to live on that?"

"Right. So we can survive—we'll sell Louise's honor."

"You always exaggerate. The solicitor has been pursuing her, it's true. That's what she told us. But she's virtuous, as you well know."

"Oh, yes! She's virtuous, and energetic, and kind! When she saw that we were having trouble with money because of your illness, she wanted to become a servant so she wouldn't be a burden to us. I've never told you how hard that was on me. Her, a servant, mistreated, humiliated? She, the one who is so naturally proud? Remember, we used to laugh and call her Princess because she always said that she would make our poor hovel look like a little palace by getting it sparkling clean? Dear child! It would have been an indulgence to myself to keep her here with us while I had to spend my nights working. And also, when I saw her in front of me at my workbench with her kind, rosy face and her pretty brown eyes, when I heard her sing—that would always lighten my load! Poor Louise, so hardworking and still so cheerful . . . Even with your mother, whom she could handle so well! Lord! When she talked to you, when she looked at you, there was no way not to agree with her. And she was so good at taking care of you! She was so good at cheering you up! And she did so much to take care of her brothers and sisters. She found the time to do everything. When Louise left, all our happiness left with her."

"Listen, Morel, drop all that. You're breaking my heart," said Madeleine, crying hot tears.

"And when I think that maybe that monster . . . You see, when I think about that, my head starts spinning. It makes me want to go kill him and then kill myself afterward."

"And then what would become of us? But there you go, exaggerating again. The solicitor may have said something to Louise—just in jest. In any case, he goes to mass every Sunday. He's always around priests. Lots of people say that it's safer to keep your money with him than in a savings bank."

"What does that prove? That he's rich and hypocritical. I know Louise well. She's virtuous, yes, but she loves us too well. Her heart bleeds for our poverty. She knows that without me you really would die of hunger. And if that solicitor threatened to throw me in prison, the poor girl might be ready to . . . Oh! My head! I'm going to drive myself crazy!"

"God! If that happened, the solicitor would have given her money and presents. Knowing her, she wouldn't have kept anything for herself. She would have brought everything to us."

"Don't say such things! I can't believe you have even thought of such things. Louise, accepting gifts . . . Louise . . ."

"Not for her. For us—"

"Be quiet! Please! Stop talking! You terrify me. If I weren't here, I don't know what would happen to you or my children, with you thinking like that."

"What did I say that was so bad?"

"Nothing."

"All right, then! Why are you afraid that—"

The gem-cutter interrupted his wife impatiently. "I am afraid because for the past three months, each time Louise comes home and gives me a kiss, I see that she blushes."

"That's because she's happy to see you."

"Or because she's ashamed. She looks sadder and sadder."

"Because she sees us getting more and more unhappy. And then, when I talk with her about the solicitor, she says that he hasn't been threatening anymore to throw you in prison."

"Yes, but at what price is he no longer threatening her? She doesn't say, and she blushes when she embraces me. Oh! God! It would already be evil for a master to say to a poor, honest girl who depends on him for her bread, 'Give in to me, or I'll fire you; if anyone asks for a reference, I'll tell them that you can't be trusted so you won't be able to find employment elsewhere.' But to say to her, 'Give in to me, or I'll throw your father in prison!'—to say that when you know that a whole family relies on the work of that father! Oh! That's a thousand times more evil!"

"And when you think that with one of those diamonds over there on your workbench you would have plenty of money to reimburse the solicitor and get our daughter out from his service and keep her here with us . . ." said Madeleine, slowly.

"Why do you go on repeating the same thing to me? What good does it do? Certainly, if I were rich, I wouldn't be poor," said Morel with an attitude of pained impatience.

This man's upright character came so naturally and so organically to him that it never entered his mind that his wife, beaten down and embittered by misfortune, could have ulterior motives and want to challenge his irreproachable honesty.

He went on bitterly. "We must resign ourselves to our fate. Happy are those who can keep their children nearby and keep them from straying. But who will protect a girl of the people? No one. If she's of an age to earn money, she goes out in the morning to her workshop and comes home in the evening. During that time the mother works, for her part, as does her father. Our time is money, and bread is so expensive that we no longer have the leisure of looking after our children. And then people complain about the loose morals of poor girls, as if their parents had the means to keep them at home, or the time to watch over them when they go out. All our poverty is nothing compared to our worries over leaving our wives, our children, and our fathers. And we are the ones who need the comfort of a healthy family life the most. But as soon as our children are old enough, we're forced to separate from them!"

At that moment a loud knock was heard on the attic door.

CHAPTER 20

THE JUDGMENT

Startled, the gem-cutter got up and went to open the door. Two men entered the attic.

One was thin, tall, and had a horrible, pimpled face that was framed by a thick, grizzled pair of black muttonchops. He held a large loaded stick in his hand. The hat he wore was misshapen, and his long green waistcoat was filthy and tightly buttoned. His worn black velvet collar revealed a long red neck that was as hairless as a vulture's. This man's name was Malicorne. The other man was shorter, but his manner was just as vulgar as the first man's. He was red, fat, and squat, and dressed in a way that was grotesquely luxurious. Shiny buttons closed his shirt of dubious cleanliness. A yellowish green overcoat left visible beneath it a plaid vest with worn fabric, around which was wound a long gold chain. This man was named Bourdin.

"Ugh! This place stinks like poverty and death!" said Malicorne, pausing at the threshold.

"Well, it certainly doesn't smell of perfume. What are they doing in here, anyway?" replied Bourdin, with disgust and contempt on his face. Then he approached the artisan, who was looking at him with as much surprise as indignation.

Gammy's wicked, watchful, and devious face was peeking through the door, which had been left ajar. Unbeknownst to them, he had followed these strangers and was watching—spying on them and listening to them.

"What do you want?" the gem-cutter asked abruptly, revolted by the vulgarity of the two men.

"Jérôme Morel?" said Bourdin.

"That's me."

"The gem-cutter?"

"That's me."

"Are you sure of that?"

"That's me, I tell you. I am losing patience with you. What do you want here? Tell me now, or get out of here!"

"How's that for decency? Thanks a lot! Hey, Malicorne," said the man as he turned back toward his comrade, "there isn't much of anything here. Not like at the Viscount de Saint-Remy's place!"

"Yes, but when there's something to be had, you always find no one home, like on rue de Chaillot. The chicken had flown the coop the day before and was still holding out. Vermin like this, on the other hand, stay in their kennels."

"It's true. This one is just asking to be thrown in the slammer so he can score some dog food."

"The loan shark better watch out. This guy's going to cost him more than he's worth, but that's his business."

"Listen!" said Morel, indignantly. "If you weren't drunk, as you seem to be, I might get angry at you. Get out of my home right now!"

"Ha, ha! He's something, this cripple!" cried Bourdin, imitating the gem-cutter's misshapen posture in an insulting way. "Can you believe, Malicorne, that he has the cheek to call this his 'home'? A hovel I wouldn't keep my dog in."

"What is going on, Morel?" cried Madeleine, who had been too terrified to speak up until then. "Call for help! What if these men are crooks? Watch out for your diamonds!"

Indeed, as he watched the two suspicious-looking strangers getting closer and closer to the workbench, where his jewels were still lying out in the open, Morel feared something of the sort. He ran to his table and covered the precious stones with his hands.

Still eavesdropping and on the lookout, Gammy caught Madeleine's words and noted the artisan's movements. He said to himself, "Hmm . . . I'd heard he was a gem-cutter who worked with fake jewels. If the gemstones were fake, he wouldn't have to worry about getting robbed. Good to know! That means that old Madame Mathieu, who's here a lot, must also be a broker in real gems. So those are real diamonds she's got in her basket. Good to know! I'll tell the Owl all about it. The Owl, the Owl, the Owl," chanted Red-Arm's son.

"If you don't leavc here this instant, I'll call the police," said Morel.

Frightened by this scene, the children began to cry and the senile old woman sat up in her seat.

"If anyone has the right to call the police, it's us! Do you understand, Mr. Cripple?" said Bourdin.

"Considering that we might call the police to help us cart you off to prison if you resist," added Malicorne. "We don't have a justice of the peace with us, it's true. But if you feel the urge to enjoy his society, we can arrange for one to be taken out of his nice warm bed. Bourdin can go to get him."

"To prison? Me?" cried Morel, stunned.

"Yes, to Clichy!"

"To Clichy?" repeated the artisan, a haggard look on his face.

"This guy's got a thick skull!" said Malicorne.

"To the debtors' prison. Is that better?" said Bourdin.

"You . . . you . . . must be . . . what? . . . The solicitor . . . Oh, no!" And the worker, pale as death, fell back onto his stool. He could not say another word.

"We are bailiffs, and we're here to nab you, if we can. Do you get it, partner?"

"Morel . . . it's Louise's boss's promissory note! We're done for!" cried Madeleine with a heartrending wail.

"Here's the warrant," said Malicorne as he took a stamped document out of his wallet. After intoning a part of the warrant in the usual way, in a nearly unintelligible voice, he pronounced its last words clearly. These were unfortunately only too meaningful for the artisan: "'As a last resort, the court sentences the aforementioned Jérôme Morel to pay the aforementioned Pierre Petit-Jean,[95] businessman, by all legal means including corporeal imprisonment, the sum of thirteen hundred francs with interest accruing from the date the protest was registered. The court also sentences him to pay all expenses of the court in this matter. Sworn and decreed in Paris this thirteenth of September 1838.'"

"And what's happened to Louise, then?" cried Morel, almost losing his mind. He seemed not to have heard the incantation. "Where is she? She must have left the solicitor, since he's throwing me into prison. Louise! My God! What has become of her?"

"Who's Louise?" asked Bourdin.

"Leave him be," Malicorne interjected brutally. "Don't you see he's got a screw loose? Come on." He approached Morel. "Come on. Left, right! Forward, march! Shake a leg! I've got to get out of this place. The air in here is killing me."

"Morel, don't go with them! Defend yourself!" cried Madeleine, deliriously. "Kill them, kill these beggars. Oh! You're a coward! You're going to let yourself be led away? You're going to abandon us like that?"

"You can act like you own the place, madame," said Bourdin, sardonically. "But if your husband raises a hand against me, I'll lay him out flat."

Thinking only of Louise, Morel heard nothing of what was going on around him. Suddenly, an expression of bitter joy illuminated his face as he exclaimed, "Louise must have left the solicitor's house! I'll go to prison happily." But then, glancing around him, he cried, "My wife! Her mother! And all my children! Who will feed them? No one's going to trust me to work with gemstones in prison. They're going to think I'm in prison

95. The clever solicitor, who didn't want to prosecute him in his own name, had forced the unfortunate Morel to sign a blank note and had had the bill made out to a third party. [SN]

because I've done something dishonest. But that's as much as a death sentence for my family! Does that solicitor want us all to die?"

"I'm counting! One . . . two . . . are we done?" asked Bourdin. "This is getting tiresome at this point. Get dressed, and let's go."

"My good sirs, I beg your pardon for what I just said to you!" cried Madeleine, still in bed. "You wouldn't have the heart to take Morel away. What will become of me with five children and my crazy mother? Look at her! She's over there, hunched on her mattress. She's crazy, my good sirs. She's crazy!"

"The old shaved lady?"

"Hey! You're right, she's shaved," said Malicorne. "You know, I thought she was wearing a white kerchief."

"Children, go and throw yourselves at the feet of these good gentlemen," cried Madeleine. As a last resort, she was hoping to move the bailiffs to pity. "Beg them not to take your poor father, our only breadwinner, away!"

Despite what their mother had asked, the children just continued to cry. They were frightened and dared not get out of their pallet.

In response to the noise and the look of the bailiffs, all of which was unusual to her, the senile old woman began to make dull howling sounds as she huddled against the wall.

Morel seemed to have lost consciousness of what was going on around him. This event had been so unexpected and so brutal, and the consequences of his arrest seemed so appalling to him, that he could not believe it all was happening. Already broken down by every sort of deprivation, he had no strength left. He sat on his stool, pale, haggard, slumped over, his arms hanging slack, his head drooping onto his chest.

"Come on already, damn it! Is this ever going to be over?" cried Malicorne. "Do you think we're on holiday here? Get moving, or I'm going to take you by force." The bailiff put his hand on the artisan's shoulder and gave him a rude shake.

These threats and this gesture terrified the children. The three little boys left their straw pallet half naked and came weeping to throw themselves at the feet of the bailiffs. Their hands joined in prayer, they cried out piteously, "Mercy! Don't kill our father!"

At the sight of these unfortunate children shivering from cold and fear, Bourdin, despite his natural hardness and despite being inured to such scenes, almost felt pity. His comrade, on the other hand, was pitiless. He jerked his leg away from the children who were clutching at him in supplication.

"All right! Get on with you, you little brats! What a lousy profession this would be if you always had to deal with beggars like this."

A horrible event made this scene even more awful than it already was. The oldest of the little girls, who had remained in bed with her sick sister, cried out suddenly, “Mama, Mama! I don’t know what’s wrong with her! Adèle is all cold! She keeps staring at me! And she’s not breathing anymore!”

The poor consumptive child had just quietly passed away without complaining. Her gaze had never left that of the sister who loved her so tenderly.

It is impossible to describe the cry of the gem-cutter’s wife when she heard this terrible statement, for she understood exactly what it meant. It was a gasping, convulsive cry, a cry that could come only from the deepest bowels of a mother.

“My sister looks like she’s dead! My God! Help! I’m scared!” cried the child as she rushed out of the pallet and ran terrified to throw herself into the arms of her mother. The latter, forgetting that her nearly paralyzed legs could not support her, made a violent effort to get up and run toward her dead daughter, but she lacked the strength to do so. She fell onto the floor, uttering a final cry of despair.

All this struck Morel to the heart. He emerged from his stupor and he leapt over to the straw pallet. He picked up his four-year-old daughter and found her dead.

The cold and deprivation had hastened the end of the fatal illness that was itself the fruit of poverty. Her poor little limbs were already growing rigid and cold.

BOOK IV

CHAPTER I

LOUISE

Morel remained frozen on the spot, his gray hair standing on end from fear and despair. He held his dead daughter in his arms and gazed at her fixedly, his eyes red and dry.

"Morel, Morel . . . Give me my Adèle!" cried the unhappy mother, holding her arms out toward her husband. "It can't be true. No, she can't be dead! You'll see, I'll warm her up."

The senile woman's curiosity was roused by the eagerness of the two bailiffs to seize the gem-cutter, who did not want to let go of his child's body. The old woman stopped shouting, got up from her bed, and slowly approached Morel. She ducked her hideous and stupid head under his shoulder and, for a few moments, contemplated the corpse of her granddaughter. Her face retained its ordinary expression of wild-eyed stupefaction. After a minute, the senile woman let out a deep, raucous cry, sounding like a famished beast. Then, returning to her pallet, she cried out, "Hungry! Hungry!"

"You see, gentlemen, you see? A poor little four-year-old girl, Adèle. Her name is Adèle. I kissed her just last night, and again this morning—look what happened! You're going to tell me that at least that's one less mouth to feed, that I should be happy about that, right?" said the artisan, a haggard look on his face. His sanity was starting to give way under the stress of so many blows.

"Morel, I want my daughter. Give her to me!" cried Madeleine.

"That's right. Everyone in turn," answered the gem-cutter. He walked over to his wife and placed the child in her arms. Then he hid his face in his hands and let out a long moan.

Madeleine, no less bewildered than her husband, covered her daughter's body up in the straw of her pallet, brooding over her with a savage kind of jealousy. The other children were on their knees sobbing.

The bailiffs had been moved briefly by the death of the child, but now they fell back into their usual manner of hard brutality. "Come on, comrade," said Malicorne to the gem-cutter. "It's too bad your daughter is dead, but we've all got to die someday. There's nothing we can do about it, and nothing you can do, either. You've got to come along with us. We've got another guy to pick up. It's good hunting out there today."

Morel didn't hear the man. Completely lost in his own gloomy thoughts, the artisan said to himself in a mute and choppy voice, "We're going to have to find a shroud for my little girl and watch over her here . . . until they come to take her away. We have to find a shroud for her! But what will we use? We don't have anything. And the coffin—who will lend us money for it? Oh! A tiny little coffin, for a four-year-old child . . . that can't be too expensive. We don't need a hearse—I could just carry her in my arms! Ha, ha, ha!" he added with a frightening laugh. "Look how lucky I am! She could have died at eighteen, as old as Louise is now, and no one would lend me enough for a larger coffin!"

"Hang on a minute. This fellow is about to lose his marbles," said Bourdin to Malicorne. "Look at his eyes. He's starting to get me scared! And that old idiot who's howling with hunger! What a family!"

"Still, we've got to finish what we started. Even though this beggar's debt is only for seventy-six francs and seventy-five centimes, we'll inflate our fee to two hundred and forty or two hundred and fifty francs, just like everybody else. The moneylender's the one who's paying."

"Really, who's lending to whom? This bird's going to have to pay the piper because he's the one who's going to have to dance to the music."

"When this guy has enough to pay his creditor two thousand five hundred francs of principal, interest, fees, and everything, it'll be a cold day in hell . . ."

"Not as cold as it is in here—it's freezing in here," said the bailiff, blowing on his hands. "Let's finish this job. Get him all wrapped up—he can cry along the way. Is it our fault his daughter croaked?"

"When you're as broke as this guy, you shouldn't have kids."

"That'll teach him!" added Malicorne. Then, hitting Morel on the back, he said, "Come on, let's get going, comrade. We don't have any more time to waste. You can't pay, so it's off to prison!"

"To prison, Morel?" a young, pure voice called out. A young, fresh-looking, rosy woman with well-coiffed brown hair strode briskly into the garret.

"Ah! Mademoiselle Rigolette," said one of the children, crying. "You are so kind! Save our papa! They want to take him to prison, and our little sister just died . . ."

"Adèle died?" cried the young woman. Her large, bright, black eyes filled with tears. "Your father has to go to prison? This can't be!" And, standing motionless, she looked at the gem-cutter, his wife, and the bailiffs, one after the other.

Bourdin came over to Rigolette. "Look, my pretty child, you're still calm, so make this good man understand what's going on here. Okay, his little girl just died. That's all well and good, but he still has to come with us to Clichy, to the debtors' prison. We're the debt collectors."

"So it's true!" cried the young woman.

"All too true! The mother has the little girl in her bed, and no one can get her away from her. That's all she's thinking about. This would be a good time for the father to hightail it out of here."

"Good Lord! What a disaster!" cried Rigolette. "What a disaster! What's to be done?"

"He's got to pay or he goes to prison. There's no other way. Do you happen to have two or three thousand francs to loan them?" asked Malicorne, in a tone of mockery. "If you do, go get the dough and fork it over—that's all we ask."

"Oh, this is dreadful!" said Rigolette indignantly. "How dare you joke in the presence of suffering like this!"

"Fine, then—we'll stop joking," said the other bailiff. "Since you want to make yourself useful, try to keep the wife from seeing we're taking her husband away. You'll help them both avoid having a bad time."

Hard as it was, this was good advice. Rigolette followed it and went up to Madeleine. The latter, driven to distraction by despair, seemed not even to see the young woman who was kneeling next to her pallet with the other children.

Morel recovered from his momentary bewilderment only to fall back into the most painful ruminations. Calmer now, he could appreciate the true horror of his position. Given that the solicitor had gone to such an extreme as this, he was sure to be utterly pitiless. The bailiffs were just doing their job. The artisan resigned himself to his fate.

"Now, then, can we finally get going?" Bourdin said to him.

"I can't leave these diamonds here. My wife is half crazy," said Morel, gesturing toward the diamonds spread over his workbench. "The broker for whom I work is supposed to come get them this morning or during the day at some point. They're worth a lot of money."

"Good!" said Gammy, who was still hovering by the partially open door. "Good, good, good! The Owl will hear all about this."

"Give me just until tomorrow," said Morel, "so I can return these diamonds to the broker."

"Impossible! We've got to go right now."

"But I can't leave the diamonds out in the open like this. They could get lost."

"Take them along with you. Our carriage is downstairs. You can pay for it along with the other fees. We'll go to see your broker. If she's not there, you can deposit the gemstones with the Clichy clerk—they'll be as safe there as if they were in the bank. Let's get going! We'll get out so your wife and children don't see us."

"Give me just until tomorrow so I can bury my child!" asked Morel in a plaintive voice that was hoarse from the tears he was holding back.

"No! We've already wasted more than an hour here."

"The burial would just make you more miserable than you already are," added Malicorne.

"Oh, yes! That would certainly make me more miserable," said Morel, bitterly. "Since when do you care about making people miserable? Let me just ask one last thing."

"Good Lord, enough already! Hurry up!" said Malicorne with brutal impatience.

"When exactly did you receive the order to arrest me?"

"The judgment against you came four months ago, but it wasn't until yesterday that the court clerk got the order from the solicitor to execute the writ."

"Just yesterday? Why did it take so long?"

"How should I know? Let's go—pack up your stuff."

"Yesterday! And Louise hasn't come home. Where is she? What's become of her?" said the gem-cutter, as he took a box of cotton out of the workbench and arranged the stones in it. "But I can't think about that right now. I'll have plenty of time to mull it over in prison."

"Come! Get packed and dressed."

"I don't have anything to pack. All I have are these diamonds to leave with the clerk."

"Get dressed, then!"

"I'm wearing the only clothes I own."

"You're going out in those rags?" asked Bourdin.

"You'll be ashamed to be seen with me, I guess," replied the gem-cutter, bitterly.

"No, we'll be in your carriage," said Malicorne.

"Papa, Mama is asking for you," said one of the children.

"Listen," Morel whispered rapidly to one of the bailiffs. "Have a heart. Show me one last kindness. I can't face up to saying good-bye to my wife or children. My heart would break. If they see you taking me away, they will run up to me. I don't want that. I beg of you, say loudly to me so they can hear you that you will come back in three or four days, then pretend to leave. You can wait for me on the next floor down. I will come out five minutes later. It will spare me those good-byes, and I won't resist, I promise. I'm going out of my mind—I almost lost it a moment ago."

"Oh, sure! You want to play a trick on me?" said Malicorne. "You'll hightail it out of here, you old joker."

"Oh, God!" cried Morel in painful indignation.

"I don't think he's trying to pull one over on us," Bourdin whispered quietly to his companion. "Let's do what he's asking. If we don't, we'll never get out of here. I'll stand right outside the door. There's no other way out of the garret. He can't get away."

"All right, then, but he can go to the devil! What a loser! What a total loser!" Then, turning to Morel, he said in a low voice, "Okay. We'll wait for you on the fourth floor. Put on your show, and be quick about it."

"I thank you," said Morel.

"Okay, let's get going!" said Bourdin, loudly, as he gave the artisan a knowing look. "Since that's the way it is and you've promised to pay us. We'll leave you for now, but we'll come back in five or six days. But you'd better have the money!"

"Yes, gentlemen, I hope to be able to pay you then," answered Morel.

The bailiffs left. Not wanting to be taken by surprise, Gammy had disappeared into the stairway as the debt collectors stepped outside the garret.

"Madame Morel, did you hear?" said Rigolette, turning to the gem-cutter's wife in order to distract her from her dismal thoughts. "They're leaving your husband alone. The two men have gone."

"Mama, did you hear? They're not taking Papa away!" repeated the eldest boy.

"Morel! Listen! Listen! Take one of those big diamonds! No one will know the difference, and we'll be saved," said Madeleine, totally delirious. "Adèle won't be cold anymore, she won't be dead anymore . . ."

Taking advantage of a moment during which none of his family was watching him, the gem-cutter carefully left the garret. The debt collector awaited him outside his apartment on a small landing that was also under the shelter of the roof. On this landing was a door that opened on a storeroom that partly extended out from Morel's garret. That was where Monsieur Pipelet kept his leather supplies. In addition, as we've pointed out, the worthy porter called this retreat his "orchestra row seat at the theater," because a hole cut into the partition between two slats sometimes allowed him to watch the sad scenes that took place at the Morels' home.

The bailiff noticed the storehouse door. For a moment he'd thought that his prisoner might be planning to take this exit to escape or hide from him. "Let's go! Forward march, you worthless soldier," he said as he put his foot on the first step of the stairway down and gestured to the gem-cutter to follow him.

"Please, one minute more!" said Morel. He got down on his knees on the floor. Through one of the cracks in the door, he cast a last glance upon his family, joined his hands together, and said very quietly, in a heartrending voice, weeping hot tears, "Adieu, my poor children . . . Adieu, my poor wife! Adieu!"

"Enough already! Are you still droning on?" said Bourdin, brutally. "Malicorne was right. What a loser! Such a loser!"

Morel got up. He was on the verge of following the bailiff when he heard these words echo in the stairway: "Father! Father!"

"Louise!" the gem-cutter cried out as he raised his arms to the heavens. "I can kiss you one last time before I leave!"

"Thanks be to God that I got here before it was too late!" said the voice as it came closer. The young woman could be heard quickly mounting the stairs.

"Take your time, dear girl," said a third voice that was sharp, wheezy, and breathless. It came from a lower floor. "I'll sit in ambush in the alley if I have to, with my broom and my dear old husband. They're not getting out of here before you've spoken with them, those wretches!"

This, the reader will surely have recognized, was Madame Pipelet, who, though less nimble than Louise, followed her at her own pace.

A few minutes later, the gem-cutter's daughter was in her father's arms. "It's you, Louise! My good Louise!" said Morel, weeping. "But you're so pale! My God! What's wrong?"

"Nothing—nothing at all," answered Louise in a stutter. "It's just that I ran so quickly! Here's the money."

"What?"

"You're free!"

"So you knew about this?"

"Yes, yes. Here, sir, take this money," said the young woman as she gave a roll of gold coins to Malicorne.

"But this money, Louise—"

"I'll tell you everything. Don't worry. Let's go calm my mother."

"No, in a moment!" cried Morel, standing in front of the door. He was thinking of the death of his younger daughter; Louise didn't know about it yet. "Wait—I need to talk with you first. But this money—"

"Wait a minute!" said Malicorne after counting out the gold pieces and putting them in his pocket. "Sixty-four, sixty-five; that's thirteen hundred francs. Is that all you've got, honey?"

"But you only owe thirteen hundred francs!" said Louise, stunned, as she turned to her father.

"Yes," said Morel.

"Just a minute," said the bailiff. "The bill is for thirteen hundred francs, it's true. So here's the bill, all paid up. But what about the fees? Not counting this arrest, they run to eleven hundred and forty francs."

"Oh, no!" cried Louise. "I thought it was only thirteen hundred francs. But, monsieur, we can pay you the rest later. This is a large sum on account, isn't it, Father?"

"Later—sure! Go and bring the money to the court clerk and they'll let your father go. Let's go already!"

"You're taking him away?"

"Right this instant. You've paid some on account. When he pays the rest, he'll go free. Go ahead, Bourdin. We're on our way!"

"Please, have mercy!" Louise cried out.

"What a bore! Now the whining's starting all over again. It's enough to make you break a sweat in the middle of winter, I swear!" the bailiff said brutally. Then, going up to Morel, he said, "If you don't start walking right away, I'll take you by the scruff of your neck and drag you down the stairs behind me. This business is getting on my nerves."

"Oh, my poor father! I thought I was going to be able to save you at least!" said Louise, overcome.

"No, no, God is not just!" cried the gem-cutter in a despairing voice, stomping his foot in rage.

"Yes, God is just. He always takes pity on good people who are suffering," said a soft and resonant voice. At that very instant, Rodolphe appeared at the door of the little retreat. Unobserved, he had been watching several of the scenes we have just recounted. He was pale and profoundly moved.

The bailiffs retreated before this sudden appearance. Morel and his daughter looked at this stranger, stupefied.

Taking a small packet of folded banknotes out of a pocket in his vest, Rodolphe withdrew three of them and, presenting them to Malicorne, said to him, "Here are two thousand five hundred francs. Give this young woman back the gold she gave you."

More and more astonished, the bailiff took the bills. He hesitated as he examined them every which way, turning them over and over again. Finally, he put them in his pocket. Then, as the mixture of surprise and fear began to subside, his vulgarity again got the upper hand. He looked Rodolphe up and down and said to him, "Your notes are good, but how do you come to have such a sum in your possession? Are they really even yours?" he added.

Rodolphe was very modestly dressed and covered with dust from having spent time in Monsieur Pipelet's storage room. "I demand you return that gold to this young woman," Rodolphe replied in a curt and hard voice.

"'I demand!' Where do you get off talking to me that way?" the bailiff yelled as he walked up to Rodolphe menacingly.

"The gold! The gold!" said the prince as he grabbed and shook Malicorne's wrist so violently that the latter bent over from the pain of his iron grip.

"Oh! You're hurting me!" he cried out. "Let me go!"

"Give her back the gold, then! You've been paid. Get lost! And without any more insolence, or I'll throw you down the stairs."

"Fine! Here's the gold," said Malicorne, handing the roll of gold coins back to the young woman. "But don't talk to me like that anymore and don't treat me rough just because you're stronger than me."

"That's right. Who are you, anyway, to put on airs like that?" said Bourdin as he took shelter behind his colleague. "Who are you?"

"You're asking who he is, you lout? Why, he's my tenant, that's who he is. He's the king of tenants, you uncouth idiots!" cried Madame Pipelet, who finally made her entrance, all out of breath and still wearing her blond Titus wig. The doorkeeper's wife was holding an earthen pot full of hot soup that she was bringing up to the Morels out of charity.

"What does that old weasel want?" asked Bourdin.

"If you insult my looks, I'll jump on you and bite you!" cried Madame Pipelet. "And on top of that, my tenant, my king of tenants, will personally pick you up and toss you down the staircase, like he told you. And I will sweep you out like the heap of rubbish that you are."

"This old lady is capable of raising the whole house against us. We've been paid, we've earned our fee—let's get the hell out of here!" said Bourdin to Malicorne.

"Here are your documents," the latter said as he threw a folder at Morel's feet.

"Pick them up! You've been paid to be honest," said Rodolphe, and, stopping the bailiff with one of his strong hands, he pointed with the other at the papers. Held once more in this viselike grip, the bailiff knew he had no chance against such an opponent. He crouched down, muttering to himself, picked up the dossier, and handed it to Morel, who took it, unthinkingly.

He thought he must be dreaming.

"You may have a grip like a dockworker's, but you better not get on the wrong side of us!" said Malicorne. And after brandishing his fist at Rodolphe, he leapt down ten steps in a single bound, followed by his accomplice, who kept looking behind him with considerable fear.

Madame Pipelet started to think about how to avenge Rodolphe for the threats of the bailiff. Looking at her pot as if inspired, she cried out, heroically, "Morel's debts have been paid! They'll have something to eat, so they won't need my scraps. Look out below!" And, leaning over the banister, the old woman emptied the contents of her pot onto the heads of the two bailiffs, who had just at that moment reached the first floor.

"And alley-oop!" added the porter's wife. "Look at them, as wet as a bowl of soup. As wet as two bowls of soup! Hee, hee, hee! Make no mistake about it!"

"A thousand million curses on you!" cried Malicorne, sopping wet with Madame Pipelet's daily fare. "Can you be more careful up there? You old slut!"

"Alfred!" rejoined Madame Pipelet, screaming bloody murder. Her voice was sharp enough to wake the dead. "Alfred! Knock them one upside the head, deary! They wanted to behave like Bedouins with your Anastasie. Those two guys have no sense of decency. They manhandled me! Beat on them with your broom! Tell the oysterwoman and the liquor salesman to help you. Go to it—have at them! Get the cat! Get the cat!

After the thief! Sss! Sss! Sss! . . . Pow! Yoo-hoo! Hit them! Deary! Wham, bam!!!"

And to cap off most impressively the onomatopoetic exclamations that she had accompanied with furious stomping about, Madame Pipelet, drunk with the success of victory, threw her earthen pot down from the top of the staircase. It shattered with a horrible noise precisely as the bailiffs, stunned by her fearsome cries, were descending the stairs four steps at a time. This last event served to add prodigiously to their fear.

"And alley-oop!" cried Anastasie, erupting into peals of laughter and crossing her arms on her chest in a triumphant pose.

While Madame Pipelet was pursuing the bailiffs with her insults and hooting, Morel threw himself at Rodolphe's feet.

"Oh, monsieur, you have saved our lives! To whom do we owe this unhoped-for help?"

"To God. You see, he always takes pity on good people."

CHAPTER 2

RIGOLETTE

Louise, the gem-cutter's daughter, was remarkably attractive; her beauty was striking. Slender and tall, she resembled Juno in the regularity of her severe features, and the huntress Diana in the elegance of her elevated stature. In spite of her tanned complexion and the rough redness of her hands—which were beautiful and shapely, even though they were toughened by domestic labor—in spite of her humble clothing, this young woman had such a noble air that the artisan, in his fatherly admiration, called her "princess manner."

We will not try to depict the gratitude and joyous bewilderment of this family, so abruptly ripped from the clutches of a horrifying fate. For a moment, in this mood of exhilaration, the little girl's death was forgotten.

Only Rodolphe noticed Louise's extreme pallor, as well as the way she seemed overcome by a gnawing preoccupation, despite her father's deliverance. Wanting both to reassure the Morels completely about their future and to explain a generosity that might compromise his disguise, Rodolphe took the gem-cutter aside onto the landing as Rigolette prepared Louise to learn of the death of her little sister. "The day before yesterday, in the morning, a young lady came to your home," he said.

"Yes, monsieur, and she seemed very distressed at our condition."

"After you thank God, you must thank her, not me."

"Is it true, then, monsieur? That young lady—"

"Is your benefactress. I often brought fabric to her home; when I came here to rent a room on the fourth floor, the doorkeeper's wife told me of your cruel situation. Knowing this lady's charity, I ran to see her about you. And the day before yesterday she came to see you so as to judge the extent of your suffering with her own eyes. She was terribly moved, but since your sorrows might have resulted from bad behavior on your part, she charged me with finding out more about you. She wanted her charity to be in proportion to how upright you were."

"What a kind and good lady! I was right when I said—"

"When you said to Madeleine, 'If only the rich knew!'—right?"

"But how—how do you know my wife's name, monsieur? Who told you that . . . ?"

"Since six o'clock this morning I've been hiding in the little storage room next to your garret."

"You? Monsieur?"

"And I heard everything—everything. You are a good and honest man!"

"But, for God's sake, why were you there?"

"For better or for worse, I could only learn about you by going to the source. I wanted to see and hear everything without your knowing it. The doorkeeper had told me about the little space here when he proposed leasing it to me to make it into a woodshed. This morning, I asked him if I could see it. I stayed there an hour, and my time there convinced me that there was no one more upright, noble, or courageously resigned as yourself."

"Good Lord, monsieur, I don't deserve any credit for that. I was born that way, so it's the only way I know how to behave."

"I know that. I'm not praising you, I'm just recognizing you for what you are. I was going to leave the little space to deliver you from the bailiffs when I heard your daughter's voice. I wanted to leave the pleasure of rescuing you to her. Unfortunately, the greed of those debt collectors stole that sweet satisfaction from poor Louise, so I made my appearance. I had received some payments yesterday that were due. I was about to make an advance payment on your benefactress's behalf by paying off that horrible debt. But your misfortune was so great, and you were so honest, so worthy, that the interest she takes in you will not end there. I am authorized by your guardian angel to assure you that a peaceful, happy future is in store for you and your family."

"Can that be possible? But at least tell me her name, monsieur! Her name, the name of that angel descended from the heavens, that guardian angel, as you call her?"

"Yes, she is an angel. And you were also right when you said that the rich have their sorrows, too, just like the poor."

"Can that lady possibly be unhappy?"

"Who doesn't have grief? But I see no reason not to tell you her name. The lady's name is . . ."

Remembering that Madame Pipelet knew that Madame d'Harville had come to the house in order to see the commandant and fearing her tendency toward gossip and indiscretion, Rodolphe was silent for a moment, and then said, "I will tell you the name of this lady—on one condition—"

"Anything, monsieur!"

"I will tell you on the condition you repeat it to no one. Do you understand? No one."

"Oh, I swear it! But will I not be able to thank this benefactor of the poor?"

"I will ask Madame d'Harville. I am sure she will be happy to comply."

"What is the lady's name?"

"Madame the Marquise d'Harville."

"Oh! I will never forget that name. She will be my saint, my idol. When I think that, thanks to her, my wife and my children are saved! Saved! Not all of them—not all of them. We'll never see my poor little Adèle again! Alas! I knew we were going to lose her one day; she was doomed . . ." The gem-cutter wiped his eyes.

"As for the last respects for your poor little daughter: if you will allow me, here's what I think you should do. I haven't yet moved into my room. It's large, airy, and clean. It already has a bed. We can move everything there that's necessary for you and your family to set up your home until Madame d'Harville finds you more comfortable lodgings. The body of your child will remain in the garret, where a priest will keep watch over her tonight according to custom. I will ask Monsieur Pipelet to take care of these sad arrangements."

"But, monsieur, how can I take your own room from you? Really, you don't have to do that. Now that we are safe, now that I no longer fear going to prison, my hovel will seem like a palace to me, especially if Louise stays with us and takes care of everything, like she used to."

"Your Louise will never leave you again. You were saying that it would be an indulgence for you to keep her with you forever. That will be best. That will be your reward."

"My God, monsieur, can it be possible? I must be dreaming! I was never very religious, but an experience like this—such a providential salvation! It would make a believer out of anyone!"

"You should always believe in God. What does it cost you?"

"You're right," replied Morel, naively. "What does it cost you?"

"If there can be any compensation for a father's loss, I would tell you that one of your daughters has been taken, but another has been returned to you."

"You're right, monsieur. We will have our Louise with us now."

"You'll accept my room, right? Otherwise, I don't know how we can accommodate the sad ritual of watching over the dead. Think of your wife, whose mental state is already so fragile. You can't leave her for twenty-four hours in the presence of such a painful sight."

"You've thought of everything! Everything! You are so kind, monsieur!"

"Your benevolent angel is the one you should be thanking—her goodness inspires me. I am saying what she would say. She will approve of this all, I'm sure. So you're accepting my offer, then—we've agreed. Now, tell me about this Jacques Ferrand." A dark cloud passed over Morel's face. "This Jacques Ferrand," continued Rodolphe, "is this Jacques Ferrand the same one who is a solicitor living on rue du Sentier?"

"Yes, monsieur. Do you know him?" And then, struck again for the moment by his fears regarding Louise, Morel cried, "Since you know him, monsieur, tell me . . . tell me . . . do I have the right to be angry at that man? And who knows . . . if my daughter . . . my Louise . . ." He could not finish his thought and hid his face in his hands.

Rodolphe understood his fears. "The very actions the solicitor has taken should reassure you," he said to him. "It's clear that he had you arrested in order to retaliate against your daughter for spurning his advances. For the rest, I have every reason to suspect that he is a corrupt man. And if that's true," said Rodolphe, after a moment of silence, "you may depend on divine justice to deal with him accordingly."

"He is very rich and a great hypocrite, monsieur!"

"You were very poor and very desperate! Did divine justice fail you?"

"Oh, no, monsieur! Great God! Don't think that I said this out of ingratitude."

"A guardian angel came to your aid. An inexorable avenging angel may well visit the solicitor—if he's guilty."

At this moment, Rigolette stepped out of the garret, wiping away her tears.

Rodolphe said to the young woman, "Isn't it true, neighbor, that Monsieur Morel would be well advised to stay with his family in my room while he waits for his benefactor—I am just her agent—to find him appropriate lodging?"

Rigolette looked at Rodolphe in astonishment. "Really, monsieur? You would be so generous?"

"Yes, but on one condition—and it depends on you, dear neighbor."

"Oh, if it's up to me—"

"I've been needing to settle several urgent bills for my boss. Someone is going to come by to find them soon. My papers are down there. If you wouldn't mind being so neighborly as to let me take care of this work in your home—all I need is the corner of a table to work on while you're doing your own work. I wouldn't disturb you at all, and the Morel family would be able to set up their household in my room right away, with the assistance of Monsieur and Madame Pipelet."

"Oh, if that's all you need, monsieur, I'll be happy to oblige! Neighbors need to help each other out. You're being a model of that in what you're doing for that good Monsieur Morel. I am happy to help, monsieur."

"Call me 'neighbor' instead of 'monsieur.' Otherwise I'll be embarrassed and I wouldn't dare accept your help," said Rodolphe, smiling.

"Oh, if that's all that's stopping you, I'll be glad to call you my neighbor. That's what you are, after all."

"Papa, Mama is asking for you. Come now!" said one of the little boys, stepping outside the garret.

"Go, my dear Monsieur Morel. When everything is ready for you downstairs, they'll come up and let you know."

The gem-cutter rushed back into his home.

"Now, neighbor," said Rodolphe to Rigolette, "I need you to do me one more favor."

"I'll be happy to do anything I can, neighbor."

"I am sure that you are an excellent little homemaker. We need to buy everything the Morel family needs, right away: comfortable clothing, comfortable places to sleep, everything they need to get settled in my room. The only furnishings in there right now are my bachelor's furniture that got delivered yesterday, and there's not much of that. What do we have to do to get everything the Morels will need right away?"

Rigolette reflected for a moment and answered, "It can all get done within two hours. I'll get good, warm, clean clothes for them, and some nice white sheets for the whole family. Two little beds for the children, a large one for the grandmother—basically, everything they need. But you know that this will cost a lot of money."

"How much?"

"Oh, at least five or six hundred francs."

"For everything?"

"Alas, yes! So, you see, it's a lot of money!" said Rigolette, her eyes widening as she shook her head.

"And when would we have it?"

"Within two hours!"

"You must be a good fairy, neighbor!"

"Lord, no—it's very easy. The Temple market is just two steps away from here, and you can find everything you need there."

"The Temple?"

"Yes, the Temple."

"What's that?"

"You don't know the Temple, neighbor?"

"No, neighbor."

"Well, that's where people like you and me, if they're thrifty types, buy their furniture and clothing. It's a lot cheaper there than elsewhere, and just as good."

"Really?"

"You better believe it. Listen: how much did you pay for this overcoat?"

"I can't tell you exactly."

"What, neighbor? How can it be that you don't know how much your overcoat cost?"

"I will confess to you in confidence, neighbor," said Rodolphe, smiling, "that I owe money on it. So you understand—I can't really be sure how much it will cost."

"Ah! Neighbor, neighbor! You're making me think you're not very organized."

"Alas, I am not, neighbor."

"We'll have to change that if you want us to become friends—and I can tell already that we will be because you seem so nice! You'll see, you won't be sorry to have me as your neighbor. You'll help me in various ways, and I'll do mending for you—that's what neighbors are for. I'll take good care of your laundry, you'll give me a hand when I polish my floor. I wake up early. I'll wake you up so you won't be late for work at your store. I'll knock on your wall until I hear you say, 'Good morning, neighbor!'"

"It's a deal. You will wake me up. You'll take care of my laundry and I'll polish your floor."

"And you'll get your affairs in order?"

"Certainly."

"And when you have things you need to buy, you'll go to the Temple, right? For example, your overcoat probably cost you eighty francs, I'm guessing. Well, you could have gotten it at the Temple for thirty francs!"

"That's incredible! So you think that with five or six hundred francs those poor Morels—"

"They'll have what they need, and it'll last a long time."

"I've got an idea, neighbor!"

"Let's hear it!"

"Are you a good judge of household goods?"

"Well, I guess you could say so," said Rigolette, with a touch of self-satisfaction.

"Take my arm, then, and let's go to the Temple together to buy everything we need to deck out those Morels. How does that sound to you?"

"What a pleasure! Those poor people! But where do we get the money?"

"I have it."

"Five hundred francs?"

"The Morels' benefactor gave me carte blanche. She wants nothing to be spared to make things right for those good people. Even if there's a place where we can find better furnishings than we could at the Temple—"

"You can't find anything better anyplace else, and besides, they've got everything and it's ready to wear. Little clothes for the children and dresses for the mother."

"Then let's go to the Temple, neighbor."

"Oh, Lord! But—"

"What's wrong?"

"Nothing—it's just that, you see . . . my time is all I own. I'm already a bit behind in my work from coming here to take care of that poor Morel woman. You understand, an hour here, an hour there—bit by bit, they add up to a whole day. A day, that's thirty sous, and when you don't earn anything on a particular day, still you need to live. But who cares, it's all the same to me. I'll catch up at night. And then again, you know, this'll be a picnic, they don't come by every day, and I'm going to make the best of it. I'll pretend like I'm really rich—rich, rich, rich!—that it's my money we're buying all those good things for the Morels with. All right, then! Let me go get my shawl and bonnet, and I'm all yours, neighbor."

"If that's all you have to do before going out, would you like me to get my papers in the meantime and bring them over to your place?"

"Gladly. You'll be able to see my room that way," said Rigolette with pride. "I've already done all my housekeeping and that'll show you that I really am an early riser, so if you plan on sleeping late and being lazy, look out! I'll be a troublesome neighbor!" At that, she skipped down the stairs, light as a bird. Rodolphe followed her and entered his own apartment to dust himself off after his time in Monsieur Pipelet's storeroom.

We will explain later on why Rodolphe was still ignorant of the fact that Fleur-de-Marie had been kidnapped the day before at the Bouqueval farm, as well as why he had not come to visit the Morels the day after his conversation with Madame d'Harville. We will also remind the reader that Mademoiselle Rigolette was the only person who knew where François Germain, Madame Georges's son, was now living and that Rodolphe dearly wanted to find out the secret of this address. He hoped that the walk to the Temple that he had just proposed to the seamstress might make her trust him. He also wanted to distract himself from the sad thoughts the death of the artisan's little girl had awakened in him. Rodolphe's own bitterly missed child would have died at about the same age—Fleur-de-Marie's age—when Jacques Ferrand's housekeeper had handed her over to the Owl's care. We will recount later why, and under which circumstances, this action was taken.

Armed with a huge roll of paper that would help him play his part, Rodolphe entered Rigolette's room. Rigolette was about the same age as Songbird, her former friend from prison. The difference between these two girls was the difference between laughter and tears; between lighthearted joy and melancholy reverie; between the boldest sort of spontaneity and a somber, incessant preoccupation with the future; between a delicate, exquisite, elevated, poetic, painfully sensitive nature, incurably hounded by remorse, and a gay, lively, happy, restless, prosaic nature that was not reflective but was nevertheless kind and obliging. Far from being selfish, Rigolette worried only about other people. Every fiber of her being went into sympathy for others; she felt for those who suffered from the bottom of her heart. But, as the vulgar say, as soon as she looked the other way, her thoughts turned elsewhere.

Often she would stop in the middle of a burst of laughter to break into the most sincere tears—and then she would stop crying to laugh again.

A true child of Paris, Rigolette preferred dizzy excitement to calm, and motion to rest. She preferred the harsh, echoing harmonies of the Chartreuse or Coliseum dance hall orchestras over the soft murmur of the wind, streams, or leaves; and the deafening tumult of Parisian intersections over the solitude of the countryside. Over the serenity of a beautiful, dark, silent, starry night, she preferred the explosion of fireworks, the blaze of the crowning burst, the giant booming sounds the explosions made.

Alas, yes! This good young woman frankly preferred the black mud of the streets of the capital to the flowing green of flowering meadows; its filthy or burning paving stones to the fresh-smelling, velvety moss found on paths through violet-perfumed woods; the suffocating dust of the turnpikes and the boulevards to the field's swaying golden stalks, ornamented with the scarlet of wild poppies and the deep azure of cornflowers.

Rigolette never left her room except on Sundays and early each morning, when she would do her daily shopping for chickweed, bread, milk, and millet for herself and her two birds, as Madame Pipelet had said. But she gladly lived in Paris, for the sake of Paris. She would have been in absolute despair if she had to live anywhere else.

Another unusual thing about Rigolette was that in spite of her taste for Parisian pleasures, in spite of her freedom—or rather, the state of abandonment in which she found herself, since she was completely alone in the world—in spite of the remarkable thrift she needed to employ in her every expense in order to make ends meet on thirty sous a day, in spite of the sauciest, most mischievous, and cutest little face in the world, Rigolette never chose her romantic partners outside of her class. We will not call them lovers: the future will tell whether or not Madame Pipelet's remarks about the seamstress's past neighbors were slanderous or indiscreet. Rigolette selected only men in her class, which is to say, she chose only her neighbors. And it was no delusion to think that equality of rent indicated equality of class.

An opulent and famous artist, a modern Raphael for whom Cabrion served as a Giuliano Romano,[96] had seen a portrait of Rigolette. Since the painter had merely copied nature, the painting did not in any way flatter her. Struck by the charming features of the young woman, the master insisted to his student that he had poeticized or idealized his model's appearance. Cabrion, proud of his pretty neighbor, suggested to his master that he come by one Sunday at the Hermitage ball to judge her as if she were an artwork. The Raphael, charmed by her ravishing face, did everything he could to supplant his Giuliano Romano. He made the most

96. Giuliano Romano (1499–1546), the Renaissance student of Raphael. [TN]

seductive and splendid propositions to Rigolette, but she refused them all heroically. And yet, she would happily accept a neighbor's offer of a modest dinner on a Sunday at the Meridian Café (a well-known cabaret on the boulevard du Temple) or a seat in the gallery at the Gaïté or Ambigu theater.

Such intimacies might seem compromising and could make one have doubts about Rigolette's virtue. Yet without going any further into this subject at present, we will point out to the reader that certain kinds of tact may harbor impenetrable secrets and abysses.

After a few words regarding the seamstress's appearance, we will accompany Rodolphe into his neighbor's room.

Rigolette was barely eighteen years old. She was of average size, or perhaps even a bit on the small side. But she was so graceful, bore herself so finely, and was so voluptuously shaped—and her figure was in such perfect harmony with her light and furtive step—that she seemed perfectly put together. If she had been one inch taller, she would have lost a great deal of her gracious allure. The movement of her little feet, always impeccably shod in black cashmere boots with a slightly thick sole, recalled the alert, flirtatious, and discreet pace of the quail or the wagtail. She seemed not to walk but rather just barely to touch the pavement; she glided rapidly over its surface.

This gait is particular to seamstresses. It is at once agile, fetching, and slightly frightening. This way of walking has, no doubt, three causes: their desire to be thought pretty; their fear of inciting any manifestation of an overly expressive show of admiration; and their constant preoccupation with losing as little time as possible in their travels.

Rodolphe had seen Rigolette only in the dim light of the Morels' garret or on the no less dim landing of the stairway. He was thus astonished to encounter the brilliance of the young woman's fresh beauty when he quietly entered the room lit by two large casement windows. He stood still for a moment, struck by the gracious picture he had before him.

Standing in front of a mirror placed above her fireplace, Rigolette had almost finished fastening the ribbons that tied her little embroidered tulle bonnet underneath her chin. The bonnet was lightly ornamented with a stitched decoration of cherry-colored silk. Of a very narrow cut and worn far back on her head, the bonnet revealed two wide, thick, glossy plaits of hair, brilliant as jet, that fell very low on her forehead. Her delicate, narrow eyebrows seemed to be drawn in ink; they arched over her two large, alert, sly-looking eyes. Her firm, full cheeks were softened by the freshest rosiness—fresh looking and fresh to the touch, too, like a reddened peach plumped by the morning's cool dew.

Her upturned little nose, mischievous looking, shameless and saucy, would have made the fortune of a Lisette or a Marion.[97] Her mouth was slightly large, with very pink, moist lips and little white teeth that were straight and pearly; it was given to laughter and mockery. Three charming dimples gave a mischievous grace to her face; two were scooped out of her cheeks, and the third was on her chin, not far from a beauty mark, a little ebony speck perched seductively close to the corner of her mouth.

Between her trimmed collar that was mostly folded back and the bottom of her little bonnet could be seen, gathered together by a red ribbon, the beginnings of a full growth of beautiful hair that was so perfectly twisted and tucked up that its roots were as neat and black as if they had been painted on the surface of the ivory of that charming neck.

A dress of purple Corinth merino wool with a plain back and tight sleeves, which Rigolette herself had sewn with love, revealed a waist that was so tiny and slender that the young woman never needed to wear a corset—merely as a matter of thrift, of course! A suppleness and uncommon freedom in the smallest movements of her shoulders and torso—recalling the soft undulations of a cat—betrayed this fact.

Imagine a dress that adheres to the round, polished form of a sculpture, and one will understand how Rigolette could perfectly well afford to do without the undergarment we have just mentioned. The belt of a little Levantine silk apron, the color of a green grape, encircled her waist, small enough to hold in one's hands.

Certain that she was alone, as indeed she believed she was—for Rodolphe, standing in the doorway, stayed motionless and unobserved—Rigolette smoothed her tresses with her adorable little hand, all white and manicured. She put her little foot on a chair and bent over it to tie the laces of her small boot. This intimate operation could not be completed without exposing to Rodolphe's indiscreetly watchful eyes a pair of snow-white bloomers, and the calf of a beautifully curved, pure, spotless leg.

The reader will be able to guess, from the detailed explanation that we have given of her preparations, that the seamstress had chosen to wear her prettiest bonnet and apron on their visit to the Temple in honor of her neighbor.

She found the supposed salesman to her liking. His face, at once benevolent, proud, and bold, pleased her very much. And then, he was so kind to the Morels, giving up his room to them so generously, that,

97. Lisette is a common name for a clever, flirtatious servant or grisette. See, for example, Marivaux's *The Game of Love and Chance*. Marion probably refers to Robin's mate in *Le jeu de Robin et Marion*, a medieval French play that may have inspired the romance in the later Robin Hood legend. [TN]

thanks to this proof of his goodness, and perhaps also thanks to his attractive appearance, Rodolphe had already, unbeknownst to him, made great strides in winning her over.

As a result of her practical ideas about forced intimacy and the reciprocal obligations of neighbors, the seamstress felt very fortunate to have such a neighbor as Rodolphe after the departures of the traveling salesman, Cabrion, and François Germain. The room had remained vacant a long time, and she had begun to fear that it would be occupied by someone less to her liking.

Rodolphe took advantage of the fact that he was unseen to cast a curious glance around the apartment. He thought the modest household's extreme tidiness exceeded even Madame Pipelet's high praise of it. There could be nothing more cheerful or more orderly than this poor little room. Gray wallpaper with green flowers covered the walls; the nicely colored red floor tiles shone like a mirror. A white earthenware pot sat in the fireplace, in which a small supply of wood was stacked symmetrically. The wood was cut so short and thin that one could compare each piece, without hyperbole, to an enormous matchstick.

Atop the stone fireplace, which looked as if it were made of gray marble, stood two ordinary flowerpots as decoration. They were painted a pretty emerald green; from springtime onward, these pots would be full of common flowers that smelled heavenly. A small hanging boxwood case held a silver watch that substituted for a standing clock. At one end stood a copper candlestick that was as shiny as gold and topped off with the remains of a candle. On the other end shone no less brightly one of those lamps made from a cylinder and a copper reflector, mounted on a steel stem and with a lead bottom. A rather large square mirror, framed in black wood, overhung the fireplace.

Gray and green chintz curtains with braided wool borders—which Rigolette had cut, created, decorated, and also hung on their light, wrought-iron curtain rods—draped the casement windows and the bed, which was covered with a matching counterpane. Two cabinets with glass windows, painted white, stood on either side of the alcove. No doubt they held cleaning utensils, a portable heater, a washing table, brooms, etc., so that none of these objects could ruin the charm of the room.

A gorgeous, shiny walnut chest of drawers of a beautiful grain; four chairs made of the same wood; a large table for ironing and working, covered with one of those green wool tablecloths one sees sometimes in the cottages of poor farmers; a straw armchair with a matching ottoman, which was the seamstress's usual chair: this was the sum of her modest furnishings. Finally, in the recess of one of the casement windows, one could see the cage of two canaries, Rigolette's faithful fellow boarders. Thanks to one of those practical improvements that only poverty can inspire, this cage was sitting in the middle of a large wooden box that was a foot tall. Placed on a table, this box, which Rigolette called her birds' garden, was full of earth covered with moss during the winter. During the spring, she grew grass and little flowers in it.

Looking at this small abode with care and curiosity, Rodolphe could understand perfectly the joyful good humor of this girl. He thought about the solitude brightened by the birds' chirping and Rigolette's singing. In the summer, she surely worked next to the open window, half hidden by a greenish curtain with pink sweet peas, orange nasturtiums, and blue and white convolvulus; in the winter, she would sit in the corner by her little stove, working under the soft light of her lamp.

Then, each Sunday, she rested from this labor by distracting herself with a good, honest day of pleasures, spent with a young, jolly, carefree neighbor, in love as was she (at this time, Rodolphe had no reason as yet to believe in the seamstress's virtuousness).

On Mondays, she would take her work up again, thinking about past pleasures and pleasures still to come. Rodolphe felt he understood the poetry of those vulgar refrains about Lisette and her little room, about those mad passions that fill attic apartments with joy. This poetry that embellishes everything, that makes a cheerful lovers' nest out of poor men's hovels, is nothing but youth—laughing, fresh, and green. No one could represent this adorable divinity better than Rigolette.

Rodolphe had reached this point in his thinking when, looking at the door absently, he noticed a large bolt—the kind of bolt that wouldn't be amiss on the door of a prison. This bolt gave him food for thought. It could mean one of two things—two very distinct things: it could serve to keep lovers locked out—or it could serve to keep lovers safely locked inside. One of this bolt's uses decisively gave the lie to Madame Pipelet's assertions, whereas the other confirmed them. Rodolphe was considering both interpretations when Rigolette, turning her head, saw him. Without batting an eyelash, she said to him, "So, neighbor, you're already here, I see."

CHAPTER 3

NEIGHBORS

Once the boot was laced, the pretty leg disappeared under the ample folds of Rigolette's purple Corinth wool dress. "Have you been there long, Monsieur Sneak?"

"I was standing there, admiring in silence."

"And what were you admiring, neighbor?"

"I was thinking this was such a nice little room. This room is fit for a queen, neighbor!"

"Well, of course. You see, it's my indulgence. I never go out, so I figure the least I can do is make it nice for myself in here."

"But I've never seen such beautiful curtains! And that chest of drawers, it looks as if it were made of mahogany! You must have spent a fortune decorating this place!"

"Not a word about that. I had four hundred and twenty-five francs when I got out of prison. I spent almost all of it on this place."

"When you got out of prison—you were in prison?"

"Yes—it's a long story. I hope you're not thinking I was in prison for doing something wrong!"

"Of course not! But what happened?"

"After the cholera epidemic, I found myself all alone in the world. I was about ten years old at the time."

"Who took care of you before that?"

"Oh, some very good people! But they died of cholera." (With this, Rigolette's large black eyes welled up with tears.) "All their worldly goods had to be sold to pay off their small debts, and there was no one who wanted to take care of me. I didn't know what to do, so I went up to a guardhouse that was across from our home and I said to the sentry, 'Monsieur soldier, my parents are dead. I don't know where to go. What should I do?' Then the officer came over and had me taken to the police chief, who committed me to prison for vagrancy. I got out when I was sixteen."

"But who were your parents?"

"I don't know who my father was. I was six years old when I lost my mother. She had retrieved me from the orphanage where she had been forced to place me earlier. The good people I mentioned before lived in our house. They didn't have any children, so when they saw that I was an orphan, they took me in."

"And what was their position in life? What did they do?"

"Papa Crétu—that's what I called him—was a house painter, and his wife was an embroiderer."

"Were they at least relatively well-off laborers?"

"Like all couples. Of course, when I say 'couples,' I don't mean to say they were married, even though they called themselves husband and wife. They had their ups and downs. Today there's work and they have plenty. Tomorrow the work dries up and they're poor. That didn't keep the couple from being happy with their lives and always cheerful." (At this memory, Rigolette's face became serene once more.) "There wasn't another couple like them in the neighborhood. Always in good spirits, always singing—and such good people as you would never believe. Whatever they had they shared with others. Mama Crétu was a jolly, fat woman of thirty—spotless as a new coin, lively as an eel, cheerful as a finch. Her husband was a Roger Bontemps:[98] he had a big nose and a big mouth, he always had a paper hat on his head, and such a funny face—such a funny face!—that you couldn't look at him without laughing. When he came home from work, all he did was sing, make faces, and gambol about like a little kid. He made me dance with him and bounced me on his knee. He played with me as if he was my age, and his wife spoiled me, saying it was a blessing! All they ever asked was that I should be cheerful, and thanks be to God, cheerfulness was one thing I had plenty of. That's why they christened me Rigolette, and that's been my name ever since.[99] As for cheerfulness, they set a good example for me. I never saw them looking sad. If they ever had any arguments, the wife would say to her husband, 'Listen, Crétu, this is stupid, you're making me laugh too hard!' Or he would be the one to say to his wife, 'Listen, Ramonette (I don't know why he called her that), you've got to shut up. You're making me ill—you're too funny!' And I would laugh from seeing them laugh. That's how I was raised. They made me who I am. I hope I've done well by their example!"

"Absolutely, my dear neighbor. So they never fought?"

"Never, ever. Sunday, Monday, sometimes Tuesday, they would celebrate their wedding (that's what they called having a good time), and they would always take me with them. Papa Crétu was a very good worker, when he wanted to work. He earned as much as he wanted—same thing for his wife. As long as they had money for these Sunday and Monday excursions and for living day to day as best they could, they

98. *Bon temps* means "good times." Roger Bontemps is a recurring figure in French literature, from the fifteenth century on, for someone who is good-humored and likes pleasure. [TN]

99. *Rigoler* means "to laugh" or "to have fun." [TN]

were happy. Even if they were out of work, they were happy anyway. When we had only bread and water, I remember how Papa Crétu would take a book out of his library . . ."

"He had a library?"

"That's what he called the little bin where he put all of his collections of new songs. He bought them and learned them all. When there was nothing but bread in the house, he would take an old cookbook out of his library and say to us, 'Let's see: what shall we eat today? This dish? This one?' And he would read us the names of all sorts of delicious-sounding things. Each of us would choose our dish; Papa Crétu would take an empty pot and, making the funniest faces and jokes, pretend to fill the pot with all of the ingredients necessary to make a good stew. Then he would pretend to dish it out onto an empty plate that he had also put on the table—all the while making faces that made us laugh so hard our sides hurt. He would take his book again, and, as he was reading the recipe for, let's say, a delicious chicken fricassee that we had selected and that was making our mouths water, we would eat our bread. We would laugh like lunatics while he read."

"And did this cheerful household have any debts?"

"Never! Whenever there was money, we celebrated. When there wasn't, we would eat 'à la tempera'—that's what Papa Crétu called it, because he was a painter."

"And didn't he ever think about the future?"

"Oh, for sure! For us, the future was Sundays and Mondays. In the summer, we would spend those days out of town; in the winter, just outside of Paris."

"Since these good people got along so well and celebrated their wedding (as they called it) so often, why didn't they get married?"

"One of their friends asked them that in front of me once."

"And what did they say?"

"They answered, 'If we have children someday, then it'll be time. But as for the two of us, we're happy the way we are. Why should we be forced to do what we want to do anyway? It would cost money, too, and we don't have extra money lying around.' But hey—I've been chattering away here. I get carried away when I start talking about that good old couple. They were so good to me that I can't help going on and on about them. Listen, neighbor, would you be kind enough to fetch my shawl on the bed there and attach it for me under the collar of my blouse with that big pin? Then we should get going, because we need time to choose what we need to buy for those poor Morels at the Temple market."

Rodolphe hurried to comply with Rigolette's request. He took the large brown tartan shawl with wide poppy-red stripes from the bed and placed it carefully around Rigolette's charming shoulders.

"Now, neighbor, lift my collar a bit, hold the dress and the shawl together, put in the pin, and do try not to stab me with it."

In order to execute these new commands, Rodolphe had almost to touch the ivory neck where Rigolette's ebony hair was so neatly gathered. Daylight was fading, and Rodolphe got closer to Rigolette—too close, it appeared, for the seamstress made a startled little cry.

We are uncertain of the cause for this cry. Was it the sharp point of the pin? Was it Rodolphe's lips that had grazed the surface of this white, fresh, smooth neck? In any case, Rigolette turned around abruptly and cried out, half in laughter and half in sadness, making Rodolphe regret the innocent liberty he had taken, "Neighbor, I will never ask you to attach my shawl again!"

"I'm sorry, neighbor. I'm so clumsy!"

"On the contrary, monsieur, and that's what I'm complaining about. Here, give me your arm—but behave yourself, or I'll get angry with you."

"Truly, neighbor, it's not my fault. Your pretty neck was so white that I was dazzled by it for a moment. My head inclined against my will and—"

"All right, all right! In the future I'll take care not to dazzle you again that way," said Rigolette, wagging her finger at him. Then she closed the door.

"Here, neighbor. Take my key. It's so heavy that it will tear my pocket apart. It's as big as a pistol." She laughed.

Rodolphe took upon himself the burden (and that's the right word for it) of her enormous key. It could have figured gloriously on one of the allegorical platters that conquered occupants of a city humbly offered their conquerors.

Although Rodolphe believed himself to have changed sufficiently over the years not to have to fear being recognized by Polidori, he raised the collar of his overcoat as he passed the charlatan's door.

"Neighbor, don't forget to let Monsieur Pipelet know that we're going to bring in things that need to go into your room," said Rigolette.

"You're right, neighbor. Let's go into the doorkeeper's rooms for a moment."

Monsieur Pipelet, his perpetual stovepipe hat on his head, dressed in his green suit as always, was sitting with a serious look on his face at a table covered with pieces of leather and the debris of shoes of every kind. He was busy resoling a boot with the same seriousness of purpose with which he did everything. Anastasie was not with him.

"So, Monsieur Pipelet," said Rigolette. "Here's some news I hope will make you happy! Thanks to my neighbor, the poor Morels are relieved from their suffering. When you think that they were going to take the poor worker to prison! Oh! Those debt collectors are really heartless!"

"And they have no manners, either, mademoiselle," added Monsieur Pipelet, angrily, as he gesticulated with the boot he was repairing and into which he had thrust his left hand and arm. "No, I am not afraid to shout it before heaven and earth: those men are completely devoid of manners. They took advantage of the shadowy parts of the stairway to dare to make indecent gestures at my spouse's person! When I heard her crying that her modesty had been offended, I gave in to my instinctive liveliness, in spite of myself. I won't deny it: my first response was to stand still and turn crimson from shame as I thought of the odious assaults of which Anastasie had just been victim. I knew things were serious from the momentary derangement she exhibited when, in her delirium, she threw her earthenware crock down the stairs from the top floor. At that moment, those appalling scoundrels passed by my quarters—"

"And you went after them, I hope, Monsieur Pipelet?" asked Rigolette, trying hard to keep a straight face.

"I tried," answered Monsieur Pipelet with a deep sigh. "When I realized that I would have to confront their brazen looks and even perhaps their licentious proposals, that nauseated me, and I was beside myself. I'm no meaner than any other man, but when those shameless individuals passed by here, my blood rose right away, and I couldn't help covering my eyes with my hands so as to spare myself the sight of those lewd evildoers. But I wasn't surprised! I knew something bad was going to happen to me today, because I'd dreamed of that monster Cabrion last night!"

Rigolette smiled, and Monsieur Pipelet's sighs blended in with the sounds of the hammer he used on the sole of the old boot he was repairing.

One would have to conclude from Alfred's reflections that Anastasie had sung her own praises quite loudly indeed. In her fashion, she had imitated the flirtatious practice of women who, in order to rekindle the passion in their husbands or lovers, portrayed themselves as being incessantly and dangerously pursued.

"Neighbor," said Rigolette quietly to Rodolphe, "let poor Monsieur Pipelet believe that they insulted his wife's honor. Really, he's secretly flattered by the idea."

Not wanting to destroy the illusion Monsieur Pipelet had labored under, Rodolphe said to him, "You chose well to restrain yourself, my dear Monsieur Pipelet. It was wise of you to choose the path of contempt. In any case, Madame Pipelet's virtue is beyond any doubt."

"Her virtue, monsieur? Her virtue?" Alfred began again to gesticulate with the boot in his arm. "I would answer for it with my head, even on the scaffold itself! The glory of the great Napoléon and Anastasie's virtue—I'd bet my honor on both of them, monsieur!"

"And how right you are, Monsieur Pipelet. But forget those miserable bailiffs. I would like to beg a favor of you, please."

"All men are meant to help each other," replied Monsieur Pipelet in a sententious and melancholy voice. "All the more in this case, when it is a matter of such a good tenant as Monsieur."

"I need to have various things we'll be bringing back here shortly taken up to my room. These things will be for the Morels."

"Don't worry about it, monsieur. I will be sure all is in order."

"In addition," Rodolphe continued, a note of sadness in his voice, "we will also need a priest to watch over the little girl they lost last night. We will need to record her death and also arrange for a decent service and funeral procession. Here's some money. Don't spare any expense. Morel's benefactor, for whom I am only the agent, wants everything to be done right."

"Count on me, monsieur. Anastasie went out to buy our dinner. When she returns, I'll have her keep watch here, and I'll go out to take care of your commissions."

At that moment, a man approached who was so completely ensconced in his overcoat, as the Spanish say, that you could barely see his eyes.[100] Without getting too close to the porter's lodgings, and remaining as much as possible in the shadows, he asked whether Madame Burette, the secondhand merchant, was at home.

"Are you from Saint-Denis?" asked Monsieur Pipelet, seeming to understand.

"Yes, in an hour and a quarter."

"That's right, then. You can go up."

The man in the coat disappeared rapidly up the stairs.

"What was that all about?" Rodolphe asked Monsieur Pipelet.

"He's scheming something with Old Lady Burette. People are coming and going all the time. She told me this morning that if anyone came for her that I should ask if they were from Saint-Denis, and that if they answered, 'In an hour and a quarter,' I should let them up, but nobody else."

"A real live password!" said Rodolphe, rather intrigued.

"Exactly, monsieur. That's why I said to myself, 'He's scheming something with Old Lady Burette.' In addition to that, Gammy—he's a nasty hanger-on, a little gimp who works for Monsieur César Bradamanti—came in last night at two with an old half-blind woman they call the Owl. She stayed until four in the morning at Old Lady Burette's place while a carriage waited downstairs. Where was that hag coming from? What was that hag doing here at that ungodly hour? Those are the questions I keep asking myself without coming up with any answers," Monsieur Pipelet said, gravely.

---

100. In French, Sue uses the word *embosser*, which doesn't really mean *covered up by* or *ensconced in*, to replace the Spanish word *embozar*, which does. Hence the interjection "as the Spanish say." [TN]

"And that woman you call the Owl left again at four o'clock in the morning by carriage?" Rodolphe asked.

"Yes, monsieur. I'm sure she'll be back, too, because Ma Burette told me that the hag didn't need the password."

Rodolphe thought, not without reason, that the Owl was scheming some new foul deed, but—alas!—he was far from realizing how much this new conspiracy concerned him.

"So it's all arranged, then, my dear Monsieur Pipelet. Don't forget everything I ordered for the Morels, and please ask your wife to have a good meal delivered to them from the best food shop in the neighborhood."

"Don't worry about it one bit," said Monsieur Pipelet. "As soon as my wife returns, I'll go to the city hall, the church, and the food shop. To the church for the dead, and to the food shop for the living," Monsieur Pipelet added, with a touch of poetry and philosophy. "It's as good as done, monsieur. As good as done."

At the entrance to the alley, Rodolphe and Rigolette found themselves face-to-face with Anastasie, who was returning from the market carrying a heavy basket of provisions.

"It's about time!" the doorkeeper's wife shouted, looking over the two neighbors with a sly, meaningful glance. "There you are, arm in arm already! That's fine! Hot! Hot! Hey, youth must have its day! Pretty girls and handsome boys—long live love! Alley-oop!"

And the old woman disappeared into the alley, crying, "Alfred, don't whine, old deary! Here comes your Stasie with something yummy for you, you big sweet-tooth!"

Offering his arm to Rigolette, Rodolphe left the house on rue du Temple with her at his side.

CHAPTER 4

RIGOLETTE'S BUDGET

A frigid wind picked up where the night's snow left off. The roadway, normally muddy, was almost dry. Rigolette and Rodolphe were headed for the immense and singular bazaar people call the Temple market. The young woman hung on the arm of her escort without any false modesty; she was as unself-conscious with him as if they had been old friends.

"Isn't she funny, that Madame Pipelet, with her remarks?" said the seamstress to Rodolphe.

"Honestly, neighbor, I think she may have a point."

"What do you mean, neighbor?"

"She said, 'Youth must have its day—long live love! Alley-oop!'"

"And?"

"That's just how I see things myself."

"What do you mean?"

"I would like to spend my youth with you. I'd like to cry, 'Long live love!' and follow you wherever you lead me."

"That's easy enough to believe. You're not choosy!"

"What would be the harm in it? We're neighbors."

"If we weren't neighbors, I wouldn't be going out with you like this."

"Are you telling me I have cause to hope?"

"Hope for what?"

"That you might like me?"

"I like you already."

"Really?"

"Why not? You're kind, you're merry. Even though you're poor yourself, you're doing what you can for those poor Morels by telling rich people about their suffering. You have an attractive face and a pleasing appearance—which is always nice and flattering as far as I'm concerned, since I'm the one who's taking your arm and I'll do that often in the future. I think I've given you plenty of reasons I should like you."

Then, breaking into laughter, Rigolette cried out, "Look over there! Look at that fat woman with her old fleece-lined shoes—she looks like she's being dragged along by two cats without any tails!" And then she laughed some more.

"I prefer to look at you, neighbor. I am so happy to think that you already like me."

"I'm telling you that because that's the way it is. If I didn't like you, I'd tell you. I am happy to say that I've never deceived anyone nor played the coquette. If I like someone, I tell him right away."

Then, stopping again in front of a store, the seamstress cried, "Oh, look at the pretty clock and the two lovely vases! I already have three pounds and ten sous saved in my piggy bank to buy things like that! In five or six years I will be able to buy them."

"You've saved money, neighbor? How much do you earn?"

"At least thirty sous a day, sometimes forty. But I only count on making thirty because it's more prudent. So I always budget myself based on that," said Rigolette in a manner that made her seem as important as if she were managing the financial balance of an enormous budget.

"But on only thirty sous a day, how do you manage to live?"

"It's not hard to do the figures. Do you want me to explain them to you, neighbor? You seem like you might be a bit of a spendthrift—it might be good for you to hear me go over them."

"Tell me then, neighbor."

"With my thirty sous a day, I earn forty-five francs a month, right?"[101]

"Yes."

"So, we take out twelve francs for my rent, and twenty-three francs for food."

"Twenty-three francs for food?"

"That much, I'm afraid! I have to admit that for a frail little person like myself, that's a lot! But I just won't deny myself anything."

"You're quite the gourmande."

"Ah! But let's not forget that that includes the cost of food for my birds."

"I suppose if all three of you are living on that, it's less extravagant. But tell me how this works on a daily basis. Just for my further education."

"Listen, then. A pound of bread costs four sous. Two sous' worth of milk make six sous. Four sous for vegetables in the winter or fruits and salad in the summer—I love salad because, like vegetables, it's not so messy to make. You don't get your hands that dirty. So that's already ten sous. Three sous for butter or oil and vinegar to season the food, and that's thirteen! A vessel of nice, clean water—oh! That's my indulgence. That makes a total of fifteen sous, if you please! Add to that two or three sous a week for hempseed and chickweed to treat my birds,

101. See note on currency. Rigolette's monthly income, in terms of twenty-first-century buying power, was worth about $250. [TN]

who most of the time eat a few bread crumbs and milk, that comes to twenty-two to twenty-three francs a month, no more, no less."

"And you never eat meat?"

"Oh, sure! Meat! It costs ten to twelve sous a pound. Can you imagine? And then it makes everything smell like cooking, like the stewpot. Whereas milk, vegetables, and fruit are ready right away. You know what I love to prepare? It's not difficult to make, and I make it perfectly."

"Tell me about this dish."

"I put some nice yellow potatoes in my pot. When they're cooked, I mash them with a bit of butter and milk. A pinch of salt—it's the food of the gods. If you're nice, I'll make some for you."

"Made by your pretty hands, I'm sure it would be delicious. But let's figure this out, neighbor. We're already at twenty-three francs for food, twelve for rent; that makes thirty-five francs per month."

"To get to the forty-five or fifty francs that I earn, I have ten or fifteen francs for the wood or oil I need over the winter, for my upkeep and laundry needs. My soap, I mean—except for my sheets, I do all my own laundry myself. It's another one of my luxuries. Paying for a laundress would cost me an arm and a leg, whereas I iron my clothes very well and do a decent job on them. During the five months of winter, I burn a rack and a half of wood.[102] And I spend four or five sous' worth of oil a day for my lamp. It costs me about eighty francs a year for heating and lighting."

"That means that at most you have a hundred francs left over for your upkeep."

"Yes, and that's where I manage to save my three francs and ten sous."

"But your dresses, your shoes, that pretty bonnet?"

"I only put on my bonnets when I go out, and they don't make me go broke anyway because I make them myself. At home, I'm happy to go bareheaded. As for my dresses and these boots, isn't the Temple there for things like that?"

"Ah, right. The glorious Temple. Well, there you can find . . ."

"Excellent and very pretty dresses. Do you realize that the great ladies are in the habit of giving their old dresses to their chambermaids? When I say 'old,' I'm talking about dresses that have been worn for one or two months in a carriage. And these chambermaids go and sell the dresses at the Temple for next to nothing. That's why I have a grape purple Corinth dress of very beautiful merino wool that I purchased for fifteen francs. It probably cost sixty; it was hardly ever worn, and I tailored it to fit. I hope it does me proud."

102. Rigolette's rack is one cubic meter of wood, or a little more than a quarter of a cord. [TN]

"I would say rather that you do it proud, neighbor. But since you have the Temple as a resource, I begin to understand how you can pay your upkeep on a hundred francs a year."

"Isn't it the truth, though? They have charming summer dresses for five or six francs, ankle boots like the ones I'm wearing, practically brand new, for two or three francs. Look, wouldn't you say they were custom made for me?" asked Rigolette, stopping and holding out her pretty foot. It truly was very nicely shod.

"Your foot is charming, it's true. But you must have a hard time finding shoes of that size. Now you're going to tell me they have children's shoes at the Temple?"

"You're such a flatterer, neighbor. But you can see that a little girl who lives all alone, and lives pretty well at that, can get by with thirty sous a day! It must be said also that the four hundred fifty francs that I got when I left the prison helped me a lot to get started. When people saw me in my furnishings, it gave them confidence in me, and it helped me to get work. It did take me a long time to find enough work, but fortunately I saved enough to live on for four months without employment."

"Did you know, neighbor, with all your giddiness, you are a very orderly and rational person?"

"Well, I should hope so! When you're all alone in the world and you don't want to owe anyone anything, you have to figure out how to get by and feather your own nest, as they say."

"And your nest is charming."

"Isn't it? I really deny myself nothing. Really, one would have to say that my home is above my means. I have my birds; in the summer, I always have two flowerpots on my fireplace, and that's not counting the crates in my window and the one under my birdcage. And as I told you, I had already saved three francs and ten sous in my piggy bank set aside for the day when I will be able to buy a set of fire irons."

"What became of your savings?"

"Good Lord, seeing those poor Morels recently, seeing how incredibly miserable they looked—so miserable!—I said to myself, 'It makes no sense to have three stupid pieces of twenty sous sitting around in a money box when there are decent people dying of starvation next door!' So I lent my three francs to the Morels. When I say 'lent,' it's just so they wouldn't be embarrassed. I would have been happy to give them to them outright."

"Of course now that they're back on their feet, neighbor, they should pay you back."

"It's true—I wouldn't say no to that! It would be a first step toward buying my fire irons. That's my dream!"

"And you also need to think a little about the future."

"About the future?"

"If you got sick, for example."

"Me? Sick?" And Rigolette exploded into laughter. She laughed so hard that a fat man walking in front of her with a dog under his arm turned around, taken aback, thinking she was making fun of him. Without ceasing to laugh, Rigolette made him a half curtsy with a look on her face that was so mischievous that Rodolphe could not keep from sharing his companion's laughter. The fat man continued on his way, grumbling to himself.

"You're crazy, neighbor! Come now!" said Rodolphe, becoming serious again.

"It's your fault, too, you know."

"My fault?"

"Yes, because you said silly things to me."

"Because I told you that you could get sick?"

"Sick? Me?" And she laughed again.

"Why is that so unlikely?"

"Do I look like someone who gets sick?"

"I've never seen a rosier, healthier-looking face."

"All right, then. So why do you think I'd ever get sick?"

"What do you mean?"

"At the age of eighteen, with the life I lead, how can it happen? Summer or winter, I wake up at five o'clock in the morning. I go to sleep at ten or eleven. I eat whatever I want, which is not much, it's true. The cold doesn't bother me, I work all day, I sing like a lark, I sleep like a marmot. I'm heart whole, joyful, happy. I make sure that I have work to do. So what do you think would make me get sick? It would be pretty funny if I got sick." And she laughed again.

Struck by her blind, cheerful confidence in the future, Rodolphe reproached himself for the risk he had taken of shaking it. He realized, with some fear, that a single month's illness could overturn this laughing, peaceful existence. But Rigolette's deep faith in her good cheer and her youth—all that she could really call her own—seemed admirable and even sacred to Rodolphe. Her confidence showed neither insouciance nor improvidence; rather it was an instinctual belief in divine love and justice. They would never abandon a good and hardworking creature, a poor girl whose only fault was to count on the youth and health she had from God. In the springtime, when the birds are on the wing, joyous and singing in the sky, grazing on pink alfalfa or parting the warm azure air, do they worry themselves over the prospect of a hard winter?

"So," said Rodolphe to the seamstress, "there's nothing you desire?"

"Nothing."

"Absolutely nothing?"

"No. Well, there's my fire irons, but I'll get them someday. I don't know when, but I've determined that I'll get them and so I will. I will take in more night work if I have to."

"And other than the fire irons?"

"There's nothing I want, at least as of now."

"As of now?"

"Before today, I had feelings for a neighbor I liked. I wanted to help keep his home for him as I always do. I wanted to do favors for him so that he could do favors for me in turn."

"It's already agreed, neighbor. You'll do my laundry and I'll polish your floor. And also, you'll wake me up early by knocking on my wall."

"And you think that's all?"

"What else is there?"

"Oh, you've only skimmed the surface. Don't you have to take me on trips to the city gates or on the boulevards on Sundays? That's the only day I get for recreation."

"Definitely. And in the summer we can go into the countryside."

"No, I hate the countryside. I only like Paris. It's true that, to be obliging in the past, I've visited Saint-Germain a few times with one of my friends from prison whose name was Songbird because she sang all the time. She was such a great girl!"

"What's become of her?"

"I don't know. She spent all her money when she got out of prison without seeming really to enjoy herself very much. She was always sad, but she was sweet and charitable. When we went out together, I didn't have work yet. When I had work, I never left my home. I gave her my address, but she never came to see me. No doubt she's busy herself. But all this is just to say that I love Paris more than anything. So it would be nice, when you can, if you would take me out for dinner or sometimes to a play on Sundays. If you don't have the money for that, we can go to see the stores in the arcades. I would like that almost as much. But don't worry: when we go out together on our little journeys, I will do you proud. You'll see how nice I can be with my pretty deep blue silk dress that I wear only on Sundays. It looks great on me. To go with it I have a little bonnet that's decorated with lace. It's got orange bows on it, and it doesn't look too bad on my black hair. I also have some Turkish satin ankle boots that I had made for me, and a charming floss-silk shawl that looks like cashmere. You'll see, neighbor—people will turn around to look at us all the time when we go by. The men will say, 'What a nice girl that little one is, honest to God!' And the women, for their part, will say, 'What a nice-looking young man he is. That tall, thin young man has a very distinguished air, and his little brown mustache suits him very well.' And I will agree with those ladies, for I adore mustaches. Unfortunately, Monsieur Germain didn't wear one because of the demands of his job. Monsieur Cabrion had one, but it was red, like his thick beard—and I don't much like thick beards. And then again, he was too much of a prankster in the streets, and he tormented poor Monsieur Pipelet. Monsieur Giraudeau (my neighbor before Monsieur Cabrion) carried himself very well, but he was cross-eyed. In the beginning, it was very annoying because he always seemed to be looking at someone next to me, and I'd turn around to see who it was." She laughed.

Rodolphe listened to this babble with curiosity. He wondered for the third or fourth time whether Rigolette guarded her virtue or not.

Sometimes the very freedom of the seamstress's speech and his memory of the large lock almost made him think that she loved her neighbors as brothers, as comrades, and that Madame Pipelet had slandered her. Then, at other times, he smiled at his own credulity. How likely was it that such a young woman, alone in the world, could have resisted being seduced by Messieurs Giraudeau, Cabrion, or Germain? Nevertheless, Rigolette's candor and her quite original familiarity aroused new doubts in him.

"Your plans for my Sundays are quite charming, neighbor," Rodolphe said gaily. "You can rest assured we will go on some wonderful outings."

"Just a minute, Monsieur Spendthrift. I warn you, I'll control the purse strings. In the summer, we can dine very nicely—very nicely indeed!—for only three francs at the Chartreuse or the Hermitage in Montmartre. A half dozen quadrilles or waltzes on top of that, and a few rounds on the carousel—I love riding horses!—and it will cost you a hundred sous, not a penny more. Do you know how to waltz?"

"Yes, very well."

"Fantastic! Monsieur Cabrion used to step on my feet all the time, and then, as a joke, he would throw firecrackers on the ground.[103] That made us less than welcome at the Chartreuse." And she laughed.

"Don't worry. I promise you, I'll be restrained in the matter of firecrackers. But in the winter, what will we do?"

"In the winter, since you don't get as hungry, we can dine perfectly well for forty sous, which leaves three francs for the play because I don't want you to spend more than a hundred sous! That's already a lot of money, but if you were alone, you would spend all of that at a cabaret, at a pool hall with suspicious types who smell horribly of tobacco. Wouldn't it be better to spend your day cheerfully with a girlfriend who behaves nicely and is always laughing, a friend who finds the time to help you save money on some of your expenses by hemming your ties and taking care of your housecleaning?"

"That's a clear improvement, neighbor. But what happens if my friends see me with my nice girlfriend on my arm?"

103. Monsieur Cabrion was throwing what are today called poppers or caps. [TN]

"Well, then they'll say, 'That lucky devil Rodolphe, he's doing pretty well!'"

"You know my name!"

"When I found out that the room next door had been let, I asked the name of the new tenant."

"So my friends will say, 'That Rodolphe is very happy!' And they'll envy me."

"So much the better!"

"And if I'm not as happy as I seem?"

"What does it matter, as long as people think you are? You men don't need more than that."

"What about your reputation?"

Rigolette burst into laughter. "A seamstress's reputation? Who believes in shooting stars like that?" she said. "If I had a father or a mother, a brother or a sister, because of them, I'd care what people said about me. But since I'm all alone in this world, it's nobody's business but my own."

"But I'll be very unhappy."

"What for?"

"I would be passing for happy, when, on the contrary, I will love you. Sort of the way you dined at Papa Crétu's place—enjoying your dried bread while reading a cookbook."

"Oh, come on. You'll be fine! I'll be so nice to you, so grateful, and I won't be any trouble at all. You'll say to yourself, 'After all, it's just as nice to spend my Sundays with her as with one of my pals.' If you are free on a weeknight and you don't mind, you can spend the evening with me. You can take advantage of my fire and my lamp. You can rent some novels and read them aloud to me. Better that than to waste your money on billiards. Or if you have to stay late for your job, or if you would rather go to a café, you can say good night to me when you come back in, if I'm still awake. If I'm asleep, I'll say good morning to you the next day through the wall to wake you up. Listen: Monsieur Germain, my last neighbor, spent all his evenings like that with me. He didn't mind! He read me all of Walter Scott's novels! That was great! Sometimes, on Sundays, when the weather wasn't good, instead of going to a play and going out, he would go to buy something. We would have a real little tea party in my room, and then afterward we would read. It was almost as good as going to the theater! I'm just saying this so you know that I'm not so hard to live with, and that I do anything anyone could ask. And then, you were talking about getting sick: if ever you got sick, I would be your very own little nurse in sister's habit. Just ask the Morels. Listen, you don't know how lucky you are, Monsieur Rodolphe. You really hit the jackpot when you moved in next to me!"

"It's true—I've always been very lucky. But as for Monsieur Germain: where is he now?"

"In Paris, I think."

"You don't see him anymore?"

"Since he left the house, he hasn't been back to see me."

"But where does he live? What's he doing?"

"Why do you ask, neighbor?"

"Because I'm jealous of him," said Rodolphe, smiling, "and I'd like to—"

"Jealous?" Rigolette burst into laughter. "There's nothing to be jealous of. Poor fellow!"

"Seriously, neighbor, I would be very interested in knowing where I could find Monsieur Germain. You know where he lives, and without singing my own praises, you must know that I'd never use the secret I'm asking you to tell me in order to do him any harm. I swear I have his best interests at heart."

"Seriously, neighbor, I believe that you may well want the best for Monsieur Germain, but he made me promise not to tell anyone his address. If I don't tell it to you, it's because I can't. Please don't be angry at me for that. If you had trusted me to keep a secret for you, you'd like to see me acting this way, wouldn't you?"

"But . . ."

"Listen, neighbor: once and for all, let's not talk about this anymore. I made a promise and I'm going to keep it. And whatever you say to me, you'll get the same answer."

Despite her giddiness and lightness, the young woman pronounced these last words with such firmness that Rodolphe understood, to his sorrow, that he would not get what he wanted to know out of her. It would disgust him, moreover, to use trickery to get her to betray her trust, so he waited and said, cheerfully, "Let's not talk about it again, neighbor. What the devil! You're so good at keeping other people's secrets that I'm no longer surprised that you keep your own so well."

"I keep my own secrets? I wish I had some—that would be fun!"

"What? You don't have any little secrets of the heart?"

"A secret of the heart?"

"Come on. You mean to tell me that you've never loved anyone?" Rodolphe asked Rigolette, looking at her intently to try to figure out the truth.

"What? Never loved anyone? What about Monsieur Giraudeau? Or Monsieur Cabrion? Or Monsieur Germain? Or you, now?"

"You never loved any of them more than you do me—or in a way different from the way you love me?"

"Good Lord, no! Less, maybe, because I had to get used to Monsieur

Giraudeau's crossed eyes, to Monsieur Cabrion's red beard and his practical jokes, and to Monsieur Germain's sadness; he was a sad one, that poor young man. You, on the other hand, I liked right away."

"Listen, neighbor, don't get angry with me. I'm going to talk with you like a real friend would."

"Fire away. I can take it. And anyway, you're so kind, you wouldn't have the heart to say anything that would cause me pain. I'm sure of that."

"Of course not. But listen. Seriously, have you never had any lovers?"

"Lovers? Yeah, right! Where would I find the time for a lover?"

"What does time have to do with it?"

"Why, everything! First of all, I would be as jealous as a tiger, and I'd always be making myself suspicious and would feel bad. Well, do I make enough money to be able to waste two or three hours a day crying or making myself unhappy? And if he cheated on me—more tears! More sorrows! Really, that would be a good one. That would set me back very nicely!"

"But not all lovers are unfaithful. Not all of them make their mistresses cry."

"It would be even worse if he was too nice a guy. Could I live for a moment without him? And since he would probably have to be at his office all day, or at his workshop or store, I would feel like a poor lost soul the whole time he was gone. I would come up with a thousand fantasies of how other women loved him and how he was hanging around with them. And if he left me! Imagine that! I don't even know all the things that could come of that. All I know is that my work would bear the brunt of it, and if that happened, what would become of me? It's all I can do, calm as I am, to keep up, working twelve to fifteen hours a day. Think about what would happen if I lost three or four days a week in tormenting myself. How would I make that time up? Impossible! I would have to work for someone, and that's not for me. I like my freedom too much for that!"

"Your freedom?"

"Yes. The mistress of the tailor's shop that gives me my work would hire me right now as her first seamstress. I would earn four hundred francs, and I would have my bed and board."

"And you wouldn't accept that?"

"No! No way. I would be earning wages working for someone else, whereas, however poor I am here, at least I'm my own boss. I don't owe anyone anything. I have energy, I'm honest, I'm healthy and cheerful. I have a good neighbor like you. What else do I need?"

"And you've never thought of getting married?"

"Married? Me? I can only marry a poor person like myself. Look at those miserable Morels. That's where that leads. On the other hand, if you're only responsible for yourself, you can always get by."

"So you never daydream or have fantasies about what could be?"

"Sure I do. I dream of my fire irons. Apart from them, what else do you think I should want?"

"But if some relative had left you a little fortune, twelve hundred francs of income, maybe—to you who live on five hundred francs?"

"Oh, dear! That could easily be a good thing, or a bad one."

"A bad thing?"

"I'm happy the way I am. I'm familiar with the life I'm living, but I don't know what my life would be like if I was rich. Listen, neighbor: when I go to bed after a good day of work, when I've extinguished my lamp, I can see, by the little glow of the embers that are still in my stove, my nice, tidy room, my curtains, my chest of drawers, my chairs, my birds, my clock, my table covered with fabrics people entrust me with. I say to myself, 'All this is mine. I don't owe anything to anybody.' Really, neighbor, these ideas lull me to sleep like a caress. And sometimes I fall asleep proud and content. Well, if I owed my home to the money I inherited from an old relative, I'm sure it wouldn't bring me as much pleasure. But here we are at the Temple! You have to admit that it's a beautiful sight!"

CHAPTER 5

THE TEMPLE

Even though Rodolphe did not share Rigolette's profound admiration for the sight of the Temple, he was nonetheless struck by the singular appearance of this enormous bazaar, with all its separate areas and small alleys. Toward the middle of rue du Temple, not far from a fountain found at an angle from a large open plaza, one could see an immense parallelogram. It was built out of timber and covered with a slate roof. This was the Temple. Bordered on the left side by rue Dupetit-Thouars and on the right by rue Perrée, it converged on a vast circular structure, a huge rotunda, surrounded by a gallery of arcades. A long passage, cutting the parallelogram in half lengthwise, split it into two equal parts. These parts were themselves divided and subdivided again in an infinite manner by a multitude of tiny lateral and transversal pathways that crossed in every direction, sheltered from the rain by the building's roof.

In this bazaar, new merchandise is generally forbidden, but the smallest scraps of any kind of fabric, the tiniest shreds of iron, copper, smelting, or steel, could find a seller or a buyer. There are merchants who sell odds and ends of fabric in every color, every shade, of every quality, of every age, destined to form the patches that repair clothing that is torn or full of holes. There are shops where one can find mountains of shoes that are worn down, full of holes, twisted, split—nameless, formless, colorless things, among which appear here and there old, fossilized soles, an inch thick, as studded with nails as a prison gate, as rigid as a horseshoe. These are the merest skeletons of shoes, whose attachments have been eaten away by time. All of these shoes are moldy, hardened, full of holes, corroded—and all of them find buyers. There are merchants who live off this commerce.

There are retailers of braids, fringes, crests, ribbons, trimmings of silk, cotton, or thread. These come from the shreds of curtains that can no longer serve their original purpose.

Other salespeople support themselves in the women's hat trade. These hats arrive at their shops only in bags of secondhand goods, after the strangest wanderings, the most violent transformations, and the most unbelievable discolorations. So that the merchandise doesn't take up too much space in a store usually no larger than an enormous box, the shopkeepers fold these hats neatly in half and then flatten and pile them up tightly. Except for the brine, it's exactly the same method used to conserve herring. Thanks to this mode of storage, one can hardly believe how many of these things can be packed into a space of four square feet.

When a buyer appears, a salesperson pulls these scraps out from under the weight they have been beneath. The merchant gives a blasé little punch to the base of the form to make it stand up again; she smoothes out the piping on her knee, and behold! You have before your eyes a peculiar, fantastic object that makes you think, in some hazy way, of those fabulous head coverings that have become the signature look of theater ushers, ballet dancers' aunts, and duennas in provincial dramas.

Further along, by the sign that says, "Today's Fashion," under the arcades of the rotunda at the end of the wide passageway that separates the Temple into two parts, a myriad of clothing is suspended like votive offerings, in colors, shapes, and styles that are even more varied and outrageous than those of the women's hats. Here you can find gray linen morning coats enhanced by three rows of military copper buttons, ornamented for warmth with a little fur collar of foxhair.

There are also waistcoats in a primitive shade of bottle green, faded by time into a pistachio color, trimmed with a black braid and brightened up by a Scottish blue and yellow lining, to hilarious effect.

Also garments once known as swallowtail coats, the color of tinder, with a rich, plush collar, ornamented with buttons that used to be silver toned but are now of a coppery red.

You can also see brown dresses à la polonaise with collars made of cat fur, ribbed with military frogging, embellished with fraying black cotton. Not far from these are dressing gowns artistically made out of driving coats from which they have removed the triple collars and which they have decorated on the interior with pieces of printed cotton. The best looking of these are a sordid blue or green, ornamented with pieces of another shade that have been embroidered with satin stitches and lined with red fabric, with orange rosettes and matching cuffs and collar. A cord of a dressing gown made of an old bellpull from twisted wool serves as the belt on these elegant housecoats that Robert Macaire[104] would have been proud to laze about in.

We will note merely as a matter of record the many Frontin outfits that were more or less suspect, more or less barbaric.[105] Here and there in the midst of these could be found, nonetheless, a few authentic royal

104. An archetypal French villain, originally a fictive knight convicted of murder in the fourteenth century. [TN]

105. Frontin was the name of a bumbling valet in a comedy by François Devienne (1759–1803). [TN]

or princely livery uniforms that all sorts of revolutions had washed up from the palace to the dark vaults of the Temple rotunda.

These exhibitions of old shoes, old hats, and old, ridiculous clothing make this bazaar grotesque. Here old rags are pretentiously embellished and disguised. Yet it must be acknowledged that this vast establishment is of great service to the poorer, less comfortable classes. There they can buy, at deep discount, excellent things that are almost brand new and that have lost none of their real value.

One of the sides of the Temple, devoted to bedding, was full of pieces of quilts, sheets, mattresses, and pillows. Further along, there were rugs, curtains, and all sorts of household tools. Elsewhere were clothes, shoes, and headwear for people from every social condition and of every age. Nothing about these objects, which were generally extremely clean, rendered them undesirable.

Without visiting this bazaar, no one would believe how little time and money would fill a cart with everything necessary to furnish homes for two or three completely destitute families. Rodolphe was struck by the manner—at once rushed, considerate, and cheerful—with which the merchants, standing outside of their shops, solicited the patronage of passersby. These practices, signs of a sort of respectful familiarity, seemed to belong to another era.

Rodolphe gave his arm to Rigolette. They had hardly set foot in the passageway where merchants who sold bedding were stationed when they were pursued by the most tempting offers:

"Monsieur, come in and see my mattress, it's just like new! I'll open one of its seams so you can see its stuffing. You'd think it was lamb's wool, it's so soft and white!"

"My pretty little lady, I have beautiful linen sheets, they're even better than new because they've been broken in. They're as soft as a glove and strong as steel wool!"

"Hey, you happy newlyweds, come on in and buy some of my blankets! Check them out, and you'll see that they're soft, warm, and lightweight. It's almost like eiderdown, it's repaired, just like new—it couldn't have been used even twenty times. Hey, little lady, get your husband to give me your business and I'll get your household set up at little cost. You'll be happy, you'll come back to see Old Lady Bouvard, you'll find everything you need here! Yesterday, I got something at a great bargain. You can come in and see! Come on in already! It's free to look around!"

"Honestly, neighbor," said Rodolphe to Rigolette, "I think that nice fat woman deserves our business. She took us for newlyweds, which flatters me. I think we should try her store."

"The fat woman's store it is, then!" said Rigolette. "I liked her looks, too!"

The seamstress and her companion went into Old Lady Bouvard's store. Thanks to a magnanimity perhaps with no equal anywhere besides the Temple, Old Lady Bouvard's rivals didn't protest against the preference they had shown her. One of her neighbors even extended this generosity so far as to say, "As long as it's Old Lady Bouvard and not someone else who's getting that windfall. She's got family members to support. She's the doyenne and the honor of this place."

It was, in any case, impossible to have a more welcoming, open, cheery face than the Temple's senior merchant.

"Listen, my pretty little lady," she said to Rigolette, who was examining several objects with a very practiced eye. "Two full sets of bedding, just like new. If by chance you're interested in a little old desk that isn't very expensive, I've got one for you right here." (Ma Bouvard pointed a desk out.) "I got it in the same lot. I don't usually buy furniture, but I couldn't turn it down. The people I got it all from seemed so sad! Poor lady! Selling this old item especially seemed to break her heart. I think it was a family heirloom."

With these words, while the merchant bargained over the price of different furnishings with Rigolette, Rodolphe considered more closely the piece of furniture that Old Lady Bouvard had just shown them. It was one of those old secretary desks made out of rosewood, in a nearly triangular shape that closed by way of a front panel. When this panel was folded back and supported by two long copper hinges, it served as a writing table. In the middle of this panel, ornamented with inlay work in different colors of wood, Rodolphe noticed some initials inlaid in ebony, an *M* and an *R* interwoven with each other, topped by the crown of a count. He guessed that the last owner of this piece of furniture must have belonged to an elevated class of society. His curiosity grew: he looked at the secretary with renewed attention, mechanically pulling out the drawers one after the other. When he had some difficulty opening the last drawer, he looked to see what was making it stick. He discovered and carefully removed a piece of paper that had been caught between the tray and the bottom of the piece of furniture.

While Rigolette completed her negotiations with Old Lady Bouvard, Rodolphe examined his find with great interest. It was clear from the number of deletions that this was the rough draft of an unfinished letter. Rodolphe read what follows with considerable difficulty:

> Sir,
>
> Please understand that only the most appalling misfortune could force me to undertake making this request of you. My scruples are not the result of some misplaced pride; rather, they stem from my knowledge that I have absolutely no right to ask you for the favor I am daring to request. The sight of my daughter, reduced like myself to the most

frightful penury, is forcing me to overcome my embarrassment. Just a few words about the cause of the disasters that have overcome me.

After the death of my husband, I had an inheritance of three hundred thousand francs invested by my brother with Monsieur Jacques Ferrand, Solicitor. With my daughter, I retired to Angers, where I received the interest on this sum via my brother. Ruined, it seemed, by secret and unlucky speculations, he killed himself eight months ago. After this fateful event, I received a few desperate lines from him. When I read these lines, the letter said, he would be no more. He ended the letter by warning that he had no papers showing ownership of the sum he had placed in my name with Monsieur Jacques Ferrand. The latter never gave out receipts, for he was honor and piety incarnate. It would suffice for me to go to him in person so that the affair could be sorted out in an acceptable way.

As soon as it was possible for me to think of anything besides the horrible death of my brother, I came to Paris, where I knew no one but you, monsieur, and even you only indirectly, through the relations you had had with my husband. As I mentioned, the sum deposited with Monsieur Jacques Ferrand constituted my entire fortune. My brother had been sending me the interest due from this money every six months. More than a year had gone by since the last payment, so I paid a visit to Monsieur Jacques Ferrand so as to ask him for the money, of which I had the most pressing need.

No sooner had I been announced to him than, showing no respect whatsoever for my sorrow, he accused my brother of having borrowed two thousand francs from him that his death had made him unable to recover. He added that not only was his suicide a crime before God and man, but that it was also an act of plunder, of which he had been the victim.

This odious language outraged me. My brother's unquestioned integrity was well known. He had, it is true, unbeknownst to me and to his friends, lost his fortune on risky investments, but he died with his reputation intact, missed by all, and leaving no debt besides the one to the solicitor.

I answered Monsieur Ferrand that I authorized him to deduct on the instant the two thousand francs my brother had owed him from the three hundred thousand francs I had on deposit with him. At those words, he looked at me in bewilderment and asked me of which three hundred thousand francs I was speaking.

"Of the money my brother deposited with you eighteen months ago, monsieur, and from which you have paid me interest through my brother," I said, not understanding his question.

The solicitor shrugged his shoulders, smiled in pity, as if my words couldn't have been serious, and answered me that, far from investing any money with him, my brother had, on the contrary, borrowed two thousand francs from him.

It is impossible to express the fear I felt when I heard this response.

"So what happened to that money, then?" I cried. "My daughter and I have no other source of income. If it has been stolen from us, we will become utterly destitute. What will become of us?"

"That's no concern of mine," said the solicitor, coldly. "Your brother probably squandered the money in the unfortunate speculations he was engaging in without anyone knowing about them, instead of investing it with me, as he told you."

"That is false and it's slander, monsieur!" I cried. "My brother was the very soul of honesty. Far from fleecing me and my daughter, he sacrificed himself for us. He never wanted to marry because he wanted to leave all he had to my child."

"Do you have the audacity to claim, madame, that I am capable of denying the existence of a deposit that had been made with me?" the solicitor asked in an attitude of indignation that seemed so honorable and so sincere that I could only say to him, "No, of course not, monsieur; your reputation for integrity is well known. But neither can I accuse my brother of such heartless embezzlement."

"What documents do you have on which to base your claim against me?" asked Monsieur Ferrand.

"I haven't any, monsieur. Eighteen months ago, my brother, wishing to take care of my affairs, wrote to me, 'I have found an excellent rate of six percent; send me your legal authorization to sell your property; I'll invest the three hundred thousand francs, which the money will come to with what I add to it, with the solicitor Monsieur Jacques Ferrand.' I sent my legal authorization to my brother, and a few days later he told me that the investment had been made with you and that you never gave out receipts. Six months later he sent me the interest due on the money."

"And do you have at least some correspondence from him on the subject, madame?"

"No, monsieur. They were all about business, so I didn't keep them."

"Unfortunately, based on this information, there is nothing I can do," the solicitor said to me. "If my integrity were not above all suspicion, and out of reach of any charges, I would tell you, 'The law is open to you. Sue me. The judges will choose between the word of an honorable man who has for thirty years enjoyed the esteem of respectable people, and the posthumous declaration of a man who, after having secretly ruined himself in the maddest of enterprises, found his only refuge in suicide.' I would finish by telling you: 'Go ahead and sue me, madame, if you dare. You will merely dishonor your brother's memory.' But I think you will have the good sense to resign yourself to what is doubtless a great hardship, but one I have nothing to do with."

"But, monsieur, I have a child! If my fortune has been stolen from me, my daughter and I have nothing left but a modest home! Once that is sold, we will be faced with poverty, monsieur! The most abject poverty!"

"You were cheated, which is unfortunate. I can't do anything to help you," the solicitor answered me. "Once again, madame, your brother deceived you. If you hesitate to take my word for it, go ahead and bring suit. The courts will decide."

I left the solicitor's office with my heart dead within me. What could I do in this extremity? Without a deed to prove the validity of my claim, convinced of my brother's unimpeachable integrity, overcome by Monsieur Ferrand's confidence, having no one to turn to for advice (you were on a journey at the time), knowing that I needed money to consult legal experts, and wanting desperately to hold on to the little bit of money that remained to me, I dared not file such a suit. It was then that . . .

The draft of the letter ended there. Some indecipherable deletions covered the few lines that followed; finally, at the bottom of the page, in a corner, Rodolphe read the following form of a reminder: "Write to Madame the Duchess de Lucenay."

Rodolphe was pensive after reading this fragment of a letter. Even though this new infamy that Jacques Ferrand seemed accused of could not be proven, this man had shown himself to be so pitiless toward the unfortunate Morel, so inhumane toward his daughter, Louise, that this wretch's denial of an investment, protected as he was by certain impunity, could hardly be seen as surprising. This mother, who claimed this fortune, which had disappeared so strangely, was no doubt accustomed to a life of ease. Ruined by a sudden blow, knowing no one in Paris, as the letter said, what must the existence of these two women be at present? They were utterly destitute, perhaps, all alone in this immense city!

As we know, Rodolphe had promised to involve Madame d'Harville in some intrigues, assigning her, at random if need be, and just to occupy her mind, a role to play in some future good deed. He was certain, moreover, that he would find some misery to relieve before his next meeting with the marquise.

He thought that luck might have put him on the trail of a noble calamity that, as he had planned, would occupy the heart and imagination of Madame d'Harville.

The intent of the letter that he held in his hands, and of which the copy had no doubt never been sent to the person whose assistance was implored, evidenced its author's proud and resigned personality, a personality that would find the prospect of receiving alms repugnant. So, he thought, how many precautions, detours, and delicate stratagems would it take to hide the source of generous assistance from the woman—or to make her accept it?

And then, one would need so much tact to get close to this woman in order to judge whether she truly merited the sympathy she seemed so clearly to inspire. Rodolphe anticipated a host of new, curious, touching emotions arising in this situation that would certainly *amuse* Madame d'Harville in the singular manner he had promised her.

"Well, *husband*?" Rigolette said to Rodolphe gaily. "What is that piece of paper you were reading there?"

"My little *wife*," Rodolphe answered, "you are very nosy! I will tell you everything in a moment. Have you finished making all your purchases?"

"I certainly have, and your protégés will have a household fit for kings. All that's left is to pay. Madame Bouvard has been very accommodating, I must say."

"My little *wife*, I have an idea! While I pay, why don't you go and choose some clothing for Madame Morel and her children? I declare my ignorance on the subject of such purchases. You can tell them to carry it all here. We can make one trip of it that way, and our poor friends can get everything at once."

"You are always right, *husband*. Wait for me here—I won't be long. I know two salespeople who I have bought from regularly. I'll find everything we need in their shops." And with this, Rigolette left. But she returned to say, "Madame Bouvard, I'm entrusting you with my husband. Don't go making eyes at him!"

She laughed, and then quickly disappeared.

CHAPTER 6

THE DISCOVERY

"Gotta say," Old Lady Bouvard said to Rodolphe after Rigolette's departure, "gotta say that you've got a great little housekeeper there. Bless my soul! She really knows how to shop, and she's so nice! All pink and white, with those big black eyes and her black hair, too—she's a rare find!"

"Isn't she charming, and aren't I a lucky husband, Madame Bouvard?"

"You're as lucky a husband as she is a wife. I'm sure of that!"

"And no one would ever say you're wrong. But tell me, how much do I owe you?"

"Your little housekeeper wouldn't give me more than three hundred and thirty francs for the whole lot. As God is my witness, I'm only making fifteen francs, because I didn't get these things as cheaply as I could have. I didn't have the heart to bargain for them. The folks who were selling them just seemed too unhappy!"

"Really? Were they the same people you bought the little secretary from?"

"Yes, monsieur. You know, it breaks your heart just thinking about it. Imagine, the day before yesterday a lady came in here who was still young and pretty but so pale and so thin that it hurt to look at her. But people like us see that all the time. Even though she was all got up proper, as they say, her old wool shawl, black and threadbare, her dress of Aleppo silk, also black and also frayed, her straw hat in the month of January (this woman was in mourning)—all of this let out that she's experiencing what we call 'genteel poverty.' I'm sure she was a very proper lady. She asked me, blushing all the while, if I wanted to buy all the bedding off the two beds along with the little old secretary. I said that I had to buy things if I wanted to be able to sell them. I told her it was fine with me and that she could count on the sale, but that I wanted to see the objects. She asked me then to come to her home, not far from here, on the other side of the boulevard, in a house on the quai of the Saint-Martin canal. I let my niece mind the store—I'm the lady in charge—we go to a house of humble folk, as they say, at the bottom of the courtyard, and we go up to the fourth floor. The lady knocks and a girl of fourteen comes to open it for us. She was also wearing mourning and was also very pale and thin. But despite that, she was pretty as the day is long—so pretty that I couldn't help staring."

"And who was that pretty girl?"

"The daughter of the lady in mourning. Despite the cold, all she had on was a flimsy black cotton dress with white polka dots on it and a worn little black shawl."

"And was their lodging wretched?"

"Imagine, monsieur, two very clean rooms, but with practically nothing in them, and so icy cold it made your heart stop. There was a fireplace, but there wasn't a speck of ash in it. It gave no sign of there having been a fire in some time. As for furniture, there were two beds, two chairs, a chest of drawers, an old trunk, and the little secretary. On the trunk there was a bundle in a scarf. This little bundle represented all of the worldly goods left to the mother and daughter once their furniture was sold. The landlord was taking the two bedsteads, the chairs, the trunk, and the table in place of money they owed him, as the porter, who came up with us, explained. Then this lady asked me frankly to appraise the mattress, sheets, curtains, and bedcovers. I swear, monsieur, that even though my job is to buy low and sell high, when I saw that poor little miss with her eyes all full of tears, along with her mother who seemed to be crying on the inside, even though she acted calm, I assessed it within fifteen francs of its actual value—its actual value, I swear. I even agreed to take the little secretary just to oblige them, even though it's not what I usually sell."

"I'll buy it from you, Madame Bouvard."

"Bless my soul! So much the better, monsieur. It would have been on my hands a long time. I only agreed to take it to do that poor lady a favor. So I told her the price I'd offer her for her belongings. I expected her to bargain with me, to ask for more. Well, that just showed me once more that she was no common type. Genteel poverty, you know, monsieur? So I said to her, 'That's a lot.' She answered, 'That's fine. Let's return to your shop and you will pay me, because I won't be coming back to this house.' Then she said to her daughter, who was sitting on the trunk, crying, 'Claire, take the bundle.' (I remember distinctly that the girl's name was Claire.) The young lady got up, but as she passed by the little secretary, she fell to her knees in front of it and started sobbing. 'My child, collect yourself. There are people here with us,' her mother said softly, which didn't stop me from hearing her. Imagine, monsieur: these people were poor, but proud nonetheless. When the lady gave me the key to the secretary, I could also see a tear in her reddened eyes. It seemed her heart was bleeding from having to part from this old piece of furniture, but she was trying to maintain her composure and her dignity in front of strangers. Finally she told the doorkeeper that

I had come to take everything the landlord wasn't keeping, and we came back here. The young lady gave her arm to her mother and carried the little bundle that contained all they owned. I gave them their money, three hundred and fifteen francs, and I haven't seen them since."

"What was their name?"

"I don't know. The lady sold her things to me with the doorkeeper there. I didn't need to ask her her name. She was definitely the owner of the things she was selling me."

"What is her new address?"

"I don't know that, either."

"Surely they would know in her old building?"

"No, monsieur. When I went there to look for the objects I had purchased, the doorkeeper, in speaking to me of the mother and her child, told me, 'Those were such quiet people—so respectable and so unhappy! I hope nothing bad has happened to them! They seem so calm, but deep down I can tell they're desperate.' 'And where are they going to live now?' I asked him. 'Bless my soul, I have no idea,' he answered me. 'They left without telling me. They certainly won't be back.'"

Rodolphe's momentary hopes were dashed. How could he locate these two unhappy women? All he had to go on was the name of the daughter, Claire, and the fragment of the draft of the letter we've discussed above, with the writing at the bottom that said, "Write to Madame de Lucenay." The only chance he had—and it was an unlikely one—to recover the trail of these unfortunate women was through Madame de Lucenay. She was, by a happy chance, a member of Madame d'Harville's social circle.

"Here, madame. Pay yourself out of this," said Rodolphe to the merchant, presenting her with a note for five hundred francs.

"I'll go and get you your change, monsieur."

"Where can we find a cart to transport these things?"

"If it isn't too far, a pushcart should be enough. Old Jérôme has one right nearby. He's my usual deliveryman. What's your address, monsieur?"

"Rue du Temple, number seventeen."

"Number seventeen on rue du Temple? Oh, I know the place!"

"You've been in that house before?"

"Several times. First, I bought some used clothes from a private pawnbroker who lives there. Her job isn't a very pretty one, it's true, but it's none of my business. She sells, I buy, and that's all we have to do with each other. Another time, it must have been less than six weeks ago, I returned there to pick up the furnishings of a young man who lived on the fourth floor there and who was moving."

"Would that man happen to be Monsieur François Germain?" Rodolphe exclaimed.

"Exactly! Do you know him?"

"Very well. Unfortunately, he didn't leave his new address at rue du Temple and I don't know where to find him now."

"If that's all you need, I can help you out."

"You know where he lives?"

"Not exactly, but I know where you'll certainly be able to find him."

"Where is that?"

"At the office of the solicitor he works for."

"A solicitor?"

"Yes, a solicitor who lives on rue du Sentier."

"Monsieur Jacques Ferrand?" cried Rodolphe.

"The very same! He's a pious man. He's got a crucifix and some holy wood in his study. It smells so much like the sacristy in there that you'd think you were in one."

"But how did you find out that Monsieur Germain works for that solicitor?"

"Here's how. The young man came to offer to sell me all his furniture at once. That time, too, even though it wasn't my line, I bought the whole lot, and then I put it up for sale piece by piece. Since this would work out well enough, I wanted to help the young man out. I bought his bachelor's furniture, right? I paid him for it, right? He must have been happy with me because two weeks later he came back to buy some bedding from me. He came with a little cart and a deliveryman. We got it all packed up, right? But at the moment he was going to pay me, he realized that he had forgotten his wallet. He seemed like such an honest young man that I said to him, 'Take the things anyway. I'll come to your place to get my money.' 'Very good,' he said to me, 'but I'm never at home. If you come tomorrow to the office of the solicitor Monsieur Jacques Ferrand on rue du Sentier, where I work, I'll pay you there.' I went there the next day, and he paid me. The only funny thing was that he sold all his furniture, to buy new stuff another two weeks later."

Rodolphe thought he could guess—and he in fact guessed correctly—the reason behind this odd behavior. Germain had wanted to erase all traces of himself so as to foil the wretches who were pursuing him. He was no doubt afraid that moving his belongings might give them a lead as to his new address. To avoid that risk, he had preferred to sell his belongings and buy new ones again later.

When he thought of how happy Madame Georges would be when she finally saw again the son whom she had sought in vain for so long, Rodolphe felt a chill of joy run down his spine.

Rigolette soon returned, her eyes gleaming and a smile on her face.

"So, didn't I tell you?" she cried. "I wasn't wrong! We will have spent six hundred and forty francs in all, and the Morels will be living like princes. Look! See the merchants who are coming—look at all they're carrying! That household will lack for nothing—they have everything they need, including a grill, two beautiful pots that have just been replated, and a coffeepot. I said to myself, 'Since we're trying to do things right, let's do things right!' And with all that, I've lost at most three hours on this. But pay the bill quickly, neighbor, and let's get going! It's almost noon. My needle is going to have to go at lightning speed to catch up for this morning's fun."

Rodolphe paid what he owed and left the Temple with Rigolette.

CHAPTER 7

AN APPARITION

Just as the seamstress and her companion were entering the alleyway of their house, Madame Pipelet, who was clearly disturbed, desperate, and somewhat deranged, ran into them and almost knocked them down.

"My goodness!" said Rigolette. "What's wrong, Madame Pipelet? Where are you running like this?"

"It's you! Mademoiselle Rigolette!" cried Anastasie. "The good Lord has sent you to me. Help me save Alfred's life!"

"What's wrong?"

"My poor old deary has fainted—have mercy on us! Run and get two sous' worth of absinthe at the spirit seller's place—get the strongest stuff he has. That's his remedy when he's indisposed—in his gut. That will revive him, maybe. You'll be good enough to go, won't you? You wouldn't turn me down! Let me go back to Alfred's side. I'm in a daze."

Rigolette let go of Rodolphe's arm and ran to the spirits shop.

"But what happened, Madame Pipelet?" asked Rodolphe as he followed the doorkeeper's wife back into her quarters.

"How would I know, monsieur? I had gone out to the city hall, the church, and the caterer's to relieve Alfred of having to do all that. I come back, and what do I see? My old deary with his four pegs in the air! Go in, Monsieur Rodolphe," said Anastasie as she opened the door to her lair. "Look and see if that doesn't break your heart!"

What a sad sight it was! Still wearing his stovepipe hat, even more covered up by it than usual, since the dubious beaver, violently crammed down on his head (to judge from a break that went from one side of it to the other), hid Monsieur Pipelet's eyes. He was sitting on the floor, his back resting against the foot of his bed.

Alfred had recovered from his fainting spell. He began to make some slight movements with his hands, as if he were trying to push someone or something away. Then he tried to rid himself of his improvised visor.

"He's wriggling about! That's a good sign! He's coming to!" cried the doorkeeper's wife. And crouching down to his level, she yelled into his ear, “What’s wrong, Alfred dearest? Your Stasie is here . . . How are you? We’re getting you some absinthe, it’ll make you feel better.” Then, in the most caressing falsetto voice, she added, “They’ve torn my poor little boy to pieces, have they? They’ve murdered him, have they?”

Alfred sighed deeply and let loose one fateful word that came out like a groan: “CABRION!!!”

And his trembling hands seemed once again to try to repel a terrifying vision.

“Cabrion? That wretch of a painter again?” cried Madame Pipelet. “Alfred had so many dreams last night that he kicked me to pieces. That monster is his nightmare! He hasn’t just poisoned his days, but also his nights. He pursues him even into his sleep! Yes, monsieur, as if Alfred were some kind of evildoer and that Cabrion—curse him!—his own remorse on his tail.”

Rodolphe smiled to himself, foreseeing some new trick on the part of Rigolette’s old neighbor.

“Alfred! Talk to me! Don’t be mute! You’re frightening me!” said Madame Pipelet. “Come on, snap out of it. Why do you think about that scoundrel all the time? You know that when you think about him it has the same effect on you as cabbage. It makes your gut hurt and it suffocates you.”

“Cabrion!” repeated Monsieur Pipelet, lifting his hat with effort. It had worked its way far down over his eyes. He rolled it about distractedly.

Rigolette entered, carrying with her a little bottle of absinthe.

“Thank you, missy! You are so kind!” said the old woman. Then she added, “Take this, old deary. Have a swig of this—it’ll make you feel better.” And Anastasie, hurrying to bring the flask to his lips, undertook to make him swallow some absinthe.

Alfred struggled valiantly but in vain as his wife, taking advantage of her victim’s weakness, held his head firmly with one hand and forced the mouth of the little bottle between his teeth with the other. She forced him to drink the absinthe, after which she cried out in triumph, “And alley-oop! Now, up on your feet, deary!”

Indeed, after wiping his mouth with the back of his hand, Alfred opened his eyes, stood up, and asked in a frightened voice, “Did you see him?”

“Who?”

“Did he leave?”

“Who, Alfred?”

“Cabrion!”

“Did he dare to come here?” cried the doorkeeper’s wife.

Monsieur Pipelet, as mute as the commander's statue, nodded his head twice like that ghost to reply in the affirmative.[106]

"Monsieur Cabrion came here?" Rigolette asked, trying to repress a strong urge to laugh.

"That monster has it in for Alfred!" cried Madame Pipelet. "Oh! If I had been there with my broom! I would have stuffed it down his throat. But tell us, Alfred—tell us what happened with him!"

Monsieur Pipelet made a gesture with his hand, signaling that he was about to speak. They all listened to the man in the stovepipe hat in total, reverent silence. He expressed himself in the following terms, with great emotion in his voice: "My wife had just left to spare me the trouble of doing what Monsieur asked me to do," here he nodded in Rodolphe's direction, "that is, of going to the city hall, the church, and the food shop."

"My old deary had nightmares all night long. I wanted to spare him," said Anastasie.

"That nightmare had been sent to me like a warning from on high," the doorkeeper continued in a prophetic tone. "I had dreamed of Cabrion . . . Cabrion would make me suffer. The day began with an attack on my wife's person."

"Alfred! Alfred! No more about that, please! It embarrasses me in front of these people," said Madame Pipelet as she simpered, made cooing noises, and lowered her eyes modestly.

"I thought that I had paid my debt of unhappiness that cursed day after those lewd evildoers left," said Monsieur Pipelet, "but then—oh, God!"

"Keep going, Alfred! Be strong!"

"I will be," Monsieur Pipelet answered heroically. "I have to . . . I will be. So I was sitting over there perfectly calmly at my table, thinking about the alteration I wanted to make to the upper of this boot that had been entrusted to my labor, when I heard a noise. There was a brushing sound on the floor of our quarters. Was it a presentiment? A warning from on high? My heart jumped, I looked up, and through the window I saw— I saw—"

"Cabrion!!!" cried Anastasie, clasping her hands together.

"Cabrion," said Monsieur Pipelet, quietly. "His hideous face was right there, up against the window, looking at me with those cat eyes of his.

---

106. A reference to the Commendatore in Mozart's *Don Giovanni*. In the opening scene, the Don kills him in a duel. Later in the opera, in an act of scornful bravado, he invites the statue of the dead man to a dinner party. The statue nods, accepting silently. When he comes to dinner at the end of the opera, he carries Don Giovanni down to hell. [TN]

What am I saying? Those are tiger's eyes! Just like in a dream. I tried to speak, but my tongue was glued to the roof of my mouth. I wanted to get up, but I was glued to my chair. My boot fell from my hands, and, as I do in every one of the critical moments of my life, I stayed completely motionless. Then the key turned in the lock, the door opened, and Cabrion came in!"

"He came in? What nerve!" said Madame Pipelet, as shocked as her husband by this act of brazenness.

"He walked in slowly," said Alfred. "He stopped for a moment at the door, as if to hypnotize me with his terrifying gaze . . . then he came toward me, stopping after each step as if to pin me to the wall with his eyes, not saying a word; he was as upright, silent, and menacing as a ghost!"

"That gets my back up," said Anastasie.

"I stayed motionless, sitting in my chair. Cabrion kept approaching me slowly, holding my eyes in his like a snake does a bird. He terrified me and, in spite of my efforts, I kept staring at him. He came right up close to me. I couldn't stand his revolting presence any longer. It was too strong for me. I couldn't keep it up. I closed my eyes. Then I felt him dare to put his hands on my hat. He took it from the top, raised it slowly off my crown, and bared my head! I began to feel dizzy. I had stopped breathing. My ears were buzzing. I was more and more stuck to my chair. I closed my eyes tighter and tighter. Then Cabrion bent over, took my bald head—that I have the right to call venerable, or at least I did before he attacked it—he took my head in his hands, which were as cold as death, and on my forehead, which was covered in a cold sweat, he planted . . . a rude kiss! That shameless scoundrel!"

Anastasie lifted her arms to the heavens.

"My most determined enemy comes to kiss me on the forehead! To force me to submit to his disgusting caresses after having hatefully persecuted me to get his hands on a lock of my hair! Such a monstrosity gave me food for thought. It also paralyzed me. Cabrion took advantage of my stupor to put my hat back on my head. Then, with a blow from his fist, he pushed it down over my eyes, as you've seen. That last outrage confused me; I was overwhelmed, everything was spinning around me, and I fainted at the moment at which I saw him from under the brim of my hat leaving our quarters—leaving as tranquilly and slowly as he had entered."

Then, as if this story had sapped his strength, Monsieur Pipelet fell back into his chair, raising his hands to the heavens and looking as if he were casting a silent curse.

Rigolette left abruptly; she had reached the end of her self-control. She couldn't breathe from holding in her laughter and could not hold herself back much longer. Rodolphe himself had a hard time trying to keep a straight face.

Suddenly, the confusing noise that signals the arrival of a popular gathering echoed in the street. A great tumult could be heard outside the gate to the alley, and soon the sound of rifle butts could be heard resonating on the door's concrete panels.

CHAPTER 8

THE ARREST

"Good God! Monsieur Rodolphe!" cried Rigolette as she came running in pale and trembling. "There's a police superintendent and officers there!"

"Divine justice will be mine!" said Monsieur Pipelet in an outburst of religious gratitude. "They've come to arrest Cabrion—unfortunately, they're too late!"

A police superintendent who was identifiable as such from the sash he wore under his black suit came into the doorkeeper's quarters. His face was grave, dignified, and severe.

"Monsieur Superintendent, it's too late! The criminal got away!" said Monsieur Pipelet, sadly. "But I can give you his description: he's got an atrocious smile, rude stares, bad manners—"

"Of whom are you speaking?" asked the officer.

"Cabrion, Monsieur Superintendent! But if you go quickly, there's still time to catch him," answered Monsieur Pipelet.

"I have no idea who this Cabrion is," said the officer, impatiently. "Does an individual named Jérôme Morel, a gem-cutter, live in this house?"

"Yes, Superintendent," said Madame Pipelet, standing at attention and saluting.

"Take me to his apartment."

"Morel the gem-cutter?" the doorkeeper's wife said, overcome by surprise. "But he's the very lamb of God! He is incapable of—"

"Does Jérôme Morel live here? Yes or no?"

"He lives here, Superintendent, with his family, in a garret."

"Take me to this garret."

Then, turning to a man who was accompanying him, he said, "Tell the two municipal guards to wait downstairs and not to move from the alley. Send Justin to get a cab."

The man left to execute these orders.

"Now," said the officer, turning to Monsieur Pipelet, "take me to Morel's place."

"If you don't mind, Superintendent, I'll go in Alfred's stead. He's not feeling well because of Cabrion's tricks, which, like cabbage, don't agree with his digestion."

"You or your husband. It doesn't matter—let's get going!"

And, preceded by Madame Pipelet, he started to go upstairs. But he quickly stopped as he noticed that he was being followed by Rodolphe and Rigolette.

"Who are you? What do you want?" he asked them.

"They're two tenants who live on the fourth floor," said Madame Pipelet.

"I beg your pardon, monsieur. I didn't realize you lived here," he said to Rodolphe.

The latter, thinking the officer's manners were a good omen, said to him, "You are going to find a desperate family, monsieur. I don't know what sort of new blow threatens this unfortunate artisan, but he was sorely tried last night. One of his daughters, already weakened by illness, died before his very eyes—dead of cold and poverty."

"Is that possible?"

"It's the truth, Superintendent," said Madame Pipelet. "If it weren't for this man talking to you now—and he is the king of renters, since he kept the poor Morel from having to go to prison—all of the gem-cutter's family would have starved."

The superintendent looked at Rodolphe with as much curiosity as surprise.

"Nothing simpler, monsieur," said the latter. "A very charitable person, knowing that Morel, whose honor and integrity I personally give you my word on, was in a position that was as deplorable as it was undeserved, charged me with paying the bill for a debt for which some bailiffs were going to take this poor worker. He's the sole wage earner for a large family."

Struck in turn by Rodolphe's noble face and dignified manners, the officer answered him, "I have no doubts about Morel's integrity. I only regret that I must fulfill an unpleasant duty in your presence that will cause you deep concern, seeing as you care so much about the family."

"What do you mean, monsieur?"

"To judge from what you have done for the Morel family and from the way you express yourself, I can see, monsieur, that you are a good man. Since I have no reason, in any case, to hide the object of the warrant that I must execute, I have to tell you that the person I am to arrest is Louise Morel, the gem-cutter's daughter."

The memory of the roll of gold coins that the young woman offered to the bailiffs returned to Rodolphe's mind.

"For God's sake, what is she accused of?"

"She is to be taken into custody on suspicion of infanticide."

"Her? Her? Oh! Her poor father!"

"From what you have told me, monsieur, I can imagine that, considering the difficult circumstances this artisan has faced, this new blow is going to be terrible. Unfortunately, I must obey the orders I have received."

"But it's just custody, right?" cried Rodolphe. "Surely there is no proof of it!"

"I can't say any more on this subject. The court has been led to take up the case of this crime—or rather, of this presumed crime—by the declaration of a man who is by all accounts respectable. He is Louise Morel's employer."

"Jacques Ferrand, the solicitor?" cried Rodolphe, indignant.

"Yes, monsieur. But why do you seem so outraged at his name?"

"Monsieur Jacques Ferrand is a wretch, monsieur!"

"I see, unfortunately, that you are not acquainted with the man of whom you speak, monsieur. Monsieur Jacques Ferrand is the most honorable man in the world. His integrity is vouched for by everyone."

"I will tell you again, monsieur: that solicitor is a wretch. He wanted to have Morel thrown into prison because his daughter refused his lewd advances. If Louise is accused only on the strength of the denunciation of such a man, rest assured, monsieur—the accusation has little merit."

"It's not up to me, monsieur, and I really do not find it suitable to argue over the value of Monsieur Ferrand's declarations," said the officer, coldly. "The prosecutor has taken up this case; the courts will decide it. As for me, I have orders to take Louise Morel into custody, and I will follow those orders."

"You are right, monsieur. I regret that my momentary indignation, legitimate as it may be, made me forget that this was indeed neither the time nor the place to have such an argument. Just a word: the body of the child Morel lost is still in the garret. I offered my room to the family to spare them the sad spectacle of the corpse. So it's at my home that you will find the gem-cutter and probably his daughter. I beg of you, monsieur, in the name of humanity, not to arrest Louise abruptly in the midst of all those unhappy people who have just barely escaped an appalling fate. Morel has undergone so many shocks this night that his sanity would not hold up. His wife is also dangerously ill—such a blow would kill her."

"I have always executed my orders with as much tact as possible, monsieur. I will do the same in this circumstance."

"Will you allow me, monsieur, to ask you one favor? Here is what I suggest: the young woman who is following us with the doorkeeper's wife lives in the room next to mine. I am sure that she will put it at your disposition. You can ask first for Louise to be sent for, and then, if you must, for Morel, so his daughter can say her good-byes to him. At least this way you will spare a poor, sick, infirm mother a heartrending scene."

"If we can arrange matters in that way, I'll be happy to oblige, monsieur."

The conversation we have just described had taken place in whispers while Rigolette and Madame Pipelet were keeping a discreet distance, several steps from the superintendent and Rodolphe. The latter walked back to the seamstress, who was trembling at the mere presence of the superintendent. He said to her, "My poor neighbor, I need to ask yet another favor of you. I need you to give me your room for an hour."

"As long as you need it, Monsieur Rodolphe. You have my key. But, dear God, what on earth is going on?"

"I will tell you shortly. That's not all. I need you to be good enough to go back to the Temple and tell them not to deliver what we bought for at least an hour."

"Of course, Monsieur Rodolphe. But has something terrible again befallen the Morel family?"

"Alas, yes! Something very sad. You'll know only too soon."

"All right, neighbor. I'll run to the Temple. Heavens! Thanks to you, I was sure those good people were out of trouble!" said the seamstress as she ran down the stairs.

Rodolphe had wanted more than anything to spare Rigolette the sorry sight of Louise's arrest.

"Superintendent," said Madame Pipelet, "since my king of tenants is leading you, may I go back to find my Alfred? I'm worried about him. It's been hardly an hour since he recovered from the shock Cabrion gave him."

"Go, go ahead," said the officer. He remained alone with Rodolphe. They both arrived on the landing of the fourth floor in front of the room that the gem-cutter and his family temporarily occupied.

Suddenly, the door opened. Louise, pale and in tears, walked out abruptly. "Good-bye! Good-bye, Father!" she cried. "I will return, but I must leave now!"

"Louise, my child; listen to me, please," said Morel, following his daughter and trying to hold her back.

At the sight of Rodolphe and the officer, Louise and the gem-cutter froze.

"Ah! Monsieur, our benefactor!" said the artisan, recognizing Rodolphe. "Help me to keep Louise from leaving. I don't know what's wrong with her, but she's scaring me. She wants to leave. She shouldn't return to her employer, should she, monsieur? Didn't you tell me, 'Louise will never leave you again—that will be your reward'? Oh! That happy promise made me forget for a moment—I admit it—the death of my little daughter Adèle. But it's also that I never want to be separated from you again, Louise! Never! Never!"

Rodolphe's heart was breaking. He did not have the strength to say a single word in reply.

The superintendent said severely to Louise, "Your name is Louise Morel?"

"Yes, monsieur," answered the young woman, taken aback.

Rodolphe had opened the door to Rigolette's room. "You are Jérôme Morel, her father?" asked the officer, turning to the gem-cutter.

"Yes, monsieur, but—"

"Enter that room with your daughter." And the officer gestured toward Rigolette's room, where Rodolphe was already standing.

Reassured by the presence of the latter, the gem-cutter and Louise, bewildered and worried, followed the orders of the superintendent, who closed the door and said to Morel, sadly, "I know that you are an honest and unfortunate man. For that reason I regret that I must tell you that I have come to arrest your daughter in the name of the law."

"Everything has been found out! I am lost!" cried Louise, horrified, throwing herself into her father's arms.

"What are you saying? What are you saying?" said Morel, stupefied. "You've gone mad. What makes you think you're lost? Why lost? Arrest you? Why would they want to arrest you? Who would want to arrest you?"

"Me—in the name of the law," the superintendent said, revealing his official sash.

"Oh! I am so miserable! So miserable!" cried Louise, dropping to her knees.

"What! In the name of the law?" said the artisan, whose reason, gravely shaken by this new blow, was beginning to crumble. "Why are you arresting my daughter in the name of the law? I will answer for Louise. She's my daughter, my worthy daughter. Isn't that true, Louise? What? Arrest you, when our guardian angel brought you back to us to console us for the death of our little Adèle? Come on! That can't be true! And besides, Superintendent, with all due respect, only criminals get arrested, right? And Louise, my daughter, is not a criminal. Surely, my child, you see, this man has made a mistake. My name is Morel; there are many Morels. Your name is Louise; there is more than one Louise. That's it. You see, Superintendent, there's been an error—certainly there's been an error!"

"Unfortunately, there has been no error. Louise Morel, say your farewells to your father."

"You're going to take my daughter away?" cried the worker, and, goaded by pain into fury, he moved toward the officer with a menacing look.

Rodolphe seized the gem-cutter by the arm and said to him, "Calm down and don't give up hope. Your daughter will be returned to you. Her innocence will be proven. She can't be guilty."

"Guilty of what? She can't be guilty of anything. I would walk through fire sooner than—" Then, remembering the gold that Louise had brought over to pay the bill of exchange, Morel cried, "But that money! What about that money from this morning, Louise?" And he gave his daughter a terrible look.

Louise understood. "Me, steal?" she cried. Her cheeks, flushing in righteous indignation, along with her tone and gestures, reassured her father.

"I knew it!" he cried. "You see, Superintendent, she denies it, and she's never lied in all her life, I swear to you. Ask anyone who knows her and they'll tell you just the same thing. Her, a liar? Yeah, sure! She's much too proud to do that. In any case, the bill of exchange was paid by our benefactor. She doesn't want to keep that gold. She was going to return it to the person who lent it to her but wouldn't allow his name to be revealed—isn't that true, Louise?"

"Your daughter is not accused of theft," said the officer.

"But, good Lord! What is she accused of, then? As her father, I swear that she is innocent of anything they could accuse her of. And I've never lied in my life, either."

"What good does it do to know what she's accused of?" said Rodolphe, moved by his pain. "Louise's innocence will be proven. The person who has taken up your cause will protect your daughter. Take heart. Providence won't abandon you this time, either. Embrace your daughter, you'll see her soon."

"Superintendent," cried Morel, not listening to Rodolphe, "you can't take a daughter away from her father without at least saying what she's accused of doing! I want to know everything. Louise, will you speak?"

"Your daughter is accused of infanticide," said the officer.

"I—I—I don't understand . . . You—" And Morel staggered, babbling senselessly.

"Your daughter is accused of having killed her child," said the superintendent, profoundly moved by this scene. "But it has not yet been proven that she has committed this crime."

"Oh, no! That's not true, monsieur! That's not true!" cried Louise loudly, getting on her feet. "I swear to you that he was dead! He wasn't breathing any longer. He was cold. I lost my head—that was my crime. But killing my child? Oh, never!"

"Your child, you wretch?" cried Morel, raising his two hands against Louise, as if he would have annihilated her with this gesture and this terrible curse if he could.

"Mercy, Father, have mercy!" she cried.

After a moment of terrifying silence, Morel said in a calm voice that was even more terrifying, "Superintendent, take her away. She's no daughter of mine."

The gem-cutter tried to leave. Louise threw herself at his knees and wrapped both of her arms around them, and, with her head thrown back, she cried out in bewildered supplication: "Father, listen to me for one moment. Listen to me!"

"Superintendent, take her away. I leave her to you," said the gem-cutter as he tried with all his strength to get out of Louise's embrace.

"Listen to her," said Rodolphe, stopping him. "Have a little pity at such a moment."

"Her? My God! Her!" repeated Morel, bringing his hands to his forehead. "She's dishonored. Oh! She's vile—vile!"

"And what if she dishonored herself to save you?" said Rodolphe, softly.

These words struck Morel like a thunderbolt. He looked at his weeping daughter, still kneeling at his feet. Then, looking at her with a questioning gaze that would be impossible to depict, he cried out in a muffled voice, his teeth grinding in rage, "The solicitor?"

Louise was on the verge of answering. She was going to speak, but, on reflection, she stopped, lowered her head in silence, and remained mute.

"But no, he wanted to have me thrown in prison this morning!" exploded Morel. "So it can't be him, then! Oh, so much the better! So much the better! She doesn't even have an excuse for her sin, so I won't bear any responsibility for her dishonor. I can curse her without remorse!"

"No, no! Don't curse me, Father! I will tell everything to you alone, and you'll see—you'll see if I don't deserve your forgiveness."

"Have pity on her and listen to her!" said Rodolphe.

"What will she tell me? About her foul deed? It will be made public, so I'll wait for that."

"Monsieur!" cried Louise, turning to the officer. "Have pity on me! Let me say a few words to my father—maybe before I leave him forever. And you can hear me, too, benefactor—but only you and my father."

"I'll allow it," said the officer.

"Are you insane, then? Will you refuse this last comfort to your child?" Rodolphe asked Morel. "If you believe that you owe me any gratitude for the good I have done you, listen to your daughter's plea."

After a moment of fierce and dismal silence, Morel answered, "Let's go."

"But where? Where are we going?" asked Rodolphe. "Your family is next door."

"Where will we go?" cried the gem-cutter with bitter irony. "Where will we go? Upstairs, to the garret, right next to my daughter's corpse. That's the perfect spot for this confession, isn't it? Let's go. We'll see if Louise dares to lie before her sister's corpse. Let's go!"

And Morel left quickly as if deranged, without looking at Louise.

"Monsieur," said the superintendent in a low voice, "have mercy. In the interest of this poor father, keep this conversation short. What you said is true: his sanity is not going to hold up. A moment ago his gaze was nearly that of a lunatic."

"Alas, monsieur! Like you, I fear a terrible new misfortune. I will keep this heartrending good-bye as short as I can."

And Rodolphe rejoined the gem-cutter and his daughter.

As strange and gloomy as Morel's choice was, the circumstances more or less determined it. The officer had agreed to await the outcome of this interview in Rigolette's room. The Morel family was in Rodolphe's room, so the only remaining space was the garret. It was to this dismal little hole that Louise, her father, and Rodolphe repaired.

CHAPTER 9

THE CONFESSION

What a cruel and somber spectacle it was!

In the middle of the garret that we have described, atop the bed of the senile woman, rested the body of the little girl who had died that morning. A shred of a sheet was covering her. The unusual and vivid brightness, filtered through the attic window, threw harsh light and shadow on the faces of the participants in this scene.

Rodolphe, standing with his back to the wall, was deeply moved. Morel, sitting on the edge of his workbench, his head lowered, his hands hanging limply, with a fixed, wild-eyed stare, could not tear his eyes away from the mattress where lay the remains of little Adèle. The anger and indignation of the gem-cutter seemed to weaken at this sight and change into an inexpressibly bitter sadness. His energy was abandoning him as he began to fail beneath this latest blow. Louise, mortally pale, felt as if she might collapse. The revelation that she had to make terrified her. And yet she chanced clasping her father's hand—that poor, shriveled hand, deformed from excessive labor—in her own trembling hand. He did not pull back, and so his daughter, breaking into sobs, covered it with kisses. She felt his hand press gently back against her lips; Morel's anger had fallen away and her tears, so long suppressed, finally began to flow.

"Father, if you only knew!" cried Louise. "If you only knew how much I am to be pitied!"

"Oh! I will feel this sorrow all my life, Louise, all my life long," said the gem-cutter, weeping. "You—my God! You, in prison? In the dock with criminals? You, who were always so proud, when you had the right to be proud . . . No!" he said in a new transport of painful despair. "No! I would rather see you under that shroud next to your poor little sister."

"So would I—I wish I were dead like her!" said Louise.

"Don't say that, unhappy child, you're hurting me. I was wrong to say that to you. I went too far. So speak. But in God's name, do not lie to me. No matter how terrible the truth is, tell it to me. I want to hear it from your lips. It will seem less cruel that way. Alas, speak! The time we have here is ticking away. They're waiting for you downstairs. Oh! How sad it is to say good-bye like this! Good heavens!"

"Father, I will tell you everything," said Louise, steeling herself. "But promise me, and I ask also that our benefactor here promise me this also: do not repeat anything I say to anyone. Not to anyone. If he found out that I spoke, you see— Oh!" she said, quivering in terror. "You would be destroyed—destroyed like me. You don't know the power and savagery of that man!"

"Which man?"

"My employer."

"The solicitor?"

"Yes," said Louise, whispering and looking around her as if she were afraid of being overheard.

"Rest assured," Rodolphe said, "however cruel or powerful that man is, we will stand up against him! As for the rest, if I were to reveal anything you're going to say to anyone, it would only be in your interest or in your father's."

"And I, too, Louise, if I speak, it would be in order to try to save you. But what more has that wicked man done to you?"

"There's one more thing," said Louise after a moment of thought. "This story involves someone who performed a great service to me. He was full of goodness for my father and our family. This person was in the employ of Monsieur Ferrand when I arrived there, and he has made me swear not to name him."

Thinking that this person was perhaps Germain, Rodolphe said to Louise, "If you want to talk about François Germain, don't worry. His secret will be completely safe with your father and me."

Louise looked at Rodolphe in surprise. "You know him?" she asked.

"What? That good, excellent young man who lived here for three months was working for the solicitor when you began there?" said Morel. "The first time you saw him here you seemed not to know him!"

"We had agreed on that beforehand, Father. He had serious reasons to hide the fact that he worked for Monsieur Ferrand. I was the one who told him there was a room to let on the fourth floor here, knowing that he would be a good neighbor to you."

"But who was it that found your daughter employment with the solicitor, then?" asked Rodolphe.

"After my wife's illness, I had said to Madame Burette, the pawnbroker who lives here, that Louise wanted to enter domestic service in order to help us. Madame Burette knew the solicitor's housekeeper; she gave me a letter for her that recommended Louise as a young woman of excellent character. May that letter be cursed! That was the cause of all of our sorrows. Anyway, monsieur, that is how my daughter came to be working for the solicitor."

"Although I know some of what caused Monsieur Ferrand's hatred for your father," said Rodolphe to Louise, "would you please be kind enough to tell me briefly what happened between you and the solicitor since you entered his service? It could help us protect you."

"In the beginning of my time with Monsieur Ferrand," Louise answered, "I had nothing to complain of about him. I had a lot of work and the housekeeper was rude to me at times; the house was gloomy, but I endured everything patiently. Being a servant is being a servant—elsewhere I would just have had other disagreeable things to contend with. Monsieur Ferrand had a severe face. He went to mass, he often received visits from priests at home—I wasn't suspicious of him. In the beginning, he barely looked at me. He spoke to me very harshly, especially in the presence of strangers.

"Other than the doorkeeper, whose lodgings looked out onto the street, in the part of the building where the study is located, I was the only servant, along with Madame Séraphin, the housekeeper. The building we lived in was a large, isolated hovel between the courtyard and the garden. My room was up on the top. Often I was afraid when I was alone at night either in the kitchen, which was underground, or in my bedroom. At night I thought I could sometimes hear strange, muffled sounds from the floor underneath me where no one lived. Only François Germain would come in there often to work during the day. Two of the windows on that floor were walled up, and one of the doors was very thick, reinforced with iron plates. The housekeeper told me since then that Monsieur Ferrand kept his safe there.

"One day I had stayed up very late to finish some mending that needed to be finished quickly. I was going to go to sleep when I heard quiet steps in the corridor that led to my room. Someone stopped at my door. At first I thought it had to be the housekeeper. But when the person didn't enter, I became frightened and didn't dare move. I listened, but no one moved. Still, I was sure there was someone at my door. I asked two times who was there, but there was no answer. More and more afraid, I pushed my chest of drawers up against the door, which had no bolt or lock. I kept listening, but the person didn't move. After a half hour that seemed endless to me, I got in bed. The night went by peacefully. The next day, I asked the housekeeper if I could put a bolt on my door because it had no lock. I told her about my fear during the night. She told me that I must have been dreaming and that, anyway, I would have to ask Monsieur Ferrand if I wanted a lock. He shrugged his shoulders when I asked him and said I was mad. I didn't dare say any more about it.

"Some time afterward the catastrophe with the diamond happened. My father was desperate and didn't know what to do. I told Madame Séraphin about his problem, and she said, 'Monsieur Ferrand is so charitable that he might do something to help your father.' That very night, I was serving at dinner, and Monsieur Ferrand said to me abruptly, 'Your father needs thirteen hundred francs. Go to him tonight and tell him to come tomorrow to see me in my study. He will have his money. He's an honest man; he deserves help.' When he showed that kindness, I melted into tears. I didn't know how to thank my employer. He said to me, with his usual terseness, 'It's fine, it's fine. This is nothing, really.' That night, after I finished working, I went to bring my father the good news, and the next day—"

"I received the thirteen hundred francs against a blank bill of exchange that I accepted in that form and that was due three months from that date," said Morel. "I did just as Louise did; I wept from gratitude and called the man my benefactor, my savior. Oh! He must be truly wicked to dishonor the praise and veneration I swore to him!"

"Didn't making you sign a blank bill of exchange with a due date that was coming up so soon that you wouldn't be able to pay make you at all suspicious?" asked Rodolphe.

"No, monsieur. I thought that the solicitor was taking the usual precautions against a loan, that's all. Anyway, he told me that I didn't have to worry about paying the money back to him for two years. Every three months I would just renew the bill of exchange to keep things in order. But then, on the first due date, he sent me notice here that the bill was not paid, and he obtained a judgment against me under someone else's name. But he said that it shouldn't worry me because it was an error of his bailiff."

"That's how he meant to keep you in his power," said Rodolphe.

"Alas, yes, monsieur! Indeed, it's from the time of that judgment that he began to . . . But you go on, Louise—you go on. I don't know where I am anymore; my head is spinning and I'm blanking out— This will drive me mad! It's all too much—too much!"

Rodolphe calmed the gem-cutter down. Louise went on: "I worked harder than ever to show my gratitude in the only way I could for the kindness Monsieur Ferrand had shown us. The housekeeper took a distinct dislike to me at that time. She enjoyed tormenting me, getting me into trouble by not telling me what Monsieur Ferrand had ordered me to do. This cruelty caused me considerable suffering and I would have preferred to work elsewhere, but the obligation my father had to my employer made it impossible for me to leave. Monsieur Ferrand had lent this money three months earlier. He continued to be abrupt with me in front of Madame Séraphin. However, he sometimes would give me secret looks that upset me, and then he would smile when he saw me blush."

"Think of it, monsieur. At exactly that time, he was in the process of obtaining an order for my arrest!"

"One day," Louise continued, "the housekeeper left after dinner, which was not normal for her. The clerks left the study; they were living elsewhere. Monsieur Ferrand sent the doorkeeper on an errand. I was all alone in the house with my employer. I was working in the antechamber. He rings for me. I enter his bedroom; he was standing in front of the fireplace. I walk up to him; he turns around suddenly and takes me in his arms. His face was as red as blood, and his eyes were gleaming. I was frightened beyond belief; at first I was paralyzed with fear, but, strong as he was, I fought against him so vigorously that I got away. I ran into the antechamber and pushed the door closed, holding it shut with all my might. He had the key."

"You see, monsieur, you see?" said Morel to Rodolphe. "That's the way this worthy benefactor conducts himself."

"After a few moments, the door gave way before his efforts," Louise said. "Fortunately, the lamp was within my reach and I had the time to extinguish it. The antechamber was some distance from the room he was in; he suddenly found himself in total darkness. He called me, but I didn't answer. Then he said to me in a voice trembling with anger, 'If you try to escape, your father will go to prison for the thirteen hundred francs he owes me and can't pay.' I begged him to have pity on me; I promised to do everything imaginable to serve him well in recognition of his kindness, but I declared to him that nothing would force me to disgrace myself."

"That's how my Louise talks, all right," said Morel. "That's the way she talked when she had the right to be proud. But how could it be that . . . ? Oh, well, go on, go on."

"I was still in darkness. After a moment, I heard the door to the antechamber close—my employer had groped his way over to it. Now he had me in his power. He ran to his room and quickly returned with a lamp. I don't dare tell you, Father, the new struggle I had to endure: his threats, his pursuit of me from room to room . . . Fortunately, despair, fear, and anger gave me strength. My resistance made him furious. He was no longer in control of himself. He manhandled me; he hit me. My face was bleeding."

"My God!" cried the gem-cutter, raising his hands to the heavens. "But these things are criminal. And that monster goes unpunished! Unpunished!"

"Maybe," said Rodolphe, who seemed to be deep in thought. Then, turning to Louise, he said, "Have courage. Tell us everything."

"This battle went on for a long time. My strength was giving out when the doorkeeper, who had returned, rang twice. He was announcing a letter that had arrived. Fearing that if I didn't go to pick it up the doorkeeper would bring it up to him himself, Monsieur Ferrand said to me, 'Get going! If you say a word, your father is ruined. If you try to leave my house, he'll still be ruined. If anyone tries to obtain a reference for you, I'll keep you from finding a position by implying that you had stolen from me, without actually saying as much. I will also say that you are a terrible servant.' The day after this scene, despite the threats my employer had made, I ran here to tell my father everything. He wanted me to leave this house that very instant, but the prospect of prison loomed. The little bit I earned had become indispensable to my family since my mother's illness, and the bad references Monsieur Ferrand threatened to give me might have prevented me from finding another position for a long while."

"Yes," said Morel, with bleak bitterness. "We had the cowardice, the selfishness to let our child return there. Oh! I told you the way it is: poverty inspires the vilest acts!"

"Alas, Father, didn't you try to obtain the thirteen hundred francs in every way you could? Since you couldn't do it, we had to accept the options open to us."

"Sure, sure. Go on with your story. Your own family served as your executioner; we are guiltier than you of the catastrophe that befell you," said the gem-cutter as he hid his face in his hands.

"When I saw my employer again," said Louise, "he was brusque and hard, the way he had been before the scene I described to you. He never said a word about what happened. The housekeeper continued to torment me. She gave me barely enough to eat; she kept the bread under lock and key. Sometimes, right in front of me, out of pure spite, she would foul the leftovers that they gave me. She almost always ate with Monsieur Ferrand, you see. At night, I hardly slept; I was afraid that at any moment the solicitor might enter my room with its door that wouldn't lock. He had the chest of drawers that I put in front of my door to protect myself taken away; all I had left was a chair, a little table, and my trunk. I tried to barricade myself the best I could with those things, and I slept fully clothed. For a while he left me alone; he didn't even look at me. I started to calm down a little, thinking that he no longer had designs on me. One Sunday, he gave me permission to go out. I came to announce this good news to my father and mother—we were all very happy! It was then I told you all that had happened up to that point. The rest of what I have to tell you," said Louise with a tremor in her voice, "is horrifying; I have always hidden it from you."

"Oh! I could tell that you were hiding a secret from me!" cried Morel in a sort of frenzy and with a singular volubility that astonished Rodolphe. "Your pallor, your features—I should have figured it out. I told your mother about it a hundred times. But she just pooh-poohed me to calm me down. And that worked out well, didn't it? That sure worked out well! To escape a bad fate, we left our daughter with this monster! And where is our daughter headed? To the criminals' dock. That worked out well, all right! Ah! But then . . . well . . . who knows? In fact . . . because we're poor . . . yes . . . but the others? Oh, forget about the others . . ." Then, stopping as if to collect the thoughts that were escaping him, Morel slapped his forehead and cried, "Listen! I don't know what I'm saying anymore! I have a terrible headache. I feel like I'm drunk." And he hid his head in his hands.

Rodolphe did not want to let Louise know how much the incoherence of the gem-cutter's language frightened him. He said, gravely, "You are not being fair, Morel. It wasn't just because of your daughter alone, but for her mother, her children, even for you yourself that your poor wife feared the terrible consequences of Louise's departure from the solicitor's house. Don't blame anyone here. All of your curses and all of your hatred should fall on one man only—on that monster of hypocrisy who has made a girl choose between dishonor and ruin. The death, perhaps, of her father and her family . . . As for this employer who vilely abused his power as an employer, be patient. As I've told you, divine justice sometimes keeps terrible and surprising punishments in store to avenge such crimes."

Rodolphe's words about providential revenge were uttered with such certitude and such conviction that Louise looked at her rescuer with surprise and almost fear.

"Go on, child," said Rodolphe, turning to Louise. "Don't keep anything from us. It's more important than you know."

"So I was starting to feel a little less frightened," said Louise, "when one evening Monsieur Ferrand and the housekeeper both left, one after the other. They didn't dine at home, and I was left alone. As usual, they left me my ration of water, bread, and wine, after locking up the cupboards. After I finished my work, I had my dinner, and then, as I was afraid to be alone in the living quarters, I went back to my bedroom after lighting Monsieur Ferrand's lamp for him. When he went out at night, we never waited up for him. I took up my work, and, little by little, I gave in to my sleepiness—which is not normal for me. Ah! Father!" cried Louise, stopping herself in fear. "You're not going to believe me! You're going to accuse me of lying! And yet, look, I swear to you on the body of my poor little sister that I am going to tell you the exact truth."

"Explain what happened," said Rodolphe.

"Alas! Monsieur, for seven months I have been trying to understand what happened that dreadful night! But I haven't been able to figure it out—I almost go mad when I try to clear up the mystery."

"My God! What is she going to tell us?" cried the gem-cutter, emerging from the fog of blank stupor that had beset him intermittently since the beginning of her story.

"In contrast to my usual practices, I had fallen asleep in my chair," said Louise. "That's the last thing I remember. Before, before—oh! Father, I am sorry! But I swear I'm not guilty!"

"I believe you! I believe you! But go on!"

"I don't know how long I had been sleeping when I awoke—still in my bedroom, but lying down. Monsieur Ferrand, who stood next to me, had stolen my honor."

"You're lying! You're lying!" cried the gem-cutter, furiously. "Swear to me that you gave in to his violence, to the fear of seeing me dragged off to prison, but don't lie like that!"

"Father, I swear to you—"

"You're lying! You're lying! But why would the solicitor have wanted to get me put in prison if you had already given in to him?"

"Given in? Oh, no, Father! My sleep was so deep that I was like a dead person. It seems extraordinary to you, it seems impossible—and, God knows, I can understand that only too well seeing as even now it's hard for me to comprehend what happened."

"But I understand everything," said Rodolphe, interrupting Louise. "This was about the only crime that man hadn't yet gotten around to. Don't accuse your daughter of lying, Morel. Tell me, Louise: when you had dinner, before going up to your room, didn't you notice a strange taste in something you drank? Try hard to remember."

After thinking about it for a moment, Louise answered, "I do remember that the mixture of water and wine that Madame Séraphin left me as usual tasted a little bitter. I didn't think about it then because the housekeeper amused herself by putting salt or pepper in my drinks."

"And that day in particular your drink seemed bitter to you?"

"Yes, monsieur, but not too bitter to drink. I thought maybe that the wine had gone bad."

His gaze fixed and haggard, Morel listened to Rodolphe's questions and Louise's answers without seeming to follow their thrust.

"Before you fell asleep in your chair, didn't your head feel heavy, and your legs feel weighed down?"

"Yes, monsieur. My temples were pounding, I had a slight chill, and I wasn't feeling very well."

"Oh! The wretch! The wretch!" cried Rodolphe. "Do you realize, Morel, what that man made your daughter drink?"

The artisan looked at Rodolphe without answering.

"The housekeeper, his accomplice, had clearly mixed opium, a soporific, into Louise's drink. This robbed your daughter of motion and consciousness for several hours. When she emerged from that lethargic slumber, she found that she had been dishonored!"

"Ah! Now I understand my misfortune," said Louise. "You see, Father, I am less guilty than I seemed. Father, Father, answer me, please!"

The gem-cutter's gaze became terrifying in its rigidity. This naive and honest man could not get his mind around an act of such horrible perversity. He could hardly understand this frightful revelation. And, moreover, it must be said that his reason had been slipping away for the past few moments. Already, his thinking was becoming cloudy, and then he would fall into a thoughtless void that is to our intelligence what night is to our eyesight, an obvious symptom of mental illness.

However, Morel said, in a quiet, choppy, hurried voice, "Oh, yes, that is truly evil—truly evil—very evil." And he fell back into his despondent state.

Rodolphe looked at him anxiously. He believed that the poor man's power of indignation was starting to weaken, in the same way that people sometimes do not cry when they experience violent sorrows.

Wanting to finish this sad interview as quickly as possible, Rodolphe said to Louise, "Be brave, my child. Finish unraveling this web of horror."

"Alas, monsieur! You have hardly heard anything yet. When I saw Monsieur Ferrand next to me, I screamed in terror. I wanted to flee, but he held me down by force. I still felt so weak, my limbs were still so heavy, no doubt due to the drink you told me about, that I couldn't get free of him. 'Why should you run away now?' said Monsieur Ferrand to me in an astonished manner that confused me. 'What whimsy is this? Am I not here because you consented to it?' 'Ah, monsieur, how unworthy!' I cried. 'You took advantage of my sleep to ruin me! My father will learn of this.' My employer burst into laughter. 'I took advantage of your sleep? Are you kidding me? Who do you think will believe that lie? It's four in the morning. I've been here for two hours. You have been sleeping deeply for a long time. Admit, rather, that I did nothing but benefit from your goodwill. Come on, don't be so capricious or I'll get angry. Your father is in my power. You have no reason to rebuff me now. Be nice and submissive and we can be good friends. Otherwise, beware . . .' 'I will tell my father everything!' I cried. 'He will know how to avenge me. There is such a thing as justice!' Monsieur Ferrand looked at me with surprise. 'But you must be mad! What are you going to tell your father? That it suited you to receive me here? Go right ahead—you'll see how he'll welcome you.' 'My God! That's not true! You know full well that you're here against my will.' 'Against your will? Will you have the shamelessness to insist on that lie, to talk about rape? Do you want a proof of your falseness? I commanded Germain, my cashier, to come back last night at ten o'clock to finish an important job. He worked here until one o'clock in the morning in a room below this one. Wouldn't he have heard your screams, the sound of a struggle like the one I had with you downstairs, you wicked girl, when you weren't as reasonable as you were today? Well, then! Ask Germain tomorrow, and he'll affirm what I'm telling you: that everything was perfectly quiet tonight in this house.'"

"Oh! He took every precaution to make sure he'd get away with it!" said Rodolphe.

"Yes, monsieur, since I was completely staggered by it all, I could find nothing to counter anything Monsieur Ferrand said. I didn't know what he had had put in my drink, and so I couldn't even explain to myself why I had stayed asleep. All appearances were against me. If I complained, everyone would think me the guilty party. People couldn't have thought anything else since, even in my own mind, that horrifying night was an impenetrable mystery."

CHAPTER 10

THE CRIME

Rodolphe was still stunned at the terrifying extent of Monsieur Ferrand's hypocrisy. "So, you couldn't bring yourself to complain to your father about the solicitor's disgusting attack on you?" he asked Louise.

"No, monsieur. He would have thought I was Monsieur Ferrand's willing partner, and, also, I was afraid that in his anger my father would forget that his liberty and the very survival of our family still depended on my employer."

"And probably," said Rodolphe, trying to spare Louise some portion of her painful confession, "having given in to his coercion and to the fear that you would condemn your father to prison by resisting the wretch, you continued on as his victim?"

Louise lowered her eyes and blushed.

"And was his conduct any less brutal toward you after that?"

"No, monsieur. To avoid suspicions, when he happened to have the priest and curate of Bonne-Nouvelle over for dinner, my employer reproached me harshly in front of them. He asked the priest to admonish me. He told him that sooner or later I would lose my virtue, that my manner with the office clerks was too free, that I was a good-for-nothing, and that he kept me on purely out of charity toward my father, an honest family man he had tried to help. Except for the favor he had done my father, all of this was false. I never saw the office clerks. They worked in a part of the building entirely separate from ours."

"And when you found yourself alone with Monsieur Ferrand, how did he explain his behavior toward you in front of the priest?"

"He assured me that he had only been joking. But the priest took his accusations seriously. He told me harshly that a person would need to be especially sinful to lose their virtue in such a religious household, with so many examples of piety before them. I didn't know what to say to that. I lowered my head and blushed. My silence and confusion made me seem even guiltier. My life was such a burden to me that several times I was on the verge of ending it all; but then I thought of my father, my mother, and my brothers and sisters whom I was helping to support a bit, and I accepted my lot. In the midst of their abasement of me, I had one consolation: at least my father was spared having to go to prison. A new misfortune overcame me: I became pregnant. I now considered myself utterly ruined. I don't know why, but I had the feeling that Monsieur Ferrand—who should have been less cruel toward me upon learning this news—would treat me instead with even greater harshness. Even so, I was still far from imagining what would really happen."

Having returned from his momentary mental lapse, Morel looked around in bewilderment. He wiped his forehead with his hand, collected his thoughts, and said to his daughter, "I think I blanked out there for a moment. It's all the fatigue and worries . . . What were you saying?"

"When Monsieur Ferrand found out that I was pregnant—"

The gem-cutter gestured in despair. Rodolphe calmed him down with a glance.

"Keep going. I'll listen to the end of your story," said Morel. "Go on."

Louise went on: "I asked Monsieur Ferrand how I might hide my shame and the consequences of a sin for which he was responsible. Alas, you will hardly believe this, Father . . ."

"Well?"

"Interrupting me with indignation and feigned surprise, he seemed not to understand me. He asked if I was crazy. Terrified, I cried, 'But good God! What will become of me now? If you have no pity for me, at least have pity on your child.' 'How dreadful!' cried Monsieur Ferrand, lifting his hands to the sky. 'How dare you, you wretch, accuse me of being so basely corrupt as to lower myself to the level of a girl like you! You have the shamelessness to connect me to the consequences of your excesses—me, the person who repeated to you a hundred times in front of the most respectable witnesses that you would ruin yourself, you vile slut! Leave this home immediately. You're fired!'"

Rodolphe and Morel were struck with horror, such infernal hypocrisy leaving them thunderstruck.

"Oh! I must say, this is beyond my worst fears!" said Rodolphe.

Morel said nothing. His eyes widened to a frightening extent and a convulsive spasm distorted his features. He got off the workbench where he had been sitting, opened a drawer abruptly, and took a very long and sturdy file from it. It was extremely sharp and had a wooden handle. He rushed toward the door.

Rodolphe, figuring out what he had in mind, grabbed him by the arm and stopped him. "Morel, where are you going? You'll destroy yourself, unhappy man!"

"Look out!" cried the furious artisan as he struggled. "I'll kill two people instead of just one!" And the madman gestured threateningly at Rodolphe.

"Father, that's our benefactor!" cried Louise.

"He doesn't care about us! Bah! He wants to protect the solicitor!"

cried Morel. Having completely lost his bearings, he struggled with Rodolphe.

In a mere second, the latter skillfully disarmed Morel, opened the door, and tossed the file into the stairway.

Louise ran to the gem-cutter, held him in her arms, and said to him, "Father, he's our benefactor! You raised your hand against him! Come to your senses!" These words recalled Morel to himself. He hid his face in his hands and, without saying a word, he fell at Rodolphe's knees.

"Get up, you poor father," said Rodolphe, with kindness. "Patience . . . patience. I understand your rage, and I share your hatred. But in the name of our vengeance, do not ruin our chances of carrying it out successfully."

"Oh, God!" cried the gem-cutter as he arose. "But what can the courts . . . the law . . . do against him? Poor as we are, when we go to accuse that rich, powerful, respected man, they're going to laugh in our faces! Ha, ha, ha!" And he was overcome with a convulsive laughter himself. "And they'll be right! Where is our proof? Yes, our proof? They won't believe us. That's why I'm telling you," he cried, his crazed rage returning with even greater force, "I have confidence only in the objectivity of the knife!"

"Be quiet, Morel. Your pain is causing you to lose yourself," Rodolphe said to him, sadly. "Let your daughter speak. The moments are precious to us now. The officer is waiting for her. I need to know everything, I'm telling you—everything. Go on, my child."

Morel fell back onto his stool, overwhelmed.

"There is no point, monsieur, in telling you of my tears or my prayers," said Louise. "I was utterly crushed. This had happened at ten o'clock in the morning in Monsieur Ferrand's office. The priest was supposed to come for lunch with him that day. He arrived at the moment my employer was heaping reproaches and outrages on me. He seemed extremely annoyed at the sight of the priest."

"And what did he say then?"

"He quickly decided how he would act. He cried out, gesturing at me, 'So, Father! I told you many times that that miserable girl would lose her virtue. Well, it's happened! Fallen forever! She has just confessed everything to me and begged me to save her. And to think that out of pity I took such a wretch into my own home!' 'What?' said the priest to me in indignation. 'In spite of all the wholesome advice that your employer gave you in my presence, you've sullied yourself to this extent? Oh! That is unpardonable. My friend, after all the good you did this girl and her family, showing her any pity would just be weakness. Remain inexorable!' said the priest, fooled like everyone else by Monsieur Ferrand's hypocrisy."

"And you didn't unmask that vile creature on the spot?" asked Rodolphe.

"Good God! Monsieur, I was terrified. I couldn't keep a clear head. I didn't dare; indeed, I couldn't say a single word! And yet, I wanted to speak, to defend myself. 'But, monsieur—' I cried. 'Not another word, you lowly creature,' said Monsieur Ferrand, interrupting me. 'You heard the priest. Pity would be tantamount to weakness. You have one hour to leave my house!' Then, without leaving me the time to respond, he led the priest into another room.

"After Monsieur Ferrand left," Louise went on, "I felt for a moment as if I were delirious. I saw myself being forced to leave his house, unable to find another position because of the state I was in and because of the bad references that my employer would give me. I had no doubt either that in his anger he would have my father imprisoned. I didn't know what would become of me. I went to hide in my room. After two hours, Monsieur Ferrand appeared. 'Have you packed your bag?' he asked me.

"'Have mercy!' I begged him, falling at his feet. 'Don't send me away in the state I am in! What will become of me! I won't be able to find a position anywhere!'

"'It serves you right. God will punish you for your promiscuity and your lies.'

"'You dare to tell me that I'm lying?' I cried, indignantly. 'You dare to say that you aren't the one who ruined me?'

"'Leave my home this instant, you loathsome creature, since you persist in your slanders!' he cried in a terrifying voice. 'And to punish you, tomorrow I will have your father thrown in prison!'

"'Oh! No! No!' I said to him, horrified. 'I won't accuse you again, monsieur! I promise I won't, but don't send me away! Have pity on my father! The little I earn here keeps my family alive! Keep me here with you—I won't say a thing. I'll try to be sure no one notices anything, and when I can't hide my sad condition anymore, then, well, all right, you can send me away.'

"After more supplication on my part, Monsieur Ferrand agreed to keep me in his home. So appalling was my condition that I regarded this as a great favor. However, during the five months that followed this cruel scene, I was very unhappy and very harshly treated. Sometimes, but only on the rare occasions on which I would see him, Monsieur Germain would ask me in a kind way what was wrong. My shame kept me from telling him anything, however."

"Wasn't that more or less around the same time he came to live here?"

"Yes, monsieur. He was looking for a room either in the neighborhood of rue du Temple or of the Arsenal. There was one for rent here. I told him about the one you are now occupying, monsieur, and it suited him. When he left it, about two months ago, he asked me not to tell anyone here his new address. People could find him working at Monsieur Ferrand's place."

Rodolphe believed that Germain's need to escape his pursuers explained these precautions.

"And you never thought of confiding in Germain?" he asked Louise.

"No, monsieur. He, too, was fooled by Monsieur Ferrand's hypocrisy. He said he was hard and demanding, but he thought he was the fairest man on earth."

"When Germain lived here, did he never hear your father sometimes accuse the solicitor of trying to seduce you?"

"My father never spoke of his fears in front of strangers. In any case, at that time, I tricked him into thinking he had nothing to worry about. I reassured him by saying that Monsieur Ferrand no longer had designs on me. Alas! My poor father, now you will forgive me those lies. I only told them to give you some peace of mind. You can see that, can't you?"

Morel did not answer. He was sobbing, his forehead supported by his arms folded atop his workbench.

Rodolphe signaled Louise not to speak further to her father directly. She went on: "I spent those five months in tears, in continual anguish. Because of the precautions I took, I managed to hide my condition from everyone's eyes. But I could not hope to hide it like that during the last two months before I inevitably came to term. The future frightened me more and more. Monsieur Ferrand had declared that he no longer wished to keep me in his employ. So I was going to be deprived of the scarce resources that helped to enable my family to survive. Cursed, cast out by my father—for, after all the lies I had told him to keep his mind at ease, he would think I was the willing accomplice and not the victim of Monsieur Ferrand—what would I do? Where could I seek refuge? Where could I go . . . in the condition I was in? I then had an idea that was completely criminal. Happily, I could not go through with it. I tell you this, monsieur, because I don't want to keep anything from you, even if it could incriminate me; I also want to show you the extremes that Monsieur Ferrand's cruelty pushed me to. If I had given in to a horrible idea, would he not have been an accomplice to my crime?"

After a moment of silence, Louise spoke again with effort, and in a trembling voice. "I had heard the doorman's wife saying that a charlatan lived in the house and—"

She could not finish her sentence.

Rodolphe remembered that in his first conversation with Madame Pipelet he had been handed, in Madame Pipelet's absence, a letter written on rough paper and in a false hand. On that letter he remembered seeing the trace of tears . . .

"And you wrote to him, unhappy child. That was about three days ago! You had cried over that letter, and your writing was disguised."

Louise looked at Rodolphe with fear. "How did you know that, monsieur?"

"Don't worry. I was alone in Madame Pipelet's office when that letter was delivered, and I happened to notice it."

"Well, then—yes, monsieur. In that letter, which I did not sign, I wrote to Monsieur Bradamanti to say that, since I dared not go to his home, I begged him to be at the Château-d'Eau that night. I had lost my mind. I wanted to get his terrible instructions. I left my employer's home with the intention of following those instructions, but after a moment I came back to my senses. I understood the crime that I had been on the verge of committing. I came back home and I missed that meeting. That very evening a scene took place that led to this most recent misfortune, which now oppresses me.

"Monsieur Ferrand thought I had gone out for two hours, even though I returned in a very short time. As I passed before the little door of the garden, to my great astonishment I saw it had been left ajar. I went in that way and carried the key back to Monsieur Ferrand's office, where it was usually kept. That room was in front of his bedroom, the most remote place in the whole house. That's where he kept his secret appointments—his daily affairs were taken up in his office. You will soon understand, monsieur, why I'm giving you these details. As I knew my way around the whole house, after I went through the dining room, which was lit up, I entered the living room without a lamp, and then the office that led to his bedroom. The door to that last room opened just as I was putting the key on a table. Hardly had my employer seen me by the light of the lamp that was burning in his room, when he abruptly closed the door on a person I could not see. Then, in spite of the darkness, he threw himself at me, seized me by the neck as if he wanted to strangle me, and said in a low voice, in a tone that was both furious and alarmed, 'You were spying on me—you were listening at the door! What did you hear? Answer me! Answer me, or I'll crush the life out of you!' But then, changing his mind, and without even giving me the chance to say a word, he pushed me out into the dining room. The pantry was open—he threw me in there brutally and locked the door."

"And you had heard nothing of his conversation?"

"Nothing, monsieur. If I had known he was in his room with someone, I would have been sure not to enter the little room. He forbade even Madame Séraphin to go there."

"And when you left the pantry, what did he say to you?"

"The housekeeper came to let me out, and I didn't see Monsieur Ferrand again that evening. The shock, the fear I had undergone made me very ill. The next day, as I was coming downstairs, I met Monsieur Ferrand. I shivered as I thought of his threats from the day before. How surprised I was when he said to me, almost calmly, 'You know very well that I forbid anyone to enter the antechamber when I have someone in my room. But considering how little time you will be remaining here, there's no point in scolding you anymore.' And he returned to his office.

"His moderation surprised me after the violence of the day before. I continued doing my work as usual, and I went to tidy up his bedroom. I had been very ill all that night. I felt weak and worn down. As I was organizing some of his clothes in his dark closet situated near the alcove, I was suddenly taken by a painful dizziness. I felt like I was losing consciousness. As I fell, I tried reflexively to hold myself upright by grabbing on to a coat that was hanging from the wall. In my fall, I pulled this garment down, and it covered me almost entirely.

"When I came to, the glass door of the alcove room was shut. I heard Monsieur Ferrand's voice speaking very loudly. Remembering the scene from the day before, I thought I was as good as dead if I so much as moved. I supposed that, hidden under the coat that had fallen on me, I had not been visible to my employer as he closed the door on this dark cloakroom. If he discovered me there, how would I make him believe this almost inexplicable accident? I held my breath, therefore, and against my will I heard the end of a conversation that had no doubt begun some time earlier."

CHAPTER II

THE INTERVIEW

"And who was the person closeted in the solicitor's room, talking with him?" Rodolphe asked Louise.

"I don't know, monsieur. I didn't recognize the voice."

"And what were they saying?"

"The conversation had been going on for some time, I'm sure, because this is all I heard: 'Nothing could be simpler,' said this voice I didn't know. 'A rogue named Red-Arm, a determined smuggler, has put me in touch with a family of freshwater pirates[107] to help us with the matter we were discussing a moment ago. This family lives at the tip of a little island near Asnières. They're the worst criminals on earth. The father and grandfather were guillotined, two of the sons have been sent to the galleys for life, but the mother still has three boys and two girls left, and each one of those is a bigger crook than the other. I've heard that to rob people at night on both banks of the Seine, they sometimes go by boat all the way down to Bercy. These people would kill any passerby just for the coins in his pocket. But we don't need them for that; all we need is for them to put up your lady from the countryside. We'll pass the Martials (that's the name of my pirate family) off to her as an honest family of fishermen. I will go on your behalf to pay two or three visits to your young lady. I'll prescribe certain special potions for her, and within a week she'll make the acquaintance of the Asnières cemetery. In villages, death is as common as a letter arriving in the mail, whereas in Paris people get too nosy. So when will you be sending your lady from the provinces to the Asnières island? I need to let the Martials know the role they'll be playing.' 'She will arrive here tomorrow, and the day after tomorrow she'll be at their place,' answered Monsieur Ferrand. 'I'll let her know that Doctor Vincent will be taking care of her on my behalf.' 'The name Vincent will do fine,' the voice said; 'it's a name as good as any other.'"

"What is this new mystery of crime and infamy?" said Rodolphe, more and more surprised.

"New? No, sir—you'll soon see that it is linked to another crime that

107. The reader will learn shortly about the mores of these Parisian pirates. [SN]

you know about," said Louise. She continued: "I heard the chairs moving; the interview was over. 'I won't ask you what your secret is,' said Monsieur Ferrand. 'I have my hold on you and you have yours on me.' 'That makes it easier for us to help each other without ever getting in each other's way,' said the voice. 'Look what an eager servant I am! I received your letter yesterday at ten o'clock at night, and here I am with you this morning. Good-bye, partner—don't forget the Asnières island, Martial the fisherman, and Doctor Vincent. With those three magic words, in one week, your lady from the provinces will be no more.'

"'Wait,' said Monsieur Ferrand. 'I bolted the door of my study as a precaution and I need to unbolt it. I also want to see if there's anyone in the antechamber so you can leave by the same little garden path you used coming in.' Monsieur Ferrand left for a moment and then came back in. I finally heard him withdraw with the person whose voice I heard. You can see how terrified I was, monsieur, during that interview, and how unhappy I was to have overheard such a secret without meaning to. Two hours after this conversation, Madame Séraphin came to look for me in my room. I had gone up there, trembling and feeling sicker than I'd ever felt up to that point. 'Monsieur is asking for you,' she said. 'You are luckier than you have any right to be. Come on, let's go. You're very pale. What he's going to tell you will put a little color in your cheeks.'

"I followed Madame Séraphin. Monsieur Ferrand was in his office. When I saw him, I shivered, despite myself. And yet his manner was less threatening than usual. He looked at me for a long time as if he were trying to read my mind. I lowered my eyes. 'You seem very ill,' he said to me.

"'Yes, monsieur,' I answered, astonished that he was not speaking to me with his usual disrespect.

"'It makes perfect sense,' he added. 'It's the consequence of your condition and your efforts to hide it. But in spite of your lies, your bad conduct, and your indiscretion yesterday,' he said, in a softer voice, 'I feel bad for you. In a few days it will be impossible for you to hide your pregnancy. Even though I treated you as you deserved in the presence of the parish priest, such an event would bring shame to a house like mine in the eyes of the public. And furthermore, your family would be in despair. So, given these circumstances, I have decided to help you.'

"'Ah! Monsieur!' I cried. 'These kind words of yours have made me forget everything!'

"'Forget what?' he asked, harshly.

"'Nothing, nothing—I'm sorry, monsieur,' I said from fear of irritating him and believing him to be thinking of my best interests.

"'Listen to me,' he said. 'You will go see your father today. You will tell him that I am sending you for two or three months to the countryside to take care of a house I've just bought. During your absence I will have your wages sent to him. Tomorrow you will leave Paris. I will give you a letter of reference to give to Madame Martial, the mother of an honest family of fishermen who live near Asnières. You will need to be careful to say that you are coming from the provinces without saying anything else. You will find out later the reason for this reference—it's all in your own interest. Madame Martial will treat you like one of her own children. The doctor who is a friend of mine, Doctor Vincent, will give you the care you need in your condition. So you see how good I am to you!'"

"What a horrible plot!" cried Rodolphe. "I understand everything now. Believing that you had heard one of his terrible secrets the day before, he decided to get rid of you. He probably had some reason of his own to deceive his accomplice by characterizing you to him as a woman from the countryside. His proposal must have terrified you!"

"It was a violent blow, and I was staggered by it. I didn't know what to say; I looked at Monsieur Ferrand in terror, and my head was spinning. I was going to put my life at risk, in all probability, by telling him that I had heard his plans that morning—but fortunately I remembered the new dangers such a confession would entail.

"'Did you not understand me?' he asked, impatiently.

"'Yes, I did, monsieur,' I said to him, trembling, 'but I would prefer not to go to the country.'

"'Why not? You will be treated very well in the place I am sending you.'

"'No! No! I won't go; I would rather stay in Paris and not be separated from my family. I would rather tell them everything and die of shame, if that's what it takes.'

"'Are you refusing my offer?' said Monsieur Ferrand, keeping his anger under control, to this point, and watching me closely. 'Why have you so suddenly changed your mind? You were ready to accept my offer just a moment ago.' I saw that I was done for if he figured out what I was thinking. I told him that I hadn't realized that I would have to leave Paris and my family. 'But you are bringing dishonor upon your family, you wretch!' he cried—and, no longer able to control himself, he grabbed me by the arm and pushed me so hard that I fell over. 'I'll give you until the day after tomorrow,'[108] he cried. 'Tomorrow you will leave

108. This appears to be a slip on Sue's part. Presumably, he meant to write "tomorrow." In the first mention of the timeline for Louise to go to Asnières, she was to arrive at Jacques Ferrand's "tomorrow," and be at Asnières the day after. In the second mention, she was to visit her father, leave Paris "tomorrow," and arrive at Asnières the day after. [TN]

here to go to the Martials' or you'll be going to tell your father that I sent you away and that he will be going immediately to prison.'

"I remained where I was on the floor, alone. I didn't have the strength to get up. Madame Séraphin ran in when she heard her employer raising his voice. With her assistance, and getting weaker with each step, I managed to get back to my room. As soon as I got there, I collapsed onto my bed. I stayed there until it was nighttime. All of these shocks had made me very ill. The atrocious pain that woke me up around one in the morning made me feel that I was about to bring that poor child into the world well before he was due."

"Why didn't you call for help?"

"Oh, I didn't dare! Monsieur Ferrand wanted to get rid of me. He would have sent for Doctor Vincent, I'm sure, who would have murdered me right then and there instead of at the Martials' place. Or maybe Monsieur Ferrand might have smothered me and said that I had died in childbirth. Alas, monsieur, these fears may have been mad, but at that moment they caused me considerable anguish. If I hadn't been so frightened, I would have faced up to my shame, and I wouldn't be accused of having killed my child. Instead of calling for help, and fearing that they would hear my horrible suffering, I gave birth—all alone, in the dark—to that unhappy creature whose death was no doubt caused by this premature delivery. Because I didn't kill him. God, no! I didn't kill him! No! In the dark of that night I had one moment of bitter joy, and that was when I held my child in my arms." And her voice was extinguished by her sobs.

Morel had listened to his daughter's story apathetically, with a gloomy indifference that frightened Rodolphe. However, seeing her burst into tears, the gem-cutter, still sitting with his elbows propped up on his worktable with his hands at his temples, fixed his gaze on Louise and said, "She's crying . . . she's crying . . . why is she crying?" Then he went on, after a moment's hesitation, "Ah, yes—I know why, I know why, it's the solicitor. Go on, my poor Louise. You're my daughter, and I still love you. A moment ago I didn't recognize you—my tears were too thick to see through. Oh, God! My head is killing me!"

"You see that it's not my fault, don't you, Father?"

"Yes, yes . . ."

"It's a terrible thing to have happened, but I was so afraid of the solicitor!"

"The solicitor? Oh! I believe you! He is so wicked—so wicked!"

"Will you forgive me now?"

"Yes . . ."

"Truly?"

"Yes, truly. Oh! I still love you, although . . . I can't . . . say . . . you see . . . because . . . Oh! My head! My head!"

Louise looked at Rodolphe anxiously.

"He's ill. Let him calm down a little. Go on."

Louise went on after looking worriedly at Morel two or three times: "I held my child close. I was surprised that I couldn't hear him breathing, but I said to myself, 'The breathing of a baby this small, you can hardly hear that.' But then he also seemed really cold to me. I couldn't get any light, because they never let me keep a lamp. I waited until it was light out. I tried to warm him up as much as I could, but he seemed to be getting colder and colder. I said to myself again, 'It's so cold out, that's what's making him numb.' When the sun rose, I brought my child over to the window. I looked at him. He was stiff and icy. I glued my lips to his to try to feel his breath, and I put my hand over his heart, but there was no heartbeat—he was dead!" She burst into tears.

"Oh! At that moment," she said, "something happened within me that's impossible to describe. I can't remember anything after that. It's all confused, like in a dream. I felt despair, terror, and rage, all at the same time, but more than any of that, I was seized with a new terror: I no longer feared that Monsieur Ferrand would crush me; but I feared that if they found my child lying dead beside me, I would be accused of having killed him. So I had only one thought: I had to hide the body from all prying eyes. That way, my dishonor would not be known, I would no longer have to fear my father's anger, and I could escape the vengeance of Monsieur Ferrand. Now that I had given birth, I could leave his house, find a position elsewhere, and continue to earn money to be able to support my family.

"Alas, monsieur, that's why I decided not to say anything to anyone and to hide my child's corpse. No doubt I was wrong to do that, but I felt so besieged on all sides in the position I was in and so broken by illness, almost to the point of delirium, that I didn't think about what would happen if I was discovered."

"What torments you have undergone! What torments!" said Rodolphe, completely overcome.

"The morning was getting on," Louise continued. "I only had a few moments left before the house would be stirring. I didn't hesitate any longer. I wrapped my child up as best I could and walked down the stairs very quietly. I went to the back of the garden to dig a hole in the earth in which to bury him, but it had been so frigid the night before that the ground was too hard. So I hid the corpse in the back of a little cellar that no one used during the winter. I covered him with an empty flower tub, and I returned to my room without anyone having seen me.

"I have only very confused recollections, monsieur, of everything I'm telling you about now. Weak as I was, I still don't know how I found the strength and the energy to do all of that. At nine o'clock, Madame Séraphin came in to see why I hadn't gotten up yet. I told her that I felt so sick that I was pleading with her to let me stay in bed all day—the next day I would leave the house, since Monsieur Ferrand was sending me away. After an hour, he came by to see me himself. 'You have become even more ill: that's what your stubbornness gets you,' he told me. 'If you had taken advantage of my kindness, today you would have been safe with good people who were seeing to all of your needs. In any case, I won't be so heartless as to let you remain in your state without any medical assistance. This evening Doctor Vincent will come to see you.'

"I shivered in fear when I heard this threat. I answered Monsieur Ferrand that the day before I had been wrong to refuse his offer and that I would now accept it, but that as I was still too ill to travel, I would not leave until the day after tomorrow to go to the Martials'. It wasn't necessary, I said, to call in Doctor Vincent. I was only trying to gain some time. I had already decided to leave the house and go home the next day to my father. I hoped that this way he wouldn't know anything about what had happened. Reassured by my promise, Monsieur Ferrand was almost affectionate toward me. He told Madame Séraphin, for the first time ever, to take good care of me.

"I spent the day in mortal fear. I was terrified that, at any moment, chance would lead someone to discover the corpse of my child. I wanted only one thing, which was for the weather to warm up so that the ground would thaw enough to let me dig a grave. Snow was falling. That gave me some hope. I stayed in bed all day.

"At nightfall, I waited until everyone was asleep. I found the strength to get up and go to the wood pile to find a hatchet for splitting wood that I could make a hole with in the snow-covered ground. With a great deal of difficulty, I finally succeeded. Then I took the body, cried some more over him, and buried him as best I could in the little flower tub. I didn't know which prayer I was supposed to say for the dead, so I said an Our Father and a Hail Mary and prayed that God would receive him in heaven. I thought my courage was going to fail me when the time came to cover the makeshift bier that I had fashioned for him with earth. Imagine a mother having to bury her child! Finally, I was finished. Oh, God, it took so much out of me. I covered the area with snow again so no one could see that anything had changed. The moon had given me light to work by. When everything was done, I could hardly get myself to leave. Poor child, buried in the frozen ground, under the snow! Even though he was dead, it seemed to me that he must be feeling the cold. Finally I went back to my room. I went to bed with a violent fever. In the morning, Monsieur Ferrand sent to find out how I was feeling. I answered that I felt a bit better and that I would surely be able to leave for the country the next day. I stayed in bed that day, too, hoping to get a little stronger. In the evening, I got up and went down into the kitchen to warm up a bit. I stayed there all alone until it was late. I went into the garden to say one last prayer.

"Just as I was going back to my room, I met Monsieur Germain on the landing of the office where he worked sometimes. He was very pale. He said to me very quickly, as he put a roll of coins in my hand, 'Your father is going to be arrested tomorrow morning for a bill of exchange of thirteen hundred francs. He won't be able to pay it. Here's the money. As soon as it's light out, run home to your father. I've only now come to know who Monsieur Ferrand really is. He is an evil man. I will unmask him. But whatever you do, don't tell anyone that you got this money from me.' And Monsieur Germain didn't even give me the chance to thank him. He was already running down the stairs."

CHAPTER 12

INSANITY

"This morning," Louise continued, "before anyone arose at Monsieur Ferrand's home, I came here with the money that Monsieur Germain had given me in order to save my father, but it wasn't enough, and without your generosity I wouldn't have been able to free him from the clutches of the bailiffs. After I left Monsieur Ferrand's, they must have gone up to my room and found the evidence that would have put them on the trail of that sad discovery. One last favor, monsieur," said Louise, removing the roll of money from her pocket. "Would you please give this money back to Monsieur Germain? I had promised him that I would not tell anyone that he worked for Monsieur Ferrand, but since you knew it already, I haven't been indiscreet. Now, monsieur, I will say again before you, before God who hears all, I have not said a single word that was not true. I have not tried to lessen my faults and—"

But, cutting herself off suddenly, Louise cried out in fright, "Monsieur! Look at my father! Look at him . . . what's wrong with him?"

Morel had heard the last part of this story with a somber indifference that Rodolphe had attributed to this unhappy man's overwhelmed state of mind. When one experiences such violent shocks in such close succession, one's tears tend to dry up and one's sensations become deadened. Rodolphe thought that Morel could hardly have had sufficient strength left to become indignant. But Rodolphe was wrong.

Just as the flame of a torch wanes and then flares back up again as it is being extinguished, Morel's sanity, already severely challenged, wavered for a while and cast a few last beams of intelligence—and then, suddenly, it went dark. Utterly removed from what was being said and what was happening around him, within the last few moments the gem-cutter had gone mad.

Although his mill was on the other side of his workbench, and although he had no gems or tools in his hands, the artisan simulated the operations of his ordinary work with the aid of imaginary instruments. He looked attentive and busy, and he accompanied this pantomime by making a noise with his tongue on his palate; he was trying to imitate the sound of the mill in its rotating movements.

"Monsieur," said Louise with growing anxiety, "look at my father!" Then, approaching the artisan, she said to him, "Father! Father!"

Morel looked at his daughter with the troubled, vague, distracted, and indecisive gaze peculiar to people who have lost their minds. Without halting his senseless labor, he answered very quietly in a soft and sad voice, "I owe thirteen hundred francs to the solicitor. It's the price for Louise's life. I have to work, to work, to work! Oh! I'll pay, I'll pay, I'll pay . . ."

"Good God, monsieur, it's not possible! This can't last! He's not completely crazy, is he?" cried Louise in a heartrending voice. "He'll come back to his senses. This can't be anything but a momentary delirium."

"Morel, my friend!" said Rodolphe. "We're here! Your daughter is right next to you; she's innocent!"

"Thirteen hundred francs!" said the gem-cutter without looking at Rodolphe, and he continued to make the motions of working.

"Father," said Louise, throwing herself at his knees and, despite his efforts, holding his hands tightly in hers. "It's me, Louise!"

"Thirteen hundred francs!" he repeated, pulling away with some difficulty from his daughter's grasp. "Thirteen hundred francs—or else," he added in a low voice, almost conspiratorially, "or else, Louise will face the guillotine." And he went back to pretending to turn his mill.

Louise let out a terrible cry. "He has gone mad! He has gone mad! And it's me! I caused it! Oh, God! God! But it wasn't really my fault! I didn't want to do anything wrong! It was that monster!"

"Come, poor child, take heart," said Rodolphe. "We can hope. This may only be a temporary insanity. Your father's suffering has been too much for him. No one could endure so many sorrows in so little time. He has lost his reason for the moment, but it will come back to him."

"But my mother, my grandmother, my sisters, my brothers—what will become of them?" cried Louise. "Here they are, deprived of my father and me. There's nothing left for them but to die of starvation, poverty, and despair!"

"I'm here, am I not? Calm down; they will lack for nothing. Take heart, I tell you! Your testimony will help punish a great criminal. You have convinced me of your innocence, and it will be recognized and proclaimed—I am sure of it."

"Ah, monsieur! Don't you see? Dishonor, madness, death: these are the evils this man has brought about. And no one can do anything to touch him! Nothing! Ah! That thought makes my suffering complete!"

"Far from it. The opposite thought should help you to bear it."

"What do you mean, monsieur?"

"You must carry with you the certainty that your father, you, and all of your family will be avenged."

"Avenged?"

"Yes! And I swear to you, I myself," said Rodolphe, solemnly, "I swear that once his crimes have been proven, this man will pay dearly for the dishonor, madness, and death he has caused. If the law is powerless to reach him, and if his deceitfulness and skill are equal to his heinous crimes, we will combat his deceitfulness with deceitfulness, his skill with skill, and his heinousness with heinousness. But these actions will be to his that which a just and avenging punishment, inflicted on a guilty person by an inexorable force, is to cowardly, clandestine murder."

"Oh, monsieur! May God hear you! But it's no longer myself I wish to avenge—it's my father who has been driven mad, it's my baby who died in childbirth."

Then, trying one last time to rouse Morel from his insanity, Louise cried out again, "Adieu, Father! They're taking me off to prison; I won't see you ever again! It's Louise, your daughter, here saying good-bye to you. Father! Father! Father!" To these wrenching appeals there was no response. There was no returning echo from this poor, annihilated soul—none at all. The paternal bonds, always the last to be broken, no longer held.

The door to the garret opened. The police superintendent entered. "My time is short, monsieur," he said to Rodolphe. "I regret to tell you that I cannot allow this discussion to go on much longer."

"This discussion is over, monsieur," Rodolphe responded bitterly as he gestured toward the gem-cutter. "Louise has nothing left to tell her father. He has nothing left to hear from his daughter—he's gone mad!"

"Good God! I was afraid of that. Ah! How dreadful!" cried the officer. Quickly going over to the worker, after a brief examination, he recognized the truth of this tragic reality.

"Ah, monsieur!" he said with sadness to Rodolphe. "From the first, I sincerely wished that the innocence of that young woman would be established! But after such a terrible misfortune, I will not limit myself to wishes. No, no—I will attest to this family's uprightness and desolate misfortune; I will attest to the appalling last blow that has beaten them down. And have no doubt, this will give their judges one reason the more to find the accused innocent."

"Good, good, monsieur," said Rodolphe. "If you do that, you will no longer merely be fulfilling your duties; you will be performing the work of God."

"Believe me, monsieur, our work is almost always so painful that when we may concern ourselves with anything honest and good, it brings us happiness and gratitude."

"One more thing, monsieur: what Louise Morel has told us has proven her innocence to me beyond any doubt. Can you tell me how the crime she has been accused of was discovered, or rather, denounced?"

"This morning," the magistrate said, "a housekeeper in the service of Monsieur Ferrand, the solicitor, came to tell me that after the abrupt departure of Louise Morel, whom she knew to be seven months' pregnant, she went up to the young woman's room and found traces of a clandestine childbirth. After some investigation, some footprints in the snow led to the discovery of the body of a newly born child who had been buried in the garden.

"After I heard that woman's declaration, I went over to rue du Sentier. I found Monsieur Jacques Ferrand there, indignant that such a scandal should have taken place at his home. The priest from the Bonne-Nouvelle church, whom he had sent for, also told me that the Morel girl had confessed her sin before him one day when she was begging her employer to be indulgent and to have pity on her in connection to this matter. He had often, furthermore, heard Monsieur Ferrand give Louise Morel the most severe warnings, predicting to her that sooner or later she would lose her virtue; this prediction had just so unfortunately come true, the priest added. The indignation of Monsieur Ferrand," the officer continued, "seemed so well founded to me that I shared in it. He told me that Louise Morel had no doubt taken refuge with her father. I came here right away; the crime was flagrant, so I had the right to proceed to an immediate arrest."

Rodolphe restrained himself as he heard this talk of Monsieur Ferrand's indignation. He said to the officer, "Thank you very much, monsieur, for being so obliging and for the support you wish to offer on Louise's behalf. I am going to take this poor man to an asylum along with his wife's mother."

Then, turning to Louise, who, still kneeling next to her father, was trying in vain to recall him to his senses, he said, "You will have to resign yourself, my child, to leaving without kissing your mother good-bye. Spare her the wrenching farewell. Don't worry about what will become of her: from now on, your family will have everything they need. We'll find a woman to take care of your mother and your brothers and sisters, under the supervision of your kind neighbor Mademoiselle Rigolette. As for your father, nothing will be spared to bring about a rapid and complete cure for him. Take heart; believe me, honest people are often rudely tested by misfortune, but they always emerge from these struggles purer, stronger, and more respected."

Two hours after Louise's arrest, on Rodolphe's orders, David drove the gem-cutter and the old senile woman to Charenton.[109] There they were to be treated in private rooms and to receive special care. Morel left the

109. Charenton was an insane asylum founded in 1645. The Marquis de Sade was a famous inmate there. Later in the novel, Morel is treated at Bicêtre. [TN]

house on rue du Temple without any resistance. He went wherever he was led, without objection. His was a gentle, inoffensive, and sad madness.

The grandmother was hungry. They showed her some meat and some bread, and she followed the meat and bread.

They entrusted the gem-cutter's stones to the care of his wife, who returned them that same day to Madame Mathieu, the broker, who came to pick them up. Unfortunately, Gammy, who knew the value of the ostensibly fake gems from the interview overheard after Morel's arrest by the bailiffs, had spied on and followed the broker. Red-Arm's son thus confirmed that she lived at number eleven boulevard Saint-Denis.

Rigolette, with great delicacy, informed Madeleine Morel of the gem-cutter's attack of insanity and of Louise's imprisonment. At first Madeleine cried a great deal and was inconsolable; she wailed in despair. Then, once this first burst of suffering had passed, the poor creature, weak and capricious, calmed down more and more, consoled by the comforts she saw surrounding herself and her children, thanks to their benefactor's generosity.

As for Rodolphe, his thoughts were bitter as he reflected on Louise's revelations. "Nothing could be more typical," he said to himself, "than this kind of corruption, visited with more or less violence by the master on the servant. Sometimes through terror or surprise; sometimes simply through the unequal relations that servitude fosters. This depraved conduct, sanctioned by their authority and merely serving to satisfy their lust—this depravation that comes down from the rich to the poor and that shows contempt for the protective sanctity of the domestic hearth—is sad enough when it is accepted willingly, but it is hideous and horrible when it is a matter of force. It is an impure and brutal servitude, an ignoble and barbaric enslavement of a living creature who, in her terror, answers the master's lust with tears and his caresses with shudders of disgust and fear.

"And then also," Rodolphe went on in his meditation, "when one considers the consequences for these women! Almost always, degradation, poverty, prostitution, theft, and sometimes even infanticide! But our laws never have any impact on these consequences! Under other circumstances, every accomplice to a crime is liable for the penalty for that crime; everyone who receives stolen goods is liable for the same punishment as the thief; it's only just. But if in his idleness, a man seduces a young, innocent, pure woman, impregnates her and then abandons her, and leaves her to face nothing but shame, poverty, and despair, and, by doing this, pushes her toward infanticide, a crime that she must pay for with her life . . . will that man be viewed as her accomplice? Oh, please!

What is this but a trifle? It's nothing—no, it's less than nothing. It's a little fling, a single day's fancy for some girl's pretty, bedraggled little face. The game is over—time to move on to another!

"Even worse, if this man is especially coldhearted (all the while remaining the best son in the world), he might go to see his victim in the criminal court. If he happens to be called as a witness, he can enjoy himself by telling the people there, all of them very eager to guillotine the young woman as soon as possible—all for the greater glory and for public morality, of course: 'I have something important to reveal to the court.' 'Speak.' 'Gentlemen of the jury, this unfortunate woman was virtuous and pure, it's true. It's also true that I seduced her. I got her pregnant—all true. After all, she was blond, and I left her for another who was a brunette; still the truth and nothing but the truth. But in doing all of this, I was availing myself of an inalienable right, of a sacred right that society recognizes and with which it endows me.'

"'The fact is that this fellow is completely within his right,' each member of the jury will whisper to another. 'There's no law that prohibits a man getting a blonde pregnant and then abandoning her for a brunette. He's just sowing his wild oats!'

"'Now, gentlemen of the jury, this unfortunate woman is claiming that she killed her child—I'll even go so far as to say our child—because I abandoned her; because, finding herself alone and in the most dire poverty, she was frightened, she lost her head. And why? She said that, since she had to take care of and feed her child, it had become impossible to go to work for any length of time in the workshop and earn a living so as to maintain herself and the product of our lovemaking. But permit me to say, gentlemen of the jury, that I find this reasoning pitiful. Couldn't Mademoiselle go and give birth at the Bourbe,[110] if there was any room there? Couldn't she have shown up at the police office in her neighborhood at the critical moment to make a public declaration of her shame, in order to be authorized to leave her child at the Foundling Hospital? Finally, while I was chasing skirts at the public house, looking out for my next mistress, wasn't there a less barbarous way for Mademoiselle to get out of her bind? For I must confess, gentlemen of the jury, that I find this too convenient and too cavalier a manner of getting rid of the fruit of a few moments' pleasure and error, thus escaping any future cares. Well, really! A girl should be able to do more than just lose her honor and face people's scorn and vilification and carry an illegitimate child in her womb for nine months! She should have to raise that child, too! She should have to take care of him, feed him, find him a profession—basically, she should make an honest man of him—like

110. The name of a Paris lying-in hospital. [TN]

his father, or if it's a daughter, an honest woman who doesn't dishonor herself like her mother. Because motherhood has its sacred duties, you know! And the kinds of miserable mothers who trample these sacred duties underfoot are unnatural and deserve a terrible punishment, one that makes a proper example of them. In that belief, gentlemen of the jury, send that criminal quickly to the executioner for me, and you will be performing the duty of virtuous, independent, firm, and enlightened citizens. So say I!'

"'This gentleman frames the question in a very moral light,' some rich hosier or some old usurer decked out as the jury foreman will say benevolently. 'Goodness, he has only done what we would have done ourselves in his place, seeing how nice this little blond girl is—even if she is a little too pale. This fellow, as Joconde[111] puts it, has courted the brunette and the blonde; there's no law against that. As for this unfortunate woman—it's her fault, after all! Why didn't she control herself? She didn't have to commit a crime—a monstrous crime that shames society right down to its foundations.'

"And this rich hosier or usurer would be right. He would be completely right. On what grounds could this gentleman be charged with any crime? With what complicity—direct or indirect, moral or material—could he be charged? This happy rascal seduced a pretty girl, then he just left her on her own; he confesses to having done these two things. Is there any law against the one act or the other? Does our society not say, much like the father in some bawdy story or other, 'Look out for your hens, my rooster is on the loose. I wash my hands of him!' But if a poor wretch buys some rag, knowing it was stolen—be it out of need, stupidity, compulsion, or ignorance of laws he can't read, anyway—well, then, if the thief is sent to the galleys for twenty years, so is he sent to the galleys for twenty years as a receiver of stolen goods. That's strong, logical reasoning, for without receivers of stolen goods, there would be no thieves, and without thieves, there would be no receivers of stolen goods.

"But there should be no more pity—in fact, there should be even less pity—for the person who instigates crime than for the person who carries it out. The slightest complicity should be punished with terrible severity! Now here is a rigorous and productive philosophy, one that is elevated and moral. One could bow to a society that dictated such a law, but then he would remember that this same society that is so inexorable toward the least complicity in crimes against property is so structured that a simple and naive man who might try to demonstrate that there is, at the very least, a moral link and material complicity

111. Joconde was a character in an eponymous comic opera by Charles-Guillaume Étienne (1778–1845). [TN]

between the wandering seducer and the seduced and abandoned girl—such a man would seem like a wide-eyed idealist.

"And if this simple man happened to suggest that, without a father, there might—perhaps—be no baby, society would protest against the outrageousness and madness of such an idea. And society would be right, absolutely right, for, after all, this man who could say so many eloquent things to the jury, as little as he might be an aficionado of tragedies, would be within his rights if he went to see the execution of his mistress for the crime of infanticide—a crime in which he is complicit, or even more correctly, a crime of which he is the author, given his despicable lack of restraint.

"Doesn't the charming protection that covers certain little acts of mischief having to do with the little god of love—this protection that gets accorded to the male segment of our society—doesn't it show that the French still make sacrifices to the Graces? And doesn't it show that the French are still the most gallant people in the universe?"

CHAPTER 13

JACQUES FERRAND

At the time the events we have been recounting were taking place, there was a long, cracked wall at one end of rue du Sentier that was covered with a layer of plaster and studded with the shards of bottles. This wall, bordering the garden of the solicitor Jacques Ferrand on this side, led to a main building that was built right on the road. It was only one floor high, and above it rose granaries. Two large escutcheons of gilded copper bore the solicitor's insignia. They flanked the worm-eaten carriage entrance whose original color could no longer be identified due to the mud that covered it. This door led to a covered passage. At the right was the lodge of an old, half-deaf doorkeeper, a man who was to the community of tailors what Monsieur Pipelet was to the brotherhood of bootmakers. To the left stood a stable that served as a storeroom, washhouse, and woodshed, as well as a hutch for a burgeoning colony of rabbits, confined to the feeding trough by the doorkeeper, who raised these domestic animals to distract himself from the sorrows of his recently having become a widower.

Next to the lodge was the entrance to a dark, narrow, winding staircase that led to the office, a fact that was announced to clients by the image of a hand painted in black with an index finger that pointed to a sign—also painted on the wall in black—that read, "The Office Is on the First Floor." On one side of a large paved courtyard surrounded by grass stood some deliveries that no one attended to; on the other, a rusted iron grille that enclosed the garden. At the back was the main building, in which the solicitor lived, alone.

A flight of eight or ten stairs composed of separate rock steps, each one unstable, mossy, greenish, and weatherworn, led to this square building, which was made up of a basement kitchen with its adjoining rooms, a ground floor, a first floor, and the attic in which Louise had lived. This building also seemed to be in a dilapidated state: there were deep cracks in its walls; the windows and blinds, once painted gray, had become nearly black with the passage of time; the six windows on the first floor, which overlooked the courtyard, had no curtains; a kind of oily, opaque rust covered the windowpanes; and on the ground floor, through the more transparent windowpanes, one could see faded yellow cotton fabric curtains with red rosettes on them. On the garden side, the building had only four windows, two of which were boarded up.

This garden, overgrown with parasitical scrub, seemed abandoned. No flower bed or shrub was anywhere to be seen. There was a cluster of elms, five or six green trees, a few acacias and elders, and a light yellow lawn that had been eaten away by moss and the summer sun. There were also some chalky dirt paths encumbered with brambles. At the back was a greenhouse that was half underground. The only view the garden had was the tall, blank, gray walls of the adjoining houses, interrupted here and there by barred windows that looked like they should be adorning a prison. Such was the sad picture formed by the solicitor's garden and home.

Monsieur Ferrand attached great importance to this appearance, or rather, to this reality. To the common man, indifference to comfort almost always seems to indicate disinterestedness, and slovenliness suggests austerity. Comparing the ostentatious expense of some solicitors, or the fabulous wardrobes of their wives, to the somber home of Monsieur Ferrand, with its disdain for elegance, sumptuousness, and detail, his clients felt a kind of respect for this man, or rather a sort of blind confidence in him. Given his large clientele and supposed fortune, he might, like so many of his confreres, have referred to "my retinue" (such people actually say such things), "my galas," "my little place in the country," "my day at the opera," etc.—but instead, he lived under conditions of the most austere thrift. Thus, deposits, placements, trusts—in short, every kind of business that relies on widely accepted integrity and on loudly trumpeted good faith—all came in abundance to Monsieur Ferrand.

The solicitor's practice of living on very little was a matter of personal taste for him. He hated high society, ostentatious displays, and all pleasures for which one had to pay dearly. Even if he had felt differently, he would have sacrificed his most burning desires for the sake of appearances, so important did he think such appearances.

A few words on this man's character: he was one of the true sons of the great family of misers. We almost always think of misers as ridiculous or grotesque. The most wicked of them do not go beyond selfishness or hardness. Most of them increase their fortune by hoarding. Some of them—a very small number—venture to lend at usurious rates. Only the most determined of them dare to cast a glance into the deep abyss of speculation. It is almost unheard of for a miser to go so far as to commit a crime in order to acquire some new wealth, let alone to go so far as to commit murder.

It's not hard to understand why this is so. Avarice is above all a negative and passive passion. The miser dreams, in his never-ending plots, of enriching himself by not spending anything, by always shrinking the limits around what he considers necessary. He does not dream of getting rich at someone else's expense. More than anything, he sacrifices himself on the altar of holding on to things.

Weak, timid, crafty, mistrustful, and above all prudent and circumspect, never aggressive, indifferent to the evils committed by his neighbor, the miser at least does nothing to cause those evils. Before all else, he wants certainty, hard matter, or to put it differently, he is greedy only because he believes only in facts, in the gold he has in his safe.

Speculations, even the safest loans, hold little allure for him, for no matter how improbable it might be, there is always a chance of loss in any speculation, and he will always sacrifice the possibility of interest to the risk of exposing his capital.

Such a timorous man, who is so contemptuous of possibilities, will thus rarely possess the savage energy of the scoundrel who will risk being sent to the penal colonies or, indeed, risk his life in order to get his hands on a fortune. "Risk" is a word that doesn't exist in the vocabulary of the miser.

It was in this sense that Jacques Ferrand was, shall we say, something of a curiosity, a hitherto perhaps unknown variety of the species *miser.* For Jacques Ferrand took risks—big risks. He counted on his subtlety, which was extreme; his hypocrisy, which was profound; his intelligence, which was supple and creative; and his audacity, which was the devil's own. He made use of all of these qualities to assure himself impunity for his crimes, which were already numerous.

Jacques Ferrand was even more of an exception. Ordinarily, the kinds of adventurous and energetic people who fear nothing in their pursuit of gold are plagued by burning passions: for gambling, luxury, fine food, or great debauchery. Jacques Ferrand had none of these violent, disruptive needs. Deceitful and patient when he committed forgery, cruel and determined when he murdered, he was as sober and orderly as Harpagon.[112] Only one passion, or rather only one appetite, was capable of working him up into a frenzy. It was a shameful, ignoble passion, almost ferocious in its animality: this passion was lust: the lust of the beast, of the wolf or the tiger. When the bitter, tainted yeast of lust bubbled up in the veins of this robust man, gusts of ravenous heat made their way up to his face, and carnal effervescence obstructed his intelligence. At such times, he occasionally forgot his usual devious caution, and he became, as we have noted, a tiger or a wolf; to wit, his initial violence against Louise.

Administering the soporific, and then the daring hypocrisy with which he had denied his crime, were more his style, if one could call it that, than open force. Coarse desire, brutal ardor, contemptuous savagery:

112. Harpagon is the name of the miser in Molière's play *The Miser.* [TN]

that was how this man experienced love. This is to say, as his conduct with Louise proved, that he had no notion of kindness, goodness, or generosity. The loan of thirteen hundred francs that he had made to Morel at high interest was, as far as Ferrand was concerned, a trap, a tool of coercion, and a good business deal, all wrapped into one. Certain of the gem-cutter's integrity, he knew he would be reimbursed sooner or later; but only the profound effect Louise's beauty had on him would have led him to lend out that strategically placed sum.

Other than this weakness, Jacques Ferrand cared only for gold. He loved gold for gold's sake. Not for the pleasures it procured, because he was a stoic. Not for the pleasures it could potentially procure, for he was not enough of a poet to enjoy such speculation as some misers do. As to what belonged to him, he loved possessing it for its own sake. As for what belonged to others: if it was a large deposit, for example, loyally confided to him thanks to his reputation for uprightness, he felt the same wrenching pain, the same despair when it came time to return it that the goldsmith Cardillac[113] experienced when he had to part from an ornament that his exquisite taste had turned into an artistic masterpiece. The solicitor regarded his sterling reputation for integrity as an artistic masterpiece in its own right. But a deposit was also a jewel from which he could not separate himself without feeling terrible regret.

How much care, shrewdness, deception, and cleverness—in other words, how much art—had he not put into attracting a particular sum of money into his coffers, into perfecting that sparkling reputation for integrity in which the most precious signs of confidence came to be embedded, like pearls and diamonds in the gold of Cardillac's diadems! The more the famous goldsmith perfected his art, it is said, the more highly he valued his ornaments, regarding each new one as his masterpiece and ruing the necessity of having to give it up. The more Jacques Ferrand perfected himself as a criminal, the more he prided himself on the brilliant, staggering signs of trust accorded to him. He, too, always considered his latest swindle to be his greatest masterpiece.

In the coming pages of this story we will see the means he used—and they were truly prodigious accomplishments of plotting and strategy—to appropriate several very considerable sums of money without having to face any consequences of doing so. His mysterious hidden life made him experience the same kind of constant terror that the gambler experiences at the height of his play. Against everyone else's fortune he staked his

113. Cardillac was a jeweler in the time of Louis XIV who was known for the beauty of the jewelry he created and also for the difficulty with which he released possession of it to the clients who paid for it, sometimes leading him to rob them. E. T. A. Hoffmann tells the story in *Mademoiselle de Scudéry*. The story is also the basis of the twentieth-century opera by Hindemith. [TN]

hypocrisy, his deceptiveness, his brain—and the game was all too easy, as they say. For, except for his fear of human justice, which he characterized in a coarse and energetic fashion as "a chimney that could fall on his head," losing meant merely not winning, as far as he was concerned. And further, he was such a talented criminal that, in his bitter irony, he could see constant profit in the limitless esteem, the confidence without boundaries that he inspired not only in his legions of rich clients but also in the lower middle classes and workers who lived in his neighborhood. A great number of them placed their money with him, saying, "He's not charitable, it's true; he's overly pious, which is unfortunate; but he's a safer bet than the government and the savings banks."

Despite his rare skill, this man had committed two errors that almost always befall even the most devious criminals. Forced by circumstances, it is true, but still, he had taken on two accomplices. This immense weakness, as he said, had been partly remediated. Neither of the two accomplices could take him down without his being taken down himself. And neither of them would have anything to gain by going to this extreme other than to open themselves and the solicitor to society's punishment of them. On this front, then, he was not anxious. In any case, since he was not done with crime, the dangers of having accomplices were counterbalanced by their criminal assistance, of which he still made use at times.

A few words now about Monsieur Ferrand's physical appearance, and then we will take the reader into the solicitor's office, where we will meet up once again with the principal characters of this narrative. Monsieur Ferrand was fifty years old, but he didn't even seem forty. He was of medium build, stooping, wide in the shoulders, vigorous, square, stocky, ruddy, and hairy as a bear. His hair was plastered to his temples; his forehead was bald, his eyebrows barely visible. His bilious complexion was hard to discern under a copious spray of freckles. Yet when a vivid emotion shook him up, this fawn-colored, earthen mask became suffused with blood and turned a livid shade of red.

His face was as smooth as the head of a corpse, to put it in vulgar terms. He had a snub nose that looked like a pushpin, and his lips were so thin, so imperceptible, that his mouth looked like it was etched into his face. When he smiled his wicked and sinister smile, one could see the bottoms of his teeth, which were almost all black and rotten. Always shaven up to the temples, his pallid face wore an expression that was at once austere and beatific, impassible and rigid, cold and reflective. His little black eyes, quick, piercing, and constantly on the move, disappeared under his large green eyeglasses.

Jacques Ferrand could see perfectly well, but hiding behind his glasses afforded him the great advantage of observing others without being observed; he knew how often a glance unwittingly gives one away. In spite of his imperturbable daring, two or three times in his life, he had encountered certain gazes that were so powerful and magnetic that he had had to lower his eyes. And yet, in certain life-and-death circumstances, it can be fatal to lower one's gaze before the man who is interrogating, accusing, or judging you. Monsieur Ferrand's large glasses were thus a sort of sheltered entrenchment, behind which he could scrutinize the smallest maneuvers of his enemies—for everyone was the solicitor's enemy, because everyone was to some degree his dupe. Accusers are after all nothing but former dupes who have been enlightened or who have risen up in revolt.

In his dress he tended toward a carelessness that verged on slovenliness, or perhaps it was just that he was naturally filthy. His face was shaven every two or three days; his scalp was dirty and rough. His flat fingernails were encased in black, and he smelled like a goat. He wore old, shredded waistcoats, greasy hats, threadbare ties, blackened wool stockings, and ungainly shoes. All of these traits recommended him singularly as a virtuous man as far as his clients were concerned. They thought he was indifferent to worldly pleasures; he had about him an odor of practical philosophy that they found charming.

People said he would have sacrificed any tastes, any passion, any weakness to the trust his clients placed in him. He earned perhaps sixty thousand francs a year, and his household was composed of one female servant and an old housekeeper. His sole pleasure was to go each Sunday to mass and vespers. He knew of no opera to equal the grave sound of the organ, no worldly society that was worth as much as an evening spent peacefully at the fireside with the parish priest after a frugal dinner. He derived all his joy from his own integrity, his pride in his honor, his pleasure in his religion. Such was the judgment of Monsieur Jacques Ferrand's contemporaries upon this rare and great man of goodwill.

CHAPTER 14

THE OFFICE

Monsieur Ferrand's office looked like any other office, his clerks like other clerks. One entered it by way of an antechamber furnished with four old armchairs. In the office itself, surrounded by racks with pigeonholes stacked with the boxes containing the files of Monsieur Ferrand's clients, five young men, hunched over black wood desks, laughed, chattered, or scribbled madly. A waiting room, also full of boxes, was customarily occupied by the head clerk. Next came another empty room that separated the solicitor's office from the waiting room, in order to provide greater privacy. Such was the arrangement of this laboratory where all kinds of transactions were executed.

An antique cuckoo clock placed between the two windows of the office had just chimed two o'clock in the afternoon. The clerks were in some kind of agitation; a few fragments of their conversation will reveal the cause of this commotion.

"Certainly, if someone had asserted that François Germain was a thief," said one of the young men, "I would have said, 'You're lying!'"

"Me, too!"

"Me, too!"

"I was so upset to see him arrested and taken away by the police, I was, that I couldn't eat my lunch. But that turned out to be for the best, seeing as I didn't have to eat Old Lady Séraphin's usual ratatouille."

"Seventeen thousand francs, now that's real money!"

"That's a good chunk of change, for sure."

"And to think that in the fifteen months since Germain had become a cashier he'd never lost track of even a centime in the boss's safe."

"I think the boss was wrong to have Germain arrested, since that poor boy swore on everything he holds holy that he had only taken thirteen hundred francs' worth of gold."

"And all the more since he brought the thirteen hundred francs in gold back this morning in order to put them back in the safe, just when the boss had sent for the police."

"That's the problem with people who are as rigidly honest as our boss. They have no heart."

"It's true, you should think twice before destroying a poor young man who had behaved well up to then."

"Monsieur Ferrand said that it was all about setting an example."

"Example of what? It's no example for people who are honest, and people who aren't know perfectly well that they run the risk of being caught if they steal."

"This house is giving the police superintendent plenty of business, at any rate."

"What do you mean?"

"Honestly! This morning, that poor Louise, and now Germain . . ."

"I don't understand what the business with Germain is all about."

"But he confessed!"

"It's true he confessed he had taken thirteen hundred francs, but he swore up and down that he didn't take the other fifteen thousand francs in banknotes and the other seven hundred francs that were missing from the safe."

"Indeed. Since he already confessed one thing, why not confess the other?"

"It's true. It's the same punishment for fifteen hundred francs as for fifteen thousand."

"Yes, but a scoundrel can tell you, you can stow the fifteen thousand francs away, and then, when you get out of prison, you can start a nice little business."

"That's not so dumb, either."

"You can say and do all you want to deny it, but there's something fishy going on."

"And to think, Germain would always defend the boss when we called him two-faced!"

"It's true, though. 'Why shouldn't the boss go to mass?' he said to us. 'That doesn't mean you have to go.'"

"Hey, here's Chalamel coming back from his errands. Isn't he going to be surprised!"

"What's up, guys? Has something new happened about that poor Louise?"

"If you hadn't dawdled on your errands, you idler, you might know what's going on."

"Hey, you think it's just a hop, skip, and a jump from here to rue de Chaillot?"

"Yeah, right. Right!"

"Well, what about that notorious Viscount de Saint-Remy?"

"He still hasn't come?"

"No."

"But his horses were all harnessed, and he let me know through his servant that he was going to come right away. The servant said he didn't seem happy. Ah! Gentlemen, that was a pretty little mansion. Real comfort—it looked like one of those little lord's castles from olden times, the kind they talk about in Faublas.[114] Ah, Faublas! Now there's my hero, my role model!" said Chalamel as he put down his umbrella and removed his clogs.

"I think that viscount must be facing debts and debtors' prison."

"There's a demand for thirty-four thousand francs that the bailiff sent here, because it's supposed to be paid at the office. The creditor prefers it that way—I don't know why."

"He'd better be able to pay now, that pretty viscount, now that he's come back yesterday evening from the countryside where he'd been holed up for the previous three days to escape the debtors' police."

"But how come they haven't already seized his property?"

"He's no dummy! It's not his house. All of his belongings are in the name of his servant, who is supposed to rent the place to him furnished, just as his horses and his carriages are in his stable manager's name. That guy says he rents a magnificent carriage and horses to the viscount for a certain amount of money per month. Oh, he's a sly one, that Monsieur de Saint-Remy. But what were you saying? That he's come back here again?"

"Would you believe that two hours ago the boss came running in here like a madman? 'Germain isn't here?' he cried. 'No, monsieur.' 'Well, that wretch stole seventeen thousand francs from me last night,' the boss went on."

"Germain, steal? Come on."

"'You'll see.'

"'How can it be, monsieur? Are you sure? It can't be possible!'—that's what we were all shouting."

"'I am telling you, gentlemen, that yesterday I had put in the drawer of the desk where he works fifteen thousand-franc notes, as well as two thousand francs in gold, in a little box. Everything is gone.' At that moment, old Monsieur Marriton, the doorman, came in saying, 'Monsieur, the police are on the way.'"

"And Germain?"

"I'm getting to that. The boss said to the doorkeeper, 'As soon as Monsieur Germain gets here, send him here, to the office, without saying anything to him. I want to catch him out in front of you, gentlemen,' said

---

114. *Les amours du Chevalier de Faublas* (*The Loves of the Knight Faublas*) was a libertine novel, published in three parts, starting in 1787. It was written by Jean-Baptiste Louvet de Couvray, a man of letters, radical philosopher, and bookseller who took an active, if fraught, role in the French Revolution. [TN]

the boss. After a quarter of an hour, poor Germain arrived like there was nothing going on. Old Lady Séraphin had just brought us the ratatouille. He greeted the boss and said hello to us, calm as anything. 'Germain, you're not having lunch?' asked Monsieur Ferrand. 'No, monsieur. Thank you, I'm not hungry.' 'You're rather late.' 'Yes, monsieur, I was obliged to go to Belleville this morning.' 'No doubt in order to hide the money you stole from me!' the boss cried out in a terrifying tone of voice."

"And what did Germain do?"

"The poor boy turned pale as a sheet, and answered right away, stuttering, 'Monsieur, I beg of you, don't destroy me.'"

"So he'd stolen it, then?"

"I'm getting there, Chalamel. 'Don't destroy me!' he said to the boss. 'Are you confessing, then, you wretch?' 'Yes, monsieur, but here is the missing money. I thought I would be able to replace it this morning before you got up. Unfortunately, a person who had a little of my money and who I thought I could meet up with yesterday evening at her home had been in Belleville for the last two days. I had to go there this morning. That's why I'm late. Have pity, monsieur, don't destroy me! When I took the money, I knew that I could replace it this morning. Here are the thirteen hundred francs in gold.' 'What do you mean, thirteen hundred francs?' cried Monsieur Ferrand. 'As if it's just a matter of thirteen hundred francs! You stole from the desk in the room on the first floor fifteen bills in a green wallet, each one for a thousand francs, and two thousand francs in gold.' 'Me? Never!' cried the poor Germain, completely staggered. 'I took thirteen hundred francs in gold from you, but not one sou more. I didn't see any wallet in the drawer. There were only two thousand francs in gold in a box.' 'Oh! You despicable liar!' cried the boss. 'You stole thirteen hundred francs, you could have stolen more besides. The courts will decide. Oh, I will show no mercy for such shameless embezzling. I will make an example of you.'

"Finally, my poor, dear Chalamel, the police arrived at that point, along with the superintendent's secretary, to draw up a report. They took hold of Germain, and that was that!"

"Could it really be? Germain, the most honest guy there is?"

"It seemed very odd to us, too."

"Well, you know, you do have to admit one thing: Germain was a little crazy. He would never let anyone ever know where he lived."

"That's true enough."

"There was always something mysterious about him."

"That doesn't prove he stole fifteen thousand francs."

"No doubt."

"I was just saying."

"Oh, well! It comes as news to me. It's like being hit upside the head. Germain . . . Germain, who seemed so honest . . . you could have given him the sacrament without his needing to confess first!"

"But sometimes it seemed he had some kind of presentiment of something bad that was going to happen to him."

"Why?"

"For some time, he seemed to have something eating away at him."

"Maybe it was related to Louise."

"Louise?"

"As to that, I'm just repeating what Old Lady Séraphin was saying this morning."

"What is it, then? What?"

"That he was Louise's lover—and the father of her child!"

"What a cad!"

"Come on, now!"

"Oh, please!"

"That can't be true!"

"How do you know this, Chalamel?"

"It wasn't even two weeks ago that Germain told me, in confidence, that he was crazy in love—but crazy, crazy in love—with a little working girl, a real virtuous one, whom he had known in the house where he had lived. He had tears in his eyes when he spoke of her."

"Look at Chalamel, look at Chalamel! What an old-fashioned softy!"

"He says that Faublas is his hero, and he's such a good little boy, such a blockhead, such an old fogey that he doesn't understand that you can be in love with one and the lover of the other!"

"I'm telling you that Germain was speaking seriously."

At that moment, the head clerk entered the office. "Well! Chalamel!" he said. "Have you finished making your rounds?"

"Yes, Monsieur Dubois. I went to Monsieur de Saint-Remy's place. He's going to come here soon to pay."

"And you went to see the Countess MacGregor?"

"That, too. Here is the answer."

"And to the Countess d'Orbigny?"

"She thanks the boss kindly. She arrived yesterday morning from Normandy; she didn't expect to have the answer so soon. Here is the letter. I also stopped by to see the Marquis d'Harville's administrator, as he had requested, for the fees for the contract that I went to have signed the other day at his mansion."

"You had told him, of course, that there was no rush?"

"Yes, but the administrator wanted to pay it anyway. Here's the money. Ah! I forgot the card that was here, downstairs with the doorkeeper. It had some writing on it (the card, not the doorman). This gentleman asked to see the boss, and he left this."

"'Walter Murph,'" the head clerk read out. "Beneath, in pencil, it says, 'Will return at three on an important business matter.' I don't recognize the name."

"Ah! I also forgot," said Chalamel, "that Monsieur Badinot said it was fine, that Monsieur Ferrand should do as he thought best, that whatever he wanted to do would be fine."

"He didn't give you a written response?"

"No, monsieur, he said he didn't have the time."

"Very good."

"Monsieur Charles Robert will also be here later today to talk to the boss. It seems he fought a duel yesterday with the Duke de Lucenay."

"Was he wounded?"

"I don't think so. They would have told me at his place if he had been."

"Look, here's a carriage, and it's stopping."

"Some beautiful horses there! And they've got spirit!"

"And that fat English coachman, with his white wig and brown livery with silver braids! And he's got epaulettes like a colonel!"

"He's got to be an ambassador, for sure."

"And his messenger boy, he's wearing a lot of silver, too!"

"And what a mustache!"

"Hold on," said Chalamel. "That's the Viscount de Saint-Remy's carriage!"

"Not too showy, huh? Lord have mercy on us!"

Soon afterward, Monsieur de Saint-Remy was on his way into the office.

CHAPTER 15

MONSIEUR DE SAINT-REMY

We have described Monsieur de Saint-Remy's charming features, his exquisite elegance, and his stylish bearing. He had arrived the day before from the Arnouville farm (the Duchess de Lucenay's property), where he had found refuge from Malicorne and Bourdin, the debtors' police who were pursuing him.

Monsieur de Saint-Remy entered the office brusquely, his hat on his head, looking haughty and proud. With his eyes half closed, he asked in a highly imperious manner, without looking at anyone, "Where is the solicitor?"

"Monsieur Ferrand is working in his office," said the head clerk. "If you wouldn't mind waiting a moment, monsieur, he will be able to see you shortly."

"What do you mean, wait?"

"But, sir—"

"I don't want to hear any 'buts,' monsieur. Go tell him Monsieur de Saint-Remy is here. This solicitor making me wait in his antechamber is really too much. It stinks of cooking in here!"

"Please follow me into the next room, monsieur," said the head clerk. "I'll go in right now to let Monsieur Ferrand know you're here." Monsieur de Saint-Remy shrugged his shoulders and followed him. After a quarter of an hour, which seemed more than long enough to Monsieur de Saint-Remy and transformed his disdain into anger, the head clerk ushered him into the solicitor's office.

The contrast between these two men was striking. Both of them were profoundly adept at comprehending faces and generally able to judge at a glance the people with whom they had business. Monsieur de Saint-Remy was seeing Jacques Ferrand for the first time. He was struck by the look of this pale, rigid, impassive face, with its eyes hidden by enormous green glasses and its skull half covered by an old black silk cap.

The solicitor was sitting at his desk on a leather armchair next to a dilapidated fireplace full of ashes, in which two blackened embers still smoked. Green percaline curtains that were almost in shreds, hanging from small iron rods over the windows, hid the inner windowpanes and cast a livid and sinister beam of light into this already somber office. Some black wood chests filled with labeled boxes, a few cherrywood chairs reupholstered in Utrecht yellow velvet, a mahogany clock, a yellow tile floor that was humid and icy, a ceiling full of cracks and ornamented with garlands of spiderwebs: such was the sanctum sanctorum of Monsieur Jacques Ferrand.

Before the viscount had taken two steps into the office or said a single word, the solicitor, who knew him by reputation, already hated him. In the first place, he saw in him a rival in deceit. And then, since Monsieur Ferrand had a lowly and ignoble-looking face, he detested elegance, grace, and youth in others, especially when these advantages were coupled with a supremely insolent attitude.

The solicitor customarily assumed a rude, nearly vulgar, abrupt tone with his clients, who only esteemed him that much more for acting like a German peasant. He determined to intensify his brutishness with Monsieur de Saint-Remy.

The latter, who also knew nothing of Jacques Ferrand except his reputation, expected him to be some kind of bookkeeper, either good-natured or buffoonish. The viscount always figured that people known for proverbial integrity, of whom Jacques Ferrand was said to be the paradigm, were ninnies.

This was far from the case here, however. The attitude of this bookkeeper aroused in the viscount an indefinable feeling of half fear, half hatred, even though he had no real reason either to fear or to hate him. And so, as a result of his own strong-willed personality, Monsieur de Saint-Remy exaggerated his usual insolence and conceit. The solicitor kept his cap on his head; the viscount kept his hat on his own head and, as he reached the door, exclaimed in a haughty, biting voice, "Really, it's not customary, monsieur, that you should be so unkind as to have me come here instead of just sending for the money for the drafts that I underwrote for that Badinot. The fool set the police on me over them. You tell me that, in addition to that, you have a very important message for me. So be it. But then you shouldn't have made me wait for a quarter of an hour in your antechamber. That's bad manners, monsieur."

Monsieur Ferrand, imperturbable, finished some sums he was doing, wiped his pen methodically on a water-soaked sponge that was wrapped around his chipped porcelain inkstand, and turned his glacial, ashen, pug-nosed, bespectacled face upon the viscount. His face looked like that of a corpse whose eyes had been replaced by large, fixed, dull, green pupils. After reflecting for a moment in silence, the solicitor said to the viscount, in a brusque and curt tone, "Where is the money?"

This sangfroid exasperated Monsieur de Saint-Remy. He, the darling of women, the envy of men, the paragon of the best society Paris had to offer, the feared duelist—he couldn't produce any more effect than this on this nobody of a solicitor! This scene disgusted him. Although he was in a conversation with Jacques Ferrand, his personal pride revolted against the situation. "Where are the drafts?" he replied, just as tersely.

From the end of one of his fingers, which were as hard as iron and covered in red hair, the solicitor, without answering, tapped on a large leather wallet that was sitting next to him.

Determined to be just as laconic, but seething with anger, the viscount took out of the pocket of his coat a little notebook made of Russian leather that fastened with gold clips, removed forty bills of a thousand francs each, and showed them to the solicitor.

"How much?" the latter asked him.

"Forty thousand francs."

"Give them to me."

"Take them and let's get this over with quickly. Do your job, take your money, give me back those drafts," said the viscount as he threw the packet of banknotes on the table.

The solicitor took them, got up, went to the window to examine them closely, and turned them over one by one with such scrupulous and insulting attention that Monsieur de Saint-Remy turned white with rage. As if he had sensed the thoughts that roiled the viscount, the solicitor shook his head, turned partially toward him, and said to him in an indefinable tone of voice, "You run into them."

Stunned into momentary silence, Monsieur de Saint-Remy replied drily, "What do you run into?"

"Counterfeit banknotes," answered the solicitor, continuing to examine with the utmost care the ones he was holding.

"And what leads to your making this remark to me?"

Jacques Ferrand stopped for a moment and looked pointedly at the viscount through his glasses. Then, shrugging his shoulders slightly, he continued to examine the notes without saying a word.

"Good God, monsieur! I'll have you know that when I ask someone a question, I expect an answer!" Monsieur de Saint-Remy, irritated by Jacques Ferrand's calm demeanor, exclaimed.

"Those are good," said the solicitor as he turned back toward his desk, where he took a little bundle of stamped papers to which were attached two bills of exchange. He then put one of the thousand-franc notes and three rolls of one hundred francs on the debt file and said to Monsieur de Saint-Remy, pointing with his fingertip to the money and titles, "There's what you get back from the forty thousand francs. My client asked me to collect the expenses."

The viscount could barely contain himself as Jacques Ferrand did his tabulations. Instead of answering him and taking the money, he cried out in a voice trembling with anger, "I asked you, monsieur, why you said, with regard to the banknotes that I gave you, that you could run into counterfeits."

"Why?"

"Yes."

"Because I sent for you here in connection with counterfeiting." The solicitor fixed his gaze on the viscount through his green glasses.

"What have I to do with counterfeiting?"

After a moment of silence, Monsieur Ferrand said to the viscount in a sad and severe manner, "Do you know, monsieur, what a solicitor does?"

"Both the calculations and the functions of the job, monsieur, are straightforward. I had forty thousand francs a moment ago, and now I have thirteen hundred left."

"You are very amusing, monsieur. I will now tell you that a solicitor is, with regard to worldly matters, what a confessor is to spiritual matters. As a matter of his occupation, he is often privy to vile secrets."

"And so, monsieur?"

"He often finds himself forced to be in contact with scoundrels."

"And from this follows, monsieur . . . ?"

"He must, to the extent that he can, prevent an honorable name from being dragged through the mud."

"What do I have to do with any of this?"

"Your father left you a respected name on which you bring dishonor, monsieur!"

"Exactly what do you presume to say to me?"

"If it weren't for the sympathy that this name inspires in all honest people, instead of being called here before me, you would be called before the magistrate at this moment."

"I don't know what you're talking about."

"Two months ago, through the intermediary of a business agent, you discounted a bill for fifty-eight thousand francs, underwritten by the house of Meulaert and Company in Hamburg, in the name of William Smith and payable in three months at the office of Monsieur Grimaldi, a Parisian banker."

"So?"

"That bill was forged."

"That isn't true!"

"The bill was forged! Meulaert and Company had never contracted an engagement with William Smith. They don't know him."

"Could that be true?" cried Monsieur de Saint-Remy with as much surprise as indignation. "I was then horribly deceived, monsieur, for I took the bill as having the value of ready cash."

"From whom?"

"From William Smith himself. The Meulaert Company is so well known, and I knew Monsieur William Smith's integrity so well myself, that I accepted the bill in payment for a sum he owed me."

"There has never been any William Smith. He's entirely imaginary."

"Monsieur, this is an insult!"

"His signature is forged and invented, like all the rest."

"I am telling you, monsieur, that Monsieur William Smith exists. But I have no doubt been the victim of a terrible fraud."

"Oh, you poor young man!"

"What does that mean?"

"In a word, the current possessor of the bill is convinced that you have committed a forgery."

"Monsieur!"

"He claims to have the proof. The day before yesterday, he came to ask me to bring you before me and to propose returning the forged draft to you in return for a transaction. Up to that point, everything was straightforward. Here's what isn't, and I'm only telling you about it for your information: he demands a hundred thousand francs, crowns, this very day. Otherwise, tomorrow at noon he will charge you with forgery in the office of the royal prosecutor."

"What an indignity!"

"And moreover it's ridiculous. You are ruined. You were pursued for a sum that you just paid me, thanks to who knows what resource. That's what I told this holder in due course. He answered me that a certain very rich great lady would not leave you in such straits."

"Enough, monsieur! Enough!"

"Another indignity, another absurdity! All right."

"So, monsieur, what do they want from me?"

"To exploit an unworthy action in an unworthy manner. I consented to tell you this proposition even as I shuddered before it as an honest man should. Now it's up to you. If you are guilty, choose between the criminal court or the blackmail. My conduct here is purely professional. I will not get involved to any further extent in such a filthy business. The holder in due course is an oil dealer named Monsieur Petit-Jean. He lives on the bank of the Seine, on the quai de Billy, number ten. Work things out with him. You should get along with him, if you're a forger, as he insists."

Monsieur de Saint-Remy had entered Jacques Ferrand's office with an insolent manner and his head held high. Although he had committed a few shameful actions in his life, he still retained a certain inbred pride, a natural courage which had never betrayed him. At the beginning of this interview, regarding the solicitor as an adversary unworthy of him, he had been happy to mock him. When Jacques Ferrand had spoken of a forgery, however, the viscount felt crushed. In turn, he found himself in the power of the solicitor.

Without the absolute control he had over himself, he would not have been able to hide the terrible blow that this unexpected revelation caused him since it could have incalculable consequences for him that the solicitor could not even suspect. After a moment of silence and reflection he resigned himself—this prideful, irritable man who was so vain in his bravura to implore the vulgar man who had so rudely spoken the austere language of probity. "Monsieur, you have given me proof of your interest, for which I thank you. I regret the harshness of my first words to you," said Monsieur de Saint-Remy, cordially.

"I have no interest in you whatsoever," the solicitor answered him brutally. "Your father was honor incarnate. I would not have wanted to see his name dragged into criminal court—that's all."

"I repeat to you, monsieur, that I am incapable of the crime of which I am being accused."

"Tell it to Monsieur Petit-Jean."

"But I swear to you, the absence of Monsieur Smith, who has so unworthily defrauded me—"

"Oh, that vile Smith!"

"The absence of Monsieur Smith puts me in a cruel bind. I am innocent. If they charge me, I will prove it, but such a charge always makes a gallant man cringe."

"And so?"

"Be generous enough to use the sum I just gave you to give the person who holds the draft less reason to go after me."

"That money belongs to my client! It's sacred!"

"But in two or three days I'll reimburse you."

"You won't be able to."

"I have resources."

"None at all—none that you can attest to, at least. Your furniture and your horses don't belong to you anymore, you say, which looks to me like a despicable fraud."

"You are very harsh, monsieur. But even admitting that, can't I liquidate everything under such desperate circumstances? It's just that, since it's impossible for me to come up with a hundred thousand francs by tomorrow at noon, I'm begging you to use the money I just gave you to get that unfortunate draft away from him. Or else, you, who are so rich, give me an advance. Don't leave me in this position."

"Me, answer for a hundred thousand francs for you? You must be crazy."

"Monsieur, I beg of you, in the name of my father of whom you spoke just now, be good enough to—"

"I am good to those who deserve it," the solicitor said rudely. "I am an honest man, and I hate swindlers. I would not be unhappy to see one of those pretty, impious, debauched boys who recognize neither faith nor the law pilloried just once to set an example for the others. But I hear your horses getting impatient out there, Monsieur Viscount," said the solicitor as he smiled, showing the tips of his black teeth.

At that moment a knock was heard on the door of the office. "What is it?" asked Jacques Ferrand.

"Madame the Countess d'Orbigny," said the head clerk.

"Ask her to be so kind as to wait a moment."

"That's the Marquise d'Harville's stepmother!" cried Monsieur de Saint-Remy.

"Yes, monsieur. She has an appointment with me. And so, if you please—"

"Don't say a word about any of this, monsieur!" Monsieur de Saint-Remy exclaimed, threateningly.

"I told you, monsieur, that a solicitor is as discreet as a confessor."

Jacques Ferrand rang; the clerk appeared.

"Have Madame d'Orbigny come in." Then, turning to the viscount, he said, "Take these thirteen hundred francs, monsieur. It will be a deposit for Monsieur Petit-Jean."

Madame d'Orbigny, formerly Madame Roland, entered at the moment at which Monsieur de Saint-Remy was leaving, his features contracted with anger at having humiliated himself to no good end before the solicitor.

"Oh! Hello, Monsieur de Saint-Remy," Madame d'Orbigny said to him. "I haven't seen you in ages."

"Indeed, madame, since Harville's marriage, for which I served as a witness, I have not had the honor of meeting you," said Monsieur de Saint-Remy, leaning forward and wearing an expression on his face that was smiling and affable. "Have you been living in Normandy since then?"

"Oh, dear, yes. Monsieur d'Orbigny can only live in the country now, and whatever he likes, I like. What you see before you is a real woman of the provinces. I haven't come to Paris since the marriage of my dear stepdaughter to the excellent Monsieur d'Harville. Do you see him sometimes?"

"Monsieur d'Harville has become very prickly and very morose. One rarely sees him in society," said Monsieur de Saint-Remy with a shade of impatience. This conversation was intolerable to him, both because it fell at an awkward moment and because it seemed to amuse the solicitor greatly. But the stepmother of Madame d'Harville, delighted to have this meeting with an elegant man, was not a woman to release her prey so quickly.

"And my dear stepdaughter," she went on, "is not as prickly, I hope, as her husband?"

"Madame d'Harville is very fashionable and is always surrounded by admirers, as pretty women always are. I fear that I am keeping you too long, madame."

"Not at all, I assure you. It's my good fortune to run into the most elegant man in Paris, the king of fashion. Ten minutes from now, I will be as up-to-date on Paris as if I'd never left. And your dear friend Monsieur de Lucenay, who was a witness to the marriage of Monsieur d'Harville along with you?"

"More eccentric than ever. He left for the Orient, and he returned just in time to receive a sword thrust—not a very deep one."

"Poor duke! And his wife is still beautiful and ravishing?"

"You know, madame, that I have the honor of being one of her best friends, so my account on this matter must be biased. Please, madame, when you return to Aubiers, do me the favor of remembering me to Monsieur d'Orbigny."

"He will be very happy, I can assure you, to receive your charming greeting. He often asks after you and your exploits. He always says that you remind him of the Duke de Lauzun."

"That comparison is an honor in itself. But unfortunately for me, it is kinder than it is true. Adieu, madame. I do not dare to hope that you will be able to receive me before you depart."

"I would be sorry if you took the trouble to come to see me! I am camped out for a few days in furnished rooms, but if, this summer or autumn, you happen to pass by our home on your way to one of those fashionable châteaux in which the great ladies fight each other over the pleasure of receiving a visit from you, spare us a few days, if only to mark the contrast between us and them. You can rest with us poor country folk from that dazzling life at the château that's always so elegant but so riotous because wherever you are, it's always a holiday!"

"Madame . . ."

"I don't need to tell you how happy Monsieur d'Orbigny and I will be to have you visit. But good-bye, monsieur. I fear this kind gruff man (she gestured toward the solicitor) won't put up with our chatter any longer."

"On the contrary, madame, on the contrary," said Ferrand in a manner that only increased Monsieur de Saint-Remy's pent-up rage.

"Don't you think Monsieur Ferrand is a terrible man?" Madame d'Orbigny asked, pretending to be a scatterbrain. "Be careful of him, though. Since you are fortunate enough to have him in charge of your affairs, he will scold you constantly. He's pitiless. But what am I saying? On the contrary, a great man like yourself, having Monsieur Ferrand as your solicitor—that's a seal of approval, for everyone knows that he never lets his clients get into trouble, or otherwise he gives up their accounts. Oh, he doesn't want to be the solicitor of just anyone . . ." And then, addressing Jacques Ferrand, she said, "You know, you Puritan you, that you've performed quite an act of conversion there. You have made the most elegant man, the king of fashion, behave himself."

"It is indeed a conversion, madame. The viscount is leaving my office completely different from when he entered it."

"When I say that you perform miracles, there's nothing surprising about it! You are a saint."

"Ah, madame. You are flattering me," said Jacques Ferrand, modestly.

Monsieur de Saint-Remy bowed deeply to Madame d'Orbigny. Then, as he left the solicitor, he tried one more time to move him. He said in a casual manner that betrayed deep anxiety nonetheless, "So you're certain, my dear Monsieur Ferrand, that you don't want to give me what I was asking for?"

"Some folly, perhaps? Be inexorable, my dear Puritan!" cried Madame d'Orbigny, laughing.

"You understand, monsieur, that I cannot go against the wishes of such a beautiful lady."

"My dear Monsieur Ferrand, let's speak seriously here . . . of serious things . . . You know that the thing I'm talking about . . . is very serious. So you're certain that you will refuse me?" the viscount asked in barely disguised anguish.

The solicitor was cruel enough to seem to hesitate for a moment. Monsieur de Saint-Remy had a moment of hope.

"What, you man of iron, are you giving in?" Madame d'Harville's mother-in-law said, laughing. "Does he cast an irresistible spell over you, too, then?"

"Honestly, madame, I was on the verge of giving in, as you say, but you have made me blush at my weakness," answered Monsieur Ferrand. Then, turning to the viscount, he said to him in a voice that made the latter understand perfectly well what he meant, "*Seriously,*" he stressed this word, "that would be impossible. I cannot tolerate that you should commit such foolishness on a mere whim. Monsieur, I think of myself as my clients' tutor. I have no other family, and I would regard myself as complicit in their follies if I let them commit them."

"Oh! You're such a Puritan! Look what a Puritan he is!" said Madame d'Orbigny.

"In any case, go to see Monsieur Petit-Jean. He will feel, I'm sure, the same way I do. Like me, he will tell you . . . no!"

Monsieur de Saint-Remy walked out, desperate.

After a moment of reflection, he said, "There's no other choice." Then, to his horseman, who was holding open the door to his carriage, he said, "To the Lucenay mansion."

While Monsieur de Saint-Remy makes his way to the duchess's home, we will let our readers listen in on the conversation between Monsieur Ferrand and Madame d'Harville's stepmother.

CHAPTER 16

THE WILL

The reader may have forgotten the portrait Madame d'Harville sketched of her stepmother. At the risk of repeating ourselves, then, Madame d'Orbigny is a small, thin, blond woman with eyelashes that are nearly white. Her eyes are round and pale blue, her speech is honeyed, her gaze is hypocritical, and her manner is both insinuating and insidious. A study of her false and perfidious physiognomy reveals in it something like underhanded cruelty.

"What a charming young man that Monsieur de Saint-Remy is!" said Madame d'Orbigny to Jacques Ferrand when the viscount had left.

"Yes, charming. But, madame, let's discuss our business. You wrote to me from Normandy to say that you wanted to consult me on some serious matters."

"Haven't you always been my advisor since that good Doctor Polidori sent me your way? Speaking of him, have you heard anything about him lately?" Madame d'Orbigny asked with what seemed like perfect disinterest.

"Since his departure from Paris he hasn't written to me once," the solicitor answered with no less indifference.

We should alert the reader that each of these two characters was shamelessly lying to the other. The solicitor had seen Polidori (one of his two accomplices) recently and had proposed that he go to Asnières, to the home of the Martials, the freshwater pirates of whom we will speak later. He asked him to go there, under the name of Doctor Vincent, we should say, in order to poison Louise Morel. For her part, the stepmother of Madame d'Harville had come to Paris precisely to confer in secret with this scoundrel, who, as we have said, hid under the name of César Bradamanti.

"But I am not here about the good doctor," Madame d'Harville's stepmother went on. "As you can see, I am very upset. My husband isn't well. His health gets weaker by the day. I have no serious fears, but his condition torments me—or rather, it torments him," said Madame d'Orbigny, as she wiped her eyes, which had teared up slightly.

"What's wrong?"

"He speaks incessantly of final arrangements to be made . . . of his will." Here Madame d'Orbigny hid her face in her handkerchief for a few minutes.

"That is certainly sad," said the solicitor, "but taking such a precaution suggests nothing in itself to cause any worries. In any case, what does Monsieur d'Orbigny intend in this regard, madame?"

"Heavens, what would I know? You will understand that when he starts talking about this subject, I don't let it go on in that direction for very long."

"But, after all, has he told you nothing concrete on the subject?"

"I believe," said Madame d'Orbigny in a perfectly disinterested manner, "I believe that he wants not only to give me everything that the law permits him to leave me but—oh, but no! I beg of you—please let us not speak of this!"

"Of what should we speak?"

"Alas! You are right, you merciless man! In spite of myself I must return to this sad subject that brings me here to you. Well, then! Monsieur d'Orbigny wants to push his goodness to me to the extent that he wants to misrepresent part of his fortune so he can make me a gift—of a considerable sum."

"But what about his daughter?" Monsieur Ferrand exclaimed, severely. "I must tell you that for the last year Monsieur d'Harville has put me in charge of his affairs. Recently I had him buy a magnificent tract of land. You know my toughness in business—it doesn't matter to me that Monsieur d'Harville is a client. What I argue for is the right thing to do. If your husband wants to make a decision with regard to his daughter, Madame d'Harville, that I do not find appropriate, I will tell you so with the most brutal honesty. You should not count on my cooperation in this matter. Clean and straightforward—that has always been my line of conduct."

"And mine as well! That's why I have been repeating endlessly to my husband exactly what you've just said: 'Your daughter has done you great wrong, yes, but that is not a reason to disinherit her.'"

"Very good. Well done. And what did he say to that?"

"He answered, 'I will leave my daughter twenty-five thousand francs in income. She had more than a million from her mother. Her husband has an enormous personal fortune of his own. Why can't I leave the rest to you, my tender friend, my guardian angel, the only support, the only consolation of my old age?' I am repeating these only too flattering words to you," said Madame d'Orbigny with a modest sigh, "in order to show you how good Monsieur d'Orbigny is to me. But in spite of that, I've always refused his offers. And so, he decided to ask me to come to see you."

"But I don't know Monsieur d'Orbigny."

"But he, like everyone else, knows your honesty."

"But why did he send you to me?"

"To cut short my refusals, my scruples, he said to me, 'I don't propose that you go to see my own solicitor because you'll think him too devoted to me personally. But I would absolutely adhere to the decision of Monsieur Jacques Ferrand, a man whose rigorous integrity is proverbial. If he finds your delicacy compromised by your acquiescence to my offer, we will speak of it no more. But otherwise, you will have to accept it.' 'I consent to that,' I said to Monsieur d'Orbigny; and that's how you became our arbiter. 'If he approves,' my husband added, 'I will give him full power to collect, in my name, my income on rents and portfolio. He will keep that sum on deposit, and after I die, my tender friend, you will at least have the existence you merit.'"

Never before perhaps had Monsieur Ferrand felt so profoundly the value of his glasses. Without them, Madame d'Orbigny would have been struck, no doubt, by the gleam that lit up his eyes at the mention of the word "deposit."

He answered, nonetheless, in a surly voice: "This is becoming truly bothersome. This must be the tenth or twelfth time someone has called me in as an arbiter. It's always on the pretext of my integrity. Everybody always says the same thing, 'Such integrity, such integrity!' Some advantage! All it ever brings me is trouble and worries."

"My good Monsieur Ferrand, please. Don't be hard on me. Just write to Monsieur d'Orbigny. He's awaiting your letter so as to be able to give you full power over his affairs, so as to be able to realize the sum he has in mind."

"How much is it, roughly?"

"He mentioned something like four to five hundred thousand francs, I think."

"Well, the sum is less considerable than I expected. After all, you're devoted to Monsieur d'Orbigny. His daughter is rich, and you have nothing. I can approve of this. It seems to me that, in all honesty, you owe it to him to accept his offer."

"Really? You think so?" asked Madame d'Orbigny, duped like everyone else as to the proverbial integrity of the solicitor. Polidori had never disabused her of this notion.

"You can accept it," he repeated.

"Then I will accept it," said Madame d'Orbigny with a sigh.

The head clerk knocked at the door. "What is it?" asked Monsieur Ferrand.

"It's Countess MacGregor."

"Have her wait a moment."

"I will leave you, then, my dear Monsieur Ferrand," said Madame d'Orbigny. "You will write to my husband, then, since that is what he wishes, and he will send you his power of attorney tomorrow."

"I will write to him."

"Good-bye, then, my good and worthy counselor."

"Oh, you have no idea, you society folk, how disagreeable it is to have to be in charge of such deposits. The responsibility weighs on us. I'm telling you, there's nothing worse than this beautiful reputation for integrity. All it does is bring on more drudgery."

"And the admiration of all honest people!"

"Thank God! I look forward to my recompense in a better world than this!" said Monsieur Ferrand, piously.

After Madame d'Orbigny left, Sarah MacGregor entered the room.

CHAPTER 17

COUNTESS MACGREGOR

Sarah walked into the solicitor's office with her usual poise and confidence. Jacques Ferrand did not know her, nor did he know the purpose of her visit. He became even more observant than usual, in the hope of acquiring another dupe. He looked very closely at the countess, and despite the calm exterior of this woman with a marble countenance, he noticed a slight quiver in her eyebrows that seemed to him to betray a hidden anxiety.

The solicitor got up from his armchair, pulled up a chair, gestured to Sarah that she should sit in it, and said to her, "You requested a meeting with me today, madame. I was very busy yesterday; I couldn't answer you until this morning. Please accept my sincere apologies."

"I wanted to see you, monsieur, about a matter of the greatest importance. Your reputation for being honest, kind, and obliging made me hope for success in the step I am taking."

The solicitor bowed his head slightly as he sat in his chair.

"I know, monsieur, that your discretion has been borne out by many tests of it."

"That's my duty, madame."

"You are an unswerving and incorruptible man, monsieur."

"Yes, madame."

"However, if someone said to you, 'Monsieur, it's up to you to save the life—no, more than the life, the sanity—of an unhappy mother,' would you have the heart to refuse?"

"Tell me the facts of the case, madame, and I will give you an answer."

"About fourteen years ago, at the end of December 1824, a man who was still young at the time, dressed in mourning, came to see you to propose your taking, as the basis for a life annuity for a three-year-old child whose parents wanted to remain anonymous, the sum of one hundred and fifty thousand francs."

"And so, madame?" said the solicitor, thus avoiding an affirmative response.

"You agreed to be responsible for this investment and to assure this child an annuity for life of eight thousand francs. Half of this revenue was to be invested for the child's benefit until it reached adulthood. The other half was supposed to be paid by you to the person who was taking care of this little girl."

"And so, madame?"

"After two years had passed," said Sarah, unable to hold back a slight expression of emotion, "on the twenty-eighth of November 1827, the child died."

"Before continuing this discussion, madame, I must ask you to tell me what your interest is in this matter."

"The mother of the little girl was . . . my sister, monsieur.[115] As proof of this statement, I have with me the death notice of the poor little girl, letters from the person who took care of her, and the receipt from one of your clients, the one with whom you placed the fifty thousand crowns."

"Let me see the papers, madame."

Somewhat surprised that she was not taken at her word, Sarah withdrew several pieces of paper from a wallet, which the solicitor examined attentively.

"So, madame, what can I do for you? The death notice is perfectly legal, and the fifty thousand crowns went to Monsieur Petit-Jean, my client, upon the death of the child. That's one of the risks of life annuities, as I told the person who arranged this matter with me. As for the income, I paid it punctually until the child's death."

"I am more than happy to attest that your conduct in this affair has been above reproach. The woman in whose charge the child was placed also deserves our gratitude. She took great pains to care for my poor little niece."

"That is true, madame. I was so satisfied with the conduct of that woman that, when I saw that once the child died, she was without employment, I even took her into my service. Since that time, she has remained in my household."

"Madame Séraphin works in your household, monsieur?"

"For fourteen years, as my housekeeper. And I have nothing but the highest praise for her."

"Since that is the case, monsieur, she could be of great assistance to us if you . . . if you were so kind as to grant a request that will seem strange to you, or perhaps even . . . criminal, at first glance. But once you knew the motives for which it was made—"

"A criminal request, madame? I don't think you are any more capable of making one than I am of hearing it."

---

115. We hardly need remind the reader that the child in question is Fleur-de-Marie, Rodolphe and Sarah's daughter. As we shall see, Sarah's claim to represent her sister was a lie necessary to her plans. Sarah was, moreover, as convinced as Rodolphe of the little girl's death. [SN]

"I know, monsieur, that you are the last person to whom such a request should be made, but I am putting all my hope—my only hope—in your pity. In any case, may I count on your discretion?"

"Yes, madame."

"Then I will continue. The death of this poor little girl threw her mother into such despair that her pain is as intense today as it was fourteen years ago, and so, having at first feared for her life, we now fear for her sanity."

"Poor mother!" said Monsieur Ferrand, sighing.

"Oh, yes, she is a very unhappy mother, monsieur, because when her daughter was first born all she could do was blush for her existence, whereas now circumstances have changed, such that if the child were still alive, my sister could legitimate her, take pride in her, and never leave her again. Thus, the endless regret she feels, combined with her other sorrows, makes us fear for her sanity constantly."

"Unfortunately, there's nothing that can be done about that."

"But there is, monsieur."

"What do you mean, madame?"

"Suppose that someone came and said to the poor mother, 'Your daughter was believed to be dead, but she lives; the woman who took care of her when she was little can attest to this.'"

"Such a lie would be cruel, madame. Why would you give such vain hopes to this poor mother?"

"But what if it wasn't a lie, monsieur? Or rather, what if this imagining became a reality?"

"Miraculously? Believe me, madame, if it required nothing more than for me to add my prayers to yours, I would pray from the depths of my heart for it to be so. Unfortunately, the death certificate is in perfect form."

"Oh, I certainly know that, monsieur. The child is dead; yet, if you helped, this unhappiness might not be irremediable."

"You are speaking in paradoxes, madame."

"Then I will speak more clearly. If my sister were reunited with her daughter tomorrow, not only would she be returned to life, but, further, she would be sure of marrying the father of the child who is today single like herself. My niece died when she was six years old. Separated from their child when she was at the most tender age, her parents don't have any memory of her. Suppose that a girl of seventeen were to be found, a girl the age my niece would be now. There are so many girls like that, girls who have been abandoned by their parents. We could say to my sister, 'Here is your daughter; you have been deceived about her death. There were important reasons for telling you she was dead. The woman who raised her and a respectable solicitor will confirm this for you and prove that this is really your daughter.'"

Jacques Ferrand, after letting the countess speak uninterrupted, got up abruptly and exclaimed in indignation, "Enough! Enough! Madame, this is vile!"

"Monsieur!"

"To dare to propose to me—to me!—that I participate in the invention of a child and in the abrogation of a death notice? Those are truly criminal acts! This is the first time in my life that I've had such an outrageous notion proposed to me. And, as God is my witness, I have done nothing to deserve it!"

"But, monsieur, who would be harmed by it? My sister and the person she wishes to marry are widowed and childless. Both of them bitterly mourn the loss of their daughter. To deceive them? Why, it's making them happy, making them value their lives again. And it means giving a happy life to some poor abandoned girl. This is no crime! It's a noble and generous thing to do."

"Truly," said the solicitor, his indignation growing, "it's amazing the way the most execrable plans can be cloaked in such beautiful colors!"

"But, monsieur, think about it—"

"I repeat, madame, that this proposal is vile. It is shameful to see a woman of your moral worth engaging in such abominable machinations—machinations I dearly hope your sister is unaware of."

"Monsieur—"

"Enough, madame, enough! I am not chivalrous. I will tell you the brutal truth to your face."

Sarah gave the solicitor one of her black looks and said to him icily, "So you refuse?"

"Please, stop insulting me, madame."

"Watch out!"

"And now threats?"

"Indeed, threats. And to prove that my threats are real, first of all, know that I have no sister."

"What, madame?"

"I am the mother of the child."

"You?"

"Me! I tried to arrive at my purpose indirectly, thinking that the story might evoke your sensibilities, but you are pitiless. So I'll remove the mask. And if it's war you want, war is what you'll get."

"War? Because I refuse to be associated with a criminal plot? What effrontery!"

"Listen to me, monsieur: your reputation as an honest man is an accepted fact, perfect, widespread, and unquestioned."

"Because I've earned it. That's why you would have to be crazy to dare to make me such a proposition as you have!"

"I know better than anyone, monsieur, how little faith one should have in reputations of austere virtue. They so often veil ladies' love affairs and men's most knavish behaviors."

"Just what are you trying to suggest?"

"Since the beginning of our conversation, I don't know why, but I have begun to doubt that you deserve the esteem and consideration you enjoy."

"Really, madame? Such doubt must do honor to your powers of perspicacity."

"Don't you think? My doubts are founded on very little—on instinct, on inexplicable gut feelings—but my insights seldom deceive me."

"Let's bring this interview to a close, madame."

"First, you will know what I have determined. Let me begin by telling you that, between you and me, I'm convinced that my poor daughter is dead. But that doesn't matter. I will claim that she is not dead. There is evidence, unlikely evidence, to back up that claim. At this moment, you are in such a position as to have many envious people lurking about you, just waiting to have the opportunity to attack you. I will provide them with one."

"You?"

"Yes, me. I'll do it by attacking you on some absurd pretext, on an irregularity in the death notice or some such thing—it doesn't matter what. I will insist that my daughter is not dead. Seeing as it is in my greatest interest to make believe she is still alive, this suit, though a lost cause, by giving this affair the widest possible dissemination, will serve me well. A mother who reclaims her child always makes for a moving story. I will have as my allies all of the people who envy you, all your enemies, and all of the sensitive, romantic souls out there."

"That's both crazy and evil! What would be my interest in claiming your daughter to be dead if she weren't?"

"It's true, your motive is a bit hard to figure out. Fortunately, we have lawyers for that! And, now that I think of it, here's an excellent motive: you wanted to split with your client the money invested as a life annuity for that poor child, so you made the child disappear."

The solicitor shrugged his shoulders, impassively. "If I were such a great criminal as to do that much, why wouldn't I just kill her instead of making her disappear?"

Sarah trembled in her surprise. She remained silent for a moment and then said, bitterly, "For a holy man, you can meditate a crime and plan it profoundly! Could I have hit my mark just now by accident? That gives me something to think about. And think about it, I will. One last word: you see what kind of woman I am. I crush any obstacle that stands in my way, without pity. Think carefully before you give me your final answer. Tomorrow I will ask you for your decision. You can do what I'm asking with impunity; in his joy, the father of my daughter will not contest the likelihood of such a resurrection if our lies, which will make him so happy, are skillfully plotted out. In any case, there is no proof of our daughter's death besides what I wrote to him fourteen years ago. It would be easy to persuade him that I deceived him about it. At the time, after all, I had well-founded grievances against him. I will say to him that in my sorrow I had wanted to break, as far as he was concerned, the last tie that bound us to each other. There's no way you can be compromised in any of this. You need only affirm, as an irreproachable man, that you, Madame Séraphin, and I had all planned this out between us, long ago—and everyone will believe you. As for the fifty thousand crowns set aside for my daughter: I'll take care of that myself, and the money can remain with your client, who will remain utterly ignorant of this whole matter. Finally, you may name your own fee for this service."

Jacques Ferrand maintained his composure, despite the peculiar character of this situation, which was both foreign and dangerous for him. The countess, believing that her daughter was truly dead, had come to propose to the solicitor that he have the child pass for living whom he had passed off as dead fourteen years before. He was too clever and knew too well the perils of his position to underestimate the importance of Sarah's threats. Admirably and meticulously constructed as it was, the edifice of the solicitor's reputation was built on sand. The public abandons beliefs as easily as it becomes enamored of them, loving as it does to have the opportunity to cast its former idols to the ground. What might the full consequences be of an initial attack on his reputation? Even if it made no sense, the very audacity of such an attack could raise suspicion . . .

Sarah's perspicacity and hardness terrified the solicitor. This mother had not shown a moment of tenderness in speaking of her daughter; she seemed to consider her death merely as a lost opportunity. Personalities such as hers are devoid of pity when they plot—and when they take revenge. Wanting to give himself time to figure out how to parry her dangerous thrust, Ferrand said to Sarah, coldly, "You have given me until tomorrow at noon, madame. I, in turn, give you until the day after tomorrow to renounce this proposition, whose gravity you clearly do not understand. If I haven't received a letter from you between now and then that attests that you have decided to abandon this criminal and insane enterprise, you will learn at your own expense that honest people who refuse to be complicit in crime are protected by the law, which can always reach out and capture those who engage in such odious machinations."

"So I take it, monsieur, that you are asking for an extra day to think it over? That's a good sign, and I grant your request. The day after tomorrow, at this same time, I'll be here. And then, as I said, it will either be peace or war for us. And when I say war, I mean war to the death, with no mercy and no pity."

And at that, Sarah left.

"Everything's going according to plan," Sarah said to herself. "That miserable girl Rodolphe became interested in on a whim and sent to the Bouqueval farm, no doubt in order to make her into his mistress later on, no longer poses any threat to me, thanks to the one-eyed hag who got her out of the way. Rodolphe's adroitness saved Madame d'Harville from the trap I laid for her, but she'll never be able to escape the next trap I have in store for her. She'll be lost to Rodolphe forever. So he'll be sad, disheartened, and removed from all affection. In that state, he'll want nothing better than to give in to a lie that I can make look completely plausible with the solicitor's help. And that solicitor will help me, because I terrified him. I can easily find some young, pitiful, poor orphan girl who, once I've told her how, will fill the place of our long-lost child, so bitterly mourned by Rodolphe. I know the largeness, the generosity of his heart. Yes, to give a name and rank to the girl he believes to be his daughter, he will renew his ties to me—ties that I had always thought unbreakable. The predictions of my old nurse will finally come true, and I will surely attain this time the object of my entire life: a crown!"

Sarah had barely left the solicitor's house when Monsieur Charles Robert came in. He got out of the most elegant gig and walked into Jacques Ferrand's office with the air of one long familiar with it.

CHAPTER 18

MONSIEUR CHARLES ROBERT

The commandant, as Madame Pipelet called him, entered the solicitor's office unceremoniously, where he found him in a dark and bilious mood. The solicitor said to him, in a harsh tone, "I reserve afternoons for my clients. When you want to see me, come in the morning."

"My dear bookkeeper (this was one of Monsieur Robert's jokes), I'm here on an important matter, first of all. But I'm also here to reassure you personally in connection with some fears you might have."

"What fears?"

"So you haven't heard?"

"What?"

"About my duel."

"Your duel?"

"With the Duke de Lucenay. What, you didn't know about it?"

"No, I didn't."

"Oh, bother!"

"And what was this duel about?"

"It was about an extremely serious matter that only blood could answer for. Imagine: in the middle of the embassy, Monsieur de Lucenay gave himself leave to tell me to my face that I had phlegm."

"That you had . . . ?"

"Phlegm, which, my dear bookkeeper, is a malady that is surely quite ridiculous."

"You fought each other over that?"

"And why else should we have fought? You think that I am obliged to stand by calmly and hear someone claim in cold blood that I have phlegm? And in front of a charming woman, moreover? In front of a little marquise whom— Well, anyway, I couldn't allow that to pass."

"Certainly not."

"We military men, you understand . . . we are always on the ready for such things. My seconds agreed with the duke's seconds on terms yesterday. I put it very clearly: either we have a duel, or I get a retraction."

"A retraction of what?"

"Of the phlegm, for crying out loud! Of the phlegm he had the audacity to diagnose me as having!"

The solicitor shrugged his shoulders.

"For their part, the duke's witnesses said, 'We will vouch for the honorable character of Monsieur Charles Robert, but Monsieur de Lucenay cannot, must not, and does not wish to retract.' 'So, gentlemen,' my witnesses responded, 'Monsieur de Lucenay is going to maintain stubbornly that Monsieur Charles Robert has phlegm?' 'Yes, gentlemen, but he does not believe that this constitutes an injury to Monsieur Robert.' 'In that case, he should retract.' 'No, gentlemen; Monsieur de Lucenay recognizes Monsieur Robert as a man of honor, but he claims that Monsieur Robert has phlegm.' You see that there was truly no other way to resolve such a serious matter."

"No other way. You were insulted to the core of your honor."

"Isn't that the truth? So they agree on a day and hour for the encounter. Yesterday morning, at Vincennes, everything occurred in the most honorable way possible. I gave a slight thrust of my sword to the arm of the Duke de Lucenay. The witnesses declared that my honor was satisfied. Then the duke proclaimed in a loud voice, 'I never take anything back before a duel, but afterward it's a different matter altogether. It is thus my duty and my honor to declare that I accused Monsieur Charles Robert falsely of having phlegm. Gentlemen, I recognize not only that my honest adversary does not have phlegm but furthermore that he is incapable of ever having it.' Then the duke held out his hand to me in the most cordial fashion and asked me, 'Are you satisfied?' 'We are friends to the death now!' I answered him. And I really owed him that much. The duke performed perfectly in every respect. He could have said nothing at all, or he could have merely said that I didn't have phlegm. But to affirm that I could never have it, now that's what I call the behavior of a true gentleman."

"That's what I call honor at its finest! So what do you want here?"

"My dear accountant (another one of Monsieur Robert's jokes), I'm here on a matter of great importance to me. You know that, in keeping with our contract, when I advanced you three hundred and fifty thousand francs in order to finish paying you your charge, it was stipulated that in giving you three months' advance notice, I could withdraw from your safekeeping the funds that you are paying me interest on."

"And so?"

"Well," said Monsieur Robert, embarrassed, "I . . . well . . . but . . . it's just that . . ."

"What?"

"You'll understand, it's just a whim, but I have taken it into my head to become a landed proprietor, dear bookkeeper."

"Get to the point already! I'm losing my patience!"

"In a word, I have been offered the opportunity to acquire some land, and if this is not too disagreeable to you, I would like—that is to say, I am desirous of withdrawing my money from your keeping. I have come to give you notice, as called for by our contract."

"Oh, I see."

"You aren't angry, I hope?"

"Why should I be angry?"

"Because you might think . . ."

"I might think what?"

"That I have heard certain rumors . . ."

"What rumors?"

"Nothing, really, just some stupid things."

"But tell me what you mean."

"Just because some silly things are being said about you is no reason for me to withdraw my money."

"What kinds of things?"

"There's not a shred of truth to them. But some malicious people have been saying that you have gotten involved, in spite of yourself, in some messy business. It's purely gossip, obviously. It's like when they said that we were speculating on the stock market together. Those rumors died down very quickly. I'd be a monkey's uncle if—"

"So you don't feel your money is safe with me?"

"Yes, I do, I do—but I'd just prefer to have possession of it."

"Stay here a moment." Monsieur Ferrand closed the drawer of his desk and got up.

"So, where are you going, then, my dear accountant?"

"I'm going to look for evidence to show you the real truth about my business troubles," said the solicitor, with irony. Opening the door to a little hidden staircase that gave him access to the back wing without having to pass through the study, he disappeared.

He had scarcely left the room when the head clerk knocked at the door. "Enter," said Charles Robert.

"Monsieur Ferrand isn't here?"

"No, my worthy member of the bar" (another one of Monsieur Robert's jokes).

"There's a veiled lady who wants to speak to the boss right away about a pressing matter."

"The boss will return in just a moment, my worthy member of the bar. I'll give him your message. Is the lady pretty?"

"You'd have to be real clever to know how to tell. Her veil is black and so thick you can't see her face."

"Fine, fine! I'll sneak a peek when I leave. I'll tell Monsieur Ferrand as soon as he returns."

The clerk left the room.

"Where the devil did that bookkeeper go?" Monsieur Charles Robert wondered. "He must be looking into the contents of his safe for me. If those rumors are absurd, so much the better! As to that, well, it could easily be malicious people spreading those rumors. Upright people like Jacques Ferrand always stir up envy. All the same, I'd like to have my money. I will buy the château they told me about. It has Gothic turrets from the time of Louis XIV, straight out of the Renaissance—everything there is pure Rococo.[116] It'll be stately without being all worm-eaten. It won't be anything like my love for that prudish Madame d'Harville. Boy, did she get me going! Good Lord! She had me going! Oh, no, I didn't get my money's worth, like that stupid doorkeeper's wife from rue du Temple told me, that woman with her childish wig. That little affair cost me at least a thousand crowns. It's true that I still have the furniture, and I still have compromising information on the marquise. But here comes my bookkeeper."

Monsieur Ferrand returned, holding in his hand several papers that he gave to Monsieur Charles Robert.

"Here," he said to the latter. "Three hundred and fifty thousand francs in treasury notes. In a few days we can settle the interest. Make me out a receipt."

"What?" cried Monsieur Robert, astonished. "At least you don't believe that—"

"I don't believe anything."

"But—"

"The receipt!"

"My dear accountant!"

"Write it out, and tell people who speak to you about the troubles I'm having with my business exactly how it is that I respond to such suspicions."

"The fact is, as soon as people know about this, your credit will be that much more solid. But really, take this money back. I have nothing to do with it now. I said I wanted it in three months."

"Monsieur Charles Robert, I don't brook suspicious remarks twice."

"You're angry!"

"Give me my receipt!"

"You're hard as iron," Monsieur Charles Robert said. Then he added as he wrote out the receipt, "There's a meticulously veiled lady out there. She wants to talk with you right away about some pressing matter. I'm going to take the pleasure of getting a good look at her on my way out. Here's your receipt. Is everything in order?"

"Very good. Now get going. Take this little staircase here."

---

116. This is a rather special château someone wants to sell to Charles Robert, combining, as it does, Gothic, Renaissance, and Rococo architecture, thus styles that differ from each other by hundreds of years. His notions of architecture may be as vague as his lovemaking is heavy-handed. [TN]

"But the lady?"

"Exactly. I don't want you to see her." And the solicitor rang his head clerk, saying to him, "Have the lady come in. Adieu, Monsieur Robert."

"Oh, well, I guess I'll have to miss out on seeing her. No hard feelings, bookkeeper. Please believc that—"

"Fine, fine! Good-bye!"

And the solicitor closed the door on Monsieur Charles Robert.

After a few moments the head clerk ushered the Duchess de Lucenay into the room. She was dressed very modestly, wrapped in a large shawl, with her face completely hidden by the thick veil of black lace that covered it, along with her matching watered silk hat.

CHAPTER 19

MADAME DE LUCENAY

Looking quite agitated, Madame de Lucenay walked slowly up to the solicitor's desk as he walked forward to meet her. "Who are you, madame, and what do you want from me?" barked Jacques Ferrand. He was already in a dark mood after having endured Sarah's threats. And Monsieur Charles Robert's irritating suspicions had only exasperated him further. In addition, the duchess was dressed so modestly that the solicitor saw no reason not to treat her harshly. Since she hesitated to speak, he said to her in a hard voice, "Will you please say what you're doing here already, madame?"

"Monsieur," she said in an emotional voice as she tried to keep her face hidden underneath the layers of her veil, "Monsieur, can I confide in you a secret of the highest importance?"

"One can always trust me with any secret. However, I must know and see to whom it is that I am speaking."

"Monsieur, maybe it's not necessary. I know that you are honor and integrity incarnate."

"Well, but in fact, madame, there is . . . well, someone . . . awaiting me. Who are you?"

"My name is not important, monsieur. One of my friends—one of my relatives—just left your office."

"And his name?"

"Monsieur Florestan de Saint-Remy."

"Ah!" said the solicitor, glancing inquisitively and attentively at the duchess. "And so, madame?" he asked.

"Monsieur de Saint-Remy has told me everything, monsieur."

"What did he tell you, madame?"

"Everything!"

"But once more, I ask you—"

"Dear God! Monsieur, you know full well."

"I know many things about Monsieur de Saint-Remy."

"Alas, monsieur, it's something awful!"

"I know many awful things about Monsieur de Saint-Remy."

"Oh, monsieur! He told me you were pitiless!"

"As far as crooks and forgers like him are concerned, yes, I'm pitiless.

If that Saint-Remy is your relative, you should be ashamed of the connection instead of admitting it. Have you come here to weep and make me feel pity? There's no point. Not even taking into account that this is a nasty business for an honest woman to be mixed up in—*if* you're an honest woman, that is."

The duchess's pride and patrician blood rose up in the face of this brazen insolence. She sat upright and pushed her veil back on her head; then, with a lofty attitude, imperious gaze, and steely voice, she said, "I am the Duchess de Lucenay, monsieur."

This woman looked so grand and her manner became so imposing that the solicitor fell instantly under her charm and domination. Struck silent, he stepped backward and automatically removed the black silk cap that covered his head, bowing deeply before her.

There could be nothing prouder nor more graceful than the face and bearing of Madame de Lucenay. It is true that she was a good thirty years old at the time, and her face was pale and a bit tired looking. But she had large brown eyes that were sparkling and bold, magnificent black hair, an arched and delicate nose, red and disdainful lips, a glowing complexion, and dazzlingly white teeth. Tall and thin, she was graceful and full of nobility. She had the step of a goddess on a cloud, as the immortal Saint-Simon put it.[117]

In eye shadow and grand eighteenth-century attire, Madame de Lucenay would have been, from a physical and moral perspective, just like one of those libertine[118] duchesses of the Regency period who devoted at once so much daring, carelessness, and seductive fellow feeling to their numerous love affairs, admitting their errors from time to time with so much candor and naiveté that the most rigid moralists would say, smiling, "Certainly her morals are too light and she is guilty of many things, but she is so good, and so charming! She loves those she loves with such devotion, such passion, such faithfulness, for as long as she loves them, that it's hard to be too angry with her. After all, it's only herself she damns, and she makes so many people happy!"

Apart from the makeup and the hooped petticoats, that was precisely Madame de Lucenay—that is, when she was not overcome by more somber preoccupations.

She had entered the solicitor's office looking like a timid middle-class woman, but she had become all of a sudden a grand, haughty, and

---

117. A slight paraphrase of Saint-Simon's description of the Duchess of Burgundy. The Duke de Saint-Simon (1760–1825) was an early French social theorist associated with utopian socialism. [TN]

118. At that time, "libertinism" signified independence of mind and an indifference to what people said of you. [SN]

irritated lady. Never in his life had Jacques Ferrand met a woman of such insolent beauty, of a bearing at once so noble and so bold.

The duchess's slightly tired face, her lightly circled beautiful eyes, her rosy, dilated nostrils, all indicated an ardor that men who are not given to platonic admiration tend to adore with wildness and abandon. Although he was old, ugly, vulgar, and sordid, Jacques Ferrand was as much a man to appreciate Madame de Lucenay's particular type of beauty as any other.

His hatred for Monsieur de Saint-Remy and rage against him increased on account of the savage admiration he felt for the man's proud and beautiful mistress. Jacques Ferrand, gnawed at by all sorts of barely contained fury, was enraged that this gentleman who was a forger, whom he had almost forced to abase himself before him by threatening him with criminal proceedings, inspired such love in this great lady that she would risk taking a step that could ruin her. With these thoughts, the solicitor felt his boldness, which had abandoned him for a moment, return. Hatred, envy, and a ferocious and burning resentment lit up his gaze and brought fiery color to his forehead and cheeks. They glowed with the most shameful fires and the wickedest passions.

Seeing Madame de Lucenay on the verge of opening such a delicate discussion, he expected her to speak circuitously and emotionally. Judge, then, his astonishment! She spoke with as much assurance and condescension as if she were speaking about the most natural thing in the world, as if she could have no reason to be reserved or observe any of the decorum with a man of his status that she would have employed addressing her equal. In effect, by wounding her to the quick, the solicitor's insolent vulgarity had forced Madame de Lucenay to leave behind the role of humble supplicant she had adopted, with great difficulty, to begin with. Returning to herself, she felt it beneath her dignity to be in the slightest bit reticent with this scribbler of deeds.

Madame de Lucenay was intelligent, charitable, and generous. She was full of goodwill, devotion, and kindness, in spite of her faults. But she was also her mother's daughter, and her mother was a revoltingly immoral woman who had managed to degrade even the noble and holy misfortune of having had to emigrate.[119] Madame de Lucenay, in her naive contempt for certain kinds of people, would have said, much like the Roman empress who bathed in front of a slave, "This isn't a man."

And so the duchess said resolutely to Jacques Ferrand, "Listen, Mister Solicitor. Monsieur de Saint-Remy is one of my friends. He confided to me the troubles he is in owing to the accident of having been the victim

119. An émigré in this context was an aristocrat who had emigrated from France in the 1790s to escape the French revolutionary government. [TN]

of a double swindle. Money can take care of anything. How much will it take in order to make these miserable worries go away?"

Jacques Ferrand was dumbstruck by the casual and deliberate way she got to her point. "They are asking for a hundred thousand francs!" he said in a surly manner, once he had mastered his astonishment.

"Then you will have your hundred thousand francs, and you will return those false documents immediately to Monsieur de Saint-Remy."

"Where are the hundred thousand francs, Madame Duchess?"

"Have I not told you that you will have them, monsieur?"

"They must be received tomorrow before noon, madame, or else the charge of forgery will be entered against him in court."

"Fine, then. Pay that sum, and I will stand good for it. As for you, I will pay you well."

"But, madame, that's impossible."

"You aren't going to tell me, I hope, that a solicitor like yourself can't find a hundred thousand francs from one day to the next."

"And on what collateral, madame?"

"What do you mean? Explain yourself."

"Who will be responsible for this sum?"

"I will."

"But, madame—"

"Is it really necessary to say that I own property, forty leagues from Paris, that earns eighty thousand pounds of revenue? That should suffice, I imagine, for what you call collateral?"

"Yes, madame, pending a written deed of mortgage."

"And what, pray tell, might that word mean? Some formality, no doubt. Go ahead, monsieur—get it done."

"Such a deed cannot be formalized in less than two weeks, madame, and it must be agreed to by your husband."

"But the property is mine. It is mine alone," said the duchess, impatiently.

"That doesn't matter, madame. Your husband is financially responsible for you, and mortgage deeds are very long and very detailed."

"But once again, monsieur: you cannot expect me to believe that it is so difficult to come up with a hundred thousand francs in two hours."

"Well, then, madame, you should turn to your family solicitor or to your stewards. As for me, I can't do it."

"I have my reasons, monsieur, for keeping this a secret," said Madame de Lucenay, haughtily. "You know the scoundrels who want to blackmail Monsieur de Saint-Remy, and that's why I've come to you."

"Your faith in me does me infinite honor, madame, but I cannot do what you ask of me."

"You don't have the money?"

"I have much more than that in banknotes or in good, solid gold, here in my safe."

"That's big talk! Is it my signature that you need? I'll give it to you. Let's put an end to this."

"Supposing that you are Madame de Lucenay . . ."

"Come in an hour to the Lucenay mansion, monsieur. I will sign, in my own home, what needs to be signed."

"Will Monsieur the duke be signing as well?"

"I don't understand, monsieur."

"Your signature on its own is worthless to me, madame." Jacques Ferrand savored the painful impatience of the duchess with delectable pleasure. Beneath her appearance of calm and disdain, she felt terrible anguish.

For the moment, she had reached the end of her resources. The day before, her jeweler had advanced her a considerable sum on her gems, some of which had been given to Morel, the gem-cutter. This sum had served to pay for Monsieur de Saint-Remy's bills of exchange and thus to pay off other creditors. Monsieur Dubreuil, the farmer at Arnouville, was ahead on his farm rent by more than a year, and in any case, there wasn't enough time to send to him. Moreover, unfortunately for Madame de Lucenay, two friends whom she could have turned to in such a dire situation were not currently in Paris. She thought that the viscount was innocent of forgery. He had claimed that he was the victim of two swindles, and she had believed him. But that did not make his position any less terrible. Monsieur de Saint-Remy, charged with a crime! Him, dragged off to prison! And even if he fled, would he not still have his name dishonored by such suspicion?

Madame de Lucenay trembled in terror at these thoughts. And her love for this man, who was at once so wretched and so deeply seductive, was completely blind. She felt the sort of reckless passion for him that women of her character and background frequently experience when the first bloom of their youth has passed and they are in the fullness of their years.

Jacques Ferrand scrutinized attentively the slightest changes in Madame de Lucenay's expressions. She seemed more and more beautiful and attractive to him. His hate-filled admiration and restraint added to the ardor of his feelings. He felt a bitter pleasure at tormenting this woman with his refusals, this woman who could feel nothing for him but disgust and contempt.

She could not abide the thought of saying anything to the solicitor that might sound like a plea. And yet, because she had recognized the futility of all other means, she had resolved to turn to him. This man alone could save Monsieur de Saint-Remy. She said to him, "Since you have the sum I am asking you for in your possession, monsieur, and since the collateral I offer is completely sufficient, why do you refuse me?"

"Because men have whims, just like women do, madame."

"But what kind of whim makes you act against your interests? As I just told you, monsieur, you can name your conditions? Whatever they are, I accept them!"

"You would accept any condition whatsoever, madame?" said the solicitor with a singular expression on his face.

"Any at all! Two, three, four thousand francs—more, if you want! Because, I must say," added the duchess candidly in a tone that was almost affectionate, "I have no one to turn to but you. Monsieur, no one but you! It's impossible for me to find anywhere else what I am asking you to get for tomorrow. And it must be done—do you understand? It absolutely must be. So I repeat to you, whatever condition you stipulate: I accept it. No matter what the cost—no matter what."

The solicitor's breathing grew forced, his temples were pounding, and his forehead was turning red. Fortunately, the lenses of his glasses blocked out the impure gleam burning in his eyes. Over his thinking, normally so clear and so calculating, hung a fiery cloud. He was losing his ability to think clearly. In his indecent blindness, he interpreted Madame de Lucenay's last words in a vile manner. Through his clouded perception, he vaguely glimpsed an emboldened woman much like some ancien régime ladies of the royal court. Like a woman pushed to her limits out of fear that the one she loved might be disgraced, she might be capable of making the most terrible sacrifices to save her lover. This was worse than a vile idea; it was a stupid one, but, as we've said, Jacques Ferrand would sometimes become a tiger or a wolf, and then the beast in him overcame the man.

He got up abruptly and approached Madame de Lucenay. Taken aback, the latter got up as well and looked at him in astonishment.

"No matter what the cost?" he cried in a trembling, uneven voice, coming closer still to the duchess. "Well, then, I will lend you this sum on one condition—on one condition only. And I swear that—" He could not finish making his declaration.

Thanks to one of the peculiar contradictions of human nature, at the sight of Monsieur Ferrand's hideously inflamed face, and guessing the strange and grotesque thoughts that his amorous hopes raised in him, Madame de Lucenay burst into laughter, in spite of all of her anxieties and anguish. This laughter was so frank, so uproarious, and so irrepressible that the solicitor recoiled in shock. Then, without giving him the chance to say a single word, the duchess laughed harder and harder. She covered her face again with her veil, and between two gales of laughter, she said to the solicitor, who was overcome with hatred, rage, and fury, "Frankly, I would prefer asking for this service from Monsieur de Lucenay."

She left, continuing to laugh so loudly that the solicitor could still hear her even through the closed doors of his office.

Jacques Ferrand began to think clearly again only to curse himself bitterly for his imprudent behavior. But little by little he became calmer at the thought that, after all, the duchess could hardly speak of this adventure without seriously compromising herself.

Still, this day had gone badly for him. He was plunged into dark thoughts when the hidden door of his office opened and Madame Séraphin entered in a state of great emotion.

"Ah! Ferrand!" she exclaimed, clasping her hands together. "You were right when you said that we might be ruined one day for having let her live!"

"Who?"

"That cursed little girl."

"What do you mean?"

"A one-eyed woman whom I don't know and to whom Tournemine gave the little one to get her off our hands fourteen years ago, when we passed her off for dead—oh, God, who would have believed it?"

"So tell me—tell me!"

"That one-eyed woman just arrived. She was downstairs just now. She told me that she knew that I was the one who gave up the little girl."

"Damnation! Who could have told her? Tournemine is on a convict ship."

"I denied everything and treated the one-eyed woman like a liar. But she insists that she's found the little girl, who's grown now. She says she knows where she is and that she is ready to tell everything and denounce us."

"This is a day from hell!" cried the solicitor in a burst of rage that made him look hideous.

"Good Lord, what am I supposed to tell this woman? What can I promise her to shut her up?"

"Does she seem like a person of means?"

"When I treated her like a beggar, she had me call for her basket to be brought in. It had money in it."

"And she knows where the girl is now?"

"She claims that she knows."

"It's Countess Sarah MacGregor's daughter," the solicitor said to himself in a daze. "And just now she was offering me so much money to say that her daughter wasn't dead! And she really is alive. I could return her to her! Yes, but what about that false death notice? If an investigation were to take place, I'd be finished. That crime could lead them to uncover the others."

After a moment of silence, he said to Madame Séraphin, "This one-eyed woman knows where the girl is?"

"Yes."

"And this woman says she'll come back?"

"Tomorrow."

"Write to Polidori and ask him to come see me tonight at nine."

"Would you like to get rid of the girl—and the old lady? That would kill two birds with one stone, Ferrand!"

"I told you to write to Polidori and tell him to come tonight at nine!"

At the end of this day, Rodolphe said to Murph, who had not been able to get in to see the solicitor, "Tell Monsieur de Graün to send a messenger this instant. Cecily must be in Paris within six days."

"That wicked she-devil again? The execrable wife of our poor David, as beautiful as she is vile! What on earth for, Your Lordship?"

"What for, Sir Walter Murph? In a month you can ask Jacques Ferrand, the solicitor, that very question."

CHAPTER 20

DENUNCIATION

On the same day the Owl and the Schoolmaster kidnapped Fleur-de-Marie, a man on horseback arrived at about ten o'clock at night at the Bouqueval farm. He came, he said, on behalf of Monsieur Rodolphe, to calm Madame Georges about the disappearance of her young protégée. She would be returned within a day or two. For important reasons, the man added, Monsieur Rodolphe asked Madame Georges not to write to him in Paris if she had something to ask of him, but rather to give a letter directly to the messenger, who would make sure he got it.

Sarah had sent this emissary. By means of this ruse, she calmed Madame Georges's fears, thus delaying by a few days the moment at which Rodolphe would learn of Songbird's kidnapping. In this interval, Sarah hoped to force the solicitor Jacques Ferrand to take up the vile hoax (the substitution of the child) that we have spoken of. But that wasn't all. Sarah also wanted to get rid of Madame d'Harville, who still seemed a serious threat to her and whom she would have already ruined if it hadn't been for Rodolphe's presence of mind.

The day after the marquis had followed his wife into the house on rue du Temple, Tom showed up and easily got Madame Pipelet gossiping. He learned that a young lady who was on the verge of being caught in flagrante by her husband had been saved thanks to the quick thinking of a tenant in the house named Monsieur Rodolphe.

Knowing this, and with no material proof of the rendezvous that Clémence had given Charles Robert, Sarah conceived another odious plan: it consisted in sending yet another anonymous letter to Monsieur d'Harville that would bring about a complete rupture between Rodolphe and the marquis, or would at least sow such suspicions in the mind of the marquis as to make him forbid his wife ever to receive visits from the prince.

This letter read as follows:

> You have been shamefully deceived; the other day your wife, warned that you were following her, invented the pretext of an imaginary act of charity. She was headed for a rendezvous with an august personage who had rented, under the name of Rodolphe, a room on the fourth floor in this house on rue du Temple. If you doubt the veracity of this

information, strange as it may seem to you, go to rue du Temple and find out for yourself. Describe the features of the august personage of whom you have been told and you will discover quickly enough that you are the most credulous and good-humored husband who has ever been so royally deceived. Do not ignore this note. Otherwise, people will say that your—friendship—for the prince is excessive.

Sarah mailed this note at five o'clock on the day of her interview with the solicitor. That same day, after having told Monsieur de Graün to expedite as best he could Cecily's arrival in Paris, Rodolphe went out in the evening to visit Madame the Ambassador of ***. He meant to visit Madame d'Harville at her home afterward to tell her that he had found a charitable intrigue worthy of her.

The reader will now follow us to the home of Madame d'Harville, where he will find, from the conversation that ensued, that this young woman, by showing herself to be generous and compassionate toward her husband, whom she had up until that point treated only with extreme coldness, was already following Rodolphe's noble advice.

The marquis and his wife were getting up from the table. The scene was taking place in the little salon of which we have spoken; Clémence's expression was affectionate and sweet; Monsieur d'Harville looked less sad than usual. We must hasten to say that the marquis had not yet received this new, vile, anonymous letter from Sarah.

"What are you doing this evening?" he asked his wife carelessly.

"I will be staying in. And what will you be doing?"

"I don't know," he answered, sighing. "Society is intolerable to me. I will spend this night the way I spend so many others: alone."

"Why spend it alone? Won't I be here?"

Monsieur d'Harville looked at his wife in surprise. "Well, yes, but . . ."

"But what?"

"I know that you often prefer to be alone if you're not going out into society."

"Yes, but since I am capricious," Clémence said with a smile, "today I would very much like to share my solitude with you—if it suits you, that is."

"Really?" cried Monsieur d'Harville with emotion. "How kind you are; you anticipated a desire I didn't even dare to utter aloud!"

"You know, dear, your surprise almost seems like a reproach!"

"A reproach? Oh, no, no! But after those unfair and cruel suspicions I had the other day, finding you so in such a kind mood is a surprise to me, I have to admit. It's the loveliest surprise imaginable, though."

"Let's forget the past," she said to her husband with a smile of angelic sweetness.

"Clémence, do you think you could?" he answered with sadness. "Didn't I dare to suspect you? If I were to tell you what things I imagined in my blind jealousy . . . but they are really nothing in comparison with my greater—and incurable—injustices."

"Let's forget the past, I'm telling you," said Clémence, holding back her painful feelings.

"What is this you say? Could you too forget that past?"

"I hope to."

"Can it be true? Clémence, can you really be that forgiving? But no, I can't possibly believe in such happiness—I had given up on it forever."

"You were wrong, as you see."

"Dear God, what a transformation! Am I dreaming? Oh, tell me that I'm not imagining things . . ."

"No, you aren't imagining things."

"Yes, you don't look so coldly at me, and your voice is almost affectionate. Oh, tell me this is true! Tell me I'm not hallucinating."

"No . . . because I, too, need forgiveness."

"You?"

"Yes, all too frequently. Haven't I been hard to you, maybe even cruel? Shouldn't I have realized that you would have needed singular courage, indeed more than human virtue, to act differently than you've acted? Isolated, unhappy, how could you resist the desire to find some consolation in a marriage that might make you happy? Alas, when one suffers, one is so disposed to believe in the generosity of others. Your fault was only that you counted on my generosity. Well, henceforward, I will try to make you right to have done so."

"Oh! Please go on!" said Monsieur d'Harville in a sort of ecstasy, his hands clasped together.

"Our existences are forever linked one to the other. I will do everything I can to make your life less bitter."

"Heavens! Clémence, am I really hearing you correctly?"

"I beg you, don't be so surprised. You're making me feel bad. It's a bitter reproach for my past conduct. Who else should feel your pain, who else should offer you a friendly, helping hand, if not me? I have come to a new realization. I've thought long and hard about the past and about the future. I have come to recognize my errors, and I think I've found the way to make things right."

"Your errors, you poor woman?"

"Yes. The day after our marriage, I should have appealed to your honor and asked you frankly for us to live separately."

"Ah, Clémence! Have pity on me!"

"Otherwise, having accepted my position, I should have made it more noble with my devotion instead of blaming you all the time with my haughty and silent coldness. I should have tried to console you for having such a frightful malady and thought only about your misfortune. Little by little, I would have become attached to you through my commiseration with you. Your gratitude would have repaid me for any trouble, even any pain my compassion cost me. And then—but what's wrong? You're crying!"

"Yes, I'm crying—crying from happiness. You can't know what new emotions in me your words bring to life. Oh, Clémence! Let me cry a bit. I understand better than ever right now how guilty I was to chain you to my sad life!"

"And never before have I been more determined to forgive. These sweet tears of yours make me see the kind happiness I have been missing. Take heart, my dear! Take heart! Rather than seeking lives of glory and happiness, let's find our satisfaction in the accomplishment of the serious duties life imposes on us. Let's be indulgent with each other. If we feel too weak, we should look to our daughter's cradle and concentrate all of our affection on her. In this way, we will still experience some joy, a melancholy and holy joy."

"You are an angel—an angel!" Monsieur d'Harville exclaimed, clasping his hands and contemplating his wife with a passionate admiration. "Oh! You have no idea of the pleasure and the pain you are giving me, Clémence. You don't realize that your harsh words from before, your most bitter reproaches—alas, completely deserved reproaches—have never overwhelmed me to the extent of your adorable gentleness, your generous resignation right now. And yet, despite myself, I feel myself begin to hope again. You wouldn't believe the future I now dare to see for us."

"And you can have complete, indeed blind faith in what I tell you now, Albert. I have made the firmest kind of resolution. I will never falter, I swear to you. Later, I may well be able to give you new assurances of the strength of my word."

"Assurances?" cried Monsieur d'Harville, more and more exalted by this happiness that he had so little anticipated. "Assurances? Why would I need any? Your look, the way you speak, that divine expression of goodness that makes you even more beautiful than ever, the ecstatic beating of my heart: doesn't all of that tell me that you're speaking the truth? But you know, Clémence, that men are insatiable in their desires," added the marquis as he came closer to his wife's armchair. "Your noble and touching words give me courage, they make me dare to hope—to hope for heaven, yes, to hope for things that yesterday I regarded as mad dreams!"

"Please, what do you mean by all this?" said Clémence, a little upset by her husband's passionate speech.

"I'll explain gladly!" he exclaimed as he seized his wife's hand. "Yes, through tenderness, care, and love—you understand, Clémence?—love,

I hope to make you love me! Not with a pale, lukewarm affection, but with an ardent affection, like mine. Oh! You don't know that kind of passion! Do I dare even speak of it to you? You have always acted so coldly toward me. Never a word of kindness. Never a word like the ones you just spoke a moment ago that made me weep, that are now making me drunk with happiness. And I deserve that happiness . . . I have always loved you so! And I suffered so much, without telling you! This was the sorrow that was devouring me! Yes, my disdain for society, my somber, taciturn character—all of it was because of this. Think of it this way: to have in your home an adorable and beloved wife who belonged to you, a wife you desire with every transport of a suppressed passion, and to be condemned forever by her to lonely, aching nights of insomnia! Oh! No, you don't know the tears of despair I cried, my senseless rages. I can tell you, you would have been moved. But what am I saying? You have been moved. You have guessed the pain I was in, haven't you? You will have pity on me. Seeing your ineffable beauty and your enchanting grace will no longer be both my happiness and my torture every day. Yes, the treasure that I consider my most precious belonging, this treasure that belongs to me and that I didn't possess—this treasure will soon be mine. Yes, my heart, my joy, my intoxication, everything tells me this. Isn't it true, my dear one, my tender love?"

As he said these words, Monsieur d'Harville covered his wife's hand with passionate kisses.

Though heartsick at her husband's misunderstanding, Clémence could not keep herself from making an instinctive movement of repugnance, almost of fright, and from pulling her hand back from him abruptly. Her face expressed her feelings too clearly for Monsieur d'Harville to be deceived. And the blow was a terrible one.

His features then took on a heartrending expression. Madame d'Harville quickly held out her hand to him and cried, "Albert, I swear to you, I will always be the most devoted of friends to you, the most tender of sisters . . . but nothing more. I ask your pardon if, without meaning to, I gave you hopes—hopes that I can never make real for us!"

"Never?" cried Monsieur d'Harville, fixing his desperate, pleading gaze on his wife.

"Never," said Clémence.

This single word, and the way the young woman said it, showed irrevocable resolution.

Led to her noble resolutions by Rodolphe's influence, Clémence had made the firm decision to shower Monsieur d'Harville with touching care and affection, but she felt herself incapable of ever feeling love for him. A feeling more inexorable than fear or contempt or hatred separated Clémence forever from her husband: an unconquerable feeling of repugnance.

After a moment of painful silence, Monsieur d'Harville passed his hand over his tearstained eyes and said to his wife, with heartbreaking bitterness, "I'm sorry for misunderstanding. I ask your pardon for having given in like that to a senseless hope."

And then, after a new silence, he cried, "Oh! I am so unhappy!"

"My friend," said Clémence softly to him, "I don't want to reproach you. But do you consider my promise to be the most tender of sisters worth nothing at all? Our devoted friendship will bring you care and attention that you could never hope for from love alone. Have hope—have hope that there will be better days ahead. Up until now, you have found me almost indifferent to your sorrows. You will see how well I sympathize with them. You will see the kind of consolation you can take in my affection."

A valet entered the room and said to Clémence, "His Highness, the Grand Duke of Gerolstein asks whether Madame the marquise is able to receive him."

Clémence gave her husband a querying look. Recovering his composure, Monsieur d'Harville said to his wife, "But of course."

The valet left the room.

"Pardon me, my friend," Clémence said, "but I hadn't said I wasn't receiving. In any case, it has been a long time since you saw the prince. He will be very happy to see you again."

"I would have been happy to see him as well," said Monsieur d'Harville. "However, I must tell you, at this moment I am so overwrought that I would have preferred his visit to be on another day."

"I understand. But what can we do? Here he is."

At that moment, Rodolphe was announced.

"I am so very happy, madame, to have the honor to see you again," said Rodolphe. "And my good luck is that much greater since it has allowed me the happy opportunity of seeing you, too, my dear Albert," he added, turning toward the marquis, whose hand he shook cordially.

"It certainly has been a long time, my lord, since I've had the chance to offer you my services."

"And whose fault is that, my invisible friend? The last time I came here to see Madame d'Harville, I asked for you, but you were absent. You've ignored me for more than three weeks since then. That's hardly very friendly."

"Show him no pity, Your Highness," said Clémence, smiling. "Monsieur d'Harville is all the more guilty because he feels the most profound devotion to your highness—a devotion that could perhaps be doubted because of his neglect."

"Well, then, madame! You can see how vain I am; whatever d'Harville does, it will never be possible for me to doubt his affection. But I shouldn't say that—I'll only encourage him to go on pretending to be indifferent to me."

"Please believe me, my lord, that it has only been a few unforeseen circumstances that have kept me from benefiting more often from your goodwill toward me."

"Just between us, my dear Albert, I believe you to be just a bit too platonic in your friendship. Although you are confident that you are loved, you do not hold much store in giving or receiving tokens of one's attachment."

In a lapse of etiquette that Madame d'Harville found slightly annoying, a valet entered the room holding a letter addressed to the marquis. This was Sarah's anonymous letter of denunciation that accused the prince of being Madame d'Harville's lover. Out of deference for the prince, the marquis pushed away with his hand the small silver tray that the servant had brought him. He whispered, "I'll get to that later."

"Dear Albert," said Rodolphe, affectionately, "are you standing on ceremony with me?"

"My lord . . ."

"If Madame d'Harville permits, I beg you: read the letter."

"I assure you, my lord, I am in no hurry to do so."

"Please, Albert, read the letter!"

"But, my lord—"

"I beg of you. Indeed, that's an order."

"Since your highness commands me to do it . . ." said the marquis as he took the letter from the tray.

"I certainly do command you to treat me as your trusted friend."

Then, turning toward the marquise as Monsieur d'Harville removed the fatal letter—whose contents Rodolphe could never have imagined—from its envelope, he added, with a smile, "What a triumph for you, madame, always to make this stubborn man give way to your will!"

Monsieur d'Harville walked up to one of the candelabras of the fireplace and opened Sarah's letter.

BOOK V

CHAPTER I

ADVICE

Rodolphe and Clémence were talking together while Monsieur d'Harville read Sarah's letter over, twice. The marquis's features remained calm, except that an almost imperceptible nervous tremor stirred in his hand. After a moment of hesitation, he put the letter in the pocket of his vest.

"At the risk of seeming like a complete barbarian," he said to Rodolphe, smiling, "I would like to ask your permission, my lord, to go off to respond to this letter. It turns out to be more important than I originally thought."

"Won't I see you again this evening?"

"I do not think I will have that honor, my lord. I hope that your highness will be so good as to excuse me."

"What a mysterious man!" Rodolphe said, cheerfully. "Won't you try, madame, to keep him with us?"

"I do not dare to try my own powers where your highness has tried in vain."

"Seriously, my dear Albert, do try to come back to us as soon as you've finished writing your letter. Otherwise, promise me that you will give me a few moments of your time some morning. I have so many things to tell you."

"Your highness is too good to me," said the marquis, bowing deeply. He left the room, leaving Clémence with the prince.

"Something is bothering your husband," Rodolphe said to the marquise. "His smile seemed forced to me."

"When your highness arrived, he was in a very emotional state. He had a hard time keeping it from you."

"Did I come at an awkward moment?"

"No, Your Highness. You actually spared me the end of a painful conversation."

"How is that?"

"I told Monsieur d'Harville about my decision to act differently toward him. I promised him my support and comfort."

"How happy he must have been!"

"Yes, at first, as much as I was. His tears and his joy made me feel a kind of emotion I've never known before. In the past, I thought I could avenge myself by reproaches or sarcastic comments to him. What a sorry revenge! My sorrows grew only more bitter as a result. But just now—what a difference! I had asked my husband if he was going out; he had answered me sadly that he would spend the evening alone, as he does so often. When I offered to stay here with him, you should have seen his astonishment, my lord! How radiant his usually somber features suddenly became! Ah! You were right: there is nothing more charming to arrange than these happy surprises!"

"But how did these signs of kindness on your part end up as the painful conversation to which you referred?"

"Alas, Your Highness," said Clémence, blushing. "After the hopes I inspired in him that I meant to make realities, he came to believe in some more tender hopes, even though I had been careful to guard against them, since I knew I could never satisfy them."

"I understand. He loves you so dearly."

"As much as I was at first moved by his gratitude, I was frozen, frightened even, once his language turned passionate. Finally, when in his exaltation he put his lips to my hand, I felt a devastating coldness, and I could not hide my fear. I caused him real pain by showing the incurable alienation his love causes me. I'm truly sorry for it. But at least Monsieur d'Harville is convinced, finally, that in spite of my warmer feelings toward him, he should not expect more of me than the most devoted friendship."

"I pity him, even though I cannot blame you. There are feelings that are, if one might say it, sacred. Poor Albert—so good, so honest, even! He has such a brave heart and such a devoted soul! If you knew how long I had been preoccupied with the sadness that was eating away at him, even though I didn't know the cause . . . Let's allow time and reason to do their work. Gradually, he'll recognize the value of the affection you're offering him, and he will resign himself to it, just as he resigned himself before without the touching consolations you are offering him now."

"And which he will never be without, I swear to you, my lord."

"And now, let's think about other misfortunes. I promised you a good deed that would have all the charm of a novel in full swing. I have come to fulfill my promise."

"Already, Your Highness? How wonderful!"

"Ah! I was more inspired than I knew when I praised that little room on rue du Temple of which I've told you. You can't imagine what fascinating and touching things happened there. First, your protégés in the garret are enjoying the good fortune that your presence foretold for them. They still have some terrible hardships ahead of them to endure—but I don't want to sadden you. One day you will know how many dreadful evils can befall a single family."

"How grateful they must be to you!"

"It is your name that they bless."

"You saved them in my name, my lord?"

"In order to make the charity sweeter to them. In any case, all I did was bring your promises to fruition."

"Oh! I will have to go tell them the truth and let them know what they owe you."

"Don't do that! You know that I have a room in that house. We must beware of new cowardly anonymous messages from your enemies, or mine. And the Morels are now taken care of. Let's think about our intrigue. There's a poor mother and her daughter who lived in ease a while ago. Today, they have been reduced, as a consequence of an atrocious act of plunder, to the most horrendous circumstances."

"Poor women! And where do they live, my lord?"

"I don't know."

"But how did you come to know about their misery?"

"Yesterday, I went to the Temple. You don't know what the Temple is, do you, Marquise!"

"No, my lord."

"It's the most amusing bazaar. I was going there to do some shopping with the woman who is my neighbor from the fourth floor."

"Your neighbor?"

"Well, don't I rent a room in rue du Temple?"

"I had forgotten, my lord."

"This neighbor is a ravishing little seamstress. Her name is Rigolette. She's always laughing, and she's never had a lover."

"How virtuous, for a seamstress!"

"She's not well behaved just because she's virtuous. It's just as much a matter of having no leisure time, as she puts it, to fall in love. It would cost her too much time, because she has to work twelve to fifteen hours a day in order to earn the twenty-five sous she lives on."

"Can she live on so little?"

"And how! She even allows herself the luxury of two birds that eat more than she does. Her little room is sparkling clean, and she dresses herself in the prettiest way."

"Living on twenty-five sous a day takes real talent!"

"Real talent, yes. A talent for order, work, economizing, and practical wisdom, I can tell you. And so I'm recommending her to you. She tells me she is a very clever seamstress. In any case, you wouldn't be obliged to wear the dresses she would make you."

"I will send work for her starting tomorrow. Poor girl! To live on such a pittance and to be so invisible, so to speak, to us rich people who spend a hundred times more than that on our slightest whims!"

"So it's agreed that you'll take an interest in my little protégée. Let's return to our adventure. I had gone to the Temple with Mademoiselle Rigolette to make a few purchases for your poor people in the garret, when, riffling by chance through the drawers of an old office desk that was for sale, I found the draft of a letter written by a woman who was complaining to a third party about how she and her daughter had been reduced to poverty through the dishonesty of an agent. I asked the merchant where the piece of furniture had come from. It had been part of a modest set of furniture that a woman, who was still young, at the end of her resources, had sold her. This woman and her daughter, the merchant told me, seemed to be of the respectable classes and were bearing up proudly under their distress."

"And you don't know where they live, my lord?"

"No, unfortunately, not yet. But I have ordered Monsieur de Graün to try to find out, even going, if necessary, to police headquarters. It's likely that, given their utter destitution, the mother and daughter will have gone to find shelter in some miserable furnished room. If that's how it is, we have reason to hope, seeing as the managers of those houses keep a record each night of all the strangers who pass through during the day."

"What a singular set of circumstances!" said Madame d'Harville in astonishment. "How compelling it is!"

"And that's not all. In a corner of the draft of the letter that was in that old piece of furniture, one could read the words, 'Write to Madame de Lucenay.'"

"Wonderful! Maybe we can find out more from the duchess!" Madame d'Harville exclaimed, excitedly. Then she said, sighing, "But since we don't know the name of this woman, how will we be able to identify her to Madame de Lucenay?"

"We will need to ask her if she knows a widow who is still young, looks distinguished, and whose daughter, who is sixteen or seventeen, is named Claire. I remember that name."

"That's the name of my daughter! It seems I have yet another motive to care about these unfortunate women."

"I forgot to tell you that the brother of this widow killed himself a few months ago."

"If Madame de Lucenay knows this family," said Madame d'Harville as she reflected on this news, "such information will suffice to put her on the right track. Indeed, the sad death of this poor man must have struck the duchess. Heavens, I need to go see her right away! I will write her a note this evening so I can be sure to meet her tomorrow morning. Who could these women be? From what you know about them, my lord, they seem to belong to the upper classes of society. And to see themselves reduced to such conditions of distress! Ah! For them, poverty must be doubly appalling."

"And it was caused by the thievery of a solicitor, a certain Jacques

Ferrand, an abominable scoundrel who has, to my knowledge, committed other crimes already."

"My husband's solicitor!" cried Clémence. "He's my stepmother's solicitor, too! You must be wrong, Your Highness. He has the reputation of being the world's most honest man."

"I have proof to the contrary. But please, don't tell anyone of my suspicions, or rather of my knowledge, of the crimes of that wretch. He is as clever as he is criminal, and in order to expose him I need him to believe for a few more days that he is above suspicion. Yes, he's the one who fleeced those poor, unfortunate women. He denied that he had a deposit that, to all appearances, had been put in his keeping by the widow's brother."

"And what was the amount?"

"It was all the money they had in the world!"

"What a dreadful crime!"

"One of those crimes," Rodolphe exclaimed, "that have no excuse—neither need, nor passion. Frequently hunger makes people steal, and revenge drives them to commit murder—but this solicitor, already rich, this man endowed by society with a nearly holy character, with a character that demands and compels trust—this man is pushed to crime by pure, cold greed. A murderer can kill you only once, and quickly, with a knife; this man kills you slowly, with all of the tortures of despair and misery he plunges you into. For a man like this Ferrand, nothing is sacred! Not the orphan's inheritance, not the last farthing that the poor man has so laboriously amassed. You put your gold in his keeping: he's tempted by it, so he steals it. This man transforms you from a rich and happy person into a poor and miserable one—by his mere will. Through self-deprivation and hard work, you earn your bread and shelter for your old age. This man rips that bread and that shelter from you in your old age—by his mere will.

"And that's not all. Look at the frightening consequences of these vile acts of plunder. That widow of whom we were speaking is dying of sorrow and distress, and her daughter, young and beautiful, without resource or support, accustomed, as she is, to a life of ease, with no training in how to earn her living, will soon find herself forced to choose between dishonor and hunger! If she strays, if she succumbs to need—she'll be ruined, degraded, dishonored. Because of his act of plunder, Jacques Ferrand is the cause of the mother's death and the daughter's prostitution! He has killed the body of the one and the soul of the other. And that, once again, happens not in one blow, as in other homicides, but slowly and cruelly."

Clémence had never before heard Rodolphe speak with so much indignation and bitterness. She listened to him in silence, struck by his words that were of an eloquence that, though surely gloomy, also revealed a vigorous hatred of evil.

"Please excuse me, madame," Rodolphe said to her after a few moments of silence. "I couldn't contain my indignation at the thought of the horrible misfortunes that could befall your future protégées. Ah! Believe me, it is impossible to exaggerate the terrible consequences that so often develop in the wake of ruin and poverty."

"Oh! On the contrary, I must thank you, my lord, for having, with your unsparing words, increased—if possible—the tender pity I felt already for that unfortunate mother. Alas! It's for her daughter that she must suffer the most. Oh! It's dreadful! But we will save them; we will make their future secure—won't we, my lord? Thank heavens, I'm rich—not as rich as I'd like to be, now that I can see a new way to use my riches, but if need be, I can ask Monsieur d'Harville for help. I will make him so happy that he will not be able to refuse any of my new whims, and I can foresee that I will have many of these indeed. You say our protégées are proud, my lord. I like them even more for that. Pride in misfortune always indicates an elevated soul. I will find a way to save them without their even realizing that my help is an act of benevolence. It will be difficult, but so much the better! Oh! I already have a plan; you'll see, my lord—you'll see that I will not lack in cleverness or delicacy."

"I can already see that you have some of the most Machiavellian schemes imaginable up your sleeve," said Rodolphe, smiling.

"But we have to find them first. I can't wait for tomorrow! Once I leave Madame de Lucenay's home, I'll go directly to where they lived before and interview the neighbors. I'll see for myself; I'll ask everyone there for information. I will compromise myself, if need be! I will be so proud to achieve my desired end all by myself and on my own. Oh! I'll succeed! This adventure is so moving. Poor women! I almost feel as if thinking about them makes me care even more for my daughter."

Moved himself by this charitable passion, Rodolphe smiled in sorrow as he contemplated this woman who was twenty years old, so beautiful, so loving, trying to forget the domestic misfortunes that had befallen her by taking up such noble distractions. Clémence's eyes shone brightly, her cheeks were slightly flushed, and her movements and speech were so animated that her ravishingly beautiful face became even more attractive.

CHAPTER 2

THE TRAP

Madame d'Harville saw that Rodolphe was silently contemplating her. She blushed, lowered her gaze, and then, looking up in charming confusion, she said to him, "You're laughing at my enthusiasm, my lord! It's just that I can't wait to taste the sweet joys that will make my life so much more exciting, instead of what it's been until now: sad and pointless. To be sure, this is not the fate I had always dreamed about. There is a kind of sentiment, a kind of happiness, the most vivid emotion of all, that I will never know. Although I am still very young, I must renounce it forever!" Clémence added with a suppressed sigh. Then she continued, "But, at last, thanks to you, my savior, always thanks to you, I will remake my life with other interests. Charity will replace love. I already owe such touching feelings to your counsel! Your words have so much influence over me, my lord! The more I think about them, and the more I explore your ideas, the more I find them great, just, and fruitful. And when I think, then, that instead of remaining content merely with commiserating with me over problems that really ought to be matters of indifference to you, you have, rather, given me the soundest advice, guiding me, step by step, on this new path that you have opened to a poor, beaten-down, and sorrowing heart! Oh, my lord, what a wealth of human kindness you have! How did you learn to feel so much generous pity?"

"I have suffered greatly. I am suffering still. That's why I know the secret of so many sorrows!"

"You, my lord? You are unhappy?"

"Yes. You might say that in order to prepare me to sympathize with everyone else's misfortunes, fate saw to it that I would undergo all of them myself. As a friend, I was struck through my friend; as a lover, I was struck through the first woman I loved with the blind confidence of youth; as a husband, I was struck through my wife; as a son, I was struck through my father; as a father, I was struck through my child."

"I thought that the grand duchess had not left you a child, my lord."

"Indeed. But before my marriage I had had a daughter who died very young. Well, then, as strange as this seems, the loss of this child whom I had barely ever seen is the great sorrow of my life. The older I get, the deeper my sorrow grows. Every year my sorrow grows more bitter. It seems it grows in proportion to the age my daughter would be now. She would be seventeen years old by now!"

"And her mother, my lord? Is she still alive?" asked Clémence after a moment of hesitation.

"Oh! Don't speak to me of her mother!" cried Rodolphe, whose face grew black at the thought of Sarah. "Her mother is an unworthy creature, a soul hardened by selfishness and ambition. Sometimes I wonder whether perhaps it wasn't for the best that my daughter died than remain in the care of such a mother."

Clémence felt a sort of satisfaction when she heard Rodolphe express himself in this way. "Oh! I can understand now how deep your sorrow is, my lord, for your daughter!" she exclaimed.

"I would have loved her so much! And besides, it seems to me that we princes always have some self-interest in our love for our sons: we have hopes for our bloodline and name, and we have ulterior political motives. But a daughter! A daughter you love just for herself. And also because when we've seen humanity, alas, in its most sinister aspects, it is so delightful to sit in contemplation of a pure and honest soul! To breathe in her virginal perfume, to observe her trembling youth with an anxious tenderness! The mothers maddest in their love, the mothers proudest of their daughters, do not experience these pleasures; they are too similar to their daughters to be able to appreciate them, to be able to taste this inexpressible sweetness. They think much more of the masculine qualities of a brave and fearless son. For in the end, don't you think that the thing that makes the love of a mother for her son or the love of a father for his daughter so moving is that in these affections there's a weak being who always needs protection? The son protects his mother, the father protects his daughter."

"Oh, that's too true, my lord."

"But alas! What's the good of understanding such inexpressible joys if one can never experience them?" said Rodolphe, despondently.

Clémence could not stop herself from shedding a tear, so profoundly had Rodolphe's tone bespoken heartbreak.

After a moment of silence, almost blushing from the emotion he had allowed himself to display, he said to Madame d'Harville, smiling sadly, "I am sorry, madame, that my sorrows and memories carried me away in spite of myself. You will forgive me, won't you?"

"Ah! My lord, please believe me when I say that I share your sorrows. Don't I have the right? Haven't you shared in mine? Unfortunately, it's little enough consolation I can give."

"No, no! Your expression of interest is sweet and good for me. It's almost soothing to admit one's suffering. And I would not have told you about it if it weren't for the nature of our conversation, which evoked painful memories in me. It's a weakness, but I cannot hear anyone speak of a girl without thinking of the one I lost."

"Such preoccupations are completely natural. Listen, my lord: since I last saw you, I accompanied a friend of mine, who volunteers to work with young women prisoners at Saint-Lazare, on one of her visits to the prisons.[120] This institution has some very guilty creatures in custody. If I hadn't been a mother, I would have judged them, no doubt, much more severely. But instead I feel the most sorrowful pity for them when I think about how they perhaps might not have fallen if they had not been abandoned, or if they had not been left in poverty from their earliest childhood. I don't know why, but after having these thoughts, I felt as if I loved my daughter even more."

"Come now, take heart," said Rodolphe with a melancholy smile. "This conversation leaves me feeling much better about you. A salutary path has been opened to you. Following it, you will survive, without faltering, years of the kind of testing that can be so dangerous for women, and especially for a woman of your abilities. In the end, you will have deserved much; you will still have to struggle and to suffer, for you are still young, but you will take heart in thinking of the good you will have done, and the good you will have yet to do."

Madame d'Harville broke out into tears. "At least," she said, "I'll always have your support and your advice—right, my lord?"

"From near or far, I will always care deeply about anything that involves you. Always, as long as it will be in my power, I will strive to contribute to your happiness—and to the happiness of the man to whom I have sworn my lifelong friendship."

"Oh! Thank you for this promise, my lord," said Clémence as she wiped away her tears. "Without your generous support, I believe my strength would abandon me. But believe me when I swear to you that I will accomplish my duty bravely."

At these words, a little door hidden in the tapestry suddenly opened. Clémence cried out in fright, and Rodolphe started.

Monsieur d'Harville appeared, pale and full of emotion. He looked profoundly moved; his eyes were full of tears.

Once their first surprise subsided, the marquis said to Rodolphe as he gave him Sarah's letter, "My lord, here is the vile letter that I received a short time ago in your company. Would you do me the kindness of burning it after you have read it?"

Clémence looked at her husband in shock.

"Oh! This is vile!" cried Rodolphe in indignation.

"Well, my lord, there's something I must confess to that is even more cowardly than this piece of anonymous cowardice, and that's my conduct!"

---

120. Saint-Lazare, originally a leper colony, became a prison during the Reign of Terror and a women's prison shortly after that. It was mostly destroyed in 1936. [TN]

"What do you mean?"

"Just a moment ago, rather than boldly showing you this letter straight out, I hid it from you. I pretended to be calm while in fact I was enraged, jealous, in despair. That's not all: do you know what I did, my lord? Shamefully, I went to hide myself away behind that door in order to spy on you. Yes, I was so wretched as to doubt your loyalty and your honor. Oh! The author of these letters knows his mark! He knows my weakness. Well, my lord, tell me, after having heard what I just heard—for I didn't miss a word of your conversation, for I know what concerns drew you to rue du Temple—tell me, after having been so base as to mistrust you and to make myself the accomplice of such a horrible calumny by believing it, don't you think I should get down on my knees to beg for your forgiveness and your mercy? And that's what I am doing right now, my lord, and that's what I'm doing, Clémence—for I have nothing now but faith in your generosity."

"Good Lord, dear Albert, what on earth must I pardon you for?" said Rodolphe as he held out both hands to the marquis with the most touching cordiality. "Now you know the secrets Madame d'Harville and I have been keeping. I am delighted that this has happened, for now I can lecture you as I please. Now I am your forced confidant. And what's even better is that you are Madame d'Harville's confidant. Now you know everything you can expect from this noble heart."

"And you, Clémence," Monsieur d'Harville said to his wife, sadly, "will you forgive me for this, too?"

"Yes, but only on the condition that you help me to make you happy."

And she held out her hand to her husband, who pressed it with great feeling.

"Really, my dear marquis!" cried Rodolphe. "Our enemies are clumsy oafs! Thanks to them, here we are even closer than we have ever been. You have never valued Madame d'Harville more than you do now, and she has never been more devoted to you. You have to admit that we have gotten our revenge on these envious and wicked people! It's always like that, and we can expect more where that came from, for I have an idea where this thrust originated, and I am not one to suffer patiently those who do my friends evil. But that's my business. Good-bye, madame; our plot has been discovered, so you will never be alone in helping your protégés. Don't worry: we'll meet up again soon to find some new and mysterious affair to engage in, and the marquis will have to be very sly to uncover it."

After accompanying Rodolphe to his carriage to thank him some more, the marquis returned to his chambers, without seeing Clémence again.

CHAPTER 3

REFLECTIONS

It would be difficult to portray the tumultuous and contradictory feelings that agitated Monsieur d'Harville once he found himself alone.

He was overjoyed to recognize the extraordinary falsehood of the accusation made against Rodolphe and Clémence. But at the same time, he was convinced that he had to give up his hopes of being loved by her. The more Clémence, in her conversation with Rodolphe, had shown herself resigned, brave, and resolved to do good, the more he castigated himself bitterly for having chained an unfortunate young woman to his own fate out of a sinful selfishness.

Far from being consoled by the conversation he had overheard, he fell instead into a melancholy, a depression of inexpressible depths.

Idle wealth has one thing terrible about it: nothing can distract the wealthy, and nothing can protect them from painful feelings. Because the wealthy are never truly preoccupied by future needs or by everyday labors, they are prey at any moment to the greatest moral afflictions. With the ability to have anything that can be bought for money, they constantly want what money cannot buy or violently regret not having it. Monsieur d'Harville was in desperate pain since what he wanted, after all, was merely his just and legal due: the possession, if not the love, of his wife. Now, in the face of Clémence's inexorable rejection, he wondered whether there was nothing but bitter derision to the legal formula: "The wife belongs to her husband." To what power could he appeal for help, and what sort of intervention could he seek, in order to conquer the coldness and repugnance that would change his life into one long torture, since he could not, should not, and did not want to love anyone besides his wife? He was forced to recognize that in this matter, as in so many others in conjugal life, the simple will of a husband or wife imperiously and without appeal overruled the sovereign will of the law.

These waves of powerless rage sometimes alternated with a gloomy state of despondency. A bleak, icy cold future weighed heavily upon him. He had the presentiment that his sorrow would bring on more frequent attacks of his frightful illness. "Oh!" he cried out, both in tenderness and in sorrow. "It's all my fault! It's my fault! Poor, unhappy woman! I deceived her—vilely deceived her! She may—she must—hate me! Yet just now, she displayed the most touching concern for me. And instead of being content with that, my insane passion carried me away. I became amorous, I spoke of love. And scarcely had my lips brushed against her hand when she recoiled in horror. If I had had any doubts about her invincible repugnance for me, the conversation she had with the prince put them to rest. Oh, it's dreadful! Dreadful!

"And what right did she have to confide in him about this hideous secret? Wasn't this an unworthy betrayal? By what right did she do this? Alas! By the right all victims have to complain of their tormentors. Poor girl, so young, so affectionate; the worst thing she could say against the horrible fate I've consigned her to was that it wasn't the end she had dreamed of and that she was much too young to have to give up on love. I know Clémence. The promise she made to me, to the prince, is one she will keep forever. She will be the sweetest of sisters to me. So, then! Isn't my position enviable? The cold and forced connection we two had will be replaced by gentle and affectionate relations. She could have treated me with icy disdain, and I wouldn't have been able to say a word against her conduct.

"So I will console myself by enjoying what she offers me. Will it not make me only too happy? Too happy! Oh! I am so weak; I am such a coward. But isn't she my wife, after all? Isn't she mine? All mine? The law recognizes my power over her, doesn't it? My wife resists me—fine, then, I have the right to—" He interrupted himself with a sardonic laugh. "Oh, right, it's violence now, is it? Sure! Now I'm thinking about violence? One more crime. So what should I do, then? Because I love her, I love her like a madman—I love only her, I want only her. I want her love, and not her cool, sisterly affection. Oh! In the end, she will have pity on me. She's so kind, and she'll see how unhappy I am. But no—no! Never! There are some kinds of estrangement that women can never overcome. Disgust—yes, disgust! Do you understand? Disgust! You have to get this into your head: your horrible illness will always inspire her with horror. Do you understand? Always!" Monsieur d'Harville shouted in melancholy excitement.

After a moment of fierce silence, he went on: "This anonymous denunciation that accused the prince and my wife came from the hand of an enemy. But just now, before having overheard her, I suspected for a moment that it could be true! I imagined him capable of such a cowardly betrayal! And I regarded my wife with the same suspicion! Oh! Jealousy knows no cure. And yet, I cannot fool myself. If the prince, who is my closest and most generous friend, encourages Clémence to occupy her thoughts and feeling with charitable works, if he promises her his advice, his support, it's because she needs advice and support. In fact, with her beauty and youth and all of her admirers, without a love to anchor her, having my faults, which are atrocious, to excuse hers, could she avoid straying?

"Another torment! Dear God, how I've suffered when I thought her guilty! What terrible agony! But no, this is a vain fear. Clémence swore not to fail in her duties. She will keep her promises. But at what price? At what price? Just now, when she came back to me with her words of affection, her smile, sweet, sad, resigned, gave me nothing but pain. How much it must have cost her to return to her torturer! Poor woman! She looked so beautiful and so touching at that moment! For the first time I felt the overwhelming sting of remorse, for until then, her haughty disdain toward me had been vengeance enough for her. Oh! I am miserable—miserable!"

After a long night of insomnia and bitter reflection, Monsieur d'Harville's restlessness ended as if by magic. He impatiently awaited the break of day.

CHAPTER 4

PLANS FOR THE FUTURE

As soon as morning broke, Monsieur d'Harville rang for his valet. Upon entering his master's quarters, old Joseph heard him, to his great surprise, humming a hunting tune, a sure if rare sign that Monsieur d'Harville was in a good mood. "Ah, Monsieur le Marquis," said the faithful servant, moved at the sight. "What a nice voice you have! It's a shame you don't sing more often!"

"Truly, Monsieur Joseph, you think I have a nice voice?" Monsieur d'Harville said, laughing.

"If the marquis's voice were as raspy as a hoot owl's or grated like a rattle, I'd still think it a nice voice."

"Oh, stop it, you flatterer!"

"Indeed! When you sing, Marquis, it's a sign that you're happy. And when that happens, your voice seems to me the most beautiful music ever heard."

"If that's true, my dear Joseph, prepare to get an earful of it."

"What do you mean?"

"You will be able to enjoy this charming music you seem to like so much all the time."

"Does that mean you'll be happy all the time, Monsieur le Marquis?" Joseph cried out, clasping his hands together in joyous astonishment.

"Every day, my dear Joseph, I'll be happy each and every day. Yes, we're done with sorrow and sadness. I know I can tell you this: you, the discreet, the only confidant of my troubles. I am at the height of happiness. My wife is an angel of kindness; she begged me to forgive her for her past estrangement. Do you know what she attributed it to? Guess! To jealousy!"

"Jealousy?"

"Yes, to absurd suspicions caused by anonymous letters."

"How dreadful!"

"Women are so proud, you understand. That's all it took to separate us. But, happily, last night she explained in all frankness why she was upset. I disabused her of her suspicions. I cannot possibly tell you how happy she was, for she loves me! Yes! She loves me! The coldness she showed toward me was weighing as heavily on her as it was on me.

Finally, our cruel separation has come to an end. You can't imagine how delighted I am!"

"Is it really true?" cried Joseph, his eyes moist with tears. "If only it is really true, Monsieur le Marquis, I think you will be happy forever, for the only thing lacking in your life was the marquise's love. Or rather, as you said, it was only her estrangement that made you unhappy."

"And to whom would I say this, my poor Joseph? Don't you possess an even sadder secret? But let's not talk about sad things. This is too beautiful a day for that. Maybe you can see that I was crying? It's because I was overcome with happiness, you see. I so little expected it! I'm so weak, am I not?"

"Come on, Monsieur le Marquis, you have every right to cry from happiness; you've certainly cried enough from sadness. And look at me! I'm doing the same thing as you! These are honest tears. I wouldn't trade them for ten years of my life. I have only one fear, and that's that I may not be able to keep myself from throwing myself at Madame la Marquise's feet the first time I see her."

"Crazy old man, you are as unreasonable as your master. Now I've got something I'm afraid of, too."

"What's that?"

"I'm afraid it won't last. I'm too happy. What does my life lack now?"

"Nothing at all, Monsieur le Marquis—absolutely nothing."

"That's why I'm afraid. I distrust such a perfect and complete happiness."

"Alas! If that's all you're worried about, Monsieur le Marquis—no, I don't dare say it."

"I understand. Well, I believe your fears are needless. The upheaval that this happiness is causing in me is so sharp, so profound, that I am sure I am nearly cured!"

"What do you mean?"

"Hasn't my doctor told me a hundred times that often a violent moral shake-up would be enough either to cause or to cure this terrible malady? Why shouldn't happy emotions be powerful enough to save me?"

"If you believe that, Monsieur le Marquis, it will be true. It is true. You are cured! This must be a blessed day! Ah, as you said, Madame la Marquise is an angel come down from heaven. I begin to be almost afraid myself, monsieur; this is perhaps too much happiness for one day. But I've got a solution: if you just need one little worry to reassure you, well, then, thank God! I've got just the ticket!"

"What's that?"

"One of your friends has happily, conveniently—funny how this came up just in time!—has received a sword thrust—really not a serious one, it's true. But still, that will do to make you sad enough for there to be a flaw in this otherwise perfect day, which is what you want. It's true that the wound really ought to have been more serious for your purposes, but you have to take what you can get."

"Really, that's a bit too much! And who are you talking about?"

"The Duke de Lucenay."

"Is he wounded?"

"Just a scratch on the arm. The duke came here yesterday to see Monsieur, and he said that he would return this morning to ask for a cup of tea."

"Poor Lucenay! Why didn't you tell me before?"

"Yesterday I did not get to see Monsieur le Marquis."

After a moment of thought, Monsieur d'Harville said, "You are right. This bit of sadness will surely assuage the jealous fates. But I've just had an idea. I'm thinking of putting together a stag party—for all of Monsieur de Lucenay's friends—to celebrate the happy outcome of his duel. He'll be thrilled, since he won't be expecting a party."

"Great idea, Monsieur le Marquis! Here's to happiness! You need to make up for lost time. How many people will be attending? I need to let the butler know."

"Six people, in the little winter dining room."

"And the invitations?"

"I'll write them. One of the stableboys can mount up and deliver them right away. It's early, so everyone will still be home. Ring the bell."

Joseph rang.

Monsieur d'Harville entered his office and wrote the following letter several times, changing only the name of the guest:

Dear ***,

This is a group invitation to an impromptu event. Lucenay is supposed to come over for lunch with me this morning. He thinks he is coming to see me only. Please help me give him a delightful surprise by joining me and some of his other friends whom I will also invite. Be here at twelve sharp.

A. d'Harville.

A servant entered the room. "Please send someone on horseback to deliver these letters immediately," said Monsieur d'Harville. Then, turning to Joseph, he said, "Write these addresses: the Viscount de Saint-Remy—Lucenay can't do without him," Monsieur d'Harville said to himself, "Monsieur de Montville—one of his travel partners—Lord Douglas—his loyal whist partner—and the Baron de Sézannes—his childhood friend. Have you got all of that?"

"Yes, Monsieur le Marquis."

"Send out those letters this minute," said Monsieur d'Harville. "Oh, Philippe, please ask Monsieur Doublet to come to see me."

Philippe left the room.

"So, what's wrong with you?" Monsieur d'Harville asked Joseph, who was looking at him in amazement.

"I still haven't gotten over it, monsieur. I haven't ever seen you looking so well, so cheerful. And also, you're normally so pale, but now you have such good color, and your eyes are shining."

"It's just happiness, dear Joseph; nothing but happiness. Oh, by the way, I need your help in a plot. I need you to go get some information from Mademoiselle Juliette, Madame d'Harville's servant who is in charge of her diamonds, I believe."

"Yes, Monsieur le Marquis, Mademoiselle Juliette is the one who takes care of them. I helped her clean them less than a week ago."

"Go ask her the name and address of her mistress's jeweler. But she must not breathe a word of this to the marquise!"

"Ah! I understand, monsieur. It's a surprise!"

"Run along. Here's Monsieur Doublet."

And in fact the steward entered the room as Joseph was leaving. "I await your orders, Monsieur le Marquis."

"My dear Monsieur Doublet, I am going to shock you," said Monsieur d'Harville, laughing. "I am going to make you squeal in distress."

"Me, Monsieur le Marquis?"

"Yes, you."

"I will do everything in my powers to satisfy Monsieur le Marquis."

"I am going to spend a lot of money, Monsieur Doublet—a huge amount of money."

"There's nothing shocking in that, Monsieur le Marquis. We can spend lots. Thank the Lord, we can spend lots."

"For a long while I've had an itch to build something: I would like to add a gallery to the garden, at the right wing of the mansion. I've been hesitating to undertake this folly which I've never told you about until now, but I've decided to go ahead with it. We must let my architect know about it so he can come here to discuss the plans with me. Well, Monsieur Doublet? You're not groaning at the prospect of this expense?"

"I can attest to Monsieur le Marquis that I am not groaning."

"This gallery will be for hosting parties; I would like it to be built as if by magic. Now, since magic tends to be expensive, it will be necessary to sell fifteen or twenty thousand pounds of income property so as to be able to afford to pay for the project because I want work on it to start as quickly as possible."

"That makes perfect sense. Best to enjoy it right away. I have always said, 'The only thing the marquis lacks is a taste for something or another.' The good part about a taste for buildings is that they last. As for money:

Monsieur le Marquis shouldn't worry. Thank the Lord, if that's what he wants, this fantasy of a gallery is well within his power."

Joseph returned. "Monsieur le Marquis, here is the jeweler's address. His name is Monsieur Baudoin," he said to Monsieur d'Harville.

"My dear Monsieur Doublet, you will now go to this jeweler and ask him to bring here, in an hour, a river of diamonds worth about two thousand louis. Women can never have too many gems, especially since they put them on their dresses nowadays. You will work out the arrangements for payment with the jeweler."

"Yes, Monsieur le Marquis. I won't be groaning about this, either. Diamonds are like buildings—they last. And this surprise will also make Madame la Marquise so happy—not to mention the happiness you'll get from doing it. As I had the honor of saying the other day, no one has a more beautiful life than Monsieur le Marquis."

"Good old Monsieur Doublet," said Monsieur d'Harville, smiling. "Your congratulations always have the knack of being inconceivably apt."

"That's their only merit, Monsieur le Marquis, and if they have it, that's maybe only because they come from the depths of my heart. I'm going to run over to see the jeweler," said Monsieur Doublet. He departed.

As soon as he was alone, Monsieur d'Harville walked around in his office, his arms folded across his chest, his gaze fixed and thoughtful.

His face changed suddenly. No longer did it express the contentment that had fooled the marquis's steward and old servant. It expressed, rather, a calm, somber, and cold resolution. After having paced the room for a short while, he sat down heavily, as if overwhelmed by the weight of his sorrows. He put his elbows on his desk and hid his face in his hands. After a moment, he sat up abruptly, wiped a tear that had wet his reddened eyelid, and said, with effort, "Let's go. Courage. Let's go."

He wrote then to many different people on essentially insignificant subjects, but in each of these letters he made or deferred appointments for several days from then. The marquis was finishing his correspondence when Joseph returned. Joseph was so cheerful that he forgot himself so far as to hum himself.

"Monsieur Joseph, you have a very nice voice," his master said to him, smiling.

"My lord, you can joke about it, Monsieur le Marquis. I don't care. I'm singing so loudly in my heart that I can't help it if you can hear it on the outside."

"Please send these letters for me."

"Yes, Monsieur le Marquis. But where will you be receiving the gentlemen arriving shortly?"

"Here, in my office. They will smoke after lunch, and Madame d'Harville won't be bothered by the smell in her chambers that way."

At this moment, the sound of a coach could be heard in the court of the mansion.

"That's Madame la Marquise, who is going out. She asked for her horses this morning very early," said Joseph.

"Run over, then, to ask her to please stop by here before leaving."

"Yes, Monsieur le Marquis."

Right after the servant left the room, Monsieur d'Harville walked up to a mirror and studied himself attentively. "Good, good," he said to himself in a soft voice. "That's it—rosy cheeks and shining eyes. Joy or fever, it doesn't matter, as long as it misleads people. All right, it's time to put a smile on my face. There are so many different kinds of smiles. But who can distinguish the real ones from the fakes? Who can penetrate this mask of lies and say, 'Your laugh hides bleak despair; your hearty cheer hides the thought of death'? Who can guess at such a thing? No one—fortunately, no one. No one? Oh, yes, there is someone. Love wouldn't make such an error. Its instinct would bring it knowledge. But I hear my wife. My wife! Let's go. Back to your role, you sinister playactor."

Clémence entered Monsieur d'Harville's office. "Good morning, Albert, my dear brother," she said in a sweet and affectionate voice as she offered him her hand. Then, noticing the smiling expression on her husband's face, she said, "What happened to you, my dear? You look radiant."

"It's just that as you walked in the room, my dear little sister, I was thinking of you. In addition to that, I was under the impression that we had come to an excellent resolution."

"That doesn't surprise me."

"What happened yesterday—your admirable generosity, the noble conduct of the prince—all of that gave me much to think about, and I have come around to your way of thinking. And I mean I've come around completely, and I'm sorry for yesterday's slight impulses toward rebellion. You'll forgive me, even just out of flirtatiousness?" he added, smiling. "I'm sure you wouldn't have wanted me to give up on your love too easily."

"This is so wonderful to hear! What a happy transformation!" Madame d'Harville exclaimed. "Ah! I was sure that if I spoke to your heart and your mind, you would understand. Now I have no more doubts about the future."

"Nor do I, Clémence, I can assure you. Yes, since I made my determination last night, the future which seemed so vague and somber to me now seems singularly clear, and so much simpler."

"Nothing can be more natural, my dear. Now we're both going in the same direction, supporting each other like brothers and sisters do. At the end of our journey, we will be to each other just what we are today. This sentiment will never change. Ultimately, I want you to be happy—and that's what will happen, because I've committed my desire here," said Clémence, touching her forehead with her finger. Then she went on with a charming expression, lowering her hand to put it on her heart. "No, I am wrong. Here's where it is. That's where that good thought will constantly keep watch—over you, and over me, too. You'll see, my good brother, what the stubbornness of a devoted heart can bring."

"Dear Clémence!" answered Monsieur d'Harville, containing his emotion.

Then, after a moment of silence, he went on, gaily: "I asked you to be so good as to come here before leaving in order to let you know that I won't be able to have tea with you this morning. I have several people coming to lunch. It's a kind of impromptu party to celebrate the happy outcome of the duel that poor Lucenay had. By the way, he was only very lightly wounded by his adversary."

Madame d'Harville blushed as she remembered the cause of this duel: a ridiculous comment Monsieur Lucenay had made in front of her to Monsieur Charles Robert. This was a cruel memory for Clémence; it reminded her of a lapse that made her feel ashamed. To turn her attention from this painful thought, she said to her husband, "What an odd coincidence: here is Monsieur de Lucenay coming to have lunch with you, and I was just going to invite myself over, perhaps a little rudely, to see Madame de Lucenay this morning. I have a great deal to discuss with her in connection with my two unknown protégées. From there I'm planning on going to the Saint-Lazare prison with Madame de Blainval. You don't know all I plan on doing. Right now, I'm plotting to get myself allowed to participate in the rehabilitation of young female detainees."

"You are truly insatiable," said Monsieur d'Harville with a smile. Then he added, with a sudden tremor of painful emotion that, in spite of his efforts to hold it back, revealed itself slightly in his voice, "So that means I won't see you again," and then he was quick to add, "today?"

"Does it bother you that I'm going out so early?" Clémence asked him quickly, surprised to hear his tone of voice. "If you like, I can put off my visit to Madame de Lucenay."

The marquis had been on the verge of giving himself away. He took up again his most affectionate tone. "Yes, my dear little sister, your leaving me bothers me so much that I can't wait for you to come back. That's one flaw I will never get rid of."

"That's good, my dear, because if you did, I wouldn't like it one bit."

A gong announced the arrival of a visitor to the mansion.

"Here is one of your guests, no doubt," said Madame d'Harville. "I'll leave you now. By the way, what will you be doing tonight? If you haven't made plans yet, I demand that you accompany me to the Théâtre des Italiens. Maybe now you will be more interested in music."

"I put myself at your service with great pleasure."

"Will you be going out soon, my dear? Will I see you again before dinner?"

"I'm not going anywhere. You'll find me—here."

"I'll stop by when I return to find out whether your stag party went well."

"Good-bye, Clémence."

"Good-bye, my dear—see you soon! I am giving you full rein to do whatever you like while I'm gone—any tomfoolery you like! Have fun!"

And after clutching her husband's hand warmly, Clémence walked out one door just a moment before Monsieur de Lucenay entered through another.

"She gave me full rein for tomfoolery. She urged me to have fun. When I said good-bye, in my soul's last cry of agony, she understood me as if I meant, in that word of final and eternal separation, nothing more than 'See you soon.' And now she's running off feeling calm and happy. Good. That means I've done a good job pretending. Heavens! I never knew I was such a good actor! But here's Lucenay."

CHAPTER 5

STAG PARTY

Monsieur de Lucenay entered Monsieur d'Harville's quarters. The duke's wound was so slight that he didn't even have his arm in a sling. His expression was just as ironic and haughty, his nervous energy just as constant, his unreasonable pleasure in worrying the people around him just as limitless as ever. Yet despite his bad habits and his jokes that were always in the worst of taste, and despite his outsize nose that gave his face an almost grotesque character, Monsieur de Lucenay, as we've said, was not a vulgar person, thanks to a strain of natural dignity and brave impudence that never abandoned him.

"You must think I don't care about you at all, my dear Henri!" said Monsieur d'Harville as he extended his hand to Monsieur de Lucenay. "It was only this morning that I learned of your unfortunate adventure."

"Unfortunate? Oh, come now, Marquis! I got my money's worth, as they say. I've never laughed so hard in my life! That excellent Monsieur Robert was so resolutely determined not to be seen to have phlegm. Really, didn't you know about that? The other evening, at the embassy of ***, I asked him, in front of your wife and Countess MacGregor, while he was conducting her about, how his phlegm was. *Inde irae*;[121] for, between you and me, he wasn't suffering from that at all. But it doesn't matter. You understand—to hear someone say so in front of pretty women is very provoking."

"What silliness. That's just like you. But who's this Monsieur Robert?"

"I don't know anything about him, honestly—nothing at all. He's a gentleman I met at the waters. He was walking before us in the winter garden at the embassy. I called him over to make this stupid joke at his expense. He paid me back two days later with a gallant little scrape of his sword. That's the sum total of our relations. But let's not talk anymore about such silliness. I'm here to ask you for a cup of tea."

As he said this, Monsieur de Lucenay flung himself onto the sofa and stretched out. Once there, inserting the end of his cane between the wall

121. Latin for "hence this resentment." [TN]

and a painting that was hanging over his head, he began to fiddle with the frame and make it sway back and forth.

"I was expecting you, dear Henri, and I have arranged for a surprise for you," said Monsieur d'Harville.

"Oh, bother. What sort of surprise?" asked Monsieur de Lucenay as he started to make the frame sway quite alarmingly.

"You're going to end up knocking that painting off the wall, and it's going to fall right on your head."

"By Jove, you're right! You've got an eagle's eye. But, so tell me, what is the surprise you have in store for me?"

"I've asked some of our friends to come to lunch with us."

"Oh, well, that's something else. As to that, Marquis, bravo! Bravissimo! Archibravissimo!" Monsieur de Lucenay cried out at the top of his lungs as he gave the cushions of the sofa some good whacks with his cane. "So who's coming? Saint-Remy? No, he won't be here. He's been in the countryside for the past few days. What on earth can he be up to in the countryside in the dead of winter?"

"Are you sure he isn't in Paris?"

"Absolutely sure. I had written to him to ask him to serve as my second. He wasn't here, so I was left to Lord Douglas and Sézannes."

"That works out perfectly. They'll be joining us for lunch."

"Bravo! Bravo! Bravo!" Monsieur de Lucenay shouted anew. Then, twisting and turning around on the sofa, he accompanied his uncouth cries with a series of twists and turns that would be the envy of a mountebank. The Duke de Lucenay's acrobatic performance was interrupted by the arrival of Monsieur de Saint-Remy.

"I didn't have to ask whether Monsieur de Lucenay was here," said the viscount, gaily. "You can hear him from downstairs!"

"What? You're here, you beautiful faun, you rustic, you werewolf?" cried the duke, as he sat up abruptly in astonishment. "We thought you were in the country."

"I have been back since yesterday. I just received d'Harville's invitation and I ran right over here, thrilled about this great surprise." And Monsieur de Saint-Remy held out his hand to Monsieur de Lucenay and then to the marquis.

"And I am very grateful to you for your speedy arrival, my dear Saint-Remy. Isn't it natural? Shouldn't Lucenay's friends be delighted at the outcome of this duel which, after all, might have led to a terrible tragedy?"

"But what in the name of God were you doing in the country in the middle of winter, Saint-Remy? I'm dying to know," said the duke, refusing obstinately to change the subject.

"Isn't he curious!" said the viscount, turning to Monsieur d'Harville. Then he answered the duke: "I want to wean myself from Paris little by little because I'm going to have to leave it soon."

"Oh, right! You had that beautiful fantasy of joining the French delegation to Gerolstein. We don't want to hear about your cockamamie notions about diplomacy! You'll never go there—that's what my wife says and everyone else agrees with her."

"I can assure you that Madame de Lucenay is as much in error as everyone else."

"She told you right in front of me that it was folly."

"I've been known to commit many follies in my life."

"Yes, elegant and charming follies, of just the right sort, as one who thought you had practically ruined yourself with your magnificence worthy of Sardanapalus[122] might say, I'll admit to that. But the idea of burying yourself in a hole of a court like that—in Gerolstein? There's a nice move! That wouldn't be a folly—it would be stupid. You are too intelligent for stupidities like that."

"Be careful, my dear Lucenay. When you speak ill of that German court, you're going to find yourself in trouble with d'Harville, who's the close friend of the reigning grand duke. And for that matter, he received me the other day, with the utmost of grace at the embassy of *** when I was presented to him."

"Really! My dear Henri," said Monsieur d'Harville, "if you knew the grand duke as I know him, you would understand that Saint-Remy shouldn't have any hesitation about spending time in Gerolstein."

"I believe you, Marquis, even though they say your grand duke is a real original. That doesn't mean a gallant like Saint-Remy, our finest flower, could live anywhere but Paris. Only Paris appreciates him at his full worth."

Monsieur d'Harville's other guests had just arrived when Joseph entered the room and whispered a few words to his master.

"Gentlemen, will you excuse me?" said the marquis. "It's my wife's jeweler, and he has diamonds I have to choose from for her. It's a surprise. You understand about this, Lucenay: we're both husbands of the old school."

"Ah! A surprise!" cried the duke. "My wife gave me a surprise yesterday, and it was a really remarkable one!"

"Some splendid gift?"

"She asked me for a hundred thousand francs."

"And since you're so magnificently openhanded, you gave her the money."

"Lent it! Her Arnouville property has been mortgaged for the money.

---

122. For Sardanapalus, see Book II, Chapter 13, footnote 59. He was notorious for self-indulgence, and his death was preceded by the destruction of his property and harem. That death is the subject of Eugène Delacroix's famed painting *The Death of Sardanapalus*, which Sue may have had in mind. [TN]

Short reckonings make long friends. But it doesn't bother me; loaning a hundred thousand francs with two hours' notice to someone who needs it is a nice thing to do, and a rare enough occurrence. Isn't that true, you dissipated fop? You're an expert in borrowing, aren't you?" the duke asked Monsieur de Saint-Remy, laughing, hardly suspecting the true relevance of what he said.

Despite his audacity, the viscount at first blushed slightly; then he said, shamelessly, "A hundred thousand francs! That's a bundle! How could a woman ever need a hundred thousand francs? We men—now that's another story."

"Honestly, I don't know what my wife wants to do with that money. And, truth be told, I don't really care. Probably some old bills for clothing. Impatient shopkeepers are so insistent. It's her affair. And you can surely see, Saint-Remy, that once I agreed to lend her the money, it would have been in the worst possible taste to ask what she wanted it for."

"And yet, people who lend money are usually especially curious to know what the people borrowing it plan to do with it," said the viscount, laughing.

"Remy, you have such wonderful taste, by God," said Monsieur d'Harville, "so you have to help me choose the set of jewels for my wife. If it meets your approval, I'll know I made the right choice. Your judgment reigns supreme in the world of fashion."

The jeweler entered the room bearing several cases of jewels in a large leather pouch.

"Look, it's Monsieur Baudoin!" said Monsieur de Lucenay.

"Here at your service, Duke."

"I know for a fact that you're the one who is ruining my wife with those gleaming, infernal temptations of yours," said Monsieur de Lucenay.

"This winter, the duchess wished merely to have her diamonds remounted," said the jeweler, slightly embarrassed. "And I brought them to the duchess just now, right before coming here to see the marquis."

Monsieur de Saint-Remy knew that Madame de Lucenay had exchanged her diamonds for paste in order to help him and so this encounter was decidedly unpleasant for him. Yet he said, without shame, "Husbands are so curious! Don't answer him, Monsieur Baudoin."

"Curious? Oh, no, not at all," said the duke. "My wife is the one who's paying. She can do whatever she has a mind to—she's richer than I am."

During this exchange, Monsieur Baudoin had spread out on a desk several stunning ruby and diamond necklaces.

"How they sparkle! And how beautifully those gems have been cut!" said Lord Douglas.

"Alas, monsieur," said the jeweler, "I had one of the best gem-cutters in Paris working for me. Unfortunately, he's gone insane—I will never find one like him again. My gem broker told me that he probably lost his mind because of his poverty, poor man."

"Poverty? You entrust your diamonds to people in poverty?"

"Absolutely, monsieur. I've never known a gem-cutter to steal anything. And yet, that job is a hard one and you don't make much at it."

"How much is this necklace?" asked Monsieur d'Harville.

"The marquis will notice that the gems are of a magnificent water and cut, and all nearly of the same size."

"This preparatory rhetoric threatens the worst for your wallet," said Monsieur de Saint-Remy, laughing. "My dear d'Harville, get ready for an exorbitant price."

"Come now, Monsieur Baudoin, in all good conscience, what will you take for it?" asked Monsieur d'Harville.

"I would not like to force the marquis to bargain. The best price I can give is forty-two thousand francs."

"Gentlemen!" cried Monsieur de Lucenay. "Let all us husbands admire d'Harville in silence. To arrange a surprise for his wife that costs forty-two thousand francs! Heavens! Let's not let this get around. It sets a terrible example."

"Laugh all you like, gentlemen," said the marquis, gaily. "I am in love with my wife and won't hide it. I admit it—indeed I boast of it!"

"We can certainly see that," said Monsieur de Saint-Remy. "Such a gift makes your point more than all of the protestations in the world."

"I will take this necklace, then," said Monsieur d'Harville. "At least if you think this black enamel setting is in good taste, Saint-Remy?"

"It makes the sparkle of the gems stand out even more. It's marvelously effective!"

"I've decided on this necklace," said Monsieur d'Harville. "My business manager, Monsieur Doublet, will make the financial arrangements with you."

"Monsieur Doublet has already let me know that, Monsieur le Marquis," said the jeweler. He left after having put back in his pouch, without having counted them (such was his confidence), the different gemstones he had brought and that Monsieur de Saint-Remy had handled and examined for a long time and with some attention during their discussion.

As he handed the necklace to Joseph, who was awaiting his orders, he said to him softly, "Mademoiselle Juliette should be careful to place these diamonds with her mistress's others without her noticing. I want the surprise to be as complete as possible."

At this moment, the butler announced that luncheon was served.

The marquis's guests moved into the dining room and sat down at the table.

"You know, my dear d'Harville," said Monsieur de Lucenay, "this house is one of the most elegant and best situated in all of Paris?"

"It's comfortable enough, I guess, but it's a little cramped. I'm planning to add a gallery in the garden. Madame d'Harville would like to give some large balls, and our great rooms are not big enough to accommodate them. But there's also nothing more bothersome than the encroachments parties make in the rooms one lives in. Now and again, they end up exiling you from your own home."

"I agree with d'Harville," said Monsieur de Saint-Remy. "There's nothing shabbier or more bourgeois than being forced to move out of one's quarters to make way for a ball or concert. In order to host truly beautiful parties without being put out, you really need to provide a separate space for them. And furthermore, large, dazzling rooms, the kind designed for a grand ball, must be of a very different character than our ordinary great rooms. There is the same difference between those two different kinds of quarters as there is between a monumental painted fresco and an easel painting."

"He's right," said Monsieur d'Harville. "What a shame, gentlemen, that Saint-Remy doesn't have twelve to fifteen thousand pounds in income! Imagine the marvels he would build for our admiration!"

"Since we have the good fortune to live under a representative government," said the Duke de Lucenay, "shouldn't the country vote to set aside a million per year for Saint-Remy and to give him the job of representing French taste and elegance here in Paris? He would set the standards for taste and elegance for all of Europe—and for the world!"

"Hear, hear!" cried out all of the guests in unison.

"And this million should be levied as a tax on those abominable skinflints who possess great fortunes. They would be notified, pursued, and convicted of living like misers!" added Monsieur de Lucenay.

"And as such," said Monsieur d'Harville, "condemned to defray the magnificence they should have been displaying."

"And on top of that, the functions of head priest, or rather, of master of elegance," Monsieur de Lucenay went on, "once they had devolved upon Saint-Remy, would, by inspiring imitation, have a prodigious influence on the general taste."

"He's exactly the kind of person we should all want to be like."

"Clearly."

"And in trying to copy him, we would all purify our taste."

"In the time of the Renaissance, the general taste was superb because it was modeled after the taste of the aristocracy, which was exquisite."

"Given the serious turn this conversation has taken," said Monsieur d'Harville, gaily, "the only thing left to do, it seems to me, is to address a petition to the chambers calling for the establishment of the office of a grand master of French elegance."

"And since the deputies, without exception, pass for having very grand, very artistic, and very magnificent ideas, this motion will be approved by acclamation."

"While we await the decision that will legally confer the right of supremacy that Saint-Remy already exercises in practice," said Monsieur d'Harville, "I will request his advice regarding the gallery that I'm going to build. I've been struck by his ideas about the requisite splendor of parties."

"My feeble glimmers of inspiration are at your service, d'Harville."

"And when will we inaugurate your magnificence, my dear friend?"

"Next year, I suppose. I want the work to start immediately."

"You're quite a planner!"

"I have many other projects in mind, honestly. I'm thinking of completely redoing Val-Richer."

"Your property in Burgundy?"

"Yes. I'd like to do something large there, if—God lets me live long enough."

"Oh, you poor old man!"

"But didn't you buy a farm near Val-Richer recently in order to expand your property?"

"Yes. And a good piece of business it was, one my solicitor recommended."

"And who is this rare and precious solicitor who gives such good business advice?"

"Monsieur Jacques Ferrand."

At this name, a light shudder wrinkled Monsieur de Saint-Remy's brow. "Is he really as honest a man as they say he is?" he asked casually of Monsieur d'Harville, who remembered then what Rodolphe had told Clémence about the solicitor.

"Jacques Ferrand? What a question! He has the old-fashioned kind of integrity one doesn't come by these days," said Monsieur de Lucenay.

"He's as respected as he is respectable."

"A very pious man—that certainly doesn't hurt."

"An excessively miserly man—which is a good guarantee for his clients."

"He's one of those old-school solicitors who asks who you think they are when you try to ask them for a receipt for the money you've placed with them."

"I'd trust him with my whole fortune for that alone."

"But how the devil did Saint-Remy come to suspect anything about this worthy man, whose integrity is proverbial?"

"I'm just passing on vague rumors. Other than that, I have no reason to challenge the greatness of this phoenix among solicitors. But let's get back to your plans, d'Harville. What do you want to build at Val-Richer? The château is said to be admirable."

"I will consult you; rest assured of that, my dear Saint-Remy, and maybe sooner than you may think, for I take great enjoyment in such work. It seems to me that there is nothing more exciting than to have one project after another so that years to come are all planned out and occupied. Today, this project; in a year, that one. Later on, it's something else. Put that together with a charming wife one adores who is half the point of all of your inclinations and designs, and life is sweet indeed."

"Good Lord, I believe it! Really, that's heaven on earth."

"Now, gentlemen," said d'Harville when the meal was finished, "if you would like to smoke a cigar, you will find some excellent ones in my office."

The men got up from the table and went back into the marquis's office. The door was open to his bedroom, which was attached to it. As we have said, the only ornament in this room was two displays of very beautiful weapons.

Having lit his cigar, Monsieur de Lucenay followed the marquis into his room. "You know, I'm still an aficionado of weapons," said Monsieur d'Harville to him.

"These really are some magnificent English and French rifles. Indeed, I would be hard-pressed to decide between them. Douglas!" cried Monsieur de Lucenay. "Come in here and tell me if these rifles don't stand up to your best Mantons."

Lord Douglas, Saint-Remy, and two other guests entered the marquis's bedroom to examine the weapons.

Monsieur d'Harville, taking a combat pistol, cocked it and said, laughing, "Here, gentlemen, is the universal panacea for all ills. No more irritation, no more ennui . . ." And, joking, he put the barrel of the gun close to his lips.

"Not for me! I prefer another remedy," said Saint-Remy. "That one's only good in desperate cases."

"Yes, but it's so quick," said Monsieur d'Harville. "Boom! It's over. It's faster than the will itself. Really, it's marvelous."

"Be careful there, d'Harville. Jokes like that are always dangerous. A disaster can happen so quickly!" said Monsieur de Lucenay as he watched the marquis bringing the pistol closer to his lips.

"Good Lord, my dear friend, do you think that I would play this way with it if it were loaded?"

"I'm sure you wouldn't, but it's still not a good idea."

"Look, gentlemen: here's how you do it. You put the barrel delicately between your teeth and then . . ."

"Good Lord! Don't be such a fool, d'Harville, putting that gun there!" said Monsieur de Lucenay, shrugging his shoulders.

"You bring the finger closer to the trigger . . ." continued Monsieur d'Harville.

"You're too old to behave like such a child!"

"A little squeeze of the trigger," the marquis continued, "and you go straight to meet your maker."

With these words, the shot rang out. Monsieur d'Harville had blown his brains out.

We will not attempt to portray the stupor or the shock that Monsieur d'Harville's guests felt. The next day, one could read the following story in a newspaper:

> Yesterday, an event as unexpected as it was tragic sent the entire Faubourg Saint-Germain into mourning. One of those careless acts that lead each year to such tragedies caused a devastating accident. The following are the facts of the case that we have been able to gather on reliable authority: Monsieur le Marquis d'Harville, the owner of an immense fortune, aged barely twenty-six, known for his kind heart, married for only a few years to a woman he idolized, had assembled some of his friends for a luncheon. After leaving the table, they went into Monsieur d'Harville's bedroom where he kept several valuable weapons. While allowing his guests to examine some rifles, Monsieur d'Harville took a pistol that he did not believe to be loaded and jokingly brought it to his lips. Secure in this belief, he squeezed the trigger, and the pistol fired! The unfortunate young man fell dead, his head blown to pieces! The consternation of Monsieur d'Harville's friends, who had seen him, only moments before, so full of youth, happiness, and plans for the future, is indescribable. Finally, as if all of the circumstances of this painful event conspired to make it even more cruel in their painful contrasts, that very morning, intending to arrange a surprise for his wife, Monsieur d'Harville had bought a very expensive set of jewels that he meant to give to her. It was at this moment, at which life had perhaps never seemed more beautiful and full of joy for him, that he fell victim to this terrible accident.
>
> Before such misfortune, all reflection is futile. We can only remain crushed before the impenetrable works of divine providence.

We cite the newspaper in order to record the general belief that attributed the death of Clémence's husband to a fatal and deplorably careless act. Need we say that Monsieur d'Harville took the mysterious secret of his voluntary death with him alone to his tomb?

Yes, a death that was voluntary and calculated, and indeed premeditated, with as much coolness as generosity so that Clémence could not have had the slightest suspicion of the real cause of this suicide. Thus all of the projects that Monsieur d'Harville had discussed with his manager and friends, his happy confidences to his old servant, the surprise that he had arranged for his wife that very morning: all of these were so many snares designed to take in a credulous public. How could it be that a man who was so preoccupied with the future, so eager to please his wife, was thinking of killing himself? His death was thus not attributed, and could not be attributed, to anything besides carelessness.

As for his decision, it had been dictated by incurable despair. By becoming just as affectionate and tender toward him as she had previously been cold and haughty, by returning nobly to him, Clémence had caused her husband to feel the most painful remorse. Seeing her melancholy resignation to a long life without love, a life spent with a man struck with an incurable and frightening malady, convinced by the solemn certitude of her pronouncements that she would never overcome the repugnance she felt toward him, Monsieur d'Harville was filled with a profound pity for his wife, and terrible disgust with himself—and indeed, with life.

In the height of his agony, he said to himself, "I only love, I can only love, one woman in the world—and that's my wife. Her conduct, so generous and so transcendent, would only intensify my insane passion for her—if such a thing were possible. And this woman who is my wife can never truly be mine. She has the right to scorn me, to hate me; I tricked her in the most vile way into chaining herself, young as she was, for life to me and my detestable fate. I repent having done this. What is my duty toward her now? I must deliver her from the odious bonds that my selfishness imposed on her. Only my death can break these bonds. Thus, I must kill myself."

And this is why Monsieur d'Harville had carried out this grand and sorrowful sacrifice.

If such a thing as divorce existed, would this unhappy man have killed himself?

No! He could have partially repaired the damage he had caused by giving his wife back her liberty. This would have permitted her to find happiness in another union. The inexorable immutability of the law thus sometimes renders some harm irreparable, or, as in this case, it does not allow it to be undone except through a new crime.

CHAPTER 6

SAINT-LAZARE

We believe it incumbent upon us to alert the more squeamish of our readers that the Saint-Lazare prison, set aside especially for female thieves and prostitutes, is the site of daily visits by several women whose charitable nature, reputation, and social position command the respect of all. These women, brought up amid the splendors of wealth, who are rightly said to belong to the choicest ranks of society, come each week to spend long hours among the miserable prisoners of Saint-Lazare. If they observe in these degraded souls the slightest yearning toward the good, the slightest regret for a criminal past, they encourage the women's better tendencies, lay the groundwork for repentance, and, through the powerful magic of the words "duty," "honor," and "virtue," manage, from time to time, to wrest one of these abandoned, vilified, and scorned creatures from the mire.

Accustomed to the courtesies of high society and to the exquisite manners of the best company, these women leave their worldly mansions, kiss the virginal foreheads of their daughters who are pure as heavenly angels, and go into the dark prisons to face the brazen indifference or vile remarks of these female thieves or prostitutes. Faithful to the mission the highest morality imposes, they descend valiantly into this infected swamp and lay their hands on these gangrenous hearts. If they detect there the weakest throb of honor in its pulse, the slightest indication of even the slimmest chance of salvation, these women declare war against eternal damnation to rip from its clutches the sick soul for whom they have not lost all hope. The squeamish readers whom we are addressing should calm their sensitivities with the realization that they will hear and see nothing, after all, that these venerable women to whom we refer don't see and hear every day.

Without presuming to draw a too ambitious parallel between their mission and our own, might we not at least say that we are sustained in this long, painful, difficult work by the conviction that we may have awakened noble feelings of sympathy for those unfortunate people who, upright and courageous, do not deserve to be in this condition, as well as sympathy for sincere repentance and simple honesty? We hope also to have inspired disgust, aversion, horror, and a healthy fear of all that is absolutely impure and criminal. We have not recoiled before the most hideously true scenes, thinking that, like fire, moral truth purifies everything. Our words have too little value, our opinion too little authority, for us to claim that we can either teach or reform. Our only hope is to call the attention of thinkers and people of means to these great social problems; one may deplore them, but their reality cannot be denied.

Nevertheless, among those who are fortunate in this life, there are some who, disgusted by the coarseness of these sorrowful depictions, have claimed that these scenes are exaggerated, unrealistic, and impossible. In this way, they will not have to pity (we will not say "have to ameliorate") so much evil. This is easy enough to understand. The selfish man who is well fed and stuffed to the gills with gold wants above all to be able to digest his meal in peace. He finds the sight of poor people shivering with hunger and cold tiresome. He prefers to sleep off his wealth or fine food with drooping eyes, basking in the voluptuous experience of a ballet in an opera.

Most rich and happy people, on the contrary, have generously shown compassion for misfortunes of which they were unaware. Some have even thanked us for having pointed them toward new ways of employing their charity. We have been greatly sustained and encouraged by such support.

We can easily concede that this work is not good, from an artistic perspective, but we would maintain that it is not a bad book, from a moral perspective. Were this work, in its brief moment in the public eye, to have merely the outcome we have just mentioned, that would be enough to make us very proud of it and consider it to be an honor to us. What compensation could be more glorious for us than the blessings of a few poor families who will have owed some small material relief to the thoughts we have provoked?

This being said with respect to the latest tour we will take our readers on, after having—we hope—appeased their scruples, we will now conduct them into Saint-Lazare, an immense building with an imposing and gloomy appearance, situated on rue du Faubourg-Saint-Denis.

Unaware of the awful tragedy that was taking place in her own home, Madame d'Harville had gone to the prison after having obtained information from Madame de Lucenay on the subject of the two unhappy women who had been plunged into distress by the greed of the solicitor Jacques Ferrand. Madame de Blainval, one of the patronesses of the charity benefiting young imprisoned women, could not accompany Clémence to Saint-Lazare on this day, so Clémence went alone. She was warmly welcomed by the director and several women who were inspectors there. The inspectors could be identified by their black uniforms and by the blue ribbons with silver badges on them that they wore around their necks.

One of these inspectors, a woman of mature years with a serious and kind face, remained behind with Madame d'Harville in a small room adjoining the clerk's office. One cannot imagine the untold devotion, intelligence, commiseration, and wisdom of these respectable women who perform the modest and obscure functions of guards to these prisoners. There is nothing wiser or more practical than the notions of order, work, and duty that they impress upon the prisoners in hopes that these teachings will outlast their prison stay. By turns indulgent and firm, patient and severe—but always fair and impartial—these women, in constant contact with the prisoners, end up acquiring a real understanding of the prisoners' expressions after years of experience with them. They are almost always capable of sizing them up accurately at first glance, and they can classify them instantly as to their degree of immorality.

Madame Armand, the inspector who had remained alone with Madame d'Harville, possessed to a very high degree this almost prophetic knowledge regarding the character of the prisoners. Her words and judgments carried considerable authority in the institution. She said to Clémence, "Since the marquise has asked me to designate which of our prisoners, as a result of good conduct or sincere repentance, might most merit her interest, I believe I can recommend a poor woman who is, I think, more unfortunate than guilty. I do not think I am wrong when I say that it is not too late to save this young woman, an unfortunate child who is at most sixteen or seventeen years old."

"And what did she do to end up in prison?"

"She is guilty of having been on the Champs-Élysées at night. As it is forbidden to people like her to frequent certain public places either day or night, and since the Champs-Élysées is one of the places where it is forbidden to walk, they arrested her."

"And she seems to you to merit my attention?"

"I have never seen such regular or more innocent features. Imagine, Marquise, the face of a virgin. The thing that gave her face an even more modest expression was that when she arrived here, she was dressed like a peasant girl from the environs of Paris."

"So she's a country girl, then?"

"No, Madame la Marquise. The inspectors knew her. She had lived in a horrible house in the Cité from which she was absent for two or three months. But since she had not requested that she be struck from the official lists of such persons, she remained subject to the special authority that sent her here."

"But perhaps she had left Paris in order to try to rehabilitate herself?"

"I think so, madame, and that's what interested me immediately in her. I asked her about her past; I asked her if she came from the countryside, and I told her to have hope if, as I believed, she wished to return to a moral life."

"What was her answer?"

"Looking up with her big, sad, blue eyes that were full of tears, in an angelic voice she said, 'I thank you, madame, for your kindness, but I can't speak about my past. I was arrested; I was in the wrong, and I have nothing to complain about.' 'But where do you come from? Where have you been staying since you left the Cité? If you went to the countryside to seek an honorable existence, say something, prove it to us. We will write to the prefect to obtain your freedom. You will be taken off the official list of designated persons and people will help you in your good resolutions.' 'I beg of you, madame, please do not ask me any more questions. I won't be able to answer them,' she said. 'But when you leave this place, do you want to return to that frightful house?' 'Oh, never!' she cried. 'What will you do, then?' 'God only knows,' she answered, letting her head fall back down on her chest."

"That is strange! And how well does she express herself?"

"She speaks very well, madame. She is timid and respectful, but without anything low about her. I will go even further: despite the extreme sweetness of her voice and expression, there is occasionally in her tone and attitude a sort of proud sadness that confuses me. If she did not belong to the unfortunate class of which she is a member, I would almost think her pride shows that her soul is aware of its higher worth."

"This is just like a novel!" cried Clémence, interested in the last observation and finding, as Rodolphe had told her, that often nothing could be more entertaining than doing good. "And how does she get along with the other prisoners? If she is endowed with the elevated spirituality that you suppose, she must suffer greatly from her proximity to such wretched companions."

"Good Lord, Marquise, everything about this young woman comes as a surprise to me, even though I am a seasoned and professional observer. She has hardly been here for three days, but she already has considerable influence over the other prisoners."

"So quickly!"

"They feel not only sympathy for her, but also something close to respect."

"How can that be? These unfortunate women—"

"These unfortunate women sometimes have an uncanny instinct for recognizing—you could even say divining—the noble qualities in others. It's just that they sometimes hate people whose superiority they are obliged to acknowledge."

"And they don't hate this poor girl?"

"Far from it, madame. None of them knew her before she came here. At first they were struck by her beauty. Although her features are of a rare purity, they are veiled, you could say, by a sickly pallor that is quite touching. Her melancholic, sweet face at first inspired in them more a feeling of sympathy than of jealousy. And then she kept very silent—another source of astonishment for these creatures who, for the most part, are always trying to drown their sorrows with noise, speech, and constant movement. In the end, even though she is dignified and reserved, she showed herself to be compassionate, which kept her companions from being put off by her aloofness. That's not all. There's an uncontrollable creature who has been here for the past month whose nickname is the She-Wolf because of her violence, daring, and savagery. She's twenty years old, tall, virile, with a face that's rather pretty, but hard. We have often been forced to put her in solitary to restrain her. Only the day before yesterday, she left her cell, still angry from the punishment she had just been subject to. It was time for the meal, and the poor girl I was speaking of wasn't eating. She said sadly to her companions, 'Who wants my bread?' 'Me!' said the She-Wolf at first. 'Me!' another creature, who was almost deformed, said a moment later. Her name is Mont-Saint-Jean; she serves as a laughingstock and sometimes, in spite of our best intentions, as a butt of the other prisoners' jokes, even though she's several months' pregnant. The young woman gave her bread first to Mont-Saint-Jean, to the She-Wolf's considerable anger. 'I'm the one who asked for your ration first,' she cried, furiously. 'That's true, but this poor woman is pregnant. She needs it more than you,' answered the young woman. The She-Wolf ripped the bread out of Mont-Saint-Jean's hands anyway and began to swear while waving her knife about. As she is very mean and greatly feared, no one dared to take poor Songbird's side, even though all of the prisoners thought in their hearts that she was right."

"What did you say was her name, madame?"

"Songbird. That's the name, or rather the nickname, under which my protégée—who will hopefully soon be your protégée, Madame la Marquise—was brought in here. Almost all the girls here have nicknames of some sort."

"That one is unusual."

"In their hideous parlance, the name means 'singer.' That girl has a very pretty voice, they say. I have no difficulty believing that, for her speaking voice is enchanting."

"And how did she manage to escape that terrible She-Wolf?"

"Made even more furious by Songbird's calm, she ran toward her, swearing and brandishing her knife. All of the other prisoners cried out in fear. All alone, Songbird, looking upon this fearsome creature without fear, smiled at her bitterly and said to her in her angelic voice, 'Yes! Kill me—kill me, please! I want to die. Just don't make me suffer too much!' According to those who were there, she pronounced these words with a simplicity that was so heartbreaking that almost all of the prisoners had tears in their eyes."

"I can believe that," said Madame d'Harville, terribly moved.

"Fortunately, the worst characters," continued the inspector, "sometimes undergo sudden changes for the good. Upon hearing these words, which showed heartbreaking resignation, the She-Wolf was moved to the core of her soul, as she said later. She threw her knife to the floor, trampled on it with her feet, and cried, 'I was wrong to threaten you, Songbird, just because I'm stronger than you. You weren't afraid of my knife; you're brave. I like brave people. So from now on, if anyone tries to harm you, they'll have to answer to me.'"

"What a strange person!"

"The example the She-Wolf set served to increase Songbird's influence so that now—and this is almost unheard of around here—almost none of the prisoners speak to her in a familiar fashion. Most of them respect her, and they even offer to do all the little favors for her that prisoners can do for each other. I spoke with a few of the prisoners from her dormitory to learn the cause for the deference they show her. 'It's not a feeling we can control,' they answered me. 'We can tell that she's not just any old person, like the rest of us.' 'But who told you that?' 'No one told us—you can just tell.' 'But how?' 'From many things. First of all, yesterday, before going to bed, she got on her knees and said her prayers. To be able to pray, as the She-Wolf says, you have to have a right to it!'"

"What a strange idea!"

"These poor women have no religious feelings, and yet they never allow themselves a sacrilegious or impious word. You will see, madame, in all of our rooms, a kind of altar with the statue of the Virgin surrounded by offerings and ornaments they have made. Every Sunday, they burn a certain number of votive candles. Those who come to the chapel act with perfect respect, but generally the view of holy places is daunting to them or frightens them. To return to Songbird, her companions went on to tell me, 'You can tell that she's not one of us from her gentle manner, her sadness, and her manner of speaking.' 'And also,' added the She-Wolf brusquely—for she was there during this conversation—'it can't be that she's one of us, because this morning in the dormitory, without knowing why, we were all ashamed of dressing in front of her.'"

"What odd delicacy in the midst of such degradation!" cried Madame d'Harville.

"Yes, madame; they show no shame in front of men and among themselves, yet they're painfully modest if they're seen by us when they're not fully dressed or when charitable women like you, Marquise, visit the prisons. Thus this profound instinct of modesty that God has put in us reveals itself once again, even in these creatures, at least in the presence of the only people to whom they feel they owe respect."

"It is at least of some consolation to find even here that some of our good natural sentiments are stronger than depravity."

"No doubt about it. These women are capable of acts of dedication that would be very honorable if they had honest recipients. There is still one sentiment that is sacred for them, even though they respect and fear nothing, and that is the sentiment of motherhood. They honor it among themselves and rejoice in it. There are no better mothers. They will stop at nothing to keep their children with them. They make the greatest sacrifices in order to raise them, for, as they say, this little person is the only person who does not scorn them."

"So they have a deep sense of their own abjectness, then?"

"No one despises them as much as they despise themselves. For those of them who have repented sincerely, the original stain of their sin cannot be erased, even when they find themselves in better circumstances. Others go insane, so much is the idea of their original abjectness both unshakeable and implacable. That's why, madame, I would not be surprised if Songbird's deep sadness resulted from some remorse of this kind."

"If that is the case, what a terrible torture it must be for her! A remorse that nothing can assuage!"

"Fortunately, this remorse is more common than one thinks, madame, since it speaks well of the human race. The avenging conscience never goes completely to sleep. Or rather—and this is strange!—it could be argued that the soul sometimes keeps watch while the body sleeps. I made this observation again just last night in connection with my protégée."

"Songbird?"

"Yes, madame."

"How did that happen?"

"Quite often, when the prisoners are asleep, I go to make my rounds in the dormitories. You can't imagine, madame, how different the expressions of these women are when they are asleep. A good number of them who appear arrogant, mocking, bold, and rude during the day seem to me completely changed when sleep strips their features of all their exaggerated cynicism. Because vice, alas, has its pride! Oh! Madame, these dejected, gloomy, and somber faces now make only sad revelations. Now there are only shudders and painful sighs, involuntarily elicited by dreams that have no doubt shown them only the inexorable realities of their lives! I spoke to you a moment ago, madame, of that girl nicknamed the She-Wolf, an unbroken, unbreakable girl. About two weeks ago, she cruelly insulted me in front of all the prisoners. I shrugged my shoulders, and my indifference made her even angrier. Then, to get back at me, she came up with who knows what sort of vile insults about my mother, whom she had often seen visiting me here."

"How terrible!"

"I confess, as stupid as her attack on me was, it hurt me. The She-Wolf could tell, and she exulted in her victory. That night, toward midnight, I went to inspect the dormitories. I came close to the She-Wolf's bed; she wasn't supposed to be put in solitary confinement until the next morning. I was struck by what I can only call the sweetness of her face, compared to its usual hardness and insolence. Her features, full of sadness and contrition, seemed to be pleading. Her lips were half open, her chest heavy. And then something that seemed unbelievable, for I thought it impossible, two tears—two big tears—fell from the eyes of this woman who had a character of steel! I had been contemplating her in silence for a few minutes when I heard her say, 'I'm so sorry! Her mother!' I listened more attentively, but all I could make out from her almost unintelligible murmuring was my name—Madame Armand—pronounced with a sigh."

"She repented in her sleep for having insulted your mother."

"That's what I thought, and that made me less hard on her. No doubt, because of her awful pride, she had wanted to exaggerate her natural vulgarity in front of her companions. Maybe it was an instinctive goodness that made her repent during her sleep."

"And the next day, did she show any regret for her prior conduct?"

"None whatsoever. She acted in just as vulgar, fierce, and ill-tempered a fashion as always. But I can tell you, madame, nothing makes me have more pity than what I saw and told you about. I am absolutely persuaded—it's an illusion, perhaps!—that during their sleep these unfortunate women regain their innocence, or rather, they become themselves again, with all their flaws, it's true, but sometimes also with some good instincts that have not been dissimulated by vice's detestable and impudent braggadocio. From all of this I have been led to believe that these creatures are generally less evil than they try to appear. Acting on this conviction, I have often obtained results that would have been impossible if I had completely lost hope in them."

Madame d'Harville could not hide her surprise at encountering so much good sense, so much intelligence combined with such elevated, practical feelings of humanity, in this obscure inspector in a prison for fallen women.

"Heavens, madame," said Clémence. "The way you go about your sad work shows how much care you put into it. What incredible observations, what curious studies, but most of all, what great good you can and must be doing here!"

"It is very difficult to achieve good results. These women stay here only a short time, and so it is difficult to have an effective influence on them. One must be contented to plant the seeds in the hope that a few of the good ones will bear fruit someday. And sometimes, this hope does come true."

"But, madame, you must have a lot of endurance and virtuousness not to give in, considering the ingratitude elicited by this work that so rarely ends well!"

"My consciousness of fulfilling my duty sustains and encourages me, and in addition, I am repaid sometimes with fortunate discoveries. One finds enlightenment now and again in hearts that one would have thought absolutely hidden in darkness."

"Still and all, women like you must be very rare, madame."

"No, no, I assure you. There are others who do what I do but with greater success and more intelligence. One of the prison inspectors in another part of Saint-Lazare intended for those arrested for very different crimes would be much more interesting to you. She told me this morning about the arrival of a young woman arrested for infanticide. I have never heard anything more heartbreaking. The father of this unhappy girl, an honest worker, a gem-cutter, went mad from the pain of learning of his daughter's shame. I don't think that there could be anything more appalling than the misery of this whole family living in a garret on rue du Temple."

"On rue du Temple?" cried Madame d'Harville, astonished. "What is the name of this worker?"

"His daughter's name is Louise Morel."

"Is it really her?"

"She was in the service of a respectable man, Monsieur Jacques Ferrand, the solicitor."

"Someone recommended this poor family to me as an object of charity," said Clémence, blushing. "But I hardly expected to hear that such a horrible new event had befallen them. And what does Louise Morel say?"

"She says she is innocent. She swears that her child had died. And it seems that what she says has the ring of truth. Since you've taken an interest in her family, Marquise, if you would be so good as to deign to see her, your goodness might calm her despair, which people say is horrifying."

"I will certainly go see her. So I will have two protégées here instead of one. Louise Morel and Songbird—everything you've told me about this poor girl touches my very heart. But what must be done to free her? To do that, I would find her a position and take responsibility for what becomes of her."

"With the connections you must have, Marquise, it will be very easy to get her out of prison between today and tomorrow. It depends absolutely on the decision of the prefect of police. The recommendation of a well-placed person would be decisive for him. But I've lost the thread of what I wanted to say, which was what I saw when I saw Songbird sleeping. And I must say about that that I would not be surprised if she had another sorrow, no less cruel, on top of her profoundly painful sense of abjectness."

"What do you mean, madame?"

"I might be wrong, but I would not be surprised if this young woman, having escaped, I don't know how, from the degradation in which she had been raised, would have felt—did feel, perhaps—an honest love that would be at once her happiness and her torment."

"And what makes you think such a thing?"

"Her obstinate silence with respect to the place she spent the three months following her departure from the Cité makes me think she fears that the people with whom she had found refuge will seek to find her."

"Why should she be afraid?"

"Because she would have to tell them about a past they surely don't know about."

"Indeed, those peasant girl's clothes . . ."

"And then something else happened that gave support to my initial suspicions. Yesterday at night, as I went to carry out my inspection in the dormitory, I came up to Songbird's bed. She was fast asleep. Unlike her companions, she had a calm and serene face as she slept. Her long blond hair, half fallen out of her cap, was falling in profusion over her neck and shoulders. She had her two little hands clasped, crossing her chest as if she had fallen asleep while she was praying. I had been contemplating her angelic face with tenderness for a few moments when I heard her say someone's name in a quiet voice and in a tone that was at once respectful, sad, and emotional."

"And this name was?"

After a moment of silence, Madame Armand said, gravely, "Although I consider what one overhears from someone sleeping to be sacred, your interest in this unfortunate young woman is so generous, madame, that I may tell you this secret. The name was Rodolphe."

"Rodolphe!" cried Madame d'Harville, thinking of the prince. Then, figuring that, after all, his royal highness, the Grand Duke of Gerolstein could have nothing to do with the Rodolphe of poor Songbird, she said to the inspector, who seemed surprised at her exclamation, "That name took me by surprise, madame, because, by a singular coincidence, I have a relative with the same name. But everything you tell me about Songbird interests me more and more. Couldn't I see her today, right now?"

"Of course, madame. I will go to find her, if you wish. I will also find out about Louise Morel, who is in the other part of the prison."

"I will be in your debt, madame," said Madame d'Harville, staying behind. "This is odd," she said to herself. "I can't make sense of the strange impression that the name of Rodolphe created in me. I must truly be mad! What sort of relations could possibly exist between him and such a creature as this?" Then, after a moment of silence, the marquise added, "He was right! How interesting this all is! The mind and the heart expand when they are employed in such noble occupations! As he says, it seems that one is participating a bit in the work of divine justice when helping those who deserve it. And then again, these excursions into a world that we had no idea even existed are so fascinating, so entertaining, as he likes to say! Where is the novel that could ever create such touching emotions in me? Which one could ever capture my curiosity to this extent? That poor Songbird, for example, because of what I've just heard: she inspires me with such profound pity. I can give in blindly to my feeling sympathy for her because the inspector has too much experience to be fooled regarding our protégée. And that other unfortunate girl, the daughter of the worker whom the prince so generously rescued in my name! Those poor people! Their appalling poverty served as a pretext for him to save me! I escaped my shame, and death, too, perhaps, by means of a hypocritical lie. This deceit weighs on me, but I will expiate it by doing good. It will be so easy for me! It is so sweet to follow Rodolphe's noble advice! Obeying him is just like loving him! Oh, this feeling is intoxicating! It is Rodolphe alone whose breath has animated this new life he has created for me in order to console those who suffer. I feel a wonderful joy because I act only through him, with ideas that come only from him. I love him—oh! Yes! I love him! And he will never know of my life's eternal passion."

While Madame d'Harville awaits Songbird, we will take the reader into the prisoners' quarters.

CHAPTER 7

MONT-SAINT-JEAN

The clock in the Saint-Lazare prison rang two.

A gentle, mild, almost springlike warmth had come on the heels of the cold that had been in force for several days. The water reflected the sun's rays in a large, square basin with stone edges that stood at the center of a courtyard planted with trees and surrounded by towering dark walls. Numerous barred windows pierced those walls. Wooden benches were fastened to various spots in this vast paved enclosure that served as the site of the prisoners' recreation.

The ringing of a clock signaled the beginning of the recreation period. The prisoners poured out of the building through a thick, closely watched door that was opened to let them out. These women, dressed all alike, wore black caps and long, blue wool smocks fastened with a belt with an iron buckle. In all, there were two hundred prostitutes among them, charged with violations of the special regulations that applied to them and kept them isolated from society. On first glance, there was nothing about them that looked unusual, but if you looked more closely you could see that almost all of their faces bore the nearly ineffaceable stigma of vice, and above all, the signs of debasement that ignorance and poverty produce.

At the sight of such an assembly of fallen creatures, you can't avoid thinking with sadness that many of them were pure and honest once, at least for a time. We specify "many" because, as we will show further on, a great many of them were indeed debased, corrupted, and depraved—not only since their youth, but since their earliest childhood, and even since their birth, if such a thing were possible.

One might wonder, with a sad sort of curiosity, what fatal chain of events could have led those women who were once modest and chaste to this place. So many different channels empty into this sewer! Rarely does a passion for debauchery develop for its own sake. No; it is neglect, bad examples, perverse education, and, most of all, hunger that lead so many unfortunate girls into vice. For it is from the lower classes alone in all our civilization that we collect this tax on body and soul.

When the prisoners rushed out en masse, running and shouting into the courtyard, it was clear that it was not only the joy of leaving their workshops that made them so noisy. After having burst out of the one door that led into the courtyard, the crowd spread out and formed a circle around a deformed being whom they showered with jeers. She was a small woman who was between thirty-six and forty years old; she was short, stocky, and deformed, and her neck was wedged between her lopsided shoulders. The other prisoners had torn off her cap; her blond, or rather pale yellow, hair, bristly, tangled, and streaked with gray, fell limp across her low, unintelligent forehead. She wore a blue smock like the other prisoners, and she had under her right arm a little packet wrapped in a dingy plaid handkerchief that had holes in it. She was trying, with her left elbow, to parry the blows she was receiving.

There could be nothing more sadly grotesque than the features of this unfortunate woman. Her face was ridiculous and hideous, looking like nothing so much as a muzzle. Wrinkled, weathered, sordid looking, and earthen colored, it was punctuated by two nostrils and two raw little red slits for eyes. One moment angry, the next moment pleading, she growled and implored in turns. But the women only laughed harder when she begged than when she threatened.

This woman was the butt of the prisoners' games. One thing should have protected her from this malicious treatment: she was pregnant. Yet her ugliness and stupidity, along with their habit of treating her as if she were there solely for their mass entertainment, made these persecutors implacable despite their customary respect for maternity.

The She-Wolf stood out as one of the bitterest enemies of Mont-Saint-Jean (this was the scapegoat's name). The She-Wolf was a tall girl. She was twenty years old, agile, with a masculine build. Her face had even features, and her thick black hair had ruddy glints in it. Her hot blood made her skin blotchy. A dark down cast a shadow over her fleshy lips; her chestnut-colored eyebrows, thick and close-set, joined together over her large, wild eyes. There was something violent, ferocious, and bestial in the expression on this woman's face. A habitual grimace when angry that drew her top lip back to bare her white, widely spaced teeth accounted for the nickname of She-Wolf.

But her face was marked more by boldness and insolence than by cruelty. In a word, one could see that, more tainted with vice than essentially evil, this woman still had natural impulses toward goodness in her, as the inspector had just told Madame d'Harville.

"God! What have I done to deserve this?" cried Mont-Saint-Jean as she tussled with her companions. "Why are you picking on me like this?"

"Because it's fun."

"Because being tormented is all you're good for."

"It's your role in life."

"Look at yourself. You can see that you've no right to complain."

"But I don't complain for as long as I can, as you well know. I stand it for as long as I can."

"Well, we'll leave you alone if you tell us why your name is Mont-Saint-Jean."

"Yes, yes, tell us why!"

"I've told you a hundred times already. It was because of an old soldier I used to love, back in the day. They called him that because he had been wounded in the battle of Mont-Saint-Jean. I took his name. Are you happy now? Now that you keep making me repeat the same thing?"

"If he looked like you, he must have been a fresh-faced one, your soldier!"

"He must have been a cripple."

"The butt end of a man."

"How many glass eyes did he have?"

"And how many tin noses?"

"If he liked you, he must have had no arms and no legs and have been deaf and blind."

"I'm ugly. I'm a monster. Fine. I know that already. So go on, say stupid things, tease me all you like; it's all the same to me. But just stop beating me up—that's all I ask."

"What do you have there in that old handkerchief?" asked the She-Wolf.

"Yes, what does she have in there?"

"Show us!"

"Let's see what it is!"

"Oh, no! I beg of you!" the wretched woman cried out as she held her little packet in her hands as tightly as she could.

"We should take it away!"

"Yes, get it from her! What do you say, She-Wolf!"

"God! If you have to be mean, go ahead, but leave that alone. Leave it alone!"

"What is it?"

"All right. It's the beginning of some baby clothes for my child. I'm making it with old bits of laundry I've collected that no one wants. That can't make any difference to you, can it?"

"Oh! Mont-Saint-Jean's little one's baby clothes! That will be too funny for words!"

"Let's see it!"

"The baby clothes . . . the baby clothes!"

"She must have used the guard's little dog to measure it by!"

"Here are the baby clothes!" cried the She-Wolf as she tore the packet from Mont-Saint-Jean's hands. Almost in tatters, the handkerchief tore open, and a large number of scraps in fabrics of every color and old pieces of half-shaped clothing flew out into the courtyard. The prisoners trampled them under their feet, intensifying their jeers and laughter.

"What a bunch of rags!"

"It looks like the bottom of a ragpicker's basket!"

"There are samples of old rags in there!"

"That's quite a shop you've got there!"

"And to think, you're going to sew all of that?"

"You'll need more thread than fabric."

"It'll be embroidered!"

"Hey, pick up your scraps, Mont-Saint-Jean!"

"Do you have to be so mean? My God, do you have to be so mean?" cried the poor creature as she ran to and fro after the rags she was attempting to gather in spite of their shoving her about. "I never hurt anyone," she added, in tears. "I offer to do anything just to be let alone. I've offered half of my ration even though I was hungry—but no, it's always the same. What do I have to do to be left in peace? These people can't even feel sorry for a poor pregnant woman! Do you have to be more cruel than wild animals? It was really hard for me to pick up all of those little pieces of fabric. How else can I make baby clothes for my child? I don't have money to buy things with. What is it to you if I pick things up that people don't want and just throw away?" Then, suddenly, Mont-Saint-Jean cried out in hope, "Oh! There you are, Songbird! I'm saved! Talk to them for me. They'll listen to you, for sure, because they love you as much as they hate me."

Songbird, the last of the prisoners to arrive, entered the courtyard. Fleur-de-Marie was wearing the blue smock and black cap of the prisoners, but even in this coarse outfit, she was still charming. However, since her abduction from the Bouqueval farm (the outcome of which we will explain later), her features seemed profoundly changed. Her pale complexion, once tinged with pink, was now as white as alabaster. Her expression had also changed. It was now stamped with a sad dignity. Fleur-de-Marie felt that accepting the painful sacrifices of expiation with courage would help her attain redemption more completely.

"So ask them to have mercy on me, Songbird," Mont-Saint-Jean went on, pleading to the girl. "Look at them dragging everything around that I worked so hard at to collect so I could start baby clothing for my child! What kind of pleasure can they get from that?"

Fleur-de-Marie didn't say a word, but she began actively to pick up all of the rags she could find, one by one, from underneath the feet of the prisoners.

One prisoner was maliciously holding a sort of undershirt of rough, grayish-brown cloth under her clog. Fleur-de-Marie, still bent over, raised her eyes, with their power of enchantment, and said to her in her sweet voice, "I beg of you, let me take this back to that poor woman over there who is crying." The prisoner picked up her foot.

Songbird recovered the undershirt, along with almost all the other shreds, which she got back piece by piece. The only thing left for her to retrieve was a small child's bonnet that two prisoners were fighting over, laughing. Fleur-de-Marie said to them, "Please, be kind. Give her back this little bonnet."

"Oh, sure! This bonnet's for a harlequin in swaddling! It's made from a piece of gray fabric with bits of green and black fustian, and a lining from a mattress cover." This, in fact, was an accurate description of the bonnet, point by point. And it was greeted with endless jeers and laughter.

"Go ahead and make fun of it, but give it back to me," said Mont-Saint-Jean, "and please don't drag it through the stream like you did everything else. I'm sorry you had to dirty your hands for me, Songbird," added Mont-Saint-Jean, gratefully.

"Bring me the harlequin bonnet!" said the She-Wolf, laying hold of it and brandishing it in the air like a trophy.

"I beg of you, give it to me," said Songbird.

"No, that's just so you can give it back to Mont-Saint-Jean!"

"Indeed, yes."

"Oh, come on! It's not worth the bother, that shred of a rag!"

"Well, but Mont-Saint-Jean can only get rags for her baby clothes. You should feel sorry for her, She-Wolf," said Fleur-de-Marie as she reached toward the bonnet.

"You can't have it!" the She-Wolf said, savagely. "Why do I always have to give in to you, just because you're weak? You're taking advantage of that, you know!"

"What would be the merit in giving in to me if I were stronger than you?" answered Songbird with a gracious half smile.

"No, no. You want to twist me around your finger again with your soft little voice. No, you can't have it!"

"Come on, She-Wolf. Don't be mean."

"Leave me alone. You're irritating me."

"Please!"

"Listen—you're getting tiresome. I said no, and I meant no!" cried the She-Wolf, having become well and truly angry.

"Take pity on her. Look how she's crying!"

"What do I care? Too bad for her! She's our whipping boy."

"That's right—that's right! We should never have given her back those rags," murmured the prisoners, carried away by the She-Wolf's example. "Too bad for Mont-Saint-Jean!"

"You're right: too bad for her," said Fleur-de-Marie, bitterly. "She's your whipping boy, and she should just accept the fact. Her moans amuse you, and her tears make you laugh. You have to find some way to pass the time, right? If you killed her right here on the spot, she wouldn't have a thing to say about it. You're right, She-Wolf, it's simple justice! This poor woman has done nothing to hurt anyone, she can't defend herself, she's alone against the lot of you. You're beating her down. Isn't that really brave, isn't that the height of generosity?"

"So we're cowards, are we?" cried the She-Wolf, beside herself now, because of her natural violence and her impatience at being contradicted by anyone. "Answer me! We're cowards, huh?" she said, growing angrier by the moment.

The prisoners started making threatening noises about Songbird. Offended, the prisoners came closer to her and circled around her, shouting. They had forgotten the power she had had over them up until then, or rather, they were rising up against it.

"She calls us cowards!"

"What right does she have to say bad things about us?"

"Is she any better than we are?"

"We were too nice to her."

"And now she thinks she can act all high and mighty."

"If we want to torment Mont-Saint-Jean, what does she have to say about it?"

"Since that's the way it is, you're going to get more beatings than you got before—do you hear, Mont-Saint-Jean?"

"And here's one for starters," said one of them as she punched her.

"And if you meddle in things that aren't any of your business again, Songbird, it'll be the same for you."

"Yes! Yes!"

"That's not enough!" cried the She-Wolf. "Songbird has to apologize to us for calling us cowards! It's true: if we let her get away with that, she'd end up walking all over us. We're real idiots for not seeing this in the first place."

"Apologize!"

"Get on your knees!"

"On your knees!"

"Both knees!"

"Or else we'll give her what we give Mont-Saint-Jean, her protégée."

"On your knees! On your knees!"

"We'll see if we're cowards!"

"Just try saying it again!"

Fleur-de-Marie remained calm in the face of all this furious shouting. She let the tumult die down. Then, when she could make her voice heard, casting her beautiful, calm, melancholic gaze over all the prisoners, she answered the She-Wolf, who once again was yelling: "Just you dare to tell us we're cowards again!"

"You? No, no, it's that poor woman whose clothes you've torn, whom you've beaten and dragged in the mud. She's the one who's the coward. Don't you see how she's crying and trembling when she looks at you? I'll say it again, she's the coward, since she's afraid of you!"

Fleur-de-Marie's instincts were perfect. If she had invoked justice or duty against the brainless, cruel fury of the prisoners toward Mont-Saint-Jean, they wouldn't have listened to her. She reached them by addressing the sentiment of natural generosity that is never completely extinguished, even in the most corrupted mobs.

The She-Wolf and her companions muttered some more, but they recognized their cowardice and acknowledged it to themselves.

Fleur-de-Marie did not want to take unfair advantage of this first triumph, so she continued: "Your whipping boy doesn't deserve pity, you say, but what about her child? It surely does! Don't you think it can feel the blows you gave his mother? When she asks you for mercy, it's not for her, it's for her child! When she asks for a little of your bread, if you have some to spare, when she tells you she's hungrier than usual, it's not for herself, it's for her child! When she begs you, with tears in her eyes, to spare the shreds of fabric that she gathered up with such effort, it's not for herself, it's for her child! That poor little bonnet made up of scraps and shreds, lined with mattress cover fabric, that you were making so much fun of, maybe it's funny. But when I see it, the only thing I want to do is cry, I swear to you. Make fun of me and Mont-Saint-Jean, if you want."

The prisoners laughed no longer.

The She-Wolf was even looking sadly at the little bonnet that she still held in her hand.

"Good Lord!" Fleur-de-Marie continued as she wiped her eyes with the back of her delicate white hand. "I know you're not wicked. You torment Mont-Saint-Jean because you've got nothing else to do, not because you're cruel. But you're forgetting that there are two of them, her and her child. If she could hold it in her arms, it would protect her against you. Not only would you stop beating her out of fear of harming the poor, innocent child—but if it was cold, you'd even give its mother everything you could to cover it, wouldn't you, She-Wolf?"

"It's true. Who wouldn't feel sorry for a baby?"

"That's as clear as day."

"If he was hungry, you'd give him the bread out of your mouth, wouldn't you, She-Wolf?"

"With all my heart. I'm no meaner than anyone else."

"Us, neither!"

"A poor little innocent kid!"

"Who would have the heart to hurt him?"

"You'd have to be a monster!"

"Or heartless!"

"Or a wild animal!"

"I told you so—I knew you weren't wicked," said Fleur-de-Marie. "You're good, it's just that you didn't think. Instead of having her child in her arms for you to pity, she has it in her belly. And that's the only difference."

"That's the whole difference!" said the She-Wolf, excitedly. "But no, it's not the whole difference. You're right, Songbird, we were cowards. And you were brave to dare to tell us as much, and you were brave not to be frightened of us when you did tell us. You know, we can say and do what we want, we can argue against it—but you're not like us and we just have to give in to that. It bugs me, but that's the way it is. Just then, we were wrong. You were braver than us."

"It's true. That little blondie must be a brave one to tell us those truths like that to our face."

"Oh! It's because those blue eyes, those sweet blue eyes, once she claps them on you . . ."

"They become real little lions!"

"Poor Mont-Saint-Jean! She really ought to light a candle or two for you."

"But the thing about it is, it's true. When we were beating Mont-Saint-Jean, we were beating her child."

"I didn't think of that."

"Me, neither."

"But Songbird thinks of everything."

"Beating a baby—that's disgusting!"

"Not a single one of us could really do that."

There is nothing more volatile than the passions of a mob. Nothing is faster or more sudden than their turnings from evil to good and from good to evil. A few simple, touching words from Fleur-de-Marie had provoked an instant reaction in favor of Mont-Saint-Jean, who was crying from gratitude. Every heart was moved because, as we've said, sentiments related to maternity are always raw and powerful among the unfortunate women we have been discussing.

Suddenly, the She-Wolf, violent and excited in everything she did, took the little bonnet that she held in her hand, made a sort of purse out of it, dug into her pocket, pulled out twenty sous, threw them in the bonnet, and cried out as she presented it to her companions, "I've put twenty sous in there to buy something to make baby clothes for Mont-Saint-Jean's little one. We'll measure and sew it all ourselves, and that way making it will cost her nothing!"

"Yes! Yes!"

"A great idea! Let's take up a collection!"

"Count me in!"

"Great idea!"

"Poor woman!"

"She's as ugly as a monster, but she's still a mother like any other."

"Songbird was right. In fact, looking at those wretched baby clothes made of rags makes me want to cry my eyes out."

"I'm putting in ten sous."

"I'm in for thirty."

"I'm in for twenty."

"I'm in for four sous. That's all I have."

"I have nothing, but I'll sell my ration tomorrow to put something in. Who will buy it from me?"

"Me!" said the She-Wolf. "I'll put in ten sous for you. But you keep your ration, and Mont-Saint-Jean will have baby clothes fit for a princess."

Mont-Saint-Jean's surprise and joy were beyond description. Her grotesque and ugly face, inundated with tears, became something close to touching. Her expression beamed happiness and gratitude.

Fleur-de-Marie was very happy, too, even though she was obliged to say to the She-Wolf, when she held out the little bonnet for her contribution, "I have no money, but I'll work harder than anything."

"Oh! My good little angel of paradise!" cried Mont-Saint-Jean, falling at Songbird's feet and trying to take her hand in order to kiss it. "What did I ever do for you to make you so generous to me, and all of these ladies, too? Is this possible, God, my savior? Baby clothes for my child—good baby clothes, everything we'll need! But who would have ever believed it? I'm going mad with joy. Me, just now, I was the butt of everyone's jokes. And then all at once you say—well, you say something—with your dear little angel's voice, and now you've turned them good instead of mean, and now suddenly they like me. And me, too, I like them! They're so kind! I was wrong to get mad. I was so stupid and unfair and ungrateful! Everything they were doing to me was just a joke. They didn't mean to hurt me. It was all for the best—here's the proof! Oh! Now they could knock me dead here and now, and I wouldn't make a peep. I was just too soft."

"We have eighty-eight francs and seven sous," said the She-Wolf as she finished counting the total they had collected. She wrapped it up in the little bonnet. "Who will be our treasurer until we spend the money? We can't give it to Mont-Saint-Jean, she's too brainless."

"Songbird should hold on to it," they all said in unison.

"If you ask me," said Fleur-de-Marie, "we should ask the inspector,

Madame Armand, to take responsibility for the money and to make the purchases necessary for the baby clothes. Who knows? The good deed you're doing could touch Madame Armand, and maybe she will ask for a reduction of a few days' prison sentence for the women she notes as having been involved. So, She-Wolf," added Fleur-de-Marie as she took her companion by the arm, "aren't you happier now than when you were scattering Mont-Saint-Jean's poor rag shreds to the winds?"

The She-Wolf didn't answer at first. The generous exaltation that had animated her features for a moment had been succeeded by a sort of wild, animal mistrust.

Fleur-de-Marie looked at her with surprise, not understanding this sudden change at all.

"Songbird, come with me. We need to talk," said the She-Wolf in a somber voice.

And, pulling away from the group of prisoners, she abruptly led Fleur-de-Marie over to the basin with the grooved stone edges that was in the middle of the yard. A bench was nearby.

The She-Wolf and Songbird sat down and found themselves nearly isolated from their companions.

CHAPTER 8

SHE-WOLF AND SONGBIRD

We believe strongly in the influence of certain dominant individuals over the masses. The masses understand their feelings, and they have enough power over them to move them for good or ill. Some of these individuals are audacious, fiery, and indomitable; they appeal to the lower passions, stirring them up the way tempests stir up sea foam. But just like all other storms, these ones are not only furious but also ephemeral. Their gloomy effervescence is followed by the quiet return of feelings of sadness and malaise that gain the upper hand over even the most miserable conditions. Setbacks in the wake of violence are always bitter; awakening after excess is always painful. This is just the kind of baneful influence the She-Wolf personifies.

Other individuals—and they are much rarer, for their generous instincts must be infused with intelligence, and they need to have a mind as developed as their heart—inspire people toward the good, the same way the first kind inspires them toward evil. Their action penetrates souls gently, just as the warm rays of the sun may penetrate bodies with life-giving heat, just as the fresh dew of a summer's night gives life to arid, burning earth. Fleur-de-Marie could be said to personify this benevolent influence.

The reaction of the masses toward the good is not as abrupt as their reaction in favor of evil. The effects of the good last longer, however. This influence has something immaterial to it that smoothes, relaxes little by little, calms, makes the most hardened hearts expand, and lets them taste an inexpressible sensation of serenity. Unfortunately, such a spell is temporary.

After having glimpsed heavenly lights, people who have become depraved fall back into the darkness of their normal lives. Their memories of the gentle emotions that had caught them by surprise for a moment gradually subside. Sometimes, however, they make vague attempts to try to remember them, the same way we try to sing ourselves the lullabies of our happy childhoods.

Thanks to the charity she had inspired in them, Songbird's companions had just experienced the fleeting sweetness of these feelings, and the She-Wolf had shared them, too. But the latter, for reasons we will reveal shortly, could not remain under this beneficent impression as long as the other prisoners.

If it seems surprising to hear and see Fleur-de-Marie, who earlier was so passive and so full of painful resignation, now acting and speaking with courage and authority, it is because the noble teachings she had received during her stay at the Bouqueval farm had rapidly developed the rare qualities of her excellent nature. Fleur-de-Marie understood that it was not enough to lament an irreparable past and that the only path to rehabilitation was through doing good or inspiring others to do good.

As we said earlier, the She-Wolf was sitting on a wooden bench next to Songbird. The juxtaposition of these two young women offered a striking contrast. The pale rays of the winter sun shone on them both. The pure blue sky was dappled here and there with little cottony white clouds. A few birds, cheered by the warming temperature, were chirping on the black branches of the tall chestnut trees in the courtyard. Two or three sparrows, bolder than the others, came to drink and bathe in a little stream into which the basin overflowed. Green moss covered the stone casings of the basin's edges. In between their separate rows of bricks grew a few tufts of grass and wall-growing plants that had been spared by the frost.

This description of a prison basin might seem banal, but Fleur-de-Marie noticed each one of these details. She fixed her eyes sadly on this little corner of green and on this clear water in which the transient whiteness of the clouds was reflected as they moved across the blue of the sky and in which the golden rays of a beautiful sun broke apart into a luminous brilliance. Sighing, she thought about the magnificence of this nature that she loved so much and admired so poetically, and of which she was once more deprived.

"What did you want to tell me?" asked Songbird of her companion, who was sitting next to her and who had remained somber and silent.

"We need to have this out!" cried the She-Wolf, harshly. "Things can't go on this way!"

"I don't understand, She-Wolf."

"A moment ago, in the courtyard, I said to myself, thinking about Mont-Saint-Jean, 'I don't want to give in to Songbird again,' and yet I have just given in to you again."

"But—"

"But I'm telling you that this can't go on."

"What's your problem with me, She-Wolf?"

"I . . . I'm not the same person I was before you came here. No—I've lost my courage, my strength, and my daring."

Then, cutting herself short, the She-Wolf lifted the sleeve of her dress and showed Songbird her white arm. It was sinewy and covered with black hair. She showed her an indelible tattoo on the front of her arm that represented a blue dagger plunged halfway into a red heart. Underneath this emblem could be read the following words:

Death to cowards!
Martial
F.L. (for life)

"Do you see that?" asked the She-Wolf.

"Yes. It's sinister, and it frightens me," said Songbird, looking away.

"When Martial, my lover, inscribed these three words—Death to cowards!—on my arm with a needle that was red-hot from the fire, he believed me to be brave. If he knew how I've behaved for the last three days, he would plant his knife in my body the same way this dagger is planted in this heart. And he'd be right, because he wrote here, 'Death to cowards!'—and I'm a coward."

"What makes you a coward?"

"Everything."

"Are you sorry you were kind just a little while ago?"

"Yes."

"Ah. I don't believe you."

"Because it's yet another proof of the power you have over us all. Didn't you hear Mont-Saint-Jean when she was on her knees and thanking you?"

"What did she say?"

"She said, speaking of us, that 'in no time at all, you turned them good instead of mean.' I should have strangled her when she said that. Because, to our shame, it was true. Yes, in no time at all, you changed black into white. We listened to you, we followed our better instincts, and we're your dupes again, like a moment ago."

"My dupes? For having generously helped that poor woman?"

"That's not what I'm talking about," cried the She-Wolf angrily. "I've never bowed down to anyone before. I am called She-Wolf, and that's a good name for me. I have left my mark on more than one woman—more than one man, too. No one will ever say that a little girl like you can walk all over me."

"Me? How have I done that?"

"How would I know? You come here and you start off by insulting me."

"Insulting you?"

"Yes. You ask who wants your bread, and I am the first to respond. Me! Mont-Saint-Jean doesn't ask you until after I do. And you choose her over me. I run at you in a rage with my knife out."

"And I say to you, 'Go ahead, kill me if you want—just don't make me suffer too much,'" said Songbird. "And that was it."

"That was it? Right, that was it! But your words alone made me drop the knife from my hands. Your words made me apologize to you—to you, who had insulted me. Is that normal? Listen: when I had my wits about me again, I felt sorry for myself. And the evening you arrived here, when you got on your knees to pray, why, instead of mocking you and getting everybody else in the dormitory against you—why did I say, 'Leave her be. She's praying, and she can because she has the right'? And the next day, why did all of us feel ashamed to dress in front of you?"

"I don't know, She-Wolf."

"Really!" said this violent creature, with irony. "You don't know? No doubt, it's as we've said jokingly before: you're of a different species from us. Maybe you believe that?"

"I never said I believed that."

"No, you never say it, but you act it."

"Please, listen to me."

"No, listening to you isn't good for me—or looking at you. Until now, I've never envied anyone. Well, two or three times I've caught myself envying your holy virgin face, your soft and sad demeanor—it's stupid and it's cowardly. But I've even gotten to the point of envying your blond hair and your blue eyes—and I've always hated blondes. After all, I'm a brunette! Why would I want to look like you? Me, the She-Wolf? A week ago I would have left my mark on anyone who would have dared to say that. But it's not your fate that tempts me. You look as sorrowful as a Magdalene. Tell me: is that normal?"

"How am I supposed to know what impression I make on you?"

"Oh, you know what you're doing, looking like butter wouldn't melt in your mouth."

"But what evil plan do you think I'm up to?"

"How would I know? It's precisely because I don't understand any of it that I don't trust you. And another thing: up to now I've always been either happy or angry, but never thoughtful. And now you make me thoughtful. Yes, some of the words you said touched my heart against my will and made me start wondering about all sorts of sad things."

"I'm sorry I may have made you sad, She-Wolf, but I don't remember having told you—"

"For God's sake!" cried the She-Wolf, interrupting her companion in impatient rage. "Sometimes the things you do make me feel things just as much as the things you say! You're a sly one!"

"Don't get mad, She-Wolf. Tell me what you mean."

"Yesterday, in the workshop, I was watching you good. You had your eyes and face lowered over your sewing work. A big tear fell onto your hand. You looked at it for a minute, and then you brought your hand up to your lips, as if to kiss it and wipe it away. Isn't that true?"

"It's true," said Songbird, blushing.

"That wasn't such a big deal, but just then you seemed so unhappy—so unhappy—that I felt sick to my stomach, all turned upside down. Tell me, do you think that's funny? Really! I have always been as hard as a rock as far as feelings go. No one can say they've ever seen me cry. But all I have to do is look at your little mug and I start feeling all cowardly inside! Yes, because this is all just pure cowardice. The proof of it is that for the past three days I haven't dared write my lover, Martial, because I've had a bad conscience about it. Yes, being around you is making me all watery. This has to stop. I've had enough. This is not going to end well. I know myself. I want to stay the way I am. I don't want people to make fun of me."

"Why would people make fun of you?"

"For God's sake! Because they would see me being nice and playing the innocent—me, who used to make everyone around here quake in their boots! No, no. I'm twenty years old, I'm as pretty as you, in my own way. I'm mean. People are afraid of me, and that's the way I like it. I don't care about anything else. Anyone who says otherwise can drop dead!"

"Are you angry with me, She-Wolf?"

"Yes. Knowing you is bad for me. If this goes on another couple of weeks, instead of calling me She-Wolf, they'll start calling me Lamb Chop. No, thanks! No one castrates me like that. Martial would kill me. So it comes to this: I don't want to be around you. To get away from you completely, I'm going to request a change of placement. If they don't let me have it, I'm going to do something really bad to get my spirit back and to get sent to solitary until I'm freed. So now I've said what I wanted to, Songbird."

Fleur-de-Marie understood that her companion, whose heart was not completely corrupted, was essentially at war with her better impulses. Fleur-de-Marie had no doubt aroused these vague tendencies toward goodness by inspiring sympathy and charity in the She-Wolf, despite herself. Fortunately for humanity, there are rare but dramatic examples that prove that there are chosen souls who are blessed, almost unbeknownst to themselves, with such a power of attraction that they force more rebellious souls to enter their sphere and to emulate them. The prodigious results of certain missions, of certain kinds of apostolizing, cannot be explained in any other way.

On a much smaller model, that was the nature of the relationship between Fleur-de-Marie and the She-Wolf. But because of an odd contradiction, or rather, as a consequence of her intractable and perverse character, the She-Wolf was trying with all her might to fend off the positive influences that were gaining a hold on her in just the same way that honest people struggle with all their force against bad influences.

When you consider the fact that vice often has its own infernal pride, it is not surprising to see the She-Wolf making such an effort to preserve her reputation as an unbreakable and feared creature—and to keep from changing from a wolf into a lamb chop, as she put it. Still, all of these hesitations, rages, and combative gestures were interspersed with some generous impulses; they revealed signs in this wretched woman that were too favorable and too clear for Fleur-de-Marie to abandon the hopes she had, for a moment, held out for her.

Yes, sensing that the She-Wolf was not completely fallen, she wanted to save her, just as she had been saved herself. "The best way to prove my gratitude to my benefactor," thought Songbird, "would be to give to others, if they are capable of hearing it, the noble advice he gave me."

Timidly taking the hand of her companion, who was looking at her with dark defiance, Fleur-de-Marie said to her, "I can tell you, She-Wolf, that the reason you care about me is not because you're cowardly, but because you're generous. Only brave hearts are moved by the sorrow of others."

"There's nothing generous or courageous about it," said the She-Wolf, brutally. "It's cowardice. And another thing: I don't want you saying I was moved by other people. It's not true."

"I won't say it again, She-Wolf. But since you were kind to me, you won't mind if I'm grateful for it, will you?"

"I don't care one way or another, since tonight I'll be in another room, away from you. Or I'll be alone in solitary, and soon I'll be out of here, thank God!"

"And where will you go when you get out?"

"What do you think? I'll go home, of course, to rue Pierre-Lescot. I've got my own place."

"And Martial?" said Songbird, hoping to keep the conversation going by speaking with the She-Wolf about something she cared about. "What about Martial? Will you be happy to see him again?"

"Yes, oh, yes!" she answered, passionately. "When I was arrested, he was just getting better from some sickness, a fever that he'd gotten from living for so long by the water. For seventeen days and seventeen nights, I didn't once leave his side. I sold half of my junk to pay for the doctor, the drugs, and everything. You could say, and I will say, that if my man is alive, it's because of me. I lit a candle for him again yesterday. It's silly, but that's all right. Sometimes you see things like that helping people get better."

"And where is he now? What's he doing?"

"He's still living near the Asnières bridge, by the water."

"By the water?"

"Yes, he lives there with his family, in a house far away from anything else. He's always at war with the fishery police, but once he's in his boat, with a loaded rifle, it's not a good idea to get near him!" said the She-Wolf, full of pride.

"So what's his job?"

"He fishes illegally at night. Then, since he's brave as a lion, when some bum is looking for a fight, he's right there. His father has had run-ins with the law. He still has his mother, two sisters, and a brother. He'd be better off without the brother since he's a scoundrel who's going to end up getting his head chopped off one of these days. His sisters, too, for that matter. Anyway, it doesn't matter—it's their necks."

"And where did you and Martial meet?"

"In Paris. He wanted to learn how to be a locksmith. It's a good trade, always a red-hot iron and fire around you. Always danger, you know! That suited him, but like me, he's got a short fuse and he couldn't get along with his boss. So he went back to his parents and went marauding along the river with them. He comes by to see me in Paris, and I go to see him during the day in Asnières. It's not that far. Even if it was further away, I'd go anyway, even on my hands and knees."

"You'll be happy in the countryside, She-Wolf!" said Songbird, sighing. "Especially if you love walking around the fields, like I do."

"I'd like it better to be walking in the woods, in big forests, with my man."

"In forests? Aren't you afraid?"

"Afraid? Really? Is a she-wolf ever afraid? The more deserted and thickly grown the forest is, the better I like it. A hut in the middle of nowhere where I would live with Martial, who would be a poacher; to go with him at night to lay traps for the game, and then, if the guards came to arrest us, to shoot at them with our rifles, me and my man, hiding in the bushes. Oh! Lord, that would be so great!"

"Have you ever lived in the woods, She-Wolf?"

"No, never."

"So who gave you these ideas?"

"Martial."

"How?"

"He was a poacher in the Rambouillet forest. A year ago, they pinched him for shooting at a guard who had shot at him. Lousy guard! Well, they couldn't prove it in court, but Martial had to leave the territory. Then he came to Paris to learn the locksmith's trade. That's where I met him. Since he was too hotheaded to get along with his boss, he preferred to return to Asnières to be with his family and go marauding down the river. Fewer cages there. But he still misses living in the woods. He'll go back there someday. Talking about poaching and forests, he put those ideas in my head. Now I feel like I was born to live that way. But it's the same for everyone: whatever your man wants is what you want. If Martial had been a thief, I would have been a thief. When you've got a man, you do anything to be like him."

"And your parents, She-Wolf? Where are they?"

"How would I know?"

"So you haven't seen them in a long time?"

"I don't even know if they're dead or alive."

"So they weren't nice to you?"

"They weren't nice or mean. I think I was eleven when my mother ran off with a soldier. My father, who was a day laborer, brought a mistress back with him to our attic, with her two sons, one who was six years old and the other who was my age. She sold apples from a wheelbarrow. It wasn't too bad in the beginning. But later, while she was out with her cart, my father cheated on her with an oysterwoman who came over—and she found out about it. From then on, they fought so furiously almost every night that we got sick about it, me and the two boys I was sleeping next to, because where we lived only had one room, and the three of us had to share a bed in the same bedroom as my father and his mistress. One day—it was actually her saint's day, Saint Madeleine—she gave my father what-for for not having wished her a happy saint's day. One thing led to another, and my father ended up crushing her skull with a broom handle. I thought for sure that was it. Ma Madeleine fell over like a sack of lead, but she had lived hard, and she had a hard head, too. After that, she paid my father back in kind. Once she bit his hand so hard that she pulled a piece of him off between her teeth. I have to say that those massacres were like theater day at Versailles: on working days, the fights weren't as worth watching—there were bruises but no blood."

"And was that woman hard on you?"

"Ma Madeleine? No, on the contrary, she was just a bit sharp. Other than that, she was a good woman. But in the end, my father had had enough of her. He left her the little bit we had, and he never came back. He was from Burgundy. I guess he went back to where he came from. I was fifteen or sixteen then."

"So you stayed with your father's old mistress?"

"Where else was I going to go? So then she took up with a roofer who moved in with us. One of Ma Madeleine's sons, the older one, drowned on Swan Island. The other apprenticed himself to a carpenter."

"And what did you do when you lived with her?"

"I helped her pull her cart, I made meals, I brought food to her man, and when he came home tipsy, which happened more than his share of the time, I helped Ma Madeleine to slap him around and keep him quiet, because we still all lived in the same room. He was as mean as a junkyard dog when he was in his cups. He'd kill anybody. One time, if we hadn't taken his hatchet away from him, he would have killed us both. Ma Madeleine got a blow in her shoulder from that that she bled from like a stuck pig."

"And how did you become . . . what we are?" asked Fleur-de-Marie, hesitantly.

"Madeleine's son, little Charles, the one who drowned later on Swan

Island, him and me had been . . . well, together . . . more or less since the time that he, his mother, and his brother came to live with us, when we were both kids. Oh, well. Then, after him, the roofer—that was all the same with me, but I was afraid of getting kicked out by Ma Madeleine, if she figured anything out. And she did, of course. Because she was a kind woman, she said to me, 'Since this is the way it is, you're sixteen years old, you can't do anything on your own, you're too headstrong to work as a servant or to learn a trade, you come with me and I'll put you on the government list. Since you don't have parents, I'll answer for you. All you'll have to do is party. I'll rest easy about you, and you'll no longer be a burden on me. So what do you say to that, my girl?' 'You know, you're right,' I answered her. 'I never thought of doing that.' We were at the Bureau of Public Morals,[123] she recommended me for a brothel, and since then I've been registered. I saw Ma Madeleine again about a year ago. I was drinking with my man, and we invited her to join us. She said that the roofer was sent to the galleys. I haven't seen her since then. I don't know who it was—someone claimed lately that she was taken to the morgue three months ago. If it's true, it's too bad, you know? She was a good woman, that Ma Madeleine. She was openhanded, and she had no more malice in her than a pigeon."

Although she had been immersed from a young age in an atmosphere of corruption, Fleur-de-Marie had since then breathed such pure air that the oppression she felt from the She-Wolf's horrible story was physically painful. And if we have had the sad courage to write this story, it is because people need to know that, hideous though it is, it is still a thousand times better than real occurrences beyond number.

Yes, ignorance and poverty often lead the poor classes into this frightening human and social degradation. Yes, there are many dens in which children and adults, girls and boys, legitimate and illegitimate offspring, all roll around together on the same mattress, like animals from the same litter. They constantly have before them abominable examples of drunkenness, violence, debauchery, and murder. And yes, incest adds, too frequently, yet another horror to this already stupendous set of horrors.

The rich can cover their vices in shadow and mystery, thus preserving the sanctity of the domestic hearth. But the most honest workers, who almost always occupy a single room with their entire families, are forced, by lack of beds and space, to make their children, brothers and sisters, sleep together with husbands and wives sleeping just a few feet away. If one already shudders to think of the fatal consequences of the conditions faced almost inevitably by poor but upright workers, imagine the situation for

123. From the time of Napoléon up until the middle of the twentieth century, prostitution was legal in France but was regulated by the government. To be a prostitute legally, a woman was inscribed on a list and registered with the Bureau of Public Morals. [TN]

workers who are depraved because of their ignorance or their loose living. What appalling examples would this not create for unfortunate, abandoned children? Or rather, how could they not incite in them, from their earliest childhood, the most brutal tendencies, the most beastly passions? Would they even have the vaguest concepts of duty, honesty, or modesty? Wouldn't our social laws be as foreign to them as they are to savages from the New World? These poor creatures are corrupted at birth, and when they often end up in prison through vagrancy and neglect, they are already branded with the vulgar and terrible expression "prison fodder." And the expression has some truth to it. This sinister prediction almost always comes true. The galleys or the brothel: each sex has its own future path.

We are not trying to justify dissipation here. We are just asking that one compare the voluntary degradation of a woman piously raised in the bosom of a prosperous home, a home in which she would be provided with nothing but the most noble examples, with the degradation of someone like the She-Wolf, a creature raised, one might say, amid vice, by vice, and for vice, a young woman who was shown the path toward prostitution, not unreasonably, as if it were a trade authorized by the government. Which it is.

There is an office at which one registers, becomes certified, and signs on the dotted line: an office at which mothers often authorize the prostitution of their daughters, and husbands the prostitution of their wives. This office is called the Bureau of Public Morals!

A society must have an urge to organize things that amount to a deep and even incurable vice when it makes laws to govern the condition of men and women such that power—power, that grave and moral abstraction—is obliged not only to tolerate but to regulate, legitimate, and protect this sale of body and soul, which, multiplied by the untrammeled appetites of an immense population, grows exponentially every day. And society thinks it will make it less dangerous this way!

CHAPTER 9

BUILDING CASTLES IN THE AIR

Overcoming the emotion that her companion's sad confession had evoked in her, Songbird said to her timidly, "Listen to me, and don't get angry."

"Go ahead. I think I've chattered on enough. But, really, it doesn't matter, since this is the last time we'll ever speak."

"Are you happy, She-Wolf?"

"What do you mean?"

"Are you happy with the life you're leading?"

"Here, at Saint-Lazare?"

"No, when you're home, when you can do what you want."

"Sure, I'm happy."

"Always?"

"Always."

"Wouldn't you like to trade lives with someone else?"

"Trade for what kind of life? This is the only kind I'll ever get."

"Tell me, She-Wolf," said Fleur-de-Marie after a moment of silence. "Don't you like to build castles in the air? It's fun to do that in prison!"

"What kind of castles in the air?"

"Like about Martial."

"About my man?"

"Yes."

"I swear, I've never daydreamed about him."

"Let me build a nice castle for you and Martial."

"What good will that do?"

"It will help pass the time."

"All right, then. Let's see what this castle looks like."

"Let's imagine, for example, that by chance, as can happen sometimes, you come to meet someone who says to you, 'You were abandoned by your mother and father, and your childhood was full of so many bad examples that you should be pitied instead of blamed for becoming—'"

"Becoming what?"

"What we've become, you and I," said Songbird, softly. She continued: "Suppose that this person goes on and says to you, 'You love Martial, he loves you. You and he should leave behind this wicked life. Instead of being his mistress, become his wife.'"

The She-Wolf shrugged her shoulders. "Why should he want me to be his wife?"

"Other than the poaching, he hasn't committed any other crime, has he?"

"No. He poaches on the river the same way he did in the woods, and he's in the right to do it. Aren't fish just like game—there for anyone? Where's their owners' brand on them?"

"So let's suppose that he renounces his dangerous trade of being a river pirate and decides to become completely upright. Let's suppose that he's so honest about his new resolutions that he inspires enough trust in an unknown benefactor to make the benefactor find him a job—as a game warden, for example. A game warden instead of a poacher; that would suit his tastes, don't you think? It's the same job, but on the right side."

"That would work! You're still living in the woods."

"But they'll only give him this job on the condition that he marry you and take you with him."

"Martial would take me with him?"

"Yes. You were saying that you'd be so happy to live together deep in the forest. Wouldn't you both rather have a nice little thatched cottage to live in, where you could be an active, hardworking housekeeper, instead of having to live in a nasty poacher's hut and have to hide away in it like criminals?"

"You're making fun of me. That's not a real possibility."

"Who knows? Luck happens. And anyway, we're just building castles in the air."

"Ah, well—all right, then."

"What do you think, She-Wolf? I can almost see you already, set up in your little house, deep in the forest, with your husband and two or three children. Children! Wouldn't that make you happy?"

"My man's children?" cried the She-Wolf with fierce passion. "Oh, yes, I would love those kids more than anything!"

"They'll keep you company when you're alone. Then, when they're a little older, they'll start to help out with things. The littler ones will collect dead branches for the fire. The older one will take the cows out to pasture in the forest grasses, because someone will give you cows to reward your husband for his hard work. Because he was a poacher, he'll make a great game warden."

"That's really true. These castles in the air are really fun. Tell me some more, Songbird!"

"Everyone will be very pleased with your husband. His boss will arrange some nice extras for you. You'll have a poultry yard, a garden . . . but you know, you'll have to work hard yourself, She-Wolf! From morning to night."

"Oh, as to that, as long as I were by my man, work wouldn't scare me. I've got good, strong arms."

"And you'd have plenty to keep them busy, I can tell you. There's always so much to do—so much to do! There's the stable to take care of, the meals to prepare, the family's clothes to mend . . . one day it's the washing, the next day it's bread to bake, or you have to clean every corner of the house so the other forest guards say, 'Oh! There's no housekeeper like Martial's wife! Her house is a miracle of cleanliness, from top to bottom. And her children are always so well groomed! It's because she's so proud and hardworking, that Madame Martial.'"

"Wow, Songbird—it's true, I would be called Madame Martial," said the She-Wolf with a sort of pride. "Madame Martial!"

"That sounds better than She-Wolf, don't you think?"

"Sure, I'd rather have the name of my man than the name of an animal. But—oh, nonsense. I was born a she-wolf, I'll die a she-wolf."

"Who knows? Who knows? If you don't flinch in the face of an honest, hardworking life, some good can come of it. So the work wouldn't scare you?"

"Oh! No, not at all. It would take more than my man and three or four little kids to take care of to be too much for me!"

"And, of course, it wouldn't be all work. There would be moments of rest. In the winter, at night, while the children are asleep and your husband smokes his pipe and cleans his rifles or pets his dogs . . . You would get to have some good times."

"Bah! Who needs good times like that? Just sitting there with my arms folded? Not me. I'd rather be mending the family's clothes in the evening by the fire. It's not that tiring. During the winter, the days are so short!"

Gradually, Fleur-de-Marie's words were making the She-Wolf forget the present for the dream of the future. She was as vitally interested as Songbird had been earlier when Rodolphe had spoken to her of the rustic pleasures of the Bouqueval farm.

The She-Wolf did not hide the savage tastes that her lover had inspired in her. Remembering the profound impression for the good that Rodolphe's cheerful paintings of life in the country had inspired in her, Fleur-de-Marie thought to try the same means of persuasion on the She-Wolf, believing—and rightly believing—that her picture of a rude, poor, solitary existence would sufficiently move her companion to make her ardently desire such a life. And the She-Wolf would then merit pity and compassion.

Enchanted to see her companion listening to her with curiosity, Songbird went on, smiling, "So, Madame Martial—you don't mind if I call you that—how do you feel about that?"

"No, really, on the contrary, I'm flattered." Then the She-Wolf shrugged her shoulders and smiled as well. "I feel silly pretending to be a married lady. Are we little children? Oh, well, it doesn't matter. Go on. It's fun. What were you saying?"

"I was saying, Madame Martial, that when we were just speaking of your life in the winter, deep in the woods, we were only considering the worst of the seasons."

"My word, no, it's not the worst! I wouldn't find it bothersome at all to listen to the wind rustling at night in the forest, or to hear the wolves howling from time to time, from far away, far away . . . so long as I was in the corner by the fire with my man and my kids, or even all alone without my man, if he had to go on his rounds. Oh! Guns don't scare me, especially if I had to defend my children. I would be good at that. Oh, you can be sure that the She-Wolf would defend her little wolf cubs!"

"Oh, I can well believe that of you. You're very brave. But, weakling that I am, I prefer the spring to the winter. Oh, spring! Madame Martial, spring, when the leaves become green, when the pretty flowers of the wood blossom and smell so good—so good that the air is perfumed by them: that's when your children will delight in rolling around on the new grass. And the forest will be so thick with greenery that it will be hard to make your house out through the foliage. I feel as if I can see it from here. In front of the door, there's a bower made of vines that your husband planted. It shades the grassy bank where he likes to nap during the hottest hours of the day, while you come and go, asking your children not to wake up their papa. I don't know whether you've noticed, but in the dead of summer, around noon, it gets as quiet in the woods as it does at night. There's no sound from either the rustling of the leaves or the singing of the birds."

"That's true," the She-Wolf said, mechanically. Forgetting more and more the reality around her, she almost thought she could see the pictures Fleur-de-Marie had drawn for her unroll before her eyes, pictures that Fleur-de-Marie had made from her imagination fueled by her instinctive love for natural beauty.

Thrilled with the profound attention her companion was paying to her words, Fleur-de-Marie continued, letting herself get swept up as well by the charm of the thoughts she was evoking: "There is one thing that I love almost as much as the silence of the woods, and that's the sound of big drops of summer rain falling on the leaves. Do you like that, too?"

"Oh, yes! I love the summer rain, too."

"Don't you just? When the trees, moss, and plants are all soaking wet, it smells so fresh! And then, when the sun passes through the trees and makes all those little drops of water that are hanging from the leaves after the rain sparkle! Have you noticed that, too?"

"Yes, but I can only remember it because you're telling me about it now. It's so funny—you talk so well, Songbird, that I feel like I can really see everything as you speak. And then also, I don't know how to explain this, but what you're saying—well . . . it makes you feel good. You make things seem new again, like the summer rain we were just talking about."

Just like the beautiful and the good, poetry can often be contagious. The She-Wolf, this violent and fierce nature, couldn't have helped but become entirely subject to Fleur-de-Marie's influence. The latter went on, smiling: "We can't be the only ones who love the summer's rain. What about the birds? They're so happy! They shake out their feathers and chirp joyously. Not any more joyously, though, than your own children, those children who are as free, joyful, and without care as the birds. Can you see, as the day ends, the littlest ones running through the woods in front of the eldest, who brings the two heifers back from the pasture? They have recognized the ringing of the faraway little bells almost right away!"

"You know, Songbird, I almost think I can see the littler, bolder one, who has gotten himself put astraddle on the back of one of the cows with the help of his older brother, who's holding him."

"And you would think, to judge from the careful way that heifer is walking, that the poor animal knows the burden she's carrying. But now it's time for supper. Your eldest has amused himself by filling a basket with beautiful strawberries while bringing his livestock to pasture. He's brought them back nice and fresh to you underneath a thick layer of wild violets."

"Strawberries and violets! That should smell wonderful! But, heavens! Where the devil do you come up with these ideas, Songbird?"

"In the woods where the strawberries grow, where the violets bloom, as soon as you look for them, there they are for the picking, Madame Martial. But let's talk about housekeeping. It's nighttime, so you have to milk your cows and then prepare supper under the vine arbor, because you can hear your husband's dogs barking and soon afterward comes the voice of their master, who, tired as he is, comes in singing as he returns. And how can you not want to sing when, on a beautiful summer's evening, your heart full, you look at the house in which your good wife and two children are awaiting you? Isn't that true, Madame Martial?"

"It's true: all you could do is sing," said the She-Wolf, becoming more and more lost in thought.

"Unless you weep from joy instead," said Fleur-de-Marie, herself moved. "And tears like that are as sweet as song. Then, when it gets completely dark out, how lovely it is to stay under the bower to enjoy the serenity of a beautiful evening! You can breathe in the scents of the forest . . . listen to the children chattering . . . look up at the stars . . . Then your heart is so very full that you need to let it overflow in prayer. How can you not thank the one to whom we owe the freshness of the evening, the scent of the woods, the soft light of the starry sky? After this thanksgiving, or this prayer, you go peacefully to sleep until the next morning, when, again, you thank your Creator, because this life, so poor and hardworking, but also so tranquil and honest—this is your normal everyday life!"

"My normal everyday life?" said the She-Wolf, her head lowered to her chest, her gaze fixed, her breathing heavy. "Well, it's true, God is good to give us enough to live on and be so happy with so little."

"So tell me now," said Fleur-de-Marie, gently. "Don't you think that person blessed who would give you this peaceful and hardworking life instead of the miserable one you lead in the mud of the streets of Paris?"

The word "Paris" called the She-Wolf abruptly back to reality.

A strange phenomenon had just taken place in the soul of this creature. Fleur-de-Marie's naive depiction of a humble and rugged way of life, her simple story, lit up one moment by the soft glow of the domestic hearth, gleaming the next moment with joyous rays of sunlight, refreshed by the breeze of the great woods or perfumed by the scent of wildflowers, had made a deeper and more compelling impression on the She-Wolf than any exhortation to moral transcendence could have possibly done. As Fleur-de-Marie's story progressed, the She-Wolf more and more wished to become that tireless housekeeper, that valiant wife, that pious and devout mother.

To inspire—even for a moment—a violent, immoral, tainted woman with the love of family, the respect for duty, the taste for work, and gratitude toward the Creator, and this simply by promising her what God gives to everyone, namely, the sun and the sky and the shade of the forests, and what any human being who works has earned, namely, a roof over his head and bread to eat: doesn't this speak to the goodness and beauty of Fleur-de-Marie's storytelling? Would the most severe moralist or the preacher fullest of fire and brimstone have obtained more with chastising and threatening predictions of human vengeance and divine thunderbolts?

The sad anger into which the She-Wolf felt herself descend when she came back to reality, after having let herself be charmed by the new and salutary reverie into which, for the first time, Fleur-de-Marie's story had immersed her, proved the influence of her words on her unhappy companion. The more bitter the She-Wolf's regrets in having to return from this comforting mirage to the horror of her real condition, the more effective Fleur-de-Marie's storytelling showed itself to be.

After a moment of silence and reflection, the She-Wolf raised her head abruptly, passed her hand across her forehead, got up angrily, and, looking down on Fleur-de-Marie menacingly, said, "See? You see I was right not to trust you and not to listen to you! This is going to turn out badly for me! Why did you talk to me that way? To make fun of me? To torment me? This all comes from having been stupid enough to tell you that I would have liked to live deep in the woods with my man! Who are you, anyway? Why did you turn my life upside down like that? You don't know what you've done, you wretch! Now, even though I don't want to, I'm going to dream about that forest always, and about that house and those children, and all of the happiness I'll never have—never! And if I can't forget what you've just told me about, my life is going to be utter torture; it will be a living hell! And it's all your fault! Yes, your fault!"

"So much the better," said Fleur-de-Marie. "Oh, yes, so much the better!"

"So much the better, you say?" cried the She-Wolf, her eyes menacing.

"Yes, so much the better. If the wretched life you lead now looks like a hell to you, you'll prefer the one I described."

"And what good does it do to prefer it, since it can never be mine? What good does it do to regret being a streetwalker seeing as I'll live and die a streetwalker?" cried the She-Wolf, angrier and angrier. She seized Fleur-de-Marie's little wrist in her strong hand. "Answer me! Answer me! Why did you just make me want what I can't have?"

"Like I told you, wanting an honest and hardworking life means you're worthy of such a life," Fleur-de-Marie said, without trying to pull her hand away.

"Oh, great! What does being worthy of it get me? What does that prove? How will that help me?"

"It will help you see that you can make your dream come true," said Fleur-de-Marie in a tone that was so serious and so convincing that the She-Wolf, once more under Fleur-de-Marie's spell, let go of her hand and sat there, stunned.

"Listen to me, She-Wolf," said Fleur-de-Marie in a voice that was full of compassion. "Do you think I'm so mean that I would awaken such thoughts and hopes in you if I weren't sure that, in making you blush for your present state, I'd give you the means to escape it?"

"You . . . you can do that?"

"Me? No. But I know someone who is as kind, great, and powerful as God himself."

"As powerful as God?"

"Listen, She-Wolf. Three months ago, I was, like you, a poor, lost, abandoned creature. One day, the man of whom I speak to you with tears of gratitude"—and here, Fleur-de-Marie wiped her eyes—"one day this man came to me. He wasn't afraid—vile as I was, scorned as I was—to comfort me, the first comfort anyone ever gave me! I told him about my suffering, my poverty, my shame, without hiding anything from him, just like you just told me about your life, She-Wolf. After listening to me with kindness, rather than blaming me, he pitied me. He didn't blame me for my degradation; instead, he extolled the calm and pure life that one leads in the countryside."

"Just like you a moment ago."

"So then, just as the future he showed me seemed more beautiful, so my degraded life seemed to me more horrifying!"

"Good Lord! Just like me!"

"Yes, and just like you, I said, 'What good does it do, alas, to show a glimpse of this paradise to me—to me, condemned as I am to hell?' But I was wrong to despair, because the man of whom I speak is, like God, supremely just, supremely good, and incapable of raising a false hope in a poor creature who wasn't asking anyone for pity or happiness or hope."

"And what did he do for you?"

"He treated me like a sick child. I was just like you, trapped in a foul atmosphere. He sent me away to breathe healthy, life-giving air. I, too, was living among people who were hideous and criminal. He sent me to the care of people made in his image, people who purified my soul and raised my spirit, for, like God once more, he gives a spark of his divine intelligence to those who love and respect him. Yes, if my words move you, She-Wolf, if my tears raise tears in you, it's because his spirit and thought have inspired me! If I speak to you of a happier future, one available to you through repentance, it's because I can promise you this future in his name, even though he doesn't know now what I'm committing him to! So if I say to you, 'Hope!' it's because he always hears the voices of those who want to become better people, for God sent him on this earth to make us believe in divine providence."

As she spoke, Fleur-de-Marie's face became radiant, inspired. Her pale cheeks colored for a moment with a light, rosy tint. Her beautiful eyes shone gently. She was radiating a beauty that was so noble and so stirring that the She-Wolf, already profoundly moved by this conversation, looked on her companion with respect and admiration. She cried out, "My Lord! Where am I? Am I dreaming? I have never heard or seen anything like this. It's not possible! But who are you, anyway? Oh! I was right when I said you were different from us! But how is it that you, who speak so well, who can do so much, who know such powerful people—how is it that you're here, a prisoner with us? But . . . but . . . it must be to tempt us! You're here to tempt us to goodness, the way the devil tempts us to evil!"

Fleur-de-Marie was going to answer her when Madame Armand came to interrupt her, looking for her to take her back to see Madame d'Harville. The She-Wolf was still stunned from this encounter. The inspector said to her, "I am pleased to see that Songbird's presence in this prison has brought happiness to you and your companions. I know that you have taken up a collection for that poor Mont-Saint-Jean. That was good, it was charitable, She-Wolf. It will be remembered. I was quite sure you were better than you wanted to appear. As a reward for your good behavior, I believe I can promise you that your remaining time here will be considerably shortened." And Madame Armand walked away, followed by Fleur-de-Marie.

No one should be surprised by Fleur-de-Marie's nearly eloquent language. It should be remembered that her character, so gifted to begin with, had been rapidly developing, thanks to the education and teachings that she had received at the Bouqueval farm.

And furthermore, more than anything else, the young woman had been strengthened by her own experience. The sentiments she had awakened in the She-Wolf's heart had been awakened in her own by Rodolphe, and in very similar circumstances. In the belief that she had recognized some good instincts in her companion, she had tried to bring her over to an honest life by showing (according to the theory Rodolphe had applied at the Bouqueval farm) that it was in her own interest to become honest, by painting her rehabilitation in cheerful and attractive colors.

And while we are on this subject, we should repeat that, in the way that they try to inspire the poor and ignorant classes with a horror of evil and a love of good, people proceed in an incomplete and, it seems to us, unintelligent and inefficient manner. In order to turn them away from the wrong path, we threaten them incessantly with divine and human revenge; we incessantly cause them to hear that sinister clanging—of prison keys, of iron collars, of penitentiary chains. Finally, far away, at the extreme horizon of crime, in its frightening penumbra, we show them the executioner's guillotine, gleaming with the flames of eternal damnation . . .

It is plain to see that the role of this intimidation is constant, formidable, and terrible. The person who does evil will meet with captivity, infamy, and torment. This is just; but does our society promise to reward honorable gifts and glorious distinction to the person who does good? No.

Does our society encourage the great mass of laborers, who are fated to a life of work, deprivation, and, almost always, deep poverty, to resignation, order, and honesty by rewarding them with beneficent remunerations? No.

As for the scaffold up which the guilty climb: does it constitute a bulwark for the good man? No.

What a strange and fatal symbol! We represent justice as blind, holding in one hand a sword with which to punish and, in the other, scales on which the accusation and defense are weighed. This is not an image of justice. It is an image of the law, or rather, of the man who condemns or absolves according to his lights.

JUSTICE would hold in one hand a sword and in the other a crown. One would serve to punish the wicked, and the other would serve to reward the good. The people would see, then, that if evil ends in terrible punishment, good brings about its own shining rewards. Instead, at present, the people search in vain, with their naive, native good sense, for the counterbalance to the courts, convict ships, and scaffolds. The people can see our criminal justice [*sic*] clearly enough, the work of upright, enlightened men with integrity who are always busy searching for, discovering, and punishing villains. The people don't see a virtuous justice,[124] the work of upright, enlightened men with integrity who are always busy searching for and rewarding those who do good. All men hear is, "Tremble!" They never hear, "Hope!" Everything threatens, nothing consoles.

The state spends many millions every year on a sterile punishment of crimes. With this enormous sum, it funds prisoners and jailers, galley

124. A few days after writing these lines, we were rereading *The Memorial of Saint Helena*, the immortal book that strikes us as a sublime treatise of practical philosophy. We noticed the following passage that had escaped us previously: "Thus, one of my dreams (the emperor is speaking here), once the great events of war are accomplished and paid for, and we can turn within again to rest and catch our breath, would have been to seek a dozen true philanthropists, the kind of honest people who live only for the good and exist only to practice it. I would have dispatched them throughout the empire and have had them travel everywhere in secret in order to report back to me. These people would have been the 'spies of virtue.' They would have reported to me directly. They would have been my confessors, my spiritual directors. The decisions I would have made with them would have been my secret good works. My great occupation, during the time of my rest, would have been, to the extent my powers enabled me, to have busied myself with the betterment of society. I would have concerned myself with everything, down to individual pleasures" (*Memorial*, edition of 1824, vol. V, p. 100). [SN]

Edited by Emmanuel, Count of Las Cases, *The Memorial of Saint Helena* is a collection of transcriptions of Napoléon's statements while in exile on Saint Helena. It was immensely popular during the Restoration as a memorial to the First Empire, and it served to keep Bonapartism alive. [TN]

slaves and overseers, scaffolds and hangmen. Granted, this is all necessary. But how much does the state spend on the salutary and fruitful compensation of good people? Nothing.

And that's not all. As we will demonstrate when this story takes us into men's prisons, many workers of irreproachable morals would be thrilled if they knew they could one day enjoy a standard of living like the one prisoners enjoy, with good food, a good bed, and a decent lodging! And yet, shouldn't people like Morel the gem-cutter—who have lived a laborious, upright life of resignation for twenty years amid poverty and temptation—have the right, in the name of their dignity as honest men whom their hard life has harshly challenged over a long period, to claim title to the same well-being as criminals? Do such people not deserve enough from our society that we should take the trouble to seek them out, if not to compensate them, in the name of glorifying humanity, at least to sustain them in the painful and difficult path they travel so valiantly?

Is the righteous man, however modest he might be, so much better than the thief or the assassin at hiding himself? And are the latter not always discovered by the criminal justice system? Alas, this is a utopia, but it is a utopia that can only console us.

Imagine, as a thought experiment, a society organized in such a way as to offer a court of virtue, much the same as it has a criminal court. A public minister would record noble actions and announce them before all, much the same as crimes are currently announced for legal prosecution.

Here are two examples, two kinds of justice. Let it be decided which of the two is the more productive in terms of education, consequences, and positive results:

A man has killed another man in order to rob him. At dawn, the guillotine is set up without notice in a remote area of Paris, and the head of the murderer gets lopped off in the presence of the dregs of the people, who laugh at the judge, the condemned man, and the executioner. This is society's last word. Here we have the greatest crime that can be committed against society, and its greatest punishment. This is the most terrible and salutary lesson that it can offer the people. And it is the only one—for there is no counterweight to this executioner's block, dripping with blood. No, our society offers no gentle and beneficent spectacle to oppose this gloomy one.

To continue with our utopian vision: wouldn't it be different if almost every day the people had in front of them examples of various very virtuous people whose glory the state trumpeted and to whom it gave remuneration? Wouldn't it be a constant encouragement to do good if people saw frequently an august, imposing, venerated court recognizing a poor and honest worker standing up before a crowd, a worker whose long, upright, intelligent, and hardworking life it would recount and to whom it would say, "For twenty years, more than anyone, you have worked, suffered, and courageously struggled against misfortune. You have raised your family to follow the principles of righteousness and honor. Your superior virtues have marked you for great distinction. Through this, let your merits be known and rewarded. Vigilant, just, and all-powerful, our society never allows evil or good to languish unnoticed. Society repays each person according to his good works. The state awards you a pension sufficient to your needs. Showered with public recognition, you will live the rest of your life in comfort and ease, and that will be instruction for all. And thus are exalted, and will be exalted in the future, all those who, like yourself, will have justified and given proof of rare and great moral virtue, doing good over many years with admirable perseverance. Your example will encourage others in great number to imitate you. Hope will lighten the heavy burden that fate imposes on them during their long time on this earth. Inspired with the laudable desire to emulate you, they will struggle energetically to accomplish the most difficult tasks in order to be distinguished publicly and rewarded like you."

We ask the following question: which of these two spectacles—the murderer beheaded or the good man rewarded—would make the masses react in the wholesome and most productive way? It is surely the case that many people of delicate sensibilities will be indignant at the mere thought of giving filthy material recognition for that most ethereal quality in the world: virtue. They will find all sorts of reasons of various philosophical, platonic, theological, but most of all economic stripes to contest these ideas, to wit: "Doing good is its own reward"; "Virtue is priceless"; "A clear conscience is beyond recompense." And then, finally, this definitive objection, to which there is no reply: "The eternal happiness that awaits the just in the next life ought alone suffice to inspire good deeds in this life." To the last observation, we will say that our society does not seem to rely exclusively on the divine judgment that awaits the guilty in the next life when we wish to intimidate and punish them. Society prefaces the Last Judgment with its own human judgments. In anticipation of the inexorable arrival of the archangels with their hyacinth armor, the sounding trumpets, and the flaming swords, our society modestly makes do with the services of the police.

To repeat our points here: in order to terrify the wicked, we give material embodiment to the anticipated effects of celestial anger, or rather, we reduce it to human, perceptible, visible proportions. Why should it not be the same with the effects of divine remuneration when it comes to good people?

But let us turn away now from these mad, absurd, inane, impractical utopias for being just that: veritable utopias. Our society already works so well as it is! You have only to ask, rather, the kinds of people who, laughing raucously, their legs unsteady with drink, their eyes glazed over, come stumbling out from their joyous feasts!

CHAPTER 10

THE PROTECTOR

The inspector, accompanied by Songbird, soon came into the small salon where Clémence awaited them. The girl's pale complexion had colored slightly in the wake of her conversation with the She-Wolf.

"The marquise was touched by the excellent references I have given you and wishes to see you," said Madame Armand to Fleur-de-Marie. "She may be able to help to win an earlier release for you."

"I thank you, madame," Fleur-de-Marie answered her, timidly, as the inspector left her alone with the marquise.

The latter, struck by the innocent features and the graceful and modest demeanor of her protégée, could not keep from remembering that Songbird had pronounced Rodolphe's name in her sleep, and further, that the inspector believed that the poor prisoner was in the grips of a deep and secret passion. Even though she was completely convinced that there was no possibility that this Rodolphe could be the grand duke, Clémence recognized that Songbird was worthy of a prince's love, at least as far as her beauty was concerned.

Fleur-de-Marie, seeing how her protector's expression, as we have noted, radiated a charming kindness, felt drawn to her in sympathy.

"My child," Clémence said to her, "while Madame Armand gives high praise to the gentleness of your character and your unusually good behavior, she also complains of how little you trust her."

Fleur-de-Marie lowered her head and did not respond.

"The peasant's clothing that you were wearing when you were arrested, along with your silence regarding the place where you were living before being brought here, proves that you are hiding something from us."

"Madame . . ."

"I have no call on your trust, my poor child, nor do I want to ask you awkward questions. It's only that I have been assured that if I ask for your release from prison, my request might be granted. Before I act, I would like to speak with you about your plans and about your resources for the future. Once you're set free, what will you do? If, as I do not doubt, you mean to follow the excellent path you've begun to follow, please trust me that I will help you to make an honest living."

Songbird was moved almost to tears by the care that Madame d'Harville showed for her. After a moment's hesitation, she said to her, "You deign, madame, to show such kindness and generosity toward me that it may be that I should break the silence that I have kept until now about the past. I was held back by an oath."

"An oath?"

"Yes, madame. I swore not to tell judges or the employees of this prison anything about the events that brought me here. But, madame, if you felt you could promise . . ."

"Promise what?"

"To keep my secret. With your help, madame, I could calm certain respectable people who are no doubt very worried about me without breaking my oath."

"You may rely on my discretion. I will say only what you authorize."

"Oh! Thank you, madame! I was so afraid that not telling my benefactors anything would seem ungrateful!"

Fleur-de-Marie's sweet tone of voice and careful choice of words struck Madame d'Harville anew. "I will not hide from you the fact that your demeanor and your words astonish me greatly," she said to her. "How, with an education that seems to have been an excellent one, could you . . ."

"Have fallen so far, madame? Isn't that what you want to say?" said Songbird, bitterly. "My education, alas, began only recently. I owe this gift to a generous protector who, like you, madame, took pity on me, without knowing me and without even having been given the positive references that you have received."

"And who is your protector?"

"I don't know, madame."

"You don't know?"

"He makes himself known only by his inexhaustible goodness. I thank the heavens that I fell across his path."

"And where did you meet him?"

"One night, in the Cité, madame," said Songbird, lowering her gaze. "A man was trying to beat me. This unknown benefactor defended me courageously. That was my first encounter with him."

"So this was a man of . . . the people?"

"The first time I saw him, he was dressed like a worker and spoke like one, but later . . ."

"Later?"

"The way he spoke to me, the profound respect with which the people he placed me with treated him, all of that showed me that he had disguised himself as a man who hangs about the Cité."

"But why would he do that?"

"I don't know."

"And do you know the name of this mysterious protector?"

"Oh, yes, madame," said Songbird, ecstatically. "Thank God that I do, for this way I can bless and adore his name forever. My savior is named Monsieur Rodolphe, madame."

Clémence turned scarlet.

"And does he have no other name?" she asked Fleur-de-Marie, sharply.

"I don't know it, madame. On the farm where he sent me, they know him only as Monsieur Rodolphe."

"And how old is he?"

"He is still young, madame."

"And handsome?"

"Oh! Yes, he's handsome and noble, like his heart."

The grateful and impassioned tone with which Fleur-de-Marie pronounced these words produced a painful impression on Madame d'Harville. An invincible, inexplicable, instinctive response told her that Fleur-de-Marie was speaking about the prince.

What the inspector had said was correct, thought Clémence. Songbird was in love with Rodolphe. It was his name that she had pronounced while she was sleeping. Under what strange set of circumstances could the prince and this unfortunate girl have met? Why had Rodolphe gone into the Cité in disguise? The marquise could not answer these questions. She only remembered what Sarah had wickedly and falsely told her previously about what she claimed were Rodolphe's eccentricities, his strange love affairs. Was it not strange, after all, that he should have pulled this ravishingly beautiful and uncommonly intelligent creature out of the mire?

Clémence had noble qualities, but she was a woman all the same, and, even if she had determined to bury her love in the deepest part of her heart, she loved Rodolphe deeply.

The marquise did not realize that this was doubtless one of the generous actions that the prince was accustomed to performing in secret, nor that she might well be confusing love with a feeling of intense gratitude. No more did she consider, finally, that, even if Songbird's feelings toward him were of that more tender kind, Rodolphe might not be aware of it, and so, in a moment of bitterness and injustice, she could not help but regard Songbird as her rival.

Her pride bridled as she realized that she was blushing and that she suffered, in spite of herself, from such a detestable jealousy. As a result she took up the conversation again now in a harsh voice that contrasted cruelly with the affectionate benevolence of her first words: "How is it possible, mademoiselle, that your protector has left you in prison? How do you come to be here?"

"Good heavens, madame!" said Fleur-de-Marie, timidly, struck by her sudden change in tone. "Did I do something to make you unhappy with me?"

"How could you possibly make me unhappy with you?" asked Madame d'Harville, haughtily.

"It's just because, it seems to me that a moment ago—well, you spoke with more kindness to me, madame."

"Really, now, mademoiselle, must I weigh each word I use with you? If I consent to interest myself in your case, I have the right, I think, to ask you certain questions." As soon as she had said these words, Clémence regretted their harshness, for more reasons than one. First of all, she returned, and in this she deserves praise, to her original generosity, and then, also, she realized that if she offended her rival, she would learn from her nothing of what she wished to know.

Indeed, Songbird's expression, open and confiding moments before, had turned suddenly fearful. Just as a sensitive plant shuts its delicate petals at the first sign of attack and closes in on itself, so did Fleur-de-Marie's heart close up in pain.

Clémence continued on more gently so as not to make her protégée more suspicious by changing tone so suddenly. "I repeat, I truly cannot understand how you can be a prisoner here when you are so happy in having a praiseworthy protector. How, after having sincerely returned to the righteous path, could you have gotten arrested at night in an area that was off-limits to you? I confess that all of this seems extraordinary to me. You speak of an oath that has, up to now, condemned you to silence. But even this oath is so strange!"

"I have told you the truth, madame."

"I'm sure you have. All I have to do is see you and hear you to believe you incapable of lying. But the incomprehensible aspect of your situation is making me even more impatient in my curiosity. That's the only reason my words were so sharp a moment ago. All right, I admit that I was in the wrong, for although I have no right to your trust aside from my strong desire to be useful to you, you offered to tell me what you had not told anyone else. Believe me, poor child, I am very moved to receive this proof of your faith in the interest I take in you. I promise you that I will be scrupulous in keeping your secret if you trust me with it. I will do everything in my power to carry out your intention."

With this rather skillful job of damage containment (please forgive us this vulgarity), Madame d'Harville won back Songbird's trust after having momentarily frightened her away. Fleur-de-Marie, in her innocence, blamed herself for having misinterpreted the words that had wounded her. "Forgive me, madame," she said to Clémence. "I was surely wrong for not having told you immediately what you wanted to know. You had asked me for the name of my savior, and in spite of myself, I couldn't resist giving in to the happiness of talking about him."

"There's nothing I would rather hear. It proves how grateful you are to him. But under what circumstances did you leave the good people with whom he surely had placed you? Is the oath you told me of related to that event?"

"Yes, madame. But thanks to you, I think I can now reassure my benefactors as to my disappearance without betraying my promise."

"Let's hear what you have to say, my poor child. I'm listening to you."

"About three months ago, Monsieur Rodolphe had placed me in a farm located four or five leagues away from here."

"He brought you there . . . himself?"

"Yes, madame. He had put me in the care of a kind and venerable lady. I came quickly to love her as if she were my mother. She and the village priest took charge of my education on Monsieur Rodolphe's recommendation."

"And did Monsieur . . . Rodolphe come often to the farm?"

"No, madame. He came three times over the period I was there."

Clémence could hardly repress a tremor of joy.

"And when he came to see you, it made you very happy, didn't it?"

"Oh, yes, madame! It made me more than happy. I felt a mixture of gratitude, respect, admiration, and even a little fear."

"Fear?"

"Between him and me, and between him and everyone else, there was such a great distance!"

"But what rank did he occupy, then?"

"I don't even know whether there's a rank that corresponds to him."

"Yet you speak of the distance that exists between him and everyone else."

"Oh, madame! The thing that puts him so far above everyone else is the elevation of his character, his inexhaustible generosity toward those who suffer, the enthusiasm he inspires in all. The wicked can't even hear his name pronounced without trembling. They respect him as much as they fear him. But I'm sorry, madame, for talking about him again. I should hold my tongue. I will give you an inadequate idea of a man one should be content to adore in silence. It's like trying to express God's grandeur in the words of mere mortals."

"That comparison—"

"Is perhaps sacrilegious, madame. But I don't think I'm offending God when I compare him to the man who made me aware of right and wrong, the man who took me out of the abyss, the man to whom I owe what is ultimately my rebirth."

"I cannot blame you, my child. I understand your noble exaggerations. But how did you come to abandon the farm where you must have been so happy?"

"Alas! It was not by choice, madame!"

"Who forced you to leave, then?"

"One evening, a few days ago," said Fleur-de-Marie, still trembling as she told her story, "I was on my way to the village rectory, when a wicked woman, who had tormented me in my childhood, along with a man who was her accomplice, threw themselves on me in an ambush in a sunken road. After they wrapped me up, they took me away in a cab."

"Why did they do that?"

"I don't know, madame. My abductors were following the instructions, I believe, of some powerful people."

"What happened after this kidnapping?"

"The cab had hardly started on its way when the wicked woman, whose name is the Owl, cried, 'I have acid here with me. I'm going to rub it into Songbird's face to disfigure her.'"

"How terrible! You unfortunate child! And who saved you from this danger?"

"Her accomplice, a blind man named the Schoolmaster."

"He defended you?"

"Yes, madame, that time and another one, too. The first time, a struggle broke out between him and the Owl. Using his strength, the Schoolmaster forced her to throw the bottle of acid out the window. That's the first favor he did for me, after having assisted her, however, in kidnapping me. The night was dark. After an hour and a half, the car stopped on the main road, I think, that crosses the Saint-Denis plain. A man on horseback was waiting there. 'Well?' he asked. 'Did you get her, finally?' 'Yes, we've got her!' answered the Owl, who was furious that she'd lost the opportunity to disfigure me. 'If you want to get rid of this little girl, I know a good way to do it. I'll lay her down on the ground, on the road, and I'll roll the wheels of the car over her head. It will seem like she was killed in an accident.'"

"But that's dreadful!"

"Alas! Madame, the Owl was absolutely capable of doing what she said. Fortunately, the man on horseback told her that he didn't want to do me any harm, that he just wanted me to be held for two months in a place I couldn't leave or from which I couldn't write to anyone. Then the Owl proposed to take me over to a man named Red-Arm, who's the owner of a tavern on the Champs-Élysées. There were several underground rooms in that tavern. One of them could serve as my prison, the Owl said. The man on horseback accepted her proposal. Then he promised me that after I stayed for two months with Red-Arm, he'd make sure I had a life that would be so nice that I'd never miss the Bouqueval farm."

"What a strange mystery!"

"The man gave money to the Owl and promised her more when the time came to take me back from Red-Arm. He galloped away on his horse. Our cab continued on its way toward Paris. A little while before we reached the gate, the Schoolmaster said to the Owl, 'You want to lock Songbird up in one of Red-Arm's cellars, but you know full well that these caves are always flooded in the wintertime! Are you trying to drown her?' 'Yes, I am,' answered the Owl."

"But, good God! What had you done to that horrible woman?"

"Nothing, madame. Since my childhood she had always had it out for me that way. The Schoolmaster answered her, 'I don't want Songbird to be drowned. She's not going to Red-Arm's.' The Owl was just as astonished as I was to hear this man defend me in this manner. She became terribly angry and swore that she would take me to Red-Arm's place in spite of anything the Schoolmaster wanted. 'I dare you to try,' he said. 'I've got Songbird here by the arm, and I'm not going to let go. I'll strangle you if you get anywhere near her.' 'But what do you want to do with her, then?' cried the Owl. 'We've got to get rid of her for two months without letting anyone know where she's gone!' 'I know what to do,' said the Schoolmaster. 'We'll go to the Champs-Élysées and park the cab somewhere near a guard station. You'll go to find Red-Arm in his tavern. It's midnight. You'll get him, you'll bring him over, he'll take Songbird, and he'll turn her in to the police, saying that she's a Cité streetwalker whom he found wandering around in front of his tavern. Since streetwalkers are sentenced to three months of prison when they're found on the Champs-Élysées, and since Songbird is still registered with the police, they'll arrest her and put her in Saint-Lazare. There she'll be guarded and hidden just as well as she would be in Red-Arm's cellar.' 'But Songbird won't allow herself to be arrested,' said the Owl. 'Once she's turned over to the guard, she'll tell them that we've kidnapped her and she'll give us up. Even supposing she gets put in prison, she'll write to her protectors and everything will be revealed.' 'No, she'll go to prison willingly,' said the Schoolmaster. 'And she'll swear not to denounce us to anyone while she's in Saint-Lazare or after she leaves, for that matter. She owes me this, because I prevented you from disfiguring her, Owl, and from drowning her at Red-Arm's place. But if, after swearing never to squeal on us, she were to be so unfortunate as to attempt to do so anyway, we would turn the Bouqueval farm into a scene of fire and bloody carnage.' Then, turning to me, the Schoolmaster added, 'It's up to you. Make the oath I'm asking of you. You will get off with two months in prison. Otherwise, I leave you to the Owl, who will take you to Red-Arm's cellar, where you'll drown. Make up your mind. I know that if you make an oath, you'll abide by it.'"

"And you swore to it?"

"Alas! Yes, madame, for I was so afraid of being disfigured by the Owl or being drowned by her in a cellar. That seemed so terrifying to me. Another kind of death might have seemed less scary, and I might not have tried to escape it."

"What a sinister prospect, at your age!" said Madame d'Harville, looking at Songbird in surprise. "Once you leave this place and you're back in the hands of your benefactors, won't you be happy? Won't your repentance efface the past?"

"Can the past ever be effaced? Can the past be forgotten? Does repentance kill one's memory, madame?" cried Fleur-de-Marie in such a desperate tone that Clémence trembled.

"But all sins can be redeemed, poor child!"

"And the memory of one's defilement? Madame, it becomes more and more terrible the more one's soul is purified, the more one's spirit is elevated! Alas! The higher you ascend, the deeper seems the abyss from which you have emerged."

"So you give up all hope of rehabilitation and forgiveness?"

"Not for others, madame, no. Your kindness proves to me that remorse will never lack forgiveness."

"So, according to you, you're the only person for whom there is no pity?"

"Other people can be ignorant of, or forgive, or forget what I was. But I can never forget it, madame."

"Do you want to die sometimes?"

"Sometimes?" said Songbird, smiling bitterly. Then she was silent for a moment. "Yes, madame, sometimes."

"However, you feared becoming disfigured by that horrible woman. You cared about your beauty, didn't you, poor little one? That shows that life still holds out some promise for you. Take courage, dear; take courage!"

"Perhaps it's a weakness in me to think this, but if I was pretty, as you say, madame, I would want to die pretty with the name of my benefactor on my lips."

Madame d'Harville's eyes filled with tears. Fleur-de-Marie had said these last words with such simplicity. Her pale, worn, angelic features and her sad smile matched her words so perfectly that there was no doubting the reality of her grim desire.

Madame d'Harville was too sensitive not to intuit the inexorable and fatal logic of Songbird's train of thought. "I will never forget what I was . . ." This was clearly an implacable idée fixe that would dominate and torment Fleur-de-Marie to the end of her days. Ashamed at having momentarily mistaken the disinterested nature of the prince's interest,

Clémence also regretted having allowed herself to be carried away by an absurd impulse of jealousy toward Songbird. The young woman expressed her praise of her protector in such naive terms. Strangely, the admiration that this poor prisoner felt so profoundly for Rodolphe served perhaps to increase the intense love Clémence had always had to hide from him.

In order to escape this line of thought, she said, "I hope that in the future you will be less hard on yourself. But let's discuss the oath you took. Now I understand why you didn't want to speak. You didn't want to denounce those wretches."

"Although the Schoolmaster took part in my abduction, he defended me twice. I would seem ungrateful toward him."

"And you went along with the plans of those monsters?"

"Yes, madame. I was so afraid! The Owl went off to look for Red-Arm. He took me over to the guardhouse and said that he had seen me lurking around his cabaret. I didn't deny it, so they arrested me and brought me here."

"But your friends at the farm must be dying of anxiety!"

"Alas, madame, in my first moments of shock, I didn't think about the fact that my oath would keep me from being able to ease their worries. Now I regret this. But I think that I can ask you to write to Madame Georges without breaking my oath, don't you think? She's at the Bouqueval farm. You can tell her that there's absolutely no reason to worry about me. Just don't tell her where I am, however, for I promised not to tell."

"My child, your precautions will become unnecessary if they grant my recommendation that you be released. Tomorrow you can return to the farm without having betrayed your oath in any way. Later you can consult your benefactors in order to decide the extent to which you are bound by that oath, considering the fact that you made it under coercion."

"So you think, madame, that I have cause to hope, thanks to your kindness, that I might be able to leave this place soon?"

"You are such a deserving young woman that I will surely succeed. I have no doubt that you will be able to reassure your benefactors yourself the day after tomorrow."

"Good Lord, madame, how is it possible that I deserve so much kindness on your part? How can I thank you?"

"By continuing to follow the path you have chosen. I only regret not being in a position to do anything for your future. Your friends have already claimed that pleasure for themselves."

Madame Armand entered suddenly with a worried look on her face. "Marquise, I regret that I must relay a message to you," she said to Clémence, hesitantly.

"What do you mean, madame?"

"The Duke de Lucenay is downstairs. He has come from your home, madame."

"Heavens! You are frightening me! What has happened?"

"I don't know, madame, but Monsieur de Lucenay has been sent to bring you news, he says, that is sad and unexpected. He learned from his wife, the duchess, that you were here, and thus he rushed over here."

"Sad news?" thought Madame d'Harville. Then, suddenly, she cried in a heartrending voice, "My daughter! It could be my daughter! Oh! Tell me, madame!"

"I don't know what has happened, madame."

"Oh! Have mercy, madame! Take me directly to Monsieur de Lucenay!" cried Madame d'Harville as she left in a panic, followed by Madame Armand.

"Poor mother!" said Songbird in sadness as she followed Clémence with her gaze. "No, it's impossible! That she should be struck by such a blow at the very moment at which she was showing such kindness to me! No, no, and no again! That's just not possible!"

CHAPTER II

A FORCED INTIMACY

We now lead the reader into the house on rue du Temple on the day of Monsieur d'Harville's suicide. It was about three in the afternoon. Monsieur Pipelet, alone in his lodge, was hard at work restoring the boot that had more than once fallen from his hands since Cabrion's latest and most audacious prank. The face of the noble doorkeeper was beleaguered and seemed much more melancholy than usual. In the manner of a soldier who touches the scars of his battle wounds as he feels the humiliation of his defeat, Monsieur Pipelet would sigh deeply, pausing in his work, and touch the transverse crease in his top hat, dug out by the insolent hand of Cabrion. All of Alfred's worries, anxieties, and fears thus came back to him as he reflected on the marauder's inconceivable and unceasing harassment.

Monsieur Pipelet had neither an extensive nor an elevated intelligence. Nor was his imagination terribly vivid or poetical, but he did have firm, upright, logical common sense. Unfortunately, as a natural consequence of the rectitude of his judgment, unable to comprehend the eccentric and exaggerated nature of what is called, in the language of the art studio, a caricature, Monsieur Pipelet was always trying to find rational and plausible motives behind Cabrion's exuberant conduct, and he had, on this subject, masses of questions for which he had no answers. And so, sometimes, like a latter-day Pascal, he felt himself overcome with vertigo as he attempted to sound the infinite depths of the abyss that the infernal genius of the painter had dug out from under his feet. How many times, wounded by his emotional effusion, had he been forced to withdraw into himself, thanks to Madame Pipelet's unbridled skepticism, which, accepting only hard fact and refusing to seek deeper meaning, vulgarly estimated Cabrion's baffling behavior toward Alfred as a simple farce!

Monsieur Pipelet, a grave and serious man, could not admit such an interpretation. He bemoaned his wife's blindness. His belief in his human dignity rebelled at the thought that he could be the plaything of such a vulgar scenario. A farce! He was absolutely convinced that Cabrion's peculiar conduct hid some sort of dark conspiracy under the guise of a frivolous appearance. As we've said, it was in hopes of solving this dark conundrum that the man in the stovepipe hat had endlessly plumbed his powers of dialectical reasoning.

"I would sooner put my own head in the noose," said this austere man in whose mind the questions only grew larger as he considered them. "I would sooner put my own head in the noose than admit that Cabrion has hounded me so relentlessly merely in order to play a stupid trick on me. One only writes comedies for an audience. Now, this malicious creature had no witnesses for his latest enterprise. He acted alone and in the dark, as he always does. He crept into the solitude of my lodge on the sly in order to place his hideous kiss on my mortally offended forehead. And I ask any disinterested observer, to what end? It was not out of bravado: no one saw him. It was not for pleasure: it offends the laws of nature. It was not for friendship: I have only one enemy in the world, and it's him. We must accept, then, that there's some mystery here that my reason cannot penetrate! So where does this diabolical plan—which he follows through devious paths and carries out with a fearful persistence—lead? The impossibility of lifting the veil slowly saps my strength and consumes my very being!"

Such were the painful reflections of Monsieur Pipelet at the moment we rejoin him. The honest doorkeeper had just that instant reopened his still bleeding wounds by touching the damaged spot on his hat with a melancholy gesture, when a piercing voice came from one of the higher floors of the house and the following words rang out in the echo chamber of the staircase: "Quickly, Monsieur Pipelet! Come up now! Hurry!"

"I do not recognize that voice," said Alfred after a moment of contemplative listening. He dropped his forearm, still encased in the boot he was mending, to his knee.

"Monsieur Pipelet, come quickly already!" said the voice in an urgent tone.

"That voice is completely foreign to me. It's a male voice, and it's calling me. That much I am able to say for certain. That is not a sufficient reason for me to leave my rooms. To leave them unoccupied, to desert them in the absence of my spouse!" cried Alfred, heroically. "That I will never do!"

"Monsieur Pipelet!" the voice repeated. "Come up quickly! There's something wrong with Madame Pipelet!"

"Anastasie!" cried Alfred, leaping up from his seat. Then he fell back down into it, saying to himself, "Innocent that I am. That can't be. My spouse went out an hour ago. Yes, but could she not have returned without my noticing it? That would be unusual, but I must allow that it's possible."

"Monsieur Pipelet! Come up here right away! Your wife is in my arms!"

"Someone is holding my spouse in his arms!" cried Monsieur Pipelet, rising instantly to his feet.

"I can't undress Madame Pipelet all by myself!" added the voice.

These words produced a magic effect on Alfred. He turned scarlet; his chastity was outraged. "This strange male voice speaks of undressing Anastasie!" he cried. "I stand against that! I forbid it!" And he flew out of the lodge—but at the threshold, he stopped.

Monsieur Pipelet found himself in one of those horribly critical and eminently dramatic positions that poets so often exploit. On the one hand, his duty called for him to remain in his lodge. On the other, his modest conjugal sensibility called him upstairs.

Amid these terrible perplexities, the voice returned, "So you're not coming, Monsieur Pipelet? Too bad—I'm cutting the laces and closing my eyes."

This threat pushed Monsieur Pipelet into action. "Monsieuuuur!" he cried in a stentorian voice, running like a madman out of his lodge. "For pity's sake, I call on you, Monsieuuur, to cut nothing whatsoever and to leave my spouse intact! I am coming up!" And Alfred lunged into the darkness of the stairway, in his panic, leaving open the door to his rooms.

No sooner had he left the rooms than a man suddenly entered them, quickly took the cobbler's hammer off the table, jumped on the bed, and by means of four nails that had been driven in in advance at each corner of a thick cardboard panel that he had in his hand, nailed the panel to the back of Monsieur Pipelet's dark alcove, and then disappeared. This operation was completed so quickly that the doorkeeper, who had remembered almost immediately that he had left his door open, came back down, locked it, took the key, and went back upstairs without suspecting that someone had entered his rooms. After taking this precaution, Alfred ran back up to rescue Anastasie, crying with all his might, "Monsieuuuur! Do not cut anything! I'm coming up! Here I am! I place my spouse in the safekeeping of your delicacy!"

The worthy doorkeeper went from one shock to another. For no sooner had he mounted the first steps in the staircase than he heard Anastasie's voice—coming not from the top floor, but from the alley. This voice, more shrill than ever, was crying, "Alfred! How could you leave your post unattended? Where are you, you old ladies' man?"

At this moment, Monsieur Pipelet was about to put his right foot on the landing of the first floor. He stood there petrified, with his head turned toward the bottom of the staircase, his mouth agape, his eyes staring, and his foot in the air.

"Alfred!" Madame Pipelet yelled again.

"Anastasie's downstairs. So she isn't up there in danger!" said Monsieur Pipelet to himself, holding faithfully to his tight, logical reasoning. "But then, that unknown man's voice that was threatening to undress her—who was that? Was it an impostor, then? Someone's making cruel sport of my anxiety. But to what end? Something extraordinary is happening here. Well, no matter. 'Do your duty, come what may.' Once I have answered my spouse, I shall go back upstairs to clear up this mystery and determine whose voice I heard."

Monsieur Pipelet walked back downstairs feeling very uneasy. He found himself face-to-face with his wife. "It's you!" he said to her.

"Of course it's me. Who else are you expecting?"

"It's you; my eyesight is not deceiving me?"

"Oh, come on. What's got you making googly eyes at me again? You're looking at me as if you wanted to eat me."

"It's just that your presence here makes clear that there are things happening here . . . things happening . . ."

"What things? Look, give me the key to the rooms. Why did you leave them empty? I've just come back from the Normandy stagecoach office. I went there in a cab to carry over Monsieur Bradamanti's suitcase. He doesn't want anyone to know that he's leaving tonight. He doesn't trust that little Gammy brat—and he's right about that!"

Upon saying this, Madame Pipelet took the key that her husband was holding in his hand, opened the door, and walked in before him. Just as the couple returned, someone quietly descended the staircase and passed by the apartment quickly, without their noticing. This was the male voice that had given rise to Alfred's anxiety so effectively.

Monsieur Pipelet sat down heavily in his chair and said to his wife in an emotional voice, "Anastasie, I sense something odd going on. Things are happening here . . . things . . ."

"Here you go again, going on and on about the same thing. Things happen everywhere! What's wrong with you? Look! Oh, you're bathed in perspiration! You're swimming in it! Did you just work hard at something? It's pouring off you! You old dear!"

"Yes, sweat is pouring off me and for good reason." Monsieur Pipelet passed his hand across his face, which was quite wet. "Things are going all topsy-turvy here."

"What's wrong with you now? You can never just sit still. I don't know why you always have to run around like an alley cat instead of sitting tranquilly in your chair, guarding our apartment."

"Anastasie, it is very wrong of you to say that I run around like an alley cat. If I run around, it's for you."

"For me?"

"Yes, to spare you an outrage that would have caused us both to blush and bemoan our fate, I abandoned a post that I consider as sacred as a soldier's lookout."

"Someone wanted to outrage me?"

"It wasn't you, seeing that the outrage that threatened you was supposed to happen upstairs, and you had gone out, but—"

"The devil take me if I can make out a single thing you're going on about! Have you completely lost your marbles? Listen, I'm going to start thinking you're losing it—maybe from a hammer's blow to your head, thanks to that scoundrel Cabrion, damn him! Since his caper from the other day I don't know you anymore. You seem like you're in a daze. Is that guy going to go on giving you nightmares forever?"

Anastasie had hardly gotten these words out of her mouth when something strange happened. Alfred was still seated with his face turned toward the bed. The apartment was lit by the wan rays of a winter sun and by a lamp. Monsieur Pipelet thought, at the moment his wife pronounced the name "Cabrion," that, by the light of these two dim sources, he could see, lurking in the shadows, the motionless, derisive face of the painter.

It was him, with his pointy hat, his long hair, his thin face, his satanic laugh, his tapered beard, and his hypnotic gaze. For a moment, Monsieur Pipelet thought he was dreaming. He rubbed his eyes, thinking he was imagining things. But it was no illusion; there was nothing more real than this apparition. The frightening part was that the body was invisible; you could see only a head, with its bright coloring standing out from the darkness of the alcove.

At this sight, Monsieur Pipelet suddenly fell backward, without saying a word. He raised his right arm toward the bed and pointed at this terrible vision with such an expression of shock that Madame Pipelet turned around to look for what had caused this fright, one which she would come to share herself, shortly, in spite of her habitual pluck. She recoiled, taking two steps backward, seized Alfred's hand with all her strength, and screamed, "CABRION!"

"Yes," murmured Monsieur Pipelet in a hollow, deadened voice as he closed his eyes.

The stupor of both spouses paid the best of tributes to the talent of the artist who had so admirably painted Cabrion's features on the cardboard panel.

Once past her first moment of shock, Anastasie, as intrepid as a lion, ran over to the bed, got onto it, and—not without a certain chill—tore the panel off the wall onto which it had been nailed. The Amazon crowned this valiant achievement by giving forth her favorite war cry: "And alley-oop!"

Alfred, his eyes closed and his hands stretched out in front of him, stood motionless, as he always had in the critical moments of his life. The intermittent convulsive oscillation of his stovepipe hat was the only thing that showed the restrained turmoil of his inner emotions.

"Come on, open your eyes, my old deary," said Madame Pipelet, triumphant. "It wasn't anything—just a painting. It's just a portrait of that scoundrel Cabrion! Look at me stomping all over it!" And Anastasie, in her indignation, threw the painting on the floor and trampled it under her feet, crying, "That's what I'd like to do to you in the flesh, you rogue!" Then, picking up the portrait, she said, "Look, now I've put my mark on him! See?"

Shaking his head, Alfred denied this without saying a word and gestured to his wife that she should remove this hateful image from his sight.

"Have you ever seen such shamelessness? That's not all! He wrote on the bottom of it, in red letters, '*Cabrion, to his good friend Pipelet, for life*,'" said the doorkeeper's wife, examining the board in the light.

"His good friend . . . for life!" murmured Alfred. And he raised his hands to the heavens in witness to this latest, outrageous irony.

"But, now we're on it, how did this happen?" asked Anastasie. "This portrait wasn't here this morning when I made the bed, that's for sure. You took the key to the apartment with you just now. No one could get in there while you were gone. So really, how could that portrait have gotten here? Oh, you old dear, could it be that you put it up yourself?"

This monstrous hypothesis made Alfred jump out of his chair. He glared at her with a furious, menacing look in his eyes. "Me? Me? You think I would hang the portrait of this evildoer in my own alcove? No longer content to persecute me with his odious presence, now he pursues me at night in my dreams and during the day in a painting! Do you want to drive me crazy, Anastasie? Do you want to make me stark, raving mad?"

"Oh, come on. If you had decided to make it up with Cabrion during my absence to get a little peace, what would have been the harm?"

"Me, make it up with . . . do you hear what she's saying, God?"

"And maybe he gave you his portrait as a sign of his friendship. If that's what happened, you don't have to deny it."

"Anastasie!"

"If that's what happened, you'd have to admit that you're as fickle as a pretty woman."

"Are you my wife?"

"After all, it really must have been you who put this portrait up, right?"

"Me? My God!"

"But who was it, then?"

"You, madame."

"Me?"

"Yes!" cried Monsieur Pipelet, driven to distraction. "It was you! I have to believe it was you. This morning, in bed with my back turned, I wouldn't have seen anything."

"But my old deary—"

"I tell you, it had to be you. Otherwise, it could only be the devil, I think, since I never left the apartment, and when I went upstairs to answer the male voice, I had the key. The door was locked, and you were the one who opened it. Can you deny that?"

"It's true enough!"

"So you admit it?"

"All I admit is that I don't understand a thing. It's a prank, and it's a well-played one, to boot! You have to give it that."

"A prank!" cried Monsieur Pipelet, carried away by a delirious indignation. "Ah, there you go again—a prank! I'm telling you, there's some abominable plot behind all of this. There's something underneath the surface. It's some kind of setup—a conspiracy. They're hiding the pit under the flowers. They're trying to distract me so I won't see the edge of the hole they're going to throw me into. The only thing left for me to do is to seek out the protection of the law. Fortunately, France is protected by God." At this, Monsieur Pipelet walked over to the door.

"Where are you going, old deary?"

"To the police superintendent to file charges. This portrait will serve as evidence of how they persecute me."

"But what charge will you make?"

"What charge will I make? What? My most dogged enemy has found a way, by means of the most fraudulent machinations, of forcing me to have his portrait in my home, indeed, above my nuptial bed. How can the police not take me under their protection? Give me the portrait, Anastasie. Give it to me—but don't let me see it on the portrait side—the sight of it disgusts me! The traitor cannot deny he did it, because it has his handwriting on it: *'Cabrion, to his good friend Pipelet, for life.'* For life! Yes, that's what it's all about. He wants to take my life, and that's surely why he's been pursuing me. And he'll end up taking it, because I'm living in a continual state of alarm. I'll think, pretty soon, that I'm seeing that infernal being everywhere! Under the floor, in the walls, on the ceiling! At night, he can see me lying in the arms of my spouse; during the day, he's standing behind me with his satanic grin always on his face! And who's to say that he isn't here right now, hiding somewhere like some poisonous insect? Let's see. Are you there, monster? What about over there?" cried Monsieur Pipelet, accompanying his furious imprecations with a swiveling of his head that made him look as if he wanted to look into and question every part of the room.

"I'm here, my good friend!" said the well-known voice of Cabrion, affectionately.

These words seemed to emerge from deep within the alcove, thanks to the simple trick of ventriloquism. The infernal scoundrel was actually standing outside of the door to the lodge, enjoying this scene down to its smallest details. After pronouncing these last words, though, he prudently made off—not, as we will see later on, before having left something new to cause anger, astonishment, and much reflection on the part of his victim.

Madame Pipelet, courageous and skeptical as always, looked under the bed and in the most remote corners of the lodge without finding anything. She went out to look in the alley but was no more fortunate in that search. Meanwhile, Monsieur Pipelet, staggered by this latest blow, had fallen back into his chair overcome with desperation.

"It's nothing, Alfred," said Anastasie, demonstrating once again her strength of character. "That scoundrel was hiding next to the door, and while we were looking in one direction, he ran away in the other. Be patient! I'll catch him at it one day, and then he'd better beware! I'll put my broomstick down his throat!"

The door opened, and Madame Séraphin, housekeeper to the solicitor Jacques Ferrand, came into the apartment.

"Hello, Madame Séraphin," said Madame Pipelet. She wanted to hide her domestic worries from an outsider, so she suddenly adopted a gracious and pleasant tone. "How can we help you?"

"First, tell me about your new sign."

"Our new sign?"

"The little placard."

"What little placard?"

"The black one that has red letters on it. It's hanging over the door to your alley."

"What? In the street?"

"Yes, in the street, just over your door."

"My dear Madame Séraphin, I swear on everything holy that I don't know a thing about any of this. What about you, old deary?"

Alfred stayed silent.

"Well, really, the sign refers to Monsieur Pipelet," said Madame Séraphin. "He's the one who should explain it."

Alfred moaned softly and inarticulately, shaking his stovepipe hat. This pantomime meant that Alfred realized that there was no way he could explain anything to others given how preoccupied he was with problems each of which was infinitely less amenable to solution than the last.

"Don't pay any attention, Madame Séraphin," said Anastasie. "Poor

Alfred has a pyloric cramp again. It gives him all kinds of pain. But what is this little placard you're talking about? Maybe it belongs to the liquor salesman next door?"

"No, definitely not. I'm telling you that it's a little placard that's hanging right over your door."

"Come on, you're joking."

"Not at all. I just saw it on my way in. It says in big letters, 'PIPELET AND CABRION PARTNERS IN THE FRIENDSHIP BUSINESS, ETC. *See Doorkeeper Within.*'"

"My God! That's written over our door? Did you hear that, Alfred?"

Monsieur Pipelet looked at Madame Séraphin with a deranged stare. He didn't understand, and he didn't want to understand.

"That's what it says—on the street—on a placard?" said Madame Pipelet, flabbergasted at this new bit of audacity.

"Yes, as I said, I just read it coming in. So I said to myself, 'What a funny notion! Monsieur Pipelet is a cobbler by trade, and he's advertising to passersby with a sign that he's engaged in 'the business of friendship' with a Monsieur Cabrion. What does that mean? There's something there that isn't clear. But since it said, 'See doorkeeper within,' I figured Madame Pipelet would explain it all to me. But look!" cried Madame Séraphin suddenly, interrupting herself. "Your husband looks like he's sick. Look out! He's falling over backwards!"

Madame Pipelet caught Alfred, nearly passed out, in her arms. This last blow had been too much for him. The man in the stovepipe hat more or less lost consciousness as he murmured these words. "The wretch! He has postered me up in public!"

"As I was telling you, Madame Séraphin, Alfred is suffering from this pyloric cramp, not to speak of an unleashed scamp who is killing him with a thousand pinpricks. This poor old dear can't hold out against it! Fortunately, I have a bit of absinthe here to give him. That should put him back on his feet."

Indeed, thanks to Madame Pipelet's infallible remedy, Alfred gradually came back to his senses. But alas: hardly had he regained consciousness when he was subjected to a cruel new trial.

A person of advanced age, decently dressed and with a face that was so innocent, or rather, so clearly that of a ninny, that one could never suspect him of having the slightest ironic ulterior motive common to a certain kind of Parisian street idler, opened the glass part of the door that moved and said in a singularly intrigued tone, "I just saw something written on a placard over your alley, 'Pipelet and Cabrion partners in the friendship business, etc. See doorkeeper within.' Could you please be so kind as to explain to me what this means, since you're the doorkeeper here?"

"What it means?" cried Monsieur Pipelet in a thundering voice, finally giving way to his long-suppressed rage. "It means that Monsieur Cabrion is a vile impostor, *monsiiiieur.*"

The street idler took a step backward at this sudden, furious explosion. Exasperated, his eyes aflame, his face scarlet, Alfred was halfway out of the apartment. He was supporting himself with his two hands clutching at the lower panel of the door as the faces of Madame Séraphin and Anastasie were floating in the dim background of the apartment.

"You should know, *monsiiiieur,*" cried Monsieur Pipelet, "that I have no business with that villain Cabrion—and least of all the business of friendship!"

"That's true, and you must have been on the shelf for a long time, you old pickle, to come in here and ask such a thing!" cried Madame Pipelet, bitingly, showing her snarling mug over her husband's shoulder.

"Madame," the street idler said in a sententious manner as he backed up another step, "signs are made to be read. You display it, I read it. I am within my rights, and you are not within yours to address me with such coarseness!"

"Coarseness yourself, you old skinflint!" Anastasie snapped back, baring her teeth.

"You're a coarse peasant!"

"Alfred, give me your bootstrap and I'll take this guy's measure. I need to teach him not to be a joker at his age—the old bumpkin!"

"You insult one who comes in merely to ask for the information you offer on your sign! Things don't work like that, madame!"

"But, *monsiiiieur* . . ." cried the unhappy doorkeeper.

"But, monsieur," said the street idler, exasperated. "Be friends with Monsieur Cabrion as much as you like, but good heavens, don't post it in big letters for all passersby to read! On that note, I am obliged to warn you that you are a prideful lout, and that I am going to press charges with the police superintendent." And the street idler walked out in a rage.

"Anastasie," said Pipelet in a pained voice, "I can't survive this, I can tell you that. I have been struck a death blow. I no longer have any hope to escape him. You see, my name is publicly linked with the name of that wretch. He dares to advertise that I am engaged in the friendship business with him, and the public believes it. I find out about it, I tell them about it, I inform them of it . . . It's monstrous! It's obscene! It's an idea from hell! But it has to end . . . this is the last straw. One or the other of us must succumb in this struggle to the death!" Roused beyond his habitual apathy, Monsieur Pipelet seized Cabrion's portrait and strode toward the door, determined to find a vigorous resolution to his plight.

"Where are you going, Alfred?"

"To the police superintendent. I'm going to take down that blasted sign. With that sign in one hand and this portrait in the other, I will proclaim, 'Protect me! Avenge me! Deliver me from Cabrion!'"

"Well said, my old deary. Look sharp! Pull yourself together! If you can't get the placard down yourself, ask the liquor salesman to help you and to lend you his little ladder. That villain Cabrion! Oh! If I had him in my grips and if I could, I swear I'd fry him up in my frying pan. That's how much I'd like to see him suffer. Yes, there are people they guillotine who haven't deserved it as much as he does. That scoundrel! I'd like to see that crook at the Place de Grève!"[125]

Given the circumstances, Alfred exhibited sublime forbearance. Despite the terrible grievances he held against Cabrion, he still had the generosity to display some feelings of pity toward the painter. "No," he said, "no, even if I could, I wouldn't ask for his head!"

"Well, I would! I would! I would! It would just be too bad for him. And alley-oop!" cried the fierce Anastasie.

"No," said Alfred. "I have no taste for blood, but I have the right to demand that that miscreant be condemned to life imprisonment. My well-being requires it. My health demands it. Justice must grant me this remedy. Otherwise, I will leave France—my beautiful France! That's what will end up happening."

And Alfred departed his apartment majestically, overcome by his sorrows like one of those imposing victims of fate in antiquity.

125. Until 1830, public executions were held on the Place de Grève, which was a public square in front of the Paris city hall. [TN]

CHAPTER 12

CECILY

Before we allow our reader to overhear the conversation between Madame Séraphin and Madame Pipelet, we should let him know that although Anastasie had no suspicions whatsoever about the solicitor's virtue and piety, she did feel he was extremely wrong to treat Louise Morel and François Germain so harshly. Naturally, the doorkeeper's wife included Madame Séraphin in this condemnation. Being the skillful politician she was, however, Madame Pipelet, for reasons we will reveal further on, managed to mask the estrangement she felt from the housekeeper with a warm and cordial welcome.

After expressing her strict disapproval of Cabrion's behavior, Madame Séraphin said, "That was something! So what's become of Monsieur Bradamanti? Yesterday evening I wrote to him, but no answer. This morning I came to look for him, but nobody was home. I hope this time I'll have better luck."

Madame Pipelet acted as if she were highly annoyed. "That man!" she cried. "What bad timing!"

"What do you mean?"

"Monsieur Bradamanti hasn't returned yet."

"That's intolerable!"

"Isn't it? It's detestable, is what it is, my poor Madame Séraphin!"

"And I have a lot to talk over with him!"

"Isn't that just your luck?"

"All the more since I had to come up with excuses to come here. Because if Monsieur Ferrand ever suspected that I knew a charlatan—he being so pious and religious—well, you can guess the scene there'd be!"

"He's like Alfred. He's so straitlaced—so straitlaced!—that he ends up getting shocked by everything."

"And you don't know when Monsieur Bradamanti will return?"

"He has an appointment with someone at six or seven o'clock this evening, and he asked me to tell the person he's expecting to come back if he hadn't returned yet. Come back this evening and you'll be sure to find him." And Anastasie added mentally, "You can count on it; he'll be on his way to Normandy in an hour."

"I'll come back this evening, then," said Madame Séraphin, annoyed. Then she added, "I had something else to tell you, my dear Madame Pipelet. You know what happened to that fool Louise, that girl everyone thought was so honest?"

"I don't want to hear about it," said Madame Pipelet, raising her eyes in sorrow. "It makes my hair stand on end."

"I just was going to tell you that we don't have a servant anymore, so if you happen to hear of a well-behaved young woman who's very hard-working and very honest, I'd appreciate it very much if you came to tell me. It's so difficult to find good help these days. One has to search everywhere."

"Rest assured, Madame Séraphin. If I hear of someone, I'll let you know. You know as well as I do that good positions are as hard to find as good help." And then Anastasie added, but to herself again, "But you'll find them sooner than I'd send a poor girl to starve in your hovel! Your boss is too much of a miser and too mean. The idea of denouncing both poor Louise and poor Germain at one fell swoop!"

"I don't need to tell you," said Madame Séraphin, "how peaceful our house is. A young woman has everything to gain by being placed with us. Louise had to have been the very soul of wickedness to have turned out so badly in spite of the good and saintly advice she got from Monsieur Ferrand."

"Of course. And so you can trust me—if I hear of the kind of young person you're looking for, I'll be sure to send her to you right away."

"There's one more thing," said Madame Séraphin. "If it's possible, Monsieur Ferrand would like for this servant not to have a family. That way, you understand, she won't have any reason to go out and will thus have fewer chances of being disturbed. It follows that, I'm guessing, if it could possibly be arranged, Monsieur would prefer an orphan. It would be a good deed, first of all, but also because, as I just said, without dependents or hangers-on, she wouldn't have any excuse to leave. That wretched Louise was a real lesson for Monsieur. Really, my poor Madame Pipelet! That's what makes it so hard now to choose a good servant. To have such a scandal in as pious a house as ours! How dreadful! So tonight, then, I'll come to see Monsieur Bradamanti, and on my way I'll go to see Old Lady Burette."

"Till tonight, then, Madame Séraphin. You'll find Monsieur Bradamanti in then, for sure."

Madame Séraphin departed.

"She seems determined to see Bradamanti!" said Madame Pipelet. "What can she want with him? And he, on the other hand, seems determined not to see her before he leaves for Normandy! I was really afraid that that Séraphin woman wasn't going to leave, all the more since Monsieur Bradamanti is waiting for the lady who already came yesterday evening. I couldn't see her very well, but this time I'm really going to try to get a good look at her, just the same as I did the other day with that two-farthing commandant's honey. He hasn't set foot here since! I'll burn his wood—that'll teach him. Yes, I'm going to burn all his wood! That ill-mannered whippersnapper. Get out of here, with your lousy twelve francs and your silk dressing gown! That did you a lot of good, didn't it? But who is Monsieur Bradamanti's lady? Is she a middle-class woman, or is she just riffraff? I'd really like to know, because I'm as curious as a magpie. It's not my fault: God made me this way. That's his problem. It's just the way I am. Hey . . . I've got an idea, a really good one, for finding out that lady's name. I'll have to try it. But who's here now? Oh, it's my king of tenants. Hello, Monsieur Rodolphe!" said Madame Pipelet as she gave a military salute with the back of her left hand touching her wig.

This was indeed Rodolphe. He still had not heard of Monsieur d'Harville's death.

"Hello, Madame Pipelet," he said as he entered. "Is Mademoiselle Rigolette at home? I need to talk with her."

"Her? That poor little kitten, isn't she always? And always working—is there ever a time she isn't at it?"

"And how is Morel's wife? Is she doing a bit better?"

"Yes, Monsieur Rodolphe. Heavens, thanks to you or to the protector whose agent you are, she and her children are so happy now. They're like fish in the water. They have a fire, air, good beds, good food, a helper to take care of them—and that's not counting Mademoiselle Rigolette, who works like a busy little beaver but still keeps track of them as if she had nothing else to do. And a black doctor came whom you sent to see Morel's wife. Hee, hee, hee! You know, Monsieur Rodolphe, I said to myself, 'Hey, this darkie must be the coal miners' doctor! He can take their pulse without getting his hands dirty.' But it's all the same, color doesn't mean anything. He seems to be an excellent doctor, all the same. He ordered a potion for Morel's wife that helped her right away."

"Poor woman! She must still be very sad!"

"Oh, yes, Monsieur Rodolphe. What do you expect? Her husband's mad, and then her Louise is in prison. You know, the whole affair with Louise is a heartbreak for her. For an honest family, it's terrible. And when I think that just a moment ago Old Lady Séraphin, the solicitor's housekeeper, came here and said such horrible things about that poor girl! If I hadn't been trying to get that Séraphin woman to swallow the bait, things would have gone differently. But for a moment, at least, I walked the line. Doesn't she have a lot of nerve to come and ask me if I know a young person to replace Louise for that skinflint of a solicitor? What rakes and misers those people are! Can you believe that they're looking for an orphan to be their servant, if one should turn up? Do you know why, Monsieur Rodolphe? Supposedly because an orphan doesn't have relatives and therefore doesn't have any occasion to go out and see them, and so she'll be quieter. But that's really not what it's about. That's a sham. The real reason is that they want to catch a poor girl who has nothing, because if she doesn't have anyone to advise her, they can skimp on her wages as much as they like. Isn't that true, Monsieur Rodolphe?"

"Yes . . . yes," he responded, distractedly.

Hearing that Madame Séraphin was looking for an orphan to replace Louise as a servant for Monsieur Ferrand, Rodolphe had a sudden plan for how he might devise a certain punishment for the solicitor. While Madame Pipelet was speaking, he was making slight modifications to the role he had been planning to assign to Cecily, who was to be the principal instrument of the just punishment he would inflict on Louise Morel's torturer.

"I was sure you would think the same thing as me," said Madame Pipelet. "Yes, I'll say it again: they only want a young person who is alone in the world to work for them so they can cut down on her wages. You'd have to kill me before I'd recommend anyone to them. First of all, I don't know anyone, but if I did, no matter who it was, I would be sure to keep them from ever entering that hovel. Don't you think I'm right, Monsieur Rodolphe?"

"Madame Pipelet, would you like to do me a great favor?"

"Good Lord! Monsieur Rodolphe, what do you want me to do? Walk through fire? Curl my wig with boiling oil? Would you rather that I bit someone? Just say the word! I'm yours, heart and soul—unless it has anything to do with playing tricks on Alfred."

"Don't worry, Madame Pipelet. Here's what I want you to do. I have a young orphan, a foreigner. She's never been to Paris, and I'd like to place her with Monsieur Ferrand."

"You must be kidding. Really? In that hovel, with that old miser?"

"It's still a position. If the young woman I'm talking about doesn't do well there, she'll leave later. But at least she'll earn a living right away. I won't have to worry about her."

"Heavens, Monsieur Rodolphe! It's up to you, and now you've been warned. If in spite of all this you think it's a good opportunity, it's up to you. And anyway, you have to be fair to the solicitor. If there are things against him, there are things going for him, too. It's true that he's as miserly as a dog, as harsh as a donkey, and he has the religiosity of a sexton. But he's the most honest man there is. He pays poorly, but he pays cash on the barrelhead. The food is bad, but it's there every day. In the end, it's a house where you have to work like a horse, but you can't find a more boring place. There's no chance of a girl finding things to do and places to go. Louise was just an accident."

"Madame Pipelet, I am going to entrust you with a secret."

"On the word of Anastasie Pipelet, née Galimard, as sure as there's a God in heaven, and as sure as Alfred wears only green clothing: I will be as silent as the grave."

"You can't tell Monsieur Pipelet anything about this."

"I swear on my old dear's head, as long as it's for an honest cause."

"Oh, Madame Pipelet!"

"We'll trick him five ways from Sunday, he won't know a thing that's going on. Think of him as being as innocent as a six-month-old baby, and having about as much malice."

"I trust you. Listen to me."

"It's cradle to grave for us, my king of tenants. So go right ahead."

"The young woman I'm talking about has done something wrong."

"Understood! If I hadn't married Alfred when I was fifteen, I might have done fifty, even a hundred somethings wrong! The person you see before you today, I used to be a real firecracker in the day, heaven knows! Fortunately, Alfred extinguished me with his virtue. If it hadn't been for him, I would have done all sorts of crazy things for men. All this is just to say that if your young woman has committed only one something wrong, there's room for hope."

"I think so, too. This young woman was a servant in Germany with one of my relatives. The son of this relative was her partner in her sin. You catch my drift?"

"Alley-oop! And now I understand just as well as if I'd been the one who did the something wrong."

"The mother sent the servant away, but the young man was foolish enough to leave his father's home and to take this poor girl to Paris."

"What do you expect? Young people . . ."

"After he got over his head having been turned, he started considering his position and these considerations were that much more prudent because he had gone through all his money. My young relative turned to me. I agreed to give him money to return to his mother with, but on the condition that he leave the girl here and I would try to find her a job."

"I couldn't have done better for my own son, if Pipelet had seen fit to give me one."

"I am delighted that you approve. But since the young woman has no references and she's a foreigner, it's difficult to find a position for her. If you could tell Madame Séraphin that one of your relatives who lives in Germany wrote to you and recommended this young woman, the solicitor might take her into his service. I would be particularly pleased if this worked out. Cecily has always been rather wild. She would surely straighten up in a house as severe as the solicitor's. That's the main reason I would like to see this young woman enter Monsieur Jacques Ferrand's service. I need hardly say that if she were presented by you, such a respectable person—"

"Oh, Monsieur Rodolphe!"

"Such a worthy person—"

"Oh, you're my king of tenants!"

"So, if this young woman were presented by you, she would certainly be accepted by Madame Séraphin, whereas if she were presented by me—"

"Understood! It would be as if I were presenting a cute young man! Done! This suits me fine. Alley-oop! We'll show that Séraphin woman. And since I've got a bone to pick with her, that makes it even better. You can count on me, Monsieur Rodolphe! I'll take her in but good! I'll tell her that I have a cousin who's been in Germany for I don't know how long, a Galimard. I'll say that I just found out that she died, along with her husband, and that their daughter, who's now an orphan, is going to be on my hands at any moment now."

"Very good! You'll bring Cecily yourself to Monsieur Ferrand without saying anything else about her to Madame Séraphin. You haven't seen your cousin in twenty years, so there's really nothing you can say besides the fact that since she moved to Germany, you haven't heard a word about her."

"Oh, but there's a problem. What if the young person can only jabber away in German?"

"She speaks perfect French. I'll tell her what she has to do. Don't worry about anything except recommending her as soon as you can to Madame Séraphin. But wait, as I think about it, no—she might get suspicious and think you're doing something to force her hand. You know how it is: often, you get turned down just because you asked."

"Are you kidding me? Don't I know! That's why I've always snubbed sweet-talkers. If they hadn't asked me for something—well, I won't say that . . ."

"That's the way it always works. So don't make any proposals to Madame Séraphin and you'll see, she'll come to you. Just tell her Cecily is an orphan, a foreigner, very young, and very pretty. Say that she's going to be a heavy burden on you and that you don't have any real feelings for her since you had had a falling-out with your cousin and you don't think much of this gift she's sent your way."

"Good Lord! You're a sly one! Don't worry, between the two of us, we'll be one too many for them. Say, Monsieur Rodolphe, we really understand each other, don't we? When I think what it would have been like if you were my age when I was a real firecracker! Honestly, I don't know what would have happened! What about you?"

"Shhh! If Monsieur Pipelet heard—"

"You're right! My poor dear, he has a one-track mind. You have no idea. Some new prank of Cabrion's and . . . but I'll tell you about it later. As for your young woman, just relax. I'll bet anything I can bring the Séraphin woman along into asking me to let them hire my relative."

"If you succeed, my dear Madame Pipelet, there'll be a hundred francs in it for you. I'm not rich, but—"

"Don't you believe in anything, Monsieur Rodolphe? Do you think I'm doing this out of self-interest? Good Lord, it's purely out of friendship! Honestly, a hundred francs!"

"But consider the fact that if I had to take care of this young woman for a long time, it would cost me much more than that in only a few months."

"Just as a favor to you, then, I'll take the hundred francs, Monsieur Rodolphe. But having you in the house has been one winning number in the lottery. I want to shout it to the rafters: you're the king of tenants! Hey, look, it's a cab! No doubt that's Monsieur Bradamanti's little lady. She came here yesterday but I couldn't see her. I'm going to make her hang around so I can get a good look at her, not to mention that I've also come up with a good way to find out her name. You'll see how I work. You'll be amused!"

"No, no, Madame Pipelet. This woman's name and face are none of my concern," said Rodolphe, stepping far back into the apartment.

"Madame!" cried Anastasie as she rushed before the person who was entering. "Where are you going, madame?"

"To see Monsieur Bradamanti," said the woman, visibly annoyed at having been stopped at the entrance.

"He isn't there."

"You must be wrong."

"No, I am not wrong," said the doorkeeper's wife, maneuvering adroitly to catch a glimpse of the woman's face. "Monsieur Bradamanti left. He's gone, long gone—except for a certain lady, that is."

"Well, that would be me. You are irritating me. Let me by."

"Your name, madame? I need to know whether it's the name of the person that Monsieur Bradamanti asked me to let in. If it's not your name, you'll have to step over my dead body before you'll be allowed to come in."

"He told you my name?" cried the woman, as surprised as she was anxious.

"Yes, madame."

"How imprudent!" murmured the young woman. Then, after a moment's hesitation, she impatiently added in a quiet voice, as if she were afraid of being overheard, "Very well. My name is Madame d'Orbigny."

At the sound of this name, Rodolphe trembled. It was the name of Madame d'Harville's stepmother. Instead of staying in the shadows, he came forward, and the daylight and lamp together gave him enough clarity to verify that this was in fact the woman he recognized from the portrait Clémence had once sketched for him.

"Madame d'Orbigny?" repeated Madame Pipelet. "That's the name Monsieur Bradamanti gave me. You can go up, madame."

Madame d'Harville's stepmother quickly moved past the lodge.

"And alley-oop!" cried the doorkeeper's wife triumphantly. "Down goes the fancy lady! I know her name—her name is d'Orbigny! Not a bad job—huh, Monsieur Rodolphe? But what's got into you now? You look all lost in thought!"

"Has that woman already been here before to see Monsieur Bradamanti?" Rodolphe asked the porter's wife.

"Yes. Yesterday evening, as soon as she departed, Monsieur Bradamanti went out right away, probably to reserve his spot in the stagecoach for today. Yesterday when he returned he asked me to take his suitcase to the depot because he didn't trust that little crook Gammy to do it."

"And where is Monsieur Bradamanti going? Do you know?"

"To Normandy, on the Alençon highway."

Rodolphe remembered that the Aubiers property where Monsieur d'Orbigny lived was in Normandy. He had no doubt that the charlatan was going to see Clémence's father with the most sinister of intentions.

"Monsieur Bradamanti's departure is what's really going to drive Madame Séraphin crazy!" said Madame Pipelet. "She's rabid about seeing Monsieur Bradamanti, who's been trying his best to avoid her. He asked me not to let her know that he was leaving this evening at six. So when she comes back here, she'll find herself facing a closed door! I'll use that opportunity to talk with her about your young person. By the way, what's her name again? Cissy?"

"Cecily."

"It's like Cécile, but with a *y* on the end. Fine with me, but I'd better write myself a note so I can remember that darned name. Cissy? Cassie? Cecily—all right, I've got it."

"I'm going up to see Mademoiselle Rigolette now," said Rodolphe to Madame Pipelet as he left the lodge.

"When you come back down, Monsieur Rodolphe, would you say hello to my poor old deary? He's very upset. He'll tell you all about it. That Cabrion monster has been up to tricks again."

"I will always listen to your husband's problems, Madame Pipelet." And at that, still preoccupied with thoughts of Madame d'Orbigny's visit to Polidori, he went upstairs to see Mademoiselle Rigolette.

CHAPTER 13

RIGOLETTE'S FIRST SORROW

Rigolette's room sparkled, as it always did, with the same charming cleanliness. The large silver watch, placed on the fireplace in a boxwood case, read four o'clock. With the worst of the winter's cold past, the thrifty worker had not lit her stove. From the window one could barely see a corner of blue sky through the irregular mass of roofs, attic gables, and tall chimneys that formed the horizon from the other side of the street. Suddenly a ray of sun that one might say had lost its way entered between two raised gables. For a few moments it turned the floor of the young woman's room a resplendent shade of scarlet. Rigolette was sitting next to the window, hard at work. The soft chiaroscuro of her alluring profile stood out against the luminous transparency of the window like a cameo of rosy whiteness against a bright red background. Brilliant glints played across her black hair that was twisted back behind her head. They tinted her hardworking little ivory hands a warm shade of amber. Her hands were moving the needle back and forth with incomparable agility. The long folds of her brown dress, overlaid by the lace of her green apron, partially hid her straw armchair. Her pretty feet, always perfectly shod, were poised on the edge of a stool placed in front of her.

Just as a grand lord amuses himself sometimes on a whim by deciding to cover the walls of a thatched cottage with glorious draperies, the setting sun illuminated this little room for a moment with a thousand iridescent fires and made the gray and green Persian curtains glow with golden reflections. It made the polish on the chestnut furniture sparkle and the tiles of the floor glow like red copper, and it wrapped the seamstress's birdcage in a scaffolding of gold.

But alas! Despite the enticing joyfulness of this ray of sunlight, the two canaries, male and female, were fluttering about in an anxious manner, and, in contrast to their usual practice, they were not singing. This was because Rigolette, in contrast to her usual practice, was not singing. The three hardly ever chirped except in unison. Almost always, Rigolette's fresh morning song awakened the songs of the two birds, who, lazier than the young woman, didn't like to leave their nest so early. Thus they issued challenges to each other; their battles were in clear, sonorous, pearly silver notes, and the birds did not always carry the day.

Rigolette was not singing herself because, for the first time in her life, she was experiencing sorrow. The Morel family's poverty had, until now, often affected her, but such scenes are too familiar to the poorer classes of people to cause lasting feelings. After having helped these unfortunate people almost every day as much as she could, and having wept sincerely with them and for them, the girl felt both moved and satisfied at once: she was moved by their misfortune and satisfied to have shown her commiseration. But nothing in this was a matter of sorrow for her. Soon enough, Rigolette's native cheerfulness would always regain the upper hand over her feelings. And not out of selfishness but as a simple response to the reality of the comparison, she would feel so happy in her own little room after leaving the Morels' horrible hovel that her fleeting sadness would quickly dissipate. This changeability of feeling was so far removed from selfishness that, by a touching logic that showed her tact, the seamstress felt it almost a duty to take the part of those less fortunate than herself if she was to enjoy her own existence—one that was certainly precarious enough, and that was earned entirely by her labors—without feeling guilty. Compared to the shocking poverty of the gem-cutter's family, her own existence felt almost luxurious to her. "To sing without guilt when there are people nearby who have so much to grieve over," she would say innocently to herself, "one must first have been as generous as one can."

Before we tell the reader the cause of Rigolette's first sorrow, we wish to reassure and complete his edification with regard to this young woman's virtue. We regret having to use the word "virtue," since it is such a grave, pompous, and solemn word that almost always implies the ideas of painful sacrifice, of difficult struggles against the passions, or of austere meditations on the end of our life here below. This was not Rigolette's kind of virtue. She had neither struggled nor meditated. She had worked, laughed, and sung. Her good behavior, as she had said to Rodolphe, so simply and sincerely, was essentially a matter of limited time. She did not have the leisure to fall in love. Cheerful, hard-working, orderly above all, it was order, work, and good cheer that had, without her even knowing it, protected her, sustained her, and saved her. Some may think this a light, easy, cheerful kind of morality; but what does its cause matter, so long as its effect is a lasting one? What difference does it make which way the roots of the plant grow, so long as the flower blossoms with a pure, brilliant, sweet-smelling bloom?

In our discussion of a utopian scheme for the encouragement, assistance, and compensation that our society should offer workers who are remarkable for their outstanding social qualities, we spoke of the spies of virtue, one of the Emperor's projects. Let us suppose that the great man's promising plan had been realized. One of those true philanthropists, charged by him to locate the good, has discovered Rigolette. Abandoned, with no counsel, with no support, exposed to all of the dangers of poverty, to all of the seductions youth and beauty entail, this charming girl has remained pure. Her honest, hardworking life would be able to serve as an edification and example.

If this child does not merit reward or assistance, has she not at least earned a few heartfelt words of praise and encouragement, words that would make her aware of her own worth, words that might raise her in her own eyes and possibly help her stay on the same course for the future? For she would know that she was being watched over with care and solicitude as she walked her difficult path with so much courage and serenity. She would know that if one day a loss of employment or unexpected illness were to threaten to overturn the delicate balance of her impoverished and busy life—a balance resting entirely on her work and health—thanks to her past virtue, at least some slight aid would come her way.

Some will say, no doubt, that it would be impossible to implement this protective surveillance with which the plan means to oversee those who were deemed particularly worthy of interest because of their excellent behavior in the past. But it seems to us that our society has already solved this problem. Have we not come up with a method—and a very useful one—for police oversight for life or for a defined term, for people whose danger has been evidenced by their deplorable past conduct? Why can our society not find a way to enact a surveillance plan aligned with the highest moral charity?

But let us leave the realm of utopias once again and return to the cause of Rigolette's first sorrow.

Except for Germain, that innocent and serious young man, the seamstress's neighbors had first taken her striking familiarity and offers of neighborliness as very meaningful flirtation. But these gentlemen had all been obliged to realize, with as much surprise as disappointment, that in Rigolette they had found an amiable and cheerful companion with whom to spend their free time on Sundays and a helpful and good-tempered neighbor—but not a mistress. Their surprise and disappointment, sharp enough at first, fell away little by little, thanks to the seamstress's frank and charming disposition. And then, as she had perceptively noted to Rodolphe, her neighbors were proud to have a pretty girl on their arms on a Sunday who made them look good in more ways than one (Rigolette had no care for what impression she gave) and who cost them no more than their share of the modest entertainments, the value of which her presence and friendliness more than doubled. And then, the dear girl could be made so happy so easily! On days of want, she dined with so much pleasure and cheer on a nice hot piece of griddle cake that she bit her little white teeth into with all her strength. And afterward, she could enjoy herself so thoroughly by taking a stroll on the boulevards or in the walkways!

If our readers feel even a little sympathy for Rigolette, they will admit that one would have to be either stupid or barbaric to turn down this gracious creature's offer of modest distractions once a week, especially, considering that, since she had no right to be jealous, she never stopped her gallants from consoling themselves for her rigors with other less cruel beauties.

François Germain alone based no illusory hopes on the young woman's familiar manners. Whether it was a heartfelt instinct or a tactful understanding, he understood immediately what kinds of pleasures Rigolette's singular camaraderie offered.

What was destined to happen, happened. Germain fell passionately in love with his neighbor but dared not utter a word of his feelings. Far from following in the footsteps of his predecessors who, once convinced of the futility of any pursuit of Rigolette, moved on to console themselves with other loves, without, for all that, experiencing any rupture with their neighbor, Germain had savored his intimacy with the young woman. He had spent not only his Sundays with her but also every other free evening he had. Over those long hours, Rigolette had shown herself, as always, full of laughter and fun, while Germain was tender, attentive, serious—and often even a little sad.

This sadness was his only awkwardness; his naturally distinguished manners were far preferable to the ridiculous pretentions of Monsieur Giraudeau, the traveling salesman, or the turbulent eccentricities of Monsieur Cabrion. Yet Monsieur Giraudeau, with his tireless loquaciousness, and the painter, too, with his no less tireless mirth, both had the advantage over Germain, whose gentle gravity sometimes overawed his neighbor. Up to this point, Rigolette had never shown a marked preference for any of her three worshippers. But as she was not lacking in judgment, she could tell that Germain was the only one who brought together all the qualities necessary to make a sensible woman happy.

All this background being established, we can now say why Rigolette was dejected and why neither she nor her birds were singing. Her round and fresh face had grown a bit pale. Her large black eyes, normally so cheerful and shining, were somewhat dim and had light circles under them. Her features revealed unusual fatigue. She had been busy working through much of the night.

From time to time, she gazed sadly at a letter that was lying open on a table next to her. This letter had just been sent to her by Germain, and its contents read as follows:

Conciergerie prison

Dear Mademoiselle Rigolette,

The place from which I write to you will tell you how unhappy I am. I have been imprisoned as a thief. I am guilty in the eyes of everyone, yet I still dare to write to you!

It would be terrible to believe that you as well could think of me as criminal and degraded. I beg of you not to condemn me before reading this letter. If you were to reject me, it would be the straw that broke the camel's back.

Here is what happened: For some time, I have not lived on rue du Temple, but I knew through Louise that the Morel family that we both care about so much had grown more and more wretched. Alas! My pity for these poor people destroyed me! I regret nothing, but my fate is cruel.

Yesterday, I had stayed at Monsieur Ferrand's place quite late, busy with urgent accounts. In the room in which I was working stood a desk. My boss would lock it up every day with the work I had done stowed inside it. That evening, he seemed nervous and agitated. He said to me, "Don't leave here until these accounts are finished. You can put them in the desk drawer, and I'll leave you the key." And he walked out.

Once my work was done, I opened the drawer to lock it up inside. But my gaze was automatically drawn to an opened letter on which I read the name of Jérôme Morel, the gem-cutter.

I must admit that, seeing that the letter concerned our unfortunate friend, I was indiscreet enough to read it. I learned from it that the artisan was due to be arrested the next day for a bill of exchange for one thousand, three hundred francs that was pursued by Monsieur Ferrand, who, under an assumed name, was getting Morel thrown into prison. The letter was from my boss's business agent. I understood the Morel family's situation enough to know what a blow it would be for its sole source of support to be incarcerated. I was both devastated and indignant. Unfortunately, I saw in the same drawer an open box that had gold in it. It contained two thousand francs. At that moment, I heard Louise going upstairs. Without thinking about how serious my actions were, I took advantage of the opportunity fate gave me and took one thousand, three hundred francs. I waited for Louise in the hallway. I put the money in her hand and said to her, "Your father is going to be arrested tomorrow at dawn for a thousand three hundred francs. Here they are. Save him, but don't tell anyone that I'm the one who gave you this money. Monsieur Ferrand is a wicked man!"

You understand, mademoiselle, that I had good intentions but that my conduct was criminal. I am hiding nothing from you. Here, however, is my excuse. For a long time, I had managed to save money by living thriftily and setting aside a little sum of one thousand, five hundred francs in the care of a banker. One week ago, he told me that his obligation to me had come to term and that he would put my funds at my disposition if I didn't wish to keep them with him. I thus had more than I took from the solicitor. I could retrieve my thousand five hundred francs the next day, but the banker's cashier did not come to work before noon, and Morel was going to be arrested the next day at dawn. But I had to enable him to pay his debt very early in the day. Otherwise, even if I were to go during the day to redeem him from prison, he would still have been arrested and led off to prison in front of his wife, which could have killed her. Also, the considerable cost of the arrest would be charged to the gem-cutter. So, you see, I could prevent all these misfortunes by taking the thirteen hundred francs, which I thought I would be able to put back in the desk the next morning before Monsieur Ferrand noticed anything. Unfortunately, I was wrong about that.

When I left Monsieur Ferrand's place, I was no longer feeling as full of the indignation and pity that had made me act the way I did. I reflected on all the danger of my position. I was then assailed by a thousand fears. I fully knew how severe the solicitor could be. After I left, he could have rummaged around in my desk and noticed the theft. In his eyes, after all, and in everyone else's besides, it is a theft.

Thinking all this made me all upset. Although it was late, I ran to the banker to beg him to give me my money on the spot. My motive behind this extraordinary demand was to go back and replace the money I had taken at Monsieur Ferrand's place. By a fatal coincidence, the banker had been in Belleville for the past two days at a country house where he was supervising the planting. I awaited the dawn of day with growing anguish. Finally, I arrived in Belleville. Everything seemed stacked against me: the banker had just left to return to Paris. I ran there to see him and got my money, finally. I went to Monsieur Ferrand's place, only to find that everything had been found out!

But that is only part of my misfortune. Now the solicitor is accusing me of having stolen fifteen thousand francs in banknotes, which were, he says, in the desk drawer along with the two thousand francs in gold. This is an obscene accusation, a heinous lie! I admit full guilt for taking the first money, but I swear, on everything sacred, mademoiselle, that I am innocent of the second theft. I never saw any banknote in that drawer. All there was were the two thousand francs in gold, of which I took the thirteen hundred francs that I was going to bring back.

That is the truth, mademoiselle. I am being charged with a staggering crime. And, yet, I think you ought to know that I am incapable of lying—but will you believe me? Alas! As Monsieur Ferrand said to me, the person who stole a small sum can steal a larger one, and no one can believe a thief.

You have always seemed so kind and so devoted to unfortunate people, mademoiselle. I know that you are so faithful and so honest that your heart will guide you, I hope, toward an appreciation of the truth. That is all I ask. Believe what I'm telling you, and you'll find that I am as worthy of pity as I am of blame. For—I repeat!—my intentions were good, and I was ruined by circumstances that were impossible to predict.

Ah! Mademoiselle Rigolette, I am terribly unfortunate! If you knew the kinds of people with whom I am destined to live until the day of my trial! Yesterday they brought me to a place they call the holding cell of the police prefecture. I cannot tell you what I felt as I went up a dimly lit staircase and found myself standing in front of a door with an iron grate that they opened and that soon shut on me. I was so troubled that at first I couldn't tell where I was. A warm, nauseating breeze brushed my face. I heard a din of sinister laughter, angry voices, and vulgar songs. I stayed fixed to my spot near the doorway, looking at the room's sandstone floor tiles. I didn't dare move forward or raise my eyes, feeling everyone examining me.

No one seemed to care about me. One prisoner more or less doesn't interest those people very much. Finally, I dared to raise my head. What horrible faces—good God! Their clothing was in shreds! They were wearing rags that were stained with mud! All of the trappings of wretchedness and vice were there. There were forty or fifty of them, seated, standing, or lying on benches nailed into the wall. There were vagabonds, thieves, and assassins—basically, everyone who had been arrested that night or during the day.

When they noticed me, I took sad comfort in the fact that they recognized that I was not one of them. Some of them looked at me in an insolent and mocking way. Then they began to talk among themselves quietly in some hideous language that I did not understand. After an instant, the boldest of the lot came over to clap me on the shoulder and ask for money to pay for my welcome. I gave a few pieces of change, hoping to buy myself some peace and quiet in this way. It wasn't enough for them, and they asked for more. I refused. Then several of them surrounded me as they flung insults and threats at me. They were going to gang up on me when, fortunately, a guard arrived, tipped off by the tumult. I appealed to him. He demanded that they return the money that I had given them. He told me that for a modest sum I could be put in a place they call "the pistole."[126] That is, I could be alone in a cell. I accepted the offer with gratitude, and I left the bandits amid their threats for the future. For they were saying that we would meet again, and that then I would stay where I was put.

The guard led me to a cell where I spent the rest of the night. It is from there that I write to you this morning, Mademoiselle Rigolette. Eventually, after my inquest, I will be taken to another prison called La Force,[127] where I fear I will be reunited with many of my companions from the holding cell.

The guard, moved by my sadness and tears, promised to get this letter to you, even though he is strictly forbidden to take such liberties. I would like to ask one last favor of you in view of our former friendship—if our past friendship does not make you blush with shame. If you wish to do me this favor, it is this: with this letter you will receive a small key and a message for the doorkeeper of the house in which I live, number eleven, boulevard Saint-Denis. I am letting him know that you may make free use of anything I own, and that he must execute your orders. He will take you to my room. Please open the desk with the key I am sending you. You will find in it a large envelope that contains different documents that I would like you to keep for me. One of them was to be sent to you, as you will see from your name on it. The others were written about you in happier times. Don't be angry about them. You weren't supposed to know about them. I ask you also to take the small amount of money that is in the desk, as well as a little satin sack that contains a little orange silk bow you were wearing on our last Sunday promenades and that you gave me the day I left rue du Temple.

Finally, I would like you to arrange to have all of the furnishings and my personal effects sold, with the exception of the few pieces of clothing that you should send me at La Force prison. Whether I'm acquitted or convicted, I will be a ruined man and I will have to leave Paris. Where will I go? What resources will I have? God only knows.

Madame Bouvard, who has already sold and bought several of my belongings, might be able to take care of everything. She's an honest woman. This arrangement will spare you a great deal of trouble, for I know how precious your time is. I had paid my rent in advance, so I ask you only to give the doorkeeper a small tip. I apologize, mademoiselle, for imposing on you with all of these details, but you are the only person in the world to whom I dare—and to whom I can—turn. I would have asked one of Monsieur Ferrand's clerks with whom I'm very

126. A private cell, for which one paid one pistole, or ten francs. [TN]

127. Originally the home of the Duke de la Force, the building was converted into a prison in 1780. There was also, originally, a prison called La Petite Force, for prostitutes. These two prisons were combined into a prison for men in 1830. [TN]

friendly to do this, but he might be indiscreet with respect to the many papers. Many concern you, as I've mentioned. Some of the others concern the sad events of my life.

Oh, Mademoiselle Rigolette! Please believe me: if you do this last favor I ask of you—proof of your former affection for me—it will be my only comfort amid the great misfortune that has beset me. I am hoping, in spite of myself, that you will not turn me down.

I ask also your permission to allow me to write to you sometimes. It would be so sweet, so precious, to be able to confide my overwhelming sadness to a benevolent heart! Alas! I am alone in the world; no one cares about me. This isolation was already very painful to me; imagine how I feel now!

And yet I am honest, and I am not conscious of ever having harmed a soul. I have always demonstrated an aversion toward anything evil, even when it came to risking my life to do so, as you will see when you read the papers I am asking you to keep for me. But when I say this, who will believe me? Monsieur Ferrand is respected by everyone. His reputation for probity was established long ago, and his accusation against me is well founded. He will destroy me. I resign myself in advance to my fate.

In the end, Mademoiselle Rigolette, if you believe me, you will not, I hope, feel contempt for me. I hope you will pity me, and think from time to time of your most sincere friend. And if you pity me, perhaps you will be so generous as to come one day, some Sunday (alas, what memories that word triggers in me!), to brave the parlor of my prison. But no, no—seeing each other again in such a place? I would never dare—but you are so kind that—

I must cut this letter short now and send it to you along with the key and a message for the doorkeeper that I must write hastily. The guard has come to let me know that I'm going to be brought before the judge. Adieu, adieu, Mademoiselle Rigolette! Do not reject me! You are my only hope, my only hope in the world!

FRANÇOIS GERMAIN.

P.S. If you answer this letter, address it to La Force prison.

Now the reader will understand the cause of Rigolette's first sorrow. Her excellent heart was profoundly moved by a misfortune that she had never before known to exist. She believed entirely in the complete veracity of the story told her by Germain, the unfortunate son of the Schoolmaster. Not inclined to be harsh, she even thought that her former neighbor had greatly exaggerated his crime. In order to save a wretched father who supported a whole family, he had taken money that he knew he could return. This action, in the seamstress's eyes, was nothing but generous.

Thanks to one of the contradictions so natural to women, and especially to women of her class, this young woman, who had never before felt for Germain, nor for her other neighbors, anything but a cordial and cheerful friendship, began to feel a sharp preference for him. As soon as she knew him to be unfortunate—unjustly accused and incarcerated—her memory erased all recollection of his former rivals.

This still wasn't love that Rigolette was feeling as yet. It was, rather, a lively, sincere affection, full of commiseration and resolute devotion. It was a very new sentiment for her, especially since it came to her accompanied by bitterness.

This was Rigolette's emotional state when Rodolphe entered her room after knocking discreetly on the door.

CHAPTER 14

FRIENDSHIP

"Hello, neighbor," said Rodolphe to Rigolette. "Am I disturbing you?"

"No, neighbor. On the contrary, I'm very happy to see you, because I'm quite upset at the moment."

"Indeed, you look pale. You seem to have been crying."

"Indeed I have been! And there's every reason I should be crying! Poor Germain! Here, read this." And Rigolette handed Rodolphe the prisoner's letter. "Doesn't that just break your heart? You told me you were concerned about him. Now's the time to show it!" she said, as Rodolphe read attentively. "Does that rotten Monsieur Ferrand have to go after everyone? At first it was Louise, and now it's Germain. Oh! I'm not a wicked person, but if something bad happened to that solicitor, I wouldn't mind one bit. To accuse such an honest boy of having stolen fifteen thousand francs from him! Germain? He's honesty itself! And besides that, he's so well-behaved, sweet, and sad. You really have to feel for him! Good Lord! In the midst of all of those scoundrels in that prison! Oh, Monsieur Rodolphe, today I've begun to learn that there's more to life than I've seen through my rose-colored glasses."

"And what do you plan to do now, neighbor?"

"What do I plan to do? Well, everything Germain has asked me to do, and as soon as possible. I'd already have left if it weren't for this last urgent piece of work that I'm finishing and will take right now to rue Saint-Honoré on my way over to Germain's room to find the papers he told me about. I spent half the night working so I could get a jump on the morning. I'm going to have so many things to do besides my work that I'll need to get organized. First, Madame Morel would like me to go to see Louise in prison. That might be difficult, but I'll try. Unfortunately, I just don't know who I need to ask to get in."

"I had given that some thought."

"You, neighbor?"

"Here's a pass."

"That's wonderful! Could you give me one for the prison where our poor Germain is being kept, too? It would make him so happy."

"I will also arrange for you to be able to see Germain."

"Oh, thank you, Monsieur Rodolphe!"

"So you're not afraid to go to his prison?"

"Well, of course my heart will be pounding the first time I go there, but that's all right. When Germain was happy, wasn't he always ready to do more than I asked? Didn't he take me to plays and on walks, read to me in the evenings, help me arrange my flower boxes, and wax my floors? Well, he's in trouble, and now it's my turn. A poor little nothing like myself can't do very much, I know, but I'll do anything I can—I'll be there for him. He'll see that I'm a good friend. You know, Monsieur Rodolphe, there's one thing that makes me unhappy, and that's that he doesn't trust me. How could he think me capable of despising him? Me! Now, I ask you, is that right? That old miser of a solicitor accuses him of being a thief. Why would that make any difference to me? I know very well that it's not true. Even if Germain's letter hadn't made it as clear as day that he was innocent, I never would have believed that he was guilty. All you have to do is look at him! Anyone who knows him can see for sure that he'd never be capable of such a crime. You'd have to be as evil as Monsieur Ferrand to tell such lies."

"Bravo, neighbor! I admire your indignation."

"Oh, I wish I were a man so I could go and say to that solicitor, 'Ah! You say that Germain has stolen from you? Well, here's a little something for you, you old liar! He'll never take this away from you!' And pow! Pow! I'd beat him into a pulp."

"Your notion of justice is very efficient," said Rodolphe, smiling at how excited Rigolette was.

"It's just that it really turns my stomach. As Germain said in his letter, everyone will take his employer's side against him because his employer is rich and respected, and Germain is just a poor young man with no one to protect him. That is, unless you go to his aid, Monsieur Rodolphe. You know such generous people. Isn't there something we can do?"

"He needs to await his trial. Once he's acquitted, as I believe he will be, he'll get plenty of offers from people who care about him, I assure you. But listen, neighbor. I know from experience that your discretion may be counted on."

"Oh, Monsieur Rodolphe, of course! I've never been a chatterbox!"

"Well, no one can know—even Germain himself can't know—that he has friends looking out for him. Because he does have friends."

"Really?"

"Very powerful and very devoted friends."

"It would buck him up so much to know that!"

"No doubt, but he might not be able to keep it to himself. And then Monsieur Ferrand might be frightened and put himself on guard. His suspicions would be raised, and since he's very clever, it would be difficult to catch him. That would be terrible, for this is not only about proving Germain's innocence. We also have to reveal Germain's accuser for what he truly is."

"I see what you mean, Monsieur Rodolphe."

"It's the same with Louise. I'm bringing you this pass to see her so you can ask her not to tell anyone what she told me. She will know what that means."

"Understood, Monsieur Rodolphe."

"In a word, it's very important that Louise not complain in prison of her boss's wickedness. But she shouldn't hide anything from a lawyer I'm arranging for her. They need to work together for her defense. Make sure she understands everything I'm suggesting."

"Don't worry, neighbor—I won't forget a thing. I have a good memory. But speaking of goodness! You are so good and generous! When someone is in trouble, you're right there!"

"I've told you, neighbor, I'm just a poor salesman. But when, on my wanderings about town, I find good people who deserve protection, I tell a generous person who trusts me about them, and that person helps them. There's nothing more to it than that."

"And where are you staying, now that you've given your room to the Morels?"

"I'm staying in a furnished room."

"Oh, how I'd hate that! It's as if everyone has been in your home when you live where everyone else has lived."

"I'm only there at night, so . . ."

"I can understand that that would be less distasteful. But look at our lives, Monsieur Rodolphe! My home made me so happy! I had put together a life that was so tranquil that I never would have believed it possible for any trouble to come to me, and you see how that's worked out! No, I can hardly express how hard Germain's misfortune has hit me. I can see that the Morels and others have a lot that they have a right to complain about, but in the end, poverty is poverty. Poor people are used to it, so no one's surprised by it, and we all help each other the best we can. Today it's one person, tomorrow it's another. Work at things with a will and good cheer, and you get along. But when you see a poor, honest, good young man, a longtime friend, accused of theft and thrown in prison all higgledy-piggledy with scoundrels! Oh, dear! There's nothing I can do against that. That's something I never thought about and it's thrown me for a loop." And Rigolette's big eyes filled with tears.

"Take heart! Your cheerfulness will return when they find your friend innocent."

"Oh, they'll have to find him innocent! All anyone needs to do is read that letter he wrote me to the judges. That will be enough, won't it, Monsieur Rodolphe?"

"Well, really, that letter, simple and moving as it is, does have the ring of truth to it. You should let me make a copy of it, for it will be necessary for Germain's defense."

"Certainly, Monsieur Rodolphe. If my writing weren't the merest scrawl, in spite of all the lessons Germain, good as he was, gave me, I would offer to copy it for you myself. But my handwriting is so bad, so scratchy, and so full of errors!"

"I would ask you, then, just to let me have the letter until tomorrow."

"Here it is, neighbor, but you'll take good care of it, right? I burned all of the love letters that Monsieur Cabrion and Monsieur Giraudeau wrote me starting out, with flaming hearts and doves circling at the top of the paper when they thought I would give in to their cajoling. But I'm keeping this poor letter from Germain somewhere safe, along with any others he might write me. For in the end, Monsieur Rodolphe, doesn't it speak well of me that he asks me to do these favors for him?"

"No two ways about it. It proves that you are the best little friend anyone could ever wish for. But, now that I think about it, instead of going to Monsieur Germain's place now on your own, would you like me to go with you?"

"Yes, I would, neighbor. It's getting dark, and I'd just as soon not walk around the streets all alone at night. And besides, I have some work to bring to a place near the Palais-Royal. But you might get tired or bothered from all that walking, don't you think?"

"Not at all. We'll take a cab."

"Really? Oh! How I'd enjoy going there in a carriage if I wasn't so troubled! And I really must be in a sad mood, since this is the first time since being here that I haven't sung all day. My birds are all confused about it. Poor little animals! They don't know what's going on. Two or three times Papa Crétu sang to me to get me started. I really wanted to answer his song, but after a minute I just started crying. Ramonette took up the song again, but I couldn't sing along with her any better."

"What odd names you've given your birds! Papa Crétu and Ramonette!"

"You know, Monsieur Rodolphe, my birds make me happy when I'm alone. They're my best friends. I've named them after those good people who made me happy when I was a child and who were my best friends as well. And what makes the names perfect is that Papa Crétu and Ramonette were cheerful and sang like God's own little birds."

"Oh, now I remember. Those are the names of your adoptive parents."

"Yes, neighbor. These names may be ridiculous for birds, I realize that. But I'm the only one who has any reason to care. You know, this was one of the ways I could tell Germain had a good heart."

"How is that?"

"It's true. Monsieur Giraudeau and Monsieur Cabrion—Monsieur

Cabrion most of all—used to make jokes about the names of my birds. 'Calling a canary Papa Crétu, that's a good one!' Monsieur Cabrion couldn't get over it, and he just kept on making fun of me, to no end. 'If it was a rooster,' he said, 'well, then—you could call him Crétu.[128] It's the same with the name of the female canary, Ramonette, it's like Ramona.' In the end he bugged me so much that I didn't go out with him for two Sundays in a row to teach him a lesson, and I told him straight out that if he started making fun of my birds again, which hurt my feelings, I would never go out with him again."

"That's telling him!"

"It wasn't easy, I can tell you, Monsieur Rodolphe, seeing as I wait for my Sundays out as if they were the Messiah. It made me really sad to have to stay alone when it was so nice out. But it was fine with me. I'd just as soon give up my Sundays instead of having to go on listening to Monsieur Cabrion make fun of something I cared about. Besides, if it weren't for the feelings I connected with them, I certainly would have preferred to give my birds different names. You know what name I really love? Colibri.[129] Well, I did without that name, because I will never have birds named anything other than Crétu and Ramonette. Otherwise, I would feel as if I were sacrificing the memory of my kind adoptive parents, as if I were just forgetting them. Don't you think so, Monsieur Rodolphe?"

"You're absolutely right. And Germain never made fun of those names?"

"On the contrary. They only seemed funny to him the first time, the same way they do to everyone: that's to be expected. But when I explained to him why they have those names, just as I did to Monsieur Cabrion, he got tears in his eyes. From that day on, I said to myself, 'Monsieur Germain has a good heart. The only thing you can hold against him is his sadness.' And you know, Monsieur Rodolphe, I feel bad that I held his sadness against him. I didn't understand at the time that one can be sad. Now I understand that all too well. And look, my package is all finished now, and my work ready for delivery. Could you hand me my shawl, neighbor? It's not cold enough for me to put on a coat, is it?"

"We'll be taking a carriage, and I'll bring you back here, too."

"That's right. We'll go and come back more quickly that way. We'll be saving time, at any rate."

"But you know, I'm wondering: how will you get along? Won't your work suffer from your visits to the prisons?"

"No, no, and no. I've got everything figured out. First, I've still got

---

128. Cabrion is making a pun on *crête*, which refers to the crest or comb of a bird. If one doesn't care about spelling and if one makes up verbs, *crétu* could be taken for "crested" or "coxcombed." [TN]

129. French for "hummingbird." [TN]

my Sundays. I'll go to see Louise and Germain on those days and that will take the place of walks and distractions. Then, during the week, I'll go back to the prison another time or two. Each visit will take me at least three hours, right? Well, I'll work an hour extra every day to stay on top of everything. I'll go to bed at midnight instead of eleven. That will give me an extra seven or eight hours a week that I can spend going to see Louise and Germain. You see, I'm richer than I look!" added Rigolette, smiling.

"Aren't you afraid you'll get tired?"

"Nonsense! I'll get by. You can get used to anything. And it's not going to go on forever."

"Here's your shawl, neighbor. I won't be as indiscreet as I was yesterday; my lips won't get anywhere near your charming neck."

"Oh, neighbor! Yesterday was yesterday, and now we can laugh about it. But today things are different. Be careful not to poke me with the pin."

"Hey, this pin is twisted."

"Well, then take another from the pincushion over there. Ah! I almost forgot—would you like to do me a favor, neighbor?"

"Just ask, neighbor."

"Cut me a nice quill, a fat one, so when I get back I can write to that poor Germain to tell him that I've done what he asked. He'll get my letter early tomorrow in prison, and that will be a nice way for him to wake up."

"And where are your quills?"

"There, on the table. The penknife is in the drawer. Wait, I'll light my candle for you. It's starting to get dark."

"I can't say no to a request to cut a quill."

"And then I have to put on my bonnet." Rigolette ignited a phosphorus match and lit a candle-end in a very shiny little candlestick.

"Honestly, neighbor! A candle! What luxury!"

"For what I burn of it, it costs me scarcely more than a tallow candle, and it's much tidier."

"It's not more expensive?"

"Good Lord, no! I buy these candle-ends by the pound, and a half pound of them lasts me almost a year."

"You know, I don't see anything here for your dinner," said Rodolphe as he carefully cut the quill while the seamstress fastened her bonnet in front of the mirror.

"I'm not the slightest bit hungry. I had a cup of milk this morning, and I'll have another tonight with a little bread. That will be plenty for me."

"Would you like to come for a simple dinner with me after we leave Germain's place?"

"Thank you, neighbor, but I'm feeling too sad right now. Another time, I'd love to. Listen: the day after Germain gets out of prison, I'll be your guest, and after that, you can take me to a play. Is it a deal?"

"It's a deal, neighbor. I won't forget that promise, I can tell you. But you won't come today?"

"Not today, Monsieur Rodolphe. I would be gloomy company for you, and it would take too much time. Especially now, when I can't afford to get lazy. I don't have a quarter of an hour to waste."

"All right. I'll put this pleasure aside . . . for today."

"Here's my sack, neighbor. You go out first, and I'll shut the door."

"Here's a good quill for you. Now give me your sack."

"Be careful not to rumple it. It's plain silk, so it wrinkles easily. Hold it in your hand lightly, like that. Good. Now go ahead. I'll light the way." And Rodolphe walked down the stairs behind Rigolette.

As the neighbors passed in front of the doorkeeper's apartment, they saw Monsieur Pipelet, who was coming toward them from the back of the alley with his arms hanging down. In one hand he held the sign that announced to the public that he was engaged in the friendship business with Cabrion. In the other hand he held the portrait of the cursed painter. Alfred was so overcome with despair that his chin was touching his chest, and only the immense base of his stovepipe hat was visible above it. Approaching Rodolphe and Rigolette in this posture, with his head lowered, he might be taken for a ram or a brave Breton champion preparing himself for combat.

Anastasie appeared shortly in the doorway of the apartment. At the sight of her husband, she cried, "Well, there you are, old deary! So what did the police superintendent tell you, Alfred? Alfred! Be careful! You're going to bonk into my king of tenants, who's right there in your face. Excuse us, Monsieur Rodolphe, it's just that rascal Cabrion again whose turning him more and more into a brute beast. He's going to turn him into a donkey, for sure! Alfred, can you please say something?"

Hearing this voice so dear to his heart, Monsieur Pipelet lifted his head. His features bore the traces of great bitterness.

"What did the superintendent say to you?" asked Anastasie.

"Anastasie, we must gather together the little we have, say good-bye to our friends, and prepare our suitcases. We need to leave Paris—indeed, we need to leave France. My beautiful France! For now that that monster knows that he can do anything he likes with impunity, he is capable of following me anywhere, through every corner of the kingdom!"

"What? What about the superintendent?"

"The superintendent?" cried Monsieur Pipelet, indignantly angry. "The superintendent laughed in my face."

"In your face? A man of your age, who looks so respectable that he'd look as silly as a goose to anyone who didn't know his good qualities?"

"Well, in spite of that, when I respectfully laid out before him my mass of complaints and grievances against that infernal Cabrion, that officer, after looking at the sign and the portrait I brought as evidence and laughing—yes, I tell you laughing, and I'll even say laughing indecently—that officer said to me, 'My good man, this Cabrion is a strange one. He's a real joker. I'll tell you straight out, you should just laugh at him, and there's plenty there to laugh at!' 'You say I should laugh at him, *monsiiieuuurrr*?' I cried. 'To laugh at him? But I am being eaten up by anxiety. That scoundrel is poisoning my life. He makes a mockery of me. He'll make me lose my mind! I demand that he be put in prison, that he be sent into exile—at least in exile from my street.' At these words, the commissioner smiled and showed me the door, politely. I understood what he was saying to me. And here I am."

"Superintendent of nothing!" cried Madame Pipelet.

"It's all over, Anastasie. It's all over. I have no hope left. There's no justice in France. I have been atrociously sacrificed!" And, as his peroration, he flung the sign and the portrait with all his might into the back of the alley.

Standing in the shadows, Rodolphe and Rigolette smiled a little at Monsieur Pipelet's despair. After addressing a few words of consolation to Alfred, whom Anastasie was calming as best she could, the king of tenants left the house on rue du Temple with Rigolette, and they both got into a cab in order to go to François Germain's home.

CHAPTER 15

THE WILL

François Germain lived at eleven boulevard Saint-Denis. We will remind the reader, who has no doubt forgotten it, that Madame Mathieu, the diamond broker of whom we have spoken in connection with Morel the gem-cutter, lived in the same house as Germain.

On the long trip from rue du Temple to rue Saint-Honoré, where the head dressmaker to whom Rigolette wanted first to bring her work lived, Rodolphe had the chance to appreciate the young woman's excellent character anew. Like all people who are instinctively kind and dedicated, she had no awareness of the delicacy or generosity of her conduct, which seemed very straightforward to her.

Nothing could have been easier for Rodolphe than to generously support Rigolette's present and future well-being and to thus give her the ability to visit Louise and Germain and offer them charitable consolation, without worrying about the amount of time her visits took away from her work, her only resource. However, the prince feared that he would undermine the seamstress's meritorious dedication if he made her life too easy. Already having decided to reward the rare and charming qualities he had discovered in her, he wanted to follow her in this new and interesting test until it had reached its outcome. Needless to say, if the young woman's health had been even slightly affected by the excess of work she imposed so valiantly on herself in order to be able to set aside a few hours each week for the gem-cutter's daughter and the Schoolmaster's son, Rodolphe would have instantly come to the rescue of his protégée. He was as moved as he was made happy by his study of this personality, so naturally happy, so little accustomed to sorrow that even now, from time to time, a spark of gaiety managed to brighten her mood.

After about an hour, the carriage, returning from rue Saint-Honoré, stopped at eleven boulevard Saint-Denis, in front of a house of modest appearance. Rodolphe helped Rigolette out of the carriage. She went in to see the doorkeeper and gave him Germain's message, without omitting also to give him the promised tip. Thanks to his friendliness, the Schoolmaster's son was universally loved. Monsieur Pipelet's colleague was upset to learn that the house had lost such an honest and peaceful tenant and said so.

The seamstress, equipped with a lantern, rejoined her companion since the doorkeeper could not come upstairs until a while later in order to receive her final instructions.

Germain's room was on the fourth floor. Arriving at the door, Rigolette said to Rodolphe, as she gave him the key, "Here, neighbor—you open the door. My hand is trembling too much. You'll make fun of me, but when I think that poor Germain won't be coming back here, I feel like we're in the room of a dead person."

"Don't give in to thoughts like that, neighbor. You can't let ideas like that control you."

"I know it's wrong, but I can't help it." And she wiped away a tear.

Although he was not as emotional as his companion, Rodolphe nonetheless also experienced a painful sensation as he entered the modest abode. Knowing the heinous obsessiveness with which the Schoolmaster's accomplices had pursued and perhaps were still pursuing Germain, he had the impression that this unfortunate young man must have spent many sad hours alone here.

Rigolette placed the lantern on a table.

The furnishing of this bachelor's room could not have been more spare. There was a cot, a chest of drawers, a walnut desk, four wicker chairs, and a table. White cotton curtains draped the windows and the alcove. The only decoration one could see was a carafe and a glass on the fireplace.

From the impression in the bed, which was still made, one could see that Germain must have flung himself onto it for a few moments fully dressed during the night that preceded his arrest.

"Poor boy!" said Rigolette, sadly, as she examined the interior of the room with interest. "You can tell that he didn't have me as his neighbor any longer. It's tidy, but it's not cared for. There's dust everywhere, the curtains are smoky, the windows need shining, and the floor isn't waxed. Ah, what a difference! The place on rue du Temple wasn't a better room, but it was more cheerful because everything was sparkling and clean, like my room."

"You were also there to give him your advice."

"Look at this!" cried Rigolette, gesturing toward the bed. "He didn't sleep the other night. That's how anxious he was! Look, that handkerchief he left there, it's all wet with his tears. It's perfectly obvious." And she took it, adding, "Germain kept a little orange tie that I gave him when we were happy. I'm going to keep this handkerchief as a memento of his misfortunes. I'm sure he wouldn't mind."

"On the contrary, he will be happy to have this evidence of your affection."

"But now let's deal with serious matters. I'll look in the chest for clothing to put in a packet to take to the prison for him. Old Lady Bouvard, whom I'll send here tomorrow, will take care of the rest. First I'll open the desk so I can take the papers and money that Germain has asked me to keep for him."

"Come to think of it, Louise Morel gave me those thirteen hundred francs in gold that Germain had given her in order to pay off the gem-cutter's debt that I had already paid. I have that money. It belongs to Germain, since he reimbursed the solicitor. I'll give it to you, and you can put it together with the money you'll be keeping for him."

"As you wish, Monsieur Rodolphe. But really, I'd almost rather not have such a large amount of money in my home. There are so many thieves around these days! The papers are fine, I'm not worried about them. But money, that's dangerous."

"You might be right, neighbor. Do you want me to take care of the money? If Germain needs anything, you can let me know right away. I'll give you my address and I will send you what he asks you for."

"Listen, neighbor, I wouldn't have dared ask you to do us this favor, but it would be much better that way. I will also give you the money the sale of his belongings brings in. Now, let's have a look at his papers," said the young woman as she opened the desk and its several drawers. "Ah, it's probably this one. Here's a big envelope. Oh, good Lord! Monsieur Rodolphe, look what's written here. It's so sad!" And she read in an emotional voice, "'In the case of my death by violence or otherwise, I ask the person who opens this desk to bring these papers to Mademoiselle Rigolette, dressmaker, number seventeen rue du Temple.'

"Can I unseal this envelope, Monsieur Rodolphe?"

"Of course. Didn't Germain say that there was a letter that he had written especially to you in his papers?"

The young woman broke the seal. Several writings were enclosed in the envelope. One of them carried the following address:

To Mademoiselle Rigolette,

Mademoiselle, when you read this letter, I will no longer be alive. If, as I fear, I have died a violent death by falling into an ambush similar to the one I've recently escaped, certain information included here under the title "Notes on My Life," can be of use to track down my murderers.

"Ah! Monsieur Rodolphe," said Rigolette, cutting herself short. "I am no longer surprised that he should have been so sad! Poor Germain! Always tormented by thoughts like that!"

"Yes, he must have suffered terribly, but his worst days are over: believe me."

"Alas! I want to believe it, Monsieur Rodolphe, but all the same, he's in prison, accused of theft."

"Don't worry. Once his innocence is established, instead of falling back into loneliness, he will find himself among friends. You, first of all, but then also his beloved mother, from whom he has been separated since his childhood."

"His mother? She's still alive?"

"Yes. She thought that he was lost to her. Imagine her joy when she sees him again, but shown to be innocent of the heinous accusation made against him! You see that I was right when I told you that his worst days were behind him. Don't speak to him about his mother, though. I'm confiding this secret in you because you care so much for Germain and so, at the very least, your devotion to him won't be accompanied by cruel worries about his future fate."

"I am grateful to you, Monsieur Rodolphe. You don't have to worry. I will keep your secret." And Rigolette continued to read Germain's letter:

> If you wish to glance over these notes, mademoiselle, you will see that I have been very unhappy my whole life, except for the time I spent with you. What I never would have dared tell you, you will find written in a kind of memento entitled "My Only Days of Happiness."
>
> Almost every evening, when I left you, I poured out the comforting thoughts your affection inspired in me, thoughts that were the only ones to sweeten the bitterness that is my life. What for you was friendship was, for me, love. I have hidden my love from you in this way until that time at which I am no more for you than a sad memory. My destiny was so unhappy that I never would have spoken to you of my feelings. Sincere and profound as they were, they would have brought you nothing but unhappiness.
>
> I have only one wish left, and I hope you will consent to carry it out.
>
> I have seen the admirable courage with which you work, and how organized and careful you have to be in order to live on the modest salary you earn with such difficulty. Often, without ever telling you, I trembled to think that an illness, caused perhaps by excessive work, could reduce you to such a terrible position that I cannot imagine it without shrinking in fear. It is very sweet for me to think that I can at least spare you a good share of the torments and perhaps the poverty that your carefree youth, fortunately, does not foresee.

"What's he saying, Monsieur Rodolphe?" asked Rigolette, astonished.

"Keep reading. We'll see."

Rigolette went on:

> I know how little you live on and how important even the most modest sum might be for you in difficult times. I am quite poor, but by saving assiduously, I've set aside fifteen hundred francs, which I've deposited with a banker. This is everything I own. According to my will, which you will find here, I am leaving the money to you. Accept this from a friend, from a good brother who is no more.

"Oh! Monsieur Rodolphe!" said Rigolette, melting into tears and giving the letter to the prince. "This is too painful! Germain was so kind to think of my future like that! What a heart he has, good Lord! The best heart in the world!"

"A worthy, brave young man!" said Rodolphe, with emotion. "But calm down, my child. Germain is not dead, thank God. This premature testament at least will have served to let you know how much he loved you—how much he loves you."

"And to think, Monsieur Rodolphe," Rigolette continued, "that I never suspected it! In the beginning of our time living as neighbors, Monsieur Giraudeau and Monsieur Cabrion always went on and on to me about their burning passion for me, as they put it. But when they saw it led them nowhere, they stopped saying such things to me. Germain, on the other hand, never spoke to me of love. When I proposed that we be good friends, he gladly accepted my offer, and since that time we lived as real comrades. But you know—I can surely tell you this now, Monsieur Rodolphe—I would not have been angry if Germain had told me, like all the others, that he was in love with me."

"But you're surprised to learn of it now?"

"Yes, Monsieur Rodolphe. I thought it was his sadness that made him act like that."

"And that sadness put you off a little?"

"It was the only thing wrong with him," said the seamstress, naively. "But now I forgive him for it. I'm angry with myself for having held it against him."

"First because you know that unfortunately he had only too many reasons to be unhappy, and then, perhaps because you are now certain that, despite this sadness, he was in love with you?" asked Rodolphe, smiling.

"It's true. It's flattering to be loved by such a brave young man, don't you think, Monsieur Rodolphe?"

"And one day, perhaps you will return this love."

"Heavens! Monsieur Rodolphe, it's very tempting. This poor Germain really is to be pitied. I'm putting myself in his shoes. If at the moment at which I thought myself to be completely abandoned, scorned by everyone, there was one person, a good friend, who came to me in an even more tender spirit than I'd hoped, I would be so happy!"

After a moment of silence, Rigolette said with a sigh, "On the other hand, we are both so poor that it might not be very prudent. You know, Monsieur Rodolphe, I don't want to think about this because I might be wrong. What's certain is that I will do everything I can for Germain as long as he's in prison. Once he's free, there will still be time to find out whether it's love or friendship I feel for him. Then, if it's love . . . well, then, neighbor, what can I say? It will be love. Up until that point it would get in the way of deciding what to do. But it's getting late, Monsieur Rodolphe. Would you mind gathering those papers together while I go to make up a bundle of linens for him? Oh! I forgot the little bag that contains the little orange tie I gave him. It's in the drawer, no doubt. Yes, here it is. Oh, look how pretty the little bag is! It's all embroidered! Poor Germain, he kept that little tie like a relic. I remember the last time I put it on, and when I gave it to him, he was so happy—so happy!"

At that moment, someone knocked on the door to the room.

"Who is it?" asked Rodolphe.

"Is *Ma'am* Mathieu there?" asked a high-pitched, hoarse voice in an accent that marked its speaker as one of the lowest classes of society. (Madame Mathieu was the diamond broker of whom we have spoken.)

Something about the voice, with its particular accent, evoked vague memories in Rodolphe's mind. Wanting to clear things up, he took the light and went himself to open the door. There he found himself face-to-face with one of the people who frequented the ogress's joint, a man he recognized immediately from the deep, fatal stamp of vice on his beardless juvenile face: this was Fishhook.

This was Fishhook, the phony cabdriver who had driven the Schoolmaster and the Owl to the sunken road at Bouqueval; Fishhook, the murderer of the husband of the unfortunate dairywoman who had led the uprising of the laborers of the Arnouville farm against Songbird. Either because this wretch had forgotten what Rodolphe looked like, perhaps because he had seen him only once at the ogress's joint, or because the change in his appearance kept him from recognizing the Slasher's victor, he showed no surprise at seeing his face.

"What do you want?" Rodolphe asked him.

"I have a letter for *Ma'am* Mathieu. I have to give it to her personally," said Fishhook.

"This isn't where she lives. Look across the hall," said Rodolphe.

"Thanks, boss. They told me the door on the left. I got it wrong."

Rodolphe did not remember the name of the diamond broker, which Morel had mentioned only once or twice. He thus had no reason to be especially interested in the woman to whom Fishhook had come as messenger. Nevertheless, although he was unaware of all this criminal had done, his face showed such perversity that Rodolphe stayed in the doorway, curious to see the person to whom Fishhook was bringing this letter.

Fishhook had scarcely knocked at the door across from Germain's when it opened, and the broker, a large woman of about fifty, appeared with a candlestick in her hand.

"*Ma'am* Mathieu?" said Fishhook.

"That's me, my boy."

"Here's a letter. I need an answer." And Fishhook took a step, in order to enter the broker's room. But she signaled him to stay where he was. She opened the letter while holding her light, read it, and said in a satisfied manner, "You can say that it's fine, my boy. I will bring what they're asking for. I will go at the same time as I did before. My compliments to the lady."

"Yes, boss. Don't forget the messenger."

"Go and ask the people who sent you. They are richer than I am." And the broker shut her door.

Rodolphe went back into Germain's room, seeing Fishhook run rapidly down the stairs.

On the boulevard, the outlaw found a man with a low and savage-looking face who was waiting for him in front of a shop. Even though they were within earshot of several people—although, to be sure, they couldn't understand what he said—Fishhook seemed so happy with himself that he couldn't stop himself from saying to his companion, "Come on and let's get drunk on the hard stuff, Nicolas—the old bird's falling right into our clutches. She'll go to the Owl's. Old Lady Martial will give us a hand in heisting the rocks from her and then we'll haul the carcass to your rust bucket."

"Let's hit the road, then. I've got to be at Asnières soon. I'm afraid my brother Martial might think something's up." And the two criminals, having finished this conversation that would have been unintelligible to anyone who might have overheard it, headed toward rue Saint-Denis.

A few moments later, Rigolette and Rodolphe left Germain's home, got back into the cab, and returned to rue du Temple. The cab stopped. The moment the doorkeeper's wife opened up for them, Rodolphe could see, in the glow of the liquor store's oil lamp, his faithful Murph waiting for him in the entrance to the alley. Since the squire was the only one who knew where to find the prince, his presence always meant that something serious or unexpected had happened.

"What is it?" Rodolphe asked him quickly as Rigolette was gathering together several bundles in the car.

"A terrible misfortune, Your Highness!"

"In heaven's name, speak!"

"The Marquis d'Harville . . ."

"You frighten me!"

"He was hosting a lunch this morning for several of his friends. Everything was going swimmingly. He had never been happier, when a bit of fatal carelessness—"

"Get to the point!"

"As he was playing with a pistol that he didn't think was loaded—"

"Was he seriously injured?"

"My lord!"

"Well?"

"Something terrible has happened."

"What are you saying?"

"He is dead!"

"D'Harville? Oh, that's too horrible!" cried Rodolphe with such a heartbreaking wail that Rigolette, who was just then getting out of the carriage with her bundles, cried out, "My God! What's wrong, Monsieur Rodolphe?"

"I've just told my friend some very sad news, mademoiselle," Murph told the young woman, seeing that the prince was himself incapable of speaking.

"Some great sorrow?" said Rigolette, trembling.

"Yes, something terrible," answered the squire.

"Oh! How dreadful!" said Rodolphe after a few minutes of silence. Then, remembering Rigolette, he said, "Pardon me, my child, if I don't accompany you back to your place. Tomorrow I will send you my address and a pass so you can be admitted to see Germain in prison. I will see you again soon."

"Oh, Monsieur Rodolphe, truly, I feel for you in this sorrow. Thank you so much for having come along with me. I'll see you soon, won't I?"

"Yes, my child. We'll see each other soon."

"Good evening, Monsieur Rodolphe," Rigolette said, sadly, and then disappeared into the alley with the different things she had brought from Germain's home.

The prince and Murph got into the carriage and were driven to rue Plumet. Rodolphe immediately wrote the following message to Clémence:

Madame,

I have just learned how you have been stricken by this unexpected blow, one which deprives me of one of my best friends. My shock and sorrow are beyond words.

All the same, I must speak to you of some matters that have nothing to do with this cruel circumstance. I have just found out that your stepmother, who has been in Paris for several days, it seems, is leaving this evening for Normandy and bringing Polidori with her.

This means that your father is surely threatened with great danger. Please excuse my presumption in giving you the following advice, but I believe it is in your best interest. After this morning's horrifying misfortune, no one will have any problem understanding your need to leave Paris for a while. And so believe me when I say that you must leave—and leave quickly—for Les Aubiers so you can arrive there at the very least at the same time as your stepmother, if not before her. Do not worry, madame; whether near or far, I am watching over you. We will defeat your stepmother's abominable plans.

Adieu, madame. I am writing these words to you in haste. My heart breaks when I think of how I last saw him yesterday evening . . . calmer and happier than I'd seen him in such a long time.

Your faithful servant,

RODOLPHE.

Three hours after receiving this letter, Madame d'Harville, acting on the prince's advice, was on her way to Normandy with her daughter beside her.

A postal carriage, having left Rodolphe's residence, followed the same route.

Unfortunately, amid the worries caused by this turn of events and the hurried nature of her departure, Clémence forgot to let the prince know that she had met Fleur-de-Marie in Saint-Lazare.

The reader will perhaps remember that, the day before, the Owl had come to threaten Madame Séraphin with the prospect of revealing Songbird's existence. She had claimed (accurately) that she knew where the girl then was. The reader will also remember that, after this meeting, the solicitor Jacques Ferrand, fearing the revelation of his criminal intrigues, believed he had a powerful motive to get rid of Songbird, whose existence, were it to become known, could be dangerously compromising. He had therefore sent for Bradamanti, one of his accomplices, in order to construct a new conspiracy, of which Fleur-de-Marie would be the victim. Bradamanti was busy with the no less pressing interests of Madame d'Harville's stepmother, who had sinister reasons for bringing the charlatan to see Monsieur d'Orbigny. No doubt considering it more advantageous to serve his old friend, Bradamanti had not responded to the solicitor's request, and he had left for Normandy without seeing Madame Séraphin.

A storm was brewing over Jacques Ferrand. During the day, the Owl had returned to reiterate her threats, and, to prove that they were not idle, she had declared to the solicitor that the little girl who had previously been abandoned by Madame Séraphin was currently a prisoner of Saint-Lazare named Songbird and that if he did not give her ten thousand francs within three days, this girl would receive papers that would inform her that she had been entrusted as an infant to the care of Jacques Ferrand.

As was his wont, the solicitor boldly denied everything and sent the Owl away, calling her a shameless liar, convinced as he nevertheless was of the dangerous extent of her threats. Thanks to his numerous connections, the solicitor was able, the very same day, to verify that Songbird was indeed a prisoner of Saint-Lazare and that her good conduct had been so noted that she was expected to be released any moment from her detention. Armed with this information, Jacques Ferrand worked out a diabolical plan. In order to execute it, he felt that Bradamanti's assistance was even more indispensable. Hence Madame Séraphin's vain attempts to meet the charlatan.

When he learned that evening of Bradamanti's departure, the solicitor, pressured as he was into action by his fears and the imminent danger he was in, remembered the Martial family, the freshwater pirates who were stationed near the Asnières bridge, the people to whom Bradamanti had proposed sending Louise Morel in order to get rid of her with impunity. Absolutely unable to accomplish his sinister designs on Fleur-de-Marie without an accomplice, the solicitor took the most careful precautions not to be compromised in the event of a new crime, and so the day after Bradamanti's departure for Normandy, Madame Séraphin hastily betook herself to the Martial residence.

CHAPTER 16

THE SCAVENGER'S ISLAND

The following scenes will take place during the evening of the day on which Madame Séraphin, on the orders of the solicitor Jacques Ferrand, went to see the Martial family, the freshwater pirates who had taken residence at the tip of a little island on the Seine, not far from the Asnières bridge.

Old Martial, put to death on the scaffold like his father before him, had left behind a widow, four sons, and two daughters. The second of these sons had already been condemned for life to the galleys. Of the numerous members of this family, there still lived on the Scavenger's Island (the name the local inhabitants had given to this retreat, for reasons we will see) the Old Lady Martial, along with her three sons, of whom the eldest (the She-Wolf's lover) was twenty-five years old, the next was twenty, and the youngest was twelve; and two daughters, one of whom was eighteen, and the other nine.

Examples of families such as this one, in which inherited crime perpetuates itself in a frightening way, may be found in abundance. This cannot help but be the case. As we keep repeating: our society thinks always to punish but never to prevent evil. One criminal will be thrown in prison for life, another will be decapitated. These condemned men leave young children. Does society take care of these orphans—orphans that society has itself created either by rendering their father legally nonexistent[130] or by cutting off his head? Will society give these children a healthy, protective upbringing after the fall of him who the law has declared shameful or vile, after the fall of the man whom the law has killed? No. "When the beast dies, the venom dies with it," says our society. But our society is wrong. The venom of corruption is so subtle, so corrosive, and so contagious that it is almost always hereditary. But if it is combated in time, it will never be incurable.

Here is a strange contradiction:

Does an autopsy prove that a man has died of hereditary disease? With preventive care, the descendants of this man may be shielded from the

130. One could be sentenced in the nineteenth century to a *mort civile*, or "civil death," which entailed the loss of all of one's legal rights. [TN]

illness of which he was the victim. The same situation obtains in the moral order. Were we to show that a criminal almost always bequeaths to his son the germ of his precocious perversity, would we do for the health of this young person what the doctor does for the body when it is a matter of fending off a hereditary ailment? No. Instead of curing these unfortunate people, we let the gangrene develop until they die. And then, in the same way that the masses expect the son of the executioner to become an executioner, so they believe that the son of a criminal must be a criminal. And so they consider the corruption caused by society's selfish negligence as if it were the product of an inexorably fatal heredity. And the result is, if the orphan that the law created manages, by some stroke of luck, and despite the grim education he has received, to remain hardworking and honest, a barbarous prejudice will bring the paternal stigma back to life to work against him. Always the target of undeserved reprobation, he will hardly ever be able to find work.

And instead of coming to his assistance by saving him from the demoralization and despair and, especially, the dangerous resentment injustice causes, all of which sometimes push the most generous souls to rebellion and wrongdoing, our society says, "If he turns bad, we'll know it. Don't we have jailers, prison guards, and executioners to take care of people like that?"

Thus, for the man who, in spite of the horrible examples before him, manages to keep himself pure (a rare and beautiful thing), there is no support, no encouragement! And thus, for the man who has been immersed from birth in an environment of domestic deprivation, and has been degenerate from his youth, there is no hope of a cure!

"Yes! There is! I'll cure the orphan I made," our society answers, "but in my own time and place, in my own way, later. The wart cannot be excised nor the abscess drained until they are ready for such actions."

A criminal asks for medical attention and is told, "Prisons and galleys: these are my hospitals. For incurable cases, I've got the guillotine. As for taking care of my orphan, as I've said, I'm aware of the problem. But be patient, let the seed of hereditary corruption ripen and grow so as to spread its damages far and wide. Be patient. When our man is rotten to the core, when he oozes criminality out of every pore, when a real theft or murder puts him in the dock of infamy on which his father sat—oh, then we'll cure this heir of evil, just like we cured the man who left him his legacy. Whether he ends up in the penitentiary or on the scaffold, the son will find the father's seat still nice and warm for him."

Yes, this is how our society reasons in these matters. And then we are surprised, indignant, appalled to observe practices of theft and murder passed down inexorably from generation to generation.

The dark portrait of freshwater pirates that follows is meant to demonstrate what the inheritance of evil can do in a family when our society does nothing either legally or unofficially to preserve those unfortunate orphans the law creates from feeling the terrible consequences of the death sentence brought down upon the father.

The reader will excuse us for prefacing this new episode with a sort of introduction. Here is why we have done this: the further we get in this publication, and the more single-mindedly and, in our opinion, unjustly its moral ends are attacked, the more we feel entitled to stress how serious and honest the thinking is that sustains and guides us. We owe it to various known and unknown friends, grave, delicate, lofty souls who have wished us well in our attempts and have sent flattering testimonials of their admiration to respond one last time to these blind, obstinate recriminations that have reached as far as the legislative assembly. To proclaim the odious immorality of our work is to proclaim, implicitly, it seems to us, the odiously immoral tendencies of people who honor us with their vibrant sympathy. It is thus in the name of their sympathy as much as our own that we will try to prove by an example, chosen from among several, that this work is not completely devoid of generous and practical ideas.

Last year, in one of the first parts of this book, we offered the outline of a model farm founded by Rodolphe to encourage, teach, and reward poor, upright, and hardworking farmworkers. In this regard, we added the following observation: "People who are honest but unfortunate deserve at least as much of our concern as criminals. However, whereas there are numerous societies devoted to the patronage of young people who have been detained or released, there are none founded in the interest of saving poor young people whose conduct has always been exemplary. As a result, one must commit some transgression in order to enjoy the benefit of these institutions, which are otherwise so meritorious and productive."[131]

And we put these words in the mouth of a peasant from the Bouqueval farm: "It's human and charitable to never lose faith in the wicked. But you also have to give hope to the good. Suppose an honest young man, robust and hardworking, wanted to do good work and learn. He comes to this farm of ex-thieves, and they say to him, 'My friend, have you stolen a little something and been a vagabond?' 'No,' he says. 'Well,' they would say, 'there's no place here for you.'"

Sharper intelligences than ours have been struck by this discordant note. Thanks to them, what we considered a utopia has recently come into existence. Under the authority of one of the most eminent and honorable men of these times, Monsieur the Count Portalis, and under the

131. This observation does not appear in this precise form in the text, but it repeats the ideas already put forward in Book III, Chapter 6, pp. 324–25. Rodolphe's "model farm" at Bouqueval was founded on the principles discussed again here. [TN]

intelligent direction of a veritable philanthropist with a generous heart and a practical and enlightened mind, Monsieur Allier, a society has just been founded with the aim of coming to the assistance of poor, honest young people in the department of the Seine and putting them to work in agricultural colonies.[132] This single, simple parallel is enough to establish the morality of our work. We are very proud and happy to have found that we share the same ideas, wishes, and hopes as the founders of this new patronage organization. We are one of the propagators, perhaps the most obscure, but also the most convinced, of these two great truths: that it is our society's duty both to prevent evil and to encourage and reward the good as much as we can.

Inasmuch as we have spoken of this new work of charity, whose just and moral concept will surely have productive and salutary consequences, let us hope that its founders will perhaps think to fill another gap by extending their tutelary patronage, or at least their private solicitude, to the young children whose fathers have been tortured or condemned to an ignominious penalty that entails the loss of legal identity[133] and who, we repeat, have been made orphans by the court in its application of the law.

These unfortunate children who would already be worthy of concern because of their healthy inclinations and because of their poverty would deserve even more special attention precisely because of their exceptional, painful, difficult, and dangerous position. Yes: their position is painful, difficult, and dangerous.

Let us say it once more: almost always the victims of cruel expulsions, the family members of a condemned man, as they vainly seek work, find themselves forced to leave the places where they can find the means of existence as a result of the general disapproval of the community. And so, embittered, stung by injustice, already marked with the stain of sins they didn't commit as if they themselves were criminals, sometimes having reached the end of honest sources of income, are these unfortunate people not set up for failure, if they remain honest? If, on the other hand, they have already undergone an almost inevitably corrupting influence, must we not try to save them while there is still time?

In addition, the presence of these orphans of the court in the midst of other children of whom we have spoken, who are also under the care of society, would serve as a useful lesson for all of us. It would show that

---

132. Joseph-Marie, Comte de Portalis (1778–1858) was a French diplomat and politician. He and Régis Allier, the author of *Études sur le système pénitentiaire et les sociétés de patronage* (Paris, 1842), founded the colony of Petit-Bourg in 1844. It was already in the planning stages as Sue was writing this. [TN]

133. See Book V, Chapter 16, footnote 130 on *mort civile.* [TN]

if the guilty man is inexorably punished, his family members will not lose anything as a result but, rather, will gain in the esteem of the community if, by dint of courage and virtue, they managed to rehabilitate a dishonored name.

Do we really want to say that the law means to make the punishment even more severe by virtually striking the criminal father in terms of the future of his innocent son? That would be barbarous, immoral, and irrational. Is it not, on the contrary, morality of the highest order to prove to the masses that there is no hereditary transmission of evil, and that the original sin is not impossible to remove? Let us hope that these reflections appear worthy of some notice from yet another patronage society.

It is undoubtedly painful to think that the state never takes the initiative in all of these pressing questions that concern our social organization so vitally. Could it be otherwise? At one of the more recent legislative sessions, a petitioner who was struck, he said, by the misery and suffering of the poor, proposed, among other methods of remediation, the "foundation of homes for disabled workers." This plan, while certainly defective in its form, contained nonetheless a valuable philanthropic idea that was worthy of more serious consideration to the extent it addressed the immense question of the organization of labor; this plan, we are sorry to report, "was met with general and prolonged laughter."

Having said all this, let us move on.

Let us return to the freshwater pirates and the Scavenger's Island. The head of the Martial family, the first to establish himself on this little island that charged a moderate rent, was a scavenger. These scavengers, like stevedores and ship dismantlers, stand submerged in the water up to their waist all day in order to practice their trade. Stevedores unload floating wood; ship dismantlers demolish the rafts that brought this wood. Just as aquatic in nature as the preceding jobs, the scavenger's job has a different purpose.

Walking as far into the water as he can go, the scrap metal scavenger drags the river's sand, under the sludge, with the help of a long dredger. Then, collecting it in large wooden bowls, he washes it like iron ore or gravel with gold dust in it, removing in this way a great quantity of metallic bits of all sorts: iron, copper, smelting, lead, tin, all coming from the debris of numerous tools. Often the scavengers even find fragments of jewelry, gold, or silver in the sand, carried down by the Seine, either by way of the sewers into which the streams empty or by way of the masses of snow and ice that collect in the streets over the winter and get thrown into the river. We do not know how or in what manner these laborers, generally honest, peaceful, and hardworking, came to be known by this formidable title. Because the Martial patriarch, the first person to live on this hitherto uninhabited island, was a scavenger (a distressing exception to the rule), the residents of the river's coast called it the Scavenger's Island.

The freshwater pirates' residence is situated on the southern part of the island. In the daytime, one can read on a sign that hangs over the door:

THE SCAVENGERS' MEETING PLACE
GOOD WINE, GOOD FISH STEW, AND FRIED FOOD
Punts rented here for pleasure trips

From the above, one may see that the head of this cursed family had combined his formal or illegitimate trades with those of innkeeper, fisherman, and boat renter.

The widow of this executed criminal continued to run the house. Vagrants, vagabonds on the lam, animal trainers, and traveling charlatans all came by to spend their Sundays, as well as other days that weren't holidays, on pleasure trips.

Martial (the She-Wolf's lover), the eldest son of the family, the least criminal of the bunch, was a poaching fisherman. A veritable cutthroat when he needed to be, he would take up the cause of the weak against the strong, but only for pay. One of his other brothers, Nicolas, Fishhook's future accomplice in plotting the murder of the diamond broker, seemed to be a scavenger, but in fact conducted sorties of freshwater piracy along the Seine and its banks. Finally, François, the youngest son of the executed criminal, took the curious on boat trips. We will note here that Ambrose Martial was condemned to the galleys for burglary and attempted murder. The older daughter, nicknamed Calabash, helped her mother to cook and serve food to the guests. Her sister, Amandine, nine years old, also tended to the household needs, as far as her abilities allowed.

The night is dark this particular evening. Stars can be seen twinkling in the dark azure sky, but only in isolated spots, through strangely shaped openings in the thick, opaque gray clouds chased about by the wind. The island's silhouette, bordered by tall, denuded poplars, stands out distinctly in black against the diaphanous obscurity of the sky and the whitish transparency of the river. With its irregular gables, the house is completely shrouded in darkness. Only two windows on the ground floor are lit. Their glass panes look as if they are aflame. These red glows are reflected like long trails of fire in the little waves lapping at the wharf that lies close to the residence. The chains of the boats moored there make a sinister sound as they clang together. This noise blends ominously with the gusts of icy wind through the branches of the poplars and with the low grumbling of the waters.

Part of the family has gathered in the kitchen. This room is large and low. Across from the door are two windows, underneath which stretches a long furnace. To the left is a tall fireplace, and to the right, a staircase that goes up to the upper floor. Next to this staircase is the entrance to a large room furnished with tables for the use of the tavern's guests.

Together with the flames of the fire, the light of a lamp makes the many pots and other copper utensils glow as they hang along the walls or stand on shelves with various earthenware bowls. A large table stands in the middle of the kitchen.

Surrounded by three of her children, the executed man's widow is seated at the corner of the hearth. This woman, tall and thin, looks to be about forty-five years old. She is dressed in black. Over her forehead she wears a mourner's kerchief, tied in the manner of a merchant; it hides her hair and frames her flat, pale forehead that is already creased with wrinkles. Her nose is long, straight, and pointed; she has prominent cheekbones, hollow cheeks, and bilious, pallid, deeply pockmarked skin. The corners of her mouth, which are always turned down, make her cold, sinister expression, as impassive as a marble mask, look even harsher. Her gray eyebrows arch over her dull blue eyes.

The executed man's widow is busy sewing, as are her two daughters. The eldest, dried up and tall, looks very much like her mother, thanks to her calm, hard, and wicked-looking face, thin nose, severe mouth, and blank gaze. The sole difference is her jaundiced complexion, which makes her look as yellow as a quince and has earned her the nickname of Calabash. She is not dressed in mourning. Her dress is brown, and her black tulle bonnet leaves visible two dull, faded blond plaits of thin hair.

François, the youngest of the Martial sons, crouched on a stool, mends an aldret, a particularly destructive kind of fishing net, the use of which is strictly prohibited on the Seine. In spite of his weather-beaten tan, the child's complexion is rosy. A forest of red hair covers his head. His features are rounded, with plump lips, a prominent forehead, and piercing, sharp eyes. He looks nothing like either his mother or his older sister. He seems shifty and fearful. From time to time, through the mop of hair that falls across his forehead, he glares defiantly at his mother or exchanges a meaningful, affectionate glance with his little sister Amandine.

This sister, seated next to her brother, is busy at work. She is not sewing initials but rather removing identifying marks from clothing stolen the day before. She is nine years old. She looks as much like her brother as her sister resembles her mother. Her features are no more regular than François's but are less coarse than his. Even though her skin is covered with freckles, it is bright and fresh. Her lips are thick, but rosy; her hair is red, but fine, silky, and shiny; her eyes are small, but they are of a soft, pure blue. When Amandine's glance meets her brother's, she gestures toward the door. At this sign, François answers with a sigh. Then, attracting his sister's attention with a rapid gesture, he counts deliberately ten strands of the net from one end of his netting needle. In the symbolic language of these children, this signifies that their brother Martial will not be home until ten o'clock.

At the sight of these two silent, wicked-looking women and these two poor little children who seem so anxious, mute, and fearful, one would conclude that this group comprises two torturers and two victims.

Taking note of the fact that Amandine had ceased working for a moment, Calabash said to her in a harsh voice, "Are you going to be finished taking the identifications out of that shirt anytime soon?"

The child lowered her head without responding. With her fingers and scissors, she hastily finished removing the threads of red cotton that formed letters on the fabric. A few moments later, Amandine turned timidly to the widow and showed her the work she had done. "Mother, I've finished," she said.

Without saying a word, the widow threw another piece of clothing at her. The child could not catch it in time and dropped it. With a hand as hard as wood, her big sister gave her a sharp blow on the arm, shouting, "Little idiot!"

Amandine took her place again and gave all her attention to her needlework after giving her brother a look with a tear in her eye.

The same silence continued to reign in the kitchen. Outside, the wind still moaned and shook the tavern's sign. This sad groaning and the mute bubbling of a pot placed in front of the fire were the only sounds to be heard. The two children observed with hidden fear that their mother was not speaking. Although she was customarily silent, this complete lack of speech and a certain pinching of her lips told them that the widow had gone white, as they called it. By this they meant that she was in the grip of an intense anger.

The fire was about to go out for lack of wood. "François! Throw in another log!" yelled Calabash.

The young darner of illegal nets looked behind the pillar of the fireplace and answered, "There aren't any more there."

"Go out to the woodshed," said Calabash.

François muttered a few unintelligible words and did not move.

"Hey, François. Did you hear me?" Calabash said in a sharp voice.

The executed man's widow put a napkin down on her lap from which she, too, was removing identifying marks. She glanced at her son. The latter was keeping his head down, but he knew—he could almost feel—the terrible glare of his mother weighing on him. Fearing to look at this terrifying face, the child did not move. "Are you deaf, then, François?" said Calabash, irritated. "Look at this, Mother." The big sister's job seemed to be accusing the two children and demanding the punishments for them that the widow would then apply without pity.

Without anyone noticing, Amandine gave a little nudge to her brother with her elbow, silently urging him to obey Calabash. But François did not move.

The older sister looked at her mother to ask her to punish the guilty one. The widow took note. With her long, bony finger she pointed her toward a strong, supple willow stick that was stored in the corner cupboard of the fireplace. Calabash leaned backward, took this instrument of correction, and gave it to her mother.

François had perfectly understood his mother's gesture. He quickly got up and leapt out of range of the menacing rod. "Do you want our mother to beat you black and blue?" Calabash cried out.

The stick still in hand, the widow, her pale lips pinched tighter and tighter together, looked at François with an unwavering stare, without saying a word. From the light trembling of Amandine's hands and the redness that suddenly covered her neck, it could be seen that, even though she was accustomed to such scenes, the child, whose head was down, was dreading the fate that awaited her brother. The latter, having taken refuge in a corner of the kitchen, looked fearful and angry.

"Watch out! If you don't obey by the time our mother gets up, that'll be it for you!" said the older sister.

"I don't care," said François, growing pale. "I'd rather be beaten like I was the day before yesterday than go out to the woodshed, out again into the night . . ."

"And why is that?" asked Calabash, impatiently.

"I'm afraid to go into the woodshed," answered the child, shuddering against his will.

"You're afraid, you imbecile? What are you afraid of?"

"I don't know, but I'm afraid."

"You've been in there a hundred times. You were there again yesterday evening."

"I don't want to go back there now."

"Our mother is getting up!"

"Too bad!" cried the child. "Let her beat me—let her kill me. She can't make me go into the woodshed, especially at night."

"I'll ask one more time: why?" asked Calabash.

"All right, it's because . . ."

"Because?"

"Because there's someone in there."

"There's someone in there?"

"Someone buried there," said François, shivering.

The executed man's widow could not repress a sudden shudder, in spite of her general imperturbability. Her daughter did the same. These two women looked as if they had been struck by the same bolt of electricity.

"There's someone buried in the woodshed?" Calabash went on, shrugging her shoulders.

"Yes," said François, so softly that he could hardly be heard.

"Liar!" cried Calabash.

"I'm telling you that when I was looking for wood, I saw a bone from a corpse in a dark corner of the woodshed. It was poking out a little from ground that was wet around it," answered François.

"Did you hear, Mother? Is he stupid or what?" said Calabash, making a secret sign to the widow. "Those are sheep bones that I put there to make into detergent."

"Those were no sheep bones," said the child, in a fearful voice. "Those were buried bones, bones from a dead person. There was a foot coming out of the earth. I had a good look at it."

"And you told your brother, your pal Martial, all about your nice discovery right away, didn't you?" asked Calabash with a savage irony.

François did not answer.

"You're a nasty little stoolie," cried Calabash, furious. "He's as cowardly as a cow. He has it in him to get us cut down like they cut our father down!"

"Since you call me a stoolie," cried François, exasperated, "I'll tell everything to our brother Martial. I hadn't said anything about it yet because I haven't seen him for a while. But when he comes back tonight, I—"

The child did not dare finish his sentence. His mother was coming toward him, calmly but inexorably.

Although she tended to hunch over, she was very tall for a woman. Holding her rod in one hand, the widow grabbed her son by the arm with her other hand. Despite the child's terror, resistance, pleadings, and tears, she dragged him after her, forcing him to go up the staircase in the back of the kitchen.

After a moment, the sound of muffled trampling came from upstairs, mixed with cries and sobs. A few minutes later, this noise stopped. A door slammed loudly. The widow came back downstairs. Then, still impassive, she put the willow stick back in its place, sat back down next to the hearth, and took her needlework back up again without saying a single word.

BOOK VI

CHAPTER I

THE FRESHWATER PIRATE

After a few moments of silence, the widow of the executed man said to her daughter, "Go and get some wood. Tonight, when Nicolas and Martial come home, we'll fix up the woodshed."

"Martial? So you're going to tell him, too, about—"

"Get some wood," said the widow, interrupting her daughter abruptly.

The latter, accustomed to having to submit to her mother's iron will, lit a lantern and went outside. When she opened the door, the pitch-black night became visible and one heard the crackling of the tall poplars shaking in the wind, the clanging of the boats' chains, the whistling of the north wind, and the low groaning of the river. These were profoundly sad sounds.

During the previous scene, Amandine had been painfully moved by François's plight, as she loved him tenderly. She had dared neither to look up nor to wipe away the tears that were falling drop by drop onto her knees. Her suppressed sobs were suffocating her. She tried to contain even the pounding of her heart, which was palpitating in fear.

She could not see for her tears. In hurrying to remove the identifying marks from the shirt they had given her, she had cut her hand with her scissors. The wound was bleeding copiously, but the poor child was thinking less of her pain than of the punishment she was going to get for having stained the piece of clothing with her blood. Fortunately, the widow had not noticed it, as she was deeply absorbed in some reflection of her own.

Calabash came back in carrying a basketful of wood. She responded to a look from her mother with a nod. This meant that the dead man's foot was indeed coming up out of the ground.

The widow pursed her lips and continued working. The only difference was that she seemed to work her needle even more quickly.

Calabash stoked the fire, took a look at the boiling pot that was cooking in the corner of the fireplace, and then sat back down again next to her mother. "Nicolas still hasn't come back yet!" she said. "I hope that old woman from the morning didn't get him involved in some bad business when she arranged a meeting for him with a rich guy for Bradamanti.

There was something about her that seemed so underhanded. She didn't want to say what she was doing, what her name was, or where she was from."

The widow shrugged.

"You don't think Nicolas is in any danger, do you, Mother? Maybe you're right, after all. The old woman asked him to show up at seven in the evening on the quai de Billy in front of the station and to wait there for a man who wanted to talk with him and who would say 'Bradamanti' as a password. That really shouldn't be too dangerous. If Nicolas is late, it's probably because he found something along the way, like the day before yesterday when he nicked this clothing from a boat full of laundry." And she showed one of the pieces Amandine was removing the stitches from. Then, addressing the child, she asked her, "What does 'nick' mean?"

"It means 'to take,'" said the child without looking up.

"It means 'to steal,' you little fool. Do you understand? To steal."

"Yes, sister."

"And when you know how to nick things like Nicolas does, there's always a way to make some money. The clothes he stole yesterday have given us a boost and only cost us the trouble of taking the identifications out—right, Mother?" said Calabash with a burst of laughter that revealed her shrinking gums and teeth that were as yellow as her skin.

The widow didn't react to this joke.

"Speaking of giving us a boost for free," continued Calabash, "we can maybe get ourselves some more wares to sell. Did you know that a few days ago an old man came to live in the country house of Monsieur Griffon, the doctor at the Paris hospice? It's the one standing all alone, a hundred feet from the water, facing the brick kiln."

The widow lowered her head.

"Nicolas was saying yesterday that there might be a good job there to pull off," said Calabash. "And I've known since this morning that there's loot for us in there, for sure. We'll have to send Amandine over to stroll around the house. No one will pay any attention to her. She'll act like she's playing, have a good look around, and then she'll come back and tell us what she's seen. Do you hear what I'm saying to you?" added Calabash harshly as she turned to Amandine.

"Yes, sister, I'll go," said the child, trembling.

"You always say, 'I'll do it,' and you never do, you sly devil. Remember the time I told you to take a hundred sous from the counter at the Asnières grocery while I was on the other side of the store? That was easy. No one suspects a child. Why didn't you obey me?"

"I didn't have the courage to do it, sister. I didn't dare."

"The other day you dared well enough to steal a handkerchief from the peddler's pack while he was selling things in the tavern. Did he notice anything, you imbecile?"

"You forced me to do it, sister. The handkerchief was for you, and, besides, it wasn't money."

"What difference does that make?"

"Well, taking a handkerchief isn't really as bad as taking money."

"I'd give my word on it, it's that Martial who taught you that virtuous claptrap, isn't it?" said Calabash, with irony. "You're going to tell him everything, aren't you, you little stoolie? Do you think we're afraid your Martial is going to eat us?" Then she turned to the widow, adding, "Do you see, Mother? It's going to end badly for him. He wants to lay down the law around here. Nicolas is up in arms against him, and so am I. He's egging Amandine and François on against us, against you. How long can it go on?"

"It can't," said the mother curtly, in a hard voice.

"Especially since his She-Wolf has been in Saint-Lazare, it's like he's had it in for everyone. Is it our fault if his mistress is in prison? Once she's out, she'll just come back here, and I'll give her just what she deserves and in good measure. Even if she acts tough . . ."

After reflecting for a moment, the widow said to her daughter, "So you think there's a good job to pull off with that old guy who's living in the doctor's house?"

"Yes, Mother."

"He looks like a beggar."

"That doesn't keep him from being an aristocrat."

"An aristocrat?"

"Yes, and it doesn't keep him from having gold in his wallet, even though he walks to Paris on foot every day and returns in the same manner, with a big cane as his only horse cart."

"How do you know he has gold?"

"I was just at the Asnières post office to see if there was a letter from Toulon."[134] At these words, which reminded her of her son's time in prison, the widow of the executed man frowned and stifled a sigh. Calabash went on: "I was waiting my turn when the old guy who's living at the doctor's place came in. I recognized him right away from his beard as white as his hair, his face the color of boxwood, and his black eyebrows. He doesn't look like he'll be easy. Despite his age, he looks like a tough old bird. He said to the woman at the counter, 'Do you have any letters from Angers

134. Toulon was the earlier site of galley ships to which prisoners were condemned. By this time, it was the site of a prison, known as a *bagne*, that functioned in the place of the ships. Other famous fictional characters imprisoned there were Jean Valjean in *Les Misérables* and Vautrin in *Le Père Goriot*. [TN]

for the Count de Saint-Remy?' 'Yes,' she answered. 'Here's one.' 'It's for me,' he said. 'Here are my identity papers.' While the woman was examining them, the old man took out his green silk wallet to pay the fee. At one end of it I could see gold shining through the stitches. It made a bulge as big as an egg. There were at least forty or fifty louis in there!" Calabash shouted, her eyes gleaming with greed. "All the same, though, he dresses like a tramp. He's one of those old misers who's loaded with money. You know, Mother, we even know his name. That might come in handy for getting us into his place once Amandine tells us whether he has servants."

Calabash was interrupted by violent barking. "There! The dogs are crying out," she said. "They can hear a boat coming. It's Martial or Nicolas." At the sound of Martial's name, Amandine's features expressed constrained joy. After several minutes waiting, during which she kept her eyes glued impatiently and anxiously on the door, the child watched, with regret, as Nicolas, Fishhook's future accomplice, entered.

Nicolas Martial's face was both debased and vicious. Small, frail, and sickly, he hardly appeared to be up to the demands of his dangerous, illegal occupation. Unfortunately, the wretch's savage will and energy made up for what he lacked in physical strength.

Over his blue overalls, Nicolas wore a sort of sleeveless goatskin jacket with long brown fur on it. As he entered, he threw a copper ingot on the floor that he had carried on his shoulder with difficulty. "Good evening, Mother, and good hunting!" he cried, in a hollow and hoarse voice, after unloading his burden. "There are three ingots just like this one in my punt, a bundle of rags, and a trunk full of who knows what. I didn't have the time to open it. Maybe I've stolen a— We'll see!"

"What about the man on the pier at Billy?" asked Calabash as the widow observed her son in silence. To answer, the latter plunged his hand into the pocket of his trousers and shook it, causing a large number of silver coins to jangle.

"You took that all off him?" cried Calabash.

"No, he forked over two hundred francs all by himself, and he'll hand over another eight hundred when I— But that's enough! Let's unpack my punt first, and we can chatter later. Is Martial here yet?"

"No," said his sister.

"So much the better! We can stow away the booty without him, so long as he doesn't find out about it."

"Are you afraid of him, you coward?" asked Calabash, bitterly.

"Afraid of him? Me?" He shrugged. "I'm just afraid he might sell us out, that's all I'm afraid of. As for fearing him—Throatslitter here has a tongue that's too well sharpened for that."

"Oh, whenever he's not here, you like to swagger. But whenever he's here, that shuts your trap right up."

Nicolas seemed unaffected by this insult and said, "Come on, quickly! Let's go out to the boat. So where's François, Mother? He can help us."

"Mother locked him upstairs after giving him a drubbing. He's going to bed without his supper," said Calabash.

"Fine, but I still need him to come anyway to help unload the boat. All right, Mother? With me, him, and Calabash, we'll get it done in one trip and be right back inside."

The widow pointed her finger toward the ceiling. Calabash understood her and went to fetch François.

Old Lady Martial's somber face had relaxed somewhat at Nicolas's arrival. She loved him more than she loved Calabash; she loved him less, however, than she loved her son who was imprisoned in Toulon, as she always said. The maternal love of this ferocious creature grew in proportion to the criminality of the child in question. This perverse preference is sufficient to explain the widow's antipathy for her two young children who showed no disposition toward crime, as well as her deep hatred for Martial, her eldest son. His life had not been beyond reproach, but compared to Nicolas, Calabash, and their brother, the convict in Toulon, he looked like an honest man indeed.

"What did you manage tonight?" the widow asked Nicolas.

"Coming back from the quai de Billy, where I met the rich guy I had an appointment to see this evening, I spotted a small sailboat docked to the pier right near the Invalides bridge. It was dark out. I say to myself, 'No light in the cabin—the sailors are on shore. I get on board. If I find someone asking questions, I say I need some rope to repair my oar.' I enter the cabin. No one there. So I swipe what I can: the rags, a big trunk, and, on the bridge, four copper ingots. I made two trips, since the sailboat was full of copper and iron. Now, here's François and Calabash. Quick, let's go to the punt! Come on, you, too, Amandine! You can carry the rags. You have to learn to walk before you can run."

Left on her own, the widow made preparations for the family supper. She put out glasses, bottles, earthenware plates, and silverware on the table. As she finished her preparations, her children returned, heavily weighed down with cargo. The weight of the two copper ingots that little François was carrying on his shoulders looked like it would crush him. Amandine was barely visible beneath the heap of stolen rags she was carrying on her head. Finally, Nicolas was carrying a white wooden trunk with the assistance of Calabash. On top of it he had put the fourth copper ingot.

"The trunk! The trunk! Let's crack it open already!" cried Calabash, wildly impatient. They threw the copper ingots to the floor. In order to lift off the cover of the trunk, which was sitting in the middle of the kitchen, Nicolas took up the heavy iron hatchet that he carried on his belt and inserted it under its top. The shifting, reddish glow of the fireplace lit up this scene of pillage. Outside, the wind howled ever more violently. Dressed in his goatskin, crouched over the coffer, Nicolas attempted to break it open, hurling blasphemous curses as he saw that the thick cover stood up to his vigorous pressure.

Her eyes inflamed with greed, her cheeks reddened by the thrill of the pillage, Calabash knelt on the trunk and applied all the weight of her body to anchor it so as to give Nicolas a stable point of leverage. The widow, separated from this group by the width of the table, stretched out over it, leaning in the direction of the stolen object, her eyes gleaming with feverish avarice.

And then, by a cruel but unfortunately all too human impulse, the two children, whose good natural instincts had often triumphed over the cursed influence of this abominable domestic corruption, forgot all their scruples and fears and gave in as well to their fatal curiosity. Holding each other tight, with bated breath and shining eyes, François and Amandine were just as impatient as the others to find out what the trunk contained, and they were just as irritated by how long it was taking Nicolas to break it open.

Finally, the top burst open. "Ah!" cried the family in unison, panting and gleeful. And each one of them, from the mother down to the little girl, rushed with savage ardor to pounce on the crushed trunk. No doubt shipped to Paris by a novelty merchant from a riverside village, it contained a large quantity of fabric for women's clothing.

"Nicolas is no fool!" cried Calabash as she unrolled a piece of wool muslin.

"No," answered the bandit as he unfolded a bundle of scarves in turn. "This was worth the trouble."

"Levantine fabric! It'll sell like hotcakes," said the widow as she dug around herself in the trunk.

"Red-Arm's fence, the lady who lives on rue du Temple, will buy this fabric," added Nicolas. "And Old Micou, the landlord of the furnished apartments in the Saint-Honoré neighborhood, will take care of the brass."

"Amandine," François whispered to his little sister, "won't one of those beautiful silk handkerchiefs Nicolas is holding make a pretty necktie?"

"It would make an awfully pretty headscarf, too," answered the child, full of admiration.

"I have to say, you sure were lucky to get on that small sailboat, Nicolas," said Calabash. "Hey, look! Look at these shawls we have here! There are three of them—real floss silk. Look, Mother!"

"Old Lady Burette will give us at least five hundred francs for the lot," said the widow after close inspection.

"Really, this must be worth at least fifteen hundred francs," said Nicolas. "But like they say, all fences are thieves. Oh, well. I don't want to quibble. I'll still allow myself to be duped this time and let Old Lady Burette and Old Micou call the shots. At least Old Micou's a buddy."

"It doesn't matter. That old seller of secondhand iron scrap is a thief like all the rest of them. That lousy crew of fences know we need them," said Calabash, draping herself in one of the shawls, "and they take advantage of the fact!"

"That's it," said Nicolas as he reached the bottom of the trunk.

"Now we have to bundle it all up again and put it away," said the widow.

"I'm keeping that shawl," said Calabash.

"You're keeping this, you're keeping that," said Nicolas, brusquely. "You'll keep it if I give it to you. You're always taking things, little Madame Shameless."

"Come on! Are you saying you don't take things?"

"I nick things, and I risk my skin to do it. You're not the one who'd be nabbed if they'd caught me on that sailboat."

"Oh, take your shawl back, then. As if I care," said Calabash bitterly as she threw it back into the trunk.

"It's not so much the shawl. I'm not so stingy that I need to haggle over a shawl. One shawl more or less—Old Lady Burette will pay the same. She buys by the lot," answered Nicolas. "But instead of saying you'll take that shawl, you could have asked me to give it to you. Go ahead, keep it. Keep it, I'm telling you, or I'll throw it into the fire to make the pot boil faster." These words calmed Calabash down. She took the shawl without resentment.

Nicolas must have been in a generous mood, because, tearing off the top of one of the pieces of silk with his teeth, he pulled two scarves from it and threw them at Amandine and François, who had not stopped contemplating the fabric with envy.

"Here you go, kids! That little mouthful will give you the taste for nicking things. Eating gives you more of an appetite. Now go upstairs to bed. I've got to talk with our mother. You'll get your supper upstairs."

The two children clapped their hands joyously and triumphantly brandished the stolen scarves they had just gotten.

"So, you little numbskulls," said Calabash. "Are you still going to listen to Martial? Has he ever given you scarves as nice as that?"

François and Amandine looked at each other and then lowered their heads without answering.

"Answer me," Calabash said, harshly. "Has Martial ever given you presents?"

"Indeed, no. He never has," said François, looking down happily at his red silk scarf.

Amandine added in an undertone, "Our brother Martial doesn't give us presents because he doesn't have anything."

"He'd have something if he stole," said Nicolas, angrily. "Isn't that so, François?"

"Yes, brother," answered François. Then he added, "Oh! My scarf is so beautiful! It will make such a nice tie to wear on Sundays!"

"And I have such a pretty headscarf!" said Amandine.

"We haven't even mentioned the fact that the children of the guy who runs the pottery kiln will go nuts when they see you go by," said Calabash. She looked attentively at the children's faces to see if they understood the nasty significance of her words. The abominable creature was appealing to their vanity in order to help her snuff out any remaining scruples these unfortunate children might have. "The pottery kiln guy's kids," she went on, "will look like beggars. They'll just die of jealousy, because you two are going to look like little rich kids in your beautiful silk scarves!"

"Hey, that's true!" said François. "Well, then, my beautiful tie really makes me happy—the little pottery kiln kids will go crazy for not having one like it. Right, Amandine?"

"Me, I'm just happy with my headscarf."

"And so you'll never be anything but a ninny," said Calabash, disdainfully. Then, taking some bread and cheese off the table, she handed it to the children and said, "Go up to bed. Here's a lantern. Be careful of the flame and be sure to put it out before you fall asleep."

"That's right!" added Nicolas. "Don't forget that if you are stupid enough to tell Martial about the trunk, the copper ingots, and the rags, I'll light a fire under your feet that will make you dance. Plus, I'll have to take those scarves away from you."

After the children went upstairs, Nicolas and his sister hid the rags, the trunk of fabric, and the copper ingots at the bottom of a little cellar that was down a few steps and opened onto the kitchen not far from the fireplace.

"Now, then, old lady! Something to drink—and the good stuff!" cried the bandit. "Some real wine, some brandy! I've earned my keep today, good and proper. Serve up dinner, Calabash. Martial can have our leavings—that's good enough for him. Let's talk now about the rich guy on the quai de Billy, because we're going to have to get things moving tomorrow or the day after tomorrow. I want to lay hands on the money he's promised. I'll tell you all about it, Mother, but let's have some drink, blast it! Some drink—it's on me!" And Nicolas again jangled the hundred-sou pieces that he had in his pocket. Then, tossing his goatskin and black wool cap across the room, he sat down at the table in front of an enormous plate of lamb stew, a cold piece of veal, and a salad.

When Calabash brought out the wine and the eau-de-vie, the widow, as always impassive and somber, sat at one side of the table with Nicolas at her right and her daughter to her left. Facing her were the empty seats of Martial and the two children.

The bandit took from his pocket a long, wide Catalan knife with a sharp blade on it and a handle made out of horn. Contemplating this murderous weapon with a ferocious sort of satisfaction, he said to the widow, "Throatslitter still slices just fine! Pass me the bread, Mother!"

"Speaking of knives," said Calabash, "François found something in the woodshed."

"What?" said Nicolas, not understanding what she had said.

"He saw one of the feet."

"The man's?" cried Nicolas.

"Yes," said the widow as she put a slice of meat on her son's plate.

"That's funny! The pit was plenty deep," said the criminal. "I guess with time, the earth must have got packed down."

"We've got to throw the whole thing into the river tonight," said the widow.

"That's the safest plan," said Nicolas.

"We can attach a brick to him with a piece of an old boat chain," said Calabash.

"Not a bad idea!" said Nicolas as he filled his glass. Then, turning to the widow and holding the bottle high, he said, "Come on, drink with us! It'll cheer you up, Mom!"

The widow shook her head, held back her glass, and said to her son, "What about the man from the quai de Billy?"

"Here's what happened," said Nicolas, without ceasing to eat or drink. "As I got to the station, I attached my punt and got out onto the pier. The clock at the Chaillot military bakery was ringing seven o'clock. You couldn't see the nose in front of your face. I had been walking along the parapet for a quarter of an hour when I heard someone walking quietly behind me. I slowed down. A man wrapped up in a coat came up to me, coughing. I stopped, he stopped. All I know of his face is that his coat was hiding his nose and his hat was hiding his eyes." (We remind our reader that this mysterious person was Jacques Ferrand, the solicitor who, wanting to get rid of Fleur-de-Marie, had that very morning bid Madame Séraphin to hurry over to see the Martial family, hoping they would be the instruments of his latest crime.)

"The rich man said, 'Bradamanti,'" said Nicolas. "That was the password the old lady and I agreed on so I'd be able to recognize this individual.

"'Scavenger,' I answered him, as we'd agreed.

"'Your name is Martial?' he asked me.

"'Yes, boss.'

"'A woman came to your island this morning. What did she tell you?'

"'That you had a message for me from Monsieur Bradamanti.'

"'Do you want to make some money?'

"'Yes, boss, always.'

"'You have a boat?'

"'We have four, boss. It's our business. Boatmen and scavengers, father and son, at your service.'

"'Here's what I need done, as long as you're not afraid.'

"'Afraid of what, boss?'

"'Of seeing someone drown by accident—except you may have to help the accident along. Do you understand?'

"'Sure, boss, I get it. You want someone drinking his fill of the Seine, but as if by accident? I can do that. But since that's a dangerous stew, the seasoning is going to cost much more.'

"'How much . . . for two?'

"'For two? There are two people who have to be put in the river's soup?'

"'Yes.'

"'Five hundred a piece, boss. That's not so much!'

"'It's a deal, then—a thousand francs.'

"'Paid in advance, boss.'

"'Two hundred francs in advance, the rest afterward.'

"'You don't trust me, boss?'

"'No. You could pocket my two hundred francs without keeping your end of the bargain.'

"'What about you, boss? Once the job is done, when I ask you for the eight hundred francs, you can always say, "No, thanks, been there, done that!"'

"'Those are the risks. Are you in or not? Two hundred francs on deposit, and the night after tomorrow, here, at nine o'clock, I'll pay you the eight hundred francs that's owing.'

"'And how will you know that I've put the two people in the drink?'

"'I'll know. Anyway, that's my business. Is it a deal?'

"'It's a deal, boss.'

"'Here are two hundred francs. Now listen carefully: will you be able to recognize the old woman who came to see you this morning?'

"'Yes, boss.'

"'Tomorrow or the day after tomorrow, at latest, you'll see her come to the riverbank across from your island at around four o'clock with a young blond woman. The old woman will signal to you by shaking a handkerchief.'

"'Yes, boss.'

"'How long does it take to get from the riverbank to your island?'

"'A good twenty minutes.'

"'Do your boats have flat bottoms?'

"'As flat as my hand, boss.'

"'You need to outfit one of your boats carefully with a kind of large valve at the bottom that will allow you to open it and let the water flow in in a blink of an eye. Do you get it?'

"'I get it, boss. You're a sly one! I've got just the thing, an old half-rotten boat. I've been wanting to break it up. It's just the thing for this last trip.'

"'You'll leave your island, then, on this boat with the valve. Have a good boat follow you, piloted by one of the members of your family. You dock, you take the old woman and the young blond woman onto the boat with the hole in it, and you head back toward your island. But some way from shore, you pretend to lean over to fix something. You open the valve and jump quickly into the other boat, while the old woman and the blond girl . . .'

"'Into the drink! Got it, boss!'

"'But are you sure nothing will get in your way? What if you have customers at your bar?'

"'There's nothing to worry about there, boss. At that hour, especially in the winter, no one ever comes. Things are dead that time of year. And even if someone came, it wouldn't be any bother. On the contrary, it would be a friend we could trust.'

"'All right, then! In any case, there's nothing here to get you in trouble. The boat will be presumed to have sunk from disrepair, and the old woman who brings you the young woman will disappear right along with her. In the end, in order to be sure they are both properly drowned (by accident, of course), you can always seem to try to save them if they come up to the surface or if they get near your boat, and then . . .'

"'And then I can help them . . . go back under. Fine, boss!'

"'This trip will have to take place after sunset so it's dark out when they fall in the water.'

"'No, boss, that won't work. If I can't see clearly, how will I know if the two women have drunk their fill or want some more?'

"'That's right. Well, then, the accident will take place before dusk.'

"'Sounds good, boss. But won't the old woman suspect something?'

"'No. When she gets there, she's going to whisper to you, "Drown the little one. A little before you sink the boat, give me a sign so I'll be ready to escape along with you." You'll answer her so that she won't be suspicious.'

"'So she'll think she's bringing the little blonde to be tossed in the drink . . .'

"'And she'll go in with the little blonde.'

"'You thought that one out good, boss!'

"'But above all, don't let the old woman think anything's up!'

"'Don't worry, boss. She'll lick it up like honey.'

"'All right, then. Good luck, my boy! If I like your work, there might be more where that came from.'

"'At your service, boss!' At that point," said the bandit, finishing his story, "I left the man in the coat, I got back in my boat, and, passing by that little sailboat, I cleaned out the booty you've just seen."

Nicolas's story makes clear that the solicitor was hoping to get rid of Fleur-de-Marie and Madame Séraphin at once by means of a double crime. The latter would be caught in the trap she'd thought to have been set only for Songbird. Need we repeat that having good cause to fear that at any moment the Owl might tell Fleur-de-Marie that she had been abandoned by Madame Séraphin, Jacques Ferrand thought that he had only too good a reason for making this young woman disappear? Her claims could strike a mortal blow to both his fortune and his reputation. As for Madame Séraphin, the solicitor was ridding himself of one of the two accomplices (Bradamanti was the other) who could ruin him. It's true that they would be ruining themselves at the same time if they did, but Jacques Ferrand believed his secrets would be better kept by the tomb than by the power of personal interest.

The executed man's widow and Calabash had listened to Nicolas attentively. He had interrupted his tale only to toss back excessive quantities of alcohol. And then he began to speak in a singularly elated tone: "That's not all," he continued. "I got my hands on another job with the Owl and Fishhook on rue aux Fèves. It's a great job, really well planned. If we don't muff it, I'll say we'll get something big from it. We'll be fleecing a diamond broker who sometimes has something like fifty thousand francs' worth of gemstones in her shopping bag."

"Fifty thousand francs!" cried mother and daughter, their eyes sparkling with avarice.

"Yes, only that little bit. Red-Arm's in on it, too. He'd already taken in the broker yesterday with a letter we two had Fishhook bring her at the boulevard Saint-Denis. That Red-Arm is a gutsy guy! Since he already has plenty, you can trust him. To bait the broker, he's already sold her a diamond for four hundred francs. She won't have a second thought about coming to his tavern on the Champs-Élysées at nightfall. We'll be in ambush there. Calabash will come, too. She can guard my boat along the

Seine. If we have to take the broker somewhere dead or alive, it will be a useful wagon for us, one that won't leave any traces. Now there's a plan! That dirty Red-Arm, what a brainy guy!"

"I still don't trust Red-Arm," said the widow. "After the business on rue Montmartre, your brother Ambrose ended up in Toulon and Red-Arm ended up being let go."

"Because there was no evidence against him. He's so clever! But betray others, never!"

The widow shook her head as if she had never been fully convinced of Red-Arm's trustworthiness. After a few minutes of reflection, she said, "I prefer the job on the quai de Billy for tomorrow or the day after tomorrow, the one where you drown the two women. But Martial's going to get in our way, the way he always does."

"Why the devil can't we get rid of him?" cried Nicolas, half drunk, planting his long knife into the table in rage.

"I've told our mother that we've had enough and that this can't go on," said Calabash. "As long as he's around, we can't get anywhere with those children."

"I'm telling you, he's capable of turning us in one of these days, the villain!" said Nicolas. "Look, Mother. If you had listened to me before," he added, with a fierce and meaningful glance at his mother, "everything would have been taken care of."

"There are other ways."

"That's the best way!" said the bandit.

"Not now," answered the widow in such an absolute tone of finality that Nicolas went silent, dominated by his mother's influence. He knew she was just as criminal and just as wicked as he was, but also more determined. "Tomorrow morning he will leave the island forever," the widow added.

"What?" said Calabash and Nicolas, in unison.

"He'll come back in. Start a fight with him. But straight up and in his face, the way you've never had the guts to do it before. You can even come to blows, if you have to. He's strong, but there are two of you, and I'll help you. But no knives, do you hear me? No blood. You can beat him, but I don't want there to be any wounds."

"And what happens then, Mother?" asked Nicolas.

"Afterward, we'll have words. We'll tell him to leave the island tomorrow. Otherwise, he'll go through the same thing that happened tonight every day. I know him. These continual brawls will disgust him. We've let him alone too much until now."

"But he's as stubborn as a mule. He's capable of wanting to stay just for the sake of the children," said Calabash.

"He's a complete tramp, but he's not afraid of a beating," said Nicolas.

"One beating, yes," said the widow. "But every day? That would be hell. He'll give in."

"What if he doesn't?"

"Well, then I have another surefire way to get him to leave tonight, or tomorrow morning at latest," said the widow, smiling strangely.

"Really, Mother?"

"Yes, but I would prefer to wear him down with beatings. If I don't succeed that way, well, then there's the other way."

"And what if the other way doesn't work, either, Mother?"

"There's one last method that always works," said the widow.

Suddenly the door opened, and Martial entered. The wind was so strong outside that they had not heard the barking of the dogs announce the return of the eldest son of the executed man's widow.

CHAPTER 2

MOTHER AND SON

Martial walked slowly into the kitchen, knowing nothing of his family's malicious plans. A few things the She-Wolf said in her conversation with Fleur-de-Marie have already suggested how unusual this man's life was. Having an instinctively good nature, incapable of committing an openly low or wicked act, Martial nonetheless led an irregular existence. He fished illegally, and his strength and audacity made the game wardens afraid enough of him to turn a blind eye to his poaching on the river. To this already hardly honest activity, Martial added another that was completely illegal: a well-known street tough, he voluntarily took it upon himself, more from too much courage or bravado than from greed, to avenge the victims of stronger adversaries in fist or cudgel fights. It must be said, in any case, that Martial chose the causes he pleaded with his fists with complete rectitude. Generally, he took the part of the weak against the strong.

The She-Wolf's lover looked very much like François and Amandine. He was of average size but robust, with broad shoulders. His thick red hair, which was cut short, formed five points on his open forehead. His short, thick, heavy beard, his wide cheeks, his prominent, jutting nose, and his bold blue eyes all gave his masculine face a singularly resolute expression.

He wore an old rain hat on his head. Despite the cold, he had on only a shabby blue smock over his jacket and trousers, which were made of very worn and bulky cotton velvet. He held an enormous knotty stick in his hand that he put down next to him on the sideboard.

A fat basset hound with bandy legs, a black coat, and bright fawn-colored spots had come in along with Martial, but he stayed near the door, daring neither to approach the fire nor the company already seated at the table. Experience had taught old Miraut (this was the name of the basset hound, Martial's old poaching companion) that, like his master, he was no favorite with the family.

"So, where are the children?"

These were Martial's first words upon sitting at the table.

"They are where they are," said Calabash, in a sour tone.

"Mother, where are the children?" asked Martial again, without paying any attention to his sister's answer.

"They went to bed," said the widow, drily.

"Didn't they have any supper, Mother?"

"What do you care?" cried Nicolas, brutally, after having drunk a large glass of wine in order to embolden himself. His brother's force and character intimidated him greatly.

Martial, as indifferent to Nicolas's attacks as he was to Calabash's, once again addressed his mother, "I don't like it that the children are already in bed."

"Too bad," said the widow.

"Yes, too bad! I like to have them next to me while I have my supper."

"Well, they get on our nerves, so we sent them away!" cried Nicolas. "If you don't like it, go and get them!"

Martial, surprised, stared at his brother. Then, realizing the pointlessness of quarreling, he shrugged his shoulders, cut a piece of bread, and served himself a piece of meat. The basset hound came toward Nicolas, though keeping a very respectful distance. The bandit, irritated at the disdainful imperturbability of his brother and hoping to make him lose patience by striking his dog, gave Miraut a furious kick. The dog howled miserably.

Martial turned scarlet, squeezed the knife he had in his closed fist, and hit the table violently, but, containing himself still, called to his dog and said to him gently, "Come here, Miraut." The basset hound came to lie at his master's feet.

This restraint ran against Nicolas's plans. He wanted to push his brother over the edge so as to trigger an explosion. Thus, he added, "I don't like dogs. I don't want your dog staying here!"

Martial responded merely by pouring a glass of wine and drinking it slowly.

Exchanging a rapid glance with Nicolas, the widow encouraged him with a sign to continue his aggression against Martial, hoping, as we have said, that a violent quarrel would lead to a rupture and then to a complete separation. Nicolas went over to pick up the willow stick that the widow had used to beat François, and, advancing on the basset hound, he struck him viciously as he said, "Get out of here, Miraut!"

Up until this point Nicolas had often employed an underhanded aggressiveness toward Martial, but never had he dared to provoke him with such daring and persistence. The She-Wolf's lover, thinking that they were trying to push him over the edge for some ulterior motive, intensified his self-restraint. In response to the howl of the dog, beaten by Nicolas, Martial got up, opened the door of the kitchen, put the basset hound outside, and returned to eat his supper. This unbelievable patience, so out of character with Martial's habitually passionate personality, confused his aggressors.

They looked at each other, profoundly surprised. He, meanwhile, seemed utterly unaffected by what had happened, ate his meal with gusto, and remained completely silent.

"Calabash, put the wine away," said the widow to her daughter.

"Wait. I haven't finished my supper yet."

"Too bad!" said the widow as she took the bottle away herself.

"Ah! That's different!" answered the She-Wolf's lover. And, pouring himself a big glass of water, he drank it, smacking his lips and saying, "Now that's real water!"

This unflappable calm irritated further Nicolas's hate-filled anger, which his heavy drinking had already exacerbated. Nevertheless, he still held back from a direct attack, knowing his brother's uncommon strength. Suddenly, in a moment of happy inspiration, he cried out, "It's good that you gave in on the matter of your basset hound, Martial. It's a good habit to learn. Because you're going to have to watch us kick your mistress out of here the same way we kicked out your dog."

"Oh, yes. If the She-Wolf is unlucky enough to set foot on this island once she's out of prison," said Calabash, who understood what Nicolas was up to, "it'll be me who'll be slapping her around something fierce."

"And I'll give her a nice dip in the mud, next to the hut at the tip of the island," added Nicolas. "And if she comes up, I'll push her back down, kicking her with my shoes, the old shrew."

This direct insult of the She-Wolf, whom he loved with a wild passion, overcame Martial's resolution to remain peaceful. He scowled, his face turned red, the veins in his forehead expanded and stood out like rope from his face. Nevertheless, he retained enough self-control to say to Nicolas, in a voice only slightly changed by his constrained anger, "Be careful. You're looking for a fight, and you'll get a beating you aren't bargaining for."

"Me? A beating?"

"Yes. Worse than the last."

"What? Nicolas," said Calabash in mock astonishment, "Martial beat you up. Tell me, Mother, did you hear that? Now I see why Nicolas is so frightened of him."

"He beat me up . . . because he took me by surprise," cried Nicolas, turning white with fury.

"You lie. You jumped me from behind, I gave you a beating, and I took pity on you. But if you take it into your head again to talk about my mistress—my mistress, let's be clear about that—there'll be no mercy for you this time. I'll leave my mark on you good and proper."

"And what if I want to talk about the She-Wolf?" asked Calabash.

"I'll box your ears as a warning, and if you start again, well, then I'll start in warning you again."

"And if I talk about her?" said the widow, slowly.

"You?"

"Yes, me."

"You?" said Martial, making a violent effort to contain himself. "You?"

"You'll beat me up, too, won't you?"

"No, but if you speak to me of the She-Wolf, I'll thrash Nicolas. So go on, that will get to you as well as him."

"You?" cried the criminal in fury, picking up his dangerous Catalan knife. "You're going to give me a thrashing?"

"Nicolas! No knives!" cried the widow, getting up quickly to seize her son by the arm. But the latter, drunk with wine and anger, got up, pushed his mother aside harshly, and threw himself upon his brother. Martial took a quick step back, seized the large, knotty stick he had put on the sideboard when he came in, and went on the defensive.

"Nicolas! No knives!" repeated the widow.

"Let him alone!" cried Calabash, picking up the scavenger's hatchet.

Nicolas, still brandishing his formidable knife, looked for his chance to throw himself on his brother. "I'm telling you," he cried, "that I'm going to kill you and your slut She-Wolf, the two of you, and I'm starting now. Help me, Mother! Help me, Calabash! Let's take him out! This has been going on for too long!"

And, thinking he saw his chance, the bandit flung himself at his brother, his knife upraised.

Martial, an expert singlestick fighter, feinted back quickly, raised his stick, and, fast as lightning, flourished it in a figure eight and struck Nicolas's right forearm so heavily that the latter, suddenly paralyzed with pain, let his knife fall to the floor.

"You scoundrel! You've broken my arm!" he cried, seizing his right arm with his left hand. The arm hung limp at his side.

"No, I felt my stick recoil," Martial responded as he sent the knife under the sideboard with a kick. Then, taking advantage of Nicolas's pain, he took him by the collar and pushed him forcefully backward to the door of the little cellar we've mentioned. He opened the door with one hand and, with the other, threw his brother, still stunned by the sudden attack, into the cellar, and then closed the door.

Coming back then for the two women, he seized Calabash by the shoulders, and, in spite of all her resistance, cries, and a hatchet blow that injured him lightly on the hand, he managed to shut her into the lower room of the bar off the kitchen.

Then, turning to the widow, still in shock from this unexpected and skillful maneuver, Martial said to her, coldly, "Now, Mother, it's between the two of us now."

"Well, all right, then! It's between the two of us!" cried the widow. Her impassive face grew animated, her pasty skin reddened, and a dark fire illuminated her previously dull eyes. Anger and hatred gave her features a terrible aspect. "Yes! It's between the two of us!" she said in a threatening voice. "I've been waiting for this moment. Now, finally, you'll know what I have on my mind."

"And I'm going to tell you what I have on my mind, too."

"You'll remember this night, even if you live a hundred years."

"I'll remember it, all right! My brother and sister tried to murder me and you did nothing to stop them. But let's hear what you have to say. What is it you have against me?"

"What do I have against you?"

"Yes."

"Since your father's death, you've been nothing but a coward."

"Me?"

"Yes, you coward! Instead of staying with us to help us, you've gone off to the safety of Rambouillet. You've gone poaching in the woods with the game merchant you met in Bercy."

"If I had stayed here, I'd be in the galleys by this point like Ambrose, or almost there, like Nicolas. I didn't want to be a thief like the rest of you. That's why you hate me."

"And what do you do for a living? You steal game and fish. Theft without any danger—a coward's theft!"

"Fish and game don't belong to anyone. They belong to one person one day, someone else the next. They belong to whoever knows how to catch them. I don't steal. As for being a coward—"

"You take money to beat up people who are weaker than you!"

"Because they've beaten up people who were weaker than themselves!"

"A coward's profession! A coward's profession!"

"There are more honest professions, it's true. But you're no one to talk!"

"Why didn't you take up one of those honest professions, then, instead of coming back here to be a do-nothing who sponges off his mother?"

"I give you the fish I get and the money I have! It's not a lot, but it's enough. I don't cost you anything. I tried to be a locksmith to earn more money, but when you've been a vagabond on the river and in the woods since childhood, it's hard to get used to another way of living. That's it for life. And then," added Martial in a somber tone, "I've always preferred to live alone on the water or in the forest. No one asks me any questions there. Everywhere else, on the other hand, people talk to me about my father and I have to tell them he was guillotined. And my brother? He's a convict! And my sister? She's a thief!"

"And your mother, what do you say then?"

"I say . . ."

"What?"

"I say she's dead."

"That's the right answer. It comes to the same thing. I renounce you, you coward! Your brother is in the penitentiary! Your grandfather and your father ended their lives bravely on the scaffold, mocking the priest and the executioner! Instead of avenging them, you quake in your shoes!"

"Avenging them?"

"Yes. Show that you're a real Martial. Spit on Charlie's[135] knife and on the red robe,[136] and end up like your father and mother, brother and sister."

Even though he was well accustomed to his mother's ferocious diatribes, Martial couldn't help getting the chills now. The face of the executed man's widow had become terrifying as she pronounced these last words. Her fury increasing, she went on: "Oh, you coward! You're even more of a cretin than a coward! You want to be honest! Honest? You'll always be scorned and rebuffed as the son of a murderer, the brother of a convict! But instead of that making you enraged and hungry for revenge, it makes you afraid. Instead of striking back, you save your own hide. When they guillotined your father, you left us, you coward! And you knew that we couldn't leave our island to go into town without people chasing us and throwing stones at us as if we were rabid dogs! Oh! We'll get even for that—we'll get even!"

"I'm not afraid of anyone, not of any ten men. But to be jeered at by everyone as the son and brother of a condemned man—I couldn't take it. I preferred to go into the woods to poach with Pierre, the game salesman."

"You should have stayed there, in your woods."

"I came back because of my run-in with that guard, but most of all because of the children. They were of an age to be corrupted by your example."

"What's it to you if they were?"

"I care, because I don't want them to become worthless beggars like Ambrose, Nicolas, and Calabash!"

"You can't be thinking that!"

"And they would have, if they'd been left alone with all of you. I put myself out to apprentice so I could try to earn enough to take those children with me and leave the island. But everyone knows everything

135. A nickname for the guillotine. Named after Charles-Henri Sanson, who started as the executioner under Louis XVI and then became the executioner during the Revolution, performing the executions of Louis XVI and Marie Antoinette. [TN]

136. Priest. [TN]

in Paris. I was always the son of the condemned man and the brother of the convict. I got into fights every day. I got tired of it."

"But you didn't get tired of being honest! You've done such a good job of that! Instead of having the courage to come back to us, to be just like us, to be like the children will be despite you—yes, despite anything you can do—you think you can cajole them with your preaching. But we're already way ahead of you. We've already got François, or almost. Just give him the chance and he'll be one of us."

"I tell you that won't happen."

"You'll see that I'm right. I know what I'm talking about. At bottom, he's a criminal. It's just that you get in his way. As for Amandine, once she's fifteen, she'll go out on her own. Oh! They threw stones at us! They ran after us like we were rabid dogs! Well, they'll see what our family is made of—except for you, you coward, for you're the only one who makes us feel ashamed."[137]

"That's too bad."

"And since you've gotten spoiled here with us, you'll have to leave tomorrow and never come back."

Martial looked at his mother in surprise. After a moment of silence, he asked her, "Is this why you were trying to quarrel with me at supper?"

"Yes, we wanted to let you know what awaited you if you wanted to stay here against our will. It will be hell. Do you understand? Hell! Every day, another fight, more blows, more scuffles. We won't always be on our own as we were tonight. We'll get friends to help us. You won't last a week."

"Do you think you're scaring me?"

"I'm just telling you what will happen to you."

"Fine with me. I'm staying here."

"You're staying here?"

---

137. The appalling truth of this scene is unfortunately not exaggerated. We read the following in the excellent report of Monsieur de Bretignères regarding the penal colony at Mettray (session dated March 12, 1842): "It is important to note the official status of the inmates. Among them we count 32 illegitimate children, 34 children whose father and mother have remarried, 51 whose parents are in prison, 124 whose parents have not been subjects of criminal investigation but have fallen into dire poverty. These figures are eloquent and extremely instructive. They allow us to trace the effects to the causes and give us the hope of rooting out the evil whose origin has thus become clear to us. The number of criminal parents allows us to appreciate the education that their children must have received under the teaching of such instructors. Educated in the ways of crime by their fathers, the sons have come to no good under their direction, thinking that they would do well by following their examples. Caught up in the justice system, they have resigned themselves to prison as the lot of their families. All they bring there is the imitation of vice. A spark of divine grace must reside within the heart of such a coarse and vulgar being if any decency is to remain in it." [SN]

"Yes."

"Against our wishes?"

"Against your wishes, and Calabash's and Nicolas's wishes, and the wishes of all the losers like him."

"You make me laugh." Coming out of the mouth of this woman, with her sinister and ferocious face, these words were horrifying.

"I tell you, I'll stay here until I find a way to make my living somewhere else, with the children. I could make do on my own living in the woods, but I'll need more time to be able to take care of them. More time to find what I'm looking for. Until then, I'm staying."

"Oh, so you're staying until you're ready to take the children away?"

"Exactly."

"You're going to take the children away?"

"When I tell them to come, they'll come. They'll come running—I guarantee it."

The widow shrugged and said, "Listen, I've just told you that even if you live to be a hundred, you'll never forget this night. Now I'm going to tell you why. But first, have you made up your mind you won't leave?"

"Yes! I'll say it a thousand times!"

"In a moment, you'll say no a thousand times. Listen to me carefully. Do you know what your brother does for a living?"

"I have my suspicions, but I don't want to know."

"You know now . . . he steals . . ."

"The worse for him."

"And for you."

"For me?"

"At night he commits breaking and entering, a crime he could get sent to the galleys for. We're the receivers of what he steals. If it gets discovered, as receivers of stolen goods, we all get condemned to the same penalty as he is, and you, too. They'll round up the family, and the children will be out on the street, where they'll learn the trade of your father and grandfather just as well as they'd learn it here."

"How would I get arrested a receiver of stolen goods, as your accomplice? On what evidence?"

"No one knows how you live. You wander around on the water, you have the reputation of being a bad man, you live with us. Who do you think will believe you don't know all about our thefts and receiving of stolen goods?"

"I will prove that I don't."

"We'll accuse you as our accomplice."

"You'd do that? Why?"

"To pay you back for staying where you're not wanted."

"A moment ago you tried to scare me one way, and now you're trying another. It won't work. I'll prove that I've never stolen anything. I'm staying."

"Oh, so you're staying? Listen to some more, then. Do you remember what happened on Christmas Eve last year?"

"Christmas Eve?" asked Martial, searching his memory.

"Think hard."

"I don't remember."

"You don't remember that Red-Arm brought a man here who looked rich and who needed a place to hide?"

"Yes, now I remember. I went up to bed and I left him at supper with you. He spent the night in our house, and Nicolas took him to Saint-Ouen before dawn."

"Are you sure that Nicolas took him to Saint-Ouen?"

"That's what you told me the next morning."

"So you were here on Christmas Eve, then?"

"Yes, so what?"

"That night, that man who had all that money was murdered in this house."

"Him? Here?"

"We robbed him and buried him in the woodshed."

"That's not true," cried Martial, turning pale with terror, not wanting to believe his own family had committed this latest crime. "You're trying to scare me! It's not true!"

"Go and ask your pet François what he saw in the woodshed this morning!"

"François? What did he see?"

"One of the man's feet poking up from the ground. Take the lantern, go ahead. You can see for yourself."

"No," said Martial, wiping the cold sweat off his forehead. "No, I don't believe you. You're saying this to—"

"To prove to you that if you go on living here against our wishes, you are risking being arrested at any moment on charges of being an accomplice to theft and murder. You were here on Christmas Eve. We will say you helped us carry out the crime. How will you prove you didn't?"

"My God!" said Martial, hiding his face in his hands.

"Now will you agree to leave?" said the widow, a sardonic grin on her face.

Martial was staggered. Unfortunately, he did not doubt the truth of what his mother had just told him. The vagabond life he had led, together with his living among such a criminal family, would indeed allow terrible suspicions to weigh against him. These suspicions could turn into certainty in the eyes of the court if his mother, brother, and sister accused him of being their accomplice.

The widow gloated over her son's fall. "You have one way out of this problem: you can rat on us!"

"I should, but I won't do that. You know that perfectly well."

"That's why I told you everything. So are you going to leave now?"

Martial tried to appeal to this shrew with tenderness. "Mother, I don't believe you capable of murder."

"Whatever you like. But go."

"I will leave on one condition."

"No conditions!"

"You must put the children in apprenticeships far away from here, in the provinces."

"They're staying here."

"Listen, Mother: when you've succeeded in making them end up just like Nicolas, Calabash, Ambrose, and my father, what good will that do you?"

"They'll be able to help us pull off some good jobs. There aren't too many of us around here. Calabash stays with me here to work the bar, so Nicolas has to go out alone. Once they're trained, François and Amandine will be able to help him. People threw stones at them, too, even though they were so little! They have to get their revenge!"

"Mother, you love Calabash and Nicolas, don't you?"

"And if I do, so what?"

"If the children imitate them, and if your crime and theirs get discovered . . ."

"So?"

"They'll go to the scaffold, just like my father."

"So?"

"Doesn't that fate make you tremble?"

"Their fate will be mine as well, neither better nor worse. I steal, they steal. I kill, they kill. Whoever takes the mother will take the children as well. We won't abandon each other. If our heads fall, they'll fall into the same basket, where they'll bid each other good-bye. We won't retreat. You're the only coward in the family. We want you out of here. Get out!"

"But the children! The children!"

"The children will grow up. I'm telling you, if it weren't for you, they'd already be properly trained. François is almost there. When you leave, Amandine will make up for lost time."

"Mother, I beg of you, please send the children into apprenticeships far away from here."

"How many times do I have to tell you that they're in apprenticeships right here?"

The executed man's widow pronounced these last words in such an inexorable manner that Martial lost all hope of softening her steely heart. "Since that's the way it is," he said in a curt and resolute voice, "it's your turn to listen: I'm staying."

"Oh!"

"Not in this house. I'd be murdered by Nicolas or poisoned by Calabash. But since I don't have any money to pay for rent anywhere else, the children and I will live in the shed on the tip of the island. The door is solid, and I'll reinforce it even more. Once I'm barricaded in there with my rifle, my stick, and my dog, I'm not afraid of anyone. Tomorrow morning I'll take the children away. During the day, they'll come with me, either in my boat or outside. At night, they'll sleep next to me in the cabin. We will live off my fishing, and that's the way it will be until I find places for them—and I will find places for them."

"So, that's the way it is?"

"None of you—not you, not my brother, not Calabash—can keep this from happening. Do you understand? If they discover your thefts or the murder you committed while I'm still on the island, too bad—I'll take that risk! I'll explain that I came back and stayed on account of the children, to keep them from turning into bums. The courts will decide who to believe. But may I be struck down dead if I leave this island and those children stay one more day in this house! So you and the others can just try to chase me off the island!"

The widow knew well how resolute Martial was. The children loved their older brother as much as they feared him. They would, therefore, follow him anywhere, without hesitation. As for Martial, well armed, determined, always on his guard, in his boat during the day, sheltered and barricaded in his cabin on the island at night, he had nothing to fear from the evil designs of his family.

Martial thus would be able to carry out his plan in every detail, but the widow had many reasons to hinder its execution. First of all, just as honest artisans sometimes consider the number of their offspring to be a form of wealth because of the help they get from them, so too did the widow count on Amandine and François for their assistance in crimes she hoped to carry out. Also, what she had said about her desire to avenge her husband and son was true. Certain beings who are bred to crime, who grow up and harden into it, end up in open revolt against society, waging bitter war on it. They believe that committing new crimes can avenge the just punishment inflicted on them or their family members. And finally, Nicolas's sinister designs against Fleur-de-Marie, and later against the diamond broker, could be compromised by Martial's presence. The widow had hoped to achieve an immediate separation between herself and Martial, either by inciting a quarrel between him and Nicolas or by revealing to him that if he insisted on staying on the island, he risked being seen as an accomplice to several crimes.

The widow was crafty, but also shrewd. Grasping that she had been wrong, she felt that she would have to resort to treachery to get her son to fall into a bloody trap. Thus, after a rather long silence, she said, with affected bitterness, "I see what you're trying to do. You don't want to turn us in yourself. You want to get the children to do it."

"Me?"

"They know now that a man is buried here. They know that Nicolas has stolen. Once they're apprenticed, they'll talk. They will come for us—you, too, right along with us. That's what would happen if I listened to you, if I let you find a place for the children somewhere else. And yet you say that you mean us no harm! I'm not asking you to love me, but just don't hasten the moment of our being taken."

The softened tone of the widow made Martial believe that his threats had produced a positive effect on her. He fell into a terrible trap.

"I know the children," he said, "and I am sure that if I told them not to say anything, they wouldn't say anything. In any case, I would be with them all the time, one way or another, so I would watch over their silence."

"Who can watch over the words of a child? Especially in Paris, where people are so curious and talkative. I want them here as much because I want them to help us pull off our jobs as because I want to prevent them from selling us out."

"Don't they go into town sometimes or into Paris? Who could keep them from talking if they had anything to talk about? If they were far away from here, it would be much better! There wouldn't be any danger no matter what they might say."

"Far from here? And where would that be?" said the widow, staring at her son.

"Let me take them away. Where doesn't matter to you."

"How will you and the children get by?"

"My old boss, the locksmith, is a good man. I will tell him what it's necessary to tell him and then maybe he'll lend me something for the children. With that, I'll put them in apprenticeships far away from here. We'll leave in two days and you'll never hear from us again."

"No. After all, I want them to stay with me. I'll be surer of them that way."

"In that case, I'm moving into the shed on the island until something better comes along. I'm stubborn, too, you know?"

"Yes, I know that. Oh! I wish you were far away from here! Why didn't you stay in your woods?"

"I'm offering to take myself and the children off your hands."

"You'd leave the She-Wolf behind here, your mistress whom you love so much?" the widow said suddenly.

"That's my business. I know what I have to do. I know what I'm doing."

"If I let you take François and Amandine away, you'll never set foot in Paris again?"

"Within three days we'll be gone and we'll be as good as dead as far as you're concerned."

"I like that better than having you here and always being on edge about them. All right, since there really isn't any choice, take them. And get out of here as soon as you can. I never want to see you again!"

"It's a deal!"

"It's a deal. Give me the key to the cellar so I can let Nicolas out."

"No, he can sleep off his wine down there. I'll give you the key back tomorrow morning."

"What about Calabash?"

"That's different. You can let her out as soon as I go upstairs. It turns my stomach to have to look at her."

"Go. And may you go to hell!"

"That's how you say good night, Mother?"

"Yes."

"Happily, that will be the last time I have the pleasure of hearing it," said Martial.

"Yes, the last," said the widow.

Her son lit a candle and then opened the kitchen door and whistled for his dog, who bounded in joyously from outdoors and followed his master up to the top floor of the house.

"Go ahead. You've paid for this in full," muttered the mother as she brandished her fist at her son, who had just gone upstairs, "and now you're going to get it."

Then, assisted by Calabash, who went to find a ring of skeleton keys, the widow picked the lock of the cellar and freed Nicolas.

CHAPTER 3

FRANÇOIS AND AMANDINE

François and Amandine were lying in a room situated directly over the kitchen at one end of a corridor. There were several other rooms off this corridor that were used as meeting rooms for people who frequented the bar.

After having shared their frugal supper, instead of putting out their lantern as the widow had told them to do, the two children had stayed up, leaving their door ajar to watch out for Martial on his way back to his room. Sitting on a rickety stool, the lantern projected pale beams of light through its transparent shade. Plastered walls striped with brown planks, a pallet for François, an old, small, far too short children's bed for Amandine, a heap of debris from the chairs and benches broken by rowdy guests of the bar on the Scavenger's Island: such was the interior of this shabby room.

Seated at the edge of the pallet, Amandine looked at herself as she arranged her hair in the bandanna she had made of the stolen scarf, her brother Nicolas's gift to her. François, kneeling, was holding up a fragment of a mirror for his sister. With her head turned to one side, she was busy fluffing out the large bow she had made by knotting the corners of the scarf. Rapt in contemplation at this hairstyle, and quite dazzled by it, he neglected momentarily to hold the piece of mirror in such a way that she could see her reflection. "Hold the mirror higher," said Amandine. "I can't see myself now. There . . . good . . . wait a minute . . . all right, I'm done. Now look! How do you like how I've done my hair?"

"Oh, it's beautiful! Lord, what a beautiful bow you've made! Will you make me one just like that for my tie?"

"Sure, in just a moment. But let me walk around a little first. You can walk ahead of me. Back up, holding the mirror high as you do, so I can see myself walking."

François executed this difficult maneuver as best he could. Amandine was greatly satisfied and lolled about, glorious and triumphant, under the scarf's ends and enormous knot.

Under any other circumstance, this coquettishness would have been very innocent and very naive. But it became blameworthy in association with the theft of which both François and Amandine were aware. This shows yet again the frightening ease with which children, even the most honest, may be corrupted almost unwittingly when they are continuously immersed in a criminal atmosphere. And furthermore, the only mentor these poor little children had, their brother Martial, was, as we have noted, hardly without flaw himself. Incapable of committing theft or murder, he nevertheless led the irregular life of a vagabond. Certainly, he was revolted by the crimes of his family; he loved both children tenderly; he defended them from mistreatment; he tried to remove them from the pernicious influence of his family; but, with no support from any rigorous, positive moral teachings, his guidance was weak protection for his protégés. They refused to commit certain crimes, not because they were honest, but more to obey Martial, whom they loved, and to disobey their mother, whom they feared and hated.

As for their notions of justice and injustice, they had none, habituated, as they were, to the detestable examples they had every day before their eyes. As we have said, this country tavern, frequented by the dregs of the lowest of the low, served as the scene of obscene orgies, of criminal debauches. And Martial, opposed as he was to all theft and murder, showed a striking indifference to these filthy saturnalia. This indicates how uncertain, vacillating, and precarious were the moral instincts of these children. François in particular had arrived at the dangerous moment at which a wavering soul, hovering between good and evil, could at any moment be either lost forever, or saved.

"That red scarf looks so nice on you, sister!" said François. "It's so pretty! When we go out to play on the beach in front of the pottery kiln guy's place, you'll have to do up your hair like that. When those kids who won't stop throwing stones at us and calling us little gallows-fodder see us, it'll drive them crazy! I'll put on my nice red tie, and we'll say to them, 'Yeah, yeah, but you don't have the nice silk scarves that we do!'"

"But you know, François," said Amandine, after a moment of reflection. "If they know the scarves we're wearing are stolen, they'll call us little thieves."

"With these scarves, they can go right ahead and call us thieves."

"When it's not true, I don't care, but now . . ."

"Since Nicolas gave us the scarves, we didn't steal them."

"Yes, but he took them off a boat, and our brother Martial told us that we should never steal."

"But since it was Nicolas who did it, that has nothing to do with us."

"Do you really think so, François?"

"Of course."

"All the same, I'd feel better if we'd been given the scarves by the person who owned them. What do you think, François?"

"I don't care either way. We got them as gifts. They're ours."

"Are you really sure?"

"Yes, yes, stop worrying already!"

"All right. It's okay, then. We haven't done what Martial told us not to do—and we've got these beautiful scarves!"

"Hey, Amandine, what if he knew that the other day Calabash made you take that checkered neckerchief from the salesman's pack when he had his back turned?"

"Oh, François, don't say that!" said the poor child, her eyes filling with tears. "Our brother Martial might stop loving us. And then, don't you see, he'd leave us here alone."

"Don't be afraid! I would never tell him about it. I was just joking."

"Oh! Don't joke about that, François! I've had enough to feel bad about, you know! But I had to do it. Our sister pinched me until I was bleeding, and then she looked at me in such a mean way! And still I got scared twice and I thought I'd never be able to do it. In the end, the salesman didn't notice anything, and our sister kept the kerchief. Yet if they'd caught me, François, they would have put me in prison."

"They didn't catch you, so it's just as if you'd never stolen."

"Really?"

"Swear to God!"

"It must be really sad to be in prison."

"Yeah, right! It's just the opposite."

"How can you think it's just the opposite, François?"

"You know that big gimp who lives in Paris where Old Micou, Nicolas's fence, lives? The one who has a furnished room in Paris on the passage de la Brasserie?"

"A big gimp?"

"Yeah, Old Micou sent him here once at the end of autumn. He was with a guy who had performing monkeys, and two women."

"Oh, right, right—the big gimp who spent a whole lot of money."

"I'll say he did—he paid for everyone. Do you remember those trips he took on the water? I was the one who took them. The monkey guy even brought his organ along to play music in the boat!"

"And then that night they set off such nice fireworks, didn't they, François?"

"The big gimp was no cheapskate! He gave me ten sous to keep! He never drank any wine that wasn't the best. They ate chicken at every meal. He had to have eaten at least eighty francs' worth."

"That much, François?"

"Oh, yes."

"So was he really rich?"

"Not at all. The money he was spending was money he'd earned in prison. He'd just gotten out."

"He earned all that money in prison?"

"Yes. He said that he still had another seven hundred francs, and that when he didn't have any more, he'd find some job to pull off. If they caught him, that was fine with him, because he would just return to all the friendly guys in jail, he said."

"So he wasn't afraid of prison, François?"

"No, just the opposite. He was telling Calabash that they're all a bunch of friends and guys who like to have a good time. He said he'd never had a better bed or better food than when he was in prison: good meat four times a week, heat all winter, and a nice pile of money when you leave. And all the while, there are stupid, honest workers out there, dying of hunger and cold from not having enough work."

"The big gimp really said that, François?"

"I heard him say it myself, because I was the one rowing the boat while he was telling his story to Calabash and the two women, who were saying that it was just the same in the women's prisons they'd just gotten out of."

"Well, then, François, it can't be so bad to steal if prison is such a nice place."

"Lord, how would I know? Our brother Martial is the only one around here who says it's bad to steal. Maybe he's wrong."

"All the same, we have to believe him, François. He loves us so much!"

"It's true that he loves us. When he's here, there's no chance we'll be beaten. If he had been here tonight, our mother wouldn't have beaten me up. Old beast! She's so mean! Oh, how I hate her! I hate her! I wish I was big so I could pay her back for all the beatings she's given us. The ones she's given you, especially, since you're much less tough than I am."

"Oh, François, be quiet. It frightens me to hear you saying that you'd like to beat our mother!" cried the poor little girl as she cried, throwing her arms around the neck of her brother and kissing him tenderly.

"But it's true, all the same," said François, pushing Amandine away gently. "Why do our mother and Calabash always have it in for us?"

"I don't know," said Amandine, wiping her eyes with the back of her hand. "Maybe it's because our brother Ambrose got put in the galleys and our father got guillotined that they're so hard on us."

"Is that our fault?"

"Of course not, but what do you expect?"

"Well, really, if I'm going to be beaten all the time, in the end I'd rather steal like they do. What good is it doing me not to steal?"

"And what would Martial say about that?"

"Oh, if it weren't for him, I would have given in a long time ago, because a person gets tired of being beaten, too. You know, our mother was never meaner than she was tonight. She was like a fury. It was dark, really dark. She didn't say a word. All I felt was her cold hand holding me by the neck while she beat me with the other. And I thought I saw her eyes light up."

"Poor François. Just because you said you'd seen the bone of a dead man in the woodshed."

"Yes, a foot coming out of the ground," said François, shuddering in terror. "I'm sure of it."

"Maybe there used to be a cemetery here. That could be it."

"I'd like to believe it. But then why would our mother say to me that she would beat me up again if I told Martial about the dead man's bone? You see, it must be someone who got killed in an argument and who got buried there so no one would know what had happened."

"You're right. Hey, do you remember another time something like that almost happened?"

"When?"

"You know, the time Monsieur Fishhook stabbed the tall guy who was so bony—so bony that he used to show his body for money."

"Oh, yeah, they called him the Walking Skeleton. Our mother came and separated them. Otherwise, Fishhook might have killed that tall, bony guy! Did you see how Fishhook was foaming at the mouth and how his eyes were jumping out of his head?"

"Oh, he's not at all afraid of sticking a knife in you. He's a proud one!"

"He's so young and so wicked, François!"

"Gammy is even younger, and he would be at least as wicked as him if he were stronger."

"Oh, yeah, he's really mean. The other day he hit me because I didn't want to play with him."

"He hit you? Fine. The next time he comes here . . ."

"No, no, François, he was just joking around."

"Are you sure?"

"Yes, I swear."

"All right, then. Otherwise . . . But I don't understand what that kid is up to. How does he always manage to have so much money? He's lucky! The time he came here with the Owl, he showed us twenty-franc gold pieces. He really seemed to be taunting us when he said, 'You would have some of these, too, if you weren't such saps.'"

"Saps?"

"Yes, in slang, that means dummies or imbeciles."

"Oh, right."

"Forty francs, in gold . . . Boy, I'd buy some nice things with that. What about you, Amandine?"

"Oh, me, too!"

"What would you buy?"

"Let's see," said the child, putting her head down in an attitude of contemplation. "I would first buy our brother Martial a good, warm smock so he wouldn't get cold in his boat."

"But what about for you?"

"I'd like to have a little wax Jesus with his lamb and his cross, like that plaster-figure street seller had on Sunday. You know, under the porch of the Asnières church?"

"By the way, let's hope that no one tells our mother and Calabash that they saw us in church!"

"You can say that again. She's always telling us we aren't allowed to go in there. It's too bad, because it's really nice inside a church. Don't you think, François?"

"Yes, they had such beautiful silver chandeliers!"

"And the portrait of the Holy Virgin. She looks so kind."

"And those beautiful lamps! Did you see them? And the nice tablecloth on that big buffet in the back, where the priest was saying the mass with his two friends who were dressed like him, the ones who gave him water and wine?"

"Tell me, François, do you remember that year during the Corpus Christi when we saw all of those little girls on the bridge who were taking their communion in their white veils?"

"Their bouquets were so nice!"

"They were singing so sweetly as they held the ribbons of their banner."

"And the silver embroidery on their banner was shining in the sun! It must have cost a lot of money!"

"Good Lord, that was so pretty, François, wasn't it?"

"I'll say. And the communicants with their little white satin bows on their arms, and their candles with red velvet handles and with gold, too."

"The little boys had their own banner, didn't they, François? Oh, Lord, I got beaten so badly that day for having asked our mother why we couldn't be in the procession like the other children!"

"That was when she told us we could never enter a church, whether we were at the market town or in Paris—and then Calabash showed her old yellow teeth, laughed, and added, 'Unless it was to steal from the poor box or pickpocket the parishioners while they were hearing mass.' What a vicious animal she is."

"Oh! To steal in a church? I'd rather die. Wouldn't you, François?"

"Stealing there or somewhere else—what do you care where you do it, once you've decided to do it?"

"Heavens! I don't know. I'd be more afraid. I could never do it."

"Because of the priests?"

"No. Maybe because of that portrait of the Holy Virgin. She seems so gentle and so kind."

"What's a portrait going to do to you? It's not going to eat you, you silly goose!"

"That's true. But I really couldn't do it. I can't help it."

"Speaking of priests, Amandine, do you remember that day when Nicolas gave me two huge swats because he saw me wave at the priest on the riverbank? I saw him wave, so I waved. I didn't think I had done anything wrong."

"Yes, but that time, really, our brother Martial said the same as Nicolas, that there was no need to wave at priests."

At this moment, François and Amandine heard footsteps in the corridor. Martial was returning to his room without suspicions after his conversation with his mother. He believed that Nicolas was going to remain locked up until the next morning. Seeing a ray of light beam out from the children's room through the partially opened door, Martial came in to see them. They both ran to him, and he kissed them tenderly.

"What? You're not asleep yet, you little chatterboxes?"

"No, brother. We were waiting to see you come to your room so we could say good night to you," said Amandine.

"And we heard people shouting down there, too, as if there was an argument going on," added François.

"Yes, I had words with Nicolas. But it's nothing. In any case, I'm happy to see you still up because I have some good news to tell you."

"To tell us, brother?"

"Would you be happy to leave here and come with me somewhere far, far away?"

"Oh, yes, brother!"

"Yes, brother."

"Well, in two or three days all three of us will be leaving this island."

"That's so wonderful!" cried Amandine, clapping her hands with joy.

"Where will we be going?" asked François.

"You'll see, you nosy boy. But it doesn't matter. Wherever we go, you'll learn a good trade that will let you earn a living. That, at least, is certain."

"Won't I get to go fishing with you anymore, brother?"

"No, my boy. You'll enter an apprenticeship with a carpenter or a locksmith. You're strong and skillful. If you put your all into it and work hard, you'll already be able to earn something by the end of your first year. So, what's wrong? You don't look happy about this."

"It's just that . . . brother, I . . ."

"Come on, tell me."

"I would rather not have to leave you. I would rather stay with you, fish and fix your nets, than learn a trade."

"Really?"

"Lord! To be cooped up in a workshop all day, that's a sad life. And being an apprentice would be boring."

Martial shrugged his shoulders. "You'd rather be a lazy vagabond strolling the streets, right?" he said to him severely. "While you wait so you can become a thief."

"No, brother, but I'd like to live with you somewhere else the way we live here—that's all."

"Right. You want to drink, eat, sleep, and have fun fishing, just like a rich man, right?"

"I'd like that better."

"It's possible, but you will like something else. Listen, you know what, my poor François? It's really time I took you away from here. Without realizing it, you could become a worthless beggar, like the others. Mother was right. I'm afraid you might have vice in you. What about you, Amandine? Would it make you happy to learn a trade?"

"Oh, yes, brother. I would love to learn something. I would like that better than staying here. I would be so happy to leave with you and François!"

"But what's that you have on your head, my girl?" said Martial as he noticed Amandine's marvelous hairstyle.

"It's a scarf Nicolas gave me."

"He gave me one, too," said François, proudly.

"And where did those scarves come from? I can't believe Nicolas bought them for you as gifts."

The two children lowered their heads and did not answer him.

After a second, François said resolutely, "Nicolas gave them to us. We don't know where he got them, do we, Amandine?"

"No, no, we don't, brother," added Amandine, stuttering, turning scarlet, not daring to look up at Martial.

"Don't lie to me," said Martial, severely.

"We're not lying," said François, boldly.

"Amandine, my child, tell me the truth," said Martial, gently.

"All right. The truth is," said Amandine, timidly, "that these nice handkerchiefs came from a trunk of fabrics that Nicolas brought home tonight in his boat."

"And that he'd stolen?"

"I think so, brother. From a small sailboat."

"So you were lying to me, François!" said Martial.

The boy kept his head down and did not respond.

"Give me that scarf, Amandine. Give me yours, too, François."

The small girl took the scarf off her head, looked one last time at the enormous bow that had not come undone, and gave it to Martial, repressing a sigh of regret. François slowly pulled his handkerchief out of his pocket and, like his sister, handed it over to Martial.

"Tomorrow morning," he said, "I'll give these scarves back to Nicolas. You shouldn't have taken them, children. Profiting from theft is the same as stealing yourself."

"It's too bad. Those handkerchiefs were so pretty," said François.

"When you have a trade and earn money by working, you can buy scarves that are just as nice as that one. Come on, time for bed. It's late, children."

"You aren't mad at us, are you, brother?" asked Amandine, timidly.

"No, no, my girl, it's not your fault. You live with thieving beggars, so you do the same thing they do without realizing it. When you're with good people, you'll do what they do. And the devil take me if that doesn't happen soon! So let's get on with it. Good night!"

"Good night, brother!"

Martial kissed the children. He left them alone in their room.

"What's wrong, François? You look sad!" said Amandine.

"Well, our brother took away my beautiful scarf. And also, didn't you hear?"

"What?"

"He's going to take us away to put us in apprenticeships."

"Doesn't that make you happy?"

"Hell, no."

"You'd rather stay here and get beaten every day?"

"I get beaten, but at least I don't have to work. I spend all day in the boat or fishing. Or else I play, or I serve the guests who sometimes give me tips, like that big gimp. It's much more fun than being cooped up in a workshop from morning to night and having to work like a dog."

"But didn't you hear? Our brother said that if we stayed here any longer we'd turn into thieving beggars!"

"I don't care. The other kids already call us little thieves and gallows-fodder. And working is just too boring."

"But we get beaten every day here, brother!"

"They beat us because we listen to Martial more than we listen to them."

"He's so good to us!"

"He's good, he's good, I'm not saying he isn't. And I do love him. No one dares to hurt us when he's around. He takes us walking around, it's true, but that's all he ever does. He never gives us anything."

"Heavens! He doesn't have anything to give us! Whatever he earns he gives our mother for his food."

"But Nicolas has money. If we listened to him and our mother, for sure they wouldn't make our life so difficult. They would give us nice clothes, like the ones we got today. They wouldn't distrust us anymore. We would have money, like Gammy."

"But, heavens, we'd have to steal for that to happen, and our brother, Martial, would be hurt by that!"

"Oh, well, too bad for him!"

"Oh, François! And if we got caught, we'd have to go to prison."

"Being in prison or being shut up in a workshop all day, what's the difference? Anyway, the big gimp said it's fun to be in prison."

"But that would make Martial sad. You didn't think of that, did you? You know, he only comes back and stays here for us. If it was just him, he wouldn't bother. He would go back to being a poacher in the woods he loves so much."

"Well, let him take us with him into the woods," said François. "That would be better than anything. I would be with him, which is what I like, and I wouldn't have to work at some trade that bored me."

François and Amandine's conversation was interrupted. Someone outside locked the door and bolted it. "They're locking us in!" cried François.

"Oh, my God! Why are they doing that, brother? What are they going to do to us?"

"Maybe it's Martial?"

"Listen . . . listen to how his dog is barking!" said Amandine, pricking up her ears.

After a few seconds, François added, "It sounds like they're banging at his door with a hammer. Maybe they're trying to break it down."

"Yes, yes, his dog is still barking."

"Listen, François! Now it sounds like they're nailing something. My God! I'm afraid! What are they doing to our brother? His dog is howling now!"

"Amandine, I can't hear anything anymore," said François, getting closer to the door. The two children were listening anxiously, holding their breath.

"Here they come back from our brother's room," whispered François. "I hear them walking in the corridor."

"Let's get in bed! Our mother would kill us if she found us awake!" said Amandine, terrified.

"No," François went on, still listening, "they just passed by our door. They're running down the stairs."

"My God! What's going on?"

"They're opening the kitchen door . . . now . . ."

"You think so?"

"Yes, yes, I know that noise."

"Martial's dog is still howling," said Amandine, listening. Suddenly she cried out, "François! Our brother is calling us!"

"Martial?"

"Yes. Don't you hear? Don't you hear?" Indeed, despite the thickness of the two closed doors, Martial's booming voice could be heard from his room, calling to the two children.

"God, we can't go to him. We're locked in here!" said Amandine. "Since he's calling us, they must be trying to hurt him!"

"Oh! If I could keep them from doing that," cried François resolutely, "I'd stop them, even if it meant being cut into little pieces!"

"But our brother doesn't know they locked us in! He's going to think we didn't want to help him! Yell to him that we're locked in, François!"

The boy was about to act on his sister's advice when a violent blow outside rattled the blinds on the little window of the children's room.

"They're coming through the window to kill us!" cried Amandine, and in her fear, she threw herself onto her bed and hid her head in her hands.

François stayed still, even though he shared in his sister's terror. And yet, after the violent shock just described, the shade was not opened. The deepest silence reigned in the house.

Martial had stopped calling to the children.

Slightly reassured and propelled by a sharp curiosity, François took the risk of opening the casement slightly and trying to look through the slats of the blinds. "Be careful, brother!" whispered Amandine, who, hearing François open the window, had sat up in bed. "Do you see anything?" she asked.

"No, it's too dark."

"You don't hear anything?"

"No, the wind's too strong."

"Come back! Come back, then!"

"Ah! Now I see something."

"What is it?"

"The glow of a lantern, swaying."

"Who's holding it?"

"I can only see the light. It's coming closer! Someone's talking."

"Who is it?"

"Listen . . . it's Calabash."

"What's she saying?"

"She's telling someone to hold on tight to the bottom of the ladder."

"Ah! See, it's by taking the big ladder that was leaning against our blinds that they made that noise a moment ago."

"I can't hear anything else."

"And what are they doing with the ladder now?"

"I can't see anything anymore."

"And you can't hear anything more?"

"No."

"My God, François! Maybe they've taken the ladder around to get into our brother Martial's room through the window!"

"Could be."

"If you open the blind a little to look . . ."

"I'm afraid to."

"Just a little."

"Oh, no! What if our mother noticed?"

"It's so dark that there's no danger."

François did what his sister asked, though he didn't like it. He opened the blind slightly and looked through it.

"Well, brother?" said Amandine, overcoming her fears to tiptoe over to where François stood.

"I can see Calabash by the lantern's light," he said. "She's holding the foot of the ladder. They've leaned it up against Martial's window."

"What's happening now?"

"Nicolas is going up on the ladder, he has his hatchet in his hand. I can see it gleaming . . ."

"Ah! You're not asleep, and you're spying on us!" cried the widow, suddenly, addressing François and his sister from outside. As she was coming back into the kitchen, she had noticed the light coming through the partially opened blind. The unfortunate children had neglected to put out their light.

"I'm coming up," said the widow in a terrible voice. "I'm coming up for you, you little spies!"

Such were the events that were taking place on the Scavenger's Island the day before Madame Séraphin was to bring Fleur-de-Marie there.

CHAPTER 4

A ROOMING HOUSE

The passage de la Brasserie, a dark and not very well-known thoroughfare, situated though it was in the center of Paris, began at rue Saint-Honoré cross street and ended at the Saint-Guillaume courtyard. Toward the middle of this small, humid, muddy, dark, and sad street that was almost never touched by the rays of the sun lay a rooming house (known vulgarly as just a "furnished room" because of its low rents). On a shabby sign appeared the words "Furnished Rooms and Offices." To the right of a dark alley, no better lit, was a store whose door stood open. Here the head tenant of the rooming house could generally be found.

This man, whose name we heard pronounced several times on the Scavenger's Island, was named Micou. Officially, he was a merchant of old iron wares, but secretly he purchased and received stolen metals such as iron, lead, copper, and steel.

To say that Old Micou was an intimate of the Martial family as well as one of their business associates gives a sufficient understanding of the state of his morals.

This network, this mysterious communion that ties together the whole Parisian criminal class, is a curious and frightening phenomenon. Public prisons are major centers in and out of which waves of corruption flow incessantly. Bit by bit, these waves of corruption invade the capital, leaving blood all over its cobblestones.

Old Micou is a fat man of fifty with a vulgar, sly, pinkish face with a pimply nose and cheeks flushed from drink. He wears an otter cap and is wrapped in an old green frock coat.

Above the little smelting pot at which he warms himself may be seen a numbered plank attached to the wall. On it hang the keys to the rooms whose tenants are absent. The panes of the glass shop window that opened onto the street behind thick iron bars were painted—and for good reason—so that outsiders couldn't see what took place within the store.

An extreme darkness hovered over this large store. From the blackish, humid walls hung rusty chains of all sizes and all lengths. The floor had almost entirely disappeared underneath heaps of debris from iron and cast iron.

Three distinctive knocks on the door alerted the receiver-fence-cum-head-tenant. "Enter!" he cried. And someone came in. It was Nicolas, the son of the executed man's widow. He was very pale. His face seemed even more sinister than it had the day before, yet, during the following conversation, he feigned an intense good cheer. (This scene took place the day after the quarrel the bandit had had with his brother Martial.)

"Ah, here you are, my good fellow!" the head tenant said to him, cordially.

"Yes, Old Micou. I'm here to do business with you."

"Close the door, then. Close the door."

"Well, it's just that my dog and my little wagon are there . . . with the thing."

"What do you have for me? Double thicks?"[138]

"No, Old Micou."

"It can't be scavenged stuff. You're too much of a do-nothing these days. You haven't been working. Is it hard stuff,[139] maybe?"

"No, Old Micou. It's red stuff[140]—four ingots' worth. There must be at least a hundred and fifty pounds there. It was all my dog could do to haul it."

"Go and get me the red stuff. We'll weigh it."

"You've got to help me, Old Micou. My arm's hurt."

And at this memory of his struggle with his brother Martial, the criminal's features simultaneously expressed a resurgence of hatred and ferocious joy, as if his lust for revenge had already been satisfied.

"What's wrong with your arm, my boy?"

"Nothing—just a simple sprain."

"You should heat up an iron in the fire, put it in the water, and stick your arm in the near-boiling water. It's a scrap merchant's remedy, but it's a good one."

"Thank you, Old Micou."

"Let's go and get the red stuff. I'll help you, you lazybones!"

In two trips, the ingots were retrieved from a small cart pulled by an enormous mastiff and hauled into the shop. "That cart of yours is a good idea!" said Old Micou as he adjusted the wood platforms of enormous scales suspended from one of the beams in the ceiling.

"Yes, whenever I have something heavy to carry, I put my cart and my mastiff in my punt and I harness him up when I dock. A cabdriver might spill the beans, but my dog never will."

---

138. Lead plates, generally stolen from roofs. [TN]

139. Iron. [TN]

140. Copper. [TN]

"And how's everything going at your place?" asked the fence as he weighed the copper. "Are your mother and sister in good health?"

"Yes, Old Micou."

"And the children, too?"

"The children, too. How's your nephew, André? Where is he?"

"Don't ask. He was out carousing yesterday. Fishhook and the big gimp brought him back to me. He didn't come home until this morning. He's already on his way to the big post office on rue Jean-Jacques Rousseau. And your brother Martial, what about him? Is he still at large?"

"Lord, I have no idea."

"Really! You have no idea?"

"No," said Nicolas, affecting indifference. "For the last two days we haven't seen him. Maybe he went back to poaching in the woods, unless his boat—which was old, very old—sank in the middle of the river, with him in it."

"That wouldn't bother you, you rogue, would it? You could never stand your brother."

"That's true. Sometimes you just think this way or that way about some people. How many pounds of copper do we have here?"

"You've got a good eye. It's a hundred and forty-eight pounds, my boy."

"What do you owe me?"

"Exactly thirty francs."

"Thirty francs, when copper is going for twenty sous a pound? Thirty francs?"

"Let's just say thirty-five francs and call it a deal, okay? Or I'll tell you and your copper and your mastiff and your cart to all go to hell."

"But, Old Micou, you're robbing me blind! It's just not a fair price!"

"You show me how you come to own the copper and I'll give you fifteen sous a pound."

"It's the same old song. You're all alike, you bunch of thieves! I don't know how you can rip off your friends like that! But I've got more. If I bring you merchandise to swap, you'll give me a good deal, at least, won't you?"

"I'll be fair. What do you need? Chains or clamps for your punts?"

"No, I need four or five sheets of very strong metal, the kind you need to line shutters."

"I've got what you're looking for. Four notches thick—a bullet from a pistol wouldn't get through it."

"That's exactly what I want!"

"And what size do you need?"

"All in all, seven to eight square feet."

"Good! What else do you need?"

"Three iron bars of three to four feet in length and two inches around."

"The other day I took apart a window grille—it would be just the thing for you. What else?"

"Two strong hinges and a latch to adjust and close a two-square-foot valve whenever necessary."

"So you want a trapdoor?"

"No, a valve."

"I don't understand what you could need a valve for."

"Could be. But I understand it."

"Very good. You have plenty of choices; I have a whole pile of hinges. Anything else you need?"

"That's all."

"That's not much."

"Get my purchases packed up right away, Old Micou. I'm going to pick it up on my way back. I've got some more shopping to do."

"With your cart? Come on, you joker, I saw a bundle at the bottom of it. You've got some other little delicacy you took from the world's serving table, you little gourmand, you!"

"Since you say so, Old Micou. But you won't be eating any of it. Don't take too long getting my metal materials ready because I have to be back on the island before noon."

"Calm down. It's eight o'clock. If you're not going too far, you can come back in an hour and everything will be ready—all your money and supplies. Do you want to have a drop to drink?"

"Anytime. You owe me!"

Old Micou took a bottle of spirits, a cracked glass, and a cup without a handle out of an old cabinet and poured some out. "To your health, Old Micou!"

"To yours, my boy, and to the health of the ladies of your house!"

"Thank you. And are things going well at your furnished rooms?"

"Just so-so. I still have a few renters I'm afraid the police will come after, but they pay more because of that."

"Why?"

"Are you stupid? Sometimes I rent places out the way I buy things. I don't ask those guys for a passport any more than I ask you for a sales receipt."

"Got it. But you make those guys pay rent as high as the prices you give me are low."

"You've got to make ends meet. One of my cousins has a nice rooming house on rue Saint-Honoré, even though his wife is a good seamstress who employs as many as twenty workers on site or as pieceworkers."

"Hey, you old curmudgeon, there must be some lookers in there, huh?"

"You bet! There are two or three that I've seen bringing in their work now and then. Lordy, those girls are nice! One little one in particular who works in her own room, who's always laughing—her name's Rigolette. Good Lord, sonny boy, what I'd give to be twenty again!"

"All right, pops, cold showers or I'll pull the fire alarm!"

"But it's only natural, my boy. Only natural."

"Old letch! All right, you were saying that your cousin . . ."

"My cousin keeps an orderly house. And since he lives in the same place as that little Rigolette . . ."

"Is that true?"

"As the day is long."

"Letch!"

"He only accepts tenants with passports or papers. But if someone comes along without any, he knows that I'm less choosy and he sends their business my way."

"And those people pay more as a result?"

"Always."

"But those who don't have papers must all be jailbirds and the like!"

"Oh, no! You know, as to that my cousin just sent me someone like that a few days ago. Devil take me if I knew what it was all about. Another round?"

"Sure. It's good drink. To your health, Old Micou!"

"To yours, my boy! I was telling you that the other day my cousin sent me some customers, and I can't make out the business at all. Can you imagine, a mother and her daughter who looked like their gooses were plucked, feathered, and cooked. They were carrying all they were worth around in a little scarf. Well, it can't have been much, since they don't have any papers and they live on the fifth floor; since they've been here they haven't stirred one bit. No men ever go in to see them, sonny boy, no men. But if they weren't so thin and pale, they'd be two nice pieces—the girl, especially! She's maybe fifteen or sixteen at most. She's as white as a white rabbit, with eyes that are this big. Golly, what eyes! What eyes!"

"You're gonna get your fires burning again. And what do these two women do?"

"I'm telling you, I have no idea. They seem to be respectable, yet they don't have any papers. There's also the fact that they receive letters without addresses. There must be something wrong with their name."

"What do you mean?"

"They sent my nephew André to the post office this morning to pick up a letter addressed to Madame X. Z. The letter was to come from Normandy, from a market town called Les Aubiers. They wrote it out on a piece of paper so André could have the information to retrieve the letter. You see, they can't be worth much, women who go by the name of X and Z. But all the same there are never any men around!"

"They won't pay you."

"You don't play tricks on old dogs like me. They rented a room without a fireplace that I charged them twenty francs every two weeks and made them pay in advance for. They might be sick, because they haven't left in two days. But whatever they've got, it isn't indigestion, because I don't think they've ever lit a fire to cook with since they arrived. But I keep coming back to the fact that there are no men and no papers."

"If that's the only kind of clients you get, Old Micou . . ."

"Oh, they come and go. I may rent to people without passports, you know, but I also rent to people who know what they're about. Right now I've got two traveling salesmen, a clerk from the post office, the conductor of the orchestra from the Blind Man's Café, and a woman of independent means. They're all honest people. They're the ones who'll make the reputation of the house if the inspector starts looking too closely at things. They're not tenants who you keep in the dark. They're full light-of-day tenants."

"When you have enough light to see your way, you mean. Right, Old Micou?"

"You joker! Another round?"

"All right, but this is the last one. I've got to get going. By the way, does Robin, the big gimp, still live there?"

"Up top, the door next to the mother and daughter. He's gone through all the money he got in prison. I don't think he has hardly any more."

"Hey, you should watch out. He's breaking probation!"

"I know, but I can't get him off my back. I think he's planning some heist. Little Gammy, Red-Arm's kid, came here looking for him the other evening with Fishhook. I'm afraid that damned Robin might do something bad to my good tenants. Once his two weeks are up, I'm throwing him out. I'll tell him that I'm renting his room to an ambassador or to the husband of Madame de Saint-Ildefonse, my lady with the property."

"Lady with property?"

"You bet! Three bedrooms and another room that looks out on the street, and nothing less. Her rooms are all newly refurnished, and on top of that, there's the attic apartment her servant lives in. Eighty francs a month, paid in advance by her uncle. She keeps a room for him too when he visits from country property and needs a pied-à-terre. I think his country property is somewhere around rue Vivienne or rue Saint-Honoré, somewhere in that area."

"I get it. She's a lady with property because the old guy pays her her interest."

"You be quiet! Here comes her servant right now!"

A woman of advanced age wearing a white apron of dubious cleanliness entered the dealer's shop.

"What can I do for you, Madame Charles?"

"Old Micou, is your nephew around?"

"He's running errands at the main post office. He'll be back soon."

"Monsieur Badinot would like him to take this letter right away to the address on it. He needn't wait for an answer, but it's very urgent."

"He'll be on his way in a quarter of an hour, Madame Charles."

"He should hurry."

"Don't worry." The servant left.

"Is that the servant of one of your tenants, Old Micou?"

"Oh, no, silly. She's the servant of my propertied lady, Madame de Saint-Ildefonse. But Monsieur Badinot is her uncle. He came yesterday from the countryside," said the landlord as he examined the letter. Then he added as he read the address, "Hey, listen to this! He's got some fancy acquaintances! When I tell you we've got some people who know what they're about, this is what I'm talking about. He's writing to a viscount."

"Yeah, right!"

"Look for yourself: 'To Monsieur the Viscount de Saint-Remy, rue de Chaillot. Very urgent. Confidential.' When you rent to property owners who have uncles who write to viscounts, I should think you can afford not to look too closely at the passports of a few tenants who live on the top floors of the house, no?"

"You sure can. All right, Old Micou, I'll see you in a little bit. I've got to tie my dog to your door along with the cart. I'll carry what I need on foot. Get my purchases and my money ready. That way I can just leave straightaway from here."

"Don't worry. Four good pieces of sheet metal measuring two square feet apiece, three iron bars of three feet, and two hinges for your valve. That valve seems funny to me. Oh, well, whatever. Is that it?"

"Yes. And my money?"

"And your money. But tell me, before you go, I have to tell you something, since you're here. I'm looking you over . . ."

"And so?"

"I don't know, but it looks like something's up with you."

"Me?"

"Yes."

"You're crazy. If something's up with me, it's that I'm hungry!"

"You're hungry . . . Hmm. That's possible, but it looks like you're trying to act all happy, while deep down something's grating your gut. You've got something gnawing at your conscience, as they say. If there's something itching at you like that, it must be pretty fierce, because you're no shrinking violet."

"I tell you, Old Micou, you're crazy," said Nicolas, giving out a shiver in spite of himself.

"It looks like you were just trembling, you see."

"My arm's hurting me."

"So don't forget my remedy. It'll fix you up in no time."

"Thanks, Old Micou. See you soon." And the bandit left.

After concealing the copper ingots behind the counter, the receiver of stolen goods was busy putting together the different objects Nicolas had ordered from him, when a new customer entered his shop. This was a man of approximately fifty. He had a sharp, shrewd face and wore thick, bushy whiskers and gold spectacles. He was dressed with great care. The long sleeves of his brown overcoat had black velvet cuffs; beneath them one could see that he was wearing straw-colored gloves. His boots looked as if they had been polished the day before to a brilliant shine. This was Monsieur Badinot, the uncle of the propertied lady, the same Madame de Saint-Ildefonse whose social position was the pride and joy of Old Micou.

Perhaps one will remember that Monsieur Badinot, who was once an attorney who had been disbarred and then became a swindler and agent for businesses of dubious propriety, was now serving as a spy for the Baron de Graün and had given this diplomat considerable and precise information on a number of characters in this story.

"Madame Charles just gave you a letter to deliver," said Monsieur Badinot to the landlord.

"Yes, sir. My nephew will be back in just a moment, and he'll take it right away."

"No, give the letter back to me. I changed my mind. I'll go myself to see the Viscount de Saint-Remy," said Monsieur Badinot, pronouncing this aristocratic address emphatically and pompously.

"Here's the letter, monsieur. Do you need anything else?"

"No, Old Micou," said Monsieur Badinot, patronizingly. "But I do have some complaints to make to you."

"To me, monsieur?"

"Yes. Serious complaints."

"Really, monsieur?"

"It is certainly the fact that Madame de Saint-Ildefonse pays a great deal for your first floor. My niece is the kind of tenant to whom one owes the greatest deference. She came to this house in all confidence, wanting to avoid the noise of traffic, hoping to live here as if it were the countryside."

"And she does live that way. It's like a little hamlet here. You must see that, monsieur, because you live in the country. It's like a real hamlet here."

"A hamlet! That's a pretty notion! There's always an infernal racket here!"

"Yet it would be impossible to find a more tranquil house. Over Madame live the conductor of the orchestra of the Blind Man's Café and a traveling salesman. Over them, there's another traveling salesman. Over him, there's a—"

"I'm not talking about those people. They're quiet and decent. They suit my niece well enough. But on the fourth floor there's a big fellow whom Madame de Saint-Ildefonse met yesterday drunk again on the staircase. He was shouting like a wild animal. She was almost beside herself, she was so frightened. If you think your house is anything like a quiet hamlet with tenants like that—"

"Monsieur, I swear to you that I am just looking for the right opportunity to show that lame guy the door. He paid me his last fortnight in advance; otherwise, he'd already be out the door."

"You shouldn't have taken him in as a tenant."

"But other than him, I don't think Madame has anything to complain of. There's a clerk from the small post office who's the most respectable person imaginable. Over him, next to the big gimp, there are a woman and her daughter who never stir."

"I say once more, Madame de Saint-Ildefonse is only complaining about the lame fat man. That character is a nightmare to have around here! I'm warning you: if you keep him, he'll make all your respectable people leave."

"I'll get rid of him, don't worry. I have no interest in having him around."

"And you'll be doing the right thing, because no one would have any interest in staying in your house otherwise."

"Which wouldn't be in my interest. And so, monsieur, you can consider the fat lame man as someone who's already gone, for he only has four more days left here."

"That's too long. Well, it's your business. At the next outburst, my niece will be moving out."

"Don't worry, monsieur."

"I tell you this for your own good. Take advantage of this warning. I'm only telling you once," said Monsieur Badinot, in a patronizing fashion. At this, he left.

Need we say that this woman and this girl, living in such solitary circumstances, were the two victims of the solicitor's greed? We will now lead the reader into the sad hovel where they lived.

CHAPTER 5

VICTIMS OF EMBEZZLEMENT

(For convictions of embezzlement, the average penalty is two months in prison and a twenty-five-franc fine. Art. 406 and 408 of the Penal Code.)

When charity is given from the soul to those who suffer,
it is worth as much as the gift of bread . . .

The reader should picture a small room situated on the fourth floor of the sad house on the passage de la Brasserie.

A pale and somber day was barely making its way into this narrow room through a small window with just one casement that had three filthy, cracked panes in it. Dilapidated yellowish wallpaper covered the walls. From the corners of the cracked ceiling hung thick spiderwebs. The floor was missing tiles in many spots, exposing the beams and slats that underlay the tiles. A white wooden table, a chair, an old trunk without a lock, and a trestle bed equipped with a wooden headboard and a thin mattress, rough, unbleached linen sheets, and an old brown wool blanket: such were the furnishings that came with the room.

The Baroness de Fermont sat on the chair. Mademoiselle Claire de Fermont lay in the bed (these were the names of Jacques Ferrand's victims). Having only one bed between them, the mother and daughter took turns sleeping in it, dividing the hours of the night into shifts.

Too much anxiety and worry tormented the mother for her to be able to sleep very often. Her daughter, however, managed to find at least some relief and abandon in slumber. At this moment, she was asleep.

Nothing could be more touching or more painful than this portrait of poverty imposed upon the two women by the solicitor's greed. Until recently, they had been accustomed to the modest cushioning of a life of ease; they had been treated in their native city with all of the consideration befitting a family that was honorable and honored. Madame de Fermont was about thirty-six years old. Her face was full of sweetness and nobility. She had been considered a remarkable beauty earlier in her life, but her features were now pale and altered. She wore her black hair parted and flattened into plaits that were twisted up behind her head. Her sorrow had already turned some of her locks silver. Wearing a mourning dress that had been mended in several places, Madame de Fermont held her forehead in her hands, with her elbows on her daughter's miserable bedside. She looked at her daughter in inexpressible pain.

Claire was only sixteen years old. The ingenuous, soft profile of her face, gaunt like her mother's, stood out against the gray of the rough sheets that covered her bolster that was filled with sawdust. The girl's complexion had lost its brilliant beauty. The double fringe of long black eyelashes reached out from her large closed eyes to rest on her hollow cheeks. Once pink and moist but now dry and pale, her partly open lips revealed the white enamel of her teeth. The rude contact with the rough sheets and the wool bedcover had left the delicate skin of the girl's neck, shoulders, and arms red and blotchy in many spots.

From time to time, a light shudder brought her thin, velvety eyebrows together, as if she had been oppressed by a painful dream. The appearance of this face, already stamped with a morbid look, was painful to see. One could read on it the sinister symptoms of a lurking, threatening illness.

Madame de Fermont's tears had dried up long ago. She looked at her daughter with a dry eye inflamed by the slow fever that was silently eating away at her. Each day, Madame de Fermont grew weaker. Like her daughter, she felt the presence of a crushing unease that was the certain precursor of a grave and latent illness. Fearful of alarming Claire, though, and above all wishing not to alarm herself, if such a thing may be said, she struggled with all of her forces against the first signs of illness.

From the same generous motives, Claire tried to hide her suffering in order not to worry her mother. These two unfortunate creatures, who experienced the same sorrows, would have to experience the same pains as well. When misfortune reaches its supreme moment, the future shows itself in such a frightening fashion that the boldest individuals, not daring to look it in the face, close their eyes and try to fool themselves with irrational illusions. Such was the state of Madame and Mademoiselle de Fermont.

To describe the torments of this woman during the long hours that she contemplated her sleeping child in this way, thinking of the past, the present, and the future, would be to depict that which the noble and holy suffering of a mother has in it that is most poignant, desperate, and irrational: enchanting memories, sinister fears, terrible premonitions, bitter regrets, mortal despondency, outbursts of impotent rage against the author of so many evils, vain supplications, violent prayers, and in the end—in the end, terrifying doubts as to the omnipotent justice of the one who remains inexorable in the face of this cry, torn from the maternal entrails—this sacred cry that must nevertheless echo to the skies: "Have mercy on my daughter!"

"She's so cold now!" said the poor mother as she lightly touched the icy arms of her child with her own icy hand. "She's really cold. An hour ago she was burning up. It's the fever! Fortunately, she doesn't know she has it. My God, she's cold! This cover is so thin, too . . . I would put my old shawl on the bed, but if I took it off the door where I've hung it, those drunken men would come back again and look through the holes around the lock or through the disjointed boards of the doorframe . . . Good God, what a dreadful house! If I had known what kind of people were living here before I paid our fortnight in advance, we never would have stayed here. But I didn't know. Without papers, other boarding-houses won't accept you. How could I predict that I would ever need a passport? When I left Angers in my carriage, not thinking it a good idea for my daughter to travel by public transportation, who would have believed that—"

Then, breaking off, she said, in a burst of anger, "But this is really an outrage! Because that solicitor decided to fleece me, here I am, reduced to the most appalling extremities, and there is nothing in my power I can do to oppose him! Nothing! If I had had any money, I could have taken him to court . . . Taken him to court . . . only to hear the memory of my good and noble brother dragged through the mud, to hear people say that, having ruined himself, he killed himself after having wasted all of the fortune belonging to me and my daughter. To go to court, only to hear it said that he had reduced us to this poverty! Oh! Never! Never!

"Yet if my brother's memory is sacred, the life and future of my daughter are also sacred to me. But I have no proof against the solicitor, so I would just be creating a useless scandal.

"But what's really appalling," she said, after a moment of silence, "is that sometimes, when this atrocious fate makes me feel bitter and angry, I reach the point of accusing my brother and thinking that the solicitor was right about him, as if, by having two names to curse, my pain could somehow be assuaged. Then I get angry at myself for having such unfair, odious suspicions against the best and most loyal of brothers. Oh! That solicitor does not know all of the frightful consequences of his theft. He thought he was only stealing money, but he is torturing two souls, two women whom he's killing slowly, by degrees.

"Alas! I don't dare to tell my poor child all of my fears, because I don't want to make her miserable. But I'm in pain. I have the fever myself. I hold myself up only by force of will. I can feel the beginnings of disease in me. Maybe even a dangerous illness; yes, I feel it coming on. It's getting closer: my chest is burning and my head is splitting. These symptoms are more serious than I'm willing to recognize. My God, if I were to fall sick . . . if I were to die . . . No! No!" cried Madame de Fermont with fervor. "I don't want to die. To leave Claire, at sixteen, without any resources, alone, abandoned in the middle of Paris . . . I can't do that! No! I'm not sick, after all. What are my symptoms, after all? My chest's a little hot, my head's a little heavy. It's because of all this worrying, insomnia, cold, and anxiety. Anyone in my shoes would feel as beaten down by it as I do. But there's nothing really serious going on. Enough of this weakness. God! When I give in to ideas like that, when I hear myself going on like that, that's how I'm going to get sick! As if I had the leisure to do that, really! Shouldn't I be trying to find work for myself and Claire, since that man who gave us engravings to tint . . ."

After a moment of silence, Madame de Fermont added, in indignation, "Oh! It's abominable! Taking this work at the cost of Claire's dishonor! To take this puny means of subsistence away from us, without pity, all because I didn't want my daughter to go to work alone at night at his home! Maybe we'll find work elsewhere, sewing or embroidering. But it's so difficult when you don't know a soul! I've tried again recently, but to no avail. When you're living in such miserable conditions, you don't exactly inspire confidence in people. Yet once the small sum we have left is spent, what will we do? What will become of us? We will have nothing—absolutely nothing left to our names on this earth, not one farthing. And to think I was rich! Better not to think about that. Those thoughts make me lose my grip. They'll drive me crazy. That's my problem. I dwell too much on these things instead of trying to distract myself. That's what must have made me sick. No, no, I'm not sick. I think I'm even running less of a fever now," added the unhappy mother as she took her own pulse.

But alas, the racing, uneven, irregular pulse she felt under her cold, dry skin left her no room for any illusion of health. After a moment of gloomy, dark despair, she said, bitterly, "Oh, Lord! God! Why do you overwhelm us this way? What wrongs are we guilty of? Wasn't my daughter a model of honesty and piety? Her father, honor itself? Didn't I always bravely fulfill my duties as a wife and mother? Why have you let this wretch make us his victims? This poor child, most of all? When I think about the fact that, were it not for this solicitor's theft, I wouldn't have any fears about the fate of my daughter . . . We would be in our own home right now with no worries for the future, just sad and unhappy over the death of my poor brother. In two or three years, I would have looked to find a husband for Claire, and I would have found a man worthy of her, kind, charming, beautiful as she is! Who wouldn't have been happy to win her hand in marriage? I had thought to give her all I possessed upon her marriage, one hundred thousand crowns at least, only reserving a small pension for myself so that I could live near her. Because I could skimp on myself a bit, and when a young lady as pretty and well raised as my beloved child has a dowry of more than a hundred thousand crowns . . ."

Then, returning to the painful contrast of her present state, Madame de Fermont cried out in a sort of delirium, "But I can't just stand by and watch patiently as my daughter—my daughter, who deserves so much happiness—is reduced to the most frightful poverty, just because the solicitor will have it so. The law may allow this crime to go unpunished, but I will not. Because ultimately, if fate pushes me to the end of my rope, if I don't find any way out of the atrocious state to which that wretch has condemned me and my child, I don't know what I'll do . . . I would be capable of killing that man with my own two hands. They can do what they like to me afterward. All the mothers in the world would be on my side . . . Yes . . . But what about my daughter, then? My daughter! Could I leave her all alone, abandoned? That's my fear; that's why I don't want to die. That's why I can't kill that man. What would become of her? She's sixteen years old. She's young and as pure as an angel. But she's so beautiful! Abandonment, poverty, hunger: what frightening perils could all these terrifying hardships bring to a child of her age! And then . . . and then, what abyss might she fall into?

"Oh, it's horrifying! The more I dwell on this word, 'poverty,' the more I find it appalling in so many ways. Poverty! Poverty treats everyone atrociously, but it may be most cruel to those who have always led a life of ease. The thing I can't forgive myself for is my failure to overcome my miserable pride in the face of such perilous evil. Before I could resign myself to begging, I needed to see my daughter absolutely in the throes of starvation. What a coward I am!"

And then she added, with dark bitterness, "That solicitor has reduced me to begging, but I must cease to attend to all the demands of my position in life. I need to abandon my scruples and my delicate feelings. Those were fine before, but now I need to hold out my hand on my daughter's behalf, and my own. If I can't find any work, I'll just have to beg for the charity of strangers, since that's what the solicitor will have left us to.

"There's surely a skill in begging, an art to it that comes with experience. I will learn it. It's a trade like any other," she added in a delirious outburst. "It seems to me that my story has everything necessary for evoking sympathy: horrible, undeserved misfortunes; a sixteen-year-old daughter who's an angel. I just have to figure out how to make the most—how to be bold enough to make the most—of these advantages. But I'll get there. After all, what do I have to complain of?" she shouted with a sinister burst of laughter. "Wealth is precarious and apt to be short-lived. The solicitor has at least taught me an occupation."

Madame de Fermont remained absorbed in thought for a moment. Then she continued, more calmly, "I have often thought of asking for a job. I envy the lot of the servant of the woman who lives on the first floor. If I had her position, perhaps I would be able to meet Claire's needs with my wages. Perhaps, with that woman's care, I would be able to find some work for my daughter, who could stay here. That way, I wouldn't have to leave her. How happy I would be if things could work out that way! Oh, no, no, it's too much to hope for—it would be a dream come true. And then, to take her place, I'd have to somehow get that servant fired, and then her fate might be as unhappy as our own. Oh, well, too bad, too bad. Has anyone had any scruples about fleecing us? My daughter comes before everything else. All right: how do I manage to get myself introduced to the woman on the first floor and inside her home? And by what means can I turn her servant out? That position would be beyond our wildest dreams."

Two or three violent knocks on the door made Madame de Fermont start and jolted her daughter awake as well.

"Goodness, Mother, what's wrong?" cried Claire, sitting up abruptly. Then, in an automatic movement, she threw her arms around her mother's neck. Her mother, also frightened, pressed herself against her daughter as she looked at the door in terror.

"Mama, what is it?" repeated Claire.

"I don't know, my child. Don't worry. It's nothing. It's only someone knocking. Maybe it's someone bringing us a response from general delivery."[141]

At that instant, the worm-eaten door shook anew under the shock of several vigorous blows.

"Who's there?" said Madame de Fermont in a trembling voice.

A base, raucous, angry voice answered, "So, are you people deaf? Hey, neighbors! Hey!"

"What do you want? Monsieur, I don't know you," said Madame de Fermont, trying to cover up the tremor in her voice.

"It's Robin, your neighbor. Give me a light for my pipe! Come on! Get a move on!"

"Oh, God! It's that lame man who's always drunk," whispered the mother to her daughter.

"Come on! Give me a light for my pipe, or I'll knock your door down, I swear to God!"

"Monsieur, I don't have any lights."

"You've got to have some lucifers. Everyone has lucifers. Open your door! Come on!"

"Go away, monsieur."

"You don't want to open your door? One . . . two . . ."

"I beg you to go away or I will call—"

---

141. Called *poste restante* in both France and England. It is a service by which the post office holds mail addressed to someone until he or she calls for it. [TN]

"One . . . two . . . three . . . no? You're not going to open the door? Fine. I'll wreck everything. Here we go!" And the wretch gave the door such a furious blow that it fell open, the miserable lock that closed it having given way.

The two women cried out in fear.

Madame de Fermont, despite her weakness, rushed in front of the criminal as he put one foot into the room, and she barred him from entering. "Monsieur, this is outrageous! You will not enter!" cried the unfortunate mother as she held shut the partially open door with all her strength. "I'm going to cry for help!" She shivered at the sight of this man with his hideous, wine-reddened face.

"What's your problem?" he said. "Don't neighbors help each other out? You should have opened the door for me. I wouldn't have knocked it in if you had." Then, with the stupid obstinacy of drunkenness, he added, as he teetered on his legs of unequal length, "I want to come in, so I'll come in. And I'm not going to leave until I've gotten a light for my pipe."

"I don't have any lights, and I don't have any lucifers. In heaven's name, monsieur, leave!"

"That's not true. You're saying that so I won't see the little one who's sleeping there. Yesterday you plugged up the holes in the door. She's nice. I want to have a look at her. Take care. I'll crack your skull if you don't let me in. I'm telling you that I'm going to get a look at the little girl in her bed and that I'm going to get a light for my pipe. Otherwise, I'm going to break everything apart, and you along with it!"

"Help! Help us, God! Help!" cried Madame de Fermont, feeling the door give way under the pressure of a violent blow from the shoulder of the fat lame man.

Intimidated by her cries, the man backed away from the door, raised his fist to Madame de Fermont, and said to her, "You'll pay for this. I'll come back tonight and I'll take hold of your tongue so you can't scream." And at this, the big gimp, as they called him on the Scavenger's Island, went downstairs, making terrible threats along his way.

Seeing the broken lock and fearing that he might return, Madame de Fermont dragged the table against the door in order to barricade it. Claire was so moved, so shaken from this scene that she had fallen back onto her pallet and was lying there almost immobile, in the grips of a nervous fit. Madame de Fermont ran to her daughter, forgetting her own fear. She held her in her arms, made her drink some water, and managed to bring her back to consciousness through her caring and caresses. Soon, she saw her slowly returning to her senses and said to her, "It's all right . . . Calm down, my poor child. That bad man went away."

Then the unfortunate mother cried out in indignation and unspeakable pain, "But it's that solicitor who is the source of all our pain!"

Claire looked around the room, as much in bewilderment as in fear. "Don't worry, my child," said Madame de Fermont as she kissed her daughter tenderly. "That wretch has left."

"But heavens, Mama, what if he comes back? You saw that you cried out for help and no one came. Oh! Please, let's leave this house! I'm going to die of fear here!"

"You're shivering! You have a fever."

"No, no," said the girl to reassure her mother. "It's nothing. It's just fear. It'll pass. And you? How are you? Give me your hands. Heavens! They're so hot! Look at you—you're the one who's in pain. You're trying to hide it from me."

"Don't you believe any such thing. I'm feeling better than ever! It's just the emotion that man caused me that's making me look like this. I was sleeping very soundly on the chair. I woke up at the same time as you."

"But, Mama, your poor eyes are so red and inflamed!"

"Oh, you know, sleep is less restful on a chair, my child. You understand, don't you?"

"Really, you're not in pain?"

"No, no, I assure you I'm not. What about you?"

"Me, neither. I'm just shivering from fear, still. Please, Mama, I beg you: let's leave this place!"

"Where would we go? You know how hard it was to find this nasty little room. Unfortunately, we don't have papers, and also, we paid two weeks in advance, which they won't return to us. We have so little money left that we'll have to stretch it as much as we can."

"Maybe Monsieur de Saint-Remy will answer you one of these days."

"I have no hope left that he will. I wrote to him so long ago."

"He must not have received your letter. Why don't you write to him again? It's not so far from here to Angers. We'll get his answer quickly."

"My poor child, you know how hard it was to write to him in the first place."

"What do you have to lose? He's so kind, in spite of his brusqueness. Wasn't he one of my father's best friends? And then, he's our relative, too."

"But he's poor himself. His fortune is quite modest. Perhaps he has not answered us in order to avoid the pain of turning us down."

"But what if he never got your letter, Mama?"

"And if he did get it, my child? It's one of two things: either he is in too tight a position himself to be able to help us, or he doesn't care about us at all. So what good does it do us to set ourselves up for rejection or humiliation?"

"Come on, Mama. Take heart. We still have one hope left. Maybe we'll have a positive answer today."

"From Monsieur d'Orbigny?"

"Surely. The letter you drafted before was so simple, so touching. You portrayed our misfortune in such a natural way that he'll have to take pity on us. Honestly, something tells me that you're wrong to give up on him."

"He has so little reason to care about us! It's true that he knew your father long ago, and I often heard my poor brother talking about Monsieur d'Orbigny as a man with whom he was on very good terms before he left Paris to retire to Normandy with his young wife."

"That's exactly what makes me have hope. He has a young wife, and she'll be compassionate. And then, in the country, there's so much good you can do! I suppose he can hire you as a housekeeper, and I can work in the laundry. Since Monsieur d'Orbigny is very rich and lives in a big house, there will always be work."

"Yes, but we have so few claims upon him."

"We're so unhappy!"

"That gives us a claim on very charitable people, it's true."

"Let's hope that Monsieur d'Orbigny and his wife are very charitable people, then."

"Well, if it turns out we can expect nothing from him, I'll overcome my false shame once again and I'll write to the Duchess de Lucenay."

"Isn't that the lady Monsieur de Saint-Remy talked so often about with us, the one he kept saying had such a good heart and was so generous?"

"Yes, she's the daughter of the Prince de Noirmont. He knew her when she was a little girl, and he treated her almost as if she were his daughter, for he was very close to the prince. Madame de Lucenay must know many people. She might be able to help us find positions."

"I'm sure she will, Mama. But I understand your reservations. You don't know her at all, whereas at least my father and my poor uncle knew Monsieur d'Orbigny a little."

"In the end, if Madame de Lucenay can't do anything for us, I still have one last hope."

"What is that?"

"It's a long shot. It might be folly to have any hopes for its success. But why shouldn't we give it a try? Monsieur de Saint-Remy's son is—"

"Monsieur de Saint-Remy has a son?" cried Claire, interrupting her mother in her surprise.

"Yes, my child, he has a son."

"He never mentioned it. The son never came to Angers."

"Well, in fact, for reasons that I can't tell you, Monsieur de Saint-Remy hasn't seen his son in fifteen years, ever since he left Paris."

"Fifteen years without seeing his father? Heavens, how can that be?"

"Alas, yes, so you can see . . . I will say that Monsieur de Saint-Remy's son has made quite a splash in society, and he's very rich."

"He's very rich? And his father is poor?"

"All of Monsieur de Saint-Remy's fortune comes by way of his mother."

"But that shouldn't matter. How can he leave his father—"

"His father wouldn't take anything from him, anyway."

"Why is that?"

"That's another question I'm not at liberty to answer, my dear child. But I've heard from my poor brother that people say the young man is very generous. If he's young and generous, he must be kind. So when he learns from me that my husband was his father's close friend, perhaps he'll take an interest in us and try to find us some work or a position. He has so many and such brilliant social connections that it would be easy for him to help us."

"And then perhaps we may find out through him whether his father, Monsieur de Saint-Remy, had left Angers before you wrote to him. That would explain his silence."

"I don't believe, my child, that Monsieur de Saint-Remy has kept any contact with any of his relatives, my child. Well, we can always give it a try."

"Unless Monsieur d'Orbigny answers you in a positive fashion. And I'll tell you again: I don't know why, but I have high hopes."

"But I wrote to him several days ago, my child, telling him all about our misfortune. And he's written nothing back—nothing yet. A letter put in the mail before four o'clock in the afternoon should arrive the next morning at the Aubiers estate. We could have had an answer from him five days ago."

"Maybe he's trying to figure out how he might help us before writing back."

"May God hear your prayers, my child!"

"It seems perfectly clear to me, Mama. If he couldn't do anything to help us, he would have written back right away to tell us so."

"Unless he doesn't wish to do anything for us."

"Oh, Mama! How could that be possible? Could he refuse to answer us and leave us hoping for four days, maybe even a week—for when you're unhappy, you keep on hoping?"

"Alas, my child, people are sometimes so uncaring about the suffering of strangers."

"But your letter . . ."

"My letter gave him no idea of our anxiety, of our constant suffering. Could my letter depict our unhappy life, all of the different humiliations we undergo, our existence in this appalling house, the fear we had again just now? Could my letter depict for him the horrible future that awaits us if— But come, my child, let's not speak of this any longer. My God, you're trembling . . . you're cold!"

"No, Mama. Don't pay any attention to that. But tell me: suppose that all our chances fail us? Suppose that the little bit of money we have left in this suitcase is all spent? Is it possible that in a city as rich as Paris, we could both die of hunger and poverty? All because we can't find work and because a wicked man took everything you had?"

"Be quiet, unhappy girl."

"But, Mama, tell me: is it possible?"

"Alas!"

"But God knows everything and can do anything. How could He abandon us like this when we've never done anything to offend Him?"

"I beg of you, child, not to dwell on such depressing thoughts. I would rather see you have hope, even if it's irrational. Come now, reassure me with your dear illusions. I get discouraged too easily as it is, as you know all too well."

"Yes! Yes! Let's not give up hope. That's the best thing. The porter's nephew is going to come back from general delivery today with a letter for us, for sure. Another errand we had to pay for out of your little stash, and it's my fault. If I hadn't been so weak yesterday and today, we could have gone to the post office ourselves, like the day before yesterday . . . but you didn't want to go there yourself and leave me alone."

"How could I, my child? Come on, think about it. A little while ago, that wretch broke our door down. What if you had been alone in here?"

"Oh, Mama! Don't talk about it! Even thinking about it scares me."

At this moment there was a sudden knock at the door. "Heavens! It's him again!" cried Madame de Fermont, still recovering from her first terrifying encounter with him. She pushed the table against the door with all her might. Her fears abated when she heard the voice of Old Micou.

"Madame, my nephew André has come back from general delivery. He's picked up a letter addressed to an X and a Z. It comes from far away. It's eight sous for the postage, plus the commission. It comes to twenty sous."

"Mama, a letter from the provinces! We're saved! It's from Monsieur de Saint-Remy or Monsieur d'Orbigny! Poor mother, you won't have to suffer any longer. You won't have to worry about me—you'll be happy. God is just; God is good!" cried the girl, and a ray of hope illuminated her sweet and charming face.

"Oh, thank you, monsieur! Give it to me—give it to me right away!" said Madame de Fermont, knocking the table aside in her haste and opening the door partway.

"It comes to twenty sous, madame," said the receiver of stolen goods as he waved the long-awaited letter in front of her.

"I will pay you, monsieur."

"Ah, madame, indeed! There's no rush. I'm going up to the garret upstairs. I'll be back down in ten minutes. I can pick up the money on my way down." The dealer gave the letter to Madame de Fermont and disappeared.

"The letter is from Normandy. The stamp says Les Aubiers: it's from Monsieur d'Orbigny!" cried Madame de Fermont as she examined the address: "To Madame X. Z., poste restante, Paris."[142]

"Well, Mama, wasn't I right? Heavens, how my heart is pounding!"

"Our fate, for better or for worse, is in here," said Madame de Fermont in an emotional voice, pointing at the letter. Twice her trembling hand approached the seal in order to break it, but lacked the courage. How can one hope to depict the terrible anguish to which people in Madame de Fermont's position are prey when they know that a letter will lead to hope or despair?

The burning and feverish emotion of the gambler, panting, eyes aflame, who has staked his last chips on a card, awaiting the decisive moment that will bring him ruin or salvation: this violent emotion barely gives an idea of the terrible anguish of which we speak. In one second the soul may ascend to the most glorious heights or fall into mortal despair. This unfortunate individual moves quickly from one violent emotion to another, depending on whether he believes himself to be rescued or repulsed. From indescribable bursts of happiness and gratitude toward the generous heart that has felt sorry for the victim of a miserable fate, bitter and painful resentment against selfish indifference!

When it comes to the deserving poor, those who give money often would perhaps give money always, and those who refuse always would perhaps give often, if they knew or if they saw the hope of benevolent support or fear of a dismissive refusal—if they only knew the ineffable happiness or terror their whim produced in the hearts of those who begged their assistance.

"What weakness!" said Madame de Fermont, smiling sadly as she sat on her daughter's bed. "Once again, my poor Claire, our fate is there." She gestured at the letter. "I'm dying to know what's in it, but at the

142. Madame de Fermont had written this letter in her last place of residence. Since she did not know at the time where she would be living, she had asked Monsieur d'Orbigny to answer her at the general delivery. However, without a passport to retrieve her letter with at the post office, she had given an address using initials that one had only to identify in order to retrieve the letter so addressed. [SN]

same time I don't dare. If it's a rejection, alas, it will always be soon enough to know."

"But if it's an offer of assistance, Mama? If this poor little letter contains good and consoling news for us that will reassure us as to our future? If it promises us a humble position in Monsieur d'Orbigny's house, isn't every minute we wait a minute of lost happiness?"

"Yes, my child; but if, on the contrary . . ."

"No, Mama, you're wrong. I'm sure you are. When I told you that Monsieur d'Orbigny would never have taken so long to answer you unless he wanted to be able to give you an answer that was definitely favorable . . . Let me read the letter, Mama. I'm sure I can guess just from looking at the handwriting whether the news is good or bad. Come now, I'm sure of it now," said Claire as she took the letter. "All you have to do is look at this good, simple, upright, firm writing to see that it's the work of an honest and generous hand, one that is in the habit of offering help to those who suffer."

"Claire, I beg of you: no more groundless hopes, or I'll be even more afraid to open this letter."

"Heavens! My dear little Mama, I can tell you more or less what it contains even without opening it. Listen to me: it says, 'Madame, your fate and that of your daughter are so worthy of my attention that I beg you to do me the favor to come to see me on the chance that you might wish to be my housekeeper.'"

"Have mercy, my child! I beg you once more: no more senseless hope. Awakening from it would be too frightful. All right, take heart," said Madame de Fermont, taking the letter from her daughter's hands and getting herself ready to open the seal.

"Take heart, indeed, and it's about time!" said Claire, smiling. She was carried away by the kind of confident outburst that is so natural in someone of her age. "As for me, I don't need to. I'm sure of what I'm telling you. Come on, would you like me to open the letter? Would you like me to read it? Give it to me, you scaredy-cat."

"Yes, I think I'd like it better that way. No, no—I should be the one to read it." And Madame de Fermont tore open the seal as her heart stood still.

Her daughter, just as emotional as her mother in spite of her apparent confidence, could hardly breathe. "Read it aloud, Mama," she said.

"The letter is not long. It's from the Countess d'Orbigny," said Madame de Fermont as she looked at the signature.

"So much the better. That's a good sign. You see, Mama? That excellent young lady must have wanted to answer you herself."

"We'll see." And Madame de Fermont read the following letter in a trembling voice:

Dear Madame,

As the Count d'Orbigny has been suffering terribly for some time, he could not answer you during my absence . . .

"You see, Mama? It's not his fault."
"Listen! Listen!"

Having just returned from Paris this morning, I wanted to write to you right away, madame, after having conferred with Monsieur d'Orbigny on the subject of your letter. He can only vaguely remember the friendship you say he had with your brother. As for your husband, madame, he recognizes his name but cannot remember the circumstances under which he heard him spoken of. The claimed ruination, which you impute with so little ground to Monsieur Jacques Ferrand, whom we have the happiness to employ as our family solicitor, M. d'Orbigny considers a cruel calumny whose implications you have surely not considered. Like myself, madame, my husband knows and admires the sterling honesty of the respectable and pious man whom you attack so blindly. This is to say, madame, that Monsieur d'Orbigny, while sympathizing with you over the unfortunate situation in which you find yourself—a situation whose true cause he is not in the position to investigate—is incapable of assisting you.

With Monsieur d'Orbigny's regrets,
and your humble servant,

The Countess d'Orbigny.

The mother and daughter looked at each other in a painful daze, incapable of saying a word.

Old Micou knocked at the door and said, "Madame, can I come in? I'm here to collect the postage and commission. It's twenty sous."

"Oh, of course! Such good news is surely worth what two days of subsistence costs us," said Madame de Fermont, smiling bitterly. And, leaving the letter on her daughter's bed, she went over to an old trunk without a clasp, bent over it, and opened it.

"We have been robbed!" cried the unfortunate woman in shock. "Nothing. There's nothing left," she added in a dejected voice. Crushed, she supported herself on the trunk.

"What are you saying, Mama? The sack of money . . ."

But, getting up suddenly, Madame de Fermont left the room and turned to the dealer, who was thus standing with her on the landing. "Monsieur," she said to him, her eyes aflame, her cheeks flushed with indignation and horror, "I had a sack of money in this trunk. I must have been robbed the day before yesterday because I went out for an hour with my daughter. We need to find that money. Do you understand? You are responsible for it."

"You've been robbed? That's not true. I run a respectable house," said the receiver of stolen goods with insolence and brutality. "You're saying that so you won't have to pay the postage and the commission."

"I am telling you, monsieur, that the money was all I possessed in the world, and that it has been stolen. It must be recovered, or I will file charges. Oh! I will show neither restraint nor respect, I'm warning you."

"That's a nice one, coming from someone who has no papers! Go ahead, file your complaint! Go on, do it right now! I dare you!"

The unhappy woman was stunned. She could not go out and leave her daughter alone in bed, where she had remained since the large lame man had frightened her that morning, and especially after the threats the dealer had just made to her.

The latter went on: "This is a scam. You don't have a bag of money any more than you have a bag of gold. You just don't want to pay me for the postage—isn't that what this is about? Fine! Fine with me. When you pass by my door, I'll just tear your old black shawl from off your shoulders. It's ratty, but it's still worth at least twenty sous."

"Oh, monsieur!" cried Madame de Fermont as she broke into tears. "Have mercy! Have pity on us! That small sum was all we possessed, my daughter and I. With that stolen, we have nothing left in the world. Nothing, do you understand? Nothing for us except to starve to death!"

"What do you want from me? If it's true that someone robbed you, and of money, no less (which seems suspicious to me), it got spent a long time ago . . . that money!"

"My God!"

"The fellow who did it wouldn't have been so agreeable as to mark the pieces and keep them here so he could get caught with them, if it's someone from this house, which I doubt. For, like I was telling the uncle of the lady on the first floor just this morning, this house is a real peaceful hamlet. If you got robbed, it's unfortunate. You could file a hundred thousand complaints and you wouldn't get a centime back for your trouble. You'd get nowhere. I'm telling you—believe me. Hey!" cried the receiver of stolen goods, breaking off as he saw Madame de Fermont staggering. "What's wrong with you? You're pale! Take care! Mademoiselle, your mother is ill," added the receiver of stolen goods as he stepped forward in enough time to catch the unhappy woman, who, struck to the heart by this last blow, felt herself going under. The artificial energy that had been sustaining her for so long had given way before this new blow.

"Mother! My God! What's wrong?" cried Claire, still in bed.

The receiver of stolen goods, still strong despite his fifty years, was seized for a fleeting moment with pity and took Madame de Fermont in his arms, pushed the door with his knee to enter the room, and said, "Mademoiselle, I apologize for entering while you are in bed, but I need to bring your mother in here to you. She's fainted. It can't last long."

When she saw this man enter the room, Claire cried out in fright, and the unfortunate child hid herself as best she could under her blanket.

The dealer placed Madame de Fermont in a chair next to the trestle bed and withdrew from the room, leaving the door ajar, the large lame man having broken the lock.

One hour after this last shock, the violent illness that had been developing and threatening Madame de Fermont broke out in full force. With a burning fever and in a terrible delirium, the poor woman lay in her daughter's bed. Her daughter, bewildered, in shock, all alone, and almost as sick as her mother, had no money and no one to turn to, and was afraid that at any moment she would see the criminal who lived on the same floor entering their room.

CHAPTER 6

RUE DE CHAILLOT

We will take an advance of a few hours on Monsieur Badinot, who was rushing from the passage de la Brasserie to see the Viscount de Saint-Remy. As we have said, the latter lived alone on rue de Chaillot in a charming little house built between a courtyard and a garden. Despite its proximity to the Champs-Élysées, the most fashionable area to stroll about in Paris, the neighborhood in which the house was located was isolated.

There is no need to enumerate the advantages that Monsieur de Saint-Remy, a man especially devoted to amorous conquests, could derive from the location of such a carefully selected home. Let us merely say that a woman could enter his home very conveniently through the little door off his large garden that opened on an absolutely deserted alley beginning at rue Marbeuf and ending at rue de Chaillot. And in addition, by an incredible stroke of fortune, one of Paris's most beautiful horticultural establishments had a seldom-used exit onto this passage. On the chance that Monsieur de Saint-Remy's mysterious female visitors met anyone unexpected or ran into any other surprises, they had a perfectly plausible and bucolic excuse at the ready for venturing onto the fateful little street. They could say that they were on their way to pick out some rare flowers at the establishment of a well-known gardener-florist who had a reputation for having beautiful hothouses.

These attractive visitors would have lied only in part, for the viscount, a man endowed with a taste for refined luxury, had a charming hothouse that extended partway down the little street we have mentioned. The little secret gate opened on this delicious winter garden that led into a boudoir (if we may be forgiven this outdated expression) situated on the ground floor of the house. Thus, one could say without employing the language of metaphor that a woman who crossed this dangerous threshold into Monsieur de Saint-Remy's home was led down a garden path to her destruction. For especially in the winter, this elegant alley was lined with bush after bush of brilliant, sweet-smelling flowers.

Jealous, as most passionate women are, Madame de Lucenay had demanded a key to this little gate.

If we devote even a little space to describing the general character of this unique dwelling, it is because it reflected the kind of degrading existence that is happily becoming rarer by the day, but one that should nonetheless be mentioned as one of the curiosities of the period. We are speaking here of the existence of men who are to women what courtesans are to men. For want of a better expression, we could call these fellows male courtesans, if such an expression might be permitted to us.

The interior of Monsieur de Saint-Remy's house was, from this perspective, rather curious in that its interior was divided into two completely separate zones: the ground floor, where he received women, and the first floor, where he hosted the male companions with whom he gambled, ate, and hunted—people one calls friends. Thus, there was a bedroom on the ground floor that was all gold, mirrors, flowers, satin, and lace, a little music room in which a harp and piano could be found (Monsieur de Saint-Remy was an excellent musician), a room containing paintings and curios, the boudoir that was connected to the hothouse, a dining room for two in which meals were served and dishes removed on a revolving platter, a luxurious bathroom modeled with Oriental refinement, and, close by, a little library whose contents partially followed the catalogue that La Mettrie had put together for Frederick the Great of Prussia.[143]

Of course, all of these rooms, furnished in exquisite taste and with a care worthy of Sardanapalus,[144] were decorated with little-known paintings by Watteau[145] or Boucher,[146] sculptures of unglazed porcelain or terra-cotta by Clodion,[147] and, on plinths of jasper or antique marble, several precious copies, in white marble, of the prettiest sculptures one could find in museums. In the summer all this was coupled with views of the green depths of a thickly planted, solitary garden, packed with flowers, full of birds, watered by a little brook of running water through it that, before showering the fresh lawn, fell from a rustic black boulder above, shining as it fell like a sheet of silver gauze and melting in a pearly blade into a limpid basin where beautiful white swans were gracefully playing. And of a warm, serene night, how the shadows, perfumes, and silence filled the fragrant groves where thick leaves served as a dais for the rustic sofas made of rushes and Indian mats! During the winter, on

143. Julien Offray de la Mettrie (1709–1751) was a French physician and materialist philosopher. In response to the outrage caused by his materialism and hedonism, La Mettrie fled France for Berlin, where he was welcomed by Frederick the Great, who made him a court reader. [TN]

144. See Book II, Chapter 13, footnote 59 and Book V, Chapter 5, footnote 122. [TN]

145. See Book II, Chapter 11, footnote 49. [TN]

146. François Boucher (1703–1770), also a Rococo painter, also known for sensual subject matter. [TN]

147. Claude Michel (1738–1814), known as Clodion, a Rococo sculptor whose preferred subject matters were nymphs, satyrs, and bacchantes. [TN]

the other hand, everything except for the glass door that led to the hothouse was tightly shut up. The transparent silk of the window blinds and the lace netting of the curtains made the daylight seem even more mysterious. An abundance of exotic plants seemed to overflow from large, sparkling, gold and enamel cups poised atop the furniture. In this silent retreat full of sweet-smelling flowers and voluptuous paintings, one inhaled a sort of amorous, intoxicating atmosphere that plunged the soul and senses into burning languors.

Lastly, to do the honors to this temple that seemed to be dedicated to ancient love or to the naked divinities of Greece, a young, handsome, elegant, and distinguished man, by turns spiritual or tender, romantic or libertine, one moment mocking and gay to the point of folly and the next full of charm and grace, an excellent musician, endowed with the kind of vibrant, passionate voice that women cannot hear in song without being deeply moved by it in an almost physical way, a man who was above all amorous, always amorous: such was the viscount. In Athens he would surely have been admired, exalted, deified as was Alcibiades.[148] In our days, and in the period of this story, the viscount was nothing more than a base forger, a miserable swindler.

The first floor of Monsieur de Saint-Remy's house, as opposed to the ground floor, had a completely virile look to it. This is where he received his numerous friends, all of whom belonged to the highest ranks of society. Here there was nothing coquettishly stylish, nothing effeminate. Simple and severe furnishings with handsome weapons as decoration, portraits of racehorses that had won many a magnificent gold or silver trophy for the viscount, all of which could be seen on the furniture. The smoking room and the game room were next to a cheerful dining room in which eight people (the number of guests being strictly limited when he was holding a dinner for the cognoscenti) had many times appreciated the excellence of his cook and the no less excellent quality of the viscount's cellar before playing a tense hand of whist against him for five or six hundred louis, or noisily shaking the dice cup in an infernal game of craps.

With these sharply contrasted areas of Monsieur de Saint-Remy's home exposed, the reader will perhaps be kind enough to follow us into the humbler parts of the house, to enter the coach yard and go up the little stairway that led to the very comfortable apartment of Edwards Patterson, Monsieur de Saint-Remy's stablemaster. This illustrious coachman had invited Monsieur Boyer, the viscount's trusted valet, to lunch. A very pretty English servant having withdrawn from the room after bringing them a teapot, our two characters remained alone.

Edwards was about forty years old. Never had a cleverer or more

148. See Book II, Chapter 13, footnote 55. [TN]

portly coachman made his seat groan under a more imposing rotundity, nor encased in his white wig a more florid face, nor held more elegantly the quadruple reins of a four-in-hand in his left hand. Edwards was as fine a connoisseur of horses as Tattersall in London, having been in his youth as good a trainer as the old and famous Chifney. The viscount had found in him something very rare: an excellent coachman and a man very capable of directing the training of the several racehorses he had acquired to take bets on.[149]

When he wasn't on display in his sumptuous brown and silver livery on the emblazoned cover of his seat, Edwards strongly resembled an honest English farmer. It is in this appearance that we present him to the reader, adding nonetheless that, under his large and colorful face, one could divine the pitiless and diabolical savvy of a horse dealer.

His guest, Monsieur Boyer, the viscount's trusted valet, was a tall, thin man, with flat gray hair, a receding hairline, a piercing gaze, and a cold, discreet, and reserved expression. He chose his words carefully, had polite, gracious manners, and had at least a little reading. He had conservative political opinions and could honorably hold his own as the lead violin in an amateur string quartet. From time to time, in the most distinguished manner imaginable, he took a pinch of snuff from a gold tobacco case covered in fine pearls, after which, with the back of his hand (that was as manicured as his master's), he negligently shook out the wrinkles from his fine Dutch linen shirt.

"Did you know, my dear Edwards," said Boyer, "that your servant Betty makes an acceptable home-cooked meal?"

"Indeed, she's a good girl," said Edwards, who spoke French perfectly, "and I'll bring her along with me if I decide to start a business. Speaking of which, since we're alone, my dear Boyer, can we talk business? You understand business matters quite well, I believe?"

"Me? Oh, yes, a bit," said Boyer modestly as he took some tobacco. "When one takes care of other people's business, one naturally picks it up."

"I would like your advice on a very important matter, then. That's why I've asked you to have a cup of tea with me."

"At your service, my dear Edwards."

"You know that, apart from taking care of the racehorses, I had a contract with the viscount to oversee his entire stable, animals and staff. That's to say, I manage eight horses and five or six grooms and am paid twenty-four thousand francs a year to do so, which includes my salary."

---

149. Richard Tattersall (1724–1795) began the organization that has become Tattersalls horse auction company. He may have meant Tattersall's cousin Edmund (1816–1898), who carried on the business. Samuel Chifney (1753–1807) was a famous English jockey. He invented the bit that was named after him. [TN]

"That's reasonable."

"For four years, the viscount paid me precisely what he owed me. But toward the middle of last year, he said to me, 'Edwards, I owe you about twenty-four thousand francs. How much would you estimate my horses and carriages to be worth, at a minimum?' 'Monsieur, the eight horses cannot be sold for less than three thousand francs each, on average, and that's dirt cheap,' which is true, Boyer, for the pair of carriage horses cost five hundred guineas. 'That means the horses are worth twenty-four thousand francs. As for the carriages, there are four; let's say twelve thousand francs, which together with the twenty-four thousand francs from the horses comes to thirty-six thousand francs.' 'Well!' said the viscount. 'Buy the whole lot of them from me at that price, on the condition that for the twelve thousand francs that you will owe me in return, that will be an advance on your salary and you'll manage and leave my horses, staff, and carriages at my disposition for six months.'"

"And you wisely accepted the deal, Edwards? The offer was highly advantageous."

"Of course. In two weeks, the six months will have passed, and I will come into ownership of the horses and carriages."

"Nothing could be clearer. The contract was executed by Monsieur Badinot, the viscount's business manager. Why do you need my advice?"

"What should I do? I can sell the horses and carriages in consequence of the viscount's departure, and I'll get a good price, for he is known to be the best connoisseur of horseflesh in Paris. Or should I establish myself as a horse dealer with that stable, which would give me a strong start in the business. What do you think I should do?"

"I advise you to do what I intend doing myself."

"What do you mean?"

"I am in the same position you are in."

"You?"

"The viscount hates petty details. I came here with savings and an inheritance of about sixty thousand francs or so, and I took care of the house expenses the same way you took care of the stable, and every year the viscount paid me, no questions asked. At about the same time as he made the offer to you, my condition was that I was owed about twenty thousand francs, and the suppliers were owed about sixty thousand. So, making the same offer to me as he made to you, the viscount proposed to reimburse me by selling me the furniture of the house, including the silver, which is very beautiful, the excellent paintings, etc. All told, it was estimated to be worth a hundred and forty thousand francs. He owed me eighty thousand francs, leaving sixty thousand francs that I would have to spend for the cost of meals, wages for the staff, etc., until they ran out. That was a condition of the deal."

"Because you made money on those expenses?"

"As a matter of course, for I made arrangements with the suppliers, whom I wouldn't pay until after the sale," said Boyer as he took a big pinch of snuff. "Thus, at the end of this month . . ."

"The furniture belongs to you, just as the horses and cars belong to me."

"So it seems. The viscount has managed in this way to live, during these last few months, the way he likes to live—like a lord—and he's done this in the face of his creditors. For the furnishings, silver, horses, cars, all had been paid for in cash when he came of age, and it has become our property."

"So the viscount will have bankrupted himself?"

"He's done it in five years."

"And the viscount inherited . . . ?"

"A measly million francs in cash," said Monsieur Boyer disdainfully as he took another pinch of snuff. "Add to that million two hundred thousand francs in debt, more or less, which is no small amount. So this is just to tell you, my dear Edwards, that I had planned to rent this admirably furnished house just the way it is to some Englishmen—linen, crystal, porcelain, silver, hothouse: some of your compatriots would have paid dearly for it."

"Surely they would. Why don't you do it?"

"Well, but unproductive property is risky. So I've decided to sell the furnishings. The viscount is so well known as a connoisseur equally of precious furnishings and of artworks that anything of his will always get twice its value. That way, I will make a nice round sum. Do what I'm doing, Edwards. Sell it, and don't risk your profits in speculation. You are the first coachman of the Viscount de Saint-Remy, so it's just a matter of who will want to hire you. I just heard yesterday about an emancipated minor, a cousin of the Duchess de Lucenay, the young Duke de Montbrison, who will be arriving from Italy with his tutor and who is putting together his household staff. At least two hundred and fifty thousand pounds of income in property, my dear Edwards, two hundred and fifty thousand pounds in income. Add to that, he's just starting off in life. Twenty years old, all the illusions that come with confidence, all the intoxication that comes with the money he has to spend, and as prodigal as a prince . . . I know the manager. I can tell you this in confidence: he has already almost agreed to take me on as first valet. He's treating me as a protégé, the fool!" And Monsieur Boyer shrugged his shoulders as he snorted a pinch of snuff.

"Are you hoping to drive him out?"

"Well, goodness, he's either a knave or a fool. He thinks of placing me there as if he had nothing to fear from me! Before two months are up, I'll occupy his place."

"Two hundred and fifty thousand pounds in income from the land rents!" said Edwards, lost in thought. "And he's a young man—it's a good position . . ."

"I'm telling you, you can get something out of this. I'll put in a good word for you with my patron," said Monsieur Boyer, sardonically. "If you enter service there, you're associating yourself with a fortune that has deep roots, the kind you can cling to for a long time. It's not like that viscount's measly million, a mere snowball finished off by one ray of the Parisian sun. I saw from the first when I came here that I would only be passing through. It's too bad, because this house did us proud, and I'll serve Monsieur the viscount with the respect and esteem he deserves until the very end."

"Well, I must say, my dear Boyer, I am grateful to you and I accept your proposition. But I'm thinking, what if I offer the viscount's stable for sale to this young duke? It's all ready, and it's well known and admired all over Paris."

"That's true. You can make some real money there."

"But what about you? Why don't you suggest that he move into this house? It's so beautifully done up in every respect. Where could he find a better place?"

"Heavens, Edwards! You're a clever man, which hardly surprises me, but, all the same, you've given me an excellent idea. We should talk to the viscount. He's such a good master that he won't mind talking to the young duke on our behalf. He'll tell him that since he's leaving for the Gerolstein legation, where he'll be an attaché, he wants to divest himself of his entire household. Let's see: a hundred sixty thousand francs for the furnished house, twenty thousand francs for the silver and the paintings, fifty thousand francs for the stable and the carriages. That comes to two hundred thirty thousand francs. That's a good deal for a young man who wants to have everything arranged at once. He'd spend three times that amount trying to put together something as elegant and tasteful as what we have here. For it must be said, Edwards, there's no one else quite like the viscount for knowing the good life."

"Such as the horses!"

"And the delicious food! Godefroi, his chef, is leaving this place a hundred times better at what he does than when he got here. The viscount has given him excellent advice and helped him become much more refined."

"In addition to that, they say that the viscount is a successful gambler."

"Yes, an admirable one. He has won great sums with more indifference than he's shown when he's lost. Yet I've never seen anyone lose with greater grace."

"And what about those women! Boyer, the women! Ah! There must be some stories you could tell, considering that you had access to the apartment on the ground floor."

"I have my secrets, just like you have yours, my dear friend."

"Mine?"

"When the viscount ran his horses, didn't you also have secrets to keep? I don't want to cast aspersions on the honesty of the jockeys of your adversaries, but you know, I've heard rumors . . ."

"We don't talk about that, my dear Boyer. A gentleman does not compromise the reputation of an opponent's jockey when he has had the weakness to listen to him . . ."

"Any more than a gallant man compromises the reputation of a woman who has granted him her favors. So, as I said, let's keep our secrets, my dear Edwards—or rather, the secrets of the viscount."

"As to that, what's he going to do now?"

"He'll leave for Germany with a good traveling carriage and seven or eight thousand francs he'll manage to come up with. Oh! I'm not worried about the viscount. He's the kind of person who always lands on his feet, as they say."

"And he's got no more inheritance coming to him?"

"None, because his father has just a small amount of money to live on."

"His father?"

"Certainly."

"The viscount's father isn't dead, then?"

"At least he wasn't five or six months ago. The viscount wrote him to request certain family papers."

"But he is never seen here?"

"No, and for a good reason. For fifteen years or so, he's been living in the provinces, in Angers."

"But doesn't the viscount go to visit him?"

"His father?"

"Yes."

"Never! Never! Really!"

"So they quarreled, then?"

"What I'm about to tell you isn't a secret, for I've heard it from the Prince de Noirmont's former business manager."

"The Prince de Noirmont, Madame de Lucenay's father?" said Edwards, giving him a significant and sly look that Monsieur Boyer, true to his habits of reserve and discretion, affected not to comprehend.

Accordingly, he replied, coldly, "The Duchess de Lucenay is indeed the daughter of the Prince de Noirmont. The viscount's father was a close friend of the prince. The duchess was very young at the time, and the elder Monsieur de Saint-Remy, who loved her very much, treated her as warmly as if she were his own daughter. I've heard these details from Simon, the prince's business manager. I need not scruple to tell you about this because the story I'm going to tell you about was the talk of the town at the time. Even though he's sixty years old, the viscount's father is a man of iron character, with the courage of a lion, whose integrity was the stuff of legend. He possessed almost nothing, and he married the viscount's mother for love. She was quite a rich young woman who possessed the million whose evaporation we have had the honor to witness." Monsieur Boyer bowed his head, and Edwards did the same.

"The marriage was very happy until, they say, the viscount's father, by accident, saw some terrible letters that evidently proved that, during one of his absences three or four years after their marriage, his wife had shown a weakness for a certain Polish count."

"That often happens with the Poles. When I was working for the Marquis de Senneval, Madame la Marquise, a woman given to fanatical passion—"

Monsieur Boyer interrupted his companion. "My dear Edwards, you must learn the connections of our great families before you speak. Otherwise, you will make some terrible errors in judgment."

"What do you mean?"

"The Marquise de Senneval is the sister of the Duke de Montbrison, the household you wish to enter."

"Oh, Lord!"

"Just imagine if you had spoken of her that way before her detractors or those who envy her. You wouldn't stay in that house for twenty-four hours."

"You're right, Boyer. I'll try to familiarize myself with all family connections."

"To get back to my story, then: the viscount's father discovered that after twelve or fifteen years of what had been, until then, a happy marriage, he had reason to feel aggrieved by a Polish count. Unfortunately or fortunately, the viscount was born nine months after his father—or, let us say, after the Count de Saint-Remy—had returned from his fateful trip, such that he could not be certain, even though it was highly probable, that the viscount was the result of this adultery. All the same, the count separated from his wife immediately and did not want to touch a sou of the fortune she had brought him. He withdrew to the provinces with the approximately eighty thousand francs he had in his possession. But you will see the bitterness of this diabolical personality. Although the outrage dated back fifteen years when he discovered it, and even though it had passed the statute of limitations, the viscount's father went, accompanied by Monsieur de Fermont, one of his relatives, in hot pursuit of the Polish seducer. He found him in Venice after searching for him for eighteen months in almost every town in Europe."

"What a stubborn man!"

"The bitterness of a demon, I tell you, dear Edwards. In Venice there was a terrible duel in which the Pole was killed. Everything happened honorably, but the viscount's father displayed such ferocious joy, they say, upon seeing the Pole mortally wounded that his relative, Monsieur de Fermont, had to pull him away from the place of combat. The count, he had said, had wanted to watch his enemy expire before his very eyes."

"What a man! What a man!"

"The count came back to Paris then, went to see his wife, told her that he had just killed the Pole, and left. Since then, he has never seen her nor their son, and he has remained in Angers. That's where he lives, they say, like an absolute savage, on what's left of his eighty thousand francs, a lot of which he had burned through in pursuit of the Pole, as you might imagine. In Angers he doesn't receive any visitors except for the wife and daughter of his relative, Monsieur de Fermont, who died a few years ago. And that family has had its sorrows, it must be said. Madame de Fermont's brother blew his brains out, they say, several months ago."

"And what about the viscount's mother?"

"He lost her a long time ago. That's why the viscount, when he came of age, came into possession of his mother's fortune. Now you understand, my dear Edwards, why the viscount has nothing or next to nothing to look forward to from his father, as far as inheritance is concerned."

"Who, as far as that goes, must detest him."

"He has never wanted to see him again since he found out what he did. No doubt, he is quite sure that the viscount is the Pole's son."

The conversation of these two people was interrupted by a giant footservant who was meticulously powdered, even though it was barely eleven o'clock. "Monsieur Boyer, the viscount has rung twice," the giant said.

Appearing quite sorry to have neglected his position, Boyer got up immediately and followed the servant, showing just as much deference and obeying with as much speed as he would have if he weren't the owner of his master's house.

CHAPTER 7

COUNT DE SAINT-REMY

About two hours after Boyer left Edwards, he appeared before Monsieur de Saint-Remy when Monsieur de Saint-Remy's father came and knocked at the door to the main entrance of the house on rue de Chaillot. A tall man, the Count de Saint-Remy was still alert and vigorous in spite of his age. The almost copperish tone of his skin contrasted strangely with the brilliant whiteness of his beard and hair. His thick eyebrows, still black, partially covered his piercing, deep-set eyes. Although he was almost obsessively misanthropic and wore clothes that were almost in tatters, his calm, proud presence commanded respect.

The door to his son's house opened, and he went in. A doorman in formal brown and silver livery, perfectly powdered and wearing silk stockings, appeared on the threshold of an elegant entranceway that bore as much resemblance to the Pipelets' smoky den as a rag seller's cart bears to the sumptuous boutique of a stylish linen saleswoman. "Monsieur de Saint-Remy?" asked the count, sharply.

Instead of responding, the doorman, with bemused disdain, examined the white beard, threadbare waistcoat, and old hat of the stranger, who held a large cane in his hand.

"Monsieur de Saint-Remy?" the count repeated, impatiently, shocked at the way the porter so impolitely gave him the once-over.

"The viscount is not in." With these words, Monsieur Pipelet's confrere rang the bell and with a meaningful gesture invited the stranger to leave.

"I shall wait," said the count as he walked past the porter.

"Hey, pal, you don't walk into people's houses like that!" cried the doorman as he ran after the count and took him by the arm.

"What? You fool!" answered the old man in a threatening manner as he raised his cane. "How dare you touch me?"

"Oh, I'll dare plenty if you don't leave this instant. I told you that the viscount was not in, so just get out of here."

At this moment, Boyer, hearing raised voices, appeared on the steps in front of the building. "What's all this noise?" he asked.

"It's this man, Monsieur Boyer. He's determined to enter the house even though I told him that the viscount isn't here."

"Enough of this nonsense!" said the count, turning to Boyer, who had come up to him. "I want to see my son. If he isn't here, I'll wait for him."

As we've said, Boyer was not unaware either of the existence of his master's father or of the count's misanthropy. In addition, as a shrewd reader of faces, he had not a moment's doubt as to the count's identity. He greeted him respectfully and answered, "If the count will be so good as to follow me, I am at his service."

"Let's go," said Monsieur de Saint-Remy, following Boyer, leaving the doorman completely flabbergasted.

Still preceded by the valet, the count arrived on the first floor and followed his guide, who had him pass through Florestan de Saint-Remy's study (we will henceforth designate the viscount by his Christian name in order to distinguish him from his father) and took him into a little salon situated just off this room, immediately over the boudoir on the ground floor.

"The viscount was obliged to go out this morning," said Boyer. "If the count would be so kind as to wait for him, he will return before long." With this, the valet withdrew.

Left on his own, the count looked at his surroundings with more than a little indifference. Suddenly, however, he made an abrupt movement. His face grew animated, his cheeks became scarlet, and his features contracted in anger. He had just caught sight of the portrait of his wife—Florestan de Saint-Remy's mother.

He crossed his arms over his chest, lowered his head as if to avoid this sight, and began to pace up and down with large steps.

"It's strange," he said to himself. "This woman is dead, and I've killed her lover, but my own wound is still as fresh and painful as it was the first day I received it. My thirst for revenge has yet to be slaked. My ferocious misanthropy has almost completely isolated me from all society, but it has left me alone with thoughts of my outrage. Yes; because even though the death of this vile woman's accomplice avenged my outrage, it didn't erase my memories. Oh, I know what makes me unable to get past my hatred. It's the thought that for fifteen years I was a dupe. For fifteen years I showered esteem and respect on a miserable wretch who basely betrayed me. It's the thought that for fifteen years I loved her son, the son of her crime, as if he had been my own child—because the aversion that I feel right now toward this Florestan only shows me too well that he was the fruit of their adulterous union! And yet I have no absolute proof of his illegitimacy. It's possible, after all, that he's my son. This doubt terrifies me at times.

"What if he were my son? Then my abandonment of him, the distaste I have always shown for him, and my refusal ever to see him would be unpardonable. But after all, he's rich, young, and happy. What need could he have had of me? Yes, but his affection might have been able to soften the suffering his mother caused me!"

After a moment of deep reflection, the count shrugged his shoulders and said, "Still, these maddening and pointless doubts serve merely to re-awaken my suffering! I should be a man and overcome these stupid, painful feelings that plague me again when I think that I'm about to see him, the child whom I loved to the point of idolatry for ten years—whom I loved as my son! Him! Him! The child of the man I watched fall before my sword with such happiness, of the man whose blood I joyfully watched pour from his body! And they wouldn't let me stand over him and watch his death agony! Oh! They had no idea what it was like to be struck as cruelly as I had been. And then, to think that my name, still respected and honored, must have been uttered so frequently with insult and derision, the way they refer to cuckolded husbands! To think that my name—a name of which I've always been so proud—belongs now to the son of the man whose heart I would have liked to have ripped out! Oh, I don't know how I stop myself from going mad just thinking about it!"

And Monsieur de Saint-Remy, continuing to walk in an agitated fashion, unthinkingly lifted the door curtain that separated the salon from Florestan's study, and took several steps into this room. He had just left it when a little door that was hidden in the drapery opened softly and Madame de Lucenay, wrapped in a large green cashmere shawl and wearing a very simple hat of black velvet, entered the salon that the count had just left for a brief moment.

Allow us to explain this unexpected appearance. Florestan de Saint-Remy had arranged a rendezvous the day before with the duchess for the next morning. The latter had, as we've mentioned, a key to the little gate on the side street, so she let herself in, as usual, through the greenhouse, expecting to find Florestan in the ground-floor apartment. When she didn't find him there, she thought the viscount to be busy writing in his office, as had been the case at other times. A hidden staircase led from the boudoir to the first floor. Madame de Lucenay had gone upstairs without any fear, figuring that, as usual, Monsieur de Saint-Remy had not allowed anyone entrance to his home. Unfortunately, a rather threatening visit from Monsieur Badinot had obliged Florestan to leave abruptly, and he had forgotten that he had arranged a rendezvous with Madame de Lucenay. The latter, seeing no one, was about to go into the office when the curtains on the salon door parted and the duchess found herself face-to-face with Florestan's father. She could not help herself from crying out in fear.

"Clotilde!" the count cried out, stupefied.

A close friend of the Count de Noirmont,[150] Madame de Lucenay's father, Monsieur de Saint-Remy had long ago spoken to her with familiarity,

150. A prince in France can be any noble who holds lands designated as a principality and could thus also be a duke or a count. It was to an extent a courtesy title. [TN]

having known her as a child and girl. Thus he addressed her by her Christian name.

The duchess stood still, contemplating this old man with his white beard and ratty clothing in surprise. Still, she had a confused memory of his features.

"You, Clotilde?" repeated the count in a reproachful and painful voice. "You . . . here . . . with my son?"

These last words helped Madame de Lucenay's hazy memories. She recognized Florestan's father, finally, and exclaimed, "Monsieur de Saint-Remy!"

Her present position was so clear-cut and obvious that the duchess—whose eccentric and stubborn character we are familiar with already—did not deign to have recourse to a lie about her reason for being at Florestan's house. Counting on the warm paternal affection that the count had formerly shown her, she held out her hand to him and said to him in that manner, at once gracious, cordial, and bold, that was hers and hers alone, "Come now, don't scold me. You're my oldest friend. Remember that twenty years ago you used to call me your dear Clotilde."

"Yes, I used to call you that, but—"

"I already know everything you're going to say to me, but you know my motto: 'Whatever is, is; whatever will be, will be.'"

"Oh, Clotilde!"

"Spare me your scoldings, and, instead, let me tell you how happy I am to see you again. Your presence calls up so many memories for me! My poor father, first of all, and then being fifteen again! Oh, it's so wonderful to be fifteen years old!"

"It was because your father was my friend that—"

"Oh, yes, I know," said the duchess, interrupting Monsieur de Saint-Remy, "he loved you so much! You remember, he used to joke around with you and call you 'the man with the green ribbons.' You always used to tell him, 'You're spoiling Clotilde, watch out!' And he would answer you by hugging me. 'I hope I'm spoiling her good and proper, and I had better hurry up about it and redouble my efforts because soon enough the world will take her away from me and take its turn at spoiling her.' What a wonderful father! What a friend I lost in him!" A tear shone in Madame de Lucenay's beautiful eyes. Then, extending her hand to Monsieur de Saint-Remy, she said to him in an emotional voice, "Truly, I am very, very happy to see you again. You bring back such precious memories, memories that are so dear to my heart!"

Although the count had long been familiar with the original and resolute character of this woman, he was still astonished at the ease with which Clotilde accepted the delicate position she was in: meeting her lover's father at her lover's house!

"If you have been in Paris for a while," Madame de Lucenay went on, "it's really not right for you not to have come to see me before this. We could have had such a nice time talking about the past. You know, I have reached the age at which there is a rare charm in saying to old friends, 'Do you remember this or that?'"

The duchess could hardly have spoken with a more tranquil nonchalance if she had received a morning visit from him at her home.

Monsieur de Saint-Remy could not prevent himself from saying to her, severely, "Instead of speaking of the past, it would be more appropriate to speak of the present. My son may return any moment, and—"

"No," said Clotilde, interrupting him. "I have the key to the little door of the greenhouse, and they always announce his arrival with a bell when he returns through the main door. When I hear that noise, I'll disappear as mysteriously as I appeared, and I'll leave you to your joy in being reunited with Florestan. What a sweet surprise you'll give him when he sees you! It's been so long since you've seen him! You know, I'm the one who should be scolding you."

"Me? Me?"

"Absolutely. What guidance, what support did he have as he made his way into society? The advice of a father is indispensable in a thousand different ways. So, quite frankly, it is very bad of you to—" Here Madame de Lucenay, giving in to her eccentricity, could not keep from interrupting herself, laughing like a crazy woman, and saying to the count, "You have to admit that our position is, at the least, a singular one, and the fact that I'm the one preaching to you certainly is rather rich."

"It is indeed strange, but I deserve neither your preaching nor your praise. I'm here to see my son, but it's not for his sake. At his age, he has no need, or no longer has need, of my counsel."

"What do you mean?"

"You must know the reasons for which I abhor society—and especially Paris," said the count with a pained and constricted expression. "Only the most serious circumstances could bring me to leave Angers and come here, to this house. But I have had to overcome my repugnance and turn to every person who could help me or give me information regarding matters of great importance to me."

"Oh, well, then," said Madame de Lucenay with the most affectionate eagerness, "please don't hesitate to let me know if I can help you in any way! Do you have requests to make of people? Monsieur de Lucenay must have a certain amount of credit, because the days on which I dine with my great-aunt de Montbrison, he has deputies over to our home for a meal. One never does that without a reason. There must be some kind of compensation for the bother of having them over, like being able to influence people who are said to be influential these days. Once again, if we can help you, consider us at your service. There's also my young cousin, the little Duke de Montbrison, who, himself a peer, has ties to all the young nobility. Can he do anything for you? In that case, I offer his services to you. In a word, make use of me and my family. You'll see if I can't call myself a loyal and devoted friend!"

"I know, and I won't refuse your support, although—"

"Listen, my dear Alceste, we are worldly people. Let's act like the worldly people we are. It doesn't matter much, I suppose, whether we're here or elsewhere, as far as the business you're interested in is concerned—business that's now of real concern to me because it's important to you. Let's talk about it now, seriously. I demand it."

Saying this, the duchess drew close to the fireplace, leaned against it, and held out the prettiest little foot in the world, which at the moment was ice-cold, in front of the hearth.

With perfect tact, Madame de Lucenay had seized the opportunity to have done with talking about the viscount and to engage Monsieur de Saint-Remy on a subject to which he attached so much importance. Clotilde's conduct would have been different in the presence of Florestan's mother. Proudly, happily, and at great length, she would have confessed to her how precious her son was to her.

Despite his strictness and prickliness, Monsieur de Saint-Remy felt himself submitting to the influence of the courtly and cordial grace of this woman he had known and loved as a child, and he almost forgot that he was speaking to his son's mistress. How, in any case, could one resist the contagion of the example, when the protagonist of a terribly embarrassing position seems not even to suspect or to want to suspect the difficulty of the circumstances in which he finds himself?

"You didn't know, perhaps, Clotilde," said the count, "that I have lived in Angers for a long time?"

"No, I knew it."

"In spite of the kind of seclusion I was seeking, I chose that city because one of my relatives, Monsieur de Fermont, lived there. After the terrible misfortune that struck me, he acted toward me like a brother. After accompanying me through all of the cities of Europe in which I hoped to find . . . a man I wanted to kill, he served as my witness in a duel."

"Yes, a terrible duel. My father told me all about it a long time ago," said Madame de Lucenay, sadly. "But, fortunately, Florestan does not know about this duel. Nor does he know what caused it."

"I wanted him to continue to respect his mother," the count responded, stifling a sigh. He continued: "After a few years, Monsieur de Fermont died in Angers in my arms, leaving a daughter and a wife that, despite my misanthropy, I could not choose but to love, so pure, so noble were those two excellent creatures. I was living alone in a neighborhood outside of town, but when my fits of black melancholy let up a bit, I went to see Madame de Fermont to speak with her and her daughter of the man we all had lost. Just as when he was alive, I had come to immerse and calm myself in the sweet intimacy in which I had previously concentrated all of my affections. Madame de Fermont's brother lived in Paris. He took care of all of his sister's affairs after the death of her husband and placed approximately one hundred thousand crowns—the widow's entire fortune—with a solicitor. After a time, a new and horrible misfortune struck Madame de Fermont. Her brother, Monsieur de Renneville, killed himself—this was about eight months ago. I consoled her as best I could. When she had recovered from her first sorrow, she left for Paris in order to put her affairs in order. After a while, I learned that she had ordered the sale of the modest furnishings from the house she was renting in Angers and that this sum had been used to pay several outstanding debts she had. This circumstance made me anxious, so I looked into her situation, and I was given vaguely to know that this unfortunate woman and her daughter were in distress, victims no doubt of bankruptcy. If Madame de Fermont could have counted on anyone in such an extreme situation, it would have been me. Yet I never heard any news from her. It was in losing that sweet intimacy that I recognized how much I valued it. You cannot imagine how much I've suffered or how anxious I've been since Madame de Fermont and her daughter left. Their father, their husband was a brother to me. I absolutely had to find them. I had to know why in their ruined state they didn't turn to me, poor as I was. I left to come here, leaving behind me a person in Angers who would let me know if anyone should learn anything new about them."

"And so?"

"Yesterday, again, I received a letter from Anjou. They haven't heard anything. On my arrival in Paris, I began my investigations. I went first to the old home of Madame de Fermont's brother. There they told me that she lived on the quai of the Saint-Martin canal."

"And that address?"

"She had lived there, but no one knew where she had moved to. Unfortunately, my investigations have led me nowhere up to this point. After numerous fruitless attempts, before despairing altogether, I decided to come here. Perhaps Madame de Fermont, who, through some inexplicable motive, had not asked for my aid or support, might have turned to my son as the son of her husband's best friend. No doubt this last hope is unfounded, but I didn't want to neglect any possibility in order to find this poor woman and her daughter."

In the last few minutes, Madame de Lucenay's attention to this story had increased markedly. Suddenly, she said, "Truly, it would be a strange coincidence if these were the same people Madame d'Harville was concerned about."

"Which people?" asked the count.

"The widow of whom you speak is still young, isn't she? Her bearing is quite noble?"

"Certainly, but how do you know—"

"Her daughter, pretty as an angel, is at most sixteen years old?"

"Yes! Yes!"

"And her name is Claire?"

"For heaven's sake! Tell me, where are they?"

"Alas, I don't know."

"You don't know?"

"Here's what happened. A woman among my acquaintances, Madame d'Harville, came to see me to ask whether I knew a widow whose daughter was named Claire and whose brother had killed himself. Madame d'Harville was turning to me because she had seen the words 'Write to Madame de Lucenay' at the bottom of a draft of a letter that the unfortunate woman had written to an unknown person whose help she was asking for."

"She wanted to write to you . . . Why to you?"

"I don't know. I don't know her."

"But she knew you!" cried Monsieur de Saint-Remy, struck suddenly with an idea.

"What are you saying?"

"She heard me speak of your father and you, and of your generous and excellent heart, a hundred times. In her misfortune, she must have thought of turning to you."

"Indeed, that would make sense."

"And Madame d'Harville—how did she come into possession of this draft of a letter?"

"I don't know. All I know is that, even though she didn't know yet where this poor mother and her daughter had taken refuge, I believe she was already on their trail."

"Well, then, I must count on you, Clotilde, to take me to see Madame d'Harville. I need to see her today."

"Impossible! Her husband has just been the victim of an appalling accident. A weapon that he didn't believe was loaded went off in his hands. He was killed on the spot."

"Oh! How horrible!"

"The marquise has just gone to spend the first days of her mourning at her father's home in Normandy."

"Clotilde, I beg you: write to her today, and ask her for the information that she already has. Since she's concerned for the fate of these poor women, tell her that she could have no more enthusiastic a second to her efforts than myself. My only desire is to find my friend's widow and to share the little I possess with her and her daughter. They're my only family now."

"Still the same, still generous and devoted! You can count on me. I'll write to Madame d'Harville this very day. Where shall I send my answer?"

"To Asnières, general delivery."

"What eccentricity is this! Why are you staying there, instead of in Paris?"

"I abhor Paris because of the memories it evokes in me," said Monsieur de Saint-Remy, somberly. "My old physician, Doctor Griffon, with whom I have remained in correspondence, has a little country house on the shore of the Seine, near Asnières. He doesn't live there during the winter, so he offered it to me. It's practically a suburb of Paris. After having given myself over to my investigations, I could find there the seclusion I prefer. I took him up on his offer."

"I will write to you, then, in Asnières. I can already tell you something that might be useful to you, something I know from Madame d'Harville. Madame de Fermont's downfall was caused by the crookedness of the solicitor with whom her entire fortune was placed. This solicitor denied that he had received the deposit."

"The wretch! What is his name?"

"Monsieur Jacques Ferrand," said the duchess, unable to stifle her urge to laugh.

"You are a strange one, Clotilde. This is a very serious and sad matter, and you're laughing!" said the count, surprised and displeased.

Indeed, Madame de Lucenay, remembering the amorous declaration of the solicitor, could not repress her sense of humor. "I apologize, my friend," she said. "It's just that this solicitor is a singular character, and I've heard people say some extremely ridiculous things about him. But seriously, if he deserves his reputation for honesty as little as he deserves his reputation for saintliness (and I can testify that the latter is absolutely undeserved), he is a great scoundrel!"

"And where does he live?"

"On rue du Sentier."

"He may expect a visit from me. What you're telling me would accord quite well with certain suspicions I've had."

"Which suspicions?"

"According to certain information I've received regarding my poor friend's brother's death, I would almost be tempted to believe the poor man a victim of murder, rather than suicide."

"Good Lord! And who would make you suppose—"

"Several reasons that would take me too long to explain. I'll leave now. Don't forget the offers you made in your own name and in Monsieur de Lucenay's."

"What? You're going to leave without seeing Florestan?"

"Our meeting would be too painful. Surely, you understand. I was going to go through with it in the sole hope of finding more information regarding Madame de Fermont here because I didn't want to leave any stone unturned in my attempts to find her. And now, good-bye."

"Oh! You have no pity!"

"And you didn't know that?"

"I know that your son has never needed your advice more than now."

"What? Isn't he rich and happy?"

"Yes, but he doesn't understand people. He's blindly prodigal because he's trusting and generous; he plays the great lord in all things, everywhere and always. I fear that people take advantage of his kindness. If you knew how noble his heart is! I have never dared to preach to him about his expenditures and his chaotic finances, first of all because I am at least as mindless as he, and also . . . for other reasons. You, on the other hand, could . . ."

Madame de Lucenay did not finish her sentence. Suddenly they heard the voice of Florestan de Saint-Remy. He had abruptly entered the office next to the salon. After having closed its door brusquely, he said in a haggard voice to someone who was accompanying him, "But it's impossible!"

"I repeat," said the clear, sharp voice of Monsieur Badinot, "I repeat to you that, otherwise, you will be arrested within four hours. For if he does not have his money by then, our man will file charges at the court of the king's prosecutor, and you know what the penalty is for a forgery like this one: the galleys, my poor viscount!"

CHAPTER 8

THE CONVERSATION

It would be impossible to describe the look that Madame de Lucenay and Florestan's father exchanged as they heard those terrible words: "That's it for you . . . it will be the galleys!" The count turned white. He leaned on the back of an armchair, his knees giving way under him. His venerable and respected name—his name dishonored by a man he thought to be the result of his wife's adultery!

After this initial blow subsided, the angry features of the old man and a threatening gesture he made as he approached the office revealed such a frightening resolve in him that Madame de Lucenay grabbed his hand, stopped him, and whispered to him in an expression of the deepest conviction, "He is innocent! I swear to you that he is! Keep still and listen."

The count paused. He wanted to believe what the duchess had told him. And she was, in fact, convinced of Florestan's honesty.

To get this woman who was so blindly generous to him to make further sacrifices for him—sacrifices that were the sole means of keeping him from being arrested and further pursued by Jacques Ferrand—the viscount had sworn to Madame de Lucenay that he had been duped by a wretch from whom he had received a forged bill as a payment, and that he risked now being seen as the accomplice of the forger, since he himself had put the bill in circulation. Madame de Lucenay knew the viscount to be imprudent, lavish, and without order in his life. But she would not for a moment consider him capable of the slightest indelicacy, let alone a base or villainous act.

By twice lending him considerable amounts of money under very difficult circumstances, she had wanted to offer him the favor one friend does for another. The viscount never accepted these advances without promising to reimburse her, for he was owed—he said—more than twice what she'd lent him.

The evident wealth of his manner of living made this assertion believable. In any case, Madame de Lucenay, ceding to the impulse of her natural kindness, had only thought of how she could be useful to Florestan without at all caring to know whether he had the wherewithal to repay her. He claimed that he did, and she didn't doubt him. Would he have accepted so much money from her otherwise? When she vouched for Florestan's honor and begged the old count to listen in on his son's conversation, the duchess thought that it would reveal the confidence trick of which the viscount claimed himself to be the victim. She thought that he would be completely exculpated in his father's eyes.

"But I say again," said Florestan with emotion in his voice, "that Petit-John is a scoundrel. He swore to me that he only had the bills that I had taken from him yesterday and three days ago. I thought the one that was in circulation wasn't payable until three months from now, in London, with Adams and Company."

"Yes, yes," said Badinot, bitingly. "I know, my dear viscount, that you have very skillfully plotted out this business. Your forgeries shouldn't have been discovered until you were already long gone. But you were trying to fool those who were one too many for you."

"Oh, now's a fine time to tell me that, you wretch!" cried Florestan, furious. "Weren't you the one who put me in touch with the person who negotiated those bills for me?"

"Come now, my dear lord," Badinot responded coldly. "Calm down. You are clever at forging business signatures. You do it beautifully, but it's no reason to treat your friends with such disagreeable familiarity. If you keep this up, I'll leave you and you can settle things out on your own."

"And do you think it's possible to maintain my calm under these conditions? If what you tell me is true, if this charge is going to be filed today with the king's prosecutor, I'm finished."

"That's exactly what I'm telling you—unless, that is, you can turn once again to your charming blue-eyed angel of mercy."

"That's impossible."

"Well, then, you'll just have to accept what happens to you. It's too bad. It was the last note. And for twenty-five thousand lousy francs, you're going to have to learn to take the midday air of Toulon. This whole affair is clumsy, absurd, and stupid. How could such a clever man as you let yourself get cornered this way?"

"My God, what can I do? What should I do? Nothing here belongs to me anymore. I don't even have twenty louis to my name."

"What about your friends?"

"I am in debt to anyone who could lend me money. Do you think I'm stupid enough to have waited until now to ask them to lend me money?"

"Of course. Forgive me. All right, then, let's talk this over calmly. That's the best way to come up with a rational solution. I was trying to tell you a while ago how you were going up against someone who was too many for you, but you didn't listen to me."

"All right, say what you have to if any good will come of it."

"Let's review the situation: you told me two months ago, 'I've got one hundred thirteen thousand francs' worth of notes drawn on different banking houses, each with long due dates. My dear Badinot, find me someone who will buy them from me.'"

"And so?"

"I'm getting there. I asked you to let me see these notes. Something about them told me that these were counterfeits, even though they were forged perfectly. It's true that I didn't suspect that you were such a talented calligrapher, but as I had been managing your fortune since you had no fortune left, I knew that you were completely bankrupt. I had executed the deed by which your horses, carriages, and the furnishings of this mansion belonged to Boyer and Edwards. So it was hardly indiscreet of me to be surprised when I found you in possession of commercial notes of such considerable value, no?"

"Be so kind as to spare me your expressions of surprise, and get to the point."

"I'm there. I am experienced enough, or cowardly enough, to know that I should steer clear of any business of that kind. So I sent you to someone else, someone who, no less insightful than I, suspected that you were going to swindle him."

"That's impossible. He wouldn't have discounted those notes if he'd thought they were forged."

"How much cash did he give you for those hundred thirteen thousand francs?"

"Twenty-five thousand francs in cash, and the rest in available credit."

"And what have you drawn on from that credit?"

"Nothing. You know that full well. There was none. But he still put out twenty-five thousand francs."

"You are still young, my dear viscount! Since I stood to receive a commission from you of a hundred louis if the affair went off, I was careful not to tell the third party the real state of your affairs. He thought you were still in good shape, and he knew above all that you were very much adored by a great lady who was terribly rich and who would never leave you in trouble financially. He was thus fairly sure of getting a good return on the transaction. There was risk, certainly, but there was also the chance of making a good profit, and his calculations turned out to be good ones given that the other day you already gave him a cool hundred thousand francs to settle the forged bill of fifty-eight thousand francs, and yesterday thirty thousand francs on the second one. With the latter, he was satisfied for face value, it's true. How did you manage to procure those thirty thousand francs yesterday? The devil take me if I know! You are certainly a rare individual. You see now that, to finish off the deal, if Petit-Jean forces you to pay for the last bill of twenty-five thousand francs, he will have received from you a hundred and fifty-five thousand for the twenty-five thousand that he gave you in cash. Now you see that I was right when I said you had gone up against someone who was too many for you."

"But why did he say that that last note, which he presented today, had been sold to someone else?"

"So as not to frighten you. He also told you that, except for the fifty-eight-thousand-franc bill, the others were in circulation. Once the first was paid, the second one came due yesterday, and today it was the third."

"The wretch!"

"Oh, come now, it's each man for himself, as a famous legal expert once said, and it's a maxim I greatly admire. But let's talk calmly. This proves to you that Petit-Jean—and between the two of us, I wouldn't be surprised to find out that Jacques Ferrand, in spite of his famous saintliness, had his part in these speculations—it just proves that Petit-Jean, whose mouth your first note made water, is speculating on that last bill the same way he speculated on the others, fairly sure, as he is, that your friends won't let you get hauled into criminal court. It's up to you to see if there's anything left to be hoped for from those friends, whether you've squeezed them dry or whether there aren't a few more drops of gold to wring out of them. For if in three hours you don't have the twenty-five thousand francs, my noble viscount, you're up the creek."

"You keep going on about that."

"So I can get you to maybe agree to try plucking one last feather out of the wing of your generous duchess."

"I'm telling you, you have to give up on that. It's madness to think there's twenty-five thousand more francs to be had from her in three hours after all the sacrifices she's made."

"To please you, you happy mortal, she might attempt the impossible."

"Oh, she's already attempted the impossible. It was a matter of borrowing a hundred thousand francs from her husband, and she managed it. But that's the kind of phenomenon that doesn't come about a second time. Come now, my dear Badinot. Up until now you've never had anything to complain of from me. I've always been generous. Try to win me some kind of reprieve from that wretched Petit-Jean. You know that I always find a way to pay people who are of use to me. Once this latest business dies down, I'll turn a new leaf. You'll be happy with the way I treat you."

"Petit-Jean is as unbending as you are unreasonable."

"Me?"

"Why don't you just try to get your generous friend to care about your sad fate one more time. The devil take me, tell her what's really happening. Not just what you've already said, that you were the dupe of forgers, but that you are a forger yourself."

"I'll never make such a confession to her. It would shame me and to no good end."

"Would you prefer that she learn of it tomorrow in the *Court Gazette*?"

"I still have three hours ahead of me. I can flee."

"And where will you go without any money? But consider the alternative. With that last forged note withdrawn, you'll find yourself in a superb position—you'll only have debts. Come now, promise me that you'll speak once more to the duchess. You're such a slick one! You know how to make yourself sympathetic in spite of all your faults. At the worst, she'll respect you a little less, maybe even not at all, but at least she'll get you out of this business. Come on, promise me that you'll go see your pretty friend. I'll go see Petit-Jean, and I'm sure I can get an hour or two of reprieve."

"Damn! I'll have to drink my shame to the dregs!"

"Come on! Take heart. Be tender, passionate, and charming. I'll run to see Petit-Jean. You'll find me there until three o'clock. Later than that, and time will have run out. The court is only open until four o'clock." And Monsieur Badinot left.

When the door was closed, Florestan could be heard crying aloud in profound despair, "My God! My God!"

During this conversation, which revealed to the count the vileness of his son and to Madame de Lucenay the vileness of the man she had so blindly loved, they both had remained still, hardly able to breathe under the weight of this appalling revelation. It would be impossible to represent the mute eloquence of the painful scene that had just taken place between this young woman and the count when there was no longer any doubt as to Florestan's crime. Extending his arm toward the room where his son was, the old man smiled with bitter irony and cast a withering glance at Madame de Lucenay that seemed to say to her, "Here's the man for whom you braved so many humiliations and performed so many sacrifices! Here's the man you blame me for having abandoned!"

The duchess understood the reproach. For a moment, she lowered her head under the weight of her shame. It was a terrible lesson. But little by little, the cruel anxiety that had contracted Madame de Lucenay's features gave way to a sort of haughty indignation. The inexcusable faults of this woman were at least palliated by the faithfulness of her love, the boldness of her devotion, the generosity of her largesse, her candor, and her inexorable aversion toward anything that was base or cowardly.

Still too young, too beautiful, and too fashionable to feel humiliation at having been exploited, this haughty and resolute woman felt neither hatred nor anger once the glamour of love had suddenly vanished in her. Instantly, without any transition, a mortal disgust, a glacial disdain, killed off her affection, hitherto so passionate. She was no longer the mistress of a lover who had vilely deceived her; she was now a woman of respectable society who, upon discovering that a man of her circle was a swindler and counterfeiter, now determined to rid herself of his company.

Even if she thought that extenuating circumstances might lessen the ignominy of Florestan's behavior, Madame de Lucenay would not have allowed their relevance. In her view, a man who went beyond certain limits of honor—whether as a result of vice, outside pressure, or weakness—simply did not exist for her. Honor was for her a question of being or nonbeing.

The only painful feeling that the duchess experienced was triggered by the terrible effect this unexpected revelation had produced on the count, her old friend. For the past few minutes, he had seemed no longer to see or hear what was going on around him. His eyes stared in a fixed way, his head was bowed, his arms hung at his sides, and his complexion was ghostly pale. From time to time his chest heaved with a convulsive sigh.

In a man both resolute and energetic, such dejection was more frightening than fits of rage. Madame de Lucenay looked at him anxiously. "Have courage, my friend," she whispered to him. "For you, for me, for that man—I know what I must do."

The old man stared fixedly at her. Then, as if he had been shaken out of his stupor by a violent commotion, he raised his head, his features became menacing, and, forgetting that his son could hear him, he cried, "And I also, for you, for myself, and for that man, I also know what I must do."

"Who's there?" asked Florestan, surprised.

Madame de Lucenay, not wanting to be in the company of the viscount, disappeared through the little door and went down the hidden staircase. Florestan asked again who was there, and when no one answered, he entered the room. He found himself alone with the count.

The old man's white beard had changed his appearance so radically, and he was dressed so shabbily, that his son, who had not seen him in several years, did not recognize him at first. He approached him in a threatening manner. "What are you doing in here? Who are you?"

"I am the husband of that woman!" answered the count, pointing at the portrait of Madame de Saint-Remy.

"Father!" cried Florestan, recoiling in fear. He recognized the count's features, so long forgotten.

Upright, formidable, with a look of irritation in his eyes, his face scarlet with anger, his white hair brushed back off his head, and his arms crossed over his chest, the count intimidated his son, who, crushed, his head lowered, did not dare to meet his father's gaze. However, for reasons of his own, Monsieur de Saint-Remy made a supreme effort to calm himself and mask his furious resentment.

"Father!" said Florestan in an emotional voice. "Were you there?"

"I was there."

"Did you hear?"

"Yes, everything."

"Oh, no!" cried the viscount in pain, hiding his face in his hands.

There was a moment of silence. At first as surprised as he was chagrined at the unexpected appearance of his father, Florestan, resourceful as he was, quickly considered how he might make the best of the situation. "All is not lost," he said to himself. "The presence of my father is a stroke of fate. He knows everything, and he doesn't want his name to be tarnished. He's not rich, but he still must have twenty-five thousand francs. We'll have to play our cards close to the vest. This calls for skill, spirit, and feeling. I can leave the duchess alone. I'm saved!"

Then, transforming his charming features into an expression of painful dejection, making his eyes well up with tears of repentance, speaking in the most vibrant and pathetic tone, he cried out, joining his hands in a desperate gesture, "Oh, Father, I am so miserable! To see you again after so many years, and at such a moment! It must look to you as if I were completely guilty! But please, allow me a word, I beg of you! Let me, if not to justify myself, at least to explain my conduct to you. May I, Father?"

Monsieur de Saint-Remy did not say a single word. His features remained impassive. He sat in a chair, his elbows poised on its arms, his chin in the palm of his hand, regarding the viscount in silence.

If Florestan, shocked by the count's apparent calm, had had any idea of the reasons his father had for the hatred, fury, and revenge that were filling his mind, he surely would not have tried to dupe him as one tries to dupe any simple Géronte.[151] But as he knew nothing of the dark suspicions his father had about the legitimacy of his birth nor of his mother's sin, Florestan did not doubt that his tricks would succeed, thinking he could bring around a father who, both very misanthropic and very proud of his family name, would, rather than accept dishonor, be capable of the greatest sacrifices.

"Father," Florestan said, timidly, "will you let me try, not to exculpate

151. Géronte was a stereotypical figure of an aged fool always duped and cheated by other characters. Among other plays, he appears in Corneille's *The Liar* and Molière's *A Doctor Despite Himself.* [TN]

myself, but to tell you how I came to be drawn, almost against my will, into taking actions that were—I admit—vile?"

The viscount, taking his father's silence as tacit permission to proceed, continued: "When I had the misfortune of losing my mother, my poor mother who loved me so much, I wasn't yet twenty years old. I found myself alone, without anyone to turn to, without anyone to support me. Heir to a considerable fortune, and accustomed to luxury since my childhood, luxury became a way of life for me—a necessity. I didn't understand how hard it was to earn money, so I wasted it as if it grew on trees. Unfortunately—and I say 'unfortunately' because it's the thing that brought me to ruin—my purchases, as out of control as they were, were remarkable for their elegance. By the strength of my good taste, I put in the shade men ten times richer than I. My first success went to my head, and I became a man of luxury, the way others become soldiers or statesmen. Yes, I loved luxury, not out of any vulgar tendency to ostentation, but as the painter loves painting and the poet loves poetry. Like any artist, I was passionate about my work, and my work was my life of luxury. I sacrificed everything to its perfection. I wanted everything to be beautiful, grand, complete, and splendidly harmonious in every respect: everything, from my stable to my table, from my clothing to my house itself. I wanted my life to be an object lesson in taste and elegance. Like an artist, as well, I hungered for the applause of the masses and the admiration of the elite. This rarified form of success is hard to come by, and I won it."

As he spoke, Florestan's features gradually lost their hypocritical expression. His eyes blazed with enthusiasm. He was telling the truth. He had been seduced in the beginning by this rather uncommon manner of conceiving of luxury.

The viscount looked questioningly at his father. It seemed to him as if he had softened a little.

He went on with growing excitement: "As an oracle and regulator of fashion, my criticism or my praise passed for law. I was quoted, copied, praised, and admired, all by the best society of Paris, which is to say, the best society of Europe, of the world. Women shared in the general fascination with me. The most charming of them vied for the pleasure of attending some very exclusive parties I gave. People everywhere were always going into ecstasies over the incomparable elegance and the exquisite taste of these parties. Millionaires couldn't equal, let alone surpass, my parties. In the end, I was considered the king of fashion. That name tells you everything you need to know, Father, if you understand what it means."

"I understand what it means, and I'm sure that in the hulks you'd invent some refined and elegant new way to carry your chains. It would be all the rage among your fellow inmates and they'd call it 'à la Saint-Remy,'" said the old man, with savage irony, and then he went on: "And Saint-Remy is my name, too!" He became silent, his elbows still resting on the arms of the chair, his chin still propped in the palm of his hand.

Florestan needed to use all his self-control to keep hidden the pain caused by this stinging sarcasm. He went on, in a more humble tone: "Alas! Father, it's not out of pride that I bring up my success. As I said, this success is what brought me down. I was highly sought after, envied, flattered, and adored—not by self-interested parasites but by people whose positions were much higher than mine and over whom I had no other advantage besides the one given me by my elegance, which is to luxurious living what taste is to art. It all went to my head. I no longer paid attention to the money I was spending. My fortune would run out within a few years, but I didn't care. Could I give up this frenzied, dazzling life in which pleasures gave way to new pleasures, indulgences to new indulgences, parties to new parties, and every sort of inebriation gave way to a new kind of enchantment? Oh, Father, if you only knew what it's like to be hailed everywhere as the hero of the moment, to hear the murmurs that accompany your entrance into a salon, to hear women saying to each other, 'It's him! He's here!' Oh! If you only knew—"

"I know," said the old man, interrupting his son without changing his demeanor. "I know. Yes, the other day, in a public square, there was a crowd. Suddenly, you could hear a murmur just like the one that greets you when you go somewhere. The glances of women, most of all, converged on a very attractive boy, the same way they converge on you. And the women were pointing him out to each other and saying, 'It's him! Here he is!' just as you say they do when you arrive."

"But who was that man, Father?"

"He was a counterfeiter that they were putting into chains."

"Oh!" Florestan cried out, in pure rage. Then, feigning even deeper affliction, he added, "Father, you have no pity. What do you want me to say? I am not trying to deny my errors. I am only trying to explain to you the fatal pressure that led me to make them. Oh, well! Go ahead. Even if you feel you must crush me with cutting sarcasm, I'll try to get to the very end of my confession. I'll try to get you to understand the feverish excitement that brought me down because then, maybe, you'll pity me. Yes, because one pities a fool. And I was a fool. With eyes shut, I abandoned myself to the dazzling whirlwind, carrying the most charming women and the most amiable men along with me. Could I stop myself? You might as well tell the poet who's draining his strength, whose health is being sacrificed on the altar of his genius, 'Stop right now, just as you're being carried away by your inspiration!' No, I couldn't do it! How could I give up the reign I exercised to return in shame, ruined and mocked, to live among the unknown masses? How could I let those who envied me triumph over me when, up until then, I had defied, dominated, and crushed them? No, no, I couldn't do it! Not of my own free will, at least. The fatal day came when for the first time I lacked money. I was shocked, as if such a thing could never have happened. Nevertheless, I still had my horses, my carriages, my household furniture. Once my debts were paid, I had sixty thousand francs left—maybe. What could I do with such a pittance? So, Father, I took the first step into criminality. I was still an honest man at this point; I hadn't spent money I didn't have. But then I started to take on debts I could never repay. I sold everything I possessed to two of my staff in order to do right by them and in order to enjoy the luxury that intoxicated me for another six months, in spite of my creditors. In order to fund my gambling needs and extravagant expenses, I began by borrowing from Jews. Then, to pay the Jews, I borrowed money from my friends. Then, to pay my friends, I borrowed from my mistresses. Once these resources were exhausted, I reached a new turning point in my life. I had gone from being an honest man to a swindler, but I still wasn't a criminal yet. Still, I hesitated. I wanted to end it all in violence. I proved in several duels that I wasn't afraid of death. I wanted to kill myself!"

"Oh, come now. Really?" said the count, with fierce irony.

"You don't believe me, Father?"

"It was either much too soon or much too late!" added the old man, still impassive and maintaining the same attitude.

Thinking that he had moved his father by speaking to him of his plan to commit suicide, Florestan thought it advisable to re-create the moment with a theatrical gesture. He opened a drawer, took out of it a small green crystal bottle, and said to the count as he placed it on the table, "An Italian charlatan sold me this poison."

"And that poison . . . it was for you?" asked the old man, his elbows still on the armchair.

Florestan understood the intention behind his father's words. His features now expressed real indignation, because he was telling the truth. One day, he had had the fantasy of killing himself. It was fleeting fancy. People of his kind are too cowardly to resolve coldly, without an audience, to kill themselves, though they can face death in a duel as a matter of honor. And so he cried out in real pain, "I fell very low, but at least I didn't fall that low, Father! The poison was for me!"

"And you were too afraid?" said the count, sitting immobile.

"I admit that I shrank in the face of such an extreme action. Things were still not yet that desperate. The people I owed money to were rich and could wait. At my age, with my connections, I hoped that at some point, if I couldn't regain my fortune, I could at least find myself an honorable, independent position which would give me a place in the world. Several of my friends, perhaps less talented than myself, had made rapid advances in the diplomatic corps. I had a moment of capricious ambition. I had only to ask and I became a member of the Gerolstein legation. Unfortunately, a few days after this nomination, a gambling debt that I had contracted toward a man that I hated put me in a cruel bind. I had drained all my resources. A dreadful idea occurred to me. Thinking I would certainly get away with it, I committed a criminal act. You see, Father, I haven't hid anything from you. I admit that my conduct was disgraceful. I'm not trying to make it sound better than it was. I have two options open to me, and I don't know which one to take. The first is to kill myself—and thus to bring dishonor to your name, for if I don't pay the twenty-five thousand francs this very day, the charge is going to be filed, scandal will break out, and, dead or alive, I'm ruined. The second option is to throw myself at your mercy, Father, and to say, 'Save your son, save your name from infamy. I promise to leave for Africa tomorrow, where I will become a soldier and either die or return to you one day, fully rehabilitated.' You see, I'm telling you the truth, Father. In this moment of crisis, I have nowhere else to turn. Decide now: I can die in shame or, thanks to you, I can go on living to make restitution for my sins. These are neither threats nor the idle words of a young man, Father; I'm twenty-five years old, I bear your name, and I have enough courage to kill myself or to become a soldier, because I don't want to go into penal servitude."

The count rose. "I don't want my name to be dishonored," he said coldly to Florestan.

"Oh, Father! My savior!" the viscount cried, warmly. He was about to throw himself into his father's arms when the latter, with a glacial gesture, put him off.

"The man who has the forged bill has given you until three o'clock?"

"Yes, Father. It's two o'clock now."

"Let's go into your study. Give me something to write with."

"Here, Father."

The count sat at Florestan's desk and wrote, in a firm hand, "I undertake to pay the twenty-five thousand francs that my son owes at ten o'clock this evening. The Count de Saint-Remy."

"Your creditor only wants money. In spite of his threats, my promise will make him consent to a new delay. He will go to see Monsieur Dupont, the banker at seven rue de Richelieu. He'll guarantee the value of this note."

"Oh, Father! How will I ever—"

"You will await me this evening at ten o'clock. I will bring you the money. I want your creditor here."

"Yes, Father, and the day after tomorrow, I'll leave for Africa. You'll see that I won't be ungrateful. Maybe when I'm rehabilitated, you'll accept my thanks."

"You owe me nothing. I have only ensured that my name will not be dishonored further. It will not be," said Monsieur de Saint-Remy simply, taking the cane he had placed on the desk. He headed for the door.

"Father, give me your hand, at least!" said Florestan, begging him.

"Here, tonight, at ten o'clock," said the count, withholding his hand. And he left.

"Saved!" cried Florestan, radiant. "Saved!" Then he said, after a moment of reflection, "Almost saved. No matter. That's how these things always are. Maybe tonight I'll confess the other business to him. He's on the road now. He wouldn't want to stop in the middle of his journey, and he wouldn't want his first sacrifice to be useless for lack of a second one. And then again, why should I tell him? Who will ever know? Indeed, if nothing is discovered, I will keep the money he gives me to pay off this last debt. It took some trouble for me to move him to pity me, that devil. The bitterness of his ironies gave me doubts about his determination. But my threat of suicide and his fear of having his name tarnished won the day. That was the right place to hit him. He's surely much less poor than he pretends to be. If he has about a hundred thousand francs, he must have saved up a lot from living the way he lives. Once again, his arrival is a stroke of good luck. He seems ferocious, but, deep down, I think he's a good man. Off I go to see that bailiff!" He rang, and Monsieur Boyer appeared.

"Why didn't you warn me that my father was here? Such negligence!"

"I tried to say something to Monsieur twice as he was returning with Monsieur Badinot through the garden. But Monsieur, in all probability preoccupied with his conversation with Monsieur Badinot, gestured that I shouldn't interrupt him. I couldn't permit myself to insist. I would be truly sorry if the viscount thought me guilty of negligence."

"That's all right, then. Tell Edwards to get Orion—no, make that Plower—harnessed up immediately to the gig."

Monsieur Boyer bowed his head respectfully. As he was on his way out, a knock was heard at the door. Monsieur Boyer gave the viscount a querying glance.

"Come in!" said Florestan.

A second valet appeared, holding in his hand a small ruby red platter. Monsieur Boyer took the platter from him with a consideration mixed with jealousy and a respectful urgency. He brought it over to the viscount. The latter took a rather heavy envelope that was sealed with a black wax insignia from the platter. The two servants withdrew discreetly.

Florestan opened the envelope. It contained twenty-five thousand francs in treasury notes. There was no accompanying message.

"This really is my lucky day!" he cried, joyously. "Saved! This time, and for real, I'm completely saved! I'll run to the jeweler, and then," he said to himself, "perhaps . . . No, wait a minute. No one will suspect me. Twenty-five thousand francs are a good nest egg. Good Lord! I was a fool ever to doubt my lucky star! The moment I thought it had burned out, there it was again, shining even more brightly! But where does this money come from? I don't recognize the writing on the envelope. Let's look at the seal. The number . . . But yes! Yes! I was right: an *N* and an *L*—it's Clotilde! How did she know? And she doesn't say a word—that's strange! What timing! Ah! My God! I remember, I arranged a rendezvous with her this morning. Badinot's threats shook me so much I forgot about Clotilde. Did she leave after waiting for me on the ground floor? No doubt, this missive is her delicate way of letting me know that she's afraid of being forgotten because of my financial troubles. Yes, it's an indirect reproach to me for not having asked her help, as I always had before. Good old Clotilde, always there for me! She's as generous as a queen. What a shame to have come to this pass with her . . . she who's still so pretty. Sometimes I regret what's happened—but I only went to her when there was no other choice. I really was forced to do it."

"Monsieur's gig is ready," said Monsieur Boyer.

"Who brought this letter?" Florestan asked him.

"I don't know, monsieur."

"Well, then, I will ask them downstairs. But tell me, is there anyone on the ground floor?" added the viscount, giving Boyer a meaningful glance.

"There's no one there anymore, monsieur."

"I wasn't wrong, then," thought Florestan. "Clotilde came to see me, and then she left."

"If Monsieur would be so good as to give me two minutes of his time," said Boyer.

"Yes, but be quick about it."

"Edwards and I have learned that the Duke de Montbrison would like to set up a household. If the viscount would be so good as to propose his own, entirely furnished, as well as his complete stable, it would provide a very good opportunity to wind up our deal, and, as for the viscount, perhaps it would offer him a good reason for having sold his things at this moment."

"What an excellent idea, Boyer. For my part, I prefer this arrangement. I'll see Montbrison, and I'll speak with him. What are your conditions?"

"Monsieur understands that we must try to make the most of his generosity."

"And make a profit from our arrangement. That's as a matter of course. What's your price?"

"For everything, two hundred and sixty thousand francs, monsieur."

"Are you and Edwards making any money on this?"

"About forty thousand francs, monsieur."

"Nice work! So much the better. After all, you've served me well. If I had drawn up a will, I would have left you two that much."

At this, the viscount left to see his creditor, first of all, and then Madame de Lucenay, whom he did not suspect of having been present during his conversation with Badinot.

CHAPTER 9

THE SEARCH

The Lucenay mansion was one of those royal residences in the Faubourg Saint-Germain that seem so grand because of their sheer expanse. A modern house would easily fit inside the stairway of one of those palaces, and one could build a whole neighborhood on the plot they occupy.

Around nine o'clock in the evening of the same day, the double doors of this mansion opened before a gleaming brougham that, after having made a skillful turn in the immense courtyard, came to a stop in front of a large, covered set of doorsteps that led to the first antechamber.

As the stamping of two eager and spritely horses resounded on the pavement stones, a gigantic footman opened the carriage door, with its coat of arms. A young man nimbly got out of this brilliant carriage and agilely climbed the five or six steps of the entryway. This young man was the Viscount de Saint-Remy.

Upon leaving his creditor, who was satisfied with Florestan's father's promise to pay and had thus accorded him the requested delay and was going to return to receive his money at ten o'clock that evening on rue de Chaillot, Monsieur de Saint-Remy presented himself at Madame de Lucenay's home in order to thank her for the latest favor she had done for him. But since he had not met the duchess that morning, he was arriving triumphant, certain that he would find her, at *prima sera*, the hour she appointed for his customary visits.[152]

From the promptness of the two footmen of the antechamber who ran to open the glass door as soon as they recognized Florestan's carriage, from the profoundly respectful attitude the rest of the staff displayed, standing up spontaneously as Florestan went by, and, finally, from several almost imperceptible nuances, one would think him the second or even, really, the true master of the house.

When the Duke de Lucenay came home to his residence, his umbrella in hand and his feet shod in enormous clogs (he hated to travel by car during the day), the same domestic maneuvers were repeated in just as respectful a fashion. Nevertheless, an observer would see that

152. *Prima sera* is in Italian in the French text. It is pidgin Italian, evidently meaning here something like the first hour in the evening for visiting. [TN]

there was a large difference in the faces of the servants in the welcome they accorded the husband and the one they reserved for the lover.

The duchess's personal servants showed the same promptness when Florestan entered. One of them walked immediately ahead of him to announce his arrival to Madame de Lucenay.

Never had the viscount been more glorious; never had he felt happier, more sure of himself, more the conqueror. The victory he had had this morning over his father, the new proof of Madame de Lucenay's attachment to him, the joy of having been saved so miraculously from such a terrible situation, and his renewed faith in his lucky star all gave his attractive face an expression of daring and good humor that made it even more attractive than usual. He had never felt better in his life. And he had every reason to feel that way. Never had he carried his slender, supple figure with more nonchalant confidence. Never had he held his head so high. His pride had never been more deliciously flattered than it was when he thought, "This very great lady, the mistress of this palace, is all mine, she throws herself at my feet . . . This very morning, she was waiting for me in my home."

Florestan was indulging himself in such singularly vain reflections as he passed through the three or four rooms that led to the small room in which the duchess customarily received people. A last glance at his reflection in the mirror confirmed his own excellent opinion of himself.

The valet opened the doors to the salon and announced, "Monsieur the Viscount de Saint-Remy!"

The duchess's astonishment and indignation were inexpressible. She believed that the count had not hidden from his son that she had, like him, heard everything. As we have said, Madame de Lucenay's love for Florestan, when she learned of his baseness, was abruptly extinguished and had changed into a glacial contempt. We have also said that amid all of her frivolity and flaws, Madame de Lucenay retained, pure and whole, her sense of justice and honor, and a chivalric loyalty whose vigor and tenacity were the equal of any man's. She had all of the qualities that came with her weaknesses, all of the virtues that came with her vices. In treating love with manly chivalry, she went just as far as a man would—and even farther—in matters of devotion, generosity, courage, and, most of all, in contempt for everything base.

Planning to go out into society this evening, Madame de Lucenay had dressed—albeit without her diamonds—with her habitual taste and magnificence. Her splendid makeup, the bright rouge she wore so confidently, so boldly, like a woman of the court, up to her eyelids, her beauty, most dazzling in the light, and her bearing, of a goddess walking on clouds, made her matchless hauteur—that she could turn up, if necessary, to the point of thundering insolence—all the more striking.

The reader is familiar with the duchess's haughty and resolute character.

Imagine her expression, her gaze, as the viscount approached her, looking smart, smiling, and confident, and said to her with love, "My dear Clotilde, how good you are! How beautiful—"

He did not have the chance to finish his sentence. The duchess was sitting and had not moved, but her gesture and her gaze revealed a contempt that was both so calm and so utterly overwhelming that Florestan stopped short. He could not say another word or take another step.

Never had Madame de Lucenay behaved in this manner to him. He could not believe that this was the same woman whom he had always found so sweet, tender, and passionately submissive, for nothing is more humble or timid than a resolute woman before the man she loves and who dominates her.

Once his initial surprise subsided, Florestan was ashamed of his weakness. His ordinary daring took hold of him. Taking a step toward Madame de Lucenay in order to take her hand, he said to her in the most caressing voice, "Heavens! Clotilde, what's wrong? I've never seen you looking more beautiful, and yet—"

"What impudence!" cried the duchess as she recoiled with so much disgust and disdain Florestan was once again struck by surprise and completely floored.

"Tell me, at least, what has happened to produce such a sudden change in you, Clotilde! What have I done? What is it you want?"

Without answering him, Madame de Lucenay looked him up and down, as people say crudely, with an expression that was so insulting that Florestan felt his face turning red with anger. He cried, "I know, madame, that you like things to end quickly. Is it a breakup you seek?"

"What curious pretension!" said Madame de Lucenay with a burst of sardonic laughter. "Please know that when a servant steals from me, I don't break up with him. I throw him out."

"Madame!"

"Let's put an end to this," said the duchess in a curt and insolent tone. "Your presence disgusts me. Why are you here? Didn't you get your money?"

"So it was true. I thought it was you. Those twenty-five thousand francs—"

"Your last *forged note* has been withdrawn, am I not correct? The honor of your family has been salvaged. That's good. Get out of here."

"Oh! Believe me—"

"I dearly regret the loss of that money. It could have helped so many honest people. But I had to think about the disgrace you were bringing to your father and to me."

"Does that mean, Clotilde, that you know everything? Oh! I see that the only thing left for me to do now is to die," cried Florestan in the most pathetic and desperate tone.

The duchess greeted this tragic exclamation with an impertinent burst of laughter. To this, she added, between two peals of laughter, "My God! I never could have imagined that dishonor could be so ridiculous!"

"Madame!" cried Florestan, his features contracting with rage.

The doors opened noisily as a servant announced: "Monsieur the Duke de Montbrison!"

In spite of his self-control, Florestan could hardly contain his violent resentment. A man more experienced than the duke would certainly have noticed. Monsieur de Montbrison was barely eighteen years old. Picture the ravishing face of a young blond girl, white and pink, with crimson lips and a satiny chin just beginning to show the downy shadow of a nascent beard; add to this a pair of big brown eyes, still slightly timid, lacking only a saucy gleam, a figure as slender as that of the duchess, and you may perhaps imagine the appearance of this young duke, the most ideal cherub that a countess and her assistant ever dressed up in a woman's bonnet, after having remarked on the whiteness of his ivory neck.[153]

The viscount had either the weakness or the audacity to stay.

"How kind of you, Conrad, to have thought of me this evening!" said Madame de Lucenay in the most affectionate tone as she held out her beautiful hand to the young duke.

The latter was going to shake his cousin's hand,[154] but Clotilde lifted her hand cheerfully and said to him, "Kiss it, cousin. You are wearing your gloves."

"Pardon me, cousin," said the adolescent, and he pressed his lips on the charming bare hand that she had presented to him.

"What are you doing this evening, Conrad?" Madame de Lucenay asked him, without seeming to give Florestan the least notice in the world.

"Nothing, cousin. When I leave you, I'll be going to the club."

"Absolutely not. You'll come with us, with Monsieur de Lucenay and myself, to see Madame de Senneval. It's her day to receive guests. She has already asked me several times to introduce you to her."

"Cousin, I will be only too happy to put myself at your service."

"And then, frankly, I don't like to see you already taking on the habits and tastes of the clubs. You have everything you need to be perfectly welcome and even sought after by the best society, and you should frequent it all the time."

"Yes, cousin."

"And since my standing with you is practically that of a grandmother,

---

153. Surely a reference either to Beaumarchais's Cherubin in *Le mariage de Figaro* (first staged in 1784) or to Mozart's version of him in *Le nozze di Figaro* (1786), Cherubino, an adolescent whom the Countess Almaviva and her maid Susanna dress up as a girl. [TN]

154. Sue writes that he went to give her a "*shake-hands*" (in English). [TN]

my dear Conrad, I will allow myself to be rather demanding. You are an adult, legally, it's true, but I believe that you will still need a mentor for a long time. And you will just have to give in and accept me as yours."

"With joy, with happiness, cousin!" the young duke said, eagerly.

It is impossible to portray the mute rage of Florestan, still leaning on the fireplace. Neither the duke nor Clotilde paid him any attention. Knowing how rapid were Madame de Lucenay's determinations, he thought that she now pushed her audacity and disdain to the point of wanting to begin a flirtation right away, before his very eyes, with Monsieur de Montbrison.

But it was really nothing of the sort. The duchess felt a completely maternal affection for her cousin, having practically been present at his birth. But the young duke was so attractive and seemed so happy to receive such a gracious reception from his cousin that Florestan's jealousy, or rather his pride, was provoked. His heart was in agony from all of the cruel bites and stings of envy brought on by Conrad de Montbrison, who had wealth and charm and was about to embark on the life of pleasures, inebriation, and parties from which he was about to depart—ruined, tarnished, disdained, and dishonored.

Monsieur de Saint-Remy had party courage, if such a thing may be said, the kind of courage that leads men, from anger or vanity, to fight duels. But vile and corrupted as he was, he lacked the courage of conviction that triumphs over bad tendencies or that at least gives you the energy to escape infamy by choosing your own death instead.

Made furious by the infernal contempt of the duchess, believing that he was seeing his own successor in the young duke, Monsieur de Saint-Remy resolved to contest Madame de Lucenay's insolence with his own and, if necessary, to provoke a duel with Conrad.

The duchess, irritated by Florestan's audacity, did not look at him. And Monsieur de Montbrison, in his eagerness to please his cousin, forgot his usual manners and neglected to greet or say a single word to the viscount, whom he nevertheless knew. The latter, coming up to Conrad, who had his back turned to him, touched his arm lightly and said, in a dry and ironic tone, "Good evening, monsieur. A thousand pardons for not having noticed you."

Monsieur de Montbrison, sensing that he had indeed just shown a lack of courtesy, turned around quickly and said cordially to the viscount, "Monsieur, I'm truly embarrassed. But I dare to hope that my cousin, the cause of my distraction, will be so good as to excuse my bad manners toward you."

"Conrad," said the duchess, pushed to her limit by the impudence of Florestan, who insisted on remaining at her home and braving her contempt, "Conrad, it's all right. There's nothing to apologize for. Don't bother."

Thinking that his cousin was reproaching him jokingly for being too formal, Monsieur de Montbrison said cheerfully to the viscount, who was livid with rage, "I won't insist, then, monsieur, since my cousin forbids it. You see, her mentoring of me has already begun."

"And it won't stop there, my dear monsieur, you can be sure of that. And foreseeing that—and her grace, the duchess will be eager to make this expectation a reality—foreseeing that, as I said, the idea has occurred to me to make you a proposition."

"To me, monsieur?" said Conrad, starting to be alarmed at Florestan's sardonic tone.

"To you yourself. I'm leaving in a few days for the Gerolstein legation, to which I've been attached. I would like to unburden myself of my completely furnished house and my well-equipped stable. This works out very well for you." The viscount put insolent stress on his final words while looking at Madame de Lucenay. "It would add a certain spice to things, don't you agree, madame?"

"I do not understand your meaning, monsieur," said Monsieur de Montbrison, more and more surprised.

"I must tell you, Conrad, that you cannot accept the offer that is being proposed to you," said Clotilde.

"And why shouldn't Monsieur accept my offer, madame?"

"My dear Conrad, the property being offered to you has already been sold to others. You understand: you're being set up to be robbed as if by highwaymen."

Florestan bit his lips in rage. "Be careful what you say, madame!" he cried.

"What? Do I understand you to make threats here, monsieur?" cried Conrad.

"Come, Conrad—let's just ignore him," said Madame de Lucenay as she removed a lozenge from a candy dish with unflappable composure. "A man of honor must not and cannot allow himself to attend to Monsieur. If he insists, I'll tell you why!"

There might have been a terrible clash but the double doors opened again and Monsieur de Lucenay made his usual noisy, violent, and thoughtless entrance. "My dear, are you already dressed? Why, that's a shocker! Good evening, Saint-Remy. Hello, Conrad. Ah! You're looking at the most desperate man in the world. I haven't been able to sleep or eat. I've been staggered by what's happened. I just can't get used to it. Poor Harville. What a tragedy!"

And Monsieur de Lucenay, dropping on his back into a double-backed sort of settee, tossed his hat far across the room in a gesture of hopelessness. Crossing his left leg over his right knee, he grabbed his foot and held it in his hand, in his usual manner, continuing to exclaim sorrowfully. Conrad's and Florestan's emotional states had the chance to cool off without Monsieur de Lucenay—incidentally, the least perceptive man in the world—having noticed a thing.

Not out of embarrassment, for she was not a woman who ever felt embarrassed, as we know, but because Florestan's presence was both repugnant and intolerable to her, Madame de Lucenay said to the duke, "Whenever you're ready, we can leave. I'm going to introduce Conrad to Madame de Senneval."

"No, no, no!" the duke began to yell, dropping his foot in order to seize one of the cushions of the settee to beat his fists on violently, to Clotilde's great consternation, who, at the sound of her husband's unexpected cries, had jumped out of her chair.

"Good heavens, monsieur, what's wrong with you?" she said to him. "You've given me a terrible fright."

"No!" the duke repeated. Pushing the cushion away, he got up suddenly and began gesticulating as he walked about. "I can't get used to the idea that our poor d'Harville is dead. Can you, Saint-Remy?"

"Indeed, it was a dreadful thing!" said the viscount. With hatred and rage in his heart, he was trying to catch Monsieur de Montbrison's eye, but the latter had turned away—not out of cowardice, but out of pride—from the sight of a man who had been so cruelly branded.

"I beg of you, monsieur," said the duchess to her husband as she arose, "try to mourn Monsieur d'Harville in a less loud and especially a less peculiar manner. Please ring for my servants, if you will."

"But still, it's true," said Monsieur de Lucenay as he pulled the cord for the bell, "that three days ago he was so full of life and good health, and today what remains of him? Nothing! Nothing! Nothing!"

These last three exclamations were accompanied by three jerking movements that were so violent that the bell cord he held in his hand as he continued gesticulating had yanked free of its fixture, fallen on a candelabra full of lit candles, and pushed two of them over. One of them, coming to rest on the fireplace, broke a charming little antique Sèvres cup on its way. The other rolled onto an ermine rug on the floor and burst momentarily into flame before Conrad put it out with his foot.

At the same moment, two servants who had been summoned by the formidable clapping of the bell rushed in, only to find Monsieur de Lucenay with the bell cord in his hand, the duchess laughing hysterically over the ridiculous little cascade of candles, and Monsieur de Montbrison partaking in his cousin's hilarity. Monsieur de Saint-Remy was the only person who was not laughing.

Monsieur de Lucenay, long accustomed to such accidents, maintained perfect gravity as he handed the bell cord to one of his servants, saying to them, "Madame's carriage."

Calmed to some extent, Clotilde said, "Honestly, monsieur, there's no one like you to provoke laughter from something so sad."

"Sad? Call it instead frightful, call it instead dreadful! Listen: since yesterday, I've been thinking how many people there are—even in my own family—that I'd prefer to have died instead of that poor d'Harville. My nephew d'Emberval, for example, who's so annoying with his stutter, or maybe your aunt Merinville, who's always talking about her poor nerves and her migraines and who takes up whole days keeping you waiting for dinner and then it will just be some leavings she serves you, as if she were a doorman's wife. Do you really care for your aunt Merinville?"

"Come on, monsieur, that's enough. You're behaving like a madman," said the duchess with a shrug of her shoulders.

"But it's true!" said the duke. "Wouldn't you trade twenty people you don't care about for a real friend, Saint-Remy?"

"Certainly."

"It's like that old story about the tailor. Do you know that one, Conrad?"

"No, cousin."

"You'll get the point right away. A tailor has been condemned to hang. He's the only tailor in town: what are the townspeople going to do? They tell the judge, 'Your honor, we only have one tailor, and we have three shoemakers. If you don't mind, can't you hang one of the shoemakers instead of the tailor? Two shoemakers would be enough for us.' You get the point, Conrad?"

"Yes, cousin."

"What about you, Saint-Remy?"

"I do, too."

"Madame's carriage has arrived!" said one of the servants.

"Oh, honestly! Why aren't you wearing your diamonds?" said Monsieur de Lucenay, suddenly. "They'd go so well with what you're wearing!"

Saint-Remy shuddered.

"For the little we ever go out together into society," continued the duke, "you could have at least done me the honor of wearing your diamonds. The duchess's diamonds are beautiful. Have you seen them, Saint-Remy?"

"Yes, Monsieur knows them very well," said Clotilde. Then she added, "Give me your arm please, Conrad."

Monsieur de Lucenay followed the duchess with Saint-Remy, who could not restrain his rage.

"Aren't you coming with us to see the Sennevals, Saint-Remy?" asked Monsieur de Lucenay.

"No. I can't," he said, brusquely.

"You know, Saint-Remy, Madame de Senneval's another one of those people. What am I saying, another one? I mean another two I'd be happy to sacrifice. Because her husband is another one on my list."

"What list?"

"The list of people I wouldn't mind seeing dead if only d'Harville were still with us."

As Monsieur de Montbrison was helping the duchess on with her cape in the waiting chamber, Monsieur de Lucenay turned to his cousin and said, "Since you're coming along, Conrad, tell your driver to follow ours—unless you're coming, Saint-Remy, you can give me your place, and I can tell you another good story, one that's just as good as the one about the tailor."

"Thank you very much," said Saint-Remy drily. "I cannot accompany you."

"Oh, well. It's good-bye, then, my friend. Are you and my wife squabbling? She just got in the carriage without saying a word to you." Indeed, the duchess's carriage had moved toward the base of the doorsteps, and she was stepping into it.

"Cousin?" said Conrad as he waited deferentially for Monsieur de Lucenay.

"Go ahead! Get in!" said the duke, who, pausing for a moment at the top of the doorsteps, was looking at the elegant harnessing of the viscount's carriage.

"Are those your chestnut horses, Saint-Remy?"

"Yes."

"And there's your fat Edwards. What bearing he has! Now, that's what the coachman of a well-appointed house looks like. Do you see how well he keeps his horses in control? One must give credit where credit is due: there's no one like that devil of a Saint-Remy for getting his hands on the best of everything."

"Madame de Lucenay and your cousin are waiting for you, dear friend," said Monsieur de Saint-Remy, bitterly.

"Goodness gracious, you're right! I'm so vulgar! Good evening, then, Saint-Remy. Ah! I almost forgot," said the duke as he stopped in the middle of the steps in front of the door. "If you have nothing better to do, come and have dinner with us tomorrow. Lord Dudley sent me some grouse" (chickens that live on the heather) "from Scotland. They must be quite awful, don't you think? So I'll see you there, right?" And at that, the duke rejoined his wife and Conrad.

Left alone on the stairs, Saint-Remy watched the carriage depart. His own came up. He got in, casting a look of anger, hatred, and despair at this house into which he had entered as if he were the master and which he was leaving having been ignominiously shown the door.

"Take me home!" he said, brusquely.

"To the residence!" said the footservant to Edwards as he closed the door of the carriage.

It is not hard to imagine the bitter and hopeless thoughts that filled

Saint-Remy's head as he returned home. As he walked in, Boyer, who had been awaiting him under the peristyle, said to him, "The count is upstairs waiting for Monsieur the viscount."

"Good."

"There's another man there with whom Monsieur the viscount had an appointment at ten o'clock, a Monsieur Petit-Jean."

"Good, good . . . Oh! What an evening!" said Florestan as he went up to see his father, whom he found in the first-floor salon, the same room in which their morning conversation had taken place.

"A thousand pardons, Father, for not being present when you arrived here, but I—"

"Is the man who is in possession of the forged bill here?" asked the count, interrupting his son.

"Yes, Father. He's downstairs."

"Have him come up."

Florestan rang, and Boyer appeared. "Tell Monsieur Petit-Jean to come upstairs."

"Yes, monsieur." Boyer withdrew.

"How good you are, Father, to be true to your word."

"I always keep my word."

"I am so grateful to you! How can I ever prove to you—"

"I didn't want my name to be dishonored. It won't be."

"It won't be! No, it won't ever be dishonored again, I swear to you, Father."

The count gave his son an odd look and repeated what he had said. "No, it won't ever be again." Then he added, sarcastically, "Are you a prophet?"

"It's just that I know in the depth of my heart the strength of my resolve."

Florestan's father did not respond to this statement. He paced back and forth in the room, his two hands in the pockets of his long waistcoat. He was pale.

"Monsieur Petit-Jean," said Boyer, announcing a man with a vulgar, sordid, devious-looking face.

"Where is the note?" asked the count.

"Here it is, monsieur," said Petit-Jean (this was the front man of the solicitor, Jacques Ferrand), as he presented the document to the count.

"Is this the actual note?" the latter asked his son, gesturing with a glance toward the note.

"Yes, Father."

The count removed from the pocket of his vest twenty-five one-thousand-franc bills. He gave them to his son and said to him, "Pay him!"

Florestan paid and took the note back with a deep sigh of satisfaction.

Monsieur Petit-Jean placed the bills carefully in an old wallet and took his leave.

Monsieur de Saint-Remy left the room with him as Florestan prudently tore the note into little pieces.

"At least I still have Clotilde's twenty-five thousand francs. If I don't get caught, that's at least something. But how she treated me! Oh, really, now what can my father have to say to Monsieur Petit-Jean?"

The sound of a key turning twice in a lock made the viscount shiver. His father came back into the room. His pallor had increased.

"If I'm not mistaken, Father, I heard someone lock the door to my study."

"Yes, I locked it."

"You, Father? Why?" asked Florestan, bewildered.

"I'm going to tell you." The count positioned himself where his son could not get to the hidden staircase that led to the ground floor.

An anxious Florestan began to notice the sinister look of his father's face, and he followed all of his movements distrustfully. Without being able to say why, he felt a vague fear.

"Father, what's wrong?"

"This morning, when you saw me, your only thought was this: 'My father will not let his name be dishonored. If I manage to fool him with a few feigned words of repentance, he'll pay.'"

"Ah! How can you think that—"

"Don't interrupt me. I wasn't fooled by you. You haven't any shame, regret, or remorse. You're corrupt through and through. You've never had an honest feeling in your life. So long as you had enough money to finance your whims, you didn't steal. That's what they call the integrity of rich people of your type. After that, though, came awkward moments, followed by acts of dishonor, then crime, your forgeries. This is just the first stage of your life. You're still in a state of purity in comparison to what would become of you later—"

"If I don't change my ways, I admit it's true. But I'll change them, Father, I've sworn that to you already."

"You'd never change."

"But—"

"You'd never change. Rejected by the society you've lived in until now, you'd become a criminal soon enough, just like those wretches among whom you'd be thrown. You'd inevitably become a thief, and, if need be, you'd become a murderer. That's your future."

"A murderer? Me?"

"Yes, because you're a coward."

"I've fought duels! I've proven my—"

"And I say you're a coward. You preferred infamy to death. A day will come along when you'll prefer getting away with your latest crimes over the life of another human being. That cannot happen—I won't tolerate it. I've come just in time at least to save my name henceforth from public disgrace. I need to put a stop to this."

"What do you mean, 'put a stop to this,' Father? What do you mean?" cried Florestan, more and more terrified by the ominous expression on his father's face and by his ever growing pallor.

Suddenly someone knocked violently on the door of the study. Florestan went to open it in order to put an end to this frightening scene, but the count seized him with an iron grip and held him.

"Who's there?" asked the count.

"In the name of the law, open the door! Open up!" said a voice.

"So that forged note wasn't the last?" said the count quietly, giving his son a terrible look.

"It was, Father, I swear to you," said Florestan, trying in vain to escape the vigorous hold his father had on him.

"Open up, in the name of the law!" repeated the voice.

"What do you want?" asked the count.

"I'm the police inspector. I've a search warrant in connection with a diamond theft of which Monsieur de Saint-Remy is accused. Monsieur Baudoin, the jeweler, can prove the truth of this charge. If you don't open the door, monsieur, I will be obliged to break it down."

"A thief, already! I wasn't wrong about you," said the count in a whisper. "I had come to kill you, but I waited too long."

"To kill me?"

"Enough of the disgrace you've brought on my name. Let's put an end to it. I have two pistols here. You're going to blow your brains out with one of them, or else I'll do it for you myself, and I'll say that you killed yourself out of despair and in order to escape your shame." And with incredible composure, the count took a pistol out of his pocket and, with his free hand, offered it to his son, saying, "Go ahead! Get it over with, if you're not a coward!"

After making renewed and futile efforts to escape the count's grip, his son stepped backward with terror and turned white. From the terrible and inexorable gaze of his father, he understood that he could expect no mercy from him. "Father!" he cried.

"You must die!"

"I repent!"

"It's too late! Do you understand? They're breaking down the door!"

"I will expiate my crimes!"

"They're about to come in! So am I going to have to kill you myself?"

"Mercy!"

"The door is about to give way! Since this is the way you wanted it!" At this, the count stuck the barrel of the gun into Florestan's chest.

The noise from outside showed only too clearly that the door to the study could indeed withstand the assault no longer. The viscount saw that he was done for.

A sudden, desperate resolution occurred to him: he no longer struggled with his father, and said to him both firmly and with resignation, "You're right, Father. Give me the gun. I've brought enough dishonor upon our name. The life that awaits me is appalling. It's not even worth fighting over. Give me the gun. You'll see if I'm a coward." And he reached for the pistol. "But say at least one word, just one word of comfort, of pity, of farewell," said Florestan.

His trembling lips, his pallor, the disturbed look of his face: all testified to the terrible emotion of this ultimate moment.

"What if he really is my son after all?" thought the count with a shudder, hesitating to hand him the pistol. "If he's my son, I should hesitate even less before this sacrifice."

A long crunching sound from the study door revealed that it had just been successfully broken into. "Father, they're coming in . . . Oh! I know now that death is the right thing . . . Thank you . . . thank you . . . Give me your hand, at least, and tell me you forgive me!"

Despite his hardness, the count could not keep himself from shuddering and saying to him, in an emotional voice, "I forgive you."

"Father, the door's been opened. Run to them. At least they won't suspect you. And if they get in here, they'll stop me from ending it all. Farewell."

The steps of several people could be heard in the next room.

Florestan placed the barrel of the pistol over his heart.

The shot rang out at the moment at which the count, in order to avoid having to witness the horrible spectacle, turned away and rushed out of the salon. The double doors closed behind him. At the sound of the explosion, seeing the count pale and wild-eyed, the inspector stopped suddenly in the door's threshold, gesturing to his agents to stay where they were. Alerted by Boyer that the viscount was locked up with his father, the officer understood everything, and he showed respect in the presence of this great sorrow.

"Dead!" cried the count, hiding his face in his hands. "Dead!" he repeated, overcome. "It was the right thing to do. Death is better than dishonor . . . but it's awful!"

"Monsieur," said the officer with sadness after a few moments of silence, "spare yourself this painful sight. Leave the house now. I must now fulfill an even sadder duty than the one that brought me here to begin with."

"You are right, monsieur," said Monsieur de Saint-Remy. "As for the victim of the theft, you may tell him to apply to Monsieur Dupont, the banker."

"Rue de Richelieu, of course. He's well known," answered the officer.

"How much were the stolen diamonds estimated to be worth?"

"Thirty thousand francs, approximately, monsieur. The person who bought them and reported the theft gave your son that sum for them."

"I can still afford to cover that sum, monsieur. Have the jeweler go tomorrow to see my banker. I'll arrange matters with him."

The inspector made a bow to him, and the count left.

After the latter departed, the magistrate, profoundly moved by this unexpected scene, made his way slowly toward the salon. The door curtains were lowered. He raised them with emotion.

"No one's here!" he cried, stupefied, gazing around the room and seeing no trace of the tragic event that was supposed to have taken place in it.

Then, noticing the little door hidden in the drapery, he ran over to it. It was locked from the side of the hidden staircase. "It was a ruse! He escaped through that door!" he cried, angrily.

Indeed, the viscount had pointed the pistol at his heart in front of his father, but he had subsequently managed cleverly to shoot underneath his arm and had quickly made his escape. Despite a very thorough search of the house, the men could not find Florestan. During the conversation between his father and the inspector, he had speedily gotten to the boudoir, from there to the greenhouse, then the deserted passageway, and finally onto the Champs-Élysées.

The picture of this ignoble depravity amid such opulence is a sorry one. We are well aware of the fact. Yet when they lack upbringing, the rich inevitably have as a consequence forms of poverty, vice, and crime particular to themselves. There is nothing more frequent or more affecting than the mad and fruitless sorts of profligacy we have just depicted. They always lead to ruin, loss of respect, base deeds, or dishonor. The spectacle is deplorable, even gruesome. One might feel the same upon seeing a flourishing field of wheat senselessly ravaged by a horde of wild animals.

Certainly, one's wealth and property are and must be inviolable and sacred. Riches, either earned or inherited, should be allowed to shine, without fear of punishment or reproof before the eyes of the poor and suffering classes. The appalling inequality in fortune that exists between the millionaire Saint-Remy and the artisan Morel will have to be with us for a very long time. But precisely because these inevitable disproportions continue to be preserved and protected by the law, those who possess so much wealth ought to act morally, just as those who possess no more than their righteousness, resignation, courage, and habits of hard work must do.

From the perspective of reason, human rights, and even the interests of society, of course, a great fortune should be a hereditary deposit, entrusted to prudent, firm, intelligent, generous caretakers who are charged simultaneously with spending the fortune and making it a productive one; they should know how to fertilize, enhance, and improve everything upon which the splendid and life-giving rays of this fortune may fall.

This is the way matters unfold sometimes, but such cases are rare. How many young people like Saint-Remy, possessed at twenty years old of a considerable inheritance, proceed to fritter it away foolishly in idleness, boredom, and vice, even to the point of vileness, having no idea how better to employ their fortunes both for themselves and for others! Others, fearing the transience of all things human, hoard their money sordidly. In the end, aware that a fortune that stagnates decreases, they become either dupes or knaves, engaging in the random and immoral speculation encouraged and patronized by those in power. How could it be otherwise? Who teaches the knowledge, the rudiments of personal economy—and thereby, of social economy—to inexperienced youth? Nobody. The rich man is thrown into society with his riches just as the poor man is thrown into it with his poverty. No more attention is paid to the excesses of the former than to the needs of the latter. We consider neither fortune nor misfortune from a moral standpoint.

Is it not the duty of those in power to fulfill this great and noble responsibility? If finally they took pity on the poor, the ever growing sorrows of the workers who remain resigned to their fate, and, suppressing the kind of competition that is disastrous for everyone—if finally they took on the pressing question of the organization of labor, they would create the healthy example of cooperation between capital and labor. But this would be an honest, intelligent, equitable cooperation, one that would guarantee the well-being of the artisan without threatening the fortune of the wealthy, one that would safeguard forever the tranquility of the state by establishing bonds of affection and gratitude between these two classes.

How powerful the consequences of such practical instruction would be! Who among the rich would hesitate, then, between, on the one hand, the shady, disastrous wages of speculation, the savage joys of avarice, the senseless vanity of a ruinous dissipation and, on the other, an investment that would be both productive and beneficent, that would spread comfort, morality, happiness, and joy, for twenty families?

CHAPTER 10

SAYING FAREWELL

. . . I believed—I saw—I weep . . .

—WORDSWORTH[155]

The day following the evening on which the Count de Saint-Remy had been so outrageously duped by his son, a touching scene was taking place in Saint-Lazare during the inmates' recreation period. On this day, while the other prisoners were strolling about, Fleur-de-Marie was sitting on a bench next to the pool in the courtyard. This bench had already been christened "Songbird's bench" by the inmates, who, in an unspoken agreement, had taken to saving it for her to sit on. The girl liked the spot. Her gentle influence over them had only increased.

Songbird was fond of this bench by the pool because at least the little moss covering the curbstones in the reservoir reminded her of the greenery of the fields, just as the clear water it contained made her think of the little river that ran through the village of Bouqueval. From the gloomy perspective of a prisoner, a tuft of grass is a meadow, and a single bloom is a flower bed.

Trusting in Madame d'Harville's warm promises, Fleur-de-Marie had been expecting to leave Saint-Lazare for these past two days. Although she had no reason to worry over her delayed departure from prison, the girl was so used to being unhappy that she hardly allowed herself the luxury of believing she would be freed. Ever since she had come back among these creatures—whose looks and speech at every moment reawakened in her soul the incurable memory of her early shame—Fleur-de-Marie's melancholy had overwhelmed her even more than before. And in addition to this, the passionate exaltation of her gratitude toward Rodolphe had given birth to a new source of anxiety, of sorrow—of something approaching terror. Strangely, she had never sounded the depths of the abyss into which she had sunk until she began to measure the distance that separated her from the seemingly superhuman grandeur of this man—of this man who embodied at one and the same time such august goodness and immense

155. Even given the vagaries of checking by translating French back into English, concordances to Wordsworth show no such line in his poetry. The translators do not know whether Sue is misquoting someone else or inventing. [TN]

powers so fearful to evildoers. Despite the respectful adoration she felt for him in her heart, Fleur-de-Marie was frightened when she thought she recognized in this adoration the characteristics of being in love, though a love as hidden as it was profound, and as chaste as it was hidden, and as hopeless as it was chaste. The poor child had not thought to discover this despairing truth of her heart's feelings until she met with Madame d'Harville, who was herself in the throes of a secret passion for Rodolphe.

After the marquise's departure and her promises, Fleur-de-Marie should have been beside herself with joy as she thought of how she would soon be reunited with her friends from Bouqueval and with Rodolphe. But this was not the case. Her heart was painfully torn. She kept remembering Madame d'Harville's stinging words and haughty, scrutinizing gaze as the poor prisoner had waxed enthusiastic in speaking of her benefactor.

A singular intuition on Songbird's part had partially uncovered Madame d'Harville's secret. "My exalted gratitude toward Monsieur Rodolphe wounded that young woman of such elevated rank and beauty," thought Fleur-de-Marie. "Now I understand the bitterness of her words. She was expressing a disdainful jealousy. Her, jealous of me! She must be in love with him. And am I in fact in love with him, too? Have I been in love with him despite myself? For me to love him—me, me, a creature as abject, unworthy, and miserable as I am—oh! If it's true, I'd be a hundred times better off dead!"

Let us hasten to say that the poor child—who seemed to be fated for every kind of martyrdom—had exaggerated to herself what she was calling her love for Rodolphe. Combined with the profound gratitude she felt toward him, there was also an involuntary admiration for the grace, force, and beauty that distinguished him from all others. This admiration was absolutely spiritual and pure, but it was sharp and powerful. Physical beauty is always alluring in this way. And in addition, the voice of the blood—a voice so often neglected, silent, unacknowledged, or poorly understood—sometimes manages to make itself heard. The bursts of passionate affection that Fleur-de-Marie felt toward Rodolphe, and that frightened her in her ignorance because she distorted their meaning, stemmed from a mysterious sympathy that was just as obvious but also just as inexplicable as the resemblance of their features. In a word, Fleur-de-Marie would have understood instantly the powerful pull she felt toward Rodolphe if she learned that she was his daughter. If she fully understood the nature of their relationship, she would have admired her father's beauty without any fear.

This is why Fleur-de-Marie was so dejected, in spite of the fact that she should have been looking forward to being released from Saint-Lazare at any moment, thanks to Madame d'Harville's promise.

Melancholic and pensive, Fleur-de-Marie was thus sitting on a bench next to the pool, watching the games of several emboldened birds that had come to perch on the curbstones with a sort of mechanical interest. She had stopped working for a moment on a small children's jacket that she was almost done hemming. Need we say that this jacket was part of the new set of baby clothes that the prisoners had so generously offered to Mont-Saint-Jean, thanks to Fleur-de-Marie's moving intervention?

Songbird's poor, deformed protégée was sitting at her feet; as she busily put the finishing touches on a little bonnet, she looked up from time to time to gaze up at her benefactress. Her look was full of gratitude, timidity, and devotion; she looked at her the way a dog looks at its master.

Fleur-de-Marie's beauty, charm, and adorable gentleness made this debased woman feel as much attraction toward her as respect. There is always something sacred and great in the aspirations of even a degraded heart when it opens itself for the first time to gratitude. Until this moment, no one had given Mont-Saint-Jean the opportunity to experience the religious ardor of this sentiment that was so new to her.

After a moment or two, Fleur-de-Marie trembled slightly, wiped a tear from her eye, and returned to her sewing with renewed purpose. "Why don't you take a break from your work during our rest time, my good guardian angel?" Mont-Saint-Jean asked Songbird.

"I didn't have any money to contribute to the baby clothes. I have to put in my share in terms of work," answered the girl.

"Your share? Good God! Without you, instead of having this nice white linen and this nice warm fustian to clothe my baby in, I would just have those rags that they dragged through the mud of the courtyard. I'm very grateful to my companions. They've been so good to me, it's true. But you? Oh, you! How can I say this?" said the poor creature, hesitant and embarrassed as she tried to express her thoughts. "Listen," she went on, "do you see the sun? There, the sun?"

"Yes, Mont-Saint-Jean, it's all right, I'm listening," answered Fleur-de-Marie as she leaned her enchanting face toward the hideous countenance of her companion.

"My goodness, now you're going to make fun of me," the latter said, sadly. "I'd like to be able to talk well, but I don't know how."

"Say it anyway, Mont-Saint-Jean."

"Look at your beautiful angel's eyes!" said the prisoner as she took in Fleur-de-Marie in a kind of ecstasy. "They give you courage, those angel's eyes. All right, I'll try to say what I mean. So there's the sun, right? It's nice and warm, it brightens life in the prison, it's good to see and feel, right?"

"No doubt."

"But let's think about it: that sun didn't make itself on its own, and if we can be grateful for it, all the more reason we should be grateful to—"

"The being who created it, right, Mont-Saint-Jean? You're right—and also we should pray to that being and adore him. It is God."

"That's it! That's what I wanted to say!" the prisoner cried out, joyously. "That's it! I should be grateful to my companions, but I should pray to you and adore you—you, Songbird, because it's you who made them good to me instead of mean like they used to be."

"It's God you need to thank, Mont-Saint-Jean, not me."

"No, it's you. I can see you. You have been good to me and you made others be good to me."

"But if I am as good as you say, Mont-Saint-Jean, it's God who made me that way. So He's the one you should thank."

"Oh, heavens! Well, it could be. If you say so," said the prisoner, indecisively. "If it makes you happy to do it that way, well, then, all right."

"Yes, my poor Mont-Saint-Jean. Pray to Him often. It's the best way to show me you love me a little bit."

"Love you, Songbird? Good God! But don't you remember what you said to the other prisoners to keep them from beating me? 'It's not just her that you're hitting. It's her child, too.' Well? It's just the same with my loving you. It's not just for myself I love you, but for my child, too."

"Thank you, Mont-Saint-Jean, thank you. You make me happy when you say that." And Fleur-de-Marie reached out to her companion, full of emotion.

"What a pretty little fairy's hand you've got! It's so cute and white!" said Mont-Saint-Jean, backing away from it as if she were afraid to touch such a charming hand with her own nasty, red, sordid ones. Still, after hesitating a moment, she respectfully grazed the tip of Fleur-de-Marie's tapered fingers with her lips. Then, getting down on her knees suddenly, she fixed her with a contemplative gaze, in deep, attentive reflection.

"Why don't you come and sit over here next to me?" Songbird asked her.

"Oh, no, that can't be! Never! Not me, no!"

"Why not?"

"Discipline must be maintained, as my brave Mont-Saint-Jean used to say. Soldiers with soldiers, officers with officers. Each one where he belongs."

"You're being foolish. There's no difference at all between us."

"No difference? Good Lord! And you're saying that even as I see you the way I see you, as beautiful as a queen? Oh! Please, I'm not doing any harm. Let me stay on my knees here, where I can gaze up at you the way I was just looking at you a moment ago. Heavens, who knows? Although

I'm an ugly monster, maybe my child will look like you. They say that a look—sometimes, well, it can make that happen."

Then, with a delicacy of discernment hard to believe in a creature of her sort, fearing that she had perhaps humiliated or wounded Fleur-de-Marie with this unusual and almost religious wish, Mont-Saint-Jean added sadly, "No, no, I'm just joking. Go on, Songbird. I wouldn't allow myself to think about you that way—anyway, not without your permission. My child will be as ugly as I am. What does it matter? I won't love him any the less. Poor little unhappy child, he never asked to be born, like they say . . . And if he lives, what will become of him?" she said in a somber, dejected voice. "Alas, yes, what will become of him, Lord?"

Songbird shuddered at these words. And, in fact, what could become of the child of this wretch who was so debased, degraded, poor, and despised? What fate could be in store for such a person? What kind of future? "Don't think about that, Mont-Saint-Jean," said Fleur-de-Marie. "Let's hope your child will encounter charitable people on his path."

"Oh! No, lightning doesn't strike twice, you know, Songbird," Mont-Saint-Jean said bitterly, shaking her head. "I met you. You, you're a great stroke of luck already. And listen: I don't want to offend you, but I wish my child had had the good fortune of meeting you instead of me. This wish is the only thing I have to bequeath him."

"Pray, pray; God will answer you."

"All right, I'll pray, if it makes you happy, Songbird. Maybe it will bring me luck. Indeed, who'd have believed, when the She-Wolf was hitting me and when I was everyone's punching bag, that there would turn up a good little guardian angel who, just with her soft, pretty voice, would be stronger than everyone? Stronger even than the She-Wolf, who's so strong and so mean?"

"Yes, but the She-Wolf was very good to you when she realized that you were doubly to be pitied."

"Oh! That's true, thanks to you, and I'll never forget it. But tell me, Songbird, why did she ask after that day to change her living quarters? In spite of her moodiness, it seemed she couldn't do without you."

"She's a little temperamental."

"That's funny. A woman who came this morning from the part of the prison the She-Wolf moved into said that she's a changed woman."

"How is that?"

"Instead of quarreling or threatening everyone, she's sad. She's sad, and she keeps to herself in the corner. If you talk to her, she turns her back on you and doesn't answer. To think of seeing her silent now, when she used to yell so much all the time: it's surprising, isn't it? And the woman told me something else, too, but I don't believe it."

"What was that?"

"She said she saw the She-Wolf crying. The She-Wolf crying? Not likely."

"Poor She-Wolf! It's because of me that she moved to the other wing. I made her sad, without meaning to," said Songbird with a sigh.

"You made someone sad? My good guardian angel!"

At this moment, the inspector, Madame Armand, entered the courtyard. After looking for Fleur-de-Marie, she came over to her, smiling and seeming satisfied about something.

"I have good news for you, my child."

"What is it, madame?" cried Songbird, rising.

"Your friends have not forgotten you. They have obtained your liberty. The director just received the order."

"Can this be true, madame? Oh! What happiness! Good Lord!" Fleur-de-Marie's emotions were so violent that she grew pale, placed her hand over her heart, which beat violently, and sank back onto her bench.

"Calm down, my child," said Madame Armand to her with kindness. "Fortunately, shocks like these don't do any harm."

"Oh, madame! I am so grateful!"

"It must have been Madame d'Harville who obtained your release. There's an old lady over there who will bring you back to the people who care about you. Wait for me. I'll come back to get you. I just have to tell them something in the workshop."

It would be difficult to depict the expression of gloomy desolation that darkened Mont-Saint-Jean's features as she learned that her dear guardian angel, as she called Songbird, was about to leave Saint-Lazare. The woman's sadness came less from her fear of becoming the prison's punching bag once again than from the sorrowful prospect of being separated from the only being who had ever shown her any kindness. Still seated at the foot of the bench, Mont-Saint-Jean brought her hands up to the two tufts of bristly hair that had escaped from her old black bonnet, as if she were going to tear them out. Then, her feelings of violent affliction gave way to dejection. Her head drooped down and she sat in silence, motionless, with her forehead in her hands and her elbows on her knees.

In spite of her joy upon leaving the prison, Fleur-de-Marie could not prevent herself from shivering at a momentary memory of the Owl and the Schoolmaster. She remembered that these two monsters had made her swear never to inform her benefactors of her sad fate. But these bleak thoughts soon gave way to Fleur-de-Marie's happiness at the thought of seeing Bouqueval, Madame Georges, and Rodolphe, to whom she meant to recommend the She-Wolf and Martial. It even seemed to her now that the exalted sentiment she had been reproaching herself for feeling toward her benefactor, once it was no longer being fed by sorrow and isolation, would become calmer as soon as she once again took up the rustic occupations that she had so enjoyed sharing with the good and simple inhabitants of the farm.

Surprised at the silence of her companion, a silence of which she did not suspect the cause, Songbird touched her lightly on the shoulder and said to her, "Mont-Saint-Jean, since I'm about to be freed, isn't there something I can do for you?"

Feeling Songbird's hand on her, the prisoner trembled. Her arms fell to her knees and she turned her face, streaming with tears, toward the girl. The pain on Mont-Saint-Jean's face was so bitter that her ugliness had disappeared.

"Heavens! What's wrong?" said Songbird. "You are crying so much!"

"You're going away!" murmured the prisoner in a voice choked with sobbing. "I never thought that, at any moment, you might leave here, and that I wouldn't see you . . . ever, ever again!"

"Rest assured, I will always remember our friendship, Mont-Saint-Jean."

"Lord, Lord! And to think that I already loved you so much! When I was sitting there on the ground at your feet, I felt as if I had been saved . . . as if I had nothing more to fear. It's not because of the beatings the others might start up giving me again that I say this. My life has been hard. But it's just that it seemed like you were my stroke of good luck and that you would bring happiness to my child, if only because you had pity on me. Well, you know, it's like that, it's true. When you're used to being mistreated, you're more sensitive than other people to acts of kindness."

Then, interrupting herself to burst into tears again, she cried, "All right, it's over! It's over! Well, it had to happen one of these days. But I should've known. It's over. Over. There's nothing more—nothing more."

"Come on. Keep your head up. I'll remember you, just like you'll remember me."

"Oh, they'd have to cut me into tiny pieces before I'd disown or forget you. When I'm old—as old as the hills—I'll still be able to see your beautiful angel's face in my mind's eye. The first word I will teach my child will be your name, Songbird, since it's because of you that he won't have died of the cold."

"Listen to me, Mont-Saint-Jean," said Fleur-de-Marie, touched by the affection of this wretched girl. "I can't promise anything about you, even though I know some very charitable people. But for your child, that's something else. He's totally innocent, and the people I'm telling you about might be able to see that he is raised well as soon as you can separate yourself from him."

"Separate myself from him? Never! Oh, never!" cried Mont-Saint-

Jean, passionately. "What would become of me, when he's all I've been living for?"

"But . . . how will you raise him? Girl or boy, he'll have to be honest, and in order for that to happen—"

"He'll have to earn his keep honestly, right, Songbird? I know that, and that's what I hope for him. I tell myself that every day. And so, when I get out of here, I'll never set foot again under a bridge. I'm going to become a ragpicker, a street sweeper, just something respectable. You have to do that—if not for yourself, then at least for your child. That is, if you have the honor of having one," she said with some pride.

"And who will look after your child while you're working?" asked Songbird. "If it can be arranged as I hope, wouldn't it be better to place the little one with some good folks who live in the countryside who would make a good farm girl or farmer out of the child? You could come by from time to time to visit him, and one day you might find a way to live nearby. You can get by on so little in the country!"

"But I'm supposed to separate myself from him? Separate myself from him? This child was the source of all the joy in my life, me, who nobody loves."

"You have to think of his well-being before your own, my poor Mont-Saint-Jean. In two or three days I'll write to Madame Armand, and if the request I plan on making on your child's behalf is granted, you'll never have to say those words that broke my heart a moment ago, 'Alas, what will become of him, Lord?'"

The inspector, Madame Armand, interrupted this conversation. She had come to take Fleur-de-Marie away.

After bursting once again into sobs and bathing the young woman's hands in her desperate tears, Mont-Saint-Jean slumped back onto the bench in dazed dejection, no longer even considering the promise Fleur-de-Marie had just made her with respect to her child.

"Poor creature!" said Madame Armand as she left the courtyard, followed by Fleur-de-Marie. "Her gratitude toward you makes me think much better of her."

When the other prisoners learned of Songbird's reprieve, far from showing any jealousy of this preferential treatment, they displayed only joy. Several of them surrounded Fleur-de-Marie and said their farewells to her in the most cordial fashion possible, offering her their heartiest congratulations on her speedy release from prison. "It's fine with me," said one of them. "That little blond girl made us feel something we'll always remember. It was when we took up a collection for Mont-Saint-Jean's baby clothes. That's something they'll never forget at Saint-Lazare."

When Fleur-de-Marie left the prison building alongside the inspector, the latter said to her, "Now, my child, go report to the cloakroom. There you'll leave your prisoner's uniform and put your peasant's clothing back on. Their simple, rustic style suits you so well. Farewell, my dear! You're going to be happy because you will find yourself under the protection of good people, and you'll leave this place and never come back. Wait just a minute. Now I'm just being foolish," said Madame Armand, whose eyes were filling with tears. "There's no hiding how fond I've become of you, poor little one." Then, seeing that Fleur-de-Marie was growing teary as well, the inspector added, "I hope you won't be angry with me that I've made your leaving a sad one?"

"Ah, madame! Isn't it thanks to your recommendation that the young woman to whom I owe my freedom became concerned with what happened to me?"

"Yes, and I'm delighted that I did what I did. My premonition turned out to be right."

At that moment a bell chimed. "It's time for the workshops to pick up again. I must go back inside. Farewell, my dear child! Again, farewell!" And Madame Armand, just as emotional as Fleur-de-Marie, gave her a tender kiss. Then she said to one of the prison employees, "Take Mademoiselle to the cloakroom."

A quarter of an hour later, Fleur-de-Marie, in the same peasant's dress we saw her wearing at the Bouqueval farm, entered the clerk's office, where Madame Séraphin was waiting for her. The housekeeper of Jacques Ferrand, the solicitor, had come to pick up the unfortunate child in order to convey her to the Scavenger's Island.

CHAPTER II

MEMORIES

Jacques Ferrand had obtained Fleur-de-Marie's freedom quickly and easily, it being a matter only of a simple administrative decision. Having learned from the Owl that Songbird was being held in Saint-Lazare, he immediately visited one of his clients, an honest and influential man, and told him that a girl who had once gone astray but had since sincerely repented was now being held at Saint-Lazare, where her contact with the other prisoners might weaken her resolve. Since the girl had come to him highly recommended by respectable people who would take responsibility for her when she left prison, Jacques Ferrand added, he begged his highly influential client, in the name of morality, religion, and the rehabilitation of this poor unfortunate soul, to ask the authorities for her freedom. And then, to protect himself from any consequent investigations, the solicitor had pointedly and insistently requested his client to keep his name out of the execution of this good deed. Knowing Jacques Ferrand as a pious and respectable man and attributing this wish to his philanthropic humility, the client scrupulously respected this desire. He requested and obtained Fleur-de-Marie's freedom entirely in his own name and then, to cap off his helpfulness, he alerted Jacques Ferrand immediately upon her exit so that the solicitor could go to the girl's protectors.

In delivering this order to the prison director, Madame Séraphin added that she had been charged with conveying Songbird to the people who would take care of her. Given the excellent recommendation the inspector had given Madame d'Harville for Fleur-de-Marie, no one thought anything other than that the latter owed her freedom to the marquise's intervention. Nothing about the solicitor's housekeeper therefore was likely to incite her victim's distrust. Madame Séraphin could, when the occasion demanded it, put on the manner of a simple old biddy, as such a woman is vulgarly called. One would need a sharp eye to detect the insidiousness, falseness, and cruelty beneath her flattering look and hypocritical smile. Despite her profound villainy, which had made her the accomplice of or confidante in her employer's crimes, Madame Séraphin could not help herself from being struck by the touching beauty of this girl whom she had turned over to the Owl when she was still an infant and whom she was now delivering to a certain death.

"Well, then, my dear young lady," Madame Séraphin said to her in a honeyed voice, "you must be very happy to be leaving prison."

"Oh, yes, madame, and it must be because of Madame d'Harville's protection. She has been so good to me."

"You're not wrong about that. But come along. We're already a little late and we have a long journey before us."

"We're going to the Bouqueval farm and Madame Georges—isn't that right, madame?" Songbird exclaimed.

"Yes . . . of course, we are going to the country . . . to see Madame Georges," the housekeeper said to ward off any suspicion Fleur-de-Marie might have. And then, out of a cruel sense of humor, she added, "But before you see Madame Georges, there's a little surprise waiting for you. Come on, come on, our hackney is downstairs. Well, you're going to breathe one big sigh of relief to be getting out of here, my dear young lady! Well, let's get going. Sirs, your humble servant." And, having made her farewells to the clerk and his assistants, Madame Séraphin went downstairs with Songbird.

A guard accompanied them to order the doors to be opened. The last door had closed and the two women found themselves under the vast porch that gave onto rue du Faubourg-Saint-Denis when they ran into a girl who had probably come to visit some prisoner.

It was Rigolette, graceful and stylish as ever: her little face was framed with a simple bonnet, but it was new and ornamented with cherry-colored ribbons that set off her black braids beautifully. A very white collar was pulled down over a long brown tartan. On her arm, she carried a straw shopping bag. Because she walked with the clean, careful carriage of a cat, her boots with their thick soles were unbelievably clean, even though, alas, the poor thing had come a long way.

"Rigolette!" Fleur-de-Marie cried out, recognizing her old companion from prison and trips to the country.[156]

"Songbird!" the seamstress called in turn. And the two girls threw themselves into each other's arms.

Nothing could be more enchanting than the contrast between these two sixteen-year-old children in their affectionate embrace, both charming and yet so different in the types of their beauty. One was blond with melancholy blue eyes and a slightly sad, slightly otherworldly profile of angelic, ideal purity, like those of the adorable peasants of Greuze, with

156. The reader will perhaps remember that in the story Songbird told Rodolphe of her early years in her conversation with him at the ogress's joint, she had spoken of Rigolette, who, like her a child vagabond, had been locked up, like her, in a house of detention until the age of sixteen. [SN]

their fresh and clear complexion.[157] She was an indescribable mix of dreaminess, innocence, and grace. The other was dark, saucy, with round ruby cheeks, pretty black eyes, an innocent laugh, and a lively expression; she was a ravishing example of careless gay youth, a rare and touching example of happiness combined with indulgence, honesty with abandon, joy with work.

After their innocent embrace, the two girls looked at each other. Rigolette was ecstatic at this meeting, Fleur-de-Marie embarrassed. The sight of her friend recalled to her the short period of calm happiness that had preceded her initial debasement.

"It's you. What a pleasure!" the seamstress said.

"Heavens, yes, what a pleasant surprise! It's been so long since we've seen each other," Songbird answered.

"Well, now I understand why I haven't seen you for six months," Rigolette said, noticing Songbird's peasant clothing. "So you're living in the country?"

"Yes, for some time now," Fleur-de-Marie said, lowering her eyes.

"And you've come here like me to visit someone in prison?"

"Yes, I came . . . well, I was just visiting someone," Fleur-de-Marie stuttered, blushing with shame.

"And now you're returning home? Far from Paris, I'm sure. Dear little Songbird, still doing good. I can see you haven't changed. Do you remember that poor woman in her confinement whom you gave your mattress, some linens, and the little money you had left that we were going to spend in the countryside? You were already crazy for the countryside then, weren't you, little Miss Village Girl?"

"And you didn't think much of it, Rigolette. But you indulged me! Still and all, you would go there for my sake."

"Oh, I did it for my sake, too. You were always a little serious, and you would become so happy, so gay and playful once you were in the middle of a field or some woods that it did my heart good just to see you. But let me look at you a little. How that pretty round bonnet suits you! You look so nice that way! It's clear you were meant for a peasant bonnet just as I was meant for a seamstress's bonnet. Here you are, just as you always wanted. You must be happy. And, really, that doesn't surprise me. When I didn't see you around anymore, I said to myself, 'That good little Songbird wasn't made for Paris. She's a real woodland flower, like the song says. And those flowers don't grow in the capital. The air isn't good for them. So Songbird must have found her place among the honest people of the countryside.' And that's what you did, right?"

---

157. Jean-Baptiste Greuze (1725–1805) made his reputation as a genre painter and a painter of natural scenes, though he was also known for portraits. He wanted to be known as a painter of historical subjects but failed at that endeavor. [TN]

"Yes," Fleur-de-Marie said, blushing.

"But I fault you for one thing."

"Me?"

"You should have let me know. You don't just up and leave somebody from one day to the next. At least you send them a little news."

"I . . . well, I left Paris in such a hurry," Fleur-de-Marie said, becoming more and more embarrassed, "that I couldn't . . ."

"Oh, I don't hold it against you—I'm too happy to see you again. You were quite right to leave Paris. Really, it's so hard to live here in peace. And that doesn't even take into account the fact that poor girls who live alone, like us, can get into trouble without even wanting to. When you have no one to turn to for advice, there's so little protection. Men make such pretty promises, and then sometimes poverty can be so hard . . . Well, do you remember little Julie, who was so nice? And Rosine, the blonde with black eyes?"

"Yes, I remember them."

"Well, then, my poor Songbird, both of them were taken advantage of, then abandoned, then they went from bad to worse until they finally became some of those bad women they imprison in here."

"Good God!" Fleur-de-Marie exclaimed, lowering her head as she went crimson.

Rigolette, mistaking the meaning of her friend's exclamation, went on, "They're guilty, despicable, even. If that's what you think, I won't say no. But don't you see, my dear Songbird, just because we've been lucky enough to keep our virtue—you because you went off to live in the countryside with honest peasants, me because I didn't have time for lovers, and because I preferred my birds and the nice little household I've had so much pleasure keeping, thanks to my work—well, we shouldn't be too hard on other people. Heavens, who can say what role the spirit of the moment, deception, and poverty had to play in Rosine's and Julie's going bad? Who's to say whether we wouldn't have done the same thing they did if we'd been in their shoes?"

"Oh!" Fleur-de-Marie said bitterly. "I don't blame them. I feel sorry for them—"

"Come on, come on, we're in a hurry, my dear young lady," Madame Séraphin said, offering her arm impatiently to her victim.

"Give us another few moments, madame. It's been so long since I've seen my poor Songbird," Rigolette said.

"It's just that it's late, young ladies; it's already three o'clock and we have a long journey ahead of us," Madame Séraphin answered. She was extremely put out by this meeting, but she conceded, "I'll give you another ten minutes."

"And you," Fleur-de-Marie went on, taking her friend's hands in hers, "you're such a cheerful type—are you still happy, still joyful?"

"I was happy and joyful until a few days ago. But now . . ."

"Is something troubling you?"

"Me? Yeah, right. You know me, a real Roger Bontemps.[158] I haven't changed a bit. But unfortunately, not everyone else is like me. And since things bother other people, they bother me, too."

"You're still a kind person."

"What would you have me do? Would you believe that I've come here to see a poor girl, a neighbor and a real innocent little lamb who's being falsely accused? She sure deserves our pity. Her name's Louise Morel, and she's the daughter of an honest worker who was made so miserable that he's been driven insane."

When she heard the name of Louise Morel, one of the solicitor's victims, Madame Séraphin shivered a little and looked quite closely at Rigolette. She had never seen the seamstress's face before. Nevertheless, the housekeeper started paying close attention to the conversation of the two girls at this point.

"The poor woman!" Songbird said. "But she must be happy that you haven't forgotten her in her misfortune."

"And that's not all. That's not all. It's like everything at once. Just as you see me now, I've come from a long way and from yet another prison, this one a men's prison."

"A men's prison? You?"

"Goodness, yes, I have someone else I'm taking care of who's also unhappy. You can see my shopping bag," and Rigolette held it up, "and it's divided in two, one for each of them. Today I'm bringing Louise a little bit of linen and a little while ago I brought something to that poor Germain—my prisoner's name is Germain. Well, you see, I can't think about what just happened to him without wanting to cry. It's stupid. I know it doesn't do any good. But that's just the way I am."

"And why do you want to cry?"

"Imagine, Germain is so unhappy being mixed up with all these bad men in prison that he's completely miserable, he's lost his taste for everything, he doesn't eat, and he's getting thinner and thinner before your eyes. I can see this and I say to myself, 'He's not hungry, I'll make him some little treat that he liked when we were neighbors. That'll bring his appetite back.' When I say a treat, you understand, it's really just some yellow potatoes that I've mashed with a little milk and sugar. So I fill a nice clean cup with it and I bring it right away to him in prison and tell him I made this poor little feast myself just like I used to during the good times, you know? I figured that might make him want to eat a little. Yeah, right."

"What happened?"

---

158. See Book IV, Chapter 3, footnote 98. [TN]

"It made him want to cry. When he recognized the cup as the one I drank my milk from so often in his company, he broke down in tears. And to make matters worse, I ended up doing the same thing, even though I wanted to stop myself from crying. You see what luck I had. I wanted to cheer him up, and I just made him sadder still."

"Yes, but those tears must have been sweet to him."

"That doesn't make any difference. I'd much rather have cheered him up better. But here I am, talking about him to you without telling you who he is. He's an old neighbor of mine and he's the most honest guy in the world, just as gentle and timid as a young girl. I loved him like a friend, like a brother."

"Oh, now I understand why his sorrows are yours, too."

"Isn't that how it works? But you'll see what a good soul he is. When I went away, like always, I asked him if he had any errands for me, laughing to try to make him a little more cheerful and saying that I was his little housekeeper and I'd be a watchful and loyal guardian of his affairs. So, forcing himself to be cheerful, he asked me to bring him one of the Walter Scott novels he used to read to me at night while I was working. That novel was called *Ivan . . . Ivanhoe* . . . yes, that's it.[159] I liked that book so much he read it to me twice. Poor Germain, he's so obliging."

"He wanted something to remember those happy times with."

"Absolutely. That's why he asked me to go to the same reading room, not to rent but to buy the same volumes we used to read together.[160] Yes, buy them, and you can guess what a sacrifice that was for him since he's as poor as we are."

"What a good soul!" said Songbird, who was really moved.

"Now you're feeling soft about him, just like I did when he sent me on that errand, my good little Songbird. But you see, the more I felt I wanted to cry, the more I tried to laugh, because crying twice in the same visit when you're there to cheer someone up, well, that's a bit much. And so to hide all that, I began to tell him funny stories about a Jew, one of the characters in the novel that entertained us so much before. But the more I talked, the tearier his eyes got as he looked at me. Well, Lord, that was just breaking my heart. For a quarter of an hour, I tried in vain to keep myself from crying, but I ended up just like him. When I left him, he was

159. Sir Walter Scott had, if possible, a larger influence in France than in England, importantly on both Balzac and Dumas. His historical novels were a great success there, especially the ones set in the late medieval period, like *Ivanhoe*. The Jew, referred to a few lines down, is a secondary character in the book, the father of one of Ivanhoe's two love interests. [TN]

160. In the eighteenth and nineteenth centuries in France, reading rooms (*cabinets de lecture*) were places one could go to read current newspapers, brochures, and novels, for a small fee. [TN]

sobbing. I was so mad at myself for my silliness that I said to myself, 'If that's how I'm going to comfort him and cheer him up, I shouldn't bother going. I'm the one who's always promising myself to make him laugh. I was a real success at it, I was!'"

On hearing the name Germain, another of the solicitor's victims, Madame Séraphin had started paying even more attention.

"So what did this young man do to get sent to prison?" Fleur-de-Marie asked.

"Him?" Rigolette asked, as her tenderness gave way to indignation. "What he did was he got persecuted by an old beast of a solicitor, the same one who denounced Louise."

"The same Louise you're coming to see here?"

"Absolutely. She was the solicitor's servant and Germain was his clerk. It would take too long to explain how he accused the poor boy unjustly. But what's for sure is that he's a wicked man and he was on those two poor people like a mad dog, and they never did him any harm. But we need to bide our time. What comes around, goes around."

The expression Rigolette gave these words made Madame Séraphin anxious. Joining in the conversation, rather than keeping herself apart, she said to Fleur-de-Marie with her hypocritical sweetness, "My dear young lady, it's late. We have to leave, there are people waiting for you. I can well understand how much you care about what this young lady is telling you because even me—and I don't know the girl and the young man you're talking about—it makes me sad. My God! Is it possible there are such wicked people in the world! And so what's the name of this villain of a solicitor you're talking about, mademoiselle?"

Rigolette had no reason to distrust Madame Séraphin. Nevertheless, remembering what Rodolphe had recommended and that he had called upon all her discretion on the subject of the secret actions he was taking to protect Germain and Louise, she regretted having said, "We need to bide our time. What comes around, goes around." "This wicked man's name is Monsieur Ferrand, madame," Rigolette said, adding, quite cleverly, to make up for her slight indiscretion, "and what makes it even worse for him to persecute Germain and Louise is that no one cares about them except me, and I won't do them a lot of good."

"How terrible!" Madame Séraphin said. "I was hoping the opposite when you said, 'We need to bide our time.' I thought you were counting on some protector to offer support for those two unfortunate people against the wicked solicitor."

"Alas! No, madame," Rigolette added, in order to allay Madame Séraphin's suspicions completely. "Who would be noble minded enough to side with these two poor young people against a man as rich and powerful as Monsieur Ferrand is?"

"Oh, there are people noble minded enough to do that," Fleur-de-Marie said after a moment of reflection and with constrained exaltation. "Yes, I know someone who makes it his duty to protect those who suffer and defend them, because this person I speak of is as much a savior to honest people as he is a scourge to the wicked."

Rigolette looked at Songbird with astonishment and was on the verge of telling her, thinking of Rodolphe, that she also knew someone who courageously took the side of the weak against the strong. But staying true to the recommendations of her neighbor (that is what she called the prince), the seamstress answered Fleur-de-Marie, "Really? You know someone noble minded enough to come to the aid of poor people?"

"Yes, and even though I have already called upon his pity and his benevolence for other people, I'm sure that if he knew about the undeserved suffering of Louise and Germain, he would offer them succor and punish their persecutor, because his justice and his goodness are as inexhaustible as God's."

Madame Séraphin looked at her victim with surprise: "Could this little girl be even more dangerous than we thought?" she asked herself. "If I were likely to have felt pity for her, what she has just said would make the accident that will take her off our hands absolutely unavoidable."

"My good little Songbird, since you know such a good person, I beg of you, tell him about my good Louise and my Germain, because they do not deserve the evil befalling them," said Rigolette, thinking that her friends had nothing to lose by having two defenders instead of one.

"Don't worry, I promise to do what I can for your protégés with Monsieur Rodolphe," Fleur-de-Marie said.

"Monsieur Rodolphe!" Rigolette exclaimed, strangely surprised.

"Of course," Songbird said.

"Monsieur Rodolphe! A traveling salesman?"

"I don't know what he does. But why this surprise?"

"Because I know a Monsieur Rodolphe, too."

"Could it be the same one?"

"Let's see. What about yours—what's he like?"

"Young!"

"The same."

"A face full of nobility and goodness."

"The same again. But, good God, he sounds just like my Monsieur Rodolphe," said Rigolette, more and more astonished. Then she added, "Does he have brown hair and a small mustache?"

"Yes."

"And finally, is he tall and slender, very good-looking, and well dressed—that is, for a traveling salesman? Does this still sound like your Monsieur Rodolphe?"

"There's no doubt it's him," Fleur-de-Marie answered, "except, what surprises me is that you think he's a traveling salesman."

"As for that, I'm sure of it. He told me that."

"You know him?"

"Do I know him? He's my neighbor."

"Monsieur Rodolphe?"

"He has a room on the fourth floor, just next to mine."

"Him? Him?"

"What's so surprising about that? It's simple, really. He can't make more than fifteen to eighteen hundred francs a year. He can only afford a modest place to live, even if he doesn't seem to be careful with his finances. Because my dear neighbor, he doesn't even know what his clothing costs."

"No, no, it's not the same one," Fleur-de-Marie said, thinking it over.

"Oh, then, yours is a paragon of orderliness?"

"The one I'm talking about, you see, Rigolette," Fleur-de-Marie said enthusiastically, "is all-powerful. One speaks his name only with love and veneration. His gaze is awe-inspiring and commanding. One is tempted to kneel before his grandeur and his goodness."

"Well, now I'm completely lost, my poor Songbird. I agree with you, they don't sound the same anymore, because mine is neither all-powerful nor imposing; he's a nice fellow, really cheerful, and you wouldn't kneel before him at all. He's the exact opposite: he promised to help me wax my floors and I haven't even mentioned that he's supposed to take me out for walks on Sundays. You can see he's not some grand lord. But what am I thinking? That's really something to be thinking about, walking out on Sundays! What about Louise and my poor Germain? As long as they're in prison, there won't be any fun for me."

Fleur-de-Marie had been contemplating profoundly for a few moments. She had suddenly remembered that when she and Rodolphe first met at the ogress's, he looked and spoke like all the other clients in that joint. Wouldn't he be quite capable of playing the role of a traveling salesman with Rigolette? But what could be the purpose of this new disguise?

The seamstress, seeing Fleur-de-Marie's pensive expression, started up again: "There's no need for us to rack our brains over this, my dear Songbird. We'll know soon enough if we know the same Monsieur Rodolphe. When you see yours, tell him about me; when I see mine, I'll tell him about you. That way, we'll know what's what right away."

"So where do you live, Rigolette?"

"Seventeen rue du Temple."

"Now this is strange and it's good that I know about it," Madame Séraphin said to herself. She had listened quite carefully to this conversation. "This mysterious and all-powerful Monsieur Rodolphe character, who is surely disguising himself as a traveling salesman, lives in a room next to this little seamstress—and she certainly seems to know more than she's saying—and this defender of the oppressed, like her therefore, lives in the same house as Morel and Bradamanti. This works out fine—if the seamstress and the so-called traveling salesman keep on getting themselves mixed up in matters that don't concern them, we'll know where to find them."

"When I speak to Monsieur Rodolphe, I'll write to you," said Songbird, "and I'll give you my address so you can answer. But tell it to me again, I'm afraid I might forget it."

"Hold on, I just happen to have one of the cards I leave with my clients." She gave Fleur-de-Marie a small card on which was written, in a magnificent slanted, round hand, "Mademoiselle Rigolette, Dressmaker, 17 rue du Temple." "It's like it was printed, don't you think?" the seamstress added. "It was that poor Germain who wrote up these cards for me, back before all this happened. He's so good, so considerate. You know, it's almost like it was meant to be—you'd think the only way I'd come to see all his excellent qualities was once all this misfortune happened to him, and now I'll always blame myself for waiting so long to love him."

"So you love him?"

"Oh, goodness, yes! I need some excuse to go see him in prison. You have to admit I'm one peculiar girl," said Rigolette, stifling a sigh as she laughed through her tears, as the poet says.[161]

"You're just as good and generous as you always were," Fleur-de-Marie said, grasping her friend's hands warmly.

Madame Séraphin must have learned all she wanted to from the conversation of the two girls because she said, almost brusquely, to Fleur-de-Marie, "Come on, come on, my dear young lady, let's go. It's late and we've just lost another quarter of an hour."

"Boy, she's a grumpy one, this old woman is! I don't like her looks one bit," Rigolette whispered to Fleur-de-Marie. Then she said out loud, "When you get back to Paris, my dear Songbird, don't forget me. A visit from you would give me such pleasure! I'd be so happy to spend a day with you, to show you my little household, my room, my birds . . . I have birds; it's my one luxury."

"I'll try to visit you, but I'll definitely write to you. Well, then, farewell, Rigolette, farewell. If you only knew how happy I am to have run into you."

"Me, too! But it won't be the last time, I hope. And besides, I can't

161. The poet to whom Sue refers is Homer. In Book VI of the *Iliad*, Andromache smiles through her tears as Hector leaves her to return to battle. [TN]

wait to find out if your Monsieur Rodolphe is the same as mine. Write me as soon as you can about that, I beg of you."

"Yes, absolutely. Farewell, Rigolette."

"Farewell, my dear Songbird."

And the two girls kissed each other tenderly, hiding their emotions from each other.

Thanks to the permit Rodolphe had acquired for her, Rigolette went into the prison to see Louise.

Fleur-de-Marie got into the hackney with Madame Séraphin, who ordered the coach driver to go to Batignolles and to stop at the barrier. A very short crossroad went almost directly from there to the edge of the Seine, not far from the Scavenger's Island. Fleur-de-Marie didn't know Paris very well, so she had not noticed that the carriage was following a route different from the one that led to the Saint-Denis barrier. Only when the hackney stopped at Batignolles and Madame Séraphin gestured to her to get out did she say, "But, madame, this doesn't look like the road to Bouqueval. And besides, why would we go on foot all the way to the farm?"

"All I can tell you, my dear young lady," the housekeeper said cordially, "is that I am following your benefactors' orders and you would make them quite unhappy if you hesitated to follow me."

"Oh, madame, I would never do that!" Fleur-de-Marie exclaimed. "You have been sent by them and so I won't ask a single question. I'll follow you blindly. Just tell me if Madame Georges is still in good health."

"She's in wonderful health."

"And Monsieur Rodolphe?"

"Perfect health as well."

"So you know him, madame. But just a moment ago, when I was speaking about him with Rigolette, you didn't say anything."

"Because I wasn't supposed to say anything . . . apparently. I have my orders."

"And was it he who gave you your orders?"

"You're one curious young lady, you are," the housekeeper said, laughing.

"You're right. Forgive my questions, madame. Since we're going on foot to the place you're taking me to," Fleur-de-Marie added, smiling sweetly, "I'll know everything I'm so looking forward to finding out soon enough."

"As a matter of fact, my dear, we'll get there in a quarter of an hour."

Having left the last houses of Batignolles behind them, the housekeeper, with Fleur-de-Marie, followed a grassy road lined with walnut trees. It was a warm and beautiful day. The sky was covered with clouds colored purple by the twilight. The sun, which had just begun to set, threw slanting rays across the heights of Colombes on the other side of the Seine.

As Fleur-de-Marie came closer to the river's edge, her pale cheeks became lightly colored as she breathed in the delicious, lively, pure air of the countryside. Her touching expression showed such sweet satisfaction that Madame Séraphin said to her, "You seem very happy, my dear young lady."

"Oh, yes, madame. I'm going to see Madame Georges again, and maybe Monsieur Rodolphe, too. I have some poor, very unhappy people to recommend to their care. I hope they will relieve them. How would I not be happy? If I were sad, how would my sadness not fall away? And then, look, the sky is so cheerful, with its pink clouds. And then the grass—even in this season, it's green. And over there, over there, behind the willows, the river! Heavens, it sure is big! The sun shining on it is dazzling—it looks like shimmering gold. It was shining like that just a while ago in the little prison pool. God doesn't forget poor prisoners; he gives them the rays of the sun, too," Fleur-de-Marie added in a sort of pious gratitude. Then, led by her memories of captivity to appreciate even more the happiness of being free, she cried out in a burst of naive joy, "And, madame, over there, in the middle of the river, look at that pretty little island, bordered with willows and poplars, with that white house at the edge of the water. How charming that place must be in the summer when all the trees are covered with leaves. It must be so silent, so cool there."

"My goodness," said Madame Séraphin with a strange smile, "I'm pleased beyond words that you find that island pretty."

"Why is that, madame?"

"Because you're going there."

"To that island?"

"Does that surprise you?"

"A little, madame."

"And what if you were to meet your friends there?"

"What are you saying?"

"Your friends gathered to celebrate your getting out of prison? Wouldn't that be an even nicer surprise?"

"Is that really possible? Madame Georges, Monsieur Rodolphe?"

"Hold on a bit, my dear young lady. I have no more self-discipline than a child. With your innocent little ways, you've made me say more than I ought to have."

"I'm going to see them again. Oh, madame, my heart is beating so fast!"

"Don't walk so fast, then. I understand how impatient you are, but I can hardly keep up with you, silly girl."

"I'm sorry, madame, it's just that I'm so eager to get there."

"That's understandable enough. I can't blame you. On the contrary."

"Here's the road leading down. It's not a good one. Would you like my arm, madame?"

"That's an offer I can't say no to, my dear young lady. After all, you're nimble and agile, and I'm old."

"Lean on me, madame. Don't be afraid of tiring me out."

"Thank you, my little lady. Your help is much appreciated. This is really a steep descent. Now the road is better here."

"Oh, madame, is it true that I'm going to see Madame Georges again? I can hardly believe it."

"Be patient a little longer. Fifteen more minutes and you'll see her, and then you'll believe it."

"What's hard to believe," Fleur-de-Marie added, after thinking about it for a few seconds, "is that Madame Georges is waiting to meet me here rather than waiting for me at the farm."

"So curious, this young lady! She's always curious."

"It's true, madame. I'm really being nosy," Fleur-de-Marie said, smiling.

"That's why, to please you, I'd really like to tell you about the surprise your friends have waiting for you."

"A surprise? For me, madame?"

"Hold up, you little slyboots. You're going to make me say more, despite myself."

Here we will leave Madame Séraphin and her victim on the road leading to the river. We will arrive on the Scavenger's Island a few moments ahead of them.

CHAPTER 12

THE BOAT

> "What, already leaving?"
> "Leaving! No longer to hear your noble speech!
> No, by the heavens, I'll stay here, master . . ."
>
> —*WOLFGANG,* SCENE II[162]

During the night, the island on which the Martial family lived seemed sinister, but in the brilliant, clear light of the sun, nothing seemed more cheerful than this cursed place. Bordered with willows and poplars, covered with thick vegetation through which paths of yellow sand threaded their way, the island also featured a small vegetable garden and a fairly large number of fruit trees. In the middle of this orchard stood the shed with the thatched roof to which Martial wanted to withdraw with François and Amandine. The island, on this side, ended at a point with a sort of landing place with large stakes designed to hold in the collapsed earth.

In front of the house, reaching almost to the wharf, swelled a tunnel-shaped green trellis. During the summer, this trellis supported the climbing vines of hop and Virginia creeper to serve as a green bower under which customers could sit at tables and drink. At one end of the house, painted white and covered with tiles, stood a wing made up of a woodshed built under a storehouse. That wing was much lower than the main part of the house. Nearly at its top, one could see a window with shutters covered in sheet metal, shut up from the outside by two iron bars held into the wall with strong studs.

Three skiffs, attached to the piles of the wharf, swayed back and forth. Squatting in the bottom of one of them, Nicolas made sure the safety valve he had fashioned was working well. Standing on a bench, outside the trellis, with her hand over her eyes as a sun visor, Calabash was looking into the distance, toward the path Madame Séraphin and Fleur-de-Marie would have to follow to come to the island. "No one in sight: no one young, no one old," Calabash said to Nicolas as she got down from the bench. "It'll be just like yesterday. We'll have waited

---

162. It seems Sue invented this play. We have not been able to locate it. [TN]

around for nothing. If those women aren't here in half an hour, we'll just have to leave. Red-Arm's job pays better and he's waiting for us. The broker's going to be at his place in the Champs-Élysées at five o'clock. We have to be there before she arrives. The Owl went over it all again this morning."

"You're right," Nicolas said as he left the boat. "The devil take that old woman, making us hang around here for nothing! The safety valve works like a charm. But we may not get to pull off even one of these jobs . . ."

"And besides, Red-Arm and Fishhook need us. They can't do anything by themselves."

"True enough. Because Red-Arm needs to stay out back of his cabaret to keep watch while the job is being pulled off, and Fishhook isn't strong enough to drag the broker down into the cellar himself. That old lady will put up a fight."

"Didn't the Owl tell us, laughing about it, that she was boarding the Schoolmaster in that cellar?"

"Not that one. Another, much deeper one that floods up when the river is at high tide."

"That Schoolmaster must be moaning and groaning in that cellar, all alone and blind down there."

"He'll see well enough seeing nothing at all. It's black as a pit in that cellar."

"All the same, he can sing every song he ever knew to keep himself busy. The time is still going to seem to pass really slowly."

"The Owl says he keeps himself entertained hunting rats and that that cellar is well stocked with them."

"Hey, Nicolas, speaking of people who must be getting bored and be moaning and groaning," Calabash said, pointing to the window covered with sheet metal and smiling viciously, "there's someone up there who must be eating his guts out."

"Nah, he's sleeping. He hasn't banged against the walls since this morning, and his dog is quiet."

"Maybe he strangled it to have something to eat. The two of them must be rabid with hunger and thirst, up there for the last two days."

"That's their problem. Martial can stay up there for a long time if that makes him happy. When it's over, we'll say he got sick and died. And he won't leave a ripple."

"You think so?"

"Sure. While she was going to Asnières this morning, our mother ran into Old Férot, the fisherman. When he said he was surprised not to have seen his friend for two days, our mother told him that Martial was so sick he had to stay in bed and that she was losing all hope for him. Old Férot swallowed it whole. He'll tell others about it, so when it happens, everything will seem perfectly normal."

"Yes, but he won't die right away. That way takes a long time."

"So what do you want to do? There's no other way to do this. When that mad dog Martial sets his mind to it, he's as mean as the devil and as strong as a bull on top of it. He wouldn't have trusted us; we wouldn't have been able to get near him safely. On the other hand, as long as his door was good and nailed up from the outside, what could he do? The window was barred."

"But listen, he could pull out the bars by digging them out of the plaster with his knife. And he would have done it too if I hadn't gotten up on the ladder and hacked away at his hand with my hatchet every time he started up at it."

"What a job of guarding that was," the thief said, chuckling. "You must have enjoyed yourself doing that."

"I had to give you time to come back with the sheet metal you got from Old Micou."

"Our dear brother must have been frothing at the mouth."

"He was gnashing his teeth like someone possessed. Two or three times he tried to beat me back by hitting at me with his cudgel through the bars. But then, with only one hand free, he couldn't dig out the bars. And that's what he needed to do."

"We're lucky there's no fireplace in the room."

"And that the door is solid and his hands are hacked up. Otherwise, he'd be able to open a hole in the floor."

"And what about the beams? Is he going to get through them? No, no, don't worry, there's no chance he'll escape. The shutters are lined with sheet metal and backed up with two iron bars. The door's nailed up from the outside with three-inch boat nails. He's in a coffin as solid as if it were lead-lined oak."

"And what'll happen, do you think, when the She-Wolf gets out of prison and comes here looking for her man and comes calling for him?"

"That'll be fine. We'll tell her, 'Go look for him.'"

"Speaking of that, you know if our mother doesn't lock up those two good-for-nothing children, they're capable of gnawing down that door like rats to free Martial. That little scoundrel François has been a veritable demon since he began suspecting that we boxed up his big brother."

"Well, yeah. But can we leave them in the upstairs room when we get ready to leave the island? Their window isn't barred. All they have to do is climb out."

Just at that moment, sobbing and shouting from the house caught Calabash's and Nicolas's attention. They saw the ground-floor door, which had been open up to then, violently shut closed. A minute later, Old Lady Martial's pale, sinister face appeared through the bars of the kitchen window. The executed criminal's widow signaled her two children with her long, bony arm to come over to her.

"Come on, there's a scrap going on. I'll bet François is stirring up trouble again," said Nicolas. "That bum Martial. If it weren't for him, that kid would have been all alone. Keep a good watch here. If you see the two females coming, let me know."

While Calabash got back up on the bench and looked into the distance for the arrival of Madame Séraphin and Songbird, Nicolas went into the house. Little Amandine, on her knees in the middle of the kitchen, was sobbing and begging for mercy for her brother François. He was backed up against one of the corners of the room. Angry, threatening, and brandishing Nicolas's hatchet, he seemed determined this time not to give in to his mother one inch. Impassive and silent as always, the widow signaled to Nicolas to lock François in the cellar, which opened on the kitchen and whose door was ajar.

"No one's locking me up down there!" the child cried out with determination. His eyes were shining like those of a savage young cat. "You want to leave me and Amandine to die of hunger, like our brother Martial."

"Mama, for the love of God, leave us upstairs in our room, like yesterday," the little girl implored, putting her hands together in prayer. "It's too scary down there in that dark cellar."

The widow looked at Nicolas impatiently, as if to blame him for not having yet carried out her orders; then, gesturing imperiously yet again, she pointed to François. Seeing his brother coming toward him, the young boy brandished his hatchet desperately and exclaimed, "If anyone wants to lock me up there—I don't care if it's my mother, my brother, or Calabash—that'll be just too bad for them because I'll fight back and I'll cut them down."

Nicolas felt the immediate need just as much as the widow did to stop the two children from going to Martial's rescue when there was nobody in the house. He also knew he had to hide from them the knowledge of what was going to happen, for their window looked out on the river, where they planned to drown Songbird. But since Nicolas was just as cowardly as he was savage and didn't care much for being chopped up by the dangerous hatchet his brother was brandishing, he hesitated to come near him. The widow, angered at her son's hesitation, pushed him roughly by the shoulder toward François. But Nicolas, backing away once more, exclaimed, "What am I going to do if he wounds me, Mother? You know very well that I'm going to need my arms in a minute, and I can still feel the blow that cur Martial gave me."

The widow shrugged her shoulders contemptuously and took a step toward François.

"Don't come any closer, Mother," François cried out furiously, "or I'll pay you back for every blow you ever gave us two, me and Amandine."

"Oh, brother, let them lock you up rather than that. Oh, God! Don't attack our mother!" Amandine cried out in fear.

Just then, Nicolas saw a large woolen blanket that was being used for doing the ironing. He grabbed it, folded it in half, and skillfully threw it over François's head. Despite his efforts, François got caught up in its thick folds and couldn't use his weapon. Then Nicolas threw himself on him and, with the help of his mother, carried him into the cellar. Amandine had remained on her knees in the middle of the kitchen. As soon as she saw what happened to her brother, she got up quickly and, despite her terror, went of her own accord to join him in the tiny dark room. The door was closed, locked, and bolted on the brother and sister.

"It's all that wretch Martial's fault, after all, that these children are on us now like wild animals," Nicolas exclaimed.

"Since this morning, there hasn't been a sound coming out of his room," said the widow, pensively, with a shiver. "Not a sound."

"That goes to show, Mother, that it was smart of you to tell Old Férot, the Asnières fisherman, right away that Martial had been sick in bed for two days and was about to croak. This way, when it's all over, no one will be surprised."

After a moment of silence, as if she wanted to get away from some nagging thought, the widow said, abruptly, "Has the Owl come here since I've been to Asnières?"

"Yes, Mother."

"Why didn't she stay here so she could go with us to Red-Arm? I don't trust her."

"Yeah, but you don't trust anybody, Mother. Today it's the Owl, yesterday it was Red-Arm."

"Red-Arm is at large, my son is at Toulon, and they both committed the same robbery."

"You keep saying that. Red-Arm escaped because he's as slippery as an eel and that's all there is to it. The Owl didn't stay here because she had a meeting at two o'clock near the Observatory with the tall gentleman in mourning she kidnapped the young country girl for, with Schoolmaster and Gammy. Fishhook was the one who drove the hackney that the tall gentleman in mourning had rented for that business. So look, Mother, how do you figure the Owl's going to denounce us, inasmuch as she's told us all the jobs she's planned and we haven't told her any of ours. She doesn't know anything about the drowning that's about to happen. Calm down, Mother. Really, the wolves aren't at each other's throats. Everything's going to turn out fine. When I think about the fact that that broker can be carrying around twenty, even thirty thousand francs in diamonds in her bag and that we'll have her shut tight in Red-Arm's cellar before two o'clock . . . Thirty thousand francs in diamonds—just think about it!"

"And while we're holding on to the broker, Red-Arm will be staying outside his cabaret?" the widow said suspiciously.

"And where do you want him to be? If someone comes to his place, doesn't he have to take care of him and keep him away from the place where we're doing our business?"

"Nicolas! Nicolas!" Calabash cried out suddenly from outside. "The two women are here."

"Come on, Mother! Quick! Put on your shawl. I'll take you to the mainland and that'll be out of the way, at least," said Nicolas.

The widow had changed her mourning cap for a bonnet of black tulle. She wrapped herself up in a large tartan shawl with white and gray squares on it, closed the kitchen door, put the key behind one of the shutters on the ground floor, and followed her son to the landing dock. Almost despite herself, before leaving the island, she gave Martial's window a long look, frowned, and pursed her lips. Then, after another quick shiver, she murmured underneath her breath, "It's his fault, it's his fault."

"Nicolas, do you see them—there, along the small hill? There's a peasant girl and a missus," Calabash cried out, pointing at Madame Séraphin and Fleur-de-Marie on the other side of the river. They were coming down a small path that skirted a fairly high escarpment hanging above the kiln for finishing pots.

"Wait for the signal—don't blow the job," said Nicolas.

"Are you blind? Don't you recognize the fat woman that came the day before yesterday? Can't you see her orange shawl? And that peasant girl—boy, she's in a hurry! She still seems all happy—you can tell she doesn't know what's waiting for her."

"Yes, I recognize the fat woman. Let's go, things are on the move. Wait, though, let's each make sure we know what we have to do, Calabash," Nicolas said. "I'll take the old woman and the young one into the skiff with the safety valve and you follow me in the other, end to end, and be sure to row straight so I can heave myself into your boat with one jump when I've opened the valve and mine sinks."

"Don't be afraid—this isn't the first time I've handled an oar, is it?"

"I'm not afraid of drowning, I can swim. But if I don't jump into the other skiff in time, the women, when they're fighting not to drown, might get ahold of me. And—thanks but no thanks—I don't have any desire to be splashing around in the middle of the river with them."

"The old woman is giving the signal with her handkerchief," Calabash said. "There they are on the beach."

"Come on, come on, get aboard, Mother," Nicolas said, casting off. "Get onto the skiff with the safety valve. That way the two women won't suspect anything. And you, Calabash, jump into the other one and put some muscle in it, my girl, row hard. Oh, hold on, take my hook and keep it next to you. It's as sharp as a lance and it could come in handy for you. Now, on our way!" said the bandit, placing a long hook armed with sharpened steel in Calabash's boat.

In a few moments, the two boats, one rowed by Nicolas, the other by Calabash, reached the beach where Madame Séraphin and Fleur-de-Marie had been waiting for the last few minutes. While Nicolas tied his boat up to a pike at the river's edge, Madame Séraphin came up to him and whispered quickly, "Say that Madame Georges is waiting for us." Then the housekeeper said out loud, "We're a little late, aren't we, my boy?"

"Yes, my good lady, Madame Georges has already asked after you a number of times."

"There, you see, my dear young lady, Madame Georges is waiting for us," said Madame Séraphin, turning toward Fleur-de-Marie, who, despite her trust, had felt her heart skip a beat at the sinister look on the faces of the widow, Calabash, and Nicolas.

But the mention of Madame Georges's name calmed her down, and she answered, "I'm just as eager to see Madame Georges. Lucky the crossing isn't long."

"That dear lady is really going to be happy!" Madame Séraphin said. Then, speaking to Nicolas, "Come on, my boy, bring your boat closer so we can climb on." And she added in a whisper, "It's absolutely necessary that we drown the little girl. If she comes up from the water, push her right back down."

"Understood. And you, don't be frightened. When I give you the sign, take my hand. She'll go down all alone—it's all set up and there's nothing to be afraid of," Nicolas answered in a whisper. Then, with his savage impassiveness, touched neither by Fleur-de-Marie's beauty nor by her youth, he reached his arm over to her. The girl held on to it lightly and got into the boat. "You're next, my good woman," Nicolas said to Madame Séraphin. And he offered her his hand next.

Whether she had a bad feeling, didn't trust him, or just was afraid of jumping so briskly from the skiff Nicolas and Songbird were on while the water was flowing into its bottom, Jacques Ferrand's housekeeper said, as she backed up, "No, I think I'll go in Mademoiselle's boat." And she got in next to Calabash.

"That's fine," Nicolas said, exchanging a meaningful look with his sister. And with the end of his oar he gave a strong thrust to his skiff. His sister did the same when Madame Séraphin was beside her.

Standing motionless beside the river, indifferent to this scene, the widow kept her pensive, absorbed watch on Martial's window, which could be seen from the beach through the poplars. At the same time, the two skiffs, the first carrying Fleur-de-Marie and Nicolas, the other Madame Séraphin and Calabash, withdrew slowly from the river's edge.

BOOK VII

CHAPTER I

THE HAPPY REUNION

Before informing the reader of the outcome of the events occurring on Martial's boat with the safety valve, we will go backward a little in time. Only moments after Fleur-de-Marie had left Saint-Lazare with Madame Séraphin, the She-Wolf also left the prison. Thanks to both Madame Armand's recommendation and that of the director, who wanted to reward her for the kindness she had shown Mont-Saint-Jean, Martial's mistress had been given a reprieve of several days that were remaining on her sentence. This creature, whose thinking up to now had been corrupted, debased, and uncivilized, had, in any case, undergone a complete change of heart.

With the picture of the peaceful, rustic, solitary life painted by Fleur-de-Marie constantly in her thoughts, the She-Wolf had come to view her past life with horror. To retreat to the depths of the forests with Martial was now her one goal, her obsession. Even as this strange woman had separated herself from Songbird, whose crushing influence she meant to flee by withdrawing into another part of Saint-Lazare, all her old and evil instincts had struggled in vain against the picture she had drawn.

To effect this rapid and sincere conversion, made only stronger and more solid by the powerless struggle her companion's perverse practices waged against it, Fleur-de-Marie, following the impulses of her native good sense, had reasoned in the following way: the She-Wolf, violent and determined as she is, loves Martial passionately. She thus ought to welcome with joy the possibility of getting away from the ignominious life of which, for the first time, she felt ashamed, in order to devote herself entirely to this uncivilized, savage man. She shares the desires of this man, who seeks solitude as much as a matter of taste as to escape the reprobation that pursues his vile family everywhere they go. Aided only by the elements of the She-Wolf's personality that she could detect in their conversation, Fleur-de-Marie had given a praiseworthy direction for the savage love and bold character of this creature, and had thus changed a lost girl into an upright woman. For how else can one characterize her dream of marrying Martial, withdrawing to the dark of the forest, and living a life of work and hardship together, except as the resolution of an upright woman?

Confident in the support Fleur-de-Marie promised her in the name of her unknown benefactor, the She-Wolf came, then, to offer this praiseworthy proposition to her lover. She was not without bitter fears of rejection because Songbird, by bringing her to blush for her past, had also made her aware of her position with regard to Martial.

Once she was free, the She-Wolf thought of nothing but getting back to her man, as she called him. She had received no news from him for a number of days. Hoping to meet up with him again at the Scavenger's Island and determined to wait there for him if she didn't find him there, she got into a public carriage, which she paid generously to take her in all speed to the Asnières bridge. She crossed the bridge about fifteen minutes prior to Madame Séraphin and Fleur-de-Marie, who, coming on foot from the barrier, had arrived on the beach near the pottery kiln. When Martial did not come to take the She-Wolf in his boat, she decided to turn to an old fisherman named Old Férot who lived near the bridge to ask to take her to the island. So, at four o'clock in the afternoon, a carriage stopped at the entrance to a small street in the village of Asnières. The She-Wolf gave the driver a hundred sous, jumped out, and went as fast as she could to where Old Férot, the boatman, lived.

Having taken off her prison clothes, the She-Wolf was wearing a dress of dark green merino with a red cashmere-like shawl that was bordered in palm leaves, as well as a tulle bonnet with ribbons. Her thick, curly hair had barely been touched. In her impatient eagerness to see Martial, she had dressed with more speed than care. After such a long separation, any other woman would no doubt have taken the time to make herself beautiful for this first meeting, but the She-Wolf cared little for such delicacies or for the slowness they entailed. More than anything, she wanted to see her man as soon as she could, and this impetuous desire came not only from her passionate love but also from her need to confide in Martial the salutary resolution that her discussion with Fleur-de-Marie had led her to make.

The She-Wolf arrived quickly at the fisherman's house. Sitting in front of his door, Old Férot, a white-haired old man, was repairing his nets. When she was only just near enough to see him, the She-Wolf cried out, "Your boat, Old Férot—quick, quick!"

"Oh, it's you, mademoiselle. And a big hello to you! We haven't seen you in these parts for a long time."

"Yes, yes, but the boat—quick—to the island!"

"Well, as the fates would have it, nothing doing today."

"What do you mean?"

"My boy has taken my skiff to go to Saint-Ouen with the others to take part in rowing contests. There's only one boat on the shore here from here to the station."

"Damn!" the She-Wolf exclaimed, stomping and clenching her fists. "I'm done for!"

"It's true! I give you my word. And I don't like it one bit that I can't take you to the island, because he's probably doing much worse."

"Worse? Who? Martial?" the She-Wolf cried, grabbing Old Férot by the collar. "Is my man sick?"

"Didn't you know?"

"Martial?"

"No doubt about it. But you're going to rip my shirt. Calm down."

"He's sick? Since when?"

"Since two or three days ago."

"That can't be true! He would have written me."

"Sure he would! He's too sick to write."

"Too sick to write? And he's on the island? You're sure about that?"

"I'll tell you how I know. So, you know, this morning I ran into the widow Martial. Usually if I see her on one side of the street, well, you know, I cross over to the other because I don't much care for her company, but this time—"

"But what about my man? What about him? Where is he?"

"Just wait, I'm getting there. This time I was caught eyeball-to-eyeball with his mother and I didn't dare try to get out of speaking to her. She has such a rotten way about her that she always scares me. I can't do anything about it. 'I haven't seen your son Martial in two days,' I say to her. 'Did he leave for the city?' At that, she gives me this look . . . this look . . . well, if looks could kill, I'd be dead, as they say."

"I'm going to burst. What happened then? What then?"

Old Férot kept silent a moment and then said, "Well, hold on a moment. You're a good girl—promise me to keep it secret and I'll tell you the whole thing, as much as I know."

"About my man?"

"Yes, because, you see, Martial is a good fellow, even if he's a bit rough around the edges. And I'd be sorry if that old witch of a mother or his wretch of a brother did something rotten to him."

"But what's going on? What have his mother and brother done to him? Speak up already, speak up!"

"Oh, great—now you're back to tearing at my shirt. Let me go already! If you keep interrupting me and tearing up my things, I might never be able to finish and you won't know anything."

"Oh, my patience is wearing thin!" the She-Wolf exclaimed, stamping her foot in anger.

"You won't repeat what I'm telling you to anyone?"

"No, no, no!"

"Word of honor?"

"Old Férot, you're going to give me an apoplectic fit."

"What a girl! What a girl! Boy, do you have a temper on you! Look, here it is. First, you have to know that Martial is more and more at loggerheads with his family, and if they did something bad to him, it wouldn't surprise me. That's why I'm sorry not to have my skiff, because you better not count on anyone from the island to take you there. Neither Nicolas nor that rotten Calabash will take you there."

"I know that only too well. But what did his mother say about my man? Did he get sick on the island?"

"Don't get me confused. Here's how it went: This morning I say to the widow, 'I haven't seen Martial for two days, and his skiff is tied to the stake. So is he in the city?' Then the widow gives me the evil eye and says, 'He's sick, on the island—so sick he won't get better.' I say to myself, 'How did that happen? Only three days ago—' What now?" Old Férot said, interrupting himself. "What now? Where are you going? Where the devil is she running off to this time?"

Thinking Martial's life in danger from those on the island, out of her head with fear and mad with anger, the She-Wolf ceased listening to the fisherman and ran along the bank of the Seine.

Some topographical detail will be necessary to make the following scene intelligible: the Scavenger's Island was closer to the left bank of the river than to the right bank, where Fleur-de-Marie and Madame Séraphin had embarked. The She-Wolf was on the left bank. Without being very steep, the heights of the island hid the view of one bank from the other along its entire length. Consequently, Martial's mistress had not seen Songbird embark, and the scavenger's family had not been able to see the She-Wolf, running that very moment down the opposite bank. Finally, let us recall to the reader that Doctor Griffon's country house, where the Count de Saint-Remy was living at the moment, stood halfway up the hill from the beach at which the She-Wolf arrived, no longer seeing straight. She passed by two people without seeing them, and, struck by her haggard looks, they turned around to follow her from a distance. These two people were the Count de Saint-Remy and Doctor Griffon.

On learning that her lover was in danger, the She-Wolf's first thought had been to run impetuously to where she knew the danger was. But the closer she got to the island, the more she considered the difficulty of getting there. Just as the old fisherman had told her, she could not count on any boat belonging to a stranger and no one from the Martial family would want to come pick her up. Out of breath, her face all flushed, her eyes ablaze, she arrived at a place facing the tip of the island, which, forming a curve at this point, came fairly close to the riverbank.

The She-Wolf saw the roof of the house through the leafless branches of the willows and the poplars—the house where Martial might be dying. Seeing this and letting out a savage wail, she tore off her bonnet and let her dress fall to her feet, leaving on just her slip. She threw herself fearlessly into the river, walking as far as her feet would take her, and then, when she lost her footing, she started swimming with all her might toward the island.

Her untamed energy was a sight to behold. At every stroke, the She-Wolf's long, thick hair, which had shaken loose from the violent agitation of her activity, fluttered around her head like a double mane with copper glints in it. If it were not for the heated fixity of her look, which held the Martial house constantly in view, and the contraction of her features, distorted as they were by her terrible anguish, one might have believed that the poacher's mistress was playing in the waves, so freely and easily did the woman swim. Tattooed with her lover's motto, her muscular white arms, with a completely masculine vigor, slashed through the water, which sprayed back and rolled in wet pearls over her large shoulders and across her firm, sturdy breast, which glistened with water like a half-submerged marble bust.

Suddenly, a cry of distress rang out from the other side of the island, a desperate, terrible cry of agony. The She-Wolf trembled and came to an abrupt stop. Then, holding herself up in the water with one hand, she held her hair back with the other and listened. The cry broke out again, but weaker, more imploring, more convulsive, dying. And then everything fell back into a deep silence.

"My man!" the She-Wolf cried, and returned to swimming furiously. In her distress, she thought she had recognized Martial's voice.

The count and the doctor, whom the She-Wolf had run past, had not been able to follow her closely enough to try to stop her rashness. They came to the place facing the island just in time to hear the two frightening cries ring out. They stopped, as terrified as the She-Wolf. Seeing her struggle intrepidly against the current, they cried out, "That poor woman is going to drown!" But their fears were needless. Martial's mistress swam like a fish. In a few strokes, the intrepid creature had reached the island.

She found her footing and then, with the aid of one of the pikes that formed a sort of landing area that stood out from the end of the island, she climbed out of the water. Suddenly, the body of a young woman dressed in peasant clothing came floating slowly by one of the piles, carried on by the current. The peasant clothing held the body above the water still. As rapid in thought as in her movement, the She-Wolf grasped a pike with one hand and with the other abruptly took hold of the woman's dress as she passed. But she pulled the unfortunate woman she was saving so violently toward her and inside the wharf's stakes that, for a moment, the body went underwater, even though there was footing there. Endowed with uncommon strength and adroitness, the She-Wolf lifted

Songbird (that is who it was, though she had not yet recognized her) up in her strong arms as one lifts up a child. Taking a few more steps in the river, she placed her finally on the island's grassy bank.

"Keep at it! Take heart!" Monsieur de Saint-Remy cried out to her. Like the doctor, he had witnessed this bold rescue. "We're going to cross the Asnières bridge and come to your aid with a boat." And then both of them went quickly toward the bridge. But the She-Wolf did not hear these words.

Allow us to repeat that from the right bank of the Seine, where Nicolas, Calabash, and their mother remained after having committed this despicable crime, one could see absolutely nothing of what happened on its other side, thanks to the island's cliff. Fleur-de-Marie, whom the She-Wolf had suddenly pulled inside the landing area, having once gone under the water, did not reappear within sight of her murderers, and so they thought their victim had been swallowed by the river and drowned.

A few minutes later the current carried another corpse along near the surface of the water, without the She-Wolf seeing it. This was the body of the solicitor's housekeeper, and she was well and truly dead. Nicolas and Calabash had as much interest as Jacques Ferrand in doing away with this witness to and accomplice in their latest crime. And so, when the boat with the safety valve had been sunk with Fleur-de-Marie aboard, Nicolas jumped into the boat his sister was rowing and in which Madame Séraphin also sat, thus giving that craft a violent shaking, and, taking advantage of a moment at which the housekeeper lost her grip, he threw her into the river and finished her off there with a blow from his hook.

Exhausted and out of breath, the She-Wolf knelt down on the grass next to Fleur-de-Marie to recover her strength and examine the features of the woman she had just ripped from the jaws of death. Imagine her amazement when she recognized her prison companion. In the grip of this astonishment, she forgot Martial for a moment.

"Songbird!" she cried.

Her body bent and leaning on her knees, her hair disheveled, her clothing dripping with water, she contemplated this unfortunate child, stretched out on the grass, near death. Fleur-de-Marie was pale, motionless, her eyes half open and unseeing, her beautiful blond hair glued to her temples, her lips blue, her cold hands already stiff and icy. She certainly seemed to be dead.

"Songbird!" the She-Wolf repeated. "What a terrible coincidence! Here I am, just come to tell my man about the influence she had on me—both the good and the bad—with her speeches and promises and about the decision I've made. And here I find the poor little thing dead!

But no! It isn't true!" the She-Wolf exclaimed as she came closer yet to Fleur-de-Marie and felt an imperceptible breath escape her lips. "No! God, no! She's still breathing. I've saved her. I've never had the chance to save anybody's life before. That really feels good. That brings your strength back. Yes, but I have to rescue my man, too. He may be breathing his last at this very moment. His mother and his brother are fully capable of murdering him. Still, I can't leave this poor little thing here; I'll take her to the widow's. She's just going to have to take care of her and take me to Martial or I'll destroy that house and kill everyone in it. No brother, no mother, no sister is going to stop me once I can tell my man is there."

And as soon as she said this, the She-Wolf got up and carried Fleur-de-Marie off in her arms. Bearing this light burden, she ran toward the house, not imagining for an instant that the widow and her sister, evil as they might be, would fail to give first aid to Fleur-de-Marie.

By the time Martial's mistress had arrived at the far end of the island, from which she could see both banks of the Seine, Nicolas, his mother, and Calabash had departed. Confident that they had successfully murdered both women, they were going as fast as they could to Red-Arm's place.

At that same moment, a man who, waiting in ambush in the hollows of the riverbank, hidden by the pottery kiln, had watched the horrible scene play out was now making himself scarce, believing from what he had seen that the crimes had been accomplished. This man was Jacques Ferrand.

One of Nicolas's boats was swaying on the waves, tied to a pike on the riverbank where Songbird and Madame Séraphin had climbed on board.

Jacques Ferrand had barely left the pottery kiln to get back to Paris when Monsieur de Saint-Remy and Doctor Griffon rushed past the Asnières bridge, running toward the island, meaning to get there with the aid of Nicolas's boat, which they had seen from a distance.

Coming up to the scavengers' house, the She-Wolf, to her great surprise, found the door locked. Putting Fleur-de-Marie, who was still in a faint, down on the ground under the barrel of the trellis, she went up to the house. She recognized Martial's window. Imagine her surprise at seeing the shutters of that window covered with sheet metal and held shut from the outside by two iron bars! Guessing at least part of the truth, the She-Wolf let out a hoarse, ringing cry and started to yell with all her power, "Martial! My man!"

There was no response.

Terrified by this silence, the She-Wolf set to pacing, pacing around the house like a wild animal looking for a scent, growling as she searched for the entrance to the lair where her mate was hidden. From time to time she called out: "Are you there, my man? My man!!!" And in her rage she shook the bars of the kitchen window, struck the walls, and rammed herself against the door. Suddenly, from the inside of the house, a low sound answered her.

The She-Wolf trembled as she listened. The sound died away. "My man heard me. I'll get into this place if I have to gnaw a hole through the door with my teeth." And she started in again with her wild howl.

From inside Martial's shutters, the sound of knocking—but weak knocking—responded to the She-Wolf's roaring. "He's there!" she cried, as she stopped suddenly under her lover's window. "He's there! I'll open those shutters if I have to rip that metal off with my fingernails."

So saying, she noticed a large ladder half secured behind one of the lower room's shutters. Pulling this shutter toward her violently, the She-Wolf shook loose the key the widow had hidden on the edge of the window.

"If this works," the She-Wolf said as she tried the key in the main door's lock, "I'll be able to get up to his room. It works!" she cried out joyously. "My man is saved!"

Once she was in the kitchen, the cries of the two children, who were shut up in the cellar, stopped her in her tracks. The children, hearing loud noises, started calling out to be rescued. The widow had thought it enough to close François and Amandine in with lock and bolt, but she had left the key in the lock, never thinking that anyone would come to the island or into the house while she was gone.

Freed by the She-Wolf, François and Amandine exploded from the cellar. "Oh, She-Wolf, save our brother Martial! They want to kill him," François shouted. "They've kept him walled up in his room for the last two days."

"They didn't injure him?"

"No, I don't think so."

"Then I've gotten here in time!" the She-Wolf exclaimed, running up the stairs. Then, after climbing a few steps, she stopped and said, "I've forgotten Songbird! Amandine, get a fire going right away. You and your brother, go and get a poor girl who was drowning and bring her next to the fireplace. I saved her. She's under the trellis. François, get me an ax, a hatchet, an iron bar—something for me to break down my man's door!"

"Over there is the ax for splitting logs, but it's too heavy for you," the young boy said as, with great trouble, he dragged behind him an enormous hammer.

"Too heavy?" the She-Wolf exclaimed and, with no effort, picked up the large piece of iron, which, under other circumstances, she might indeed have had trouble lifting. Then, as she climbed the stairs four at a time, she said again to the two children, "Go run and get the young woman and bring her up by the fire."

In barely two leaps, the She-Wolf was at the end of the corridor, in front of Martial's door. "Take heart, my man, your She-Wolf is here!" she yelled, and, lifting the hammer with two hands, she shook the door with a tremendous blow.

"It's closed from the outside. Tear out the nails," Martial cried out in a weak voice. Immediately throwing herself on her knees in the corridor and setting to work with the hammer's claw and with her fingers—tearing wounds in them—the She-Wolf managed to rip several enormous nails that had barred the door from the planks and the doorframe. Finally, the door opened. Martial, pale, with bloody hands, fell almost limp into the She-Wolf's arms.

CHAPTER 2

THE SHE-WOLF AND MARTIAL

"Finally, I have you before my eyes! I'm holding you—you're here!" the She-Wolf exclaimed with joy and wild enthusiasm as Martial fell into her arms and she held him there. Then, holding him up, almost carrying him, she helped him sit down on a bench in the corridor. For a few minutes, Martial was still weak, haggard, trying to recover from the violent shock that had depleted his failing strength. The She-Wolf had saved her lover just when, completely exhausted and desperate, he felt himself to be dying, less from lack of food than from lack of air. That small room was nearly airtight. Without a fireplace or exit of any kind, it was hermetically sealed, thanks to Calabash. With sadistic foresight, she had thought to plug even the smallest slits in the door and the window with old linen.

Quivering with both happiness and anguish, her eyes wet with tears, down on her knees, the She-Wolf was watching attentively for the least little movement in Martial's expression. He seemed to be coming back to life bit by bit as he drew in long breaths of pure, healthful air. After trembling slightly, he lifted up his heavy head, let out a long sigh, and opened his eyes.

"Martial, it's me. It's your own She-Wolf. How are you doing?"

"Better," he said in a weak voice.

"Good God! Is there anything you want? Water? Some vinegar?"

"No, no," Martial said as the heaviness gradually lifted from him. "Air, air—nothing but air!"

Heedless of the risk of cutting up her fists, the She-Wolf punched through the window's four panes, which she could not reach to open without moving a heavy table aside.

"I can breathe now—I can breathe. My head is clearing up," Martial said as he returned to complete consciousness. Then, as if he had just recalled what his mistress had done for him, he cried out in a burst of inexpressible gratitude, "I would be dead without you, my good She-Wolf!"

"Yeah, yeah—but how do you feel right now?"

"I'm getting better and better."

"Are you hungry?"

"No, I feel too weak. The hardest part of being in there was the lack of air. At the end, I was suffocating, suffocating—it was awful."

"And now?"

"I'm alive again, I've come back from the dead, and it's thanks to you!"

"But your hands, your poor hands! These cuts. God, what did they do to you?"

"Nicolas and Calabash didn't dare fight me face-to-face a second time so they walled me up in my room to leave me to die of hunger. I tried to stop them from nailing my windows shut and my sister cut my hands with her hatchet!!!"

"What monsters! They told people that you were dying of an illness. Your mother spread rumors that you were in a desperate state. Your mother, my man, your own mother!"

"Please don't talk about her to me," Martial said bitterly. Then, noticing for the first time the She-Wolf's wet clothing and the strange getup she was in, he exclaimed, "What happened to you? Your hair's dripping wet, and you're in your slip . . . and it's all wet!"

"What does that matter since you're safe—you're safe!"

"But tell me how you got all wet like that."

"I knew you were in danger and I couldn't find a boat."

"You swam here?"

"Yes. But give me your hands so I can kiss them. You're in pain. Those monsters! And I wasn't here!"

"Oh, my brave She-Wolf!" Martial cried out in exaltation. "The bravest of all the brave!"

"You wrote, 'Death to cowards,' didn't you?" And the She-Wolf showed him her tattooed arm, with those words indelibly written on it.

"You are the daring one! But you're shivering with cold."

"It's not the cold."

"It doesn't matter. Go in there, get Calabash's cloak, and wrap it around yourself."

"But—"

"That's an order." In one second, the She-Wolf had wrapped herself in the tartan cloak and had come back. "You risked death—for me!" Martial repeated, looking at her exaltedly.

"Not really. But a poor girl was drowning. I saved her while I was coming ashore on the island."

"You saved her, too? Where is she?"

"Downstairs with the children. They're taking care of her."

"And who is this girl?"

"My God, if you knew what dumb luck it was. What a lucky bit of chance! She's one of the girls I knew in prison—an extraordinary girl, really."

"How so?"

"Can you believe that I loved her and I hated her at the same time? She struck the fear of God in me and made me happy all at once."

"She did that?"

"Yes, and it was all because of you."

"Because of me?"

"Listen, Martial—" Then, stopping herself, the She-Wolf added, "No, no, I'll never have the courage."

"What are you talking about?"

"I wanted to make a request of you. That's why I came to see you, because when I left Paris, I didn't know you were in danger."

"So, then, go ahead."

"I can't. Now I'm afraid to."

"Afraid to—after what you've just done for me!"

"That's just it. It would be like trying to get something in return."

"Get something in return! What don't I already owe you? Didn't you take care of me night and day last year when I was sick?"

"Aren't you my man?"

"I am your man and I'll always be your man, and that's why you have to speak frankly to me."

"Always, Martial?"

"Always, as sure as my name is Martial. For me, you see, She-Wolf, there will never be another woman in the world but you. It doesn't matter to me what you've been. This, that, or the other thing, it's my business and no one else's. I love you, you love me, and I owe you my life. There's just one thing: since you've been in prison, I'm not the same anymore. Something really has changed. I've thought about it, and you're going to change from being what you were."

"What do you mean?"

"I don't want to leave you now, but I also don't want to leave François and Amandine."

"Your little brother and sister?"

"Yes, from now on I'm going to have to be like a father to them. You understand, that means I have obligations, I have to shape up, I have to take care of them. They wanted to make complete thieves out of them. To save them from that, I'm going to take them away."

"Where to?"

"I don't have any idea. But far from Paris, that's for sure."

"And what about me?"

"You? I'm taking you, too."

"You'll take me, too?" the She-Wolf cried out in joy and astonishment. She couldn't believe in such happiness. "I won't have to live without you?"

"No, my good She-Wolf, never. You're going to help me raise these children. I know you. When I say to you, 'I want my poor little Amandine to be a good girl; treat her that way,' I know you'll be a good mother to her."

"Oh! Thank you, Martial, thank you!"

"We'll live together like honest workers. Don't worry, we'll find work, and we'll work like slaves. But at least these children won't be miserable wretches like their mother and father. I don't mean to be known any longer as the son and brother of executed criminals. I won't live anywhere anymore where everybody knows me . . . But what's up with you? What's up with you?"

"Martial, I'm afraid I'm going mad."

"Mad?"

"Mad with joy."

"Why?"

"Because, you see, it's just too much."

"What is?"

"What you're asking me . . . Oh, no, you see, it's just too much. Unless saving Songbird did it and that's brought me luck. That must be it, for sure."

"But again, what's up with you?"

"What you're asking me Martial, oh! Martial! Martial!"

"What about it?"

"It's what I was going to ask you!"

"To leave Paris?"

"Yes," she said, in a flurry. "To go with you to the forest, where we would have a nice, clean little house and children that I would love—oh, I would love them! How your She-Wolf would love her man's children! Or even, if you would like it," the She-Wolf said, trembling, "instead of calling you my man, I could call you my husband. Because I don't think we could get the job without that," she hastened to add, sharply.

It was Martial's turn to look at the She-Wolf with surprise. He didn't understand what she was talking about. "What job are you talking about?"

"Working as a gamekeeper."

"I'd be doing that?"

"Yes."

"And who's going to get me that job?"

"The benefactors of the girl I saved."

"They don't know me!"

"But I've told her about you and she's going to recommend us to her benefactors."

"And how did I come up as a topic of conversation?"

"How do you think?"

"My good She-Wolf."

"And in prison, you understand, people get to telling each other things.

And that girl is so nice, so gentle, that, despite myself, I felt a connection with her. I realized right away that she wasn't like the rest of us."

"So who is she?"

"I have no idea. I don't understand it at all, but I've never seen or heard anyone like her in my life. She reads what's in your heart like she was a spirit or something. When I told her how much I loved you, for no particular reason, really, she took an interest in us. She made me feel ashamed of my past life, not by speaking harshly, you know, as if that would have done any good with me, but by speaking to me of a life of hard work, a hard life but one spent peacefully with you, living the way you want, in the depths of the forest. Except her idea was that instead of being a poacher, you'd be a gamekeeper, and instead of being your mistress, I'd be your real wife. And then we'd have beautiful children who'd run to meet you at night when you'd return from your rounds with your dogs, your rifle on your shoulder. And then we'd have our supper at the door of our shack, in the cool of the evening, under the big trees. And then we'd go to bed and we'd be so happy, so peaceful. What can I tell you? I couldn't help myself, I listened to her. It was so appealing. If you only knew . . . she speaks so well—so well that I could picture everything she said just as she said it. I was wide awake and I was dreaming at the same time."

"Oh, yes! That would be a good and beautiful life," Martial said, sighing as well. "Although he's not gone completely bad, François has been around Calabash and Nicolas so much that the pure atmosphere of the woods would be much better for him than city air. Amandine would help you with the housework. And I would be that much better a gamekeeper because I've been one skilled poacher. You would be my housekeeper, my good She-Wolf, and then, as you say, with children, we'd have everything we could want. Once you get used to the forest, it feels just like home. You could live a hundred years there and it would feel like a day. But really, I'm getting soft in the head. Really, I have no business talking about that kind of life. All it does is make you more unhappy."

"I was letting you carry on because you've been saying just what I said to Songbird."

"What?"

"Yes, listening to her fairy tales, I told her, 'It's really unfortunate that these castles in the air, as you call them, Songbird, aren't real!' And you know what she said, Martial?" the She-Wolf said, her eyes sparkling with joy.

"No!"

"'You and Martial get married, and you both promise to live like honest people, and I'll do my best to help get you this place that you want so much,'" she answered.

"I could be a gamekeeper?"

"Yes, that's what you could be."

"But you're right, that's daydreaming. If all I had to do to get such a position was to marry you, my brave She-Wolf, we'd do it tomorrow, if I had any money. Because from this day forward, you know, you are my wife, my true wife."

"Martial, I'm your true wife?"

"My one, my only true wife. And I want you to call me your husband. Because it's just as if the mayor had already married us."

"Oh, Songbird was right! It does the heart good to say, 'My husband!' Martial, you'll see your She-Wolf doing housekeeping, working—well, you'll see . . ."

"But do you really believe in this job?"

"Poor little Songbird, if she's making a mistake, it's on someone else's account. Because she really seemed to believe what she was telling me. Besides, just as I was leaving prison, the inspector told me that Songbird's benefactors, who are very highly placed people, had gotten her released this very day. That proves that she has powerful benefactors and that she can keep her promise to me."

"Oh!" Martial suddenly cried out. "I don't know what we've been thinking."

"What now?"

"This girl is downstairs, dying maybe, and instead of helping her get better, here we are—"

"Calm down. François and Amandine are by her side. They would have come up if there had been any further danger. But you're right. Let's go to her. You need to meet the person to whom we might owe our future happiness."

And Martial, leaning on the She-Wolf's arm, went down to the ground floor. Before we follow them into the kitchen, we will recount what has happened since Fleur-de-Marie was entrusted to the care of the two children.

CHAPTER 3

DOCTOR GRIFFON

François and Amandine had just moved Fleur-de-Marie near the kitchen fire when Monsieur de Saint-Remy and Doctor Griffon, who had come ashore onto the island by means of Nicolas's boat, came into the house. As the children stoked the fire, throwing on some bits of poplar that lit up quickly and blazed brightly, Doctor Griffon gave the girl his most assiduous care.

"This unfortunate child is barely seventeen years old!" the count exclaimed, profoundly moved. Then, turning to the doctor, he said, "What do you think of her condition, my friend?"

"I can hardly feel her pulse. But the strange thing is that the facial color on this patient has not turned blue, as normally occurs after asphyxiation via submersion," the doctor answered with imperturbable sangfroid as he looked upon Fleur-de-Marie with an air of profound meditation. Doctor Griffon was a tall, thin man. Except for two tufts of sparse black hair, carefully combed from the back of his skull around his temples, he was completely bald. His face, gaunt and furrowed from the fatigue of long study, was cool, intelligent, and reflective. He had immense knowledge and consummate experience, and was an adroit and famous practitioner, the chief of medicine at a state hospital (where we will see him later). Doctor Griffon had only one flaw, and it was that he made a complete abstraction of the patient, so to speak, and attended only to the illness. Whether the patient was young, old, male, female, rich, or poor was of no concern to him. He looked only at the medical facts, which, from a scientific viewpoint, might be more or less curious or interesting, according to the case. And for him there were only cases.

"What a charming face! How beautiful she still is, despite her frightening pallor!" Monsieur de Saint-Remy said, contemplating Fleur-de-Marie sadly. "Have you ever seen sweeter, more innocent features, my dear doctor?"

"Her age is of no importance," said the doctor brusquely, "and neither is the water in the lungs, which used to be thought the cause of death. But this was a gross error. The admirable experiments of Goodwin—the remarkable Goodwin—proved that definitively."

"But, Doctor—"

"But it's a fact," Monsieur Griffon replied, absorbed as he was by the love of his art. "To determine the presence of foreign liquid in the lungs, Goodwin immersed cats and dogs several times in small tubs of ink for a few seconds, pulled them out while they were still alive, and then dissected the fellows a little while later. Well, the dissection convinced him that that ink had penetrated the lungs and that the presence of this liquid in the organs of respiration had not been the cause of the subjects' deaths."

The count knew that the doctor was basically an excellent man, but his untrammeled passion for science often made him seem unfeeling, indeed almost cruel. "Do you at least hold out any hope?" Monsieur de Saint-Remy asked him impatiently.

"The patient's extremities are very cold," the doctor said. "There is little reason to hope."

"To die at that age . . . poor child! How dreadful."

"Pupils fixed and dilated," the doctor went on without emotion, lifting one of Fleur-de-Marie's eyelids, which was ice-cold, with one of his fingertips.

"What a strange man you are!" the count exclaimed, almost indignantly. "One would think you pitiless, and yet I have seen you watch over my sickbed for many nights running. Even if I had been your own brother, you could not have shown a more admirable devotion to me."

As he continued focusing his efforts on saving Fleur-de-Marie, the doctor answered the count with unshakeable composure and without looking at him, "My word, do you think that marvelously complicated ataxic fevers just begging for careful study, such as the one you had, are things you come upon every day? It was wonderful, my dear friend, just wonderful! Stupor, delirium, twitching of the tendons, blackouts: your obliging fever presented a whole variety of symptoms. You even had something rare, very rare, and eminently worthy of interest: you even displayed a state of partial, momentary paralysis, if you please. That element of your illness by itself claimed my most devoted attention. Studying your fever was really magnificent. Frankly, my dear friend, the only thing I want in life is the chance to come into contact with a fever as beautiful as that one again. But that kind of luck happens only once in a lifetime."

The count shrugged impatiently.

At this moment, Martial, supported by the She-Wolf, who, as we have seen, had covered her wet clothing with a tartan cloak belonging to Calabash, came into the room. Taken aback by the pallor of the She-Wolf's lover and noticing his hands caked with blood, the count cried out, "Who is this man?"

"My husband," the She-Wolf answered with an indescribable expression of happiness and noble pride.

"Your wife is a good and courageous woman, monsieur," the count said to him. "I saw her save this unfortunate child, and it was an act of rare courage."

"Oh, you are right there, monsieur—she is good and courageous, my wife is," Martial answered, placing special stress on these last words and regarding the She-Wolf, in return, both tenderly and passionately. "Courageous, oh, yes! She just saved my life, too."

"You, too?" the count said, surprised.

"Take care of his hands—his poor hands!" the She-Wolf said as she wiped tears from her eyes. Those tears gave the untamed glint in her eyes a more tender expression.

"Oh, those poor chopped-up hands, it's horrible! Look at them, Doctor."

Turning his head slightly, looking over his shoulder and glancing at the numerous wounds Calabash had inflicted on Martial's hands, Doctor Griffon said to him, "Open and close your hand." Martial executed this movement, though with some pain. The doctor shrugged his shoulders as he continued to attend to Fleur-de-Marie and said, disdainfully, as if he regretted the fact, "There is absolutely nothing serious about these wounds. There has been no injury at all to any tendon. In one week, the patient will have complete use of his hands."

"Is that true, monsieur? My husband won't be crippled?" the She-Wolf cried out in gratitude. The doctor shook his head to say no. "And what about Songbird, monsieur? She'll live, won't she?" the She-Wolf asked. "Oh, she has to live! Me and my husband, we owe her so much!" And then she turned to Martial and said, "Poor little thing. She's the very person I was telling you about. Really, she may bring about all our happiness. She's the one who gave me the idea to come to you and tell you everything I told you. What luck that I saved her. And it happened here, even!"

"It was an act of divine intervention for us," said Martial, struck by Songbird's beauty. "What an angelic face! Oh! She will live, won't she, Doctor?"

"I really can't say," the doctor said. "But first of all, can she stay here? Will she get all the care she needs?"

"Here?" the She-Wolf exclaimed. "They murder people here!"

"Be quiet! Be quiet!" Martial said.

The count and the doctor looked at the She-Wolf in surprise. "This hardly surprises me. This house has a bad reputation in these parts," the doctor said to the count in a lowered voice.

"So have you been the victim of violence?" the count asked Martial. "How did you get those wounds?"

"It's nothing, monsieur. We had an argument, then we had a fight, and I was wounded. But this young country girl can't stay here," he added in a somber tone. "I'm getting out myself, with my wife and my brother and sister over there. We're getting away from this island and never coming back."

"Oh, that's wonderful!" the two children exclaimed.

"So what should we do?" the doctor asked, looking at Fleur-de-Marie. "You can't even think of moving the patient to Paris in her present state of prostration. But, come to think of it, my house is right close by. My gardener and her daughter make excellent nurses. Since you take an interest in this case of asphyxiation via submersion, my dear Saint-Remy, you will watch over the care she is given, and I'll come and look in every day."

"And you like to pretend that you're unfeeling and without pity!" the count exclaimed. "But in fact you are the most generous soul there is, and this offer proves it."

"If the patient succumbs, which is quite possible, an interesting autopsy will take place. It will allow me to confirm yet again Goodwin's claims."

"What a dreadful thing to say!" the count cried.

"For those who know how to read it, a cadaver is a book from which one may learn how to save the lives of sick people," Doctor Griffon said stoically.

"Well, after all, you do good," the count said, bitterly, "and that's what matters. Why worry about where it comes from as long as one gets the benefit? Poor child, the more I see her, the more I care about her."

"And she deserves your care, monsieur, I can tell you," the She-Wolf said excitedly as she came up to him.

"You know her?" the count cried.

"Indeed I do, monsieur. I owe all the happiness I have in life to her. In saving her, I didn't do nearly as much for her as she did for me." And the She-Wolf looked passionately at her husband, whom she no longer called "my man."

"Who is she, then?" the count asked.

"She's an angel, monsieur. She's everything there is that's good in the world. Yes, and even though she's dressed like a peasant lady, there's no missus and no great lady who can talk nearly as well as she does, with her little voice that's as sweet as music. She's some girl, I'll tell you. She's brave and good!"

"How did she come to fall in the water?"

"I don't know, monsieur."

"So she isn't a peasant woman?" the count asked.

"A peasant woman? Just look at those little white hands, monsieur."

"That's true," Saint-Remy said. "Now here's an interesting mystery. But what's her name? Who is her family?"

"Let's go," the doctor said, interrupting this conversation. "We have to move the patient into the boat."

A half hour later, still unconscious, Fleur-de-Marie was taken to the doctor's house, where she was put in a good bed and placed under the maternal care of the doctor's gardener, who was assisted by the She-Wolf. The doctor promised Monsieur de Saint-Remy, who showed more and more concern for Songbird, that he would return that very evening to look in on her.

Martial left for Paris with François and Amandine. The She-Wolf didn't want to leave Fleur-de-Marie until she saw that she was out of danger. The Scavenger's Island was now deserted.

We will shortly meet up again with its sinister inhabitants at Red-Arm's, where they are to meet up again with the Owl to murder the diamond broker. Before that, though, we will bring our reader to the meeting that Tom, Sarah's brother, had appointed with the horrible shrew who was the Schoolmaster's partner in crime.

CHAPTER 4

THE PORTRAIT

Half snake and half cat . . .

—*WOLFGANG*, BOOK II

Thomas Seyton, Countess Sarah MacGregor's brother, was walking impatiently along one of the boulevards neighboring the Observatory when he saw the Owl arrive. The horrible old woman was wearing a white bonnet and wrapped in her large red tartan. The point of a stiletto, round as a large quill and very sharp, had cut through the bottom of a straw shopping bag she was carrying on her arm. The tip of this murderous weapon, which had belonged to the Schoolmaster, was jutting out. Thomas Seyton did not see that the Owl was armed.

"Luxembourg tolls three o'clock," the old woman said. "Here I am, just like May flowers after April showers, I hope."

"Come," Thomas Seyton answered. And, walking in front of her, he crossed some empty fields and came to a deserted alley near ruc Cassini. He stopped in the middle of the alley, where it was blocked by a turnstile, opened a small door, and directed the Owl with a gesture to follow him. He took a few steps with her down a walk thickly lined with trees and then told her, "Wait here." And he disappeared.

"As long as he doesn't make me hang around too long," the Owl said. "I have to meet up with Martial at Red-Arm's at five to knock off that broker. Speaking of that, where's my blade? Oh, the little beggar, sticking its nose out the window," the old woman said when she saw the point of the dagger coming through the weave of her shopping bag. "That's what I get for not having stuck a cork on its tip." And, pulling the wooden-handled stiletto from the bag, she replaced it so that it was entirely hidden. "This is my Killer's tool," she went on. "And didn't he ask me for it, supposedly so he can kill the rats that come up to grin at him in his cellar? Poor little things! Most of the time, they have nobody but that old guy without eyes to entertain them and keep them company. The least you can do is allow them to munch on him a little, and since I don't want him to hurt the little rats any, I'm holding on to the knife. Besides, it might come in handy for me when it comes to the broker. Thirty thousand francs in diamonds! That's a nice share for each of us! This day will end well. Not like the other day with that thief of a solicitor I tried to blackmail. A lot of good it did me to threaten him that unless he gave me some money, I would accuse his housemaid of having given Songbird to Tournemine to give me when she was a little baby. Nothing doing there. He called me an old liar and gave me the boot. Okay, then! I'll get an anonymous letter written to the people on that farm Miss Lowlife went to and tell them that it was the solicitor who abandoned her long ago. Maybe they know her family, and when she gets out of Saint-Lazare, that should make things hot for that scoundrel Jacques Ferrand. But someone's coming. Well, look at that, it's the little pale lady who came to the ogress's joint disguised as a man with the tall guy who was just here. They're the ones my Killer and I robbed in the ruins around Notre-Dame," the Owl added when she saw Sarah appear at the end of the walk. "This is going to turn into another job to do. It must be because of her we kidnapped Songbird from the farm. As long as she pays well for this new one, it suits me just fine."

As she approached the Owl, whom she was seeing for the first time since the events at the joint, Sarah's expression manifested the disdain and the disgust that people from a certain social class feel when they have to be in contact with the wretches they make their tools or their accomplices. Thomas Seyton, who up to this point had actively aided his sister's criminal machinations although he thought them fairly pointless, had refused to continue on in this wretched activity. He had nevertheless agreed to put his sister into contact with the Owl once and for all, intending to steer clear, in the meantime, of any new schemes she was going to cook up.

Having had no success in bringing Rodolphe back to her by destroying his relationships or ties with people she thought dear to him, the countess hoped, as we have said, to make him the victim of a despicable deception. If her plan succeeded, the dreams of this stubborn, ambitious, and cruel woman might come true. The idea was to make Rodolphe believe that the daughter he had had with Sarah was not dead and to substitute an orphan for that child. We have seen that Jacques Ferrand, having categorically refused to enter into this conspiracy, despite Sarah's threats, had determined to do away with Fleur-de-Marie, fearing as much what the Owl could reveal as he did the countess's obstinate insistence. But she was not going to give up her almost flawless plan to corrupt or intimidate the solicitor until she was convinced that she had a girl able to fulfill the role she intended for her.

After a moment's silence, Sarah said to the Owl, "Are you clever, discreet, and determined?"

"Clever as a monkey, determined as a bulldog, silent as the tomb—that's the Owl for you, just as the devil made her. Ready to do you any service she can. And she can do anything," the old woman answered blithely. "I hope we got that young country girl out of the way good and proper for you. She's locked up in Saint-Lazare for at least two months."

"It's not about her, it's about something else."

"Whatever you wish, my little lady! As long as there's money to be had for what you propose, we'll be just like two fingers of the same hand."

Sarah could not suppress a gesture of disgust. "You must know people of the lower classes, unfortunate people—don't you?"

"There are a lot more of those than there are millionaires. You have your choice of them, thank God. When it comes to poverty, Paris is an embarrassment of riches."

"I need a poor orphan girl, and she has to have lost her parents when she was a baby. Plus, she needs to have an attractive face, a sweet personality, and she can't be more than seventeen years old." The Owl looked at the countess in astonishment. "It can't be difficult to find an orphan girl like that," the countess went on. "There are so many foundlings."

"But, really, my little lady, you're forgetting Songbird. She'll do for you perfectly."

"What is this Songbird?"

"The girl we kidnapped from Bouqueval!"

"This isn't about her, I tell you!"

"Just listen to me, and then be sure to pay me what my advice is worth. You want an orphan girl, gentle as a lamb, beautiful as sunshine, and no older than seventeen, right?"

"That's what I said."

"Well, then, when Songbird gets out of Saint-Lazare, there you have it. She's just what you want. It's as if someone made her up for you on purpose. She was about six when that wretch of a Jacques Ferrand (this was about ten years ago) gave me a thousand francs to get rid of her for him. All right, so it was Tournemine—who's in the Rochefort prison now—who brought her to me, telling me it was some child someone wanted to get rid of or pass off as dead."

"Jacques Ferrand, you say?" Sarah cried out, in a voice so distorted that the Owl pulled back in bewilderment. "The solicitor Jacques Ferrand," Sarah went on, "gave you this child, and—" She couldn't finish her sentence. Her feelings were too violent. She stretched her two hands out toward the Owl, trembling convulsively as surprise and joy contorted her features.

"I don't know what's getting you all worked up like this, my little lady," the Owl said. "It's really very simple. Ten years ago, an old acquaintance of mine, Tournemine, said to me, 'Do you want to take on a little girl that someone wants to get rid of? It's all the same whether she croaks or lives. There's a thousand francs in it and you can do with the child what you want.'"

"Ten years ago!" Sarah cried.

"Ten years."

"A little blond girl?"

"A little blond girl."

"With blue eyes?"

"Eyes as blue as cornflowers."

"And that's her . . . that at the farm . . ."

"She's the one we packed up and sent to Saint-Lazare. I have to say that I hardly expected to see that little Miss Lowlife again in the countryside."

"Oh, God, God!" Sarah cried out, falling to her knees, looking upward and raising her hands to the heavens. "How mysterious are your ways! I bow down before your divine justice. That such good fortune is even possible . . . but no, I can't believe it even now. It would be too good—no!" Then, getting up quickly, she said to the Owl, who looked at her completely taken aback, "Come." And Sarah hurried ahead of the old woman.

At the end of the walk, she climbed several steps that led to the glass door of a sumptuously furnished study. Just as the Owl was about to enter, Sarah gestured to her to remain outside. Then the countess rang loudly. A servant appeared.

"If anybody calls, I'm not in. And don't let anyone come in here, do you understand? Absolutely nobody." The servant left. To secure her privacy even more, Sarah bolted the door. The Owl had heard the directions given to the servant and had seen the door bolted. The countess, turning to her, said, "Come in quickly and shut the door."

The Owl came in. Sarah opened a small writing desk quickly and took out an ebony chest that she carried to the office desk in the middle of the room. She motioned to the Owl to come over to her. The chest contained a number of jewelry trays, one on top of the other, each holding magnificent jewelry. Sarah was in such a rush to get to the bottom of the chest that she flung the bins full of necklaces, bracelets, and tiaras willy-nilly all over the table. The rubies, emeralds, and diamonds of this jewelry sparkled brightly.

The Owl was dazzled. She was armed, she was alone, she was shut up with the countess, and her escape would be easy and certain. A hellish idea crossed this monster's mind. But to carry out this new crime, she had to get her stiletto out of her basket and get near Sarah, all without inciting her suspicions. With the cunning of a jungle cat slinking on its belly to get treacherously closer to its prey, the old woman took advantage of the countess's preoccupation to move, imperceptibly, around the desk that separated her from her victim. The Owl had already begun this underhanded course when, suddenly, she had to stop in her tracks.

Sarah took a locket out of the false bottom of the box, leaned across the table, and, holding out her trembling hand, showed it to the Owl and said to her, "Look at this portrait."

"That's Miss Lowlife!" the Owl exclaimed, struck by the closeness of the resemblance. "That's the baby they turned over to me. I can almost see her standing there, just like what she was when Tournemine brought her to me. There they are, the thick curls in her hair that I immediately cut off and sold, by God!"

"You recognize her—that's really her? Oh, don't deceive me! I implore you, don't deceive me!"

"I tell you, my little lady, that's Miss Lowlife, as clear as day," said the Owl, trying to get closer to Sarah without her noticing it. "Even now, she still looks like that portrait. If you saw her, you wouldn't believe it."

Sarah did not cry out a single time in pain or shock upon learning of her daughter's ten years of misery and abandonment. No pang of remorse disturbed her when she considered that she herself had been responsible for fatefully tearing the girl away from the peaceful retreat Rodolphe had found for her. This unnatural mother's first impulse was not to question the Owl, in painful anxiety, about her child's past. No, for Sarah, ambition had long ago snuffed out any maternal tenderness. Her transports now had nothing to do with the joy of finding her daughter again but rather with the sure expectation of seeing the proud dream of her whole life come true. Rodolphe had come to care for this unhappy child and saved her from the streets without knowing who she was. What would be his feeling when he knew that she was . . . HIS DAUGHTER? He was free, and the countess was a widow. Sarah could already see her royal crown gleaming before her eyes.

The Owl, step by slow step, had finally reached one end of the table and had placed her stiletto upright in her bag, the handle just brushing the opening, in easy reach. No more than a few steps separated her from the countess.

"Do you know how to write?" the countess suddenly asked her. And, sweeping away the chest and the jewels with her hand, she opened up a blotter that stood before an inkwell.

"No, madame, I don't know how to write," the Owl responded, just in case.

"Then I'll write at your dictation. Tell me all the circumstances surrounding the abandonment of this little girl." And Sarah, sitting down in a chair in front of the desk, took a pen and gestured to the Owl to come over beside her.

The old woman's eyes were ablaze. Finally, she stood right next to Sarah's chair. The latter, bent over the table, prepared to write. "I'll read aloud," the countess said, "and as we go along, you can correct my errors."

"Yes, madame," the Owl said, keeping track of Sarah's slightest movements. Then she slid her hand into her bag so that she could get to her stiletto without being seen.

The countess began to write. "'I declare that—'" But, stopping herself and turning toward the Owl, who already had her hand around the knife handle, Sarah asked, "When was this child delivered to you?"

"In February 1827."

"And by whom?" Sarah asked, still facing the Owl.

"By Pierre Tournemine, currently in the Rochefort prison. It was Madame Séraphin, the solicitor's housekeeper, who gave the little one to him."

The countess returned to writing and read aloud, "'I declare that in the month of February 1827 the person named . . .'"

The Owl had taken out her stiletto. She had already stood up to stab her victim between the shoulder blades. Sarah turned around to her once again. The Owl, so as not to be taken by surprise, pressed her right hand quickly on the back of Sarah's chair and leaned over so she could respond to her new question.

"I've forgotten the name of the man who delivered the child to you," the countess said.

"Pierre Tournemine," the Owl answered.

"'Pierre Tournemine,'" Sarah repeated, then went on writing, "'currently in the Rochefort prison, placed the child in my hands. She was given to him by the housekeeper of—'"

The countess was unable to finish her sentence. The Owl, after having gently let her bag slip and drop to her feet, threw herself upon the countess in rapid fury, seized the back of her neck with her left hand, pushed her face onto the table, and with her right hand planted the stiletto between her shoulder blades.

The Owl carried out this abominable attack with such speed that the countess didn't cry out or even moan. Still seated, her upper body and forehead were still on the table. Her pen had fallen out of her hand.

"That's the same way my Killer did it with the little old man from rue du Roule," the monster said. "And here's another one who won't be telling any tales. I've closed her account." Hastily gathering up the jewels and throwing them in her bag, the Owl didn't notice that her victim was still breathing.

Having completed this attack and theft, the horrible old woman opened the glass door and disappeared down the tree-lined path. She exited by the little door opening on the back alley and reached the empty fields. Near the Observatory, she flagged down a hackney, which took her to Red-Arm's place in the Champs-Élysées. As we know, the Martial widow, Nicolas, Calabash, and Fishhook had arranged to meet the Owl in this den to rob and kill the diamond broker.

CHAPTER 5

THE POLICE DETECTIVE

The reader is already acquainted with the Bleeding Heart cabaret, which is located on the Champs-Élysées near the Cours-la-Reine park in one of those large ditches that ran along that avenue a few years ago. The residents of the Scavenger's Island had not yet shown up.

Since Bradamanti's departure (as we know, he had accompanied Madame d'Harville's stepmother to Normandy), Gammy had returned to his father. Standing watch at the top of the stairs, the little lame boy was supposed to signal the Martials' arrival with an agreed-upon cry. Red-Arm, meanwhile, was in a secret conference with a police detective named Narcisse Borel. The reader may remember seeing him at the ogress's joint when he came to arrest two scoundrels accused of murder.

This detective, who was about forty years old, was vigorous and stocky, with a ruddy complexion and a sharp, piercing gaze. His face was clean-shaven to facilitate the various disguises his dangerous raids demanded. To overcome the outlaws he was up against required craft and determination; he often had to combine the supple transformations of an actor with the courage and energy of a soldier. In short, Narcisse Borel was one of the most useful and active instruments of that small-scale version of divine justice that we vulgarly and modestly call the police.

Let us attend, then, to this conversation between Narcisse Borel and Red-Arm, a conversation that seemed to be quite animated.

"That's right, Red-Arm," said the police detective. "We suspect you're taking advantage of your role as an undercover agent to go in on the thefts of a band of very dangerous criminals with impunity, and of then giving false evidence about it to the police. Take care, Red-Arm. If that turns out to be the case, it will go very badly for you."

"Alas! I know that's what people suspect, and it saddens me, my good Monsieur Narcisse," Red-Arm answered, contorting his weasel's face into a hypocritical expression of chagrin. "But today, I hope, the truth will out and my good faith will be recognized."

"We'll see about that."

"How can anybody distrust me? Haven't I proven myself more than once? Was it me or wasn't it—yes or no—who, back in the day, put you on the path to arrest Ambrose Martial, one of the most dangerous criminals in Paris, and catch him in the act? Like they say, the fruit doesn't fall far from the tree, and Martial's fruit grows in hell, and hell will have its harvest if God is just."

"That's all well and good, but someone tipped Ambrose off that he was going to be arrested. If I hadn't come an hour ahead of the time you fixed, he would have gotten away."

"Monsieur Narcisse, can you really think I would have secretly warned him of the time of your arrival?"

"All I know is that that thief shot me at point-blank range and it was just my good luck that the bullet only went through my arm."

"Well, really, Monsieur Narcisse, such misunderstandings are an occupational hazard in your line of work."

"You call that a misunderstanding!"

"Well, of course, since that scoundrel certainly intended to put his bullet in your heart."

"In the arm, in the heart, in the head, it doesn't matter, and that's not what I'm complaining about. Every job has its drawbacks."

"And its pleasures, Monsieur Narcisse, and its pleasures! Because you've got to admit, really, that when someone as sharp, skilled, and courageous as you has been on the track of a nest of thieves for a long time, when he chases them from one neighborhood to another, from one lair to another, with a faithful bloodhound like your own Red-Arm, and then ends up catching them in a trap from which there is no escape—well, you have to admit that's a great pleasure. That's the joy of the hunt. Not to speak of the fact that you're acting in the pursuit of justice," the Bleeding Heart's innkeeper added gravely.

"I would agree with you if the bloodhound were reliable, but I fear he is not."

"Oh, Monsieur Narcisse, could you really think that—"

"What I think is that, instead of putting us on the right path, you entertain yourself by leading us astray, and you take advantage of our trust in you. Every day you promise to help us get our hands on this band of thieves, and that day never comes."

"And what if that day came today, Monsieur Narcisse, as I'm sure it will? What if I help you round up Fishhook, Nicolas Martial, the widow, the daughter, and the Owl? Won't you think that to be a good day's work? Yes or no? Will you still not trust me then?"

"No, if that happens, I will trust you, and you will have rendered society a great service. We have a lot of suspicions about this pack, and some of them are almost certain to be true, but unfortunately we have no hard evidence at all."

"And if they just happen to be in the act when you pinch them, that would help something fierce in undoing their game, wouldn't it, Monsieur Narcisse?"

"No doubt about it. And you can swear to it that you didn't do anything that would be entrapment to get them to pull off this job?"

"My word of honor, I did no such thing! It was the Owl who came to me with the idea of getting the broker to come here. My son told that infernal one-eyed hag that Morel, the gem-cutter, worked with real stones, not fake ones, and that Old Lady Mathieu often had jewelry worth considerable sums of money on her. I accepted my part in the business and I suggested to the Owl that we join up with Martial and Fishhook so you can get your hands on all the hangers-on as well."

"And what about the Schoolmaster, that strong, dangerous man who was always with the Owl? He was one of the regular clients of the joint."

"The Schoolmaster?" Red-Arm asked, feigning astonishment.

"Yes, the escaped convict from the Rochefort prison, one Anselme Duresnel, serving a term of life imprisonment. We know now that he disfigured himself so as to make himself unrecognizable. You don't know anything about him?"

"Not a thing," Red-Arm answered boldly. We know that the Schoolmaster was, at that moment, imprisoned in the cellar of the cabaret, but Red-Arm had his own reasons for lying.

"We have good reason to believe that the Schoolmaster is behind some recent murders. This would be an important arrest."

"It's been six weeks since anyone has known what's become of him."

"And you're to blame for having lost track of him."

"Always finding fault, Monsieur Narcisse, always finding fault."

"It's not as if there aren't good reasons for it. And what about the smuggling?"

"Don't I have to know all kinds of people, smugglers as well as others, to put you on the right path? And I told you about the pipe for carrying liquids that was built outside the Trône barrier and going into a house on rue—"[163]

"I know all about that," Narcisse said, interrupting Red-Arm. "But for every guy you turn in, you let maybe ten more get away, and you continue your activities with impunity. I'm sure you're serving two different masters, as they say."

"Oh! Monsieur Narcisse, I would never be so dishonest in my employment arrangements."

"And that's not all. There's a woman named Burette who lends

163. Taxes were levied on alcohol at the barriers of Paris, at the city limits. Red-Arm is describing a device designed to allow smugglers to avoid having to pay this tax. [TN]

money against wages. She lives at seventeen rue du Temple, and people say she is also your own private fence."

"What am I supposed to do about that, Monsieur Narcisse? People make things up all the time, and there are so many people in the world with evil minds. And as I said, I have to mix with as many rogues as I can and I have to look like I do all the things that they do—and worse than they do—so I don't make them suspicious. But it always breaks my heart to act that way. It just breaks my heart. You have to really care about serving justice to allow yourself to do those things."

"You poor, dear man. I pity you with all my heart."

"You're laughing at me, Monsieur Narcisse. But if you believe all that, why not arrest Old Lady Burette and me?"

"You know the answer to that as well as I do. We don't want to scare off the thieves that you've been promising to turn over to us for so long."

"And I am going to turn them over to you, Monsieur Narcisse. In an hour's time, you'll have them all tied up. And it won't be too hard to do since three of them are women. As for Fishhook and Nicolas, they're as fierce as tigers but as yellow as chickens."

"Tigers or chickens," Narcisse said, partially opening his long overcoat and showing the handles of two pistols sticking out of the pockets of his pants, "I have what I need to take care of them."

"You'd still do well to take two of your men with you, Monsieur Narcisse. When their backs are up against the wall, even the biggest cowards fight like crazy."

"I'll place two of my men in the small room at the bottom, next to the one you'll have the broker go into. As soon as we hear a thing, I'll be at one door and my two men at the other."

"You'd better hurry up because the thieves are due here at any moment now."

"That's fine. I'll go put my men in position. But this better not be all for nothing this time."

The conversation was interrupted by a special whistle meant to serve as the warning sign. Red-Arm went up to the window to see whose approach Gammy was warning them of.

"Well, now, here's the Owl already. Maybe now you'll believe me, Monsieur Narcisse."

"It's at least something. But it's not everything, yet. We'll know soon enough. I'll run out and get my men in position." And the police detective disappeared through a side door.

CHAPTER 6

THE OWL

The Owl's hideous face had turned crimson, in part because she had been walking so quickly, but also because her constitution was still operating at a feverish pitch in the wake of the theft and murder. Her green eye glittered with savage joy. Gammy followed her, limping and hopping as he went. Just as she was coming down the last steps, in a mean-spirited prank Red-Arm's son stepped on one of the folds dragging from the Owl's dress. This sudden stop made the old woman stagger. Unable to hold herself up with the banister, she fell to her knees with her hands sprawling out in front of her and dropping her precious shopping basket. Out fell a gold bracelet, ornamented with emeralds and real pearls. Having only slightly chafed her fingers in the fall, the Owl grabbed the bracelet, which had not escaped Gammy's sharp eye, got up, and flung herself furiously on the little lame boy, who came up to her and said with a hypocritical expression, "Oh, dear! Have we lost our footing?"

Without answering, the Owl grabbed hold of Gammy's hair and, stooping to the level of his cheek, bit him in a rage. The blood spurted out under her tooth. And then something strange happened. Despite his wickedness, despite his anger at the sharp pain, Gammy neither groaned nor cried. He wiped his bleeding face and said, with forced laughter, "I'd like it better if you didn't kiss me quite as forcefully as that next time—all right, Owl?"

"You vicious little monkey, why did you put your foot on my dress on purpose to make me trip?"

"Me? Oh, come on now, really. I swear to you I didn't do it on purpose, my dear Owl. As often as your little Gammy might want to hurt you, he loves you too much for that. You can beat him, push him around, bite him, he'll still follow you about like a dog does his master," the child said in a falsely sweet, sugary tone of voice.

Taken in by Gammy's hypocrisy, the Owl believed him and said, "That's all right, then! If I was wrong for biting you this time, it can be for all the other times you deserved it, you thief. So come on. Today, everybody's happy! Today, I hold no grudges. So where's your father, the old swindler?"

"In the house. Do you want me to go look for him?"

"No. Have the Martials come yet?"

"Not yet."

"So I have time to go down and visit my Killer. We have things to talk about, me and old no-eyes."

"You're going to the Schoolmaster's cellar?" Gammy said, hardly able to hide his diabolical glee.

"What's it to you?"

"Me?"

"Yes, you. You asked me in a funny way."

"Because I was thinking about something funny."

"What?"

"That you really ought to at least bring him some playing cards to relieve his boredom," Gammy said, in a sly way. "That would at least be a change for him. Now his only game is to be bitten by rats. And he wins that game every time, so in the end it gets tiresome."

The Owl guffawed at this jibe. "Come to Mama, you love of a monkey. I don't know another kid who can match this one for being bad to the bone. Go look for a candle. You can light my way down to see my Killer. And you'll help me open his door. You know that I can't even push it a little way by myself."

"Oh, no, not me. It's too dark in the cellar," said Gammy, shaking his head.

"What is this? Really! You're as bad as they come, and now you're playing a coward? That I'd like to see. Go on now, quick, and tell your father I'll be back in an instant, that I'm with my Killer and that we're talking about announcing our wedding—ha, ha, ha!" the monster added, chuckling. "Go on now, hurry up! You'll be the page boy at our wedding, and if you're good, I'll let you be the one who takes off my garter."

Gammy went off sullenly in search of a light. While waiting, the Owl, still drunk with the success of her theft, thrust her right hand into her basket in order to finger the precious jewelry it contained. Indeed, it was because she wanted to find a temporary hiding place for this treasure that she was going down into the Schoolmaster's cellar, and not for her usual reason, which was to take pleasure in the pain of her latest victim. We will soon explain why the Owl, with Red-Arm's consent, had consigned the Schoolmaster to the same tiny subterranean space into which the thief had earlier thrown Rodolphe.

Gammy reappeared at the cabaret's door, holding a lit torch. The Owl followed him into the lower room, which contained the double-paneled trapdoor with which we are already familiar. Red-Arm's son, cupping the light with his hand, went ahead of the old woman, making his way slowly down a stone staircase that led to a steep incline. At the bottom was the thick door to the cellar that had very nearly become Rodolphe's tomb. When they arrived at the bottom of the staircase, Gammy seemed to hesitate at following the Owl further.

"Oh, come on, you wicked slowpoke, keep going," she told him, turning around.

"Well, really! It's so dark, and you're walking so fast, too, Owl. You know what? I think I'd rather go back upstairs. I'll leave you the candle."

"And what about the cellar door, you imbecile? Do you think I can open it myself? Will you come already?"

"No, I'm too frightened."

"If I have to come and get you, you won't be happy."

"Well, if you're going to threaten me, I'm going back up." And Gammy backed up a few steps.

"All right. Listen—be a good boy," the Owl said, suppressing her anger, "and I'll give you something."

"Great!" Gammy said, coming closer. "Talk to me like that and you can get me to do anything, Mother Owl."

"Come on, come on, I'm in a hurry."

"All right, but promise me you'll let me torment the Schoolmaster?"

"Another time. I don't have any time today."

"Just a little bit. Let me just make him foam at the mouth."

"Another time. I tell you, I have to go back up right away."

"So why do you want to open his apartment door?"

"That's none of your business. So, are you finished playing around? The Martials may already be upstairs and I have to talk to them. Be a good boy and you won't be sorry for it. So come on."

"I must really love you a lot, you know, Owl, because you can get me to do anything," Gammy said as he came toward her slowly.

The pale, blinking light of the candle, illuminating the dark corridor only slightly, outlined the hideous child's black silhouette against the cracked greenish walls that were sweating water from the dampness. At the end of the passage, through the shadows, the low broken-down arch, the entry to the cellar, could be seen. Also visible were the thick door, reinforced with iron strips, and, standing out from the shadows, the Owl's red tartan and white bonnet.

Thanks to the combined efforts of the Owl and Gammy, the door opened, grinding on its rusted hinges. A puff of damp steam blew out of the lair, which was dark as night. The torch, resting on the ground, threw some light on the top steps of the staircase, but the lower steps disappeared completely in the shadows. A cry or, rather, a savage bellowing came up from the depths of the cellar.

"Ah, there's my Killer, saying hello to his mommy," the Owl said, ironically.

"I'm hungry!" the Schoolmaster cried out, his voice trembling with rage. "Are you trying to kill me like a wild animal?"

"You're hungry, my fat kitten?" the Owl said, bursting into laughter. "Well, then, suck your thumb." The sound of a chain could be heard, suddenly jerking tight, followed by a sigh of mute, suppressed rage.

"Take care! Take care! You'll give your leg another boo-boo, like at the Bouqueval farm. Poor, dear Papa!" Gammy said.

"He's got a point, this child does. Calm down, Killer," the old woman said. "The ring and the chain are strong, old no-eyes. They come from Old Micou, and he only sells good stuff. And it's your fault, after all. Who told you to go to sleep and let yourself be tied up? All we had to do was get the ring and the chain around one of your stems and drag you down here where it's cool—just to keep you nice and fresh, you old flirt."

"It's too bad he's going to get all moldy," Gammy said.

And then the chain made another noise.

"Ha, ha! You're hopping around like a June bug tied up by its leg, Killer," the old woman said. "I can almost see it."

"June bug! Fly! Fly! Fly! The Schoolmaster is your husband!" Gammy chanted.[164]

This variation on her words made the Owl laugh even more. Having placed her bag into a hole made by the rotting of the staircase wall, she got up and said, "So, you see, Killer—"

"No, he can't see," Gammy said.

"This kid is right again! Very well. So listen to me, Killer. When we were returning from the farm, you shouldn't have been such a ninny, playing at being a nice doggy and stopping me from making Miss Lowlife ugly with my acid. And on top of that, you started talking about your inner voice and getting altogether too moralistic. I could see that your out-and-out beggar's constitution was going bad and that you were becoming honest, like someone who'd talk to a police spy, and that one day or the other, sooner or later you'd turn stoolie, old no-eyes, and so—"

"And so old no-eyes is going to have something to eat—you, Owl, because he's hungry," Gammy cried out as he suddenly pushed the old woman from behind with all his strength. The Owl fell forward, unleashing a fearsome curse as she toppled. The sound could be heard of her rolling to the bottom of the stone staircase. "Go to it! Go to it! Go to it! The Owl's all yours! All yours! Jump on her, old man!" Gammy said. Then, grabbing the basket out from under the stone where he had seen the old woman put it, he climbed quickly up the stairs, crying out in a burst of cruel laughter, "Now that push sure beat the one I gave you before, don't you think, Owl? This time you won't bite me and make me bleed. Oh, you thought I didn't hold a grudge. Thanks, but no thanks. I'm still bleeding."

---

164. Gammy is riffing here on a popular children's song. [TN]

"I've got her! Oh, I've got her now!" the Schoolmaster cried out from the bottom of the cellar.

"If you've got her, I'll split her with you," Gammy said, chuckling. And he stopped on the last step of the staircase.

"Help me!" the Owl cried in a strangulated voice.

"Thank you, Gammy," the Schoolmaster said. "Thank you!" And he let out an audible sigh of frightening joy. "Oh! I forgive you all the evil you did me, and in payment for this kindness, you're going to hear the Owl sing! Listen to the song of the bird of death."

"Bravo! And I get to sit in the mezzanine," Gammy said, settling down at the top of the stairs.

CHAPTER 7

THE CELLAR

Seated on the top step of the staircase, Gammy held up his candle to try to illuminate the appalling scene that was taking shape in the depths of the cellar. The darkness was too complete, however, for such a puny source of light to dissipate. Red-Arm's son couldn't see a thing. The struggle between the Schoolmaster and the Owl was mute and desperate; not a word was spoken, nor a cry heard. The only sounds that emerged from time to time were those of the labored panting or muffled breathing that accompany violent and restrained exertions.

As Gammy sat on the stone step, he began stomping his feet in the cadence particular to theatergoers who are impatient for the play to begin. Then he shouted a phrase that would be familiar to anyone who patronizes the balconies of boulevard theaters: "Come on already! Raise the curtain! Start the play! Music!"

"Oh, now I've got you where I want you," murmured the Schoolmaster, deep in the cellar, "and you're going to—"

A desperate move on the Owl's part cut him off. She was fighting him with the strength that comes from the fear of death.

"Louder! You can't be heard up here!" cried Gammy.

"You can try all you like to eat my hand, but I've got you where I want you," said the Schoolmaster. Then, no doubt having succeeded at restraining the Owl, he added, "That's it. Now listen—"

"Gammy, call your father!" exclaimed the Owl, in a breathless, exhausted voice. "Help! Help!"

"Go to the door, old woman! It's keeping people from hearing you," said the little lame boy, bursting into laughter. "Down with the cabal!"[165]

The Owl's cries could not penetrate these two underground floors. The wretched woman, seeing that she could not hope for the assistance of Red-Arm's son, decided to make one last effort. "Gammy, go and get help, and I'll give you my shopping basket. It's full of jewelry. It's there, under a rock."

"What generosity! Thank you, madame! But I already have the basket, don't you know? Hey, can you hear how all the gems are clicking

---

165. Gammy is quoting a line from *Agésilas*, a tragedy by Pierre Corneille. [TN]

against each other?" Gammy said as he shook the bag. "But come on—give me some worthless hotcakes, and then I'll go and get Papa!"

"Have pity on me, and I'll—" The Owl could not finish her sentence. Silence set in again.

The little lame boy started stomping again on the stone step upon which he was crouching, shouting repeatedly in time with the sound of his feet, "When is it going to start? Hey, pull up the curtain or I'll have to put on the show myself. On with the show! Start the music!"

"This way, Owl, you won't be able to deafen me anymore with your cries," said the Schoolmaster after a few minutes. No doubt he had managed to gag the old woman in this interval. "You can tell only too well," he went on in a slow, hollow voice, "that I don't want to get this over with too quickly. You tortured me, now I'll torture you. You made me suffer a lot. I have a lot to say to you before I kill you. Oh, yes, quite a lot. And it's going to be dreadful for you. Real agony, you hear me?"

"Oh, no, don't go too far, old man!" cried Gammy, rising slightly from his perch. "You can punish her a little, but don't hurt her too much. You're talking about killing her? You're kidding, right? I like my Owl. I've lent her to you, but you need to give her back to me. Don't mess her up for me. I don't want anyone to destroy my Owl. If you don't listen to me, I'm going to get Papa."

"Calm down. She's only going to get what she deserves—a lesson she'll never forget," said the Schoolmaster, attempting to reassure Gammy. He feared that the little lame boy was going to go seek help.

"All right, then! Bravo! Now the show's going to start," said Red-Arm's son, not believing that the Schoolmaster posed a serious threat to the horrible old woman's life.

"So let's talk things over, Owl," said the Schoolmaster calmly. "First of all, you know, since I had that dream on the Bouqueval farm that made me relive all the crimes we committed together as if they were happening again—since I had that dream that almost made me go mad and will end up making me go mad because here in my solitude, in the profound isolation in which I've been living, all of my thoughts keep leading, no matter what I do, to that dream—a strange change has come over me. Yes, I developed a repugnance for my own past savagery. First, I didn't let you torture Songbird. But that was nothing. By chaining me up in this cellar and making me suffer from cold and hunger but relieving me of my obsession with you, you've abandoned me to the horror of my reflections. Oh! You have no idea what it's like to be alone, all alone, with a dark veil over your eyes, as the implacable man who punished me put it. It's terrifying! Do you see? This is the cellar I threw him into to kill him, and now this cellar is the site of my torture. It may well be my grave. I'll tell you again: it's terrifying. Everything that man predicted to me has come true. He told me, 'You have taken advantage of your strength; you will become the plaything of the weakest.' That's exactly what happened. He said to me, 'Isolated from now on from the external world, face-to-face with the eternal memory of your crimes, you will one day repent of those crimes.' And that day has come. Isolation has purified me. I never would have thought it possible.

"Another thing that shows that I may be less of a criminal than before is that, even though I feel infinite joy in having you here in my grip, you monster, it's not because I want revenge against you myself, but because I want to avenge our victims. Yes, I will have fulfilled my duty when I punish my accomplice with my own two hands. Something tells me that if you had fallen into my clutches earlier, a lot of blood, a lot of innocent blood, would not have been shed. Now I'm horrified by the murders I've committed in the past, and yet—don't you find it peculiar?—I feel no hesitation or fear in murdering you gruesomely with all the most horrible refinements, as I'm about to do. So tell me, what do you think about that?"

"Bravo! Bravo! That's what I call acting! Old no-eyes, you're bringing down the house!" Gammy exclaimed, applauding. "This is still just joking around, right?"

"Still just joking around," answered the Schoolmaster, in a hollow voice. "So listen, Owl, I have to finish explaining to you how, little by little, I came around to repenting for what I have done. Learning this will be odious to you because you have no heart. It will show you how merciless I need to be when I take revenge on you in the name of our victims. I need to hurry up. The joy of holding you here gets my blood going. My temples are pounding violently the way they do when thinking about that dream makes me go crazy. One of my fits might come on now, but I'll have the time to make your impending death terrifying by forcing you to listen to me."

"Come on, Owl! Be bold!" Gammy cried. "Answer back without fear! Don't you know your part? Tell the devil to give you your line, old woman!"

"Oh, you can struggle and bite all you want," said the Schoolmaster after another period of silence. "You won't get away from me. You've cut my fingers to the bone, but I'll tear your tongue out if you move. Let's return to our conversation. When I found myself all alone in the darkness and silence, I started to have fits of furious, impotent rage. For the first time, I lost my reason. Yes: even though I was awake, I saw the dream all over again. You know? That dream . . . the little old man from rue du Roule . . . that woman who drowned . . . the livestock merchant . . . And there you were, floating over these ghosts. I'm telling you, it was terrifying. I'm blind, and my thoughts take on body and form so that they can represent the features of our victims to me—incessantly, and in a visible, almost palpable way. I wouldn't have had that terrifying dream if my mind, absorbed as it always is by the memory of my past crimes, had been obscured by its usual vision. It must be that when you're deprived of your eyesight, obsessive thoughts take an almost material form in your brain. Still, sometimes, when I think them over with a resigned terror, it seems to me that these threatening specters have pity on me. They get pale, disintegrate, and disappear. Then I think I'm waking up from a gloomy dream, but I feel weak, beaten down, broken, and—you wouldn't believe this—you're going to laugh, Owl! I cry. Do you understand? I cry! You aren't laughing? Go ahead, laugh! Laugh!"

The Owl let out a quiet, stifled moan.

"Louder!" exclaimed Gammy. "You can't be heard up here!"

"Yes," continued the Schoolmaster, "I cry, because I suffer—and my anger is in vain. I say to myself, 'Tomorrow, the day after tomorrow, I'll still be tormented by the same attacks of delirium and deadly desolation.' What a life! Oh, what a life! And to think that I didn't choose death over being buried alive in this abyss that my thoughts keep digging for me! Blind, alone, and imprisoned—what could possibly distract me from my remorse? Nothing—nothing at all. When for a moment the ghosts stop moving in front of the black veil I have before my eyes, there are still other tortures, and those are the crushing comparisons I make. I say to myself, 'If I had remained an honest man, at this moment I would be free, at peace, happy, loved, and honored by my family—instead of being blind and chained up in this dungeon at the mercy of my accomplices.'

"Alas! The regret you feel for happiness lost on account of a crime is a first step toward repentance. And when this repentance is accompanied by a terrifyingly hard expiation—an expiation that changes your life into a long bout of insomnia full of vengeful hallucinations or desperate reflections—then perhaps human forgiveness will follow the remorse and expiation."

"Be careful, old man!" cried Gammy. "You're stealing Monsieur Moëssard's[166] lines. We've heard them all before!"

The Schoolmaster ignored Red-Arm's son. "Does it surprise you to hear me talking this way, Owl? I know only too well that if I had continued to numb myself, either by new blood-soaked crimes or by the savage drunkenness of life in the galleys, this healthful change never would have taken place in me. But alone and blind, racked by remorse that I always see before me, what else can I think about? New crimes? How would I be able to commit them? Escape? How can I escape? And if I escaped, where could I go? What would I do with my liberty? No, I must live henceforward in eternal darkness, caught between the anguish of repentance and the terror of those horrible apparitions that are pursuing me. Nevertheless,

166. Simon-Pierre Moëssard (1781–1851) was a well-known actor, first in the provinces and then in Paris. He stopped acting in 1821 and became better known for his charitable endeavors. The lines Gammy accuses the Schoolmaster of stealing refer more to these charities than to any drama he acted in. [TN]

sometimes a feeble ray of hope comes shining in amid the gloom. A moment of calm follows my torments. Yes, for sometimes I manage to exorcise the ghosts that obsess me by contrasting them to the memories of an honest and peaceful past. I return in my thoughts to the earliest years of my youth, of my childhood.

"Fortunately, you see, the greatest criminals have at least a few years of peace and innocence to contrast to their criminal and bloodthirsty years. No one is born evil. The most perverse among us have known the lovable innocence of childhood; they've known the sweet joys of that charming age. And so, I say again, I sometimes feel a bitter consolation in telling myself, 'I'm cursed at this moment by all, but there was a time at which I was loved or protected because I was harmless and good.' Alas! I really have to take refuge in the past, when I can. It's the only place I can find any rest."

As he pronounced these last words, the Schoolmaster's tone had lost its hardness. This incorrigible man seemed profoundly moved. He added, "You know, the healthful influence of these thoughts is calming my anger. I've lost the courage, the strength, the will to punish you. No, it's not for me to spill your blood."

"Bravo, old man! Do you see, Owl, that it was all playacting?" cried Gammy, applauding.

"No, it's not for me to spill your blood," continued the Schoolmaster. "It would be another murder. Perhaps an excusable one but another murder nonetheless. And the three ghosts haunting me already are plenty. And then, who knows? You yourself might repent someday, right?" As he was speaking, the Schoolmaster had unconsciously allowed the Owl some freedom to move. She took advantage of this freedom to seize the stiletto she had placed in her blouse after Sarah's murder and violently stab the bandit with it in order to get free of him.

He gave a piercing cry of pain. The ferocious ardor of his hatred, vengeance, rage, and bloodlust, abruptly awakened and exasperated by this attack, burst out in a sudden, terrible explosion in which he lost all control of his reason, which had already been strongly undermined by so many shocks. "Oh, you viper! I felt your tooth!" he exclaimed in a voice that trembled with furor. He gripped the Owl, who thought she had escaped him, with all his might. "You were crawling around the cellar, weren't you?" he added, more and more deranged. "But I'm going to crush you, whether you're a viper or an owl. You were expecting my ghosts to return, no doubt. Yes, for my temples are beating with blood and my ears are ringing. My head is swimming the way it does when they're going to come. Yes, there's no mistaking it. Oh, here they are! They're coming from the depths of the darkness. They're coming closer. Look how pale they are . . . See how their blood is flowing, red and steaming . . . You're getting scared—you're struggling. Well, don't worry! You won't see those ghosts—

no, you won't see them. I feel sorry for you, because I'm going to blind you. You'll be like me, without eyes."

Here the Schoolmaster paused. The Owl screamed so horribly that Gammy, struck with fear, jumped up from his stone step and stood upright. The Owl's terrible cries seemed to bring the Schoolmaster's mindless fury to a climax. "Sing," he said in a whisper. "Sing, Owl. Sing your death song. You're lucky, you won't see the three ghosts of the people we murdered anymore—the little old man from rue du Roule, the drowned woman, the livestock merchant . . . I can see them, though. Here they come . . . they're touching me . . . Oh! They're so cold! Ah!" This wretch's last glimmer of intelligence flickered out in this cry of horror, this cry of a damned soul.

From that point on, the Schoolmaster could no longer think rationally or speak. He acted and growled like a wild animal. He acted only on the most primitive instinct of destruction for the sake of destruction.

And then something terrifying took place in the dark depths of the cellar. Hurried trampling could be heard, interrupted at different intervals by a dull noise, echoing like the sound of a skull hitting a stone one wanted to use to break it open. Sharp, convulsive groans and an outburst of infernal laughter accompanied each of these blows. Then there was a death rattle—and then nothing more could be heard. Nothing more than furious trampling—nothing more than the dull and echoing blows that kept on going . . .

Soon, the distant sound of footsteps and voices reached the depths of the cellar. Bright lights shone at the edge of the underground passage. Gammy, frozen in terror at the horrifying events he had just witnessed without seeing, could perceive several people carrying lanterns and rapidly coming down the stairs. In a moment, the cellar was overrun by several police officers, led by Narcisse Borel. Municipal guards were bringing up the rear.

They seized hold of Gammy at the top stairs of the cellar, still holding the Owl's shopping basket. Narcisse Borel, followed by several of his officers, went down into the Schoolmaster's cellar. Everyone stopped in their tracks, struck by a hideous spectacle. Chained at the leg to an enormous rock placed in the middle of the cellar, the Schoolmaster—horrible, monstrous, with a disheveled mane and overgrown beard, foaming at the mouth, wearing shreds of clothing soaked in blood—was going back and forth like a wild animal in his lair, dragging the Owl's cadaver behind him by its two legs. Her head had been horribly mutilated, broken, and crushed.

It took a violent struggle to tear the bloody remains of his accomplice away from the Schoolmaster and tie him up. After overcoming his vigorous resistance, they managed to carry him up to the lower room of Red-Arm's tavern, a vast, dark space lit only by a single window. There, handcuffed and under close watch, were Fishhook, Nicolas Martial, his mother, and his sister. They had just been arrested at the very moment they were trying to drag the diamond broker in and slit her throat. The latter was returning to consciousness in another room.

Stretched out on the ground and only barely kept under control by two officers, the Schoolmaster, lightly wounded on the arm by the Owl but completely out of his mind, was snorting and bellowing like a bull being slaughtered. At times he would raise himself up, all of a piece, in a convulsive jolt.

Fishhook was sitting on a bench. His head was down, his complexion livid and leaden, his lips discolored, his eyes glaring and ferocious; his long, smooth black hair was falling on the collar of his blue smock, which had gotten torn in the scuffle; his wrists, tightly held in handcuffs, were resting on his knees. The youthful appearance of this wretch (he was barely eighteen years old) and the regularity of the features on his beardless face, which was already withered and degraded, made all the more deplorable the hideous imprint with which debauchery and crime had marked him. He sat there impassively, not saying a word. It would be impossible to guess whether this apparent imperturbability was due to shock or cold determination. His breathing was fast; from time to time, he wiped off the sweat that bathed his pale forehead with his manacled hands.

Calabash sat next to him. Her bonnet had been torn; her yellowish hair, tied at the nape of her neck with a bit of string, hung from the back of her head in several sparse and uneven locks. More angry than overcome, her thin, bilious cheeks drained of color, she contemplated her brother Nicolas's dejection with disdain. He had been placed on a chair across from her. Foreseeing the fate that awaited him, the bandit was sitting, slumping, his head hanging down, his knees trembling and knocking into each other. He was beside himself with fear. His teeth were chattering convulsively, and he was making dull groaning noises.

Alone among them, the Martial matriarch had lost none of her audacity. The widow of the executed man was standing up against a wall. Her head held high, she glanced around the room with self-assurance. Her iron countenance did not betray the slightest emotion. Nevertheless, at the sight of Red-Arm, whom they led into the low room after having made him accompany the police superintendent and his clerk on the thorough search they conducted of the entire house—in front of Red-Arm, as we said, the widow's features contracted in spite of herself. Her little eyes, normally dull, lit up like those of a viper in a fury. Her pursed lips became pale and she tensed her pinioned arms. Then, as if she had regretted this mute display of anger and impotent hatred, she overcame her emotion and recovered her glacial calm.

While the superintendent was reading the charges, assisted by his clerk, Narcisse Borel, rubbing his hands together, gazed with satisfaction at the important arrests he had just made. These arrests would rid Paris of a band of dangerous criminals. However, recognizing how helpful Red-Arm had been in this operation, he could not help but give him a meaningful and grateful glance.

Gammy's father would have to share the fate and imprisonment of those he had denounced until after their trial. Like them, he wore handcuffs; he seemed even more frightened and upset than they were. He was contorting his weaselly face into a grimace for all he was worth so as to look desperate, and heaving great sighs of lamentation. He kissed Gammy as if he was seeking comfort in these paternal caresses. The little lame boy did not care much for these demonstrations of affectation. He had just learned that he would be transferred for the time being to a prison for juvenile offenders. "What a dreadful misfortune to be separated from my dear son!" exclaimed Red-Arm as he feigned emotion. "The two of us are the unhappiest, Old Lady Martial, for they're taking our children away from us."

The widow could not keep her calm for much longer. Not doubting for a moment that Red-Arm had betrayed them, as she had foreseen, she exclaimed, "I was certain you had sold out my son in Toulon. You Judas!" At this she spat in his face. "You've sold us out to the executioner—so be it! You're going to see how dying is done. You'll see how real Martials die!"

"Yes—we won't sulk before the grim reaper!" added Calabash, in a savage outburst.

The widow, gesturing at Nicolas with a withering, disdainful look, said to her daughter, "That coward is going to dishonor us on the scaffold!"

A few moments later, the widow and Calabash, accompanied by two officers, got into a carriage to be turned over to Saint-Lazare. Fishhook, Nicolas, and Red-Arm were taken to La Force. The Schoolmaster was taken into custody at the Conciergerie, where there are special cells set aside for the temporary housing of the insane.[167]

167. The Conciergerie was originally a royal palace, built near the Notre-Dame Cathedral. During the Reign of Terror, it was famously the prison in which one was held prior to being guillotined. After the Restoration, it remained a prison for prestigious prisoners. It became a national historical monument in 1914. [TN]

CHAPTER 8

AN INTRODUCTION

The evil that the wicked do unwittingly is sometimes more cruel than the evil they do intentionally.

—SCHILLER, *WALLENSTEIN*, ACT II[168]

Several days after the murder of Madame Séraphin, the death of the Owl, and the mass arrest of the gang of villains taken by surprise at Red-Arm's tavern, Rodolphe showed up at the house on rue du Temple. As we've said earlier, Rodolphe had summoned a mixed-race Creole woman, the unworthy wife of the black man David, from her prison cell in Germany. This he did in order to pursue Jacques Ferrand through subterfuge, reveal his hidden crimes, force him to make reparation to those he had harmed, and punish him in a terrible way if the wretch, through skill and hypocrisy, managed to escape the long arm of justice. As beautiful as she was perverted, and as charming as she was dangerous, Cecily had arrived the day before, having received detailed instructions from the Baron de Graün.

As we saw in Rodolphe's last conversation with Madame Pipelet, she had very adroitly offered Cecily to Madame Séraphin to replace Louise Morel as a servant to the solicitor. The housekeeper had gladly taken up her suggestion and promised to talk it over with Jacques Ferrand. This she did the very morning she was drowned off the Scavenger's Island, having represented Cecily to him in the most favorable terms possible.

Rodolphe had come to learn the result of Cecily's introduction to the solicitor. To his great surprise, when he came into the apartment, he found Monsieur Pipelet lying down with Anastasie standing next to his bed, offering him something to drink. His forehead and eyes barely visible beneath a very large cotton cap, Alfred was not responding to her. She had concluded that he was asleep and closed the drapes around the bed. Turning around, she saw Rodolphe. She stood up immediately and adopted her usual soldier's stance, saluting him by drawing the back of her left hand to her wig. "I am at your command, my king of tenants. You've

168. Friedrich Schiller (1759–1805) was a German Enlightenment intellectual who wrote poetry, plays, history, and criticism. *Wallenstein* (1799) was a trilogy based on the tragic demise of a commander by that name during the Thirty Years' War. [TN]

caught me at a bad moment. I'm bewildered and exhausted. There have been shocking events in the house. And that's on top of the fact that Alfred took to bed yesterday."

"What's wrong with him?"

"Do you really need to ask?"

"What do you mean?"

"It's always the same thing. That monster has been pursuing Alfred relentlessly. I'm so exhausted by it that I don't know what to do anymore."

"Cabrion again?"

"Him again."

"Is he the devil himself?"

"That's what I'm going to end up thinking, Monsieur Rodolphe. That rogue always knows exactly when I've gone out. I've hardly got my back turned when *bang!* he's here and has jumped on my old deary again. Alfred is as defenseless as a baby. Yesterday he came again when I had gone to see Monsieur Ferrand, the solicitor. And there's news from there, too."

"And what about Cecily?" asked Rodolphe, eagerly. "I came to find out—"

"Hold on, my king of tenants, don't get me mixed up. I have so many things to tell you that I'll lose my train of thought if you interrupt me."

"All right. I'm listening."

"First of all, as far as what's going on in the house is concerned: can you believe they came to arrest Old Lady Burette?"

"The woman who lends against wages from the second floor?"

"Goodness, yes. It seems she had some strange businesses going on besides being a loan shark! In addition to that, she was a receiver of stolen goods, a two-bit peddler, a smelter, a thief, a streetlamp lighter, a wheedler, a secondhand dealer, a trafficker—basically, everything you can imagine that ends in 'er.' The worst thing is that her old lover, Monsieur Red-Arm, the man who holds the lease, has also been arrested. This is a real shake-up, I'm telling you."

"Red-Arm was arrested, too?"

"Yes, in his tavern on the Champs-Élysées. They threw everybody in the clink right down to his son Gammy, that nasty little lame boy. They're saying that there were tons of massacres that took place there, that they were in a gang of criminals, that the Owl, one of Old Lady Burette's pals, was strangled. If the authorities hadn't gotten there in time, they would have murdered Old Lady Mathieu, the gem broker who gave work to that poor Morel. Is that enough news for you?"

"Red-Arm is arrested! The Owl is dead!" Rodolphe said to himself in astonishment. "That horrible old woman got what she deserved. At least that poor Fleur-de-Marie has been avenged."

"That's what's been going on around here. But I haven't gotten to Cabrion's latest outrage. I'll tell you about him in just a second. You'll see how absolutely shameless he is! When they arrested Old Lady Burette and we found out that our leaseholder, Red-Arm, had been nabbed, too, I said to my old deary, 'You'd better go right away to the landlord to let him know that Monsieur Red-Arm has been thrown in the clink.' Alfred left. In two hours, he came home, but in a state—such a state—he was as white as a sheet and snorting like a bull."

"What happened then?"

"I'll get to that, Monsieur Rodolphe. You know that there's a big white wall about ten steps away from here? My old deary happened by chance to look at that wall as he left the house. What did he see written there in charcoal, in large letters? 'Pipelet-Cabrion.' The two names were connected by a big hyphen. The hyphen joining his name with that scoundrel's is really what threw my poor deary for a loop. Okay, so that starts to get him all befuddled. Ten steps further, what does he see on the big Temple gate? Once again, 'Pipelet-Cabrion'—still with a hyphen. He walks on, and every step he takes, Monsieur Rodolphe, he sees these cursed names written on the walls of houses and doors. Everywhere, 'Pipelet-Cabrion.'[169] My old deary's head was really starting to spin. He thought everyone was staring at him. He pulled his hat down over his eyes out of embarrassment. He took the boulevard, thinking that that wretched Cabrion would have limited his indecencies to rue du Temple. Guess again! All along the boulevards, wherever there was space to write, you could see endless 'Pipelet-Cabrions.' Finally, the poor, dear man arrived at the landlord's so confused that after mumbling, floundering, and muddling for a quarter of an hour to the landlord's face, he couldn't make any sense out of what Alfred had just been babbling about. He sent him away, calling him an old fool, and told him to send me over to tell him what had happened. All right! So Alfred leaves, comes home by a different route to avoid the names that he'd seen written on the walls, and—well, guess what?"

"More 'Pipelet and Cabrions'?"

---

169. The reader will perhaps remember that a few years ago one could read the name Crédeville on all the walls in every quarter of Paris, written as an art studio caricature. [SN]

Sue is referring to two bits of graffiti common at the time. One was the words "Crédeville, thief." According to a common story, Crédeville was an escaped thief who, when the police were hunting for him, wrote his name on the walls of cities he went through, leading others to write his name all over Paris walls. The art studio caricature probably refers to "Bouginier's nose." Bouginier worked in an artist's studio and irritated his fellow workers, who painted his caricature on walls, with a prominent nose. It was also frequently copied. In *Les Misérables*, Hugo refers to the same graffiti, writing of "that expansive genius that we call Paris, transfiguring the world with its light, sketching the nose of Bouginier on the wall of the Temple of Thesis and writing 'Crédeville, thief' on the Pyramids." [TN]

"Exactly, my king of tenants. So my poor, dear man came home to me dazed and exhausted, talking about leaving the country. He tells me the story, I try to calm him down as best I can, I leave him, and I set out with Mademoiselle Cecily for the solicitor's place, before going to see the landlord. You think that's it? I only wish! I'd hardly turned my back when that Cabrion, who had been waiting for me to leave, had the effrontery to put two tall hussies on Alfred's tail. You know, it makes my hair stand up on end. I'll tell you all about it in just a minute. Let me finish telling you about the solicitor.

"So I left in a carriage with Mademoiselle Cecily, just as you'd asked me to do. She was wearing her nice German peasant girl's clothing, seeing as she'd just arrived and she hadn't had the time to order anything else, as I had to tell Monsieur Ferrand. Believe it or not, my king of tenants, I've seen a lot of pretty girls in my time, including me in my salad days, but I've never seen a girl—myself included—who could lay a finger on Cecily in terms of beauty. More than anything else, she has a look in those killer black eyes of hers—they have something—something . . . well, I can't put it into words, but it's something that really gets to you. What eyes!

"So anyway, Alfred didn't suspect a thing. And *bam!* The first time she looked at him, he turned as red as a carrot, my poor old deary. He wouldn't look at that little miss again for anything in the world. Afterward, he was fidgeting in his seat for an hour from it, as if he was sitting on stinging nettles. He told me later that he didn't know how it was, but that Cecily's gaze made him think of all the stories that shameless Bradamanti used to tell about native women, stories that made him blush so deeply, my old prude of an Alfred."

"But what about the solicitor? The solicitor?"

"I'm getting there, Monsieur Rodolphe. It was about seven o'clock in the evening when we arrived at Monsieur Ferrand's place. I asked the doorkeeper to tell his employer that Madame Pipelet was there with the servant Madame Séraphin had told him of and whom she'd told her to bring. At that, the doorkeeper sighed and asked me if I knew what had happened to Madame Séraphin. I told him I didn't, and that's when I had another shock!"

"What now?"

"That Séraphin lady drowned on a trip to the countryside she went on with one of her relatives."

"Drowned? A trip to the countryside, in the dead of winter?" said Rodolphe, surprised.

"Goodness, yes, Monsieur Rodolphe. Drowned. As for me, I was more surprised than sad. Since the terrible stuff that happened to Louise, whom she'd brought up on charges, I'd hated that Séraphin woman. So that's why, really, I said to myself, 'She's drowned, well, then, she's drowned. So what? I'm not going to die from it.' That's just who I am."

"And Monsieur Ferrand?"

"At first, the doorkeeper told me that he didn't think I could see his employer, and he asked me to wait in his apartment. But a moment later he came to get me. We crossed the courtyard and entered a room on the ground floor. There was nothing but one lousy candle in there to light the place. The solicitor was sitting by a fire in which the last bit of a burning brand was smoldering. What a dump! I'd never seen Monsieur Ferrand before. Boy, was he an ugly one! He's another guy you couldn't get me to cheat on Alfred for, even for all the gold in Arabia."

"And did the solicitor seem struck by Cecily's beauty?"

"Who can tell, with those green eyeglasses? An old monk like him wouldn't know anything about women. Still, when the two of us came in, he almost jumped out of his chair. It must have been that Cecily's Alsatian clothing surprised him, for she looked like one of those women who sell little brooms, with her short petticoats and her nice-looking legs in those blue stockings with red patches on them—except she looked a hundred billion times better. Wow, what calves she has! And such slender ankles! And such cute feet! When all's said and done, the solicitor looked absolutely flummoxed when he saw her."

"So it must have been the strangeness of Cecily's clothing that made him act that way?"

"That's what it must have been. We're getting to the good part. Fortunately, I remembered the maxim you quoted to me, Monsieur Rodolphe. That was my salvation."

"Which maxim?"

"You know: 'It's enough for one person to want something for another person not to want it, or for one person not to want it for another to want it.' So I say to myself, 'I need to help my king of tenants get rid of his German girl by pawning her off on Louise's employer.' Bold as brass, I decide to put on an act. So I say to the solicitor, without giving him time to think, 'I apologize, monsieur, that my niece here is dressed in the fashion of her country. She just arrived. These are the only clothes she has and I don't have the money to order new ones made for her, and what's more, it's not worth my trouble. We're only here because you told Madame Séraphin that you would agree to meet Cecily because of the good reference I'd given her. But I doubt that she'd suit you, monsieur.'"

"Well done, Madame Pipelet."

"'Why wouldn't your niece suit me?' asked the solicitor, who had taken up his spot by the fireplace again and seemed to be looking at us from under his glasses. 'Because Cecily has begun to feel homesick, monsieur. She's only been here three days, and she already wants to go back, even if she had to beg at the side of the road and sell little brooms like other women from her country.' 'And you who are her relative, you would stand for that?' 'Heavens, monsieur, I'm her relative, it's true, but she's an orphan and she's twenty years old and she's responsible for herself.' 'Humbug! Responsible for herself! At that age you have to obey your relatives,' he said, brusquely. At that point Cecily starts to cry and tremble, clutching at me. The solicitor was frightening her, to be sure."

"And what did Jacques Ferrand do?"

"He was grumbling still, still ranting around. 'If you abandon a girl at that age, you're just asking for her to go bad! What a great idea, returning to Germany by begging! And you, her aunt, are going to allow such conduct?' 'This is great,' I say to myself. 'You're falling for it, you old skinflint. I'll palm Cecily off on you or my name's mud.' 'I'm her aunt, it's true,' I say peevishly, 'but it's not a family relation I'm happy to have. I already have enough to take care of. I would rather my niece leave than have her on my hands. The devil take the kind of parents who send you a big girl like that without so much as paying for her!' So now Cecily, who's figured out the game, bursts into tears . . . At that point, the solicitor gets ready to speechify like a preacher and starts saying to me, 'You will owe an accounting to God for this deposit Providence has placed in your hands. It would be criminal to expose this young woman to eternal damnation. I agree to help you in a charitable deed. If your niece promises to be hardworking, honest, and pious and, most of all, promises me never, but never, to leave my home, I will take pity on her and take her into my service.' 'No, no, I prefer to go home to my own country,' said Cecily, still crying."

"Her dangerous hypocrisy hasn't failed her," thought Rodolphe. "That diabolical creature has understood the Baron de Graün's orders perfectly, I see." Then, speaking aloud, the prince asked, "Did Cecily's resistance seem to annoy Monsieur Ferrand?"

"Yes, Monsieur Rodolphe. He was muttering angrily between his teeth, and then he said to her brusquely, 'It's not a matter of what you prefer, mademoiselle. What matters is what's appropriate and decent. God will not abandon you if you behave well and do your religious duty. Here, you will be in a house that is as austere as it is pious. If your aunt really loves you, she'll take advantage of my offer. You won't make much to begin with, but if you show you deserve more through your good behavior and conscientiousness, I may eventually raise your salary.' 'Good!' I exclaim to myself. 'We've got the solicitor in the palm of our hand! Here's Cecily palmed off on you, you old skinflint, you heartless old man! That Séraphin woman was in your service for years, and you don't even seem to notice that she drowned the day before yesterday.' And then I said aloud, 'The position is certainly a good one, but if the young lady is homesick, what can you do?' 'That pain will pass,' the solicitor answered me. 'Come now. Decide what you want to do. Is it yes or no? If you consent, bring me your niece tomorrow night at the same time, and she'll start working for me right away. My doorkeeper will explain her duties to her. As for wages, I will begin by paying twenty francs a month, in addition to full board.' 'Ah, monsieur, won't you pay five francs more?' 'No. Later, if I'm satisfied, we'll see. But I must warn you that your niece will never leave this house and that no one may come here to visit her.' 'Well, really, monsieur, who do you think is going to come to see her? I'm the only person she knows in Paris, and I have my own door to guard. It was enough of a bother to have had to come here with her. You won't see me again. She'll be as much a foreigner to me as if she'd never left her own country. As for her never leaving your house, there's an easy way to take care of that: just keep her in her native dress. She won't dare to walk around in the streets dressed like that.' 'You're right,' the solicitor said to me, 'and anyway, it's respectable to maintain the traditions of one's homeland. She'll continue to dress as an Alsatian.' 'Come,' I say to Cecily, who was hanging her head and still sniveling. 'You have to make a decision, my girl. A good position in an honest house isn't so easy to find. And, moreover, if you turn this down, you'll have to take care of yourself as you will. I wash my hands of the matter.'

"At this point Cecily answers with a sigh and a heavy heart that she consents to stay, on the condition that she can leave in a fortnight if her homesickness gets to be too much for her. 'I don't want to keep you by force,' said the solicitor, 'and it isn't so hard for me to find new servants. Here is your down payment: all your aunt has to do is bring you back here tomorrow night.' Cecily had not stopped sobbing. I accepted the down payment of forty sous on her behalf from that old miser, and we came back here."

"Excellent work, Madame Pipelet! I won't forget my promise. Here's what I promised you if you managed to place that poor girl who was a burden on me."

"Wait until tomorrow, my king of tenants," said Madame Pipelet, refusing Rodolphe's money. "It's possible, you know, that Monsieur Ferrand might change his mind when I bring him Cecily this evening."

"I don't think he'll change his mind. But where is she?"

"She's in the office off the commandant's apartment. Just as you've ordered, she hasn't moved from there. She seems as obedient as a sheep, in spite of those eyes—ah, what eyes! But as far as that commandant is concerned: isn't he a schemer? When he came here himself to oversee the packing of his furniture, he told me that if letters addressed to a Madame Vincent were to come here that they were for him, and that I should send them to him at rue Mondovi, number five. He has people write to him under a woman's name, that pretty bird! He's a sly one! But that's not all. He's had the audacity to ask what had become of his wood! 'Your wood? Why stop at that? Why don't you ask where your forest is?' I answered him. You know, it's true, he'd gotten nothing but two lousy bundles. Hardly anything. One was driftwood, the other was brand-new wood—for he hadn't gotten all new wood, that moneygrubber.

What a fuss he made! His wood! 'I burned your wood,' I tell him, 'to keep your belongings from getting too damp. If I hadn't done that, you'd have mushrooms growing on your embroidered skullcap and on your silk dressing gown that you were so nice as to wear, all in vain, waiting for that little lady who made a fool of you.'"

A dull, plaintive moan from Alfred interrupted Madame Pipelet. "There's my old deary, chewing something over. He's going to wake up. Will you excuse me, my king of tenants?"

"Certainly. But I do have a few more things I want to ask you about."

"Hello, old deary! How are you doing?" Madame Pipelet asked her husband, opening the curtains to his bed. "Here's Monsieur Rodolphe. He knows all about Cabrion's latest outrage and feels bad for you from the bottom of his heart."

"Oh, monsieur!" said Alfred as he turned his head languidly toward Rodolphe. "This time I won't get over it. The monster struck me to the heart. I am the mockery of Paris. My name can be read on every wall in the city, connected to the name of that wretch. 'Pipelet-Cabrion,' with an enormous hyphen. A hyphen, if you please. Me! Connected with that infernal scapegrace in the eyes of everyone, in the capital of all Europe!"

"Monsieur Rodolphe knows about that. But what he doesn't know about is your adventure last night with those two tall hussies."

"Ah, monsieur, he saved his most monstrous outrage for last. This one went beyond all bounds of decency," said Alfred, mournfully.

"Come now, my dear Monsieur Pipelet. Tell me this latest misfortune."

"Everything he's done up to the present was nothing compared to this, monsieur. He's achieved his ends, thanks to the most shameful means. I don't know if I am going to be strong enough to tell you this story. Confusion and modesty hold me back at each step of the way."

Having sat up with great effort in his bed, Monsieur Pipelet modestly folded over the lapel on his woolen vest and began telling his story in the following words: "My spouse had just gone out. Drowning in bitterness because of this latest prostitution of having my name written on all the walls of the capital, I was trying to distract myself by taking care of the resoling of a boot I'd taken up twenty times before to fix and put down twenty times, thanks to the persistent persecutions of my torturer. I was sitting at a table when I saw the door to my apartment open and a woman walk in. This woman was wrapped up in a hooded coat. I got up from my seat respectfully and touched my hand to my hat. At that moment a second woman, also wrapped up in a hooded coat, entered my apartment and closed the door from the inside. Although I was surprised at the familiarity of their behavior and the silence of the two women, I got back out of my chair once more and again touched my hat with my hand. Then, monsieur—no, no, I can't ever—my modesty rises up to stop me."

"Come on, you old prude. This is one man to another. Go ahead."

"So," continued Alfred, turning crimson, "the coats fell off, and what do I see? Two kinds of sirens or nymphs wearing nothing but tunics made of leaves, with their heads also crowned with leaves. I was petrified. Then both of them advanced on me and held out their arms to me as if to ask me to throw myself into them . . ."[170]

"What naughty trollops!" said Anastasie.

"I was revolted by the advances of these shameless hussies," continued Alfred, in excited, chaste indignation. "And in accordance with the same response that has never abandoned me in the most critical moments in my life, I remained completely immobile in my chair. Then, taking advantage of my stupor, the two sirens approached me keeping a kind of beat, making circular movements with their legs and winding their arms in circles. I was more and more paralyzed. They reached me—and took me in their arms."

"Taking a man of his age in their arms, a married man—such scoundrels! Ah, if I'd been there, with my broomstick!" cried Anastasie. "I'd have given you a beat and circular leg movements to remember, you harlots!"

"When I felt myself wrapped up in their arms," Alfred continued, "my blood ran cold in my veins. I passed out. Then, one of the sirens—the bolder one, a big blonde, leaned on my shoulder, took off my hat, rendering my head naked, still keeping time, with her circular leg movements and winding arms. Then her accomplice, taking a pair of scissors out of her foliage, pulled together in an enormous hank all the hair I had left on the back of my head, and cut it all off, monsieur—all of it—still doing those circular leg movements. Then she said to me, singing softly and keeping rhythm, 'This is for Cabrion . . .' And the other hussy repeated, in chorus, 'This is for Cabrion . . . this is for Cabrion!'"

After a pause accompanied by a mournful sigh, Alfred went on: "As this impudent spoliation was taking place, I looked up and I saw Cabrion's infernal face, with his beard and pointy hat—right up against the windows of the apartment. He was laughing and laughing. He was hideous. I closed my eyes to escape this odious vision. When I opened them again, everything was gone. I found myself back in my chair, with my head bare and completely denuded of hair. You see, monsieur, through trickery, stubbornness, and daring, Cabrion has achieved his ends at last. And, by God, by what means! He wanted to make me seem to be his friend! He started by hanging a sign here that said we were trading in friendship together. Not content with that, he paired his name with mine on every wall of the capital, with an enormous hyphen.

---

170. Two dancers from the Porte Saint-Martin, friends of Cabrion who were wearing the tights of their ballet costume. [SN]

There's not a single inhabitant of Paris at this point who would doubt my intimacy with that wretch. He wanted my hair, and he got it. He has all of my hair, thanks to the efforts of those shameless sirens. Now, monsieur, you see, the only thing I can do is to leave France . . . my beautiful France . . . where I always thought I would live and die." And Alfred fell back onto his bed, clasping his hands together.

"But on the contrary, old deary. Now that he has your hair, he'll leave you alone."

"Leave me alone?" exclaimed Monsieur Pipelet, in a convulsive jolt. "But don't you know him by now? He's insatiable. Now who knows what he'll want from me?"

Rigolette, appearing at the entrance to the apartment, put an end to Monsieur Pipelet's lamentations. "Don't come in, mademoiselle!" cried Monsieur Pipelet, expressing, as always, a chaste susceptibility. "I'm in bed, in my underwear." As he said this, he pulled one of his sheets up to his chin. Rigolette stopped discreetly at the threshold of the door.

"I was just about to come see you," Rodolphe said to her. "Please wait for me for a moment." Then, turning to Anastasie, he said, "Don't forget to bring Cecily to Monsieur Ferrand this evening."

"Don't worry, my king of tenants. At seven o'clock she'll be there. Now that Morel's wife can walk, I'll ask her to keep watch over our apartment, because Alfred won't want to stay alone, for all the world."

CHAPTER 9

NEIGHBORS

Rigolette's rosy complexion was becoming paler by the day. Her charming face, which had always been so youthful and round, was becoming drawn. Her saucy expression, usually so animated, had become serious and even sadder than it was at the time of the last meeting between the seamstress and Fleur-de-Marie at the gate of the Saint-Lazare prison.

"I'm so happy to see you, neighbor," said Rigolette to Rodolphe as the latter left Madame Pipelet's apartment. "Really, I have so many things to tell you."

"First of all, neighbor, how are you doing? Let's have a look at your pretty face. Is it still pink and gay? Alas, no! You're looking pale to me. You must be working too hard."

"Oh, no, Monsieur Rodolphe! I swear to you, by now I'm completely up to the slight increase I've had in my work. It's just plain and simple sadness that's changed me. Heavens, every time I see that poor Germain, I get sadder and sadder."

"So he's still dejected?"

"More than ever, Monsieur Rodolphe. And the really sad thing is that everything I do to try to cheer him up just backfires. It's as if it were fate . . ." At this, Rigolette's large black eyes filled with tears.

"Explain what you mean, neighbor."

"Yesterday, for example, I go to see him and bring him a book he'd asked me to get for him because it was a novel we used to read together back in happier times when we were neighbors. When he saw the book, he burst into tears. It didn't surprise me—Lord! It was only natural. When you compare the memory of our sweet, quiet evenings by the stove in my pretty little room to his horrible life in prison, well, it's just too cruel. Poor Germain!"

"Don't worry," said Rodolphe to the young woman. "When Germain gets out of prison and his innocence is established, he'll be reunited with his mother and his friends, and when he's with them and you he'll quickly forget all about these hard, soul-trying times."

"Yes, but until that happens, Monsieur Rodolphe, he's going to continue to be tormented. And that's not all of it . . ."

"What else is going on?"

"He's the only honest man among the criminals, and they have it in for him because he can't bring himself to associate with them. The visiting room guard—a really good guy—told me to get Germain to see that it was in his interest to be less proud and to try to act more friendly to those wicked men. But he can't, because it's just too much for him. I'm afraid that one of these days something bad is going to happen to him." After stopping to wipe away a tear, Rigolette went on: "But I can't believe it. All I think about is myself. I forgot to talk to you about Songbird."

"About Songbird?" said Rodolphe, surprised.

"The day before yesterday, on my way to see Louise at Saint-Lazare, I ran into her."

"Songbird?"

"Yes, Monsieur Rodolphe."

"At Saint-Lazare?"

"She was leaving with an old lady."

"That's impossible!" exclaimed Rodolphe, stupefied.

"I can tell you for sure that it was definitely Songbird, neighbor."

"You must be wrong."

"No, no. Even though she was dressed like a peasant girl, I recognized her right away. She's still very pretty, even though she's pale, and she has the same sweet, sad mood about her as she used to."

"Songbird, in Paris? Without my being kept informed? I can't believe it. And what was she doing at Saint-Lazare?"

"She must have been there to see a visitor, just like me. I didn't have the chance to ask her much. The old lady she was with seemed so grouchy and rushed. So you know Songbird, too, Monsieur Rodolphe?"

"I certainly do."

"Well, that settles it, it must be you she was talking about."

"Me?"

"Yes, neighbor. Here's how it happened. I told her the sad story of Louise and Germain, both of them so good, so respectable and both so unfairly persecuted by that horrible Monsieur Jacques Ferrand. Because you had told me not to, I didn't tell her that you were helping them. Then Songbird told me that if a generous person of her acquaintance were to know the unhappy and undeserved fate of my two poor prisoners, he'd definitely come to their aid. I asked her the name of that person, and she said your name, Monsieur Rodolphe."

"That's Songbird all over."

"As you can imagine, we were both astonished to find out we knew the same person, or at least that the people we knew had the same names. Each of us promised to write the other to let her know if you were the same Rodolphe. And it seems you are indeed the same Rodolphe, neighbor."

"Yes, I care about that poor child as well. But when you say she is in

Paris, that surprises me so much that if you hadn't gone into your conversation in detail, I would still have thought you were mistaken. But farewell, neighbor. What you've just told me about Songbird makes it necessary for me to leave you. As far as Louise and Germain are concerned, please continue to keep it to yourself that in the fullness of time they will turn out to have unknown friends who will defend them. It is more essential than ever that you keep this a secret. By the way, how is the Morel family doing?"

"Better and better, Monsieur Rodolphe. The mother is completely back on her feet now. You can see the improvement in the children just by looking at them. The whole household owes you their lives and their well-being. You have been so generous to them! And how is that poor Morel doing?"

"Better. Yesterday I heard some news about him. He seems to be experiencing moments of clarity from time to time. They see reason to hope that they can cure his madness. So for now, stay strong, neighbor, and we'll see each other soon. Do you need anything? Is your income from your work still enough for you?"

"Oh, yes, Monsieur Rodolphe. I work a little longer into the night, but that really isn't a problem, after all, because I don't sleep much anymore anyway."

"Alas! My poor little neighbor, I'm afraid that Papa Crétu and Ramonette aren't doing much singing these days if they wait for you to start."

"You've got that right, Monsieur Rodolphe. My birds and I aren't doing much singing anymore—heavens, no. But you know what? You're going to make fun of me, but I think they understand I'm sad. Yes, instead of chirping away happily when I come in, they just warble a little in such a sweet and plaintive way that I could swear they're trying to cheer me up. I must be crazy to think that, don't you think, Monsieur Rodolphe?"

"Not at all. I'm sure your good friends the birds love you too much not to notice your sorrows."

"It's true, those poor little animals are so intelligent!" Rigolette said innocently, quite content to be confirmed in her beliefs about the intelligence of her companions in solitude.

"There is nothing more intelligent than gratitude, that's for certain. Farewell for now. Soon, neighbor, not long from now, I hope, your pretty eyes will become bright again, your cheeks nice and rosy, and your song cheerful—so cheerful that Papa Crétu and Ramonette will hardly be able to keep up with you."

"I hope you're right, Monsieur Rodolphe!" said Rigolette, sighing deeply. "All right, then. Farewell, neighbor."

"Farewell, neighbor. We'll see each other soon."

Rodolphe went home immediately to send a messenger to the Bouqueval farm. He could not understand how Madame Georges could have taken or sent Fleur-de-Marie to Paris without letting him know. Just as he was returning to rue Plumet, he saw the mail coach stop in front of the gate of the mansion. It was Murph, returning from Normandy. The squire had gone there, as we've said, in order to foil the sinister plans of Madame d'Harville's stepmother and her accomplice Bradamanti.

CHAPTER 10

MURPH AND POLIDORI

Sir Walter Murph's face was beaming. As he stepped out of the coach, he handed one of the prince's men a pair of pistols, took off his long traveling coat, and, without taking the time to change his clothes, followed Rodolphe into his rooms. Impatient, the prince had walked in ahead of him. "Good news, Your Lordship, good news!" exclaimed the squire once he was alone with Rodolphe. "The wretches have been exposed and Monsieur d'Orbigny is safe. You had me set out just in time. If I'd left an hour later, yet another crime would have been committed!"

"And Madame d'Harville?"

"She's beside herself with joy because her father's affections toward her have returned, and she's deliriously happy that she arrived, thanks to your advice, in time to keep him from a certain death."

"And so Polidori . . . ?"

"Was yet again the worthy accomplice of Madame d'Harville's stepmother. But what a monster that stepmother is! What cold-blooded daring! And that Polidori! Ah, Your Lordship, you know how at various times you have wanted to repay me for what you've called my 'proof of devotion'?"

"I've always said the 'proof of your friendship,' my good Murph."

"Well, anyway, Your Lordship, that friendship has never, ever had to contend with a more difficult test than in this particular circumstance," said the squire, half joking and half serious.

"How is that?"

"That coal miner's disguise, those wanderings in the Cité, and *tutti quanti*:[171] all that was nothing, Your Lordship, absolutely nothing in comparison with the trip I just took with that infernal Polidori."

"What are you saying? Polidori . . ."

"I've brought him here."

"With you?"

"With me. Imagine what kind of company he was. For twelve hours, I had to sit next to the man I hate and despise more than anyone else in

171. Everything or everyone like that. In Italian in the original. [TN]

the world. It was as bad as having to travel with a snake—and you know how much I hate them."

"And where is Polidori right now?"

"In the house on the allée des Veuves, under careful guard."

"And he made no fight about coming along with you?"

"None whatsoever. I gave him the choice of being arrested on the spot by the French authorities or of being my prisoner on the allée des Veuves. He didn't hesitate for a second."

"That was good thinking. It's better to have him in our control. You're worth your weight in gold, old Murph. But tell me about your trip. I'm impatient to hear how that despicable woman and her no less despicable accomplice were finally exposed."

"Nothing could have been easier. All I had to do was follow your instructions to the letter, and those unspeakable villains were stricken with terror and completely undone. In this instance, as usual, my lord, you have saved the good and punished the wicked. You are doing God's work!"

"Sir Walter, Sir Walter, don't forget what flattery got the Baron de Graün," said Rodolphe, smiling.

"Very well, then, my lord. So I'll begin what I have to tell you, or maybe, you might prefer first to read this letter from the Marquise d'Harville. It will tell you everything that had happened before my arrival foiled Polidori."

"A letter? Let me see it right now."

As he gave Rodolphe the marquise's letter, Murph added, "Just as we planned, instead of accompanying Madame d'Harville to her father's home, I had gone into an inn that served as servants' quarters right near the château, where I was supposed to wait until Madame the marquise asked for me."

Rodolphe read the following letter with tender and impatient solicitude:

Your Lordship,

On top of everything I already owe you, I now owe you the life of my father!

I will let the facts speak for themselves. They will tell you better than I what a new wealth of gratitude I have in my heart for you.

I understood completely the importance of the advice you sent Sir Walter Murph to communicate to me, when he joined me as I was leaving Paris for Normandy. So I quickly made my way over to the Aubiers château. For some reason, the faces of the people who received me seemed sinister. I didn't see any of the old servants of the house among them. No one recognized me. I was obliged to identify myself. I learned that my father had been suffering greatly for the last few days and that my stepmother had just brought a doctor in from Paris. As you can easily guess, it was Doctor Polidori.

Wanting to be taken immediately to see my father, I asked to see the old valet to whom my father was very attached. That man had left the château some time before. This information was given me by a servant who had taken me to my rooms, saying that he was going to alert my stepmother to my arrival.

Was it an illusion or was I being detained? It seemed to me that my father's servants were treating my arrival virtually as an intrusion. Everything about the château seemed gloomy and sinister to me. In the state of mind I was in, you see the least circumstance as evidence of something. I noticed everywhere the signs of disorder and neglect, as if they had figured it was pointless to care for a residence that would soon be abandoned. My worries and anxiety were increasing by the second. After having taken my daughter and her governess to our rooms, I was about to go in to see my father, when my stepmother entered.

In spite of her ability to disguise her feelings, in spite of her usual self-control, she seemed staggered by my sudden arrival. "Monsieur d'Orbigny was not expecting your visit, madame," she said to me. "He is so ill that such a surprise could be harmful to him. I think it would be better, therefore, to keep him in the dark about your presence. He wouldn't be able to understand why you were here, and—"

I didn't let her finish her sentence. "A terrible thing has happened, madame," I said to her. "Monsieur d'Harville is dead, the victim of a dreadful accident. After something like that, I couldn't go on living in my house in Paris, and I have come to spend the first period of my mourning with my father."

"You're a widow? Ah! What shameless good luck!" exclaimed my stepmother, enraged. From what you know about the unhappy marriage that this woman had arranged in order to take her revenge on me, you will understand, Your Lordship, how horrifying her exclamation was.

"It's because I fear that you want to be as shamelessly lucky as myself, madame, that I've come here," I told her, perhaps unwisely. "I want to see my father."

"That is impossible at the moment," she said to me, turning pale. "Seeing you would cause his condition to worsen."

"If my father is so gravely ill," I exclaimed, "why has no one told me about it?"

"That was Monsieur d'Orbigny's wish," my stepmother answered me.

"I don't believe you, madame, and I'm going to find out the truth," I said to her, taking a step toward the door of my room.

"I repeat: seeing you unexpectedly might cause a horrible worsening of your father's condition!" she exclaimed, planting herself in my way in order to keep me from passing. "I will not allow you to go in to see him without warning him first of your return, at the same time taking the measures his condition makes necessary."

I was in a cruel bind, Your Lordship. A sudden surprise could be genuinely dangerous to my father. But this woman, ordinarily so cold and so aloof, seemed so shocked at my presence, and I also had so many reasons to doubt the sincerity of her solicitude for the health of the man she had married out of greed—and there, too, was Doctor Polidori, the murderer of my mother, whose presence terrified me so much that I thought my father's life was in danger—so I did not hesitate between the hope of saving him and the fear of causing an emotional response that would be injurious to his health.

"I will see my father this instant," I said to my stepmother. And even though she grabbed me by the arm, I walked right by. Now this woman completely lost her composure and tried a second time, almost by force, to keep me from leaving my room. Her incredible resistance made me even more afraid, and I pried her hands off me. I knew where my father's rooms were, and I ran to him as fast as I could. I entered his room—and oh, Your Lordship! As long as I live, I will never forget the picture that scene set for me. My father, almost unrecognizable, pale and emaciated, his features racked with suffering, was stretched out in a large armchair, his head thrown back on a pillow.

By the fireplace, standing by him, Doctor Polidori was preparing to pour several drops of a liqueur from a large crystal flask into a cup a nurse was handing him. His long red beard gave his face an even more sinister expression. I came in so quickly that he made a movement of surprise, exchanged a knowing look with my stepmother, who was on my heels, and, instead of making my father take the potion he had just prepared for him, he abruptly put the flask on the mantelpiece.

Guided by an instinct I still cannot account for, the first thing I did was to take hold of that flask. The moment I did so, I saw the surprise and fear on the faces of my stepmother and Doctor Polidori and knew it had been the right thing to do. My father, bewildered, seemed irritated to see me, as I expected. Polidori gave me a savage look. Despite the presence of my father and that of his nurse, I was afraid that this wretch, knowing that his crime was all but uncovered, might be carried away into some extreme measure against me. I felt the need of reinforcement at this decisive moment, and so I rang the bell. One of my father's servants hurried in. I asked him to tell my valet (who was forewarned) to get a few objects I had left in the inn. Sir Walter Murph knew that I would use this ruse to summon him if I needed to allay my stepmother's suspicions, while giving these orders in her presence.

The surprise of my father and stepmother was such that the servant was able to leave the room before they could say a word. I felt more secure knowing that in a few moments Sir Walter Murph would be at my side.

"What is the meaning of this?" my father said to me, finally, in a voice that was weak but still imperious and angry. "I have not requested your presence, Clémence, and yet here you are? And then when you've just come in the room, you seize the flask with the potion in it that the doctor was going to give me. Explain this madness to me!"

"Leave the room," said my stepmother to the nurse. The woman obeyed.

"Calm down, dear," said my stepmother, addressing my father. "You know that the slightest emotion can be harmful to you. If your daughter is going to come here against your will and despite the fact that her presence is disagreeable to you, give me your arm and I'll take you into the small salon. While we're there, our good doctor will explain to Madame d'Harville how imprudent—to say the least—her conduct has been." And at this, she gave a meaningful glance to her accomplice.

I understood my stepmother's plan. She wanted to take my father away and leave me alone with Polidori, who, in this extreme situation, would have used violence, no doubt, in order to prize from me this flask that could provide clear proof of his criminal plans.

"You are right," said my father to my stepmother. "Since she follows me down even to my own home without any respect for my wishes, I will leave the room to this unwelcome visitor." And, rising with difficulty, he accepted the arm my stepmother held out to him and took several steps toward the small salon. At this moment, Polidori approached me. However, I got closer to my father and said to him, "I will explain to you why I come unannounced and also why I am behaving so strangely. Yesterday, I became a widow. And yesterday I also learned that your life is threatened, Father."

He was painfully hunched over as he walked. At my last words, he stopped and straightened himself up sharply. Looking at me with profound astonishment, he exclaimed, "You're a widow? And my life is threatened? What do you mean?"

"And who would dare threaten the life of Monsieur d'Orbigny, madame?" my stepmother asked impudently.

"Yes, who is threatening him?" added Polidori.

"You, monsieur, and you, madame," I answered.

"How horrible!" cried my stepmother, taking a step toward me.

"I will prove what I'm saying, madame," I answered.

"This is an appalling accusation!" cried my father.

"I'm leaving this house this instant since I'm being exposed to such atrocious slander here!" said Doctor Polidori with the indignation of a man who has had his honor questioned. Beginning to sense the danger of his position, he was surely trying to escape. But just as he was opening the door, he found himself face-to-face with Sir Walter Murph.

Rodolphe interrupted his reading of the letter and held out his hand to the squire, saying to him, "Very well done, old friend! Your presence must have crushed that wretch."

"Crushed is the right word, Your Lordship. He became pale, and took two steps backward, looking at me in bewilderment. He looked devastated. Seeing me in the middle of Normandy at such a moment! He must have thought he was having a nightmare. But go on reading, Your Lordship. You'll see that that infernal Countess d'Orbigny would be crushed next, thanks to what you had told me about her visit to the charlatan Bradamanti-Polidori at the house on rue du Temple. After all, you were the one who was acting here; I was but the instrument of your will. That's why I swear to you that you have never better played the role of that lazy divine justice than on this occasion."

Rodolphe smiled and continued to read Madame d'Harville's letter:

At the sight of Sir Walter Murph, Polidori was struck dead in his tracks. My stepmother fell victim to one surprise after another. My father, moved by this scene, weakened by illness, had to sit down on an armchair. Sir Walter locked and bolted the door through which he had entered. Standing in front of the door that led to another set of rooms so that Doctor Polidori could not escape, he said to my poor father, in a tone of the most profound respect, "I am profoundly sorry, Count, that I am taking such liberties. Only the greatest urgency and your interest alone (as you will soon recognize) could have forced me to take this action. My name is Sir Walter Murph, as this wretch who is trembling from head to toe can confirm to you. I am the private aide of his royal lordship, the reigning Grand Duke of Gerolstein."

"That is true," said Doctor Polidori, stuttering and quaking with fear.

"But, monsieur, what are you doing here, then? What do you want?"

"Sir Walter Murph," I said, addressing my father, "has come to help me expose these wretches whose victim you almost became." Then, handing the crystal flask to Sir Walter, I added, "I was alert enough to take hold of this flask at the moment Doctor Polidori was about to pour a few drops of the liqueur it contains into a potion he was giving my father."

"A physician from the neighboring town will analyze the contents of this flask in front of you, and if it is proven that it contains a slow-acting, effective poison," said Walter Murph to my father, "you will no longer have any doubt as to the dangers you were facing and how much your daughter, who has fortunately warded them off, cares for you."

My poor father looked at his wife, Doctor Polidori, me, and Sir Walter Murph, one after another, as if he were completely lost. His face manifested the most indefinable anguish. I could see on his grief-stricken features the violent struggle that was breaking his heart. No doubt he was resisting with all his strength the growing, terrible suspicions he had, afraid of having to acknowledge my stepmother's villainy. Finally, hiding his head in his hands, he cried, "Oh, my God! This is all so horrible! It's impossible! Is this a bad dream?"

"No, this is not a dream," my stepmother had the audacity to exclaim. "Nothing could be more real than this atrocious calumny designed expressly to destroy an unfortunate woman whose only crime was to devote her life to you. Come, come, my friend. We shouldn't stay here a single second longer," she added, turning to my father. "Perhaps your daughter will not be insolent enough to keep you here against your will."

"Yes, yes, let's go," said my father, beside himself. "This is all untrue. It cannot be true. I don't want to hear another word. My sanity will not tolerate it. Horrible doubts would arise in my heart and poison the few days I have left to live, and nothing could console me for such an abominable discovery."

My father seemed to be suffering so much and to be so desperate that I wanted, at all costs, to put an end to this scene that was so hard on him. Sir Walter guessed what I was thinking, but, wanting to bring about complete and entire justice, he answered my father, "Just a few words more, Count. You will have to endure the no doubt very painful sorrow of learning that a woman whom you thought attached to you by ties of gratitude has always been a hypocritical monster. But you will find certain consolation in the affection of your daughter, affection that she never ceased to feel."

"This has gone beyond all bounds of decency!" cried my stepmother, enraged. "And by what right, monsieur, and on the basis of what proof do you level such appalling slander? You say that that flask contains poison? I deny it, monsieur, and I will go on denying it until you prove otherwise. And even if Doctor Polidori had, by mistake, confused one medication with another, is that any reason to accuse me of wanting to—of conspiring with him to— Oh! No, no, I can't finish my sentence. The idea of the thing is so horrible as to be a crime in itself. So once more, monsieur, I challenge you to tell me what proof you or Madame has for this frightful, slanderous charge," said my stepmother, with incredible audacity.

"Yes. Where is your proof?" cried my unhappy father. "There must be an end to your torturing me!"

"I have not come here without proof, Count," said Sir Walter. "And this proof will be supplied to you immediately by the answers of this wretch." Then Sir Walter spoke in German to Doctor Polidori, who seemed to have recovered some of his self-assurance but who immediately lost it again.

"What did you say to him?" Rodolphe asked the squire, breaking off his reading.

"I just made a few significant remarks, Your Lordship. More or less, I said, 'By fleeing, you escaped the condemnation you had received from the court of the grand duchy. You live on rue du Temple under the assumed name Bradamanti. We know the abominable practices by which you make your living. You poisoned the count's first wife. Three days ago, Madame d'Orbigny went to get you in order to bring you back to poison her husband. His royal highness is in Paris, and he can prove every claim I make. If you admit the truth, in order to disconcert this wretched woman, you can expect not a pardon but a reduction of the severe punishment you deserve. You will accompany me to Paris, where I will put you in a secure place until his highness decides what to do with you. Otherwise, one of two things will happen: either his royal highness will ask for and obtain your extradition, or I'll call this very instant for someone to find a magistrate in the neighboring town. This flask containing poison will be given to him, and you'll be arrested on the spot. A search will be conducted of your home on rue du Temple. You know how compromising such a search will be. French justice will follow its usual course. It's up to you. Make up your mind, one way or the other.'

"These revelations, these accusations, these threats that he knew were completely founded, coming one on top of the other, overcame that villain. He wasn't expecting me to be so well informed about him. In hopes of reducing the sentence that awaited him, he didn't hesitate to sacrifice his accomplice. He answered, 'Question me. I'll tell you the truth about this woman.'"

"That's good, that's good, my worthy Murph. I expected no less of you."

"During my conversation with Polidori, Madame d'Harville's stepmother's face fell in a frightening way, even though she didn't understand German. She could see from her accomplice's growing dejection, from his manner of supplication, that I had complete power over him. She tried, with terrible anxiety, to make eye contact with Polidori, in order to give him encouragement or to implore his continuing discretion, but he kept avoiding her glance."

"And the count?"

"His emotional state was inexpressible. With clenched fingers, he clutched convulsively at the arms of his chair, his forehead covered in sweat. He was hardly breathing. His gaze, fiery and unmoving, never wavered from my own eyes. His anguish was just as painful as his wife's. What's left of Madame d'Harville's letter will tell you the end of this difficult scene, Your Lordship."

CHAPTER II

PUNISHMENT

Rodolphe continued to read Madame d'Harville's letter:

After Sir Walter Murph and Polidori spoke for a few minutes in German, Sir Walter said to the latter, "Now, answer me. Is it not Madame"—and he pointed at my stepmother—"who brought you in as a physician when Monsieur the count's first wife was sick?"

"Yes, it was she," answered Polidori.

"In order to bring the awful plan of this lady to fruition, did you not commit the crime of prescribing poison as medicine to make Countess d'Orbigny's illness, which was not serious at first, a fatal one?"

"Yes," said Polidori.

My father groaned painfully, raised his hands to the sky, and then, in despair, let them fall again.

"Malicious lies!" exclaimed my stepmother. "That is completely false. They are conspiring to destroy me."

"Silence, madame!" said Sir Walter Murph in a commanding voice. Then, continuing to speak to Polidori, he said, "Is it not true that, three days ago, Madame came to see you where you live at seventeen rue du Temple, under the assumed name Bradamanti?"

"That is true."

"Did Madame not ask you to come here to murder the Count d'Orbigny, just as you had murdered his wife?"

"Alas! I cannot deny it," said Polidori.

With this crushing revelation, my father stood up with a threatening look on his face. With a powerful gesture, he showed my stepmother the door. Then, holding out his arms to me, he cried in a hoarse voice, "In the name of your poor mother, I beg you to forgive me! Forgive me! I made her suffer terribly, but I swear to you that I had nothing to do with the crime that brought her to her grave." And before I could stop him, my father had thrown himself at my knees.

When Sir Walter and I picked him up, he had lost consciousness. I called the servants, and Sir Walter took Doctor Polidori by the arm and left the room with him. He said to my stepmother as he did so, "Listen to what I am about to say, madame: you must leave this house in one hour.

Otherwise, I'll turn you over to the forces of justice." The wretch left the room in a state of terror and rage that you can easily imagine, Your Lordship.

When my father regained consciousness, everything that had just happened seemed like a horrible dream to him. I had the sad duty to tell him of my earlier suspicions regarding the premature death of my mother, suspicions that your knowledge of Doctor Polidori's prior crimes, Your Lordship, had changed into certainties. I had to tell my father also about how my stepmother's hatred of me had led her to persecute me in ways that even included my marriage, and about what her motives had been in arranging for me to marry Monsieur d'Harville.

As much as my father had shown himself to be weak and blind with regard to this woman, he now wanted to show himself merciless toward her. In despair, he blamed himself for having nearly been the accomplice of this monster by giving his hand to her after the death of my mother. He wanted to see Madame d'Orbigny tried for her crimes. I pointed out to him the odious scandal such a trial would create, a scandal that would cause him more than a little grief. I urged him to send my stepmother away forever, merely—and only because she bore his name—giving her enough to live on.

It was quite difficult to get my father to agree to these moderate resolutions. He wanted me to send her away. This mission was doubly painful for me. I thought that perhaps Sir Walter might agree to take care of it. He agreed to do so.

"And, by God, it gave me real joy to agree to that, my lord," said Murph to Rodolphe. "Nothing brings me greater pleasure than giving that kind of extreme unction to the wicked."

"And what did that woman say?"

"Madame d'Harville had gone so far as to extend her mercy to the point of asking her father to provide a pension of a hundred louis for that villain. That seemed more like weakness than mercy to me. It was already bad enough to protect such a dangerous creature from the law. I went to see the count, and he agreed completely with my observations. It was decided that the villain would get a lump sum payment of twenty-five louis to help her toward finding herself a position or a job. 'And what kind of position or job do you expect me, the Countess d'Orbigny, to take?' she asked me, insolently. 'Honestly, that's your problem, not mine. You can be a sick nurse or governess, but my advice to you is to find the most humble and obscure profession you can. For if you have the audacity to tell anyone your name—the name you owe to your crime—people will be surprised to find the Countess d'Orbigny reduced to such a condition. They will ask about you, and you can imagine what the consequences will be if you are so mad as to let anyone know about your past. Go hide somewhere far away and, most importantly, make everyone forget about you. Become Madame Pierre or Madame Jacques and repent of your crimes—if you can.' 'And do you believe, monsieur,' she said to me, 'that, having produced this bit of stage managing, I will not claim the rights owing to me from my marriage contract?' 'Oh, of course, madame! How right you are. It would be unworthy of Monsieur d'Orbigny not to honor his promises and not to recognize all you've done—most of all, all you intended to do—for him. Go, go and make your case to the courts. I have no doubt that they will find for you against your husband.' A quarter of an hour after this conversation, the creature was on her way to the neighboring town."

"You're right. It's terrible to let this loathsome harpy go on her way virtually unpunished, but the scandal of a trial, with that old man already so weakened—it was unthinkable."

Rodolphe then continued to read Madame d'Harville's letter:

> I had no difficulty persuading my father to agree to leave Aubiers this very day. Too many sad memories would haunt him here. Although his health was weakened, the doctor who had been replaced by Polidori and for whom I sent immediately from the neighboring village told me that the distractions of a journey and the change of scene could only do him good. My father wanted him to analyze the contents of the flask without telling him anything that had happened. The doctor answered that he could only perform this task at his home, and that we would have the results of his test within two hours. It turned out that several doses of that liqueur, concocted with devilish skill, would have led to death in a given period of time, without leaving any traces other than those of a common illness the doctor named.
>
> In several hours, Your Lordship, I will be leaving with my father and daughter for Fontainebleau. We will stay there for a while, and then, as my father wishes, we will return to Paris. We will not, however, return to my home, for it would be impossible for me to stay in it after the awful accident that took place there.
>
> As I mentioned earlier in this letter, Your Lordship, the facts speak for themselves. I believe I owe everything to your inexhaustible solicitude. Forewarned by you, aided by your advice, strengthened by the support of your excellent and courageous Sir Walter, I managed to save my father from certain death, and I can count now on the return of his affection for me.
>
> Farewell, Your Lordship. It is impossible to say more than this to you right now. My heart is too full; it is disturbed by too many emotions. I could only express all I feel very poorly.
>
> D'ORBIGNY D'HARVILLE.

I am returning to this letter quickly, Your Lordship, to correct an oversight that troubles me. Acting on your noble inspiration and looking for some good act I could do, I went to Saint-Lazare to visit the poor prisoners. There I found an unfortunate child in whom you had taken an interest. Her angelic sweetness and pious resignation had earned the admiration of the respectable women who oversee the prisoners. To tell you where Songbird is (that was her nickname, if I'm not mistaken) is at the same time to put you on the way to obtain her liberty. The unfortunate girl will tell you the sinister circumstances that led to her being kidnapped from the place of protection in which you had placed her and cast into that prison where at least everyone recognized her innocent character for what it was.

May I also recall to you my two future protégées, Your Lordship, that unhappy mother and her daughter, left destitute by the solicitor Ferrand? Where are they? Have you had any news of them? Oh, please, try to discover where they are so that once I've returned to Paris, I can pay the debt I have toward all the unfortunate!

"So Songbird left the Bouqueval farm, Your Lordship?" exclaimed Murph, just as astonished as Rodolphe by this new revelation.

"I was told just a little while ago that she was seen leaving Saint-Lazare," said Rodolphe. "I don't know what to make of it. Madame Georges's silence baffles and alarms me. Poor little Fleur-de-Marie! What new miseries have befallen her? Have a man on horseback sent right away to the farm, and write to Madame Georges that I want her to come to Paris immediately. Tell Monsieur de Graün, too, that I need a pass to get into Saint-Lazare. According to what Madame d'Harville says, Fleur-de-Marie must be being held there. But that can't be true," said Rodolphe, reflecting. "She can't be a prisoner there any longer, because Rigolette saw her leaving the prison with an old woman. Could that have been Madame Georges? If not, who was that woman? Where has Songbird gone?"[172]

"Be patient, Your Lordship. Before tonight you'll know enough to be able to decide what to do next. Then, tomorrow, you will have to question that wretch Polidori. He says he has important revelations to make to you and to you alone."

"That will be a painful conversation," said Rodolphe, sadly. "I haven't seen that man since the fatal day . . . on which I . . ." Rodolphe could not finish his sentence. He hid his forehead in his hands.

"Well, blast it, Your Lordship! Why must we give in to Polidori's

172. The reader will remember that Madame Georges was not worried about her protégée because she had been deceived by Sarah's emissary, who had told her that Fleur-de-Marie had left Bouqueval on the prince's orders. She expected her to return any day. [SN]

request? Just threaten to turn him over to French law or to extradite him immediately. He'll just have to accept telling me what he says he wants to tell only you."

"You are right, my poor friend, for the presence of that wretch would make those memories, which have already caused me so much incurable grief, that much more painful. From the death of my father to the death of my poor little girl—I can't say why, but the older I get, the more I miss that child. How I would have adored her! How dear and precious the charming fruit of my first loves, of my first pure beliefs—or, I should say, of my youthful illusions—would have been to me! I would have showered on that innocent creature all the affection of which her odious mother was unworthy. And then it seems to me that the beauty of that child's soul and the charm of her personality in the form she takes as she comes to me in my dreams would have softened or assuaged all of the sorrow and remorse her fateful birth caused."

"Really, Your Lordship, it is painful to see the constantly increasing hold these pointless and cruel regrets have on your mind."

After a few moments of silence, Rodolphe said to Murph, "I can now make a confession to you, old friend: I love . . . yes, I deeply love a woman worthy of the most noble and devoted affection. And since my heart has opened up again to all the sweetness of love, since I've become open to feelings of affection, I am feeling the loss of my daughter ever more sharply. I might have feared that a romantic attachment would have lessened the bitterness of my regrets, but that's not at all the case. I find I have even more love in me. I feel better and more charitable, and more than ever I feel the cruelty of not having my daughter to adore."

"It makes perfect sense, Your Lordship. Forgive me the comparison, but just as, in some men, drunkenness brings out joy and benevolence, love makes you kind and generous."

"In contrast, my hatred of the wicked has also grown sharper. My aversion toward Sarah grows greater, no doubt because of the sorrow that our daughter's death causes me. When I think about how that horrible mother neglected her and that once her ambitious hopes were dashed by my marriage, the countess, in her pitiless selfishness, must have abandoned our child to mercenary hands, with our daughter probably dying from neglect—Well, it's my fault, as well. At the time I did not sense the extent of the sacred duties that paternity imposes. When Sarah's true character suddenly became clear to me, I should have immediately taken our daughter away from her and watched over her with care and affection. I should have known that the countess could only be an unnatural mother. So it's my fault, you see, my fault . . ."

"Your Lordship, your sorrow is confusing you. Could you, after the fateful event—the one you know I mean—have deferred by even a day the long journey you had to make as—"

"As expiation? You are right, my friend," said Rodolphe, dejectedly.

"Have you heard anything about the Countess Sarah since my departure, Your Lordship?"

"No. I haven't heard anything about her since those letters informing on Madame d'Harville that twice almost ruined her. Her presence here weighs heavily on me; indeed, it's becoming an obsession. I feel as if my bad angel is following my every step, as if some new misfortune is looming."

"Have patience, Your Lordship, have patience. Fortunately, she has been exiled from Germany, and Germany awaits us."

"Yes, we will leave soon. At least during my short stay in Paris I've kept a sacred promise. I've made some progress in the worthy path that an august and merciful will indicated to me as part of my redemption. As soon as Madame Georges's son is returned to her affections, exculpated and free, as soon as Jacques Ferrand is convicted and punished for his crimes, as soon as I've made arrangements for the future of all the honest, hardworking people who have earned my care by their resignation, courage, and integrity, we'll return to Germany. At any rate, my trip will not have been for naught."

"Most of all if you manage to expose that abominable Jacques Ferrand, Your Lordship. He's the keystone, the pivot on which so many crimes have turned."

"Although the ends justify the means, and although scruples have little place when it comes to that villain, sometimes I regret having involved Cecily in this just and avenging reparation."

"So she'll be here any day now?"

"She's already here."

"Cecily?"

"Yes. I didn't want to see her. De Graün gave her very detailed instructions, and she promised to follow them."

"Will she keep her promise?"

"First of all, she has every reason to do so. It gives her the hope of lessening her future sentence, and also she's afraid of being sent back immediately to her prison in Germany. De Graün won't let her out of sight. At the least misbehavior, he'll obtain her extradition."

"That much is certain. She came here as an escapee. When the crimes for which she received her life sentence become known, her extradition will be granted immediately."

"And even if it weren't in her own interest to cooperate with us, the task we've given her can only succeed by means of deceit, perfidy, and diabolical seduction. Cecily must be thrilled (and she was, the baron told me) to have this opportunity to make use of the loathsome talents she has in such abundance."

"Is she still extremely pretty, Your Lordship?"

"De Graün said she was more attractive than ever. He was dazzled by her beauty, he told me, which the Alsatian clothing she wore made particularly racy. The gaze of that demon still has the same truly magical expression, he said."

"Well, I'll tell you, Your Lordship: I've never been what they call brainless, a man without heart or decency. But if I'd met Cecily when I was twenty years old, even if I'd known how dangerous and perverted she is now, I wouldn't have been able to guarantee my sanity if I had to stay for any length of time near the fire of those big, blazing black eyes that sparkle in the middle of her pale and ardent face. Yes, by the heavens, I don't dare think about where a fatal love like that might have taken me."

"It wouldn't surprise me, my worthy Murph, since I know the woman. In any case, the baron was almost shocked at the canniness with which Cecily comprehended, or rather intuited, the simultaneously alluring and platonic role she had to play with the solicitor."

"But do you think Madame Pipelet's help will really get her into that household so easily? People like Jacques Ferrand are so suspicious!"

"I had counted—and rightly so—on the sight of Cecily to combat and conquer the solicitor's distrust."

"He's already seen her, then?"

"Yesterday. And Madame Pipelet's account leaves no room for doubt: he was fascinated by the Creole, for he took her into his service on the spot."

"Well, then, my lord, we've already gotten what we want."

"I hope so. His ferocious greed and wild lust have led Louise Morel's torturer to the most disgusting crimes. It's in his lust and greed that he'll meet with a terrible punishment for his crimes, a punishment that, most of all, will not be without benefit for his victims, given the aims of the Creole's activities."

"Cecily! Cecily! Never has such wickedness and corruption nor a blacker, more dangerous soul been of service in a more just project or one with a higher moral end. And what about David, Your Lordship?"

"He approves of everything. He holds that creature in such contempt and horror that he sees in her nothing but the instrument of a just revenge. 'If that cursed woman could ever merit any kind of commiseration after all the evil she did to me,' he said to me, 'it would be by giving herself over to the pitiless punishment of that scoundrel. She must be his exterminating angel.'"

When a servant knocked quietly on the door, Murph left the room, and returned shortly with two letters, only one of which was for Rodolphe. "It's word from Madame Georges!" the latter exclaimed as he read it rapidly.

"So, Your Lordship, what about Songbird?"

"There's no longer any room for doubt!" Rodolphe exclaimed after reading the letter. "There's another deep conspiracy going on. The evening of the day on which that poor child disappeared from the farm, and at the moment Madame Georges was going to tell me about that event, a man she didn't know, sent as a messenger on horseback, came to reassure her on my behalf. He told her that I knew about the sudden disappearance of Fleur-de-Marie and that in a few days I would bring her back to the farm. Despite this information, Madame Georges was worried at my silence regarding her protégée. She says she couldn't help herself from wanting to know the latest news of her darling daughter, as she calls the poor child."

"That's strange, Your Lordship."

"Why would anyone want to kidnap Fleur-de-Marie?"

"Your Lordship," said Murph, suddenly, "Countess Sarah has something to do with this kidnapping."

"Sarah? And what makes you think so?"

"Put this event together with her denunciations of Madame d'Harville."

"You're right!" exclaimed Rodolphe, struck with a sudden flash of enlightenment. "It's obvious. I understand now. Yes, it's the same logic. The countess persists in believing that if she manages to destroy every affectionate relationship she thinks I have, she will make me feel the need to reconcile with her. This prospect is as odious as it is mad. In any case, this base persecution must end. It's not just me this woman is attacking, but everything that deserves respect, care, and pity. You will send Monsieur de Graün officially in my name to see the countess. He will inform her that I am certain of the part she played in Fleur-de-Marie's kidnapping, and that if she doesn't give us the information we need to recover that unfortunate child, I'll show her no mercy and Monsieur de Graün will turn her over to the authorities."

"According to Madame d'Harville's letter, Songbird should be in Saint-Lazare."

"Yes, but Rigolette says she saw her free and leaving the prison. We need to clear up this mystery."

"I'm going right now to give your orders to the Baron de Graün, Your Lordship, but permit me first to open this letter. It is from my correspondent in Marseille to whom I recommended the Slasher. He is supposed to facilitate the poor devil's passage to Algeria."

"Well, then, has he left?"

"Your Lordship, that's the strange part."

"What do you mean?"

"After waiting for a long time in Marseille for a vessel to take him to Algeria, the Slasher, who seemed more and more sad and worried, suddenly declared, on the very day he was due to depart, that he would prefer to return to Paris."

"That's odd!"

"Even though my correspondent had put a large sum of money, as had been arranged, at the Slasher's disposal, the latter took only the very least amount he absolutely needed to get back to Paris, where he will soon certainly arrive, I am told."

"So he will explain to us himself why he changed his mind. But send de Graün right now to see the Countess MacGregor, and go yourself to Saint-Lazare to find out about Fleur-de-Marie."

An hour later, the Baron de Graün came directly from the Countess Sarah MacGregor's. Despite his habitual, official sangfroid, the diplomat seemed shattered. As soon as the butler announced him, Rodolphe noticed his pallor. "Well, de Graün, what's wrong? Did you see the countess?"

"Oh, Your Lordship!"

"What's wrong?"

"Your royal highness must prepare to be informed of something very painful."

"What is it already?"

"Madame the Countess MacGregor . . ."

"Well?"

"Your royal highness must forgive me for informing him so suddenly of an event that is so fateful, so unforeseen, so—"

"Is the countess dead, then?"

"No, Your Lordship, but no one holds out any hope for her. She has been stabbed with a dagger."

"Oh, how dreadful!" cried Rodolphe, moved to pity in spite of his aversion toward Sarah. "And who committed this crime?"

"No one knows, Your Lordship. The murder was accompanied by a theft. Someone broke into Madame the countess's apartment and took a great quantity of gemstones."

"How is she at this moment?"

"Her condition is all but desperate, Your Lordship. She has not yet regained consciousness. Her brother is beside himself."

"You will need to go every day to inquire after the countess's health, my dear de Graün."

At this moment, Murph was coming back from Saint-Lazare. "I must tell you a sad bit of news," Rodolphe said to him. "The Countess Sarah has just been attacked, and her life is hanging by a thread."

"Oh, Your Lordship! Despite her great guilt, it's hard not to feel sorry for her."

"Yes, such an end would be dreadful. And Songbird?"

"Since yesterday, she's been free, Your Lordship. They believe she is under the protection of Madame d'Harville."

"But that's impossible! Madame d'Harville has asked me, on the contrary, to take the necessary steps to get the unfortunate child out of prison."

"No doubt, Your Lordship. All the same, an elderly woman with a respectable face came to Saint-Lazare with the order for Fleur-de-Marie's release. They left the prison together."

"That's what Rigolette told me. But who is that elderly woman who came to pick up Fleur-de-Marie? Where did they go together? What is this latest mystery? The Countess Sarah may well be the only one who could clear this up, and she is not in any condition to give us information. Let's hope she doesn't take this secret with her to the grave!"

"But her brother, Thomas Seyton, would certainly be able to shed some light on the matter. He has always been the countess's advisor."

"His sister is dying. If this is connected to another conspiracy, he won't talk to us. But," said Rodolphe, upon reflection, "we need to know the name of the person who concerned himself in Fleur-de-Marie's release from Saint-Lazare. That way, we would certainly learn something."

"That's true, Your Lordship."

"Try to learn who this person is and see him as soon as possible, my dear de Graün. If you do not succeed, put your Monsieur Badinot to work. Spare no effort to discover the whereabouts of that poor child."

"Your royal highness can count on my diligence."

"Well, heavens, Your Lordship, it might be a good thing that the Slasher is returning to us. His services may be of use to you in this investigation."

"You're right, and now I can't wait to see my brave savior back in Paris. I will never forget that I owe my life to him."

CHAPTER 12

THE OFFICE

Several days had gone by since Jacques Ferrand had taken Cecily into his service. We will bring the reader, who already knows the place well, into the solicitor's office during the clerks' lunch hour. An unheard-of and marvelous extravaganza was occurring there. Instead of the thin and rather unappetizing stew the late Madame Séraphin had made to feed these young people every morning, an enormous cold turkey, served in an old file box, reigned proudly in the middle of the office desks, braced up by two loaves of soft bread, a Dutch cheese, and three bottles of vintage wine. An old lead inkwell filled with a mix of salt and pepper served as a saltcellar. Such was the menu for this meal.

Each clerk, armed with a knife and a hearty appetite, awaited the appointed hour for the feast with famished impatience. Some of them were even chewing with empty mouths as they cursed the absence of the head clerk, without whom they could not begin their meal, according to the rules of the hierarchy. This development, or rather this radical upheaval in the ordinary lives of Jacques Ferrand's clerks, indicated an enormous domestic disturbance. The following eminently Philistine conversation (if we may borrow the expression from the very intellectual writer who popularized it)[173] will cast some light on this important matter.

"Here's a turkey that never dreamed when he was born that he would end up as lunch for the boss's clerks."

"Just the same way our boss never dreamed when he began his life as a solicitor that he'd end up giving his clerks a turkey for their lunch."

---

173. The word being translated as "Philistine" is actually the French for Boeotian (*béotien*), which, like "Philistine" in English, can describe someone who is vulgar and uncultured. The history, however, is entirely different. Boeotia, a state in Greece of which Thebes was the capital, was, in the eyes of Athens, less civilized, a prejudice resulting from both political rivalry and the fact that Boeotians spoke a different dialect of Greek. The use of the word *béotien* in France to designate someone vulgar and uncultured well predates the nineteenth century. It was indeed popularized, though by the journalist Louis Desnoyers (1805–1868), who, in 1831, published *Les Béotiens de Paris*, which described Parisian mores. [TN]

"And still and all, that turkey is ours now!" exclaimed the errand boy with the greed of a gourmand.

"Errand boy, my friend, you're forgetting your place. This turkey will be foreign to you."

"And furthermore, as a true Frenchman, you must hate foreigners."

"The only thing we can do is give you the feet."

"They can serve as an emblem of your speed at running office errands."

"I thought I would at least have a right to the carcass," muttered the errand boy.

"That can be granted to you, but you have no right to it, just like it was for the Charter of 1814, which was but another carcass of liberty," quipped the office Mirabeau.[174]

"Speaking of the carcass," said one of the young men with a brutally insensitive streak, "may God bless the soul of Madame Séraphin! Since she drowned on her trip to the countryside, we are no longer condemned to a life sentence of ratatouille."

"And for a blessed week now, the boss, instead of giving us lunch—"

"Has been giving each of us a stipend of forty sous a day!"

"That's why I'm saying, 'May God bless the soul of Madame Séraphin!' "

"Indeed, when she was here, the boss would never have given us the forty sous."

"It's great!"

"It's fabulous!"

"There's no other office in Paris . . ."

"In all of Europe . . ."

"In the entire universe, where they give a simple clerk forty sous for his lunch."

"Speaking of Madame Séraphin, have any of you seen the servant who's replacing her?"

"That Alsatian woman that the wife of the doorkeeper where that poor Louise used to live brought here one evening, according to our doorkeeper?"

"Yes."

"I haven't seen her yet."

"Me, neither."

"Good Lord! It's simply impossible to see her since the boss is more ferocious than ever about not letting us go into the building on the courtyard."

174. Honoré Gabriel Riqueti, the Count de Mirabeau (1749–1791), was a moderate leader in the Revolution. Famous for his speeches, he presided over the National Constituent Assembly. [TN]

"And then it's the doorkeeper who cleans the office now. How can we see what the little lady looks like?"

"Well, I've seen her."

"You?"

"Where?"

"What does she look like?"

"Is she tall or short?"

"Young or old?"

"Let me say first of all that I am sure that she does not have as attractive a face as that poor Louise—such a good girl she was!"

"So, since you've had a look at her, what's that new servant like?"

"When I say that I've seen her, what I mean is that I've seen her bonnet. It was a funny-looking bonnet."

"Only that! Well, what was it like?"

"It was bright red and made of velvet, I think. It was the kind of hood those women who sell little brooms wear."

"Like the Alsatians? That would make sense, since she's Alsatian."

"Come on."

"Honestly! What's surprising about it? Once bitten, twice shy!"

"Oh, stop it, Chalamel. What does your proverb have to do with that Alsatian bonnet?"

"Nothing at all."

"Why did you say that, then?"

"Because 'a good deed never goes for naught,' and 'lizards are friends to men.'"[175]

"Listen, once Chalamel gets started on those proverbs of his, which have neither rhyme nor reason, he'll go on for an hour. So come on, tell us what you know about this new servant."

"I was passing through the courtyard the day before yesterday. She had her back to one of the windows on the ground floor."

"The courtyard?"

"No, silly, the servant![176] The lower windowpanes were so dirty that I couldn't see much of the Alsatian, but the ones in the middle of the window were less filthy. That's how I saw her cherry-colored bonnet and a whole slew of jet-black curls, because she seemed to have her hair bobbed and curled."

"I'm sure the boss hasn't seen any more through those glasses of his than you have, because he's the kind of guy who—well, if he was the

---

175. A saying in Provence, where it was believed that lizards would wake sleeping humans by jumping on their faces when snakes were nearby. [TN]

176. In French, the word *cour* (courtyard) is feminine. The gendering of nouns in French allows for the confusion of the courtyard for the woman, thus enabling Sue to make this joke. [TN]

last man on earth and there was one woman, the world would come to an end."

"That's not surprising. 'He who laughs last laughs best,' and furthermore, 'Punctuality is the courtesy of kings.'"

"Lord, that Chalamel, once he gets going, he just starts to fly!"

"Indeed: 'Birds of a feather flock together.'"

"That's a good one!"

"I personally think that our boss's superstitions are starting to deaden his brain."

"Maybe he's giving us those forty sous for our lunch as penance."

"The fact of the matter is that he must be mad."

"Or sick."

"I've personally found him pretty distracted over the past few days."

"It's not like we see him very much. The guy who used to give us such a hard time from dawn to dusk, that same guy who was always on our backs, hasn't put his nose in here for the past two days."

"And so the head clerk's buried in extra work."

"And that's why this morning we have to sit here dying of hunger while we wait for him."

"Things have really changed in this office!"

"That poor Germain would have been totally amazed if we'd told him, 'Can you believe it, my boy? The boss is giving us forty sous for our lunch!' 'Oh, no, that's impossible.' 'It sure is possible. He told me, Chalamel, *personally*, that he was doing it.' 'Are you joking?' 'Me, joking! Here's what happened: for two or three days after the death of Old Lady Séraphin, we got nothing at all for lunch. In some ways, we liked it better that way, because the food was less disgusting. But on the other hand, our meals were costing us money. Nevertheless, we were patient, saying, "The boss doesn't have a servant or housekeeper anymore. When he replaces one of them, we'll get our foul chow back." Well, that's not what happened at all, my poor Germain. The boss hired a servant, but our lunch was still submerged in the Lethean waters of forgetfulness. So I was basically deputized to bring a complaint to the boss on behalf of the sufferings of our stomachs. He was with the head clerk. "I don't want to feed you any more in the mornings," he said in a churlish tone and as if he were thinking of something else. "My servant doesn't have the time to take care of your lunch." "But, monsieur, we had an agreement that you would supply us with our morning meal." "All right! You may have your lunch elsewhere, and I'll pay for it. How much do you need? Will forty sous apiece cover it?" he said, seeming more and more preoccupied with something else, saying forty sous as randomly as he might have said twenty sous or a hundred sous. "Yes, monsieur, forty sous will be enough for us," I exclaimed, jumping at the deal. "So be it. The head clerk will be in charge of the expense. I'll do the accounting with him." And with that, the boss shut the door in my face.' You have to admit, gentlemen, that Germain would have been highly shocked to hear of the boss's generosity."

"Germain would think that the boss had been drinking."

"And that we were taking advantage of him."

"Chalamel, stick to your proverbs."

"Seriously, I think the boss is sick. He hasn't looked like himself for the past ten days. His cheeks are hollow enough to fit your fist in."

"And he's so distracted! It has to be seen to be believed. The other day, he raised his glasses in order to read a deed, and his eyes were so red and inflamed they looked like burning embers."

"It's his right. 'Short debts make long friendships.'"

"Let me speak. I'm telling you, gentlemen, that this is very odd. I was presenting this deed to the boss for him to read, but he kept hanging his head down."

"The boss? The fact is, this is all very odd. How can he do anything with his head hanging down like that? He must have been suffocating, unless he really had changed his practices."[177]

"Oh, that Chalamel is so tiresome! I'm telling you that I gave him the deed to read upside down."

"Ah! He must have grumbled at you!"

"You'd think! But he didn't even notice it—he looked at it for ten minutes, staring at it with his big red eyes, and then he gave it back to me and said, 'It looks fine!'"

"With his head still down?"

"Yes."

"So he didn't read the deed, then?"

"You bet he didn't, unless he was reading it upside down!"

"That's peculiar!"

"The boss seemed so somber and nasty at that moment that I was afraid of saying anything, and I left as if nothing happened."

"As for me, I was in the head clerk's office four days ago. A client came, and then a second, and then a third. All of them had appointments with the boss. They were starting to get tired of waiting. At their request, I went to knock on his door. No one answered, so I went in . . ."

"And?"

"Monsieur Jacques Ferrand had his arms folded on his desk and his bald, uninviting head resting on them. He wasn't moving at all."

"Was he asleep?"

"That's what I thought. I went up to him and said, 'Monsieur, there are clients with appointments waiting for you out there . . .' He didn't stir. 'Monsieur!' No answer. Finally, I tapped him on the shoulder. He jumped

177. The French for hanging one's head is *tête en bas*, which literally means he had his head at the bottom of his body. This is the basis of Chalamel's feeble joke. [TN]

as if the devil had bitten him. That quick motion knocked his big green glasses off his nose and I saw—you'll never believe what I saw."

"Well? What did you see?"

"Tears."

"You've got to be kidding!"

"That's a strange claim."

"The boss, crying? Come on!"

"I'll believe that when pigs fly."[178]

"And when cows jump over the moon."[179]

"Yeah, yeah, yeah. Kid around all you like, but I'm telling you that's what I saw."

"You really saw him crying?"

"Yes, crying. Then he got so furious at being taken by surprise in that lachrymose moment that he put his glasses back on quickly and shouted at me, 'Get out! Get out!' 'But, monsieur—' 'Get out!' 'There are clients you have appointments with, and—' 'I don't have the time for them. They can go to hell, and so can you!' At that point, he got up, looking so furious that I thought he was going to throw me out the door. I didn't wait any longer. I got myself out of there and told the clients to leave. They didn't seem any happier about it than you'd expect. For the honor of our office, I told them that the boss had the whooping cough."

This interesting conversation was interrupted by his honor, the premier clerk, who entered the room looking very busy. He made his entrance to general acclaim, and all eyes turned longingly toward the turkey in impatient anticipation.

"I mean no disrespect, Your Lordship, but we have had to wait a devilishly long time for you," said Chalamel.

"Watch out. If this happens again, our appetite won't be so forgiving."

"Gentlemen, it's not my fault! I've been more worried than you. Honestly, the boss must be mad!"

"I told you so!"

"But that doesn't mean we can't eat!"

"On the contrary!"

"We can talk about it just as well with our mouths full."

"We can talk about it better that way," said the errand boy as Chalamel, taking the turkey apart, said to the head clerk, "By the way, what do you think is driving the boss mad?"

"We already had the impression that he was going soft in the head when he allocated forty sous apiece for our daily lunch."

"I can tell you, gentlemen, that that surprised me as much as it

178. Literally, "when May bugs play the cornet." [TN]

179. Literally, "when chickens wear their boots backward." [TN]

surprised you. But all of that is nothing—absolutely nothing—compared with what just happened a moment ago."

"What now?"

"Has that sad sack there become so insane that he's going to force us to dine every night at his expense at the Blue Dial?"

"And after that, to go to a show?"

"And then to a café, to finish the evening off with some punch?"

"And then . . ."

"Gentlemen, you may laugh all you like, but the scene I just witnessed was more scary than funny."

"Come on, then, tell us all about it."

"Right. Don't worry about the meal," said Chalamel. "We're all ears."

"And you're all teeth, too, boys! I can see how it will work. While I talk, you're thinking you'll be chewing away. That turkey will be gone before my story is over. Be patient. I'll save it for dessert."

We do not know whether it was the pangs of hunger or their curiosity that motivated these young professionals, but they conducted their gastronomic operation so speedily that the time for the head clerk's story arrived almost immediately. In order to not get caught by the boss, they sent the errand boy, to whom they had generously allotted the carcass and feet of the bird, to serve as their lookout in the next room.

The head clerk said to his colleagues, "First of all, you need to know that the doorkeeper has been concerned over the boss's health for the last few days. Since the good fellow stays up very late, he had seen Monsieur Ferrand go into the garden several times at night, in spite of the cold or rain, and pace around it. He took the chance once of leaving his post to ask his employer if he needed anything. The boss sent him off to go to bed in such a manner that the doorkeeper has held his tongue ever since, whenever he hears the boss go into the garden. And this happens almost every night, no matter what the weather."

"Could the boss be sleepwalking?"

"I don't think that's likely. But nightly walks like that show some kind of major agitation. Let me get to my story. A little while ago, I go down to the boss's office to get some signatures from him. Just as I was putting my hand on the handle of the lock, I seem to hear someone talking. I stop. I make out two or three dull cries, which sound like muffled sobs. I hesitate to enter for an instant, but—well, I'm really afraid something terrible is happening—so I open the door . . ."

"And?"

"What do I see but the boss on his knees, on the floor."

"On his knees?"

"On the floor?"

"Yes. Kneeling on the floor, his head in his hands, leaning with his elbows resting on the seat of one of his old armchairs."

"I know what he was doing! We're stupid. He's so sanctimonious that he was getting in an extra prayer."

"It must have been some odd prayer, if that's what it was! All I heard were muffled groans, except for when he murmured, from time to time, 'My God! My God!' like a man in the grips of despair. And then—this is the other peculiar thing—he made a motion as if he was trying to tear his chest with his fingernails. His shirt opened, and I could see on his hairy skin a little red wallet hanging from a little steel chain . . ."

"Wow! Go on!"

"So then, when I saw that, honestly, I didn't know anymore whether I should stay or leave."

"That would have been my well-considered opinion as well."

"So I stayed there. And I was quite embarrassed when the boss got up and turned around suddenly. He had an old checkered handkerchief between his teeth. His glasses were still on the chair. No, no, gentlemen, I have never seen such a face as his in my life. He looked like one of the damned. I backed up, terrified. I swear, I was terrified. Then he—"

"Lunged to strangle you?"

"No, wrong guess. He looked at me for a moment, seeming to be dazed, but then, dropping the handkerchief that he had been gnawing and tearing at with his grinding teeth, he exclaimed, as he threw himself into my arms, 'Oh, I'm so unhappy!'"

"What a comedy!"

"What a comedy, indeed. Still, despite his face looking like a death mask when he pronounced those words, that didn't stop his voice from being heartrending—I would almost call it gentle . . ."

"Gentle? Oh, come on! A rattle or an owl with a cold sounds like a lullaby compared with our boss's voice!"

"That's possible, but that doesn't change the fact that, at that moment, his voice was so plaintive that I almost felt moved by him, especially since Monsieur Ferrand is not ordinarily expansive. 'Monsieur,' I said to him, 'believe me that—' 'Get out! Get out!' he said, interrupting me. 'It soothes me so much to be able to tell someone how I'm suffering.' It seems he mistook me for someone else."

"He talked to you down-to-earth like that? That means you owe us two bottles of Bordeaux! The proverb says so, and proverbs are sacred. Proverbs represent the wisdom of nations."

"Come on, Chalamel, enough with your riddles. You understand, gentlemen, that when I heard the boss speak to me in a familiar manner, I realized all of a sudden that he was either mistaken or that he was feverish. I pulled myself away from him and said, 'Monsieur, calm down! Calm down! It's me.' Then he looked at me as if stupefied."

"Finally, now you're talking sense."

"His eyes were wild. 'Huh?' he said. 'What is this? Who is it? What do you want from me?' And he put his hand up over his eyes with each question, as if to part the clouds that were obscuring his ability to think."

"'That were obscuring his ability to think . . .' As the saying goes! Bravo, head clerk! Let's write a melodrama together!"

When one speaks so well, I must say—
It's time to write a play!

"Shut up, Chalamel."

"So what could be wrong with the boss?"

"I have no idea, I swear. But the one thing I know for sure is that, once he pulled himself together, he was singing another tune. He frowned in a nasty way and said to me sharply, without giving me the chance to answer him, 'What are you doing in here? Have you been here a long time? I can't even stay in my own home without having people coming in here to spy on me? What did I say? What did you hear? Tell me! Tell me!' Honestly, he looked so mean that I answered him, 'I didn't hear a thing, monsieur. I just walked in right now.' 'You aren't lying to me?' 'No, monsieur.' 'So what is it you want?' 'I wanted to get some signatures from you, monsieur.' 'Give me the papers.' And he started signing and signing, without reading any of the half dozen notarized deeds. And this is the same man who would never put his initials on a deed without spelling it out letter by letter, from one end to the other, twice. I noticed that from time to time his hand slowed down in the middle of his signature, as if he had gotten absorbed in some obsessive idea—and then he picked up where he'd left off and signed very quickly, almost convulsively. When everything was signed, he told me to leave, and I heard him go down the little staircase that leads from his office into the courtyard."

"It keeps coming back to that. What could he be doing there?"

"Gentlemen, it might be the case that he is mourning Madame Séraphin."

"Oh, stop it. Like he could ever miss anyone!"

"That reminds me—the doorkeeper said the priest from Bonne-Nouvelle and his curate came several times to see the boss, and he wouldn't receive them. And that's surprising. We could never get those guys out of here."

"The thing I'd like to know is what kind of work he had the carpenter and locksmith do in the detached building."

"The fact is, they've been working out there three days in a row."

"And then one evening they brought in furniture, in a big covered wagonette."

"Honestly, gentlemen, tra la la! In the words of the Swan of Cambrai, I don't have a clue!"[180]

---

180. The Swan of Cambrai is a nickname for François de Salignac de la Mothe-Fénelon, known simply as Fénelon (1651–1715). He was the archbishop of Cambrai; hence the nickname. He was an author and theologian, originally an ally of Bossuet (see below) and later an opponent. [TN]

"Maybe it's the remorse he feels over sending Germain to prison that's tormenting him."

"Remorse? Him? He's too hard-boiled and blackened by time for that, as the Eagle of Meaux says."[181]

"Chalamel, you're such a joker!"

"Speaking of Germain, he's going to have to reckon with some real fine new recruits in prison, poor guy!"

"What do you mean?"

"I read in the *Court Gazette* that the gang of thieves and murderers that they arrested on the Champs-Élysées in one of those little underground taverns—"

"Those are some real caverns—"

"That that gang of villains has been thrown into La Force prison."

"Poor Germain! They'll be nice company for him!"

"Louise Morel will also have her share of new friends, because there's a whole family of thieves and murderers in the gang. From father to son, and from mother to daughter . . ."

"So they're sending the women to Saint-Lazare, where Louise is."

"One of that gang might have murdered that countess who lived near the Observatory, one of the boss's clients. He's sure sent me enough times to find out what was going on with that countess! He seems awfully interested in her health. To be fair, though, it's the only thing he doesn't seem to be in a daze about. He asked me once again yesterday to go find out what Madame MacGregor's condition was."

"And how was she?"

"She's still the same. One day there's reason to hope, and the next day, none. No one knows whether she'll make it through the day. The day before yesterday they didn't think she'd make it, but yesterday there was, they say, a glimmer of hope. The complicating factor there is that she had a brain fever."

"Did you manage to enter the house and see the place where the attack took place?"

"Sure, right! I couldn't get any further than the main entrance, and the concierge didn't seem to want to talk—far from it."

"Gentlemen, to your places! The boss is coming up here!" cried the errand boy as he entered the room, still holding the turkey carcass. Immediately, the young men hurried to their respective desks, hunching over and scribbling furiously, while the errand boy put the turkey carcass down temporarily in a box full of files. Jacques Ferrand had indeed appeared.

His gray-streaked red hair was coming loose from his old black silk

181. Jacques-Bénigne Bossuet (1627–1704), an influential conservative Catholic theologian. He was the bishop of Meaux; hence his nickname. [TN]

bonnet, falling messily out the sides at each temple. Some of the veins that marbled his head appeared to be injected with blood, while his snub-nosed face and his hollow cheeks were deadly pale. They couldn't see the expression in his look, given the large green glasses he had on, but the profound alteration of his features suggested that they had undergone the ravages of an all-devouring passion.

He slowly walked through the office without saying a word to his clerks, without even seeming to notice that they were there. He entered the room in which the head clerk was stationed, walked through it as well, and then through his own office, and immediately walked back down the small staircase that led to the courtyard.

Since Jacques Ferrand had left all the doors open as he passed through them, the clerks were quite understandably astonished to observe the strange wandering of their boss. He had walked up one staircase and down another, without stopping in a single one of the rooms through which he had walked, as if he were an automaton.

CHAPTER 13

THOU SHALT NOT LUST . . .

But instead of staying true to that which is luminous and pure in the union of hearts and minds to which friendship is limited, the filthy depths of my depravity, accentuated by the heightening of sensuous feeling that characterizes the age I was at that time, shrouded my discernment in billows of fog.

I abandoned myself without any limits to my sensual pleasures, which burned in my heart like boiling pitch and consumed everything vigorous and strong within it.

When I heard my friends boasting of their debaucheries and saw that the more obscene they were, the more they congratulated each other for them, I was ashamed of not having done as much as they had.

—*THE CONFESSIONS OF SAINT AUGUSTINE*, BOOK II, CHAPTERS II AND III

Night had fallen. The profound silence that reigned in the building in which Jacques Ferrand lived was interrupted from time to time by the howling of the wind and the squalls of rain that were falling in torrents. These melancholy sounds made the solitude of this residence that much more complete.

In a very comfortably and newly furnished bedroom on the first floor, on which there lay a thick rug, a young woman stood before a fireplace. A healthy fire was burning in it. Oddly, in the middle of the carefully locked door facing the bed, there was a small spyhole that measured five or six square inches and opened from the outside. A reflecting lamp cast a partial glow over this red, wallpapered bedroom. The draperies around the bed and the window, as well as the upholstery of an enormous sofa, were of the same color and made of damask silk and wool. We must report this minor luxury recently brought into the solicitor's residence in such minute detail because it suggested a complete change in Jacques Ferrand's habits. Until now, he behaved with sordid avarice and a spartan indifference (especially when it came to others) regarding everything that had to do with his well-being.

Cecily's face, which we will here try to depict, was outlined against this background of red wallpaper of a deep, warm tone. Tall and svelte, the Creole was in the flowering prime of her beauty. The development of her beautiful shoulders and her large hips made her round waist look so marvelously thin that one might imagine that she could use her collar as a belt. As flirtatious as it was simple looking, her Alsatian clothing was in questionable taste; it was rather theatrical, and thus perfectly suited to the effect she wished to produce. Her spencer jacket, made of fine black wool, lay partly open on her prominent bust. It had a very long bodice, tight sleeves, and a smooth back, and it was lightly embroidered with scarlet wool on the seams and raised with a row of little silver-embossed buttons. A short skirt of orange merino that seemed to be too full even though it adhered to her statuesque form allowed one to catch glimpses of the Creole's charming knees the way the old Flemish masters would so casually reveal the garters of their robust heroines. These knees were encased in scarlet stockings with blue dots on them.

The curve of Cecily's legs was beyond the dreams of any artist. Sinewy and fine beneath their rounded calves, they terminated in sweet little feet, perfectly comfortable and beautifully arched in their little black morocco shoes with silver buckles. Cecily was standing with her left hip slightly jutting out in front of the mirror that was hanging over the fireplace. The plunge of her spencer jacket gave a glimpse of her elegant, sculpted neck that was dazzlingly white but not transparent.

Taking off her red velvet cap to replace it with a madras scarf, the Creole uncovered her magnificent thick jet-black hair, which, parted in the middle of her forehead and naturally curly, hung down only to the point where her neck met her shoulders. One would have to be familiar with the inimitable taste with which Creoles twist brightly colored scarves around their heads in order to envision Cecily's gracious nighttime hairstyle and the striking contrast the spotted scarlet, azure blue, and orange fabric made against her black hair. Tendrils of her hair were escaping the tight madras folds, framing her pale but firm round cheeks with an array of perfect curls. With rounded arms raised over her head, she finished tying a large bow placed very low on the left side, almost atop her ear, with fingertips as supple as ivory spindles.

Cecily's face was impossible to forget. A bold, slightly dominant forehead rose above her almost perfectly oval face. Her matte white complexion had the satiny freshness of a camellia leaf backlit imperceptibly by the sun. Her almost disproportionately large eyes had a singular expression, for their extremely large, black, shining pupils hardly allowed the bluish white of the eye to be seen at the corners of her long-lashed eyelids. Her chin was quite pronounced, and her nose, straight and delicate, ended in two quivering nostrils that dilated at the slightest emotion. Her mouth, insolent and voluptuous, was bright crimson in color.

The reader should picture this pale face with its sparkling black eyes and its moist, smooth red lips that shone like wet coral. We would say that this tall Creole, at once svelte and fleshy, vigorous and supple as a panther, was the perfect exemplar of the kind of brutal sensuality that comes alive only in the heat of the tropics. Everyone has heard of those women of color, as they might be called, who are fatal to European men, those vampiric enchantresses who intoxicate their victims with their terrible seductions and suck them dry of their last pieces of gold or drops of blood—leaving them, as is said in the striking folk idiom, nothing but their own tears to drink and their own hearts to gnaw on. Such was Cecily.

Though her detestable instincts, which her real affection for David had contained for a while, had developed only in Europe, the civilization and influence of the northern climate had tempered their violence and modified their expression. Instead of pouncing violently on her prey and thinking only, like others of her kind, of annihilating a life and taking its fortune as soon as possible, Cecily would attach her magnetic gaze upon her victims, commencing her attack by luring them slowly into the blazing whirlwind that seemed to emanate from her. Then, when she saw them panting, overcome, suffering the tortures of an insatiate lust, in a refinement of ferocious coquetry, she took pleasure in prolonging their ardent delirium. Finally, she would return to her basic instinct and devour them in a murderous embrace.

And this was not the worst of it. The famished tiger who pounces on and carries off the prey he tears apart as he growls is less terrifying than the snake who silently hypnotizes his prey, sucks it up a little at a time, winds it in his inextricable coils, crushes it over a long period of time, feels it throbbing as he devours it slowly, and seems to feed as much on its pain as on its blood.

Cecily, as we've said, had barely arrived in Germany when, having first been corrupted by an appallingly depraved man, she managed to open up and exercise her dangerous seductions without David, who loved her with as much idolatry as blindness, having the slightest suspicion for a while. But soon, the fatal scandal of her adventures was revealed. Horrible discoveries were made, and there was nothing to do but condemn the woman to life imprisonment.

With these characteristics, she combined a supple, clever, insinuating mind, an intelligence so marvelous that in one year she already spoke French and German with the greatest ease, sometimes even with a natural eloquence. If you can imagine a woman as corrupt as the courtesan queens of ancient Rome, with daring and courage equal to any challenge, coupled with instincts of a diabolical wickedness, you have, in a nutshell, Jacques Ferrand's new servant, the determined creature who had dared to set foot into the wolf's den.

And yet, through some strange anomaly, when she learned from Monsieur de Graün of the provocative and PLATONIC role she would have to play with the solicitor and the vengeful ends that her seductions would serve, Cecily had promised to play her character with love—or, rather, with a terrible hatred against Jacques Ferrand, having been sincerely indignant when she heard the narrative of the foul misdeeds he had committed against Louise, a narrative Monsieur de Graün had had to provide the Creole in order to put her on her guard against the hypocritical practices of this monster.

A few retrospective words about the latter are absolutely necessary. When Madame Pipelet had introduced Cecily to the solicitor by describing her as an orphan over whom she wished to retain no rights or caretaking responsibilities, he had perhaps been less struck by the Creole's beauty than fascinated by her irresistible gaze, a gaze that, from the first moment he saw her, set his senses afire and obscured his reason. For, as we have mentioned in regard to the insane daring of some of his statements during his conversation with Madame the Duchess de Lucenay, this man—ordinarily so self-disciplined, so calm, so sly, so wily—forgot all his cold calculations and deep dissimulation once the demon of lust had obscured his thinking.

In any case, he was powerless to resist Madame Pipelet's protégée. After her conversation with Madame Pipelet, Madame Séraphin had proposed to Jacques Ferrand a nearly friendless young woman for whom she could vouch as a replacement for Louise. The solicitor had swiftly accepted the offer in hopes of taking advantage of the isolation and insecurity of his new servant with absolute impunity. And so, far from being predisposed to suspicion, Jacques Ferrand found that the prospect offered him additional reasons for feeling safe. Everything was to his liking. Madame Séraphin's death had relieved him of a dangerous accomplice. Fleur-de-Marie's death (he believed her to be dead) relieved him of the living proof of one of his earliest crimes. Finally, thanks to the Owl's death and the unforeseen murder of Countess MacGregor (her condition was considered hopeless), he no longer had to worry about these two women whose revelations and pursuits could have proven fatal to him.

And so, we repeat, since no feeling of suspicion counterbalanced the sudden and irresistible impression that Cecily had made on Jacques Ferrand, he eagerly seized the opportunity to lure the supposed niece of Madame Pipelet into his isolated home. Given the character, habits, and past behavior of Jacques Ferrand and taking into account the provoking beauty of the Creole as we have tried to depict her, we hope that several additional facts that we will reveal later will allow the reader to understand the sudden, unrestrained passion of the solicitor for this seductive and dangerous creature. It must also be said: even if they inspire nothing but aversion, nothing but repugnance in men who are endowed with tender and elevated sentiments, delicate and purified tastes, women of Cecily's type enact sudden changes and exercise magic omnipotence over men of brutal sensuality like Jacques Ferrand. From the first time they see these women, they understand what they are and they covet them. A fatal force draws them to the women and, soon, mysterious affinities, magnetic sympathies no doubt, chain them irrevocably to the feet of their monstrous ideal, for these women alone have the ability to put out the impure fires they ignite.

A just and avenging fate was thus drawing the solicitor to the Creole. A terrible expiation was beginning. His ferocious lust had impelled him to commit odious crimes, to pursue an indigent and honest family with pitiless persistence, reducing them to misery, madness, and death. His lust would serve as this great criminal's fearsome punishment. For it seems that an inevitable sort of justice causes certain warped and unnatural passions to reap their own rewards. A noble love, even when it is not returned, can be comforted by the sweetness of friendship and the esteem that a woman worthy of being adored always offers when she cannot feel more tender sentiments. If this compensation does not assuage the sorrows of an unhappy lover, if his despair is as incurable as his love, he can at least proclaim and almost take pride in his desperate love. But what kinds of compensations are available for those wild passions that a mere physical attraction excites to a frenzy? And let us say, further, that a physical attraction is just as irresistible for vulgar constitutions as a moral attraction is for elite souls. No, the serious passions of the heart are not the only passions that are sudden, blind, and exclusive, the only ones that, concentrating all their faculties on the chosen person, render any other affection impossible and determine an entire destiny. Physical passion can burn with incredible intensity, as it did in Jacques Ferrand's case, and then all of the phenomena that characterize irresistible, unique, absolute love in the moral order are reproduced as well in the physical order.

Although Jacques Ferrand was destined never to be happy in his lust, the Creole was careful not to dash all his hopes. But the vague, distant hopes that she nurtured in him fluctuated in accordance with her many caprices and so were a new source of torture for him, wrapping him in the burning chains he wore even more inescapably.

Anyone who is surprised that a man of this vigor and daring should not have already had recourse to deception or violence in order to triumph over Cecily's calculated resistance has forgotten that Cecily was not just another Louise. In addition, the day after her introduction to the solicitor, she had taken on a completely different role from the one for which she had been hired by her employer. Indeed, the latter would not have been deceived by his servant two days in a row.

The Creole had been told of Louise's fate by the Baron de Graün, and she had therefore learned of the abominable means by which the gem-cutter Morel's unfortunate daughter had become the solicitor's prey. Upon entering the isolated house, she had, therefore, taken wise precautions in order to spend her first night there in complete safety. The very evening of her arrival, she was left alone with Jacques Ferrand, who, in order not to frighten her, pretended barely to notice her and ordered her brusquely to go to bed. She naively allowed that she was very afraid of thieves at night but that she was strong, determined, and ready to defend herself. "With what?" asked Jacques Ferrand.

"With this," answered the Creole as she withdrew a small, perfectly sharpened stiletto from the full fur-lined cloak in which she was wrapped. The sight of this weapon gave the solicitor pause. Nevertheless, persuaded that his new servant was only afraid of thieves, he led her to the bedroom she was to occupy (Louise's old bedroom). After having examined her surroundings, Cecily said to him, trembling and lowering her eyes, that, because of this same fear, she would spend the night in a chair since she saw neither a lock nor a bolt on the door. Jacques Ferrand, already completely under Cecily's charm but not wanting to compromise himself in any way by raising her suspicions, said to her in a gruff tone that she was silly and foolish to have such fears but he promised that a bolt would be installed the next day.

The Creole did not go to bed that night. In the morning, the solicitor went up to see her to tell her what her duties would be. He had decided to maintain a hypocritical reserve toward his new servant during her first days in order to inspire her with false confidence. But, struck by her beauty, which seemed even more dazzling to him in the daylight, he was blinded by the desires that were already carrying him away and blurted out a few compliments as to Cecily's figure and beauty. Of a rare acuity, Cecily had judged the solicitor to be besotted from their very first meeting. His declaration of passion made her believe that she had best drop her pretense of timidity immediately, and, as we've said, she put on a new mask. The Creole suddenly took on an air of shamelessness.

Jacques Ferrand once again expressed his rapture over his new maid's beautiful face and enchanting physique. "Look closely at my face," Cecily said to him firmly. "Even though I'm dressed like an Alsatian peasant, do I look like a servant to you?"

"What do you mean?" exclaimed Jacques Ferrand.

"Look at this hand. Does it look like the hand of someone who does hard work?" At this, she displayed a charming white hand with slender, tapered fingers and pink nails that were polished like agate but that had a slightly swarthy cast that betrayed her mixed blood. "And this foot: is it the foot of a servant?" She put forward a ravishing little foot that was coquettishly shod and that the solicitor had not yet noticed. He could not take his eyes off it except to contemplate Cecily in wonder.

"I told my aunt Pipelet what it suited me to tell her. She doesn't know about my past life. She could believe that I was reduced to such a condition by the death of my parents, and she took me to be a servant. But you are too wise, I hope, to make the same error, my dear master, are you not?"

"And who are you, then?" cried Jacques Ferrand, increasingly surprised by her words.

"That's my secret. For reasons only I need to know, I had to leave Germany in these peasant's clothes. I wanted to stay hidden in Paris for a while, as much in secret as possible. My aunt, supposing I had already been reduced to utter poverty, had suggested that I work for you. She described the solitary life I would necessarily live in your house, and she warned me that I would never get out of here. I quickly accepted the position. Unwittingly, my aunt had gone beyond my most cherished hope. Who would be able to look for me and find me here?"

"You're in hiding? What have you done, then, to necessitate your hiding?"

"I've committed some sweet sins, perhaps . . . but that also is my secret."

"And what are your intentions, mademoiselle?"

"They remain the same. If not for your revealing compliments on my figure and beauty, I might not have made you this confession, even though your shrewdness would in any case sooner or later have gotten it out of me. Listen to me carefully, dear master: I have accepted for the moment the condition, or rather the role, of a servant. Circumstances have obliged me to do so. I will have the strength to fulfill this role completely and I will submit to all its consequences. I will serve you conscientiously, energetically, and respectfully to keep my place, which is to say, a safe and hidden retreat. But at the least expression of gallantry on your part—at the least liberty you try to take with me, I will leave you—not from prudishness, for there is nothing prudish about me, I believe." At this, she gave the solicitor a look charged with sensual electricity that went to the depths of his soul and made him shudder. "No, I'm no prude," she went on, with a provocative smile that revealed her dazzling teeth. "Good Lord! When I feel Cupid's arrow, the bacchantes are virtual saints next to me. But be fair and you'll agree that your unworthy servant can want nothing more than to fulfill her servant's job respectably. Now you know my secret, or at least a part of my secret. Perhaps you would like to act like a gentleman? Do you find me too beautiful to serve you? Would you like to change roles and become my slave? So be it! Frankly, I would prefer it that way. But only on the condition that I'll never leave and that you will have only paternal feelings for me. That won't keep you from telling me that you find me charming. That will be the reward for your devotion and discretion."

"The only one? The only one?" Jacques Ferrand stuttered.

"The only one—unless solitude and the devil drive me crazy. Neither of which can happen, for you will be keeping me company, and, as a saintly man, you will keep the devil at bay. Come now, you must decide what it will be. I will brook no compromises. Either I will serve you or you will serve me—or else I'll leave your house and beg my aunt to find me another position. All of this must seem strange to you. So be it. But if you take me for a penniless adventuress, you're making a big mistake. In order to make my aunt my unwitting accomplice, I let her think I was so poor that I had no money to buy any clothes beyond these. Instead, I have, as you see, a well-lined purse. On this side I've got gold, and on the other, diamonds." (Here Cecily showed the solicitor a large red purse full of gold, through which several gems gleamed.) "Unfortunately, all the money in the world wouldn't provide me with a retreat as safe as your house, isolated as it is by your solitary ways. So accept one of my offers or the other. You will be doing me a great service. You see, I'm almost putting myself in your power, for, by saying to you, 'I'm in hiding,' I'm also saying, 'Someone is looking for me.' But I'm sure you wouldn't betray me, even if you had any idea how to do so."

This fantastic confidence and sudden change in character upended Jacques Ferrand's ideas. What kind of woman was this? Why was she in hiding? Was it mere chance that had brought her here? If instead she had come to him with some hidden motive, what was that motive? Among all the hypotheses this peculiar adventure suggested in the mind of the solicitor, he could never have stumbled upon the real reason for the Creole's presence in his home. He had no enemies—or rather, he believed he had no enemies—besides the victims of his lust and greed. And all of them were in such distressed and painful conditions that he could not suspect them of being capable of laying a trap for him for which Cecily would be the bait. In any case, what would be the point of this trap?

No, Cecily's sudden transformation made Jacques Ferrand afraid of only one thing: he thought that if this woman was not telling the truth, it was perhaps because she was an adventuress who, thinking him rich, had wormed her way into his home in order to mislead and exploit him, and maybe to get him to marry her. But although his avarice and greed made this idea turn his stomach, he realized with a shiver that these suspicions, these reflections were too late—for if he wanted, merely by saying the word, he could put his doubts to rest by sending this woman away. And yet he did not say that word. These thoughts could hardly tear him away even for a few moments from the ardent ecstasy into which the sight of this gorgeous woman, with her completely overpowering sensual beauty, plunged him. In any case, since the day before he had felt dominated and utterly fascinated by her. He already loved her with a passion—in the only way he knew how to love.

Already the prospect of seeing this seductive creature leave his house seemed unthinkable to him. Already feeling maddened by fierce jealousy when he imagined that Cecily might shower on others the rich sensual pleasures she would withhold from him perhaps forever, he experienced a gloomy comfort in thinking, "As long as she's locked away here with me, no one else can have her."

The boldness of this woman's language, the fire in her eyes, the provoking freedom of her manners revealed well enough that she was no prude, as she had told him. This conviction, which gave the solicitor vague hopes, also secured Cecily's power over him even more. In short, since his lust had silenced his cold reason, Jacques Ferrand gave himself over blindly to the torrent of unbridled desire that was carrying him away.

They agreed that Cecily would be his servant in appearance only. This way, there would be no scandal. In addition, in order to assure the safety of his guest even further, he would not hire any other domestic help. He would give in both to serving himself and to serving her. A nearby caterer would provide his meals, he would pay for his clerks' lunch in cash, and the doorkeeper would handle the upkeep of the office. Finally, the solicitor would have a bedroom on the first floor furnished promptly according to Cecily's taste. Cecily wanted to pay for this expense, but he wouldn't hear of it and spent two thousand francs. This extravagant generosity showed only too well the unheard-of violence of his passion.

Thus began a life of misery for this wretch. Holed up in the impenetrable solitude of his house, unavailable to anyone, more and more subjugated to the yoke of his unrestrained love, giving up on learning the secrets of this strange woman, he was transformed from master into slave. He became Cecily's manservant, waiting on her meals and cleaning her rooms.

Forewarned by the baron that Louise had unwittingly been slipped a narcotic in her wine, the Creole drank only perfectly clear water and ate only foods that were impossible to tamper with. She had chosen the bedroom that she would occupy, so she had already made sure that its walls did not conceal any secret doors. Moreover, Jacques Ferrand had quickly understood that Cecily was not a woman he could take by surprise or rape with impunity. She was strong, agile, and dangerously armed. Only a frenzied delirium might lead him to make some kind of desperate attempt upon her, and she had put herself completely out of reach of any such danger.

Nevertheless, so as not to tire or repulse the solicitor's passion, the Creole seemed sometimes to be touched by his care and flattered by the terrible domination she exerted over him. Then, suggesting that by proving his devotion and abjection he could finally make her forget his ugliness and age, she amused herself by portraying for him, in boldly explicit terms, the inexpressible sensuality with which she could intoxicate him, if, by some miracle, such a love ever came to be.

Such speech, coming from such a young and beautiful woman, made Jacques Ferrand feel sometimes that he was losing his mind. His mind was eaten up by images that pursued him wherever he went. The ancient symbol of the shirt of Nessus[182] became a reality to him. Amid these nameless tortures, he lost health, appetite, and the ability to sleep. Sometimes at night, despite the cold and the rain, he would go downstairs into the garden, hoping to calm himself and break the chains of his lust by taking a quick walk. At other times, he watched the sleeping Creole in her bedroom with his fiery gaze, for, with hellish indulgence, she had allowed her door to be fitted with a small window that she opened often—very often, because Cecily had only one goal, and that was to incite the passion of this man incessantly without satisfying it, to exasperate him in this way almost to the point of madness, thus executing the orders she had been given. The moment she was waiting for seemed fast approaching.

With every new day, Jacques Ferrand's punishment became worthier of his crimes. He was suffering the torments of hell. By turns absorbed, distracted, drifting, indifferent to his most profound interests, to the maintenance of his reputation as an austere, grave, and pious man—an unearned reputation, but one acquired over long years of dissimulation and deception—he stunned his clerks by the wanderings of his intelligence, made his clients angry by refusing to see them, and distanced himself brutally from the priests who, fooled by his hypocrisy, had been up to this point his most fervent advocates.

Raging fits followed upon overpowering languidness that brought him to tears. When his frenzy reached its climax, he took to moaning in solitude in the dark, like a wild beast. His fits of rage would end in a sort of painful shattering of his entire being. He could not even enjoy the calm of death that the annihilation of thought often produces. The blood burning in this man's veins, in all the strength of his age, as he was, left him no respite, no rest. His mind was incessantly tormented by a profound and torrid agitation.

And so, as we've said, Cecily was brushing her hair at night before her mirror. When she heard a quiet sound come from the corridor, she turned around to look at the door.

---

182. The poisoned shirt Hercules was given unwittingly by his wife, leading to his death. [TN]

CHAPTER 14

THE SMALL WINDOW

Despite the noise she had just heard at her door, Cecily calmly continued preparing herself for bed. She withdrew a stiletto, five or six inches long, from her blouse, where it had been placed as if it were a whalebone in a corset. It was sheathed in a black goatskin covering, with a handle of black, silver-lined ebony, its simple handle fitted perfectly to the hand. This was no ornamental weapon. Cecily drew this stiletto from its sheath with the greatest care and placed it on the marble mantel of the fireplace. The blade, of the most finely tempered laminated steel, was triangular with fine cutting edges and a point that was as sharp as a needle and that was capable of piercing a piastre[183] without becoming blunt. Its point doused in a subtle, unyielding poison, this dagger's least prick was fatal. One day, when Jacques Ferrand expressed doubt about the weapon's fatal properties, the Creole performed an experiment *in anima vili*,[184] that is to say, on the unfortunate house dog. When lightly pricked on the nose, he fell to the floor and died in horrible convulsions.

Having placed the stiletto on the fireplace and removed her black wool spencer jacket, with her shoulders, décolletage, and arms bared, Cecily looked just like a woman dressed for a ball. As was the custom of most women of color, rather than a corset, she wore a second blouse of thick cloth cut tightly at the waist. She continued to wear her orange skirt, which, under this species of sleeveless white camisole with a plunging neckline, made up a much more revealing outfit than her original one and went beautifully with her scarlet stockings and the madras scarf she wore wrapped so jauntily around her head. There could be nothing more pure or perfect than the curves of her arms and shoulders. Two dimples and a small black velvety and flirtatious beauty mark made them only that much more enticing.

A deep sigh caught Cecily's attention. She smiled and rolled a lock of hair that escaped her scarf around one of her slender fingers.

183. Italian for "thin metal plate," the word refers to any number of silver coins of different nationalities. [TN]

184. Latin for a subject of little worth, usually designating an animal to be experimented upon. [TN]

"Cecily! Cecily!" murmured a voice at once grating and plaintive.

And Jacques Ferrand's pallid, snub face appeared through the narrow opening of the small window. His eyes were sparkling in the shadows. Cecily, who had remained silent up to now, began to sing a Creole melody in a soft voice. The words to this slow melody were sweet and expressive. Although restrained, Cecily's almost manly contralto dominated the noise made by the torrents of rain and violent gusts of wind that seemed to shake the old house to its very foundations.

"Cecily! Cecily!" Jacques Ferrand pleadingly repeated.

The Creole suddenly cut herself short, brusquely turned her head, and, seeming to hear the solicitor's voice for the first time, casually walked up to the door. "Goodness! My dear master"—a term she used derisively—"you're here." This she said with a slightly foreign accent that made her scathing and sonorous tone that much more charming.

"Oh! You are beautiful like that," the solicitor murmured.

"Do you think so?" the Creole answered. "This scarf goes beautifully with my black hair, don't you think?"

"I find you more beautiful every day."

"And look at how white my arm is."

"You monster! Get out of here! Get out of here!" Jacques Ferrand cried out in fury. Cecily broke out in bursts of laughter. "No, no—I can't bear this pain any longer. Oh! If only I weren't afraid of dying!" the solicitor exclaimed in a hollow voice. "But if I die, I won't be able to see you anymore, and you are so beautiful! I'd rather bear the pain and look at you."

"So look at me. That's the purpose of this small window. Also it allows us to talk together like friends and so it gives some charm to our solitude, which, by the way, does not bother me that much. You are so good, master! Now just wait and see what dangerous things I say to you with this door between us."

"And don't you want to open this door? Just look at how meek I am. I could have tried to come into this room with you—but I didn't."

"You're meek for two reasons. First, you know that the necessities of a vagrant life have given me the practice of arming myself with a stiletto. I know how to use this little knickknack, and its poison is stronger than a viper's. You also know that the day you give me any cause for complaint is the day I will leave this house forever, leaving you even more deeply besotted by me—since you have been so kind to your unworthy servant as to have become besotted by her."

"My servant! Say, instead, that I am your slave, your mocked and despised slave."

"Indeed, that is the case."

"And doesn't that have any effect on you in the least?"

"It helps pass the time. The days, and especially the nights, can feel so long."

"Oh, you witch!"

"But seriously, you seem to be completely beside yourself. Your features are so obviously distorted, it really is flattering. It's a small enough triumph, but you're all there is here."

"To have to put up with this! And there's nothing I can do but eat my gut—I'm powerless."

"You're really not very smart! That may be the most affectionate thing I've ever said to you."

"Go ahead—mock me, mock me!"

"I'm not mocking you. I have never yet seen a man of your age in love in the way you are, and one must admit that a young and handsome man would hardly be capable of such a mad passion. An Adonis thinks as well of himself as he does of you. He loves you only at arm's length. And if you show any preference for him, well, really, he thinks, it's only natural. It's his due—and he's barely grateful for it. But to show a preference for a man such as you, master . . . oh! That would take him to the very heavens, it would fulfill his wildest fantasies, his most impossible dreams! Because, really, the being who could say to you, 'You love Cecily to distraction. If I wish it, she will be yours in a second,' you would think that being had supernatural powers, wouldn't you, my dear master?"

"Yes! Oh! Yes . . ."

"Well, then! If you were only better at convincing me of your passion, I might have a strange impulse to play this supernatural role myself for you. Do you understand me?"

"I understand that you're still mocking me, the way you always do, without pity!"

"Perhaps. Solitude gives birth to such strange fantasies." Up to then, Cecily's tone had been sardonic. But she said these last words in a serious, meditative tone and accompanied them with a long look that made the solicitor tremble.

"Stop saying those things! And don't look at me that way—you'll drive me mad. I would rather you said, 'Never!' At least then I could have hated you and turned you out of my house!" Jacques Ferrand exclaimed, still in the thrall of vain hope. "Yes, because that way I would expect nothing from you. But, alas, alas, I know you well enough now to hope that, despite myself, one day you might give me, in a moment of idleness or disdainful impulsiveness, that which I could never get from you through your love. You tell me to convince you of my passion, but, my God! Don't you see how miserable I am? And yet I do everything I can to please you. You want to be hidden from everyone; very well, I hide you from everyone, at the risk, perhaps, of seriously compromising myself. Because, after all, I don't know who you are. I respect your secret; I never mention it to you. I have questioned you about your past, and you have not answered me."

"All right, then! I was wrong. I will give you a sign of my blind trust in you, O my master! So listen to me."

"Another mean-spirited joke, right?"

"No, I'm completely serious. You should at least know the life story of the person to whom you give such generous hospitality." And Cecily added, in a tone of hypocritically tearful compunction, "I am the daughter of a brave soldier, Madame Pipelet's brother, but I received an education above my station in life. I was seduced and abandoned by a rich young man. Then, to my father's outrage (he was completely inflexible when it came to matters of honor), I fled my native land." Then, in a burst of laughter, Cecily went on, "Now there, I think, is a completely acceptable life story. It's certainly a very likely one given how often one hears it told. You can always satisfy your curiosity with that one while you wait for some more spicy revelation."

"I knew it was another cruel joke," the solicitor said, with intense anger. "You have no feelings—none at all. What am I supposed to do? Tell me that, at least. I wait on you as if I were the lowliest servant. I neglect my most important business for you. I don't know where my head is at anymore. My clerks play tricks on me and laugh at me. My clients now think twice about letting me handle their business. I have broken off relations with several pious people I used to see. I don't even want to think about what people say about all these upheavals in my daily life. You don't know—no, you really don't know—all the dire consequences that this mad passion may have for me. All the same, I demonstrate my devotion all the time, and I make all these sacrifices. Isn't that enough? Tell me! Is it money you want? People think me richer than I am, but I—"

"Why do you think I want your money?" Cecily said, interrupting the solicitor and shrugging her shoulders. "What good does money do me when I live in this room? Really, you aren't very creative in your thinking!"

"But it isn't any fault of mine if you are a prisoner here. Don't you like this room? Do you want a more luxurious one? Just say so. Your wish is my command."

"And yet again: what's the point? What's the point? Oh, if I had to wait here for someone I adored, burning with love for him and loved in return, then I would want money, silk, flowers, perfumes. No marvel of luxury would be too much; there could never be anything too sumptuous or too enchanting to set off my ardent loves," Cecily said in a tone of passion that made the solicitor jump.

"So, then, marvels of luxury! Just say the word and—"

"What's the point? What's the point? What good is a setting without a jewel? And this adored someone, where would he be, O master of mine?"

"It's true!" the solicitor exclaimed bitterly. "I'm old, I'm ugly. The only thing I make people feel is disgust and repulsion. She heaps disdain on me. She trifles cruelly with me. And I don't have the strength to run her out of the house. I don't have the strength to do anything but suffer."

"Oh, this constant sniveling! This vapid character and his endless complaints!" Cecily cried out in irony and disdain. "All he knows how to do is whine and act desperate. And for ten days he's been locked away alone with a girl in the depths of a deserted house."

"But this woman has contempt for me. And this woman is armed. And this woman is behind a locked door!" the solicitor cried out in anger.

"So then overcome the contempt of this woman, wrest the dagger from her hand, force her to open the door that separates you from her! But not by brute strength, because that would avail you nothing."

"So by what?"

"By the strength of your passion."

"Passion? Good God, can I inspire passion?"

"Really, you're nothing but a solicitor with the heart of a monk. I pity you. But is it my place to teach you how to act? You're ugly. Be awe-inspiring, and your ugliness will be forgotten. You're old. Be energetic, and your age will be forgotten. You're repulsive; be threatening. If you can't be the noble steed, snorting fiercely in the midst of his amorous gallops, at least don't be the stupid camel who bends his knee and offers his back. Be the tiger. An old tiger roaring amid his carnage still has a certain beauty. His tigress still answers to his call in the depth of the desert."

Never had she seemed more beautiful to him. "Keep on talking—don't stop!" he cried out in excitement. "Now you say what you mean. Oh, if only I could!"

"One can always do what one wants to do," Cecily said brusquely.

"But—"

"But I tell you that if I were as old and as repulsive as you are, I would like to be in your place and have a beautiful, fiery young woman to seduce, a woman who solitude would have delivered into my hands, a woman who understands everything—because then she might be capable of anything. Oh, yes, I would seduce her. And once I had done so, then everything that had worked against me would now make my victory that much sweeter. What pride, what triumph, to be able to say to myself, 'I knew how to make her overlook my age and my ugliness! The love she shows for me, I owe it not to her pity or to her depraved caprice, but to my wit, my daring, my energy. I owe it, finally, to my unbridled passion. Yes, and now let there be as many handsome young men, full of grace and charm, as you want. This woman who is so beautiful and whom I have conquered with unlimited proof of my unbridled passion won't give them so much as a look. No, because she will know that these elegant dandies would be afraid to wrinkle the knots in their neckties or muss a lock of their hair to obey one of her capricious commands, whereas if she so much as threw her handkerchief into a burning fire and made the slightest gesture to him, her old tiger would heave himself into that pyre roaring with joy.'"

"Yes, I would do that! Try me, try me!" Jacques Ferrand exclaimed, growing more and more excited.

Coming ever closer to the small window and holding Jacques Ferrand with a fixed and penetrating look, Cecily continued, "Because this woman would know only too well that if she had an exorbitant caprice she wanted fulfilled, those young men would hesitate to spend their money if they had any or would hesitate to commit a vile act if they had none, while her old tiger—"

"He would stop at nothing, that one. Isn't that what you mean? Nothing, not fortune, not honor. He would sacrifice everything, he would!"

"Is that true?" said Cecily, resting her charming fingers on the bony, hairy fingers of Jacques Ferrand, whose gnarled hands reached through the small window, straining against the thickness of the door. For the first time he felt the touch of the Creole's cool, smooth flesh. He grew paler and let out a raspy breath. "How could this young woman not feel ardent passion?" Cecily added. "Were she to have an enemy, she would have only to point him out with a look to her old tiger. She would say: 'Strike him dead, and—'"

"And he would strike him dead!" Jacques Ferrand exclaimed, straining with his dried-out lips to touch Cecily's fingertips.

"Is that true? The old tiger would strike him dead?" the Creole said, pressing Jacques Ferrand's hand gently with her own.

"To have you," the wretch cried, "I believe I could commit any crime."

"Well, then, master," Cecily said, suddenly withdrawing her hand, "now it's my turn to say, 'Get out of here.' I didn't recognize you there for a minute and you didn't seem so ugly. Get out of here."

And she abruptly drew back from the small window. This detestable creature knew how to give her actions and these last words a seeming sincerity that was not to be believed. Her ardent, surprised, furious expression seemed to show such real spite at having for a moment forgotten Jacques Ferrand's ugliness that he, now with frenzied hope, cried out as he grasped the bars of the small window, "Cecily, come back to me—come back, command me, I will be your tiger."

"No, no, master," Cecily said, drawing further and further back from the small window. "And to conjure away the devil who tempts me, I'm going to sing a song from my native land. Master, can you hear? The wind is howling even more outside, the storm is even more intense. Isn't it a beautiful night for two lovers to be sitting side by side, near a beautiful, crackling fire?"

"Cecily, come back to me!" Jacques Ferrand cried out, pleading.

"No, no, later, when I can do it safely. Right now that lamp hurts my eyes and my eyelids feel weighed down with a sweet languor. I don't understand what I'm feeling. Partial darkness is better for me. You might say I'm in the twilight of pleasure." And Cecily went to the fireplace, put out the lamp, pulled down a guitar that was hanging on the wall, and stirred the fire, whose blazing flames still lit up this vast room.

Here was the scene Jacques Ferrand saw as he stood, motionless, at the narrow little window. In the middle of the illuminated area created by the trembling light of the fireplace, Cecily, in a pose of soft abandonment, half reclining on the spacious couch of crimson damask, held a guitar on which she warmed up, playing some harmonious chords. The blazing fireplace bathed the Creole in bright red so that she seemed thus lit up in the middle of the rest of the room's darkness. To complete the effect of this scene, the reader should recall the mysterious, almost fantastic appearance of an apartment in which the flames in a fireplace make war with large black shadows quivering on the ceiling and walls.

The tempest outside redoubled its violence, and one could hear its moaning. Still warming up on the guitar, Cecily stubbornly held Jacques Ferrand in her magnetic stare and he, hypnotized, could not take his eyes off her. "So, now, master," the Creole said, "let's have a song from my native land. We don't write verses, we just recite simple, unrhymed recitatives, and at each rest we improvise as well as we can a cantilena fitting to the stanza's theme. It's very naive and very pastoral, and I'm sure you'll like it, master. This song is called 'The Woman in Love' and it is she who is speaking."

And Cecily began a kind of recitative much more accented by the expression of her voice than by the tempo of the melody. It was accompanied by various quavering and gentle chords. Here is what Cecily sang:

Flowers, flowers everywhere.
My lover is coming! This anticipation of happiness both shatters and unsettles me.
Let us dim the daybreak; sensuality seeks a transparent shadow.
To the flower's fresh perfume my lover prefers my hot breath.
The break of day will not irritate his eyes because his lids will stay closed under my kisses.
Come, O my angel! My breast heaves, my blood boils.
Come . . . come . . . come . . .

These words, spoken with such impatient ardor that one would have said that the Creole had been addressing an invisible lover, were then translated, if we may use that word, into the theme of an enchanting melody. Her charming fingers made her guitar, an instrument that rarely has much resonance, sing with smooth and harmonious sound. Cecily's animated expression, her veiled and moist eyes, still fixed on those of Jacques Ferrand, manifested the burning languor of anticipation.

Words of love, intoxicating music, inflamed eyes, a perfect sensual beauty, the storm outside, the night . . . they all combined at that moment to carry Jacques Ferrand beyond the voice of reason. Losing his bearing, he cried out, "Enough, Cecily, have mercy! I'm losing my mind. Be silent before I die from it. Oh, I would rather be mad!"

"So now let's have the second stanza, master," the Creole said, again warming up on the guitar. And she went on with her passionate recitative:

If my lover were here and his hand merely brushed my naked shoulder,
I would feel myself quiver and die.
If he were here and his hair merely brushed my cheek, my pale cheek
would become crimson.
My cheek, pale as it is, would be in flames.
Soul of my soul, if you were there, my dried-up lips, my hungry lips
would not say a word.
Love of my life, if you were there, it would not be me, even if I were
dying, who first cried out for mercy.
Those whom I love, as I love you, I kill.
Come, O my angel! My breast heaves, my blood boils.
Come . . . come . . . come . . .

If the Creole had stressed languorous sensuality in the first stanza, in these last words she spoke with the rage of the loves of past ages. And then, as if the music had been useless in expressing her ardent delirium, she threw the guitar aside and, partially rising and stretching out her arms toward the door where Jacques Ferrand was standing, she repeated in a distraught and dying voice, "Oh, come . . . come . . . come . . ."

It would be impossible to describe the magnetic look with which she accompanied these words. Jacques Ferrand let out a terrible cry. "Oh, death—death to whomever you would love like that, to any man to whom you would utter those fiery words!" he cried out, rattling the door in a rage of jealousy and furious ardor. "Oh, my fortune, my life for one minute of this devouring sensual pleasure! You describe it with such fire."

Supple as a panther, in a single bound Cecily was at the small window and, as if she had difficulty holding in her feigned ardor, she said to Jacques Ferrand in a low, thick, palpitating voice, "Well, then, I admit it. The ardent words of this song have inflamed me as well. I didn't want to come back to this door and yet here I am again, despite myself. Because I can still hear the words you spoke a moment ago: 'If you tell me to strike him dead, I'll strike him dead.' You really love me that much?"

"Do you want my money, all my money?"

"No, I have money."

"Do you have an enemy? I'll kill him."

"I have no enemies."

"Do you want to be my wife? I'll marry you."

"I'm already married!"

"But what do you want, then? God! What do you want?"

"Show me that your passion for me is blind, mad, that you'll sacrifice everything to it."

"Everything! In a moment! But how?"

"I don't know. But there was a moment there when the gleam in your eyes dazzled me. If at this moment you were to give me one of those signs of a love in frenzy that heightens a woman's imagination even to delirium, I don't know what I would be capable of! But be quick about it! I am capricious. Tomorrow, this hour's impulse might be gone forever."

"But what proof can I give you here, this moment?" the wretch cried out, wringing his hands. "I can't bear this torture! What proof? Tell me, what proof?"

"You're nothing but a fool!" Cecily answered, drawing back from the door looking disdainful and irritated in her spite. "I was wrong! I thought you could show a strong devotion! Good night. It's a shame, though."

"Cecily! Oh, don't go! Come back. But what should I do? At least tell me. Oh, I'm losing my mind. What should I do? What should I do?"

"Figure it out."

"God! God!"

"I was only too ready to give in to seduction if you had wanted it. You'll never have such a chance again."

"But really—you can tell me what you want!" the solicitor exclaimed, almost out of his mind.

"Guess."

"Tell me. Command me."

"Bah! If you wanted me as passionately as you say, you would figure out a way to win me over. Good night."

"Cecily!"

"Instead of opening this door, I'm going to close this window."

"Have pity, listen—"

"For a moment there I really thought I was getting excited. The fire was dying, the darkness would have fallen, I would have thought only of your devotion. And then this bolt . . . But no, you didn't want to. Oh, you don't know what you're missing. Good night, you holy man."

"Cecily, listen—stay, I've figured it out!" Jacques Ferrand exclaimed after a moment of silence, in an explosion of joy impossible to render. The wretch was plunged into a kind of vertigo. An impure mist darkened his mind. Given over to blind appetite, as mad as a beast, he lost all prudence, all discretion. He lost his instinct of moral self-preservation.

"Well, all right, then! What is this proof of your love?" the Creole asked after, having gone to the fireplace to take up her dagger, she returned to the window, gently bathed in the fire's glow. Then, without the solicitor's seeing her, she checked the working of a small iron chain which held two pegs together, one of which was screwed into the door, the other into the doorframe.

"Listen," Jacques Ferrand said in a hoarse, choppy voice. "If I were to put my honor, my fortune, my life at your feet, here, this moment, would you believe that I loved you? Would that show a mad enough passion to satisfy you? What do you say?"

"Your honor, your fortune, your life? I don't understand."

"If I entrusted you with a secret that could send me to the gallows, then would you be mine?"

"You, a criminal? You're putting me on. And your austerity?"

"A lie."

"Your integrity?"

"A lie."

"Your piety?"

"A lie."

"People think you're a saint and you want to say you're a demon! Now you're boasting. No, no man has enough skillful deceit, enough cool determination, enough luck and daring to capture people's trust and respect that way. It would be the most infernal mockery. It would be a terrible challenge thrown out to society."

"I am that man. I have mocked and thrown out that challenge to society."

"Jacques! Jacques! Don't talk that way!" Cecily said in a shrill voice, her breast quivering. "You'll make me go mad."

"I'll trade you my life for your caresses. What do you say?"

"Now, finally, there's real passion," Cecily exclaimed. "Here, take my dagger. You have disarmed me."

Jacques Ferrand took the dangerous weapon carefully through the small window and tossed it far away down the corridor. "So you believe me, Cecily?" he cried out, beside himself.

"Yes, I believe you," the Creole said, pressing her two charming hands forcefully against the gnarled hands of Jacques Ferrand. "Yes, I believe you because now I can see again your look of a moment ago, that look that had me hypnotized. Your eyes glitter with savage ardor. Jacques, I love them. I love your eyes!"

"Cecily!"

"But you must be telling the truth."

"I'm telling the truth! Oh, you'll see."

"Your face is menacing. Your expression is fearful. Really, you are as handsome and terrifying as a raging tiger. But you are telling the truth, right?"

"I have committed a lot of crimes, I tell you!"

"So much the better if by confessing them to me you can prove your passion."

"And if I tell you everything?"

"I will give you everything. Because if you show such blind, courageous trust, well, you see, Jacques, that would make you that ideal lover I was calling to in the song. It's to you, my tiger, to you that I would say, 'Come . . . come . . . come . . .'" And, saying these words with an avid and ardent look, Cecily came so close to the window, so close that Jacques Ferrand could feel the fiery breath of the Creole on his cheek and the electric pressure of her cool, firm lips on his hairy fingers.

"Oh, you will be mine! I will be your tiger!" he cried out. "And after that, if you want, you can destroy my honor and send me to the gallows. My honor, my life—it's all yours now."

"Your honor?"

"My honor! Now listen. Ten years ago someone entrusted me with a child and two hundred thousand francs set aside for it. I abandoned the child. I had it declared dead with a false death certificate. And I kept the money."

"Bold and skillful. Who would have thought you capable of it?"

"Listen some more. I hated my cashier. One night he took a little money from me that he replaced the next morning. But, to ruin the wretch, I accused him of having stolen a considerable sum. People believed me. He was thrown in prison. Now, isn't my honor at your mercy?"

"Oh, Jacques, how you must love me! To reveal your secrets to me this way! What power must I have over you! I won't be an ingrate. Give me that forehead that bore such hellish ideas. Let me kiss it."

"Oh!" the solicitor exclaimed, stuttering. "If the gallows were there, standing before me, I wouldn't retreat an inch. So listen some more. That child that I had abandoned years ago found herself once again in my way. So I had her killed."

"You? How? Where?"

"A few days ago, near the Asnières bridge, at the Scavenger's Island. A person named Martial drowned her in a boat with a safety valve. Are those enough details? Do you believe me?"

"Oh, you demon from hell! You terrify me and yet I'm drawn to you. You make my blood boil. What is your power over me?"

"Listen some more. Before that, a man entrusted me with a thousand crowns. I led him into an ambush and I blew his brains out. I proved that he had committed suicide, and when his sister came to claim the money, I denied that there had been any deposit. And now my life is yours to do with as you will. Open up."

"Jacques, oh, how I adore you!" the Creole said with exaltation.

"Now I could face a thousand deaths," the solicitor exclaimed in a state of intoxication beyond any description. "Yes, you were right. If I were young and charming, I would not feel this joy in triumph. The key! Throw me the key! Open the bolt."

The Creole took the key from the lock, which was closed from the inside, and gave it to the solicitor through the small window, saying to him, wildly, "Jacques, you've driven me mad with desire."

"Finally, you're mine," he cried with a savage roar, quickly turning the bolt in the lock. But the door, secured with a dead bolt, was not yet opened.

"Come, my tiger, come!" Cecily said, in a fading voice.

"The bolt, the bolt!" Jacques Ferrand cried out.

"But what if you were deceiving me?" the Creole suddenly exclaimed. "If you invented these secrets to take advantage of me?"

The solicitor was for a moment stunned into bewilderment. He had thought he had finally attained what he desired. This latest pause brought his furor to its breaking point. He quickly put his hand on his chest, opened his vest, rapidly broke a steel chain from which hung a red wallet, took it, and, showing it to Cecily through the small window, in a breathless, heavy voice, he said, "Here is all you need to send me to the guillotine. Pull the bolt and the wallet is yours."

"Give it to me, my tiger!" Cecily cried out. And as she noisily pulled the bolt with one hand, she grabbed the wallet with the other.

But Jacques Ferrand would not let go of it until he felt the door give way under his pressure. But though the door gave way, it was still ajar with only a six-inch opening, since it was still secured at the height of the lock by the chain and pegs. At this unforeseen obstacle, Jacques Ferrand threw himself at the door, ramming against it in a desperate effort to break it down.

With lightning speed, Cecily took the wallet between her teeth, opened the casement window, threw a cloak into the courtyard, and, with an agility that matched her daring, using a knotted rope secured beforehand, she slid from the first floor down into the courtyard as lightly and rapidly as an arrow falling to earth. Then, quickly wrapping herself in the cloak, she ran to the doorkeeper's rooms, opened them, pulled the rope for the carriage entrance, exited into the street, and jumped into a carriage that, from the time Cecily had entered Jacques Ferrand's home, had come every evening, rain or shine, and, by Baron de Graün's order, parked twenty feet from the solicitor's house. This carriage, pulled by two energetic horses, went on its way at a brisk pace. Before Jacques Ferrand realized that Cecily had fled, she had already reached the boulevard.

We will now return to this monster. Through the narrow opening of the door, he could not see the window the Creole had used to prepare and effect her flight. With one last furious blow from his large shoulders, Jacques Ferrand burst the chain that held the door ajar. He threw himself into the room. He found no one there. The knotted rope still swayed from the window's balcony as he leaned over it. Then, on the other side of the courtyard, by moonlight escaping through the clouds the storm had piled up, in the opening of the vaulted entry, he saw that the carriage entrance was open.

Jacques Ferrand figured out all that had happened. He still had one last ray of hope. Strong and determined, he climbed out on the balcony, made use of the rope in his turn to slide down into the courtyard, and then quickly ran out of the house. The street was deserted. He couldn't see anyone. He couldn't hear any sound except, from far away, the rolling wheels of the carriage that was rapidly carrying the Creole away. The solicitor thought it was some carriage that had been delayed and gave it no further thought. And so he didn't have any chance to catch up with Cecily, who carried away with her the evidence of all his crimes!

Coming to this dreadful realization, stricken, Jacques Ferrand collapsed on a boundary stone near his door. He lay there a long time, silent, motionless, petrified. Haggard, his eyes fixed, his teeth clenched, his mouth foaming, he unconsciously dug his fingernails into his chest until he drew blood. He felt himself losing all ability to think, as if he were plunging into a bottomless pit.

When he came out of his stupor, he walked heavily and with an unsteady step. Everything seemed to be in motion, as if he were coming out of a profound intoxication. He slammed the street door closed and came back into the courtyard.

The rain had stopped. The wind continued to blow hard, sweeping heavy gray clouds across the sky. Those clouds veiled the moonlight without blotting it out completely. Slightly calmed by the sharp, cold night air, Jacques Ferrand thought to overcome his internal agitation with brisk movement. So he plunged into the muddy pathways of his garden, walking with rapid, jerky steps. From time to time, he grasped his forehead with his clenched fists.

Walking thus aimlessly, he came to the end of an alley, near a green house that was fallen into ruin. Suddenly, he staggered violently against a pile of freshly dug earth. He bent down, without thinking, and saw some bloodstained linens.

He was standing next to the grave Louise Morel had dug to hide her dead child . . . her child, which was also Jacques Ferrand's. Despite his stony heart, despite the fearful stress he was under, Jacques Ferrand shivered in terror. There was something fateful about this conjunction of events. Even as an avenging justice was about to catch up with his lust, chance had brought him to the grave of his child, the unhappy fruit of his violence—and his lust!

Under any other circumstance, Jacques Ferrand would have stomped across this grave with atrocious indifference. His savage energy was exhausted, however, by the scene we have described. He felt himself in the grip of a sudden weakness and terror. His forehead was bathed in sweat and his trembling knees gave way beneath him. He collapsed, motionless, beside this open tomb.

CHAPTER 15

LA FORCE PRISON

Inexplicable error, unjust error! Cruel error!

—*WOLFGANG*, BOOK II

Because of the space we will give to the following scenes, we may be accused of damaging the unity of our plot with these few episodic descriptions. But we think, especially now when important penitentiary questions that go to the heart of what our society is are about to be, if not resolved (our legislators will never allow that), at least debated, it would be an opportune moment to study the interior of a prison, that terrifying pandemonium, that gloomy thermometer of civilization. In brief, the variety of prisoners from every social class, the family or affective ties that keep them attached to the world from which they are separated by the prison walls, seem to us worthy of interest. We hope we will be excused, thus, for having mixed other secondary figures in with several prisoners who are characters already known by the reader. They are there to give life to certain critical ideas or to put them into relief and thus to complete this initiation into prison life.

And so, let us enter La Force.[185] From the outside, there is nothing dark or sinister in the look of this building that stands on rue du Roi-de-Sicile in the Marais district. In the middle of one of the first courtyards stand a few banks of earth planted with shrubs at the base of which, here and there, the first green shoots of primrose and snowdrop are already starting to grow. An entry stairway, over which hangs a trellis porch knotted with vine branches, leads to one of seven or eight covered walkways intended for the prisoners.

The gigantic buildings surrounding these courtyards look very much like those of a well-maintained military barracks or factory. They have large walls punctuated by high, wide windows through which plenty of crisp, pure air circulates. The tiles and sidewalks of the inner courtyards are kept scrupulously clean. On the ground floor there are large rooms, heated in

185. See Book V, Chapter 13, footnote 127. [TN]

the winter and well aired in the summer, that serve during the day as places for conversation, workshops, and cafeterias for the prisoners.

The upper floors are occupied by immense dormitories, ten or twelve feet high, with clean, gleaming tiles. They are equipped with two rows of iron cots, excellent beds made up of soft, thick straw mattresses, a bolster, very white canvas sheets, and warm woolen blankets.

People are used to thinking of prisons as sad, filthy, unhealthy, dark dens, and so they might be surprised, in spite of themselves, at the sight of these establishments and their hygienic and wholesome conditions. But this is a mistake. What are really sad, filthy, and dark are the hovels where so many poor, honest workers like Morel the gem-cutter languish in exhaustion, forced to abandon their pallets to their ill wives and to leave their gaunt, starving children to shiver in the cold of their foul straw beds, powerless to do anything about it.

And the same contrast exists between the expressions on faces of the inhabitants of these two residences. Constantly preoccupied with the needs of his family, for whom he can just barely provide on a day-to-day basis, watching unbridled competition reduce his salary, the hardworking artisan will always be sad and downcast. There is no period of rest for him, except for a kind of somnolent daze interrupting his endless work. And then, upon awaking from this painful daze, he finds himself once again faced with the same oppressive thoughts about the present, the same anxieties about what tomorrow will bring.

In contrast, the convict is always carefree and cheerful. He is emboldened by vice, indifferent to the past, happy in the life he leads, assured of his future (which he may always guarantee by committing some crime or offense that will return him to prison). He misses his freedom, no doubt, but finds ample compensation in the material well-being he enjoys, and he is certain to take a large sum of money away when he leaves prison, money he has earned by appropriate, moderate labor. Finally, he is respected, which is to say feared, by his companions for his cynicism and perversity.

Indeed, he wants for nothing. Prison offers him reliable shelter, a good bed, good food, high wages,[186] easy work, and, most important, companionship of his choice, people who, as we have said, measure his worth by the greatness of his crimes.

Hardened prisoners, therefore, do not know want, hunger, or cold. And why should they care about the fear they instill in honest people? They don't see or know any honest people. They glory in their crimes, which

186. High wages if one takes into account that, with all his living expenses paid for, a prisoner can make five to ten sous a day. How many workers could save a like amount from their wages? [SN]

give them influence and standing among the criminals in whose company they will henceforth spend their lives. Why would they feel any shame?

Rather than being subjected to serious and charitable remonstrances, which might lead them to feel shame and to repent their past lives, they hear wild applause encouraging theft and murder. No sooner have they entered prison than they are already considering their next crime. And what else, logically, could one expect? If they are caught and arrested yet again, they merely return to the comfort and material well-being prison affords and to their bold, merry companions in crime and debauchery. If, on the contrary, they have been less corrupted than others, if they show the slightest remorse, they are greeted by abominable mockery, infernal hooting, and awful threats.

If, finally—and this is so rare as to be the exception rather than the rule—a prisoner leaves this frightening pandemonium with the firm will to mend his ways, which he does by dint of painstaking labor, courage, patience, and honesty, and if he also manages to hide his scandalous past, then merely meeting one of his old prison companions is enough to dash this whole, painfully erected structure of rehabilitation.

Here is how it happens. If a hardened ex-convict proposes some illegal activity to a repentant ex-convict and the latter, in the face of all dangerous threats, spurns this criminal association, an informant immediately exposes the past life of this unhappy man, whose only wish was to hide it at any price and so to expiate his early transgression by leading an honest life. In this manner, exposed to the contempt or, at the very least, the distrust of those whose good opinion he has won through his work and his integrity, embittered by the injustice of it all, led astray by need, this man will finally give in to his fateful inclinations. Although he is almost rehabilitated, he will tumble once more and forever into the abyss he had climbed out of with such difficulty.

In the following scenes, we will attempt to demonstrate the monstrous and inevitable consequences of imprisoning criminals in communal spaces. After many centuries of the most barbarous experiences and the most pernicious hesitation, we seem finally to have understood how unreasonable it is to immerse people who can be cured only by pure, healthy air into an abominably filthy atmosphere. How many more centuries will it take to recognize that by keeping corrupted beings infected with moral gangrene together, we only multiply the spread of the infection, which hence becomes incurable!

Solitary confinement is the method we must adopt! We will consider ourselves fortunate if our feeble voice, even if no one takes it seriously, is at least heard as yet one more among all those with voices more influential and eloquent than ours who ask, with such just and impatient insistence, for the complete and absolute application of the system of solitary confinement.

We may also hope that perhaps one day society will come to understand that evil is an accidental illness and not an organic condition, that crimes almost always arise from the perversion of our instincts, that our inclinations, which are always essentially good, may be led astray and vitiated by ignorance, selfishness, and social indifference. The health of the soul, like that of the body, is ineluctably subject to the laws of a wholesome and preventive hygiene. God gives us powerful faculties, healthy appetites, and the desire for well-being. It falls to society to balance our competing needs and satisfy them justly. The man who has only his share of strength, goodwill, and health has a right, a sovereign right, to a justly compensated labor that guarantees him not discretionary income, but the necessary amount for staying strong and healthy, active, and able to work. When his condition in life is a happy one, an individual will remain honest and good.

The sinister regions of wretchedness and ignorance are populated by morbid beings with withered souls. Clean out these cesspools by spreading education and the opportunity for work rewarded by equitable and just compensation, and one will immediately see these unhealthy faces and vitiated souls being reborn into goodness, which is the health and life of the soul.

We will now bring our reader to the visiting room of La Force prison. It is a dark room, separated along its length into two equal parts by a narrow fenced-off corridor. One part of the visiting room connects with the interior of the prison; this is where the prisoners enter. The other part connects with the prison office; this is where outsiders who come to visit prisoners enter. The interviews and conversations between prisoners and visitors take place across the double fencing of the visiting room, in the presence of a guard, who stands inside the corridor at one of its ends.

The appearances of the prisoners who came together in the visiting room on this day contrasted with each other in numerous ways. Some wore wretched clothing, others seemed to belong to the working classes, still others to the wealthy bourgeoisie. One saw the same contrasts among the visitors, almost all of whom were women.

Generally, for a strange, fateful reason, the prisoners seem less sad than the visitors. Experience proves that after three or four days in the company of other prisoners, a new detainee has little sorrow or shame left. Even those who are most frightened by this hideous community quickly become used to it. They become infected: surrounded by degraded beings, hearing nothing but the vilest speeches, a wild desire to imitate carries them away, and, either because they want to impress their companions by equaling them in cynicism or because this moral intoxication makes them lose their bearings, the newcomers nearly always show as much depravity and insolent gaiety as the prison's habitués.

So let us return to the visiting room.

Despite the noisy din of the many conversations going on across the corridor in lowered voices, after a little time prisoners and visitors became used to these conditions. They were able to talk among themselves by absolutely refusing to let themselves be distracted for a moment or pay attention to the conversations of their neighbors. This created a kind of secrecy in the middle of the noisy exchange of surrounding conversations, each person being forced to hear his partner by not listening to one word of that which was said around them.

Among all the detainees called to the visiting room, Nicolas Martial was the prisoner seated farthest from the guard. The sullen despondency into which he had fallen when he was arrested had given way to cynical self-assurance. The detestable and contagious influence of his fellow prisoners had already done its work.

Surely, if he had been immediately placed in solitary confinement, this wretch, still in the original throes of dejection, faced with the thought of his crimes, terrified of the punishment that awaited him, would have felt, if not repentance, at least a salutary fear from which nothing would have distracted him. And who knows what good might be accomplished in a guilty person by an incessant, forced meditation on the crimes he had committed and the punishments they would result in? Instead of that, the criminal is thrown among this rabble of scoundrels who consider the least indication of repentance a form of cowardice or, more accurately, a betrayal. In their hardened savagery and mindless suspicions, they thought anyone who looked sad and dejected, who regretted his crimes, who did not share their bold indifference and recoiled from contact with them, must be willing to spy on them.

Thrown among these bandits, as we were saying, Nicolas Martial, who had long known and been told of these prison attitudes, overcame his weakness, wanting to appear worthy of his family name, which was already renowned in the annals of theft and murder. Several old ex-convicts had known his father, who had been executed. Others knew the brother who had been condemned to the galleys. He was thus well received by these veterans of crime and welcomed with their own savage brand of care.

This brotherly welcome from murderer to murderer elated the widow's son. The praise for his family's hereditary perversity bedazzled him. This terrible intoxication soon led him to forget his dire future. His only care for his past crimes was to glorify himself with them and even to exaggerate them further in the eyes of his companions.

Martial's facial expression was thus as insolent as his visitor's was anxious and dismayed. This visitor was Old Micou, the fence and the renter in the house at the passage de la Brasserie where Madame de Fermont and her daughter, victims of Jacques Ferrand's greed, had been obliged to shelter themselves. Old Micou knew only too well the price he could pay for having acquired the fruits of Nicolas's and many other people's thefts so cheaply. With the widow's son in prison, the fence was practically at his mercy since the thief could name him as his usual buyer. Even though this accusation would have little obvious evidence to support it, it was no less dangerous or frightening for Old Micou, who had thus followed to the letter all the orders that Nicolas had sent him through a freed prisoner.

"So, how are things going, Old Micou?" the thief said to him.

"I am at your service, my good man," the fence answered him eagerly. "As soon as I saw the person you sent me, right away I—"

"Now hold on. Why are you speaking to me so hoity-toity?" Nicolas said, interrupting him sardonically. "Do you have contempt for me now that I'm in trouble?"

"No, my boy, I don't have contempt for anybody," the fence said, though he really did not care to make a show of his past familiarity with this wretch.

"Well, then, speak to me like a pal, like you used to, or I'll think you don't like me anymore, and that would really break my heart."

"Sure, great," Old Micou said, sighing. "So I right away took care of all the little errands you gave me."

"Now that's talking, Old Micou. I knew for sure that you wouldn't forget your friends. And what about my tobacco?"

"I left two pounds of it in the prison office, my boy."

"Is it any good?"

"Only the best."

"And the ham hock?"

"I left that there too and four pounds of white bread. And I added a little surprise you didn't expect—a half dozen hard-boiled eggs and a round of Holland cheese."

"Now that's what I call acting like a friend! What about wine?"

"Six bottles of the good stuff, but, as you know, they'll only give you one bottle a day."

"Well, what can you do? I'll have to make do with that."

"I hope you are pleased with me, my boy."

"Sure I am and I will be again, Old Micou, because the ham hock, the cheese, the eggs, and the wine only last as long as it takes to swallow them down. But, like they say, when you don't have any more, there's always some more to be had, thanks to Old Micou, who will bring me more treats if I'm a nice boy."

"What! You expect that—"

"I expect that in two or three days you'll stock me up again with this little bit of provisioning, Old Micou."

"Devil take me if I will. Once was plenty."

"Once was plenty? Get on with you! Ham and wine is good plenty more than once, as you well know."

"That may be, but it's not my responsibility to keep you stocked in treats."

"Now, Old Micou, that's mean, and it's just not right to deny me some ham, me who always kept you supplied with stolen lead."

"Be quiet, you silly fool!" the fence said in fear.

"No, I'll give the beak something to think about. I'll say to him, 'Do you know that Old Micou—'"

"All right! All right!" the fence cried out, seeing with both fear and anger that the wretch was completely willing to take advantage of the power his complicity had given Nicolas over him. "I'll agree to it. I'll restock your provisions when you run out."

"That's fair. That's only fair. Don't forget to get coffee delivered to my mother and Calabash, who are in Saint-Lazare. They like their cup in the morning and they would miss it."

"More! You want to ruin me, you scoundrel?"

"Whatever you like, Old Micou. Let's drop the subject. I'll just ask the beak if—"

"I'll agree to the coffee, too," the fence said, interrupting him. "But the devil take you. I curse the day I met you!"

"Why, my old friend, I feel just the opposite. This moment I'm ecstatic that we know each other. I look up to you as if you were the father who nursed me."

"I hope you have no more demands to make on me," Old Micou said bitterly.

"But I do. You will tell my mother and sister that I was frightened when they arrested me but that I'm not frightened anymore and that now I'm as resolute as the two of them."

"I'll tell them. Is that all?"

"Wait. I forgot to ask you for two pairs of warm wool socks. You wouldn't want me to catch cold, would you?"

"I'd like you to croak!"

"Thank you, Old Micou, maybe some other day. Today I'm more up for something else. I'd like to have a sweet time of it. If they're going to shorten me by a head like they did my father, I'd like to have some joy in life."

"Your life is pretty good right now."

"It's great! Ever since I got here, I've been treated like a king. If they had had them, they would have lit up Chinese lanterns and set off fireworks in my honor once they knew I was the son of the famous Martial who went to the guillotine."

"That's really touching. What a beautiful heritage!"

"Well, really, we've got dukes and marquises. So why shouldn't we have our own aristocracy, we criminals?" the thief said with savage irony.

"Oh, yes, it'll be Mama Guillotine, on the Place du Palais, who'll give you your letters of nobility."

"Well, you can bet it won't be some holy-roller father. All the more reason. In prison you have to be of the aristocracy of high thiefdom to get any respect. Without that, people think you're just a big nothing. You should see what they do with them, the ones who aren't lords among thieves. How they sulk! You know, there's one just like that named Germain. He's a young little nothing who acts like he's disgusted, like he despises us. Well, he'd better watch out for his hide! He's a sly one, and people think he's a stoolie. If that's the case, they'll have his head, just as a way of getting the word out."

"Germain? This young man's named Germain?"

"Yes, do you know him? Is he a thief? Well, then, despite his acting like an idiot—"

"I don't know him. But if he's the Germain I've heard about, his goose is cooked."

"What do you mean?"

"He already just barely escaped falling into the trap that Hairy and the Big Gimp set for him a little while back."

"Why were they after him?"

"I don't know anything about it. They said that in the country he ratted out someone in their mob."[187]

"I knew it. Germain is a stoolie. Well, we know what happens to stoolies. I'll go tell my friends. That'll set them off. Well, now. Is the Big Gimp still playing pranks on your renters?"

"Thank God, that useless beggar is off my back. You'll see him here today or tomorrow."

"Here's to good times! Will we ever laugh it up! He knows how to have fun."

"It's because he'll find Germain here that I told you that that young man's goose is cooked. If he's the same one."

"What did they pick up the Big Gimp for?"

"For a theft he committed with an ex-convict who wanted to work

187. The reader will remember that Germain, who was raised to be a criminal by a friend of his father's, refused to cooperate in a theft that they wanted to commit on a banker in Nantes for whom Germain worked. Instead, he warned his boss of the plot that was being set against him and then went into hiding in Paris. Sometime after that, having met there the wretch whose accomplice he had refused to be in Nantes, Germain, who had been followed by the wretch, had very nearly been the victim of a nighttime ambush. It was to escape these new threats that he had left rue du Temple and kept his new residence a secret. [SN]

and go straight. Much chance of that! The Big Gimp did for him good and proper. He's such a bad one, that beggar. I'm sure it was him that broke into the trunk of those two women who lived at my place in the office on the fourth floor."

"What women? Oh, right, those two women. The younger one got you all hot, you liked her so much, you old dog."

"They won't be getting anyone all hot anymore. By this time, the mother must be dead and the daughter not far behind her. I have two weeks of advance rent from them, but the devil take me if I give a sou toward getting them buried! I've had enough losses, and that's not even counting the little treats you *request* from me for you and your family. That's all I needed at this point. Some luck I've had this year."

"Oh, enough! All you do is complain, Old Micou. You're as rich as Croesus. Come now. Well, I shouldn't keep you any longer."

"That's a good one!"

"So you'll come and tell me what's going on with my mother and Calabash when you bring me more provisions."

"Yes, since I have no choice."

"Oh, I forgot. While you're at it, buy me a new hat, a Scottish velvet one with a tassel. Mine isn't fit to be seen anymore."

"Come on now. Are you kidding me?"

"No, Old Micou, I want a new hat made of Scottish velvet. I have my heart set on it."

"Are you determined to see me sleeping in the streets?"

"Now look, Old Micou, don't get all worked up. Just say yes or no. I'm not going to make you do anything. But . . . well, you know what . . ."

Knowing he was at Nicolas's mercy, the fence got up to leave, not wanting to be subject to any new requests if he prolonged his visit. "You'll get your hat," he said. "But take care—if you ask for anything more, you won't get anything at all. You can do what you want. It'll be as bad for you as for me."

"Calm down, Old Micou, I won't squeeze you any more than I have to to help you keep in shape. But I have to squeeze you a little, 'cause you wouldn't want to lose your figure."

The fence left, shaking his head in anger. The guard led Nicolas back into the prison.

Just as Old Micou left the prisoners' visiting room, Rigolette came in. The guard, who was about forty years old, was a former soldier with a hard, strong face. He was dressed in a shortcoat, a cap, and blue pants. Two silver stars were sewn into the coat's collar and lapel. When he saw the seamstress, this man's face lit up with an expression of benevolent affection. He had always been struck by the grace, the kindness, and the touching goodness with which Rigolette tried to make Germain feel better when she came to visit and have a talk with him in the visiting room.

Germain, for his part, was hardly an ordinary prisoner. His reserve and his gentle, sad mien led the prison's employees to take a real interest in him. They took care not to let that interest show, however, since they feared to make him liable to mistreatment from his hideous companions, who, as we have said, both distrusted and hated him.

It was pouring rain outside, but, thanks to her thick-heeled clogs and her umbrella, Rigolette had bravely gone out in the wind and the rain.

"What a rotten day, my poor little missy!" the guard said in a kindly way. "Only a good person would come out in weather as lousy as this."

"When all you can think of the whole way here is how much pleasure you're going to give some poor prisoner, the weather hardly bothers you at all, monsieur."

"No need to ask who you've come to see."

"I should hope not. And how's my poor Germain doing?"

"Well, you know, my dear little missy, I've seen a lot of prisoners in my time. They're sad for a day, maybe two days, and then, little by little, they get into the daily routine of the place and then those who came here the saddest end up being the most cheerful of them all. But Monsieur Germain isn't like that. He seems to get more and more dejected."

"That's what's getting me down."

"When I'm on duty in the courtyard, I keep an eye on him. He's always alone. I've already told you about that. You have to tell him not to hold himself aloof like that. He has to go out of his way to talk to the others. He'll end up becoming their bugbear. We watch over the courtyards pretty well, but you can stick a knife in someone real quick."

"God, monsieur! Is he in more danger?" Rigolette cried.

"Not exactly. But these criminals see that he isn't like them and they hate him because he looks respectable and proud."

"And yet I've tried to tell him to do what you say, monsieur, and to try to talk to the least rotten of them. But he doesn't have it in him. He can't get over his disgust."

"He's wrong. He's wrong. It's just too easy to start a fight."

"Oh, my God! My God! But can't they keep him apart from the others?"

"For the last two or three days, ever since I realized that they didn't mean well by him, I've advised him to do what we call paying the pistole[188]—in other words, to get a private cell."

"And what happened?"

"There's one thing I didn't think of. A whole row of cells can't be used because of the restoration work they're doing on the prison and the others are all occupied."

"But these awful men could kill him!" Rigolette cried out, her eyes

188. See Book V, Chapter 13, footnote 126. [TN]

filling with tears. "And what if he had any benefactors, monsieur, what could they do for him?"

"Nothing really, except to get for him what prisoners get: a private cell."

"Alas, then he's done for if he's an object of hatred in the prison."

"Calm down, we'll be watching over him closely. But like I said, my dear little missy, you need to tell him to act a little friendlier. It gets easier once you've started."

"I'll try as hard as I can to get that across to him, monsieur. But for a good, honest soul, you know, it's hard to act friendly with people like that."

"You have to choose the lesser of two evils. Well, then, I'll go call for Monsieur Germain. But wait—I have an idea," the guard said, changing his mind. "There are only two more visitors here. Wait until they're gone. No one else is going to come today. It's already two o'clock. I'll send for Monsieur Germain and then you two can talk together more privately. Since you'll be alone, I can even have him brought into the corridor. That way, there'll only be one fence between you instead of two. It's at least something."

"Oh, monsieur, you're too good. I can't thank you enough."

"Shh. If anyone hears you, they'll get jealous. Sit down over there, at the end of the bench. As soon as that man and that woman have left, I'll send for Monsieur Germain." The guard went back to his post in the interior of the corridor. Rigolette went sadly to sit at one end of the visitor's bench.

While the seamstress is awaiting Germain's arrival, we will allow the reader to listen in on each of the conversations, one after the other, of the prisoners who were still in the visiting room after Nicolas Martial left.

BOOK VIII

CHAPTER I

BITTERS

The prisoner next to Fishhook was about forty-five years old. He was small and spindly, but he had a sharp, intelligent, cheerful, ironic look to him. He had an enormous, nearly toothless mouth. As soon as he started talking, he looked left and right in a manner common to people in the habit of addressing large groups in public squares. He had a pug nose. His head was disproportionately large and almost completely bald. He had on an old gray knit vest and pants of an indeterminate color, which had holes and patches in numerous places. He wore wooden shoes over bare feet that were red with cold and half covered in old rags.

This man, whose name was Fortuné Gobert, was known as Bitters. He was an old master of the shell game, a convict released on parole after a sentence for counterfeiting. Now he was accused of having violated his parole, and of burglary and breaking and entering.

Locked up in La Force only a few days earlier, Bitters had already become the recognized storyteller, and he filled the role to the entire satisfaction of his prison companions. Today, such storytellers are quite rare. But in the past, every prison barracks had an official storyteller to whom they all gave small contributions. His improvised tales made the interminable winter nights—prisoners had to go to bed at nightfall—seem shorter. If this need for fictions, for moving stories, strikes us as curious, it should still give food for thought to serious thinkers. These people who are corrupt right down to the marrow of their bones, these thieves and murderers, display an especially marked preference for stories containing elevated, heroic sentiments, stories in which the weak and the good are avenged for the terrible oppression they undergo. It's just the same with fallen women. They are singularly given to the reading of naive, touching, sentimental novels and will always spurn any readings that are obscene. What could explain how these intellectual sympathies and aversions we have just described can be so common among these unhappy people, except for their natural instinct for goodness, joined with the need to escape, at least in their imaginations, anything that reminds them of the degraded conditions in which they live?

Bitters had a real talent for these kinds of heroic stories in which the weak, after endless trials, finally triumph over their persecutors. He was endowed, in addition, with a great wealth of irony, as well as sardonic and witty repartee, and it was this that had won him his nickname.

He had just come into the visiting room. Facing him was a woman who was about thirty-five years old. Her face was pale, sweet, and touching. Her dress was poor but clean. She was crying bitterly, holding her handkerchief in front of her eyes. Bitters looked at her with a mixture of impatience and affection. "Now, see here, Jeanne," he said to her. "Don't act like a child. We haven't seen each other for sixteen years. If you keep your handkerchief over your eyes, we'll never be able to recognize each other."

"My brother, my poor Fortuné, I can't catch my breath. I can't speak."

"Stop being silly. Why are you crying like this?"

His sister, because that is what she was, stopped sobbing, wiped her eyes, looked at him as if dazed, and said, "Why am I crying like this? How can you say that? You've already spent fifteen years in prison and now here I find you there again!"

"It's true. It's just six months ago today that I got out of the center at Melun. I didn't come to see you in Paris because the capital was off-limits to me."

"And now they've already got hold of you again! God, what did you do this time? Why did you leave Beaugency, where they were keeping you under watch?"

"Why? It would be better to ask why I ever went there."

"You're right about that."

"First of all, my poor Jeanne, since we've got these fences between us, let's pretend that I've hugged and kissed you like you're supposed to do when you see your sister after an eternity apart. Now, let's talk: one of the prisoners at Melun, who was called the Big Gimp, told me that he knew an ex-prisoner of the galleys at Beaugency. This man employed paroled prisoners in a factory that made white lead. Do you know what it's like to make white lead?"

"No, brother."

"It's a really great job. After a month or two on the job, you get painter's colic. One out of three cases croaks from it. Well, actually, to be accurate, the other two will also croak. But they'll do it more at their leisure. They'll take some time, they'll go easy on themselves, and it will take about a year, eighteen months at the most. Because of that, it's a job that's less badly paid than most others. And there are some people who are born to it who don't get ill for two or three years. But those are the old men, the grandfathers of white lead makers. It's true you die of it, but at least you don't get tired out."[189]

---

189. White lead was prized for its opaque qualities and was used in making white paint and a kind of makeup face powder called Venetian ceruse. It is highly toxic, causing lead poisoning, and is now mostly banned. [TN]

"Oh, my poor Fortuné, why did you choose a job that's so dangerous that you die from it?"

"What do you want me to do for a living? When they sent me to Melun because of that counterfeiting job, I had been playing the shell game. Well, in prison they don't have workshops for that job, and since I was as weak as a baby, they put me to work making children's toys. There was a Paris manufacturer who found it cheaper to have prisoners make his puppets, wooden trumpets, sabers, and the like. Wooden sabers—you can say that again! I cut out, sharpened, and shaped those things for fifteen years! I bet I made enough to arm all the kids in a whole neighborhood of Paris. But I really worked away at wooden trumpets. And the rattles, I tell you! I pride myself that with two of those instruments you could make a whole battalion grind their teeth. So when I got out of prison, here I was, a past master at making wooden trumpets for two sous. They let me choose where to live from three or four villages that were forty leagues from Paris. My only resource was my skill at making children's toys. So even if it had been the case that everyone who lived in a village, from the littlest kid to the oldest codger, was just mad to go *tootlelootleloo* on my trumpets, it still would have been no easy thing to make a living. But I could hardly have tried to sell a whole village on blowing on trumpets from morning till night. They would have thought I was up to something."

"God, everything's a joke with you."

"Better to laugh at it than cry about it. So, in the end, seeing as playing the shell game forty leagues from Paris wouldn't get me any more than my trumpets, I made my request to go to Beaugency and go to work making white lead. That's one pastry shop that gives you indigestion fit for a miserere.[190] But up until you croak from it, it's a living. That's always something. I'd rather do that than be a thief. I'm not strong enough or brave enough to steal and it's pure chance that I did the thing I'll tell you about in a minute."

"Even if you were brave and strong, your conscience still would never have let you steal."

"Really! You think so?"

"Yes, I do. You're not bad deep down. You were dragged, almost forced, into that rotten counterfeiting business, as you well know."

"Yes, my girl. But you know, fifteen years in the big house, that blackens you up like the inside of this pipe, and that's true even if you went to jail as white as a new pipe. When I left Melun, I thought I was too much a coward to be a thief."

"But you were brave enough to take up a job that was deadly. Really,

190. A Latin prayer for mercy frequently set to music. [TN]

Fortuné, I tell you, you always want to make yourself out to be worse than you are."

"I don't know what I was thinking, but you see, I always figured, shrimp that I am, the devil take me if I know why, I'd just thumb my nose at painter's colic, that there wouldn't be enough meat on me for it to make it worthwhile for the illness and it would look elsewhere. I thought I'd end up like one of the old men white lead makers. When I left prison, I began eating into my money pile, fattened up as it was by my telling stories at night in the sleeping barracks."

"Like the ones you used to tell us in the old days, brother. You remember how much that kept our poor mother entertained?"

"My Lord! That good old woman! She never suspected for a moment, before she died, that I was at Melun."

"Right up to the last moment, she always thought you had gone off to the islands."

"Well, what could I do, my girl? All my foolery was my father's fault. He raised me to be a clown, to help him when he was cheating at the shell game, to be a rope swallower and a fire-eater. So that meant I didn't have the time to rub elbows with the children of the aristocracy and I made some bad acquaintances. But, to get back to Beaugency, once I got out of Melun, I ate up my savings for real. After fifteen years in the pen, you have to give yourself some breathing room, to liven things up a little. That was even more true because, even though I wasn't given to overeating, white lead could give me fatal indigestion. So, in short, I got to Beaugency without a penny to my name. I asked for Hairy, the Big Gimp's friend and the owner of the factory. At your service! There was no more white lead factory than would fit in the palm of your hand. Eleven people had died that year and the ex–galley slave had closed up shop. So there I am in the middle of this village with my trumpet-making as my only calling and my parole papers as my only recommendation. I asked for work suited to my abilities, and, as I had no abilities, well, you can guess what people said: "thief" here, "beggar" there, "jailbird!" In short, as soon as I showed up anywhere, people started checking their pockets for their wallets. I couldn't stop myself from starving to death in a hole like that, and I wasn't supposed to leave it for five years. Seeing that's how it was, I broke my parole and came to Paris to put my talents to work. Since I didn't have a coach and four, I came begging as best I could all the way, staying away from the police like a dog stays away from a club. I was lucky. I got just to Auteuil without any difficulty. I was exhausted, hungry as the devil, dressed as you see me, hardly in high fashion." Bitters gave a mocking glance at his rags. "I didn't have a penny on me. I could have been arrested for vagrancy. Well, Lord, the opportunity arose, the devil tempted me, and despite my cowardice—"

"Enough, brother, that's enough," his sister said, fearing that the guard, even though he was fairly far away from Bitters at the moment, might hear this dangerous admission.

"Are you afraid someone's listening?" he said. "Don't worry, I'm not hiding anything. I was caught red-handed and there was no way of denying it. I confessed everything. I know what my future holds. My goose is cooked."

"My God!" the poor woman said, weeping. "You talk about it so calmly!"

"If I got all worked up about it, what good would it do me? Now look, Jeanne, don't cry. Really, am I the one who has to comfort you, instead of the other way around?" Jeanne wiped away her tears and sighed. "So to get back to what happened to me. I had arrived at Auteuil at twilight. I was exhausted. And I didn't want to enter Paris except during the night. I sat down behind a hedge to rest and consider what I should do next. Thinking so hard ended up putting me to sleep. The sound of a voice woke me up. It was the dark of night. I listened. It was a man and a woman talking on the road on the other side of the hedge. The man was saying to the woman, 'Who do you expect to rob us? Haven't we left the house with no one there a hundred times?' 'Yes,' the woman says, 'but we didn't have a hundred francs in our dresser.' 'But who knows about it, you little fool?' says the husband. 'You're right,' says the wife, and they get going. Well, Lord, that was too good to pass up. There wasn't any risk at all. Before I come out from behind my hedge, I wait for the man and the woman to move a little farther along. I look around and twenty feet from me I see a little peasants' house. That had to be the house with the hundred francs. This was the only shack on the road and Auteuil was five hundred feet farther on. So I say to myself, 'Be brave, old friend. There's no one here, it's night, and if there's no watchdog (I've always been afraid of dogs, you know), this is in the bag.' I was lucky and there wasn't any dog. Just to be sure, I hammer on the door. Nothing. That made me feel better about it. The shutters on the ground floor were closed. I get my cane between the two panels and force them open. I come in through the window into a room. There was still a little fire in the fireplace and that gives me some light. I see a dresser without any key in the lock. I take the fire tongs and force open the drawers. There, under some linen, I find the dough wrapped up in an old wool sock. I don't waste time taking anything else. I jump out the window and fall down . . . guess where? You'll never believe it!"

"Well, God, tell me already!"

"Square onto the back of the local policeman, who was coming back to the village."

"What terrible luck!"

"The moon was up. He sees me leave by the window. He grabs me. It was one of those guys who could eat ten of me for breakfast. I'm too much a coward to resist, so I give in. I was still holding the sock in my hand. He can hear the coins jingling, so he takes it all, puts it into his shoulder bag, and makes me follow him to Auteuil. We come to the town hall followed by street children and policemen. They send some people to wait for the owners at their place. They file charges. There's no way I can deny anything. I confess it all, I sign the statement, they put me in handcuffs, and off we go."

"And here you are back in prison, and maybe for a long time."

"Listen, Jeanne, I don't want to deceive you, my girl. Best to tell you everything straight out."

"God, what more!"

"Come on, buck up!"

"But tell me already!"

"It's not a matter of prison anymore."

"What does that mean?"

"Being it's a second offense, and it's burglary of an occupied house, the lawyer said to me, 'This is all cut-and-dried.' I'm in for fifteen or twenty years in the galleys, and public exposure to top it off."

"The galleys! But you're so weak it will kill you!" the unhappy woman cried, breaking into sobs.

"And if I had signed up to be a white lead worker?"

"But the galleys, my God! The galleys!"

"It's prison out of doors, with a red smock rather than a brown one. And besides, I've always wanted to see the ocean. What an idle Parisian gawker I'll make, huh?"

"But exposure, that's awful. To be held up to the whole world's scorn. Oh, God! God! My poor brother!" And the unfortunate woman started weeping again.

"Come now, Jeanne, don't cry. It's a bad time, but then there's an end to it. And besides, I think you get to sit down. And then, I'm used to seeing crowds, right? When I played the shell game, I always had tons of people around me. I'll pretend that I'm doing my tricks and if that's too much for me I'll close my eyes and it will be exactly the same as if nobody could see me." This unfortunate man did not speak so cynically to make a show of criminal indifference, but because he wanted to comfort and reassure his sister by seeming not to care.

For someone used to the ways of prisons, and who thus no longer feels any shame, the galleys really are only a change of place and, as Bitters said with frightening accuracy, a change of prison smocks. Many prisoners even prefer the galleys because of the raucous atmosphere there, and they often try to commit murder to get sent to Brest or Toulon. And it's easy enough to understand, given that the work they did before they were sent to the galleys was almost as hard, depending on their jobs. The life of the most honest dockworker isn't any less demanding than that of galley slaves. They keep the same hours at their places of work. The pallets on which they rest their bodies, almost broken with fatigue, are frequently no better than those of the galley slaves.

"But," you say, "at least they're free!"

Yes they have one day of freedom—Sunday. And Sunday is also a day of rest for the galley slaves.

"But," you say, "what about the shame, what about the stigma?"

What does that mean? What's shame or stigma for these wretches who every day roast their souls in that hellish oven, who take every degree of infamy available in that school of mutual instruction[191] in damnation where the worst criminals are the most decorated? Such are the consequences of our current penal system: prison is sought after, and the galleys are often requested.

"Twenty years in the galleys, my God! My God!" Bitters's poor sister kept repeating.

"Don't feel too bad, Jeanne. They'll only give me work I'm fit for. I'm too weak for them to put me at hard labor. If there aren't workshops making wooden swords and trumpets like at Melun, they'll give me some easy labor like putting me to work in the infirmary. I'm not recalcitrant, I'm a good boy. I'll tell stories like the ones I tell here. I'll make the bosses fall in love with me and my comrades think well of me. And then I'll send you carved-up coconuts and straw baskets for my nephews and nieces. After all, I made my bed, so now I have to sleep in it."

"If you had only written to tell me you were coming to Paris, I would have tried to hide you, to give you a place to live until you could find work."

"Lord! I sure meant to come to your place, but I preferred not to come empty-handed. Besides, by the way you're dressed, I can see that you aren't driving around in carriages, either. Now, then: what about your husband and children?"

"Don't talk to me about my husband."

"Still the party animal! It's too bad, because, all the same, he was a good worker."

"He's no good to me. I had enough troubles before the ones you've brought me now."

"What do you mean? What about your husband?"

"He left me three years ago, after having sold all our household goods, leaving me and my children nothing but a straw mattress for furniture."

"You never told me that!"

"What good would it have done? It would have just made you feel bad."

---

191. Sue refers to monitorial schools. These were introduced by Joseph Lancaster in the beginning of the nineteenth century. As the name indicates, they entailed the instruction of younger students by older ones. [TN]

"Poor Jeanne! And how have you managed, all alone with three children?"

"Lord, I've had my share of troubles. I worked at my job as a fringe-maker as much as I could. The neighbors helped me some, watching over the children when I was out. And then, me, who's never been lucky a day in her life, I had a stroke of luck for the only time in my life, but I didn't get anything from it because of my husband."

"How did it happen?"

"My boss the furniture manufacturer had told one of his clients about my troubles, telling him how my husband had left me penniless, having sold our household goods, and how, despite that, I worked as hard as I could to raise my children. One day, when I got back home, what do you think I found? The place was completely furnished with new stuff, a good bed, furniture, linens. My boss's client had done it as an act of charity."

"Bravo for the client! Poor sister! But now I ask you, why the devil didn't you write me to tell me about your problems? Instead of spending all my savings, I could have sent you money!"

"I'm free and you're a prisoner, and I'm supposed to ask you for things?"

"Yes, you are. I was given food, clothing, and shelter, all on the government's tab. All the money I made was on top of that. Since I knew my brother-in-law was a hard worker and that you were a hard worker and a good housekeeper, I didn't worry about you, and so I used up all my savings, mouth open, eyes shut."

"It's true, my husband was a good worker. But he went away. In any case, finally, thanks to this unexpected help, I recovered my good spirits. My eldest daughter began to make some money. Except for the pain of knowing you were in Melun, we were happy. Work was going along fine. The children were decently dressed and they didn't want for hardly anything. That made me feel human again. It made me feel human! And then I had almost managed to save thirty-five francs, when all of a sudden my husband came back. I hadn't seen him for over a year. When he saw we were well housed and in decent clothing, he didn't blink an eye before he took all my money, moved himself in with us, stopped working, got drunk every day, and beat me when I complained."

"The louse!"

"And that isn't all. He kept an evil woman he was living with in a small room where we were staying. So I had to put up with that for a second time. Little by little, he started selling my furniture. Seeing how this was going to turn out, I went to a lawyer who lived in the same house to ask him what I needed to do to keep my husband from putting me and the children out in the streets."

"Well, that's easy enough. You just had to kick your husband out."

"Yes, but I didn't have the right to do that. The lawyer told me that my husband had rights to everything as if he owned the place and that he could move himself into the house and not do a lick of work. He said it was too bad but there was nothing I could do about it. He said that the fact of his mistress living under our roof gave me the right to request a legal separation and division of property, as he called it. And my case was that much stronger because I had witnesses who could say my husband beat me. He said I could bring suit against him, but that it would cost me, at the very least, four or five hundred francs to get my separation. Well, you know what that means! That's almost as much as I make in a whole year! Where could I borrow that kind of money? And if you borrow, you have to pay it back. Five hundred francs at one fell swoop, it's a fortune."

"Still and all, there's an easy enough way to pile up five hundred francs," Bitters said acerbically. "All you have to do is put your stomach on furlough, live off fresh air, and work all the same. I can't believe the lawyer didn't tell you to try that."

"You make everything a joke."

"Not this time, I don't!" Bitters exclaimed indignantly. "Because, really, it's scandalous that the law is too expensive for poor people. After all, there you are, a good, honest mother of a family, working as hard as you can to raise your children right. Your husband is a complete scoundrel. He beats you, deceives you, steals everything, and spends everything you make in the taverns. So you ask the law to protect you and keep you, your earnings, and your children out of the clutches of this good-for-nothing. And the forces of the law say, 'Yes, you're right. Your husband is a bad character. We'll give you the protection of the law. But that protection will cost you five hundred francs.' Five hundred francs! That's what it costs you and your family to live for a whole year. Really, you know, Jeanne, it's like the proverb says: 'There are two kinds of people: those who hang and those who deserve to hang.'"

Rigolette was sitting alone and thoughtful. Because she didn't have anyone she was talking to or listening to, she heard every single word of what this poor woman confided to her brother. And she was deeply touched by her misfortunes. She promised herself that she would tell Rodolphe about this unfortunate woman as soon as she saw him again, not doubting for a moment that he would come to her aid.

CHAPTER 2

A COMPARISON

Rigolette, who took great interest in the sad fate of Bitters's sister, was keeping her eye on her and trying to get closer to her when a new visitor unfortunately came into the visiting room; this visitor then asked to see one of the prisoners and sat on the bench between Jeanne and the seamstress. Upon seeing this man, Rigolette could not repress a start of surprise, even of fear. She recognized him as one of the two bailiffs who had come to arrest Morel, thus executing the order Jacques Ferrand had obtained for the gem-cutter's detention. This connection recalled to Rigolette Germain's stubborn persecutor and so made her feel sad all over again. She had been momentarily distracted from her sorrows by the touching and painful story Bitters's sister had told him. The seamstress got as far away from this new visitor as she could. She leaned against the wall and fell back into her own painful thoughts.

"You know, Jeanne," Bitters went on, his good-humored and mocking expression having suddenly become somber, "maybe I'm weak and cowardly, but if I had been there when your husband was making your life miserable that way, things might not have gone so well between us. But you were also much too nice about it yourself."

"What would you have had me do? I just had to put up with it since I couldn't do anything about it. As long as there was anything he could sell, my husband sold it to get money to go to the tavern with his mistress—anything, including my little daughter's Sunday dress."

"But why did you give him the money from your day's work? Why didn't you hide it?"

"I did hide it, but he beat me so much that I had to give it to him. I didn't really give in to him so much because of the beatings themselves. But I thought, 'Ultimately, if he hurts me badly enough, if he breaks my arm, say, and I can't work for a long time, what will become of us then? Who will feed and take care of the children? They might die of hunger if I had to go to a hospital.' So you can see for yourself, my brother, why I thought it best to give my husband the money. I tried to avoid being too badly beaten so I could keep on working."

"You poor woman! People talk about martyrs; you really were a martyr!"

"All the same, I never did anybody any harm. All I asked for was a job and to be able to take care of my husband and children. But what can you do? Some people are happy, some aren't, the same way some people are good and some are wicked."

"Yes, and doesn't it always get you how the good ones are always happy! But did you finally get rid of that beggar of a husband of yours?"

"I sure hope so, because he didn't leave finally until he'd sold my bedstead and my little children's cradle. But what really gets me is that he wanted to do worse yet."

"What, more?"

"When I say him, I really mean that rotten woman, who egged him on. That's why I'm telling you about all this. One day he said to me, 'When you've got a pretty fifteen-year-old girl in the house, like we do, you'd be a fool not to make money off her beauty.'"

"Oh, great! Now I get it. First he wants to sell the clothes off your backs, and then he wants to sell your bodies!"

"When he said that, I tell you, Fortuné, my heart stopped for a moment and then I really let him have it. And to be fair, he went red with shame from what I said. And when that awful woman decided to get mixed up in our quarrel, arguing that my husband could do anything he wanted to with his daughter, I treated that wretch so badly that my husband beat me. I haven't seen any more of them after that business."

"I tell you, Jeanne, I know men condemned to ten years in prison who've done less than your husband. At least they only strip the bones of strangers. He's one rotten scoundrel!"

"He wasn't so bad, really, you know. He got into bad company in the taverns and that got him off on the wrong track."

"Yes, he wouldn't hurt a child. But once they're grown up, that's different."

"Well, really, what do you expect? You've got to take what God gives you. At least with my husband gone, I didn't have to be afraid that when he beat me he might accidentally cripple me. So I took heart again. But I need money to buy back a mattress. You need to make a living and pay your way, and, between the two of us, my poor Catherine and me, we can hardly make forty sous a day, my two other children are too little to make anything yet, and we need a mattress. We're sleeping on a straw mat with straw we pick up from around the door of a packer who lives on our street."

"And I blew all my savings! I blew all my savings!"

"You couldn't help it. There was no way you could've known since I didn't tell you anything. Finally, we got back to work harder than ever, me and Catherine. That poor girl, if you knew how honest, hardworking, and good she is! She always has her eyes on me to figure out what I want her to do. She never complains one bit, even though she's already seen her share of misery, and she isn't even fifteen years old! You know, Fortuné, having a daughter like that, it really makes up for a lot."

"She's just like you, as far as I can tell. Someone like her is the least you deserved."

"I swear to you, really, that I feel much sorrier for her than I do for myself. Because it goes without saying, you know, that she hasn't stopped working a single moment for the last two months. Once a week, she gets out to wash the few shreds of clothing my husband left us at three sous an hour by the ships at the Pont au Change. The rest of the time, she's chained up inside like a dog. She is really too young to know such misery. I know well enough that it always comes sooner or later. But she could have at least had a year or two of ease. It also really made me sad, you know, Fortuné, that all this meant that I could hardly help you at all. But I'll try."

"Come now. Do you think I would have accepted your help? On the contrary, I've been asking for one sou from everyone I told my nonsense stories to. I'll ask for two sous or they can do without Bitters's stories. And that will provide you with a little extra for your housekeeping. But, now that I think about it, why don't you rent a furnished apartment? That way, your husband couldn't sell anything."

"A furnished apartment? Think about it. For the four of us, that would cost at least twenty sous a day. What would we have left to live on? Right now our room only costs us fifty sous a year."

"Go on, then, that's right, my girl," Bitters said, with bitter irony. "Work, wear yourself out, buy a few things again for your household. Then, as soon as you have a little something again, your husband will steal everything from you all over again. Then, one fine day, he'll sell your daughter just the way he sold your old clothes."

"Oh, no, that'll be over my dead body. My poor Catherine!"

"He'll sell your poor Catherine and it won't have to be over your dead body. He's your husband, isn't he? He's the boss of the place, like your lawyer told you, just as long as you're not legally separated. And you don't have five hundred francs to spare for that, so you'll just have to put up with it. Your husband has the right to take his daughter away from you and bring her anywhere he wants. Once he and his mistress really take it into their heads to ruin that poor child, it's just going to happen."

"God! God! But if such despicable things are possible . . . isn't there any justice?"

"Justice!" Bitters said, with a burst of sardonic laughter. "It's like meat—too expensive for poor people to eat. Unless, you know, it's a matter of sending them to Melun, putting them in a chain gang, or throwing them into the galleys. That's another matter. Justice does that for you, no charge. Cutting your head off, that's also on the house. Always for free. Come on up and take a ticket," Bitters added in his carnival barker's voice. "They don't cost ten sous or two sous or one sou. Not even one single centime. No, ladies and gentlemen, it costs only the little trifle of nothing at all. Everyone can afford it! All you need is to give them your head. The blade and the slicing, they're both at the government's expense. Now there's free justice. But the justice that would prevent an honest mother of a family from being beaten and robbed blind by a beggar of a husband, a husband who means to make money by selling his daughter and certainly will do so, that justice costs five hundred francs. And you're going to have to do without it, my poor Jeanne."

"Please, Fortuné," the unhappy mother said as she broke into tears, "you're breaking my heart."

"That's because, when I think about what's in store for you and your family, and that I can't do anything about it, my heart breaks, too. I always seem to be laughing, but don't make any mistake. There are two kinds of funny: happy funny and sad funny. I'm not strong enough or brave enough to be wicked, angry, or hateful, like the others here. With me that comes out in more or less joking speeches. My bodily cowardice and weakness have kept me from being worse than I am. It took the chance of that isolated shack, without even a dog or cat, to get me to the point of stealing. And it had to be a night with bright moonlight, because alone on a dark night, I'm afraid of anything that peeps."

"That's why I always say you're better than you think, my poor Fortuné. And that's why I hope the judges will take some pity on you."

"Pity on me? A repeat offender on parole? Don't count on it! And besides, I don't hold it against them. Whether I'm here or somewhere else, it's all the same to me. And also, you're right—I'm not wicked. And I hate those who are wicked and I show it, in my own way, by making fun of them. I'm always telling all those stories in which, to make my audience happy, I make things turn out so that those who persecute people out of pure cruelty end up getting a really terrible beating and the result is that I'm getting used to feeling the way my stories are supposed to make you want to feel."

"The people you're with, they like stories like that, my poor brother? I would never have believed it."

"Hang on! If I told them stories where some fellow who stole or killed people in the course of stealing was squished in the end, they wouldn't let me finish it. But if it's about a woman or a child or maybe, for instance, some poor devil like me who gets stomped down and trampled and who some bad guy in a black hat pursues and persecutes beyond all measure, just for the pleasure of persecuting him? Oh, then they stamp their feet with joy when in the end black hat gets what's coming to him. So you know, I have this story called 'The Runt and Chops-Him-in-Two' that was the delight of Melun prison that I haven't told yet here. I promised it for tonight, but they're going to have to fill up my piggy bank for real, and you'll get the money. And furthermore, I'll write it down for your children. They'll like 'The Runt and Chops-Him-in-Two.' Even a nun could read that story, so you have nothing to worry about."

"You know, one thing that makes me feel a little better, my poor Fortuné, is that I can see, thanks to your good attitude, that you aren't as wretched as the rest of them."

"Well, it's sure true that if I acted like one of the prisoners in our sleeping barracks I'd be shooting myself in the foot. Poor kid! I'm really afraid that, before the day is out, they're going to get him one way or the other. Things are really heating up for him. There's something rotten being planned for him tonight."

"Oh, my God! They're going to hurt him? Don't get mixed up in that, all right, Fortuné?"

"I'm not as dumb as all that! I'd just get in trouble from it. It's just that, by coming and going, I heard one person jabbering to another. They were going to gag him to stop him from making any noise. And then, to stop anyone from seeing what was happening, they meant to make a circle around him, acting as if they were listening to one of them who would act like he was reading a newspaper or something out loud."

"But why do they want to do him harm?"

"Well, he always keeps to himself, he doesn't talk to anyone, and he acts as if they all disgust him, so they think he's a police informer, which is really stupid, because, on the contrary, you have to slither in everywhere to be an informer. But what matters in the end is that he acts all respectable and that offends them. It's the captain of the sleeping barracks, the one called the Walking Skeleton, who is leading the plot against him. But he's a skeleton that has no heart, either, the way he goes after poor Germain. Germain, that's the name of the guy they hate so much. Honestly, they'll have to sort it out on their own. There's nothing I can do about it. But you see, Jeanne, that's what acting sad gets you in prison. All of a sudden they suspect you of something. And that's why no one has ever suspected me of anything. But that's enough talking, my girl. Go home and see if I'm right about things. Coming here is costing you time. Me, I don't have anything to do except chitchat. But for you, it's different. So, good-bye already. Come back once in a while; you know how I'll like that."

"Just a few more minutes, brother, please."

"No, no, your children need you. Come to think of it, I hope you haven't told them that their old uncle has taken rooms here?"

"They think you're in the islands, like our mother used to. That way, I can talk to them about you."

"That's great. But come on now, you have to get out of here."

"Yes, but listen, my poor brother. I don't have much, but I can't leave you here like this. You must be cold all the time with no socks and that worn-out vest. Catherine and I will get some rags together. Lord, Fortuné, you know it's not that we don't want to do things for you."

"Do what? Do what? Make some rags? But I have suitcases full of them. As soon as they get here, I'll be able to dress like a prince. Oh, come on, laugh a little. No? Well, seriously, my girl, I wouldn't say no while I'm waiting for the Runt and Chops-Him-in-Two to fill up my piggy bank. Then I'll give you all that money. So good-bye, dear Jeanne. The next time you come, if I can't make you laugh, they can stop calling me Bitters. But get out of here already. I've kept you too long."

"But listen to me for a moment, brother!"

"My man. Hey, my man!" Bitters called out to the guard, who was at the other end of the corridor. "We've finished talking and I'm ready to go back in. Enough talking."

"Oh, Fortuné, it's not nice to send me away like this," Jeanne said.

"On the contrary, it's very nice. So go on, good-bye, good luck, and tomorrow morning tell your children that you had a dream about their uncle in the islands and that he asked you to kiss them for him. Good-bye."

"Good-bye," the poor woman said, breaking down in tears as she saw her brother go back into the interior of the prison.

Although from the time the bailiff had sat down beside her, Rigolette had not been able to hear Bitters and Jeanne's conversation, she had nevertheless not taken her eyes off Jeanne. She was hoping to come up with a way to procure her address because she wanted to recommend her to Rodolphe's benevolence, as she had first thought to do. When Jeanne got up to leave the visiting room, the seamstress went over to her and said, timidly, "Madame, just a moment ago, without meaning to listen in on you, I overheard you saying that you made fringe and trimmings."

"Yes, mademoiselle," Jeanne said, a little surprised but well disposed to Rigolette because of her gracious manner and charming face.

"I'm a dressmaker," the seamstress said. "Now that fringe and trimmings are all the rage, I sometimes have customers who ask me for ornaments to their dresses made especially to their taste. I thought it might be less expensive to come to an arrangement with you since you work out of your home than with some merchant. I also thought I might be able to give you more business than your manufacturer does."

"Well, it's true, mademoiselle. Relieving me of the need to buy the silk first would be a slight advantage for me. You're very good to think of me. I can't get over it."

"Listen, madame, I'll be frank with you. I'm waiting for the person I came to see. Before that gentleman sat between us, I didn't have anyone to talk to and so, not meaning to listen, I swear, I heard you telling your brother about your troubles and your children. I said to myself, 'Poor people have to stick together and help each other.' So I thought, given that you were a fringemaker, I could do you a good turn. So, if what I'm suggesting really suits you, here's my address. If you give me yours, when I have a little business to turn your way, I'll know where to find you." And Rigolette gave one of her cards to Bitters's sister.

The latter, deeply touched by what the seamstress had done, said to her effusively, "Your face didn't deceive me, mademoiselle. And then—not to boast about it—you bear a striking resemblance to my eldest daughter, which is why, when I came in here, I was looking you over so much. I thank you very much. If you give me work, you will be happy with my workmanship; it will be done with great care. My name is Jeanne Duport and I live at number one rue de la Barillerie."

"Number one. That shouldn't be hard to remember. Thank you, madame."

"No, thank you, my dear young lady—it was so good of you to have thought of doing me a good turn. Once again, I can't get over it."

"But, really, it's not that hard to understand, Madame Duport," Rigolette said with a charming smile. "Since I bear a striking resemblance to your daughter Catherine, you shouldn't be surprised by what you call my goodness."

"My dear young lady, aren't you nice! You know, thanks to you, I'll be leaving here a little less troubled than I would have believed possible. And maybe we'll see each other again sometime, since you're visiting a prisoner here, like I am."

"Yes, madame," Rigolette said, sighing.

"Well, then, until we meet again, or at least I hope so, Mademoiselle . . . Rigolette," Jeanne Duport said, after she cast a glance at the seamstress's address.

"Until we meet again, Madame Duport."

Going back to sit on the bench, Rigolette thought, "At least now I know this poor woman's address. Surely Monsieur Rodolphe will take an interest in her when he learns how unhappy she is, because he's always said to me, 'If you know anyone who is worthy of our pity, tell me about it.'" And, going back to her seat, Rigolette waited impatiently for the end of her neighbor's conversation so she could have the guards call for Germain.

And now we have a few things to say about the scene we have just described.

Unfortunately, it cannot be denied that the indignation of Jeanne Duport's wretched brother was absolutely justified. Yes; when he said that justice was too expensive for poor people, he was speaking the truth. Bringing suits before the courts entails enormous costs, costs that are well beyond the means of workers, who can barely live from day to day on their inadequate salaries. If a mother or father of a family belonging to this class of people wanted, in fact, to obtain a legal separation, and if they had every right to one, would they obtain it? No, they would not. There is not a worker in the world who is in a position to lay out four or five hundred francs to meet the demanding requirements for securing such a judgment.

And yet the poor have no life beyond their domestic condition. For the head of a working household, good or bad conduct isn't only a moral question. It is a question of BREAD. Isn't the situation of a woman of the people, one such as we have just tried to depict, as worthy of our care and our protection as is that of a rich woman who suffers from her husband's bad conduct or infidelities? It cannot be denied that the sufferings of the soul are as worthy of our pity as anything can be. But when in the case of an unfortunate mother these sufferings are combined with the poverty of her children, isn't it monstrous that this woman's poverty places her outside the law and delivers her over, along with her family, defenseless, to the odious treatment of her corrupt, good-for-nothing husband? And such monstrous events take place regularly.

And an ex-convict could, with considerable justice and logic, deny the impartiality of the institutions that have condemned him with respect to this situation as well as others. Need it be said that it is dangerous for society to have to justify itself against such accusations? What power, what moral authority could laws have if we knew their application to be absolutely dependent on questions of money? Must not civil justice, just like criminal justice, be available to everybody? When people are too poor to call upon the benefits of a law designed to preserve and protect, ought not society, at its own cost, ensure its application, out of respect for the law and the tranquility of the family?

But let us turn our attention from this woman who will remain, for her entire life, the victim of a brutal and perverted husband because she is too poor to obtain a judgment of legal separation.

Let us turn to Jeanne Duport's brother. This released convict leaves a den of corruption to reenter the world. He has done his time and paid his debt to society. What precautions does society take to prevent his falling back into crime? Not a single one. If he shows himself to be incorrigible, it can crack down on him in the most terrible way. But does society first, with charitable foresight, make it possible for him to go straight? No, it does not.

The perverse contagion of our prisons is so well known and so justly feared that anyone who is released from one is everywhere an object of contempt, aversion, and fear. No matter how upright he might be, he wouldn't be able to find work anywhere. Furthermore, your withering system of parole oversight exiles him to small villages where his background must immediately be known and where he has no chance to exercise the rather special abilities so often imposed on prisoners by the work farms in the larger institutions.

If the ex-convict has had the courage to resist all evil temptation, he will have to accept one of those deadly positions about which we have spoken.

He will have to work in the preparation of certain chemical products whose fatal effects decimate those who engage in these dreadful occupations.[192] Or, as an alternative, if he has the strength for it, he may work at extracting sandstone from the Fontainebleau forest, a job that, on the average, kills its workers in six years.

An ex-convict is thus in a much more dangerous, painful, and difficult condition than he was before he committed his first crime. Wherever he goes, he is surrounded by obstacles and reefs to founder on. He has to face repulsion, disdain, and sometimes even the deepest poverty. And if he succumbs to all these frightening criminal opportunities, if he commits a second crime, we behave a thousand times more harshly toward him than we did for his first crime.

This is unjust because it is almost always the circumstances we impose on him that lead to a second crime. And this injustice occurs because, as it has been demonstrated, instead of rehabilitating, our penal system depraves. Instead of improving, it degrades. Instead of curing minor moral afflictions, it makes them incurable.

The increased penalties we mete out to recidivists is, therefore, iniquitous and barbaric since the recidivism is basically the direct consequence of our penal system. The terrible punishment inflicted on recidivists would be just and logical if our prisons made their inmates more moral, purified them, and if it offered them, at the expiration of their sentences, a possible way for them, if not an easy one, to go straight. If these contradictions in the law seem surprising, what should we think when we compare certain transgressions with certain crimes, either in terms of their inevitable consequences or in terms of the widely disproportionately punishments meted out to them? The conversation with the prisoner whom the bailiff had just come to visit will offer us a case in point of one such painful contrast.

192. We are told that a method for protecting the unfortunate workers in these terrifying industries has just been discovered. See *Memorandum Describing a New Process for Manufacturing White Lead*, presented before the Academy of Sciences by J.-N. Gannal. [SN]

CHAPTER 3

MAÎTRE BOULARD

The prisoner who came into the visiting room at the same moment Bitters was leaving was about thirty years old, with golden blond hair and a full, ruddy, jovial face. The fact that he was of average height made his extreme corpulence all the more striking. This prisoner, extremely red in the face and extremely obese, was bundled up in a long, warm coat of gray flannel that matched his long footed pants. A red velvet combination hood and cap of the Périnet Leclerc[193] variety, along with his excellent furry slippers, completed the outfit of this individual. Although fobs had gone out of fashion long ago, the gold chain of his watch sported a good number of signets made of precious gems. In addition, several rings studded with fairly fine gemstones shone on the big red hands of this prisoner named Maître Boulard, a bailiff who had been arrested for embezzlement.

As we mentioned earlier, the man he was speaking to was Pierre Bourdin, one of the debt collectors charged with executing the arrest of Morel, the gem-cutter. This bailiff was ordinarily in the service of Maître Boulard, the bailiff of Monsieur Petit-Jean, Jacques Ferrand's front man. Bourdin, shorter than the bailiff but just as plump, modeled himself, as far as he might, after his employer, whose magnificence he admired. Just like him, he had a soft spot for jewels. On this day he was wearing a stunning topaz pin, and a long golden chain wound its way in and out of the buttonholes on his vest.

"Hello, my faithful Bourdin. I knew you wouldn't shirk the call of duty," Maître Boulard said joyously in a puny little voice that contrasted pointedly with his fat body and his large, florid face.

"Shirk the call of duty?" said the bailiff. "I could never do that, General." This was how Bourdin, making a joke that was at once familiar and respectful, referred to the bailiff under whose orders he operated, this

193. Périnet Leclerc was a gatekeeper's son who stole his father's keys, letting the troops of the Duke of Burgundy into Paris in 1418. A statue in his memory was erected by Charles VI. By tradition, strollers would throw a stone at the statue as they passed it. [TN]

military locution being in any case in frequent use among certain classes of civil employees and administrators.

"I am delighted to see that friendship can withstand misfortune," said Maître Boulard with cordial cheer. "Still, I was starting to worry. It's been three days since I wrote you, and no Bourdin."

"As you can imagine, General, it's a long story. Do you remember that handsome viscount from rue de Chaillot?"

"Saint-Remy?"

"That's the one. Do you remember how he thumbed his nose at our attempt to arrest him?"

"That was indecent of him."

"You're telling me! Malicorne and I were just about done in by it, if you can believe it."

"That's not possible, my brave Bourdin."

"Fortunately, that's true, General. But here's the latest news: the handsome viscount has moved up in the world."

"He's become a count?"

"No! He's graduated from being a swindler to being a thief."

"Oh, that's hardly news."

"They're after him for the diamonds he made off with. And by the way, they belonged to the jeweler who employed that vermin Morel, the gem-cutter, the one we were going to arrest on rue du Temple when a tall, thin guy with a black mustache came in, paid for that down-and-outer, and nearly threw me and Malicorne both down the stairs."

"Oh, right! I remember. You told me that, my poor Bourdin. That was really funny. The best part of the comedy was when the doorkeeper's wife emptied a bowlful of boiling soup down your back."

"With the bowl, General. It burst apart like a bomb at our feet. That old witch!"

"You'll get combat pay for that. But what about that handsome viscount?"

"I was telling you that Saint-Remy was being pursued for theft after having made his schoolboy of a father believe he wanted to blow his brains out. A police officer, a friend of mine who knew that I had been after this viscount for a long time, asked me if I could give him any information about the viscount to put him on the dandy's trail. And I did. Last time, I found out too late, after the last arrest he'd escaped, that he'd hidden out at a farm in Arnouville, five leagues away from Paris. But when we got there, we were too late. The bird had flown."

"In any case, he paid off that bill two days later, thanks to a certain lady, they say."

"Yes, General. But that didn't matter. I knew where his hiding place was because he had already holed up there once before. He could have easily been hiding there a second time. That's what I told my friend, the police officer. He asked me to give him a hand, as a connoisseur of the sport, by bringing him to the farm. I had nothing else to do, and it was like a country outing for me. I agreed to go."

"Really? And the viscount?"

"He was nowhere to be found! After we prowled around the farm a bit and then went inside, we came back empty-handed. That's why I couldn't come to your call sooner, General."

"I was sure that there was something holding you back, my good man."

"But—if I may be so indiscreet—what on earth are you doing here?"

"Some riffraff, my dear man. A swarm of riffraff who, for a lousy sixty thousand francs or so of which they claim to have been fleeced, have charged me with embezzlement and are forcing me to step down."

"Really? General! Alas! That's a real tragedy! So we won't be working for you anymore?"

"I'm on half pay, my good Bourdin. I've been let go."

"So who are these relentless persecutors?"

"If you can believe it, one of the guys who's most vehemently against me is an ex-con who had asked me to recover the funds for a bill of seven hundred bad francs that it would be necessary to track down. I tracked it down, I was paid, I deposited the money—and after some failed speculations, I squandered that money and a lot more. That whole mob was squealing so much that they took out a warrant for me, and here I am, my good man, nothing more or less than a crook."

"If that doesn't send a chill down your spine—you, General, of all people!"

"Lord, yes. But what's even stranger is that this ex-con wrote to me a few days ago to say that that money was all he had set aside for a rainy day and that it was raining hard right now. I don't know what he meant by that. He's claiming that I was responsible for the crimes he might have to commit in order to escape poverty."

"That takes the cake, I swear!"

"Doesn't it just, though? How convenient for him. The joker can use that as his excuse. Fortunately, the law does not recognize that kind of complicity."

"After all, you've only been charged with embezzlement, right, General?"

"Certainly! Do you take me for a thief, sir?"

"Oh, come on, General! I was just trying to say that that's not anything serious enough to worry about. In the end, it's not worth getting worked up over."

"Do I look like I'm desperate, my good man?"

"Not at all. I've never seen you looking better. In fact, if you're found guilty, you'll just have two or three months to serve in prison and twenty-five francs to pay as a fine. I know my code."

"And for those two or three months, I'll get myself sent to a sanitarium. I have a legislator in my pocket."

"Oh! Then you're all set."

"You know, Bourdin, the funny thing is that it won't do those imbeciles who got me put in here any good. They're never going to see any of the money they're claiming from me. They've forced me to sell my office, which is fine by me. I supposedly owe it to my predecessor, as you say. You see, those dupes are the ones who will be the butt of this joke, as Robert Macaire says."[194]

"That's the way it looks to me, General. Too bad for them."

"Come, my good man, let's get to the reason I asked you to come to see me. There's a delicate mission to carry out here involving a woman," said Maître Boulard with an air of self-satisfied mystery.

"Oh, you scoundrel of a general! That's just like you! What's this about? You can count on me."

"I take particular interest in a young actress at the Folies-Dramatiques theater. I pay her rent, and in exchange she gives me back what my investment is worth, or at least I think so. But, as you know, my good man, when you're not around, things can go wrong. Now I have a good reason to want to know if things are going wrong: Alexandrine (that's her name) has asked me for more money. I've never been stingy with women, but, you know, I don't like to be played for a fool. So before I give the little dear a lot of money, I would like to know whether she's been faithful enough to deserve it. I know there's nothing more old-fashioned or out of style than fidelity, but it's a weakness of mine. You would do me a favor as a friend, my dear comrade, if you could keep an eye on my love affairs for a few days and let me know what I need to know, whether it be by talking up the wife of Alexandrine's doorkeeper or by—"

"Got it, General," answered Bourdin, interrupting the bailiff. "That's no harder than keeping watch over, spying, and tracking down a debtor. I'm your man. I'll find out whether Mademoiselle Alexandrine is giving you the horns, which seems hardly likely to me anyway because—if I may be so bold—General, you're too handsome and too generous a man not to be adored."

"I may be handsome, but I'm not around, my dear comrade, and that's always a fault. So I'm counting on you to find out the truth."

"You will know it. I guarantee that."

"Oh, my dear comrade, how can I express my gratitude to you?"

"Come now, General!"

"It's understood, of course, my good Bourdin, that your compensation here will be the same as what you get for an arrest."

"I won't hear of it, General. For as long as I've worked for you, haven't

194. See Book IV, Chapter 5, footnote 104. [TN]

you always stripped the debtors' bones clean—doubling, tripling the arrest fees? You've gone after the payment of those fees as doggedly as if you were the one owed the money."

"But, my dear comrade, this is different, and for my part I will not hear of—"

"General, I would be insulted if you didn't allow me to offer you information on Mademoiselle Alexandrine as a trifling proof of my gratitude."

"That's really fine! I won't fight your generosity any longer. Besides, your devotion will be a sweet reward for the easygoing way I've always conducted our business."

"That's how I mean it, General. But can't I do anything else for you? You must be suffering horribly in here, you who like the easy life! You're paying your pistole, I hope?"[195]

"Certainly. And I got here just in time, for I got the last free room. The others are under renovation. I'm as comfortable as possible in my cell. I'm not doing too badly there. I've got a stove, I got a good armchair brought in, I have three good meals, I rest and digest them, I walk around and I sleep. So you see, apart from the nagging doubts I have about Alexandrine, my life isn't too bad."

"But for someone like you who likes to eat so much, General, it must be really meager pickings here."

"Isn't there a grocer on my street almost as if he were there just for me? I have an account with him, and every two days he sends me a nicely turned-out hamper. For that matter, since you're about to do me a favor, can you ask the grocer's wife, that good little Madame Michonneau—who, by the way, isn't a bad looker—"

"Oh, General, you're such a bad, bad boy!"

"Now, now, comrade—get your mind out of the gutter," said the bailiff with a complacent wink. "I'm just a good customer and a good neighbor. So ask dear Madame Michonneau to put some marinated tuna pâté in my basket tomorrow. It's in season, it'll be a nice change, and it will wet my whistle."

"That's an excellent idea."

"Madame Michonneau should also send me a basket of assorted wines—a mix of Burgundy, Champagne, and Bordeaux like she did last time. She'll know what I want. Tell her to throw in a couple of bottles of her old 1817 cognac and a pound of freshly roasted and ground java."

---

195. Prisoners who can afford single rooms obtain this advantage. [SN]

Sue has discussed this just a few chapters prior (see Book VII, Chapter 15, footnote 188, which refers back to Book V, Chapter 13, footnote 126), but this is the first time he footnotes it. [TN]

"I'll write the date of the eau-de-vie down so I don't forget," said Bourdin as he took his notebook out of his pocket.

"Since you're already writing things down, dear comrade, will you also be so kind as to ask at my place for my eiderdown?"

"Everything you've asked will be accomplished, right down to the letter, General. Don't worry. Now I'm not so worried about your meals. But what about your daily walks? Do you have to take them in the company of all the scoundrels in prison here?"

"Yes, and it's quite lively and cheerful. I leave my place after lunch, I walk right into one courtyard and then into another, and, as they say, I rub shoulders with the riffraff. It's just like the Regency, like the Porcherons![196] I can tell you that deep down they seem like very good people. Some of them are very amusing. The most savage among them get together in a place they call the Lions' Den. Oh, comrade! Such sinister faces! There's one of them named the Skeleton. I've never seen anyone like him before."

"What a funny name!"

"He's so thin, or rather so wasted, that it's not even a nickname. I'm telling you, he's scary looking. On top of that, he's the provost of his barracks. He's the worst criminal here. He's just gotten out of the galleys, and he's also stolen and committed murder. The last murder he committed was so horrible that he knows full well that he'll be condemned to death with no possibility of appeal, but he couldn't give a damn."

"What a villain!"

"All of the prisoners venerate him and tremble before him. I put myself in his good graces right away by giving him some cigars. As a result, he's taken a liking to me, and he's even teaching me thieves' slang. I'm making good progress!"

"Ha, ha! That's hilarious! The general is learning thieves' slang!"

"I'm telling you, I'm as happy as a clam. Those guys in there love me. Some of them even talk to me like I'm an old pal. I'm not proud, you know, not like that little gentleman in there named Germain, a tramp who can't even buy a pistole. He acts all disgusted by them and then plays the great lord with them."

"But if he's disgusted with the others, he must be thrilled to find someone as stylish as you to talk with?"

"Bah! He didn't even seem to notice who I was. But even if he had noticed me, I would have taken good care not to respond to his advances. He's the prison bête noire. They'll play him a dirty trick sooner or later, and I have no desire to share in the hatred they have for him."

"And you're quite right."

"It would spoil my break—for my stroll among the prisoners is a real

196. The Porcherons were a wealthy bourgeois Parisian family who built an enormous château for themselves in 1310. The château was mostly destroyed in the Revolution. [TN]

break. The only thing is, those criminals in there don't think too highly of me from a moral perspective. You understand, I'm just here for embezzlement. That's just nothing for guys like that. That's why they don't think I'm worth much, as Arnal says."[197]

"Indeed, next to these matadors of crime, you're—"

"A veritable sacrificial lamb, dear comrade. All right! Since you're being so obliging, don't forget the errands I've asked you to carry out."

"Don't worry, General. First, Mademoiselle Alexandrine. Second, the fish pâté and the wine basket. Third, the old cognac from 1817, the ground coffee, and the eiderdown. You'll get it all. Anything else?"

"Oh, yes! I forgot. Do you know where Monsieur Badinot lives?"

"The business agent? Yes."

"Good. Please tell him that I'm still relying on his kindness to find me the appropriate lawyer for my case. Money is no object."

"I will see Monsieur Badinot, you can be sure, General. Don't worry. I'll take care of everything you've asked for by tonight, and tomorrow you'll get it all. Until then, stay strong, General."

"Good-bye, dear comrade."

At that, the prisoner left the visiting room out one door, and his visitor out the other.

And now, let us compare the crime of Bitters, the repeat offender, with the offense of Maître Boulard, the bailiff. Let us compare the motivations of both men and the reasons and needs that led them to commit their crimes. And let us compare, finally, the punishment that awaits each of them.

Leaving prison, inspiring only fear and repulsion everywhere he went, the ex-convict can work at what he knows only in the place assigned to him. He hoped to take up a dangerous job for the rest of his life, one that was appropriate to his strength, but the position turned out not to exist. So he breaks his parole and returns to Paris, thinking he can cover up his past more easily and find work there. He arrives exhausted and starving. By chance, he discovers that there is some money kept in a neighboring house. He gives in to a detestable temptation, forces open a window, opens a drawer, steals a hundred francs, and flees. He gets arrested and is imprisoned. He will be tried and convicted.

As a repeat offender, he can look forward to fifteen or twenty years of hard labor, preceded by public display. This much he knows. He deserves this formidable sentence. Property is sacred. He who breaks into your home in the middle of the night to take your belongings must receive a terrible punishment.

The guilty can object all he likes that he faces unemployment, poverty,

---

197. Étienne Arnal (1794–1872) was a comic actor. [TN]

and the exceptional, difficult, intolerable position and need that the conditions of his parole impose on him. Too bad for him. The law is the law. For its safety and peace, society wants to be—and must be—armed with limitless power. It must be able to suppress such bold attacks on the goods of others without pity. Yes, this ignorant and foolish wretch, this corrupt and disdained repeat offender deserves his fate.

But what does this person who is intelligent, rich, educated, esteemed by all, and cloaked in official authority deserve when he steals—not in order to eat, but to satisfy his sumptuous cravings or to try his luck at speculation? When he steals not a hundred francs but a hundred thousand? A million? When he steals—not at night, risking his life, but tranquilly, in broad daylight, in full view of everyone? When he steals—not from a stranger who has stowed away his money under lock and key, but from a client who has put his money, of necessity, under the safeguard of a public officer whose integrity the law guarantees, thus calling forth his trust?

What kind of terrible punishment does the man deserve who, instead of stealing a small sum almost out of necessity, steals a considerable sum out of mere excess? Would it not be a crying injustice not to apply a penalty equal to that applied to the repeat offender who has been pushed to the limit by poverty and to theft by need?

"Oh, come now!" says the law. "How can we even think of applying the same penalty to a respectable man as we apply to a vagabond? Fancy that! To compare the kind of offense respectable people commit to vulgar breaking and entering? Fancy that!"

"After all, what's the problem?" a fellow like Maître Boulard will answer, agreeing with the law. "In view of the powers vested in me by my office, I deal with a sum of money for you. I've made off with the money and squandered it. There's not a penny left. But don't think that poverty led me to this pillage! Do I look like a beggar or a vagrant? Thank God, no; I had and still have plenty to live well on. Oh, rest assured that my goals were higher and loftier. Equipped with your money, I hurled myself boldly into the dazzling sphere of speculation. I could have doubled or tripled that money, in my own interest, if fortune had smiled on me. Alas, she looked the other way! You see, I've lost as much as you!"

Once again, the law seems to say, what does this offhand, brisk, neat, quick act of plunder, committed in broad daylight, have to do with those nighttime raids, those broken locks, those jimmied doors, those skeleton keys, those crowbars, the crude and vulgar equipment of wretched thieves of the lowest orders? Don't crimes deserve different penalties, even different names, when they are committed by certain privileged people?

An unfortunate man steals a loaf of bread from a baker, breaking a window to do it. A servant girl steals a handkerchief or a louis from her employers. Such acts are rightly called theft with aggravating and dishonorable circumstances and are the jurisdiction of criminal court. And that is just, especially in the latter case. The servant who steals from his employer is doubly culpable. He is practically a member of the family. The house is always open to him, so his betrayal of the trust bestowed on him is of the most unworthy kind. It is this sort of betrayal that we condemn as dishonorable. Once again, there is nothing more just or more moral than this.

But if a bailiff or any other public official steals the money that you, of necessity, had entrusted to him in his official capacity, not only is this not considered domestic theft or burglary, but the law doesn't even call it theft. How can this be?

Because they're obviously not the same thing! "Theft" is too brutal a word. It has the smell of foul places. "Theft"? For shame! Let's call it "embezzlement" instead! That's more delicate, more decent, more in keeping with the social position and consideration of the people who are liable to commit this . . . infraction. For "infraction" is what we call it. To call it a crime would also be too brutal. And an additional distinction must be drawn: crime is the jurisdiction of the criminal court, embezzlement that of the magistrate's court.

This is the essence of equality before the law; this is the essence of distributive justice! Let us repeat: a servant steals a louis from his employer, a starving man breaks a window to steal a loaf of bread—those are crimes. Off they go to the criminal court. A public official squanders or diverts a million francs—that's embezzlement. A simple tribunal in the magistrate's court must deal with it. Does the dissimilarity in the crimes justify the appalling difference between these penalties as a matter of facts, rights, logic, humanity, or morality? How, exactly, does domestic theft, punished with a dishonorable penalty, differ from embezzlement, punished with a minor penalty? Is it because the embezzlement almost always implies the ruin of families?

But what is embezzlement, then, if not an act of domestic theft aggravated many times over by its horrifying consequences and by the official position of the individual who commits it? And furthermore, why is a theft with breaking and entering guiltier than a theft by embezzlement?

What? Do you dare to suggest that the moral violation of the vow you took never to forfeit the trust society must have in you is less criminal than the material violation of a door? Yes, people will dare to say such a thing. That's the way the law is written. Yes, the more serious the crime, the more it compromises the survival of families, the more it challenges safety and public morals—the less it is punished. In this way, the more enlightened, intelligent, well-off, and respectable the guilty parties are, the more indulgent the law is toward them. In this way, the law reserves the most terrible and degrading penalties for the wretches who have, we won't say the excuse, but at least the explanation of ignorance, debasement, or the poverty in which they have been allowed to languish. This unequal justice is barbaric and profoundly immoral. Strike the poor man without pity if he harms another's property, if you will, but strike also without pity the public official if he harms the property of his clients.

May we never hear any more lawyers excuse, defend, and win absolution (punishing so mildly is absolution, after all) for people guilty of dishonorable plundering schemes in terms such as these: "My client does not deny squandering the sums at issue. He knows the appalling distress his embezzlement has caused an honorable family. But what do you expect? My client has an adventurous spirit. He likes to bet on risky enterprises, and once he's begun speculating, once the gambling fever seizes him, he no longer knows the difference between what's his and what belongs to others." This is, clearly, a perfect consolation to those who have been fleeced, and it is singularly reassuring to those who are in the position to be so in the future.

It seems to us, however, that a lawyer would be quite poorly received in criminal court if he presented a defense that went more or less like the following: "My client does not deny having broken into a desk in order to steal from it the sum at issue. But what do you expect? He likes good food, he adores women, he holds dear his well-being and luxury. Now, once he feels the need for these pleasures, he can't tell the difference between what's his and what's not." And we maintain that the comparison between the thief and the plunderer is perfectly just. The latter gambles only in the hopes of gain, and he desires this gain only in order to augment his fortune or his pleasures.

Let us, then, come to the point of this argument: we would like a legislative reform to categorize embezzlement committed by a public official as theft and for it to be brought into line at minimum with the penalty for domestic theft and at maximum with the penalty for burglary and recidivism. The company to which the public official belongs would be responsible for the sums the individual has stolen in his capacity as its representative and its employee.

Here is a juxtaposition of two cases that will serve as a corollary to this digression. After we have stated the facts of the cases, all further commentary will be unnecessary. It will be left to us only to ask whether we live in a civilized society or a barbarous world.

We read in the *Court Bulletin* of February 17, 1843, about an appeal lodged by a bailiff found guilty of embezzlement:

> The Court concurs with the verdict of the lower court:
>
> Recognizing that the writings produced for the first time before the Court, by the accused, are powerless to counter or even to attenuate the facts asserted before the lower court;

Recognizing that it is proven that the accused, in his capacity as bailiff, representative and employee, has received sums of money from three of his clients; that, when requests on the part of the latter were addressed to obtain them, he answered all of them with subterfuge and lies;

And, finally, that he diverted and squandered the sums of money to the detriment of his three clients; that he embezzled their money; and that he has committed the said infraction, punishable by articles 408 and 406 of the Penal Code, etc., etc.;

This Court confirms the sentence of two months of prison and the fine of twenty-five francs.

On the same day, the same newspaper reported a few lines below:

Fifty-three years of hard labor.

On the thirteenth of September, a nighttime burglary was committed climbing into and forcing entry into a house inhabited by the Bresson couple, wine merchants in the village of Ivry.

Evidence left attested to the fact that a ladder had been leaned against the wall of the house, and one of the shutters of the room, in which the theft occurred and which overlooked the street, had given way to vigorous efforts to break and enter.

The objects had little value but their number was considerable. These included discarded used clothes, old bed linens, worn-out shoes, two pots with holes in them, and, finally, two bottles of white absinthe from Switzerland.

These deeds attributed to the accused, Tellier, having been fully established in the proceedings, the public prosecutor has called for the most severe sentence to be given to the accused, in view especially of his particular legal status as a repeat offender.

Thus, the jury having rendered a guilty verdict on every count, without attenuating circumstances, the Court sentences Tellier to twenty years of hard labor and public exhibition.

Thus, for the plundering public official: two months of prison. For the recidivist ex-convict: twenty years of hard labor and public exhibition. What can one add to these facts? They speak for themselves. What sad and serious reflections must they evoke! At least we hope that will be their effect.

Faithful to his promise, the old guard had had Germain called in. When the bailiff Boulard had returned to the interior of the prison, the door to the corridor opened, Germain entered, and Rigolette was no longer separated from her poor protégé by anything more than a light wire fence.

CHAPTER 4

FRANÇOIS GERMAIN

Although Germain's facial features were irregular, one could hardly imagine a more interesting face. He carried himself with dignity and had a slender build. His simple but clean clothes (gray pants and a black waistcoat buttoned up to the neck) did not in any way manifest the signs of the sordid neglect that prisoners generally fall into. His neat white hands testified to a care for personal cleanliness that had only increased the other prisoners' hatred of him. Moral perversity is almost always accompanied by physical filth. The naturally curly chestnut-colored hair that he wore long and stylishly parted to one side of his forehead framed his pale and downcast face. His beautiful blue eyes told of his honesty and kindness. His smile, at once sweet and sad, expressed his benevolence and habitual melancholy—for, although he was still quite young, this unfortunate man had already been cruelly tried. In brief, nothing could be more moving than this suffering, affectionate, resigned face, just as nothing could be more honest or more loyal than this young man's heart.

Even the reason for his arrest (minus the slanderous exaggeration due to Jacques Ferrand's hatred of him) proved Germain's kindness, and showed only that he had gotten carried away and been imprudent. If we remember that Madame Georges's son could, the next morning, replace the sum he had temporarily removed from the solicitor's till in order to save Morel the gem-cutter, we will find his behavior, if surely guilty, nevertheless also pardonable.

Germain blushed slightly when he perceived Rigolette's fresh and charming face through the wire fence in the visiting room. The latter, as was her wont, was trying to look cheerful in order to encourage her protégé and brighten him up a bit, but the poor child was not very good at hiding the worry and emotion she always felt as soon as she entered the prison. Sitting on a bench on the other side of the fence, she held her straw basket on her knees.

The old guard, instead of staying in the corridor, went to position himself next to a stove at the other end of the room. After a few moments, he fell asleep. Germain and Rigolette could thus converse in total freedom.

"Let's have a look at you, Monsieur Germain," said the seamstress as she got her face as close as she could to the fence in order to examine her friend's features. "Let's see if I approve of your face today. Is it less sad? Hmm . . . If you're not careful, I'm going to get angry at you."

"You're so kind to come back to see me again today!"

"Again? Are you trying to scold me?"

"I should be scolding you, actually, for doing so much for me when I can't do anything for you besides thank you."

"Wrong, monsieur. These visits make me just as happy as they make you. So I would just have to thank you back. Ha, ha! Got you there, smarty-pants. Now I'm thinking I should punish you for your nasty ideas by not giving you what I've brought you."

"Something else? You're spoiling me! Oh, thank you! I'm sorry I keep saying that since you don't like it, but you leave me no alternative."

"First of all, you don't know what I've brought you."

"What does it matter?"

"Well, that's not a nice thing to say!"

"Whatever it is, doesn't it come from you? Doesn't your touching kindness fill me with gratitude and . . . ?" Germain could not finish his sentence and averted his gaze.

"And what?" asked Rigolette, blushing.

"And . . . devotion," stuttered Germain.

"Why not just say 'respect,' like at the end of a letter?" Rigolette asked impatiently. "You're not telling me the truth. That's not what you were going to say. You stopped yourself all of a sudden."

"I swear . . ."

"You swear, you swear . . . I can see you blushing through the fence. Am I not your little friend, your cheerful companion? Why are you keeping something from me? Be frank with me. Tell me everything," the seamstress said timidly. She was really just waiting to hear Germain tell her that he loved her before making a naive and loyal declaration of her own to him. Germain's misfortune had given rise to her honest and generous love.

"I swear," the prisoner went on with a sigh, "that I wasn't going to say anything else. I'm not hiding anything from you!"

"What a liar!" exclaimed Rigolette, stamping her foot. "Fine. Do you see this big white woolen scarf I brought you?" She removed it from her basket. "Well, to punish you for being so dishonest, you can't have it. I had knit it especially for you. I'd said to myself, 'It must be so cold and damp in those big prison halls. At least he'll be nice and warm with this. He's so sensitive to cold!'"

"What, you . . . ?"

"Yes, monsieur, you're sensitive to cold," said Rigolette, interrupting him. "Maybe I don't have such a bad memory! Not that it stopped you from always wanting to stop me from putting wood in my stove when you spent the evening with me. Oh, I have a good memory!"

“As do I . . . too good a memory!” said Germain in an emotional voice, covering his eyes with his hand.

“There you go again! Here you are getting sad again, even though I absolutely forbid it.”

“How could all you’ve done for me since I came to this prison not bring tears to my eyes? And this latest care for me is so charming, too. Don’t you think I know that you’re taking extra work in at night in order to have the time to come see me? You really are working far too much because of me.”

“Right! You should feel sorry for me for having to take a nice walk to see my friends every two or three days And I love a good walk. It’s so much fun to look at the shops along the way!”

“And today you’ve gone out in this wind and rain!”

“Even more reason to go out! You have no idea how many funny-looking people you meet on a day like today. Some of them hold their hats down with both hands so the storm doesn’t blow them away. Others make unbelievable faces, squinting as the rain whips them in the face when their umbrellas snap inside out. You know, this morning it was real theater the whole way here. I promised myself I would make you laugh telling you about it, but you’re not up for being cheerful, obviously.”

“It’s not my fault. I’m sorry. It’s just that the beautiful impression your kindness makes has turned into deep feeling for you. You know full well that I’m not a happy-go-lucky fellow. I can’t help it.”

Rigolette did not want Germain to perceive that, in spite of her gentle prattle, she felt pretty much the same way he did. She hurried to change the subject and said, “You always say you can’t help it, but there are too many things you can’t help, either, even though I’ve asked—no, begged—you to do them,” said Rigolette.

“What are you talking about?”

“About your stubbornness in keeping yourself apart from the other prisoners and never speaking to them. The guard just told me again that you should really take it upon yourself to do something about this. It’s in your own interest. I’m sure you haven’t done anything about what he said. You’re silent. See, it’s always the same with you! You won’t be happy until those horrible men have done you harm!”

“You don’t understand how horrible they are. You don’t know all the personal reasons I have for fleeing them, for cursing them and everyone like them!”

“Alas, I think I know your reasons only too well. I read the papers you wrote for me that I retrieved from your room when you were first imprisoned. I learned there about the dangers you were in when you came to Paris because, in the provinces, you had refused to participate in the crimes of the scoundrel who had raised you. In fact, it was after his last attempted ambush that you left rue du Temple in order to throw him off your trail, telling no one but me where you were going to live. I also read something else in those papers," added Rigolette, blushing again and lowering her eyes. "I read some things that . . ."

"Oh, things you would never have known about, I swear to you," exclaimed Germain energetically, "if it hadn't been for this latest trial. But I beg of you: please be kind to me. Forgive me such childishness—forget I ever said anything. It's just that, in the past, I could allow myself to indulge in those dreams, even though they were madness."

Rigolette had just tried a second time to make Germain declare his love for her by alluding to the tender, passionate thoughts he had previously written and dedicated to his memories of the seamstress. For, as we have said, he had always felt for her a strong and sincere love. In order to enjoy the cordial intimacy of his kind neighbor, however, he had disguised this love as friendship. His misfortune had made him even more wary and more timid than before, however, because he could not imagine that Rigolette might really love him now that he was a prisoner, stained as he was by a terrible accusation, when before these troubles had struck she had manifested nothing toward him but the most sisterly attachment. Seeing that Germain had misunderstood her meaning, the seamstress stifled a sigh, waiting and hoping for a better opportunity to get Germain to reveal what was at the bottom of his heart. Thus she made an effort and went on, "Heavens! I certainly understand that the company of those vile people must be awful, but that's still no reason to risk unnecessary danger."

"I swear to you that I tried to do what you told me. I have tried several times to speak to the ones who seemed the least evil, but if you only knew the way they spoke! What men!"

"Alas! It's true. It must be awful."

"What's even more awful, you see, is that I can see myself, little by little, becoming more used to the appalling conversations that I can't help but hear, despite my best efforts. Yes, I can now listen with a gloomy apathy to horrors that on my first days here would fill me with indignation. And so, you know, I've begun to doubt myself," he said, bitterly.

"Oh, Monsieur Germain, what are you saying?"

"By living in these horrible places, your mind gets used to criminal thoughts, just like your ears get used to the vulgar words if they're always reverberating around you. Dear Lord! I understand now how one can enter this place an innocent man, though you're an accused man, and leave it corrupted . . ."

"Yes, but not you! Not you!"

"Yes, me, too, and others who are worth a thousand of me. Alas! Those who condemn us to this odious company before we are tried have no idea how painful and fateful this experience is! They have no idea that the air one breathes in here is contagious. It can kill your sense of honor."

"Please, stop talking this way. You're making me feel so bad."

"You've asked me why I'm getting sadder and sadder, and that's why. I didn't want to tell you this, but I have only one way to show my gratitude for your pity for me."

"My pity . . . my pity . . ."

"Yes, and I don't want to hide anything from you. Well, it frightens me to admit it, but I don't recognize myself anymore. For all that I've felt contempt for those wretches and avoided them, their presence, their contact is having an effect on me, in spite of myself. You could say they have poison in them that can corrupt the atmosphere around them. It seems to me that I can feel their corruption seeping through all my pores. If I were to be absolved of the wrongdoing I committed, seeing and living among honest people would fill me with confusion and shame. I haven't yet gotten to the point of enjoying the company here, but I have begun to fear the day on which I find myself once again in the midst of honorable people. And that's because I know my weakness."

"Your weakness?"

"My cowardice."

"Your cowardice? But heavens, where did you come up with these foolish ideas about yourself?"

"Isn't it cowardly and blameworthy to rationalize about your duty and your integrity? That's what I've done."

"You? You?"

"Me. When I came here, I didn't delude myself about the magnitude of my transgression, however excusable it might have been. Well, now it seems less terrible to me. Because all I hear is these thieves and murderers talking about their crimes with cynical laughter and fierce pride, I surprise myself sometimes by envying them their bold indifference, and I mock myself bitterly for the remorse that torments me over an act that is so insignificant in comparison to crimes."

"But you're right! Far from being blameworthy, your act was generous. You were sure that the next morning you could put back the money that you took for a few hours to save a whole family from ruin—and, possibly, from death."

"That doesn't matter. In the eyes of the law, in the eyes of honest people, it's theft. It may be less wicked to steal for such a reason than for some others, but you see, it's a bad sign when you have to look beneath yourself in order to excuse yourself in your own eyes. I will no longer be able to see myself as like those people who have no stain on their honor. Here I am already forced to compare myself to the degraded people I live with. And I can already tell that my conscience will ultimately get hard and numb. The next time, I might steal something—not with the certainty that I will be able to return the sum I took with a worthy end in mind, but out of greed, and I'll surely think I'm innocent compared to people who kill so they can steal. And yet, I'm as different from a man beyond reproach at this point as I am from a murderer. So because there are people who are a thousand times more degraded than myself, I will start looking less and less degraded to myself. Instead of being able to say, as I used to, 'I'm as honest as the most honest of men,' I will console myself by saying, 'I'm the least degraded of all the wretches among whom I'm destined to live forever!'"

"Forever? But what about when you get out of here?"

"What then? Even if I were acquitted, those guys know me now. If they run into me when they get out of prison, they'll speak to me as an old prison buddy. If people aren't aware of the just charge that led to my imprisonment, those wretches will threaten to tell them. So now you see how I am tied to them now in the most damned and unbreakable way. If I had been locked alone in my cell until the day of my trial, unknown to them as they would have been unknown to me, I wouldn't have been assailed by these fears that can paralyze the best resolution. And then, all alone with the thought of my crime, it would have grown larger instead of diminishing in my eyes. The more serious it would have seemed to me, the more serious the expiation I would have imposed on myself in the future. Also, the more I had to seek pardon for, the more I would have tried in my humble way to do good. For it takes a hundred good deeds to expiate onc bad one. But why would I ever think about expiating a crime that right now hardly causes me to feel any remorse? You know, I feel that I am obeying an irresistible influence against which I have long struggled with all my might. I was brought up to be bad; I'm just giving in to my destiny. After all, isolated, without a family, what does it matter whether I end up leading an honest life or a life of crime? And yet, my intentions were always so good and pure. That's why, even though they tried to make me into a criminal, I felt such a deep satisfaction in saying to myself, 'I've never done anything dishonorable, even though it's been harder for me than for anyone else.' But today—oh, it's horrible! It's too horrible!" exclaimed the prisoner in an explosion of sobbing that was so heartrending that Rigolette, deeply moved, could not hold back her tears.

She also found the expression on Germain's face heartbreaking. Who could help but sympathize with this despair on the part of this good-hearted man who was struggling against the encroachment of a fatal contagion, even as his delicacy exaggerated the danger that threatened him so? But it's true, danger did threaten him.

We will never forget the following words from a man of rare intelligence, words given all the more weight from twenty years' experience in the administration of prisons: "Even if we allow that an unjustly accused man enters prison completely pure, he always leaves it less honest than when he entered it. What one could term the first flower of honorableness disappears forever at the first contact with that corrosive air."

We must say, however, that Germain, thanks to his healthy and robust integrity, had for a long time been victorious in his struggle and that, even now, he felt the coming on of a malady with which he was not yet really infected. His fears of seeing his crime diminishing in his own eyes proved that at this moment he was still aware of its full gravity. But the fear, the apprehension, the doubts that roiled this honest and generous soul so cruelly were not any less alarming as symptoms, for all that.

Guided by her own upright spirit, by her feminine wisdom, and by the instinct of love, Rigolette instinctively guessed at what we have just said. Although she was fully convinced that her friend had not lost any of his delicate integrity, she feared that, in spite of his natural goodness, Germain might one day become indifferent to what was currently tormenting him so cruelly.

CHAPTER 5

RIGOLETTE

. . . As certain as is today's happiness, one will sometimes be tempted to
desire impossible misfortunes in order to contemplate
the noble grandeur of certain kinds of devotion with gratitude and veneration.

—*WOLFGANG, THE HOLY SPIRIT*, I, ii

Wiping her eyes and turning to Germain, who had his forehead pressed against the fence, Rigolette said to him in a touching, serious, almost solemn tone, which he had never heard from her before, "Listen to me, Germain. I might express myself poorly, because I don't speak as well as you. But what I'm about to say is right and I mean it sincerely. First of all, you are wrong to complain of being abandoned and alone."

"Oh! Don't think I will ever forget the things your pity makes you do for me!"

"A moment ago I didn't interrupt you when you spoke of pity. But since you've repeated this word, I must tell you that it's not pity at all that I feel for you. I will explain this to you as best I can. When we were neighbors, I loved you like a kind brother, like a good friend. You did me small favors and I returned them with some of my own. You shared your Sunday activities with me, and I tried to be cheerful and nice to you in order to thank you for that. That made us all even."

"Even? Oh, no, I . . ."

"Let me have a chance to speak. When you were forced to leave the house we lived in, your departure made me much more unhappy than the departures of my other neighbors."

"If only that were true!"

"It is, because those others were carefree fellows who would certainly miss me much less than you would. And they never gave in to just being friends before they made me say a hundred times over that they'd never be anything else. You, on the other hand—you understood right away the kind of relationship we had to have. Despite that, you spent all the time you had in my company. You taught me to write. You gave me good advice—advice that was a bit serious, because it was good advice. In the end, you were the most devoted of my neighbors, and the only one who never asked anything of me for what you did. That's not all: when you left the house, you gave me a great token of your trust in me. For you to have entrusted a little girl like me with such an important secret, well, that made me really proud! So when I was separated from you, I always remembered you more than I did any of my other neighbors. What I'm telling you is true. You know that I never lie."

"Can that really be? You saw a difference between me and . . . the others?"

"Certainly I did. Otherwise I would have been heartless. 'Yes,' I said to myself, 'there's no one better than Monsieur Germain. Maybe he's a little serious—but that's all right. If I had a friend who wanted to find someone to marry who would make her very, very happy, certainly I would advise her to marry Monsieur Germain, because he would be paradise for a good little housewife.'"

"You thought about me for someone else?" Germain couldn't help himself from saying, sadly.

"It's true. I would have been delighted to see you happily married, because I loved you like a good friend. You see, I'm being honest. I'm telling you everything."

"And I thank you from the bottom of my heart. It comforts me to learn that among your friends I was the one you liked best."

"That's how things stood when your troubles began. That's when I received that sad, kind letter in which you told me about what you've called a fault. It's the kind of fault that I, uneducated as I am, find beautiful and kind. That's when you asked me to go to your room to find those papers that told me that you had always loved me, without daring to tell me so. Those papers in which I read"—and here Rigolette could not hold in her tears—"that, thinking of my future and how much illness or loss of work might make it a hard one, you were making me your heir in the event of your dying violently, which you feared was only too likely. So you left me the little you had managed to set aside through hard work and saving."

"Yes, for if you had been sick or without work when I was alive, I'd be the one you'd turn to before anyone else, right? I counted on that—tell me, I wasn't wrong, was I?"

"Well, that's obvious! Who else would I turn to?"

"Now those are the kinds of words that make a person feel better. They make up for any amount of troubles!"

"I can't tell you what I felt when I read your will—what a sad word that is—every line of which reminded me of something or showed you thinking about my future. And yet you did not mean me to know this proof of your attachment unless you no longer existed. So what do you expect? After someone acts so generously, you can't be surprised if I fall in love just like that! It's the most natural thing in the world. Don't you think so, Monsieur Germain?"

The young woman said these last words with such a touching and frank naiveté, staring with her big black eyes into Germain's own, that the latter did not understand right away, so little did he believe that Rigolette could actually love him. However, her words were so crystal clear that they echoed in the prisoner's soul. He blushed and turned pale in quick succession, and then exclaimed, "What did you say? I'm afraid . . . Oh, God! What if I've misunderstood? I—"

"I'm saying that from the moment at which I saw how good you were to me, from the moment I saw how unhappy you were, my feelings for you became completely different from those one has for a friend. If one of my friends were looking for a man to marry now," said Rigolette, smiling and blushing, "I would no longer be recommending you to her, Monsieur Germain."

"You love me! You love me!"

"I have to come right out and say it myself, since you'll never ask me."

"Could it be true?"

"It's not for lack of trying to get you to see what's in front of you. But Monsieur can't take a hint. He has to have things spelled out. It might not have been quite proper of me, but since you're the only one who might scold me for having no shame, I wasn't so afraid. And then, also," Rigolette added in a more serious and more tender tone, "you seemed so overwhelmed a moment ago, so desperate, that I couldn't worry about being proper. I thought well enough of myself to believe that if I made that declaration frankly and from the bottom of my heart, it might keep you from being unhappy in the future. I said to myself, 'Up to now, I haven't been lucky in my attempts to distract or console him. The treats I made for him to eat took away his appetite; my cheerfulness made him weep. This time, at least—' Oh, no! What's wrong now?" cried Rigolette as she saw Germain hiding his face in his hands. "Come on, don't you think that's mean?" she exclaimed. "Whatever I do, whatever I say, you just keep being unhappy! That's just too mean and it's selfish, too! Do you think you're the only one in the world who feels for your pain?"

"Alas! How unhappy I am!" cried Germain in despair. "You love me when I am no longer worthy of you!"

"No longer worthy of me? Now you're just talking foolishness. It's as if I'd said back then that I wasn't worthy of your friendship because I had been in prison. Because I've been in prison, too, you know. Does that make me any less a respectable girl?"

"But you went to prison because you were a poor, abandoned child, while I—good God, what a difference!"

"As far as prison goes, we're still both on an equal footing. In fact, I'm really the one who's out of my league here. Someone in my position shouldn't think of marrying anyone but a worker. I'm a foundling. All I've got is my little room and my spunk, and here I am coming right out and asking you to take me as your wife!"

"Alas! At any other time, this would be a dream come true, the happiest day of my life! But now that I'm accused of a vile crime, I would be taking advantage of your praiseworthy generosity and your pity—which may be confusing you. No! no!"

"Oh, for God's sake!" cried Rigolette with irritation and impatience. "I'm telling you that it's not pity I feel for you! It's love. All I can think about is you! I can't sleep anymore, I can't eat. Your sad, sweet face follows me everywhere I go. You call that pity? When you speak to me right now, your voice and look go straight to my heart. There are a thousand things about you that I never noticed until now and that are driving me to distraction this very moment. I love your face, I love your eyes, I love your bearing, I love your mind, I love your good heart. Is that what you call pity? Why, after having loved you as a friend, should I now love you as a beloved? I have no idea! Why was I carefree and cheerful when I loved you as a friend, and now that I love you as a lover, I'm all preoccupied all the time? I have no idea! Why did it take me so long to see how handsome and good you are, to love you with my eyes and my heart at the same time? I have no idea, or rather, yes, I do too know, and it's because I discovered how much you loved me without your ever having told me, how generous and devoted you were. That's when love rose from my heart into my eyes, the way a sweet tear goes there when you're moved."

"Really, I feel as if I must be dreaming when I hear you talk this way."

"How about me? I would never have believed I could dare to tell you all of that, but your despair forced me to tell you. So, now, monsieur! Now that you know I love you like a friend! like my lover! like my husband!—are you going to tell me again that that's pity?"

Germain's generous scruples gave way momentarily before this declaration that was at once so naive and so brave. An unhoped-for joy thrilled him and took him away from his painful preoccupations. "You love me!" he cried. "I believe you. Your voice, your look—everything says it's true! I don't want to know what I've done to deserve such happiness. I'm just going to let myself revel in it blindly. My life, my entire life, will not be enough to repay the debt I feel toward you! Ah! I've suffered greatly, but this moment makes up for all of it!"

"Finally, you've cheered up. Oh! I was sure I'd manage to do it!" exclaimed Rigolette in a charming burst of joy.

"And it's in the midst of all the horrors of a prison and when everything is crushing me down that such happiness . . ." Germain could not finish this thought. It had brought him back to the reality of his position.

His scruples, which he had momentarily forgotten, returned more cruelly than ever, and he said, in despair, "But I'm a prisoner, charged with theft, and I'm going to be convicted—and perhaps dishonored! How can I accept your brave sacrifice or take advantage of your generous exaltation? Oh! No, I'm not vile enough to do that!"

"What are you saying?"

"I might be sentenced to years in prison."

"Well, then," answered Rigolette, calmly and firmly, "they'll see that I'm a respectable girl, and they won't forbid us getting married in the prison chapel."

"But I may be imprisoned far from Paris."

"Once I'm your wife, I'll follow you. I'll set myself up in the city you're in. I'll find work to do there, and I'll come to see you every day!"

"But I will be branded in everyone's eyes."

"You love me more than everyone, don't you?"

"How can you even ask me such a thing?"

"Then why do you care? Far from being branded in my eyes, you will appear to me as martyred by your kind heart."

"But everyone will accuse you, everyone will condemn you, they'll slander you for your choice . . ."

"Everyone? It's me for you and you for me. We'll let them talk."

"Finally, when I get out of prison, my life will be wretched and dangerous. No matter where I go, people won't want to come near me, and it's possible I won't ever find a job. And then—and this is horrible to think—but if this corruption I fear were to win me over in spite of my efforts . . . that's no kind of future for you!"

"You won't get corrupted. No, because now you know I love you, and that thought will give you the strength to resist the bad company you keep. Even if everyone disdains you when you get out of prison, you will have it in mind that your wife will welcome you with love and gratitude, absolutely certain you've remained an honest man. My language shocks you a little, doesn't it? It shocks me, too. I don't know where I find the things I say to you. It must be from the depths of my soul . . . and that should convince you. Otherwise, if you turn your nose up at an offer that has been made to you from the bottom of my heart . . . if you aren't interested in the affection of a poor girl who—"

Germain interrupted Rigolette in a passionate ecstasy. "All right! I accept! Yes, I understand that it is sometimes cowardly to refuse some kinds of sacrifice. To accept them, you have to recognize that one is unworthy of them. I accept, you noble and courageous girl!"

"Really? This time it's true?"

"I swear it to you. And then, you just said something to me that struck me, that gave me the courage I lacked."

"I'm delighted! And what was that?"

"That for your sake I will have to remain an honest man. Yes, in that thought I will find the strength to resist the vile influences all around me. I will face that contagion, and I will learn how to keep my heart, which belongs to you, worthy of your love!"

"Ah, Germain! How happy I am! If I did anything for you, you've paid me back a thousand times over!"

"And then, you know, although you excuse my fault, I will never forget its gravity. The future has two labors in store for me: to expiate the past and to deserve the happiness I owe to you. For that, I will do good. No matter how poor one is, opportunities to do good are never lacking."

"Alas! Good Lord, it's too true! One can always find someone more unhappy than oneself."

"If you can't give money . . ."

"You can give your tears, like I did with those poor Morels."

"And those alms are holy. Charity from the soul is worth as much as the gift of bread."[198]

"So, after all that, you accept me? You're not going to change your mind?"

"Oh! Never, never, never, my love, my wife. Yes, hope is returning. It seems I'm coming out of a dream. I'm no longer filled with self-doubt. I was wrong about myself. Yes, I'm glad to say, I was wrong about myself. My heart would not be beating this way if it had lost its noble energy."

"Oh! Germain, you're so handsome when you speak that way! You're making me feel so much better—not for my own sake, but for yours! So you'll promise me, right, now that you have my love to protect you, that you won't be afraid to talk with those wicked men so you don't get them mad at you?"

"Don't worry. When they saw me looking all sad and downcast, they must have thought I was in the grips of remorse. Now, when they see me looking proud and happy, they'll think I've learned their cynicism."

"That's true. They won't be suspicious of you anymore, so I can feel less anxious. So, no carelessness, right? You belong to me now. I'm your little wife, right?"

At this moment, the guard moved. He was waking up.

"Hurry!" said Rigolette, whispering with a smile full of grace and bashful tenderness. "Quick, husband, give me a nice kiss on my forehead through the fence! It will be the sign of our engagement." At this, the young woman, blushing, put her forehead up against the iron trellis.

Profoundly moved, Germain grazed her pure white forehead with his lips through the fence. One of the prisoner's tears rolled down onto it

---

198. Sue cites nearly this phrase as the epigraph to Book VI, Chapter 5, without giving it any source. [TN]

like a wet pearl. A touching baptism for this chaste, melancholy, charming love!

"Uh-oh, it's three o'clock already!" said the guard as he arose. "The visitors were supposed to leave at two. Come along, my dear little lady," he added, addressing the seamstress. "It's too bad, but it's time to go."

"Oh! Thank you, thank you, monsieur, for letting us talk alone. I really cheered Germain up. He will try to be less morose so he won't have to fear his wicked companions anymore. Isn't that true, my love?"

"Don't worry," said Germain, smiling. "I'll be the happiest guy in prison from now on."

"That's good. Then they won't pay any more attention to you," said the guard.

"Here's a scarf I brought for Germain, monsieur," said Rigolette. "Do I need to leave it at the clerk's office?"

"Normally, yes. But after all, since I've already violated the rules, a little more won't matter. Go ahead. Let's make the day complete. Quick, give him the present yourself." And the guard opened the door to the corridor.

"This good man is right. The day will now be complete," said Germain as he took the scarf from Rigolette's hands, squeezing them tenderly. "Farewell, and we will see each other soon. Now I have no fear in asking you to come to see me as soon as possible."

"Nor am I afraid to promise you that I will. Farewell, good Germain."

"Farewell, my good little love."

"And make sure you use my scarf. You shouldn't get cold. It's so damp!"

"What a beautiful scarf! When I think that you made it for me! Oh! I won't ever take it off," said Germain, holding it to his lips.

"That's better! And now, maybe you'll eat something, I hope? Do you want me to make you my little treat?"

"Certainly, and this time I'll give it its due honors."

"So be happy, Monsieur Gourmand. And next time, you'll give me all the news. All right. Again, farewell. Thank you, monsieur. Today I am leaving this place happy and at peace. Farewell, Germain."

"Farewell, my little wife . . . See you soon!"

"For always!"

A few minutes later, Rigolette, having bravely recovered her rain clogs and umbrella, left the prison much more cheerfully than she had ever entered it.

During Germain's conversation with the seamstress, other scenes were taking place within one of the prison halls. This is where we will now take the reader.

CHAPTER 6

THE LIONS' DEN

The outward appearance of a large house of detention, built according to humane standards of well-being and health, may not strike an onlooker as sinister, but the sight of its inmates creates an entirely different impression. When we are in the midst of a group of women prisoners, we are typically seized with pity and sadness, because we realize that these unfortunate women are almost always led astray less of their own free will than by the pernicious influence of the first men who seduced them. Furthermore, even the most criminal of women holds two ties sacred, deep within her soul, two ties that the lashings of the most vile and stormy passions never entirely sever: love and motherhood! To speak of love and motherhood is to say that, even in these wretched creatures, pure and sweet rays of light can still occasionally illuminate the black shadows of the most deeply corrupted souls. But among men of the kind that prison creates and then casts back out into the world, there is nothing comparable. Here it's crime from start to finish, like a lump of iron that only the most hellish passions redden. Thus, when one sees the criminals who populate our prisons, one is seized immediately with a tremor of fear and shock. Only the powers of reflection allow one to think more charitably about them. Even then, these thoughts are filled with great bitterness. Yes, with great bitterness—for one knows that the sinister populations in jails and galleys, the bloody harvest of the executioner, always develop in the mire of ignorance, poverty, and debasement.

To understand this first impression of horror and shock of which we speak, the reader will have to follow us into the Lions' Den. Such is the name of one of the halls in La Force prison. There society generally brings together the most dangerous inmates, those with the worst criminal history, the most violent, or those who are accused of the most serious crimes. However, as a consequence of urgent repairs undertaken in one of the other structures in La Force, several other prisoners had been obliged temporarily to join them. Although these prisoners were being held as a result of equally well-founded criminal accusations, they were almost gentlemen in comparison with the usual residents of the Lions' Den.

The somber, gray, and rainy sky cast a gloomy aspect on the scene we are about to depict. It occurred in the middle of a courtyard, a rather large quadrilateral formed by high white walls pierced in several places by a few barred windows. At one end of this courtyard stood a narrow fenced door. At the other end was the entrance to the furnace room, a large tiled room in the middle of which was a cast-iron stove surrounded by wooden benches on which several prisoners were lazily stretched out as they gossiped among themselves. Others, preferring exercise to rest, were walking around the yard, arm in arm, in tight ranks of four or five abreast.

We would need the lively and bleak brush of a Salvator or a Goya[199] to sketch these diverse specimens of physical and moral ugliness, to render in all its hideous freakishness the variety of apparel these unfortunate men wore. For the most part, they were covered in wretched clothing, for, since they were still only accused men—that is, they were officially presumed innocent—they did not wear prison uniforms. Some of the detainees wore them, for upon entering the prison their rags had appeared so sordid, so filthy, that after the customary bath[200] they were given the convict's uniform of a coarse gray cloth jacket and trousers.

A phrenologist would take real interest in these gaunt and weather-beaten faces, with their flattened or sunken foreheads, their cruel or insidious gazes, their wicked or stupid-looking mouths, and their huge necks. Almost all of them offered some kind of terrifying resemblance to animals. Beneath the sly features of this one could be found the perfidious subtlety of the fox; of that one, the bloodthirsty rapacity of the bird of prey; of another, the ferocity of the tiger; of still another, finally, just brute, animal stupidity.

There was something strangely sinister about the circular walk of this band of silent beings, with their bold and hate-filled looks, their insolent and cynical laughter, pressing against each other at the back of this courtyard that was shaped like a kind of square well. It sent chills up one's spine to think that this savage horde would, at a certain point, be released back into the very world upon which it had declared unrelenting war. How many bloodthirsty plots of revenge, how many homicidal plans were still incubating beneath their looks of mocking and impudent perversity!

Let us portray only some of the salient physiognomies of the Lions'

199. Salvator Rosa (1615–1673), Naples painter, known for paintings of witches and criminals, had a major influence on the Spanish Romantic Francisco Goya (1746–1828), known for his dark and disturbing paintings. [TN]

200. Thanks to a rule that is also an excellent hygienic measure, each prisoner is taken to the prison baths upon his arrival and then two times a month; his clothes are subsequently put through a process of sanitary fumigation. For an artisan, a hot bath is a sought-after and unheard-of luxury. [SN]

Den, leaving others in the background. While a guard was watching the men who were walking, a kind of secret meeting was taking place in the furnace room. Among the prisoners who were there were Fishhook and Nicolas Martial, whom we mention only for the record. The prisoner who seemed to be presiding over and leading the discussion, so to speak, was a man nicknamed the Skeleton,[201] a name we have heard mentioned several times in the Martials' home on the Scavenger's Island. The Skeleton was the provost or captain of the furnace room. This man, of rather tall stature, about forty years old, lived up to his nickname by being thinner than one could imagine. We might almost call it osteological thinness.

If the faces of the Skeleton's companions could be said more or less to bear comparison to those of the tiger, vulture, or fox, his features, with his forehead sloping backward, his bony, flat, and elongated jaws that were supported by a disproportionately long neck, looked entirely like the head of a snake. His total baldness increased this hideous resemblance because one could see, underneath the rough skin of his almost reptilian forehead, the smallest protuberances, the smallest sutures of his skull. As for his hairless visage, one need only imagine an old piece of parchment glued straight onto the bones of his face, with only a slight tightness from the jutting of the cheekbone to the angle of the lower jaw, whose joint one could very distinctly see. His small, squinting eyes were so deeply embedded, and his eyebrows and cheekbones were so prominent, that one could see two orbs literally filled with shadow beneath his highlighted, jaundiced forehead. From a short distance his eyes seemed to disappear into the depths of these two dark cavities, of these two black holes that gave such a sinister aspect to his skeleton's head. His long teeth, with their alveolar protrusions perfectly visible under the tanned skin of his flattened, bony jaws, were almost incessantly revealed by his habitual death's head grin. Although the wasted muscles of this man were almost reduced to the state of tendons, he was extraordinarily

201. About this name, we feel a pang of conscience. This year, a poor devil named Decure, who was guilty only of being a vagabond, was sentenced to a month of prison. His occupation was in fact that of being a walking skeleton in a fair, thanks to his unbelievable and shocking thinness. His type seemed curious to us, so we have made use of it. However, the real skeleton has nothing morally in common with our fictional character. Here is a fragment from Decure's deposition:

The presiding judge: What were you doing in the community of Maisons at the moment of your arrest?

R.: I was engaged in the usual practices of my occupation of Walking Skeleton, performing all sorts of exercises to amuse children. I starve my body to a skeletal condition; I flex my bones and muscles; I eat arsenic, corrosive sublimate disinfectant, toads, spiders, and all insects generally; I also swallow fire, I swallow boiling oil and bathe in it; at least once a year I am summoned to Paris by such celebrated doctors as Messieurs Dubois and Orfila who have me do all sorts of experiments with my body, etc., etc., etc." (*Court Bulletin*). [SN]

strong. Even the most robust of men had a hard time breaking the grip of his long arms and his long, fleshless fingers. One might call it the fearsome grip of an iron skeleton. He wore a blue workman's shirt with sleeves that were far too short and that revealed, to his great pride, his knotty hands and half of his forearms, or rather two bones (called the radius and the ulna, if we may be forgiven the anatomy lesson), two bones wrapped in rough, grimy skin, separated by a deep furrow along which serpentined several hard, dry, ropy veins. When he put his hands on a table, his knucklebones looked like a set of jacks, to borrow Bitters's apt metaphor.

After having spent fifteen years of his life in the galleys for theft and attempted murder, the Skeleton had broken his parole and then been caught red-handed committing theft and murder. This last murder had been committed under such vicious circumstances that, considering the fact he was a repeat offender, this criminal rightly considered himself as already condemned to death.

The influence that the Skeleton had on the other prisoners due to his strength, energy, and perversity had made the director of the prison choose him as the dormitory provost. This is to say that the Skeleton was responsible for policing his barrack room with respect to the order, arrangement, and cleanliness of the room and beds. He did this job perfectly, and no prisoner dared to fail to fulfill duties that fell under his purview.

This brings us to consider a strange and significant fact: even the most intelligent prison directors, after having tried to vest the functions we've mentioned in the prisoners who recommended themselves by virtue of some remnants of honesty, or in the ones whose crimes were least serious, found themselves forced to give up this choice, no matter how logical or moral, in favor of the most corrupt and dreaded leaders among the prisoners. These were the only ones who could wield a positive influence over their companions. So, let us say it again: the more a guilty party demonstrates cynicism and audacity, the more he will be accepted, and the more he will be respected, in a manner of speaking. Does not this fact, proven by experience, enforced by the compulsory choices of which we speak, constitute an irrefutable argument against the vice of group confinement? Does it not demonstrate, to the point of constituting absolute evidence, the intensity of the contagion that fatally infects those prisoners for whom one could yet hope for some chance at rehabilitation? Yes, for how can we hope for repentance and improvement when in the pandemonium in which one must spend long years, one's life perhaps, one sees influence measured by the number of heinous crimes one has committed? Again, do we not know that the outer world, that honest society no longer exists for the prisoner? Indifferent to the moral laws that govern them, he can only assume the customs of those who surround him. All of the distinctions of jail being assigned on the basis of the superiority of the crime, he will always and inevitably radiate toward this fierce aristocracy.

Let us return to the Skeleton, leader of the barrack room, who was talking with several prisoners, among whom were Fishhook and Nicolas Martial.

"Are you completely sure of what you're saying?" the Skeleton asked Martial.

"Yes, yes, a hundred times yes. Old Micou got it from the Big Gimp, who already wanted to kill that guy because he had ratted someone out."

"So let's beat him to a pulp and have done with it!" added Fishhook. This showed how much the Skeleton was already in favor of making things hot for poor, innocent Germain.

The leader took his pipe out of his mouth for a moment and said, in a voice that was so quiet and so sordidly hoarse that he could hardly be heard, "Germain did whatever he pleased. He was bugging us. He was spying on us, because the less you talk, the more you listen. We should have forced him to leave the Lions' Den right after we first let a little of his blood. They would have taken him out of here."

"So, then," said Nicolas, "what's changed?"

"Here's what's changed," said the Skeleton. "If he ratted, like the Big Gimp says, it won't be enough to just let his blood a little."

"That's talking," said Fishhook.

"We need to make an example of him," said the Skeleton, getting more and more animated. "Now it's not the coppers who are after us—it's stoolies. Jacques and Gauthier, the guys who were guillotined the other day—ratted out. Roussillon, the guy who got sent to the galleys for the duration—ratted out."

"And me? And my mother? And Calabash? And my brother at Toulon?" exclaimed Nicolas. "Didn't Red-Arm rat all of us out? We know that now since instead of locking him up here, they've taken him to the Roquette prison! They didn't dare throw him in here with us—you could smell what he did a mile off, the bum."

"Me, too. Didn't Red-Arm rat me out, too?" asked Fishhook.

"And what about me?" said a young prisoner with a frail voice, lisping in an affected manner. "I was skunked by Jobert, a man who had come up with a job for me on rue Saint-Martin."

This last character had a fluted voice, a pale, fat, effeminate face, and an insidious and cowardly look. He was dressed in a singular way: in the place of a hat, he wore a red scarf on his head that revealed two strands of blond hair that were stuck to his temples. The two ends of the handkerchief formed a bouffant bow over his forehead. As a tie, he wore a white merino shawl with green palm trees on it across his chest. His brown cloth jacket disappeared beneath the narrow belt of his wide plaid trousers with large multicolored squares.

"What an indignity! You'd have to be a worthless scoundrel!" said this character in a precious tone of voice. "I wouldn't have guessed that about Jobert for anything in the world."

"I knew full well that he denounced you, Javotte," said the Skeleton, who seemed to be protecting this prisoner with special care. "The proof of that is that they did the same thing with that stoolie as they did with Red-Arm. They didn't dare leave Jobert in here. They locked him up at the Conciergerie. Well, we've got to put an end to it. We have to make an example of someone. False friends are doing the job of policing. They don't worry about their hides because they've been put in another prison from the guys they ratted out."

"It's true!"

"To stop this from happening, all prisoners have to look upon every stoolie as an enemy to the death. Whether he ratted on Pierre or on Jacques, here or somewhere else, it makes no difference—let him have it. When we've put four or five of the ones we find in the courtyard into the deep freeze, others will think twice before they rat out any more of us heisters."

"You're right, Skeleton," said Nicolas. "So Germain will have to die."

"He will die," said the leader. "But let's wait until the Big Gimp arrives. When he shows everyone that Germain is a stoolie, we'll know what we need to and we'll have our example. The sheep won't bleat again. We'll suffocate him."

"And what will we do about the guards who are watching over us?" asked the prisoner whom the Skeleton called Javotte.

"I have a trick up my sleeve. Bitters will help us."

"Him? He's too much of a coward."

"And he's as weak as a flea."

"Doesn't matter. I know what I need. Where is he?"

"He came back from the visiting room, but they just came in to get him so he could chew things over with his mouthpiece."

"And is Germain still in the visiting room?"

"Yes, with that little girl who comes to see him."

"As soon as he comes in, be careful! But we have to wait for Bitters. We can't do anything without him."

"Without Bitters?"

"No."

"And we'll ice Germain?"

"That's my lookout."

"But what will we use? They took away our knives."

"What about these pincers? Would you put your neck in them?" asked the Skeleton, opening his long fingers, fleshless and strong as iron.

"You'll strangle him?"

"Just a little."

"But what if they know you did it?"

"So what? Am I a calf with two heads like the ones they show at the fair?"

"It's true. You can only have one head chopped off, and since you're sure you're going to be—"

"Super sure. My mouthpiece told me so again yesterday. I got nabbed with my hand in the patsy's bag and my knife in his throat. I'm on a return ticket, so it's all over. I'm going to send my head to the executioner's basket to see if it's true that he swindles condemned men and puts wood shavings in there instead of the sawdust that the government allows us."

"That's true. The guillotined man has the right to his sawdust. They robbed my father, too. I remember it!" cried Nicolas Martial with a savage chuckle. This abominable joke made the prisoners break out laughing.

While this exchange may be frightening, far from exaggerating, we are toning down these conversations that happen so commonly in prison. We repeat that it is nevertheless important that one have an idea, even toned down, of what is said and what is done in these appalling schools of perdition, cynicism, theft, and murder. It is important that one know the kind of bold disdain with which almost all great criminals speak of the most terrible punishments to which society subjects them. Then, perhaps, one will understand the urgency of substituting for these impotent penalties, these contagious confinements, the only punishment that is capable of terrifying the most determined scoundrels, as we will amply show.

So, as we were saying, the prisoners in the furnace room had been overcome by laughter. "Damn!" exclaimed the Skeleton. "I'd like that passel of beaks who think they're making us shiver and shake before their guillotine to see us joking around. They won't have to go any further than the Saint-Jacques barrier the day of my benefit performance.[202] They'll hear me making fun of the crowd and saying to Old Charlie[203] in a jaunty voice, 'Old Samson,[204] pull the rope, please!'"[205]

There was more laughter.

"The fact is you can swallow tobacco faster . . . Charlie pulls the rope . . ."

"And he opens the devil's door for you," said the Skeleton, continuing to smoke his pipe.

"Oh, come on! There's no such thing as the devil."

---

202. From 1832 until 1851, executions were carried out at the Saint-Jacques barrier. [TN]

203. See Book VI, Chapter 2, footnote 135. [TN]

204. Meaning Sanson, as explained in note 135. This misspelling may be Sue's error. In French, Sanson and Samson sound nearly identical. [TN]

205. To understand the meaning of this horrible joke, one must know that the blade slides between the grooves of the guillotine after having been set in motion by the loosening of a spring by means of a rope attached to it. [SN]

"Imbecile! I was just saying that to be funny. There's a blade, a head they put under it, and that's it."

"As for me, now that I know where I'm going and that the next stop is the Abbey on Scaffold Mountain, it doesn't much matter to me whether it's today or tomorrow," said the Skeleton, with savage joy. "I'd like to be there already. My mouth waters—with blood—when I think of the crowd that will be there to see me. There will be four or five thousand people who will be pushing and shoving each other for the best seats. People will rent out their windows and chairs as if it were a parade. I can already hear them yelling, 'Seat for rent! Seat for rent!'—and then there will be troops, cavalry and infantry, and all the trimmings, all laid out and ready . . . all for me, for the Skeleton. They don't do that kind of thing for the patsies—huh, guys? That's how you get a guy to go up there. If he's a coward like Bitters, that puts some iron in your spine. All of those eyes looking at you puts the fire in your belly. And besides, it's just one bad moment you have to get through, and you die in a jaunty way. It gets to the patsies and the judges, and it encourages us heisters to laugh in the grim reaper's mug."

"It's true," said Fishhook, trying to imitate the Skeleton's frightful braggadocio. "They think they're scaring us, and they think they get the last word when they send Old Charlie to open up his shop for us."

"Oh, really!" said Nicolas in turn. "We do a pretty good job mocking Old Charlie's shop! It's like prison or the galleys. We make fun of them, too. As long as you've got your friends around you, long live joy until death do us part!"

"That's for sure," said the prisoner with the precious tone of voice. "What would be really grating is if they put us alone in a cell day and night. They say that it'll come to that."

"In a cell?" exclaimed the Skeleton in an angry sort of fear. "Don't talk about that. A cell, all alone? Just shut your trap. I'd rather they cut off my arms and legs. All alone? Stuck between four walls? All alone, without any old thieves to laugh with me? I couldn't bear that! I like the galleys a hundred times better than the prisons, because in the galleys, instead of being locked up, you're outside, you see people, you come and you go, you crack wise with the crew. Well, I'd rather have my head chopped off a hundred times than be put in a cell for even one year. Yes, at this point, I'm sure I'm going to be mown down, right? Well, if they were to ask me, 'Do you want a year in a cell?' I'd stretch my neck right out for them to chop. A year alone! Is it even possible? What do they expect you to think about when you're all alone?"

"What would you do if they forced you into a cell?"

"I wouldn't stay there. I'd kick and scream until I got out," the Skeleton said.

"But if you couldn't . . . if you were sure you couldn't get out?"

"So then I'd kill the first guy who came along and get myself guillotined."

"But if instead of condemning cutthroats to death, they condemned them to a cell for the rest of their lives?"

The Skeleton appeared to be struck by this idea. After a moment of silence, he said, "Then I don't know what I would do. I'd crack my skull open against the walls. I'd starve to death rather than be in a cell. What? All alone, all my life alone, with . . . myself? Without any hope of getting away? I'm telling you, you can't do it. Look, there's no one that's got more sand than me. I would stick a shiv in a guy for six centimes—I'd even do it for nothing, for honor. They think I've only murdered two people, but if the dead could speak, there would be five guys in the deep freeze who could tell you how I get the job done."

The criminal was bragging. These bloody boasts are another trait that most characterizes hardened criminals. A prison director would tell us, "If these wretches had ever killed as many as they said they did, the population would be decimated."

"Just like me," said Fishhook in order to boast in his own right. "People think I've only offed the husband of the milk vendor from the Cité. But I've done the same for plenty of others just like Big Robert, the guy who was mown down last year."

"I was just telling you," said the Skeleton, "that I don't fear hell or high water. Well, if I were in a cell, and completely certain that I would never escape—well, damn, I think I'd be afraid."

"Of what?" asked Nicolas.

"Of being all alone," answered the provost.

"So if you had to start stealing and killing all over again, and if, instead of prisons, galleys, and the guillotine, there were only cells and solitary confinement, would you think twice before you went bad?"

"My Lord, yes . . . maybe—[this is historically accurate[206]]," answered the Skeleton. And he was telling the truth. It is impossible to imagine the unutterable terror that the mere idea of absolute isolation inspires in such criminals. Isn't this terror yet another eloquent argument in favor of this penalty? But that's not all. The sentence of solitary confinement, so feared by scoundrels, will, perhaps, have as its necessary consequence the abolition of the death penalty. Here is how: The criminal generation that currently populates our prisons and galleys will regard condemnation to solitary confinement as an intolerable torture. Accustomed to the perverse liveliness of group imprisonment that we have tried to sketch, toning down a few of its features—for, we repeat, we must recoil before monstrosities of every sort—these men, we say, seeing themselves facing the threat, if they are recidivists, of being sequestered from the vile world in which they expiate their crimes so blithely, and being put in a solitary

206. In brackets in the French text. [TN]

cell with only the memories of the past . . . these men will revolt at the idea of this terrifying punishment.

Many will prefer death. And to incur capital punishment, they will not hesitate to commit murder. For, strangely, of every ten criminals who want to stop living, there are nine who will kill in order to be killed for every one who will commit suicide. And so, we repeat, surely, the last vestige of a barbarous law will disappear from our codes. In order to deprive murderers of this last refuge that they believe they will find in nothingness, we will be forced to abolish the death penalty.

But will a life sentence of solitary confinement offer reparation or a punishment severe enough for certain serious crimes such as parricide, among others? People can escape from the most securely guarded prison—or at least they can hope to escape. The criminals of whom we speak must not be allowed this possibility or this hope.

But in the same way, the death penalty, which has no other purpose than to rid society of harmful individuals; the death penalty, which rarely gives condemned men a chance to repent, and never the time to rehabilitate themselves through expiation; the death penalty, which some undergo in a faint, almost without being conscious, and others brave with appalling cynicism; the death penalty will perhaps be replaced by a terrible punishment, but one that gives the condemned man the time for repentance and expiation, and one that will not violently cut off from this world one of God's children.

Blinding[207] will deprive the murderer of the possibility of escaping and harming anyone ever again. The death penalty will be thus effectively replaced in this, its only purpose. For our society does not kill in the name of *lex talionis*.[208] It does not kill to make someone suffer, for it has chosen, from among all possible ways, the method that it believes the least painful of all with which to do it.[209] It kills in the name of its own safety.

---

207. We use this barbarous expression because the noun form, "sightlessness," refers to that which is caused by accidental illness or natural accident. On the other hand, this noun deriving from the verb expresses our thought more accurately: the action of blinding someone. [SN]

The noun *aveuglement* for "blindness" is obsolete. The usual word is *cécité*. We have artificially rendered the first as "blinding" and the second as "sightlessness." Behind Sue's pedantry here is his comparison of Rodolphe's earlier blinding of the Schoolmaster with his argument for solitary confinement. Without that justification (and what Rodolphe says about what he does tracks Sue's argument here almost point for point), one might share the Slasher's unspoken sense of its barbarousness. [TN]

208. The law of an eye for an eye. [TN]

209. My father, Doctor Jean-Joseph Sue, believed the opposite. He published a series of profound and interesting observations on this subject which tended to show that consciousness lasts several minutes after the instantaneous decapitation. This probability alone makes one shiver in terror. [SN]

Now, what can it fear from someone imprisoned in blindness? Finally, the prospect of a life sentence of solitary confinement, leavened by charitable visits from honest and pious people who will devote themselves to this noble mission of soul-saving, would permit the murderer to redeem his soul through long years of remorse and contrition.

A great tumult and raucous exclamations of joy raised by the prisoners who were walking in the yard interrupted the secret meeting over which the Skeleton was presiding. Nicolas got up quickly and advanced to the doorstep of the furnace room in order to find out the cause of this unusual noise. "It's the Big Gimp!" cried Nicolas on his return.

"The Big Gimp!" cried the provost. "Has Germain left the visitors' room?"

"Not yet," said Fishhook.

"Let him come quickly," said the Skeleton, "so I can give him a voucher for a brand-new coffin."

CHAPTER 7

THE CONSPIRACY

The Big Gimp, whose arrival the prisoners of the Lions' Den had greeted with such joy and whose denunciation could be so fatal to Germain, was a man of average height. In spite of his stoutness and disability, he appeared to be agile and vigorous. His animal-like face, like that of the majority of his companions, had much in common with a bulldog's. His sunken forehead, his small, wild eyes, his jowly cheeks, his heavy jaws, the lower of which was quite prominent and full of long teeth, or rather of jagged fangs that jutted out in spots past his lips, made his resemblance to the animal all the more striking. He wore a beaver cap on his head, and over his clothes he wore a blue coat with a fur collar.

The Big Gimp had come into the prison in the company of a man who was about thirty years old, whose browned and sunburned face looked less degraded than those of the other prisoners, although he was trying to look as tough as his companion. At some moments his face darkened and he gave a bitter smile.

The Big Gimp found himself back on familiar territory, as the saying goes. He could hardly respond to all of the shouts of congratulation and welcome that the inmates volleyed at him from all sides.

"Here you are, then, finally, you jolly guy! This is great—now we'll have a good time!"

"We missed you."

"It took you long enough!"

"But I did what you're supposed to to get back in here and see my friends. It's not my fault if the coppers didn't get to me sooner."

"That's true enough, old buddy. You can't lock yourself up by yourself. But once you're here, the time passes and you might as well enjoy it!"

"You're in luck: Bitters is in here!"

"Him, too? An old pal from Melun! Fantastic! Fantastic! He'll help us pass the time with all his stories, and he won't lack for customers, either. We've got some new recruits."

"Who are they?"

"In the office, a moment ago, while they were locking me up, they brought in two new types. One of them, I don't know, but the other one, a guy in a blue cotton hat and a gray work shirt, him I seem to remember.

I think I saw him at the ogress's joint, the White Rabbit. He's a strong fellow."

"So, Big Gimp, do you remember at Melun when I bet you that you'd be picked up again within a year?"

"It's true—you win the bet. I've had more chances to get my return ticket than to be declared May Queen. But what about you? What have you done?"

"I did a sting on someone."

"Still playing the same game, huh?"

"The very same. Little by little, I make my way. It's an old trick, but there's a sucker born every minute, and if it weren't for my partner's stupidity, I wouldn't be here. It's all right. I'll learn from this lesson. When I start up again, I'll be more careful. I've thought the thing out."

"Hey, there's Cardillac," said the Gimp as he saw a little man coming over to him who was wretchedly dressed. He had a low, mean, and devious-looking face that resembled that of the fox and the wolf. "Hello, buddy!"

"Howdy there, you straggler," the prisoner named Cardillac said gaily to the Big Gimp. "We kept saying, 'He'll come,' and then, 'No, he won't come.' Monsieur acts like a beautiful woman: he makes us come after her."

"But of course."

"You joker!" said Cardillac. "Are you here for something a little racier this time?"

"Honestly, my friend, I'm here for burglary. Before that, I'd done some very good jobs, but the last one turned into a mess. It was a terrific deal—one that's still there for someone to pull off. But unfortunately, Frank and I blew it." And the Big Gimp gestured toward his companion, to whom all eyes turned.

"Hey, it's true! It's Frank!" said Cardillac. "I would never have recognized him in that beard of his. Is that really you? I thought you'd be the mayor of your place by now. Didn't you mean to go straight?"

"I was stupid and got punished for it," said Frank, brusquely. "But there's mercy for every sin, and I won't make that mistake twice. Now I'm a thief—I'm a thief till I die! When I get out of here, watch out!"

"That's great. That's the way to talk."

"So what happened to you, Frank?"

"The same thing that happens to any ex-con who's enough of a ninny to go straight, as you put it. It's just what they deserve! After I got out of Melun, I had a pile of nine hundred francs and change."

"That's true," said the Big Gimp. "All his troubles come from saving his money instead of frittering it away as soon as he got out of prison. You'll see what repentance gets you, and that's if you get only what you paid for it."

"They paroled me to Étampes," Frank continued. "As a locksmith by training, I was working under a master of the trade. I said to him, 'I'm an ex-convict. I know that people don't like to hire folks like me, but here are nine hundred francs I've piled up. Give me work; my money will be your collateral. I want to work and go straight.'"

"Honest to God, leave it to Frank to come up with an idea like that one."

"He was always a little cracked."

"Ha! Like a locksmith cracking a lock!"

"Joker."

"And you'll see how that worked out for him."

"So I offer my money as collateral to the master locksmith so he'll give me work. 'I'm not a banker where you can deposit money and get interest,' he says to me. 'And I don't want an ex-convict in my shop. I work in houses and open doors for which people have lost their keys. I have a reputation to uphold, and if people knew that one of my workers was an ex-convict, I'd lose all my business. Good evening, neighbor.'"

"Didn't he get just what he deserved, Cardillac?"

"He sure did."

"What a child!" Big Gimp added as he turned to Frank with a paternal gesture. "All that, instead of just breaking parole right away, coming to Paris, blowing your wad, not having a sou, and needing to steal in the first place! That's how you come up with such great ideas."

"You're always saying the same thing!" Frank said, impatiently. "It's true, I was wrong not to spend my pile right away, since I didn't get to enjoy it. To return to my parole: since there were only four locksmiths in Étampes, the first one I went to see blabbed to all the others, so when I went to ask the others for work, they all said the same thing as their colleague. Thanks a bunch. Everywhere, the same tune."

"Do you see, friends, what good it does? We're branded for life, you see?"

"So here I am locked out on the streets of Étampes. I live on my savings for a month or two," Frank said. "The money was running out, the work wasn't coming in. Parole or not, I leave Étampes."

"That's what you should have done right way, silly."

"I come to Paris. There, I find work. My boss didn't know who I was. I tell him I've come from the provinces. No one worked harder than I did. I place seven hundred francs I have left with a business agent who gives me a note for it. When the note comes due, he won't pay me. I give the note to a bailiff, who goes after the agent and gets the note paid. I leave my money with him, and I say, 'That'll be there for a rainy day.' That's when I meet the Big Gimp."

"Yes, friends, I was the rainy day, as you'll see. Frank was a locksmith who made keys. I had a job in mind and he could be of use to me, so I offered him a part in it. I had some imprints. All he needed to do was make keys out of them; that was his part. The little baby refused me because he wanted to go straight this time. I say to myself, 'I'm going to have to do what's best for him whether he likes it or not.' I write an anonymous letter to his boss and another to his companions telling them that Frank is an ex-convict. The boss throws him out and his companions turn their backs on him. He goes to another boss and works for him for a week. Same thing happens. If he'd gone to ten of them I would have kept on doing the same thing."

"And I still didn't suspect that you were the one who was ratting on me," said Frank. "If I had, you would have had a hard time of it."

"Yes, but I'm not so stupid, so I told you that I was leaving for Longjumeau to see my uncle, but I had stayed in Paris, and I knew everything you were doing through little Ledru."

"Finally, I got kicked out of my last locksmith job, like I wasn't fit to be hanged. You try to get a job and mind your own business and still all anyone says to you is not 'What do you do for a living?' but 'What were you before?' Once I was back on the streets, I say to myself, 'It's a good thing I have some money set aside.' I go to the bailiff, but he'd hotfooted it out of town. My money was down the hatch, I didn't have a single sou, I didn't even have the money to pay for a week of lodging. You should have seen how angry I was! At that point, the Big Gimp acts like he's come back from Longjumeau. He takes advantage of my anger. I was really between a rock and a hard place. I could see there was no way to go straight, but that once you took up lifting things again, that would be it for life. And my Lord, the Big Gimp was spurring me on so hard . . ."

"So our good Frank stopped turning up his nose at me," the Big Gimp said. "He does his part for real. He gets involved in the jobs, and it looks like it's going to work like a house afire, but unfortunately, just as we're about to get our hands on the dough, we get picked up by the police. What can you do, my boy? It's a pain, but the business would be too good to be true without that part of it."

"It's all right. If that crook of a bailiff hadn't robbed me, I wouldn't be here," said Frank, simmering with anger.

"Well, well!" said the Big Gimp. "You've really caught the bug. Were you really happier when you were breaking your back working?"

"I was free."

"Yes, on Sundays, and when there wasn't too much work, but the rest of the week you're chained up like a dog and you never know when you'll have work. You don't know what's best for you."

"You'll teach me," said Frank, bitterly.

"Well, let's be fair, after all. You have the right to be peeved. It's too bad that the job didn't come off. It was a brilliant plan, and it will be again in a month or two. The rich folks will let down their guard, and they'll be good for the taking again. It's a rich house—a rich one! I'm in for good for breaking parole, so it's not for me anymore. But if I find an aficionado, I'll sell him my idea on the cheap. The imprints are with my woman. All you need to do is make new counterfeit keys. With the information I can provide, it'll work by itself. There was—and there still is—ten thousand francs for the taking. That should make you feel better anyway, Frank."

The Big Gimp's accomplice shook his head, crossed his arms over his chest, and didn't answer.

Cardillac took the Big Gimp by the arm and drew him into a corner of the yard. He said to him, after a moment of silence, "That business that went bad: is it still worth doing?"

"In two months, it'll be as good as new."

"Can you prove it?"

"Hell, yes!"

"How much do you want for it?"

"A hundred francs in advance, and I'll give you the word for my woman so she gives you the imprints for the counterfeit keys. Then, if the job pans out, I want a fifth of the profit, which you'll give to my woman."

"That seems fair."

"And I'll know who got the imprints from her, so I'll denounce anyone who tries to rip me off for my share. It'll be too bad for them."

"You'd be in the right if someone tried to take you like that. But honor among thieves. We have to be able to count on each other. Otherwise, no job would ever get pulled off."

Here was another anomaly of prison morality: this wretch was telling the truth. It is very rare for thieves to go back on their word for these kinds of deals. These criminal transactions operate under a sort of good faith—or rather, so that we don't degrade this word, let's say that necessity forces these bandits to keep their promise. For if they do not, as the Big Gimp's friend said, no job would ever get pulled off. A great number of jobs are passed along, bought, and planned in this way in prison: another disgusting consequence of group confinement.

"If what you're saying is solid," said Cardillac, "I could pull the heist off. There is no real evidence against me. I'm sure to get off. I have my trial in two weeks. In twenty days, say, I'll be released. The time it will take to return, get skeleton keys made, and get information, let's say about a month to six weeks."

"That's all you need for the bosses to let their guard down. And besides, someone who's attacked once thinks it'll never happen to him again. You know how it works."

"I know. I'll do it. It's a deal."

"But do you have anything to pay me with? I want to see a deposit."

"Look, here's my last button. There are more where that one came from," said Cardillac as he tore off one of his fabric-covered buttons that ornamented his dingy blue waistcoat. Then he tore the covering with his fingernails and showed the Big Gimp that, instead of an empty mold, there was a forty-franc piece inside the button. "You see," he added, "I can give you a deposit when we've worked out the details."

"Well, then, let's shake on it, pal," said the Big Gimp. "Since you're leaving soon and you have the money for the job, I can give you something else that's a real beauty. I've got a little heist I thought up a long time back, that my woman and I have been hatching for two months and is just ready to go. Just think, an isolated house in an out-of-the-way neighborhood. There's a ground floor that looks out on one side on a deserted street, and on the other side, on a garden. Two old people who sleep like the dead. Since the riots, for fear of being looted, they have hidden a big jam jar full of gold in their paneling. My woman found all this out by making their servant blab. But I have to tell you, this job will cost you more than the last one. It's money in the bank, all dressed up and ready to go."

"We'll come to terms, don't worry. But I see you've really been at it since you got out of prison."

"Yes, I've been lucky. I've put together one thing and another and come up with fifteen hundred francs. One of my best hauls was the cash box of two women who were living in the same house as me, on the passage de la Brasserie."

"At the house of Old Micou, the fence?"

"That's right."

"And how's your woman, Joséphine?"

"She's still a real bloodhound. She was doing housework for those old people I was telling you about. She's the one who smelled out the pot of honey."

"What a great woman!"

"I'm proud of her. Speaking of great women, did you hear about the Owl?"

"Yes, Nicolas told me about it. The Schoolmaster bashed her brains out. And he's gone nuts."

"Maybe from having gone blind, I don't know how. So, Cardillac, old pal, it's a deal. Since you want to pull off my jobs, I won't tell anyone else about them."

"Tell no one. I'll take them on as part of getting out of here. We'll talk about them tonight."

"So, really, what do you guys do in here?"

"We laugh and we blather on forever."

"Who's provost of the barrack room?"

"The Skeleton."

"That guy's a tough cookie! I saw him at the Martials' place on the Scavenger's Island. We had a night of it with Joséphine and Chubs."

"Speaking of them, Nicolas is here."

"I know, Old Micou told me. He's complaining that Nicolas is blackmailing him, the old beggar. I'll teach him to dance to my music, too—that's what fences are for."

"We were speaking of the Skeleton, and there he is now," said Cardillac as he pointed out the provost, who had appeared in the doorway to the furnace room, to his companion.

"Answer to the call, soldier," said the Skeleton to the Big Gimp.

"Present, sir," the latter answered as he entered the room accompanied by Frank, whom he took by the arm.

During the conversation among the Big Gimp, Frank, and Cardillac, Fishhook had gone, on their leader's orders, to recruit twelve or fifteen handpicked prisoners. These men, so as not to arouse the suspicions of the guard, had come into the furnace room one at a time.

The other prisoners remained in the yard. A few of them, at Fishhook's request, were even talking loudly and in angry tones in order to distract the guard from what was going on in the furnace room, where the Skeleton, Fishhook, Nicolas, Frank, Cardillac, the Big Gimp, and about fifteen prisoners had gathered, all waiting eagerly to hear what the provost had to say.

Fishhook, who was placed on the lookout so he could announce the approach of the guard, stood next to the door. The Skeleton, taking his pipe out of his mouth, said to the Big Gimp, "Do you know a little young man named Germain, with blue eyes, brown hair, and the look of a patsy?"

"Germain is here?" exclaimed the Big Gimp, whose face instantly expressed surprise, hatred, and anger.

"So you know him?" asked the Skeleton.

"Do I know him?" said the Big Gimp. "My friends, I denounce him. He's a stoolie. We've got to work him over."

"Yes! Yes!" said the prisoners.

"But, really, are you sure he's ratted on anybody?" asked Frank. "What if you're wrong? Working over a guy who doesn't deserve it . . ."

This observation displeased the Skeleton, who leaned toward the Big Gimp and asked him, in a whisper, "Who is that guy?"

"A guy I worked with."

"Do you trust him?"

"Yes, but he's got no guts. He's spineless."

"Got it. I'll keep an eye on him."

"Tell us how Germain is a stoolie," said a prisoner.

"Tell us in detail, Big Gimp," said the Skeleton, who did not let Frank out of his sight.

"Here's how it is," the Big Gimp said. "A guy from Nantes called Hairy, an old ex-convict, educated the young man, whose parents were unknown. When he was of age, he placed him with a moneybags banker in Nantes, thinking he would be putting the fox in the henhouse and using Germain to pull off a brilliant heist that he had been hatching for a long while. He had two arrows in his quiver: a forgery and the sure thing of the moneybags' safe. Maybe a hundred thousand francs to be made in two separate parts. Everything was ready. Hairy trusted the little young man as he trusted himself. That scamp was sleeping in the building that housed the safe. Hairy told him his plan. Germain didn't answer yes or no. He told his boss the whole story and got out that very night for Paris."

The prisoners let out violent oaths of indignation and threats under their breaths. "He's a stoolie. We should skin him alive!"

"If you want, I'll get into a fight with him, and I'll finish him off!"

"Let's carve an admission slip to the hospital for him on his face!"

"Silence in the joint!" cried the Skeleton in an imperious voice. The prisoners went silent. "Go on," the provost said to the Big Gimp. And then he went on smoking.

"Thinking that Germain had said yes, counting on his help, Hairy and two of his friends tried the job that very night. The moneybags was waiting for them. One of Hairy's friends was pinched as he was climbing into a window, and he was lucky enough to escape. He comes to Paris, furious at having been ratted out by Germain and for having been tripped up on a great job. One fine day, he meets the little young man. It was broad daylight. He doesn't dare do anything, but he follows him. He sees where he lives, and one night, Hairy and me and little Ledru, we all jump Germain. Bad luck; he gets away. He scrams from rue du Temple, where he's been living. Since then, we haven't been able to find him again, but if he's here, I request—"

"You have nothing to request," said the Skeleton with authority.

The Big Gimp fell silent.

"I'll take charge of this. Grant me Germain's skin and I'll flay him alive. My name isn't the Skeleton for nothing. I am already dead. My grave's already been dug in Clamart. It doesn't cost me a thing to work for the good of all of us thieves. These stoolies are eating us alive, even worse than the police. They put the stoolies from La Force prison in the Roquette prison, and the stoolies from the Roquette in the Conciergerie. They think they're safe. But just wait. When each prison has killed its stoolie, it doesn't matter who he's ratted out, it'll make them think twice about doing it again. I'll set the example. The rest will follow."

All of the prisoners, admiring the Skeleton's determination, crowded around him. Fishhook himself, instead of staying next to the door, joined the group. He didn't notice that a new prisoner had entered the visiting room. The latter, dressed in a gray worker's shirt and wearing a blue cotton cap embroidered in dark red wool pulled down over his eyes, made a movement when he heard the name Germain. Then he went to mix among the Skeleton's admirers and clearly demonstrated his approval of the provost's criminal decision, both in voice and action.

"He's a sharp one, that Skeleton," one of them said, "a real professor!"

"The devil himself couldn't make him show the white feather!"

"That's a real man!"

"If every thief had his sand, we'd all be the judges and we'd send the patsies to the guillotine!"

"That's only right—turnabout is fair play."

"Yes, but they aren't working together on this."

"That doesn't matter. He's doing us a great service. When they see that they'll get killed, there won't be any more stoolies."

"That's for sure."

"And since it's dead certain that they'll guillotine the Skeleton, killing the stoolie costs him nothing."

"Me, I think it's harsh," said Frank, "killing that young man."

"What? What are you saying!" the Skeleton said in an angry voice. "Are you saying we don't have the right to knock off traitors?"

"Well, yes, he is a traitor. Too bad for him," said Frank, after a moment of reflection. These last words and the Big Gimp's assurance calmed the distrust Frank had aroused for a moment in the prisoners. The Skeleton alone continued to distrust him.

"Now, then! What are we going to do with the guard? Tell us, Dead Already—for that's your name just as much as Skeleton," said Nicolas, snickering.

"Well, we'll keep the guard busy and out of the way."

"No, let's restrain him by force."

"Yes!"

"No!"

"Silence in the joint!" said the Skeleton.

Again, a deep silence fell in the room.

"Listen up," said the leader in his husky voice. "There's no way to attack him while the guard is in the furnace room or in the yard. I don't have a knife. There'll be some stifled cries. The stoolie will struggle."

"So how . . . ?"

"Here's how. Bitters has promised to tell us his story of the Runt and Chops-Him-in-Two after dinner today. It's raining out, we'll all come back here, and the stoolie will sit down over there in the corner, where he always sits. We'll give Bitters a few sous to start his story. It's dinner hour in the jail, and the guard sees us all peacefully occupied in listening to that Runt and Chops-Him-in-Two nonsense. He won't suspect a thing. He'll go and make his rounds in the kitchen. As soon as he leaves the courtyard, we'll have a quarter of an hour to ourselves. I'll have the stoolie iced before the guard comes back. This is my job. I've taken out plenty tougher than him. But I don't want anyone helping me."

"Just a minute," cried Cardillac. "What about the bailiff who always comes around here to joke with us at the dinner hour? If he comes into the furnace room to hear Bitters and sees you kill Germain, he might call for help. He's not tough like us. He's got his own cell. We have to watch out for him."

"That's true," said the Skeleton.

"There's a bailiff here?" cried Frank. Maître Boulard had embezzled his money, as we know. "There's a bailiff here?" he said in astonishment. "What's his name?"

"Boulard," said Cardillac.

"That's him!" exclaimed Frank, shaking his fists. "He's the guy who stole my pile!"

"The bailiff?" the provost asked.

"Yes. Seven hundred and twenty francs that he had in keeping for me."

"Would you know him? Has he seen you?" asked the Skeleton.

"You better believe I'd know him, worse luck for me. If not for him, I wouldn't be here."

The Skeleton didn't like the sound of these complaints. He stared at Frank for a long time with his beady eyes as Frank was answering a few of his comrades' questions. Then, leaning toward the Big Gimp, he said to him in a whisper, "That's a kid who's capable of warning the guards about us."

"No, I vouch for him. He'll never denounce a soul. He's just still antsy about crime. It would be just like him to want to help Germain. Better keep him out of the yard."

"That'll do," said the Skeleton, and he said aloud, "Hey, Frank, don't you want to do a number on that thief of a bailiff?"

"Just watch. If he comes in here, it's the end of the story for him."

"He'll come, so get ready."

"I'm ready. I'll put my mark on him."

"So now there'll be a fight. They'll send the bailiff back to his bought cell and Frank to solitary," whispered the Skeleton to the Big Gimp. "We'll get rid of the two of them in one fell swoop."

"What a genius! You are such a sharp one, Skeleton!" said the criminal admiringly. Then he said aloud, "Now, then! Will we let Bitters know that his story will be helping us to get the guard out of the way and ice the stoolie?"

"No. Bitters is too spineless and too much of a coward. If he knew that, he wouldn't want to tell his story. But once we've done it, he'll know which side to choose."

The dinner bell rang. "Time for the feed bag, boys!" said the Skeleton. "Bitters and Germain are going to come back into the yard. Listen, friends: I'm the one they call Dead Already, but the stoolie is dead already, too."

CHAPTER 8

THE STORYTELLER

The new prisoner whom we've mentioned, the one wearing a cotton cap and a gray worker's shirt, had listened attentively to the plot on Germain's life and had approved of it enthusiastically. This man, of an athletic build, left the furnace room with the other prisoners without anyone having noticed him. He soon blended in with the different groups in the yard that were crowding around the servers who were distributing food, carrying cooked meat in copper pans and bread in large baskets. Each prisoner received a serving of deboned boiled beef that had been used to make the rich morning soup. This was to be sopped up with half a loaf of bread of better quality than the kind soldiers typically get to eat.[210] The prisoners who had money could buy wine in the canteen and, according to the prison rules, get their ration of it there. And those who, like Nicolas, had received supplies from the outside put together an impromptu feast to which they invited the other prisoners. The guests of the executed man's son were the Skeleton, Fishhook, and, under the latter's watchful eye, Bitters, so that he would be in the mood to tell his story.

The knuckle of ham, hard-boiled eggs, cheese, and white bread, supplied by the forced generosity of Micou, the fence, were spread out on one of the benches in the furnace room, and the Skeleton prepared himself to give this meal its due honors, without worrying a bit about the murder he was going to commit.

"Go and see if Bitters has arrived yet. While I wait to do Germain in, I'll do in my hunger and thirst. Don't forget to tell the Big Gimp that Frank has to jump the bailiff so we can get the two of them out of the Lions' Den."

"Don't worry, Dead Already. If Frank doesn't work the bailiff over, it won't be anything we did." And Nicolas left the furnace room.

---

210. The following is the dietary regime in our prisons: For the morning meal, each prisoner receives a bowlful of thin or rich soup diluted with a half liter of broth. For the evening meal, a quarter-pound portion of beef, deboned, or a portion of vegetables, beans, potatoes, etc. The same vegetables are never served two days in a row. Prisoners, in the name of humanity, surely have a right to this healthy and almost abundant food. But most workers, even the hardest-working ones who lead the most well-ordered lives, we repeat, don't get meat and rich soup ten times a year. [SN]

At this very moment, Maître Boulard was entering the yard, smoking a cigar, with his hands deep inside his long flannel waistcoat. His peaked hat was pulled down over his ears, and his face was beaming with a smile. He caught sight of Nicolas, who, for his own part, immediately scanned the room for Frank. Frank and the Big Gimp were eating their dinner on one of the benches in the yard. They had not seen the bailiff because they had their backs to him. Nicolas, following the Skeleton's advice, pretended not to notice Maître Boulard as he saw him coming near, and he went over to Frank and the Big Gimp.

"Hello, my good man," said the bailiff to Nicolas.

"Oh, hello, monsieur! I didn't see you. You've come to take your little walk, as usual?"

"Yes, my boy, and today I have two reasons for it. I'll tell you why. First, take these cigars. Come on, go ahead. Don't make a big deal about it—hell, it's between friends!"

"Thank you, monsieur. Now, then, why do you have two reasons for wanting to take a walk?"

"I'll tell you, my boy. I don't feel much appetite today. I say to myself, 'If I hang around you guys at dinner, watching you eat may make me hungry.'"

"Well, that's not so dumb, really. But if you want to see two types who are real trenchermen," said Nicolas, taking the bailiff little by little right over to where Frank, who still had his back turned, was sitting, "get a look at those two hogs over there. You'll get hungry again as fast as if you'd just eaten a jar of pickles."

"Oh, lordy. Let's get a look at that," said Maître Boulard.

"Hey! Big Gimp!" cried Nicolas.

The Big Gimp and Frank turned their heads quickly. The bailiff stood there stupefied, his mouth agape, recognizing the man he'd fleeced. Tossing his bread and meat on the bench, Frank jumped on Maître Boulard in a single bound, took him by the throat, and exclaimed, "My money!"

"What? What's going on? Monsieur, you're strangling me. I—"

"My money!"

"Listen to me, my friend—"

"My money! But it's too late, since I'm already here and it's your fault."

"But—I—but—"

"If I go to the galleys, it's your fault, understand? If I had had what you stole from me, I wouldn't have had to steal. I would have stayed honest, like I wanted to be. And they may find you not guilty. They won't do anything to you, but I will! I'll put my mark on you! Ah! I see you have some jewelry, some gold chains—and you steal from the poor! Had enough yet? No? Here's some more."

"Help! Help!" cried the bailiff as he fell beneath Frank's feet. The latter was kicking him furiously.

The other prisoners, quite indifferent to this scuffle, made a circle around the two combatants, or rather, around the attacker and his victim, for Maître Boulard, winded and terrified, was no longer giving any resistance. He was trying to ward off the blows his adversary was raining down on him as best he could. Fortunately, the guard ran over to them at the bailiff's cries and pulled him from Frank's clutches.

Maître Boulard got up, pale and frightened, with one of his eyes bruised. Without taking the time to gather up his hat, he ran toward the barred door and cried out, "Guard! Open up! I don't want to stay here a second longer! Help!"

"And you, since you attacked this monsieur, you must follow me to the director's office," said the guard as he took Frank by the collar. "You'll get two days in solitary for this."

"That's fine with me. He got what was coming to him," said Frank.

"Now, then!" said the Big Gimp to him in a whisper as he pretended to help him pull himself together. "Not a word of what we're planning to do to the stoolie."

"Don't worry. Maybe if I'd been here, I might have tried to help him, because killing a guy for that . . . it's a bit much. But I'd never denounce you!"

"Let's get moving—are you coming or not?" asked the guard.

"We've gotten rid of the bailiff and Frank . . . Now it's going to heat up for the stoolie!" said Nicolas.

Germain and Bitters came into the yard just as Frank was leaving it. As he walked into the yard, Germain no longer looked like the same man. His face, until then sad and dejected, looked radiant and proud. He carried his head high and looked around himself with joy and confidence. He was loved. The horror of this prison was disappearing before his eyes.

Bitters was following him, looking quite embarrassed. Finally, after hesitating to address him two or three times, he steeled himself and tapped Germain lightly on the arm before the latter could rejoin the groups of prisoners who were examining him from afar with sullen hatred. Their victim would not escape them. In spite of himself, Germain shuddered at the contact with Bitters. The face and rags of the former shell game player did not predispose one favorably toward the unfortunate man. But remembering Rigolette's advice and feeling too happy in any case not to be kind, Germain stopped and said gently to Bitters, "What can I do for you?"

"I'd like to thank you."

"For what?"

"For what your pretty little visitor wants to do for my poor sister."

"I don't understand," said Germain, surprised.

"I'll explain it to you. A moment ago, at the clerk's office, I met the guard who was in the visiting room . . ."

"Ah, yes. He's a good man."

"Usually jailers aren't like that. They're not what you could call 'good men.' But Old Roussel is a different story. He deserves being called that. Just a little while ago, he whispered in my ear, 'Bitters, my boy, do you know Monsieur Germain?' 'Yes, the bête noire of the prison yard,' I answered him."

Then, stopping himself, Bitters said to Germain, "I apologize. I'm sorry if I called you a bête noire. Don't pay any attention. Let me finish what I was saying. So I answer him, 'Yes, I know Monsieur Germain, the bête noire of the yard.' 'Maybe he's yours, too, Bitters?' the guard asked me severely. 'Guard, sir, I am too much a coward and too well behaved to allow myself any sort of bête noire, or a white one or a gray one, either.[211] And I would hardly be likely to have Monsieur Germain as a bête noire since he doesn't seem at all bad and people are unfair to him.' 'Well, then, Bitters, you are right to be on Monsieur Germain's side, because he's done you a good turn.' 'Me, sir? How?' 'Well, it's not him, exactly, and it's not for you, but except for that, you owe him a real debt of gratitude,' Old Roussel answered me."

"Tell me more. Can you explain a little more clearly what you mean?" said Germain, smiling.

"That's just what I said to the guard. 'Stop talking in riddles.' So he answered me, 'It's not Monsieur Germain but rather his pretty little visitor who was very kind to your sister. She heard her telling you her family troubles, and when the poor woman was leaving the visiting room, the girl offered to do anything she could to help.'"

"How kind Rigolette is!" exclaimed Germain, moved. "She made sure not to tell me anything about this!"

"'Oh, as to that,' I answered the guard, 'I'm just a silly goose. You're right, Monsieur Germain has done me a good turn, for his visitor might as well be Germain himself, and my sister Jeanne might as well be me, except she's much better than me.'"

"Poor little Rigolette!" said Germain. "It doesn't surprise me. She has such a good and compassionate heart!"

"The guard said, 'I heard everything without seeming to. So now you know. If you don't try to do Monsieur Germain a good turn, if you don't let him know if you know there's some plot brewing against him, you'd be nothing but a miserable bum, Bitters.' 'Guard, sir, I may be on the way to becoming a miserable bum, but I haven't got there yet. All told, since Monsieur Germain's visitor wanted to help my poor sister Jeanne, who is a good, honest woman, even if I do say so myself, I will do what I can for Monsieur Germain. Unfortunately, that won't be a lot.' 'All the same, do

211. Bitters is punning here on the expression *bête noire*, which means "black beast." [TN]

what you can. I'm going to give you some good news to convey to Monsieur Germain, too. I just now heard about it.'"

"What is it?" asked Germain.

"Tomorrow there will be a vacant single cell for sale. The guard told me to let you know."

"Really? But that's great!" exclaimed Germain. "That good man was right. You bring good news indeed."

"Without being presumptuous, I think so, too. Someone like you has no business being with people like us, Monsieur Germain."

Then, stopping himself, Bitters hastened to add in a quick whisper as he stooped as if he were picking something up off the ground, "Listen, Monsieur Germain: look at those prisoners over there staring at us. They're surprised to see us talking together. I'm going to leave you now. Be careful. If they try to start a quarrel with you, don't answer back. They're looking for a pretext to start a fight with you and beat you up. Fishhook will start the fight. Be careful of him. I'll try to change their minds." And Bitters got up as if he had found the thing he had seemed to be looking for for the last few moments.

"Thank you, my kind friend. I will be careful," said Germain sincerely as he parted ways with his companion.

Knowing only about the earlier plot from that morning to provoke a quarrel in which Germain would be beaten up in order to force the prison director to transfer him to another yard, Bitters remained ignorant not only of the Skeleton's recent plans to murder him but also of the fact that they were counting on his tale of "The Runt and Chops-Him-in-Two" to deceive the guard and turn his attention away from them.

"Come on already, you lazybones," said Nicolas to Bitters as he came to greet him. "Don't bother with your ration of tough meat. There's a feast on tonight, and you're invited."

"Where is it? At the Flower-Basket? At Little Ramponneau?"[212]

"You joker! No, in the furnace room. The table is all laid out on a bench. We've got pig knuckle, eggs, and cheese. I'm the host."

"Fine with me. But it's a pity to waste my ration, and I hate it even more that my sister can't have it. She and her children don't get to see meat very often, unless they stand at the door of the butcher shop."

"Come on, get going. The Skeleton's getting irritable. He and Fishhook might eat it all."

Nicolas and Bitters entered the furnace room. The Skeleton was straddling the end of the bench upon which Nicolas's dishes were displayed. He

212. In the nineteenth century, the Flower-Basket (Le Panier Fleuri) was a well-appointed brothel. Little Ramponneau's was the name of a restaurant and dance house at the barriers of Paris, established in 1790. But there was also a well-known Jean Ramponneau, who became a wine seller in Paris in 1740 and whose name became slang for cabarets. [TN]

was cursing and grumbling as he awaited the host. "There you are, you snail! You laggard!" exclaimed the criminal at the sight of the storyteller. "What were you up to?"

"He was talking with Germain," said Nicolas as he pulled the ham apart.

"So, you were talking with Germain?" said the Skeleton, looking closely at Bitters without ceasing to stuff himself.

"Yes!" said the storyteller. "He's a few fries short of a meal, that one (and I can say that because I love fries). He's stupid, that Germain guy, really stupid! And here I thought he might be a police spy here—but he's much too dumb for that!"

"Really? You think so?" said the Skeleton as he exchanged a quick and pointed look with Nicolas and Fishhook.

"I'm as sure of it as I'm sure this is ham! And besides, how could he spy on anyone here? He's always all alone, he doesn't talk to anyone, and no one talks to him. He treats us like we had cholera. He'd have to be really sharp to make any reports based on what he knows. In any case, he won't be ratting very long. He's on his way to a paid cell."

"Him?" exclaimed the Skeleton. "When?"

"Tomorrow morning there will be a vacant cell."

"It's clear we have to kill him now. He doesn't sleep in my room, and tomorrow it'll be too late. We only have till four o'clock today and here it is, practically three," said the Skeleton in a whisper to Nicolas while Bitters was chatting with Fishhook.

"Makes no difference to me," said Nicolas out loud, seeming to be responding to an observation made by the Skeleton. "Germain seems to have contempt for us."

"On the contrary, guys," said Bitters. "You intimidate that young man. He thinks of himself as worse than any of you. Do you know what he just told me?"

"No, tell us."

"He said to me, 'You're so lucky, Bitters, that you get to speak to that notorious Skeleton (he said 'notorious') as if you were equals. As for me, I'd love to be able to speak to him, but he has an effect on me that makes me so respectful, so respectful that when I see Monsieur Provost, I couldn't be more speechless than if I had to speak with the chief of police in the flesh and in uniform.'"

"He said that to you?" said the Skeleton, pretending to believe he evoked a feeling of admiration in Germain and that he was moved by it.

"He told me that, just as sure as you're the greatest villain on earth."

"Oh, then—well, that changes things. I'll patch things up with him. Fishhook wanted to pick a fight with him. He'd do just as well to leave him alone."

"That would be better!" Bitters exclaimed, persuaded that he had turned aside the danger that had been threatening Germain. "That would be better, since that poor boy wouldn't respond to a quarrel. He's like me—about as brave as a rabbit."

"Still, it's really too bad," said the Skeleton. "We were looking forward to that beating to amuse us after dinner. The evening's going to pass awfully slowly now."

"Yeah, what are we going to do now?" asked Nicolas.

"Since that's the way it is, Bitters should tell the barracks room a story. And I won't pick a fight with Germain," said Fishhook.

"All right, all right," said the storyteller. "That's my first condition. But I have another, and unless you agree to both, I'm not telling any stories."

"What's your other condition?"

"It is that this honorable company that reeks of financiers," said Bitters, taking on his old street hawker's style of speaking, "must pay me the trifling sum of twenty sous. Twenty sous, messieurs! To hear the famous Bitters, who has had the honor of working before the most renowned cutpurses and the most notorious cutthroats in all of France and Navarre, who is incessantly in demand in Brest and Toulon, where he will soon be on tour on the orders of the government. Twenty sous! That's nothing at all, messieurs!"

"It's a deal! We'll give you your twenty sous after you tell us your stories."

"After? Oh, no. Before," Bitters exclaimed.

"Now, then! Come on, do you think we're the kind who would cheat you out of your twenty sous?" the Skeleton said, as if he were shocked.

"Oh, not at all!" answered Bitters. "I honor all cutpurses with my confidence, and it's only to spare you expenses that I'm asking twenty sous in advance."

"Word of honor?"

"Yes, messieurs. Afterward, you'll be so happy with my story that twenty sous won't be enough and you'll force me to take twenty francs—what am I saying, a hundred francs! I know myself: I'd be petty enough to accept the money. You can see that you'll be saving money by giving me twenty sous in advance!"

"Well, you certainly don't lack for nerve, that's for sure."

"All I have is my tongue, so I have to make the best of it. And the bottom line is my sister and her children are in real hard times, and twenty sous goes a long way in a little household."

"Why don't your sister and her kids rip things off, if they're old enough?" asked Nicolas.

"Don't talk to me about her. She's such a disappointment. She's a stain on my good name. I'm too good for her."

"You should say you're too stupid, because you encourage her."

"It's true. I encourage her in the vice of being honest. But that's the only thing she's any good at. I feel sorry for her, you know? Now, then, is it a deal? I'll tell you my famous story of 'The Runt and Chops-Him-in-Two,' but you'll give me twenty sous, and Fishhook won't pick a fight with that Germain imbecile," Bitters said.

"We'll give you twenty sous, and Fishhook won't pick a fight with that Germain imbecile," said the Skeleton.

"So, then, get ready. You're going to hear something rich. But here's the rain! That will make the customers come inside. I don't have to go out to get them now."

Indeed, rain had begun to fall. The prisoners left the yard and came into the furnace room to stay dry, still accompanied by a guard.

As we have said, this furnace room was a large, long, tiled hall, lit by three windows that overlooked the courtyard. In the middle stood the furnace, next to which were the Skeleton, Fishhook, Nicolas, and Bitters. At a sign given by the provost, the Big Gimp came and joined the group.

Germain was one of the last prisoners to enter the room, absorbed as he was in his delightful thoughts. He walked over automatically to sit on the edge of the last window in the room, the same place he usually sat and one that no one would ever challenge him for, since it was far from the stove around which the prisoners liked to hover. As we've said, about fifteen prisoners had been told in advance of the betrayal with which Germain was charged and of the murder that would be his punishment. But as soon as the word got out, this plan had as many supporters as there were prisoners. These wretches, in their blind cruelty, saw this ambush as a legitimate revenge and considered it as insurance against future stoolies and their denunciations. Germain, Bitters, and the guard were the only ones who did not know what was going to happen.

The general attention of the prisoners was split among the executioner, the victim, and the storyteller who was going to deprive Germain unwittingly of the only recourse he had. For it was almost certainly the case that the guard, seeing the prisoners listening raptly to Bitters's stories, would think his attendance was not necessary and take advantage of this moment of peace to go eat his meal. And indeed, when the prisoners entered, the Skeleton said to the guard, "Listen, pal: Bitters has had a bright idea. He's going to tell us his story 'The Runt and Chops-Him-in-Two.' The weather's so rotten, you wouldn't put a dog out in it. We'll wait quietly in here until it's time to go back to our cages."

"In fact, when he starts chattering, you guys are pretty quiet. At least you don't need anyone to keep an eye on you."

"Right," said the Skeleton. "But Bitters is asking a lot to tell his story. He wants twenty sous."

"Yes, for the small trifle of twenty sous—that's practically giving it away!" exclaimed Bitters. "Yes, messieurs, it's giving it away, because you wouldn't want even a penny left in your pocket if it meant you wouldn't get to hear the tale of the adventures of the poor little Runt and the terrible Chops-Him-in-Two and that villain Gunpowder. It'll break your heart and make your hair stand on end. Now, messieurs, who wouldn't want to spend the pittance of four pennies, or, if you prefer to count in kilometers, the trifle of five centimes, to have your heart broken and your hair stand on end?"

"I'll put in two sous," said the Skeleton, and he threw a coin to Bitters. "Come on! Are you thieves going to get cheap when we can have a story like that?"

Several sous fell from all directions, to the great joy of Bitters, whose thoughts were of his sister as he took up this collection.

"Eight, nine, ten, eleven, twelve, thirteen!" he cried as he picked up the change. "Come on, rich guys, financiers, and moneybags, dig a little deeper. You can't stop at thirteen—that's an unlucky number. All you need is seven more sous—nothing but seven more sous! Really, gentlemen, are you going to let people say that the thieves of the Lions' Den can't even scrape seven sous together? Seven lousy sous? Oh, gentlemen, you're going to make people think you've been put in here unjustly or that you've been very unlucky."

Bitters's piercing voice and street performer's humor had drawn Germain out of his reverie. As much to follow Rigolette's advice by becoming a little more popular as to give some slight charitable contribution to a poor devil who had expressed such a desire to do him some good, he got up and threw a ten-sou piece at the feet of the storyteller, who exclaimed as he pointed out his generous donor to the crowd, "Ten sous, gentlemen! You see? I said there were financiers here. My respects to Monsieur. He's behaving like a moneybags, an ambassador who wants to please the present company. Yes, messieurs, you will owe most of the story of 'The Runt and Chops-Him-in-Two' to him, and you'll thank him for it. As for the three extra sous here from this coin, I will earn them by imitating the voices of the characters instead of speaking like you and me. You will owe this extra seasoning of the dish to the rich financier here, whom you should adore."

"Come on. Stop joking and start your story," said the Skeleton.

"One moment, gentlemen," said Bitters. "It is only fair that a financier who has given me ten sous should get the best seat in the house—except, of course, for our provost, who gets first choice."

This proposition fitted in with the Skeleton's plot so nicely that he shouted, "That's right! After me, he should have the best seat!" And the criminal cast another meaningful look at the prisoners.

"Yes, yes, he should move up," they said.

"He should sit in the front row."

"You see, young man, you are rewarded for your generosity. The honorable society recognizes that you have the right to the best seat," Bitters said to Germain.

Thinking that his generosity had really influenced his odious companions to feel more positively disposed toward him and delighted to be doing what Rigolette had asked of him, Germain, despite his quite strong repugnance, left his preferred spot and moved closer to the storyteller.

Bitters, having arranged the four or five benches of the furnace room around the stove with the assistance of Nicolas and Fishhook, said with emphasis, "Here are the orchestra seats! Lords and ladies get the best seats. First, the financier. Now, everyone who paid should take their seats," said Bitters gaily, firmly believing that, thanks to him, Germain no longer had anything to fear. "And those who haven't paid," he added, "may sit on the ground or stand, as it pleases them."

We will now describe the placement of the characters in this scene: Bitters was standing next to the stove, preparing to tell his story. Next to him, the Skeleton was also standing, gazing longingly at Germain as he waited to spring on him the moment the guard left the room. A short distance from Germain, Nicolas, Fishhook, Cardillac, and other prisoners, including the man in the blue cotton cap and gray worker's shirt, sat on the remaining benches. Most of the prisoners, clustered here and there, with some sitting on the floor and others standing and leaning against the walls, composed the background of this picture, lit up like a Rembrandt painting by the three side windows that cast sharp light and deep shadows on these faces of such diverse character and such hardened casts. We should say, finally, that the guard, who, without knowing it, was supposed to give the signal for Germain to be murdered, was standing next to the half-open door.

"Are we ready?" Bitters asked the Skeleton.

"Silence in the joint!" said the latter, turning halfway around. Then, addressing Bitters, he said, "Begin your tale now. We're listening."

All fell silent.

CHAPTER 9

THE RUNT AND CHOPS-HIM-IN-TWO

There is nothing sweeter, more life-giving
or dearer than your words;
they charm, they encourage, they improve.

—*WOLFGANG*, BOOK IV

Before we begin Bitters's story, we must remind the reader that, in strange contrast with what one might expect, most prisoners, in spite of their cynical perversity, almost universally favor naive, not to say puerile, stories in which an inexorable fate, after trials and travails without number, avenges the oppressed on those who tyrannize against them. Far be it from us to try to establish any sort of parallel between these corrupt beings and the poor and honest masses, but we all know with what deafening applause the common audiences in the theaters of the boulevard greet the victim's deliverance and the hissing and booing they rain down on the villain or the traitor.

People often look down upon these vulgar manifestations of sympathy toward those who are good, weak, and persecuted, and of aversion toward those who are powerful, unjust, and cruel. We think this to be an error. There is nothing more inherently encouraging than these popular feelings. Is it not clear that this healthy instinct could become firm principles to these unfortunate people whose ignorance and poverty expose them constantly to a subversive obsession with evil? How can we not have high hopes for a people whose good moral sense manifests itself so consistently? Of a people who, in the face of any pompous claims of artistic value, would never stand for a dramatic work to conclude with the triumph of the scoundrel and the agony of the good?

This fact, which is often greeted with mockery and disdain, seems highly significant to us because of the tendencies it evidences, tendencies often found, we repeat, among the most corrupt creatures in their moments of reprieve, so to speak, when they are untroubled by the prodding of criminal necessity. In brief, since hardened criminals still sympathize now and again with the recounting and expression of elevated sentiments, shouldn't we conclude that all people contain within them some appreciation of the beautiful, the good, and the just and that, by distorting and stifling these divine instincts, poverty and degradation are the first causes of human depravation? Isn't it clear that people generally become wicked only because they are poor? If we remove someone from the terrible temptations of neediness by the just improvement of his material condition, do we not restore to him the ability to practice the virtues of which his conscience already knows?

The impression Bitters's story created will demonstrate or rather expose—we hope—some of the ideas we have just laid out.

Amid the hushed silence of his audience, Bitters began his story this way: "No small time has passed since the story I am about to tell the honorable assembly took place. What they used to call Little Poland had not been destroyed yet. Is the honorable assembly familiar with what Little Poland was?"

"We know it," said the prisoner in the blue cap and gray worker's shirt. "They were the hovels on the side of rue du Rocher and rue de la Pépinière."[213]

"Exactly, my boy," said Bitters, "and the Cité neighborhood, which is not quite filled with palaces itself, would look like rue de la Paix or rue de Rivoli compared to Little Poland. What a hole! But in any case, a notorious den of thieves. There were no streets, only alleys. No houses, only shacks. No paving stones, just a little path of mud and dung, which would have made the noise of the carriages less disturbing if they passed by—which, however, they never did. From dawn to dusk, and even more from dusk to dawn, what one heard constantly were the cries 'Police!' 'Help!' 'Murder!'—but the police didn't bother with this place. The more people were killed in Little Poland, the fewer they'd have to arrest! The place was swarming with people. You had to see it to believe it. There weren't many jewelers, goldsmiths, or bankers there, but, on the other hand, there were tons of organ-players, clowns, buffoons, and animal-handlers. Among the latter, there was one named Chops-Him-in-Two because he was so mean. He was meanest of all to children. People called him Chops-Him-in-Two because he was said to have chopped a little chimney sweep in half with his ax."

At this moment in Bitters's story, the prison clock rang three fifteen.

213. In the eighteenth century, when this area was not built up, it took its name from a local cabaret named Little Poland. By Sue's time, it had become known as a place inhabited by the poor and the criminal. Balzac also refers to it, for instance, in *La Cousine Bette*. [TN]

Since the prisoners would return to their barracks at four o'clock, the Skeleton's crime had to be completed before that time.

"Damn it! The guard isn't leaving!" he whispered to the Big Gimp.

"Don't worry. Once the story gets going, he'll take off."

Bitters went on with his story: "No one knew where Chops-Him-in-Two came from. Some said he was Italian, others said he was from Bohemia, and still others said he was a Turk or an African. The simple women said he was a magician, though it seemed a funny thing to say at the time. Still, I myself would have been very tempted to agree with those simple women. The thing that made it believable was that he always had a big reddish-brown monkey with him named Gunpowder. That monkey was so sly and so mean that you would say he had the devil in his belly. I'll tell you more about Gunpowder in a moment. As for Chops-Him-in-Two, I'm going to give you a good look at him: he had skin the color of your boot sole, red hair that matched the fur of his monkey, and green eyes. And the thing that would make you believe, along with the simple women, that he was a magician, was that he had a black tongue."

"A black tongue?" asked Fishhook.

"Black as ink," answered Bitters.

"Why was that?"

"Because when his mother was pregnant, she probably spoke of a black person," said Bitters with modest certainty. "Along with that charming feature, Chops-Him-in-Two was a keeper of I don't know how many tortoises, monkeys, guinea pigs, white mice, foxes, and marmots. For every animal, there was a missing little chimney sweep or an abandoned child. Every morning, Chops-Him-in-Two would give each child one of his animals and a piece of black bread and send him on his way to beg for change or earn their expenses. The ones who didn't bring back at least fifteen sous were beaten—and badly! At first you could hear the children cry from one end of Little Poland all the way to the other. I have to say also that there was a man in Little Poland they called 'the elder' because he was the oldest resident in the neighborhood. He was something like the mayor, the provost, and the justice of the peace—or rather, of war—for it was in his courtyard (he was a wine merchant and served terrible food, too) that they went to make their cases when there was no other way to work things out or to come to an understanding. Although he was already old, the elder was as strong as Hercules and very imposing. He was a name to swear by in Little Poland. When he said, 'It's good,' everyone else said, 'It's very good.' When he said, 'It's bad,' everyone said, 'It's bad.' He was a good man deep down, but terrifying. When, for example, the strong tormented the weak—well, then, look out! As the elder was Chops-Him-in-Two's neighbor, he had heard the children cry in the beginning from the beatings the animal-handler was giving them. But he had said to him, 'If I hear the children cry again, I'm going to make you cry right along with them, and since you have a louder voice, I'm going to hit you harder.'"

"What a character that elder was! I like that elder!" said the prisoner in the blue cap.

"So do I," said the guard as he drew closer to the group.

The Skeleton could not contain his impatience and anger.

Bitters continued: "Thanks to the elder, and his threatening of Chops-Him-in-Two, no one heard the children cry at night in Little Poland. But the poor little children didn't suffer any less for all that, because if they didn't cry anymore when their master beat them, it was because they were afraid of being beaten even worse. As to going to tell the elder about it, the thought didn't even enter their heads. With the fifteen sous that each little animal trainer had to bring back, Chops-Him-in-Two lodged, fed, and clothed them. At night, a piece of black bread, just like in the morning. So much for the cost of food. He didn't give them any clothing—so much for the cost of clothing them. And he locked them in at night along with the animals, on the same straw, in a granary which one entered by a ladder and a trapdoor: and there was the cost of their lodging. Once the animals and children were all inside, he would remove the ladder and lock the trapdoor. You can guess what kind of life those monkeys, guinea pigs, foxes, mice, tortoises, marmots, and children led and what kind of din they made in the dark in that attic that was as big as anything. Chops-Him-in-Two slept in a bedroom down below, with his big monkey, Gunpowder, attached to the foot of his bed. When the milling about and the screaming in the granary got to be too much, the animal-handler got up without lighting a candle, took a big whip, climbed the ladder, opened the trapdoor, and, without looking, cracked it about. As he always had about fifteen children with him and some of them brought him in—those poor innocents—sometimes as much as twenty sous a day, Chops-Him-in-Two, once his expenses were paid—and he had few enough of those—had about four francs or a hundred sous a day to himself. With that money he went on drinking binges, for you should know that he was also the biggest drunk on earth. He was dead drunk at least once a day. That was his diet. He claimed he would have a headache all day long if he didn't drink. You should also know that, with what he made, he bought sheep hearts for Gunpowder, for his big monkey ate raw meat with gusto. But I see that the honorable assembly is asking for the Runt. Here he comes, gentlemen."

"Yes, let's see what the Runt is like, and then I can go eat my soup," said the guard.

The Skeleton traded a glance of savage satisfaction with the Big Gimp.

"Among the children to whom Chops-Him-in-Two assigned his animals," Bitters continued, "there was a poor devil nicknamed the Runt. No father, no mother, brother, or sister, and nary a penny to his name or a place to call home, he was all alone in a world he hadn't asked to be born into, a world he could depart without anyone noticing. He took no pleasure from the name Runt, you can be sure. He was so puny, sickly, and needy, it broke your heart. He looked at most seven or eight years old, but he was thirteen. If he looked half his age, it wasn't his doing. He could only find anything to eat roughly one day out of every two, and so little each time, and so poorly, that he had to be making the best of his situation to look even seven."

"Poor kid! It feels like I can see him now!" said the prisoner in the blue cap. "There are lots of children like that on the streets of Paris, little starvelings."

"They have to start young and learn how to do it so they can get good at it," said Bitters with a bitter smile.

"Let's go, get on with it, hurry up," said the Skeleton brusquely. "The guard's getting impatient. His meal is getting cold."

"Nah, it's all the same to me," said the guard. "I want to get to know the Runt a little better. I'm enjoying this."

"Really, it is very interesting," said Germain, caught up as he was in the story.

"Ah! Thank you for saying so, my dear financier," answered Bitters. "That gives me more pleasure even than your ten-sou coin."

"Damn, you're a slowpoke!" cried the Skeleton. "You're tiring us all out."

"So here it is!" said Bitters. "One day, Chops-Him-in-Two had picked up the Runt in the street, dying of cold and hunger. He would have done just as well to let him die. Since the Runt was weak, he was afraid, and since he was afraid, he became the punching bag and the laughingstock of all the other little animal-handlers. They beat him and made him so miserable that they would have made him mean if he hadn't lacked strength and courage. But no. When they beat him up, he would cry, saying, 'I haven't hurt anyone, and everyone hurts me. It's unfair. Oh, if I were strong and brave!' You might think that the Runt would add, 'I'll get back at them for what they did to me.' But no, not at all. He only said, 'Oh! If only I were strong and brave, I would stand up for the weak against the strong because I'm weak, and the strong have made me suffer!' In the meantime, since he was too little a flea to be able to keep the strong from oppressing the weak, starting with himself, he kept the big animals from eating the littler ones."

"Now that's a funny idea!" said the prisoner in the blue cap.

"And what made it even funnier," said the storyteller, "was that it seemed that with that idea the Runt managed to console himself for being beaten. That proves that, deep down, he didn't have a bad heart."

"Heavens! Just the opposite, I'd say," said the guard. "Damn, Bitters is entertaining!"

At this moment, the clock chimed three thirty. Germain's executioner and the Big Gimp exchanged a meaningful glance. It was getting late, the guard wasn't getting up to leave, and some of the prisoners, the least hardened among them, seemed almost to have forgotten the Skeleton's sinister plan for Germain as they listened avidly to Bitters's story.

"When I say," the latter went on, "that the Runt kept the big animals from eating the little ones, you understand that the Runt wasn't messing around with tigers, lions, wolves, or even the foxes or monkeys in Chops-Him-in-Two's menagerie. He was too timid to do that. But as soon as he saw a spider lying in wait in its web to take some poor fool of a fly that was buzzing gaily under the good Lord's sun, without hurting anyone—*pow!* the Runt would hit the web with a stick, deliver the fly, and crush the spider like a real Caesar. Yes, a real Caesar! He would become as white as a sheet from touching those vile animals, so he must have had real determination, this child who was afraid of a May bug, this child who had taken a long time to feel comfortable with the tortoise Chops-Him-in-Two gave him every morning. In this way, overcoming his fear of spiders in order to keep the flies from getting eaten, the Runt showed himself to be—"

"Showed himself to be as bold in his own way as a man who'd attack a wolf to take a sheep out of its mouth," said the prisoner in the blue cap.

"Or a man who'd attack Chops-Him-in-Two in order to get the Runt out of his clutches," added Fishhook, also caught up in the story.

"Exactly," said Bitters. "So that, after many mighty blows like that, the Runt didn't feel so bad anymore. He, who never laughed, started to smile. He got cocky, wearing his cap backward (when he had a cap) and humming the Marseillaise to himself like he owned the whole world. In that moment, there wasn't a spider alive capable of daring to look him in the eye. Another time, it was a cricket drowning and struggling in a brook. Quick like that, the Runt stuck two fingers bravely into the current and picked up the cricket, whom he placed straightaway on a piece of grass. A champion, gold-medal swimmer who'd just rescued his tenth drowning victim for fifty francs a head couldn't have been prouder than the Runt when he saw his cricket hop up and run off. And yet that cricket didn't give him money or a medal, didn't even say so much as a thank-you, any more than the fly did. 'But, Bitters, my friend,' the honorable assembled will say to me, 'what kind of pleasure could the Runt, who was beaten by everyone, find in being the liberator of crickets and the scourge of spiders? Since people were mean to him, why didn't he get back at them by being as mean as his weakness allowed? For example, why didn't he feed the flies to the spiders or let the crickets drown—or even drown the crickets himself, on purpose?'"

"Yes, in fact, why didn't he get back at them that way?" asked Nicolas.

"What good would that have done him?" asked another.

"Well, because you do bad things because people do bad things to you!"

"No! Oh, well, I understand why he liked to come to the rescue of flies, that poor little kid!" said the man in the blue cap. "Maybe he said to himself, 'Who knows? Maybe someone will come to my rescue someday?'"

"Our friend here is right!" exclaimed Bitters. "He read in my heart what I was going to ramble on about to the honorable assembled. The Runt wasn't very clever. He couldn't see any further than the end of his own nose. But he said to himself, 'Chops-Him-in-Two is my spider. Maybe someday someone will do for me what I did for all those poor little flies. Maybe they'll tear down his web and take me out of his clutches.' Because, up to that moment, he would never have dared run away from his master for anything in the world. He thought he would have been struck dead. But one day, when he and his tortoise had no luck and they earned only two or three sous between the two of them, Chops-Him-in-Two began to beat the poor child so hard—so hard—that, I swear, the Runt couldn't take it anymore. Tired of being everyone's butt and victim, he waited for the trapdoor to the attic to be opened, and, while Chops-Him-in-Two was feeding his animals, he slipped down the ladder—"

"Ah! That's more like it!" said a prisoner.

"But why didn't he go and tell the elder?" said Blue Cap. "He could have gotten Chops-Him-in-Two the thrashing coming to him."

"Yes, but he didn't dare. He was too afraid. He preferred to try to run away. Unfortunately, Chops-Him-in-Two saw him. He takes him by the neck and carries him back to the attic. This time, the Runt, thinking about what awaited him, shivered from top to toe, for this was not the end of his suffering. Speaking of the Runt's suffering, I have to tell you about Gunpowder, Chops-Him-in-Two's favorite big monkey. This evil animal was, I swear, taller than the Runt. Think how big that means that monkey was! Now I'm going to tell you why they didn't show him on the streets like the other animals in the menagerie. It's because Gunpowder was so mean and so strong that there was only one child from the Auvergne, a strong, determined type of fourteen years, who, after having wrestled and done battle with Gunpowder several times, had managed to bring him to heel, lead him around, and lead him by a chain. And even then, there were frequent battles in which Gunpowder drew blood. Tired of this treatment, the little Auvergne boy said to himself one fine day, 'Fine, fine, I'll get revenge on you, you nasty monkey!' So one morning he leaves with his animal as usual. To bait him, he buys him a sheep's heart. While Gunpowder is eating, he threads a rope through one end of his chain, attaches the rope to a tree, and once the awful monkey is good and tied up, he gives him a shower of blows with his stick. A real shower of blows, the kind that could start a fire."

"Well done!"

"Bravo, Auvergne boy!"

"Give him a good one, my boy!"

"Pound that damned Gunpowder into the dust!" said the prisoners.

"And beat on him he did, as hard as he could," said Bitters. "You should have seen how Gunpowder was crying, gnashing his teeth, jumping and leaping from side to side. But the boy from Auvergne just kept answering him with that stick. 'Want some more? Take that!' Unfortunately, monkeys are like cats; they're hard to kill. Gunpowder was as sly as he was mean. When he realized where his bread was buttered, so to speak, at the high point of the shower of blows, he jumped about one last time, fell flat at the base of the tree, twitched a little, and then played dead, as still as a log. That was all the Auvergne boy wanted. Thinking the monkey is dead, he gets out, never to set foot again at Chops-Him-in-Two's place. But that wretch of a Gunpowder watched him out of the corner of his eye. Even though he was all beaten up, as soon as he sees that he's alone and that the Auvergne boy is far away, he bites through the rope that attached his chain to the tree with his teeth. The boulevard Monceaux, where he had been put through his paces, was very close to Little Poland. The monkey knew his way home like the back of his hand. So he takes off, dragging his haunch, and gets home to his master, who's fuming from seeing his monkey in this condition. But that's not all. From that moment on, Gunpowder had such a serious grudge against all children in general that Chops-Him-in-Two, who wasn't any softy, after all, no longer dared to give him to anyone to lead around from fear that something bad would happen. Gunpowder was quite capable of strangling a child or eating him whole, and all of the little animal-handlers, knowing this, would rather have been hacked to pieces by Chops-Him-in-Two than get close to the monkey."

"I should really go eat my soup," said the guard, taking a step toward the door. "That devil Bitters can make the birds come out of the trees to hear his stories. I don't know where he comes up with these stories."

"Finally, the guard is leaving," said the Skeleton in a whisper to the Big Gimp. "I'm going crazy. It's burning me up, I'm so angry inside. Just be careful to make a wall around the stoolie. The rest is on me."

"Now, then! Behave yourselves," said the guard as he made his way toward the door.

"We'll behave like angels," answered the Skeleton as he drew closer to Germain, while the Big Gimp and Nicolas, after getting the sign, took two steps in the same direction.

"Oh, most venerable guard! You're leaving at the best part," said Bitters in a reproachful manner.

If the Big Gimp had not foreseen his movement and rapidly seized him by the arm, the Skeleton would have pounced on Bitters.

"What do you mean, the best part?" said the guard as he turned back toward the storyteller.

"You better believe it," said Bitters. "You don't know what you'll be missing. The most captivating part of my story is about to start."

"Don't listen to him," said the Skeleton, barely containing his furor. "He's not on his game today. Me, I think this story is dumb as anything."

"My story is dumb as anything?" exclaimed Bitters, offended in his vanity as a storyteller. "All right, then! Guard, I ask you—no, I beg you—to stay until the end. I have enough to last another good quarter of an hour. Your soup is cold anyway. Now, what do you have to lose? I'll speed up the story so you still have the time to go eat before we return to our barracks."

"All right, I'll stay, but hurry up," said the guard, coming back.

"And you are right to stay, guard. I don't mean to brag, but you've never heard the likes of this—especially the end. You'll hear the triumph of the monkey and the Runt, escorted by all the little animal-handlers and all the inhabitants of Little Poland. You have my word of honor. It's not because I'm proud—it's really a thing of beauty."

"So tell us the story quickly, my boy," said the guard, returning to his spot next to the stove.

The Skeleton was shaking with rage. He despaired of accomplishing his crime. Once it was time to go to bed, Germain would be safe. He did not sleep in the same barracks as his implacable enemy, and the next day, as we've said, he was to move to one of the vacant single-occupancy cells. And finally, the Skeleton had to admit, judging from the interruptions of several prisoners, they had been transported by Bitters's story to a state of mind that was really pathetic. It might be that they would not even stand by in fierce indifference while a terrible murder took place—a murder in which their impassive behavior was to make them complicit. The Skeleton could prevent the storyteller from finishing his story, but then he would lose his last hope of seeing the guard leave before the time Germain would be safe.

"Ah! My story is stupid as anything?" said Bitters again. "Well! The honorable assembled will be the judges of that. So, there was no meaner animal than that big monkey Gunpowder, and he was just as relentless about the children as his master was. So what does Chops-Him-in-Two do to punish the Runt for trying to escape? I'll tell you that in a minute. First, though, he grabs the child and stuffs him back up in the attic for the night, saying to him, 'Tomorrow morning, when all of your friends are gone, I'm going to take you by the scruff of the neck and you'll see what I do to anyone trying to get out of here.' You can just imagine what a terrible night the Runt spent. He hardly closed his eyes. He wondered what Chops-Him-in-Two was going to do to him. He finally fell asleep from all the wondering. But what kind of a sleep it was! He had a dream—a terrible dream—at least it began that way. You'll see. He dreamed that he was one of those flies he'd saved so often from the spiderwebs and that now he himself was falling into a big, strong web in which he was struggling with all his might without being able to get free. Then he saw a kind of monster coming toward him, slowly, treacherously; the monster had Chops-Him-in-Two's face with a spider's body. The poor Runt started struggling again, as you can well imagine. But the harder he tried, the more twisted up in the web he became, just like the poor flies. Finally the spider gets up to him . . . it touches him . . . and he feels the big, cold, hairy paws of the horrible beast drawing him in and wrapping itself around him to devour him. He thinks he's dead for sure. But all of a sudden, he hears a small, clear, sonorous, sharp buzzing sound, and he sees a pretty golden fly, with a kind of fine, brilliant stinger like a diamond needle. This fly is fluttering around the spider in fury, and says to him in a tiny voice (when I say a tiny voice, imagine the voice of a fly!), 'Poor little fly, you have saved flies, the spider won't—' Unfortunately, the Runt wakes up with a jolt, and he doesn't see how the dream ends. Still, at first he felt a little better and said to himself, 'Maybe the golden fly with the diamond stinger would have killed the spider if I had gotten to the end of the dream.' But whatever calm or consolation the Runt might have gotten from comforting himself like that, as the night ended, his fear returned with such force that he eventually forgot all about the dream, or rather, he remembered only the scary part, the big web in which he had been trapped and the spider with Chops-Him-in-Two's face. You can imagine how he must have been trembling in fear. Lord, just imagine it! He's alone, all alone, without anyone to protect him. When morning broke, as he watched the daylight appear little by little from the little attic window, he became more and more scared. His moment alone with Chops-Him-in-Two was drawing nearer. So he threw himself on his knees in the middle of the attic, and, crying hot tears, he begged the other children to ask for mercy from Chops-Him-in-Two or to help him run away, if that was possible. Oh, sure! Some, out of fear of the master, others out of indifference, still others out of sheer malice—all refused the Runt the help he was asking them for."

"Lousy brats!" said the prisoner with the blue cap. "They had no hearts and no guts!"

"That's for sure," said another. "It really gets me to see that little kid completely abandoned."

"And he's all alone and defenseless," said the prisoner with the blue cap. "You have to pity someone who can't fight back and just has to turn on his back and take it. When you have teeth and claws, that's different. Damn, if you have any fangs, better bare them now, my boy, and save your tail!"

"That's right!" said several prisoners.

"That's enough!" exclaimed the Skeleton, no longer able to hide his rage. He turned to the man in the blue cap and said to him, "Will you shut up? Didn't I just say, 'Silence in the joint?' Am I the provost here or not?"

In answer, Blue Cap looked directly at the Skeleton and then made the mocking gesture that every street urchin knows by heart, the one where you put the thumb of your right hand to your nose, with your hand open like a fan, and you put the little finger of that hand to the thumb of your left hand, also spread out in the same fashion. Blue Cap accompanied this mute response with an expression that was so grotesque that several prisoners burst out laughing, while others, on the contrary, were stupefied at the audacity of the new prisoner, so greatly feared the Skeleton was.

The latter brandished his fist at Blue Cap and said to him, grinding his teeth, "We'll settle this tomorrow."

"I'll pay what I owe right on your kisser—seventeen smackers—and I won't ask for any change back."

Afraid he might give the guard a new reason to stay, in order to prevent a possible fight, the Skeleton responded, calmly, "That's not what I mean. I supervise the furnace room, and everyone must listen to me. Isn't that true, guard?"

"It's true," said the guard. "Stop interrupting. And you, Bitters, go on. But hurry it up, my boy."

CHAPTER 10

THE VICTORY OF THE RUNT AND GUNPOWDER

"As I was saying, then," said Bitters, continuing his story, "the Runt, seeing that he's all alone in the world, resigns himself to his sorry fate. It's daytime, and all the children start getting ready to head on out with their animals. Chops-Him-in-Two opens the trapdoor and gives the signal to give each one of them his piece of bread. They all go down the ladder, and the Runt, more dead than alive, cowered in the corner of the attic with his tortoise, as motionless as it was. He watched his companions leave one after the other. He would have given anything to be able to do the same. Finally, the last one leaves the attic. The poor child's heart was beating as hard as it could. He was hoping that maybe his master might have forgotten about him. Much chance of that! Now he hears Chops-Him-in-Two, who was standing at the foot of the ladder, yelling in a coarse voice, 'Runt! Runt!' 'Here I am, master.' 'Come down right now or I'll come up and get you,' Chops-Him-in-Two says. The Runt thought his time had come, for sure. 'All right,' he says to himself, trembling from head to toe and remembering his dream. 'Here you are in the web, little fly. The spider's going to eat you.' After gently putting his tortoise on the floor, he said a sort of farewell to it, for he had grown attached to the animal. He approached the trapdoor. He was stepping on the top rung of the ladder in order to climb down when Chops-Him-in-Two, taking him by his poor, spindly leg, pulled him so hard and so sharply that the Runt came clattering down, bouncing his head off of every rung of the ladder."

"Too bad the elder of Little Poland wasn't there! He'd make Chops-Him-in-Two dance to his tune!" Blue Cap said. "Times like that, it's good to be strong."

"Yes, my boy. But, unfortunately, the elder wasn't there! So Chops-Him-in-Two takes the child by the seat of his pants and carries him over to his lair, where he kept the big monkey tied to the foot of his bed. The mere sight of the child makes the animal start hopping up and down and grinding his teeth in rage, straining at the end of his chain to get at the Runt, as if he wanted to eat him."

"Poor Runt! How's he gonna get out of this one?"

"Yeah, if he falls into the clutches of that monkey, he's done for!"

"Damn! I can't stand this," Blue Cap said. "Right now, I couldn't hurt a fly. What about you guys?"

"I swear, not me."

"Me, neither."

At this moment the prison clock chimed a quarter to four. The Skeleton, getting more and more afraid that his time was running out, exclaimed, furious over these interruptions that seemed to announce that several prisoners had truly been moved to pity, "Silence in the joint already! This unhappy story won't ever end if you keep talking as much as the storyteller does!"

Those who were interrupting fell silent.

Bitters continued: "When you remember that the Runt had had a very hard time getting used to his tortoise, and that the bravest of his comrades trembled at the mere name of Gunpowder, you can imagine how terrified he was when he saw himself dragged by his master right over to that rotten monkey. 'Have mercy, master!' he cried as his teeth chattered as if he had a fever. 'Have mercy, master! I won't do it again, I promise you!' The poor little boy was crying, 'I won't do it again,' without knowing what he was saying, because he hadn't done anything wrong. But Chops-Him-in-Two didn't care about that. Despite the struggling child's cries, he put him in reach of Gunpowder, who leapt upon him and laid hold of him."

A sort of shudder went through the audience. They were on the edge of their seats.

"I would have been stupid to leave," said the guard as he came closer to the cluster of men.

"And you haven't heard anything yet. The best is still to come," said Bitters. "As soon as the Runt felt the cold, hairy paws of the big monkey seizing him by the neck and head, he thought he was sure to be eaten. He was delirious, and started crying, moaning so as to move a tiger to pity, 'It's the spider from my dream, dear God! The spider from my dream . . . Little golden fly, help me!' 'Shut up! Shut up!' Chops-Him-in-Two said to him, kicking him hard, because he was afraid that someone would hear his cries. But after a minute there was no more risk of that, for the poor Runt was no longer crying or struggling. On his knees and as white as a sheet, he was closing his eyes and quivering from head to toe as if he were out of doors on a cold day in January. All the while, the monkey was hitting him, pulling his hair, and scratching him. And from time to time the evil animal stopped to look at his master, just as if they had some understanding between them. Chops-Him-in-Two was laughing so hard! So hard that if the Runt had cried out, his master's laughter would have blocked out the sound of his cries. It seemed as if this was encouraging Gunpowder to go after the child even more."

"Ah! You rotten monkey!" exclaimed Blue Cap. "If I had you by the tail, I'd swing you around like a sling and I'd break your head open on a paving stone."

"Nasty monkey! He's as evil as a human!"

"No man can be as mean as that!"

"Not that mean?" said Bitters. "What about Chops-Him-in-Two? Think about it. Here's what he does next: he detaches Gunpowder's chain, which was quite long, from the foot of his bed, he takes the half-dead child out of his clutches for a moment and chains him up to the other end, so that the Runt was on one end of the chain and Gunpowder on the other, the two of them attached at the waist and separated by a distance of approximately three feet."

"Now there was an idea!"

"There really are some men who are meaner than the meanest beasts. When Chops-Him-in-Two finished doing this, he says to his monkey, who seemed to understand him—and they really deserved each other, those two—'Listen to me, Gunpowder! They exhibited you, so now it's your turn to exhibit the Runt! He'll be your monkey. Come on—upsy-daisy! Get up, Runt, or I'll sic Gunpowder on you.' The poor child had fallen back to his knees and was clasping his hands, but he could not speak. All you could hear was the chattering of his teeth. 'Come on, make him walk, Gunpowder,' Chops-Him-in-Two started saying to his monkey. 'And if he refuses, do what I'm doing to him.' As he said this, he rains down blows on the child with a switch, and then gives the stick to the monkey. You know that those animals are imitators by nature, but Gunpowder was better than any of them. He takes the switch in one hand and sets to work on the Runt, who now has to get up. Once on his feet, he was—I swear—about the same height as the monkey. Then Chops-Him-in-Two left his room and went downstairs and called to Gunpowder. Gunpowder followed him, driving the Runt out in front of him with great strokes of the switch as if he were his slave. They arrive this way at the courtyard of Chops-Him-in-Two's shanty. That's where he planned to have some fun. He closes the door to the alley and signals to Gunpowder to make the child run in front of him all around the courtyard while hitting him hard with the switch. The monkey obeys, and he sets the Runt to running his paces, hitting him while Chops-Him-in-Two held his sides in laughter. You think this meanness would have been enough for him? Not a chance! That was still nothing. If this had been all, the Runt would have gotten off, after his terror, with just some scratches and blows from the switch. Here is what Chops-Him-in-Two had in mind: to make the monkey angry at the child, who, unable to breathe, was already more dead than alive, he takes the Runt by the hair, pretends to rain blows down on him and to bite him, and then he hands him over to Gunpowder, crying to him, 'Sic him! Sic him!' Then he showed him a piece of sheep's heart, as if to say to him, 'This will be your reward.' Oh! My friends, this was really a terrible scene. Picture a big reddish-brown monkey with a black snout, gnashing his teeth like someone possessed, pouncing furiously, almost in a rage, on this poor little unhappy boy who, unable to defend himself, had fallen down at the first blow and had flung himself facedown on the ground so as not to have his face ripped off. Seeing this, Gunpowder, egged on all the while by his master, climbs on his back, takes him by the neck, and starts to bite hard enough at the back of his head to draw blood. 'Oh! The spider from my dream! The spider!' the Runt cried in a stifled voice, thinking he was really and truly done for this time. Suddenly, there was a knock at the door. *Bam! Bam! Bam!*"

"Ah! It's the elder!" exclaimed the prisoners with joy.

"Yes, this time it was him, my friends. He was crying through the door, 'Open up, Chops-Him-in-Two! Will you open this door? Don't pretend you don't hear me, because I can see you through the keyhole!' The animal-handler, forced to answer, goes over grumbling to open the door to the neighbor, who was a guy who was as solid as a bridge, despite being fifty years old. You didn't want to mess with him when he was angry. 'What do you want from me?' Chops-Him-in-Two asks him as he opens the door a crack. 'I want to talk to you,' said the elder, who entered the little courtyard almost by force. Then, seeing the monkey still after the Runt, he runs, grabs Gunpowder by the scruff of his neck, tries to pry him off the child and throw him ten feet away. But just then he sees that the child is chained up to the monkey. Seeing this, the elder gives Chops-Him-in-Two a terrible look and yells at him, 'Get over here right away and unchain this poor little boy!' You can imagine the joy and surprise of the Runt, who, half dead from fear, sees that he has been saved just in time, as if by a miracle. He could not keep from remembering the golden fly of his dream, even though the elder did not look like a fly. That guy, far from it."

"Come on," said the guard as he took a step toward the door. "Now that the Runt has been rescued, I can go and eat my soup."

"Rescued!" exclaimed Bitters. "Oh, sure, rescued! His trials are far from over, though, the poor Runt."

"Really?" said some of the prisoners, with interest.

"But what's going to happen to him next?" said the guard, coming back over to him.

"Stay here, guard, and you'll find out," said the storyteller.

"That devil of a Bitters! He wraps you around his little finger," said the guard. "I guess I'll stay a little longer."

The Skeleton, speechless, was seething with rage.

Bitters continued: "Chops-Him-in-Two, who the elder put the fear of God into, detached the child from the chain, grumbling as he did so. When he was done, the elder throws Gunpowder in the air and stops his fall with an enormous kick to the kidneys, sending him rolling ten paces away. The monkey cries like he's been burned and gnashes his teeth, but he runs away quickly and goes to the top of a little toolshed to protect himself. Once there, he shakes his fist at the elder. 'Why did you hit my monkey?' said Chops-Him-in-Two to the elder. 'You should be asking me why I don't hit you yourself. To make a child suffer like that! You've gotten yourself drunk nice and early this morning, huh?' 'I'm no drunker than you. I was teaching my monkey a trick. I want to put on a show, and he and the Runt are going to appear in it together. I was doing my job. Why don't you mind your own business?' 'This is my business. This morning, when I didn't see the Runt go by my door with the other children, I asked them where he was. They wouldn't answer and they seemed embarrassed about it. I know you, and I figured that you would do something bad to him, and sure enough, I was right. Listen to me carefully! Every time I don't see the Runt going by with the others in the morning, I'll be over here right away, and you'll have to produce him and show him to me, or I'll beat you up good.' 'I'll do what I want. I don't have to take orders from you,' answered Chops-Him-in-Two, irritated at this threat of oversight. 'You won't beat up anything at all, and if you don't get out of here, or if you return, I'll—' *Pow! Bam!* goes the elder, interrupting Chops-Him-in-Two with a pair of whacks that would down a rhinoceros. 'That's what you get for talking back that way to the elder of Little Poland.'"

"Two whacks isn't much," said Blue Cap. "If I were the elder, I'd have made mincemeat out of him."

"And he would have deserved every bit of it," added a prisoner.

"The elder," Bitters went on, "could eat ten Chops-Him-in-Twos just for breakfast. So the animal-handler had to take those whacks and be happy about it. But he was furious at being beaten, and especially at being beaten in front of the Runt. So at that very moment, he swore to himself that he would get revenge, and he came up with an idea that only a demon as wicked as he was could ever have dreamed up. As he was mulling over this diabolical idea and rubbing his ears, the elder said to him, 'Remember that if you get it into your head to hurt this child again, I'll force you to leave Little Poland, you and your animals, or I'll get the whole neighborhood to rise up against you. You know that everyone already hates you. So they'll give you an escort that you'll feel in each and every bone—I guarantee it.' Two-faced liar that he was and in order to be able to execute his vile plan, instead of being angry with the elder, Chops-Him-in-Two acts like a good dog and says, sweet as pie, 'Honest, Elder, you're wrong for having beaten me, and for thinking that I meant the Runt any harm. On the contrary, like I said, I was teaching my monkey a new trick. It's not pretty when he gets his back up, and in the struggle, the little one got bitten, and I was angry about it.' 'Hmm . . .' said the elder as he looked at him, askance. 'Is that really the truth? And anyway, if you want to teach your monkey a trick, why chain him up to the Runt?' 'Because the Runt is supposed to be part of it. Here's what I want to do. I'll dress Gunpowder up in a red suit and a hat with feathers in it like a Swiss ointment salesman.[214] I'll sit the Runt down in a little children's chair. Then I'll put a napkin around his neck, and the monkey, with a big wooden razor, will pretend to give him a shave.' The elder couldn't help laughing at this idea. 'Wouldn't that be a good comedy routine?' said Chops-Him-in-Two, in a sly way. 'It really would be a good routine,' said the elder. 'Especially since they say your nasty monkey is clever and skillful enough to be able to pull off a stunt like that.' 'He sure can. When he's seen me pretend to shave the Runt five or six times, he'll imitate me with his big wooden razor. But to make it work, he has to get used to the child. That's why I chained them together.' 'But why did you choose the Runt instead of any other child?' 'Because he's the smallest of the lot, and when he sits down, Gunpowder will be bigger than him. And besides, I was going to give half of the proceeds to the Runt.' 'If that's the way it is,' said the elder, taken in by the animal-handler's hypocrisy, 'I'm sorry for the beating I gave you. Well, you can take it on account.' While his master was speaking with the elder, the Runt didn't dare breathe. He was trembling like a feather, and he was dying to throw himself at the elder's feet to beg him to take him away from the animal-handler. But he didn't have the courage for it, and he began to despair again, whispering, 'I will be like the poor fly in my dream. The spider will eat me. I was wrong to believe that the golden fly would rescue me.' 'So, my boy, since old Chops-Him-in-Two is going to give you half the take, that should help you get used to the monkey. Come on, you can do it! If the money is good, you won't have anything to complain about.' 'Him, complain? Do you have anything to complain about?' asked his master, giving him such a terrible hidden glance that the child wished he was a hundred feet under the earth. 'No . . . no . . . master,' he answered, stuttering. 'So there you have it, Elder,' said Chops-Him-in-Two. 'He's never had anything to complain about. I just want what's best for him, after all. Maybe Gunpowder scratched him the first time, but it won't happen again. I promise you, I'll keep an eye on him.' 'Good idea! That way, everyone's happy.' 'The Runt most of all,' said Chops-Him-in-Two. 'You'll be happy, won't you?' 'Yes, yes, master,' said the child, crying. 'And to make up for those scratches, I'll give you your share of a nice lunch because the elder is going to send over a plate of cutlets and pickles, four bottles of wine, and a quarter pint of spirits.' 'At your service, Chops-Him-in-Two. My cellar and my kitchen are open to

214. The costume Chops-Him-in-Two describes is a standard comic getup at the time, referred to as that of a Swiss ointment salesman. [TN]

everyone.' Deep down, the elder was a good man, but he wasn't devious and he liked to sell his wine and grub, too. That scoundrel Chops-Him-in-Two knew that perfectly well. You see that he sent him off all happy, having sold him food and drink and reassured about the Runt's fate. So that's how this poor little guy fell back under the control of his master. As soon as the elder's back was turned, Chops-Him-in-Two shows the stairs to his whipping boy and orders him to climb back up into the attic. The child doesn't need to be told twice; he takes off in fear. 'Good Lord, I'm done for!' he cries as he throws himself on the straw next to his tortoise, crying hot tears. He was sobbing there for a good hour when he hears Chops-Him-in-Two's rough voice calling him. The thing that scared the Runt even more was the fact that his master's voice didn't sound the way it usually did. 'Will you get down here already?' said the animal-handler, amid a torrent of oaths. The child hurries to go down the ladder. He's barely put his foot on the ground when his master grabs him and carries him into his room, staggering with each step, since Chops-Him-in-Two has had so much to drink that he's as drunk as a skunk and can hardly stay on his feet. His body was lurching back and forth, and he looked at the Runt, rolling his eyes with an evil glint but not saying a word because his drunkenness slurred his speech. The child had never been more frightened in his life. Gunpowder was chained to the foot of the bed. In the middle of the room there was a chair with a rope hanging off its back. 'S-s-s . . . sit . . . over there,'" Bitters continued, imitating until the end of his story the thick-tongued stuttering of a drunken man whenever he made Chops-Him-in-Two speak. "The Runt sits down, all trembling. Then Chops-Him-in-Two, still without speaking, winds the big rope around him and ties him to the chair, which wasn't easy because even though the animal trainer still could see and was still conscious, you would have thought he was trying to tie a tie knot. Finally, the Runt was tied tightly to the chair. 'Good Lord! Good Lord!' he murmured. 'This time no one's going to come to save me.' Poor kid, he was right. No one could or would come, as you'll see. The elder had left feeling calm about him, and Chops-Him-in-Two had double-locked the door to his inner courtyard and bolted it. So no one could come to the Runt's rescue."

"Oh! This time, Runt, you're done for!" said the prisoners to each other, moved as they were by the story.

"Poor kid!"

"It's really too bad!"

"If you could save him for twenty sous, I'd put my money in."

"So would I!"

"That lousy Chops-Him-in-Two!"

"What is he going to do to him?"

Bitters continued: "When the Runt was tied down to the chair, his master said to him"—and the storyteller went back to imitating the voice of a drunken man—"'Ah! You scoundrel! You're the reason I . . . I . . . was beaten by the elder . . . y-you . . . are going to d-d-die . . .' And he takes a big, freshly sharpened razor blade out of his pocket, opens it, and takes the Runt by the hair with one hand—"

A murmur of indignation and horror circulated among the prisoners and interrupted Bitters for a moment. Then he went on: "At the sight of the razor, the child begins crying, 'Have mercy, master! Mercy! Don't kill me!' 'Go ahead, cry! Cry, kid! You won't be crying for long,' answered Chops-Him-in-Two. 'Golden fly! Golden fly! Save me!' cried the poor Runt, almost delirious, remembering the dream that had had such an effect on him. 'The spider that's going to kill me is here!' 'So! You're c-c-calling me a spider?' said Chops-Him-in-Two. 'Just for that, and other . . . other things too . . . you're going to die. Do you understand? But not by my hand . . . because . . . the thing is . . . and then they'd guillotine me. I'll s-s-say it's the monkey and pr-prove it t-t-too. I've got everything . . . r-r-ready to . . . Oh, whatever,' said Chops-Him-in-Two, barely holding himself upright. Then he called over to his monkey, who was pulling at the end of his chain with all his might, grinding his teeth all the while, and looking back and forth between his master and the child. 'Take it, Gunpowder,' he said, showing him the razor and the Runt whom he had by the hair. 'You're going to do this to him, do you see?' Passing the back of the razor across the Runt's neck, he made as if he was slitting his throat. The nasty monkey was such a gifted mimic and so wicked and clever that he understood just what his master wanted him to do. As if to prove it, he took his chin with his left paw, tilted his head back, and, with his right paw, pretended to cut his own neck. 'That's it, Gunpowder, you've got it!' said Chops-Him-in-Two, stuttering, with his eyes half closed and tottering so unsteadily that he just missed falling onto the Runt in the chair. 'Yes, that's it. I'm g-g-going to unch-ch-chain you, and you . . . slit his gullet, all right, Gunpowder?' The monkey shrieked and ground its teeth as if to say yes. He reached out his paw to take the razor that Chops-Him-in-Two was offering him. 'Golden fly! Save me!' murmured the Runt in a sad, weak little voice, certain this time that he was not long for this earth. For alas, he was calling to the golden fly without hoping or expecting him to come. He was saying this the way you call out to God when you're drowning. But he turned out to be wrong. Wouldn't you know it, but just at that moment, the Runt sees one of those green and gold flies, the kind you see plenty of, come in through the open window! You'd think it was a spark of fire crackling about. Just at the moment Chops-Him-in-Two had given the razor to Gunpowder, the golden fly goes straight into the eye of that wicked scoundrel. Having a fly in your eye isn't such a big deal, but in the moment it's happening, you know it stings like anything. So Chops-Him-in-Two, who was having a hard time standing up, brought his hand up to his eye in a sharp movement. This movement was so abrupt that he wobbled, fell over flat on his face, and rolled in a heap to the foot of the bed, where Gunpowder was chained up. 'Thank you, golden fly! You saved my life!' cried the Runt, for even though he was still sitting tied up in the chair, he had seen everything."

"So it's true, by golly, that the golden fly kept him from getting his neck cut!" exclaimed the prisoners, transported with joy.

"Long live the golden fly!" Blue Cap cried out.

"Yes, long live the golden fly!" repeated several other voices.

"Long live Bitters and his stories!" said another.

"Wait! Here's the most beautiful and most terrible part of the story I promised you: Chops-Him-in-Two had fallen to the ground like a ton of bricks. He was so drunk—so drunk—that he was as still as a log. He was dead drunk, you know? And completely unconscious. But when he fell, he almost crushed Gunpowder, and he had almost broken one of his back paws. You know how mean, resentful, and malicious this nasty animal was. He hadn't put down the razor his master had given him to cut the Runt's throat with. What does that beggar of a monkey do when he sees his master within his reach, stretched out on his back and as motionless as a dead fish? He jumps on him, crouches on his chest, pulls his neck skin taut with one of his paws, and with the other—presto!—he cuts his gullet clean through, just like Chops-Him in-Two had taught him to do on the Runt."

"Bravo!"

"Well done!"

"Long live Gunpowder!" cried the prisoners, enthusiastically.

"Long live the little golden fly!"

"Long live the Runt!"

"Long live Gunpowder!"

"Well, my friends," said Bitters, thrilled by the success of his story, "an hour later, all of Little Poland was yelling the same things."

"What were they saying? What?"

"I told you that in order to pull off his evil plan at his ease, that scoundrel Chops-Him-in-Two had locked his door from the inside. At dusk, here are the children coming back one by one with their animals. The first ones knock, and no one answers. Finally, when they're all there, they knock again. No answer. One of them goes off to find the elder to tell him that, hard as they knocked, their master wouldn't let them in. 'The bum must be drunk as a lord,' he says. 'I just sent him wine. We'll have to knock down his door. These children can't spend the night outside.' They break open the door with an ax. They enter, they go upstairs, they get to the room, and what do they see? Gunpowder chained up and crouched over the body of his master, playing with the razor. The poor Runt, luckily beyond Gunpowder's reach, still sitting tied up to the chair, not daring to look at Chops-Him-in-Two's body, was looking at—guess what?—the little golden fly who, after having flitted about the child as if to congratulate him, had finally come to rest on his little hand. The Runt told the whole story to the elder and all the people who came in after him. It seemed, truly, like a miracle from heaven, as they say. The elder exclaims, 'This is the Runt's victory, and Gunpowder's victory, too, for having killed that evil ruffian Chops-Him-in-Two! He chopped up others, so it was his turn to be chopped up himself!' 'Yes! Yes!' cries the crowd, because they all despised the animal-handler. 'It's Gunpowder's victory! It's the Runt's victory!' It was the dark of night now. They light the straw torches and they tie Gunpowder to a bench that four children carry on their shoulders. The scoundrel of a monkey seemed to take this honor as the least he deserved and put on the airs of the victor, showing his teeth to the crowd. After the monkey came the elder, carrying the Runt in his arms. All the little animal-handlers, each one with his own animal, followed the elder. One was carrying a fox, another a marmot, another a guinea pig. The ones who played the hurdy-gurdy played it now; there were Auvergne coal miners with their accordions, and they were playing, too.[215] Joy was ringing out everywhere; it was a party like you couldn't believe! Behind the musicians and the animal-handlers came all the inhabitants of Little Poland, men, women, and children. Almost all of them had straw torches in their hands and were crying out like crazy people, 'Long live the Runt! Long live Gunpowder!' The parade goes all around Chops-Him-in-Two's property, carrying on like this. It was some funny scene, really, all those old shanties and all those faces illuminated by the red glow of the straw torches that were flaming, flaming! As for the Runt, the first thing he did, once he was free, was to place the little golden fly in a paper cone, and he kept repeating the whole time of his celebration, 'Little flies, I'm glad I kept the spiders from eating you, because—' "

A voice interrupted the end of Bitters's story. "Hey, Old Roussel," it cried from outside the room, "come and eat your soup already. It's ten to four."

"The story's almost over, I guess, so I'm leaving now. Thank you, my boy. That was really entertaining. And it was all your doing," said the guard to Bitters as he went over to the door. Then he paused. "Now, then! Behave yourselves," he said to the prisoners as he turned to leave.

"We'll hear the end of the story," said the Skeleton, panting in

215. Popular cabarets with dancing and accordion music were founded by immigrants to Paris who had come originally from the Auvergne region. These immigrants often worked as coal merchants. [TN]

restrained rage. Then he whispered to the Big Gimp, "Go into the doorway, watch the guard, and when you see him leave the courtyard, yell, 'Gunpowder!'—and the stoolie will die."

"Consider it done," said the Big Gimp, who went along with the guard and stood at the door to the furnace room, following him with his gaze.

"I was telling you," said Bitters, "that the Runt was saying to himself, the whole time he was carried in triumph, 'Little flies, I—'"

"Gunpowder!" the Big Gimp shouted as he returned. He had just seen the guard leaving the courtyard.

"And now the Runt is mine! I'll be your spider!" cried the Skeleton instantly, throwing himself so abruptly on Germain that the latter did not have the chance to move or cry out.

His voice was cut off by the formidable grip of the Skeleton's long, iron fingers.

CHAPTER II

AN UNKNOWN FRIEND

"If you're the spider, I'll be the golden fly, you evil Skeleton!" cried a voice at the moment Germain, surprised by the violent and sudden attack of his implacable enemy, had fallen down over his bench, left to the mercy of the criminal who, with one knee on his chest, had him by the neck. "Yes, I'll be the fly, and what a fly I'll be!" repeated the man in the blue cap, of whom we have spoken. Then, in a furious leap, knocking over three or four prisoners who separated him from Germain, he leapt onto the Skeleton and let loose a shower of blows on his skull and a rain of punches between the eyes that came so fast they seemed to be the reverberations of a hammer on an anvil.

The man in the blue cap, who was none other than the Slasher, added, as he increased the speed of his hammering on the Skeleton's head, "Here's the hail of punches that Monsieur Rodolphe drummed on my skull! I've remembered them."

At this unexpected attack, the prisoners were struck with surprise, and did not take sides either for or against the Slasher. Several of them, still under the salutary impression of Bitters's story, were even happy to see someone come to Germain's rescue. The Skeleton, at first stunned, staggered like a bull under the butcher's iron sledgehammer. He put his hands out in front of himself mechanically so as to parry his enemy's blows. Germain managed to escape the mortal grip of the Skeleton, and he started to stand up.

"What's gotten into him? What's this criminal's problem?" cried the Big Gimp. Throwing himself on the Slasher, he tried to seize his arms from behind as the latter struggled violently to hold the Skeleton down on the bench. Germain's defender responded to the Big Gimp's attack with a backward kick so violent that he sent him tumbling backward to the edge of the circle formed by the prisoners.

Germain, livid, with a purplish-blue tint to his pallor, was on his knees, half suffocated, next to the bench. He seemed not to be conscious of what was going on around him. The attempt to strangle him had been so violent and painful that he could hardly breathe.

After the first shock wore off, the Skeleton, making a desperate effort, managed to get free of the Slasher and get back up on his feet. Panting, drunk with rage and hatred, he was a terrifying sight. His cadaverous face was streaming with blood. His upper lip, snarling, like the lip of a furious wolf, revealed his clenched teeth. Finally, he called out in a voice that was palpitating with anger and fatigue, for his struggle with the Slasher had been a violent one, "Kill this bandit, you bunch of sissies! You're deserting like traitors! If you don't kill him, the stoolie will get away."

During this momentary lull, the Slasher, picking up the semiconscious Germain, had maneuvered quite skillfully so as to be able, little by little, to get closer to the corner of a wall, where he put his protégé down. Taking advantage of this excellent defensive position, the Slasher could thus hold off the prisoners for a long time without having any fear of being taken from behind. His courage and the herculean strength that he had just displayed impressed those prisoners considerably.

Bitters, terrified, disappeared during the tumult. No one noticed his absence.

Seeing most of the prisoners hesitating, the Skeleton cried, "Follow me! Knock their brains out, the little one and the big one!"

"Take care!" returned the Slasher, preparing for combat, his two hands forward, his weight balanced squarely on his sturdy haunches. "Be careful, Skeleton! If you want to play Chops-Him-in-Two anymore, I'll play Gunpowder, and I'll slit your throat."

"Come on, everybody! Attack him!" cried the Big Gimp, getting up. "Why is this cur defending the stoolie? Death to the stoolie—and to him, too! If he protects Germain, he's a traitor!"

"Yes! Yes!"

"Death to the stoolie!"

"Put him to death!"

"Yes! Death to the traitor who helps him!"

Such were the cries from the most hardened among the prisoners. Another, more compassionate group exclaimed, "No, let him speak first!"

"Yes, let him tell us why!"

"You don't kill a man before you hear what he has to say!"

"And without defense!"

"That would really be like Chops-Him-in-Two!"

"So much the better!" said the Big Gimp and other prisoners on the Skeleton's side.

"That's the only thing to do to a stoolie!"

"Put him to death!"

"Attack him!"

"Let's support the Skeleton!"

"Yes! Yes! Let's give Blue Cap what for!"

"No! Let's support Blue Cap! Let's give the Skeleton what for!" retorted the Slasher's party.

"No! Down with Blue Cap!"

"Down with the Skeleton!"

"Bravo, my boys!" exclaimed the Slasher, turning to the prisoners who were lining themselves up by his side. "You have good hearts. You wouldn't want to massacre a half-dead man! Only cowards would do something like that. The Skeleton doesn't give a damn. He's already condemned to die. That's why he's pushing at you to do this. But if you help him kill Germain, you'll be charged with it straight out. Anyway, here's an idea: The Skeleton wants to knock off this poor young man. Well, he can come and get him from me, if he has the guts for it! It'll be between the two of us. We'll fight, and we'll see how that comes out. But if he backs down, he's like Chops-Him-in-Two—we'll know he'll only push around weaklings."

The Slasher's vigor, energy, and rough face could not fail to have a powerful effect on the prisoners. A rather large number of them lined up on his side and surrounded Germain. The Skeleton's party circled around him. A bloody melee was going to take place when they heard in the courtyard the sonorous and measured steps of the infantry that always stood guard at the prison. Bitters, taking advantage of the noise and the general excitement, had gone into the courtyard to knock at the barred door of the entrance gate in order to tell the guards what was happening in the furnace room. The arrival of the soldiers put an end to this scene.

Germain, the Skeleton, and the Slasher were taken to see the director of La Force prison. The first was supposed to file his charge, and the two others were to answer the charge of causing a brawl within the prison. Germain's shock and pain had been so overwhelming and his weakness so great that he had to be supported by two guards in order to get to the nearby room housing the director's office to which they were taking him. Once there, he felt ill. His neck, with its skin severely chafed, bore the livid, bloody imprint of the Skeleton's iron fingers. A few seconds more and Rigolette's fiancé would have been strangled.

The guard in charge of watching over the visiting room, who, as we've mentioned, had always been interested in helping Germain, gave him first aid. When the latter regained consciousness, when the rapid, terrible emotions that had almost robbed him of reason gave way to reflection, his first thought was for his savior. "Thank you for your care, monsieur," he said to the guard. "Without that brave man, I would have been done for."

"How are you feeling?"

"Better. Ah! Everything that just happened seems like a horrible dream!"

"Calm down a little."

"And where is the man who came to my rescue?"

"In the director's office. He's telling him how the brawl began. It seems that without him—"

"I would be dead, monsieur. Oh, tell me his name! Who is he?"

"I'm not sure what his name is. His nickname is the Slasher. He's an ex-convict."

"And on what charges is he here? Nothing serious, I hope?"

"Very serious! Breaking and entering an inhabited house," said the guard. "He'll probably get the same sentence as Bitters. Considering he's a repeat offender, fifteen or twenty years of hard labor and public exhibition."

Germain shuddered. He would have preferred ties of gratitude to a man who was less of a criminal. "Oh, that's awful!" he said. "And yet, that man, without knowing me, protected me. Such courage, and such generosity!"

"What can I say, monsieur? Sometimes there is still a bit of good in those people. The important thing is that now you're safe and sound. Tomorrow you'll have a rented cell to yourself, and tonight you'll sleep in the infirmary, on the director's orders. Come on, be strong, monsieur! Your bad times are over. When your pretty little visitor comes to see you, you can give her peace of mind, for once you're in your own cell, you won't have anything more to fear. Except I wouldn't recommend telling her about what just happened. She would be sick with fear."

"Oh, no, I certainly won't tell her about it. But I would still like to thank my defender. However guilty he may be in the eyes of the law, he still saved my life."

"Wait a moment. I can hear him now leaving the director's office. The director is going to question the Skeleton now. I will bring them both back to the prison in just a moment—the Skeleton to solitary and the Slasher to the Lions' Den. He'll be rewarded in some small way, in any case, for what he did for you. Seeing as he's a sturdy, determined fellow, the kind you have to be in order to lead the others, they'll probably have him replace the Skeleton as provost."

After walking through a small corridor off of which the director's office was found, the Slasher entered the room where Germain was. "Wait for me here," said the guard to the Slasher. "I'm going to go find out what the director has in mind for the Skeleton, and I'll come back to get you. Here's our young man. He's doing much better. He wants to thank you, and he has reason to, for without you he'd be dead meat."

The guard left the room. The Slasher's face was radiant. He came forward joyously and said, "Damn, I'm happy! I'm so happy I rescued you!" And he held out his hand to Germain.

The latter, feeling an involuntary impulse of repulsion, at first recoiled slightly instead of taking the hand the Slasher was offering him. Then, remembering that after all he owed his life to this man, he tried to make up for his initial repugnance. But the Slasher had noticed it, and his face grew somber. Recoiling as well, he said with bitter sadness, "Ah, that's right. I beg your pardon, monsieur."

"No, it is I who should be apologizing to you. Am I not a prisoner just like you? The only thing I should be thinking of is what you have done for me. You saved my life. Your hand, monsieur. Please do me the honor of giving me your hand."

"Thank you, but there would be no point now. The first movement said it all. If you had at first shaken my hand, it would have given me pleasure. But when I think about it, I realize I shouldn't have wanted to shake your hand. Not because I'm a prisoner just like you, but rather," he added in a somber and hesitant tone, "because before coming here, I was—"

"The guard told me everything," said Germain, interrupting him. "But it remains the case that you saved my life."

"I have only performed my duty, and one I took pleasure in, for I know who you are, Monsieur Germain."

"You know me?"

"A little bit, nephew! I would answer you that way if I were your uncle," said the Slasher, resuming his usual carefree tone. "And you would be quite wrong if you thought that my being here in La Force was a mere matter of chance. If I didn't know you, I wouldn't be here in prison."

Germain looked at the Slasher in astonishment. "What? It's because you knew me . . ."

"That I'm here, as a prisoner at La Force."

"I'd like to believe you, but . . ."

"But you don't believe me."

"I mean that I can't begin to understand how I could be at all involved in your imprisonment."

"Involved? You're the entire reason why."

"How could I have had this misfortune?"

"This misfortune? Just the opposite! It's me who is in your debt. And plenty more, too."

"To me? You owe me something?"

"I should light a candle for you for giving me the opportunity to visit La Force."

"Honestly," said Germain, wiping his forehead with his hand, "I don't know whether it's the terrible shock from earlier that's weakened my ability to think, but I'm finding it impossible to understand what you're saying. The guard just told me that you were here as a suspect in a . . . in a . . ." Here Germain hesitated.

"Theft, for God's sake. Oh, yes, that's a good one! Yes, burglary, with a ladder—and at night, on top of that! The meal and all the dressings!" cried the Slasher, bursting into laughter. "No detail missing! It's a good one, all right. My theft is as magical as Saint John's herbs,[216] as they say."

---

216. Saint John's herbs: a cocktail of twenty-seven traditional plants and flowers that were supposed to be included in magic potions in medieval pagan rituals. [TN]

Germain, who was quite pained by the Slasher's bold cynicism, could not prevent himself from saying to him, "What? You who are so good, so generous . . . how can you talk that way? Don't you know what a horrible punishment awaits you?"

"Twenty years or so in the galleys and the iron collar? Yeah, I know. I must be a real out-and-out bad one, no, to take this as some kind of joke? But there's nothing you can do. Once you're a criminal . . . And just think, all the same, that it's you, Monsieur Germain," added the Slasher, sighing deeply, with a pleasantly contrite tone, "that it's you who are the cause of my misfortune!"

"When you explain yourself more clearly, I'll understand. Make fun of me all you want, my gratitude to you for the service you rendered me will be no less great," said Germain, sadly.

"Listen, I'm sorry, Monsieur Germain," said the Slasher, becoming serious. "If you don't like to see me laughing about this, let's drop it. I need to make it up to you so maybe I can make you hold out your hand to me again."

"I don't doubt you will. Despite the crime you're accused of—and which you as much as admit—everything about you bespeaks your bravery and candor. I'm sure you've been unjustly suspected. Appearances might make things look very bad for you. But it can't be more than that."

"Oh, as for that, you're wrong, Monsieur Germain," said the Slasher, so seriously this time and with such sincerity that Germain had to believe him. "I swear, just as truly as I have a protector," and here the Slasher raised his cap, "who is for me what the good Lord is for priests, I committed theft at night by forcing a window, I was caught red-handed, and I was still flush with all the stuff I had just taken."

"But you must have been hungry . . . or in dire need . . . to have to resort to such extremes?"

"Hungry? I had a hundred and twenty francs on me when they arrested me, the remainder of a bill of a thousand francs. That's not even taking into account the fact that the protector I've mentioned, and who, by the way, doesn't know I'm here, never leaves me in want of anything. But since I've spoken to you of my protector, we have to be serious now, because, you see, he's someone you feel you should go down on your knees to. So listen: the hail of blows I hammered the Skeleton with is a trick of his that I copied. I only thought of committing that theft because of him. Finally, if you're here instead of having been strangled by the Skeleton, it's thanks to him, too."

"But this protector?"

"Is yours, too."

"Mine?"

"Yes, Monsieur Rodolphe is protecting you. When I say 'monsieur,' I should actually be saying 'his lordship,' because he must be at least a prince. But I got used to calling him Monsieur Rodolphe, and he lets me."

"You're making an error," said Germain, growing more and more surprised. "I don't know any princes."

"Yes, but Monsieur Rodolphe, he knows you. You don't know anything about him? That could be. That's how he does things. He knows there's a good man in trouble, and *pow!* that good man is helped. You don't know me and you've never even seen me before, so I'm confusing you. Happiness falls from the clouds like a roof tile on your head. Patience, patience: one day or another you'll get your tile."

"Honestly, what you're saying baffles me."

"You'll learn plenty more things like that! To return to my protector, a short time ago, after a favor he claims I'd done him, he procured a superb position for me. I don't need to tell you about it, it would take too long. Basically, he sends me to Marseille to send me off to Algeria to assume my brilliant position. I leave Paris, happy as a clam. Great! But soon things change. Put it this way: when I left, the sun was shining, all right? Well, the next day the sky clouded over, the day after that it was all gray, and then after that it got darker and darker the further away I got, until finally it was as dark as the devil. Do you understand?"

"Not completely."

"Well, let's see. Have you ever had a dog?"

"What an odd question!"

"Have you ever had a dog that loved you and who got lost?"

"No."

"Well, then, I'll tell you straight out that once I was away from Monsieur Rodolphe, I was anxious, downcast, frightened, like a dog who had lost his master. I was as dumb as an animal, but dogs are dumb animals, which doesn't stop them from getting attached and remembering the good treats as much as beatings with sticks that they've gotten. And Monsieur Rodolphe had given me much better than good treats, because, you know, Monsieur Rodolphe means everything to me. He took a wicked, good-for-nothing, brutal, savage wretch, and he made me into some kind of honest man, just by saying two words to me. But those two words worked on me like magic, you see."

"What were those two words? What did he say to you?"

"He told me that I still had heart and honor, even though I had been in the penitentiary—though not for theft, it's true. No, I'd never do that. But for something worse, maybe—for killing a man. Yes," said the Slasher in a somber voice, "yes, I killed in a moment of anger. Because long ago, I had been raised like a wild animal, or rather like a bum, without a father or mother, abandoned on the streets of Paris, I didn't know God from the devil, or good from evil, or the weak from the strong. Sometimes blood came up into my eyes, and I saw red, and if I had a knife in my hand, I'd slash, slash, slash. I was like a wolf, you know? I was only good enough for beggars and thieves. It's not like that bothered me any—I had to live in the mud, so live in the mud I did. I didn't even know that that's where I was. But when Monsieur Rodolphe told me that because, faced with only poverty and the world's contempt, instead of stealing, like everybody else around, I had still preferred to work hard, any way I could, when he said that meant that I had heart and honor—damn! You see, those two words had the same effect on me as if someone had grabbed me and lifted me a thousand feet into the air above the vermin I was paddling about with. That showed me the filth I was living in. So of course I said then, 'Thanks, I've had enough. I'm done with this.' Then my heart beat with something besides anger, and I swore to myself that I'd always have that honor inside me that Monsieur Rodolphe talked about. You see, Monsieur Germain, when he told me, in his goodness, that I wasn't as bad as I thought I was, Monsieur Rodolphe encouraged me, and thanks to him, I became better than I ever was."

Hearing the Slasher speak this way, Germain understood less and less how he could have committed the theft he had admitted to.

CHAPTER 12

DELIVERANCE

No, thought Germain; it is impossible that this man whom the mere words "honor" and "heart" have made so noble could have committed the theft he speaks of with such cynicism.

The Slasher went on, not noticing Germain's astonishment. "In the end, the thing that made me feel toward Monsieur Rodolphe the way a dog does toward his master was that he made me seem better in my own eyes. Before I knew him, I only felt things skin deep. But he sure changed me from top to bottom. Once I was far away from him and where he lived, I felt like a ghost. The further I got from him, the more I said to myself, 'He leads such a funny life! He gets involved with the worst scum (and I should know), he risks his life twenty times a day, and at a time like that I could act like his dog and defend my master, 'cause I have a pretty good bite to my bark.' But on the other hand, he had said to me, 'My boy, we have to make you useful to others. Go where you can be of service.' I really wanted to answer, 'For me, there's only one person I want to serve, and that's you, Monsieur Rodolphe.' But I didn't dare. He said to me, 'Go.' I went, and I did the best I could. But damn! When I had to get into that boat, leave France, and put the sea between myself and Monsieur Rodolphe, without any hope of seeing him ever again . . . well, the truth of it is, I just didn't have the courage. He'd told his agent to give me a sum of money that was practically my weight in gold when I embarked. I went to find the man. I said to him, 'Can't do it right now. I prefer solid ground. Give me enough money to get back on foot. I've got good legs. I'll return to Paris. I can't stand it. Monsieur Rodolphe can say whatever he likes. He could get angry and not want to see me. Things happen. But this way I'll see him again and I'll know where he is, and if he continues living the way he does, sooner or later, maybe I'll be there to put myself between him and a knife. And in the end, I just can't go so far away from him! I feel like I don't know what kind of devil is pulling me back in his direction.' Finally, I get enough money to make my journey, I arrive in Paris. I don't get shy easy, but once I got back, I was struck with fear. What could I say to Monsieur Rodolphe to excuse my returning without his permission? Bah! After all, he wouldn't eat me. Whatever would be, would be. I go to find his friend, a big, fat, bald guy, a real top-notch character. Damn! When Monsieur Murph came in, I said, 'My fate is going to be decided.' I felt my throat go dry, and my heart was beating like crazy. I expected to be knocked flat, for sure. Yeah, right! The worthy man receives me as if he had just seen me the day before. He tells me that Monsieur Rodolphe, far from being angry, wants to see me right away. And, sure enough, he takes me to where my protector is waiting. Damn! When I found myself face-to-face with him, with that guy who has such a good fist and such a good heart, who is terrible as a lion and as gentle as a lamb, who is a prince and who has worn a worker's shirt like me so that he could wind up getting the chance (that I bless) of knocking me out with a hail of punches that made me see stars—well, Monsieur Germain, when I thought of all he was, I got all confused, and I bawled like a baby. So what happens next? Instead of making fun of me—because you can imagine what my mug looks like when I'm sniveling—Monsieur Rodolphe says to me, seriously, 'So you've come back, my boy!' 'Yes, Monsieur Rodolphe. I'm sorry if it was wrong of me, but I couldn't stand it. Let me hang out in some corner of your yard. Give me some feed, or let me earn it here—that's all I ask. Most of all, don't be angry with me for coming back.' 'I'm all the less angry with you because you're just in time to do something important for me.' 'Me, Monsieur Rodolphe? Do you mean it? Really? Well, you see, there must be somebody up there, just like you say. Otherwise, how do you explain that I'm here just when you need me? And what can I do for you, then, Monsieur Rodolphe? Dive headfirst from atop Notre-Dame's towers?' 'Not quite that, my boy. An honest and excellent young man whom I care about as if he were my son has been unjustly charged with theft, and he's being held at La Force. His name is Germain. He is gentle and timid. The criminals with whom he's imprisoned have taken a dislike to him. He may be in grave danger. You have, unfortunately, known what the inside of a prison is like and also you know many prisoners. On the chance that some of your former associates might be in La Force (we'll find some way of knowing that), could you go to see them and promise them things or offer them money to protect this unfortunate young man?'"

"But what kind of man is this unknown, generous stranger who cares so much about my fate?" asked Germain, more and more astonished.

"You may know someday. As for me, I have no idea. But to get back to my conversation with Monsieur Rodolphe: as he was talking to me, I had an idea—an idea that was so funny, so very funny, that I could hardly keep from laughing in front of him. 'What's so funny, my boy?' he asked. 'Lord! Monsieur Rodolphe, I'm laughing because I'm happy, and I'm happy because I know how to defend your Monsieur Germain against any harm the other prisoners might do him by sending him someone who will give him the most stubborn protection. Once that young man is under the wing of the guy I have in mind, not a single one of those guys will dare to look at him the wrong way.' 'Very good, my boy. This must be one of your former associates, right?' 'Exactly right, Monsieur Rodolphe. He went into La Force a few days ago. I found out about it when I got here. But we'll need money.' 'How much?' 'A thousand francs.' 'Here it is.' 'Thank you, Monsieur Rodolphe. In two days you'll hear from me. Your troops are ready for your orders!' Damn, I'm not in the king's service, so I could serve Monsieur Rodolphe by serving you! It was brilliant!"

"I'm starting to understand—or rather, what I understand frightens me," said Germain. "Can such devotion be possible? In order to protect and defend me in this prison, is it possible that you've committed a theft? Oh! I would regret that my whole life!"

"Just a minute! Monsieur Rodolphe told me I had heart and honor. Those are the words I live by, you see? He could still say these words to me, for if I'm no better than I used to be, at least I'm no worse."

"But what about that theft? If you didn't do it, how did you get in here?"

"Wait and see. Here's how the comedy goes: with my thousand francs, I go and buy a black wig. I shave my sideburns, I put on blue glasses, I stuff a pillow in my back, and start playing a hunchback. I go to find one or two rooms on the ground floor in a nice neighborhood that I can rent starting right away. I find just what I'm looking for on rue de Provence; I put down a deposit under the name Monsieur Grégoire. The next day I go to the Temple to buy what I need to furnish the two rooms, still wearing my black wig, my hump, and my blue eyeglasses so everyone will recognize me that way. I send my purchases to rue de Provence along with six silver place settings that I buy on the boulevard Saint-Denis, still wearing my hunchback disguise.

"I return to my residence to put everything in order. I tell the doorkeeper that I won't be staying there until two days from then, and I take my key. The windows on the two rooms were closed with strong shutters. Before leaving, I left one of them unhooked on the inside, on purpose. When it's nighttime, I get rid of my wig, glasses, hump, and the clothes I used to make my purchases and rent my room. I put this stuff in a trunk that I send to the address of Monsieur Murph, Monsieur Rodolphe's friend, telling him to hold on to the togs. I buy this shirt and this cap and a two-foot-long iron bar. At one in the morning I come to prowl around on rue de Provence in front of my residence, waiting for the moment when the police come by in order to hurry up and rob myself, burgle myself, and break and enter against myself so I can get arrested." At this, the Slasher could not keep himself from laughing uproariously once again.

"Ah! I understand!" Germain exclaimed.

"But you'll see what rotten luck I have. No police came! I could have robbed myself twenty times over without any problem at all. Finally, around two o'clock in the morning, I heard some foot soldiers walking at the end of the street. I finish opening up my shutter, I break two or three panes of glass in order to make a lot of noise, I push in the window, I jump into the room, I grab the box of silver, a few rags . . . Luckily, the patrol had heard the tinkling of the breaking glass, because just as I was coming back out the window, I'm nabbed by the guard who, at the sound of the broken windows, had come racing over.

"They knock on the door, the doorkeeper opens it. They go and look for the police superintendent. He comes. The doorkeeper says that the two rooms that had been robbed were rented the day before by a hunchbacked gentleman with black hair who wore blue glasses and whose name was Grégoire. I had the blond mane you see me with here. I'm caught like a rat in a trap, with my eyes wide open, and I was standing up straight as a ramrod, so no one could take me for the hunchback with blue glasses and black hair. I confess to everything, they arrest me, they take me to the central jail and then here, and I get here just in time to pry the Skeleton's paws off the young man who Monsieur Rodolphe had said about, 'I care about him as if he were my own son.'"

"Ah! How can I ever repay such devotion on your part?" cried Germain.

"You don't have to repay me anything. It's Monsieur Rodolphe you owe something to."

"But why should he care about me?"

"He'll let you know, unless he doesn't let you know. Sometimes he's happy to do something generous for you, and if you have the cheek to ask him why, he doesn't even take the trouble to say to you, 'Mind your own business!'"

"And does Monsieur Rodolphe know you're here?"

"I'm not so stupid to have told him my idea. He might not have let me do it. Not to brag or anything, but it was really something, wasn't it?"

"But you risked so much to do it! And the risk is still great!"

"What was I risking? It's true I might not have been taken to La Force, where they're keeping you. But I was counting on Monsieur Rodolphe's influence to help me change prisons and find you. An aristocrat like that can do anything. And once I got thrown in the clink, he would at least have wanted it to do some good."

"But what happens at your trial?"

"Well, I'll ask Monsieur Murph to send me the trunk. I'll put on my black wig, my blue glasses, and my hump in front of the judge. I'll become Monsieur Grégoire again for the doorkeeper who rented me the room, for the salespeople I bought the goods from in order for me to steal them. If they want to see the thief again, I'll take off that disguise and it will be as clear as day to them that the robber and the robbed are one and the same—they're both the Slasher, no more, no less. So what the devil can they do to me when it's proven that I robbed myself?"

"Indeed," said Germain, no longer worried. "But since you were so concerned about me, why didn't you say anything to me when you came into the prison?"

"I found out right away about the plot they were hatching against you. I could have denounced it before Bitters had begun or finished his story, but to denounce even criminals like that, well, it just isn't my way. I didn't want to trust anything but my own fists when it came to prying you out of the Skeleton's grip. And then, when I saw that criminal, I said to myself, 'Here's a great chance to recall Monsieur Rodolphe's hail of punches from when I had the honor of making his acquaintance.'"

"But if all the prisoners had ganged up on you, what would you have done?"

"Well, in that case I would have cried out like an eagle and called for help! But I felt more comfortable working on my own so I could say to Monsieur Rodolphe, 'I'm the only one who was involved in this business. I came to your young man's protection and you can be sure that I'm protecting him still.'"

At this moment the guard abruptly came back into the room. "Monsieur Germain, come quickly, quickly, to see Monsieur the director. He wants to talk to you immediately. And you, Slasher, my boy, go back to the Lions' Den. You'll be the provost, if you'd like that. You have everything it takes to succeed in that job, and the prisoners won't mess around with a guy like you."

"That suits me fine. As long as I'm here, I might as well be a captain as a soldier."

"Will you still refuse to shake my hand?" Germain asked the Slasher cordially.

"No way! Monsieur Germain, no way! I think I can allow myself that pleasure now. And I'll shake hands with you with all my heart."

"We'll see each other again, because I'm now under your protection. I won't have anything to fear, and I'll come down from my cell into the yard every day."

"You can relax. If I say so, no one will even look sideways at you. But what am I thinking? You know how to write. Put the story I just told you on paper and send it to Monsieur Rodolphe. He'll know that he doesn't have to worry about you anymore and that I'm in here for a good reason. If he found out some other way that the Slasher had stolen and doesn't know what's really been going on . . . Damn, I wouldn't like that."

"Don't worry. I'll write to my unknown protector this very evening. Tomorrow you'll give me his address and the letter will be sent. Farewell again, and thank you, my brave man!"

"Farewell, Monsieur Germain. I'll return to that heap of lowlifes where now I'm the provost. They'd better keep to the straight and narrow, or watch out!"

"When I think that it's my doing that you still have to live with these wretches for the time being!"

"What do I care? There's no risk now that they'll rub off on me. Monsieur Rodolphe has scrubbed me up too good for that. I'm fireproof!" On this note, the Slasher followed the guard out.

Germain walked into the director's office. What was his surprise when he saw Rigolette there!

Rigolette was pale and wrought with emotions, and her eyes were full of tears. Nevertheless, she was smiling through those tears. Her face expressed joy and an ineffable happiness.

"I have good news for you, monsieur," the director said to Germain. "The court has just declared that there are no longer any charges against you. Pursuant to the withdrawal of the charges and pursuant furthermore to the account of the civil party to the case, I have received the order to release you immediately."

"Monsieur . . . What are you saying? Can this be true?"

Rigolette wanted to speak, but her emotions ran too high to allow her to do so. All she could do was nod at Germain and clasp her hands together.

"Mademoiselle arrived here a few moments after I received the order to release you," added the director. "A letter of overwhelming commendation that she brought me demonstrated the touching devotion that she has shown toward you, monsieur, during your stay in prison. Accordingly, it was with the greatest pleasure that I had you brought in here, because I was certain that you would be very happy to give your arm to Mademoiselle and walk out of here together!"

"This is a dream! I must be dreaming!" said Germain. "Ah! Monsieur, how I am blessed! You must excuse me if my surprise and joy keep me from thanking you properly."

"And as for me, Monsieur Germain, I can't find the words," said Rigolette. "Imagine how happy I am. When I left you, I found Monsieur Rodolphe's friend there waiting for me."

"Monsieur Rodolphe, again!" said Germain, astonished.

"Yes, now we can tell you everything. You'll understand the whole thing. Monsieur Murph says to me, 'Germain is free. Here is a letter for the director of the prison. By the time you arrive, he will have received the order to release Germain and you can take him home.' I couldn't believe what I heard, but it was true. I hired a hackney cab as fast as I could—and he's still down there waiting for us."

We will not even attempt to depict the elation of the two lovers when they left La Force or the evening they spent together in Rigolette's little room before Germain left it at eleven o'clock to find himself a modest furnished room.

To summarize briefly the theoretical and practical ideas we have tried to make clear in this episode of prison life: we will consider ourselves fortunate if we have demonstrated the insufficiency, sterility, and danger of group confinement; the disproportion that exists between our understanding of and punishment of certain crimes (domestic theft or burglary) and certain misdemeanors (embezzlement); and, finally, the material impossibility for the poorer classes to reap the benefit of laws and civil suits.

CHAPTER 13

PUNISHMENT

We will now bring the reader back to the office of Jacques Ferrand, the solicitor. Thanks to the habitual loquaciousness of the clerks, who were almost incessantly preoccupied by the increasingly peculiar behavior of their employer, we may leave it to them to expose the events that had taken place since Cecily's disappearance.

"Ten to one odds that if he keeps wasting away, the boss will be as dead as a doornail within a month!"

"The fact is, since that servant who looked like an Alsatian left the house, he's just skin and bones."

"And not much skin!"

"Really! He must have been in love with the Alsatian, because it's since she left that he's been shriveling up like this."

"Him? The boss, in love? What a joke!"

"On the contrary, he's been seeing the priests again more than ever."

"And let's not forget that when the parish priest—a very respectable man, it must be said—left yesterday he was saying to another priest who was with him (I heard him), 'How admirable! Monsieur Jacques Ferrand is the very soul of charity and generosity on this earth!'"

"The parish priest said that? All by himself? Without any prompting?"

"What?"

"That the boss was the very soul of charity and generosity on this earth?"

"Yes, I heard him say that."

"Well, I can't figure it out anymore. The parish priest has a well-deserved reputation of being what they call a truly good pastor."

"Oh! That's true, and you have to speak seriously and respectfully about that one. He's as kind and charitable as Little Blue Coat,[217] and when someone says that of someone, he's passed the test."

"That's no small thing to say."

---

217. May we be permitted here to mention with deep veneration the name of this great and generous man, Monsieur Champion, whom we have not had the honor of knowing personally but of whom all the poor of Paris speak with as much respect as gratitude? [SN]

Edmé Champion (1766–1852) was a man of the people who rose from his humble beginnings to become a millionaire through his work as a jeweler. He became a legendary figure, giving much of his money away to the poor of Paris. [TN]

"No. For Little Blue Coat and the good priest alike, the poor only have one cry, and it's a real cry from the heart."

"So let me get back to what I was saying. When the parish priest affirms something, you have to believe him, since he's incapable of lying. However, to believe, according to what he says, that the boss is generous and charitable—well, that ties my credulity into knots."

"Oh! Oh, that's a pretty picture, Chalamel! A pretty picture!"

"Seriously, I'd as soon believe in miracles. It's no more difficult to do."

"Monsieur Ferrand, generous? He'd skin a flint!"

"But, gentlemen, he did give us forty sous for lunch. What do you say to that?"

"That doesn't prove anything! It's like when you have a random pimple on your nose. It's an accident."

"Yes, but on the other hand, the head clerk told me that three days ago the boss got an enormous sum in treasury bonds, and that . . ."

"Well?"

"Go on!"

"It's just that it's a secret."

"All the more reason to tell us. What's the secret?"

"Do I have your word of honor that you won't say anything?"

"We swear on our mothers' graves."

"May my old aunt Sally become a prostitute if I tell!"

"So, gentlemen, let's remember what the great King Louis XIV said so majestically to the Doge of Venice before his assembled court:

'*When a secret a clerk doth possess,*
He must tell others about it—oh, yes.'"

"Oh, great! There goes Chalamel again with his proverbs!"

"Off with Chalamel's head!"

"A nation's wisdom is expressed through its proverbs. It is in that spirit that I demand to know your secret."

"Come now, enough silliness. I'm telling you that the head clerk made me promise not to tell anyone . . ."

"Yes, but he didn't forbid you from telling everyone, did he?"

"Really, now, it won't leave this room. Come on!"

"He's dying to tell us his secret."

"All right! The boss is selling out. It may be a done deal by now."

"Oh, come on!"

"That's a crazy bit of news!"

"It's staggering!"

"I'm dumbstruck!"

"So if he sells out, who'll take charge of the charge for which he is no longer charged?"

"Lord, that Chalamel is unbearable with his puzzles!"

"Do I know who he's selling it to?"

"If he's selling it, it's maybe because he wants to launch himself into society, to give parties, or big bashes, as the fashionable set calls them."

"After all, he's got the wherewithal."

"And he doesn't have the tiniest sliver of a family."

"I should say he's got the wherewithal! The head clerk says he's got more than a million, including the value of his business."

"More than a million? That's a sweet sum!"

"They say he was secretly playing the market with Commandant Robert and that he made a lot of money off it."

"And as we all know, he's lived like a skinflint."

"Yes, but skinflints like him, once they start spending, they become more prodigal than anyone."

"I agree with Chalamel. I would think that by now the boss wants the soft life."

"And it would be terribly wrong of him not to spoil himself with luxury and not to give himself over to the splendors of Golconda,[218] if he has the means to do so. For as the inscrutable Ossian says in the cave of Fingal,[219]

'Every solicitor who goes on a spree,
If he has money, right he will be.'"

"Off with Chalamel's head."

"That's absurd!"

"But remember also that the boss really looks like he's thinking about having some fun."

"He has a face that would raise the devil!"

"But then, the priest keeps sounding off about his charity."

"Well, charity starts at home. Don't you know God's commandments, you barbarian? If the boss asks for the greatest pleasures as alms for himself, it's his duty to get hold of them, or he wouldn't think very much of himself."

"The thing that astonishes me is this intimate friend who seemed to come out of nowhere and who sticks to him now like his shadow."

"Not to speak of his rotten face."

218. Ancient city in India, now in ruins, famous for its mines, which produced, among other treasures, the Hope diamond. [TN]

219. Ossian was the narrator of a spurious Scottish epic, actually written by James Macpherson. Fingal was Ossian's father, the bard whose tales Ossian ostensibly wrote down. Although many suspected the poem's authenticity from the first, many took it to be genuine. It was admired throughout Europe into the nineteenth century. [TN]

"He's as orange as a carrot."

"I would be rather inclined to deduce that that intruder is the fruit of a youthful indiscretion committed by Monsieur Ferrand. For, as the Eagle of Meaux said about the tender La Vallière's taking the veil,[220]

'*Whether you love a young man or an old sot,*
In the end, it's a little kid you've got.'"

"Off with Chalamel's head!"

"It's true. When he's around, you can't get a word in edgewise."

"Thinking the stranger is the boss's son is pure stupidity. He's older than the boss—it's obvious!"

"Well, strictly speaking, what difference would that make?"

"What? What difference would it make that a son should be older than his father?"

"Gentlemen, I said, 'strictly speaking, speaking only with the greatest strictness.'"

"And how does that change anything?"

"It's very simple. In that case, the intruder would have committed the youthful indiscretion and would be Monsieur Ferrand's father instead of his son."

"Off with Chalamel's head!"

"Don't listen to him. You know that once he gets going with his silliness, nothing can stop him!"

"One thing's for sure, and that's that the intruder has a rotten face and won't leave Monsieur Ferrand's side for a second."

"He's always with him in his office. They eat together, and they can't seem to do without each other."

"I have the feeling I've seen that intruder before around here."

"Not me."

"Tell me, gentlemen, haven't you noticed that for the last few days a man with a long blond mustache and a military bearing comes around here regularly, almost every two hours, to ask the doorkeeper to see the intruder? The intruder goes down to talk for a minute to the man with the mustache, after which the latter makes a half turn like an automaton and then comes back two hours later."

"It's true, I've noticed it. I also had the impression when I went out that I saw some men who seemed to be keeping a watch out on the house."

"Seriously, something extraordinary is going on here."

---

220. For Bossuet, see Book VII, Chapter 12, footnote 181. Louise de la Vallière (1644–1710) was King Louis XIV's mistress from 1661 to 1667. In 1662, Bossuet preached sermons against the king's adultery, and she briefly went into a convent. Louis, however, brought her back to court. She had four children with the king. [TN]

"Those who live will see."

"On that topic, the head clerk might know more than us, but he's being diplomatic."

"But where is he right now, in fact?"

"He's over at the place of that countess who was attacked. It seems she's now out of danger."

"The Countess MacGregor?"

"Yes. This morning she asked for the boss double quick, but he sent the head clerk in his place."

"Maybe it's to draw up her will?"

"No, because she's getting better."

"That head clerk has a hard job now that he's replaced Germain as cashier!"

"Speaking of Germain, that's another funny thing!"

"What?"

"To get him released, the boss declared that it was he, Monsieur Ferrand, who had made an accounting error and that he had found the money that he was claiming Germain had taken from him."

"Me, I don't think it's funny, I think it's justice. You remember, I always said that Germain was incapable of stealing."

"All the same, it was very unpleasant for him to have been arrested and imprisoned for theft."

"If it was me, I'd make Monsieur Ferrand pay damages and interest."

"In fact, he should have at least taken him back as a cashier, just to show that Germain wasn't guilty."

"Yes, but Germain might not have wanted that."

"Is he still at that place in the country where he went after leaving prison, where he wrote us from to tell us that Monsieur Ferrand had dropped all charges?"

"Probably, because yesterday I went to the address he had given us. They told me that he was still in the country, and that we could write to him at Bouqueval, near Écouen, in care of Madame Georges, mistress of the farm."

"Ah! Gentlemen, a carriage!" said Chalamel as he leaned toward the window. "Well, Lord! It's not a dashing team like the one that notorious viscount had. Do you remember that dazzling Saint-Remy, with his huntsman all decked out in silver and his fat driver with that white wig? This time, it's just the usual cart, some city rat."

"And who's getting out of it?"

"Wait! Ah! A black dress!"

"A woman! A woman! Let's have a look!"

"God! That errand boy is indecently lustful for his age! All he thinks about is women. He'll end up having to be tied up, or he'll carry off the

Sabine women right in front of everybody. For, as the Swan of Cambrai says in his *Treatise on Education* for the dauphin,[221]

> *'All beware the errand boy:*
> *The lovelier sex he doth too much enjoy.'"*

"Off with Chalamel's head!"

"Lord! Monsieur Chalamel, you said a black dress? I thought—"

"It's the priest, you imbecile! Let it be a lesson to you!"

"The parish priest? The good pastor?"

"The very same, gentlemen."

"There walks a worthy man."

"He's no Jesuit, that one!"

"I think so, too, and if every priest were like him, there would be only pious people."

"Silence! He's turning the doorknob."

"Back to your places, everybody! It's him!"

And all the clerks, hunched over their desks, set to scrawling with apparent ardor, noisily scratching their pens across the paper. The pale face of this priest was both sweet and serious, intelligent and venerable. His gaze was full of gentleness and serenity. A small black skullcap hid his tonsure. His fairly long gray hair fluttered over the collar of his brown waistcoat.

We should hasten to add that, thanks to the trusting nature special to all earnest people, this excellent priest had always been and still was the dupe of Jacques Ferrand's deep, clever hypocrisy.

"Is your worthy employer in his office, my children?" the priest asked.

"Yes, Father," said Chalamel, rising with respect. And he opened for the priest the door to a room next to their office.

Hearing someone speak with a certain vehemence in Jacques Ferrand's office, the priest, not wanting to eavesdrop, walked quickly over to the door and knocked on it. "Enter!" said a voice with a rather pronounced Italian accent.

The priest found himself face-to-face with Polidori and Jacques Ferrand. The solicitor's clerks seemed not to have been wrong when they forecast their boss's imminent death. Since Cecily's flight, the solicitor had become almost unrecognizable. Although his face was frightfully thin and of a corpselike pallor, a feverish redness colored his prominent cheekbones. A nervous tic, interrupted from time to time by some convulsive spasms, distorted his face almost continuously. His craggy hands

221. For Fénelon, see Book VII, Chapter 12, footnote 178. Fénelon never wrote a *Treatise on Education* but did write *The Adventures of Telemachus*, a sermon in the form of a novel, on how to rule. [TN]

were dirty and hot to the touch. His large green glasses hid his eyes full of blood that were shining with the somber fire of a devouring fever. In a word, this sinister mask betrayed the ravages of a silent, constant, consuming illness.

Polidori's face contrasted with that of the solicitor. Nothing could be more bitterly or coldly ironic than the expression on the face of this other scoundrel. A forest of flaming red hair mixed with a few silver locks crowned his pale, wrinkled forehead. His piercing eyes, transparent and green as sea algae, were closely set next to his hooked nose. His mouth, with its thin, sunken lips, expressed sarcasm and malevolence. Polidori, completely dressed in black, sat next to Jacques Ferrand's desk.

At the sight of the priest, both arose. "Well, then! How are you doing, my worthy Monsieur Ferrand?" said the priest with solicitude. "Are you feeling any better?"

"I feel just the same as always, Father. I can't get rid of the fever," answered the solicitor. "My insomnia is killing me! God's will be done!"

"Look, Father," added Polidori with compunction, "see how pious his resignation! My poor friend is always the same. He finds solace for his pains only in the good he does!"

"I do not deserve such praise. Please spare me," said the solicitor drily as he barely held back his feeling of anger and restrained rage. "To God alone belongs the evaluation of good and evil; I am nothing but a wretched sinner."

"We are all sinners," said the priest gently. "But we do not all show the charity that distinguishes you, my respectable friend. People like you, who separate themselves enough from earthly goods to be able to think of ways to use them in their lifetimes in such a Christian way, are indeed very rare. Are you still determined to sell your business so as to give yourself over more completely to religious observance?"

"I sold my business the day before yesterday, Father. A few concessions allowed me to sell it for cash, which is unusual. Added to the other sums, this one will help me to found the institution we've discussed and for which I've drawn up a definitive plan that I'm about to submit to you."

"Ah! My worthy friend!" said the priest in profound and saintly admiration. "To do so much good so simply—and if I might add, with so much naturalness! I say it again, people like you are rare. We cannot bless them enough."

"That's because very few people bring together wealth and piety, intelligence and charity, the way Jacques does," said Polidori with an ironic smile that the priest did not catch.

At this new bit of sarcastic praise, the solicitor's hand clenched involuntarily. From behind his glasses, he cast a look of infernal rage at Polidori.

"You see, Father," Jacques Ferrand's good friend hastened to say, "he always has these nervous spasms, and he won't do anything about them. He makes me so sad; he's going to end up killing himself this way. Yes, I will have the courage to say it before the priest: you will end up killing yourself, my poor friend."

At these words of Polidori, the solicitor shuddered again convulsively, but he calmed himself down. A man less naive than the priest would have noticed the anger and constraint in Jacques Ferrand's voice during this conversation and even more during the one that followed. For, needless to say, a superior will to his own—the will of Rodolphe, in short—forced upon this man words and deeds that were diametrically opposed to those of his real character. And so, sometimes, pushed to his limit, the solicitor seemed to hesitate to obey this all-powerful and invisible authority. But a look from Polidori put an end to his reluctance. Then, concentrating his most violent resentment into a single sigh of rage, Jacques Ferrand submitted to a yoke he could not break out of.

"Alas, Father!" said Polidori, who seemed to enjoy the task of torturing his accomplice by draining his blood with pinpricks, as they say. "My poor friend neglects himself terribly. So join me in telling him that he has to take care of himself, if not for his own sake, for his friends' sakes, or at least for the poor people for whom he represents hope and support."

"Enough! Enough!" murmured the solicitor in a hollow voice.

"No, it's not enough," said the priest with emotion. "We can't tell you enough that you do not belong to yourself alone and that it is wrong to neglect your health in this manner. Over the ten years I've known you, I've never seen you sick. But over the past month, you've become unrecognizable. I can see the alteration of your facial features all the more sharply because I haven't seen you in some time. That is why I could not hide my surprise after our first conversation. But the change I've noticed in you over the last several days is even more serious. You are shriveling away before my very eyes. We are really becoming very worried. I beg you, my worthy friend: think of your health."

"I could not be more grateful to you for your concern, Father, but I assure you that my condition is not as grave as you believe."

"Since you insist on being so stubborn," said Polidori, "I am going to tell the priest everything. He loves, esteems, and honors you greatly. What will he think when he learns of your new good deeds, when he knows the true reason you're wasting away?"

"What is it now?" asked the priest.

"Father," said the solicitor impatiently, "I asked you to be so good as to come to pay me a visit so I could inform you of plans of the highest importance, not to hear myself ridiculously praised by my friend here."

"You know, Jacques, that you must resign yourself to hearing me say anything," said Polidori, fixing the solicitor with his glance. The latter lowered his eyes and went silent. Polidori went on, "You have perhaps noticed, Father, that the first symptoms of Jacques's nervous malady took place shortly after the abominable scandal that Louise Morel caused in this house."

The solicitor shuddered.

"So you know about the crime that unhappy girl committed, monsieur?" asked the priest, surprised. "I thought you had arrived in Paris only a few days ago."

"Indeed, Father. But Jacques has told me everything, as his friend, as his doctor. For he almost attributes the shaken nerves he is currently experiencing to the indignation he felt at Louise's crime. That's just the beginning of it. Alas, my poor friend has had to endure additional blows that have affected his health, as you see. An old servant who had been attached to him with sentiments of gratitude for many years—"

"Madame Séraphin?" said the priest, interrupting Polidori. "I heard about the death of that unfortunate woman, drowned in an unfortunate act of carelessness, and I can well understand Monsieur Ferrand's sorrow. It is impossible to forget ten years of loyal service like that. Such sorrow does honor to the master as well as to the servant."

"Father," said the solicitor, "I beg of you, do not speak of my virtues. You are upsetting me. It's painful."

"Who else will speak of them, then? Will you?" Polidori said, affectionately. "But there will be much more to praise, Father. You do not know, perhaps, who replaced Louise Morel and Madame Séraphin here as a servant to Jacques. You must not have heard what he did for that poor Cecily—for that was her name, Father."

The solicitor bolted upright in his chair, despite himself. His eyes were blazing behind his glasses. A burning redness made his livid face turn crimson. "Shut up! Shut up!" he cried, starting to rise. "Not a word more! I forbid it!"

"Come now, calm down," said the priest indulgently. "Is there some other good deed to tell me about? As far as I'm concerned, I strongly approve of your friend's indiscretion. Indeed I don't know this servant, for it was just a few days after her arrival at the home of our worthy Monsieur Ferrand that he was temporarily forced by overwhelming obligations to break off relations with me for a little while."

"That interruption was to hide from you the new good deed that he was considering, Father. And so, even if it offends his modesty, he must hear me, and you will know everything," said Polidori, smiling.

Jacques Ferrand went silent. He put his elbows on his desk and hid his head in his hands.

CHAPTER 14

THE BANK OF THE POOR

"You have to realize, Father," said Polidori as he addressed the priest, giving special meaning to each phrase, so to speak, by casting ironic glances at Jacques Ferrand. "You have to realize that my friend found in his new servant—whose name, as I've already mentioned, was Cecily—the most worthy personal qualities: great modesty, angelic sweetness, and, most of all, tremendous piety. That's not all: as you know, thanks to his long business experience, Jacques is extremely perceptive. He quickly understood that this young woman—for she was young and very pretty, Father—that this young and pretty woman was not born to be a servant, and that along with her . . . uh . . . virtuously austere principles, she had been the recipient of a solid education and . . . uh . . . very diverse sorts of knowledge."

"Indeed, that is unusual," said the priest, who was becoming quite intrigued. "I knew nothing of these circumstances. But what's wrong, my good Monsieur Ferrand? You seem suddenly to have taken a turn for the worse."

"Well, yes," said the solicitor as he mopped the cold sweat that was dripping from his brow, for he had to restrain himself horribly. "I have a slight migraine, but it will pass."

Polidori shrugged his shoulders and smiled. "You should know, Father," he said, "that Jacques is always this way when someone reveals one of his secret acts of charity. He is so hypocritical about the good he does! Fortunately, I'm here to trumpet his deeds and do him justice. To return to Cecily: she, in turn, soon recognized Jacques's excellent heart. When he asked her about her past, she told him unguardedly that she was a foreigner without resources who had been reduced by her husband's misconduct to the most humble conditions. As such, she had considered it nothing short of miraculous to be given the chance at employment in the pious home of a man as respectable as Monsieur Ferrand. At the sight of so much unhappiness, resignation, and virtue, Jacques did not hesitate a moment. He wrote to the unfortunate young woman's homeland to make inquiries, and the responses he received corresponded in every detail with what she had told our friend. And so, certain that his benevolence would be well placed, Jacques blessed Cecily as if he were her father and sent her back to her country with a sum of money that would allow her to live comfortably while waiting for better days, when she could find an appropriate position. I will not add a word of praise for Jacques to this story: the facts speak for themselves."

"How admirable! Very well done!" the priest, who was very moved, exclaimed.

"Father," said Jacques Ferrand in a muffled and choked voice, "I don't want to waste any more of your precious time. Let's not speak any more of me, I beg you, but, instead, let's discuss the project about which I wished to speak with you and for which I have asked your benevolent assistance."

"I can understand how your friend's praise offends your modesty, so let's talk now only about your most recent good deeds and forget that you are their author. But before that, let's speak of the business you've asked me to take care of. In keeping with your wishes, I have deposited in the Bank of France, under my name, the sum of a hundred thousand crowns to be used for restitution, with you as an intermediary, and which only I can access. You preferred that this deposit not remain in your keeping, even though it would have been as secure with you, it seems to me, as it is with the bank."

"In this respect, Father, I am conforming to the intentions of the unnamed author of this act of restitution. He is doing what he does to relieve his conscience. According to his wishes, I had to confide this sum to you and ask you to repay it to the widow Madame de Fermont, née de Renneville," the voice of the solicitor trembled slightly as he pronounced these names, "when this woman is introduced to you and verifies her identity."

"I will accomplish the task you have given me," said the priest.

"It won't be the last, Father."

"So much the better, if the others are anything like this one. For, without wishing to pry into the motives behind it, I am always moved by voluntary reparations. These sovereign decrees, dictated only by one's conscience and carried out freely and faithfully by one's inner self, always show sincere repentance. These kinds of expiation are never sterile ones."

"Isn't that so, Father? You don't usually see a hundred thousand crowns restored at one fell swoop. As for me, I was more curious about it than you, but my curiosity was no match for Jacques's unshakeable discretion. So I still do not know the name of the honest man who performed this noble act of restitution."

"Whoever he is," said the curate, "I am certain that Monsieur Ferrand holds him in high esteem."

"I indeed hold this honest man in the highest esteem," responded the solicitor with a poorly disguised bitterness.

"And that's not all, Father," said Polidori, giving Jacques Ferrand a significant glance. "Wait until you hear how far the generous scruples of the unnamed author of this restitution extend. Truth be told, I strongly suspect that our friend has contributed in no small way to the awakening of these scruples and to discovering a way to ease them."

"How so?" asked the priest.

"What do you mean?" asked the solicitor.

"And what about the Morels, that good and honest family?"

"Oh, that's right. I really had forgotten about them," muttered Jacques Ferrand.

"Just imagine, Father," said Polidori, "the author of this restitution, no doubt with Jacques's advice, not content just to restore that considerable sum, wanted further— But let me allow our worthy friend to tell you about it himself. I don't want to deprive him of the pleasure."

"Please, I'm listening, my dear Monsieur Ferrand," said the priest.

"You know," said Jacques Ferrand, with a hypocritical attitude of compunction that was accompanied by momentary, involuntary signs of resistance to the role imposed on him, which took the form of changes in his voice and hesitations in his speech, "you know, Father, that Louise Morel's misconduct shocked her father so terribly that it drove him insane. This worker's large family, now deprived of its sole support, ran the risk of dying from want. Fortunately, divine justice came to their rescue and . . . the person who voluntarily makes the restitution for which you serve as intermediary, Father, felt he had not sufficiently expiated a grave act of embezzlement. He thus asked me if I knew of any worthy unfortunate person to help. I felt it my duty to point out the Morel family to him as a worthy object of generosity, and he has given me the necessary funds and asked me to give them to you right away so that you can confer an income of two thousand francs on Morel that will revert to his wife and children."

"Indeed," the priest said, "even though I am happy to accept this new mission, which is obviously one that demands our complete respect, I am surprised that the person has not asked you to do it yourself."

"The unnamed person thought—and I share his belief—that his good works would take on an even greater value—that they would be, so to speak, sanctified—if they were carried out by hands as holy as your own, Father."

"Well, I can hardly deny such a request. I will find an investment bringing in an income of two thousand francs for Morel, Louise's worthy and unfortunate father. But I suspect, as your friend, that you have not been a stranger to the resolution that dictated this new gift of expiation."

"Please believe me, Father, when I say that all I did was to point out the Morel family," Jacques Ferrand answered.

"Now," said Polidori, "you will see, Father, to what heights the philanthropic views of my good Jacques reach when it comes to the charitable establishment we have already discussed. He is going to read us the plan he has finished drafting. The money necessary to endow it is there in his cash box, but, since yesterday, he has developed one scruple that I'll tell you about if he doesn't dare to tell you himself."

"That won't be necessary," Jacques Ferrand said, preferring at times to try to benumb himself with his own language rather than having to listen in silence to his accomplice's ironic praise. "Here's what it is, Father. I thought that it would be more of an act of Christian humility if this establishment didn't bear my name."

"But this is humility carried too far!" the priest exclaimed. "You can and should legitimately pride yourself on your charitable foundation. It's a right—no, practically a duty—for you to give it your own name."

"I prefer, however, to remain unnamed, Father. I am determined to do so, and I depend upon your kindness in hoping that you will agree to complete the last formalities in total secrecy and to hire the establishment's lower-level employees. I reserve for myself only the right to nominate the director and guardian."

"Even if I didn't take real pleasure in aiding in this good work, which is yours alone, it would be my duty to accept your request. And so I do accept it."

"Now, Father, if you don't mind, my friend will read to you the final plans that he has drawn up."

"Since you are so obliging, my friend," Jacques Ferrand said bitterly, "read it yourself and spare me the pain, I beg of you."

"No, no," Polidori said, with a glance whose sarcasm the solicitor perfectly understood, "I take real pleasure in hearing you express, in your own words, the noble sentiments that guided you in conceiving this philanthropic foundation."

"Fine. I'll read it," said the solicitor brusquely, taking a piece of paper from his desk.

Polidori had been Jacques Ferrand's accomplice for a long time, so he knew the crimes and secret thoughts of this wretch inside and out. He could not, therefore, restrain a cruel smile as he saw him forced to read the note dictated by Rodolphe.

As we will see, the prince had shown inexorable logic in the punishment he had inflicted on the solicitor. For his lust, the prince had tortured him with lust; for his greed, with greed; for his hypocrisy, with hypocrisy. For if Rodolphe had chosen this particular venerable priest to be the agent of the restitutions and expiation that he had imposed on

Jacques Ferrand, it was because he wanted to punish him doubly for having earned the unguarded esteem and open affection of the good priest through his repugnant hypocrisy. After all, was it not a terrible punishment for this hideous impostor, this hardened criminal, to be forced, finally, to practice the Christian virtues he had so often simulated, and this time to merit—even as he trembled with impotent rage—the just praise of a respectable priest whom he had hitherto deceived? Jacques Ferrand read the following note, therefore, with hidden sentiments we can easily imagine:

ESTABLISHMENT OF THE BANK FOR UNEMPLOYED WORKERS

Christ said: "*Love each other.*" These divine words form the basis of every duty, every virtue, every act of charity. They have inspired the humble founder of this institution. From Christ alone comes any good it may achieve. Limited in what he could do, the founder wanted at least to allow the greatest possible number of his brothers to participate in the help he offers them.

He addresses himself first of all to the honest, hardworking laborers with families who are sometimes reduced to cruel circumstances by lack of work. These are not degrading alms that he gives to his brothers; it is a free loan that he offers them. May this loan, as is his hope, keep them from mortgaging their future indefinitely with these crushing loans they are forced to contract so they can await the return of the work that is their sole resource and is all that sustains their families for whom they are the only source of support! To guarantee this loan, he asks of his brothers only their word of honor and the assurance of a sworn oath.

During the first year, he sets aside a sum that may go as high as twelve thousand francs, to be used to make unsecured loans-in-aid of from twenty to forty francs, without interest, to married laborers who are out of work and who live in the seventh arrondissement.[222] We have chosen this neighborhood because it is the one that contains the highest number of working-class people. These loans will be made only to workers, male or female, who present a certificate of good conduct signed by their last employer that indicates the reason and the date their employment was terminated. These loans will be repayable on a monthly basis in six or twelve payments, as decided by the borrower, starting from the date on which he finds new work. He will sign a simple engagement on his honor to reimburse the loan at fixed intervals. Two of his friends will serve as guarantors to this engagement so as to develop and extend, through

222. Paris is divided into twenty *arrondissements*, or sections. [TN]

cooperation, the sense of the sanctity of the sworn oath.[223] The worker who does not repay the sum he has borrowed, along with his two guarantors, will be denied any new future loan, for he will have reneged on a sacred engagement, and will, more important, have deprived several of his brothers in succession of the advantage he has enjoyed, the sum he has not repaid having been lost to the Bank of the Poor. When these sums are, on the other hand, scrupulously repaid, unsecured loans-in-aid will be increased from year to year in number and proportion. One day it may be possible that other arrondissements might be able to enjoy the same benefits.

Never degrade a man with alms;

Never encourage idleness with an unproductive gift;

Encourage the sentiments of honor and integrity that come naturally to the working classes;

Come to the aid of the worker, your fellow human being, who, already living day to day with difficulty because of salaries that are too low, cannot suspend his needs nor those of his family when unemployment strikes, just because work has been suspended;

Such are the ideas that have presided over the founding of this institution.[224]

May he alone who said, "Love each other," be praised for it.

"Ah, monsieur!" the priest exclaimed in religious admiration. "What a charitable idea! How I understand your emotion as you read these lines with such touching simplicity!" Indeed, as he finished reading, Jacques Ferrand's voice had changed. His patience and courage had reached their limit. But under Polidori's surveillance, he did not and could not disobey even the least of Rodolphe's orders. One may easily imagine the solicitor's rage, forced as he was to spend his fortune so liberally and charitably, all on behalf of a class that he had so pitilessly hounded in the person of Morel the gem-cutter.

"Isn't Jacques's idea excellent, Father?" asked Polidori.

"Ah, monsieur, as someone who is so familiar with every kind of poverty, I can understand better than anyone how vital this loan—which

223. The reader may perhaps be unaware that the working class generally views debts with such respect that the bloodsuckers who make short-term loans at the outrageous rate of 300 to 400 percent ask for nothing in writing, and yet they are always faithfully repaid. This abominable industry is practiced most prominently at La Halle and its environs. [SN]

224. Our project, about which we have consulted with several workers who are as honorable as they are enlightened, is no doubt imperfect. However, we leave it to the reflections of people who care about the working classes, hoping that the seed of usefulness that it contains (we affirm this without fear) could be made to bear fruit by an intelligence more powerful than our own. [SN]

would seem very moderate to the wealthy of the world—can be for the poor and honest laborers who lack work. Alas! How much good might the wealthy do if they knew that with a sum of thirty or forty francs that would be scrupulously returned to them, albeit without interest—a sum so small that it would hardly defray the cost of the least of their luxurious whims—they could often secure the future, sometimes even save the honor of a family that the lack of work has put in the grips of the appalling obsessions that poverty and need bring with them! The unemployed indigent man never has credit, or, if people consent to lend him small sums without collateral, it is at the cost of monstrously usurious interest rates. He will borrow thirty sous for one week, and he will have to return forty; and even these small loans are rare and difficult to obtain. Loans from pawnshops go at a rate of almost three hundred percent in certain circumstances.[225] The unemployed worker often pawns for forty sous the only blanket that protects him and his family from the ravages of the cold in the winter nights. But a loan for thirty or forty francs without interest," added the priest enthusiastically, "reimbursable in twelve payments when the work returns . . . For honest workers, that means salvation, hope, life! And they will pay off the loan with such fidelity! Oh, monsieur, those people never declare bankruptcy! The debt they enter in order to buy bread for their wives and children is a sacred one!"

"How precious this priest's praise must be to you, Jacques!" said Polidori. "And how much more praise will he shower on you when he hears that you are going to found a free pawnshop service!"

---

225. We have taken this information from an eloquent and excellent study published by Monsieur Alphonse Esquiros in the *Revue de Paris* from June 11, 1843: "The average number of articles engaged for *three francs* with the agents in the eighth and twelfth arrondissements is at least *five hundred* a day. The working-class population, reduced to such feeble resources, thus can get from the pawnshop only advances that are insignificant in comparison to their needs. Today the interest rates the pawnshops have the right to ask have risen, in ordinary cases, to 13 percent. But these rates increase in an appalling proportion if the loan, instead of being for a year, is made for a shorter term. Now, since the articles pawned by the poorer classes are generally items of basic necessity, they end up taking them back almost immediately after they bring them in. Some items are regularly brought in and taken back once a week. In this circumstance, if we posit a loan of three francs, the interest paid by the borrower will then be calculated at the rate of 294 percent per year. The very considerable sum of money that accumulates every year in the coffers of the pawnshop goes straight into the coffers of the hospices. In 1840, a year of economic distress, the benefits rose to 422,245 francs. It cannot be denied," Monsieur Esquiros rightly says in conclusion, "that this sum has a praiseworthy destination, since it comes from the poor and returns to the poor, but a serious question should be asked nonetheless: is it really the responsibility of the poor to help the poor?" Let us note, in conclusion, that Monsieur Esquiros, even as he calls for great improvements to be made in the operation of pawnshops, pays homage to the zeal of the current director, Monsieur Delaroche, who has already put useful reforms into effect. [SN]

"What is this?"

"Certainly, Father. Jacques has not forgotten this matter, which is, in a manner of speaking, related to his idea of the bank for the poor."

"Can this be true?" the priest asked as he clasped his hands together in admiration.

"Go on, Jacques," Polidori said.

The solicitor continued, speaking quickly, as this scene disgusted him:

"'The unsecured loans-in-aid have as their purpose the remediation of one of the most serious events in the life of the working classes: the interruption of labor. They will thus be granted only to unemployed laborers. But there are other cruel trials to be considered that can afflict even the employed laborer. Often one or two days off the job, sometimes brought on by fatigue, the need to care for a sick wife or child, or a necessary change in lodging, deprive the worker of his daily income. Then his only resource is either a pawnshop where money is lent at a very high rate, or black market creditors who make loans at monstrous rates of interest. Wishing to lighten his brothers' burden as much as possible, the founder of the Bank of the Poor will set aside an amount of twenty-five thousand francs a year for loans on wages, which may not exceed ten francs per loan. Borrowers will pay neither fees nor interest, but they must prove that they are employed in an honorable position and furnish a declaration from their employers that will vouch for their moral standing. After a term of two years, unclaimed belongings will be sold without extra fees. The total profits from this sale will be invested at five percent interest, with the owner as beneficiary. If after five years the borrower has not reclaimed this sum, it will become the property of the Bank of the Poor, and, combined with additional cash inflows, will allow the number of loans to grow.[226] The administration and office of loans of the Bank of the Poor will be located at seventeen rue du Temple, in a house bought for that purpose in the heart of this working-class neighborhood. A revenue of ten thousand francs will be set aside for the fees and administration of the Bank of the Poor, whose director for life will be—'"

Polidori interrupted the solicitor and said to the priest, "You will see, Father, from the choice he has made for director of this administration, how Jacques is making reparation for the wrong he accidentally committed. You know that, due to an error he deplores, he had falsely accused his cashier of diverting a sum that was subsequently recovered?"

"Of course."

"Well! Jacques is making that honest boy named François Germain

226. We have mentioned earlier that in some of the small states of Italy there exist free pawnshops, charitable foundations that bear much in common with the establishment we are suggesting here. [SN]

the director for life of this bank. He'll earn a salary of four thousand francs. Now, isn't that admirable, Father?"

"Nothing surprises me anymore now, or rather, nothing yet has surprised me," the priest said. "The fervent piety and virtues of our worthy friend were bound to culminate in this sort of result sooner or later. To leave all one's fortune to such a beautiful institution—ah! It's so admirable!"

"More than a million, Father!" Polidori said. "More than a million accumulated through integrity, savings, and a well-ordered life! And to think there were ever wretches who went so far as to accuse Jacques of avarice! 'Look,' they said, 'his business earns him fifty or sixty thousand francs a year, and he lives so frugally!'"

"To those people," the priest said with enthusiasm, "I would answer: 'For fifteen years he has lived like a pauper so that one day he would be able to relieve paupers magnificently.'"

"Come on, show some pride and joy over the good you're doing!" exclaimed Polidori, turning to Jacques Ferrand, who, somber, dejected, his gaze fixed, seemed absorbed in deep meditation.

"Alas!" said the priest with sadness. "It is not in this world that we can hope to be rewarded for so much virtue. We must rest our hopes in a higher place."

"Jacques," said Polidori, tapping the solicitor lightly on the shoulder. "Please finish reading."

The solicitor shuddered, wiped his forehead with his hand, and then, turning to the priest, said to him, "I'm sorry, Father, but I was thinking . . . I was thinking of how much this Bank of the Poor could grow just by accumulating revenue, provided that the loans are regularly reimbursed each year and do not cut into it. After four years, it could already make about fifty thousand crowns from free loans or loans on wages. It's enormous—enormous! And I'm glad of it," he added, thinking, with suppressed rage, of the value of the sacrifice that was being imposed on him. "Where was I again?" he said.

"You were at the nomination of François Germain as director of the institution," said Polidori.

Jacques Ferrand continued:

> A revenue of ten thousand francs will be set aside for the fees and administration of the *Bank for Unemployed Laborers*, the director of which will be François Germain, and the guard of which will be the current doorkeeper of the house, named Pipelet.
>
> Father Dumont, with whom the funds necessary for the founding of the establishment will be placed, will institute a board of control composed of the mayor and justice of the peace of the arrondissement.

These men will choose other individuals they deem useful to the patronage and growth of the Bank of the Poor. The founder would consider himself repaid many times over for the little he has done if it spurred a few charitable people to participate in his work.

The opening of this bank will be announced by every means of publicity possible. The founder repeats, in conclusion, that he should be given no credit for doing what he is doing for his brothers. His thought is nothing but an echo of the divine thought: "LET US LOVE EACH OTHER."

"And your position will be marked in heaven near that of the one who pronounced those immortal words!" the priest exclaimed as he came over to take Jacques Ferrand's hands in his own and shake them effusively.

The solicitor was standing. He no longer had the strength to go further. Without responding to the priest's praise, he hastened to give him in treasury bonds the considerable sum necessary to found this institution, as well as what was necessary for the income of Morel, the gem-cutter.

"I daresay, Father," said Jacques Ferrand finally, "that you will not refuse this new mission that I confide to your generosity. In any case, a foreigner named Walter Murph who has given me some advice in the drafting of this project will lighten your burden somewhat. He will come this very day to talk with you about the practical side of this work, and he will put himself at your disposal if he can be of assistance to you. I beg of you, Father, to keep all this a secret from everyone but him."

"You are right. God knows what you are doing for your brothers. What do the others matter? All I regret is that I cannot bring anything more than my zeal to this noble institution. At the very least, it will be just as ardent as your charity is limitless. But what's wrong? You've gone pale. Are you in pain?"

"A little, Father. The long text I read and the emotion your kind words caused me . . . the sickness I have had for the last few days . . . pardon my weakness," said Jacques Ferrand as he sat down with difficulty. "I'm sure it's nothing serious, but I'm utterly exhausted."

"Perhaps you might do well to go to bed?" the priest said with deep concern. "Maybe you should have your doctor come to see you?"

"I am a doctor, Father," said Polidori. "Jacques Ferrand's condition requires the greatest care. I will make sure he gets it."

The solicitor shuddered.

"A little rest will get you back on your feet, I hope," the priest said. "I will leave now, but before I do, I'll give you a receipt for this sum."

While the priest was writing the receipt, Jacques Ferrand and Polidori exchanged a look that would be impossible to depict.

"Take heart and be of good hope!" said the priest as he gave the receipt to Jacques Ferrand. "You will be with us for a long while yet. God will not permit one of his best servants to leave behind a life so usefully, so piously employed. Tomorrow I will come back to see you. Farewell, monsieur. Farewell, my friend, my worthy and saintly friend."

The priest departed. Jacques Ferrand and Polidori were left alone.

BOOK IX

CHAPTER I

THE ACCOMPLICES

The priest had barely left when Jacques Ferrand let out a frightening oath. His long-suppressed rage and despair exploded in fury. Panting, with a contorted face and wild eyes, he paced about quickly in his office, back and forth, like a ferocious beast on a chain. Maintaining perfect calm, Polidori observed the solicitor attentively.

"Blood and thunder!" Jacques Ferrand finally cried out in a voice bursting with rage. "There goes my entire fortune, swallowed up by these stupid good works! I, who despise and execrate all men; I, who have lived only for the pleasure of deceiving them and taking them for all they're worth; I, of all people, founding philanthropic establishments! Forcing me to do this is hellish! Is your employer the devil himself?" he cried out, exasperated, as he stopped abruptly in front of Polidori.

"I have no employer," the latter answered him coldly. "Like you, I have a judge."

"Having to obey the smallest orders of that man, like a ninny!" Jacques Ferrand said with mounting rage. "And that priest, whom I'd so often secretly mocked for being taken in by my hypocrisy, just like the others . . . Every one of those words of praise that he was offering me in good faith felt like a knife in the heart. And having to restrain myself! Always having to restrain myself!"

"Or else face the scaffold."

"Oh! The idea that I can't get out from under this fatal power! I've already had to give up more than a million. I have a hundred thousand left, counting this house, at most. What more does he want out of me?"

"He isn't done with you yet. The prince knows through Badinot that your straw man, Petit-Jean, was just your cover for usurious loans you made to the Viscount de Saint-Remy, whom, besides, you so harshly extorted (also in the name of Petit-Jean) for his forgeries. The sums of money Saint-Remy paid had been lent him by a great lady—so that's probably another restitution in store for you to make. But he's put that one off, no doubt because it's a more delicate matter."

"I'm in chains here! In chains!"

"As surely as if you were bound in iron cables."

"And you are my jailer! You wretch!"

"What do you expect? The prince follows his own system with a perfect logic. He punishes crime by means of crime, accomplice by means of accomplice."

"This is infuriating!"

"Unfortunately, your rage is useless! For until he gives me the command, 'Jacques Ferrand is free to leave his house,' I'll be sticking to you like your shadow. Listen: just like you, I've committed crimes that would send me to the scaffold. If I fail to execute the orders I've received as your jailer, it's as much as my head is worth! So you couldn't have a more incorruptible guard than I am. As for the two of us escaping from here, it can't be done. We can't take a single step from here without falling into the hands of people who, night and day, are watching both the door of this residence and that of the neighboring house, by which we would have to exit if we tried to climb out by ladder."

"Death and destruction! I know that!"

"Just accept it, then: escape is impossible. Even if we did manage to escape, our chances of getting to safety are, to say the least, doubtful. They'd put the police on our trail. On the other hand, you, by being obedient to me, and me, by making sure that you obey me completely, we both at least avoid having our throats cut. So, as I say, we just need to accept it."

"Don't push me too far with that ironic sangfroid of yours, or I'll—"

"Or you'll what? I'm not afraid of you. I'm on my guard, I'm armed, and even if you found Cecily's poisoned stiletto to kill me with—"

"Shut up!"

"It wouldn't get you anywhere. You know that, every two hours, I have to report to whoever is concerned on the state of your precious health. That way, indirectly, they find out about both of us. If I don't show up, they'll suspect I've been murdered, and you'll be arrested. But, really, to think you capable of such a crime is an insult to you. You've given away more than a million to save your life, and I'm supposed to think you'd risk it for the stupid, pointless pleasure of killing me in revenge? Really, now, I know you're not that much of a fool."

"It's because you know that I can't kill you that you increase my troubles by picking at them with your sarcasm."

"Your situation is very original. You don't see yourself, but, I swear, the irony is charming!"

"Oh! What a disaster! What an impossible disaster! Whichever way I turn I face ruin, dishonor, and death! And to think that what I fear more than anything else in the world now is nothingness! A curse on me, on you, on everything in the world!"

"Your misanthropy is more extensive than your philanthropy. The first embraces the whole world and the second merely a single arrondissement of Paris."

"Go ahead, mock on, you monster!"

"Would you prefer that I complain and blame you for everything?"

"Me?"

"Whose fault is it that we're left to this? Yours. Why did you keep that letter from me about the murder we committed hanging from your neck like a relic? That murder that was worth a hundred thousand crowns to you, that murder that we had committed so cleverly that we passed it off as a suicide."

"Why? You wretch! Didn't I give you fifty thousand francs for your part in the crime? And as for the letter that I demanded, you know full well I did it to have something against you as security. I needed it to keep you from blackmailing me by threatening to betray me, didn't I? This way, you wouldn't be able to denounce me without giving yourself up at the same time. My life and everything I owned depended on that letter. That's why I carried it so carefully upon my person."

"It's true, that was clever of you, because, that way, the only thing I could get by denouncing you would be the pleasure of climbing the scaffold right next to you. All the same, your cleverness sank us, while mine would have kept us out of trouble for this crime."

"Out of trouble? And where do you think we are now?"

"Who could have guessed this would happen? In the normal way of things, we would have gotten away with our crime, thanks to me."

"Thanks to you?"

"Yes. When we blew that guy's brains out, you wanted just to forge his signature and write to his sister that he killed himself out of despair because he'd bankrupted himself. You thought it was the height of cleverness not to mention the deposit he left with you in that phony letter. That was an absurd idea. Since our victim's sister knew about that deposit, it was obvious that she was going to make a claim on it. The right thing to do, on the contrary, is what we did do. We mentioned the deposit so that if anyone had, by chance, any doubts as to whether it was really a suicide, you would have been the last person to be suspected. How could anyone think that, if you had killed a man to make off with the money he'd deposited with you, you would be stupid enough to speak of that deposit in the forged letter you were attributing to him? So what happened? They believed in his suicide. Thanks to your reputation for integrity, you could deny the deposit, and they thought that the brother had killed himself after having squandered his sister's fortune."

"But what does all of that matter now? The crime has been found out."

"And whose fault is that? Was it my fault if my letter was a double-edged sword? Why were you such a doddering ninny as to give that terrible weapon to that hellish Cecily?"

"Shut up! Do not speak that name!" exclaimed Jacques Ferrand with a terrifying expression on his face.

"Fine. I don't want to bring on an epileptic fit. You see very well that so long as we counted only on the ordinary workings of justice, our mutual precautions were sufficient. But the extraordinary justice of the man who holds us here in his awful power works in an entirely different way."

"Oh, I know that only too well!"

"This one, he thinks that cutting criminals' heads off doesn't do enough to make up for the evil they've done. With the proof he has in his possession, he could bring us both up on charges. What would come of that? Two more good cadavers whose only value would be to fertilize the lawn in the cemetery."

"Oh, yes! What that prince, that devil, wants is tears, anguish, torments. But I don't know him. I've never been anything to him. Why is he after me like this?"

"Well, first of all, he claims to feel personally the good and evil done to other men, whom the naive fool calls his 'brothers.' And then, the people you've harmed matter to him, so he's punishing you in his own manner."

"By what right?"

"Look, Jacques, just between us, we're not the ones to be talking about rights. He had the power to get your head cut off legally. What would have come of that? Your only two relatives are dead, the state would profit from your fortune, to the detriment of the people you'd fleeced. This way, on the other hand, he ransoms your life with your fortune, and Morel, the gem-cutter and father of Louise, whom you had dishonored, is free now from want, along with his family. Madame de Fermont, the sister of Monsieur de Renneville, the ostensible suicide, gets her hundred thousand crowns back. Germain, whom you falsely accused of theft, is exculpated and put in an honorable and safe position at the head of a bank for out-of-work laborers that you've been forced to found in order to expiate the outrages you have committed against society and make reparations for them. We can admit to all this, just between us two scoundrels. But frankly, from the point of view of the man who has us in his grip, society would gain nothing from your death, and it gains a lot from your continued life."

"That's what makes me so furious! And that's not the only thing that's torturing me!"

"The prince is well aware of that. So what will he do with us now? I don't know. He promised to let us live so long as we execute his orders blindly. He'll keep his promise. But if he thinks our crimes have not yet been fully paid for, he'll make the lives he leaves to us a thousand times worse than death. You don't know him. When he thinks he has the right to be pitiless, there's no executioner to stand up against him. To have figured out what I was up to in Normandy, he must have had the devil himself at his command. It's at least the case that he has more than one demon at his service. May lightning strike that Cecily dead!"

"I'll tell you one more time: shut up! Don't say that name! Don't say that name!"

"Yes, yes, I will. May lightning strike the woman who bears that name dead! She's the one who ruined everything. Our heads would be safe on our shoulders if it weren't for your imbecilic love for that creature."

Instead of exploding, Jacques Ferrand responded, with deep sorrow, "Do you know that woman? Tell me, have you ever seen her?"

"No, never. I know they say she's beautiful."

"Beautiful!" said the solicitor, shrugging his shoulders. "Listen," he added with bitterness and despair, "just shut up. Don't make remarks about things you know nothing about. Stop accusing me of things. You would have done just what I did in my place."

"Me? Put my life in the hands of a woman?"

"Of that one, yes—and I'd do it all over again, if I thought I could hope for what I hoped for that one moment."

"The devil take me if he's not still under her spell!" exclaimed Polidori, stupefied.

"Listen," said the solicitor in a calm, quiet voice that was accentuated now and then with bursts of incurable despair. "Listen: you know how much I love gold, right? You know what I risked to get my hands on it, right? All my greatest joy and happiness came from counting how much I had, watching that sum increase because of my greed and because I gladly endured every kind of privation, and finally from knowing that I owned all that treasure. Yes, possession, not spending, not enjoying my wealth—just hoarding, that was my whole life. A month ago, if you'd told me I had to choose between my money or my life, I would have told you to kill me."

"But what good does it do to have money if you're dead?"

"You might as well ask me, 'What good does it do to have money if you don't spend it?' Even though I was a millionaire, did I lead the life of a millionaire? No, I lived like a poor man. I liked having money for the mere sake of having it."

"Still, what good is it to you if you're dead?"

"To die in possession of it, to enjoy right up to the last moment that ecstasy for which I've faced privation, infamy, the scaffold. Yes, to be able to say once more, with my head on the block, 'I possess!' Oh! Can't you see that death is sweet compared to the torments you endure watching yourself despoiled in your own lifetime, despoiled as I have been of what you've amassed with so much pain and in the face of so much danger! Oh! To have to say to yourself, every moment, every minute of the day, 'I who had more than a million, I who endured the harshest privations in order to hold on to and increase my wealth, I who in ten years might have doubled it, tripled it, I have nothing left! Nothing!' It's horrible! It's worse than dying every day; it's dying every minute of the day. Yes, rather than this horrible agony that might go on for years, I would have preferred many times over the quick and certain death that gets you before your treasure is stolen from you. I tell you, at least I'd die saying, 'I possess!'"

Polidori looked at his accomplice in profound amazement. "I can't understand you at all anymore. So why obey the orders of the man who has only to say the word and get your head cut off? Why have you chosen your life over your money if that life seems so horrible to you?"

"You see, it's because," the solicitor said in a voice that was becoming more and more of a whisper, "to die is to cease to think. Death is nothingness. And what about Cecily?"

"You still have hopes?" cried Polidori, flummoxed.

"I do not hope, I possess."

"What do you possess?"

"Her memory."

"But you can never see her again. And she delivered up your head to the chopping block."

"But I still love her, and more insanely than ever!" cried Jacques Ferrand, bursting into tears and sobs that contrasted with the dejected calm of his last words. "Yes," he went on in terrifying ecstasy, "I love her still, and I don't want to die, because I want to go on immersing myself again and again, in horribly painful pleasure, into that furnace in which I'm slowly burning up. There's no way for you to understand that night, that night when she appeared to me, so beautiful, so passionate, so intoxicating. That night will always be in my memory. That image of terrible voluptuousness is there—always there—before my eyes. Whether they're open or closed, whether I am in the grips of feverish stupor or scorching insomnia, I always see her black and inflamed gaze on me, that gaze that makes my blood boil. I can still feel her breath on my face. I can still hear her voice."

"Truly, you are feeling the torments of the damned!"

"Torments? Yes, yes, torments! But death? Nothingness? The idea of forever losing this memory that is as vivid as reality? Of giving up these memories that tear me apart, devour me, and burn me alive? No! No! No! I want to live! Poor, scorned, humiliated, imprisoned—but I want to live, so that I can still think, since that infernal creature owns my thoughts and is all I think about!"

"Jacques," said Polidori in a serious tone that contrasted with his usual bitter irony, "I've seen many people suffer before, but I've never seen anyone suffer nearly as much as you. The man who holds us in his power could not be more pitiless. He has condemned you to live, or rather, to wait for death in terrible anguish. What you've just told me explains the alarming symptoms you've gradually been displaying and for which I was vainly seeking a cause."

"But these symptoms are nothing serious! It's just exhaustion, it's just the effect of my troubles. I'm not in danger, am I?"

"No, no, but your condition is serious, and we must not let it get any worse. There are certain thoughts that you need to drive from your head. Otherwise, you will be in great danger."

"I'll do anything you advise, provided I keep on living, because I don't want to die. Oh! The priests talk about damnation! They've never imagined torture like mine. Lust tortures me; greed tortures me. I've got two open wounds instead of one, and I feel them both equally. The loss of my fortune is dreadful to me, but death would be even more dreadful. I wanted to live, my life can be nothing but endless, pointless torture, and yet I do not dare hope for death, since death would annihilate my gloomy happiness, my mental mirage reflecting Cecily back to me incessantly."

"At least you have the consolation of considering the good you've done to expiate your crimes," said Polidori, resuming his customary sangfroid.

"Yes, go ahead and mock me. You're right. Send me back to burn on those hot coals. You know full well, you wretch, that I hate humanity. You know full well that these expiations being imposed on me, these expiations in which feeble minds would find some consolation, only inspire me with hatred and rage against those who require them and those who benefit from them. Blood and thunder! To think that while my appalling life drags on, while I exist for nothing more than to take pleasure in suffering that would terrify the most fearless human being, these men whom I curse will see their wretchedness lifted from them, thanks to the money that's been stripped from me; to think that that widow and her daughter will thank God for the fortune I'm returning to them; to think that Morel and his daughter will live comfortably; to think that Germain will have an honorable and secure future! And that priest! That priest who was blessing me while my heart was swimming in gall and blood! I'd like to have stuck a knife in him! Oh! It's too much! No! No!" he cried as he held his forehead in his two clenched fists. "My head is exploding. My ideas are getting confused. I can't go on against these fits of impotent rage, these constantly recurring tortures. And it's all because of you, Cecily, Cecily! Do you at least know that I suffer like this? Are you aware of it at all, Cecily, you demon out of hell?"

And Jacques Ferrand, exhausted from this frightening excitation of nerves, fell back into his chair, panting, his arms writhing as he let out low, inarticulate moans. This attack of convulsive rage did not surprise Polidori. With his vast medical experience, he could easily recognize that in Jacques Ferrand his rage at seeing himself dispossessed of his fortune, together with his passion, or rather frenzy, for Cecily, had led to a consuming fever. And that was not all. In the fit to which Jacques Ferrand was now prey, Polidori noted with anxiety certain symptoms that suggested the presence of one of the most terrifying maladies known to mankind, a malady of which Paul and Aretaeus,[227] who were just as great observers as they were moralists, so admirably traced out the basic picture.

Suddenly, someone knocked on the office door. "Jacques," said Polidori to the solicitor. "Jacques, pull yourself together. There's someone at the door."

The solicitor could not hear him. Partially stretched across his desk, he was writhing in convulsive spasms. Polidori got up to open the door. He saw there the head clerk of the office, pale and haggard, who exclaimed, "I must speak with Monsieur Ferrand immediately!"

"Silence! He is extremely ill right now. He cannot hear you," said Polidori in a whisper. Leaving the solicitor's office, he shut the door behind him.

"Ah! Monsieur!" cried the head clerk. "You are Monsieur Ferrand's best friend and you must help me. There's not a moment to lose."

"What do you mean?"

"On Monsieur Ferrand's orders, I went to tell Madame the Countess MacGregor that he could not come to her today as she had asked—"

"And?"

"This lady, who now seems to be out of danger, took me into her bedroom. She exclaimed in a threatening voice, 'Go back and tell Monsieur Ferrand that if he isn't here at my home within half an hour, before the day is out he will be arrested for giving false evidence. The child he passed off as dead is alive. I know who he gave her to and I know where she is.'"[228]

"That woman was delirious," said Polidori coldly, with a shrug of his shoulders.

"Do you think so, monsieur?"

"I'm sure of it."

---

227. The disease Polidori suspects is epilepsy. Both Paul of Aegina (625?–690?) and Aretaeus of Cappadocia (fl. first century CE) wrote lengthy treatises that discuss many diseases. But they also both wrote on epilepsy, and Paul references Aretaeus in his discussion of the disease. [TN]

228. The reader knows that Sarah thought that Fleur-de-Marie was still imprisoned in Saint-Lazare because of what the Owl had told her before stabbing her. [SN]

"That's what I thought at first, monsieur, but Madame the countess was so certain—"

"Her illness has turned her head. When people hallucinate, they always believe in their hallucinations."

"I'm sure you're right, monsieur. The threats the countess was making against a man as respectable as Monsieur Ferrand just don't make sense."

"It's beyond common sense."

"I should tell you also, monsieur, that as I was leaving the countess's bedroom, one of her servants suddenly entered and said, 'His highness will be here in an hour.'"

"The servant said that?"

"Yes, monsieur, and I was very surprised because I had no idea which highness it could be."

"No doubt it's the prince," said Polidori to himself. "He's going to see Countess Sarah, whom he meant never to see again. I don't know what's going on, but I don't like the sound of this reunion. It could make matters worse for us." Then, turning to the head clerk, he said, "Once again, monsieur, there's nothing to worry about. It's the mad imaginings of a sick person. In any case, I will let Monsieur Ferrand know right away what you've just told me."

Now we will take the reader to the home of Countess Sarah MacGregor.

CHAPTER 2

RODOLPHE AND SARAH

We now take the reader to the home of Countess MacGregor. A beneficial turn in her health had torn her from the delirium and suffering that had made people fear seriously for her life for several days. The sun was beginning to set. Seated in a large armchair and supported by her brother, Thomas Seyton, Sarah was studying herself attentively in a mirror one of her maidservants, kneeling by her side, was holding up for her. This scene took place in the room in which the Owl had attempted to murder her.

The countess was as pale as marble, which made the darkness of her eyes, eyebrows, and hair stand out all the more dramatically. A large shawl of white muslin wrapped her body from head to toe. "Give me that coral headband," she said to one of her maidservants in a voice that was weak but imperious and curt.

"Betty will put it on for you," said Thomas Seyton. "You're going to tire yourself out. It's already quite reckless of you to—"

"The headband! The headband!" Sarah repeated impatiently, taking the piece of jewelry and putting it on her head according to her desires. "Now fasten it and leave me," she said to her maidservants.

Just as the women were leaving the room, she added, "Have Monsieur Ferrand, the solicitor, wait in the little blue salon. Then," she said with a poorly disguised expression of pride, "as soon as His Royal Highness, the Grand Duke of Gerolstein arrives, have him come in here. Finally!" Sarah said as she sat back into her armchair the moment she was alone with her brother. "Finally, that crown is within my grasp. The dream of my life! The prediction really will come true!"

"Sarah, calm your excitement," her brother said to her severely. "Just yesterday, we had given you up for lost. One more disappointment would be your death blow."

"You are right, Tom. Another failure would be terrible because I have never been closer to seeing all my hopes realized. I am certain that the only thing that kept me from succumbing to my wounds was my constant thought that I could profit from the revelation that that woman made to me when she tried to kill me. That revelation gives me incredible power."

"That's what you were saying during your delirium. You kept coming back endlessly to that same idea."

"Because that idea is the only thing that has sustained me in my precarious state. What a hope! Sovereign princess . . . almost a queen!" she added in a state of intoxication.

"Once again, Sarah, you must not have these insane dreams. Your awakening from them would be terrible."

"Insane dreams? What do you mean? When Rodolphe knows that that young girl who is a prisoner right now at Saint-Lazare,[229] and who was earlier given to the care of the solicitor who passed her off as dead, is our child, do you really believe that—"

Seyton interrupted his sister. "I believe," he said, bitterly, "that princes put the affairs of state and political expediency before all natural duties."

"Do you have so little faith in my skill?"

"The prince is no longer the earnest and passionate adolescent you seduced long ago. That time is long past for him—and for you, my sister."

Sarah shrugged her shoulders lightly and said, "Do you know why I wanted to decorate my hair with this headband and why I put on this white dress? It's because the first time Rodolphe saw me at the court of Gerolstein, I was dressed in white, and I was wearing this same coral headband in my hair."

"What?" said Thomas Seyton, looking at his sister in surprise. "You want to evoke those memories? Don't you fear, instead, the effect they may have on him?"

"I know Rodolphe better than you do. No doubt my features have changed with age and suffering and are no longer those of the sixteen-year-old girl whom he loved beyond reason, who has been his only love. His only love because I was his first love, and this love, unique in a man's life, always leaves indelible traces in his heart. So, believe me, brother, the sight of this jewelry will reawaken in Rodolphe not only the memories of his love, but, even more, of his youth. And for all men, the latter memories are always sweet and dear to them."

"But those sweet memories are linked to terrible ones. What about the dark way your love affair ended? What about the odious conduct of the prince's father toward you? And your obstinate silence when Rodolphe, after your marriage to Count MacGregor, asked you once more for your daughter, who was still a small child, your daughter

229. The reader has not forgotten that the Owl, right before stabbing Sarah, believed that Songbird was still at Saint-Lazare and had told her so. She did not know that on that very day Jacques Ferrand had had her taken to the Scavenger's Island by Madame Séraphin. [SN]

whose death you told him of ten years ago in a cold letter? Are you forgetting that since that time the prince has felt only contempt and hatred toward you?"

"Pity has replaced hatred in him. Since he knew I was dying, he sent Baron de Graün every day to find out how I was doing."

"An act of humanity."

"Just now, he has sent answer to me that he would be coming here. That is an immense concession on his part, my brother."

"He thinks you are at death's door. He supposes you were requesting a final farewell, so he's coming. You were wrong not to write him of the revelation you're going to make to him."

"I know what I'm doing. This revelation will overcome him with surprise and joy, and I will be there to benefit from his first surge of tenderness. Either he will say to me, 'A marriage must legitimate the birth of our child,' today, or he never will. If he says that, his word is sacred, and the hopes of my entire life will come true."

"If he makes you that promise, yes."

"And to see that he makes it, we can neglect nothing in this moment that will decide everything. I know Rodolphe. He hates me, even though I don't know why he does, for I have never failed in the role that I determined I would play for him."

"Perhaps. But he is not a man who hates for no reason."

"No matter. Once he's certain of having recovered his daughter, he will overcome his aversion toward me and will not retreat before any sacrifice that might assure the most desirable outcome for his child. He will want to make her as magnificently happy as she must have been unfortunate up to then."

"Yes, certainly, he will assure the most brilliant destiny for your daughter; but there is a large gulf between that restoration and a resolution to marry you so as to legitimate the birth of that child."

"His father's love will overcome that gulf."

"But that unfortunate girl has no doubt lived up to now the most desperate and wretched of lives, hasn't she?"

"Her current state of abasement will make Rodolphe want to raise her up all the more."

"Think about it: will he have her sit in the ranks of the sovereign families of Europe? Will he have her recognized as his daughter before the princes and kings whose relative or ally he is?"

"Don't you know his strange, impetuous, and resolute character, his chivalrous exaggeration regarding everything he believes to be just and ordained by duty?"

"But that unfortunate child may have been so corrupted by the wretchedness of what her life must have been that the prince, instead of feeling an attraction toward her—"

"What are you saying?" exclaimed Sarah, interrupting her brother. "Isn't she as beautiful a young girl as she was a ravishing little child? Didn't Rodolphe, without knowing her, care for her enough to want to become responsible for her future? Didn't he send her to his Bouqueval farm from which we had her kidnapped?"

"Yes, thanks to your persistent wish to cut off all the prince's ties of affection in the insane hope of bringing him back to you."

"Yet, nevertheless, if it weren't for this insane hope, I wouldn't, even at the cost of my life, have discovered the secret of my daughter's existence. Wasn't it through that woman who took her away from the farm, finally, that I discovered the disgusting underhandedness of Jacques Ferrand, the solicitor?"

"It is a problem for us that they wouldn't let me in this morning to Saint-Lazare, where they told you that unhappy child is being kept. Despite my insisting strongly, they wouldn't answer any of my questions because I didn't have a letter of recommendation to give to the prison's director. I wrote to the prefect in your name, but I won't receive his answer until tomorrow, and the prince will be here shortly. I repeat, I am sorry that you won't be able to present your daughter to him yourself. It would have been better to wait until she left prison before asking the grand duke to come here."

"Wait? And can we even be sure that the improvement I feel now in my health will last until tomorrow? It may be that only the sheer energy of my ambition is holding me up."

"But what proof can you give the prince? Why should he believe you?"

"He will believe me once he reads the beginning of the confession that woman was dictating to me when she stabbed me, a confession I have happily not forgotten in the slightest detail. He will believe me once he has read your correspondence with Madame Séraphin and Jacques Ferrand up until the supposed death of the child. He will believe me once he has heard the confession of the solicitor who, frightened by my threats, will be here shortly. He will believe me once he sees the portrait of my daughter at six years of age,[230] a portrait that, the woman told me, still bears a striking resemblance to her. So much proof will be enough to show the prince that I speak true and to persuade him to take that first step that will make me almost a queen. Ah! Even if it's only for a day or an hour, at least I'll die happy!"

At this moment the sound of a carriage could be heard entering the courtyard. "It's him! It's Rodolphe!" Sarah cried to Tom Seyton.

The latter quickly walked over to the curtain, lifted it, and answered her, "Yes, it's the prince. He's getting out of his carriage."

230. It is more likely the portrait was taken when she was four, as Sarah says on p.1148.

"Leave me alone now. This is the moment," said Sarah with unshakeable calm. A monstrous ambition and a pitiless selfishness had always been, and still were, this woman's only motivations. In the nearly miraculous resurrection of her daughter, she could see only a means of finally reaching the one constant goal of her life.

After having hesitated a moment before leaving her rooms, Thomas Seyton suddenly came over to his sister and said to her, "I will tell the prince how your daughter, whom we thought dead, is still alive. This conversation would be too dangerous for you. Violent emotion would kill you, and after such a long separation, the sight of the prince, and memories from that time—"

"Give me your hand, my brother," said Sarah. Then, putting Thomas Seyton's hand over her stony heart, she added with a sinister and glacial smile, "Do I seem to be moved?"

"No, nothing, nothing—not even a quickened pulse," said Seyton, stupefied. "I know the incredible control you have over yourself. But in a moment like this, when both a crown and your death hang in the balance—because you most know, as I said, the failure of this last hope could well kill you—I truly do not understand how you can be so calm!"

"Why are you so surprised, brother? You still don't understand? Nothing—no, nothing has any effect on my heart of marble. Nothing will make it beat more quickly until the day I feel the sovereign crown placed on my head. I hear Rodolphe. Leave me now."

"But—"

"Leave me!" cried Sarah in a tone that was so imperious, so resolute, that her brother left her rooms a few moments before the prince was brought in to see her.

When Rodolphe entered the room, his look showed pity. But, seeing Sarah seated in an armchair and dressed as if to entertain, he recoiled in surprise. His face quickly became somber and distrustful.

The countess, guessing at his thoughts, said to him in a soft and feeble voice, "You thought you would find me on my deathbed and you came to hear my final farewell?"

"I have always considered the last wishes of a dying person to be sacred. But this is a sacrilegious trick—"

"Don't worry," said Sarah, interrupting Rodolphe. "Don't worry; I haven't tricked you. I believe I only have very few hours to live. Pardon me this last bit of vanity. I wanted to spare you the experience of the somber family circle that normally accompanies one's dying breath. I wanted to die dressed as I was the first time I saw you. Alas! After ten years of separation, you're finally here! Thank you! Oh! Thank you! But you should thank God as well for having moved you enough to want to listen to my dying prayers. If you had refused me, I would have carried to my grave a secret that will be the joy, the happiness of your life. It is a joy that is mixed with some sadness, a happiness mixed with some tears—like all real human joy. But you would happily give half of the life that remains to you for this joy!"

"What are you saying?" the prince asked her in surprise.

"Yes, Rodolphe, if you hadn't come, this secret would have followed me to the grave. It would have been my only revenge, and yet—no, I wouldn't have had such awful courage. Although you have made me suffer greatly, I would have shared this supreme happiness with you—and you, luckier than I, will enjoy it for a long time, a very long time, I hope."

"But again, madame: what are you talking about?"

"When you know, you will not be able to understand how long I am taking to tell you about it, for you will regard this revelation as a miracle from heaven. But the strange thing is that I, who with a single word could give you the greatest happiness you may ever have experienced, even though the minutes of my life are now numbered . . . I feel an indefinable satisfaction at prolonging your wait. And besides, I know your heart. Despite the steadiness of your character, I would be afraid to tell you about a discovery as unbelievable as this one without any preparation. The emotions associated with overwhelming joy have their own dangers."

"Your pallor is increasing, and you seem hardly able to contain some violent agitation," Rodolphe said. "I believe this is really serious and solemn."

"Serious and solemn indeed," said Sarah in an emotional voice, for, in spite of her normal impassiveness, as she thought of the immense importance of the revelation she was about to make to Rodolphe, she felt more confusion and distress than she had expected. Finally, unable to control herself for much longer, she cried out, "Rodolphe, our daughter is alive!"

"Our daughter?"

"She lives, I tell you!"

These words, and the air of truthfulness with which they were uttered, moved the prince to the bottom of his soul. "Our child?" he repeated, quickly approaching Sarah's armchair. "Our child? My daughter!"

"She is not dead. I have incontrovertible evidence. I know where she is. Tomorrow you will see her."

"My daughter! My daughter!" repeated Rodolphe in shock. "Can it be true? She lives!" Then, suddenly, reflecting on the unlikelihood of this being the case, and fearing to be the dupe of a new scheme on Sarah's part, he exclaimed, "No! No! It's a fantasy! It's impossible! You're deceiving me. It's some kind of trick, an unholy lie!"

"Rodolphe, listen to me!"

"No, I know only too well what your ambition is. I know what you're capable of. I can guess the point of this trick!"

"Well, then, what you say is true. I'm capable of anything. Yes, I had wanted to take advantage of you. Yes, a few days before I was stabbed, I had wanted to find a girl . . . a girl I would have presented to you in the place of our child whom you regretted so bitterly."

"Enough! Oh! Enough, madame!"

"After that confession, you will believe me, perhaps, or rather you will be forced to accept the evidence."

"The evidence . . ."

"Yes, Rodolphe. I'll say it again: I had wanted to deceive you by substituting some unknown girl for the one we were mourning. But God ordained that, at the moment at which I was making this unholy bargain, I should be stabbed to death."

"You . . . at that moment!"

"God willed that the girl who would replace our daughter in this lie would be . . . guess who? Our daughter."

"Are you delirious? In heaven's name!"

"I am not delirious, Rodolphe. In this little box, with the papers and a portrait that will prove to you the truth of what I'm telling you, you'll find a piece of paper stained with my blood."

"With your blood?"

"The woman who told me that our daughter was still alive was dictating this confession to me when I was stabbed with a dagger."

"And who was she? How did she know?"

"She was the person they gave our daughter to when she was a little child after making us think she was dead."

"But this woman . . . what is her name? Can she be believed? How did you come to know her?"

"I am telling you, Rodolphe, that all of this is fate. It's providential. A few months ago, you had taken a young woman out of her wretched life and sent her to the countryside, right?"

"Yes, in Bouqueval."

"Jealousy and hatred made me no longer able to think clearly. I had that girl kidnapped by the woman I mentioned—"

"And she took the unfortunate child to Saint-Lazare."

"Where she remains."

"She is there no longer. Ah! You don't know, madame, the appalling evil you have done by taking that poor child away from the retreat in which I had placed her, but—"

"That girl is no longer at Saint-Lazare?" cried Sarah in fear. "And you speak of some appalling evil?"

"It was in the interest of an avaricious monster to have her killed. They drowned her, madame. But tell me. You were saying that—"

"My daughter!" Sarah cried out, cutting Rodolphe off as she stood upright, as still as a marble statue.

"What is she saying? Oh, my God!" Rodolphe cried.

"My daughter!" Sarah repeated as her face became livid and full of despair. "They killed my daughter!"

"Songbird, your daughter!" Rodolphe repeated, recoiling in horror.

"Songbird, yes, that's the name that woman nicknamed the Owl told me. Dead! Dead!" Sarah said, still motionless, still staring fixedly. "They killed her."

"Sarah!" said Rodolphe, who was as pale and terrifying in his appearance as the countess. "Pull yourself together. Answer me. Songbird, the girl you had the Owl kidnap from Bouqueval, was—"

"Our daughter!"

"Her?"

"And they killed her!"

"Oh, no, you must be raving. This can't be. You don't know—no, you don't know how horrible that would be. Sarah! Come to your senses! Talk to me calmly. Sit down. Calm down. Often there are resemblances, appearances that deceive. We are so inclined to believe what we want. I'm not blaming you. Just explain to me clearly . . . tell me all the reasons that bring you to believe that this is true, because this can't be. No, no! That must not be! It isn't true!"

After a moment of silence, the countess pulled her thoughts together and said to Rodolphe in a failing voice, "When I learned of your marriage, and I was thinking of marrying myself, I couldn't keep our daughter with me. She was four years old then."

"But at that time I asked you for her. I begged you," cried Rodolphe in a heartrending tone, "and my letters went unanswered. The only one you wrote told me of her death!"

"I wanted to avenge myself on you for your contempt by denying you your child. It was unworthy of me. But listen to me. I feel my life slipping away. This last blow has overpowered me—"

"No! No! I don't believe you. I do not want to believe you. Songbird, my daughter? Oh, my God, that cannot be your will!"

"Stop and listen to me. When she was four years old, my brother gave her to Madame Séraphin, the widow of an old servant of his, to raise until she was old enough to go to boarding school. The sum that was set aside for the future of our daughter was deposited by my brother with a solicitor known for his integrity. The letters of this man and Madame Séraphin, addressed at that time to me and my brother, are there, in that box. A year later, they wrote to me saying that my daughter's health had taken a turn for the worse. She was dead eight months later, and they sent me her death certificate. At that time, Madame Séraphin entered the service of Jacques Ferrand, after having given our daughter to the Owl through the intermediary of a wretch who is now in the Rochefort prison. I was beginning to write the Owl's declaration down when she stabbed me. The paper is there, along with a portrait of our daughter at the age of four. Examine it all: the letters, the confession, the portrait. You have seen that unhappy child: judge for yourself."

After uttering these words, which drained all her strength, Sarah fell weakly into her armchair.

Rodolphe was still staggered by this revelation.

There are some misfortunes that are so unexpected and so abominable that one tries not to believe in them until the weight of the evidence compels belief. Rodolphe, persuaded of Fleur-de-Marie's death, had only one hope, the hope that he could convince himself that she was not his daughter. With a frightening calm that terrified Sarah, he approached the table, opened the box, and began reading the letters, one by one. He examined the papers that accompanied them with minute attention. These letters, written to Sarah and her brother by the solicitor and Madame Séraphin and stamped and dated by the post office, related to Fleur-de-Marie's birth and the placement of funds set aside for her.

Rodolphe could not doubt the authenticity of this correspondence. The Owl's declaration was confirmed by the information of which we spoke at the beginning of this story, information gathered on Rodolphe's orders, which designated one Pierre Tournemine, then an inmate at Rochefort, as the man who had received Fleur-de-Marie from Madame Séraphin and delivered her into the hands of the Owl. This was the same Owl whom the unfortunate child had recognized later in Rodolphe's company at the ogress's joint.

Rodolphe could no longer doubt the identity of these people, nor that of Songbird. The death certificate appeared to be in order, but Ferrand himself had confessed to Cecily that this forged certificate had enabled the theft of a considerable sum of money that had been placed in an annuity set aside for the girl he had had drowned by Martial on the Scavenger's Island. It was thus with a growing and terrifying anguish that Rodolphe, despite himself, came to the awful conviction that Songbird was his daughter and that she was dead.

Unfortunately for him, everything seemed to confirm this belief. Before condemning Jacques Ferrand on the proof given by the solicitor himself to Cecily, the prince, with his deep concern for Songbird, having had inquiries made at Asnières, had learned that indeed two women, one old and the other young and dressed in peasant's clothing, had drowned on their way to the Scavenger's Island. Rumor had it that Martial had committed this latest crime. We should add, finally, that, in spite of the care of Doctor Griffon, Count de Saint-Remy, and the She-Wolf, Fleur-de-Marie, who had for a long time remained in critical condition, had hardly begun to convalesce. Her psychological and physical weakness were so great that she had thus far not been able to let Madame Georges or Rodolphe know of her situation.

This set of circumstances could not offer the slightest hope to the prince. But a last trial awaited him. He finally cast his eyes upon the portrait that he had almost feared to look at. The blow was frightful. In this childish and charming face, already marked by the divine beauty we attribute to cherubs, he could already see Fleur-de-Marie's features in the most striking way. There were her fine, straight nose, her noble forehead, her little mouth already bearing a slightly serious expression. For, as Madame Séraphin said to Sarah in one of the letters Rodolphe had just read, "The child always asks for her mother and is very sad." Here, again, were those big eyes that were of such a pure and sweet blue—the blue of a cornflower, the Owl had told Sarah when she recognized in this miniature the features of the unfortunate girl she had hounded under the name of Miss Lowlife when she was a child and Songbird when she was a young girl.

At the sight of this portrait, Rodolphe's tumultuous and violent feelings gave way to tears. He fell back, broken, into an armchair, and hid his face in his hands as he sobbed.

CHAPTER 3

VENGEANCE

As Rodolphe was crying bitter tears, Sarah's composure was visibly disintegrating. At the very moment she saw the dream of her life's ambition coming true, her last sustaining hope was flickering away forever. The effect of this terrible disappointment on her health, which had briefly improved, could only be fatal. Collapsed in her armchair, shaking with feverish trembling, her hands crossed and clenched on her knees, her gaze fixed, the countess awaited Rodolphe's first words in terror. Knowing the prince's impetuous character, she foresaw that the heart-wrenching pain that tore such copious tears from this man who was as resolute as he was inflexible could only result in some fit of rage.

Suddenly, Rodolphe raised his head, dried his tears, stood up, and, turning to Sarah, with his arms folded across his chest, looking menacing and pitiless, he contemplated her for a few moments in silence. Then he said in a muted voice, "It had to be. I raised my sword to my father. I am struck through my child. A just punishment for patricide. Listen to me, madame."

"Patricide? You? Oh, my God, what a fateful day! What more are you going to tell me?"

"You must be told, in this final moment, of all the evils your implacable ambition and ferocious selfishness have caused. Do you hear me, you heartless, faithless woman? Do you hear me, you unnatural mother?"

"Mercy! Rodolphe!"

"No mercy for you who long ago, with no pity for a sincere love, in the interest of your execrable pride, exploited a generous and devoted passion that you pretended to reciprocate. No mercy for you who armed the son against the father! No mercy for you who, instead of caring piously for your child, abandoned her to mercenary hands so as to satisfy your greed through a marriage to a wealthy man, the way you had earlier sated your unrestrained ambition by leading me to marry you. No mercy for you who, having refused to give me my child to care for with tenderness, have now caused her death through your sacrilegious scheming! A curse on you—you, my evil genius and the evil genius of my entire line!"

"Oh, my God! He is pitiless! Leave me! Leave me!"

"You will hear me out, I insist! Do you remember the last day I saw you? It's seventeen years ago now. You could no longer hide the fruit of our secret marriage, that, like you, I believed to be indissoluble. I knew well how inflexible my father's character was. I knew the kind of political marriage he was envisioning for me. Braving his indignation, I declared to him that you were my wife in the eyes of God and all men, that in a short time you would bring a child into the world, the fruit of our love. My father's anger was terrible. He did not want to believe in my marriage. Such audacity seemed impossible to him. He threatened me with his wrath if I allowed myself to speak any longer about any such folly. At that time I loved you madly. Taken in by your seduction, I believed that your heart of stone beat for me. I answered my father that I would never have any other wife than you. At these words, his rage knew no limits. He showered you with the most offensive names and exclaimed that our marriage was null and void. He claimed that to punish you for your audacity he would have you pilloried before the entire town. Giving in to my mad passion and to the violence of my character, I dared to forbid my father, my king, to speak this way of my wife. I dared to threaten him. Exasperated by this insult, my father lifted his hand against me. I was blinded by rage. I drew my sword. I threw myself at him. If Murph had not stepped forward and parried the blow, I would have been a patricide in fact as I was in intention. Do you hear! Patricide! And all to defend you!"

"Alas! I didn't know about that tragedy!"

"I sought vainly until today to expiate my crime. The blow that struck me today is my punishment."

"But what about me? Didn't I suffer from your father's hardness, too, when he broke up our marriage? Why are you accusing me of not having loved you when—"

"Why?" cried Rodolphe, interrupting Sarah and glaring at her with crushing contempt. "Know then what happened, and don't be surprised any longer by the horror you inspire in me. After that fateful scene in which I threatened my father, I gave up my sword. I was put in the most absolute confinement. Polidori was arrested for helping arrange our marriage. He proved that this union was null and void, that the minister who had blessed it was only feigning to be one, and that you, your brother, and I had all been deceived. To disarm my father's anger against him, Polidori went even further. He gave him one of your letters to your brother that he had intercepted during a journey Seyton took."

"Heavens! Can this be true?"

"Can you understand my contempt now?"

"Oh! Enough! Stop!"

"In that letter, you revealed your ambitious plans with a revolting cynicism. You spoke of me with glacial disdain. You were sacrificing me to your infernal pride. I was nothing but the instrument of the sovereign fate that had been predicted as your reward. You thought, finally, that my father had been alive long enough."

"What evil luck I have had! Now I understand everything."

"And it was to defend you that I threatened my father's life. When, without a word of reproach, he showed me that letter the next day, that letter which revealed the blackness of your soul in every line, I could do nothing but fall to my knees and beg his forgiveness. Since that day I have been plagued with an inexorable remorse. Soon I left Germany and went on long journeys. Then began the expiation I imposed on myself. It will not be completed until I die. Rewarding good and punishing evil, comforting those who suffer, probing all human wounds in order to try to save a few souls from perdition: that is the task I have given myself."

"It is noble and holy. It is worthy of you."

"If I speak to you of this vow," said Rodolphe with as much disdain as bitterness, "of this vow that I have accomplished as much as I was humanly able to wherever I have gone, it is not in desire of any of your praises. So now listen to me. Recently I came to France. I was not going to lose an opportunity for expiation in this country. While I wanted to rescue honest people who were unfortunate, I also wanted to get to know the classes crushed, degraded, and depraved by poverty. I knew that help that comes at the right moment—even in the form of a few generous words—is often enough to save an unhappy soul from the abyss. In order to judge for myself, I took on the appearance and language of the people I wished to observe. It was during one of these journeys of exploration that . . . for the first time . . . I met . . ."

Then, as if he had to recoil before this terrible revelation, Rodolphe added after a moment of hesitation, "No . . . no. I can't go on; it's too much for me."

"What else do you have to tell me? My God!"

"You will find out soon enough. But," he said with sanguine irony, "you seem so keenly interested in the past that I must speak to you of the events that preceded my return to France. After long travels, I came back to Germany. I took great pains to do what my father desired. I married a Prussian princess. During my absence you had been expelled from the grand duchy. Learning later that you had married Count MacGregor, I asked you insistently to return my daughter to me. You didn't answer. Despite all of my inquiries, I could never find out where you had sent that unfortunate child, for whose future my father had liberally provided. It was just ten years ago that a letter from you informed me that our daughter had died. Alas! Could it only have pleased God that she had died then! I would never have known the endless agony that will haunt me for the rest of my life."

"Now," said Sarah in a feeble voice, "the aversion I have inspired in you, since you read that letter, no longer surprises me. I can feel that I will not survive this latest blow. Well! Yes, pride and ambition have ruined me! Beneath my seeming passion, I have hidden a heart of ice. I feigned candor and loyalty, but I was nothing but dissimulation and egoism. Not knowing how much I merited your hatred and contempt, my mad hopes had returned, more ardent than ever. Because both of us had lost our spouses and were free, I had returned to believing the prediction that promised me a crown, and when fate made me find my daughter again, I thought I could see the hand of divine will in this unhoped-for stroke of fortune! Yes, I went so far as to believe that your aversion toward me would give way to your love for your child, and that you would give me your hand in order to restore the rank that was her due."

"Well! May your execrable ambition finally be satisfied and may this be its punishment! Yes, despite the horror you inspire in me—yes, out of attachment—what am I saying? out of respect for the terrible misfortunes of my child, I would—although determined to live forever separately from you—I would have legitimized her birth by marrying you and would have made her position as brilliant and as lofty as it had been wretched!"

"So I wasn't wrong! Oh, what misery! Misery! It's too late now!"

"Oh, I know you too well! It's not the death of your daughter you mourn. It's the loss of that rank that you had pursued with such unbending stubbornness! Well, may these vile regrets be your final punishment!"

"Final, because I will not survive it."

"But before you die, know what the existence of your daughter was like after you abandoned her."

"Poor child! Very wretched, perhaps . . ."

"Do you remember," Rodolphe said with frightening calm, "do you remember that night on which you and your brother followed me into a den in the Cité?"

"I remember that. But why do you ask that question? Your look chills my heart."

"While coming to that den, did you happen to see, standing at the corners of those debased streets, some unfortunate creatures who . . . but no—no . . . I can't do it," said Rodolphe, hiding his face in his hands. "I can't say it. My own words terrify me."

"They're terrifying me, too. What more do you have to say? Good God!"

"You saw them, didn't you?" Rodolphe said, making a terrible effort to go on. "You saw them, those women, the shame of their sex? Well, among them, did you happen to notice a beautiful young girl of sixteen? Beautiful, but with the beauty with which we endow angels. A poor child who, amid all the degradation in which they had plunged her for several weeks, managed to conserve a face that was so innocent, so virginal, and so pure that the thieves and murderers who talked to her as one of their own, madame, called her by the nickname 'Fleur-de-Marie.' Did you notice that young girl? Tell me—tell me, you tender mother."

"No, I didn't notice her," said Sarah, almost mechanically, feeling oppressed by a vague terror.

"Really?" cried Rodolphe, with a burst of sardonic laughter. "That's strange. Well, I did notice her. And here's how it happened. Listen carefully. After one of the exploratory missions I mentioned a moment ago and that then had a dual purpose,[231] I found myself in the Cité. Not far from the den into which you followed me, a man wanted to beat up one of those unfortunate creatures. I defended her against the brutality of that man. You won't guess who that creature was. Tell me, you saintly and farseeing mother, tell me. Can't you guess?"

"No . . . I can't guess . . . Oh! Leave me! Leave me."

"That unhappy girl was Fleur-de-Marie."

"Oh, my God!"

"And can't you guess who Fleur-de-Marie was, you irreproachable mother?"

"Kill me! Oh, kill me!"

"It was Songbird. It was your daughter!" exclaimed Rodolphe in a heartrending outburst. "Yes, that unfortunate girl I tore from the clutches of an ex-convict was my child—my own child, the child of Rodolphe of Gerolstein! Oh! That meeting with my child, whom I rescued without knowing, was some kind of fate, some act of providential justice . . . it was a reward for the man who seeks to help his brethren. It was punishment for patricide."

"I die cursed and damned," murmured Sarah as she sank into her chair, hiding her face in her hands.

"So," Rodolphe continued, barely containing his feelings and trying in vain to hold back the sobbing that from time to time choked him up, "when I took her away from the evil things she was being threatened with, struck as I was by the inexpressible sweetness of her voice and the angelic expression of her face, it was impossible for me not to care about her. I heard the naive and poignant story of her life of abandonment, pain, and misery with the most profound emotions. For you understand, madame, that the life of your daughter was appalling. Oh! You will know the tortures your child endured. Yes, Countess. While in the midst of your opulence you still dreamed of achieving a crown, your very young daughter, dressed in rags, went at night to beg in the street,

231. To follow the trail of Germain, Madame Georges's son. [SN]

suffering from cold and hunger. During the winter nights she shivered on a bit of straw in the corner of an attic, and then, when the horrible woman who used to torture her was tired of beating the poor little girl, having nothing better to do than cook up new ways to make her suffer, do you know what she would do to her, madame? She would pull out her teeth!"

"Oh! I want to die! This agony is unbearable!"

"Keep listening. When she finally got out from under the Owl's hand, wandering without bread, with no place to go, barely eight years old, she was arrested as a vagabond and put in prison. Ah! Those were the best years of your daughter's life, madame! Yes, in her jail, each night she thanked God for no longer suffering from the cold and from hunger, and for not being beaten anymore. And it is in a prison that she spent the most precious years of a young girl's life, the years in which a tender mother always showers her with such conscientious and watchful solicitude. Yes, instead of turning sixteen surrounded by nurturing care and noble teachings, your daughter knew only the brutal indifference of the jailers. Then, one day, in its fiercely casual way, society threw her, in all her innocence, purity, beauty, and naiveté, into the mire of the big city. Unfortunate child, abandoned, without support or counsel, left to face all the accidents of misery and vice! Oh!" exclaimed Rodolphe, allowing free rein to the sobs that were choking him. "Your heart is hard and your egoism is pitiless, but you would have wept—yes, you would have wept on hearing your daughter's heartrending story! Poor child! Soiled, but not corrupted, still chaste in the middle of that horrible degradation that was for her such a terrible nightmare, for each word told of her horror for the life to which she was fatally bound. Oh! If you knew how at each instant her lovable instincts kept revealing themselves. So much kindness, so much touching charity in her! Yes, for it was in order to comfort someone whose misfortune was even greater than her own that the poor little girl had spent the little money she had left, money that separated her from the abyss of infamy in which she was thrown. Yes, because one day came—a frightful day—when she had no bread, no work, and nowhere to sleep. On that day some horrible women met her at her weakest hour, in her time of greatest need. They got her drunk and—"

Rodolphe could not finish his sentence. He exclaimed, with a heartrending cry, "And that was my daughter! My daughter!"

"A curse on me!" murmured Sarah, hiding her face in her hands as if she dreaded seeing the light of day.

"Yes!" cried Rodolphe. "A curse on you! For it's because you abandoned her that all of these horrors took place. A curse on you! For, after I took her out of that mire and placed her in a peaceful retreat, you had her taken away by your wretched accomplices. A curse on you! For that kidnapping put her into the hands of Jacques Ferrand." As he said this name, Rodolphe went suddenly silent. He shuddered as if he had pronounced it for the first time. And indeed it was the first time he had pronounced that name in the knowledge that his daughter had been that monster's victim. The prince's face then took on a frightening expression of rage and hatred. Silent, without motion, he stood as if crushed by the thought that the murderer of his daughter still lived.

Despite her increasing weakness and the shock her conversation with Rodolphe had just given her, Sarah was struck by his sinister look. She feared for herself. "Alas! What are you thinking?" she murmured in a trembling voice. "Hasn't there been enough suffering, dear God?"

"No! It's not enough! It's not enough," said Rodolphe, talking to himself and responding to his own thoughts. "I have never experienced this before—never! I am burning with the desire for revenge. I feel such a thirst in me for blood—such calm and premeditated rage! When I didn't know that one of the victims of that monster was my child, I said to myself, 'Death for that man would be pointless, whereas his life could be fruitful if he ransomed it by accepting the conditions I impose on him.' To condemn him to giving to charity to expiate his crimes seemed just to me. And then life without gold and life without the satisfaction of his all-devouring sensuality would be a long and intense torture. But it is my daughter he exposed, child as she was, to all the horrors of poverty and then, mere girl as she was, to all the horrors of dishonor!" exclaimed Rodolphe, getting more and more heated. "It's my daughter whose murder he ordered! I will kill that man!" And the prince ran toward the door.

"Where are you going? Don't leave me!" cried Sarah, rising partway out of her chair and stretching out her hands in prayer to Rodolphe. "Don't leave me alone! I'm going to die!"

"Alone? No! No! I'm leaving you with the ghost of your daughter, whose death you caused!"

Sarah, overcome, dropped to her knees and cried out in dread, as if she had seen a terrifying phantom. "Have pity on me! I'm dying!"

"So die, then, you cursed woman!" said Rodolphe, terrifying in his rage. "Now I seek the life of your accomplice, for it's you who gave your child over to her executioner!"

And Rodolphe had himself driven right away to the home of Jacques Ferrand.

CHAPTER 4

FURENS AMORIS[232]

Night had fallen as Rodolphe was making his way to the solicitor's home.

The wing of the house Jacques Ferrand lives in is plunged in deep darkness. The wind is moaning; rain is falling. The wind had been moaning and the rain had been falling also on that sinister night when Cecily, before leaving the solicitor's house forever, had excited the man's brutal passion to a fevered pitch. Lying on the bed in a room weakly lit by a lamp, Jacques Ferrand is wearing black pants and a black vest. One of his shirtsleeves is rolled up and stained with blood. A red sheet turned into a tourniquet serves as a bandage on his wiry arm, showing that Polidori has just finished letting his blood. The latter, standing next to the bed, supports himself with one hand on the bedhead and seems to be contemplating his accomplice's face anxiously.

Nothing could be more hideously frightening than Jacques Ferrand's face, which is deep in the somnolent torpor that generally follows violent outbursts. His face, with its livid purple color standing out from the alcove, is bathed in a cold sweat and has reached the last stage of decay. His closed eyelids are so swollen and full of blood that they look like two reddish lobes in the middle of this corpselike pallor.

"Another attack as violent as the one he just had will be the end of him," said Polidori in a whisper. "Aretaeus[233] said that that majority of those who are struck by this strange and terrifying malady almost always perish on the seventh day. Today is the sixth day since that infernal Creole woman lit the unquenchable fire that burns this man up."

After a few moments of thoughtful silence, Polidori withdrew from the

---

232. The Madness of Love (in Latin in Sue's text). [TN]

233. *Nam plerumque in septima die hominem consumit* (Aretaeus). See also Baldassar's translation (*Cas. med.* I.III, *Salacitas nitro curata*). See also the admirable work of Ambroise Paré on *satyriasis*—the unhealthy exacerbation (morbid or pathological) of sexual desire in a man—this strange and frightening malady that so closely resembles a punishment from God, as he says. [SN]

The Latin phrase at the beginning of the note means, "Usually, by the seventh day, the man has been consumed by it." [TN]

bed and walked slowly around the room. "A moment ago," he said, stopping, "during the attack that almost carried Jacques off, when I heard him describe, one by one and in a panting voice, the monstrous hallucinations that were coursing through his brain, I thought I was myself trapped in a dream. What a terrible, terrible sickness! It puts each organ, one after another, through phenomena that baffle science and offend nature. That's what it was like just a moment ago, when Jacques's hearing was so intensely and painfully sensitive that my words, even though I was speaking as softly as possible, pounded so hard on his eardrum that he said it seemed to him that his skull was a bell and that an enormous brass clapper that shook with the slightest sound was hammering at his head from one temple to the other with a deafening noise and atrocious shooting pain."

Polidori became pensive again before Jacques Ferrand's bed as he came closer to it. The storm was raging outside. It soon burst into long whistles and violent surges of wind and rain that shook all the windows of this dilapidated house. Despite his bold criminality, Polidori was superstitious. He was made uneasy by dark premonitions and felt ill in some way he couldn't identify. The moaning of the hurricane, which was the only thing that broke up the night's gloomy silence, inspired a vague terror in him, which he vainly tried to withstand. To distract himself from his somber thoughts, he returned to examining his accomplice's features.

"Now," he said, leaning over him, "his eyelids are filling up. It appears his calcified blood is flowing and concentrating there. Just like the auditory organs did a moment ago, the organs of sight are surely going to present some extraordinary phenomenon to observe. What suffering! How long it lasts! How it changes! Oh!" he added with a bitter laugh. "When Mother Nature takes it in her mind to be cruel and to play the role of tormentor, she outdoes any ferocious concoction humans could ever come up with. So it is that, in this illness caused by erotic frenzy, she puts each sense through unheard-of and superhuman tortures. She develops the sensitivity of each organ to its highest pitch, bringing the atrocity of pain to its highest pitch as well."

After having contemplated the features of his accomplice for a few moments, he shuddered with disgust, recoiled, and said, "Oh! What a frightful mask. These rapid tremors that he is experiencing from time to time contract his face and make him look terrifying."

Outside, the storm redoubled its fury. "What a storm!" said Polidori, falling into an armchair and holding his hands to his forehead. "What a night! What a night! Nothing could augur worse for Jacques's condition."

After a long silence, he said, "I don't know if the prince, knowing the infernal power of Cecily's seductions and Jacques's stormy sensuality, foresaw that, in a man of such energy and vigor, the ardor of a burning and unsated passion, complicated by a sort of avaricious rage, would develop the dreadful nervous disease that tortures Jacques. But this consequence was normal and inevitable. Oh, yes!" he said, getting up suddenly as if this thought had frightened him. "Yes! The prince must have foreseen that. No field of science is unknown to his uncommon, vast intelligence. His deep gaze penetrates the cause and effect of every little thing. Pitiless in his administration of justice, he must have calculated his punishment of Jacques and based it on the logical and successive developments of a brutal passion, exacerbated into a frenzy."

Polidori went on, after a long silence: "When I think of the past, when I think of the ambitious plans I had founded, along with Sarah, on the prince's inexperience! When I think of all that has happened, of the degradations that have caused me to fall into my current abject and criminal state! I had thought I could turn this prince soft and make him the docile instrument of power I always dreamed of! I thought I could go from being a tutor to being a minister. And instead, despite my knowledge and intelligence, going from one heinous crime to another, I've plumbed the depths of dishonor. Now, in the end, here I am, the jailer of my own accomplice." And Polidori lost himself in dark reflections that led him to the thought of Rodolphe.

"I hate and fear the prince," he went on, "but I must bow in fear before this imagination, before this all-powerful will that always exceeds all expectations in a single bound. What a strange contrast in this man: on the one hand, he is tender and charitable enough to imagine the bank for out-of-work laborers, and on the other, he is savage enough to snatch Jacques from the jaws of death in order to deliver him into the clutches of all the vengeful furies of lust! And yet, there's nothing more orthodox than that," Polidori added with a somber irony. "Among the paintings Michelangelo created of the seven capital sins in his *Last Judgment* at the Sistine Chapel, I saw the terrifying punishment he inflicts upon lust.[234] But the hideous, convulsive masks of those damned by the sins of the flesh who writhe under the venomous fangs of snakes were less frightening than Jacques's face during the attack he just had. He terrified me!"

And Polidori shivered as if he still had that awful vision before his eyes. "Oh, yes!" he said in a despondency mixed with fear. "The prince is pitiless. It would be far better for Ferrand to have lost his head on the

234. "Carried away by his subject, his imagination gone wild from eight years of continuous meditation on a day that is so horrible for a believer, Michelangelo, raised to the dignity of preacher and thinking only of his salvation, wanted to punish in the most striking manner the vice that was most fashionable at that time. The horror of this torture seems to me to attain the truest sublime of that genre" (Stendhal, *The History of Painting in Italy*, 22, p. 354). [SN]

scaffold. Fire, the wheel, molten lead that burns and pierces one's limbs: all of those tortures would have been better than the torture this wretch has to endure. By watching him suffer, I've come to fear for my own fate. What will he determine for me? What is he reserving for me, Jacques's accomplice? It can't satisfy the prince's desire for revenge just to have me be his jailer. He didn't keep me from the scaffold just to let me live. Maybe he has an eternal prison waiting for me in Germany. I'd prefer that to death. I had no choice but to put myself blindly in the prince's hands. That was my only chance to be saved. Sometimes, despite his promise, though, I'm afraid. Maybe if Jacques succumbs, he'll deliver me to the executioner! In threatening me with the scaffold while he lives, he was also threatening him, my accomplice—but what if he dies? All the same, I know that the prince's word is sacred. But I, who have so many times violated divine and human laws, do I have the right to invoke a sworn promise? It doesn't matter! The same way it was in my interest for Jacques not to escape, it would be in my interest to keep him alive. But the symptoms of his sickness get worse by the moment. It would almost take a miracle to save him. What can I do? What can I do?"

At this moment, the storm was at the height of its rage. A chimney that was almost tottering from decrepitude was blown over by the wind's violence and fell on the roof and into the courtyard with the echoing crash of thunder. Jacques Ferrand, torn suddenly out of his somnolent haze, made a movement in his bed. Polidori felt more and more in the power of the vague presentiment of terror that held him in its grip.

"It's silliness to believe in presentiments," he said in a disturbed tone of voice. "But this night seems made for something sinister to happen." A quiet groan from the solicitor drew Polidori's attention. "He's coming out of his torpor," he said, coming closer to the bed. "But maybe he's just going to have another attack."

"Polidori!" murmured Jacques Ferrand, still lying on his bed with his eyes closed. "Polidori, what is that noise?"

"A chimney that's falling apart," Polidori answered in a whisper, afraid of making too loud a noise for his accomplice's hearing to bear. "A frightful storm is shaking the house to its foundations. The night is horrible . . . horrible!"

The solicitor did not hear him, and said again, turning his head slightly, "Polidori, aren't you there?"

"Yes, yes, I'm here," said Polidori more loudly, "I just answered softly because I didn't want to cause you more of the pain I gave you a little while ago by speaking out loud."

"No, now your voice enters my ears without making me feel the terrible pain I experienced before, but then it seemed that the smallest sound exploded in my skull like thunder. And still, in the middle of this din, of these nameless sufferings, I could still make out Cecily's passionate voice calling to me."

"Always that infernal woman! Always! You have to get rid of those thoughts—they'll kill you!"

"Those thoughts are my life! Like my life, they are stronger than my torments."

"But, you fool, it is only these thoughts that make you suffer, I'm telling you! Your sickness is nothing but your sensual frenzy reaching its highest pitch. As I've already told you, you must empty your thoughts of those fatally lascivious images, or you'll perish."

"Get rid of those images?" exclaimed Jacques Ferrand, in an excited tone. "Oh! Never! Never! My only fear is that my mind will exhaust itself by evoking them. But, damn it, it doesn't ever get tired! The more this vivid image appears before me, the more real it seems. As soon as the pain gives me a moment's rest, as soon as I can put two ideas together, Cecily, that demon I cherish and curse, surges before my eyes."

"What unconquerable rage! It terrifies me!"

"You know, right now," said the solicitor in a strident voice, with his eyes obstinately focused on an obscure point in his alcove, "I can already see something like a vague white form coming into being. There! There!" He pointed his hairy, scrawny finger in the direction of his vision.

"Be quiet, you miserable wretch."

"Ah! There she is!"

"Jacques! This is killing you!"

"Ah! I see her," added Ferrand, clenching his teeth, without answering Polidori. "There she is! She's so beautiful! So beautiful! Look how her black hair floats down coming undone onto her shoulders! And her little teeth between her parted lips, those lips that are so red and so moist! What pearls! Oh! Her big eyes seem to sparkle and die simultaneously. Cecily!" he added in inexpressible exaltation. "Cecily! I adore you!"

"Jacques! Listen to me! Listen!"

"Oh! To be eternally damned . . . and to see her like this for all eternity!"

"Jacques!" cried Polidori, alarmed. "Do not excite your vision with these ghosts!"

"It's not a ghost!"

"Be careful! A little while ago, as you know, you thought you were hearing the voluptuous songs of that woman, too, and your hearing was suddenly stricken with intolerable pain. Be careful!"

"Leave me alone!" cried the solicitor in impatient anger. "Leave me alone! What good is hearing if not to hear her? Or sight if not to see her?"

"But what about the tortures that follow from that, you wretched madman?"

"I can brave tortures for a fantasy! I braved death for a reality. What difference does it make to me, anyway? That burning image is my whole reality! Oh! Cecily! You're so beautiful! You know full well, you monster you, that you're intoxicating. What's the good of that infernal coquetry that still sets me aflame? Oh! You execrable fury! Do you want me to die? Stop it! Stop it, or I'll strangle you!" the solicitor cried out in delirium.

"But you're killing yourself, you wretch!" cried Polidori, shaking the solicitor roughly to rouse him from his transport.

Vain efforts! Jacques continued with renewed excitement: "O cherished queen! Demon of lust! I never saw—" The solicitor broke off what he was saying. He cried out in pain and threw himself backward.

"What's wrong with you?" Polidori asked him in astonishment.

"Put out that light. It's too bright for me. I can't stand it. It's hurting me."

"What?" said Polidori, more and more surprised. "It's just a lamp covered with a lampshade, and it's hardly giving off any light at all."

"I'm telling you that it's getting brighter in here. Look, it's getting brighter and brighter! Oh! It's too much! It's becoming intolerable!" added Jacques Ferrand, closing his eyes with an expression of increasing suffering.

"You're mad! This room is hardly lit, I'm telling you. I've just dimmed the lamp. Open your eyes and you'll see!"

"Open my eyes? But I'd go blind from the waves of fiery light flooding this room, more and more. Here, there, everywhere! They're sheaves of fire, thousands of dazzling sparks!" the solicitor cried out as he sat up in his bed. Then, letting out another moan of atrocious pain, he brought his hands up in front of his eyes. "I'm being blinded! That torrid light goes right through my closed eyelids. It's burning me up; it's devouring me! Ah! Now my hands are helping me a bit. But put out that lamp. It's throwing off a hellish flame!"

"There's no longer any doubt," said Polidori. "His vision has been affected by the same exorbitant sensitivity that affected his hearing earlier. And then there was that attack of hallucination. He's beyond hope! To bleed him again in this state would be fatal to him. He's beyond hope!"

Jacques Ferrand let out another terrible, piercing cry, which echoed through the bedroom. "Torturer! Will you put out that lamp? Its burning flame is going through my hands and making them transparent! I can see the blood circulating in the network of my veins . . . I can close my eyelids all I like, as hard as I can, but that burning lava manages to get in. Oh! What torture! They're shooting pains as dazzling as if a sharp, white-hot iron were being shoved deep into my eyeballs. Help! God! Help!" he exclaimed as he writhed on his bed, prey to horrible convulsions of pain.

Polidori, terrified by the violence of this fit, quickly extinguished the light. The two of them were now in deep darkness. At that moment, one could hear the sound of a carriage stopping at the street entry.

CHAPTER 5

VISIONS

Once the bedroom he was in with Polidori became engulfed in shadows, Jacques Ferrand's sharp pains began to subside. "Why did it take you so long to put out that lamp?" he asked. "Were you trying to make me suffer the tortures of the damned? Oh! How I suffered! Lord, how I suffered!"

"Do you feel any better now?"

"I still feel a violent irritation, but it's nothing compared to what I was going through a minute ago."

"It's just as I told you: the moment the memory of that woman excites one of your senses, that sense is almost immediately struck by one of those terrible events that confound science, and that believers could take for a terrible punishment from God."

"Don't talk to me about God!" exclaimed the monster, grinding his teeth.

"I was talking about Him as a way of noting what was happening. But since you hold on to your life, as wretched as it is, get it into your head that, as I keep telling you, one of these violent attacks will end it if you continue to bring them on."

"I want to go on living . . . because the memory of Cecily is my whole life."

"But that memory is killing you, wearing you down, and eating you up!"

"I can't get away from that memory, and I don't want to. Cecily inhabits me, just as blood inhabits the body. That man took my whole fortune away, but he couldn't deprive me of the ardent and imperishable image of that enchantress. That image belongs to me. Whenever I want it, there it is, like a slave; she says what I want; she looks at me the way I want her to; she loves me as I want her to!" the solicitor cried out in a new fit of frenetic passion.

"Jacques! Don't excite yourself! Remember the attack you just had!"

The solicitor did not hear his accomplice, who could see a new hallucination coming on. Indeed, Jacques Ferrand went on, as he burst out into convulsive, sardonic laughter, "Take Cecily away from me? But don't they know you can achieve the impossible if you focus all the power of your faculties on a single object? This is how in just a moment I will . . .

go up into Cecily's bedroom, where I have not dared to go since she left. Oh! To see, to touch the clothes that belonged to her . . . the mirror before which she dressed . . . it will be like seeing her for real! Yes, by fixing my eyes with all my strength on that mirror, I will soon see Cecily before me. It won't be an illusion or a mirage; it will really be her. I'll find her there, the way the sculptor finds his statue within a block of marble. But I swear by all the fires of hell that burn me here, she won't be any pale or cold Galatea."

"Where are you going?" said Polidori suddenly as he heard Jacques Ferrand getting up, for the most profound darkness still pervaded this room.

"I'm going to find Cecily."

"No, you will not! The sight of that room would kill you!"

"Cecily is waiting for me up there."

"You will not go. I'll hold you here and I won't let you go," said Polidori, seizing the solicitor by the arm.

On his last legs, Jacques Ferrand could not overcome Polidori, who held him in a vigorous grip. "So you want to keep me from going to find Cecily?"

"Yes, and besides, there's a lamp lit in the next room. You know the effect light had on your eyes a moment ago."

"Cecily is upstairs. She's waiting for me. I would walk through burning coals to reach her. Let me be. She told me I was her old tiger. Watch out: my claws are sharp!"

"You will not leave! I will tie you to your bed like a madman before you do that."

"Polidori, listen to me: I am not mad. I am completely clearheaded. I know full well that Cecily is not up there in the flesh, but for me, the ghosts of my imagination are just as good as reality."

"Silence!" Polidori exclaimed suddenly, cocking his ear. "I thought I heard a carriage stopping at the door a moment ago. I wasn't mistaken. Now I hear the sound of a voice in the courtyard."

"You want to distract my thoughts. It's an old trick."

"I can hear people talking, I tell you, and I think I recognize—"

"You want to deceive me," Jacques Ferrand said, interrupting Polidori, "but I'm no fool."

"But listen, you wretch! Listen, all right? Don't you hear it?"

"Leave me be! Cecily is up there, and she's calling me! Don't make me angry. I'm telling you now: watch out! Do you hear me? Watch out!"

"You will not leave."

"Watch out—"

"You will not leave this room. It is in my interest that you stay—"

"You're getting in the way of my seeing Cecily again, so you'll just have to die! Take that!" said the solicitor quietly.

Polidori cried out. "You scoundrel! You got my arm, but your hand wasn't steady. The wound is a slight one. You won't escape."

"Your wound is mortal. I used Cecily's poisoned stiletto to stab you. I have kept it on my person this whole time. Wait for the effect of the poison. Ah, finally, you're letting go of me. You're going to die. You shouldn't have prevented me from going up there to see Cecily again," Jacques Ferrand added as he groped in the darkness to open the door.

"Oh!" murmured Polidori. "I'm losing feeling in my arm . . . An icy cold has come over me . . . my knees are giving way beneath me . . . my blood is congealing in my veins . . . now I'm experiencing vertigo . . . Help!" Jacques Ferrand's accomplice cried as he rallied his strength in one last cry. "Help! I'm dying!" And then he collapsed.

The clatter of a glass-paned door being opened with sufficient violence to shatter many of its panes, Rodolphe's echoing voice, and the sound of running steps seemed to respond to Polidori's cry of agony. Jacques Ferrand had finally found the door handle in the dark, and, quickly opening the door to the next room, he ran into it, his dangerous stiletto in hand. At the same moment, the prince entered the room from the other side, awful and threatening as the spirit of vengeance itself. "You monster!" cried Rodolphe as he came closer to Jacques Ferrand. "It is my daughter you killed! You will—"

The prince did not finish his sentence. He recoiled in horror. His words seemed to have struck Jacques Ferrand down. Throwing his stiletto away and bringing his hands to his eyes, the wretch fell facedown on the ground with an inhuman cry.

In accordance with the phenomenon of which we have spoken and whose action had been suspended by the deep darkness, when Jacques Ferrand entered this brightly lit room, he was struck by a blazing light that was more dizzying and more intolerable than if he had been thrown into a flood of light as incandescent as that of the sun's disk. And the agony of this man—who was writhing in appalling convulsions, scratching at the floor with his fingernails as if he had wanted to dig a hole through which to escape the atrocious tortures that this flaming brightness was causing him to endure—was a horrifying spectacle. Rodolphe, one of his men, and the doorkeeper of the house, who had been forced to take the prince to the door of this room, all stood there, frozen with horror.

In spite of his completely justified hatred of Jacques Ferrand, Rodolphe felt the beginnings of pity for his unheard-of sufferings. He ordered that he be carried to a couch. This was done, but not without some effort, for the solicitor was so afraid of being in the direct light of the lamp that he struggled violently against them. But when his face was flooded with light, he cried out anew. It was a cry that froze Rodolphe with terror.

After more long-lasting tortures, the phenomenon came to an end from its own violence. Having reached the limits of what could be endured without death ensuing, the pain in his eyes stopped. But following the normal course of this illness, a delirious hallucination came on the heels of this attack. Suddenly, Jacques Ferrand stiffened like a cataleptic. His eyelids, which had been closed up to this point, quickly opened. Instead of fleeing the light, his eyes focused on it obstinately. His pupils, in a state of extraordinary dilation and fixedness, seemed phosphorescent and lit up from within.

Jacques Ferrand seemed to be immersed in a sort of ecstatic contemplation. His body and limbs at first remained completely immobile. Only his features moved, agitated incessantly by a nervous trembling. His hideous face, thus contracted and distorted, bore no trace of anything human. One could say that the appetites of the beast, having snuffed out the intelligence of the man, stamped this wretch's face with an absolutely bestial character.

Having reached the final stage of his delirium, he remembered, in this moment of supreme hallucination, the words of Cecily when she called him her tiger. Little by little, he descended into madness. He imagined himself to be a tiger. His halting, breathless speech indicated the chaos of his thinking and the strange aberration that had seized his brain. Slowly, his limbs, until then rigid and immobile, began to relax. A brusque movement made him fall off the couch. He tried to get up and walk, but he lacked the strength to do so. One moment he was reduced to slithering like a reptile, and the next, to crawling on his hands and knees. He kept going back and forth, this way and that, as the visions that propelled and possessed him willed.

He cowered in one of the corners of the room like a tiger in its den. His raucous, furious cries, his grinding teeth, the convulsive writhing of the muscles of his forehead and face, and his flaming gaze gave him at times a vague and frightening resemblance to that ferocious beast. "Tiger, a tiger is what I am," he said in a jerky voice, gathering himself into a crouch. "Yes, a tiger. I want blood! In my lair, bodies ripped apart! Songbird, the brother of that widow, a little child, Louise's son: there are the bodies. My tigress Cecily will have her share." Then, seeing his bony fingers, whose nails had grown incredibly during his illness, he added these disjointed words: "Oh! My sharp nails! Sharp and cutting. I'm an old tiger, but I'm stronger, suppler, bolder. No one would dare challenge me for my tigress, Cecily. Ah! She's calling me! She's calling!" he said, putting his monstrous face forward and cupping his ear.

After a moment of silence, he cowered again along the wall, saying, "No . . . I thought I'd heard her, but she's not there . . . But I see her . . . Oh! Always, always! Oh! There she is. She's calling me, she's roaring, roaring over there. Here I am! Here I am!" And Jacques Ferrand crawled toward the middle of the room on his hands and knees. Although his strength was exhausted, from time to time he moved forward with a convulsive start; then he stopped and seemed to listen attentively.

"Where is she? Where is she? As I approach, she moves away. Ah! Over there . . . Oh! She's waiting for me. Go on, go on, eat some sand while you're roaring so plaintively. Ah! Her big, ferocious eyes . . . they're becoming languid and imploring . . . Cecily, your old tiger is coming!" he exclaimed. And in a last burst of energy, he had the strength to get up on his knees. But all of a sudden, falling backward in horror, his body collapsing on his heels, his hair standing up straight, his gaze demented, his mouth disfigured with terror, his hands stretched out in front of him, he seemed to be struggling with rage against an invisible object, uttering disconnected words, and crying out in a choked voice, "What a bite! Help me! Frozen knots . . . my broken arms . . . I can't lift it . . . sharp teeth . . . No, no, oh! Not the eyes . . . help . . . a black snake . . . oh! Its flat head . . . its fiery pupils. It's looking at me . . . it's the devil . . . Ah! He recognizes me . . . Jacques Ferrand . . . to the church, holy man . . . always at church . . . go now . . . at the sign of the cross . . . Go now."

And the solicitor, getting up slightly, supported himself with one hand on the floor and tried to cross himself with the other. His livid forehead was bathed in cold sweat. His eyes were starting to lose their clarity. They were becoming dull and glaucous. All the symptoms of impending death were manifesting themselves. Rodolphe and the other witnesses of this scene remained immobile and mute as if they were in the grip of an abominable dream.

"Ah!" Jacques went on, still half stretched out on the floor and holding himself up with one hand. "The devil . . . gone . . . I'm going to church . . . I'm a holy man . . . I pray . . . Huh? They won't know, will they? Do you think? No, no, tempter . . . Of course! . . . The secret? Well, let them come . . . those women . . . all . . . yes, all . . . if nobody knows about it."

And one could see, on this hideous face of a martyr condemned for lust, the last convulsions of sensual agony. His feet in the tomb that his fevered passion had opened beneath him, obsessed by his fiery delirium, he continued to dream up still more images of mortal sensual pleasure: "Ah!" he said in a panting voice. "Those women, those women! But the secret! I'm a holy man! The secret! Ah, there they are! Three. There are three of them! . . . What does this one say? I am Louise Morel . . . Ah, yes! Louise Morel, I know . . . I'm just a girl of the people . . . Hey, Jacques . . . see what a forest of brown hair falls on my shoulders . . . You used to think my face was pretty. Hey, take this, keep it. What did she give me? Her head, cut off by the executioner. That dead head is looking at me . . . That dead head is speaking to me . . . Her purple lips are moving . . . Come! Come! Come! Like Cecily . . . No, I don't want . . . I don't want . . . Demon . . . leave me . . . go away! Go away! And that other woman? Oh! Beautiful! Beautiful! Jacques, I am the Duchess . . . de Lucenay . . . Do you see my goddesslike figure, my smile, my bold eyes? Come! Come! Yes, I'm coming, but wait! And that one who is turning her face . . . Oh! Cecily! Cecily! Yes, Jacques, I am Cecily. You see the three Graces. Louise, the duchess, and me . . . choose . . . Beauty of the people, patrician beauty, savage beauty of the tropics . . . Hell is where we are! Come! Come!"

"Hell is where you are!"

"Yes!" exclaimed Jacques Ferrand as he got up on his knees and extended his arms to seize these phantoms. This last convulsive outburst was followed by a mortal commotion. He soon fell backward, stiff and inanimate. His eyes seemed to be coming out of their sockets. Atrocious convulsions had contorted his features almost supernaturally, the way a voltaic battery contorts the faces of cadavers.[235] A bloody foam burbled out from his lips. His voice was whistling and strangulated, like the voice of someone with rabies, because, in its final throes, this appalling sickness—this appalling punishment for lust—has the same symptoms as rabies.

The life of the monster was draining away in one last and horrible vision. He stammered the following words: "Black night! Black . . . ghost . . . brass skeletons reddened by fire . . . wrap yourselves around me . . . their burning fingers . . . my flesh smokes . . . my marrow is turning to ash . . . relentless ghost . . . no! . . . no . . . Cecily! . . . fire . . . Cecily! . . ."

These were Jacques Ferrand's last words. Rodolphe left the room in shock.

---

235. Sue seems to be referring to an experiment conducted in London in 1803 by a scientist named Giovanni Aldini, who had purchased from the Newgate authorities the cadaver of a man who had been hanged. Placed in contact with electricity from a voltaic battery, the cadaver gave the appearance of reacting to it with horrible facial expressions. [TN]

CHAPTER 6

THE PUBLIC HOSPITAL

The reader will remember that Fleur-de-Marie, saved by the She-Wolf, had been transported to the country house of Doctor Griffon, not far from the Scavenger's Island. He was one of the doctors who worked in the public hospital to which we will now take the reader. This medical researcher, who was employed in this hospital, thanks to his high connections, regarded its rooms as a sort of laboratory in which he could experiment with treatments on the poor that he could subsequently use on his rich clients. He would never risk a new kind of cure on the latter before having in this way already tried and repeated its application *in anima vili*,[236] as he put it with the kind of naive barbarism to which he was led by a blind passion for the art of medicine and even more the habit and opportunity to perform, on God's creatures, every capricious experiment and every scientific fantasy that might occur to his inventive mind, without fear or limit. Thus, for example, if the doctor wanted to find out the relative effects of a new and risky medication so as to deduce what favorable effects it might have on various systems in the body, he would take a certain number of sick patients and treat some of them according to the new method and others by the old one. Sometimes, he would let nature take its course on another group. Afterward, he would count the survivors. These terrible experiments were, to be sure, a human sacrifice performed at the altar of science.[237] This did not even occur to Doctor Griffon.

---

236. See Book VII, Chapter 14, footnote 184. [TN]

237. The name I have the honor of bearing, and that my father, my grandfather, my granduncle, and my great-grandfather (one of the most erudite men of the seventeenth century) made famous by beautiful and grand practical and theoretical works on every branch of the art of restoring health, would prohibit me from making the smallest attack or thoughtless allusion with regard to doctors, even if the gravity of the subject I am treating and the just and immense celebrity of the French medical school did not stand in the way of it. In the creation of Doctor Griffon I have tried only to personify one of these men, who, respectable in all other things, can let themselves be carried away at times by their passion for the art of medicine and experimentation, to the point of gravely abusing their medical power, if one may be permitted such an expression. They sometimes forget that there is something even more sacred than science: humanity.

In the eyes of this prince of science, as they call such people these days, the patients in his hospital served as nothing but subjects for study and experimentation. And since his attempts would sometimes result, after all, in a new useful fact or a further advance of scientific knowledge, when that happened, the doctor would show the same ingenuous satisfaction and triumph as a general after a victory that cost the lives of many soldiers.

No one could be more adamantly opposed to the idea of homeopathy, from the time it appeared on the scene, than Doctor Griffon. He considered this method to be absurd, deadly, and homicidal. Sure in his beliefs and wanting to put their backs to the wall, as they say, he would have been more than happy in a gesture of chivalric courtesy, to offer homeopaths a certain number of patients on which they could freely test their methods. He was already certain that of twenty patients given this treatment, at most five would survive it. Although its own minister called for such experiments, a letter from the Academy of Medicine, written at the request of the homeopathic medicine society, forbade them and rebuked such excessive zeal. As a matter of professional courtesy, he did not want to try, on his own private authority, to do what his institutional superiors had rejected. But he did continue, with the same internal contradiction as his colleagues, to declare that homeopathic prescriptions were both

---

By a happy coincidence that reinforces the truth of what we have written here, these lines had already gone to press several days earlier when an article appeared in *The Century* (August 3, 1843), signed by several surgeons from Parisian hospitals, in which we read the following: "The intrusions we deplore (the matter in question involves surgeons who, as a result of special influence, have been given the direction of parts of public hospitals) should be reconsidered from a different perspective: that of morality. An unfortunate word has been heard lately: the word 'experimental trial.' Some decrees have given rise to medical services that go against the spirit and the letter of the statute, allowing for the authorization of such people to execute an experimental method of treatment. Such language is shocking in our era in which no one has the right to consider poor patients as fodder for trials of any sort. And moreover, how long will these trials last? On how many patients will they be performed? Should they not be kept under constant surveillance by a permanent commission that will evaluate the results? It would be gross negligence to leave such important issues unresolved. And furthermore: once doctors are allowed to go down this ill-advised path of medical trials, who knows where it will end? Won't every ostensible method demand its turn to prove its efficacy in a hospital ward? And then every adept of homeopathy, hydrosudopathy, magnetism, and machines to break up ossifications you may be sure will show up in due course to claim his right to conduct a trial."

And further down, it continues: "Some very considerable sums have been paid for treatments whose value is extremely questionable, veritable excrescences in hospitals that do not always have minimal necessary resources. Thus, while hospital administrations are reduced to skimping on things like seltzer water, or syrups necessary for making medicinal teas for poor patients with fevers, or strips of linen for bandages, etc., etc., they have spent extraordinary amounts of money on equipment—very considerable sums, especially when one considers how little value is derived from them." [SN]

without effect and extremely dangerous, without considering that that which has no effect cannot also be poisonous. But the prejudices of scientists are no less tenacious than those of the vulgar masses, and it took many years until a conscientious doctor dared to experiment in a Paris hospital with the system of small doses and with the use of blood cells to save hundreds of pneumonia patients who would have been sent by bloodletting into the next world.

As for Doctor Griffon, who so cavalierly declared millionths of particles to be homicidal, he continued without pity to force his patients to ingest iodine, strychnine, and arsenic until they reached the extreme limits of physiological tolerance—which is to say, when they died from it.

Doctor Griffon would have been stupefied to be told, with respect to this free and autocratic treatment of his subjects, "Such a state of things would make one be nostalgic for the barbarous behavior of the eras in which those condemned to die were delivered over to undergo recently discovered surgical operations that doctors did not yet dare perform on the living. If the operation succeeded, the condemned man was pardoned. Compared to what you do, this barbarism was an act of charity, monsieur. After all, they gave a wretch who was awaiting the executioner a chance to live, and they made possible an experiment that was perhaps useful to the health of all.

"Those homeopaths upon whom you heap sarcasm have tried all the medications they use to combat illness on themselves in advance before trying them on others. Several of them have not survived these rash if noble trial runs, but their deaths should be inscribed in golden letters in the book of scientific martyrs. Should you not urge your students to undertake similar experiments? Instead, you tell them that the population of a hospital is matter of little worth; their highest purpose would be their use in therapeutic manipulation, like some kind of cannon fodder used to absorb the first hail of medical grapeshot which is more deadly than cannon fire. But to try your risky medications on unfortunate workers for whom the hospital is the only refuge in the face of illness, to try a potentially fatal treatment on people whose poverty delivers them to you defenseless and trusting, to you who are their last hope and for whose lives you answer to no one but God: don't you realize that this is to push the love of science to the point of inhumanity, monsieur? Is it not enough that the poor already fill the workshops, the fields, the army? In this world, they know nothing but poverty and privation, and when they fall exhausted and half dead at the end of their travails and suffering, won't even their illness preserve them from a final, sacrilegious exploitation? I call out to your heart, monsieur: is this not unjust and cruel?"

Alas, Doctor Griffon would have perhaps been touched by these severe words, but not convinced. Man is made this way. The captain gets used to considering his soldiers to be nothing more than pawns in the bloody game we call a battle. And because men are so made, society must protect those whose fate exposes them to the consequences of these necessary human frailties.

Now, with Doctor Griffon's character once recognized (and described, one must admit, without hyperbole), it follows that the population of his clinic thus had no protection, no recourse against the scientific barbarism of his experiments. For a troubling lacuna exists in the way public hospitals are run. We hope we are pointing it out here to some effect . . .

Military hospitals are visited each day by a superior officer who is charged with hearing the complaints of sick soldiers and following up on them if they seem well founded to him. This contravening oversight, completely distinct from health administration and services, is excellent. It always produces the best results. It is, moreover, impossible to find any establishment better maintained than a military hospital. Soldiers are cared for in them with extreme gentleness, and they are treated with what we might nearly call respectful compassion.

Why is there no oversight in public hospitals analogous to that practiced by the superior officers in military hospitals, by men who are completely independent of the health administration and services, by a commission chosen perhaps from among the mayors and their assistants or among all those who exercise the diverse municipal powers in Paris, powers that are always so ardently sought after? The claims of the poor (if well founded) would in this manner have an impartial outlet, an outlet that is, we repeat, totally lacking at present. The workings of our public hospitals have no contravening oversight. This seems outrageous to us.

And so, once the door of Doctor Griffon's clinic closes behind a sick person, this latter belongs, body and soul, to science. No sympathetic or disinterested ear can hear his complaints. He was clearly told that once he was admitted to the public hospital, in an act of charity, he would henceforth belong to the doctor's experimental domain. Patient and malady would have to serve as subject of study, observation, analysis, or instruction for the young students who followed Monsieur Griffon assiduously as he made his rounds. Indeed, it soon fell upon the patient to have to respond to what were often the most painful and embarrassing interrogations, not one on one with the doctor, who, like the priest, fulfills a sacred duty and has the right to know everything. No, he would have to answer these questions aloud, before an avid and curious crowd.

Yes, in this pandemonium of science, old and young men, girls and women alike were obliged to shed every sentiment of modesty or shame, to make the most intimate revelations, to submit to the most embarrassing physical examinations before numerous observers—and almost always, these cruel formalities made their illnesses worse. This was neither humane nor fair. If the poor man enters the public hospital in the holy and sacred name of charity, he must be treated with compassion and respect, for unhappiness has its own majesty.[238] When the

---

238. We have exaggerated nothing here. We cite the following passages from an article in the *Constitutional* (January 19, 1836). This article, titled, "A Visit to the Hospital," is signed by Z., and we know that this initial conceals the identity of a celebrated doctor who cannot be accused of partiality regarding public hospitals. "When a patient arrives at the hospital, people are careful to write down immediately on a chart the name of the newcomer, the number of the bed, the type of illness, the age of the patient, his profession, his current residence. This chart is then hung from one of the ends of the bed. This measure cannot but deeply embarrass those who are temporarily sharing the refuge of the poor due to unforeseen reversals of fortune. Do you believe, really, that for Gilbert, a patient, this circumstance would have no bearing on the progress of his cure? I have seen young men and improvident old people for whom this revelation of their poverty and family name inspired a deep sadness. Being admitted to a hospital is a harsh ordeal for any patient. You can imagine how tired the patient will be the day after his arrival: over the past twenty-four hours, he has been interrogated successively first by his own doctor; second, by the doctors of the administrative office; third, by the surgeon on duty; fourth, by the department intern; fifth, by the hospital's staff physician; and finally, sixth, the following morning, by the doctor who is in charge as well as by ten to twenty zealous and inquisitive students who follow the public clinical lecture. This must surely add to the experience of young doctors, which has become so advanced these days, as much as it adds to the progress of science, but it aggravates the illnesses or, at the very least, postpones the healing of the patient . . . One of these unfortunate people said to me one day, 'If I were a criminal suspect, I would not have had more interrogations over two weeks. Fifty people have harassed me with questions since yesterday, and the questions are almost all the same. All I had when I came in here was pleurisy but I fear that the insatiable curiosity of so many people has given me an inflammation of the chest.' A woman told me, 'They bother me constantly. They want to know my age, my temperament, my constitution, the color of my eyes, whether I have a dark or light complexion, my diet, my habits, the health of my forebears, the circumstances of my birth, my fortune, my condition, my most secret affections, and the supposed reason for my troubles. They go so far as to scrutinize my conduct and to ferret out feelings that I ought to keep tightly locked up in my heart, feelings that merely suspecting I have make me blush.' And farther down: 'They tap my chest in twenty places in front of everybody. They make nasty marks in ink, apparently so they can track the progress of the obstructions that affect my bowels. Doctors today,' added this woman, 'resemble inquisitors. They care for the sick these days the way they used to punish people in earlier eras, and it pains me.'" Later in this article, Monsieur Z. adds, "The doctor can easily get to the bedside of patients who have been there a while and who are recovering or convalescent. But when he arrives at one of the beds occupied by new patients or patients in danger, he cannot get close to them before making his way through a double row of students who have been maintaining their vantage points of vigilant observation since that morning. As for the patient, he remains mute and silent amid this curious, attentive crowd. Often the illness worsens in proportion to the size of the crowd, which indicates to him danger and always triggers anxiety. While the patient contemplates the doctor with the feelings of trust and anxiety, the latter looks around at his assistants with reflection and circumspection, and then lights up suddenly when he reaches the patient, thus increasing his internal anxiety." [SN]

following lines are read, it will be understood why we have preceded them with these reflections.

There could be nothing more depressing than the appearance during the night of the vast hospital room to which we now take our readers. Along the tall, somber walls pierced here and there by barred windows like the ones in prison, there are two parallel rows of beds, dimly lit up by the sepulchral glow of a lamp hanging from the ceiling. The atmosphere is so nauseating and oppressive that the new patients often acclimate themselves to it only with some danger. This additional suffering is a kind of surcharge each new patient must inevitably pay for his sinister stay in the clinic. After a certain amount of time, a particular morbid pallor shows that the patient has experienced the initial influence of this harmful milieu, and that he is, as we have said, "acclimated."[239]

The air in this immense room is thus thick and fetid. Here and there, the silence of the night is interrupted, sometimes by plaintive moans, at other times by the deep sighs produced by feverish insomnia. Then everything grows silent, and nothing can be heard besides the monotonous and regular swinging of the pendulum on the large clock that rings hours that are so very long for the suffering that keeps vigil.

One of the ends of this room was almost entirely plunged in darkness. Suddenly, a sort of tumult and the sound of quick steps could be heard in this place. A door opened and closed several times. A sister of mercy, whose vast white bonnet and black clothing could be distinguished by the glow of the light she carried, approached one of the last beds in the row on the right. Some of the women patients, awakened suddenly, sat up in their beds, attentive to what was happening.

Soon the double doors opened. A priest came in carrying a crucifix. The two sisters knelt down. In the glow of light that surrounded this bed with a pale halo, while the other parts of this room remained in the shadows, one could see the clinic's chaplain leaning over the sickbed, pronouncing a few words so quietly that they were lost in the silence of the night. After a quarter of an hour the priest lifted the end of a sheet and covered the top of the bed with it. Then he left.

One of the kneeling nuns got up, closed the curtains that squeaked on their rods, and went back to praying next to her companion. Then everything went silent again. One of the patients had just died.

Among the women who were not asleep and who had witnessed this silent scene were three people whose names we already know: Mademoiselle de Fermont, the daughter of the unfortunate widow who was made destitute by Jacques Ferrand's greed; the woman from Lorraine, the poor laundrywoman to whom, at an earlier time, Fleur-de-Marie had given

239. Unless the circumstances are very urgent, serious surgical operations are never performed until the patient is acclimated. [SN]

the little money that remained to her; and Jeanne Duport, the sister of Bitters, the storyteller of La Force prison. We know Mademoiselle de Fermont and the sister of the La Force storyteller. As for the woman from Lorraine, she was a woman of about twenty, with a sweet and regular face, but she was extremely pale and thin. She was in the last stages of consumption. There was no hope that she could be saved. She knew this and was dying slowly.

The distance that separated the beds of these women was small enough to allow them to talk in a whisper without being overheard by the nuns. "There's another one, gone," said the woman from Lorraine quietly, thinking of death and talking to herself. "Her sufferings are over! She's really lucky!"

"She's really lucky—if she doesn't have a child," added Jeanne.

"So, you're not asleep, neighbor?" the woman from Lorraine said to her. "How are you doing on your first night here? Last night, the minute you came in, they made you lie down. I didn't dare speak to you after that. I could hear you sobbing."

"Oh, yes! I cried a lot."

"Are you in great pain, then?"

"Yes, but I'm inured to pain. I was crying from worries. I had finally managed to fall asleep, and I was sleeping, when the sound of the doors woke me up. When the priest came in and the good sisters were kneeling, I could see that it was a woman who was dying, so I said a Pater and an Ave for her in my head."

"So did I. And since I have the same illness as the woman who just died, I couldn't help but exclaim to myself, 'There's another one who's out of her suffering. She's lucky!' "

"Yes, as I said to you: if she doesn't have any children!"

"So I guess you have children?"

"Three," said Bitters's sister, sighing. "And you?"

"I had a little girl, but I didn't get to keep her for long. The poor child was ill before she was born. I was too poor during my pregnancy. I work as a laundrywoman in a boat. I had worked as much as I could. But everything comes to an end. When I had no more strength, I got no more bread. They threw me out of my rooms. I don't know what would have become of me if it weren't for a poor woman who took me with her to a basement in which she was hiding from her husband who wanted to kill her. That's where I gave birth on the straw. But happily, that kind woman knew a girl who was as pretty and charitable as an angel of God. That girl had a little money. She got me out of that basement, put me up in a rented room for which she paid a month's rent in advance, and also gave me a wicker crib for my child and forty francs for myself, with some linen. Thanks to her, I could get back on my feet and take up my work again."

"What a kind little girl! You know, I, too, met someone by chance who you could say was just like that, a young workingwoman who was very willing to help. I had gone to see my poor brother who is in prison," said Jeanne after hesitating a moment. "In the visiting room I met this worker I'm telling you about. Having heard me say that I wasn't happy, she came over to me, more than a little embarrassed, to see if she could help me out as well as she might, the poor child."

"How kind of her!"

"I accepted her help. She gave me her address, and two days later, that dear little Mademoiselle Rigolette—her name is Rigolette—had placed an order with me."

"Rigolette?" exclaimed the woman from Lorraine. "What a coincidence!"

"Do you know her?"

"No, but the girl who was so generous to me mentioned the name of Mademoiselle Rigolette several times. They were friends."

"Well!" Jeanne said, smiling sadly. "Since we're bed neighbors, we should become friends like our two benefactresses."

"Gladly. My name is Annette Gerbier. People call me La Lorraine. I'm a laundress."

"My name is Jeanne Duport. I do clothing detail work. Ah! It's so good to be able to find someone in this hospital who isn't completely a stranger, especially when I'm here for the first time and I have so many troubles! But I don't want to think about that. Tell me, La Lorraine, what was the name of the girl who was so kind to you?"

"Her name was Songbird. I'm just sorry I haven't been able to see her again in such a long time. She was as pretty as the Holy Virgin, with beautiful blond hair and blue eyes that were so sweet, so very sweet. Unfortunately, despite her help, my poor child died at the age of two months. She was so frail, she could barely breathe." The woman from Lorraine wiped away a tear.

"But what about your husband?"

"I'm not married. I was doing laundry during the day at the home of a rich man from my region. I had always behaved myself well, but I let myself be sweet-talked by the son of the house, and then . . ."

"Oh, yes. I understand."

"When I saw the state I was in, I didn't dare stay in the area. Monsieur Jules, he was the rich man's son, gave me fifty francs to go to Paris, saying that he would have twenty francs sent to me every month for the baby's clothing and the childbirth. But after I left there, I never got anything from him again, not even a letter. I wrote to him once, but he didn't answer me. I didn't dare do it again. I could tell that he didn't want to hear from me again."

"And all the same, he's the one who ruined you. Is he rich?"

"His mother owns a lot where we live, but what could I do? I wasn't there any longer. He has forgotten me."

"But if only because of his child, he shouldn't have forgotten you."

"But, on the contrary, that's exactly what made him turn on me, you see? He was angry at me for being pregnant because I became an embarrassment for him."

"Poor La Lorraine!"

"I miss my child for my sake, but not for hers. Poor little girl! She would have been too poor and would have been an orphan too soon, because I don't have long to live."

"You shouldn't think like that at your age. Have you been sick for a long time?"

"Just about three months. Heavens, when I had to earn money for me and my child, I started working twice as hard. I started working on that boat again too soon. It was a very cold winter, and I developed an inflammation in my chest. That was when I lost my little daughter. Watching over her, I didn't take care of myself. And then, on top of that, I was so sad. It ended with me becoming consumptive, condemned just like that actress who just died."

"At your age, there's always hope."

"The actress was only two years older than me, and look what happened to her."

"The woman the nuns are keeping vigil over right now was an actress, then?"

"Heavens, yes. Think of her fate. She had been as beautiful as a summer's day. She had had a lot of money, horse-drawn carriages, diamonds. But unfortunately, she was disfigured by smallpox. First she didn't have enough money, then came poverty, and finally here she is, dead in the hospital. She wasn't in any way proud. On the contrary, she was very sweet and open with everyone in this room. No one ever came to see her. All the same, four or five days ago she told us that she had written to a man she used to know earlier, in better days, a man who had loved her. She wrote to him to ask him to come and claim her body, because it made her feel bad to think that she would be dissected—cut into pieces."

"And that man—did he come?"

"No."

"Ah! That's really wrong."

"The poor woman kept asking after him, always saying, 'Oh! He'll come! Oh! He'll come, of course.' But now she's dead and he hasn't come."

"She must have suffered even more at the end."

"Oh, God, yes, because what she most feared is going to happen to her poor body."

"After having been rich and happy, it's really sad to die here! At least the rest of us are only changing one kind of wretchedness for another."

"Speaking of that," said La Lorraine after a moment of hesitation, "I wonder if you could do me a favor."

"Just ask."

"If I die before you get out of here, which is quite likely, I'd like you to claim my body. I have the same fear as the actress. I've set aside the little money I have left so I can be buried."

"You shouldn't think that way."

"It doesn't bother me. Will you promise me that?"

"But, God be thanked, that won't happen."

"Yes, but if it does happen, thanks to you, I won't suffer at the end like the actress did."

"Poor lady, to end her days here that way after having been so rich!"

"The actress isn't the only one here who has been rich, Madame Jeanne."

"Call me Jeanne, please, the way I call you La Lorraine."

"You're very kind."

"So who else was rich here?"

"A young girl of at most fifteen who was brought here last night before you came in. She was so weak that they had to carry her in. The nun said that the young person and her mother are very high-society types who were made destitute."

"Is her mother here, too?"

"No, her mother was so sick that they couldn't move her. The poor girl didn't want to leave her side, and they took advantage of her fainting to bring her here. It was the owner of the nasty furnished rooms where they were living, who, fearing they would die there on him, told the police superintendent about them."

"And where is she?"

"Look. There. In the bed across from you."

"And she's fifteen years old?"

"Heavens, at most!"

"The age of my oldest daughter!" said Jeanne, unable to hold back her tears.

CHAPTER 7

THE VISIT

Jeanne Duport began to weep bitter tears as she thought about her daughter.

"Please forgive me if I hurt you without meaning to by asking you about your children," the woman from Lorraine said to her, saddened. "Maybe they're sick, too?"

"Alas! Good Lord! I don't know what will become of them if I stay here more than a week!"

"What about your husband?"

After a moment of silence, Jeanne wiped away her tears and said, "Since we're friends here, La Lorraine, I can tell you my troubles, just as you've told me yours. That will make me feel better. My husband was a good worker. He became unbalanced, and then he abandoned me and our children after having sold everything we owned. I went back to work, some good souls helped me, I started to get back on my feet, I was raising my little family the best I could when my husband came back with a wicked woman who was his mistress. He took back the little I had, and everything started all over again."

"Poor Jeanne! Couldn't you put an end to it?"

"We would have had to obtain a legal separation. The law is too expensive, however, as my brother says. Alas! Heavens, you'll soon understand what it means for the law to be too expensive for poor folks like us. A few days ago I go back to see my brother and he gives me three francs that he'd earned by telling the other prisoners stories."

"You can tell that people in your family all have their hearts in the right place," La Lorraine said, declining, with an instinctive tact one rarely sees, to ask Jeanne why her brother was in prison.

"So I take heart again because I figured my husband wouldn't come back for a long time because he had taken everything of ours that he could get his hands on. But no: I was wrong," said the unfortunate woman, shuddering. "He had left behind my daughter, my poor Catherine."

"Your daughter?"

"You'll see what I mean, you'll see. Three days ago, I was working with my children around me. My husband came in. I could tell right away just from looking at him that he had been drinking. 'I'm going to get Catherine,' he says to me. Despite myself, I grab my daughter's arm and say to Duport, 'Where are you taking her?' 'It's none of your business. She's my daughter. Just have her pack her things and come with me.' When I hear those words, my heart stops beating for a moment, because you see, La Lorraine, that wicked woman who is with my husband—I shiver just thinking about it, but—well, that's how it is—she's been pushing him for a long time to make money off our daughter, who's young and pretty. What a monstrous woman!"

"Oh, she must be a real monster."

"So I say to Duport, 'Take Catherine away? Never. I know what your evil woman wants to do with her.' 'Listen,' says my husband to me, with his lips already white from rage. 'Don't get all stubborn about this, or I'll beat you to a pulp.' At that point he takes my daughter by the arm and says to her, 'Get moving, Catherine!' The poor little girl threw her arms around my neck and burst into tears, crying, 'I want to stay with Mama!' Seeing that, Duport becomes furious. He pulls my daughter off of me and punches me in the stomach, knocking me to the ground. Once I'm on the ground . . . once I'm on the ground . . . But, well, you know, La Lorraine," said the unhappy woman, stopping herself, "he was only that mean because he'd been drinking, of course . . . Well, anyway, he stomps on me while heaping all sorts of crazy abuse on me."

"God, he's a mean one!"

"My poor children throw themselves at his feet asking for mercy. Catherine does, too. Then he says to my daughter, cursing all the while like a madman, 'If you don't come with me, I'll kill your mother!' I was vomiting blood . . . I felt like I was half dead. I couldn't move at all . . . but I cry out to Catherine, 'Let him kill me first! But don't go with your father!' 'So you won't shut your mouth?' says Duport to me as he kicks me so hard that I lose consciousness."

"How horrible! How horrible!"

"When I regained consciousness, I found my two little boys crying."

"And your daughter?"

"Gone!" the unhappy mother cried, sobbing, in a heartrending voice. "Yes, gone. My other children told me that their father had beaten her. And besides, he threatened to kill me on the spot. Well, what do you expect? The poor child lost her head. She threw herself on me to kiss me. She also kissed her little brothers, crying all the while. And then my husband dragged her away! Ah! His evil mistress was waiting for him in the stairway. I'm sure of it!"

"And couldn't you file charges with the police superintendent?"

"At first all I could do was feel sad that Catherine was gone. But soon I felt terrible all over my body, and I couldn't walk. Alas! Heavens! What I'd been dreading finally happened. Yes, just like I said to my brother, one day my husband would beat me so badly—so badly—that I would have to go to the hospital. And then what would become of my children? And here I am today in the hospital, and I say, 'What will become of my children?'"

"Lord, there's no justice for poor people!"

"It's too expensive—too expensive for us poor folks, as my brother says," Jeanne Duport said, bitterly. "The neighbors had gone to see the police superintendent. His clerk came. Denouncing Duport didn't sit well with me, but I had to because of my daughter. The only thing I said was that he had pushed me during a quarrel I was having with him because he wanted to take away our daughter. Knocking me down didn't matter, I said, but I wanted to get Catherine back, because I feared that a wicked woman who was living with my husband was going to prostitute her."

"And what did the clerk tell you?"

"He said my husband had the right to take his daughter away because we weren't legally separated. He said it would be unfortunate if my daughter went bad because of bad influences, but that these were just suppositions and that they weren't enough to bring charges against my husband. 'There's only one thing you can do,' the clerk told me. 'You can file a civil suit requesting a legal separation, and then the fact that your husband beat you and his conduct with that horrible woman will support your suit, and they'll force him to give you back your daughter. Otherwise, he's within his rights to keep her with him.' 'But bringing suit? God, I don't have the money for that! I have my children to feed.' 'What do you want me to do about it?' said the clerk. 'That's how it is.' Yes," said Jeanne, sobbing, "he was right. That's how it is. And because that's how it is, my daughter may be a streetwalker within three months! Whereas if I had the money to file for separation from my husband, this wouldn't have happened."

"But it won't happen. Your daughter must love you so much!"

"But she's so young! At that age, they can't do much to protect themselves. And then there's fear, bad treatment, bad advice, bad examples, and the way they'll hound her to make her do wrong! My poor brother knew just what would happen. He said to me, 'Do you think that if that wicked woman and your husband determine to prostitute that girl, she won't have to go along?'[240] Good God! Poor Catherine, so sweet,

240. We remind the reader that the fathers and mothers are allowed to register their daughter on the list of prostitutes at the Bureau of Public Morals. [SN]

so loving! And I had wanted to have her take first communion vows just this year!"

"Ah! You have real troubles. And to think I was complaining," La Lorraine said as she dabbed at her eyes. "What about your other children?"

"Because of them, I did what I could to overcome the pain and keep from going to the hospital, but I couldn't hold out any longer. I'm vomiting blood three or four times a day, I have a fever that is weakening my arms and legs, and I just am in no state to work. At least if I can get better quickly in here, I'll be able to go back to my children, if they haven't already died of hunger or been jailed as beggars. With me here, who do you think is going to take care of them? Who will feed them?"

"Oh! That's terrible. Don't you have any kind neighbors?"

"They're just as poor as me, and they already have five children. Two extra children on top of that! It's a lot to ask. Still, they did promise me they'd feed them a little for one week. That's all they can do, and it's taking the bread from their mouths, and they don't have much of it to spare to begin with. That's why I have to get better in one week. Oh! Yes, better or not, I'm getting out of here all the same."

"But I just had an idea: what about that kind little workingwoman, Mademoiselle Rigolette, the one you met in prison? She would take good care of them, I'm sure."

"I thought of her, and even though the poor little thing might be living hand to mouth herself, I had a neighbor tell her about my problems. Unfortunately, she is in the country, where she's going to get married. That's what the wife of her house's doorkeeper said."

"So, in one week . . . your poor children . . . But no, your neighbors won't have the heart to kick them out."

"But what can they do? They already don't have enough to eat, and feeding my children will be taking the bread from their children's mouths. No, no, don't you see? I have to be better in one week. I've asked all the doctors who have been asking me questions since yesterday, but they've answered me, laughing, 'You'll have to ask the chief physician that question.' So when does the chief physician come in, La Lorraine?"

"Shhh! I think he's here. You're not supposed to talk while he makes his rounds," La Lorraine whispered.

Indeed, during the conversation between the two women, daylight had crept in, little by little. A tumultuous whirl of activity announced the arrival of Doctor Griffon, who soon entered the room, accompanied by his friend, Count de Saint-Remy, who, as we know, though very concerned about Madame de Fermont and her daughter, hardly expected to find the unhappy girl in the hospital.

As he entered the room, Doctor Griffon's cold, severe features seemed to light up. Glancing around him with satisfaction and authority, he answered the nuns' eager welcome with a patronizing nod.

The hard, austere face of the old Count de Saint-Remy was marked with a profound sadness. The fruitlessness of his attempts to find any trace of Madame de Fermont and the ignominious cowardice of the viscount, who had preferred a life of dishonor to death, overwhelmed him with sorrow.

"Well, then!" Doctor Griffon said triumphantly to the count. "What do you think of my hospital?"

"In truth," answered Monsieur de Saint-Remy, "I don't know why I gave in to your wishes. Nothing could be more depressing than the sight of these rooms full of sick people. From the moment I walked in, I've felt sick from it."

"Bah! In a quarter of an hour, you won't think anything of it. Philosopher that you are, you'll find a lot to observe here. And also, it was shameful that you, one of my oldest friends, were unfamiliar with this scene of my greatest glory, of my work, and that you had never seen me at work. I take great pride in my profession. Is there anything wrong with that?"

"No, certainly not. And after the excellent care you took of Fleur-de-Marie, whose life you saved, I'd do anything for you. Poor child! Her face is still so charming, even after that illness!"

"She provided me with a very curious medical phenomenon. I was thrilled to have her as a patient. By the way, how did she pass the night? Did you see her this morning before you left Asnières?"

"No, but the She-Wolf, who has been taking care of her with uncommon devotion, told me that she had slept soundly. Can we let her write anything today?"

After hesitating a moment, the doctor answered, "Yes . . . So long as the subject was not completely recovered, I was wary of the slightest emotion, the slightest intellectual stress, but now I don't see any reason she shouldn't be able to write."

"At least she can let the people who care for her know—"

"Certainly. Now, then! Have you still learned nothing new about what has happened to Madame de Fermont and her daughter?"

"Nothing," said Monsieur de Saint-Remy, sighing. "All my inquiries have yielded no results. The only hope I have is in Madame the Marquise d'Harville, who, I'm told, also cares deeply about these two unfortunate women. Perhaps she has some information that can put me on their track. Three days ago I went to see her. They told me that she would be back any day now. I wrote her about this, asking her to answer me as soon as possible."

During the conversation between Monsieur de Saint-Remy and Doctor Griffon, several groups had formed slowly around a large table that occupied the middle of the room. On this table was a register which the students assigned to the hospital, who could be recognized from their long white aprons, came over to sign, one by one, in order to mark their presence. Many more young, conscientious, eager students entered, one after the other, from outside, thus swelling Doctor Griffon's scientific cortege. The latter, having come a few minutes before his ordinary visiting time, waited for the clock to strike the hour.

"You see, my dear Saint-Remy, that my general staff is quite impressive," said Doctor Griffon with pride as he gestured toward the crowd that had assembled to hear his teaching of the practice.

"And these young people follow you to the bed of each patient?"

"That's the only reason they're here."

"But all these beds are occupied by women."

"So?"

"The presence of all these men must make them painfully embarrassed."

"Come now! A patient has no sex."

"Maybe from your perspective, but for them, modesty and shame—"

"You need to leave those beautiful notions at the door, my dear Alceste. Here we begin the experiments and studies on the living that we finish in the amphitheater on the cadaver."

"Listen, Doctor: you are the best and most honest of men. I owe you my life, and I am aware of your many excellent qualities. But the way you practice your art and your love for it make you see certain things in a way that revolts me. I'll leave you now," said Monsieur de Saint-Remy, taking a step toward the exit.

"Don't be so childish!" exclaimed Doctor Griffon, holding him back.

"No, no, there are things that make me heartsick and angry. I can see that it would be torture for me to attend you on your rounds. All right, then—I won't leave, but I'll wait for you here, next to this table."

"What a man you are, with those scruples! But I'm not letting you off that easy. I'll accept that it might be hard for you to go from bed to bed. Stay there, then, and I'll call you over for two or three cases that are really interesting."

"All right, since you insist so strongly. That will be more than enough for me."

The clock rang seven thirty. "Let's go, gentlemen," said Doctor Griffon. He began his rounds, followed by a large body of students.

As they came to the first bed in the row on the right, which had its curtains drawn, the nun said to the doctor, "Monsieur, number one died last night at four thirty in the morning."

"She lasted that long? I'm surprised. Yesterday morning, I wouldn't have thought she would have made it through the day. Has anyone claimed the body?"

"No, Doctor."

"So much the better. It's a good one. I won't do the autopsy. I'll make someone happy." Then, turning to one of the students following him, he said, "My dear Dunoyer, you have wanted a body for a long time. Your name comes first, so this one is yours."

"Ah! Monsieur! You're so kind!"

"I wish I could repay your eagerness more often, my dear friend. But put your mark on the body and take possession now. There are so many of you guys after the spoils." And the doctor moved on. The student, with the aid of a scalpel, cut a very delicate *F* and *D* (for François Dunoyer) in the arm of the late actress[241] in order to take possession of her body, as the doctor suggested.

The rounds continued. "La Lorraine," Jeanne Duport whispered to her neighbor, "what's this whole crowd of people following the doctor?"

"They're pupils and students."

"Oh, my God! Will all of those young people be there when the doctor comes to ask me questions and check me over?"

"Alas, yes!"

"But it's my chest that's the problem . . . They're not going to examine me in front of all of those men, are they?"

"Yes, yes, they have to do that. And they insist on it. I cried a lot the first time. I was dying of shame. I resisted, but they threatened to throw me out. I had to make up my mind to it. But it upset me so much that it made me much more ill. Judge for yourself: almost naked in front of so many people! It's really not an easy thing, you know?"

"I can understand in front of the doctor, if you have to—and even that's hard. But why in front of all those young men?"

"They have to learn, and they use us to teach them. What can we do? That's why we're here. That's the condition for being taken into this hospital."

"Ah! I understand," Jeanne Duport said, bitterly. "There's no getting something for nothing for people like us. Still, sometimes some things just shouldn't be. So if my poor daughter Catherine, who's fifteen years old, were to come to the hospital, would they really demand that she . . . in front of all those young men? Oh! No, I think I'd rather have her die at home."

"If she came here, she'd have to put up with it like everybody else, like

241. No one is more persuaded than we are of the knowledge and humanity of the enlightened young students enrolled as apprentices in the art of curing. We only wish the instructors who taught them would more frequently serve as examples of a compassionate tact and charitable kindness that might have such a healthy influence on the morales of their patients. [SN]

you, like me. But we need to be quiet," La Lorraine said. "If that poor young girl who is there across from you heard us—that girl they say was rich, and who's maybe never been away from her mother before—it will be her turn. Imagine how terrible and unhappy she'll feel."

"Lord, that's true! I shudder just to think of it, for her sake. Poor child!"

"Be quiet, Jeanne. Here comes the doctor!" La Lorraine said.

CHAPTER 8

MADEMOISELLE DE FERMONT

After making a brief survey of several patients whose conditions had nothing unusual or interesting to recommend them, Doctor Griffon finally came up to Jeanne Duport. At the sight of the eager crowd pushing around her bed, hungry to see and to know, to recognize and to learn, the unfortunate woman, seized with a tremor of fear and shame, wrapped herself up tightly in her bedclothes. Doctor Griffon's severe, contemplative face with its piercing gaze, his mouth always frowning in reflection, and his curt, impatient, and brusque way of speaking made Jeanne even more frightened.

"A new subject!" said the doctor as he perused the chart on which the new patient's type of illness was marked. Then he gave Jeanne a long, inquiring look. There was deep silence, during which the assistants, in imitation of the prince of science, fixed their curious gazes on the patient. In order to escape as much as possible the painful emotions all of these staring eyes wrought in her, Jeanne kept her own eyes glued to those of the doctor, whom she contemplated anxiously. After several minutes of observation, the doctor, noticing something abnormal in the yellowish tinge of the patient's eyeball, came closer to her and, with a tip of his finger, pulled up her eyelid. Silently, he examined her crystalline lens. Then several pupils, responding to a kind of silent invitation from their teacher, went up one by one to have a look at Jeanne's eye. Then the doctor began the following interrogation:

"Your name?"

"Jeanne Duport," murmured the patient, more and more terrified.

"Your age?"

"Thirty-six and a half years."

"Speak more loudly. Where were you born?"

"Paris."

"Your profession?"

"Detail needlewoman."

"Are you married?"

"Alas! Yes, monsieur," answered Jeanne with a deep sigh.

"For how long?"

"For eighteen years."

"Do you have any children?"

Here, instead of answering, the poor mother gave way to the tears she had been holding back for a long while.

"It's no good crying; you have to answer. Do you have any children?"

"Yes, monsieur. Two little boys and a girl of sixteen."

Here several questions were asked that we cannot repeat but to which Jeanne could only respond with stammered answers, and then only after several injunctions from the doctor. The unhappy woman was dying of shame, obliged as she was to answer such questions aloud in front of this large audience. The doctor, completely absorbed by his scientific concerns, didn't even notice Jeanne's painful embarrassment, and he went on:

"For how long have you been sick?"

"For four days, monsieur," said Jeanne, wiping away her tears.

"Tell us how your illness came on."

"Monsieur, the problem is . . . so many people are here . . . I really can't—"

"Come now! Where have you been all your life, my dear friend?" said the doctor, impatiently. "You don't want me to bring a confessional in here, do you? Come on, speak up. And hurry up about it."

"Good Lord, monsieur, it's just that these are family matters . . ."

"Then calm down. You're among family here—a large family, as you can see," the prince of science added. He was very cheerful this day. "Come on, let's get this finished up."

More and more intimidated, Jeanne said, stammering and hesitating over each word, "I had a fight with my husband, monsieur . . . about my children . . . I mean, about my eldest, my daughter . . . he wanted to take her away . . . Well, me, you know, monsieur, I didn't want that because of an evil woman he was living with, and who might set a bad example for my daughter. So my husband, who was drunk . . . Oh! Yes, monsieur, if not for that, he wouldn't have done it . . . My husband pushed me very hard . . . I fell, and then, a little while later, I started vomiting blood."

"Now, now, now. Your husband pushed you and you fell? You're making things prettier than they are. He certainly did more than push you. He must definitely have hit you in the stomach, several times. Maybe he even trampled you under his feet. Come on, answer! Tell the truth."

"Ah! Monsieur, I swear to you that he was drunk. Otherwise, he wouldn't have been so mean."

"Kind or mean, drunk or sober, I don't care about that, my good woman. I'm not a judge in a courtroom. I just want to get one fact straight: he knocked you down and trampled you in a rage, didn't he?"

"Alas, yes, monsieur!" said Jeanne, melting into tears. "I didn't ever give him reason to complain, all the same. I work as hard as I can and—"

"The epigastrium must hurt badly. It must feel very hot there, right?" said the doctor, interrupting Jeanne. "You must be feeling sick, run down, nauseated?"

"Yes, monsieur. I only came here as a last resort, when my strength ran out. Otherwise, I wouldn't have abandoned my children. I'm going to be very worried about them because I'm all they've got. And then Catherine . . . Ah! That's what upsets me the worst . . . If you knew—"

"Your tongue!" said Doctor Griffon, interrupting the patient again.

This command seemed so strange to Jeanne, who believed she might evoke some pity in the doctor, that she did not answer at first and stared at him in bewilderment.

"Let's see that tongue that you're so good at using," said the doctor, smiling. Then he lowered Jeanne's lower jaw with the tip of his finger. After having had his pupils take a long time successively palpating and examining the patient's tongue in order to note its color and dryness, the doctor considered things for a moment. Jeanne, overcoming her fear, exclaimed in a trembling voice, "Monsieur, I must tell you. My neighbors who are as poor as I am have agreed to take care of two of my children, but only for one week. That's already a lot. At the end of that time, I have to be back home. So I beg you, for the love of God, heal me as quickly as possible, or as much as you can, just so that I can get up and get to work. I only have a week's time, because—"

"Discolored face, complete state of prostration. However, a fairly strong, hard, frequent pulse," the doctor said imperturbably as he gestured at Jeanne. "Take note, gentlemen: oppression, heat in the epigastrium. All of these symptoms certainly indicate a hematemesis . . . which is probably complicated by hepatitis caused by domestic troubles, as the yellowish coloration of the eyeball suggests. The subject received violent blows in the regions of the epigastrium and the abdomen. The vomiting of blood is necessarily caused by some organic lesion in areas of the intestines. On that matter, I call your attention to something very curious—very curious indeed: the cadaverous openings of those who die from the disease the subject has offer singularly variable results. Often the illness, very acute and serious, carries the patient off in a very few days, and no one can find any trace of its existence. Other times, the spleen, liver, and pancreas offer more or less deep lesions. It is probable that the subject we are studying at present has suffered several of these lesions. We will thus try to find out if this is so, and you will discover if this is the case yourself by examining the patient carefully."

And with a rapid motion, Doctor Griffon, pulling the cover from the foot of the bed, uncovered Jeanne almost entirely.

We are reluctant to depict the painful struggle of this unfortunate woman, who was sobbing, overcome with shame, and imploring the doctor and his following. But in response to the doctor's threat—"We will force you to leave this hospital if you do not submit to the established protocol," a threat that was so crushing for those for whom the hospital was their last and only resort—Jeanne submitted to a public examination that lasted a long time, very long indeed, for Doctor Griffon analyzed and explained each symptom, and after that, the more studious of the assistants wanted to join theory to practice and see for themselves what the physical condition of the patient was.

As a result of this cruel scene, Jeanne felt such a violent emotion that she fell into a nervous crisis for which Doctor Griffon gave a supplementary diagnosis.

The rounds continued. Doctor Griffon soon arrived at the bed of Mademoiselle Claire de Fermont, a victim, like her mother, of Jacques Ferrand's greed. Here was a new, terrible example of the sinister consequences that ensue from embezzlement, this crime that is punished so lightly by the legal system. Mademoiselle de Fermont, wearing the tulle bonnet provided by the hospital, rested her head languidly on the bolster of her bed. One could still see, through the ravages of her illness, the traces of a very distinctive beauty on her sweet, innocent face. After a night of sharp pains, the poor child had fallen into a sort of feverish stupor, and when the doctor and his scientific cortege entered the room, the noise from their rounds had not awakened her.

"A new patient, gentlemen!" said the prince of science as he skimmed the chart that a pupil handed him. "Illness, slow, nervous fever . . . Damn!" the doctor exclaimed with an expression of deep satisfaction. "If the intern on duty is not mistaken in his diagnosis, we have a real windfall here. I've been hoping for a slow, nervous fever to come by for a long time, since it's not generally an illness we encounter in the poor. These ailments are almost always the result of grave disturbances in the patient's social position, and it goes without saying that the higher the position, the more serious the disturbance. As to the ailment itself, it's one of the most remarkable for its particular characteristics. It goes back to the earliest antiquity: the writings of Hippocrates leave no doubt in this regard, and it's very clear. This fever, as I said, almost always has its cause in the most violent troubles. Now, trouble is as old as time. And yet, and this is really singular, before the eighteenth century, this illness had not been described with precision by any author. It was Huxham, who honored medicine in so many ways in that era, it was Huxham, as I was saying, who was the first to write a monograph on nervous fever, a monograph that has become a classic.[242] And yet, it's an illness of the old school," added the doctor, laughing. "Ha, ha, ha! It belongs to that grand, ancient, and illustrious family *febris* whose origin is lost in the mists of time. But let's not get too excited. Let's see if we have the good fortune to possess a sample of this curious ailment. It would be doubly desirable if we did, for I have wanted for a long time to try an internal use of phosphorus. Yes, gentlemen," said the doctor as he heard a tremor of curiosity spread through his audience. "Yes, gentlemen, phosphorus. It's an interesting experiment and I would like to try it. It is quite daring! But *audaces fortuna juvat*[243] . . . and this would be an excellent opportunity for us. We will first examine the subject to see if she has all over her body, and principally on her chest, the miliary eruption that is so symptomatic, according to Huxham, and you will discover for yourselves, by palpating the subject, the kind of roughness that this eruption causes. But let's not count our chickens before they've hatched," said the prince of science, decidedly in high spirits.

He shook Mademoiselle de Fermont's shoulder lightly to wake her up. The girl shivered and opened her big eyes, sunken from her illness.

Imagine her shock, her fear. While a crowd of men were surrounding her bed and devouring her with their eyes, she felt the hand of the doctor lift the bedsheets and slide into the bed to find her hand and take her pulse. Mademoiselle de Fermont, pulling all of her strength together in a cry of anguish and terror, cried out, "Mother! Help! Mother!"

By a chance that was virtually providential, at the moment Mademoiselle de Fermont's cries made the old Count de Saint-Remy jump out of his chair, for he recognized her voice, the door of the room opened and a young woman, dressed in mourning, entered it quickly, accompanied by the director of the clinic. This woman was the Marquise d'Harville. "Please, monsieur," she said to the director with the greatest anxiety. "Take me to Mademoiselle de Fermont."

"Please be so kind as to follow me, Madame la Marquise," answered the director, respectfully. "The young lady is in bed number seventeen in this room."

"Unfortunate child! Here! Here!" said Madame d'Harville as she wiped her tears away. "Oh! This is horrible!"

The marquise, preceded by the director, rapidly approached the

242. John Huxham (1692–1768) was an English physician. His most famous work, published in 1755, was *An Essay on Fevers and Their Various Kinds*. Doctor Griffon probably has this work in mind. [TN]

243. Fortune favors the bold (Latin in the original). [TN]

group assembled by Mademoiselle de Fermont's bed when they heard the following words pronounced with indignation: "I am telling you that this is a vile assault you are committing. You will kill her, monsieur."

"But, my dear Saint-Remy, listen to me for a moment—"

"I repeat, monsieur, that your conduct is atrocious. I regard Mademoiselle de Fermont as my daughter. I forbid you to touch her. I am going to have her taken out of here immediately."

"But, my dear friend, this is a very rare case of slow nervous fever. I wanted to try phosphorus on it. This is a once-in-a-lifetime opportunity. Promise me at least that I may attend her, wherever you take her, since you're depriving my clinic of such a precious patient."

"If you weren't a madman, you'd be a monster," said Count de Saint-Remy.

Clémence heard these words with growing anxiety, but the crowd was so dense around the bed that the director had to say loudly, "Make way, gentlemen, if you please; make way for Madame la Marquise d'Harville, who has come to see number seventeen."

At these words, the pupils stood back with as much eagerness as respectful admiration, seeing the charming face of Clémence, which was turning red from high emotion.

"Madame d'Harville!" Count de Saint-Remy exclaimed as he pushed the doctor roughly aside and rushed over toward Clémence. "Ah! God has sent one of his angels. Madame, I knew that you cared about these two unfortunate women. You had better luck than I, since you have found them, whereas in my case it's pure chance that brought me here—just in time to witness a scene of unheard-of barbarism. Unhappy child! Look, madame . . . look. And you, gentlemen, in the name of your daughters or your sisters, have pity on a girl of sixteen, I beg of you. Leave her alone with Madame and these kind nuns. When she has regained consciousness, I'll have her taken away from here."

"All right, then. I will sign her discharge notice!" the doctor exclaimed. "But I will be right on her heels. I will stick to you like glue. This patient belongs to me. And you can do whatever you want, but I will attend this case. I will not risk giving her phosphorus, of course, but I will spend nights watching over her if necessary, just as I spent nights watching over you, you ingrate, Saint-Remy. This fever is as curious as yours was. The fevers are two sisters with each the same claim on my interest."

"You cursed man, why are you so good at what you do?" said the count, knowing that he could not indeed place Mademoiselle de Fermont in more capable hands.

"Well, heavens! It's very simple!" whispered the doctor. "I am good at what I do because I study, because I experiment, because I take risks and study my subjects carefully—no pun intended. Now, then! I'll have my slow fever, right, you old curmudgeon?"

"Yes, but is this girl in a condition to be moved?"

"Certainly."

"Then, for the love of God, go away."

"Come along, gentlemen," said the prince of science. "Our clinic will be deprived of a precious study, but I'll keep you all abreast."

And Doctor Griffon, accompanied by his audience, continued his rounds, leaving Monsieur de Saint-Remy and Madame d'Harville with Mademoiselle de Fermont.

CHAPTER 9

FLEUR-DE-MARIE

During the scene we have just recounted, Mademoiselle de Fermont, still unconscious, had been left to the tender care of Clémence and the two nuns. One of them held the pale, heavy head of the girl while Madame d'Harville, leaning over the bed, used her handkerchief to wipe away the cold sweat that bathed the patient's head. Deeply moved, Monsieur de Saint-Remy was contemplating this touching sight when a gloomy thought crossed his mind. He went over to Clémence and asked her in a whisper, "What about this unfortunate girl's mother, madame?"

The marquise turned back to Monsieur de Saint-Remy and answered him, with heartbreaking sadness, "This child no longer has a mother, monsieur."

"Good God! Dead!"

"I learned last night when I came back what Madame de Fermont's address was and of how desperately ill she was. I got to her with my doctor at one o'clock in the morning. Ah! Monsieur! What a sight! Poverty in all its horror, and no hope of saving that poor, dying mother!"

"Oh! Her agony must have been appalling, if she was thinking of her daughter!"

"Her last word was, 'My daughter!'"

"What a death! My God! A mother like her, so loving, so devoted. It's horrifying!"

One of the nuns came to interrupt the conversation between Monsieur de Saint-Remy and Madame d'Harville, saying to the latter, "The young lady is very weak. She can hardly understand what is happening. Soon she may regain consciousness, to some degree. This shock has shaken her badly. If you are not afraid to stay here, madame, while we wait for the patient to return to consciousness, I can offer you my chair."

"Yes, give it to me, please, give it to me," said Clémence, sitting next to the bed. "I will not leave Mademoiselle de Fermont's side. I want her to see at least one friendly face when she opens her eyes. Then I will bring her to my home, since, fortunately, the doctor thinks we can move her without any danger."

"Ah, madame! May you be blessed for your good deeds," said Monsieur de Saint-Remy. "But forgive me for not yet having told you my name. So many troubles, so much emotion. I am Count de Saint-Remy, madame. Madame de Fermont's husband was my closest friend. I lived in Angers. I left that city because I was anxious when I didn't receive any news from those two noble and worthy women. They had until then lived in that city, and I heard that they were completely destitute. Their state was all that much more painful because, until then, their lives had been comfortable ones."

"But, monsieur, you don't know the whole story. Madame de Fermont was the victim of the most vile theft."

"Was it her solicitor? That suspicion had crossed my mind."

"That man was a monster, monsieur! Alas! This was not the only crime he committed. But fortunately," said Clémence with exaltation as she thought of Rodolphe, "a divine intelligence has brought him to justice, and I could close Madame de Fermont's eyes reassuring her as to her daughter's future. Her death was less cruel, at least to that extent."

"I can see how that could happen. Knowing that her daughter would be under the care of someone like you, madame, my poor friend must have died more peacefully."

"Not only will I now always care what happens to Mademoiselle de Fermont, but her fortune will also be returned to her."

"Her fortune? How? The solicitor?"

"He was forced to return the money that he had appropriated to himself by means of a horrible crime."

"A crime?"

"That man had killed Madame de Fermont's brother in order to make it seem as if that unfortunate man had committed suicide after having squandered his sister's fortune."

"That's horrible! It's really beyond belief! And yet, because of the suspicions I had regarding that solicitor, I always had vague doubts as to whether that was really a suicide, for Renneville was honor and loyalty itself. And the sum that the solicitor returned?"

"It has been deposited with a venerable father, the parish priest of Bonne-Nouvelle. It will be restored to Mademoiselle de Fermont."

"This restitution is not enough for human justice, madame! The scaffold calls out for that solicitor, for he didn't commit just one murder, but two. The death of Madame de Fermont and the sufferings that her daughter is enduring in this hospital bed were caused by that wretch's vile embezzlement!"

"And that wretch committed another murder that was just as horrifying and just as atrociously plotted."

"What do you mean, madame?"

"If he managed to get rid of Madame de Fermont's brother by staging a suicide, in order to keep himself safe from the law, a few days ago he got rid of an unfortunate girl he wanted to make disappear by having her drowned. He was certain that her death would be considered an accident."

Monsieur de Saint-Remy gave a start, looked at Madame d'Harville with surprise, thinking of Fleur-de-Marie, and exclaimed, "Ah! Heavens, madame, what a strange coincidence!"

"What is it, monsieur?"

"That girl! Where did he try to drown her?"

"In the Seine . . . near Asnières, I was told."

"That's her! That's her!" Monsieur de Saint-Remy exclaimed.

"Who are you talking about, monsieur?"

"It's the girl the monster wanted to get rid of."

"Fleur-de-Marie!"

"You know her, madame?"

"Poor child, I loved her dearly. Ah, if you only knew, monsieur, how beautiful and touching she was. But how did it all happen?"

"Doctor Griffon and I gave her first aid."

"First aid? To her? Where?"

"On the Scavenger's Island, when they rescued her."

"Rescued her? Fleur-de-Marie, rescued?"

"By a good creature who, at the risk of her own life, pulled her out of the Seine. But what's wrong, madame?"

"Ah, monsieur! I still don't dare to believe in such happiness. I'm afraid to be taken in by some mistake yet once more. I beg you, tell me: what does this girl look like?"

"She's very beautiful, with the face of an angel."

"Does she have big blue eyes and blond hair?"

"Yes, madame."

"And when they tried to drown her, was she with an older woman?"

"Indeed, when she was able to speak again, which was only yesterday (for she's still quite frail), she told us that. An old woman was with her."

"Praise God!" exclaimed Clémence, clasping her hands together with fervor. "I can tell him that his protégée is still alive![244] How happy he will be, especially after his last letter when he wrote to me of that poor

244. Madame d'Harville, having arrived only the day before, still did not know that Rodolphe had discovered that Songbird (whom he believed to be dead) was his daughter. A few days earlier, the prince, upon writing to the marquise, had informed her of the latest crimes of the solicitor as well as the restitutions he had forced him to make. Monsieur Badinot's work had led to the discovery of Madame de Fermont's address on the passage de la Brasserie, and Rodolphe informed Madame d'Harville of it as soon as he knew. [SN]

child with such bitter sorrow! I'm sorry, monsieur! But if you knew the joy I feel because of what you've just told me, and the joy it will bring to a person who loved and protected Fleur-de-Marie even more than I did! But, please, tell me: where is she right now?"

"Near Asnières, in the home of one of the doctors at this hospital, Doctor Griffon, who, in spite of some deplorable eccentricities, is, in many ways, an excellent man. Fleur-de-Marie was carried to his home, and since then he has showered her with the most assiduous care."

"And is she completely out of danger?"

"Yes, madame, but only for the past two or three days. And today she will be allowed to write to her protectors."

"Oh, that will be my job, monsieur! Or rather, it will be my pleasure to take her back to those who, thinking her dead, have felt such bitter sorrow."

"I can easily understand such sorrow, madame, for it is impossible to know Fleur-de-Marie without falling under the charm of that angelic creature. Her grace and sweetness exercise an indefinable power over everyone who comes near her. The woman who saved her, and who has watched over her day and night as she would watch over her own child, is courageous and devoted, but her character is so passionate that they've nicknamed her the She-Wolf. Imagine! Well, a single word from Fleur-de-Marie is enough to stop her in her tracks. I saw her sob and cry out in despair when, after a troubling attack of fever, Doctor Griffon had almost given up on Fleur-de-Marie's life."

"That doesn't surprise me. I know the She-Wolf."

"You, madame?" said Monsieur de Saint-Remy, surprised. "You know the She-Wolf?"[245]

"Indeed, you must be surprised to hear that, monsieur," said the marquise, smiling sweetly, for Clémence was happy—oh, so happy—at the thought of the sweet surprise she had in store for the prince. How intoxicated would she have been if she knew that it was a daughter whom he believed to be dead that she was going to bring back to Rodolphe! "Ah, monsieur," she said to Monsieur de Saint-Remy, "this is such a great day for me that I would like it to be as wonderful for others as well. It seems to me that there must be a lot of honest people fallen on hard times here who could use a helping hand. Doing that would be a worthy way to celebrate the excellent news you have given me." Then, turning to the nun who had just given a few spoonfuls of some medicine to Mademoiselle de Fermont to drink, she said, "Well, Sister? Is she coming to?"

245. During her visit to Saint-Lazare, Madame d'Harville had heard about the She-Wolf from Madame Armand, the supervisor. [SN]

"Not yet, madame. She is so weak. Poor young lady! It's hard to feel her pulse."

"I'll wait for her to be in a state to be moved by carriage before I take her. But tell me, Sister: among all of these unfortunate patients, do you know of any who are especially worthy of care and pity, of any to whom I could be of service before I leave this hospital?"

"Ah, madame, you must have been sent by God," said the nun. "Over there," she said, pointing at the bed of Bitters's sister, "is a poor woman who is very ill and very much to be pitied. She only came here when she couldn't hold out any longer. She mourns constantly because she was obliged to abandon her two little children for whom she is the sole support. She was saying a moment ago to the doctor that she wanted to leave whether she was cured or not in a week, because her neighbors had promised to keep her children only for a week, after which they wouldn't be able to take care of them any longer."

"Take me to her bed, I beg you, Sister," said Madame d'Harville, getting up and following the nun.

Jeanne Duport, hardly recovered from the violent attack brought on by Doctor Griffon's questions, had not noticed Clémence d'Harville's arrival in the room of the hospital. How great was her astonishment when the marquise, raising the curtains on her bed, said to her, looking at her with a gaze full of compassion and kindness, "Oh, you good mother, you do not need to worry about your children. I will take care of them. Don't worry about anything but getting better so you can get back to them as soon as possible!"

Jeanne Duport thought she must be dreaming. In the very spot in which Doctor Griffon and his following of students had forced her to undergo such a cruel examination, she now saw a ravishingly beautiful young woman speaking words of pity, solace, and hope.

Bitters's sister was so moved that she could not say a single word. She merely clasped her hands together as if she were praying, looking at her unknown benefactress in adoration.

"Jeanne! Jeanne!" La Lorraine whispered. "Answer the kind lady!" Then she added, turning to the marquise, "Ah! Madame, you are saving her life! She would die of despair, thinking of her children whom she considered as virtually abandoned already. Isn't that true, Jeanne?"

"As I said, you can relax, dear mother. You have no need to worry," the marquise said, pressing Jeanne Duport's burning hand in her own little, delicate white hands. "Relax and don't worry any more about your children. You can even leave this hospital today, if you want. You will be taken care of at your own home. You'll have everything you need. That way, you won't have to leave your dear children. If your lodgings are unhealthy or too small, we can find you better ones right away so you can be in one room and your children in another. You will have a kind sick nurse who will take care of them while caring for you. Finally, when you're back on your feet, if you are out of work, I'll put you in a position to wait until you can find some. And from today onward, I guarantee your children's future!"

"Oh! Good God, is this really happening? So cherubs really come down from the sky like in the books in church!" Jeanne Duport said, trembling, unable to think, hardly daring to look at her benefactress. "Why are you being so good to me? What have I done to deserve this? It can't be possible! Is it true I can get out of this hospital where I've already wept and suffered so much? And never leave my children? And have a sick nurse? It's like a miracle from God!"

And, indeed, the poor woman was speaking the truth. If people knew how sweet and easy it is to perform these miracles frequently, and at a very low price! Alas! For some unfortunate people who are abandoned or rejected by everyone, immediate, unhoped-for aid, accompanied by kind words and tender, charitable glances, must truly seem to have the supernatural quality of a miracle! How could someone like Jeanne Duport hope or even dream that the good fortune Madame d'Harville promised had any likelihood of befalling her?

"This is no miracle, good mother," Clémence answered, deeply moved. "What I am doing for you," she added, blushing slightly at the memory of Rodolphe, "what I am doing for you has been inspired by a generous mind who has taught me to have sympathy for those who suffer. He is the one you must thank and bless."

"Ah! Madame, I will bless you and yours!" Jeanne Duport said, weeping. "I beg your pardon for expressing myself so badly, but I am not accustomed to experiencing such great joy. This is the first time such a thing has ever happened to me."

"Well! Look, Jeanne," said La Lorraine, who was moved. "There are Rigolettes and Songbirds among the rich, too. They're grander, it's true, but when it comes to having good hearts, they're just the same!"

Madame d'Harville turned around in surprise toward La Lorraine when she heard her say these two names. "You know Songbird and a young workingwoman named Rigolette?" Clémence asked her.

"Yes, madame. Songbird, a good little angel, did for me last year—well, really, according to her small means—what you are doing for Jeanne. Yes, madame! Oh! It does me such good to say and repeat it before everyone! Songbird took me out of a basement in which I had just given birth on the straw. That dear little angel put me up, me and my child, in a room in which there was a good bed and a crib. Songbird paid for those things out of pure charity; she hardly knew me and she was poor herself. Isn't that a beautiful thing to do, madame?" La Lorraine said in exaltation.

"Oh, yes! The charity of the poor for the poor is something great and holy," Clémence said, her eyes moist with sweet tears.

"It was the same thing with Mademoiselle Rigolette, who, according to her means as a little workingwoman," La Lorraine said, "offered to help Jeanne out a few days ago."

"What an incredible coincidence!" Clémence said to herself, more and more moved, since each of these two names, Songbird and Rigolette, reminded her of Rodolphe's noble acts. "And you, my child, what can I do for you?" she said to La Lorraine. "I would like for the names you have just mentioned to bring you good luck."

"Thank you, madame," La Lorraine said with a smile of bitter resignation. "I had a child, but she's dead. I have a terminal lung disease, so I don't need anything."

"What a terrible thought! At your age, so young? There's always something to try."

"Oh, no, madame, I know my fate. I'm not complaining! I've already seen a woman with my lung disease die last night in here. You die very quietly, you know? I thank you, anyway, for your kindness."

"You're exaggerating your condition."

"I'm not wrong, madame, for I can really feel it. But since you're so kind . . . a great lady like yourself is all-powerful . . ."

"Speak. Tell me what I can do for you."

"I had asked Jeanne to do me a favor, but now, since she's leaving, thanks to God and you . . ."

"Can't I do this favor for you myself?"

"Certainly, madame. A word from you to the sisters or to the doctor would take care of everything."

"Whatever I need to say, I'll say it, of that you may be sure. What does it concern?"

"Since I saw the actress die tormented by the fear of being cut into pieces after her death, I've had the same fear. Jeanne had promised me to claim my body and have me buried."

"Ah! That's horrible!" said Clémence, shivering from dread. "Coming here makes one see that, for the poor, there is still misery and terror, even beyond the grave!"

"Forgive me, madame," La Lorraine said, timidly. "For a great, rich, happy lady such as you deserve to be, this is a very depressing request. I shouldn't have made it!"

"On the contrary, I thank you for making it, my child. It tells me of a new kind of misery I did not know of before, and I will put this knowledge to good use. Rest assured, although your end may be very far off in the distance, when it does come, you will be certain to rest in holy ground."

"Oh! Thank you, madame!" La Lorraine exclaimed. "Dare I ask your permission to kiss your hand?"

Clémence presented her hand to La Lorraine's parched lips. "Oh, thank you, madame! I will have someone to love and bless until the end, along with Songbird, and I won't be sad anymore about what will happen to me after I die!"

This detachment from life and these fears concerning matters beyond the grave had moved Madame d'Harville painfully. Leaning over and speaking into the ear of the nun, who had come to let her know that Mademoiselle de Fermont had completely regained consciousness, she said to her, "Is the condition of this young woman really so dire?" With a nod, she indicated La Lorraine's bed.

"Alas! Yes, madame. La Lorraine's condition is fatal. She might not even have a week left to live!"

A half hour later, Madame d'Harville, accompanied by Monsieur de Saint-Remy, took the young orphan back to her home. She had hidden her mother's death from the girl. That very day, one of Madame d'Harville's agents, after having visited the miserable lodgings of Jeanne Duport on rue de la Barillerie and collected strong testimonials on her behalf, immediately rented two large rooms and a very well ventilated office on the quai de l'École. He furnished the modest but healthful abode in two hours, and, thanks to the instantaneous resources of the Temple market, Jeanne Duport was moved that very evening to this residence, where she found her children and an excellent sick nurse. The same agent was charged with claiming La Lorraine's body and having her buried when she succumbed to her illness.

Once she had brought Mademoiselle de Fermont to her home and gotten her settled, Madame d'Harville left immediately for Asnières, accompanied by Monsieur de Saint-Remy, in order to collect Fleur-de-Marie and take her to Rodolphe's home.

CHAPTER 10

HOPE

The first days of spring were approaching. The sun was beginning to give off more warmth, the sky was clear and blue, and the air was mild. Fleur-de-Marie, supported on the She-Wolf's arm, was testing her strength with a walk through the garden of Doctor Griffon's little house. The invigorating heat of the sun and the exertion of walking colored Songbird's pale, gaunt face with a rosy tint. Her peasant's clothing had been torn when she had received first aid, so she was now wearing a dress of deep blue merino wool in a smock style, merely tied at her narrow, delicate waist by a woolen cord.

"What wonderful sun!" she said to the She-Wolf as she paused at the foot of a bower of green trees with a southern exposure that surrounded a stone bench. "Would you like to sit here a moment, She-Wolf?"

"Why are you asking me if I'd like to?" Martial's wife answered brusquely, shrugging her shoulders. Then, taking a shawl of silk floss off her neck, she folded it in four, knelt down, put it over the slightly wet sand of the path, and said to Songbird, "Put your feet on that."

"But, She-Wolf," Fleur-de-Marie said, having recognized what her companion intended to do too late to stop her, "She-Wolf, you're going to ruin your shawl."

"No arguments. The ground is cool," the She-Wolf said. And then, taking Fleur-de-Marie's little feet authoritatively in her hands, she put them on the shawl.

"You spoil me too much, She-Wolf."

"Yeah—and you don't really deserve it. You always complain about whatever I'm trying to do for your own good. Aren't you tired? We've been walking for a good half hour. The clock just rang noon in Asnières."

"I'm a little worn out. But I can feel that this walk has done me good."

"You see? You wore yourself out. So why couldn't you have asked to sit down earlier?"

"Don't scold me. I didn't realize I was so tired. It's so nice to be able to walk when you've been laid up in bed for so long. It's so nice to see the sun, the trees, and the countryside when you thought you'd never see them again!"

"The fact is that you were in critical condition for two days. Poor

Songbird. Yes, we can tell you that now. We didn't think you were going to make it."

"And do you know what, She-Wolf? When I realized I was underwater, in spite of myself I remembered that a mean woman who had tormented me when I was little always used to threaten to throw me to the fish. Later, she had wanted to drown me again.[246] So I said to myself, 'I'm so unlucky. It's fate. I can't escape it.'"

"Poor Songbird. That was the last thought you had when you felt you were dying?"

"Oh, no!" said Fleur-de-Marie with exaltation. "When I thought I was dying, my last thought was for the man I consider to be like God. And when I felt myself coming back to life, my first thought went up to him."

"It's a pleasure to do something nice for you, because you never forget it."

"Oh! No! It's so good to go to sleep feeling grateful and to wake up that way, too!"

"That's why people would walk through fire for you."

"Kind She-Wolf . . . Well, you know, I can tell you that one of the things that make me so happy to be alive is the hope of bringing you some happiness. I want to keep the promise I made you. You remember our castles in the air when we were at Saint-Lazare?"

"As for that, there will be plenty of time for it later. Seeing you here on your feet, I've earned my keep, as my man says."

"If only Count de Saint-Remy would tell me soon that the doctor says it's all right to write to Madame Georges! She must be so worried! And Monsieur Rodolphe might be, too!" Fleur-de-Marie added as she lowered her eyes and blushed again at the thought of her God. "Maybe they think I'm dead!"

"Just like the people who tried to drown you, poor little one. Oh! Those criminals!"

"You still don't think it was an accident, then, She-Wolf?"

"An accident? Yes, 'accidents,' that's what the Martials call them. When I say the Martials, I'm not including my man, for he's not one of that family, not him—no more than François or Amandine will ever be."

"But why would anyone want to see me dead? I've never hurt anyone, and no one knows me."

"All the same, if the Martials are big enough scoundrels to drown someone, they're not stupid enough to do it without having a good reason. Something the widow said in prison to my man proves I'm right."

"So he went to see his mother, that terrible woman?"

246. In one of Red-Arm's submerged caverns on the Champs-Élysées. [SN]

"Yes. He has no more hope for her, nor for Calabash or Nicolas. The authorities had discovered plenty to charge them with, but that lousy Nicolas, in the hopes of saving his own life, accused his own mother and sister of another murder. That finished things for all of them. The lawyer has no hopes for any of them. The legal authorities say they want to make an example of them."

"Ah! That's horrifying! It's almost an entire family!"

"Yes, unless Nicolas manages to escape. He's in the same prison as a monstrous criminal called the Skeleton who's putting together a plan to escape, him and some others. It's Nicolas who had a released prisoner tell Martial this, 'cause my man was still weak enough to go and see his lousy brother at La Force. So, encouraged by this visit, this wretch—may he rot in hell—had the effrontery to arrange for someone to tell my man that he might escape at any moment and that Martial should get money and clothes for a disguise ready with Old Micou."

"Your Martial has such a good heart!"

"As good a heart as you could ever ask for, Songbird. But the devil take me if I let my man help a murderer who wanted to kill him! Martial won't denounce the escape plot, and that's help enough for them. Anyway, now that you're healthy again, Songbird, we're going to leave—me, my man, and the children—to go on our tour of France. We will never set foot again in Paris. It really hurt Martial being called the son of the guillotined man. How will he feel now that his mother, brother, and sister all went the same way?"

"Wait at least until I've spoken about you to Monsieur Rodolphe, if I get to see him again. You've returned to the good. I said that I would get you rewarded for that, and I want to keep my word. Otherwise, how could I possibly ever repay you? You saved my life, and during my illness you showered me with care."

"Exactly! Now it would seem as if I did it because I wanted something if I let you ask your protectors for something for me. You're alive . . . like I said, that's my pay for that day's work."

"Good She-Wolf . . . don't worry. It's not a matter of your self-interest but of my gratitude."

"Hey, listen!" said the She-Wolf suddenly upon standing up. "It sounds like the noise of a carriage. Yes, yes, it's coming closer. Look, there it is. Didn't you see it pass by the gates? There's a woman inside."

"Oh, heavens!" exclaimed Fleur-de-Marie with great emotion. "I think I recognize—"

"Who is it, then?"

"A young, pretty lady I met in Saint-Lazare who was very good to me."

"So she knows that you're here?"

"I don't know, but she knows the person I'm always telling you about, the one who, if he wishes—and he will wish it, I hope—can make our castles in the air from prison come true."

"A position for my man as a gamekeeper, with a cabin for us in the middle of the woods," said the She-Wolf with a sigh. "All of that is just a bunch of fairy tales. It's too good to be true. It could never happen."

The sound of rapid steps could be heard behind the arbor. François and Amandine, who, thanks to the kindness of Count de Saint-Remy, had not left the She-Wolf's side, ran up to them, out of breath, crying, "She-Wolf! There's a pretty lady here with Monsieur de Saint-Remy! They want to see Fleur-de-Marie right away!"

"I wasn't mistaken!" said Songbird.

Almost at that very moment, Monsieur de Saint-Remy appeared, accompanied by Madame d'Harville. Hardly had she recognized Fleur-de-Marie when she cried out, running toward her and hugging her tenderly in her arms, "Poor, dear child! Here you are! Ah! You're alive! Miraculously rescued from a horrible death . . . How happy I am to find you! Just like all your friends, I thought you were dead, and I was so sad about it!"

"I am so happy to see you again, too, madame, for I never forgot how kind you were to me," said Fleur-de-Marie, responding to Madame d'Harville's tender caresses with charming grace and modesty.

"Ah! You don't know the surprise, the mad joy in store for your friends, who weep for you so bitterly at this very moment."

Taking the She-Wolf, who had been standing a distance from her, by the hand, Fleur-de-Marie said to Madame d'Harville as she introduced her, "Since my health is so dear to my benefactors, madame, permit me to ask you to show the same goodness to my companion, who risked her own life to rescue me."

"Don't worry, my child. Your friends will show the good She-Wolf that they know they owe her for their happiness in seeing you alive."

The She-Wolf, blushing and embarrassed, unable either to speak a word or even to look Madame d'Harville in the eye, for she was very intimidated in the presence of such a dignified woman, could not hide her astonishment at hearing Clémence pronounce her name.

"But we don't have a moment to lose," said the marquise. "I'm dying of impatience to take you away, Fleur-de-Marie. I've brought a shawl along in my carriage, as well as a very warm coat. Come, come, my child." Then, turning to the count, she said, "Will you be so good as to give my address to this courageous woman so she can say her good-byes tomorrow to Fleur-de-Marie? That way, you'll have no choice but to come to see us," added Madame d'Harville, speaking to the She-Wolf.

"Oh, madame! I will certainly be there," the latter answered, "since it will be in order to bid Songbird farewell. It would be too painful for me not to be able to kiss her one more time."

A few minutes later, Madame d'Harville and Songbird were on their way to Paris.

After having witnessed the death of Jacques Ferrand, who was so terribly punished for his crimes, Rodolphe had gone back to his home in inexpressible dejection. After a long and painful night of insomnia, he had sent for Sir Walter Murph in order to confide in him the crushing discovery he had made the day before regarding Fleur-de-Marie.

The worthy squire was staggered by the news. More than anyone, he could understand and share in the immensity of the prince's pain. The latter, pale and overwhelmed, his eyes red from recently shed tears, had just made his painful revelation known to Murph. "Have courage," said the squire, wiping his eyes, for, in spite of his phlegmatic character, he too had wept. "Yes, have courage, Your Lordship! Much courage! I won't offer you vain consolations. This pain must be incurable."

"You are right. What I felt yesterday is nothing compared to what I feel today."

"Yesterday, Your Lordship, you were merely stunned by the blow, but every day you will find it more and more painful. So you must be strong. The future is sad—very sad."

"And then again, yesterday, the contempt and horror I felt for that woman . . . But God have mercy on her! She is before Him now. Yesterday, the surprise, hatred, and shock—all of those violent passions kept down these outbursts of loving despair. But I can't hold them in any longer. I could hardly weep then. At least in your company, I can . . . So you see . . . I have no strength left . . . I'm weak; forgive me. More tears . . . again . . . forever . . . Oh, my child! My poor child!"

"Weep, Your Lordship, weep! Alas! Nothing can make up for this loss."

"And so much atrocious misery I would have wanted to make her forget!" Rodolphe exclaimed in a heartrending voice. "After all she suffered! To think of the fate that awaited her!"

"Perhaps the change might have been too sudden for the unfortunate girl, given how many cruel trials she had already been through?"

"Oh, no, no! Really, if you knew how carefully, how tactfully I would have told her about the circumstances of her birth! How gently I would have prepared her for that revelation! It would have been so simple, so easy. Oh! If that were all I had to do!" added the prince with a heartbreaking smile. "You see, I would have been perfectly calm. It would hardly have been awkward at all. I would have gotten down on my knees before that beloved child and said to her, 'You whose life has been such torture up to now, now be happy, forever happy. You are my daughter.' But no," said Rodolphe, recovering himself. "No. That would have been too sudden, too unexpected. Yes, I would have been very calm and self-contained, and I would have told her calmly, 'My child, you need to know something that will astonish you. Heavens, yes! Can you believe that we have discovered who your family is? Your father exists, and your father is . . . me.'"

Here, the prince interrupted himself once again. "No, no! It's still too sudden, too abrupt. But I can't help it. That revelation just comes immediately to my lips. It demands so much self-control. You understand, my friend, don't you? To be there, in front of your daughter, and to have to hold yourself back!" Then, letting himself be carried away by a new burst of despair, Rodolphe exclaimed, "But what's the good of all these pointless words? I will never have anything to tell her. Oh! The thing that's most horrible, horrible even to think about—you see?—is that I had my daughter right next to me for a whole day. Yes, for that whole day that will be forever both cursed and sacred, when I brought her to the farm, that day on which the treasures of her angelic soul were revealed to me in all their purity! I was there when that adorable creature awoke, and nothing in my heart said to me, 'She's your daughter!' Nothing, nothing! How blind, barbarous, and stupid I was! I had no idea. Oh! I was unworthy of being a father!"

"But, Your Lordship—"

"But when you take it all together," said the prince, "wasn't it my responsibility to never leave her? Yes or no? Why didn't I adopt her? I mourned my own daughter so. Why, instead of sending that unfortunate child to live with Madame Georges, did I not keep her with me? Then, today all I would have to do would be to hold my arms out to her. Why didn't I do that? Why? Ah! Because one never does more than half the good one ought to do, because one doesn't appreciate the world's wonders until they're gone forever . . . Because instead of raising this admirable girl up right away to her proper position—she, who in spite of poverty and abandonment was, in spirit and at heart, greater and more noble perhaps than the advantages of birth and education could ever have made her—I thought I was doing a lot for her by placing her on a farm, with good people, as I would have done for the first interesting beggar girl who crossed my path. It's my fault. It's my fault. If I'd done that, she wouldn't be dead. Oh! Yes, I have been punished. I deserved it. A bad son . . . a bad father!"

Murph knew that such sorrows are inconsolable. He remained silent.

After a rather long silence, Rodolphe went on, in a different voice. "I can't stay here. Paris is odious to me. Tomorrow I will leave."

"You are right, Your Lordship."

"We will make a detour. I'll stop at the Bouqueval farm. I'll go and stay for a few hours in the bedroom in which my daughter spent the only happy days of her sad life. There, with pious care, I'll gather together everything that remains of her: from the books she was using to learn to read, the notebooks in which she wrote, the clothes she wore, everything down to the furniture, to the tapestries in her bedroom, of which I'll take an exact design. And in Gerolstein, in the private park in which I raised a monument to the memory of the father I insulted, I'll build a little house in which I'll re-create her room. I'll go there to mourn my daughter. Of those two funereal monuments, one will remind me of my crime against my father, and the other of the punishment I received for it through my child."

After another silence, Rodolphe added, "So, make everything ready for tomorrow morning."

Wishing to distract the prince from his dark thoughts for a moment, Murph said to him, "Everything will be ready, Your Lordship, but you're forgetting that tomorrow the marriage of Madame Georges's son and Rigolette is to take place. Not only have you ensured Germain's future and given his fiancée a magnificent dowry, but you've promised them that you would be their witness. Only then were they to know the name of their benefactor."

"It's true, I made that promise. They're at the farm, so I can't go there tomorrow without attending their wedding. But I must confess, I won't have the heart to go through with it."

"When you see how happy those young people are, you may get a bit of relief from your sorrows."

"No, no, suffering is solitary and selfish. Tomorrow you will go and make my excuses and stand in for me with them. You'll ask Madame Georges to gather everything that belonged to my daughter. We'll have her room sketched and they'll send it to me in Germany."

"Will you leave without seeing Madame the Marquise d'Harville, also, Your Lordship?"

At the thought of Clémence, Rodolphe started. This sincere love was still alive in him, ardent and deep. Yet in this moment, it was drowned, so to speak, under the wave of bitterness with which his heart was inundated. In a peculiar contradiction, the prince felt that only Madame d'Harville's tender affection could help him bear the unhappiness that had befallen him, and he reproached himself for this thought on the grounds that it was unworthy of the seriousness of his paternal grief.

"I will leave without seeing Madame d'Harville," said Rodolphe. "A few days ago I wrote to her of the grief I felt at Fleur-de-Marie's death. When she learns that Fleur-de-Marie was my daughter, she will understand that there are some kinds of grief, or rather some fateful punishments, that one needs to confront alone. Yes, alone, if they are to do their work of expiation. And how terrible it is, the expiation that fate imposes on me! For it begins, for me, at the same moment that I begin to grow old."

Someone was knocking lightly and discreetly on the door to Rodolphe's study. He made a motion of pained impatience. Murph got up and went over to open the door. Through the partially opened door, one of the prince's assistants said a few words to the squire in a whisper. The latter responded with a nod of his head, and, turning toward Rodolphe, he said, "Will your lordship allow me to absent myself for a moment? Someone wishes to speak with me immediately on behalf of your royal highness."

"Go," the prince answered.

Murph had barely left the room before Rodolphe, hiding his face in his hands, let out a long moan. "Oh!" he cried. "What I feel frightens me! My soul is overflowing with gall and hatred. The presence of my best friend wears on me. The memory of a noble and pure love calls to me and also confuses me, and then—and this is cowardly and unworthy of me—yesterday, I felt savage joy when I learned of Sarah's death, the death of that unnatural mother who caused the loss of my daughter. It gives me pleasure to think about all the horrible agony of the monster who had my child killed. Oh, what rage! I came too late!" he exclaimed, jumping out of his chair. "And yet, yesterday, this wasn't causing me this grief, and yesterday, like today, I knew my daughter was dead. Oh, yes, but I had not yet said the words that will poison my life from now on: 'I saw my daughter, I spoke with her, I admired everything that was adorable about her.' Oh! The time I lost while she was at that farm! When I think that I only went there three times! Yes, that was all. And I could have gone there every day and seen my daughter every day . . . What am I saying? I could have kept her by my side forever. Oh! That will be my torture: to repeat this to myself over and over again, forever!" And the unhappy man found a cruel pleasure in returning to this depressing and pointless thought, for it is the nature of great sorrows to revive themselves endlessly through terrible repetition.

Suddenly, the door to the study opened, and Murph entered looking very pale, so pale that the prince started to get up and cried, "Murph, what's wrong?"

"Nothing, Your Lordship."

"But you're very pale."

"It's from . . . astonishment."

"Why are you astonished?"

"Madame d'Harville!"

"Madame d'Harville? Good Lord! More unhappiness?"

"No, no, Your Lordship. Don't worry. She's in there . . . in the sitting room."

"She's here? She's in my home? It's impossible!"

"And there's also . . . I must tell you . . . a surprise."

"Such a thing for her to do . . . But what's going on, in heaven's name?"

"I don't know . . . But I can't get ahold of what I'm feeling."

"Are you hiding something from me?"

"On my honor, Your Lordship, no—on my honor. I only know what Madame the marquise told me."

"So what did she tell you?"

"'Sir Walter,' and her voice was emotional but her look was radiant with joy, 'my presence here must be very surprising to you. But there are certain circumstances that are so demanding that they leave little time to consider matters of etiquette. Please ask his highness to give me a few minutes' worth of conversation with him—in your presence, for I know that the prince has no better friend in the world than you. I could have asked him to do me the courtesy of coming to my home, but it would have delayed this meeting by maybe an hour, and the prince will be grateful to me that I have not delayed this conversation by a single minute,' she said with a look that made me tremble."

"But I cannot imagine," said Rodolphe in a different tone, becoming even paler than Murph, "what could be the cause of your nervousness, of your emotion . . . of your pallor . . . There's something else . . . This conversation . . ."

"On my honor I don't know . . . anything more. These words that the marquise said shook me up all on their own. Why? I'm not sure. But you, too, are very pale, Your Lordship."

"Me?" said Rodolphe, leaning on his armchair, for he could feel his knees giving way beneath him.

"I am telling you, Your Lordship, that you are just as shaken as me. What's wrong with you?"

"Even if I have to die from this blow, ask Madame d'Harville to come in," said the prince.

Through a strange kind of sympathy, Madame d'Harville's unexpected and extraordinary visit had awakened in Murph and Rodolphe the same vague and irrational hope. But this hope seemed so insane to them that neither one wanted to confess it to the other. Madame d'Harville, followed by Murph, entered the prince's study.

CHAPTER II

FATHER AND DAUGHTER

Not knowing, as we have said, that Fleur-de-Marie was the prince's daughter, Madame d'Harville, completely joyous at the thought of bringing him back his protégée, had thought she could present the girl to him without having to prepare him for it. She had left her in her carriage only because she did not know whether Rodolphe would want to make himself known to the girl and receive her at his home. But when she saw the profound change in Rodolphe's appearance, which betrayed dismal despair, and noticed the trace of recent tears in his eyes, Clémence thought he had been struck by a much crueler sadness than the death of Songbird. And so, forgetting the object of her visit, she exclaimed, "Good God! Your Lordship, what's wrong?"

"You don't know, madame? Ah! All hope is lost. Your urgency . . . the conversation you had wanted to have with me immediately . . . I had believed that—"

"Oh, I beg of you, let's not discuss what brought me here, Your Lordship. In the name of my father, whose life you saved, I have the right, almost, to ask you the reasons for the grief that overwhelms you. Your dejection and your pallor frighten me. Oh! Speak, Your Lordship! Be generous and take pity on my fears."

"What good will it do, madame? My wound is incurable."

"These words frighten me even more, Your Lordship. Tell me what's going on. Sir Walter? Good Lord, what's wrong?"

"Well," said Rodolphe in a choked voice, making a violent effort to control himself, "since I told you of Fleur-de-Marie's death, I've learned that she was my daughter."

"Fleur-de-Marie, your daughter?" cried Clémence in a voice that would be impossible to reproduce.

"Yes. And a moment ago, when you came to say you needed to see me right away to tell me of a piece of news that would overwhelm me with joy, have pity on my weakness, but a father who has been driven mad from the pain of having lost his child is capable of the maddest hopes. For one moment I had believed that— But no, no, I can see that I was wrong. Pardon me, I am nothing but an insane wretch."

Rodolphe, drained from the rebound between a fleeting hope and a crushing disappointment, fell back onto his seat, hiding his face in his hands. Madame d'Harville remained stupefied, immobile, mute, hardly breathing. She was at one moment in the clutches of an intoxicating joy, and the next, in fear of the overwhelming effect of the revelation she had to make to the prince, and then the next moment, exalted by a religious gratitude toward divine providence, which had charged her with the responsibility of telling Rodolphe that his daughter was alive and that she was bringing her to him. Agitated by such violent and diverse emotions, Clémence found herself speechless.

Having momentarily shared the prince's mad hopes, Murph appeared to be as dejected as he was. The marquise, suddenly, giving in to an abrupt and involuntary impulse, forgot the presence of Murph and Rodolphe, and got down on her knees, clasped her hands together in prayer, and cried out, with an expression of fervent piety and ineffable gratitude, "Thank you, Lord! Praise God, I see in this your all-powerful will . . . Thank you once again, for having chosen me . . . to tell him that his daughter is alive!"

Although she had uttered these sincere and excited words in a whisper, Murph and the prince still heard them. The latter raised his head sharply the moment Clémence got back to her feet. It would be impossible to describe the look, the gestures, or the expression on Rodolphe's face as he gazed at Madame d'Harville, whose lovely countenance, stamped by her celestial joy, was at that moment radiating a superhuman beauty. Supporting herself with one hand on the marble of a console and holding her other hand over her quickly beating heart, she answered a look from Rodolphe, which we must again decline to describe, by nodding her head.

"Where is she?" said the prince, shaking like a leaf.

"Downstairs, in my carriage."

If not for Murph, who, as quick as lightning, threw himself in front of Rodolphe, the latter would have left the room in his overwrought state. "Your Lordship, you will kill her!" cried the squire, holding the prince back.

"She has only been convalescent since yesterday. You must take care, Your Lordship, for she is still frail," Clémence added.

"You are right," said Rodolphe, barely able to control himself. "You're right. I will be calm. I will not see her yet. I will wait for my initial emotion to subside. Ah! This is just too much for one day!" he added in a trembling voice. Then, turning to Madame d'Harville and holding out his hand to her, he exclaimed, in an effusion of indescribable gratitude, "I am forgiven . . . you are the angel of redemption."

"Your Lordship, you returned my father to me. God wanted me to bring your child back to you," answered Clémence. "But I must ask you to forgive me, as well, for my weakness. This sudden, unexpected revelation has left me bewildered. I must say that I wouldn't have the courage to go down and get Fleur-de-Marie. My emotions would frighten her."

"And how did they save her? Who saved her?" cried Rodolphe. "Can you believe my ingratitude? I had not yet asked you that question."

"A courageous woman pulled her out of the water just as she was drowning."

"Do you know her?"

"Tomorrow she will come visit me."

"I owe her more than I can say," said the prince, "but I shall repay her."

"I was right to obey my instinct not to have brought Fleur-de-Marie here with me!" the marquise said. "She would have been shocked by the gloominess of this scene."

"It's true, madame," said Murph. "It's an act of Providence that she isn't here."

"I didn't know whether his lordship wanted to be known to her, and I didn't want to present her without consulting him first."

"Now," said the prince, who had spent the last few minutes fighting down his agitation, and whose face seemed nearly calm, "now that I can assure you, Murph, that I am again calm, go and get my daughter." The words "my daughter" were pronounced by the prince in a tone that we could not possibly express.

"Your Lordship, are you completely sure you're ready?" Clémence asked. "Be careful."

"Oh, you needn't worry. I know the danger she runs, and I'll protect her from it. Good Murph, I beg of you: go, go!"

"Don't worry, madame," said the squire, who had been observing the prince attentively. "She can come now. The prince is in control of himself."

"So go, go quickly, old friend."

"Yes, Your Lordship. But a minute, if you please. I'm not made of iron," the good gentleman said as he wiped away the last of his own tears. "She must not see that I was crying."

"Most excellent man!" said Rodolphe, grasping Murph's hand in his own.

"All right, all right, Your Lordship, now I'm ready. I didn't want to cross the waiting room weeping like a Magdalene." And the squire turned toward the door. But then, changing his mind, he said, "Your Lordship, what should I say to her?"

"Yes, what should he say?" the prince asked Clémence.

"That Monsieur Rodolphe wants to see her. Nothing else, I think."

"That's it: that Monsieur Rodolphe wants to see her. Nothing more. All right, go on—go."

"That's definitely the best thing to tell her," said the squire, who felt at least as affected by all this as Madame d'Harville. "I'll tell her simply that Monsieur Rodolphe wishes to see her. That won't give her any ideas or make her suspect anything. That's the best thing to do, indeed." But Murph did not move.

"Sir Walter," Clémence said to him, smiling, "I do believe you're afraid."

"It's true, Madame la Marquise. Despite my six feet of height and my thick exterior, I'm still in a state of deep emotion."

"My friend, be careful," Rodolphe said to him. "Wait a moment longer if you're not sure of yourself."

"All right, all right; this time, Your Lordship, I've got ahold of myself," the squire said, after having rubbed his eyes with his herculean fists. "Really, this weakness is perfectly ridiculous at my age. Don't worry, Your Lordship."

And Murph left the room with a firm step, his face expressionless.

A moment of silence followed his departure. Clémence then realized, blushing, that she was alone with the prince in his home. The prince came up to her and said to her, almost timidly, "If I choose this day and this moment to make you a sincere declaration, it is because the solemnity of this day and this moment will add all the more to the seriousness of this declaration. I have loved you from the first moment I saw you. As long as I had to hide my love, I hid it. Now that you are free and you have brought me back my daughter, would you like to be her mother?"

"Me, Your Lordship?" cried Madame d'Harville. "What are you saying?"

"I beg of you, do not refuse me; let this day make my life forever happy," said Rodolphe, tenderly.

Clémence had also loved the prince passionately and for a long time. She thought she must be dreaming. Rodolphe's declaration, at once so simple, so grave, and so touching, made under such circumstances, transported her into unhoped-for bliss. She responded, hesitatingly, "Your Lordship, it is my duty to remind you of the distance between our ranks and what your position as a sovereign demands."

"Allow me to think before all else of the demands of my own heart and of that of my dear daughter. Make us both happy—oh, so happy—her and me, together. Allow me, who only a moment ago had no family, to be able now to say 'my wife' and 'my daughter.' Allow this poor child, who was a short while ago without a family herself, to be able to say 'my father,' 'my mother,' 'my sister,' for you have a daughter who will become my daughter, too."

"Ah, Your Lordship! To such noble words I can only reply with tears of gratitude!" Clémence exclaimed. Then, getting control of herself, she added, "Your Lordship, they're coming. It's your daughter."

"Oh! Don't refuse me!" said Rodolphe in an emotional, supplicating voice. "In the name of our love, call her 'our daughter.'"

"Well, then! Our daughter," Clémence murmured as Murph, opening the door, led Fleur-de-Marie into the prince's salon.

The girl, who had gotten out of the marquise's carriage before the peristyle of this immense mansion, had crossed an initial entryway with footservants in full livery all around, a waiting room in which valets were standing, the usher's room, and finally the servants' room, occupied by a chamberlain and the prince's staff, in full uniform. Imagine how astonished Songbird, who knew no splendors that exceeded those of the Bouqueval farm, must have felt going through these princely suites, sparkling with gold, mirrors, and paintings. As soon as she appeared, Madame d'Harville ran to her, took her by the hand, and, wrapping one of her arms around her as if to support her, led her over to Rodolphe, who, standing next to the fireplace, was incapable of moving.

Murph, after having handed Fleur-de-Marie over to Madame d'Harville, hastened to disappear partially behind one of the immense window drapes, fearing that he was not yet in complete control of himself.

At the sight of her benefactor, of her savior, of her God, who was gazing upon her in silent ecstasy, Fleur-de-Marie, already so shaken, began to tremble.

"Don't worry, my child," Madame d'Harville said to her. "Here is your friend, Monsieur Rodolphe, who has been awaiting you impatiently. He was very worried about you."

"Oh! Yes, yes; very, very worried," stammered Rodolphe, still immobile and whose heart was melting at the sight of his daughter's pale, sweet face. And so, in spite of his resolve, the prince was obliged to turn his head away for a moment to hide his emotion.

"But look, my child, you are still very weak. Sit down over there," Clémence said so as to divert Fleur-de-Marie's attention. She took her over to a large gilded wooden armchair. Songbird sat down in it with trepidation. She was getting more and more nervous. She was upset and could not speak. It upset her that she remained unable to say a word of gratitude to Rodolphe. Madame d'Harville was resting on her elbows on the back of the armchair, bent over Fleur-de-Marie and holding one of her hands in her own. Finally, she signaled to the prince, who came over gently to the other side of her chair. In greater control of himself now, he said to Fleur-de-Marie, who turned her enchanting face toward him, "Finally, my child, you are reunited forever with your friends! You will never leave them again. Now, most of all, you will have to forget all you have suffered."

"Yes, my child, the best way to show us your love," added Clémence, "is to forget your sad past."

"Please believe me, Monsieur Rodolphe, and believe me, madame, that if I think about it sometimes in spite of myself, it will be so that I can remind myself that, if it weren't for you, I'd still be very unhappy."

"Yes, but we will be sure you will never have any more of those gloomy thoughts. Our tenderness will not leave you any time for that, my dear Marie," said Rodolphe, "for you know that I gave you that name on the farm."

"Yes, Monsieur Rodolphe. And Madame Georges, who gave me permission to call her my mother . . . how is she? Is she doing well?"

"Very well, my child. But I have some important news for you."

"For me, Monsieur Rodolphe?"

"Since I last saw you, there have been some significant discoveries regarding the circumstances of . . . of . . . your birth."

"My birth?"

"We know who your parents were. We know your father."

Rodolphe's voice was so full of tears as he pronounced these words that Fleur-de-Marie, very moved, turned sharply around to look at him. Fortunately, he was able to turn his face away from her.

And then another bit of burlesque intervened to distract Songbird and to keep her from noticing her father's emotion too clearly. The worthy squire, who had not left his refuge behind the curtain and seemed to be looking attentively at the gardens of the mansion, was weeping like a child and could not stop from blowing his nose with an impressively loud noise.

"Yes, my dear Marie," Clémence hastened to say, "we know your father. He is alive."

"My father?" Songbird cried out with an expression that tested Rodolphe's courage anew.

"And you will see him one day," said Clémence, "perhaps soon. The thing that will astonish you, no doubt, is that he is of a very high rank in society. He is of noble birth."

"And my mother, madame? Will I see her?"

"Your father will answer that question, my child. But won't you be happy to see him?"

"Oh, yes, madame," said Fleur-de-Marie, lowering her eyes.

"You will love him so much when you know him!" the marquise said.

"From that day onward, a new life will start for you. Right, Marie?" added the prince.

"Oh, no, Monsieur Rodolphe," Songbird answered, naively. "My new life began the day you took pity on me, when you sent me to the farm."

"But your father . . . cherishes you," said the prince.

"I don't know him, and I owe you everything, Monsieur Rodolphe."

"So . . . you love me . . . as much . . . perhaps . . . maybe more than you would love your father?"

"I bless you and respect you like God, Monsieur Rodolphe, because you did for me what God alone could do," Songbird answered with exaltation, forgetting her habitual timidity. "When Madame was kind enough to speak to me in prison, I told her, just as I told everyone . . . yes, that's Monsieur Rodolphe. To those who were very unhappy, I would say, 'Have hope! Monsieur Rodolphe comforts the unhappy!' To those who hesitated between good and evil, I would say, 'Be of good cheer, be good, Monsieur Rodolphe rewards the good.' To those who were wicked, I would say, 'Beware, Monsieur Rodolphe punishes the wicked.' Finally, when I thought I was dying, I said to myself, 'God will take pity on me, for Monsieur Rodolphe has judged me worthy of his care.'"

Fleur-de-Marie, drawn out by her own gratitude toward her benefactor, had overcome her fear. A light rosiness colored her cheeks, and her beautiful blue eyes, which she raised toward the heavens as if she were praying, were shining with the softest glow. Everyone fell silent for a few seconds after Fleur-de-Marie's enthusiastic speech. All the participants in this scene were deeply moved.

"I see, my child," said Rodolphe, hardly capable of containing his joy, "that, in your heart, I have more or less taken the place of your father."

"It's not my fault, Monsieur Rodolphe. I may be wrong to feel this way, but, as I said, I know you and I don't know my father." And then she added, bowing her head in confusion, "And then, well, you know what my past is, Monsieur Rodolphe, and in spite of it you've overwhelmed me with your kindness. But my father, he doesn't know about that past. He might be sorry to have found me again," the unfortunate child said with a shudder. "And since he is, as Madame says, of a very high rank, he will surely be ashamed of me. He will blush because of me."

"Blush because of you?" Rodolphe exclaimed, holding up his head haughtily and with a proud look. "Rest assured, poor child, your father will make a position for you that is so brilliant and so exalted that the greatest of the greats in this world will look at you henceforward with only the deepest respect. Blush because of you? No, no. After the queens to whom you are related by blood, you will be the equal of the most noble princesses of Europe."

"Your Lordship!" cried Murph and Clémence in unison, terrified at Rodolphe's excitement and the increasing pallor of Fleur-de-Marie, who was looking at her father in bewilderment.

"Blush because of you?" he continued. "Oh, if I was ever happy and proud of my sovereign rank, it is because, thanks to my rank, I can raise you up just as high as you were low before. Do you hear me, my dear child? My adored daughter? It's me! I am your father!"

And the prince, no longer able to contain his emotion, threw himself at Fleur-de-Marie's feet, showering her with tears and caresses.

"Praised be God!" cried Fleur-de-Marie as she joined her hands in prayer. "I have been granted the right to love my benefactor as much as I have loved him. He's my father . . . I can cherish him without remorse . . . Praised be—" She couldn't finish. The shock was too strong; Fleur-de-Marie fainted in the prince's arms.

Murph ran to the door of the service room, opened it, and said, "Call Doctor David immediately, for his royal highness—someone has fallen ill."

"A curse upon me! I've killed her!" Rodolphe cried, sobbing, kneeling before his daughter. "Marie, my child, listen to me—it's your father . . . Forgive me . . . Oh! Forgive me . . . for not being able to keep this secret any longer . . . I've killed her! My God! I've killed her!"

"Calm down, Your Lordship," Clémence said. "There's no danger, I'm sure. Look, her cheeks are full of color. It's just the shock. Just the shock."

"But she's barely begun to recover. She'll die of it . . . Oh, what a disaster! What a disaster I've wrought!"

At this moment David, the black doctor, entered the room quickly, holding in his hands a little box full of flasks as well as a piece of paper that he handed to Murph.

"David! My daughter is dying . . . I saved your life—you must save my child!" cried Rodolphe.

Although he was bewildered at the prince's speech referring to his daughter, the doctor ran over to Fleur-de-Marie, whom Madame d'Harville was holding in her arms. He took the girl's pulse, put his hand on her forehead, and turned back toward Rodolphe, who was pale and terrified as he awaited his verdict: "There is no danger. Your highness may rest assured."

"You're telling me the truth? There's no danger? None?"

"None, Your Lordship. A few drops of ether, and this attack will be over."

"Oh, thank you, David, my good David!" the prince exclaimed, effusively. Then, turning to Clémence, he added, "She is alive . . . our daughter will live."

Murph had just glanced at the note David had given him as he entered the room. He shuddered and looked at the prince in horror.

"Yes, my old friend!" said Rodolphe. "Soon my daughter will be able to call Madame la Marquise d'Harville her mother!"

"Your Lordship," Murph said, trembling, "yesterday's news turns out to have been false."

"What are you saying?"

"A violent attack, followed by a loss of consciousness, had made them think Countess Sarah had died—"

"The countess?"

"This morning, they have hopes for her survival."

"My God! My God!" cried the prince, staggered, as Clémence watched him, bewildered, still not understanding.

"Your Lordship," said David, still attending to Fleur-de-Marie, "you need not worry in the slightest bit about her, but she urgently needs some fresh air. We can roll her armchair onto the terrace if we open the garden door. Her fainting spell will come to a complete end."

Murph quickly ran to open the glass door that gave onto an immense doorway that formed a terrace. Then, with David's help, he gently rolled outside the armchair in which Fleur-de-Marie was still sitting, unconscious.

Rodolphe and Clémence were left alone.

CHAPTER 12

DEVOTION

"Oh, madame," Rodolphe cried out as soon as Murph and David had left the room, "you don't know who Countess Sarah is, do you? She's Fleur-de-Marie's mother!"

"Good God!"

"And I thought she was dead!" There was a moment of profound silence. Madame d'Harville's heart was breaking. "And what you still don't know," Rodolphe went on bitterly, "is that that woman, who is as selfish as she is ambitious, and who wanted me only for my title, entrapped me into a marriage when I was young that was later dissolved. When she wanted to remarry, she abandoned the child to heartless people who cared for nothing but money, thus causing all her trials."

"Oh, my lord, now I understand why you always displayed such aversion toward her."

"You can now also understand why she tried to ruin your reputation twice with vile denunciations! Forever in the grip of her unyielding ambition, she thought she could compel me to return to her by isolating me from all human love."

"What a hideous idea!"

"And she is not dead!"

"My lord, that regret is not worthy of you."

"You say that because you don't know all the evil she has caused. Even at this moment, when I had rediscovered my daughter and I was going to give her a mother worthy of her . . . Oh, no! No. This woman is an avenging demon following my every footstep."

"Come now, my lord, take heart," Clémence said, wiping away the tears she was shedding, despite herself. "You have a great and holy obligation to fulfill. You yourself have said it in a true and generous outpouring of fatherly love: from now on your daughter's life must be as happy as it had earlier been wretched. She must be raised up as high as she was cast down. To do that, you must legitimate her birth, and to do that, you must marry the Countess MacGregor."

"Never. Never. That would be to reward the perjury, selfishness, and savage ambition of that unnatural mother. I will recognize my daughter and adopt her, and that way she will also know through you, I hope, motherly love."

"No, my lord, you will not do that. You will not allow the shadow of illegitimacy to hang over your daughter. Countess Sarah is of a noble and ancient line. Doubtless the alliance is unequal, but it is an honorable one. Through this marriage, your daughter will be legitimate and not merely legitimated, and so she will be able, whatever the future brings, to pride herself in her father and claim her mother openly."

"But to give you up? My God, that's impossible! Oh, you can't imagine what my life might have been if I could have shared it with you and my daughter, my only loves in this world."

"You still have your child, my lord. God has miraculously given her back to you. To find your happiness incomplete would be ingratitude!"

"Oh! You don't love me as much as I love you."

"Please believe that, my lord. Believe it. The sacrifice you make to your duty will seem less painful to you."

"But if you love me, if your regret is as bitter as mine, you will be dreadfully unhappy. What will there be left for you?"

"Charity, my lord. That beautiful sentiment that you awakened in my heart, that sentiment that has made me forget so many sorrows for some time and to which I owe much sweet consolation."

"Please, listen to me. I will agree to it. I will marry this woman. But once I have made that sacrifice, do you really think, feeling as I do nothing but contempt and disgust for her, that I could live by her side? No, no, we will never be separated from each other. She will never know my daughter. Otherwise, Fleur-de-Marie will lose you and thus the sweetest of mothers."

"She will still have the sweetest of fathers. By this marriage, she will be the legitimate daughter of a sovereign prince of Europe and so, as you said, my lord, her station in life will be as glorious as it was obscure."

"You are without pity. I am so miserable!"

"How can you speak that way, you who are so great, so just, you who so nobly recognize duty, devotion, and self-abnegation? Just a little while ago, before this miraculous discovery, when you were weeping such heart-wrenching tears for your daughter, if a voice had said to you, 'Make a wish, just one wish, and it shall be granted,' you would have cried out, 'My daughter, oh, my daughter—let her be alive!' And that miracle has taken place. Your daughter has been returned to you—and you say you are miserable. Oh, my lord! Let us be grateful that Fleur-de-Marie can't hear you."

"You are right," Rodolphe said after a long silence. "Such happiness would have been heaven on earth. And I am not worthy of that. I will do what I must. I cannot regret my reluctance, though, since it has given me one more proof of your soul's beauty."

"That soul that you have raised up and made better than it was. If what I do now is good, it is you I have to praise for it, just as it has always been you I have praised for every worthy thought I have ever had. Take heart, my lord. As soon as Fleur-de-Marie is strong enough for the journey, take her away. Once in Germany, that tranquil and serious land, her change will be complete and her past will be nothing more to her than a sad and distant dream."

"But what about you? What about you?"

"As for me, I can say this to you now, because I will always be able to say it with pride and joy: my love for you will be my guardian angel, my savior, my virtue, my future. All the good that I do will come from it and return to it. I will write to you every day. You will forgive me this demand. It is the only one I will make. And you, my lord, you will answer me now and again . . . just to tell me about her whom, for a moment at least, I was able to call my daughter," Clémence said, unable to hold back her tears. "And she will be in my thoughts always. And, finally, when long years have given us the right to proclaim aloud the unalterable affection that binds us, well, then, I swear to you on your daughter's life that, if you wish it, I will come to Germany to live in the same city as you so that we may never be parted and so we may end our lives in that fashion. Our lives might not be what we would have desired, but they will at least have been honorable and worthy."

"My lord!" Murph cried out, suddenly coming into the room. "The daughter God has returned to you has regained consciousness. She has revived. Her first words were, 'My father!' She is asking to see you."

A few moments later, Madame d'Harville had left the prince's residence, and he was traveling with all speed to the Countess MacGregor's, accompanied by Murph, the Baron de Graün, and an aide-de-camp.

CHAPTER 13

THE MARRIAGE

When Rodolphe had informed her of Fleur-de-Marie's murder, the Countess Sarah MacGregor had been crushed by the revelation. It had dashed all her hopes, and, tormented by a belated remorse, she had been subject to one violent nervous attack after another as well as a terrifying delirium. Her wound, which had only half healed, had reopened, and a long spell of unconsciousness had briefly given rise to the belief that she had died. Nevertheless, thanks to the strength of her constitution, she did not succumb to this harsh attack. A new spark of life brought her back to consciousness. Seated in an armchair in order to ease her labored breathing, Sarah had, for several moments, been immersed in dejected reflection, almost regretting her escape from death.

Suddenly, Thomas Seyton entered the countess's room. He could hardly contain his emotions. He signaled the two women waiting on Sarah to leave. She seemed hardly to have noticed her brother's presence. "How are you?" he asked.

"Still the same. I feel terribly weak, and from time to time I have painful feelings of suffocation. Why did God not take me from this world during my last attack?"

"Sarah," Thomas Seyton said, after a moment of silence, "you are hanging between life and death. A violent emotion could kill you. But it could also save your life."

"I am beyond emotions, my brother."

"Perhaps."

"Rodolphe's death would leave me indifferent. The ghost of my drowned daughter—drowned because of me—is always there, in front of me. That is not an emotion; it's an unending remorse. Only now that I no longer have a child have I really become a mother."

"I would prefer to find you once more in that state of cool ambition that made you consider your daughter as merely a means to realize your life's dream."

"The prince's terrifying reproaches have killed that ambition. The knowledge of my daughter's atrocious trials has awakened maternal feelings in me."

"Well," Seyton said, weighing each word, so to speak, "suppose by chance that something impossible had occurred, that a miracle had happened and you found out that your daughter was still alive. How would you bear up under such a discovery?"

"I would die of shame and despair upon seeing her."

"Do not believe that. You would be too intoxicated by the triumph of your ambition! Because, of course, if your daughter had lived, the prince would have married you. He himself told you as much."

"Even if such an insane thing were true, I don't think I would have the right to live. After having married the prince, my duty would be to relieve him of such an unworthy spouse, to relieve my daughter of such an unnatural mother."

Thomas Seyton's discomfort grew moment by moment. Charged by Rodolphe, who was waiting in the next room, to inform Sarah that Fleur-de-Marie yet lived, he could not decide what to do. The countess's life was so precarious that it might blink out at any moment. There was, therefore, not a moment to lose in bringing about a marriage *in extremis*, which was necessary to legitimate Fleur-de-Marie's birth. To prepare for this sad ceremony, Rodolphe was accompanied by a minister and by Murph and the Baron de Graün, as witnesses. The Duke de Lucenay and Lord Douglas, whom Seyton had hastily alerted, were to serve as the countess's witnesses and had just that moment arrived.

Time was running out. But the remorse caused by her maternal feelings, which had now replaced Sarah's pitiless ambition, made Seyton's task all the more difficult. He could only hope that his sister was deceiving him or deceiving herself and that this woman's pride would reawaken the moment the crown she had so long dreamed of was within her grasp.

"My sister," Thomas Seyton said, in a serious and solemn voice, "I'm in a horrible difficulty. With one word, I might return your life to you . . . or I might kill you."

"As I've already said, I have no more emotions for you to fear."

"Except for one, perhaps."

"And what is that?"

"What if it concerned your daughter?"

"My daughter is dead."

"And if she were not?"

"We've just gone over that hypothesis. Enough, brother. My remorse is enough for me."

"But what if it weren't a hypothesis? What if by some unbelievable, unhoped-for chance, your daughter had been torn from the jaws of death? What if she lived?"

"You are causing me pain. Don't talk this way."

"Well, then, God forgive me, and God be your judge! She still lives."

"My daughter?"

"I tell you she lives. The prince is here, with a minister. I have alerted two of your friends to serve as your witnesses. The prophecy has come true. You are a sovereign."

Thomas Seyton fixed on his sister a look filled with anguish as he said these words. He watched her face for any sign of emotion. To his astonishment, Sarah's expression remained unmoved. All she did was bring her two hands to her chest, fall back into her chair, and let out a slight cry, which, it appeared, some sudden, deep pain had torn from her. And then her face became calm again.

"What's wrong with you, my sister?"

"Nothing. Surprise. A joy I didn't dare hope for. Finally my dreams will come true!"

"I wasn't mistaken," Thomas Seyton thought. "She is still in the thrall of her ambition. She is saved." Then he said to Sarah, "So, my sister! What did I tell you?"

"You were right," she said with a bitter smile, guessing what her brother had thought. "My ambition has once again strangled all my maternal feelings."

"You will live! And you will love your daughter."

"I don't doubt it. I will live. See how calm I am."

"And this calm is real?"

"Miserable and broken as I am, do you think I have the strength for feigning?"

"So now you understand my hesitation a moment ago."

"No, I don't. I'm surprised at it. You know what my ambition is. Where is the prince?"

"He is here."

"I want to see him before the ceremony." And then she said, with feigned indifference, "My daughter is no doubt here?"

"No, you will see her a little later."

"It is true—there is time. Have the prince come in, if you please."

"My sister, I don't know how to say this, but you are acting strangely, you have a sinister air about you."

"Do you think I should be laughing? Do you think that fulfilled ambition should project a sweet and tender expression? Have the prince come in!"

Despite himself, Seyton felt anxious about Sarah's calm. He thought for a moment that he had seen her hold back her tears. After another moment's hesitation, he opened the door and left the room, leaving the door open.

"And now," Sarah said, "as long as I can see and embrace my daughter, I will be content. This won't come easily. Rodolphe will refuse me in order to punish me. But I will succeed . . . oh, I will succeed! Here he is."

Rodolphe entered and closed the door. "Has your brother told you?" the prince asked Sarah, coldly.

"Everything."

"So now your ambition is satisfied?"

"It is satisfied."

"The ministers and witnesses are there."

"I know."

"I take it they may enter."

"A word first, my lord."

"Speak, madame."

"I would like to see my daughter."

"That's impossible."

"I tell you, my lord, that I demand to see my daughter!"

"She has barely recovered. This morning she received a violent shock. She could hardly survive such an interview."

"But she may at least embrace her mother."

"What's the point? You are already a sovereign princess."

"Not yet, I'm not. And I won't be until after I have embraced my daughter."

"What?" he exclaimed. "You will put the satisfaction of your pride second to—"

"To the satisfaction of my maternal affection. Does that surprise you, my lord?"

"Alas, yes!"

"So will I see my daughter?"

"But—"

"Beware, my lord, my days, indeed my hours may be numbered. As my brother said, this crisis may cure me or kill me. As we speak, I am collecting my strength and energy—and I need every bit of it—to combat the shock this discovery has given me. I demand to see my daughter. If not, I reject your offer of marriage, and, if I die, her birth will be illegitimate."

"Fleur-de-Marie isn't here. I will have to send for her to be brought from my residence."

"Send for her to be brought here right now and I consent to all you request. As I may have very little time, the marriage will take place during the time it takes Fleur-de-Marie to get here."

"As surprising as your feelings are to me, they are too praiseworthy for me not to take them into consideration. You will see Fleur-de-Marie. I will write to her."

"There, on the desk, where I was stabbed."

While Rodolphe was writing a few hasty words, the countess wiped away the icy perspiration that bathed her forehead. Her expression, which had remained calm up to now, betrayed the violent suffering she had concealed. One might think that, in ceasing to restrain herself, Sarah was relaxing from a dissimulation that had caused physical pain.

Having written his letter, Rodolphe got up and said to the countess, "I will send this letter to my daughter by one of my aides-de-camp. She will be here within the half hour. May I come back with the minister and the witnesses?"

"You may. Or rather, ring for them, please. Don't leave me alone. Order Sir Walter to take charge of this. He'll gather the witnesses and the minister." Rodolphe rang and one of the women who waited on Sarah appeared. "Please ask my brother to send in Sir Walter Murph," the countess said. The serving woman left. "This marriage is a sad one, Rodolphe," the countess said bitterly. "Sad for me. For you it will be a happy one!" The prince made a gesture. "It will be happy for you, Rodolphe, because I will not survive it!"

At that moment, Murph entered. "My friend," Rodolphe said, "send this letter to my daughter right away by way of the colonel. He will bring her back in my coach. And ask the minister and the witnesses if they will please come into the adjoining room."

"My God!" Sarah cried out in a tone of supplication, once the squire had left. "Please give me sufficient strength to see her! Don't let me die before she gets here!"

"Oh, why weren't you always such a good mother?"

"Thanks to you, I have at least learned repentance, devotion, and selflessness. Yes, just a while ago, when my brother told me our daughter was alive—let me say 'our daughter,' I don't have long to say it, I can feel my heart giving way—I felt I had been given my death blow. I hid it, but I was happy for it. Our daughter would be made legitimate and I would die immediately after."

"Don't say such things!"

"Oh, I'm not deceiving you this time—you'll see!"

"Not a sign of that unyielding ambition that has been your ruination! Why has fate withheld repentance from you for so long?"

"If it is late, it is deep and sincere, I swear it to you. If at this solemn moment I thank God for taking me from this world, it is because my life would have been too horrible a burden for you."

"Sarah, please!"

"Rodolphe, one last request . . . Your hand . . ."

Turning his face away, Rodolphe stretched out his hand to the countess, who took hold of it quickly with both of hers. "Oh, yours are cold as ice!" Rodolphe cried out in fear.

"Yes, I feel myself dying! It may be that, as his final punishment, God will not allow me to embrace my daughter."

"Oh, yes, He will, yes! He will be moved by your remorse."

"And you, my friend, are you moved by it? Do you forgive me? Oh, please, say it! In another moment, when our daughter arrives, if she gets here in time, you won't be able to forgive me in front of her. That would be to tell her how much guilt I bear. And you wouldn't want that, would you? Once I'm dead, what harm will it do you if she loves me?"

"Rest assured, she will never know a thing!"

"Rodolphe, forgive me! Please forgive me! Have you no pity? Am I not miserable, too?"

"Well, then, unhappy woman, God forgive the evil you have done your child, as I forgive you the evil you have done me."

"You forgive me—from the bottom of your heart?"

"From the bottom of my heart," the prince, who was touched, said.

The countess pressed Rodolphe's hand warmly against her weak lips with a surge of joy and gratitude. Then she said, "Bring in the minister, my friend, and tell him not to go away afterward. I feel extremely weak!"

The scene was a heartbreaking one. Rodolphe opened the two panels of the door at the end of the room. The minister came in, followed by Murph and the Baron de Graün, Rodolphe's witnesses, and by the Duke de Lucenay and Lord Douglas, the countess's witnesses. Thomas Seyton followed next. All the participants in this unhappy event were serious, melancholy, and reflective. Even the Duke de Lucenay put aside his usual exuberance.

The marriage contract between the very noble and powerful prince, H.R.H. Gustave-Rodolphe V, the reigning Grand Duke of Gerolstein, and Sarah Seyton of Halsbury, Countess MacGregor (which contract legitimated Fleur-de-Marie's birth), had been prepared with care by the Baron de Graün. It was read by him and then signed by the spouses and their witnesses.

The minister said in a solemn voice to Rodolphe, "Does your royal highness consent to take as his wife Madame Sarah Seyton of Halsbury, the Countess MacGregor?" The prince answered yes in a loud, firm voice. And at that moment, despite her repentance, Sarah's dying features came alive: a rapid, transient expression of triumphant pride flitted across her livid features. This was the last burst of the ambition that would die only with her own death.

Those attending this sad and impressive ceremony spoke not a single word while it took place. When it was over, Sarah's witnesses, the Duke de Lucenay and Lord Douglas, came over to the prince in silence to bid him a solemn farewell and then left. Upon a sign from Rodolphe, Murph and Monsieur de Graün followed them out.

"Brother," Sarah whispered, "ask the minister if he would please accompany you to the adjoining room and to have the kindness to wait there a moment."

"How are you doing, my sister? You are very pale."

"I am certain I will live now. Am I not the Grand Duchess of Gerolstein?" she added with a bitter smile. Left alone with Rodolphe, as her face became distorted in a frightening manner, Sarah, in a drained voice, whispered, "My strength is at an end. I feel myself dying. I won't see her!"

"Yes, yes—rest assured, Sarah, you will see her."

"It's hopeless now. This self-control . . . Oh! It has taken superhuman strength. My eyesight is already fading!"

"Sarah!" the prince said, coming quickly up to the countess and taking her hands in his. "She's going to be here any moment . . . she can't be much longer now."

"God does not wish to grant me this final consolation."

"Sarah! Listen, listen. I think I hear a carriage. Yes, it's your daughter—here she is!"

"Rodolphe, don't tell her that I was a bad mother!" the countess, who could no longer hear anything, managed to say slowly. The sound of a carriage echoed across the courtyard's sonorous pavement. The countess didn't hear it. Her words were becoming more and more incoherent. Rodolphe was leaning over her anxiously. He saw her eyes glaze over. "Forgive me, my daughter! Oh, to see my daughter! Forgive me! At least, after my death, I have the honors of my rank," she finally whispered. Those were Sarah's last intelligible words. The one guiding determination of her whole life returned to her despite her repentance.

Murph suddenly entered the room. "My lord, the Princess Marie—"

"No!" Rodolphe cried out. "Do not let her come in. Tell Seyton to bring the minister." Then, pointing at Sarah, who was fading away in slow agony, Rodolphe added, "God has denied her the supreme consolation of embracing her child."

Half an hour later, the Countess Sarah MacGregor's life had ended.

CHAPTER 14

BICÊTRE

Two weeks had passed since Rodolphe, by marrying Sarah *in extremis*, had legitimated Fleur-de-Marie's birth. It was now the third Thursday of Lent. Having established the date, we now take the reader to Bicêtre. This immense establishment, which, as everyone knows, treats the insane, also serves as a place of refuge for seven or eight hundred elderly poor people who are admitted to the public retirement home[247] when they either reach the age of seventy or are stricken with some very grave infirmity.

Upon arriving at Bicêtre, one first enters a spacious courtyard planted with large trees interspersed with green grass, ornamented in summer with flower beds. Nothing could be more cheerful, tranquil, or refreshing than this walkway specially designed for the indigent old people mentioned above. It surrounds the buildings whose first floor have spacious, well-aired dormitories filled with good beds. On the ground floor, there are impressively sanitary cafeterias where Bicêtre's pensioners take their meals in common. These meals are healthy, abundant, and delicious. They are prepared with the greatest care, thanks to the paternal oversight of this fine establishment's administrators.

Such a refuge would be the dream of a widowed or unmarried worker who, after a long life of privation, honesty, and hard work, could find the kind of repose and well-being there that he had never known. Unfortunately, the favoritism characteristic of our times, which extends everywhere and pervades all places, has taken hold of Bicêtre's purse strings as well and, for the most part, it is only former domestic help who, thanks to the influence of their last employers, can currently enjoy this retreat. This seems to us a disgusting abuse of power. There is nothing more praiseworthy than honest, long-term domestic service. No one is more deserving of such a reward than these servants who, after long years of devotion, used to finish their days by becoming practically one of the family. But as praiseworthy as their background

247. It cannot be repeated enough that, at the last legislative session, a petition, emanating from the most honorable feelings and desires, whose purpose was to ask for a public retirement home for workers, was withdrawn amid general laughter in the chambers (see *The Monitor*). [SN]

is, this retirement profits their employers and not the state, which must repay them for it.

Wouldn't it be more just, both morally and as a matter of humanity, therefore, to allow the placements available in Bicêtre and other like establishments to belong by right to workers chosen from among those whose conduct has been most worthy or whose situation is most unfortunate? For them, these retreats, however limited their numbers were, would be at least a distant hope that would lighten the trials of each day, if only a little. It would be a beneficial hope, one that would encourage them to do good and would show them a future—a far-off future, to be sure, but a certain one—that brought a little rest and happiness as a reward. And as they would not be able to claim such retreats except by irreproachable conduct, their moral conduct would become, so to speak, a matter of necessity for them.

Is it really too much to demand that the small number of workers who reach very advanced years, having survived every sort of privation, might have a chance of obtaining a little bread, a little rest, and a shelter for their exhausted old age at Bicêtre?

It is, of course, true that such a law would exclude men of letters, scientists, and artists who, in their old age, had no other refuge from a place in these establishments. But even now, men whose talent, scientific knowledge, or intelligence has been esteemed in their own time can barely find any places for themselves among the domestic help sent, through their employers' influence, to Bicêtre. So, in the name of those who have won renown, to the benefit of France, and of those whose fame has been consecrated by the voice of the people, is it too much to wish for them as well that they be offered a modest but worthy retreat in their final years?

Well, yes, it must be too much to ask. And yet let us consider one example from among thousands. The state has spent eight to ten million on La Madeleine, which is neither a temple nor a church.[248] What good could be done with such an enormous sum of money! Surely one could found a retirement home where two hundred and fifty to three hundred people, people who had in the past stood out as scientists, poets, musicians, administrators, lawyers, etc., etc. (since nearly all these professions have at one time or another been represented in Bicêtre) might enjoy a dignified retirement.

---

248. La Madeleine was begun as a church in 1763, halted in 1767, and resumed in 1777. It was not finished at the time of the French Revolution, and construction was held in abeyance until, in 1806, Napoléon began working on it again as a "Monument to the Glory of the Grand Army" and gave it the design of a Greek temple. During the time of the Restoration, it was decided to make the building a church, but work was still not completed before the July Monarchy, which decided to make the building a monument to national reconciliation. It was finally consecrated as a church in 1842. [TN]

One would think this would be a question of humanity, of decency, of national dignity for a country that claims to take the lead in art, intelligence, and civilization, but no one even considers it. We know this because Hégésippe Moreau[249] and so many other rare geniuses have died in state hospitals or in conditions of indigence. We know this because so many noble minds that once burst out in pure and vibrant flame now wear the cloak of the deserving poor at Bicêtre. We know this because there is no charitable establishment here, as there is in London,[250] where a stranger without means may find at least a bed for the night, a roof over his head, and a bit of bread. We know this because workers who go to La Grève[251] to look for work and wait to be hired aren't even offered the protection against seasonal weather of a shed like those that protect wholesale and retail street markets.[252] And yet La Grève is the stock exchange of unemployed laborers, a stock exchange in which there are only honest transactions, because their end is only to obtain hard work, and the only dividend they pay is the insufficient salary with which a worker buys his bitter bread.

We know this because . . .

We could go on forever if we wanted to count all the useful foundations we have sacrificed to the grotesque idea of this Greek temple, finally destined for Catholic worship.

But let us now return to Bicêtre. And to finish our account of the number of different destinations in this establishment, let us say that, at the time

249. Born Pierre-Jacques Roulliot (1810–1838), Hégésippe Moreau was called by the name of his biological father, Moreau, from birth and, as a poet, took the pen name Hégésippe. The hard life and early death of this lyric poet made him an exemplar of the Romantic myth of the great poet dying young. [TN]

250. The Charitable Society founded in London by one of our compatriots, the Count d'Orsay, who, with this noble and worthy work, continues his generous and enlightened patronage. [SN]

251. The Place de Grève, already renamed by the time of the novel Place de l'Hôtel de Ville, was where public executions took place until 1830. In the early nineteenth century, it became a site at which workers gathered when they were in search of employment. [TN]

252. We are aware of the activity and zeal of the Prefect of the Seine and the Prefect of Police and their very good will toward the poor and working classes. Let us hope that our appeal reaches their ears and that their initiatives with the Municipal Council will put an end to such a state of affairs. The expense would be minimal and the good achieved would be very great. The same could be said for interest-free loans given by state pawnshops for sums of, let us say, less than three or four francs. Ought we not, I repeat here, reduce the exorbitant rates of interest on loans? How can the city of Paris, as powerfully rich as it is, not be able to afford the poorer classes the privileges offered them, as I have said, by many cities in the north and middle of France, where loans are interest-free or set at 3 percent or 4 percent interest? (See the excellent work of Monsieur Blaise on the *Statistics and Organization of Public Pawnshops*, a work filled with interesting facts and sincere, eloquent, and high-minded assessments.) [SN]

of this story, those who were condemned to death were imprisoned here after their trial. And so, in one of the small spaces in this building, the Martial widow and her daughter Calabash were awaiting their execution, whose hour was fixed for the next day. The mother and daughter had neither appealed their verdict nor asked for any clemency. Nicolas, the Skeleton, and several other scoundrels had managed to escape La Force the night before they were to be transferred to Bicêtre.

As we have said, there was nothing more cheerful than the entrance to this building when, coming from Paris, one entered through the Courtyard of the Poor. Thanks to an early spring, the elms and linden trees were already covered with green shoots. The large grass lawns were extremely fresh, and here and there flower beds were studded with snowdrops, primroses, and cowslips in bright, varied hues. The sun colored the bright sand of the alleys golden. Dressed in gray cloaks, the old-age pensioners walked around and about or sat on benches and talked with each other. Their serene expressions generally manifested peace, quiet, or a sort of carefree tranquility.

The clock had just rung eleven when two cabs stopped before the external fences. Madame Georges, Germain, and Rigolette got out of the first carriage, and Louise Morel and her mother, the second. Germain and Rigolette, as we know, had been married for two weeks. We will allow the reader to imagine the bubbly gaiety, the boisterous happiness with which the seamstress's fresh features glowed. Her petal-like lips only opened when she laughed, smiled, or kissed Madame Georges, whom she called her mother.

Germain's features expressed a calmer, more reflective, more serious happiness. It was mixed with a feeling of profound gratitude, almost respect, for this good and courageous young girl who had given him such helpful and charming comfort when he was in prison, a time of which Rigolette seemed not to have the least memory. Indeed, as soon as her little Germain turned the conversation to that subject, she would immediately start talking about something else, claiming that those memories made her sad. Even though she was now Madame Germain and Rodolphe had given her forty thousand francs as a dowry, Rigolette had not wanted to exchange her seamstress's headwear for a more respectable hat, and her husband was in complete agreement. It is certainly the case that coquetry had never been better served by humility, since nothing was more graceful or elegant than her little broad-brimmed bonnet, a little in the peasant style, and decorated on each side with two large orange bows, which made the striking blackness of her hair stand out. Since she now had the time for curlers, her hair was long and curly. A richly embroidered collar adorned the young bride's charming neck. A French cashmere scarf, of the same color as her bonnet ribbons, half hid her fine and supple figure. Although she wore no corset, as was her practice (and even though she now had the time to lace herself), her mauve taffeta high-necked dress did not make the slightest fold over her bust, which was as slender and round as that of the marble Galatea. Madame Georges regarded her son and Rigolette with a deep happiness that was still new to her.

After a careful investigation and an autopsy of her child, Louise Morel had been freed by the grand jury. The beauty of the gem-cutter's daughter was marked by sorrow and showed a sort of gentle and sad resignation. Thanks to Rodolphe's generosity and the care that he had provided for her, Louise Morel's mother, who accompanied her, had been restored to health.

Upon being asked by the superintendent at the outside gate what her business was here, Madame Georges answered that one of the doctors connected with the section for the insane had arranged a meeting for her and those with her at eleven thirty. The superintendent allowed her to choose to wait for the doctor either in his office, which he directed her to, or in the large landscaped courtyard that we have already mentioned. She chose the courtyard, took her son's arm, and, continuing her conversation with the gem-cutter's wife, strolled through the garden's pathways. Louise and Rigolette followed a few steps behind.

"How happy I am to see you again, my dear Louise," the seamstress said. "When we came to pick you up, just a while ago, at rue du Temple, after we got there from the Bouqueval farm, I wanted to go up to see you. But my husband didn't want me to; he said it was too high a climb. So I waited in the cab, your carriage followed mine, and now here I am seeing you again for the first time since—"

"Since you came to comfort me in prison. Oh, Mademoiselle Rigolette," Louise exclaimed, affectionately, "what a good soul you are! What—"

"First of all, my dear Louise," the seamstress said, interrupting the gem-cutter's daughter laughingly, so as to put an end to her expressions of gratitude, "I am no longer Mademoiselle Rigolette, but Madame Germain. I don't know if you knew that. And I do insist on being addressed properly."

"Oh, I knew you were married. But let me thank you again for—"

"What you certainly do not know, dear Louise," Madame Germain continued, once again interrupting Morel's daughter so as to change the direction of the conversation, "what you don't know is that I owe my marriage to the generosity of the same man who has been a beneficent providence to all of us—to you, to your family, to me, to Germain, to his mother."

"Monsieur Rodolphe! Oh, we ask God to bless him each and every day! When I got out of prison, my lawyer came to me on his behalf to offer me advice and encouragement. He told me that, thanks to Monsieur Rodolphe, who had already done so much for us, Monsieur Ferrand"—and the unhappy girl could not pronounce this name without a shiver—"Monsieur

Ferrand, to make up for the evil he had done us, had set up incomes for me and my father. My father is still here, but, thank God, he is getting better and better."

"And he's coming back to Paris with you today if what his worthy doctor expects turns out to be true."

"Please God!"

"It can't but please God. Your father is so good, so honest! And I am sure that we will be taking him back with us. The doctor thinks he needs a sharp shock and that the unexpected presence of the people whom your father was used to seeing practically every day before he went out of his mind might complete his cure. For as little as I know about it, it seems a sure thing to me."

"I can't bring myself to believe it yet, mademoiselle."

"Madame Germain. Madame Germain, if you don't mind, my dear Louise. But to return to what I was saying, do you know who Monsieur Rodolphe really is?"

"He's the savior of the unfortunate."

"Well, that's first of all. But in addition to that? You don't know. Good, then! I'll tell you." Then, turning to speak to her husband, who was walking in front of her on the arm of Madame Georges and talking with the gem-cutter's wife, Rigolette cried out to him: "Don't go so fast, my love. You'll tire our good mother out. And besides, I like to keep you closer to me." Germain turned around, and then slowed down his pace a little and smiled at Rigolette. She furtively blew him a kiss. "Isn't my little Germain a darling! Isn't he just, Louise? With his beautiful manners! And such a handsome figure. Wasn't I right to prefer him to all the other neighbors, to Monsieur Giraudeau, the traveling salesman, and Monsieur Cabrion? Oh, Lord! Speaking of Cabrion, where are Monsieur Pipelet and his wife? The doctor said that they had to be here too because he had often heard your father speak their names."

"They'll be here soon. When I left the house, they had been long gone."

"Oh, then they won't miss the appointment. As far as punctuality goes, Monsieur Pipelet is as regular as a clock. But let's get back to my marriage and Monsieur Rodolphe. First of all, he was the one who sent me to bring Germain his order of release. Can you imagine that? Well, you can imagine our joy when we left that cursed prison! We came back to my place, and, with Germain's help, I made a little tea party, but a tea party for real trenchermen. It's true that it didn't do us much good because, when it was over, neither of us had eaten a thing. We were too happy. At eleven o'clock, Germain went away. We arranged to meet each other the next morning. At five in the morning, I was up at work, because I needed to make up at least two hours. At eight o'clock, there's a knock, I open the door, and who do you think it was? Monsieur Rodolphe. First I start to thank him from the bottom of my heart for all he did for Germain. He doesn't let me finish. 'Neighbor,' he says, 'Germain is coming soon. You will give him this letter. You and he will take a cab and go right away to a little town called Bouqueval, near Écouen, on the road to Saint-Denis. Once there, you will ask for Madame Georges.' Well, with pleasure. 'Monsieur Rodolphe, I have to tell you that this will be another day lost from work, and, without casting any blame, that makes three of them.' 'Rest assured, neighbor, you'll find work with Madame Georges. I've found you an excellent position.' 'If that's how it is, then that's great, Monsieur Rodolphe.' 'Good-bye, neighbor.' 'Good-bye and thank you, neighbor.' He leaves, Germain comes, I tell him what happened. Monsieur Rodolphe would never deceive us. We get in the carriage, cheerful as two little birds. And we were so sad the day before. Guess what? We get there. Oh, my dear Louise, well, despite myself, I can't stop from crying. This Madame Georges, who is right there in front of us, is Germain's mother."

"His mother!"

"Yes, by God, his mother, from whom he was kidnapped as a little child and whom he never hoped to see again. Well, you can just imagine how happy they were. When Madame Georges had had a good cry and was done kissing her son, it was my turn. Monsieur Rodolphe must have written her good things about me because she took me in her arms and told me she knew what I had done for her son. 'And if it pleases you, Mother,' Germain says, 'Rigolette will be your daughter as well.' 'If it pleases me? My children, I want nothing better. I can tell, you will never find a better or a sweeter wife.' So there we all are, settled on a beautiful farm, Germain, his mother, and my birds—whom I'd sent for, the poor little things! They should get to be part of the party, too. Even though I don't much like the countryside, the days passed by so fast it was like I was dreaming. I only worked when I wanted to. I helped Madame Georges, I strolled around with Germain, I sang, I jumped about. I had a ball. Finally our marriage was set, and it took place, as of yesterday, two weeks ago. Two days before the wedding, who do you think arrives in a beautiful carriage? A big, fat, bald gentleman with excellent manners who's carrying wedding presents from Monsieur Rodolphe. Just imagine, Louise, a big rosewood coffer with these words written on a blue porcelain plaque on top: 'Work and Wisdom. Love and Happiness.' I open the coffer and what do I find? Little lace bonnets, like the one I'm wearing, fabric for dresses, jewelry, gloves, this scarf, a beautiful shawl. Really, it was like a fairy tale."

"Well, it's at least true that it's like a fairy tale. Being so good and working so hard brought you happiness."

"As for being good and working so hard, I didn't do it on purpose, dear Louise. It just happened that way. So much the better for me. But that's not all there was: at the bottom of the coffer, I find a pretty wallet with these words: 'From one neighbor to the other.' I open it and there are two envelopes, one for Germain, the other for me. In Germain's, I find a piece of paper naming him director of a bank for poor people with a salary of four thousand francs. In the envelope for me, he finds a note for forty thousand francs—a treasury note—yes, that's it—it's my dowry. I want to turn it down, but Madame Georges, who had talked with the big, bald gentleman, tells me, 'You may accept it, my child; indeed, you have to accept it. It's your reward for your wisdom and your hard work . . . and your goodness to those who suffer. Because it was by working nights and risking your health, and so losing your only means of making a living, that you were able to go and comfort your friends in need.'"

"Oh, that's really true," Louise exclaimed. "There's no one else like you, you have to say that, Mademoi— Madame Germain."

"It's about time! So I say to the fat, bald gentleman, 'I didn't do anything I didn't want to do.' He answers me, 'That has nothing to do with it. Monsieur Rodolphe is immensely wealthy. Your dowry is a sign of his friendship and respect. He would be very sorry if you turned it down. And in any case, he will be at your wedding and he will make you accept it.'"

"What good luck that a person as charitable as Monsieur Rodolphe is so rich!"

"It's certainly true, he's really rich. But that isn't the only thing. Oh, my dear Louise, if you knew who Monsieur Rodolphe is! And after I made him carry all my packages! Well, be patient, you'll find out. The day before my marriage, very late at night, the big, bald gentleman arrives by post carriage. Monsieur Rodolphe can't come. He is under the weather, but the big, bald gentleman is here to take his place. And that's the only way we found out, dear Louise, that your benefactor and ours was . . . guess what? A prince!"

"A prince?"

"A prince? What am I saying? A royal highness, a reigning grand duke, a minor king. Germain explained all that to me."

"Monsieur Rodolphe!"

"Uh-huh, my poor Louise! And to think I'd asked him to help me polish my floors!"

"A prince, practically a king! That's how come he can do so much good."

"You can understand my confusion, my dear Louise. And then, seeing how he was practically a king, I didn't dare refuse the dowry. We were married. One week ago, Monsieur Rodolphe sent to us to say, to Germain and me and Madame Georges, that he would be very happy if we would pay him a marriage visit. We go there. Well, heavens, you can guess how hard my heart was beating. We get to rue Plumet and we go into a palace. We go through lots of rooms, all filled with servants with stripes down their legs and gentlemen in black with gold chains on their necks and swords at their sides and officers in uniforms and who knows what all? And then there's gold decorations here, and more gold decorations there. You could hardly see, it sparkled so much. And then, finally, we find the bald gentleman with other gentlemen all decked out in rich embroidery. He takes us into a large room and announces us, and there we find Monsieur Rodolphe—I mean to say, the prince—dressed very simply and acting all nice and open and not at all proud, really acting like the old Monsieur Rodolphe, so I found myself completely put at my ease and recalling how I made him pin my shawl up, cut my quills, and give me his arm in the street."

"You weren't afraid anymore? Oh, I would have been completely petrified!"

"Well, not me! After greeting Madame Georges with a kindness you haven't seen the like of, and offering his hand to Germain, he says to me, smiling, 'So, then, neighbor, how are Papa Crétu and Ramonette doing?' That's the names of my birds; he was really nice to remember that. 'I'm sure,' he added, 'that you and Germain are vying with your pretty birds to see who can sing the happiest songs.' 'Yes, my lord.' Madame Georges lectured us the whole way, us two Germains, telling us how we had to call the prince 'my lord.' 'Yes, my lord, we are very happy and our happiness seems to be greater and sweeter because we owe it all to you.' 'You don't owe it to me, my child, but rather to your own excellent qualities and those of Germain.' Et cetera, et cetera. I'll just skip the rest of the compliments. Finally we left this lord with our hearts a little heavy because we wouldn't see him anymore. He said that he was going back to Germany in a few days. Maybe he's already left, but, whether he's gone or not, we'll always remember him."

"He must make his subjects very happy."

"I should think so! Look at all the good he's done us, and we're complete strangers. But I've forgotten to tell you that one of my old prison companions lived on this farm. She was a very good, honest girl, and, lucky for her, she'd also met Monsieur Rodolphe. But Madame Georges advised me strongly not to speak about her to the prince. I don't know why. Probably because he doesn't like people to talk to him about the good he does. What is certain is that it seems that that dear Songbird has found her parents and that they've taken her with them, far, far away. The only thing I'm sorry for is that I couldn't kiss her good-bye before she left."

"Well, so much the better," Louise said bitterly. "There's another one who's happy."

"Forgive me, dear Louise. How selfish I am. It's true, I'm only talking about happy things and you have so many reasons to still be sad."

"If I still had my child with me," Louise said, sadly, interrupting Rigolette, "that would have been a comfort to me. Because now, what honest man would want me, even though I have money?"

"On the contrary, Louise, I would say that only an honest man could understand your condition. Yes, if he knew everything, if he knew you, he could only feel sorry for you and respect you, and he would be certain to have in you a good and worthy wife."

"You say that to comfort me."

"No, I say that because it's true."

"Well, whether it's true or not, it still makes me feel better and I thank you for it. But who's that over there? Look, it's Monsieur Pipelet and his wife! Heavens, they seem happy! And he's been still so upset lately over Monsieur Cabrion's jokes."

And indeed, Monsieur and Madame Pipelet were coming up to them with a spring in their step. Alfred, as always, with his eternal stovepipe hat on his head, was wearing a magnificent meadow-green coat that was still shiny new. His tie, with embroidered corners, was buried in a formidable shirt collar that hid half of his cheeks. A large vest in deep, bright yellow with large brown stripes, a pair of slightly short black pants, dazzling white knee stockings, and shoes as shiny as an egg completed his ensemble.

Anastasie was basking in a dress of purplish merino under a deep blue shawl that clashed with it sharply. She proudly showed her freshly curled wig to all the world as she held her bonnet suspended from her arm by green ribbon strings, as if it were a purse.

Alfred's expression, which was usually so serious and collected and had recently been so dejected, was glowing, jubilant, and bubbly. As soon as he saw Louise and Rigolette, he ran toward them, crying out in his deep voice, "Saved . . . gone!"

"Well, heavens, Monsieur Pipelet," Rigolette said, "you certainly seem happy! So, what's happened to you?"

"Gone, mademoiselle, or rather madame, I mean, I should, I must say, because now you are exactly like Anastasie, thanks to matrimonification, just the same as your husband, Monsieur Germain, is exactly like me."

"You are very good, Monsieur Pipelet," Rigolette said, smiling, "but who is it who's gone?"

"Cabrion!" Monsieur Pipelet cried out, breathing in and out with indescribable satisfaction, as if an enormous weight had been lifted from his shoulders. "He has left France forever, for always, in perpetuity. He has finally gone away."

"Are you really sure?"

"I saw it . . . I saw him with my own eyes get into the stagecoach headed for Strasbourg, him and all his luggage, everything he owned—which is to say a case, a hat, a handrest, and a paintbox."

"So what's my old deary sounding off about to you?" Anastasie said, coming up, all out of breath, because she had difficulty keeping up with Alfred's sudden fast dash. "I bet he's telling you about Cabrion's departure. That's all he's been harping on, the whole way here."

"Because of it, Anastasie, I feel lighter than air. Before, it seemed to me that I weighed a ton. Now I feel like I'm about to float away. Gone—he's finally gone! And he won't be coming back!"

"Lucky for us, guttersnipe that he was!"

"Speak well about those who aren't here, Anastasie. Happiness makes me merciful. I will simply say that he was an unworthy rogue."

"But how did you know he was going to Germany?" Rigolette asked.

"From a friend, our king of renters. Speaking of that dear man, maybe you don't know? Thanks to the good recommendation he gave us, Alfred has been named the superintendent caretaker of a pawnshop and a charitable bank that's been founded in our house by some good soul that I have the impression is the person Monsieur Rodolphe works for as a traveling salesman of good deeds."

"This is working out well," Rigolette said. "My husband will be the director of that bank, also because of Monsieur Rodolphe."

"Well, alley-oop!" Madame Pipelet shouted cheerfully. "That's great! That's great! People you know are always better than strangers, and familiar faces are always better than new ones. But getting back to Cabrion, you won't believe what happened. A big, bald gentleman, who came to tell us that Alfred had been named caretaker, asked us if a very talented painter named Cabrion had not once resided in our building. When he heard Cabrion's name, there's my old deary lifting his boot up in the air and then fainting dead away. Luckily, the big, fat baldy then added, 'That young painter is going to Germany. A rich person is taking him there for a job that's going to last for years. He might just stay there.' To confirm that, the individual gave my old deary the date Cabrion was leaving and the address to forward messages to."

"And I had the unhoped-for pleasure to read in the register, 'Monsieur Cabrion, artist and painter, moved to Strasbourg and then to foreign parts.'"

"His departure was set for this morning."

"So I go to the courtyard with my wife—"

"We see the guttersnipe climb up to the upper deck next to the conductor."

"And then at the last moment, just as the carriage started to move, Cabrion sees me, recognizes me, turns around, and shouts to me, 'I'm leaving forever . . . friends for life.' Luckily, the conductor's horn almost drowned out the last words and their indecent familiarity, which I despise . . . But, finally, God be praised, he's gone."

"And gone forever, you may have faith in it, Monsieur Pipelet," Rigolette said, holding in a fierce desire to break out laughing. "But what you don't know and what's really going to surprise you is that Monsieur Rodolphe was—"

"Was?"

"A prince in disguise. A royal highness."

"Oh, come on now, you're just joking around," Anastasie said.

"I swear it to you on my husband's life," Rigolette said in complete seriousness.

"My king of renters is a royal highness!" Anastasie exclaimed. "Well, alley-oop! And after I asked him to watch our lodgings! Forgive me, forgive me, forgive me." And without thinking, she put her bonnet back on as if such a head covering was more suitable for speaking about a prince.

In a display that was formally diametrically opposed, but came from exactly the same feeling, Alfred, in contrast to all his normal habits, uncovered his head and, bowing deeply to the empty air, exclaimed, "A prince, a royal highness in our lodgings! And he saw me under the sheets when I was in bed because of Cabrion's indignities!"

At that moment, Madame Georges turned to Rigolette and her son and said, "Children, here is the doctor."

CHAPTER 15

THE SCHOOLMASTER

Doctor Herbin was a man of ripe years, with a distinguished and extremely intelligent expression, a look of remarkable wisdom and profound insight and a smile that radiated goodness. His voice, which was naturally harmonious, became almost tender when he spoke to his mentally ill patients. Similarly, the sweetness of his tone and the gentleness of his words seemed often to be able to calm the natural irritability of these unfortunate people. He was one of the first to have substituted commiseration and kindliness for the terrible, coercive methods used in the treatment of madness in earlier times. No longer were chains, blows, or cold showers employed, nor, most strikingly, was isolation (except in special cases). His acute intelligence had led him to understand that sequestration only further excited monomania, insanity, and rage, whereas, on the other hand, exposing the mentally ill to a communal experience, with its innumerable events and distractions, prevented patients from becoming too absorbed in their own obsessions, which solitude and intimidation only made darker and more gloomy.

Experience thus shows that, for the mentally ill, isolation is as fatal in its consequences as it is beneficial for criminals. The mental imbalance of the former becomes more intense with solitude, just as the moral imbalance, or rather the moral perversion, of the latter is increased and becomes incurable in the company of equally corrupt peers. It is surely true that, in a few years, our current penal system, with its galleys, its imprisonment in common spaces, its pillories, and its gallows, will seem as vicious, savage, and atrocious as the former treatment inflicted on the mentally ill seems now to us to be absurd and atrocious.

"Monsieur," Madame Georges[253] said to Monsieur Herbin, "I thought I might accompany my son and daughter-in-law, even though I do not know Monsieur Morel. But I have become so interested in the condition of this excellent man that I couldn't resist my desire to be present, with my children, at the complete reawakening of his intelli-

253. We are aware that it is only with the greatest difficulty that women gain admission to mental asylums, but we ask the reader's pardon in allowing this irregularity, necessary to our plot. [SN]

gence, which, I have been told, you hope will follow from the shock you are about to administer to him."

"At least I have great hopes, madame, for the favorable impression that the presence of his daughter and other people he used to see will create."

"When they came to arrest my husband," Morel's wife said in an emotional voice as she pointed Rigolette out to the doctor, "our good little neighbor here was in the act of helping me and my children."

"My father also knew Monsieur Germain very well, since he was always very good to us," Louise added. Then, pointing out Alfred and Anastasie, she went on, "Monsieur and Madame are the doorkeeper of our house and his wife. They also came to our family's aid in its misfortunes many times and helped us as much as they could."

"I want to thank you, monsieur," the doctor said to Alfred, "for the trouble you have taken to come here. But, given what people have told me, this visit must be an expense for you, is it not?"

"Monssssssieur," Pipelet said, bowing gravely, "we must all help each other in this world. And besides, old Morel is the most honest of men, at least before he went out of his mind as a result of them arresting him and dear Mademoiselle Louise here."

"And even though I still regret," Anastasie said, "even though I still regret that the potful of burning soup I dumped on the heads of those bailiffs wasn't boiling lead. Isn't that right, deary—pure, burning lead?"

"That is true. One must offer this homage which is proper to the affection my spouse bears for the Morels."

"If the sight of the mentally ill does not frighten you, madame," Doctor Herbin said to Germain's mother, "we will walk across several courtyards to arrive at the outside building, where I thought it best to bring Morel, and I have given orders this morning that he not be brought to the farm, as he usually is."

"To the farm, monsieur?" Madame Georges asked. "Is there a farm here?"

"Does that surprise you, madame? I can easily understand that. Yes, we have a farm here. Its produce is an important resource for the asylum, and the mentally ill cultivate it."[254]

"They work there in complete freedom, monsieur?"

"Certainly, and the work, the calm of the countryside, the view of nature are all some of the best means of effecting a cure. Only one guard brings them there, and there have hardly ever been any escape attempts. They are truly content to go there. And the small salary they earn helps to improve their condition and earn them small treats. But here we are at

254. This farm, which is an institution that is a very helpful element in the cure of the patients, is situated very near to Bicêtre. [SN]

one of the courtyard gates." Then, seeing Madame Georges show a slight expression of fear, the doctor added, "Have no fear, madame. In a few minutes, you will take this as calmly as I do."

"After you, monsieur. Come along, children."

"Anastasie," Monsieur Pipelet whispered, "just think. If Cabrion's hellish tormenting of me had gone on, your Alfred would have been driven crazy, and then I would have been sent among these unfortunate people that we are going to see. They would clothe me in the most baroque getups, chain me up to the wall, or lock me into a room like a wild beast in the Jardin des Plantes!"[255]

"Don't talk that way, old deary. They say that mad people, when it comes to love, are like real monkeys when they see a woman. They throw themselves against the bars of their cages, billing and cooing in the most horrible way. Their guards have to calm them down by beating them with whips and pouring large buckets of cold water on their heads from a hundred feet up. And that's not too little to cool them off."

"Anastasie, don't get too near the cages of these insane people," Alfred said in a grave tone. "Accidents happen so quickly!"

"And besides, it wouldn't be nice of me to seem to be taunting them. Because, after all," Anastasie added in a melancholy tone, "we women make these men act that way by being attractive. Really, Alfred, I tremble to think that if I had denied myself to you, you would probably have gone as mad from love as one of these crazy people, and you would have fastened yourself to the bars of your cage every time you saw a woman, and then have blushed afterward, my poor old dear, when now, on the contrary, you try to get away whenever one of them gets you worked up."

"My modesty is delicate, it's true, and I've never thought that was such a bad thing. But, Anastasie, the door is opening and it frightens me. We're going to see really terrifying faces and hear the clattering of chains and the grinding of teeth."

As we can see, Monsieur and Madame Pipelet had not heard the conversation with Doctor Herbin and so partook of the popular prejudices that still exist with regard to asylums for the mentally ill, prejudices which, for that matter, just forty years ago were only too horribly accurate.

The courtyard door opened. The court, in the form of a long parallelogram, had trees growing in it and benches scattered throughout. Each side had a strangely constructed gallery over it. Large, well-aired cells opened up on the galleries. Fifty men, more or less, each dressed in the same gray clothing, were walking about, talking, or seated in the sun, rapt in silent contemplation. There could be no greater contrast between

255. The Jardin des Plantes is primarily a botanical garden. It also has a small zoo and museum attached to it. [TN]

their appearance and the idea people usually have of the strange clothing and expressions of the mentally ill. Indeed, one had to have had a long experience observing such people to see on many of these faces any sure evidence of their madness.

When Doctor Herbin came into the courtyard, large numbers of these mentally ill patients gathered happily and eagerly around him, reaching out their hands and manifesting touching expressions of trust and gratitude. He responded to them cordially, saying, "Hello, hello, my children." Some of these unfortunate people, who were too far away from the doctor to take his hand, came up to the people accompanying them and, with some timidity and hesitation, offered their hands to them.

"Hello, my friends," Germain said to them, shaking their hands with a kindness that seemed to be charming to them.

"Monsieur," Madame Georges said to the doctor, "are these the mentally ill?"

"These are virtually the most dangerous ones in the asylum," the doctor said, smiling. "We allow them to be together with each other during the day. Only at night do we close them back in the cells whose doors, as you can see, are now open."

"Really, these people are completely crazy? But why aren't they violent, then?"

"At first they are, when they first show their illness and come here. Then, little by little, our treatment starts to take effect, the sight of their companions calms them and distracts them from their obsessions, gentle treatment pacifies them, and their attacks of violent behavior, which are at first quite frequent, become more and more rare. Look, here comes one of the most dangerous of them."

This man was about forty years old, robust and wiry, with long black hair, a large, bilious face, a searching gaze, and a very intelligent expression. He walked gravely up to the doctor and in a tone that was exquisitely polite, if somewhat formal, said to him, "Doctor, I ought also to have the right to take the blind man for a walk and to talk with him. I have the honor to call to your notice that it would be a flagrant injustice to deprive this unfortunate man of my conversation"—and here the insane man smiled with disdainful bitterness—"and leave him to the ramblings of some complete idiot who knows nothing—and I think I can say this with some certainty—nothing, I say, of even the most common principles of any science whatsoever. My conversation, on the other hand, would give the blind man some healthy distraction. So, for instance," he added, in his extremely voluble manner, "I would have informed him of my views with regard to isothermal surfaces and orthogonals, leading him to notice that partially differential equations, when geometrically translated into two orthogonal surfaces, may never be completely integrated with each other because of their complexity. I would have proved to him that combined surfaces are of necessity all isothermal, and, together, we would have figured out which surfaces are capable of being combined into a triply isothermal system. I don't think it is a delusion, monsieur, to ask you to compare this recreation with the foolishness that others use in talking with the blind man," the mentally ill patient added, taking a breath. "So don't you think it's a crime to deprive him of my conversation?"

"Do not take what he has just said, madame, as the wild ravings of an insane man," the doctor whispered. "He sometimes discusses the most abstract questions of geometry or astronomy in this way, with a wisdom that would do the most illustrious scientists proud. His knowledge is extraordinary. He speaks every living language. But, alas, he is a martyr to his desire for knowledge and his pride in it. He has come to believe that he alone has comprehended all human knowledge and that, by keeping him here, we will plunge humanity once again into the shadows of the most profound ignorance."

The doctor then addressed aloud the mentally ill patient, who was looking at him with a kind of respectful anxiety as he awaited his response. "My dear Monsieur Charles, your complaint seems to me to be completely justified, and this poor blind man, who, I believe, is mute but, fortunately, not deaf, would be infinitely charmed by the conversation of one as erudite as you are. I will make a point of seeing that you are done justice in this matter."

"And yet, you still persist in keeping me here and thus depriving the universe of all the human knowledge that I have mastered and assimilated," the madman said, becoming more and more excited as he began to gesticulate in an extremely agitated fashion.

"Now, now. Calm down, my good Monsieur Charles. Fortunately, the universe is not yet aware of what it's missing. As soon as it starts to demand it, we will make every effort to satisfy that demand. In any case, a man of your abilities and your knowledge will always be able to put them to service in important ways."

"But I am to science what Noah's ark was to the continuation of life on the planet," he exclaimed, his teeth grinding, his gaze wandering.

"I know that, my friend."

"You want to hide my light under a bushel," he cried out, closing his fists. "But I will shatter you like glass," he added, in a threatening tone, his face turning scarlet with rage and his veins bulging out as if they were ready to burst.

"Oh, Monsieur Charles!" the doctor answered, looking at the insane man with a calm, steady, piercing look and speaking in a sweet, flattering tone. "I thought you were the greatest scientist of our time—"

"Of all time," the madman exclaimed, suddenly forgetting his anger in favor of his pride.

"You didn't let me finish. I was about to say that you were the greatest scientist of the past, the present—"

"And the future," the madman added proudly.

"You terrible chatterbox! You're constantly interrupting me," the doctor said, smiling and clapping him on the shoulder in a friendly way. "One would think that I'm completely unaware of the admiration you inspire and deserve. Well, now, let's go see the blind man. You take us to him."

"Doctor, you are a good man. Come on, then, and you will see what he is forced to listen to, when I could tell him about so many beautiful things," the madman said, now completely calm and walking in front of the doctor in a contented manner.

"I must admit, monsieur," Germain said, as he came closer to his mother and his wife, whose fear he had noticed when the madman had spoken and gestured violently. "For a moment there, I was afraid he would have a fit."

"Good heavens, monsieur! In the past, at his first excited expressions, at the first threatening gesture this unfortunate man made, the guards would have fallen on him, tied him up, beaten him, and immersed him in cold water—which is one of the worst tortures one can imagine. You can imagine the effect such treatment would have on a sensitive and irritable physical state like his, whose strength becomes more violent the more it is suppressed. And so he would have had a frightening fit of rage that the most powerful constraints could not have withstood. He would have become more and more frustrated by those constraints and would have become almost incurable. Whereas, as you can see, if we do not suppress this sudden excitement, or if we turn it in a different direction, by taking advantage of the excessively capricious attention span one often sees among the insane, these transient agitations subside as quickly as they arise."

"But who is this blind man he keeps referring to, monsieur? Is it some delusion of his?" Madame Georges asked.

"No, madame. It's a really strange story," the doctor answered. "This blind man was arrested in a den of thieves and murderers in the Champs-Élysées. They found him chained up in the middle of an underground cellar next to the body of a woman who was beaten up out of all recognition."

"Oh! That's horrible," Madame Georges said, shivering.[256]

"This man is hideously ugly. Vitriol has eaten away his whole face. Since he has come here, he has not said a single word. I don't know if he is really mute or if he is feigning it. By a strange chance, the only fits he has

256. Rodolphe had always kept Madame Georges in ignorance of what happened to the Schoolmaster after he escaped from the Rochefort prison. [SN]

had have been during my absence and always at night. Unfortunately, he won't answer any question addressed to him, and it's impossible to acquire any information about what happened to him. His seizures seem caused by some form of rage the origins of which we cannot figure out, because he won't say a single word. The other mentally ill patients take a lot of care of him. They lead him around when he walks and they enjoy talking to him, but only according to their degree of sanity, alas. But here he is."

All the people accompanying the doctor recoiled in horror at the sight of the Schoolmaster. That is who the blind man was. He was not mad, but he was pretending to be both insane and mute. He had slaughtered the Owl not in a fit of madness, but in a heated fever like the one with which he had been previously stricken at the time of the horrible vision he had at the Bouqueval farm. Following his arrest in the Champs-Élysées tavern, coming out of his passing moment of delirium, the Schoolmaster had paid close attention while he was held in one of the cells of the Conciergerie, where the insane are temporarily detained. When he heard people around him say, "This is an enraged madman," he determined to play that role, and also imposed on himself the silence of a mute so that he would not give any compromising answers to anyone who might doubt his feigned madness. And he had been successful in this stratagem. After he was brought to Bicêtre, he feigned violent fits from time to time, always taking care to choose the nighttime for these spectacles so as to escape the penetrating observations of the doctor in chief. Although the surgeon in residence was always awakened and hastily summoned, he had never managed to arrive before the fit had come to an end.

The very small number of his accomplices who knew the Schoolmaster's real name and knew about his escape from the Rochefort prison had no idea what had become of him and, in any case, had no interest whatsoever in denouncing him to the authorities. Thus, no one was able to figure out his identity. Consequently, he hoped to remain at Bicêtre forever, continuing to feign being a mute madman. Indeed, forever: this was now this man's sole wish, his only desire, thanks to his inability to cause further harm, which had paralyzed his evil instincts. Thanks to the profound isolation he had experienced in Red-Arm's cellar, remorse, as we know, had slowly but surely taken possession of his rock-hard heart.

Deprived of all communication with the outside world, with only the memories of his past, his mind was focused on endless reflection, and so his thoughts frequently ended up taking on bodily form, creating images in his brain, as he had said to the Owl. Thus his victims often seemed to appear before him. This was not madness, however, but the power of memory intensified to its highest degree.

Thus this man, at the height of his maturity, endowed with an athletic constitution, this man who might certainly live for many more years, this man who was in full possession of his wits, would have to spend long years, completely mute, among insane people. Otherwise, if his identity were discovered, he would be taken to the gallows for his most recent murders or condemned to life imprisonment among other criminals, for whom he felt a constantly increasing repugnance as a result of his repentance.

The Schoolmaster was sitting on a bench. A forest of grizzled hair covered his large, hideous head. His elbows resting on his knees, his chin was propped in his hand. Even though his terrifying mask of a face was deprived of sight, though his nose was nothing but two holes and his mouth was twisted out of shape, still his monstrous features bore an expression of crushing, incurable despair. A mentally ill patient with a sad, kindly, youthful expression, kneeling in front of the Schoolmaster, held his strong hand in his own, looked at him sweetly, and kept repeating only these words: "Strawberries, strawberries, strawberries."

"Behold," the mad scientist said gravely, "the only conversation this idiot is able to have with the blind man. If this man's bodily eyes are shut, the eyes of his soul are surely open, and he would be grateful to be able to communicate with me."

"I have no doubt about it," the doctor said, while the poor insane man with the melancholy expression contemplated the Schoolmaster's horrible face and kept repeating in his gentle voice, "Strawberries, strawberries, strawberries."

"Since he came here, that is the only word we've heard from this poor madman," the doctor said to Madame Georges, who was looking in horror at the Schoolmaster. "What meaning he attaches to that word, the only one he says, I have not been able to figure out."

"Good Lord, Mother," Germain said to Madame Georges, "look at how despondent that poor blind man seems!"

"It's true, my child," Madame Georges answered. "It makes my heart stop beating, despite myself. The sight of him gives me such pain. Oh, how sad it is to see this dark side of humanity!"

Madame Georges had hardly gotten those words out of her mouth when the Schoolmaster shuddered. His stitched-up face became pale beneath his scars. He got up and turned his head so suddenly toward Germain's mother that she could not hold in a cry of terror, even though she didn't know who this wretch was. The Schoolmaster had recognized his wife's voice and her words informed him that she was talking to their son.

"Mother, what's wrong?" Germain exclaimed.

"Nothing, my child, but this man's movement, the expression on his face . . . it all frightened me. I'm sorry, monsieur. Please forgive my weakness," she added, turning to the doctor. "I almost regret giving in to my curiosity and accompanying my son."

"Oh, it's just this once, Mother! There's nothing to be sorry for."

"Well, it's a sure thing our good mother won't be coming here again ever, or us, either, isn't that so, Germain, darling?" Rigolette said. "It's so sad. It breaks your heart."

"Oh, come on. You're just a little scaredy-cat. Isn't that right, Doctor?" Germain said, smiling. "Isn't my wife a little scaredy-cat?"

"I must admit," the doctor answered, "that the sight of this unfortunate mute blind man upsets even me, and I've seen a lot of suffering."

"What a sweet little mug, huh, old deary?" Anastasie whispered. "Well, but really! Next to you, all men seem to me as ugly as this scary fellow. That's why no one can boast . . . you understand, right, Alfred?"

"Anastasie, I'm going to dream about that face there, I'm sure of it. I'm going to have nightmares."

"My friend," the doctor said to the Schoolmaster, "how are you doing?" The Schoolmaster stayed silent. "Don't you hear me, then?" the doctor went on, clapping him lightly on the shoulder. The Schoolmaster made no answer. He lowered his head. After a few moments, his sightless eyes let fall a tear. "He's crying," the doctor said.

"Poor man," Germain added, caringly.

The Schoolmaster trembled. Once again he heard his son's voice. His son felt compassion for him.

"What's wrong? What sorrow do you bear?" the doctor asked. Without answering, the Schoolmaster hid his face in his hands. "We won't get anything from him," the doctor said.

"Let me talk to him. I'll comfort him," the mad scientist said in his serious and pretentious way. "I am going to demonstrate to him that all the kinds of orthogonal surfaces with three isothermal systems are: one, those with second-order surfaces; two, those that are ellipsoids revolving both around a small and a large axis; three, those that— Well, maybe not," the madman went on, changing his mind as he reconsidered. "I'll talk to him about the planetary system." Then, turning to the young mentally ill patient still kneeling in front of the Schoolmaster, he said, "Be off with you . . . and take your strawberries with you."

"My boy," the doctor said to the young madman, "you all have to take your turn walking with and talking to this poor man. Let your comrade take your place." The young mentally ill man immediately obeyed, getting up and looking timidly at the doctor with his big blue eyes. He showed his deference with a wave, signaled his good-bye to the Schoolmaster, and went off, repeating in a plaintive voice, "Strawberries . . . strawberries."

The doctor, seeing the painful impression this scene made upon Madame Georges, said to her, "Fortunately, madame, we will see Morel in a moment, and if my expectations are well founded, your soul will experience the joy of seeing this excellent man returned to the affections of his worthy wife and daughter." And the doctor went off, followed by the people accompanying him.

The Schoolmaster was left alone with the scientific madman, who began to explain to him, very knowledgeably for that matter, and very eloquently, the movements of the stars, which only come out at night, silently traveling their immense curves across the sky.

But the Schoolmaster wasn't listening. He was thinking, with deep despair, that he would never hear either his son's or his wife's voice again. Knowing with certainty the well-deserved horror he inspired in them and the pain and shame the revelation of his name would cause them, he would die a thousand times over before revealing his identity to them. He had only one, final consolation: for one moment he had moved his son to some pity. And despite himself, he remembered Rodolphe's words just before he had inflicted on him a terrible punishment: "Every word you speak is a blasphemy, every word you speak will become a prayer . . . You are bold and cruel because you are strong, you will be gentle and humble because you will be weak . . . Your heart is closed to repentance, you will weep for your victims. You have turned yourself from a man into a savage beast . . . One day your intelligence will be sparked by remorse and will be lifted up by expiation . . . You have not even given the respect that wild beasts give to their females and their young; after a long life consecrated to the redemption of your crimes, your final prayer will be to beg God to grant you the unmerited happiness of dying amid your wife and child."

"We are going to walk through the idiots' courtyard, and then we'll come to the building where we'll find Morel," the doctor said, leaving the courtyard where the Schoolmaster was.

CHAPTER 16

MOREL, THE GEM-CUTTER

Despite the fear she had felt at the sight of the mentally ill patients, Madame Georges felt compelled to stop a moment as she passed before a fenced-in courtyard that enclosed incurable idiots. These poor beings often didn't even have the instincts of a wild animal. Most of the time, no one knew who they were or where they came from. Their identities unknown to all, even to themselves, they went through this life as absolute strangers to feeling or thought, experiencing only the most basic of animal needs. The hideous combination of wretchedness and debauchery, lived out in dark, vile hovels, is the usual cause of this debasement of the species, one which affects the working classes most frequently.

Although the superficial observer cannot deduce madness at first, merely from looking at the expression of the mentally ill person, it is really all too easy to recognize the physical characteristics of complete idiocy. Doctor Herbin had no need to point out to Madame Georges the moronically savage expression, the dumb insensitivity, or the stunned imbecility that gave to the features of these unfortunate people an expression that was both hideous and painful to see. Almost all of them were dressed in long, filthy, ragged smocks, because, despite constant oversight, no one could stop these creatures, absolutely deprived as they were of reason or even instinct, from soiling and shredding their clothing by crawling about or rolling like wild animals in the mire of the courtyard where they were kept during the day.[257]

Some were crouched in the hidden corners of a lean-to that gave them

---

257. We must say, in this regard, that it is impossible to see the dormitories built for these idiots without experiencing a profound admiration for the charity and intelligence with which their hygienic cleanliness has been designed. When one considers that in the past these unfortunate people rotted away on vile straw mats and that now they have excellent beds maintained in perfectly sanitary states by truly marvelous means, one can only, as I said, give all due praise to those who have devoted themselves to ameliorating such wretchedness. One can expect no gratitude from these people, not even that of the beast toward his master. These benefactors are thus doing good for the sole purpose of doing good, in the sacred name of humanity. And that makes what they do that much greater, that much more worthy of praise. We do not know how to praise highly enough the administrators and doctors of Bicêtre and the meritorious support they receive from Doctor Ferrus, who is responsible for the general inspection of

some shelter. They were curled up around themselves like animals in their dens, moaning in a quiet, constant drone. Others, braced against the walls, stood there mute and motionless, staring fixedly at the sun. One old man, who was grotesquely obese, sat in a wooden chair, wolfing down his pittance of food with animal-like voracity, looking about him all the time with angry sidelong glances. Some walked around in quick circles in the small space available to them. This strange exercise could go on for hours without interruption. Others sat on the ground, swaying incessantly, heaving the tops of their bodies first forward, then back, never stopping this vertiginously monotonous movement except to let out bursts of laughter, the strident, guttural laughter of idiots. And still others, finally, in states of complete devastation, opened their eyes only when meals were being served and otherwise remained motionless, deaf, dumb, and blind, without making any movement or sound that would indicate that they were still alive.

The complete absence of any verbal or intellectual communication of any kind is one of the most sinister elements in any group of idiots. Despite the incoherence of their thinking and speech, insane people do at least talk, recognize each other, and seek each other out. Among idiots, on the other hand, there is only dumb indifference and savage isolation. One never hears any articulate speech from them. From time to time they emit a few savage bursts of laughter, or moans and cries that have nothing at all human about them. Only a very few of them even recognize their caretakers. These unfortunate beings do not seem to be members of our species, nor even, as a result of the complete annihilation of all their intellectual faculties, any species of animal whatsoever; they are so incurably stricken that they seem more like mollusks than like any animated life-form, and frequently they live long lives in this state. And yet, we say again in admiration, the people who tend to these creatures and their well-being with the utmost kindness, out of respect for their mere existence, offer such care even though these creatures don't have the least awareness of it.

Surely it is a beautiful thing to so respect the principle of human dignity as to extend that respect even to these unfortunate people who have nothing more left of the human than its external shell. But, as we keep saying,

---

asylums for the mentally ill, and to whom we owe thanks for that excellent law concerning the mentally ill, a law based on deep scientific observations. [SN]

Guillaume-Marie-André Ferrus (1784–1861) was a French psychiatrist, a student of Philippe Pinel, and one of the reformers of the treatment of the insane in nineteenth-century France. The law Sue refers to is probably the law of June 30, 1838, which establishes systems of French mental asylums and regulations for the treatment of the insane. These reforms, Pinel and Ferrus, and this law are famously the target of Michel Foucault's reinterpretation of this period in *The History of Madness* as the period of the Great Confinement. [TN]

one ought also to consider the dignity of those who, endowed with all of their intellectual faculties, filled with energy and activity, are the living strength of our nation. We should make them aware of that dignity by encouraging them when they make it manifest by their love of work, resignation, and integrity, rather than saying, with pious self-righteousness, "Punish here; God will reward in the next world."

"These poor people!" Madame Georges said as she followed the doctor, after having given the courtyard of the idiots a last look. "How sad it is to think that there is no remedy for this disease!"

"Alas, madame, there is none!" the doctor answered. "Especially when they have reached adulthood. Thanks to scientific progress, idiot children receive a form of education that cultivates the germ of partial intelligence with which they are sometimes endowed. We have a school here which is managed with great perseverance and enlightened patience and which already achieves results that are more than one could expect.[258] By very ingenious methods specifically adapted to their particular conditions, we stimulate both the physical and moral well-being of these children, and many learn the elements of reading, as well as how to count and to recognize colors. We have even been able to teach them to sing in harmony with each other, and I can assure you, madame, there is a strange kind of charm, which is both sad and touching, in hearing these plaintive, uneven, sometimes lamenting voices being lifted toward the heavens in a hymn almost all of whose words, even though they are in French, they do not recognize. But here we are at the building in which we will find Morel. I have ordered that he be left alone this morning so that the effect I hope to produce in him can have its greatest force."

"What form does his madness take, Doctor?" Madame Georges whispered to the doctor so that Louise would not hear them.

"He is under the illusion that if he has not managed to earn the thirteen hundred francs he needs to pay a debt contracted to a solicitor named Ferrand during his day's work, Louise must die on the gallows for the crime of infanticide."

"Oh, monsieur, that solicitor was a monster!" Madame Georges exclaimed, having learned of the hatred this man bore Germain. "Louise Morel and her father were not his only victims. He persecuted my son with a pitiless single-mindedness."

"Louise Morel has told me everything, madame," the doctor answered. "God be thanked, that wretch is no longer among the living. But may I ask you to wait a moment with these good people? I will go see how Morel is doing." Then, turning to the gem-cutter's daughter, he said, "I beg you, Louise, to listen carefully. As soon as I shout 'Come!' you should

258. Again, this school is one of the most intriguing and interesting of institutions. [SN]

appear on the instant, but all by yourself. When I say 'Come!' a second time, everybody else will come in with you."

"Oh, monsieur, my courage is starting to fail me!" Louise said, wiping away her tears. "If this experiment doesn't work! . . ."

"I have high hopes that it will bring him around, and I have been treating people in this way for some time. Come now. Take heart, and attend to what I ask of you." And the doctor left the people who were accompanying him and went into a room with barred windows that opened on a garden.

Thanks to rest, a healthy diet, and the other cares with which he was showered, the face of Morel the gem-cutter was no longer pale, gaunt, and hollowed out by a sickly thinness. His full face, which had some color to it, showed that he had returned to health. But his melancholy smile and a fixed stare that still often paralyzed his features also showed that his reason had not yet been completely restored.

When the doctor came in, Morel was sitting hunched over a table, imitating the movements of his labor as a gem-cutter and saying, "Thirteen hundred francs, thirteen hundred francs. Otherwise Louise will go to the gallows! Work, work, work."

This delusion, which, however, now came upon him less and less frequently, had always been the primordial symptom of his madness. At first disheartened to find Morel at this moment under the influence of his monomania, the doctor quickly thought of a way to turn this circumstance to the benefit of his plan. He took from his pocket a purse with sixty-five louis that he had put there beforehand, poured these coins into his hand, and spoke suddenly to Morel, who was so profoundly absorbed in his work that he had not noticed that the doctor had come in. He said, "Enough work now, my good Morel. You have finally earned the thirteen hundred francs you needed to rescue Louise. Here they are." And the doctor threw the handful of coins on the table.

"Louise is saved!" the gem-cutter cried out, quickly gathering up the coins. "I'm running right to the solicitor." And, getting up quickly, he ran toward the door.

"Come!" the doctor shouted in intense anxiety, since the instantaneous cure of the gem-cutter depended on his first impression. Hardly had he called "Come!" than Louise appeared at the door, arriving at the same moment as her father. Astonished, Morel took a couple of steps back and let the coins fall from his hands. He contemplated Louise for a few minutes in deep wonderment, not yet recognizing her. Then, as, little by little, he came nearer to her, he looked at her with an anxious and fearful curiosity.

Louise, trembling with emotion, had difficulty holding in her tears. The doctor, meanwhile, signaling Louise to stay silent, surveyed the slightest changes in the gem-cutter's expression. Morel, leaning toward his daughter, began to turn pale. He wiped his forehead, which was bathed in sweat, with his hands. Then, taking another step toward his daughter, he tried to say something to her, but the words died on his lips, his pallor became more intense, and he looked around himself in surprise, as if, slowly but surely, he were emerging from a dream.

"This is good, this is good," the doctor whispered to Louise. "It's a good sign. When I say 'Come,' throw yourself into his arms and call him 'Father.'"

The gem-cutter brought his hands to his chest and looked himself over from head to toe, so to speak, as if to convince himself that he really was who he thought he was. His features were stamped with painful uncertainty. Instead of looking directly at Louise, he seemed to want to hide himself from her sight. And then he said in a halting whisper, "No! No! It's a dream. Where am I? Impossible! A dream. This isn't her." Then, seeing the coins scattered on the floor, "And these coins. I don't remember them. Am I awake or dreaming? My head is spinning. I don't dare look. I'm ashamed. This isn't Louise."

"Come," the doctor said aloud.

"Father, don't you recognize me? It's me, Louise, your daughter!" she cried out, melting in tears as she threw herself into the gem-cutter's arms. At that moment, Morel's wife, Rigolette, Madame Georges, and the Pipelets all came in.

"My God!" Morel said while Louise showered him with caresses. "Where am I? What do you want from me? What's happened? I can't believe that—" Then, after a few moments of silence, he suddenly took Louise's head between his two hands, stared at her closely, and then, after a few anguished moments, he cried, "Louise!"

"He's cured!" the doctor said.

"My husband, my poor Morel!" the gem-cutter's wife cried out, coming up to join Louise.

"My wife!" Morel said. "My wife and my daughter!"

"And here I am, too, Monsieur Morel," Rigolette said. "All your friends have met together here."

"Look, monsieur, all your friends!" Germain added.

"Mademoiselle Rigolette! Monsieur Germain!" the gem-cutter said, recognizing each of these new people with renewed astonishment.

"And your old friends from the downstairs lodging, too!" Anastasie said, coming up to them next, with Alfred. "Here are the Pipelets, the good old Pipelets, your friends till the end. So, alley-oop, old Morel. This is one good day!"

"Monsieur Pipelet and his wife! So many good people here with me! It seems like it's been so long! And you're Louise, right?" he cried, carried away as he clasped his daughter in his arms. "It is you, Louise, right? You're sure of that?"

"My poor father. Yes, it's me and it's my mother, and all your friends are here. You won't leave us anymore. You'll never be unhappy again. We're going to be happy now; all of us will be happy."

"All of us will be happy. But wait—I need to remember something. All of us will be happy. But I seem to remember that they were after you to throw you in prison, Louise."

"Yes, Father, but I'm out now. I've been found innocent. As you see, here I am, right by your side."

"But wait a little. It's coming back to me. Wait. Yes, I remember now." And then the gem-cutter said, in terror, "And what about the solicitor?"

"Dead. He's dead, Father," Louise murmured.

"Dead! Him! Well, then, I believe you. We can be happy. But where am I? How did I get here? How long have I been here? And why? I can't seem to recall things that well."

"You were so ill, monsieur," the doctor told him, "that you were brought here, to the countryside. You had a very serious fever, as well as delirium."

"Yes, yes, I remember the last thing that happened before I got sick. I was talking with my daughter, and . . . But who was it? Who was it? I've got it! A very generous man, Monsieur Rodolphe. He stopped me from getting arrested. After that, really, I can't remember a thing."

"One of the complications of your illness was a loss of memory," the doctor said. "The sight of your daughter, your wife, and your friends has brought things back to you."

"So who am I staying with, then?"

"With one of Monsieur Rodolphe's friends," Germain said quickly. "We thought that a change of surroundings would help you."

"Perfect," the doctor whispered. Then, turning to a guard, he added, "Send the cab to the end of the garden path so that he doesn't have to go across the courtyards and exit by the main gate."

As frequently happens in cases of madness, Morel had no memory and no awareness whatsoever of the mental illness with which he had been afflicted. A few minutes later, supported on the arms of his wife and daughter and accompanied by a student doctor who, as a matter of prudence, the doctor had assigned to watch over him until they reached Paris, Morel got into the cab and left Bicêtre without ever having had any idea that he had been kept there because of insanity.

"Do you believe that this poor man is completely cured?" Madame Georges said to the doctor, who accompanied her to Bicêtre's main entrance.

"I do believe it, madame. And I expressly wanted to leave him under the happy influence of this family reunion. I would have feared any further separation from them. And besides, one of my students will stay with him and instruct him in the routine he should follow. I will visit him every day until it is certain that his cure has taken hold. I am taking such care of him not only because I find his case to be a very interesting one, but also because the Grand Duchy of Gerolstein's chargé d'affaires most particularly recommended him to my attention."

Germain and his mother exchanged a meaningful glance. "I thank you, monsieur," Madame Georges said, "for the kindness you have shown in having allowed me to visit this institution. I think myself particularly fortunate to have been present at this touching scene that you so skillfully foresaw and orchestrated with your expert knowledge."

"Madame, I am even more delighted that its success returns such an excellent man to the affections of his family."

Still in a state of emotion because of what they had just seen, Madame Georges, Rigolette, and Germain set back out on the road to Paris, along with Monsieur and Madame Pipelet.

Just as Doctor Herbin came back into the courtyard, he ran into one of the upper-level employees of the asylum, who said to him, "Oh, my dear Doctor Herbin, you'd never imagine what I've just seen. An observer of human behavior like you would have found it endlessly fascinating."

"What now? What did you see?"

"You know about the two women here who are condemned to death, the mother and the daughter who will be executed tomorrow?"

"Of course."

"Well! I have never in my life seen such cold-blooded audacity as that of this mother. The woman is a demon straight from hell."

"Isn't that the Martial widow, the one who was so cynical during her trial?"

"The very same."

"So what's she done now?"

"She had asked to be kept in the same cell as her daughter until they were executed. We granted her request. Her daughter, who is much less hardened than she is, seemed to have softened more and more as the moment of her end came nearer, even as the devilish confidence of the mother grew even more pronounced, if that is possible. Just a while ago, the prison's venerable father confessor came to their cell to offer them religious comfort. The daughter seemed open to it when her mother, without losing her icy cold-bloodedness for a single moment, showered down such vile sarcasm on her and the confessor that the venerable priest, after having tried in vain to make this indomitable woman listen to a few holy words, was driven from the cell."

"The day before she climbs the gallows! Audacity like that really is frightening," the doctor said.

"It's one of those families, moreover, that you would think is hounded by the old Greek fates. The father died on the gallows, one of the sons is in the galleys, and another, also condemned to death, just recently escaped prison. Only the older brother and two young children seem to have escaped the family disease. And yet this woman has asked that the eldest son, the only honest one from this whole cursed line, come tomorrow and hear her last wishes."

"What a meeting that will be!"

"Aren't you curious to see what happens there?"

"Honestly, no. You know what my principles are with regard to the death penalty, and I have no need of a repulsive scene like that one to confirm me in what I think. If that horrible woman maintains her indomitable bearing right up to her death, it will be a deplorable example for the people!"

"There's one other thing about this double execution that seems extremely strange to me, and that's the date on which it will happen."

"Why?"

"Today is mid-Lent."[259]

"So?"

"The execution will take place tomorrow at seven in the morning. Well, crowds of people in masquerade, who have spent the night at balls in bars near the city limits, will have to cross paths with the deathly procession on their way back to Paris."

"You're right. That will be a hideous contrast."

"And that's not even considering the fact that from the execution grounds at the Saint-Jacques barrier, you can hear the music from the bars in the neighborhood in the distance. That's because people dance in the cabarets until ten or eleven o'clock in the morning to celebrate the last day of carnival."

The next day the rising sun was radiant and dazzling. At four o'clock in the morning, several infantry and cavalry pickets surrounded Bicêtre's limits and set up guard around it. We will now bring the reader to the cell in which the executed man's widow and her daughter Calabash were imprisoned together.

259. The third Thursday after Lent. There is a specifically French tradition of holding a mid-Lent carnival in addition to the more widespread pre-Lenten one. [TN]

BOOK X

CHAPTER I

MORNING PREPARATIONS

At Bicêtre, a dark corridor led to the cell that housed the prisoners who were condemned to die. This corridor was illuminated in places by several barred windows that were similar to basement windows, but situated slightly above the ground level of an upper courtyard. The only daylight this cell ever saw was from a large barred window over the door that opened on the barely lit corridor we have just described. This dark cell, with its crumbling ceiling, damp and moldy walls, and floor-stones that were as cold as tombstones, held Madame Martial and her daughter Calabash.

The angular face of the executed man's widow stands out from the shadows that pervade the cell: hard, impassive, and as pale as a marble mask. Deprived of the use of her hands by a straitjacket that she wears over her black dress, a sort of long gray canvas coat that laces up the back and which has sacklike sleeves that have no openings in them, she calls for someone to remove her bonnet, complaining that her head is getting too hot. Her gray hair falls disheveled upon her shoulders. Seated on the edge of her bed with her feet on the floor-stones, she looks pointedly at her daughter Calabash, on the other side of the cell from her. The latter, half asleep and also wearing a straitjacket, has her back to the wall. Her head is lowered onto her chest, her gaze is fixed, her breathing uneven. Apart from the light convulsive tremor that agitates her lower jaw from time to time, her face seems quite calm, in spite of its extreme pallor.

Inside and at the end of the cell, next to the door, under the open barred window, a decorated veteran with a coarse, weathered face, a bald skull, and a long gray mustache is seated in a chair. He keeps watch over the condemned women.

"It's freezing in here, but my eyes are burning! I'm thirsty, too—always thirsty," Calabash said after a few moments. Then, turning to the veteran, she added, "Some water, please, monsieur."

The old soldier arose, took a tin pitcher full of water from a stool, filled a glass with it, approached Calabash, and slowly helped her drink. Her straitjacket prevented the condemned woman from using her hands. After drinking greedily, she said, "Thank you, monsieur."

"Would you like some water?" the soldier asked the widow. The latter motioned to say no. The veteran went back to sit down. Another silent spell ensued.

"What time is it, monsieur?" asked Calabash.

"It's almost four thirty," the soldier said.

"Three hours from now!" Calabash said with a sardonic and sinister smile, alluding to the moment set for her execution. "In three hours . . ." She did not dare finish her sentence. The widow shrugged her shoulders. Her daughter understood what she was thinking and said, "You are braver than I, Mother. You never give way."

"Never!"

"I know it full well. It's easy enough to see. Your face is as calm as if you were still sitting by the fireplace in our kitchen, busy with your sewing. Ah! That time seems so far away now! So far away!"

"Stop chattering!"

"It's true. Instead of sitting quietly and thinking without saying anything, I prefer to talk. I prefer—"

"You prefer to distract yourself with your own voice, coward!"

"When all is said and done, Mother, not everyone has your courage. I've done the best I could to follow your example: I didn't listen to the priest because you didn't want me to. That doesn't mean I wasn't wrong, perhaps, for in the end," added the condemned woman, shivering, "after all, who knows? And after all, it's soon . . . it's in—"

"In three hours."

"You say that with such coolness, Mother! My God! All the same, it's still true that . . . the two of us . . . we're not sick and we don't want to die . . . and still, in three hours—"

"In three hours you'll go to your death like a real Martial. Everything will go black, that's all. A little courage, daughter!"

"It's not nice to talk to your daughter like that," the old soldier said in a slow, grave voice. "It would have been better to let her listen to the priest."

The widow shrugged her shoulders again with fierce disdain and continued speaking to Calabash again without even turning her head toward the veteran. "Be brave, my daughter. We will show that we women are braver than those men with their priests. Those cowards!"

"Commandant Leblond was the bravest officer in the Third Light Infantry Corps. I saw him riddled with wounds at the fall of Zaragoza.[260] He died making the sign of the cross," the veteran said.

"So you were his confessor?" the widow asked him, letting out a burst of savage laughter.

260. The Spanish town of Zaragoza was the site of two brutal sieges by Napoléon's armies in 1808–1809. [TN]

"I was his soldier," the veteran answered quietly. "I just meant to say that you can pray at the moment of death without being a coward."

Calabash looked attentively at this man with his weather-beaten face, the perfect image of a soldier of Napoléon. A deep scar furrowed his left cheek and trailed off somewhere beneath his large gray mustache. The simple words of this veteran, whose features, wounds, and red ribbon all seemed to bespeak calm, battle-tested bravery, struck the widow's daughter profoundly.

She had refused the priest's religious comfort more out of false shame and fear of her mother's sarcastic taunts than out of real hardness. In her uncertain, fading way of thinking, she contrasted the sacrilegious mockery of the widow to the approbation of the soldier. Strengthened by the belief he exhibited, she thought there could hardly be cowardice in following religious instincts that such intrepid men had obeyed before her. "Indeed," she said, in anguish, "why was it that I didn't want to listen to the priest? There's nothing weak about it. Well, it's true, it would have made me lose my bearings. And then, well, after all, who knows?"

"Back to that again!" said the widow in a crushing tone of contempt. "It's too late for that. Too bad. It's as if you wanted to be a nun. The arrival of your brother Martial will complete your conversion. But he won't come here, that honest man, that good son!" At the same moment the widow was saying these words, the enormous lock on the cell clanged noisily and the door opened.

"Already?" Calabash cried, leaping convulsively. "My God! They've moved up the time! They lied to us!" Her face began to fall apart in a frightening manner.

"So much the better. If the executioner's watch is fast, there's less time for you to disgrace me with your religiosity."

"Madame," said an employee of the prison to the condemned woman, with the gentle commiseration that comes from impending death, "your son is here. Do you want to see him?"

"Yes," said the widow, without so much as turning her head.

"Monsieur, you may enter," the employee said.

Martial came in. The veteran stayed in the cell; the door had been left open as a precaution. Through the shadows of the corridor, partially illuminated by the light of dawn and by a lamp, a few soldiers and guards could be seen. Some were sitting on a bench, while others were standing.

Martial was as pale as his mother. His face expressed deep anguish and horror; his knees were quaking beneath him. Despite the crimes of this woman, and despite the aversion she had always shown toward him, he believed he had a duty to fulfill her last wishes.

As soon as he entered the cell, the widow glared at him and said to him in a dull, angry voice that seemed aimed at arousing deep hatred in her son's soul, "Do you see what they're going to do to your mother and sister?"

"Ah! Mother, it's dreadful! And yet, I told you it would come to this, alas! I told you!"

The widow pursed her lips, which were white with rage. Her son did not understand her. Nevertheless, she went on, "They are going to kill us, just as they killed your father."

"My God! My God! And there's nothing I can do! It's over. What do you think I can do now? Why didn't you listen to me, you and my sister? You wouldn't be in here if you had."

"Ah! So that's the way it is," said the widow, with her habitual savage irony. "You think this is right, don't you?"

"Mother!"

"Look how happy you are. Soon you'll be able to say, without lying, that your mother is dead. You won't have to be ashamed of her any longer."

"If I were a bad son," Martial answered brusquely, revolted by his mother's unjust hardness, "I wouldn't have come here."

"You've come out of curiosity."

"I've come to obey you."

"Ah! If only I had listened to you, Martial, instead of listening to our mother, I wouldn't be here!" cried Calabash in a heartrending voice, finally giving in to the anguish and terror that she felt but had held back under the widow's influence. "It's your fault! A curse on you, Mother!"

"Now she repents and she accuses me. That must make you happy!" the widow said to her son with a burst of diabolical laughter.

Without responding to his mother, Martial approached Calabash, whose final agony was now beginning, and said to her, with compassion, "Poor sister . . . it's too late now."

"It's never too late . . . to be a coward!" their mother said in a cold fury. "Oh! What a family! What a family! Fortunately, Nicolas has escaped. Fortunately, François and Amandine will escape from you. Vice has already taken hold of them. Poverty will finish the job!"

"Ah! Martial, take good care of them . . . or they'll end up like our mother and me. Their heads will be cut off, too!" Calabash cried out, groaning softly.

"He can try to take care of them all he likes!" exclaimed the widow with savage exaltation. "Vice and poverty will be stronger than he, and one day they'll avenge their father, mother, and sister!"

"Your horrible expectations will turn out to be false, Mother," Martial answered her indignantly. "Neither they nor I will ever have to fear poverty. The She-Wolf rescued the girl Nicolas was trying to drown. The parents of that girl offered us the choice of either taking a great sum of money or less money and property in Algeria, right next to the farm they've already given to a man who also performed great services for them. We chose the property. There's some danger involved, but that's fine with me and the She-Wolf. Tomorrow we're leaving with the children, and we'll never come back to Europe as long as we live."

"Is what you're telling me true?" the widow asked Martial in a surprised and irritated tone.

"I never lie."

"You're lying today to make me angry."

"You're angry because the fate of those children is secure?"

"Yes, because you're going to make those wolf cubs into lambs. Your father's blood, my blood, and your sister's won't be avenged."

"This is no time to be talking like that."

"I've killed, so I'll be killed. So everything's fair."

"Mother, you can repent."

The widow burst out in laughter again. "I've lived in crime for the last thirty years, and they've given me three days to repent for thirty years, with death at the end of it. Would I have the time to do that? No, no; when my head falls, my teeth will be gnashing with rage and hatred."

"Save me, brother! Get me out of here! They're coming," Calabash murmured in a weakening voice, for the wretch was beginning to be delirious.

"Will you shut up?" the widow said, exasperated by Calabash's weakness. "Will you shut up? Oh! What a vile wretch! And it's my own daughter!"

"Mother! Mother!" cried Martial, torn apart by this horrible scene. "Why did you make me come here?"

"Because I wanted to make you brave and I wanted to make you hate, but if you fail at the first, you'll fail at the second, you coward!"

"Mother!"

"Coward, coward, coward!"

At this moment the loud sound of footsteps could be heard in the corridor. The veteran took out his watch and looked at the time. The sun was rising outside, dazzling and radiant. It suddenly cast a golden sheet of light through the small window from the corridor across from the cell door. This door opened and the entrance to the cell was brightly illuminated. In the middle of this lit-up space, the guards carried two chairs.[261] Then the clerk came in to say to the widow, in a voice full of emotion, "Madame, it is time . . ."

The condemned woman stood up straight, impassive. Calabash let out anguished cries. Four men came in. Three of them, rather poorly dressed,

261. Normally, the morning preparation of condemned prisoners takes place in the antechamber to the clerk's office, but some indispensable repair work had rendered it necessary to make these sinister preparations in the cell. [SN]

held in their hands small bundles of very thin but very strong rope. The largest of these four men was formally dressed in black, with a round hat and white tie. He handed a piece of paper to the clerk. This man was the executioner. The piece of paper was a written order for two women ready for the guillotine. The executioner was taking possession of these two creatures of God. From this point on, he alone was responsible for them.

Calabash's desperate terror had given way to a stunned torpor. Two of the executioner's assistants had to sit her down on her bed and brace her up there. Her jaws, clenched by a tetanus-like convulsion, barely allowed her to say a few random words. Her eyes were rolling in her head, already dull and unseeing. Her chin was touching her chest, and without the support of the two assistants, her body would have fallen forward like an inert mass.

Martial, after having kissed this wretched woman one last time, stood motionless and terrified, not daring, indeed not able, to take a single step. He seemed to be mesmerized by this terrible scene. The widow's audacious coolness did not desert her. With her head high and erect, she herself assisted in undoing the straitjacket that was keeping her from moving. Once the garment fell from her, she could be seen to be wearing an old black wool dress. "Where do you want me to go?" she asked in a firm voice.

"Please be so good as to sit down on one of these chairs," the executioner said to her, gesturing toward one of the two seats placed at the entrance to the cell.

With the door still open, one could see several guards, the director of the prison, and a few privileged, curious onlookers in the corridor. The widow was walking boldly toward the place she had been directed to, when she passed in front of her daughter. She stopped, approached her, and said to her in a slightly emotional voice, "Kiss me, daughter."

At the sound of her mother's voice, Calabash emerged from her apathy, sat up on her chair, and, with a gesture of malediction, she cried out, "If there is a hell, may you rot in it, you cursed woman!"

"Daughter, kiss me," the widow repeated, taking a step.

"Don't come near me! You've been the death of me!" the wretched woman murmured, throwing her hands in front of her to keep her mother off.

"Forgive me!"

"No! No!" Calabash said in a convulsive voice. Having used all her remaining strength in this effort, she fell almost unconscious into the arms of the assistants.

A cloud passed across the indomitable face of the widow. For a moment, her dry and fiery eyes became moist. At this moment, she met the gaze of her son. After a moment of hesitation, and as if she had given in to the effort of an internal struggle, she said to him, "What about you?"

Martial threw himself, sobbing, into his mother's arms. "Enough!" said the widow, overcoming her emotion and disengaging herself from her son's embrace. "Monsieur is waiting for us," she added, pointing at the executioner. Then she walked rapidly over to the chair, where she resolutely sat down. The flash of maternal sensibility that had momentarily lit up the black depths of this abominable soul suddenly went out.

"Monsieur," said the veteran to Martial, approaching him with sympathy, "don't stay here. Come along, come along."

Martial, lost in horror and fear, followed the soldier without thinking.

Two assistants had carried Calabash, in agony, to her chair. One of them was holding up her already almost lifeless body, while the other man, using very fine, very long whipcords, was tying her hands behind her back with bonds and knots that were impossible to undo. He knotted her ankles together with a cord that was long enough to allow her to walk by taking small steps. This process was both strange and terrible: the long, thin cords with which the men were silently encircling and pinioning the condemned woman with both speed and dexterity were almost invisible in the darkness and so they looked like nothing so much as the thread that spiders extrude for the purpose of immobilizing their victims prior to devouring them.

The executioner and his other assistant tied up the widow with the same deftness. The widow's face showed no change at all, except for an occasional light coughing. When the condemned woman was thus immobilized, the executioner, taking a long pair of scissors out of his pocket, said to her politely, "Please be so good as to lower your head, madame."

The widow lowered her head, saying, "We're good customers. You had my husband, and now you've got his wife and daughter." Without responding, the executioner gathered the long gray hair of the condemned woman with his left hand and began cutting it very short, very short indeed, especially around the neck. "This is the third time in my life I've had my hair done," said the widow, cackling in a sinister fashion. "The day of my first communion, when they put the veil on me, then the day of my marriage, when they put orange flowers on me, and now, today, I'm getting a death hairdo, right?" The executioner remained silent. Because the widow's hair was thick and rough, the operation took so long that by the time all of Calabash's hair had fallen to the floor, her mother's had been only partially shorn.

"You know what I'm thinking?" the widow said to the executioner after contemplating her daughter again. The executioner still remained silent. The only sound that could be heard was the grinding noise of the scissors and the raspy, hiccoughing sound arising from time to time from Calabash's chest. At this moment, a priest with a venerable face could be seen approaching the director of the prison and speaking quietly with him. This holy minister had come a final time to try to turn the widow's soul away from its hardened condition. “I’m thinking,” said the widow after a few minutes when she realized that the executioner wouldn’t answer her, “I’m thinking that, when she was five years old, my daughter, whose head you’re about to chop off, was the prettiest child you could imagine. She had blond hair and fair, rosy cheeks. Who would have said then that—” Then, after another period of silence, she exclaimed, with a burst of laughter and an expression that could not be described, “What a comedy fate is!”

At this moment, the last locks of the condemned woman’s gray mane fell onto her shoulders. “We’re done, madame,” said the executioner, politely.

“Thank you! May I recommend my son Nicolas to you?” said the widow. “You’ll be giving him a haircut one of these days!”

A guard came over to whisper a few words to the condemned woman. “No, I’ve already told you that. No,” she answered, shortly. The priest heard these words, raised his eyes to the heavens, joined his hands together, and went away.

“Madame, we’re ready to go. Is there anything I can give you?” the executioner offered obsequiously.

“No, thank you. I’ll have a good mouthful of earth this evening.” After this latest barb, the widow stood up straight. Her hands were tied behind her back, and a bond that was loose enough to allow her to walk attached one of her ankles to the other. Although her step was firm and resolute, the executioner and an assistant, obligingly, tried to offer her support. She made an impatient gesture and said in a hard, imperious voice, “Don’t touch me. My eyes are clear and my legs are strong. When I’m on the gallows, people will see whether I can still speak clearly and whether I’ll be saying any words of repentance.” And the widow walked out of the cell into the corridor, flanked by the executioner on one side and his assistant on the other. The two other assistants had to carry Calabash on her chair; she was barely conscious.

After they passed through the long corridor, the funereal procession went up a stone staircase that led to an external courtyard. With its warm golden rays, the sun was flooding the tops of the high white walls that enclosed the courtyard and stood out against the glorious blue sky. The air was gentle and warm; a more splendid or magnificent spring day had never been seen.

In this courtyard a picket of departmental police could be seen, along with a cab and a long, narrow carriage with a yellow chassis, pulled by three post-horses that were whinnying gaily as they shook their clanging bells. One mounted the carriage the same way one boarded a bus, through a door at the rear. This resemblance inspired the widow to offer one last mocking observation: “This driver isn’t going to say, ‘All full!’” she said. Then she ascended the steps as lightly as her bound ankles would allow. Calabash, barely conscious and supported by an assistant, was placed in the carriage across from her mother. Then they closed the door.

The cabdriver had fallen asleep. The executioner gave him a shake. "Excuse me, boss," said the driver, waking up and climbing heavily down from his seat, "but the mid-Lent carnival is a hard night for us. When you called me, I had just come back from driving a bunch of male and female dockworkers who kept singing 'Old Lady Godichon' at the Vendanges de Bourgogne."[262]

"All right, then. Follow that car to the boulevard Saint-Jacques."

"Excuse me, boss. I was at the Vendanges an hour ago, and now I'm going to thc guillotine! It just goes to show that every day's a new dawn, like they say."

The two carriages, preceded and followed by the picket of police, exited the outer gate of Bicêtre and took off at a brisk trot in the direction of Paris.

262. "Old Lady Godichon" was a popular, slightly off-color traditional song. The Vendanges de Bourgogne—the Harvests of Burgundy—was one of the cabarets at the edge of Paris that featured dancing and live entertainment. [TN]

CHAPTER 2

MARTIAL AND THE SLASHER

We have depicted the scene of the condemned women's morning preparation in all its dreadful reality because it seems to us that this rendering offers powerful arguments first against the death penalty, second against the way this penalty is imposed, and third against the consequences one expects and the example it offers the masses.

Although stripped of the impressive religious trappings that are the least capital punishment should provide, inflicted by the law, as it is, in the name of a vengeful public, still these preparations are the most terrifying aspect of the death penalty, and this is what is hidden from the multitudes.

In Spain, for example, it is different: the condemned person remains exposed for three days in a mortuary chapel, and he has his coffin always in view. The priests say the prayers for the dying, and the church bells toll a funeral knell day and night.[263] People there think that this kind of initiation into an impending death can put fear into the most hardened criminals and inspire a healthy terror in the crowds that press up against the bars of the mortuary chapel. Then the day of the execution is a day of public mourning. The bells of every parish ring for the dead. The condemned man is slowly taken to the gallows with an imposing and doleful formality. His coffin is still in front of him; the priests, saying the prayers for the dead, walk at his sides. The monastery brothers follow, and finally the alms collectors who ask the crowd for funds to say masses for the eternal rest of the executed man's soul. No crowd is ever deaf to this appeal.

All of this is no doubt horrifying, but it operates logically; it is intimidating; it shows that one does not erase from this world one of God's creatures in the fullness of life and strength as if he were nothing more than a bull brought to the slaughter. It makes the multitude, which always judges the crime by the gravity of the punishment, recognize that homicide is an abominable act, since the penalty for committing it stirs up, saddens, and upsets a whole town. We say again, this appalling spectacle can give birth to serious reflections and inspire a

263. This is the way it happened in Spain during my stay there, from 1824 to 1825. [SN]

useful fear, and the barbarous aspect of this human sacrifice is at least enveloped in the terrible majesty of the way it is carried out.

Yet given the fact that matters unfold exactly as we have reported—and sometimes with even less gravity—we must ask: what kind of example are we hoping to offer here? The condemned person is taken at dawn, tied up, thrown into a closed vehicle, the postilion rider whips the horses and gets to the gallows, the body is placed on the tilting board, and a head falls into the basket—amid the most atrocious mockery coming from the most corrupt elements of the crowd!

And once more, I repeat: in this rapid and furtive style of execution, where is there any example being set? Where is the dread? And moreover, as the execution takes place behind closed doors, as it were, in a walled-off square, no one knows of the bloody, solemn ritual that is taking place; nothing signals that *a man will be killed* that day. Laughter and song continue to fill the theaters, and the populace goes buzzing along in their carefree, noisy, merry way. Yet from a social, religious, and humane perspective, it should matter to everyone that a juridical homicide is being committed in the name of the public interest.

Ultimately, we must say once again, as we continually say: here is the executioner's blade; but where is the prize? Show the reward side by side with the punishment. Only then will the lesson be fruitful and complete. If the people who watched the day before as the blood of a great criminal stained the scaffold saw on the day that followed this day of mourning and death a great benefactor of humanity being rewarded and exalted, they would dread the prospect of execution all the more because they would aspire to this triumph. Terror barely deters crime at all; it never inspires virtue.

Do we consider the effect of the death penalty on the condemned themselves? Some brave death with bold cynicism; others, half dead from shock, are barely conscious when they submit to it; still others offer their heads in profound and sincere repentance. But this penalty is insufficient for those who flout it, useless for those who are already effectively dead, and excessive for those who sincerely repent.

Let us repeat: society kills the murderer neither to make him suffer nor to inflict upon him the law of an eye for an eye; it kills him to make it impossible for him to hurt others again; it kills him so that the example of his punishment may serve as a disincentive for future murderers. As for us, we believe that the penalty is barbaric, and that it is not frightening enough.

We believe that in some crimes such as patricide or other qualifying deeds, blinding and permanent solitary confinement would keep a condemned person from doing harm to others and would punish him in a way that was a thousand times more frightening, even as it left him the time to repent and find redemption. If anyone doubts the truth of this assertion, we would recall the many reports testifying to the invincible horror hardened criminals manifest toward isolation. Is it not well known that some prisoners have committed murders in order to be condemned to death, preferring this punishment to existence in a prison cell? Imagine their terror were blinding, joined with solitary confinement, to take from them all hopes of escape—hopes they cherish and sometimes even realize despite being weighed down with irons in prison cells. For that matter, we also think that the abolition of capital punishment may perhaps be one of the necessary consequences of solitary confinement. The dread this isolation inspires in the population that fills our prisons and galley ships being such that many of these unredeemable men will prefer death over solitary confinement, it will surely be necessary to remove this last, horrifying option for them by banning executions.

Before we go on with our story, let us say a few words about the relationship recently established between the Slasher and Martial. Once Germain left prison, the Slasher proved easily that he had robbed himself; he explained to the examining magistrate what the purpose of this singular act of deception had been, and was freed after being rightly and harshly scolded by this magistrate. Rodolphe wanted to reward the Slasher's latest act of devotion (he already owed his life to him), and, since he had not yet been reunited with Fleur-de-Marie, he fulfilled his coarse protégé's dearest wishes by putting him up in the mansion on rue Plumet. He also promised him that he would take him along when he returned to Germany. As we have said, the Slasher felt for Rodolphe the blind, stubborn attachment of a dog to his master. Living under the same roof as the prince and seeing him from time to time while patiently awaiting a new opportunity to sacrifice himself to him or his loved ones were the very summit of the Slasher's ambition and happiness. He vastly preferred this condition to the money and farm in Algeria that Rodolphe had placed at his disposition.

However, when the prince recovered his daughter, everything changed. Despite his great gratitude toward the man who had saved his life, he could not bring himself to take this witness to Fleur-de-Marie's original shame along with him to Germany. Absolutely determined, however, to grant the Slasher his every wish, he had him come to see him one last time, telling him that he hoped, because of his loyalty, he would perform one last service for him. At these words, the Slasher beamed. But he soon looked dismayed when he learned that not only would he not be able to follow the prince to Germany but that he would have to leave the mansion that very day. Needless to say, Rodolphe offered the Slasher brilliant compensation: the money that had been set aside for him, the contract of sale on the farm in Algeria, and more, if he wanted—he could have anything he asked. But, struck to the heart, the Slasher refused this, and for the first time in this man's life, perhaps, he wept. Rodolphe had to insist in order to convince him to accept what he had originally offered him.

The following day, the prince summoned the She-Wolf and Martial. Without telling them that Fleur-de-Marie was his daughter, he asked them what he could do for them. He would fulfill all their desires. Seeing their hesitation, and remembering what Fleur-de-Marie had told him about the rather primitive tastes of the She-Wolf and her husband, he offered the brave couple the choice of either a considerable sum of money or, instead, half that sum and land at the height of its productiveness, a dependency of the farm that neighbored the one he had bought for the Slasher, and which was also available for purchase. In making this offer, the prince had thought also that Martial and the Slasher, both rugged and full of energy, both endowed with good and valorous instincts, might get along well with each other. This was all the more likely since both of them had reasons to seek solitude: one because of his past, the other because of his family's crimes.

He was not mistaken. Martial and the She-Wolf accepted this offer ecstatically. Then, when Murph, having acted as intermediary, had brought them all together, the three were overjoyed to think of the relationship they would have as neighbors in Algeria. Despite the deep sadness into which he had sunk—or rather, because of this sadness—the Slasher, touched by the friendly overtures of Martial and his wife, responded to them effusively. Soon a sincere friendship brought the future colonists together. People of their temperament judge each other quickly and become friends with equal speed. For their part, the She-Wolf and Martial, having been incapable of drawing their new friend out of his somber lethargy, despite their affectionate attempts, came to believe that nothing would cheer him up except the distraction of the journey and the activities of their future life. Once they were in Algeria, they would be obliged to learn how to tend the lands they had been given, while the previous owners, according to the conditions of the sale, would have to continue to operate the farms for one more year so that the new owners could be in a position to know how to cultivate them in the future.

Knowing what has gone before, the reader will understand why the Slasher, informed of the painful interview to which Martial had to submit in order to obey his mother's last wishes, wanted to accompany his new friend to the gate of Bicêtre. He waited for him in the cab that had brought them there and that would take them back to Paris once Martial, horrified, had left the cell where the terrible preparations were being made for his mother's and sister's execution. The Slasher's expression was completely changed: the bold and good-humored expression that normally characterized his masculine features had given way to a gloomy dejection. Even his voice had lost some of its harshness. A sadness deep in his heart, a sadness he had never known before, had broken this lively man, shattering him completely.

He looked at Martial with compassion. "Have courage," the Slasher said to him. "You have done everything a good fellow could do. It's over. Think of your wife, of the children you stopped from becoming miscreants like their father and mother. And, finally, tonight we will leave Paris and never return, and you'll never again hear anyone mention the source of your sorrows."

"All the same, Slasher, you know, they were my mother and sister, after all."

"Well, what can you do? That's the way it is, and when things are the way they are, you have to put up with them," said the Slasher, stifling a sigh.

After a moment of silence, Martial said to him, cordially, "I should be the one comforting you, poor man. You're always so sad."

"Always, Martial."

"Well, my wife and I are sure that, once you're out of Paris, you'll feel better."

"Yes," the Slasher said, after a few moments and almost shivering in spite of himself. "If I get out of Paris . . ."

"Well, we're leaving tonight."

"Yes, you two are. You're leaving tonight."

"What about you? Have you changed your mind now?"

"No . . ."

"Well, then?"

The Slasher remained silent, and then he said, trying to control himself, "Listen, Martial. You're going to shake your head at this, but there's something I want to tell you. If something happens to me, at least that will prove to you that I wasn't wrong."

"So what is it?"

"When Monsieur Rodolphe asked us if we would like to leave together for Algiers and be neighbors there, I didn't want to deceive you or your wife. I told you what I had been."

"Let's not talk about that anymore. You've served your time. You are as good and brave as anyone. But I have the sense that, like me, you would prefer to live far away, thanks to our generous protector, to living here, where, however well-off and honest we might become, people would always hold our past against us—you, for a misdeed for which you have served your time and for which, moreover, you continue to repent, and me, for the crimes of my parents, even though I'm not responsible for them. But for you and us, the past is, well, past, over and done with. Don't worry. We are counting on you, and you can count on us."

"Between you and me, perhaps the past is past. But as I've said to Monsieur Rodolphe, you know, Martial, there's someone up there—and I've killed a man."

"That's a terrible thing, but at that moment you had ceased to be yourself. You were like a madman, and then, after all, you've saved the lives of other people. That must count for something."

"Listen, Martial. If I tell you about why I'm unhappy . . . Here's why: I used to have a recurring dream in which I would see the sergeant I killed. For a long time, I haven't had that dream, but last night it came back again."

"It's just a coincidence."

"No. It's an omen that something bad is going to happen today."

"You're not being rational, my good friend."

"I have a feeling that I won't be leaving Paris."

"As I said, that makes no sense. Your sorrow at having to leave our benefactor, the thought of taking me today to Bicêtre, where such sad things were in store for me—all of that must have gotten you agitated last night. So, naturally, your dream came back to you."

The Slasher shook his head, sadly. "It came back to me right on the day before Monsieur Rodolphe's departure, for he's leaving today."

"Today?"

"Yes. Yesterday I sent a messenger to his mansion. I didn't dare go there myself, since he's forbidden me to. They told me that the prince was leaving this morning, at eleven, by way of the Charenton barrier. Thus, once we're back in Paris, I'm going to stand there so I can try to catch sight of him. It will be the last time—the last!"

"He seems so good that I can well understand your affection for him."

"Affection?" said the Slasher with deep, intense feeling. "Oh, yes! You see, Martial, I would sleep on the floor, eat black bread—I'd be his dog. All I asked was to be where he might be. But that was too much to ask. He didn't want it."

"He's been so generous to you!"

"That's not what makes me love him so much. It's because he told me I had heart and honor. Yes, and at a time when I was as savage as a stupid animal, when I had contempt for myself as the scum of the earth, he made me understand that there was still goodness in me, since, my sentence completed, I had repented, and, after having suffered the greatest poverty without resorting to theft, I had worked courageously in order to earn an honest living without wishing anyone ill, even though everybody considered me the worst kind of criminal, which is hardly encouraging."

"That's true. It often takes no more than a few encouraging and uplifting words to put you on the right path or keep you there."

"Isn't that the truth, Martial? So when Monsieur Rodolphe said those words to me, damn! You see, my heart was beating high and proud. Since that time, I would walk through fire to do good. If I get the chance, people will see. And thanks to whom? Thanks to Monsieur Rodolphe."

"It's precisely because you have become a thousand times better than you were that you shouldn't have evil forebodings. Your dream doesn't mean a thing."

"Well, we'll see. It's not like I'm looking for anything bad to happen. Nothing worse could happen to me than what's happened. Never to see Monsieur Rodolphe again! I thought I'd never have to leave him. Staying in my proper place, of course, I would have been there, devoted to him body and soul, always there for him. It's all right. Maybe he's wrong. Listen, Martial, I'm just an earthworm compared to him. But still, sometimes the least of us can be of use to the greatest. If that ever happened, I would never forgive him for depriving himself of my help."

"Who knows? Maybe you will see him again someday."

"Oh, no! He told me, 'My boy, you must promise never to try to see me again. That will be a real favor to me.' You understand, Martial, that I promised him I wouldn't. On my honor, I'll keep that promise, but it's hard."

"Once you're over there, you'll forget what's making you unhappy, slowly but surely. We will work and live alone, peacefully, like good farmers, just having to exchange rifle fire once in a while with the Arabs. So much the better! That will suit me and my wife just fine. She's a brave one, you know, that She-Wolf!"

"If there's any shooting to do, I'm there, Martial!" the Slasher said, a little less dejected. "I'm your man! And I used to be a trooper."

"And I was a poacher!"

"But you, you have your wife and those two children to whom you are something of a father. Me, I have only my own skin to worry about. And since Monsieur Rodolphe won't use it for an umbrella, I hardly care about it. So if someone has to get a haircut, it'll be me."

"We'll both be in it together."

"No, I'll take care of it alone! By heaven! I'll take care of those Bedouins!"

"That's the spirit! I'd rather hear you talk like that than the way you were sounding a little while ago. Come on, Slasher. We'll be like real brothers, and then you'll be able to tell us about your sorrows if you still have them, for I'll have my own, too. Today's memory will last for a long time for me, you know? You can't see your mother and sister the way I saw them without having it stick in your mind. We're a lot alike, you and me, in too many ways, for us not to get along well. Neither one of us flinches from danger. Well, we'll be half farmers, half soldiers! There's hunting to do there, so we'll hunt together. If you want to live alone in your home, you can live there and we'll be your neighbors. But otherwise, we can all live together. We will raise the children to be good people, and you'll practically be their uncle, since we'll be brothers. Does that sound good to you?" said Martial, extending his hand to the Slasher.

"It sounds good to me, my good Martial. And then, finally, my sorrow will kill me—or I'll kill it, as they say."

"It won't kill you. We'll get old there in our desert, and every night we'll say, 'Brother, thanks to Monsieur Rodolphe . . .' That will be our prayer for him."

"You know, Martial, this makes me feel a lot better."

"Good! You're not thinking about that stupid dream anymore, I hope?"

"I'll try not to."

"Now, then! You'll come and get us at four o'clock! The stagecoach leaves at five."

"It's a deal. But we'll be in Paris soon. I'm going to stop the cab. I'll walk on foot to the Charenton barrier. I'll wait to watch Monsieur Rodolphe pass by."

The carriage stopped, and the Slasher got out.

"Don't forget—four o'clock! See you then, my good comrade!" Martial said.

"At four o'clock!"

The Slasher had forgotten that it was the day after mid-Lent. Thus he was strangely surprised by the peculiar, hideous scene that he saw as he walked along a section of the exterior boulevard he was taking to get to the Charenton barrier.

CHAPTER 3

THE FINGER OF GOD

After a few moments, the Slasher found himself being carried along against his will by a closely packed throng of people, a huge influx of the masses coming out of the Glacière neighborhood and accumulating along the approaches to this gate on their way over to the boulevard Saint-Jacques, where the execution was to take place. Although it was daytime, the music of the dance halls could be heard from afar. The reverberating sound of the trombones stood out most of all.

One would need the paintbrush of Callot, Rembrandt, or Goya[264] to depict the bizarre, hideous, almost fantasy-like aspect of this multitude. Almost all of them—men, women, and children—were wearing old masquerade outfits. Those who could not afford this luxury wore brightly colored rags on top of their clothing. Some young men were decked out in half-torn, mud-soiled women's dresses. All of these faces, withered by debauchery and vice, pallid with drunkenness, were alight with savage joy as they looked forward, after a night of foul orgies, to watching two women be put to death on the scaffold.[265] This immense cohort, the vile, fetid scum of the population of Paris, was composed of the criminals and fallen women who looked out each day for the crime that would allow them to earn their daily bread, and who returned to their lairs each evening largely sated.[266]

As the outside boulevard was quite narrow here, the accumulating crowd was backing up and completely blocking the flow of traffic. Despite his athletic strength, the Slasher was obliged to remain nearly immobile in the middle of this compact mass. He resigned himself to it.

---

264. Jacques Callot (1592–1653) was a printmaker known for etchings showing common people. For Goya, see Book VIII, Chapter 6, footnote 199. [TN]

265. The execution of Norbert and Després took place this year the day after mid-Lent. [SN]

266. According to Monsieur Frégier, the excellent historian of these criminal classes of our society, there are thirty thousand people in Paris whose only means of supporting themselves is theft. [SN]

Honoré Antoine Frégier (1789–1860) wrote *Des classes dangereuses de la population dans les grandes villes et des moyens de les rendre meilleures* (On the Criminal Classes of the Populations of Large Cities and the Means of Improving Them). [TN]

The prince, who would depart from rue Plumet at ten o'clock, he had heard, would not get to the Charenton gate until about eleven o'clock. It was only seven o'clock now.

Although he had previously lived among the degraded class of people to whom these masses belonged, the Slasher now felt the greatest disgust for them as he found himself in their midst. Pushed by the flow of the crowd as far as the wall of one of the dance halls these boulevards teem with, the Slasher involuntarily witnessed a strange spectacle through the open windows from which escaped the deafening sound of an orchestra of brass instruments.

In a vast, low room, occupied at one end by musicians, surrounded by benches and tables that were cluttered with the debris of a meal—broken plates, overturned bottles—a dozen disguised men and women, half drunk, were lustily dancing the mad and obscene dance called the cancan. A small number of the habitués of these establishments participate in this dance only at the end of the ball, when the municipal guards on watch have left. Among the ignoble couples who participated in this saturnalia, the Slasher noticed two that were being applauded in particular for the revolting cynicism of their poses, gestures, and speech. One member of the first couple was a man who was more or less disguised as a bear, in a jacket and trousers made of black sheepskin. The head of the animal, no doubt too cumbersome to wear, had been replaced by a sort of hood with long fur on it that covered his face entirely. Two holes where the eyes were and a wide slash around the mouth allowed him to see, speak, and breathe. This masked man, one of the escaped prisoners from La Force (among whom were also Fishhook and the two murderers who were arrested at the ogress's joint at the beginning of this story), was Nicolas Martial, the son and brother of the two women for whom the gallows had been put up a few steps away. Carried along in this act of senseless atrocity and impudent boasting by one of his companions, a dangerous criminal, also an escapee and also disguised, this wretch, with the assistance of this disguise, dared to give himself over to the last joys of the carnival. The woman who was dancing with him, dressed as a canteen-keeper, was wearing an embossed, hardened leather hat with tattered ribbons on it, a sort of jerkin made of red embroidered fabric that had three rows of brass hussar's buttons on it, a green skirt, and white calico pantaloons. Her black hair was falling in her face in a disheveled manner. Her gaunt, leaden features reeked of impudence and immodesty.

The couple opposite these two dancers were no less debased. The man, exceedingly tall, disguised as Robert Macaire,[267] had rubbed so much soot onto his bony face that he was not recognizable. Furthermore, a large bandage was covering his left eye, and the dull white of the right

267. See Book IV, Chapter 5, footnote 104. [TN]

eyeball, standing out from his black face, made it even more hideous. The lower part of the Skeleton's face (the reader has doubtless already recognized him) disappeared entirely into a high-rising tie made out of an old red shawl. He wore the traditional gray hat, which was worn out, flattened, shoddy, and had no top. Dressed in a tattered green coat and reddish-purple trousers that were patched in numerous places and tied at the ankles with strings, this murderer was exaggerating the most grotesque and cynical poses of the cancan. He swung his long limbs that were as tough as iron from right to left and back and forth, bending and straightening his arms and legs with so much vigor and elasticity that they looked as if they had steel springs inside them.

The worthy leader of this obscene saturnalia, his dance partner, a tall and agile creature with an impudent drunkard's face, was disguised as a stevedore, with a police cap poised atop a powdered wig that had a fat tail. She wore a threadbare green velvet jacket and trousers, cinched at the waist by an orange sash, its ends floating out behind her. A fat, ignoble, masculine-looking woman, the ogress from the joint, sitting on one of the benches, held the tartan coats of this creature and the canteen-keeper on her knees as they outdid each other in producing leaps and cynical poses with the Skeleton and Nicolas Martial.

A lame child could also be seen among the other dancers. He was dressed as the devil in a black sweater that was much too big and long for him, red leggings, and a horrible, grimacing green mask. Despite his infirmity, this little monster was surprisingly agile. His precocious depravity matched, if it did not exceed, that of his frightful companions, and he was prancing about with as much effrontery as anyone before a fat woman disguised as a shepherdess. She was egging her partner on in his profligacy by laughing uproariously.

As no charges had been brought against Gammy (the reader will also have recognized him), and as Red-Arm had been kept provisionally in prison, the child had been taken in, at the request of his father, by Micou, the fence from the passage de la Brasserie, who had not in fact been denounced by his accomplices.

As secondary figures of the picture we have been trying to paint, imagine everything that is lowest, most shameful, most monstrous in this idle, bold, greedy, bloodthirsty, godless, and dissolute mob that has increasingly shown itself to be hostile to the social order, and to whom we wish to call the attention of thinking people as we end this story. May this last horrible scene exemplify the danger that incessantly threatens our society!

Yes, we must think about this: the cohesion and alarming growth of this race of thieves and murderers is a kind of living protest against the vice of repressive laws, especially against the absence of preventive measures, of farsighted legislation, of broad-minded, protective institutions that would be set up to oversee the moral education, from childhood, of this mass of wretches who have been abandoned or perverted by bad examples. Once again, these disinherited beings, whom God made neither better nor worse than his other creatures, would not be incurably contaminated and corrupted if they had not been immersed from birth in the mire of poverty, ignorance, and brutality.

Still under the influence of the laughter and bravos of the crowd that was pressing against the windows, the protagonists in this abominable orgy that we are recounting cried out to the orchestra to play one last galop.[268] The musicians, delighted to be nearing the end of a performance that was so hard on their lungs, gave in to the general will and played an energetic galop at a lively and quick pace. At the sound of these resounding notes from the brass instruments, the excitement increased. All of the couples grabbed at each other, shook their bodies, and, taking the lead from the Skeleton and his dancing partner, began an infernal round, hurling savage cries as they did so.

A thick dust raised by their furious stomping rose from the floor of the room and cast a sort of sinister red cloud on this whirlwind of intertwined men and women who were twirling about at dizzying speeds. For these people, driven by wine, movement, and their own cries, it was soon no longer mere intoxication they were feeling, but rather delirium or frenzy. They needed more room. The Skeleton cried out, panting for breath, "Look out! There's the door! We're heading for the boulevard!"

"Yes! Yes!" cried the crowd that was amassing at the windows. "A galop to the Saint-Jacques barrier!"

"It's almost time for them to shorten those two dames by a head's length!"

"The executioner is doing a double feature! That'll be fun!"

"To the accompaniment of a slide trombone!"

"We'll dance the guillotine quadrille!"

"Let's go, headless women!" cried Gammy.

"This will cheer up the condemned women!"

"I'll invite the widow to dance."

"I'll ask the daughter."

"That'll make the old beheader happy."

"He'll be doing the cancan in his workplace with his employees."

"Death to patsies! Long live thieves and cutthroats!" the Skeleton cried in a bloodcurdling voice.

---

268. The galop is a fast dance named after the horse's gallop. It was often performed as the last dance of the evening. [TN]

The taunts and threats of these cannibals, accompanied by obscene songs, cries, whistles, and hoots, were still mounting when the Skeleton's band, through the force of its passionate violence, created a wide space for itself in the middle of this compact crowd. It was now a horrifying mob. The howling, curses, and bursts of laughter that could be heard bore no resemblance to anything that could be called human.

The tumult was suddenly pushed to its height by two new incidents. The car carrying the condemned women, accompanied by its cavalry escort, appeared from afar at the corner of the boulevard. At this point the entire mob rushed in that direction, crying out all the while in savage glee. At this moment also, the crowd was joined by a messenger coming from the boulevard des Invalides and heading toward the Charenton gate at a gallop. He was wearing a light blue jacket with a yellow collar, ornamented with silver braids at the seams. But, as a sign of mourning, he wore black pants with his heavy boots. His hat, also heavily embroidered with silver, had a crepe band on it. Finally, on the eyelets of the bridle, embellished with bells, the imprint of the sovereign coat of arms of Gerolstein could be seen.

The messenger slowed his horse to a walk, but it was getting harder and harder for him to move. When he came to the middle of the flood tide of the mob we have described, he was almost forced to come to a full halt. Although he cried "Look out!" and moved his horse forward with the greatest care, he was quickly yelled at, cursed, and threatened.

"Is this guy trying to drive his camel onto our backs?"

"It's just a silver breastplate, thank you very much!" cried Gammy under his green mask with its red tongue.

"If he gives us any trouble, let's throw him off his horse."

"And let's slice the silver off his jacket to melt it down," said Nicolas.

"And we can slice your stomach open if you have any complaints, you lousy flunky," added the Skeleton, addressing the messenger and seizing the reins of his horse. The crowd had become so tightly packed that the criminal had given up on his plan to dance all the way to the gate.

The messenger, who was strong and determined, said to the Skeleton as he raised the handle of his whip, "If you don't drop the reins of my horse, I'll slash your face."

"You, you rotten lout?"

"Yes. I'm riding slow, and I yell, 'Look out!' You have no right to stop me. His lordship's carriage is following behind me. I can already hear the whips. Let me pass."

"Your lordship?" said the Skeleton. "What do I care about your lordship? I'll brain him just 'cause I feel like it. I've never knocked off one of those lordships—and now I've sort of got a hankering to do it."

"There are no more lords! Long live the Charter!" cried Gammy. And humming these verses from "La Parisienne"[269] as he did so—"Forward! Let us march against their cannons!"—he suddenly grabbed one of the messenger's boots, pulled on it with all his might, and made him stagger in his saddle. A harsh blow from the whip handle to his head punished Gammy for his impertinence. But the furious mob immediately set on the messenger. It did no good to spur his horse to tell it to carry him forward and get away. He could not manage this, nor could he pull out his hunting knife. Dismounted, pushed down amid cries and hoots of rage, he would have been killed if not for the arrival of Rodolphe's carriage, which served to divert the delirious transport of these wretches.

For some time the prince's brougham, harnessed to four post-horses, had been traveling at a walking pace. One of the two footservants, wearing mourning (because of Sarah's death), sitting on the rear seat, had even prudently gotten down and was holding on to one of the door handles, since the carriage rode low to the ground. The postilions were crying, "Look out!" They advanced with great care.

Both Rodolphe and his daughter were dressed in full mourning. He was holding one of her hands in his own and gazing at her with happiness and tenderness. Fleur-de-Marie's sweet and charming face was framed in a little black crepe hood that made the glowing whiteness of her skin and the brilliant luster of her beautiful blond hair stand out all the more. It almost seemed that her large eyes were reflecting back the azure sky of this beautiful day. Those eyes had never been a softer or more limpid blue. Although her face, smiling sweetly, wore an expression of calm and happiness when she looked at her father, a tinge of melancholy, sometimes even of indefinable sadness, often cast a shadow on Fleur-de-Marie's features when her father's eyes were no longer upon her.

"You aren't angry at me for waking you up so early so that we could depart earlier?" Rodolphe said to her with a smile.

"Oh, no, Father! This is such a beautiful morning!"

"It's just that I thought, you know, that we would be able to time the rests in our trip better if we left earlier. That way it would be less tiring for you. Murph, my aides-de-camp, and the attending carriage which carries your ladies in waiting will join us at our first stop, where you will have the chance to rest."

"Dear father . . . you're always thinking of me."

"Yes, mademoiselle. And you can't blame me for that. It's impossible to think of anyone else," said the prince, smiling. Then he added, with a burst of tenderness, "Oh! I love you so much! I love you so much! I need

---

269. "La Parisienne" was a popular song composed after the July 1830 Revolution. It was the national anthem during Louis-Philippe's July Monarchy (1830–1848). [TN]

your forehead right now." Fleur-de-Marie leaned toward her father, and Rodolphe, enraptured, pressed his lips to her charming forehead.

It was at this moment that the carriage, approaching the crowd, had begun to move very slowly. Rodolphe, surprised, lowered the window and said in German to the footservant who was manning the door, "Well, Franz? What's happening? What is this tumult?"

"Your Lordship, there is such a crowd that the horses can't go any further."

"And why is there a crowd?"

"Your Lordship . . ."

"Well?"

"It's just that, Your Highness . . ."

"Speak already!"

"Your Lordship, I just heard that there is going to be an execution over there."

"Oh! How dreadful!" exclaimed Rodolphe, moving back inside the carriage.

"What's wrong, Father?" asked Fleur-de-Marie quickly, with anxiety.

"Nothing. Nothing, my child."

"But what are those threatening cries? Do you hear them? They're getting closer. Dear Lord, what is that?"

"Franz, order the postilions to turn around and approach Charenton by a different route—any other route," Rodolphe said.

"Your Lordship, it's too late. We're caught in the middle of the crowd. These people stopping the horses have a nasty look about them."

The footservant could no longer speak. The crowd, driven to distraction by the bloodthirsty braggadocio of the Skeleton and Nicolas, suddenly surrounded the carriage, shouting loudly. Despite the efforts and threats of the postilions, the horses were stopped, and Rodolphe could see nothing but horrible, furious, threatening faces from all sides at the level of the doors. Dominating them because of his height was the Skeleton, who approached the door.

"Father, be careful!" exclaimed Fleur-de-Marie as she flung her arms around Rodolphe's neck.

"So you're the great lord?" said the Skeleton, putting his hideous head into the carriage.

Rodolphe would have given in to the violence of his character in the face of this insolence if his daughter had not been present, but he restrained himself and instead answered him coldly, "What do you want? Why are you stopping my carriage?"

"Because we feel like it," said the Skeleton, putting his bony hands on the door handle. "Everything in good time. Yesterday you trampled on the mob. Today the mob will trample on you, if you move."

"Father, we're going to be murdered!" Fleur-de-Marie murmured in a whisper.

"Don't worry. I know what's happening," said the prince. "It's the last day of carnival. These people are drunk. I'll get rid of them."

"We have to get him to come out—and his dame, too," cried Nicolas. "Why should they get to trample on the poor?"

"You seem to have had a lot to drink already, and you want to drink some more," said Rodolphe, taking his wallet out of his pocket. "Here, this is for you. Don't hold my carriage up any longer." With that, he threw his wallet into the crowd. Gammy caught it in midflight.

"Come on, you're going on a trip, so your pockets are stuffed with cash. Cough up some more, or we'll kill you. I have nothing to lose. I'm telling you that it's your money or your life here in full daylight. What a scene!" the Skeleton said, completely drunk with wine and bloodlust. And he suddenly opened the door.

Rodolphe's patience had reached its limit. Concerned for Fleur-de-Marie, who was becoming more frightened by the second, and thinking that a show of strength would intimidate this wretch he took to be merely drunk, he jumped out of the carriage to seize the Skeleton by the neck. At first the latter stepped back quickly, pulling a long dagger out of his pocket, and then he threw himself upon Rodolphe. Fleur-de-Marie, seeing the criminal's dagger hovering over her father, cried out in a heartrending manner, leapt out of the car, and wrapped her arms around him.

It would have been curtains for her and her father if the Slasher, who from the beginning of this fight, having recognized the prince's livery, had not managed, with superhuman effort, to get to the Skeleton. At the moment the latter was threatening the prince with his knife, the Slasher held the arm of the brigand with one hand and with the other seized him by the collar and threw him over backward. Although caught off guard by the surprise attack from behind, the Skeleton was able to turn around. He recognized the Slasher and exclaimed, "The man in the gray smock from La Force! This time, I'm going to kill you!"

And, throwing himself furiously on the Slasher, he plunged his knife in his chest.

The Slasher staggered but he didn't fall. The crowd was holding him up.

"The police! The police have arrived!" cried a few frightened voices.

At these words, at the sight of the Slasher's murder, this entire crowd that had been so compact dispersed as if by magic, fearing that they would be implicated in this crime. They fled in all directions. The Skeleton, Nicolas Martial, and Gammy disappeared also.

When the police arrived, brought by the messenger, who had managed to escape when the crowd left him in order to surround the prince's carriage, the only people left on the stage of this sad scene were Rodolphe, his daughter, and the Slasher, who was bathed in blood. The prince's two footmen had placed him on the ground and leaned him up against a tree. All of this had taken place much more quickly than it is possible to record, a few steps away from the dance hall from which the Skeleton and his gang had emerged.

The prince, pale and upset, held the fainting Fleur-de-Marie in his arms while the postilions readjusted the harness traces which had been partially broken in the melee.

"Quickly," said the prince to his people who were engaged in trying to save the Slasher, "carry this poor man into this cabaret. And you," he added, turning to his messenger, "climb up on the carriage and ride back to the mansion as fast as you can go and get Doctor David. He's not going to leave until eleven o'clock. You'll find him there." Moments later, the carriage left in a gallop, and the two domestics moved the Slasher into the low room in which the orgy of dancing had taken place and in which a few of the women who had played a part in it still remained.

"My poor child," said Rodolphe to his daughter, "I'm going to take you to a room in this house, and you can wait for me there. This courageous man has just saved my life once again, and I won't leave him only to the care of my people."

"Oh, Father! I beg of you, do not leave me!" cried Fleur-de-Marie with terror as she grasped Rodolphe's arm. "Don't leave me alone! I would die of fright! I will go wherever you go!"

"But this is an appalling spectacle!"

"But thanks to this man, you still live for me, Father. At least allow me to stay with you so I can thank and comfort him."

The prince was quite perplexed. His daughter displayed such great terror at the thought of remaining alone in a room of this degraded tavern that he resigned himself to taking her along with him as he went into the lower chamber the Slasher was in.

The owner of the dance hall and several of the women who had remained there (among whom was the ogress from the joint) had quickly laid the wounded man on a mattress and then stanched and bandaged the wound with napkins. The Slasher had just opened his eyes when Rodolphe entered. At the sight of the prince, his face, which was as pale as death, became slightly more animated. He smiled painfully and said to him in a weak voice, "Ah! Monsieur Rodolphe! What luck it was that I was there!"

"Brave and devoted as always!" the prince said to him in sadness. "You've saved me again."

"I was going to head over to the Charenton barrier to try to see you as you left. But luckily, I got stuck in the crowd. This had to happen, anyway. I told Martial about it. I had a presentiment."

"A presentiment?"

"Yes, Monsieur Rodolphe. The dream about the sergeant . . . I had it, last night."

"Forget those thoughts! Keep your hope up! Your wound isn't fatal!"

"Oh, yes, it is. The Skeleton struck true. It's all right. I was right when I told Martial that an earthworm like me could sometimes be of service to a great lord like you."

"But I owe you my life—my life—yet again."

"We're even, then, Monsieur Rodolphe. You told me that I had heart and honor. What you said, then, you see— Oh! I can't breathe . . . Your Lordship . . . not to give you orders . . . but do me the honor . . . of giving me . . . your hand . . . I think this is it . . ."

"No! It's impossible!" exclaimed the prince as he bent over the Slasher and held the icy hand of the dying man in his own. "No—you will live—you will live—"

"Monsieur Rodolphe, you see, there's something . . . up there . . . I killed . . . with a knife . . . I die . . . by the knife," said the Slasher in a voice that was growing ever weaker and softer.

At this moment, his gaze fell on Fleur-de-Marie, whom he had not yet noticed. His surprise could be seen on his dying face. He gestured and said, "Oh! My God! It's Songbird—"

"Yes. She's my daughter. She blesses you for having saved her father for her."

"She . . . your daughter . . . here . . . that reminds me of how we met . . . Monsieur Rodolphe . . . and the blows that finished me off . . . but this . . . knife wound will also . . . finish me off . . . I slashed . . . and I was slashed . . . it's only just . . ."

He sighed deeply and his head fell backward. He was dead.

The sound of the horses echoed outside. Rodolphe's carriage had met up with the one carrying Murph and David, who, in their haste to rejoin the prince, had left earlier than planned. David and the squire entered the room. "David," said Rodolphe, wiping the tears from his eyes as he gestured toward the Slasher. "Good God, is there nothing else we can do?"

"Nothing, Your Lordship," said the doctor after examining him briefly.

During this brief examination, a silent and terrifying scene had just taken place between Fleur-de-Marie and the ogress, which Rodolphe didn't notice. When the Slasher had quietly uttered Songbird's name, the ogress, raising her head quickly, had seen Fleur-de-Marie. The horrible woman had already recognized Rodolphe. They were calling him "Your Lordship" and he was calling Songbird his daughter. Such a metamorphosis astonished the ogress, who had stubbornly attached her stupidly bewildered eyes upon her former victim. Pale, terrified, Fleur-de-Marie seemed fascinated by her gaze. The death of the Slasher—along with the unexpected appearance of the ogress, who had just revived, more painfully than ever, the memory of her first degradation—seemed a sinister omen to her. From this moment on, Fleur-de-Marie was struck by the kind of presentiment that often has irresistible power over characters such as her own.

A short time after these sad events, Rodolphe and his daughter left Paris forever.

EPILOGUE

CHAPTER 1

GEROLSTEIN

Prince Henri d'Herkaüsen-Oldenzaal
To Count Maximilien Kaminetz
Oldenzaal, August 25, 1840[270]

I have come from Gerolstein where I spent three months in the company of the grand duke and his family. I thought I would find a letter announcing your arrival at Oldenzaal, my dear Maximilien. Imagine my surprise and disappointment when I learned that you were still detained in Hungary for several weeks. I have not written you for four months because I did not know to where to send my letters, thanks to that haphazard mode of travel which is all your own. But you absolutely promised me, in Vienna, when we parted, that you would be at Oldenzaal by August 1. Well, I must give up the pleasure of seeing you, I suppose, and, yet, I have never had a greater need of opening my heart to you, my dear Maximilien, my oldest friend—because, after all, even if we are still young, our friendship is old, dating as it does from our childhood.

What can I tell you? In three months, I have become a completely changed man. I have come to one of those moments which can determine one's entire future existence. So you can understand how much I miss you and miss what you might say to me! But whatever keeps you in Hungary, I won't have to miss you for much longer. You will come. I beg you to come, because I will surely need all the comfort you can give me, and I can't go looking for you. My father, whose health grows weaker by the day, has called me away from Gerolstein. Every day, he gets weaker. I can't possibly leave him.

270. We remind the reader that about fifteen months have gone by since the day Rodolphe left Paris by the Saint-Jacques gate, right after the Slasher was murdered. [SN]

Modern editions of the novel change this date to 1841 to bring it into accord with the datings of Rigolette's letter in Chapter 4 and Rodolphe's letter to Clémence in Chapter 7 of the epilogue. We have kept the dating of the original edition. [TN]

I have so much to tell you that I will go on at some length. I need to tell you about the fullest and the most dramatic period I have ever gone through in my life.

It is a strange and sad happenstance that we have been inevitably kept apart from each other, given how inseparable we have been. We who have been like brothers, who have been the two most fervent apostles of thrice holy friendship! We were so proud of proving that Carlos and Posa in our Schiller weren't mere abstract ideals and that, like the divine creations of our great poet, we knew how to experience the sweet delights of an affectionate and mutual attachment.[271]

Oh, my friend, why aren't you here? Why weren't you here? My heart has been overflowing with the most inexpressibly sweet and the most inexpressibly sad feelings for the past three months. And I have been alone. And I am alone. You who know how strangely expansive my sensibility sometimes is, you should pity me. You have often seen how the most naive account of a generous act, or even the simple scene of a beautiful sunset or a peaceful, starry night, will bring tears to my eyes. Do you remember last year, the time we spent at the ruins of Oppenfeld, on the shore of the great lake and our silent reveries during that magnificent evening so full of calm, poetry, and serenity?

What a peculiar contrast! That was three days before that bloody duel for which I didn't want you to be my second because I would have suffered too much for you if I had been wounded before your very eyes. That was the duel over a gambling quarrel where my own second unfortunately killed that young Frenchman, the Viscount de Saint-Remy.[272] Speaking of that, do you know what has become of that dangerous siren Monsieur de Saint-Remy brought to Oppenfeld, the one whose name, I think, was Cecily David?

You must be smiling with pity at me, my friend, to see me wander so among vague memories of the past rather than getting to the point of the serious confidences I told you of. That's because, despite myself, I draw back every time I have to utter those confidences. I know how severe you can be, and I'm afraid you will scold me—yes, scold me—because, rather than acting upon reflection and wisely (alas, the wisdom of someone who is twenty-one!), I have acted foolishly, or rather, I have not acted at all. I allowed the current that swept me up to carry me blindly along, and it's only since I have returned from Gerolstein that I have, so to speak,

271. Don Carlos and the Marquis of Posa are friends who support each other through the various dramatic conflicts of Friedrich Schiller's play *Don Carlos* (1787). [TN]

272. Seconds oversee that both parties to a duel observe the rules that they have agreed will govern it. If Henri's second killed Saint-Remy, it will have been because Saint-Remy was breaking one of those rules to give him an unfair advantage. [TN]

returned to reality from the enchanting dream that beguiled me for three months. And that awakening has been a gloomy one.

Well, my friend, my good Maximilien, let's get to it. I'll be brave. Listen to me indulgently. I'll begin by lowering my eyes, since I don't dare look at you . . . and as you read these lines, your features must be so serious, so severe. You stoic!

Having obtained six months' leave, I left Venice and I stayed here with my father for a little while. Inasmuch as he was in good health at the time, he suggested that I go visit my wonderful aunt, Princess Juliane, the mother superior of the Gerolstein abbey. I think I have told you, my friend, that my grandmother was the first cousin of the current grand duke's grandfather and that he, Gustave-Rodolphe, has always been so kind, because of this relationship, as to treat both my father and me very warmly as cousins. You also know, I think, that during a fairly long trip the prince lately made to France, he gave my father the responsibility of taking care of the grand duchy's administration. I do not tell you these details out of any pride, as you well know. They explain why I lived in such intimacy with the grand duke and his family while I stayed in Gerolstein.

Do you remember that last year, when we were traveling along the banks of the Rhine, we learned that, in France, the prince had met up again with Countess Sarah MacGregor and married her *in extremis* in order to legitimate the daughter she bore him at the time of their secret first marriage? This marriage was later annulled as having been formally improper because it was entered into against the will of the then reigning grand duke. This young girl, whose position was so solemnly recognized by that marriage, is the charming Princess Amélie,[273] who Lord Dudley, having seen her at Gerolstein about a year ago now, talked to us about with such enthusiasm when we were in Vienna that we accused him of exaggeration. What a strange coincidence! Who could then have foreseen what would happen?

Even though you have no doubt already more or less guessed my secret, let me follow the train of events as they occurred without getting ahead of myself.

The Sainte-Hermangilde convent, of which my aunt is the abbess, is barely an eighth of a league's distance from Gerolstein. Indeed, the abbey's gardens reach just to the outer neighborhoods of the city. My aunt, who, you will remember, loved me like a mother, had given me the use of a charming house, completely separated from the cloister. The day I arrived she told me that there was going to be a solemn reception and a party at court two days later, before which the grand duke would officially announce his coming marriage to the Marquise d'Harville, who

273. Because the name Marie recalled such sad memories for Rodolphe and his daughter, he gave her the name of Amélie, one of his mother's names. [SN]

had recently come to Gerolstein in the company of her father, the Count d'Orbigny.[274]

Some found fault with the prince for not having sought out a sovereign alliance this time as he had before (the late duchess of the widowed grand duke had belonged to the House of Bavaria). Others, however, and my aunt was of their number, congratulated him for having preferred to the usual ambitious customs a young and adorable woman whom he loved and who belonged to the highest ranks of French nobility. My aunt, as you know, my friend, has moreover always felt the deepest affection for Grand Duke Rodolphe. She, more than anyone, has always been able to appreciate the prince's finer qualities.

"My dear child," she said to me with regard to this solemn reception, which I would have to attend two days after my arrival, "my dear child, the most marvelous sight you will see at this party, I can say without fear of contradiction, will be the pearl of Gerolstein."

"Of whom are you speaking, my dear aunt?"

"Of the Princess Amélie."

"The daughter of the grand duke? Indeed, Lord Dudley had spoken to us about her in Vienna with such enthusiasm that we accused him of poetic exaggeration."

"At my age, with my character, and in my position, one is not frequently given to enthusiasms, so you will believe in the impartiality of my judgment, my dear child! Well, then, I will tell you, and it is I who say it, that I have never in my life met anyone more enchanting than the Princess Amélie. I would mention her angelic beauty if she were not endowed with an inexpressible charm that is superior even to that beauty. Imagine innocence mixed with dignity, and grace with modesty. From the moment the grand duke introduced me to her, I have felt a sympathy for this young princess that was beyond my will. And besides, I'm not alone. The Archduchess Sophie has been at Gerolstein for the last few days. She is the proudest and haughtiest princess I know."

"Her irony is fearsome, it's true, Aunt. Few people escape her mordant humor. At Vienna people constantly feared being scorched by her wit. Has the Princess Amélie found her way into her good graces?"

"The other day she came here after having visited the house of refuge the young princess oversees. 'Do you know something?' the redoubtable

274. For the purposes of verisimilitude, we remind the reader that the last sovereign princess of Courland, a woman as remarkable for her unusually superior intelligence as for the charm of her character and the goodness of her heart, was Mademoiselle de Medem. [SN]

Anna Charlotte Dorothea von Medem (1761–1821) was the daughter of a German count who became Duchess of Courland (a grand duchy) upon her marriage in 1799 to its duke, Peter von Biron. Sue is justifying the verisimilitude of Rodolphe's marriage to someone not of a royal family with a historical example of such a marriage. [TN]

archduchess said to me with her brusque frankness. 'I have a singularly satiric sensibility, as you know. Well, if I were to live in the company of the duke's daughter for a sufficiently long time, I would become completely inoffensive, I'm sure of it. Her kindness is that penetrating and contagious.'"

"Is my cousin really an enchantress?" I said to my aunt with a smile.

"Her most powerful attraction, at least in my eyes," my aunt said, "is her mixture of sweetness, modesty, and dignity of which I spoke, which gives her face the most touching and angelic expression."

"Well, Aunt, modesty is certainly a rare quality when it comes to a princess who is so young, so beautiful, and so happy."

"Consider, then, my dear child, how much rarer it is in Princess Amélie's case to enjoy her high position without any vain ostentation when you consider that her elevation, which occurred without any objections, is so recent."[275]

"And in her conversation with you, Aunt, did the princess make any allusion to her past?"

"No, but when, despite my advanced years, I spoke to her with the respect which is her due, since her highness is the daughter of our sovereign, her artless embarrassment, mixed with gratitude and veneration for me, touched me deeply. Her reserve, which was filled with nobility and friendliness, showed me that her present circumstances would not make her dizzy enough to forget her past, and that she would give the same respect to my years that I would accord to her rank."

"She really must have exquisite tact," I said to my aunt, "to be able to observe such delicate nuances."

"And so, my dear child, the more I saw the Princess Amélie, the more I felt confirmed in my first impression. You wouldn't believe all the good works she has accomplished since she has been here, and these with a reflectiveness and maturity of judgment that I can barely believe possible in a person of her age. But judge for yourself: at her request, the grand duke has founded in Gerolstein an establishment for orphaned young girls of five or six years, and also for young women who have been orphaned or abandoned at sixteen, an age that is so dangerous for unfortunate girls whom no one protects against seduction, vice, and the weaknesses brought on by need. The teachers and directors of this house's pensioners are the noble sisters of my abbey. When I visit there, I have often had the occasion to see how much these poor, disinherited creatures adore Princess Amélie. She spends a few hours every day in this establishment, which has been placed under her special protection. And, as I said, my

275. Upon arriving in Germany, Rodolphe had said that Fleur-de-Marie, who had long been believed to be dead, had never left her mother, the Countess Sarah. [SN]

child, it isn't merely respect or gratitude that the pensioners and the sisters feel for her highness. It's practically fanatical adoration."

"This Princess Amélie must be an angel," I said to my aunt.

"An angel, yes; the Princess Amélie is an angel," she went on. "She must be because you cannot imagine the touching kindness with which she treats her protégés, with what pious care she showers them. I have never seen the susceptibilities of the unfortunate handled with more delicacy. You would think that some irresistible sympathy draws the princess, more than anyone else, toward this category of poor, abandoned women. On top of all that—would you believe it?—daughter of a sovereign as she is, she never calls these young girls anything else but 'my sisters.'"

Maximilien, I must admit that these last words of my aunt's brought a tear to my eye. Don't you think the conduct of this young princess really is both beautiful and holy? You know my truthfulness and I swear to you that I am telling you and will continue to tell you nearly word for word exactly what my aunt said.

"Knowing how marvelously talented the princess is," I told her, "I will be quite embarrassed when I am presented to her tomorrow. You know how hopelessly timid I am and you know how much more imposing I find elevation of mind than elevation of rank. I am, therefore, certain to seem as stupid to the princess as I will be embarrassed. I'm just warning you beforehand."

"Oh, don't worry yourself about it," my aunt said with a smile. "She will have pity on you, all the more so since you are not really a new acquaintance for her."

"Me, Aunt?"

"Yes, you."

"What makes you think that?"

"You remember that when you were sixteen and you left Oldenzaal to travel through Russia and England with your father, I had your portrait taken in the costume you wore to the first masquerade ball given by the late grand duchess?"

"Yes, Aunt, the clothing of a German page of the sixteenth century."

"Our great painter, Fritz Mocker, even as he faithfully reproduced your features, rather than merely depicting you as a sixteenth-century character, by an artistic caprice, took a fancy also to imitate the manner of painting of that period, even to the point of reproducing their dilapidation. A few days after she came to Germany, the Princess Amélie, having come to see me, along with her father, noticed your portrait and asked me innocently who that charming face from the past was. Her father smiled, and nodded at me as he answered her, 'That portrait is of one of our cousins who, even though, as you see from his clothing, my dear Amélie, would be more or less three hundred years old by now, manifested rare courage and a wonderful heart when he was young.

Really, can't you see his courage in his glance and his kindness in his smile?'"

(I beg of you, Maximilien, don't shake your head with impatience and disdain when you see me writing such things about myself. You must know how it pains me. But what follows in my narrative will show you that these childish details, whose dismaying ridiculousness I feel all too well, are unfortunately necessary. I now close this parenthesis and continue.)

"The Princess Amélie," my aunt continued, "taken in by this innocent joke after looking more attentively at the portrait, shared her father's views with regard to the sweet and proud expression on your face. Later, when I went to see her at Gerolstein, she smiled and asked of me if there was anything more I could tell her about her cousin from times past. I confessed our deception to her, telling her that the handsome page from the sixteenth century was merely my nephew, the Prince Henri d'Herkaüsen-Oldenzaal, who was now twenty-one years old, and a captain in the guards of His Majesty the Emperor of Austria and who, except for the clothing, looked exactly like his portrait. When I said this," my aunt added, "the Princess Amélie blushed and became serious again, as she nearly always is. Nevertheless, as you can see, my dear child, you will not be a complete stranger or a new face for your cousin, as the grand duke calls you. And so be calm and do honor to your portrait," my aunt added with a smile.

This conversation took place, as I told you, my dear Maximilien, the day before I was to be presented to my cousin the princess. I left my aunt and went back to where I was staying.

I have never hidden from you even my most secret thoughts, be they good or ill. And so I will confess to you some absurd and foolish imaginings I indulged in after the conversation I have just described to you.

CHAPTER 2

GEROLSTEIN (CONTINUATION)

Prince Henri d'Herkaüsen-Oldenzaal
To Count Maximilien Kaminetz

You have told me many times, my dear Maximilien, that I am completely bereft of vanity. I believe it; I have to believe it to be able to go on with this account. Otherwise, I would be opening myself to an accusation of arrogance.

When I was home alone, remembering my conversation with my aunt, I could not help myself from thinking, with some secret satisfaction, that the Princess Amélie, having noticed my portrait, painted six or seven years ago, had a few days afterward asked, jokingly, if there was any news of her cousin from days gone by. I readily admit that nothing could have been sillier than to have founded the least hope on such an insignificant circumstance. But since, as I have told you, I will be as completely truthful with you as I always am—well, then! This insignificant circumstance made me ecstatically happy. It is surely true that the praise of the Princess Amélie, coming from a woman as serious and as austere as my aunt is, raised my opinion of the princess even higher. It made me even more receptive to the recognition she had deigned to give me, or at least that she had given to my portrait. Still—what can I say?—that recognition raised such foolish hopes in me that, now that I can see the past in a calmer mood, I wonder how I could have let myself be carried away into trains of thought that would inevitably lead to despair.

Even though I was related to the prince and always made welcome by him, it was really impossible for me to hold out the least hope of marrying the princess, even if she had welcomed my love, which was, to say the least, highly improbable. Our family did honor to its rank, but, if one compared our wealth with the immense properties of the grand duke, one of the richest of the German nobility, our family was poor indeed. And, in addition, I was hardly even twenty-one years old, and I was a mere captain of the guards, without fame, without any achievement of my own. In a word, there was not the least chance in the world that the prince would even consider me for his daughter.

All these reflections should have warned me away from a passion that I might not have yet felt but of which I did have some kind of strange inkling. Alas! Instead, I gave way to new acts of childishness. At this time, I wore a ring that Thécla (the good countess, whom you know) had given me in days gone by. Even though this token of a light, naive, and thoughtless love could hardly have troubled me much, I heroically sacrificed it to my nascent love and the poor ring sank into the rapid waters of a river that flowed beneath my window.

It would be pointless to tell you how I got through that night. You can guess what happened. I knew the Princess Amélie to be blond and angelically beautiful: I tried to imagine her features, her figure, her bearing, the sound of her voice, the expression of her eyes. Then, thinking about that portrait of mine, which she had noticed, I sadly remembered that that cursed artist had flattered me outrageously. In addition, I despaired as I compared the picturesque livery of a sixteenth-century page with the severe uniform of a captain of the guards of His Imperial Majesty. These childish preoccupations were then followed by some generous considerations, I assure you, as well as some noble stirrings of my soul. I was touched, profoundly touched, as I recalled Princess Amélie's adorable kindness when, as my aunt told me, she referred to the poor abandoned girls she sheltered as her sisters.

And here is a peculiar and inexplicable contradiction: as you know, I have the humblest opinion of myself, and yet I was vain enough to believe that the sight of my portrait had struck the princess deeply. I had sufficient good sense to understand that an unbridgeable gap separated me from her forever, and yet I wondered, with real anxiety, if she would not find me unworthy of my portrait. Ultimately, I had never seen her, and I was already convinced that she would hardly notice me—and yet I believed that I had reason to sacrifice the token of my first love to her.

And so I spent both this night and a part of the next day in the veritable anguish I have described to you. The hour for the reception arrived. I tried on two or three sets of uniforms, finding one to be more ill-made than the next, and I left for the grand ducal palace very dissatisfied with myself.

Even though Gerolstein was separated from the Abbey of Sainte-Hermangilde by barely a quarter of a league, I was assailed by numerous thoughts over the course of this short journey. All the childish thoughts with which I had been preoccupied disappeared before one serious, sad, and almost threatening idea. An unconquerable foreboding announced the coming of one of those crises that can dominate one's whole life. I had something like a revelation that I was going to fall in love, to fall in love passionately and to love as one loves only once in a lifetime. And to complete this fate, this love, whose object was as high as it was worthy, could be for me only an unhappy one.

These ideas frightened me so much that, all of a sudden, I resolved wisely to stop my carriage, return to the abbey, and go back to my father, leaving to my aunt the task of excusing my abrupt departure to the duke. Unfortunately, one of those trivial events that occasionally have immense effects stopped me from doing what I originally had intended. When my carriage had arrived at the entrance to the avenue that led to the palace, I leaned out of the carriage door to order my people to turn around. Just at that moment the Baron and Baroness Koller, who, like me, were going to the court, saw me and ordered their carriage to stop. Seeing me in uniform, the baron said to me, "Can I be of help to you, my dear prince? What has happened to you? Since you are going to the palace, if some accident has befallen your horses, climb in with us."

Nothing could have been easier than to find some excuse for leaving the baron and going back to the abbey; isn't that right, my friend? Well, either out of inertia or because of some secret desire to get around the salutary decision I had just made, I answered, with some embarrassment, that I was telling my coachman to ask at the palace guardhouse whether we should enter through the new pavilion or through the marble courtyard.

"The entrance is through the marble courtyard, my dear prince," the baron answered me, "since it's a reception for a grand gala. Tell your coachman to follow my coach and I'll show you the way."

You know, Maximilien, how much of a fatalist I am. I wanted to return to the abbey to spare myself the sorrows I could foresee. The stars were opposed to this decision, and I abandoned myself to my fate. You don't know Gerolstein's grand ducal palace, do you, my friend? According to everyone who has visited the capitals of Europe, the only royal residence that exceeds the magnificence of its buildings and surroundings is Versailles. If I go into some detail on this subject, it's because, as I now remember its imposing splendors, I wonder why they didn't then recall to me my relative insignificance. For, after all, Princess Amélie's father was the ruling sovereign of this palace, its guards, and its marvelous wealth.

The marble courtyard, built in the shape of a gigantic semicircle, was so called because, with the exception of a large beltway around it for carriages, it was tiled entirely with marble in every color. These tiles formed a magnificent mosaic at the center of which an immense basin, formed of antique brèche marble, was constantly filled with abundant water falling from a large bowl made of porphyry. Rows of marble statues surrounded the perimeter of this cour d'honneur. These statues were of white marble, in an elevated style, and equipped with gilded bronze torchères from which came dazzling spurts of flaming gas. Alternating with these statues were richly sculpted Medici vases, standing on pedestals. These vases held enormous oleanders, veritable flowering hedges whose shining foliage, seen in the light, gleamed a metallic green.

The carriages stopped at the foot of a double range of banistered staircases which went up to the palace's peristyle. At the foot of this staircase, two horsemen of the duke's regiment of the guard, chosen from among the grand army's tallest noncommissioned officers, stood on display, mounted on black horses. My friend, you who so much appreciate military men, you would have been struck by the severe, martial bearing of these two giants, whose breastplates and steel helmets, in the Greek style, without crest or feather, sparkled in the lights. These horsemen wore blue uniforms with yellow collars and white buckskin pants, with heavy boots rising over the knees. Finally, for you, my friend, again in your capacity as an enthusiast of military detail, I will add that two grenadiers from the regimental infantry of the grand duke's guard stood on guard duty at the top of the stairway, one on each side of the doors. Their uniforms, except for the color of the coats and lapels, were similar, people told me, to those of Napoléon's grenadiers.

After having crossed the vestibule, where there were two halberd-bearing Swiss guards wearing the prince's livery, I went up an imposing white marble staircase that led to a portico ornamented with columns made of jasper and overhung with gilded and painted domes. Two long rows of footmen lined the portico. I then entered the guardroom. A chamberlain and a household aide-de-camp stood ready at its door. They were responsible for bringing to the prince those persons who had the right to an individual introduction. My relationship, distant as it was, earned me this honor: an aide-de-camp led me to a room crowded with men in court dress or in uniform and women in evening wear.

As I slowly walked through this brilliant crowd of people, I heard scattered sentences that increased my emotions: everybody was admiring Princess Amélie's angelic beauty, the Marquise d'Harville's charming features, and the Archduchess Sophie's truly imperial air. She had just arrived from Munich with the Archduke Stanislas and would soon be leaving again to go to Warsaw. But even as they all gave due homage to the archduchess's lofty dignity and the Marquise d'Harville's distinguished graciousness, everybody agreed that nothing compared to the enchanting face of Princess Amélie.

As I approached the grand duke and his daughter, I felt my heart start to beat violently. When I got to the door of the salon (I forgot to tell you that a ball and a concert were taking place at the court), the incomparable Liszt had just sat down to the piano.[276] Consequently, the

276. Franz Liszt (1811–1886) would have then been already famous as a virtuoso pianist in 1840 or 1841. His fame reached its stratospheric heights as *The Mysteries of Paris* was appearing serially in the *Journal des Débats*, in 1842. [TN]

light murmur of conversation gave way to the most attentive silence. I stood in the doorway, awaiting the end of the piece, which the great artist played with his usual superiority.

Then, my dear Maximilien, I saw the Princess Amélie for the first time. Allow me to describe the whole scene for you, since recalling all my memories of it gives me indescribable pleasure. Imagine, my friend, a gigantic salon, furnished in royally sumptuous style, with dazzling lights, the walls covered with crimson silk, with golden foliage embroidered in relief on it. The Archduchess Sophia sat in the first row, on a gilded armchair (the prince granted her the honors of the palace). On her left was the Marquise d'Harville, and on her right the Princess Amélie. The grand duke, wearing the uniform of a colonel in the guards, stood behind them. Happiness seemed to have rejuvenated him, and he looked to be less than thirty years old. The military uniform flattered the elegance of his figure and the handsomeness of his features. The Archduke Stanislas, in the uniform of a field marshal, stood next to him. Then came Princess Amélie's ladies-in-waiting and, finally, women of high standing at the court.

Is there any need to tell you that the Princess Amélie stood out against this sparkling crowd, more on account of her grace and beauty than her rank? Do not condemn me for saying this, my friend, until you have looked over the portrait of her I will give you. Though it will fall infinitely short of the original, you will understand my adoration, why I loved her from the moment I first saw her, and why the rapid birth of this passion could only be equaled by its strength and its duration, which will be eternal.

Princess Amélie, wearing a simple white moiré dress, was decorated, as was the Archduchess Sophia, with the grand cordon of the imperial order of Saint John Nepomucene, which the empress had recently sent her. A headband of pearls, encircling her beautiful and noble forehead, went perfectly with the two magnificent braids of ash-blond hair that framed her lightly colored cheeks. Her charming arms, whiter than the layers of lace that surrounded them, were half hidden by gloves that rose to just below her dimpled elbows. Her figure could not have been more perfect, nor her foot, in its white satin slipper, prettier. When I first saw her, her large eyes, of the purest azure blue, had a faraway look. I do not even know whether at that moment she was absorbed in the contemplation of some serious idea or whether she was deeply impressed by the dark harmony of the piece Liszt was playing. But her half smile seemed to me to express an indescribably sweet melancholy. With her head drooping slightly on her breast, she mechanically pulled the leaves from a large bouquet of carnations she held in her hand.

I will never be able to describe to you what I felt at that moment. All my aunt had told me about Princess Amélie's ineffable kindness came back to me. Go ahead and smile, my friend, but, despite myself, I felt tears coming to my eyes as I gazed upon this so wonderfully beautiful young girl, treated with the greatest honor and respect, loved to the point of idolatry by a father like the grand duke, looking about her in almost melancholy distraction.

As I have often told you, Maximilien, just as I think men to be incapable of experiencing some kinds of happiness, which are, so to speak, too complete, too expansive for our limited faculties, in just the same way I believe some people to be too divinely endowed not to feel bitterly, sometimes, how alone they are in this world. They are unable to escape so much disappointment, so much resistance from the world, that less favored types know nothing about. Well, it seemed to me at that moment that Princess Amélie was experiencing feelings that arose from her having that very thought.

Suddenly, by a strange bit of chance (fate operates everywhere in what I tell you here), she turned her head, mechanically, in my direction. You know what scrupulous observers we are of etiquette and class hierarchy here. Thanks to my title and to my family connection to the grand duke, the people among which I was at first standing had little by little withdrawn, so that I remained almost alone and very visible, in the first rank of those who stood in the gallery's doorway. It was owing to this circumstance, doubtless, that Princess Amélie, awakening from her reverie, noticed me. That would be why she made a slight start of surprise and blushed. Her reaction is easily explained. She had seen my portrait at the abbey, visiting my aunt, and she recognized me. She hardly looked at me for more than a second but her glance aroused in me a deep and violent response. I felt that my face was on fire. I lowered my eyes and stayed still for a few minutes without daring to look up again at the princess. When I finally brought myself to do so, she was whispering to the Archduchess Sophia, who seemed to be listening with the most affectionate interest.

Since Liszt had taken a break of a few minutes between the two pieces he was to play, the grand duke took advantage of the pause to express his admiration to the pianist in his most gracious manner. Returning to his place, the prince saw me, nodded to me in the kindest possible way, and said a few words to the archduchess, pointing me out with his look. After having looked me over for a moment, she turned back to the grand duke, who could not stop himself from smiling as he answered her and said something to his daughter. The Princess Amélie seemed to me to be embarrassed since she blushed all over again.

I was in torment. Unfortunately, etiquette did not permit me to move from where I was standing until the concert had ended, and it was soon about to begin again. I stole glances at Princess Amélie two or three times. She seemed sad and thoughtful. My heart skipped a beat. I was in pain at having caused her a slight irritation, without meaning to. I could guess what it was about. Doubtless, the grand duke, joking, had asked if she thought I looked at all like the portrait of her cousin from times past, and, in her naiveté, she perhaps was angry with herself for not having told her father that she had already recognized me. Once the concert was over, I followed the household aide-de-camp, who brought me over to the grand duke, who was so good as to walk a few steps toward me, take me by the arm, and say to the Archduchess Sophie, as he walked up to her, "I beg of your imperial highness permission to introduce you to my cousin, the Prince Henri d'Herkaüsen-Oldenzaal."

"I have already met the prince in Vienna and it is a pleasure to encounter him again here," the archduchess answered as I bowed deeply before her.

"My dear Amélie," the prince went on, turning to his daughter, "this is Prince Henri, your cousin. He is the son of Prince Paul, one of my most venerable friends. I regret not seeing him here today at Gerolstein."

"Would you be so kind, monsieur, as to inform Prince Paul that I entirely share my father's regrets. I am always happy to meet his friends," my cousin replied to me with a very graceful simplicity.

I had never heard the princess's voice before. You must imagine, my friend, the sweetest, the freshest, the most harmonious tone of voice, the kind of voice that resonates with what is most delicate in our souls.

"Henri, I hope you will stay for some time with your aunt, whom, as you know, I love and respect as if she were my mother," the prince said, smiling with kindness. "You will come to visit us often, informally, in the afternoon, around three o'clock. If we are going out, you will walk with us. You know I have always loved you as someone with one of the most noble hearts I know."

"The generous welcome you give me, Your Royal Highness, leaves me speechless with gratitude."

"Well, then, to prove your gratitude," the prince said with a smile, "ask your cousin to dance the second quadrille with you. The first belongs by right to the archduke."

"Will your highness grant me that pleasure?" I said to the Princess Amélie, bowing to her.

"Just call each other cousin. That's the good old German way," the grand duke said in high humor. "It's not fitting for members of the same family to stand on ceremony."

"Cousin, will you do me the honor of dancing this quadrille with me?"

"Yes, cousin," Princess Amélie answered.

CHAPTER 3

GEROLSTEIN (CONTINUATION AND CONCLUSION)

Prince Henri d'Herkaüsen-Oldenzaal
To Count Maximilien Kaminetz

I cannot adequately describe, my friend, how much the grand duke's paternal warmth toward me both pleased and pained me. The trust he displayed in me, the affectionate kindness he showed in asking his daughter and me to replace polite formality with those familiar addresses among relations that are so sweetly intimate: all these things filled me with gratitude. How much more bitterly I reproached myself, then, for feeling the fatal charm of a love that the prince neither could nor would sanction.

It is true that I had promised myself (and I had rigorously held to this resolution) never to say a word that could even lead my cousin to suspect the love I felt. But I feared that my emotions and my looks would betray me at any moment. Despite myself, moreover, this feeling, silent and hidden as it was, seemed to me a guilty one.

I was able to reflect on all this while the Princess Amélie danced the first quadrille with the Archduke Stanislas. Here, like everywhere else, the dance was nothing more than a sort of walk in time to the orchestra's tempo. Nothing could have suited my cousin's grave and serious comportment to better effect.

I looked forward both with pleasure and anxiety to my release from the ball and the brief conversation it would afford me with her. But I had enough self-control to hide my nervousness when I went to find her by the Marquise d'Harville. Thinking of the events surrounding the portrait, I expected the Princess Amélie to share my embarrassment, and I was not mistaken in this. I remember our first conversation practically word for word, and so I will recount it to you, my friend.

"Will your highness allow me," I said to her, "to call you 'cousin,' as the grand duke requests?"

"Certainly, cousin," she answered graciously. "I am always happy to obey my father."

"And, cousin, from what my aunt has told me about you, which is to say, from how highly she has taught me to think of you, I am all the more proud of this familiarity."

"My father has also often spoken about you, cousin, and this may surprise you," she added timidly, "but I knew you already, if one may call it that, by sight. The mother superior of Sainte-Hermangilde, for whom I have the highest respect and affection, showed my father and me a portrait one day . . ."

"Where I was depicted as a sixteenth-century page?"

"Yes, cousin. And my father even played the little trick on me of telling me that the portrait was of one of our relations from times past, adding, moreover, some very kind words for this cousin of the past that our family ought to congratulate itself for including among its current connections."

"Alas! Cousin, I fear I bear no more resemblance to the portrait of my character that the grand duke has deigned to sketch of me than I do to the sixteenth-century page."

"You are mistaken, cousin," the princess said to me naively, "since, at the end of the concert, when I glanced by chance at the gallery, I recognized you right away, despite your change in dress." Then, no doubt wanting to change a subject that embarrassed her, she said to me, "Doesn't Monsieur Liszt play with admirable talent?"

"His talent is admirable indeed. You seemed to take such great pleasure in listening to him!"

"That's because it seems to me that music without words has twice the charm. Not only does one enjoy the skill with which it's played, but you can fit whatever you are thinking of at the moment to the melodies you are listening to and so they could be said to provide the accompaniment to your thoughts. I don't know if I'm making myself entirely clear, cousin."

"Perfectly. In that way, your thoughts become the lyrics that you apply mentally to the melody you hear."

"That's right, that's right, you understand perfectly," she said with a gesture of gracious satisfaction. "I was afraid that I didn't explain clearly what I felt a moment ago when we heard that melody, which was so plaintive and touching."

"We must thank God, cousin," I said to her with a smile, "that you can have no words to give to such a sad melody."

Whether it was because my remark was indiscreet and she wanted to avoid responding to it or because she didn't hear it, suddenly the Princess Amélie pointed to the grand duke, who was giving his arm to the Archduchess Sophie and walking across the gallery where the dancing took place, and she said, "Look at my father, cousin! Look how handsome he is! How he seems so noble and good! How everybody looks at him with such devotion! It seems to me that people love him even more than they revere him."

"Oh!" I exclaimed. "It's not only here in the surroundings of his court that he is held dear. If the blessings of the people sounded down through posterity, the name Rodolphe of Gerolstein would be immortal, and justly so." My excitement in saying this was sincere. As you well know, my friend, people call the prince's grand duchy the Paradise of Germany, and with good reason. It would be impossible to describe for you the grateful look my cousin gave me in hearing me speak this way.

"In estimating my father this way," she said to me with emotion, "you show yourself completely worthy of the attachment he feels for you."

"No one can admire him or love him more than I do! Beyond the rare qualities he has that make for great princes, does he not have a genius for kindness that makes people adore some princes?"

"You don't know how truly you speak!" the princess said, even more moved than she had been.

"Oh, but I do know! And all those he governs know it as well as I do. People love him so much that they are pained by his sorrows as much as they take pleasure in his happiness. The eagerness all show to come offer their respects to the Marquise d'Harville does honor at once both to his royal highness's choice and to the worthiness of the future grand duchess."

"No one deserves my father's devotion more than the Marquise d'Harville. And that's the highest compliment I can give."

"And you must surely have a just appreciation of her since you probably knew her in France, did you not, cousin?" Hardly had I uttered these last words than some sudden thought that I couldn't quite read occurred to the Princess Amélie. She lowered her eyes and, for just a moment, her face took on an expression of sadness that struck me silent in my surprise.

By this time, we had reached the end of the quadrille. A last turn separated me from my cousin for an instant. When I brought her back to the marquise, it seemed to me that her features had kept their slight alteration. I believed then and I still believe now that my allusion to the princess's stay in France had recalled to her her mother's death and so caused her the painful impression I just mentioned to you.

I noticed in the course of the evening one circumstance which will seem insignificant to you but which seemed to me yet another indication of how this young girl makes everyone care for her. Her pearl headband having fallen slightly askew, the Archduchess Sophie, to whom she had then given her arm, had the kindness to ask if she could readjust this ornament on the princess's forehead. Now, for anyone who knows the archduchess's notorious haughtiness, such kindness on her part will seem hardly credible.

Furthermore, the Princess Amélie, who I was watching closely at this moment, seemed at once so confused, so grateful, I would almost dare to say so embarrassed, by this gracious attention, that I thought I saw some tears shining in her eyes.

And that, my friend, was how my first night in Gerolstein went. If I have gone into so much detail in telling you about it, it is because almost every circumstance has had a later significant consequence for me. Now I will cut matters short. I will tell you only the principal events concerning my conversations with my cousin and her father.

The grand duke and the Marquise d'Harville were married two days after this party, and I was one of the very few people who were invited to the wedding. Never have I seen the Princess Amélie wear a more radiant and serene expression than during this ceremony. She looked upon her father and the marquise with a kind of religious ecstasy, which gave a new charm to her features. It almost seemed that she reflected back the ineffable happiness of the prince and Madame d'Harville. On that day, my cousin was very cheerful and talkative. I gave her my arm during a walk around the magnificently illuminated palace gardens after dinner. On the subject of her father's marriage, she told me, "It seems to me that the happiness of those we hold most dear is sweeter for us even than our own happiness, since there is always an element of selfishness in the pleasure we take in our own personal joys." If I quote this reflection from among the thousand that my cousin uttered, it's because it will give you a better understanding of this adorable creature's heart, which, like that of her father, had a genius for benevolence.

I had a fairly long conversation with the grand duke several days after his marriage. He asked me about the past and about my plans for the future. He gave me very wise advice and the most flattering encouragement possible. He even spoke to me of various plans he had for governing, showing in me a trust that both flattered me and made me proud. And then—how shall I put this to you?—for one moment the most foolish thought occurred to me: that the prince had guessed about my love for his daughter and that his purpose in this conversation was to look me over, feel me out, and maybe bring me to make an avowal.

Unfortunately, this insane hope didn't last very long: the prince ended the conversation by telling me that the time of great wars was over and that I should take advantage of my name, my connections, the education I have received, and the close friendship between my father the prince de M. and the emperor's prime minister to begin a diplomatic rather than a military career. He thought that all questions that used to be decided on the battlefield would henceforth be determined in diplomatic meetings. Soon the torturous and perfidious ways of the old diplomacy, he said, would give way to an expansive and humanitarian politics arising from the true interests of the people, who, day by day, had become more aware of their rights. He also thought that an elevated, honest, and generous intelligence, in a few years' time, could have a noble and great role to play in political affairs and could do much good. And finally, he offered me the support of his sovereign protection to help me begin the career that he was asking me to undertake as soon as possible.

You will understand, my friend, that if the prince had had the slightest personal plans for me, he would not have made such an offer. I thanked him for his proposals with real gratitude, adding that I was keenly aware of the value of his advice and that I was determined to follow it.

I had, at first, been very reserved with regard to my visits to the palace. At the insistence of the grand duke, however, soon enough I came every day at about three o'clock. People lived there with all the charming simplicity characteristic of our German courts. It was like the life of the great English estates, but made more attractive by friendly simplicity and the sweet freedom of German mores. When weather permitted, I took long rides on horseback with the grand duke, the grand duchess, my cousin, and various members of their household. When we stayed in the palace, we entertained ourselves with music: I sang, along with the grand duchess and my cousin, whose voice had a purity and sweetness beyond compare and which I could never hear without feeling stirred to the depths of my soul. Other times still, we studied in detail the prince's marvelous collections of paintings and art objects or his impressive library. The prince, as you know, is one of the most learned and enlightened men in all Europe. I would return to the palace for dinner with considerable frequency, and when there was an opera performance, I would accompany the grand duke's family to the theater.

My days passed as if in a dream. Little by little, my cousin came to regard me almost as a brother. She did not hide the pleasure she felt in seeing me. She confided in me about anything that concerned her. Two or three times, she asked me to accompany her when she went with the grand duchess to visit the young orphans. Frequently, she also talked with me about my future, and this with a maturity of intellect and a serious and thoughtful interest that astonished me coming from a young girl of her age. She also liked to hear me talk about my childhood and about my mother, who, alas, I still sorely miss. Every time I wrote to my father, she begged me to be remembered to him. And then, since she embroidered with beautiful skill, one day she gave me a charming tapestry that she had worked on for a long time to send to him. What can I tell you, my friend? A brother and a sister who saw each other again after being separated for many years could not have enjoyed a sweeter intimacy. And that was so much the case that when, if by the rarest chance, we were alone, if a third person broke in, that would not change the subject or tone of our conversation.

When you remember the confession I have made to you, this fraternal affection between two young people may surprise you, my friend. But the more my cousin treated me with trust and familiarity, the more I kept watch over myself and constrained myself for fear of losing that precious closeness. And further, my reserve was only increased by the fact that the princess treated me with such candor, such noble trust, and, most of all, so little coquetry, that I was practically certain that she had no idea of my violent passion for her. I still have, however, one slight suspicion on this matter as a result of something I will tell you about in a moment.

If this fraternal intimacy could have gone on forever, the happiness it gave me might have been enough. But precisely because I took such intense pleasure in it, I considered that soon the career to which the prince had committed me would call me to Vienna or some foreign land. And I thought that soon enough the prince would think of marrying his daughter to someone worthy of her. The closer the time of my departure drew, the more these thoughts became painful to me. Soon, my cousin noticed the change that had come over me. The night before the day I was going to leave her, she told me that for some time she had found me more somber and more preoccupied. I tried to avoid saying anything; I attributed my sadness to vague unease.

"I cannot believe you," she told me. "My father treats you practically like a son. Everyone loves you. To feel unhappy would be ingratitude."

"Well, then, it's true!" I said to her, unable as I was to conquer my feelings. "It's not unease, but sorrow, deep sorrow, that I feel."

"But why? What has happened to you?" she asked me with great concern.

"You just told me, cousin, that your father treated me like a son, that everybody loved me. But, then, soon I will have to give up all this affection that is so dear to me. In short, I will have to leave Gerolstein and, I must confess to you, this thought makes me despair."

"And do the memories of those who are dear to us amount to nothing for you, cousin?"

"Of course not, but time and circumstance bring so many unforeseeable changes!"

"There are some kinds of affection, at least, which never change. The affection my father has shown you and that which I feel for you are among them, as you well know. We are brother and sister, and we can never forget that," she added, raising to me her big blue eyes, which were wet with tears. This look bowled me over. I was on the point of betraying my feelings, but, fortunately, I was able to contain myself.

"It's true that affections last," I told her with some embarrassment, "but positions change. And so, cousin, do you believe that when I return after some years away, this intimacy, whose charm I value so much, will really still last?"

"Why should it not last?"

"Because then, cousin, you will certainly be married. You will have other things to occupy you. And you will have forgotten your poor brother."

I swear to you, my friend, that I said nothing more than that to her. I still do not know if she saw in these words an avowal that offended her or if she was as painfully struck as I was by the inevitable changes that the future would necessarily bring to our feelings for each other. In either case, rather than answering me, she became silent and dejected for a moment. Then she quickly got up, her face pale and altered, and then left, only stopping to look for a few seconds at the tapestry on which one of her ladies-in-waiting, the Countess d'Oppenheim, was working while sitting in a window seat in the salon where our conversation had taken place.

That very evening, I received a letter from my father that called on me to return here quickly. The following morning, I went to take leave of the grand duke. He told me that my cousin did not feel entirely well and that he would take it upon himself to make my farewells to her. He embraced me paternally, adding how sorry he was that I had to leave so quickly and especially that the cause of my departure was my inquietude over my father's health. Then, recalling to me with the warmest benevolence his advice on the subject of the new career he was requesting that I begin as soon as possible, he added that when I returned from my diplomatic missions, or during periods of leave, he would always take the greatest pleasure in seeing me again at Gerolstein.

Fortunately, when I arrived here, I found the state of my father's health somewhat improved. He was still confined to bed and still extremely weak, but his health no longer gave me serious concern. Unfortunately, he took note of my dejection and my somber taciturnity. He has already more than once, though in vain, begged me to confide in him the cause of my glumness. I would not dare to tell him, despite his unbounded love for me. You know how hard he is on anything whatsoever that seems to him to lack either candor or honor.

Yesterday, I was watching over him. Believing him to be asleep, I was unable to hold back my tears as I wept silently for the beautiful times I had had at Gerolstein. As he was just barely asleep, and as I was absorbed in my sorrows, he witnessed me weeping. He asked me about my sorrows with the most touching kindness. I attributed my sadness to my concern over his health, but he was not taken in by this deception.

Now that you know all, my dear Maximilien, tell me, if you can, if my situation isn't completely desperate? What should I do? What path should I take?

Oh, my friend, I could never adequately communicate my anguish to you. God, what is going to happen? All my hopes are lost forever! If my father does not give up on what he has decided to do, I am the most miserable of men.

Here is what has just happened. I had just finished this letter when my father, who I believed to be still in bed, to my astonishment, came into his study, where I was writing at the time. He saw my first four pages, filled with my writing, lying on his desk. I was just finishing this one.

"To whom are you writing at such length?" he asked, smiling.

"To Maximilien, Father."

"Ah!" he said to me, with an expression of affectionate reproach. "I know that you confide in him completely. He is really fortunate, I must say!"

He said this in such a painfully stricken tone that, touched by his expression, I answered, almost without thinking, by giving him my letter. "Read it, Father."

He read it all, my friend. Do you know what he said then, after a few moments of reflection? "Henri, I am going to write to tell the grand duke what happened during your stay in Gerolstein."

"Father, I beg of you, don't do that."

"Is what you tell Maximilien the exact truth?"

"Yes, Father."

"In that case, your conduct, up to this moment, has been honorable. The prince will recognize that. But you cannot in the future show yourself to be unworthy of his noble trust, and that is what will happen if, taking unfair advantage of his invitation, you return to Gerolstein with the intention of making his daughter love you."

"Father, do you really think—"

"I think that you are passionately in love and that sooner or later passion will give you bad counsel."

"But really, Father! Are you going to write to the prince that—"

"That you love your cousin to distraction."

"In heaven's name! Father, I beg you, don't do anything of the kind!"

"Do you love your cousin?"

"I love her with all my soul, but—"

My father interrupted me. "In that case, I am going to write the grand duke and request for you his daughter's hand in marriage."

"But, Father, any such pretention would be insanity on my part."

"That's true. Nevertheless, I must make this request of the prince frankly, telling him the reasons that force me to do so. He welcomed you with the most honorable hospitality. He showed you paternal kindness. It would be unworthy of both me and you to deceive him. I know what a good soul he has. He will be sensitive to the fact that I have taken the course of honesty. If he refuses to give you his daughter's hand, and it is all but certain that he will, he will at least be aware that, if you return to Gerolstein, you cannot have the same intimate relationship with her." And then my father added, in a kind tone of voice, "My child, you have freely shown me the letter that you were writing to Maximilien. I now know everything. It is my duty to write to the grand duke, and I mean to write him immediately."

As you know, my friend, my father is the best of people, but his tenacity of will is unbreakable when it comes to anything he thinks of as his duty. Imagine what my anguish, my fear must be. Although the course he is taking is, after all, open and honorable, it isn't any less upsetting for me. What will the grand duke think of this mad request? Won't he be shocked, and won't the Princess Amélie be hurt that I have let my father do such a thing without her approval?

Oh, my friend! Have pity on me. I don't know what to think. I seem to be staring into an abyss, and I'm overcome by vertigo.

I am finishing this letter in haste. I will write again soon. Once more, pity me, because, in all honesty, I fear the fever that has already gone on for so long will end by driving me mad. Farewell, farewell. Your friend forever,

Henri d'H-O.

And now we will take our reader to the palace of Gerolstein, where Fleur-de-Marie has lived since her return from France.

CHAPTER 4

PRINCESS AMÉLIE

Rodolphe had made sure that the rooms Fleur-de-Marie occupied (we will refer to her as Princess Amélie only in her formal role) in the grand duke's palace had been furnished with the greatest taste and elegance. The view from the balcony of the girl's chapel included, in the distance, the two towers of the Sainte-Hermangilde, which hung over huge banks of greenery and were themselves dwarfed by a high, wooded mountain at the foot of which sat the abbey.

On a beautiful summer morning, Fleur-de-Marie allowed her gaze to wander across the splendid landscape that stretched toward the horizon. Her head bare, she wore a high-necked spring dress of white fabric with thin blue stripes on it. A very simple wide cambric collar, turned down over her shoulders, left visible the two ends and the knot of a little silk tie made of the same blue as the belt on her dress. She sat in a large sculpted ebony armchair with a high back upholstered in crimson velvet. With her elbow supported by one of the arms of this seat and her head slightly bowed, she rested her cheek on the back of her small, white, blue-veined hand.

Fleur-de-Marie's languid attitude, pallor, fixed gaze, and bitter partial smile all revealed her deep melancholy. After several moments, her chest heaved with a deep, painful sigh. Letting fall the hand on which she rested her cheek, she bowed her head even lower on her chest. The unfortunate girl looked as if she were buckling under the weight of some great sorrow.

At this moment, a middle-aged woman with grave and distinguished features, dressed with elegant simplicity, entered the chapel almost timidly and gave a quiet cough to let Fleur-de-Marie know she was present. The latter, emerging from her reverie, raised her head abruptly and said as she greeted her in a gesture full of grace, "What do you wish, my dear countess?"

"I am here to let your highness know that his lordship requests that she wait for him. He will be here in a few minutes," answered Princess Amélie's lady-in-waiting with respectful formality.

"Indeed, I'm surprised my father has not already come to kiss me good morning. I am always so impatient for him to make his visit each morning! But I hope that I do not owe the pleasure of seeing you at the palace two days in a row to an illness of Mademoiselle d'Harneim, my dear countess?"

"Please do not worry yourself over that, Your Highness. Mademoiselle d'Harneim asked me to replace her today. Tomorrow she will have the honor of resuming her attendance on your highness, who will perhaps be so good as to excuse this substitution."

"Certainly, for I stand to lose nothing by this arrangement. After having had the pleasure of seeing you two days in a row, my dear countess, I will then have Mademoiselle d'Harneim's company for the following two days."

"Your highness is too kind to us," the lady-in-waiting answered, bowing again. "Her great benevolence gives me the courage to ask her a favor!"

"Speak, speak. You know how eager I am to please you."

"Truly, your highness has long accustomed me to her kindness. But this matter touches on such a painful subject that I wouldn't have the courage to broach it if it weren't a very worthy action. This is why I dare to count on the extreme indulgence of your highness."

"You have no need of my indulgence, my dear countess. I am always very grateful when I am given the opportunity to do a bit of good."

"The matter concerns a poor creature who had unfortunately left Gerolstein before your highness had founded her charitable foundation, which has so effectively helped orphaned or abandoned girls who are left defenseless against bad influences."

"And what did she do? What do you wish for her?"

"Her father, a very reckless man, had gone to seek his fortune in America, leaving his wife and daughter in a very fragile situation. The mother died. The daughter, barely sixteen years old, left to her own devices, left the country for Vienna to follow a seducer, who quickly abandoned her there. As always happens in such cases, the first step down the path of vice led this unfortunate girl into an abyss of degradation. In hardly any time at all, she became, like so many other wretches, the shame of her sex."

Fleur-de-Marie lowered her gaze, blushed, and could not conceal a light shudder, which did not escape her lady-in-waiting. The latter, fearing that she had wounded the chaste sensibility of the princess by discussing such a creature with her, said in embarrassment, "I sincerely beg the forgiveness of your highness. I have surely shocked her by drawing her attention to such a tainted being. However, the unfortunate girl has demonstrated such true repentance that I thought I might ask you to take pity on her in some small way."

"And you were quite right to do so. Please continue," said Fleur-de-Marie, overcoming her painful feelings. "Those who stray are indeed worthy of pity when repentance follows their fall."

"That is what has happened in this case, as I noted to your highness. After two years of this abominable life, this fallen woman was touched by grace. Seized with a belated remorse, she returned here. Chance led her upon her arrival to seek lodging in a house belonging to a worthy widow whose sweetness and piety are legendary. Encouraged by the pious goodness of the widow, the poor creature confessed her sins to her, adding that she felt a true horror at her past life and that she wished, at the price of the most difficult penance, to obtain the happiness of entering a religious establishment where she might expiate her sins and merit their redemption. The worthy widow in whom she confided, knowing that I had the honor of being part of your highness's household, wrote to recommend this poor girl to me. She hopes that, with your highness's intervention with Princess Juliane, the abbey's mother superior, she might hope to enter the convent of Sainte-Hermangilde. She asks the favor of being put to the most difficult labors so that her penitence might be that much more worthy. I took care to speak with the woman several times before permitting myself to ask for the pity of your highness on her behalf, and I am firmly convinced that her repentance is a lasting one. Neither need nor age has led her back to the good. She is barely eighteen years old; she is still very pretty, and she possesses a small sum of money that she would like to donate to a charitable work if she obtains the favor she requests."

"I will take on your protégée," Fleur-de-Marie said, barely able to contain herself. Her own past life bore so many resemblances to that of the unfortunate girl on whose behalf she was being asked to intervene. Then she added, "The repentance of this unfortunate girl is too praiseworthy for us not to encourage her."

"I do not know how to express my gratitude toward your highness. I hardly dared to hope that she might deign to be so charitable as to care about such a creature."

"She was guilty, and she repents," Fleur-de-Marie said in a tone of commiseration and inexpressible sadness. "It is right to take pity on her. The more sincere her remorse, the more painful it must be for her, my dear countess."

"I believe I hear his lordship," the lady-in-waiting said suddenly without taking note of Fleur-de-Marie's increasingly anguished emotional state. And indeed, Rodolphe had entered the room that preceded the chapel, holding in his hand an enormous bouquet of roses. At the sight of the prince, the countess discreetly withdrew. Hardly had she left when Fleur-de-Marie threw her arms around her father's neck. She leaned her forehead on his shoulder and remained in this position for a few seconds without speaking.

"Good morning, good morning, my beloved daughter," said Rodolphe, pressing his daughter affectionately in his arms, not yet noticing her sadness. "Look at this rosebush! I've brought you a beautiful harvest this morning! That's what kept me from coming earlier. I don't believe I've ever brought you a more magnificent bouquet than this. Here."

And the prince, the bouquet still in his hand, retreated slightly so he could remove himself from his daughter's embrace and look at her. Seeing her tears flowing, however, he threw the bouquet on a table, took Fleur-de-Marie's hands in his own, and exclaimed, "You're crying! Heavens! What is wrong?"

"Nothing—nothing, my good father," Fleur-de-Marie said as she wiped her tears and tried to smile at Rodolphe.

"I beg of you, tell me what's wrong. Who could have made you so sad?"

"I assure you, Father, that there is no reason for you to worry. The countess had come to ask for my help for a young woman who is so deserving, so unfortunate, that I was moved to tears by her story in spite of myself."

"Really? That's all it is?"

"That's all it is," Fleur-de-Marie answered, taking the flowers Rodolphe had thrown onto the table. "You spoil me too much!" she added. "What a magnificent bouquet! And when I think that every day you bring me another one like it that you have picked yourself!"

"My child," Rodolphe said as he contemplated his daughter with anxiety, "you are hiding something from me. Your smile is sad and constrained. I beg of you, tell me what is afflicting you. Don't worry about the bouquet."

"Oh! You know how this bouquet is my greatest joy every morning; and, then, you know how much I love roses. I have always loved them so much. You remember," she added, with a heartbreaking smile, "you remember my poor little rose plant whose fragments I always kept . . ."

When he heard this painful allusion to the past, Rodolphe exclaimed, "Poor child! It is as I suspected! Even in the midst of all the brilliance that surrounds you, you still can't stop thinking about that horrible time. Alas! I had thought I could make you forget about it by showering you with love and kindness!"

"I am so sorry, Father! I spoke without thinking. I have upset you."

"I am upset, poor angel," Rodolphe said with sadness, "because these memories of the past must be terrible for you. They would poison your life if you didn't have the strength to resist them."

"Father, it was just by chance. It's the first time since we came here."

"It's true, it's the first time you've talked to me about it, but it may not be the first time that these thoughts have tormented you. I noticed your melancholy moods, and sometimes I thought it was the past that was making you so sad. But since I couldn't be sure, I didn't dare even try to combat the fateful influence of those memories, even by showing you how empty and unjust they were. For if your sorrows were caused by something else, if the past was for you what it should be—a pointless and troublesome dream—I risked awakening in you the very painful ideas I sought to destroy."

"You are so kind! These fears show me yet again your indescribable tenderness!"

"What would you expect? I was in a difficult position, a delicate one. As I said, I didn't say anything to you, but I was continually preoccupied by everything concerning you. When I entered this marriage, which gratified my deepest wishes, I had also thought I was providing yet another guarantee for your comfort. I was too familiar with the excessive delicacy of your heart to hope that you would ever stop thinking of the past, but I told myself that if, by chance, your thoughts came to rest there, that, when you felt the maternal love of this noble woman, who knew and loved you in the depths of your misfortunes, you would have to feel that the past had been expiated more than enough by your atrocious sufferings, and you would be indulgent toward yourself, or rather, you would do yourself justice. After all, doesn't my wife, thanks to her rare qualities, have the right to everybody's respect? Well, the moment you feel you are her daughter or cherished sister, shouldn't you feel reassured? Isn't her tender affection itself a complete rehabilitation? Doesn't this tell you that she knows as well as you that you were a victim and not guilty, that no one can reproach you for the misfortune that afflicted you since your birth? Even if you had committed grave sins, would they not have been expiated many times over, redeemed by all of the good things you have done, by everything excellent and lovable that you have cultivated in yourself?"

"Father—"

"Oh! I beg of you, let me tell you everything I'm thinking, since chance has led to this conversation, which in some sense we should surely be grateful for. For a long time I have wanted to talk about this, but I've also been afraid of it. May God grant that this ends well! It's my duty to make you forget so many frightful sorrows. The mission I must fulfill in your regard is so august and sacred that I would have sacrificed my love for Madame d'Harville or my friendship for Murph for your comfort, if I thought their presence might have been too painful a reminder of the past."

"Oh! My dear father, how can you even think that? Doesn't their presence, on the contrary—the presence of those two who know what

I was and who nevertheless love me so tenderly—doesn't it personify the very idea of forgetting and forgiveness? Really, Father, it would have made my life a misery to me if you had renounced your marriage with Madame d'Harville for me."

"Oh! I wouldn't have been the only one to welcome this sacrifice if it had been able to assure your happiness. You don't know the sacrifice Clémence had been willingly prepared to make. For she, too, understands the full extent of my duties toward you."

"Your duties toward me? My God! What have I done to deserve anything like that?"

"What have you done, poor, beloved angel? Up until the moment you were returned to me, your life had been nothing but bitterness, wretchedness, and desolation. And I blame myself for your past sufferings just as if I had caused them myself! So when I see you smiling and contented, I believe that I have been pardoned. My only goal in life, my only wish, is to make you as ideally happy as you have been unfortunate, to raise you as high as you had been brought low, because it seems to me that the last vestiges of the past may be erased when the most eminent and honorable people pay you the respect that is your due."

"Respect, to me? No, no, Father. To my rank, or rather to the rank you have given to me."

"Oh! It's not your rank people love and revere. It's you. You must understand this, my cherished child: it's you, it's you alone. There are some kinds of homage that one's rank demands, but there are others that originate in one's charm and attraction! You don't know how to tell the difference between them because you do not know yourself and because, with an incredible intelligence and tact that make me feel as much pride in you as I do admiration, you bring a mixture of such dignity, modesty, and grace to these ceremonious relations that are so new for you that even the haughtiest individuals are incapable of resisting you."

"You love me so much, Father, and people love you so much, that they know they will please you by showing me such deference."

"Oh! What a naughty girl!" Rodolphe exclaimed, interrupting his daughter and kissing her tenderly. "What a naughty girl! She won't allow her father's pride the slightest satisfaction!"

"Isn't that pride gratified if I attribute to you alone the benevolence people show me, Father?"

"Certainly not, little miss," said the prince, smiling at his daughter in order to banish the sadness he saw still afflicted her. "No, little miss, it is not the same thing. For it is not permitted of me to be proud of myself, and I can and must be proud of you. Yes, proud. Once again, you don't know how divinely talented you are. Fifteen months of education, amazingly, have accomplished so much that even the most difficult mother would wax enthusiastic over you. And this education has only served to increase the almost irresistible influence you exercise on everyone around you without your suspecting it."

"Father, your praise is embarrassing me."

"I'm speaking the truth, and nothing but the truth. Would you like me to give you some examples? Let's speak boldly about the past. It's an enemy I want to combat face-to-face. I must look the demon in the eye. Well, then! Do you remember the She-Wolf, that courageous woman who saved you? Do you remember the scene from prison that you told me about? A mob of prisoners, more ignorant than wicked, were persistently tormenting one of their weak and feeble peers, their whipping girl. You appear, you speak, and instantly these furies, blushing at their cowardly cruelty toward their victim, become as charitable as they had been wicked. Do you think that's nothing? And, moreover, isn't it thanks to you that the She-Wolf, that indomitable woman, came to repent and desire an honest and hardworking life? Yes or no? So believe you me, dear child, the person who had tamed the She-Wolf and her rowdy companions with only kindness and a rare elevation of spirit at her disposal is the same person, although in other circumstances and in the very opposite sphere of society, who managed, thanks to that same charm (do not smile at this comparison, little miss), to fascinate the haughty Archduchess Sophie and my entire entourage as well. For the good and the wicked, the great and the small, all of them almost always end up submitting to the influence of superior souls. I don't mean to say that you are a born princess in the meaning aristocrats give to that word, for that would be meager flattery to you, my child. But you are one of that small number of privileged beings who are born to say to a queen exactly what needs to be said in order to charm her and win her love, and also to say to poor, vilified, and abandoned creatures exactly what needs to be said in order to make them better, comfort them, and win their adoration."

"My kind father! Enough, please."

"Oh! Too bad for you, little miss. My heart has been holding this back for too long. You need to understand that, with my fears of awakening in you those past memories that I wish to annihilate, that I will annihilate from your mind forever, I didn't dare speak to you of these comparisons, of these parallels that make you so adorable to me. How many times have you left Clémence and me in ecstasies over you? How many times has she said to me, when you have moved her to tears, 'Isn't it marvelous that this dear child is who she is, after all the misfortune she endured?' Or rather, as Clémence put it, 'Isn't it marvelous that, instead of degrading her noble and rare character, misfortune has on the contrary given wings to her superior traits?'"

At this moment, the door to the salon opened, and Clémence, the Grand Duchess of Gerolstein, entered, holding a letter in her hand. "Here, my love," she said to Rodolphe, "is a letter from France. I wanted to bring it to you in order to say good morning to this lazy child whom I haven't seen yet this morning," Clémence added as she kissed Fleur-de-Marie tenderly.

"This letter comes at just the right time," Rodolphe said cheerfully after perusing it. "We were just talking about the past, that monster we are going to fight constantly, my dear Clémence, for it threatens our child's peace and happiness."

"Can that be true, my love? Those fits of melancholy we observed—"

"Had no other cause than evil memories. But fortunately we now know our enemy—and we will triumph over it."

"But who is that letter from, my love?" asked Clémence.

"From that nice Rigolette, Germain's wife."

"Rigolette!" exclaimed Fleur-de-Marie. "How wonderful to hear from her!"

"My love," Clémence whispered to Rodolphe, glancing at Fleur-de-Marie, "aren't you worried that this letter might remind her of painful things?"

"It is precisely such memories I wish to wipe out, my dear Clémence! We must face them boldly and I am sure that I will find excellent ammunition against them in Rigolette's letter. That good little creature loved our child and appreciated her just as she ought to have appreciated her."

And Rodolphe proceeded to read the following letter aloud:

Bouqueval Farm, August 15, 1841

Your Lordship,

I take the liberty to write once again to you to inform you of a very happy event in our lives and in order to ask a new favor of you, of you to whom we already owe so much—or rather, of you to whom we owe the veritable paradise in which my good Germain, his good mother, and I exist.

Here, Your Lordship, is the news: I have been practically mad with joy for the past ten days, because since ten days ago, I have been the mother of a little love of a daughter. I think she's just the picture of Germain, but he thinks she looks just like me. Our dear Mother Georges says that she looks like both of us. The fact is that she has charming blue eyes like Germain, and curly black hair just like mine. But really, my husband is grossly unfair, even though it's not like him. That's right, he always wants to hold our little one in his lap, while I say it's my right to have her—isn't that so, Your Lordship?

"What good, worthy young people! How happy they must be," Rodolphe said. "If ever a couple was well matched, it's this one."

"And Rigolette so deserves her happiness!" said Fleur-de-Marie.

"That's why I always blessed the fates that brought us together," Rodolphe said, and he continued:

But indeed, Your Lordship, you must forgive me for bothering you with these little household quarrels that always end with a kiss. And anyway, your ears must be burning up, Your Lordship, for not a day goes by when we don't look at each other, Germain and me, and say, "Heavens! We're so happy! We're so happy!"—and, naturally, your name comes up right away after that. Excuse that scratching there, Your Lordship, and that blob of ink. It's just that, without thinking, I had written "Monsieur Rodolphe," as I used to call you, and I had to correct it. Speaking of that, I hope you'll find that my writing has improved, along with my spelling. Germain is always working with me on it, and I don't write block print going every which way, like when you used to cut my quills for me.

"I must confess," said Rodolphe, laughing, "that my little protégée is fooling herself a little, and I'm sure that Germain is spending more time kissing his pupil's hand than giving it directions."

"Come, come, my dear. You're being unfair," said Clémence, looking at the letter. "It's a little uneven, but very legible."

"It's true that there's some improvement," Rodolphe said. "A while ago it would have taken her eight pages to say what she can now write in two." He continued to read:

It is, however, true that you cut my quills, Your Lordship. When we think about it, Germain and me, we're ashamed, remembering how you never acted at all proud. Ah! Heavens! Here I am, without my knowing, going on about other things than the thing we want to ask you, Your Lordship. For my husband joins me in this, and it's quite important: we're going to tell you an idea, and here it is.

We beg you, Your Lordship, to be so good as to choose a name to give to our dear little daughter. The godfather and godmother both agree. And do you know who that godfather and godmother are, Your Lordship? Two of the people you and Madame la Marquise d'Harville rescued from hardship in order to make them very happy, as happy as us. In a word, it's Morel, the gem-cutter, and Jeanne Duport, the sister of a poor prisoner named Bitters, a worthy woman I had seen in prison when I went there to visit my poor Germain, the same one the marquise later helped get out of the hospital.

Now, Your Lordship, you must be told why we chose Monsieur Morel to be the godfather and Jeanne Duport for the godmother. We said to ourselves, Germain and me, "It will be like thanking Monsieur Rodolphe again for his kindness if we name the worthy people who owe everything to him and the marquise to be the godfather and godmother of our child." And Morel the gem-cutter and Jeanne Duport are the most honest of people, to boot. They're people like us, and furthermore, like Germain and I said, they are our relatives in happiness, since they are, like us, in the family of your protégés, Your Lordship.

"Oh, Father! Don't you think this idea is really charming and delicate?" Fleur-de-Marie said, full of emotion. "To name the people who owe everything to you and my second mother as the godfather and godmother to their child!"

"You are quite right, my dear child," said Clémence. "I could not be more touched by their remembering us this way."

"And I am very happy to have chosen such good recipients for my good deeds," said Rodolphe. He continued to read:

In any case, by means of the money you had him be given, Monsieur Rodolphe, Morel is now a fine gem broker. He earns enough to raise his family in comfort and to teach a trade to his children. The good poor Louise is going to marry a worthy laborer, I believe, who loves her and respects her the way she deserves because, though she was unfortunate, she wasn't guilty of anything, and Louise's fiancé has a good enough heart to understand that.

"I was sure," exclaimed Rodolphe, turning to his daughter, "I would find ammunition against our enemy in dear little Rigolette's letter! You hear, this is the expression of an honest, upright soul's good common sense. She says of Louise, 'though she was unfortunate, she wasn't guilty of anything, and her fiancé has a good enough heart to understand that.'" Fleur-de-Marie, more and more touched and saddened by the reading of this letter, shuddered at the brief look her father gave her as he was pronouncing the final words we have emphasized. The prince went on:

I will tell you something else, Your Lordship: thanks to the marquise, Jeanne Duport was able to obtain a separation from her husband, that vile man who stole everything from her and beat her. She got her oldest daughter back, and she has a little trimmings store in which she sells what she makes with her children. Their business is prospering. They're the happiest people living. And who can we thank for all of this? You, Your Lordship, and Madame the marquise. You both know how to give wisely and how to give well.

Speaking of that, Germain will write to you at the end of the month, as he usually does, Your Lordship, about the Bank for Unemployed Laborers and Free Loans. The workers are hardly ever late in repaying their loans, and already people have noticed a great deal of prosperity spreading through the neighborhood. At least now poor families can make it through off periods in their work without having to pawn their linens and mattresses. And when they are back at work, you should also see how hard they work at their jobs. They are so proud that people trust them to work hard and to be honest! Good Lord, that's all they have. And so they bless you for having let them take out loans on that capital. Yes, Your Lordship, it's you they bless—you. For all that you kept saying you had nothing to do with this foundation except for the nomination of Germain as the director, and that it was an anonymous donor who performed this great act, we prefer to believe that it is you to whom thanks are owed. It just feels more natural!

Anyway, somebody's trumpeting it all over town that you're the one people ought to praise. That trumpeter is none other than Madame Pipelet, who repeats to everybody she meets that her king of tenants (sorry, Monsieur Rodolphe, that's what she always calls you) is the only person who could have created this charitable work, and that her old, dear Alfred thinks just the same. As for him, he is so proud and so happy in his position as bank guard that he says he wouldn't care about Monsieur Cabrion's harassment anymore. To end this account of your family of grateful people, Your Lordship, I will add that Germain has read in the newspapers that a certain Martial, a colonizer in Algeria, has been highly praised for the courage he showed in leading his tenant farmers in repelling an attack of Arab pillagers. His wife, who was just as courageous as he, was slightly wounded while fighting at his side, where she was shooting a rifle like a real grenadier. Since that time, the newspaper says, they've taken to calling her Madame Carbine.

Forgive me for this long letter, Your Lordship, but I thought you wouldn't be ill-disposed toward having some news of all the people for whom you've been such a providential blessing. I write to you from the Bouqueval farm, where we have been staying with our dear mother since spring. Germain leaves in the morning to go to work, and he comes back in the evening. In the autumn we will return to live in Paris. It's funny, Your Lordship, how much I love the countryside now when I didn't like it at all before. The only way I can explain it to myself is that it's because Germain likes it so much. Speaking of the farm, Monsieur Rodolphe, since you surely know where that good little Songbird is, if you have the chance, tell her that we always remember her as the sweetest and best person in the whole world, and, as for me, I never think of how happy we are without saying to myself, "Since Monsieur Rodolphe was also dear Fleur-de-Marie's Monsieur Rodolphe, she must be happy like us, too, thanks to him," and that makes my happiness even more complete.

Good heavens, how I've gone on! What must you be thinking, Your Lordship? But you're so nice, it doesn't matter! And then, you know, it's your fault if I chirp away as much and as joyously as Papa Crétu and Ramonette, who don't dare to compete with me at singing anymore. Well, Monsieur Rodolphe, I can tell you, I wear them out.

You won't refuse our request, will you, Your Lordship? If you name our dear little daughter, we feel it will bring her happiness; it will be her lucky star. You know, Monsieur Rodolphe, sometimes Germain and I almost congratulate each other for having known hard times, because we feel doubly how happy our child will be not to know what the wretchedness we lived through is like.

If I conclude by saying to you, Monsieur Rodolphe, that we are trying to help poor people here and there according to our means, it's not to boast about ourselves, but because I want you to know that we are not keeping all of the happiness you've given us all to ourselves. In any case, we always tell the people we help, "It's not us you should be praising and thanking. It's Monsieur Rodolphe, the best and most generous man in the world." And they take you to be a kind of saint, at the very least.

Farewell, Your Lordship. You should know that when our little daughter learns to read, the first word she will spell out will be your name, Monsieur Rodolphe, and after that, the words you had inscribed on my trousseau box: "*Work and Wisdom. Honor and Happiness.*"[277]

Thanks to those four words, along with our tender and loving care, we hope, Your Lordship, that our child will always be worthy of pronouncing the name of the one who was so providentially good to us and to all of the unfortunate people he knew.

I apologize, Your Lordship, but it's just that as I finished this letter, I had these big tears come into my eyes. But they're good tears. Excuse me, please. It's not my fault. I can't see very clearly now, and I keep scratching things out.

With respect and gratitude to Your Lordship,

Rigolette, Germain's wife.

P.S. Oh, heavens! Upon rereading my letter, Your Lordship, I've realized that I called you Monsieur Rodolphe many times. You'll forgive me, won't you? You know very well that whatever we call you, we respect you and bless you all the same, Your Lordship.

277. In an earlier mention of Rodolphe's inscription on Rigolette's trousseau box, the message read, "*Work and Wisdom. Love and Happiness.*" [TN]

CHAPTER 5

MEMORIES

"Dear little Rigolette!" Clémence said, touched by what Rodolphe had just read. "That naive letter shows so much beautiful feeling."

"No doubt about it," Rodolphe said. "We couldn't have helped anyone more deserving. Our protégée has an excellent character. She has a heart of gold—and our dear child appreciates her as much as we do," he added, turning to his daughter. Then, struck by her pallor and dejection, he cried out, "What's wrong?"

"Alas, what a depressing contrast there is between my position and Rigolette's. 'Work and Wisdom. Honor and Happiness': these four words explain what her life has been and what it surely will be. A hard-working, well-behaved young girl, a cherished wife, a happy mother, an honored woman—that is her destiny! Whereas in my case . . ."

"Good God! What are you trying to say?"

"Forgive me, dear father. Don't think me ungrateful, but despite your endless affection and that of my second mother, despite all the respect and luxury that surround me, despite your sovereign power, there is no cure for my shame. Nothing can wipe away the past. Again, I ask your forgiveness, Father. I have hidden it from you until now, but the memory of my early taint has made me lose all hope. It is killing me."

"Clémence, do you hear this?" Rodolphe cried out in despair.

"But, you poor child!" Clémence said as she took Fleur-de-Marie's hand affectionately in her own. "Doesn't our love and the affection of all those around you—which you completely deserve—doesn't all that show you that the past should be nothing to you but a bad dream?"

"Oh, it's fate—fate!" Rodolphe said. "Now I curse my fears and my silence. This deadly idea that took root in your mind so long ago has done terrible damage there without our realizing it, and it's too late now to fight against this ghastly error. Oh, I am truly miserable!"

"Take heart, my love," Clémence said to Rodolphe. "You were saying just a moment ago that it's always better to know the enemy who threatens you. Now we know the cause of our child's sorrow, and we will triumph over it because we have truth, justice, and our love on our side."

"And also because she will see in the end that if there is no cure for her affliction, that means that there won't be any for ours, either,"

Rodolphe said. "Because all justice, human and divine, would be meaningless if, after all that had happened to this unfortunate girl, she were merely to exchange one torment for another."

After a long silence, during which Fleur-de-Marie seemed to collect herself, she took Rodolphe's hand in one of her own and Clémence's in the other, and said to them in a very faint voice, "Listen to me, dear father, and you as well, my loving mother: this day is a solemn one. God has willed it to be impossible for me to hide what I feel from you any longer—and I thank him for it. I would have made the confession you are about to hear before long, in any case. After all, all suffering reaches its limit, and if mine has been hidden, I couldn't have kept quiet for much longer."

"Oh, I see it all now!" Rodolphe cried. "There is no more hope for her."

"I have hope for the future, Father, and that hope gives me the strength to talk to you like this."

"And what can you hope for in the future, poor child, since your present state brings you only sorrow and bitterness?"

"I will tell you, Father. But first, permit me to recall my past to you and to confess before God, who hears all, what I have felt up to now."

"Speak, speak; we're listening," Rodolphe said, sitting down with Clémence next to Fleur-de-Marie.

"All the time I was in Paris, by your side, Father," Fleur-de-Marie said, "I was so happy—oh, so completely happy! Those happy days would repay years and years of suffering. You see, at least I have known happiness."

"For a few days, perhaps."

"Yes, but what pure, unalloyed joy! As always, you showered me with the most tender cares! I gave myself over, without fear, to outbursts of gratitude and affection that, at each and every moment, made me love you more. The future seemed dazzling with promise. A father to adore, a mother to cherish twice over since she would replace the one I had and never knew. And then, I must confess, my pride grew, despite myself, so much was it an honor to me to belong to you. When the few people in your household in Paris happened to speak to me and called me 'highness'—I couldn't stop myself from being proud of that title. If I then thought vaguely of the past, it was only to say to myself, 'I, who was once so tainted, am now the cherished daughter of a sovereign prince whom everybody blesses and reveres; I, who was once so wretched, am now enjoying all the most luxurious of pleasures and an almost royal existence!' Alas! What could you expect, Father? My luck was so unexpected, and your power dazzled me with such splendor, that maybe I can be excused for letting myself be blinded like that."

"Be excused? But nothing could be more natural, my poor, adored angel. What sin is there in being proud of a rank that's yours by right, in enjoying the advantages of the position I have restored to you? I well remember that time too and how you were so charmingly cheerful. How many times did I see you fall into my arms, overcome with joy, and say to me with that enchanting tone, those words that, alas, I am not to hear again, 'Father, it's too much happiness, too much!' Unfortunately, those are the memories, you know, that lulled me into a false sense of security. And later, I didn't worry enough about the causes of your melancholy."

"But tell us, my child," Clémence said, "what could have changed this first joy, which was so pure and so deserved, into sadness?"

"Alas, something fatal and unforeseen happened!"

"What happened?"

"Father, you remember," Fleur-de-Marie said, unable to suppress a tremor of horror, "you remember the horrible scene that occurred just before we left Paris, when your carriage was stopped near the gate?"

"Yes," Rodolphe answered, sadly. "Brave Slasher! After he saved my life yet again, he died there right in front of us, saying to me, 'God is just. I have killed, and now I am killed.'"

"Well, Father, do you know who I saw one moment before that poor man passed away? Do you know who was staring at me? Oh, that look—that look! It has followed me everywhere since that moment," Fleur-de-Marie went on, trembling.

"What look? Who are you talking about?" Rodolphe cried out.

"The ogress from the joint," Fleur-de-Marie murmured.

"That monster! You saw her again? Where was that?"

"You didn't see her in the tavern where the Slasher died? She was one of the women standing over him."

"Oh!" Rodolphe said, overcome. "Now I understand it. You were already struck with terror at the Slasher's murder and so you must have thought you saw an act of God in that dreadful meeting."

"It's only too true, Father. When I saw the ogress, my blood went cold. It seemed to me that my heart, which had glowed with hope and joy up until then, suddenly withered under her glance. Yes, to meet up with that woman again at the exact moment when the Slasher was dying as he said, 'God is just,' it seemed to me a divine rebuke for the proud forgetfulness of my past, and that I would have to expiate it by humiliation and repentance."

"But that past was forced on you. You have nothing to answer to for it before God!"

"You had no choice, you poor, deluded, unfortunate child."

"Once you were thrown into that abyss, against your own will, thanks to the atrocious indifference of society, of which you were the victim, there was nothing you could do to get out of it, regardless of your remorse, your horror, or your despair. You were chained forever in that den. Only the stroke of luck that put you in my path allowed you to be taken away from that place."

"And after all, as your father has said, my child, when all is said and done, you were the victim, not a willing participant, in this abomination!" Clémence exclaimed.

"But, Mother, I have been subjected to this abomination," Fleur-de-Marie said dolefully. "Nothing can annihilate those dreadful memories. They haunt me ceaselessly, not like before, when I lived among the peaceful inhabitants of a farm or the degraded women who were my companions in Saint-Lazare. Now they have followed me all the way into this palace in which the elite of Germany reside. They have pursued me, in the end, all the way into my father's arms, right up to the steps of his throne." And then Fleur-de-Marie broke down into tears. Rodolphe and Clémence stayed silent in the face of this terrifying expression of invincible remorse. They were crying as well, feeling powerless to comfort her. "Since then," Fleur-de-Marie went on, wiping away her tears, "every moment of every day I say with bitter shame, 'I am honored, I am revered. The most eminent and venerable of people show me respect. Before the gaze of a whole court, an emperor's sister has deigned to adjust my headband across my forehead—and I have lived in the mire of the Cité, treated by thieves and murderers as one of them.' Oh, Father, forgive me! But the more elevated my position has become, the more I have been struck by the deep degradation into which I had fallen. Every time I am offered another homage, I feel myself guilty of profanation. My God, can you imagine it! To allow elders to bow down before me, having been what I have been . . . to allow noble young girls and justly honored women to be flattered by being in my company . . . even to allow princesses, who are doubly revered, both on account of their age and the holiness of their character, to shower considerations and praise on me: can this be other than impiety and sacrilege? And then, Father, if you only knew what I have suffered and what I must suffer every day when I say to myself, 'If God revealed my past, with what well-deserved contempt would I be treated! I, who am at this moment raised so high!' What a frightening and just punishment that would be!"

"But, my unfortunate child, my wife and I both know your past. We are worthy of our rank and yet we cherish and adore you."

"Your love for me is the unconditional love of a mother and a father."

"And what about all the good you have done since your arrival? What about that beautiful and holy institution, that refuge you opened for orphans and poor abandoned girls, and the admirable, intelligent, and devoted care you shower on them? What about your insistence on calling them your sisters and having them call you the same as well, so that you really do treat them like sisters? Does all of this count for nothing toward the redemption of failings that were not even your own? Finally, what about the affection the worthy abbess of Sainte-Hermangilde shows for you? She has only known you since you came here. Don't you owe that affection entirely to the elevation of your mind, the beauty of your soul, and your sincere piety?"

"As long as the praise of the abbess of Sainte-Hermangilde concerns only my present conduct, I take joy in it without regrets, Father. But when she holds me up as an example to the noble young women who have taken vows in the abbey, and when those young women see in me a model of every virtue, I feel myself dying of embarrassment, as if I were participating in some vile lie."

After a fairly long silence, Rodolphe, in a state of painful dejection, said, "It's clear that there is no hope of persuading you. Reason is powerless against a conviction that is that much more unshakeable because it has its basis in a generous and elevated feeling. You keep thinking about your past. The contrast between those memories and your present position must truly be a constant torment to you. It is my turn to ask you to forgive me, you poor child."

"You, dear father, asking me forgiveness? For what, for God's sake?"

"For not having foreseen your sensitivity. Given your heart's excessive delicacy, I should have expected it. And yet what could I have done? It was my duty to recognize you solemnly as my daughter. And it follows that this respect, whose homage is so painful to you, would come of necessity to you. Yes, I was at fault. You see, I was too proud of you. I was too happy to take pleasure in the charm your beauty, your mind, and your character had over everyone who came near you. I ought to have hidden my treasure away, to have lived in near retirement with Clémence and you. I should have done without these parties and constant receptions where I loved so much to see you shine, madly believing that I could elevate you so high, so high that the past would entirely cease to exist for you. But, alas, the opposite has come to pass. As you said to me, the more elevated you have become, the deeper and darker the abyss I've pulled you out of has seemed to you. As I said: it's my fault. And yet I thought I was doing well by you," Rodolphe said, wiping his tears away. "But I was wrong. And also, I believed too soon that I had been pardoned. God's vengeance is not satisfied. It continues to attack me in the happiness of my daughter!"

Someone knocked discreetly a few times on the door of the salon that led into Fleur-de-Marie's chapel, interrupting this sad conversation. Rodolphe got up and opened the door a crack. There was Murph, who said to him, "I ask your royal highness's pardon for disturbing him, but a messenger from the Prince d'Herkaüsen-Oldenzaal has just brought this letter, which, he says, is very important and must be given on the instant to your royal highness."

"Thank you, my good Murph. Don't go away," Rodolphe said to him with a sigh. "In a moment, I will need a few words with you."

And the prince, after closing the door, stayed in the salon for a moment to read the letter Murph had just given him. Here is what it said:

My Lord,

May I hope that the family bonds that connect me to your royal highness, who has always deigned to show me so much friendship, will excuse an action that would certainly show too much effrontery if it were not necessitated by an honest conscience.

Fifteen months ago, my lord, you returned from France, bringing with you a daughter who was that much more dear to you because you had thought to have lost her forever, whereas, in fact, she had never left her mother, whom you married *in extremis* in Paris in order to legitimate Princess Amélie's birth, making her thus the peer of other highnesses of the German Confederation.

Her birth is therefore that of a sovereign. My sister, the abbess of Sainte-Hermangilde, who has often had the honor of seeing the beloved daughter of your royal highness, has also written to me that her beauty is incomparable, and that the goodness of her heart equals her birth, just as the elevation of her mind equals her beauty.

And so, my lord, I will straightforwardly broach the subject of this letter inasmuch as a serious illness unfortunately keeps me at Oldenzaal and prevents me from presenting myself in person to your royal highness. During the time my son spent in Gerolstein, he saw the Princess Amélie almost every day. He loves her passionately, though he always hid his love from her. I have thought it my duty, my lord, to inform you of this. You have deigned to give my son a father's welcome and to make him promise to return to the bosom of your family and to live in that intimacy which is so precious to him. I would have been shamefully remiss, as a matter of honor, in hiding this circumstance from your royal highness, since it will surely change the reception that you meant to offer my son.

I recognize that it would be madness for us to hope to ally ourselves more closely still with your royal highness's family. I recognize that the daughter of whom you are, with good right, so proud, my lord, must certainly expect a higher destiny. But I also know that you are the most loving of fathers and that if you could ever believe my son worthy of joining your family and of making the Princess Amélie happy, you would not be stopped by the daunting inequality of the match, which would be for us such an unhoped-for good fortune.

It would not be suitable for me to sing Henri's praises, my lord. But I appeal to the encouragement and praise that you have so often deigned to bestow on him.

I dare not say more, my lord, nor can I. My feelings run too deep. Whatever you determine, please be so kind as to believe that we will receive that decision with respect and that I will always be true to the profoundly devoted feelings with which I have the honor to be

Your Royal Highness's
Very Humble and Obedient Servant,

GUSTAVE-PAUL
Prince d'Herkaüsen-Oldenzaal

CHAPTER 6

CONFESSIONS

After reading the letter from Henri's father, the prince, Rodolphe remained sad and thoughtful for a little while. Then, as a ray of hope broke out across his face, he returned to his daughter's side. Clémence was showering her with loving comfort, but to no avail. "You said it yourself, my child: God has willed that this day be one of solemn coming to terms," Rodolphe said to Fleur-de-Marie. "I didn't expect that another new and serious circumstance would come to our notice that would show even more how true those words were."

"What are you talking about, Father?"

"Yes, my love, what is it?"

"More reasons to be fearful."

"For whom, Father?"

"For you."

"For me?"

"You have only told us part of your sorrows, you poor child."

"Please be good enough to explain, Father," Fleur-de-Marie said, blushing.

"Now I can. Before, I couldn't, because I didn't know how completely you despaired of any future. Listen, my dearest daughter. You believe yourself to be, or rather you are indeed, very unhappy. When, at the beginning of our conversation, you spoke of what hopes remained to you, I understood, and my heart was broken because it meant to me that I would lose you forever. I would see you locked in a cloister, buried alive in your grave. You wanted to enter a convent."

"Father . . ."

"Isn't that true, my child?"

"Yes, if you permitted it," Fleur-de-Marie answered, almost unable to speak.

"You would leave us!" Clémence cried out.

"The Abbey of Sainte-Hermangilde is right nearby Gerolstein. I would see my father and you all the time."

"But you must realize that vows like that are eternal, my dear child. You aren't even eighteen years old, and, maybe, one day . . ."

"Oh, I will never repent of the decision I've made! I can only find rest and forgetfulness in the solitude of the cloister, at least as long as my father and you, my second mother, continue to love me."

"The burdens and comforts of the religious life," Rodolphe said, "might really, if not cure, at least assuage the pains of your torn and battered soul. And even if it cost half of my life's joy, I might come to approve of your decision. I know how you suffer, and I would never say that renouncing the world might not have to be the fatal, logical end point of your sad existence."

"What? Not you, too, Rodolphe!" Clémence exclaimed.

"Allow me to finish my thought, my love," Rodolphe went on. Then, turning to his daughter, he said, "But before taking this extreme step, we must make sure that there is no other future which would be in greater accord with your wishes and ours. If that turns out to be the case, then no sacrifice will be too costly for me, if it will assure your future." Fleur-de-Marie and Clémence both started in surprise. "What do you think of your cousin Prince Henri?"

Fleur-de-Marie trembled and blushed crimson. After a moment's hesitation, she threw herself in the prince's arms, weeping.

"You love him, you poor child!"

"You never asked me that before, Father!" Fleur-de-Marie answered, wiping the tears from her eyes.

"We were not mistaken, my love," Clémence said.

"So, you love him," Rodolphe added, taking his daughter's hands in his own. "Do you love him very much, my dear child?"

"Oh! If you only knew how hard it was to hide my feelings," Fleur-de-Marie said, "once I realized I had them. Alas! If you had asked me the slightest question, I would have confessed everything. But my shame held me back and would always have held me back."

"And do you believe that Henri knows of your love for him?" Rodolphe asked.

"Heavens! I don't think so!" Fleur-de-Marie exclaimed, fearfully.

"And what about him? Do you think he loves you?"

"No, Father, no. Oh, I hope not! It would cause him too much pain."

"And how did you come to fall in love with him, my dearest angel?"

"Alas! Practically without knowing it. You remember the portrait of the page?"

"The one that was in the abbess of Sainte-Hermangilde's apartment? It was Henri's portrait."

"Yes, Father. Thinking that painting was from another century, one day, when we were together, I revealed to the mother superior how struck I was by the beauty of the portrait. And then you said, joking, that the painting represented one of our family members from past times who had shown great courage and excellent qualities while still young. What you said about this relative's noble character in connection with his grace of expression strengthened my initial impression even more. Since then, I often took pleasure in thinking about that portrait, and I didn't hesitate to do so inasmuch as I thought that it depicted one of our cousins who was long dead. Little by little, I accustomed myself to these sweet thoughts, knowing that it would never be permitted to me to experience love in this life," Fleur-de-Marie added with a heartbreaking expression as she began to weep once more. "I took a melancholy pleasure in this strange fantasy, half joyful, half sad. I looked on this handsome page from days of yore as something like a fiancé from beyond the tomb, as someone I might meet up with again one day in eternity. It seemed to me that that was the only kind of love worthy of a heart that belonged entirely to you, Father. But please excuse this sad bit of childishness."

"On the contrary, nothing could be more touching, you poor child!" Clémence said, with deep emotion.

"Now I understand," Rodolphe said, "why you chastised me so sadly, one day, for having fooled you about that portrait."

"Alas, yes, Father! Think how embarrassed I was when, later, the mother superior gave me to understand that the portrait was of her nephew, a member of our family. That troubled me very much and I tried to forget my first impressions. But the more I tried, the more they took root in my heart, becoming stronger from the very persistence of my efforts. Even more unfortunately, Father, I often heard you praise the heart, the intelligence, and the character of Prince Henri."

"You already loved him, my dear child, even when you had only seen his portrait and heard me speak of his rare qualities."

"Although I didn't yet love him, Father, I was drawn to him, and I chastised myself bitterly for it. But I took comfort from thinking that no one in the world would ever know this sad secret, which I felt to be so shameful. For me—me—to think of loving someone and not to rest content in the affection of my second mother and you! Wasn't it my duty to you to hold you both dearest to me with all my strength and all my heart? Believe me! Among all the things for which I blamed myself, that was the most painful. Then, finally, I saw my cousin for the first time at that large affair that you gave for the Archduchess Sophie. The portrait's likeness of Prince Henri was so striking that I recognized him at once. That very evening, Father, you introduced me to my cousin, giving us permission to treat each other with the intimacy that family relationship allows."

"And so, soon you fell in love with each other?"

"Oh, Father! He spoke of how much he respected and admired you, how attached he was to you, with so much eloquence—and you yourself had spoken so well of him!"

"And he deserved it. You can't find a more elevated mind, a better heart, or a more courageous one."

"Enough, Father! Don't praise him like this. I'm already unhappy enough!"

"Yes, but I mean to convince you entirely of your cousin's rare virtue. What I say surprises you. I understand that, my child. But go on."

"I sensed how dangerous it was for me to see Prince Henri every day, but I couldn't keep myself away from that danger. Despite my blind trust in you, Father, I didn't dare tell you my fears. It took all my courage just to keep this love secret. And yet, I must admit, Father, despite all my regrets, often I would forget my past and feel in this fraternal intimacy sparks of happiness of a kind I had never experienced before. They were followed, alas, by dark despair as soon as my sad memories regained their hold over me. Because, alas, if they tormented me when people who were almost indifferent to me poured down their praise and respect, you can imagine, Father, the tortures I felt when Prince Henri showered me with the most delicate praises and expressed for me a frank and pious adoration, saying all the while that he placed the brotherly affection he felt for me under the holy protection of his mother, whom he lost when he was very young. At least I made an effort to deserve that name of sister which he gave me, by offering my cousin advice about his future, as well as I was able to, at any rate, and interesting myself in everything that related to him, always promising myself to ask you for your benevolent support for him. But often, as well, you can't imagine how greatly I was tormented, how often I had to hold back my tears, when Prince Henri asked me by chance about my childhood or my early youth. Oh, always to be deceiving him, always deceiving, always fearful, always lying, always to be trembling before the gaze of the one you love and respect, as if you were a criminal trembling before your judge's inexorable gaze! Oh, Father! I was wrong. I know it. I know I had no right to love. But I paid for this sad love with plenty of suffering. What more can I say? Prince Henri's departure, by causing me renewed, violent pain, made me recognize the truth. I saw that I loved him more than I had believed." And then Fleur-de-Marie added despondently, as if this confession had drained all her strength away, "I would have admitted all this to you soon enough, because this fatal love had brought my suffering to its limit. So now that you know all, Father, can you say that I can have any other future than the cloister?"

"Yes, there's another one, my child, and this one is as sweet, as cheerful, and as happy as the convent's future is dark and gloomy!"

"Father, what are you saying?"

"Now it's your turn to listen to me. You know that I love you too well and that my affection is too penetrating for your and Henri's love to have escaped my notice. After a few days, I was certain he loved you even more maybe than you love him."

"No, no, Father, he can't possibly love me that much."

"He loves you, I tell you. He loves you passionately, to distraction."

"Oh, my God! My God!"

"Listen a little longer. When I made that joke about the portrait, I didn't know that Henri would come soon after to see his aunt here, in Gerolstein. When he came here, I gave in to the affection he has always inspired in me. I invited him to see you frequently. After a few days, Clémence and I could no longer have any doubt about your interest in each other. If your position was the more painful one, my poor child, mine was also painful enough and, even more importantly, it was an extremely delicate one. As your father, knowing Henri's rare and excellent qualities, I couldn't but be profoundly happy at this attraction because I could never imagine a husband more deserving of you."

"Oh, Father, have pity! Have pity!"

"But, as an honorable man, I considered my child's sad past. So, far from encouraging Henri's hopes, in several conversations, I gave him advice that was absolutely contrary to what he might have expected me to say if I thought of granting him your hand in marriage. As both a father and an honorable man, in such a delicate situation, I had to keep rigorously neutral, continuing to treat your cousin with the same affability as I had done previously, without, however, encouraging him in his love for you. Up to now, my dearest child, you have been so unhappy that, seeing you, as one might say, reawakened to life because of this noble and pure love, I would not, for anything in the world, have taken from you such a rare and divine joy. Even admitting that this love would have had to be broken off later, you would at least have known a few days of innocent happiness. And then, after all, this love might ensure your future tranquility."

"My tranquility?"

"Listen just a moment longer. Henri's father, Prince Paul, has just written me. Here is his letter. Even as he sees this alliance as beyond his wildest dreams, he asks for your hand in marriage for his son, who, he says, both holds you in respect and loves you passionately."

"Oh, my God! My God!" Fleur-de-Marie said, hiding her face in her hands. "I could have been so happy!"

"Be of good cheer, my well-loved daughter! If you wish it, this happiness is yours," Rodolphe exclaimed tenderly.

"Never! Never! Have you forgotten?"

"I have forgotten nothing. But tomorrow you are entering a convent, not only burying yourself there forever, but leaving me for a straitened life, full of tears. Well, if I am to lose you, at least I'll lose you by knowing that you're happy and married to someone you love, who adores you."

"Married to him? Me, Father?"

"Yes, but on condition that, immediately after your marriage, entered into at night, with no other witnesses than Murph, standing up for you, and the Baron de Graün, standing up for Henri, the both of you leave for some quiet retreat in Switzerland or Italy where you will live unknown, as a prosperous middle-class couple. Now, my dearest daughter, do you know why I'm resigning myself to your living far away from me? Do you know why I wish Henri to abandon his title once he has left Germany? It's because I'm convinced that living in isolated happiness, focused on an existence stripped of all luxury, little by little, you will forget this odious past, which is especially painful for you because of its bitter contrast with the ceremonial obeisances that befall you constantly here."

"Rodolphe is right!" Clémence exclaimed. "Alone with Henri, always enjoying his happiness and your own, you won't have any time to think about the sorrows of your past, my child."

"And then, since we can't stay away from you for very long, Clémence and I will come visit you every year."

"And one day, when the wound that gives you so much pain has healed and scarred over, once you have found forgetfulness in happiness—and that moment will come sooner than you think—you will return to us, never to leave us again."

"Forgetfulness in happiness!" Fleur-de-Marie murmured as, despite herself, she allowed herself to be lulled by this enchanting dream.

"Yes, yes, my child," Clémence went on, "when you see yourself constantly blessed, respected, and adored by the husband of your dreams, by the man whose noble and generous heart your father has so frequently sung the praises of, how will you have any spare time to think about the past? And even if you did think of it, how could this past make you sad? How could it stop you from believing in the glowing happiness of your husband?"

"Really, it's true," Rodolphe said, hardly able to hold back his tears of joy in seeing his daughter's certitude shaken. "After all, tell me how, in the presence of your husband's adoration for you, when you will be constantly aware of the real happiness he owes you, how will you be able to hold yourself to blame?"

"Father," Fleur-de-Marie said, forgetting the past in the presence of this ineffable hope, "could there really be so much happiness in the world for me?"

"Oh, I was sure of it!" Rodolphe exclaimed in a burst of triumphant joy. "Is there any father, after all, who would not want to make his beloved child so happy?"

"She deserves every bit of happiness we can give her, my love," Clémence said, sharing in the prince's ecstasy.

"To marry Henri one day, and spend my life with him, my father and my second mother," Fleur-de-Marie repeated, giving in to the sweet intoxication of these thoughts more and more.

"Yes, my beloved angel, you will be completely happy! I am going to answer Henri's father, telling him I consent to the marriage," Rodolphe exclaimed, holding Fleur-de-Marie in his arms with inexpressible emotion. "Don't worry. Our separation will be only a brief one. The new obligations that marriage will demand of you will make your footsteps in the path of forgetfulness and joy, where you will walk forever, that much more firm. Because, you understand, if one day you become a mother, you will have to be happy not only for yourself."

"Oh!" Fleur-de-Marie burst out with a heartbreaking cry, because that word, "mother," had awoken her from the enchanting dream that was lulling her in her suffering. "Mother! Me? Oh, never! I am unworthy of that sacred title. I would die of shame before my child, if I had not already died of shame before its father, when I had to confess my past."

"Oh, God, what is she saying?" Rodolphe exclaimed, thunderstruck by her sudden change.

"Me, a mother?" Fleur-de-Marie said again, with bitter despair. "Me, respected and blessed by an innocent, pure child? Me, who was once despised by everybody? Me, to profane the sacred name of mother? No! Never! Wretched fool that I was to let myself give in to such an unworthy hope!"

"My daughter, for pity's sake, listen to me."

Fleur-de-Marie stood up, pale and beautiful with the majesty of incurable pain. "Father, we are forgetting that, before we marry, Prince Henri will have to learn about my past life."

"I had not forgotten it," Rodolphe exclaimed. "He must know everything and he will."

"And do you want me to die of shame to see myself so degraded in his eyes?"

"But he will know also the irresistible chain of events that threw you into that abyss. And he will also know of your rehabilitation."

"And in the end," Clémence said, holding Fleur-de-Marie in her arms, "he will feel that, if I can call you my daughter, he can, without shame, call you his wife."

"But, as for me, Mother, I love and respect Prince Henri too much ever to give him a hand sullied by the touch of the criminals of the Cité."

A short time after this mournful scene, the following story appeared in the *Official Gazette of Gerolstein*:

> Yesterday, in the Grand Ducal Abbey of Sainte-Hermangilde, in the presence of His Royal Highness, the reigning Grand Duke and all his court, the very high and very powerful princess Her Highness, Amélie of Gerolstein assumed the veil. The novitiate was received by his most illustrious and most reverend noble, His Lordship Charles-Maxime,

Archbishop and Duke of Oppenheim. His Lord Annibal-André Montano, of the Principate of Delphes, Bishop of Ceuta *in partibus infidelium*[278] and papal nunzio, gave the papal benediction and welcome.

The sermon was preached by the very reverend Lord Pierre d'Asfeld, Canon in the chapter of the Cologne Cathedral and Count of the Holy Roman Empire.

VENI, CREATOR OPTIME.[279]

278. The phrase means "in the territory of the infidels" and designates a bishop who is not attached to any specific diocese. [TN]

279. Come, Greatest Spirit. [TN]

CHAPTER 7

VOWS

RODOLPHE TO CLÉMENCE

Gerolstein, January 12, 1842[280]

By reassuring me about the state of your father's health, my dear, you give me hope that you will be able to bring him here before this week is out. I had warned him that in the Rosenfeld residence, which is in the middle of the forest, he would face the hard cold of our bitter winters despite any precautions he might take. Unfortunately, his passion for hunting made him impervious to any advice. I beg of you, Clémence, leave as soon as your father can bear the jostling of the coach. Leave that barbarous country and that barbarous lodging, fit only for those old Germans with iron bodies whose race has long since disappeared.

I am afraid that you will be the next to fall ill. The hardships of this sudden journey and the worries that beset you until you reached your father must have affected you cruelly. I wish I could have accompanied you. I beg of you, Clémence, take care of yourself. I know how brave and devoted you are. I know the loving care you will give your father. But he would be as driven to despair as I would be if this trip made you ill. The count's illness makes me doubly unhappy, since it takes you from me just when I could have benefited so much from the comfort of your love.

The ceremony in which our poor child takes her vows is still set for tomorrow, January 13, an ominous anniversary. JANUARY 13 was the day I drew my sword on my father. Oh, my love, I had thought myself already pardoned for that act. The alluring hope of living out my days with you and my daughter had made me forget that it was not I, but she, who had been punished up to now, and that my chastisement was still to come. Well, it did come when, six months ago, the unfortunate

280. About six months have passed since Fleur-de-Marie entered the convent of Sainte-Hermangilde as a novice. [SN]

child revealed to us her heart's double torment: her incurable shame in her past and her unhappy love for Henri.

According to a fatal logic, each of these two bitter and burning emotions must have intensified the other and led to her unshakeable decision to take the veil. As you well know, my love, fight this intention as we might, with all the strength of our adoration for her, we could not deceive ourselves into believing that this brave step would not have also been ours in her place. How could we respond to those terrible words, "I love Prince Henri too much to give him a hand stained by the criminals of the Cité"?

All there was left for her to do was to sacrifice herself to her noble scruples, to the ineradicable memory of her shame! And she has done that—bravely. She has renounced the glories of this world and climbed down the steps from the throne to wear the habit and kneel on the stone floor of a church. With her hands crossed upon her chest, she bowed her angelic head, and that beautiful blond hair that I loved so much and keep as a treasure has fallen before the blade.

Oh, my love, you know the heartrending emotion we felt at that mournful and solemn moment. That same emotion is as poignant now as it was in the past. I am crying like a baby as I write these words.

I saw her this morning. Although she seemed much less pale than usual and claimed not to be in any pain, I have deathly fears for her health. Alas! When I saw her face under the veil and wimple that cover her noble forehead, I could see that her features had become gaunt and white as cold marble, which made her big blue eyes seem even bigger. I couldn't stop thinking then of the sweet, pure brilliance with which her beauty shone when we were married. Isn't it true that we had never seen her look more charming? Her gorgeous face seemed to shine with our happiness.

So, as I was saying, I saw her this morning. She had not been informed that Princess Juliane had voluntarily resigned her position as mother superior in her favor: tomorrow, therefore, on the day she takes her vows, our child will be elected abbess, since the noble young ladies of the community are unanimously in favor of conferring that dignity on her.[281]

281. It occasionally happens that one gives a nun the position of abbess on the same day she takes her vows. See *The Life of the Very High and Very Devout Princess Madame Charlotte-Flandrine of Nassau, the Very Worthy Abbess of the Royal Monastery of the Holy Cross, Who Was Elected Abbess at the Age of Nineteen.* [SN]

Charlotte-Flandrine de Nassau (1579–1640) entered the monastery of Sainte-Croix in 1593 and became abbess in 1603 at the age of twenty-four. There is a life of her written by Claude Allard in 1653 whose title is close to the one Sue cites, but it does not include the information that she was elected abbess at nineteen. [TN]

From the beginning of her novitiate, everyone has been of the same opinion with regard to her piety, her charity, and the religious exactitude with which she fulfills all the duties of her order, the rigor of whose rules she woefully exaggerates. She has had the same influence over the convent that she has everywhere, without either desiring it or being aware of it, which only augments its power.

Our discussion this morning has confirmed my suspicions. She has found neither rest nor forgetfulness in the solitude of the cloister or the severe religious practices of monastic life. Nevertheless, she remains happy in her decision, which she regards as the fulfillment of an overriding duty. But she still suffers because she was not made for such mystical contemplations, which, for some people, allow them to forget all their feelings, all their earthly memories, and to lose themselves in ascetic ecstasy.

No, Fleur-de-Marie believes; she prays; she submits to her order's hard, rigorous observances. She showers the most ardent religious comfort and the most humble care on the poor, sick women who are patients in the abbey hospital. She has gone so far as to refuse the help of a lay sister in doing her modest housekeeping for that sad, cold, bare cell where we noted, with such mournful surprise, the dried branches of her little rosebush hanging under her crucifix, as you will remember, my love. She is, in all, cherished for her exemplariness and venerated as a model of the community. But she still confessed this morning that she is not so absorbed by the practices and rigors of the religious life for the past not to constantly appear before her, not only such as it was, but such as it might have been—and she castigates herself bitterly for this weakness.

"Father, I blame myself for it," she said with that calm, sweet resignation that you know so well. "I blame myself for it, but I can't stop myself from often thinking that if God had wanted to spare me the degradation that will stain me forever, I would have been able to live with you always, loved by the husband you chose for me. Although I wish otherwise, the whole of my life can be divided between those mournful regrets and the frightful memories of the Cité. I pray God, vainly, to deliver me from these obsessions and to fill my heart only with pious devotion and religious hope, and, finally, to take entire possession of me, since I want to give myself to him entirely. But he does not grant my prayers, doubtless because my worldly concerns make me unworthy to enter into communion with him."

"Well, then!" I exclaimed, possessed by a mad glimmer of hope. "There is still time! Today your novitiate ends, but you will not take your solemn vows until tomorrow. You are still young. Renounce this hard, austere life that gives you none of the comfort you expected. Come trade one form of suffering for another and suffer in our arms, where our love may soften your sorrows."

Shaking her head sadly, she answered me with that inflexibly strong reasoning that has surprised us so often: "Doubtless, Father, solitude is very sad to me—to me, especially since I am already so accustomed to your constant affection. Certainly, I am prey to bitter regrets and heartbreaking memories, but at least I know that I am fulfilling an obligation. And I recognize—I know—that anywhere else I would be out of place. I would find myself again in the same cruelly false position that has already given me so much pain, for your sake and for mine . . . since I have my pride, too. Your daughter will be what she must be, do what she must do, accept what she must accept. Tomorrow, everyone will know all about the filthy mire you removed me from. I hope that, in seeing me repentant at the foot of the cross, people may forgive my past in the light of my present humility. And it could never be like that, my dear father, if people continued to see me as I was a few months ago, shining amid the splendors of your court. And anyway, when I satisfy the just and severe demands of the world, I can satisfy my demands on myself, and so I thank and bless God with all the strength I have in me when I think that only he could offer your daughter a sanctuary and a position worthy both of her and of you, a position, which, after all, is not that painfully different from that of my original degradation and which might earn me the only respect owed to me: that which one grants to repentance and humble sincerity."

Alas, Clémence, what was there to say to that? It's fate! Fate! This unhappy child is endowed, if one can put it this way, with an inexorable logic regarding everything that touches on delicacies of honor and the heart. Minds and souls like that refuse to consider palliatives or false positions. Such people will submit to the most implacable consequences.

I left her as I always do, with a broken heart. Without basing the slightest hope on our conversation, our last before she takes her vows, I had said to myself, "Today she might yet renounce the cloister." But, as you can see, my love, her will is as solid as rock, and I must, alas, give in to it and repeat her words: "Only God can offer her a sanctuary and a position worthy both of her and of me."

Once again, her decision is one that our society would find admirably suitable and logical. Given Fleur-de-Marie's exquisite sensitivity, no other condition is possible for her. But, as I've often said to you, my love, if my sacred duties—more sacred even than those of family—didn't keep me among my people who love me and for whom I figure somewhat as a godsend, I would have left with you, my daughter, Henri, and Murph to live an obscure and happy life in some unknown corner of the world. That way, far from the imperious laws of a society powerless to cure the evil it does, we could surely have forced happiness and forgetfulness on that unhappy child. Here, on the other hand, amid the brilliance and ceremony of the court, that is impossible, however restrained the court might be. And so I repeat, it's fate! Fate! I can't abdicate my power without endangering the happiness of a people who depend on me. These brave and worthy people! Let us hope that they remain forever unaware of what their loyalty costs me!

I bid you an affectionate farewell, my beloved Clémence. It is almost a comfort to me to see you so pained by the fate of my child, because that way I can refer to *our* sorrow, and there is no selfishness in my suffering.

It sometimes frightens me to think what I would become if you were not with me in these painful circumstances. And then these thoughts often also make me even sorrier for Fleur-de-Marie's fate. Because I still have you. But what does she still have in this world?

Farewell again; a sad farewell, my noble love, good angel of these bad times. Come back soon. Your absence weighs on you as much as on me.

I am yours for life, my love! I am yours heart and soul!

R.

I am sending you this letter via messenger. Unless something unexpected happens, I will send you another letter tomorrow, as soon as possible after the sad ceremony. I send all my best hopes and wishes for your father's quick recovery. I forgot to tell you the news about poor Henri. His health is improving and no longer gives grounds for any serious worries. His worthy father, who is himself ill, found in himself the strength to care for his son and watch over him—a miracle of paternal love, which, nevertheless, does not surprise me at all.

And so, dear, I'll write tomorrow—tomorrow, which is a dark day of ill omen for me!

Yours, as always and forever.

R.

Abbey of Sainte-Hermangilde

Four o'clock a.m.

Don't worry, Clémence, don't worry, even if the hour at which I write you this letter and the place from which it is dated might well frighten you. Thank God, the danger has passed, although the crisis was a terrifying one.

Yesterday, after I had written you, some kind of gloomy presentiment started to make me nervous. I remembered my daughter's pallor and the pain she seemed to be in as well as the weak state in which she has languished for some time and thought that she would certainly be spending this last night before her vows in prayer in an immense and icy church. Accordingly, I sent Murph and David to the abbey to ask of Princess Juliane her permission to stay until tomorrow in the attached house where Henri usually stays. That way, my daughter might receive prompt aid and I would hear quickly if, as I feared, she lacked the strength to fulfill the stern—not to say cruel—duty to spend an excessively cold January night in prayers. Thus, I wrote to Fleur-de-Marie to say that, although I completely respected the exercise of her religious duties, I begged her to consider her health and to spend her night of watching and praying in her cell and not in the church.

Here is how she answered: "Dear Father, I thank you from the bottom of my heart for this latest, tender proof of your concern for me. Do not have any worries. I believe myself perfectly able to fulfill my duty. Your daughter, dear father, can show neither fear nor weakness. The rules are what they are and I must conform to them. If some physical pain were to come from that, I would offer it to God in all joy. I hope you will approve of this, you who have always practiced renunciation and duty with such courage. Farewell, dear father. I won't say that I will pray for you. When I pray to God, I am always praying to you because I am unable not to confuse you with the divinity I implore. On this earth, you have been for me that which God will be in heaven, should I deserve it.

"Please be so good as to bless your daughter in your thoughts this night, dear father. Tomorrow she will be the Lord's bride. She kisses your hand in pious respect,

"Sister Amélie"

This letter, which I cannot read without bursting into tears, nevertheless made me at least a little calmer. I, too, had a dark, waking night before me.

When night had fallen, I went to close myself up in the pavilion I had built not far from the monument erected in my father's memory in expiation of that fatal night. Around one o'clock in the morning, I heard Murph's voice, which made me shiver in fear. He was coming, at all speed, from the convent.

What can I tell you, my love? Just as I had foreseen, the unfortunate child, despite her courage and will, did not have the strength to fulfill that barbarous practice completely. Princess Juliane had found it impossible to relieve her of that obligation, the rules on that subject being very strict. At eight o'clock in the evening, Fleur-de-Marie knelt down on the stone of that church. She prayed right up until midnight. But then, succumbing to her weakness, the horrible cold, and her own emotion—she had been weeping silently for a long time—she fainted. Two nuns, who, by Princess Juliane's order, had shared her night of watching, came to relieve her and carried her to her cell.

David was called for on the instant. Murph got into a carriage and sped over to find me. I flew as fast as I could to the convent. Princess Juliane received me. She told me that David feared that seeing me would make too sharp an impression on my daughter. He thought that her loss of consciousness, from which she had recovered, since it had been caused only by great weakness, was really no cause for alarm. A horrible thought came to me at first. I thought that they meant to hide some great illness from me, or at least to prepare me to learn about it. But the mother superior said to me, "My lord, I can say positively that the Princess Amélie is out of danger. A light tonic that Doctor David has made her take has given her back her strength." I could not doubt what the abbess stated so positively. I believed it and awaited with painful impatience any news about my daughter.

After fifteen anguished minutes, David returned. Thank God, she was better. She had wanted to continue her prayerful watch in the church, consenting only to kneel on a cushion. When I expressed my opposition and consternation that the mother superior had given in to her wishes, adding that I was formally protesting that decision, he answered that it would have been dangerous to oppose my daughter's will at a time when she was under the influence of strong emotions, and, in any case, Princess Juliane had agreed to have the poor child leave the church when matins occurred in order to take some rest and prepare herself for the ceremony.

"So she is, then, at the church now?" I asked him.

"Yes, my lord, but she will leave within half an hour."

I had myself immediately taken to the north gallery, from which one oversees the whole choir. There, amid the vast church's shadows and lit only by the pale glimmer of a sanctuary lamp, I saw her, near the railing, kneeling with her hands joined together, still praying fervently. I kneeled myself as well, thinking of my daughter.

The clock rang three in the morning. Two sisters seated in the stalls, who had not taken their eyes off of her, came over to whisper to her. After a few moments, she crossed herself, got up, and crossed the choir with a reasonably firm step. But still, my love, when she passed beneath the lamp, her face seemed to me as white as the long veil drifting around her. I left the gallery immediately after, wanting at first to join her. But I was afraid that the emotion caused by our meeting would prevent her from experiencing a few moments of rest. I sent David to find out how she was feeling. He returned to tell me that she was feeling better and that she was going to try to sleep for a bit.

I am staying at the abbey for tomorrow morning's ceremony. Now, my love, I begin to think it pointless to send you this incomplete letter. I will finish it tomorrow, telling you what happens on this sad day.

Soon, then, my love. I am broken down by pain. Have pity on me.

CHAPTER 8

THE 13TH OF JANUARY—LAST CHAPTER

RODOLPHE TO CLÉMENCE

The thirteenth of January, an anniversary that is now doubly catastrophic. We have lost her forever, my love. Everything is over—everything! Let me tell you what happened.

It turns out to be true that there is an awful kind of pleasure to be had in recounting a horrible pain. Yesterday, I bemoaned the fate that kept you apart from me. Today, I am thankful you are not here, Clémence. It would be too painful for you.

This morning I was sleeping fitfully when I was awoken by the sound of church bells. I trembled in fear. They seemed funereal. Indeed, it sounded as if they tolled for a funeral. And indeed, my daughter is dead to us. Dead, you understand. Starting today, Clémence, you will have to mourn her in your heart—in that heart that has always beat for her like a mother's. What does it matter to us whether our child is buried in a marble tomb or a cloister's vault? What difference could it make to us?

Starting today, you understand, Clémence, we must look upon her as dead. And in any case, she is so weak that her health—so altered by so much sorrow, so many blows—is beginning to fail. Why not, then, that other death, the more complete one? Fate does not tire in its pursuit.

And then again, you can surely understand, after reading my letter from yesterday, why it might be happier for her if she were dead.

Dead . . . these four letters look odd—don't you think?—when one writes them with regard to one's adored daughter—such a beautiful, charming girl, of such angelic goodness. Hardly eighteen and dead to the world! In all honesty, what good does it do, to her or to us, for her to linger in suffering in the dismal quiet of the cloister? What does it matter whether she lives if she is lost to us? She must love this life that fate has made for her!

What I have written here is dreadful. There is such barbarous selfishness in a father's love!

She took her vows in a solemn ceremony at noon. I was there, hidden behind the curtains of our gallery. I felt even more intensely all the poignant emotions we have been feeling since she became a novice. And here's what is strange: everybody adores her. People generally believe that she is drawn to the religious life by an irresistible vocation. They ought to see her taking of vows as a joyous occasion for her, yet an oppressive sadness hung over the crowd. Sitting among the common people, in the back of the church, I saw two noncommissioned officers in my guard—two tough old soldiers—lower their heads and weep. You would have thought that everybody had a pained foreboding. If it had a basis, though, it was only partially fulfilled.

Once her vows were taken, our child was brought into the chapter room where the nomination of the new abbess was to take place. Thanks to my privilege as sovereign, I went to this room to await Fleur-de-Marie's return from the choir. She soon came back in. She was so emotional and weak that she needed the support of two other nuns. It was less her pallor or the change in her features that frightened me than the way she was smiling. To me, it appeared as if there was something of a sinister satisfaction to that smile. I'm telling you, Clémence, we will need courage—considerable courage. Something tells me that our child has received a death blow. After all, her life would be so unhappy.

This is the second time that I have said to myself, when thinking that my daughter might be dying, that death would at least put an end to her cruel existence. This thought is a horrible sign. But if we must be stricken by this tragedy, it is best to be prepared; don't you think this is so, Clémence? To prepare for that kind of tragedy, you have to sip slow anguish, drop by drop, beforehand. It's an unheard-of refinement of torture, a thousand times worse than the blow that strikes you unawares. At least stupor and annihilation spare you some of this atrocious heartbreak.

But compassion customarily demands that one be prepared for a blow. In all probability, I myself would not act in any other way, my dear, if I had to inform you of the fatal event of which I have been speaking. So, you should be frightened if you notice that I speak about her to you carefully and with sad, despairing circumlocutions after having announced that, after all I said, her health was not causing me grave concern. Yes, you should be frightened if I speak to you as I am writing now, because, even though she was calm enough when I left her a little while ago to finish this letter, I say again, Clémence, that I feel as if I can sense inside me that she is in more pain than she shows. I hope to heaven I am wrong and that what I take for presentiments are merely the result of the desperate sadness this doleful ceremony has evoked in me!

So Fleur-de-Marie came into the great chapter room. All the stalls were filled, one after the other, by the nuns. She went over, modestly, to the last seat in the row on the left. She was leaning on the arm of one of the sisters since she seemed still quite weak. Princess Juliane was seated at the head of the room, with the grand prioress on one side and another dignitary on the other. She held the golden cross, the symbol of her authority as abbess, in her hand.

A deep silence fell over the room as the princess got up, took her cross in her hand, and said, with gravity and great emotion, "My dear daughters, my advanced age forces me to entrust this emblem of my spiritual power"—and here she indicated the cross—"to younger hands than mine. A papal bull authorizes me to do this. I therefore will present for benediction to His Reverend Archbishop of Oppenheim and His Royal Highness, the Grand Duke, our sovereign, whichever of you, my dear daughters, has been chosen by you to succeed me. Our grand prioress will make the results of the election known to you, and I will pass on my ring and cross to whomever you choose."

I did not take my eyes off my daughter. Standing in the stall, her hands joined together in prayer at her chest, partially enveloped by her white veil and the long folds in the train of her black dress, she stood still and pensive. She had had no idea that she would be chosen. The abbess had told no one but me of her coming elevation.

The grand prioress took up her register and read: "Each of our dear sisters having been asked one week ago, in accordance with the convent rule, to place her vote in the hands of our holy mother and to keep her choice secret until now, I hereby declare, in the name of our holy mother, that one of you, my dear sisters, as a result of exemplary piety and angelic virtues, has earned the unanimous vote of the community. The one you have chosen is our sister Amélie, who has in this life been the very high and powerful princess of Gerolstein."

At this speech, a murmur of sweet surprise and happy satisfaction circulated in the room. All the nuns gazed upon my daughter with expressions of tender sympathy. I myself, despite the oppressive thoughts with which I was preoccupied, was extremely moved by this choice, which, made by each sister in isolation and in secret, nevertheless testified to a touching unanimity.

Fleur-de-Marie, who was stunned, became even paler yet. Her knees trembled so much that she was forced to hold herself up by resting her hand on the back of the stall in front of her.

In an elevated and serious tone of voice, the abbess said, "Dear daughters, is good Sister Amélie the choice of all of you as the one most worthy and most deserving of this office?"

Each nun responded in a loud voice, "Freely and willingly, I have chosen and I now choose Sister Amélie for my holy mother and superior."

Gripped by an inexpressible emotion, my poor daughter dropped to her knees, clasped her hands, and stayed that way until each vote had been registered. Then the abbess, putting the cross and ring into the grand prioress's hands, walked toward my daughter to take her by the hand and lead her to the seat reserved for the abbess.

My love, my dearest love, I had to break off for a moment. I needed to regain my courage to finish recounting this heartbreaking scene for you.

"Rise, my dear daughter," the abbess said to her. "Come and take your proper place. Your pious virtues, not your rank, have won it for you." While saying this, the venerable princess bent over my daughter to help her get up.

Fleur-de-Marie made a few uncertain steps and then, when she came to the middle of the chapter room, she stopped and said, in a tone whose calmness and firmness surprised me, "Forgive me, Holy Mother, but I would like to say something to my sisters."

"First take the seat of the abbess, my dear daughter," the princess said. "It is from there that your voice must reach them."

"Holy Mother, I am not fit for that seat," Fleur-de-Marie answered in a loud, trembling voice.

"What are you saying, my dear daughter?"

"Such a lofty position is not appropriate for such as me, Holy Mother."

"But you are called to it by the votes of every sister."

"Give me leave, Holy Mother, to make here, on both my knees, a solemn confession. My sisters will then see, as will you, Holy Mother, that the most humble life possible can never be humble enough for me."

"Your modesty misleads you, my dear daughter," the superior said with kindness, believing that the unfortunate child was just giving in to an exaggerated sense of modesty. I, however, realized what Fleur-de-Marie meant to confess to.

Gripped with fear, I cried out, imploring her, "My child, I beg of you—" I do not know how to describe for you, my love, everything I read in the profound look Fleur-de-Marie gave me when I said these words. As you will see in a moment, she had understood what I was saying. Yes, she had understood that I would have to share the guilt of this horrible revelation. She had understood that when she made a confession like the one she planned, I would be open to being accused—me—of lying, because I had always led people to believe that Fleur-de-Marie had never left her mother. Recognizing this, the poor child believed herself guilty of the blackest ingratitude toward me. She did not have the strength to go on and, overwhelmed, bowed her head down.

"I repeat, my dear daughter," the abbess went on, "your modesty misleads you. The unanimity with which your sisters choose you shows you how worthy you are to replace me. The very fact that you have enjoyed the pleasures of this world makes your renunciation of those pleasures that much more worthy. We have not elected Her Highness the Princess Amélie, but Sister Amélie. Your life began for us the day you set foot in this house of God, and it is that exemplary and holy life that we are rewarding. I will go further, my dear daughter. Your existence, prior to your entering our fold, could have been every bit as fallen as it is now, on the contrary, pure and praiseworthy, and, even so, the religious virtues you have exemplified during your stay here would only expiate and further redeem your past, however guilty it may be, in the eyes of the Lord. Given that, my dear daughter, you must surely believe that even your modesty ought to be satisfied."

Fleur-de-Marie felt the abbess's speech that much more deeply, as you may well believe, my love, because she believed her past to be ineradicable. Unfortunately, this scene had profoundly moved her, and, even though she put on calmness and strength, it seemed to me that her features changed in a way that was very troubling. Twice she trembled as she wiped her forehead with her poor, gaunt hand.

"I believe I have convinced you, my dear daughter," Princess Juliane went on, "and you will not want to cause your sisters the painful sorrow of refusing this mark of their trust and affection."

"No, Holy Mother," she said with a striking expression and a voice that became weaker and weaker. "I believe now that I may accept this honor. But, as I am very tired and in a little pain, if you will allow it, Holy Mother, I ask that the ceremony of my consecration be put off for a few days."

"It will be done according to your wishes, my dear daughter, but while you await the blessing and consecration of your new role, take this ring and assume your place. Our dear sisters will pay you the homage that our rules demand." And the superior, slipping her pastoral ring on Fleur-de-Marie's finger, led her to the chair of the abbess.

The ceremony was a simple and touching one. Next to the seat she occupied, the grand prioress stood on one side holding the golden cross, while Princess Juliane stood on the other. Each nun approached to bow before our child and kiss her hand with respect. I could see that her emotion was increasing moment by moment as her expression slowly broke down. This scene, in the end, was doubtless too much for her: she fainted before the procession of her sisters had been completed.

You can imagine how frightened I was! We brought her to the abbess's rooms. David had not left the convent. He hurried to her to give her medical attention. I hope he has not deceived me, but he assured me that this new trouble was caused only by an extreme weakness resulting from the wearying fasts and deprivation of sleep that my daughter had imposed on herself during her long, harsh novitiate. I believed him, because her angelic features, though frighteningly pale, did indeed show no trace of suffering when she regained consciousness. I was even struck by the serenity with which her beautiful face glowed. And this tranquility made me fearful all over again. It seemed to me that she was hiding a secret hope of an immediate deliverance.

The superior had returned to the chapter to close the ceremonies. I was there alone with my daughter. After looking at me for a few moments in silence, she said to me, "Good father, can you ever forget my ingratitude? Can you ever forget that at the moment I was going to make that painful confession, you had to plead with me to stop?"

"I beg of you, don't talk."

"And I did not consider," she went on, bitterly, "that to speak before everybody of that depraved abyss you pulled me out of was to reveal a secret that you had kept out of love for me. It was to accuse you publicly—you, my father—of an act of concealment that you would never have permitted yourself except to assure a brilliant and honored life for me. Oh, can you ever forgive me?"

Rather than responding, I pressed my lips to her forehead and she could feel my tears flow. After having kissed my hands over and over again, she said to me, "I feel better now, Father. Now that I am dead to the world, according to our rules, I would like to leave a few of my belongings to several people. But as everything I possess is yours, will you permit me to do that, my father?"

"Can you doubt it? But I implore you," I said to her, "to banish such gloomy thoughts. You can take care of such things later. You have the time, don't you?"

"Certainly, my dear father, I have a long life still ahead of me," she added in a tone of voice that made me tremble anew, though I couldn't say why. I looked at her carefully. There was no change in her features that would justify my worries. "Yes, I still have a long time to live," she went on, "but I must not busy myself with earthly things any longer since, as of today, I have renounced all that connects me to earthly concerns. I beg of you, don't refuse me."

"Give me your orders. I will do as you wish."

"I would like my dear mother to keep my work basket and the tapestry I began with her always in the small room she usually uses for herself."

"Your wishes will be followed, my child. Your rooms have stayed exactly as they were the day you left the palace. Everything that belonged to you is for us the object of religious worship. Clémence will be deeply touched by your thoughts for her."

"As for you, my dear father, you must take my big ebony chair, please, the one in which I spent so much time thinking and dreaming."

"It will be placed next to mine in my study and I will see you there every day sitting next to me, as you used to do so often," I said to her, without being able to hold back my tears.

"Now I would like to leave some remembrances from me to those who gave me so much care during my time of hardship. To Madame

Georges, I would like to leave the writing desk that I used to use. That will be a fitting gift," she added, smiling sweetly, "because she is the one who, when I was at the farm, first taught me to write. As for Bouqueval's venerable village priest, who gave me religious instruction, I would like him to have the beautiful cross that hangs in my chapel."

"Very good, my child."

"I would like also to send my pearl headband to good little Rigolette. It's a simple bit of jewelry that she can wear in her beautiful black hair. And then, if it's possible, since you know where in Algeria Martial and the She-Wolf are, I would like that courageous woman who saved my life to have my gold-enameled cross. Please give these different testaments of my memory, dear father, to these people, telling them that they are from Fleur-de-Marie."

"I will execute your wishes. But haven't you forgotten someone?"

"I don't think so, dear father."

"Think carefully. Among those who love you, isn't there one who is very unhappy, as unhappy as your mother and I? Someone who regrets your entry into a convent as painfully as we do?" The poor child understood me and pressed my hand, her pale face blushing slightly for a moment. Forestalling a question that she surely was afraid to ask, I said to her, "He is better. There is no longer any fear for his life."

"And his father?"

"He feels the effects of his son's improvement. He is better also. And Henri? What will you leave him? Some memory of you will be a dear and precious comfort for him!"

"Give him my prayer stool, dear father. Alas! I have often bathed it with my tears as I asked God for the strength to forget Henri, since I was unworthy of his love."

"How happy he will be to see that you have a place in your thoughts for him!"

"As for the asylum for orphans and young girls abandoned by their parents, I would like, dear father, for you to . . ."

Here Rodolphe's letter broke off with these almost illegible words: "Clémence, Murph will finish this letter. I am no longer able. I have gone mad. Oh, it is JANUARY 13!"

The letter, in Murph's handwriting, ended this way:

Madame,

I have been ordered to complete this sad story by his royal highness. His lordship's earlier two letters must have prepared your royal highness for the crushing news it is my duty to relate.

Three hours ago, his lordship was engaged in writing to your royal highness. I was waiting in the next room for him to give me the letter in order to send it right away by messenger. Suddenly, I saw Princess Juliana come in looking very upset. "Where is his royal highness?" she said to me in a voice full of emotion. "Princess, his lordship is writing to the grand duchess of the day's news." "Sir Walter, I must inform his lordship that something terrible has happened. You are his friend. Would you please be so kind as to tell him about it? Coming from you, the blow will cause him less pain."

I understood everything. I thought it more prudent to make the fatal revelation to him myself. Because the mother superior had added that Princess Amélie was slowly departing this life, and that his lordship had to come quickly in order to hear his daughter's last words, there was no way for me to break the news to him gently. I walked into the salon. His royal highness noticed how pale I looked.

"You are here to bring me some bad news!"

"The worst news, Your Lordship. Try to be strong."

"Ah! I knew it would be so!" he cried.

Without uttering another word, he ran into the cloister. I followed him there.

After her last conversation with his lordship, Princess Amélie had been taken from the mother superior's room to her cell. One of the nuns was watching over her. After an hour, she noticed that Princess Amélie, who had been speaking to her from time to time, was sounding weaker and weaker, and as if she was in greater pain. The nun ran to alert the mother superior. Doctor David was summoned. He hoped to curb this latest loss of strength with a tonic, but it was to no avail. Her pulse had grown so weak that it could hardly be detected. He realized with despair that the repeated emotional turmoil had probably drained Princess Amélie's remaining strength. There was no hope of saving her.

That was the situation when his lordship arrived. Princess Amélie had just received the last rites. A glimmer of consciousness remained to her. In one of her hands that she held crossed over her chest, *she held the remains of her little rose plant.* His lordship fell onto his knees at her bedside, weeping.

"My daughter! My beloved child!" he cried in a heartrending wail.

Princess Amélie heard his voice, turned her head slightly in his direction, opened her eyes, tried to smile, and then said to him, her voice barely audible, "My dear father, I beg you to forgive me. Henri, as well . . . And my kind mother . . . forgive me."

These were her last words.

Her death throes lasted an hour and were peaceful, if such a thing can be said. She gave her soul up to God.

When his daughter had breathed her last, his lordship did not speak. His calm and silent demeanor was chilling to behold. He closed the princess's eyelids, kissed her several times on the forehead, took the remains of the little rose plant with reverence, and left the cell.

I followed him. He returned to the house attached to the cloister, and, showing me the letter he had begun to write to your royal highness, and to which he tried vainly to add a few words—his hand was trembling so convulsively—he said to me, "I cannot write. I am utterly broken. I am incapable of thinking. Write to the grand duchess that I no longer have a daughter!"

I have done as his lordship ordered.

As his oldest servant, I beg the permission of your royal highness to urge her to return with all speed—as quickly as the health of the Count d'Orbigny allows her to do so. The mere presence of your royal highness may help to calm his lordship's despair. He wishes to watch over his daughter's body each night until she is buried in the grand ducal chapel.

I have performed this sad task requested of me, madame. Please excuse the incoherence of this letter.

With the most respectful and devoted
wishes of your royal highness's servant,

Walter Murph

The day before the funeral service for Princess Amélie, Clémence arrived in Gerolstein with her father. Rodolphe was not left alone for Fleur-de-Marie's funeral.

Letter from Eugène Sue to the Editor of *Le Journal des Débats*

Monsieur,

The Mysteries of Paris has now come to an end. Would you be so kind as to allow me publicly to thank you for having so kindly offered the *Journal des Débats*' large and powerful support to this work, which is unfortunately as imperfect as it is incomplete? My gratitude is that much greater, monsieur, because many of the ideas this work espouses diverge fundamentally from those you energetically and skillfully support; one rarely encounters the courageous and loyal impartiality you have shown with regard to me.

I ask that impartiality of you once more, monsieur, in the service of saying a few words in recommendation of a modest publication, founded and WRITTEN EXCLUSIVELY BY WORKERS, entitled *La Ruche Populaire* [The Hive of the People]. Several honest and enlightened artisans have created this popular forum in which they articulate their grievances with both propriety and moderation. (I cite, among others, a letter addressed to the king by Monsieur Duquesne, a working-class printer, that is both respectful and moving.) The organization of work, the regulation of competition, and the scale of wages are all addressed by the workers themselves, and for this reason alone it seems to me that their example merits the attention of all those who concern themselves with public affairs.

Unfortunately, however, many years may yet go by before these profound issues, in which workers have such a vital interest, will be resolved. Meanwhile, every day both brings and reveals to us new forms of wretchedness, new cases of individuals in distress: the founders of *La Ruche* hope that, in bringing before us each month the cases of their most unfortunate brethren, the more fortunate people of this world may hear their call.

Allow me, monsieur, to quote the first page of *La Ruche Populaire*:

LA RUCHE POPULAIRE

Saving good, unfortunate people who are to be pitied is a fine thing to do. Learning about those who struggle without losing their honor and energy and coming to their aid, sometimes without their knowledge and preventing misery or temptation from taking hold of them and leading them into crime—that's even better.

RODOLPHE, in The Mysteries of Paris

If, as we believe, the people cannot be helped or delivered with any effectiveness except through farsighted legislative measures, we do not think that that is any reason to underestimate or blindly reject tactfully offered aid.

The role that Monsieur Eugène Sue gives to Rodolphe in *The Mysteries of Paris* has inspired in us the idea of searching out honest and unfortunate families who, by that fact, merit religious fellow feeling. We appeal piously, in their name, to the humanity of the rich: even one act of charity is sometimes enough to turn aside misfortune, to ward off from wretchedness, from despair, perhaps even from crime, a family that has no resources whatsoever. And handouts are degrading. We suggest, principally, finding them work or some salaried position, sufficient, ultimately, to relieve them from the terrible grip of need.

We know of several deserving families in distress in need of relief: those who wish to act as benefactors may contact the office of this journal, or we can give them the necessary addresses so that they can give aid themselves directly.

We will take the liberty of citing one of many: a family composed of a father, a mother, and four children, the oldest of whom is six. They have looked to no avail for work that would allow them to survive; and the reason they cannot find it is the same one that would elicit the most touching concern: because their family is so large.

Another of these families has just lost its chief breadwinner. He was an honest painter who fell from four stories up. He leaves a pregnant wife and several very young children in the most profound grief and the greatest need.

I admit, monsieur, that it has given me great pleasure to quote this page, which cites my name in such flattering terms. I will always think myself rewarded beyond anything I ever hoped for every time that I have reason to believe that my writings have inspired some generous act or some charitable consideration, and such seems to me the idea given effect by the founders of *La Ruche Populaire*.

In this way, rich people who wish to subscribe to this monthly journal (six francs for one year, to the offices of *La Ruche*, 17 rue des Quatre-Fils, Marais district) will learn every month about some poor, respectable person whom relieving might bring them satisfaction. Because—let it be said loudly and clearly—there are many people in France who commiserate with the sufferings of the poor, but too often they lack for an opportunity to engage in charity in a way that enriches the heart and, if we may put it this way, engages their concern. In this connection, *La Ruche Populaire* will offer valuable information to those elevated souls who seek out the purest and most noble of joys.

Please allow me one more word, monsieur. As you have carried half the burden of this work because of the extensive dissemination you have given it, I believe that when you learn one of its effects, you will congratulate yourself on it as much, I hope, as I do. People have written to me from both Bordeaux and Lyon that, in those two cities, several rich and compassionate people are engaged in bringing to reality my project for a bank of interest-free loans for unemployed workers. And someone here who puts an immense fortune to the most generous and enlightened use has given me great hope that a like institution will be founded in Paris.

Let us now hope, monsieur, that a legislator who is a true friend of the people will turn his attention to the following needs:

Establishing lawyers for the poor;

Lowering the exorbitant interest rates charged by state pawnshops;

Establishing rehabilitative education for the children of those executed or given life imprisonment for their crimes;

Reforming the penal code with regard to embezzlement.

And then, perhaps, this book, which has recently been so bitterly attacked yet again, will at least have produced some good.

Very Sincerely Yours,

Eugène Sue

French Currency in the Nineteenth Century

The basic unit of currency from the French Revolution onward was the franc:

1 franc = 20 sous

1 franc = 100 centimes

Other units of money referred to:

The livre (French for "a pound") was the unit of French currency up until the French Revolution. In the nineteenth century the term was used interchangeably with the franc and has no relationship with the pound sterling.

The écu was also a pre-Revolutionary coin. In the nineteenth century, the term referred to a 5-franc piece.

A louis or a louis d'or was worth 20 francs.

In the nineteenth century, 5 francs = $1.

Using 1840 as a rounded-off date for the novel, $1 in 1840, in terms of buying power, is worth roughly $27 as of 2014. This figure is far from precise because we buy different things (we no longer buy horses and carriages as standard transportation; no one in the nineteenth century bought computers, stereos, or air-conditioning). One could get higher figures by comparing wages or household income figures. By this figuring, one franc in the novel would be worth about $5.50 in current buying power.